AN EPIC FANTASY PENTALOGY

THE RHENWARS SAGA

By ML Spencer

Darkmage
Darklands
Darkrise
Darkfall
Darkstorm (prequel)

AN EPIC FANTASY PENTALOGY

ML Spencer

This is a work of fiction. All of the characters, organizations, and events portrayed in this novel are either products of the author's imagination or are used fictitiously.

THE COMPLETE RHENWARS SAGA:
AN EPIC FANTASY PENTOLOGY

Maps by M.L. Spencer

STONEGUARD PUBLICATIONS

Cover by Claudia McKinney and Teresa Yeh
phatpuppyart.com
Edited by Morgan Smith

ISBN: 978-0-9997825-7-6

Printed in the United States of America

"The Rhenwars Saga" • Felix Ortiz

For Dan, Ashlynn, Cameron, and Paul.

I love you always.

Darkmage

BOOK ONE

THE Black Lands
To Bryn Calazar
Greystone Keep
Wolden
Cerulean Plains
AERYSIUS
Glen Farquist
Orien's Finger
Auberdale
Rothscard
Covendrey
THE Rhen
Isle of Titherry
Meridan
Southwark
THE Southern Continent
c. 1747 DCE

Prologue

Aerysius, The Rhen

Thunder ripped the sky, amplified to a throbbing din by the stone walls that rimmed the square beneath the Hall of the Watchers. Meiran Withersby felt the sound of it physically in her chest. Sheets of rain poured from blackened skies, pounding down on the roof of the cloistered passage above her. She glanced out through the narrow arches that lined the walkway but could make out nothing. Just a thick, choking blackness so complete that it seemed as if a dark pall had been draped down over the entire city, perhaps the entire world. The only light was the dim glow of the lantern that dangled from her fingers.

Lightning crackled and, for the briefest instant, Aerysius winked into existence around her and then disappeared again as abruptly. Meiran hastened her pace, wrapping the black cloak she wore more tightly about herself. Her feet moved with a pressing urgency, motivated by more than just the desire to find shelter from the elements.

In her right hand, she fingered a strip of parchment she'd found on the pillow in her bedchamber. It was written in the same, bold script as similar notes she had received in the past. The last one had been two years before and had contained an almost identical message: *Meet me in the greenhouse. Fourth Watch.* There was no signature—there never was. But Meiran already knew who the author must be.

She couldn't wait to share her secret with him, the one she'd been waiting two long years to whisper in his ear.

Finding that note had filled her with a dizzying thrill of anticipation. Her stomach had been in knots all day. She hadn't been able to concentrate on the simplest task. She had walked around feeling giddy, catching herself daydreaming at the worst possible moments. She couldn't help it, even though it was no way for someone of her station to behave. She was, after all, the most powerful Grand Master in all of Aerysius.

She was also a woman in love.

Lightning strobed the sky, followed immediately by a peal of thunder that shook the air. The wind was at her back, pushing her forward with icy fingers that rippled her cloak out before her. Her dark hair spilled like a fan before her face, whipping at her skin.

She reached the end of the cloister and burst through a massive, iron shod door. It was not more stone, or even cold marble, that greeted her feet. Instead, Meiran found herself on a narrow path within an old-growth forest.

There were many greenhouses in Aerysius. Most were used to grow food crops, some for herbs or even flowers. But the enormous structure she found herself within was the duplicate of a temperate rainforest. A miniature environment filled with ponds and streams, vegetation and animals.

Soft magelight glowed from behind stands of trees, filtered up from the ground, filling the forest with an ethereal glow. Overhead, rain beat distantly on the shutters drawn over the glass rooftop to protect it from the storm.

As she moved deeper into the forest, it became impossible to tell the environment was artificial. The air was warm and heavy with humidity. Meiran followed the trail around the edge of a pond to a small meadow aglow with magelight that moved like mist over the dark blades of grass. As she stepped onto the spongy lawn, Meiran halted with a sharp intake of breath.

He was there, at the far end of the meadow. Standing with his back to her.

Heart pounding, she crossed the meadow in quick, soft strides. She was so excited. It was hard not to giggle as she dashed through the swirling magelight on the grass. When she reached him, she laid her hand on the soft fabric of his shoulder, her touch hesitant. Slowly, he turned toward her.

She recoiled her hand in shock.

"Were you expecting someone else?" uttered a cold, malicious voice.

An intense feeling of horror overwhelmed her as Meiran shook her head in confused disbelief. She turned, wanting to run away, but froze instead. The lantern slipped from her fingers.

Twin shadows moved toward her over the grass. Not shadows. Something much, much worse. As they neared, the dark forms coalesced into shapes that were vaguely human but featureless, like demonic silhouettes.

Meiran tried to scream, but her throat constricted instead. An intense pang of dread spasmed her stomach. The feeling intensified, became choking, immaculate terror. She couldn't move. She couldn't breathe.

A shadowy hand rose toward her, dark fingers groping to touch her face.

Instinctively, she reached within. But the attempt was pointless. There was only silence inside. The constant rhythm of the magic field was absent, as if it had never existed at all. She was powerless against this enemy.

When the chill shadow of the necrator touched her, Meiran collapsed.

Chapter One
Acolyte of Aerysius

Aerysius, The Rhen

Fog rolled in overhead, gray wisps groping with nebulous tendrils across the sky. Darien Lauchlin measured its progress against the jagged slopes of mountain peaks. The fog appeared to move at an impossible rate when viewed against the snowy ridges. It spread misty fingers across the face of the sun, lending a chill stillness to the air that made the early morning shadows grow even deeper.

It was a strange time of year for such a heavy fog. In Amberlie, late summer days usually dawned clear and bright, redolent with the fragrance of pine and honeysuckle. But this day a cold wind had greeted the graying east, and the air felt heavy with the promise of rain. Another storm was coming, Darien suspected. But what kind of storm, he couldn't guess. A peculiar storm, both out of place and out of season. He only hoped it wouldn't arrive today.

Today, he was coming home.

The only thing Darien heard was the sound of his own footsteps as he trudged up the dusty path. His worn-out boots made scuffing noises as he walked; he was too tired to pick up his feet. He squared his shoulders wearily and drew himself up under the weight of his pack. As he did, something inside it clanked as it rattled against the scabbard of the longsword he wore slung across his back. The sound grated on his nerves. Swords were not looked upon favorably under the shadow of Aerysius.

Ahead, he could see a crossroads. As he drew nearer, the noise of other travelers made it clear he wasn't the only person awake in the dim stillness of the morning. The trail topped a low rise, and then he saw them. They came from all directions, every day of the year, to converge at this place. They brought with them their troubles, their sick, their hopes, even their dead, and usually left with nothing. There were many more pilgrims than he remembered.

Darien stepped onto the road in a space between two groups of travelers. The people in front of him seemed one family. The man had the look of a farmer. He was flanked by two boys and a woman who carried a babe in her arms. The child's weak cries were heart-rending, as was the sight of the small, blue-tinged face. Darien felt a knot tighten in his stomach, but there was nothing he could do. Frustration was a feeling he had become all too familiar with. He directed his gaze back at the dirt of the road and tried to ignore the child's wheezing.

Ahead, the forest was thinning out. The sight fed him with hope, and he picked up his pace. Through a break in the trees, he caught sight of a ramp that stretched out over the riverbed.

Darien hurried forward and took the mother by the arm. "Come with me," he said, pulling her away from the rest of her family.

The mother's eyes widened in surprise as they took in the color of his cloak. She glanced back at her husband, who stood watching her go with a mixture of hope and fear in his eyes.

Determined, Darien pulled her along after him as he bored his way through the press of bodies gathered in front of the gatehouse.

The heavy pack lent him momentum, so they quickly reached the forefront of the throng. He glanced around, at last finding the gatekeeper seated behind a small desk by the gate. Trudging toward him, he insinuated himself at the front of the line, the sight of his cloak forestalling any complaints.

When the man behind the desk looked up at him, Darien was mildly surprised. He thought he knew every mage of Aerysius. But the old man before him with thinning white hair and a face cobwebbed by wrinkles was unknown to him.

Then it dawned on him: the summons. All Masters had been recalled, including some who had never passed beneath the ancient arches since their Raising.

"Name and business," the old man grated in a monotonous tone. His mouth barely moved, as though he were unused to the most fundamental mechanisms of speech.

Darien took a deep breath, then supplied his name and title. "Darien Lauchlin, Acolyte of Aerysius."

As he spoke, he pulled back the fabric of his shirtsleeve, exposing the intricate markings that encircled his left wrist, forming what looked like a heavy metallic chain. The emblem was the mark of the Acolyte's Oath. It symbolized the first vow taken upon acceptance to the Assembly of the Hall. To serve the land and its people. With his life, if possible. If not, then by death.

The man took note of the markings and simply nodded. "You're late." He gestured at the ramp. "Get on your way, boy, and better pray that Emelda goes easy on you."

Darien suppressed a grimace. He'd gotten off to a late start after receiving the summons to return home.

"Let's go," he said to the woman, applying a slight pressure to her back. The mage who guarded the gate would have no knowledge of healing. Such study was reserved for specific orders, and no Sentinel or Querer would ever condescend to such a lackluster duty.

As Darien guided the woman and child through the gate, the crowd surged toward the opening. Immediately, guards stepped forward to press the throng back.

They had to step over a slight gap where the ramp ended, and a wood platform began. The people already gathered there were forced to shift back to make room. Darien ignored their stares, edging sideways to position himself against the platform's railing. He could feel the almost palpable tension of the people surrounding him, noticed how they backed away from the sight of his cloak.

The woman beside him dropped to her knees, gazing up at him with imploring eyes. Tears spilled down her cheeks, her mouth constricting in grief.

"Please," she begged, offering her child to him. "Help us. You can save him. Please. Oh, *please*."

Darien could only look down at her helplessly. She had mistaken him for a full Master because of the color of his cloak. It was not the first time the error had been made.

"I can't," he told her gently. "I'm just an acolyte. The only thing I can do is get you up there."

The woman collapsed over the small form in her arms. He knelt at her side, wanting to comfort her. Not knowing what else to do, Darien ran a hand over the tangled mats of her hair, clenching his jaw against a redoubled pang of frustration.

A shout rang up from below, signaling the guards to close the gate. Darien helped the woman regain her feet. He caught hold of the platform's railing and drew her against him.

The wood beneath them jolted. There was a sudden wave of panic as feet scrambled for better purchase. Then the entire platform seemed to take flight, surging backward and up. The gap between the gate and the ramp widened, exposing the swift waters of the river below.

He looked up and saw the ropes that held the platform aloft. Far below, many teams of horses labored in their traces to lift the platform up the cliff. The ground below drew farther away, the air taking on a slight chill.

Darien closed his eyes and reached out from within, tasting the flow of the magic field. Here, he had to be careful. A powerful vortex of magic surrounded Aerysius. Though he was only an acolyte, the wild cyclone of power was violent enough to hurt him if he let his mind stroke it the wrong way. For a full Master, such a mistake would be fatal—which was why the lift relied on horse power until it was well above the surging flux of magic.

There was a sharp jolt, and then the platform sped upward at a dizzying pace. They had passed into the calm eye of the vortex, and magic took over as the means of lifting them up the mountainside.

Darien noticed that the woman was hugging the child so hard, he was afraid she might crush it.

"May I hold him?" he asked.

The woman nodded, offering the child to him.

Darien received the small life softly into his arms, swaddling the babe in the folds of his cloak. He held him close against his chest, seeking to revive him with the warmth of his body. The wheezing babe stared up at him with soft brown eyes that made his heart ache.

The lift slipped silently into a bank of fog, so thick he couldn't see the child in his arms. Then, miraculously, the mist parted, and warm sunlight streamed from a brilliant blue sky, revealing the foundations of Aerysius above.

The city was carved from the side of the mountain, etched right into the vertical wall of granite. The spires of Aerysius seemed wrought from millions of glistening crystals, tendril-thin bridges arching between them thousands of feet above the Vale. To Darien, the sight was no less breathtaking than the first time he'd seen it, and this time there was added meaning.

He was finally home.

The platform slowed to a stop, halting beside an arching foundation. Above, a waterfall spilled down from the top of a soaring spire, birds diving in and out of the mist created by the spray.

But the sound of the woman sobbing beside him dampened any joy he might have felt over his homecoming. Looking down, Darien saw that the child in his arms lay completely limp, the soft eyes closed. He patted the small body with his hand, trying to prod any type of life out of it.

But the boy didn't stir.

He stood dazed as the woman removed the dead child from his grasp. The gate opened, and the crowd spilled past him off the platform. The woman fled after them, cradling the sad bundle in her arms.

Darien lingered behind on the lift, feeling numb as he stared down at his empty hands. He stood there for a while, his thoughts scattered like broken glass. It wasn't until the lift shifted under the weight of new passengers that he finally blinked, his mind snapping back into focus. He forced himself to move forward, turning sideways to forge a path through the oncoming crowd.

It took him long minutes of walking before he remembered where he was supposed to be going. He changed course, turning onto a side street that would take him into the heart of the lower terrace.

As he moved through the streets of Aerysius, Darien scarcely noticed people staring at him and moving out of his way. He didn't care. He wasn't in the mood to care and, besides, the same looks plagued him everywhere he went.

He was used to standing out in a crowd. The sight of a black-cloaked man bearing a sword on his back was a glaring contradiction that most people couldn't ignore. Masters of Aerysius swore the Oath of Harmony. They didn't walk about carrying weapons.

He climbed the wide steps in front of the Hall of the Watchers, passing beneath the ancient arches that stabbed upward into the sky like twisted spears. Inside, the circular hall was filled with a hazy amber light that filtered down from stained glass windows set high above. It was enormous, one of the largest structures ever built by man. Great pillars carved to resemble massive stone trees with spreading branches supported the weight of the domed ceiling. There were hundreds of them, row upon row.

He took a flight of steps that descended into the base of the hall. There, he found a woman seated behind a small desk, scribing something with a feathered quill. She continued to write, appearing completely engrossed in her task. Only when he stood across the desk from her did she slide her spectacles off her face, looking sideways up at him with an irritated expression.

"You're late."

Darien nodded. "I left a week after receiving the summons."

He wished he'd stopped at the Acolytes Residence to clean up a bit. The way the woman was staring at him made him conscious of every speck of dust from the road, of the week-old growth of stubble on his face. He saw her eyes come to rest on the hilt of the sword at his back. The woman's eyebrows flicked upward, her look incredulous. Not many people had the gall to come armed to an audience with the Prime Warden of Aerysius.

"I see you've grown too big for your britches, Darien Lauchlin," she said. "It might be wise to put off your Raising until you can remember you are yet an acolyte. You may be the Prime Warden's own son, but that does not excuse you. If anything, it means you must be seen as an example for others."

He didn't know whether she referred to his late arrival or the unsubtle insult of the sword. If she wanted him to remove the weapon, then she was mistaken. He had no intention of doing so. His mother would have to get used to the sight of it.

He waited as the woman merely stared at him. When it became obvious that he wasn't going to budge or offer apology, she shook her head and made a *tsk*ing sound with her tongue.

"Well, if you insist on acting like a child, so be it. Let your mother deal with you. Have no doubt, she will." She stood up, tossing her quill down with an air of finality.

"Come."

She turned her back on him, opening a door beside her desk. Darien followed her at a good distance as she led him down a hallway. He had been there before, many times. He really had no need to be shown the way. But his mother expected—or, rather, demanded—formality at all times.

The hallway ended at a white door. The woman opened it and gestured for him to wait. Darien paused just long enough to hear her announce him before brushing past her through the opening.

The room inside was filled with brilliant white light. The entire chamber was encased with windows that had scarcely a pane between them. The Prime Warden's solarium looked out from within the mountainside, the view an unspoiled panorama of the white-capped Craghorns and the Vale of Amberlie below.

Emelda Lauchlin was seated on a raised dais before the panoramic windows, her face impatiently expectant. Darien did not forget his manners. He went instantly to his knees, abasing himself until his black hair was spread out on the floor beside his face. He didn't dare move from that position until he was bid. So he waited, listening to the sound of his breath, the dead babe's face haunting his thoughts.

A long minute dragged by, followed by another. By the third, Darien had no doubt his mother was angry.

After five minutes, he knew she was livid.

"Arise."

He swallowed as he pushed himself off the floor. He felt the blood rush out of his head and, for a moment, he felt terribly dizzy. He saw that his mother had risen as well. She glared down at him imperiously from her position on the dais. She wore her ebony hair pulled back from her face, which only served to augment the stern set of her features.

For a long moment, they stood staring at each other across the distance between them. Then, more graceful than a queen, the Prime Warden of Aerysius descended the steps of the dais. She stopped before him, having to look up to meet his gaze. Her blue eyes burned fiercely, her lips pressed into a frown of barely controlled rage. Then, abruptly, she swept forward to embrace him.

Darien was taken aback. He moved awkwardly to return the gesture, which was made more difficult by the baldric he wore and the pack still slung from his shoulder. When they separated, he was surprised to see the anger on her face replaced by a warm smile of affection. Looks were not the only thing he had inherited from her; Emelda Lauchlin had a temperament just as unpredictable as his own.

"My son." She stared at him with wonder in her eyes. "You have changed a great deal."

Her gaze lowered to fix on the leather strap that crossed his chest. This was the critical moment, he knew. She would either accept him for what he was or reject him utterly, and it all hinged on whether or not she accepted the sword.

She chose to ignore it.

Taking him by the hand, she led him to a white chair and claimed the one beside it. Darien struggled out of his pack and leaned his sword against the chair's leather armrest.

He tried to gauge his mother's disposition by the way she held herself. She sat leaning forward slightly, arms open and resting on the cushions at her sides. It was a welcoming posture, one that invited him in instead of shutting him out. He took it for a good sign.

"Tell me," she pressed, "how fares the Front?"

It was time to make his case. Darien had rehearsed this speech all the way down from the Pass of Lor-Gamorth. But now, when the moment to deliver it was upon him, the carefully rehearsed phrases eluded him. Shaking his head, he decided honesty was the best thing he could offer her.

"We're dying," he said, staring down at a smear of mud on his knee.

As if sensing his struggle, his mother set a hand on his arm. The touch strengthened him enough to continue.

"The Enemy is massing in numbers never before seen. We don't have enough soldiers. We're facing a critical shortage of weapons and supplies. We're running out of ideas and, frankly, we're running out of hope. There's been precious little support from the South. The last group of men they shipped us was a pack of criminals up from Rothscard, and that's been months ago. We'll all be dead in another few months, either by the sword or by hunger, but it doesn't matter which. The fact is, you'll have Enemy hordes pouring down on top of you, and your only line of defense will be feeding the crows."

As he let the last words die, Darien felt an instant pang of regret. He hadn't meant to raise his voice. Silence followed while his mother only stared at him, her expression impossible to read. He felt drained, as though the flood of words he'd let pour from his mouth had sapped his strength.

"So, you are suggesting that the might of Aerysius should turn the tide of this war?"

Her words, though softly spoken, were deliberately chosen. His mother was trying to probe him to find out where he stood on the issue. It was a test, of sorts. Whether or not she approved his Raising might even depend on how he responded. But Darien didn't care. There was only one way he could answer her, and it was with the conviction of his beliefs.

"I'm suggesting there may not *be* an Aerysius if you don't Unbind the Sentinels," he said, the words sounding harsher than he meant. "The order exists to defend the Rhen against this very threat. I understand the need for the Oath of Harmony, but it has served its purpose. Times change, Mother. The time for the Oath has passed. If we don't Unbind the Sentinels, then there will be no hope. The Enemy will slaughter us."

Her eyes dropped to the leather-wrapped scabbard that leaned against his chair. Very carefully, she asked, "What then, Darien?"

Here was the crux of the test. Darien feared to step across this threshold. But he had already pressed too far to stop now.

"Let me receive the Transference from two Masters. Give me the strength to create a grand resonance. Then we can lure their forces southward and annihilate them."

His words were met by silence, as though they had fallen on empty space. Darien dropped his gaze and stared at the floor, knowing he'd gone too far.

It was long seconds before his mother spoke again.

"Tonight, you shall be Raised to the Order of Sentinels, as your father was before you." Her voice was cold, as icy as the mountain wind. "You will accept the Transference from Grand Master Ezras Nordric, who has decided to pass beyond and leave the trials of this war to the next generation. To you. You shall swear the Oath of Harmony in front of the full Assembly of the Hall. Before you do, you will take that thing at your side and cast it off the cliff. I will never hear the words 'grand resonance' out of your mouth again. Do I make myself clear, Darien?"

"Aye," he answered, feeling the last of his hopes dashed by his mother's resolve. Darien bowed his head, accepting defeat.

He would take the Oath, as she asked. Only, he didn't believe he could keep it. There was a harsh penalty for Oathbreakers. They would strip the power from him—a painful form of execution. Then they would hang his body from the arches as a warning, and also as a statement. The world needed to know that the justice of Aerysius was without mercy, even for its own. That was the price of betrayal, the price of Oathbreaking. Yet, if such an act could stop the war…

There was a text Darien had read once. It had been part of his curriculum: *The Mysteries of Aerysius* by Cedric Cromm. In it was a short biography of Grand Master Orien, who had stood on the crag now known infamously as Orien's Finger to bring the vast power of a vortex to bear against an invasion long ago.

Orien's desperate act had turned the tide of battle and driven the Enemy from the North. Then Orien had calmly knelt and surrendered himself to his punishment. Orien's face was among those of the Watchers in the Hall, his image carved severely in stone. He had been an Oathbreaker and had died a cruel death for his actions. Yet, he had also been a savior.

"You may go." His mother dismissed Darien curtly, waving a hand in the direction of the door. "Spend the rest of the day in solitude and reflection."

As he stood to leave, her voice stopped him.

"It's good to have you home. You remind me of your father so much. He would have been very proud to see the man you have become."

Darien nodded somberly as he gathered his things. His father had been a formidable Sentinel, and part of him was pleased at hearing his mother's words. But he also found them bitterly ironic. Gerald Lauchlin had despised the Mage's Oath yet had died preserving it. Darien had always aspired to follow the example set by his father, but he had no wish to meet such a similar, hypocritical end.

He strode back down the hallway, taking lengthy strides to put some distance between himself and his mother's solarium. He could hear his pulse pounding in his ears, almost as loud as the sound of his ringing footsteps. He mounted a flight of stairs that took him up, spiraling, into the Spire of the Hall.

He paused to catch his breath at a landing, cursing himself silently for the way he had mismanaged the interview. Heat rose to flush his cheeks as he clenched and unclenched his fists in anger. He stood still, taking slow, deep breaths until the throbbing of his pulse subsided in his ears. He started to move forward again, but a familiar voice stopped him short.

"So, the prodigal son finally returns."

Darien sucked in a sharp breath between clenched teeth. He closed his eyes, wondering just how many tests the gods would throw his way in one day. Then, opening his eyes, he slowly turned to face his only brother.

Aidan looked the same as Darien remembered. He stood leaning against the carved railing of the staircase, his black cloak flipped back over one shoulder in the manner he was accustomed to wearing it. It lent him a polished, aristocratic appearance. He stood with one hand tucked neatly behind his back, the other draped over the railing as though it were the armrest of a throne. He gazed upon Darien with eyes that were a perfect copy of their mother's.

"Still playing with your toys, I see? You should have abandoned them years ago." Aidan arched an eyebrow, strolling forward down the steps. He circled Darien slowly, eyeing the weapon on his back with an expression of distaste. "Or is it your intention to swear the Oath of Harmony upon that sword?"

Darien sighed, shaking his head. He'd hoped things would have changed over the two years of his absence. Meeting Aidan's gaze, he said, "I was thinking maybe we could just be brothers again. Perhaps it was too much to expect."

Aidan blinked, a gallant smile springing to his lips. "Not too much, I think. It was only a jest." He clapped Darien on the shoulder with a soft chuckle. The act was condescending, and the smile on his face seemed forced. "Really, Darien, you always take things much too seriously. Here, let me get that for you."

Aidan swept the pack off Darien's shoulder without waiting for a reply. He held the dusty leather away from his body, as though afraid some of the grime might smudge off and mar his appearance. He extended his hand in invitation.

As they climbed the stairs, Aidan made an attempt at conversation. "I trust your journey was safe?"

Darien nodded, thinking he didn't have the breath to waste on a reply as he considered the spiraling staircase still above them.

"Oh, I just remembered." Aidan turned to look back at him, smiling pleasantly. "I have a message for you from Grand Master Meiran. You do remember her, of course?"

Darien glared at his back. His brother was taunting him under the infuriating guise of politeness, just like he always had. Aidan knew all about the scandal that had hastened Darien's departure two years before. Everyone knew of it.

He had pursued Meiran for months, even though she was well above his station and he had no business being near her. There were no laws forbidding Masters and acolytes from associating in private, but the traditions of Aerysius were often more stringent than formal laws.

His mother had caught wind of the affair. She had Darien packed up and shipped off to the Front in all haste, without even a chance to say goodbye. Meiran had received a demerit, unheard of for a Grand Master of her status.

Aidan went on as though he were ignorant of the whole ordeal, "She sends her regards. Really, Darien, you must have made quite an impression before you left. It usually isn't considered proper for a Grand Master to be seen chasing around after acolytes."

"I won't be an acolyte much longer," Darien growled, fighting to control the anger his brother always had a way of provoking. He silently berated himself. He was feeding right into Aidan's ploy. Not wanting his brother to get the better of him, he added in a lighter tone, "Besides, I was the one who did all the chasing."

They arrived finally at a level high up in the Spire of the Hall. His brother led him down a well-lit hallway, stopping at a mahogany door about halfway down the passage. Aidan swept it open with a gallant swirl of his cloak, exposing the chambers within.

Darien stood in the doorway, surveying his new quarters with a feeling of trepidation. This was not the stark cell of an acolyte. The room was as large as his mother's solar, decorated lavishly enough to suit a nobleman. There was a fire already blazing in the hearth and a vase with cut flowers sitting on the dining table.

"Well, here you are," Aidan announced. "I trust you find your quarters adequate? I chose the location, but Mother made all the arrangements."

"It's far more than adequate," Darien muttered, feeling stunned and more than a little overwhelmed. He took a step inside, wondering if it would be possible to get used to so much space after spending the last two years freezing in the cramped cellar of Greystone Keep.

He collected himself enough to say, "My thanks, Aidan. It's wonderful."

His brother set his pack down by the door, hesitating as if uncertain whether he wanted the dirty thing to soil the floor tiles.

"I'll see you tonight, then," Aidan said. "Don't get too comfortable, now. You'll not want to miss your own Raising."

Darien barely heard the sound of the door closing as his brother took his leave. He stood gazing around the chamber, feeling too exhausted to think. Memories of the dead child kept creeping into his awareness, making him feel hollow.

Moving awkwardly, he leaned his sword against the wall beside his back. Then he slumped down into a heavily cushioned chair and found a goblet of wine already poured and waiting on the table beside him.

His hand trembled as he raised the goblet to his lips. He took the liquid into his mouth in thirsty gulps, trying to wash away the images in his head.

As he set the spent glass back on the table, his head suddenly felt too heavy to hold up any longer. He snuggled back into the soft cushions and gazed up at the painted ceiling, a soft ringing sound filling his ears.

The ceiling blurred, growing darker, the colors melting and running together.

He never remembered falling asleep. The drug in the wine acted swiftly.

Chapter Two
Two Goblets, Two Rites

Aerysius, The Rhen

The dark altar existed deep within the heart of the mountain. It was accessible only by someone with knowledge of the vast network of passages that had been formed by the natural action of running water and the hard labors of men thousands of years dead.

The man carrying Meiran's unconscious body had that knowledge, and other knowledge, besides. He had spent years of his life in preparation for this night, poring over forbidden manuscripts full of dark teachings and secrets purposefully forgotten. A perfect map of the entire cave system existed in his head, along with the methods of disarming the magical traps and devices rigged to prevent access. He had journeyed down these dark passages many times before. The ancient warren was his own personal sanctuary, the unholy shrine his private chapel.

The altar existed in a small chamber roughly hewn from the black rock of the mountain's heart. The walls wept the wet blood of the mountain down their coarse faces, glistening in the pale magelight he cast. Puddles collected on the floor, stagnant pools that splashed foul droplets up to soil the hem of his cloak as his boots disturbed their surfaces. He crossed the chamber to the far side, where he stooped to lay the woman upon the worn surface of the altar rock.

The altar was formed from a single slab of black stone with ancient, rusted chains set there to restrain a victim for sacrifice. It had been a common practice among the dark sects of ages past. He didn't bother with the chains, had even dismissed the necrators after they had served their initial purpose. The woman on the altar needed no restraint, either physical or ethereal. Meiran had been touched by hell's own shadow. She would never again awaken.

His nostrils sucked in the stale air of the chamber as he went about his business with meticulous efficiency. He removed the black cloak from Meiran's body, folding it carefully before placing it on the floor.

He then paused a moment, eyes drinking in the thin silk his action had exposed. His hand moved to caress the fabric's texture where it lay smooth against the firm curve of her hips. The touch stimulated him, inciting his heart to quicken its pace. In all his careful planning, he had never imagined this moment would be so irresistibly erotic.

With the back of his hand, he stroked aside a wayward lock of brown hair that had fallen over Meiran's pale, perfect face. He continued the motion, running his fingers down the side of her cheek, over her parted lips. He leaned down, brushing those lips with his own tender kiss.

When he bared the sword from its scabbard with a crisp ring of steel, he was pleased to find it just as sharp as he'd expected. In two quick motions, he laid open the skin of Meiran's wrists to the bone.

Stooping, he bent to catch the pulsing blood flow in a crystalline wine goblet. When it was full, he let Meiran's arm fall limply onto the surface of the altar.

He turned, then, toward the Well.

The Well of Tears stood in the center of the chamber, made of rough stone blocks and covered with a round slab of granite four inches thick. Around its rim were carved runes in an ancient, unholy script that looked like vicious slashes in the stone, as though made by the claws of a vile beast. The Well was a portal to the darkest depths of the Netherworld, a gateway that opened a conduit straight to the bowels of hell. Once opened, the Well would unleash the dark hosts of Chaos upon the world.

He would have the terror of the night at his command.

Kneeling beside the Well, he dipped a finger into the goblet of blood. The fluid dripped to the floor as he moved his hand to the first rune, tracing its form with the warm blood from Meiran's veins.

The blood took a moment to absorb into the porous stone. When it did, the marking began to glow with a pale green light. He moved around the rim to the next rune in the sequence, then another, dipping his finger into the goblet and repeating the act all around the rim. He moved carefully, taking his time, until all of the markings glowed with the same pale, sickening light.

But his work was not yet complete. The Well had to be unsealed from both sides. His action had unlocked the side of the gateway that existed in this world. But someone else would have to open it from the other side.

The lid was far too heavy to be shifted by the limited strength of a single man. So he reached within, aligning his mind with the rhythm of the magic field. As if pushed by the invisible hand of a giant, the cover of the Well of Tears lifted and slid aside, falling sharply to the floor with a resounding crash.

He turned back to Meiran.

Her blood was nearly spent, running in scarlet rivulets down the side of the altar and mixing with the pools of water on the floor. He moved to place two fingers on her neck, feeling for a pulse. It was still there, tremulous, and growing fainter. He stood over her, gazing down at her beautiful, ashen face until the tempo of her heart finally stalled in her veins.

He pressed his hands against her cheeks as she died, cupping her face as though with the tender embrace of a lover. There was a faint tingling sensation in his fingertips where they touched her soft skin, weak at first, then growing infinitely stronger. The flow of power swam up from within her, coursing into him, filling his body and mind with a shuddering ecstasy almost too great to stand.

He pulled himself on top of her, moving his hands behind her back to lift her body against his chest, hugging her fiercely as he absorbed the final spasms of current that flowed into him. When it was finished, he collapsed on top of her, spent and gasping.

He pushed himself off her, standing up. His breath still came in gasps, his body trembling from the deluge of energy from the Transference. With his newfound strength, he placed a finger on her forehead and uttered an enchantment that would have been completely beyond him only a few moments before. He pressed upon Meiran's soul a Word of Command, sending her spirit to the Netherworld with a task she would have no choice but to perform.

He lifted her body, carried the dead weight of her over to the Well. With one, smooth motion, he cast her in. The blue fabric of her dress rippled in the wind created by the speed of her fall. He watched as the sight of her was quickly lost, consumed by the shadows of the Well. He never heard her body hit the bottom. As far as he was aware, it never did.

Aidan Lauchlin knelt on the floor in the dim light of the Well's shining runes. He waited, wondering how long it would take her to complete the task he had Commanded of her soul.

Dark colors swam gradually into focus, hazing in and out across his vision. It took Darien long moments to realize it was the ceiling he was looking at and not some confused chiaroscuro that had taken on a life of its own.

Blinking, he sat up and gazed around the room in foggy bewilderment. He must have fallen asleep, though he didn't recall doing so. There was a throbbing ache in the back of his head. His mouth was dry, and his eyes ached when he rubbed them.

Beside his chair, the crystalline goblet sat empty. The bottle next to it was mostly full, completely untouched, save for the one glass that had been poured from it.

He wondered what time it was. It felt as though

he'd been sleeping a long time. He struggled out of the chair, regretting the motion instantly. The throbbing in his head turned to a stabbing pain that lanced like hot irons into his eyes. Wincing, Darien squinted as dark blotches swam across his vision.

It took him a moment to recover enough to stagger across the room to the hearth. The fire had burned out, the coals gray and cold. That was the first thing he noticed. Frowning, he glanced toward the paned window. Through glass streaked with rain, he saw only consummate darkness. Panic seized him. It was late.

Then he noticed the clock on the wall with heavy iron counterweights. The position of the bronze hands on its face made the feeling of panic in his gut wrench into a wave of nausea. It was a quarter past the stroke of midnight. He was already late for the Rite of Transference in the temple.

"Bloody hell," he growled.

His mother was going to kill him.

Darien stood frozen, groping through the fog in his head to figure out what to do first. He had no time to clean up. His clothes were worn and travel-stained, his hair unwashed, his face unshaven. He'd taken no time to prepare himself mentally.

He sprang for the bedchamber, ignoring the stabbing pain in his head. His mother would have arranged for a wardrobe—she was never one to miss a detail. Yet he still exhaled a sigh of relief when he saw fresh clothing already laid out on the bed.

Stripping the filthy rags off his body, he donned the new black robes in a matter of seconds. One glance at the looking glass told him his face was a lost cause. He cupped his hands and filled them with water from the basin, splashing it over his cheeks. The towel he used to dry his face came away stained and filthy. He dragged his fingers through his hair, ripping through most of the snarls, then tied the long strands back with a strip of leather.

That was as good as it was going to get.

As he dashed out of the bedchamber, Darien suddenly remembered the sword his mother had ordered thrown off the cliff. He had absolutely no intention of doing so—the sword was a gift from Meiran.

But the weapon wasn't where he'd left it. Someone had removed it while he slept.

The curse Darien swore as he slammed the door shut would have chilled even his mother's cold blood.

He was well beyond fashionably late by the time he reached the Temple of Athera in the upper reaches of the city. Being located on the sheer face of a mountain precipice, Aerysius was spread out more vertically than horizontally. Many of its streets were switchbacks, climbing steeply up the side of the cliff, that or granite stairs carved into the face of the mountain itself. Sky bridges linked the tops of towers at lower levels of the city with the bases of structures at higher elevations. Navigating the streets, particularly in the pouring rain, was difficult.

To Darien, the climb to the temple was a grueling punishment. His body ached at every joint, and the throbbing in his head refused to go away.

He was shaking and drenched by the time he topped the last flight of stairs. He thrust the temple door open, his long strides propelling him into a well-lit antechamber.

He stopped in the middle of the room and glanced about frantically, trying to figure out where to go. There were four doors to pick from, as well as two staircases to either side. He was about to just start trying doors when a cold voice from above halted him.

"I'm not certain who I should be more furious with: you, for arriving over an hour late, or your brother, for not bothering to present himself at all."

Darien slumped, shivering, not wanting to look up to face the wrath of his mother. She stood at the railing of the balcony, glaring down at him imperiously. At least she was alone; that was a small comfort. Darien wasn't sure he could stand the humiliation of another public dressing-down by her. He strode toward the staircase grudgingly.

His mother waited for him on the balcony. Fury radiated from her presence, sharpening her every movement. When Darien stopped in front of her, she grabbed his face, her fingers squeezing until they hurt. She jerked her hand away roughly.

"What is the matter with you?" she hissed between clenched teeth. "When I sent you away, you were ready for this. More than ready! But now I see you've come back to us with the manners of a swine and nothing but contempt for our ways."

Darien seethed with a silent rage that threatened to ignite. Emelda was Prime Warden as well as his mother, but that was no excuse for the callous way she always treated him. She showed less respect for him than she did for the lowliest kitchen scullion. He didn't care that she held the keys to his Raising in her hand, didn't care that she had the authority to send him away again, perhaps this time forever. The anger inside burned fierce, impossible to contain.

"Then make your choice," Darien demanded. "Either let's do this, or tell me now, and I'll be on my way."

Emelda stared at him as if truly seeing him for the first time in her life. She blinked slowly before dropping her gaze. It was the only time in Darien's memory he had ever seen his mother back down.

The silence between them stretched. Finally, Emelda looked up to meet his gaze. An expression of regret had replaced the anger in her eyes. Darien almost didn't recognize the emotion, it looked so foreign on her features.

"I'm sorry," she said. "I've always held the highest expectations of you. Perhaps they have been too high. I suppose it's because, for the most part, you have always lived up to them."

It was Darien's turn to drop his gaze. Her soft words had extinguished the last spark of anger left within him. He stared at the floor, thoughts and feelings running through his head in a torrent, leaving him terribly confused. He didn't notice her hand moving until he felt the touch of her fingertips against his.

"It's time," she whispered. "Are you ready?"

Darien nodded but didn't speak. He felt incapable of trusting his voice. He allowed her to guide him toward a door off the balcony. He opened it for her and waited as his mother went through first, following silently in her wake.

What he found inside the chapel looked nothing like the formal ceremony he'd been expecting. What he saw, rather, appeared to be a gathering of old friends. The High Priest of Athera appeared to be gossiping with Grand Master Ezras, an ancient-looking man seated at the far end of the room. They seemed to be swapping old stories over drinks.

Beside them were a few other Masters he recognized, and even a Grand Master, all appearing to be just participating in friendly conversation. Yet, it was who he didn't see that struck Darien most deeply. His mother had already warned him Aidan would be absent. But he'd been hoping that Meiran would be there. It was more than just hope, really.

He needed her there.

Perhaps something urgent had come up. Or, more likely, she'd moved on to someone else. Whatever the reason, Meiran's absence quenched the last spark of anticipation Darien had left. He breathed out a sigh of resignation.

No one had prepared him for the ceremony, and he didn't know what to do. Everyone was staring at him, all conversation suddenly halted. A few people were shifting uncomfortably, some exchanging looks of irritation. He glanced at his mother, who nodded her head in the direction of Ezras.

Gathering his courage, Darien crossed the room in a carefully measured pace, to where the old man sat waiting for him expectantly. He tried not to look at any of the other faces in the room, not wanting to know what was written on them. Instead, he kept his gaze fixed on Ezras.

When he reached him, Darien dropped to his knees before the ancient Sentinel, bowing his head deeply. He wasn't sure if it was the proper thing to do, but it felt right. And now that he had chosen to make a place for himself at the Grand Master's feet, he was committed. By the unwritten rules of protocol, all he could do now was wait.

The waiting seemed to last a lifetime.

There was no sound in the room, not even a rustle of fabric or the tinkling of ice in a glass. Darien stared at the floor, his apprehension growing. He was beginning to get the feeling that there must be something else he should be doing, though he couldn't imagine what. The tension in the room was growing. The silence was stretching too long, even for the witnesses. He felt their eyes boring into his back. Feeling unnerved, he almost stood up.

Then he felt a pressure under his chin. The ancient Sentinel had reached down to take Darien's face in his hand, lifting his chin with gnarled fingers, directing his gaze upward and into his own.

Darien found himself looking into a pair of clear blue eyes that blazed with an acute flame of intelligence. There was no readable expression within them. There was only that single spark that burned intensely. Darien found himself transfixed by it, unable to break away. The old man's stare held him more securely than any iron shackle, even when he became aware that those penetrating blue eyes were doing much more than merely staring.

Ezras had been scrutinizing him the entire time.

Suddenly, Darien was filled with doubt. The old man before him was one of the most powerful mages in Aerysius and was also the most accomplished. Ezras had been a prevailing force in the effort that had turned back the Enemy at the Battle of Meridan almost twenty years before. He had later gone on to do the same at the Battle of Dobson Hollow. All accomplished while maintaining his Oath of Harmony. Darien wondered if he was worthy of accepting the Transference from this old man. He thought of his own professed opinions of the Oath and began to have doubts.

He doubted, but he did not look away.

Neither did Ezras. He sat staring Darien straight in the eyes as his cracked lips moved to form words.

"Did you know I was a friend of your father's?"

Darien blinked. His shock was as much due to hearing the sound of a voice after such a long silence as it was to the sentiment in the old man's tone. When he found his own voice again, it came out as a barely grated whisper:

"No, Grand Master. I did not."

Ezras nodded slightly. His ancient hand yet lingered on Darien's chin, while his intense blue eyes continued to assess his every reaction. After another long stretch of silence, the old man spoke again.

"You have his eyes. And I sense something else of him in you as well: you have his spirit. Gerald Lauchlin was an inspiring man and a loyal friend. You would do well to model yourself after him." Ezras frowned, pausing a moment in reflection. "Come to think of it, it seems you already have. He was late to his own Raising too. Well, perhaps not quite so late as yourself."

The high priest must have taken that moment as his cue. He stepped behind the chair Ezras occupied and leaned forward to ask him, "Are you ready, Grand Master?"

Ezras turned to look up at the priest with a warm smile devoid of any sign of regret. "Quite ready. This bag of bones some would call a body has stopped serving any useful purpose I can think of. Yes, I believe it's well past time. You may begin."

The priest nodded. He looked down at Darien, who was still kneeling at the Sentinel's feet.

The priest asked, "Darien Lauchlin, are you prepared to assume the chains of servitude that will bind you forever as a guardian of the Rhen and of its people?"

"I am, Your Eminence."

Darien was able to answer without hesitation, feeling himself bolstered by the old man's indomitable spirit.

"And are you also prepared to accept accountability for your every action, so that your decisions be always tempered by wisdom, compassion, and humility?"

"Aye, Your Eminence. I am."

The priest moved forward to stand beside Ezras. He placed a hand on the Sentinel's shoulder in a warm gesture that suggested an old friendship between the two men. He held his hand there as he stated formally, "Grand Master, may your journey to the Atrament be swift. Your time of service is at an end. Depart in peace, knowing that your service has not gone unnoticed nor unappreciated. Your name will be entered into the Book of Records, so that your works will be known until the end of time."

Ezras chuckled as the priest uttered the last line of the ancient ritual and removed his hand. "My thanks, Your Eminence. Most eloquently spoken. Though you should have omitted that last part about my works. I'm certain they're not worth the waste of parchment."

He looked down at Darien then, a warm and welcoming smile on his lips. "Come, young man. Take these old hands. All this pomp and ceremony is frankly getting on my nerves. I'd like to have an end to it."

"Aye, Grand Master," Darien whispered.

His heart beat furiously as a host of conflicting emotions warred within him. These were the last moments of the old man's life. Darien had never really known Ezras but realized he was quite fond of the man. The old Master's imminent passing filled him with a bitter sense of remorse.

At the same time, he also felt singularly responsible for the ending of that life. He knew his guilt was unjustified; the transfer of power from one generation of mages to the next was simply the way it had been since the beginning of time, the only way it could ever possibly be. Deciding to pass on his gift had been Ezras' choice alone. Still, Darien found it hard to shake the guilt, all the same.

There was also an acute sense of anticipation, knowing that the moment he had always waited for had finally arrived. That feeling of excitement was mixed with an intense pang of sadness that had been lingering at the back of his mind throughout the entire ritual.

He'd wanted so much for Meiran to be there.

But she was not.

So he did as the old man bid and took the mage's age-spotted and gnarled hands into his own, closing his eyes.

Almost immediately, he felt the stir of the conduit that Ezras established between them. He could feel the surge of it, the charge of power that flowed up his arms and into his chest, spreading out to fill his body with an overwhelming gush of exhilarating energy. It was as though every fiber within him had been suddenly awakened together at once. He could feel the magic field pulsing within him, throbbing, as brilliantly radiant as the sun. The feeling swelled, became encompassing, fillling him entirely.

And then, abruptly, he felt the conduit slam closed.

When Darien opened his eyes, he found himself drained and weak. He gasped for breath as rivers of sweat streamed from his brow, his heart pounding like a stampede of horses in his chest. His cheeks were wet with spilt tears he didn't even remember shedding, and his whole body trembled.

The reality he awakened to was the same as before, and yet altogether different. It seemed more vivid, somehow, as though the world he'd known before was just a dim reflection that didn't quite do justice to the real thing. The hues of colors seemed more saturated, the shadows somehow less dense. All of his senses were overwhelmed, the experience surreal. He felt like a newborn just expelled from the womb, opening its eyes for the first time.

A shudder in the floor beneath him brought Darien's senses sharply back into focus. He pushed himself off the ground, rising to a crouch as a stab of fear lanced through him. Another tremor hit, this time big enough to rock the entire structure of the temple.

Everyone in the room surged toward the windows. Beyond the glass, the sky had taken on a pasty green hue.

Regaining his feet, he moved toward the others. As he neared the windows, Darien saw that the glow of light came from far below, from the square beside the Hall of the Watchers. A pillar of green energy had erupted from the center of the pavement, shooting straight upward into the sky.

"What is it?" he gasped.

It was his mother's voice that answered him, leaden and hollow sounding. "The Well of Tears has been opened. May the gods have mercy on us all."

Chapter Three
The Fallen

Aerysius, The Rhen

Aidan Lauchlin stared at the towering column of energy that thrust upward from the center of the square to stab the skies above Aerysius like a terrible, scintillating lance. The sight of the sickly green pillar filled him with a quivering sense of accomplishment.

The column of light stabbed into the sky, a potent signal that could be witnessed from as far away as the Black Lands. So vast was its power that the air around it shimmered. Lightning called forth from the clouds forked down to shatter against that terrible spire, wielding the might of the heavens against the vile power of the Netherworld. The very air was charged, the odor of it sickly sweet.

Aidan breathed in deeply, relishing the scent, savoring the sight of his creation with a feeling akin to rapture as he strode out into the luminous glow of the square. Against that glowing column, his form looked nothing more than a ghostly black shadow, though one with deadly purpose. His brother's sword rode at his back, still sheathed in Meiran's blood. He hadn't bothered to wipe the blade clean. He was yet hoping to give it back to its owner.

He walked toward the heart of the square, stopping yet fifty paces away from the brilliant spire of light. Aidan narrowed his eyes, finding it impossible to stare directly at the column. He waited almost casually, hands clasped behind his back, as lurid shadows danced behind him on the pavement. In the distance, the melancholy toll of a single bell rang out across the city. Aidan stared harder at the gateway, silently willing something to happen.

Eight shapes emerged from the glowing pillar, dark forms spreading out away from the gateway in a widening circle toward the eight points of the compass. Aidan squinted, trying to put features to the three figures approaching his own position. It was impossible at first; the shapes were only moving darkness eclipsed by the brilliant light.

Gradually, details began to emerge. As they neared, the figures resolved into human shapes that drew slowly out of shadow. The vague features yielded identity only slowly. It was not until the first was standing right in front of him that Aidan was able to put a name to the face no human alive had ever seen.

Zavier Renquist stopped only feet away, dark eyes considering him with sinister intensity. The tainted light of the gateway cast harsh shadows across the chiseled angles of his face. He wore his long brown hair pulled back in a manner that exaggerated the cruel effect of his narrow eyes and hawk-like nose. In life, Renquist had been the most distinguished Prime Warden to ever exist, his greatness tempered only by the greatness of his betrayal.

The histories all gave Renquist almost sole credit for the fall of Bryn Calazar, the ancient capital of Caladorn. It was Renquist's treachery that had precipitated the fall of Caladorn itself, propelling the northern empire into the darkening spiral that had eventually ended with the complete desecration of the land. In the years after, the name Caladorn had faded, only half-remembered by scholars and the wise. Most people now knew it only as the Black Lands.

But Zavier Renquist was a thousand years dead. The man now standing before Aidan was one of the Eight Servants of Xerys, God of Chaos and Lord of the Netherworld. In life, Renquist had allied himself with the forces of evil. Upon his death, he had become a true demon.

Other dark shapes drifted toward him. A man and a woman approached first. The man wore a felt hat and was garbed in a black long coat, though the fabric was tailored in a cut Aidan had never seen before.

The woman had dark skin and darker hair that flowed down her back to her waist. At her side paced two creatures that looked like enormous wolfhounds with glowing green eyes, their feet padding silently across the stone.

Aidan had no idea who the man was. Accounts of the Eight were often muddled and vague. But he knew the woman to be Myria Anassis, an ancient Querer who had sworn her allegiance to Xerys before the fall of Bryn Calazar. Her pets were not mere dogs. They were thanacrysts, creatures that fed solely on the life force of a mage. Aidan had always thought them but a figment of legend.

More dark shapes approached, moving silently around the turbulent green column. A bearded, red-haired man holding a silver morning star drew up to stand beside Renquist. Aidan took him to be Byron Connel, the Battlemage who had single-handedly destroyed Caladorn's resistance. The tall, dark-haired man with a red scar bisecting his face must be Cyrus Krane, an ancient Prime Warden of Aerysius who had turned rabid.

Another woman approached with platinum hair that glowed a pasty green in the light of the gateway, a demon-hound jogging at her side. Her wide, pale eyes lent her a sense of innocence that masked the viciousness of her nature. Aidan was not fooled; Arden Hannah had deceived the entire Assembly of Bryn Calazar, helping Renquist lead them to their doom. There were two others, a man and a woman in dark blue robes, who Aidan did not know. They halted to stand before him with the rest, silently contemplating him in the brilliant glow of the gateway.

It was Zavier Renquist who addressed him. "Your efforts have been met with gratitude by our Master. He is well-pleased. In exchange for unsealing the Well of Tears, Xerys commits to you the services of the Eight. We are yours to command, until the purpose of our summoning is fulfilled."

Aidan couldn't help the smile that formed on his lips. He was trembling with a pride and pleasure too great to be physically contained. But the distant sound of a tolling bell reminded him that he must not tarry long savoring his success. Time was running short. A greater work lay yet before him, and there was much to do.

"I command you to help me take Aerysius," he said.

Renquist simply nodded, as though the ancient Prime Warden had expected no less.

"The hour is late, and most of the Masters are asleep in the Spire of the Hall. They will only now be stirring from their beds and rushing to heed the warning bells. I need your assistance so I can use the Circle of Convergence. Hold the doors of the Hall so that my work may progress unimpeded."

Arden Hannah's eyes had been growing wider as Aidan revealed the perfection of his plans. He was certain she recognized the inspiration behind them; Aidan had derived most of his ideas from what he'd read of their own treachery.

"Then let us be about it," Zavier Renquist said, turning away. "Cyrus, I believe your friends might come in handy. Why don't you bring some along?"

Cyrus Krane grinned malevolently. Aidan felt an unnerving sensation grip the pit of his stomach. All around the square, pools of shadow emerged from the ground, melting upward to coalesce into black, nebulous shapes that vaguely resembled human forms. Aidan held his breath as he watched the dark forms solidify into a host of necrators akin to the first two he had raised. The terror they normally inspired didn't affect him at all; his bargain with darkness rendered him immune to their influence.

Most of the necrators glided soundlessly off into the night, slipping away into the shadows of the city. They would be about their own dark business, working their sinister purpose while he accomplished his own in the Hall of the Watchers.

Aidan made his way around the glowing pillar of light toward the Hall, the terror of the night gliding silently behind in the wake of his footfalls.

Darien could only stare at the green column of light that challenged the black dome of the heavens. Lightning crackled all around the pillar, stabbing at it from the sky as if all of the gods were assembled together in the clouds, marshaling their greatest might against it. From where he stood on the temple steps, he could see the Hall of the Watchers rising behind it in the square. Both the Hall and the arches in front of it were bathed in the same green light. A bell clanged in the distance, the sound of its toll a dire warning.

He was not alone on the temple steps. His mother stood beside him, staring at the towering atrocity in the sky. The other mages had gathered around them, all gaping upward.

The terrible urgency of the spear of light had driven them out into the darkness of the night, the clamor of the warning bells speeding their feet. Until they had halted on the temple steps, frozen by the dazzling abomination in the sky.

"By all the gods," someone whispered behind him.

But the gods had little to do with it. Someone had opened the Well of Tears, the ancient portal to the Netherworld that existed somewhere beneath the city—probably right under the square, judging by the location of the column.

How anyone could do that—*why* anyone would—was utterly beyond him. It had to have been a mage, one of their own number. Someone Darien probably knew. But a betrayal of such magnitude was unimaginable. He couldn't think of one person who could possibly harbor that degree of malice inside. It was unthinkable.

But if the Well of Tears had been unsealed, then the gateway to the Netherworld was open as well. It didn't matter who had accomplished the act. The forces of Chaos were now the impetus that drove that towering pillar of energy, thrusting it upward into the sky. The terror of the night would be unleashed into the heart of Aerysius. As the peal of the warning bells rang out across the darkness, Darien realized his home was under imminent attack.

"What do we do?" he asked, the sound of his voice lost somewhere in his throat. He was thinking of Meiran, wondering where she could possibly be.

"We must reach the circle." His mother's voice was shaking. "It's the only way. The Circle of Convergence was used once before to seal the Well of Tears. There must be a way to do it again."

"The last time the Well was sealed, it was open only in this world," said Master Finneus Corlan. "That's not the case this time. Before, we confronted but a mere seepage of the Netherworld's taint. The gateway now stands fully open before us. The Circle of Convergence is not the answer."

"Then what is?" the Prime Warden demanded.

"The Well must be sealed from both sides," insisted Master Lynnea. "We must split up. According to *A Treatise on the Well of Tears,* there is only one way to seal it completely: we must find the Well and deactivate the rune sequence. Then one of our Grand Masters must enter the gateway itself. It must be someone of at least fourth tier. The Well demands a sacrifice—"

"What are you saying?" Emelda snapped, cutting her off.

Master Lynnea blinked.

Finneus placed a soothing hand on the woman's shoulder. "What my esteemed colleague is trying to say, Prime Warden, is that in order to seal the Well of Tears, one of our two Grand Masters will have to enter the gateway. The mending of the seal in the Netherworld requires a sacrifice."

Darien glanced from one face to the other as his mother pondered her options. He had no desire to volunteer. He had experienced the wonder of Transference only minutes before. He'd not even had a chance to test his newfound strength.

His eyes found Grand Master Tyrius Flynn, who stood gazing up at the tall pillar of light. The man had years of experience working with magic and was vastly more prepared to face the challenges that might confront them. Darien felt his resolve solidify, knowing he should be the one to volunteer.

"I'll go down to the gateway," Tyrius announced into the night. "The only thing I ask is for a couple of good friends to come along and help me on my way." He turned to Darien. "But first I want to hear you swear the Oath of Harmony."

Darien found himself unable to look the Grand Master in the eyes. The old man had just saved his life, and knew it. What Tyrius was really asking was an easy settlement for any debt Darien might believe he owed him.

Thinking of it that way made saying the Oath an easy thing, despite his reservations. As Darien uttered the ancient phrases, they seemed to flow from his mouth of their own accord, requiring no conscious thought. He stared into Tyrius' eyes the whole while he spoke, silently admiring the old man's iron courage.

> *"I swear to live in harmony with all of creation,*
> *To use my gift with temperance and wisdom;*
> *Always to heal and never to harm,*
> *Or my life will be rightfully forfeit."*

Tyrius lay his hand on Darien's shoulder in a gesture of compassion. Then he departed, taking with him Masters Lynnea and Finneus.

The downpour had stopped. The night had become crisp and chill, but for the glowing column of energy and the lightning that licked against it. Everything around them had taken on its sickly hue, and the entire city looked otherworldly and empty. To Darien, Aerysius resembled what he imagined the Netherworld must look like: devoid of life, light, and color.

He followed in the wake of the small company that went down from the temple steps. They wound their way across a terrace and out over the narrow arch of a sky bridge that spanned the gap between the terrace and the tower of an adjacent building. As they crossed the bridge, Darien had an unimpeded view of the Hall of the Watchers, lustrous in the reflected light.

The bridge he stood on suddenly jolted as a tremor passed through the air. It was followed shortly by another. And another. The disturbances in the air were visible, coming at them in expanding, concentric rings with a focus far below in the Hall of the Watchers.

Darien didn't need anyone to explain to him what he was witnessing. Aerysius' Circle of Convergence was being put into play with malicious intent. The expanding rings of compressed air were the prelude to a structural resonance.

Darien felt his whole body shudder every time a wave of energy passed through him. And the waves kept increasing, coming faster and harder, until it was all he could do to remain standing.

He had to get his mother off the bridge.

The other mages stood as if rooted, staring down at the disturbances coming from the Hall. Darien pushed his way through them and grabbed his mother by the arm, wrenching her into motion. He could feel the bridge shuddering beneath his feet, the rhythmic vibrations increasing in frequency.

As he neared the end of the bridge, the whole structure shivered and gave way beneath his feet. Darien threw himself forward, clenching his mother's arm in a two-handed grip.

The bridge crumbled and fell, Emelda and the others falling with it. Darien spilled onto the floor of a balcony, barely managing to retain his hold on his mother as her body slapped hard against the side of the building and hung swaying in his grasp.

Darien pulled, using all the strength he possessed to drag her up and over the edge. His mother lay there beside him, panting, her eyes staring vacantly up into the sky.

The resonance was still driving the air before it. Darien pushed himself to his feet, helping his mother up after him. The air itself seemed solidified. It jarred against him, knocking him with the force of breaking ocean waves.

He staggered, trying to keep his feet, while the building they stood on swayed with the rhythms of the merciless waves. Emelda almost fell, catching herself against him as Darien struggled to keep them both standing.

From far below, a loud noise rose from the Hall of the Watchers. The very stones of the ancient structure were starting to sing as they reached their breaking point. The tone quavered in the air like a grace note with each passing ripple of energy.

"Oh, by the gods, Darien," his mother moaned into his chest.

He held her, staggering, as below the note swelled to a wailing threnody. The Hall of the Watchers shuddered, the air filled with the nerve-grating noise of stone grinding against stone. And then, so very slowly, the spire of the Hall came crashing down. The top caved in first with a gushing blast of dust and debris, the deafening roar of it ripping through the night, trembling the very mountain.

One wall of the Spire was left halfway standing, almost completely obscured by a swirling cloud of dust. Another tremor shook the structure, and the wall leaned over slowly. Then it crumbled, raining enormous chunks of rock down onto the roof of the dome. The Hall of the Watchers imploded violently. Pillars of dust were hurled into the gaping sky, illuminated by the lambent glow of the column of power.

Darien stared open-mouthed at the scene of devastation as though looking into the face of apocalypse. A chilling numbness overcame him, dampening his senses until even sound seemed to fade into obscurity. Timeless seconds crept by, and he was aware of none of them. The only thing he could do was stare out at the billowing clouds of dust as his mind grappled with the enormity of the devastation.

Aerysius was gone, though most of its structures yet remained standing. But the Hall of the Watchers was the heart of the city, and it had been ripped clean away, excised from the body. Darien didn't know how many of his brethren had died in the Hall, but he knew with a certainty that it must have been many. No one moved in the ruins of the square.

He remembered Masters Tyrius, Lynnea and Finneus, who had probably been down there somewhere. And the mages who had come with them in search of the Well were gone, their bodies fallen to the street many stories below. As far as he knew, his mother and himself could well be the only surviving mages left in all the world.

Meiran.

The thought ripped through him with the force of a death blow, the pain of it almost doubling him over. Darien's eyes scoured the ruins below until his vision blurred. But there was no movement in the scattered rubble, no sign of life. Only undulating clouds of dust swirled over the shattered remains of his home. The soaring structure of the Hall of the Watchers had been reduced to an enormous mass grave, the mounds of broken stone an immense burial cairn.

If Meiran had been there, then she was dead.

"Aidan."

The sound of his mother's trembling voice seemed to come from another world. Instantly, sound and substance came rushing back. Darien blinked as if waking from a nightmare, a cold sweat breaking out all over his body. The air was thick with rising dust, and his vision swam with tears he was too numb to shed. He wiped a hand across his eyes, restoring his sight. Then he turned to look at his mother's face.

Emelda stared at him with eyes wide with shock, shaking her head as her mouth stretched into a tight grimace of anguish. He took her into his arms, holding her against his chest as her body shook with spasms of grief.

Aidan had always been her favorite. Darien wondered why he could not summon even a fledgling tear over his brother's death. Perhaps he was past tears, past the ability to grieve.

With a last, long look at the ruins of the Hall, Darien forced himself to turn away from the sight. Delay now might cost them everything. They had to flee the city, but Darien doubted the wood platform would ever make the trip again to the valley floor.

"Mother," he whispered, gently pulling away. "We need to flee. Down the mountain. I know there's a way, but you've never told me. If it's some secret, I don't think it matters anymore."

Emelda blinked at him. Her face was a mess, all crusted in grime and smudged with tears. But deep within her eyes stirred a flicker of the strength he was used to. It was the same, innate strength that moved within himself.

"We must reach the Temple of Isap." Her gaze darted toward the southeastern part of the city, and Darien followed her stare. The sun would be rising eventually in that direction, but not for a while yet. There was definitely a chance the two of them could reach the temple if they kept low enough and made good speed.

But confusion continued to nettle him. It was another route he'd been considering. Placing his hands on his mother's shoulders, he pressed, "I don't understand. How can the priests of Death help us escape down the mountain?"

"The Catacombs," his mother whispered, shivering as if she had just revealed some dire secret. She probably had. "The Catacombs of Death exist partly in the Atrament. Distance and time have no meaning there. We can make use of the Catacombs to escape and go anywhere we like."

Darien frowned in disbelief. It seemed unimaginable that the Temple of Death could have harbored a secret of that magnitude for so long. If these Catacombs truly existed, then the priesthood of Death had found a wonder that would rival even the greatest works of the Hall.

"Then we must go," he agreed, feeling a pressing sense of urgency. He squeezed her shoulders. She was bleeding from cuts and scrapes she'd acquired during her fall from the bridge.

So Darien did what he had been trained to do all his life. He closed his eyes and reached within. Only, this time, it was different. Whenever he'd tried this same mental exercise in practice, there had always been just emptiness inside. But now his mind grasped something tangible. He could feel the song of the magic field as never before, soaring inside him like a symphony. He touched it, feeling it conform easily to his will, as though it were the most natural thing he had ever done in his life.

When he opened his eyes, he saw that his mother's injuries were healed. She looked renewed, invigorated. Her face was swept clean of grime, the torn fabric of her dress mended. She looked hale. And very much full of pride.

"Thank you," she said simply.

He took her by the hand and led her off the balcony into the shadows of the building. Emelda walked at his side down long flights of stairs and out into the empty street. They continued down and off the terrace, working their way eastward toward the bottom of the city. The night air was thick, filled with acrid smoke and choking dust.

The streets were littered with debris that had fallen from the heights. They often found themselves skirting a pile of rubble, as collapsed parts of buildings and bridges impeded almost every step. There were few people alive in the city. It was like walking in a world of the dead under the glow of that filthy green light. Every so often, the silence was pierced by distant screams.

They had been traveling for over an hour when Darien found himself confronted by an obstacle that looked impossible to cross or go around. An entire building had fallen across the road, cutting them off from the bridge on the other side.

They needed to reach that bridge. They were already at the lowest reaches of the city, at a split in the enormous rock face where the cliff bowed inward, creating a vertical crevice that cut deep into the sheer rock wall. The bridge that spanned the gap arched over a drop of thousands of feet. There was nothing but air below it, all the way down the sheer precipice to the valley floor.

A wolf howled, the sound eerie and mournful. The noise made Darien shiver with a feeling of dread; there were no wolves in all of Aerysius.

Something skirted the edge of his vision. It looked like a shadow moving on the far side of the road. But when he turned toward it, there was nothing there. Frowning, he rubbed his eyes as he pondered the situation. The only way to the bridge was up and over that wall of rubble.

So they climbed.

The going was slow, as the debris had a way of shifting underfoot. Darien let his mother go before him, picking out her own path as he trailed behind, steadying the blocks that threatened to slip out from under them with the force of his mind.

The more he exercised his power, the more he became accustomed to it. It was simply another extension of himself, just like his sword. He handled it expertly; he had trained for this all his life.

A block of rubble shifted overhead. Instantly, an avalanche of stone and marble started to slide down on top of them. Darien simply deflected the shower of debris, hardly sparing it a thought. He saw his mother turn to stare at him with respect in her eyes. Though Prime Warden, Emelda Lauchlin was still only first tier.

Darien knew why his mother had waited so long to arrange his Raising. She had been waiting for just the right time, when he could receive the Transference from an especially strong Grand Master. Ezras had contained five times the amount of power in his frail old body as Emelda was capable of wielding. It was possible she was allowing Darien to stabilize the larger pieces of rock by himself, to give him practice working with his newfound strength. Yet, he couldn't help admitting, it was also possible she couldn't do it herself.

They reached the top of the rubble and gradually worked their way down the other side. In the distance, another wolf-like cry broke the silence of the night. The sound chilled Darien's blood. He hurried his mother off the rubble and started toward the bridge.

A scraping sound from behind them made him stop. Whirling, Darien reached for the hilt of his sword and grasped only air.

A lone man was coming toward them from the

other side of the street, black cloak rippling about him as he moved, face lost in shadow.

Darien released the breath he hadn't realized he'd been holding. He stood waiting for the man to approach. His mother stood at his side, looking at the newcomer with an expression of vibrant hope.

Darien was skeptical. At least there was someone else alive in the night besides themselves. He had the feeling that his mother was studying the shadows of the approaching face for traces of familiar features. She was hoping it was Aidan, he suspected, miraculously saved from the catastrophe of the Hall. Darien just hoped it was someone useful.

When the figure stepped out of shadow, his eyes widened in surprise. His mother drew in a sharp gasp and immediately started forward. Darien thrust out his hand and held her back.

She was right. It *was* Aidan.

But there was something very different about his brother.

Aidan Lauchlin halted in the middle of the street, regarding them with a narrow blue stare that somehow seemed more arrogant than usual, supremely more confident. Darien frowned, trying to put a finger on exactly what seemed so wrong. It was something subtle, something just not right. His mother pulled against his hold on her arm, struggling to free herself and rush toward the son she had thought was lost. But Darien tightened his grip, refusing her.

Then he saw it: Aidan was wearing his sword.

Darien could think of absolutely no good reason in the world why his brother would be carrying his own weapon. A few explanations drifted across his mind, but Darien rejected them all, until the only explanation left was one too terrible to consider.

But it fit. Horribly, it made a sinister kind of sense. Like Meiran, Aidan had also missed his Raising.

"What's the matter with you?" Emelda spat at him, tugging her arm in an effort to release his grip. Darien only held on more firmly.

"He opened the Well of Tears," he said, eyes only for Aidan as he searched the shadowy face before him for confirmation of his words. But there was no reaction on his brother's face. Aidan just continued to stare at him, eyes calm and arrogant.

Darien wished his brother would do something, anything. Shout in denial, rain him with curses, lash out with the scathing sarcasm Darien always found so infuriating. Anything but his silence.

His brother's complete lack of response confirmed Darien's worst fear.

A confident smile spread slowly on Aidan's lips. Darien reached within for the magic field, the action now almost a reflex. Then he stopped himself, recalling in horror his Oath to Tyrius Flynn. *Never to harm.* The words rang bitterly within the confines of his head, along with his plea to his mother: *Unbind the Sentinels.*

He was not Unbound.

He had uttered his Oath, the Oath he had already chosen not to keep. But something had changed in him. Darien didn't know if it was his experience with Grand Master Ezras or perhaps even Tyrius Flynn. Maybe it was the destruction of the home he had always taken for granted, or witnessing Aerysius's greatness being erased from the world.

Darien realized he would keep that Oath. Gerald Lauchlin had kept it to a bitter grave. His son could do no less.

Dimly, on the edge of his vision, he saw five dark shapes approaching. They looked like nebulous silhouettes of mist gliding toward him from out of the shadows of the street. A sickening horror rose inside him, a harrowing chill that was appalling. The air around him thickened until it was hard to even breathe.

Darien felt his mother's arm grow cold in his grasp. He knew what those black forms were, had read about them in texts, heard them named in the darkest tales and myths. He knew their only chance was to run. The touch of a necrator was not death; it was something very much worse.

Darien spun his mother around, propelling her toward the bridge. He started after her, but his foot caught in a crack in the street. He stumbled, thrusting his arms out as he fell to the ground. He caught himself with the heels of his hands and rolled, barely avoiding the necrator that melted up from the street in the exact place he'd landed.

Gaining his feet, Darien glanced behind to see his mother clearing the end of the bridge. It exploded behind her. Shards of broken stone flew toward him, and he flung his arms up to shield his face. He groped desperately for the power within, but there was nothing there.

Darien froze in the steel grip of the starkest terror

he'd ever known in his life. It wrenched up from his stomach, clenching his throat, as all of the blood seemed to rush out of his head at once. He retained enough of himself to recognize the feeling for what it was: not a true emotion but, rather, the awful influence of the necrator that stood like a black wraith in front of him.

He forced his legs to move, backing away from it, stumbling over debris.

His brother walked casually toward him, a hand lifting the baldric that held Darien's sword over his head. Aidan flung the sword at him, scabbard and all. It slid toward him across the pavement, bumping along, coming to a rest at his feet. Darien reached down to retrieve it, never taking his eyes from the necrator. The other four were approaching as well. He gripped the scabbard in his right hand, the trembling fingers of his left hand closing around the hilt of the blade.

"Aren't you wondering who helped me unseal the Well of Tears?" Aidan asked, striding toward him. He stopped perhaps ten paces away, as though hesitant to come too close to the necrators.

Darien was too distracted to respond. The five dark shapes in front of him were pressing him slowly backward toward the edge of the cliff. And not just any cliff. He knew it wasn't just a simple fall to another terrace. His death wasn't going to be that clean.

Aidan took another step toward him. "I killed Meiran. It's her blood that stains your sword."

Darien looked down at the blade in its scabbard, not daring to bare the steel. It would only confirm what he already knew had to be true. Meiran had not been there at his Raising. That should have been enough to tell him something was horribly wrong.

The rage and pain that consumed him was overwhelming, a harrowing fury that swept aside every other emotion, burying him under a breaking tidal wave of wrath and grief. He almost lashed out with his mind, was on the brink of focusing his rage into a fiery spear of vengeance.

It wasn't his Oath that held him back.

It was the necrators. Three of them glided forward, their vile influence keeping his power in check.

"It won't hurt so very much," Aidan promised, moving toward him. "I've had much practice tonight. I'll even make it quick. Come, Brother."

Darien took a step back from him. And another. The necrators glided smoothly after him, maintaining their distance. Aidan strode between them as Darien looked around for anything he could use to defend himself.

There was nothing. His sword was useless against another mage, and the song of the magic field was silent inside him. There was only Aidan and the necrators, or the cliff. The choice was easy to make. Carrying out that decision, now...that was hard.

But knowing Meiran waited for him made it a little easier. He knew she would be there, somewhere in the distances that span eternity.

Darien had backed up as far as he could against the edge of the cliff. There was nowhere else to go. He held his gaze locked with his brother's eyes as he took one last step off the edge of the precipice.

Chapter Four
The Price of an Oath

Aerysius, The Rhen

Emelda Lauchlin landed roughly on the other side of the gaping chasm. Pushing herself up off the ground, she watched helplessly as her son surrendered himself to the mountain's sheer face.

There was nothing she could do.

She watched him go.

Emelda screamed Darien's name, reaching out with her mind across the distance between them—too little, too late. She collapsed forward, arms hugging her chest. A wail of mortal grief tore from the depths of her soul.

First Gerald, and now their son. It was too much to bear. And Aidan…Darien said it was Aidan who'd opened the Well of Tears. Emelda hadn't believed him at the time. Now, she did. Aidan was her child, her firstborn. He had opened the Well, destroyed the Hall of the Watchers, slain his only brother, and brought Aerysius to its knees. She couldn't understand, any more than she could stop the waves of anguish threatening to sweep her away in a harrowing current of despair.

And now he was coming for her.

Emelda watched through a blur of tears as delicate strands of energy twined across the yawning mouth of the crevice where the stone bridge had been only moments before. She gaped in shock at the span of solid light that formed, woven from silver filaments of magic. It was impossible. Such an act was well beyond the talents of even the mightiest Grand Master.

Emelda shuddered as her son mounted that glimmering span and moved toward her, flanked by five living shadows that flowed soundlessly after him. Part of her wanted to run, but she couldn't summon the strength to do more than draw breath. A paralyzing fear crept up from her stomach, seizing the motion of her chest. The necrators moved past him, gliding swiftly toward her.

She took a trembling step backward and stumbled as Aidan stepped off the glowing bridge that shimmered out of existence just as quickly as it had appeared. She shuddered as his cold blue gaze fixed on her. There was nothing left of the son she knew in those terrible, piercing eyes. Fresh tears of horror ran down Emelda's cheeks as she shook her head in denial.

"Why?" she shrieked, backing away from the demon who used to be her son.

The malevolent sneer on his face was terrifying. He advanced toward her, shaking his head as if in disgust, then paused to consider her for a moment. In a voice she barely recognized, he said, "You're so pathetic, Mother."

The shock of the insult came as a hammer blow, driving the last bit of strength from her body. She moaned, covering her face with her hands and sobbing into them. That was all she could do. He advanced the last few steps toward her, reaching a hand up to caress her face.

She recoiled from the touch, backing away from him. "How *could* you? He was your *brother!*"

Aidan only chuckled. "You would be surprised at what I'm capable of."

Emelda whirled away from him, tears spraying

from her cheeks as she sprinted in the direction of the ruined street. She didn't get far. Her body hit a solid wall of air and rebounded to the ground. She lay there, panting in the dust and dirt, staring up at the green-infected sky. Chest heaving, she saw him moving toward her again. Only, now, she knew there was nowhere to run. She was helpless. Her Oath prevented her from doing anything to protect herself. The dark presence of the necrators insured that she kept it.

She rolled onto her stomach, forcing herself to her knees and then to her feet. Fists balled at her sides, Emelda shrieked, "You destroyed the Hall! You killed *all of them!*"

Aidan shrugged offhandedly, turning his face toward the pillar of light and the ruins of the Hall of the Watchers. Ever so softly, he said, "They were weak. So was Darien...so are you."

His eyes locked on hers as he took a confident step toward her. "You've played at power nearly your entire life. Only, you have never truly understood its nature. I do.

"Always, you've taken me lightly. When it was time for my Raising, you chose a pitiful first-tier Master to initiate my Transference. You crippled me for life. But when it came time for my dear brother, you arranged it so he would receive the Transference from a strong Grand Master. Darien was a coward, and he was also a fool. He didn't lift a hand to save his own life—just see how he squandered that gift! I might have made use of that strength to create something truly meaningful. Instead, you chose to waste it on him. And just look what he accomplished with it."

"Darien kept his Oath!" Emelda shouted, filled with a sudden gush of pride tempered only by the grief she felt inside.

"Father kept his Oath as well," Aidan reminded her, "and see what came of it. My father *burned* because of your pathetic doctrine! He died *screaming,* tied to a stake. He begged you to Unbind the Sentinels before Meridan, but you denied him. Father's death was another meaningless waste. You've made a career out of sacrificing our family's blood in the name of righteousness."

He was lecturing *her* about sacrificing the blood of their family? Aidan blamed her for Gerald's death, but even that explanation didn't suffice. Nothing could come close to justifying the atrocities he had committed in that single, terrible night.

Darien's words came back to torment her: *Unbind the Sentinels.* Gerald's words. Uttered just before he had left her for Meridan by the Sea. Her husband had martyred himself to uphold a vow he didn't believe in, only because she had told him it was the right thing to do. Now their son had chosen to do the same. Could Aidan possibly be right? Was it really all her fault?

She knew that couldn't be true. She was not wrong. And that still didn't explain why Aidan had committed such heinous acts. He was deranged. There was no other explanation. And he was advancing toward her once again.

Emelda glanced at the cliff, knowing there was nowhere else to run. Darien had chosen to make an end on the rocks so far below. Perhaps she could do the same. It seemed fitting. The fall would be terrible, but at least death would come instantly.

Emelda dismissed the thought. She didn't have that kind of strength. Aidan was right; she was weak. The cliff was not an option.

He regarded her suspiciously. Predator-like, he stalked the short distance toward her, fixing her with the malevolent intensity of his gaze.

She allowed his approach. There was nothing left for her to do. But as he reached out for her, Emelda realized she was not yet ready to end her life. Tears of panic welled in her eyes as a shiver ran through her body. Aidan's hand froze an inch away from her cheek, a hungering smile on his lips.

She had wanted a cleaner death, something she could face with the dignity befitting a Prime Warden of Aerysius. But she was warden of nothing, and there was no dignity in this end. Emelda couldn't stop the tears that flowed down her cheeks, couldn't hide the despair and terror in her heart. The touch of Aidan's hand on her face was not comforting. It felt soiled, like a clod of dirt torn up from a grave. Emelda closed her eyes, knowing exactly what was coming.

A stabbing slap of air exploded between them.

Emelda flew backward as Aidan was hurtled in the opposite direction. Strong arms wrapped themselves around her and hauled her toward the street. She willed her legs into motion, stumbling after the black-cloaked man who had saved her life.

They ran through the crumbled streets of Aerysius, up a flight of broken stairs. The green light of the gateway was not enough to repel the shadows, and Emelda had no idea who it was she followed in that wild flight. It wasn't until he pulled her into the dim light of an archway that he turned around enough for her to catch a glimpse of his face.

At first, she'd imagined it was Darien, miraculously alive and hale enough to save her. But the features she encountered were completely familiar and yet utterly forgotten. Tyrius Flynn grabbed her shoulders and shook her until she regained her senses enough to realize she was still under the appalling influence of the necrators.

Emelda screamed. As she did, Tyrius clamped a hand over her mouth, muffling the sound. She kept screaming into his hand, over and over again, sucking breath in through her nostrils and wailing until there was only emptiness left inside. She collapsed into his arms, weeping helplessly.

"Emelda."

The sound of her name brought her back from the edge. She gazed up into the comforting brown depths of the Grand Master's eyes, knowing her old friend had now saved her twice.

"It—it was Aidan," she stammered. "He opened the Well of Tears. He killed Darien."

"I saw."

Tyrius' eyes were full of sympathy. She collapsed into his arms, pouring out her anguish into the soft folds of his cloak. Her body shook as he wrapped his arms around her, drawing her head against his chest.

"We cannot stay here, Emelda."

She didn't want to run anymore. She threw her head back, lips constricting against her teeth. But the scream she felt in her heart was stillborn; she knew he was right. Collecting herself, she pulled away from his embrace.

"Where are Lynnea and Finneus?"

Tyrius shook his head. "They're dead, the both of them. We came across a darkmage down by the Citadel. Emelda, Aidan is not alone. The Eight walk abroad again. There are vile beasts ranging all over the city and more necrators than I ever knew existed in the world."

"More must have come through the gateway. Tyrius, we were trying to reach the Temple of Isap. The Catacombs—"

"Yes," the Sentinel breathed, eyes widening. But then his brow furrowed, and he paused, considering. "The temple is only a short distance from here. But the journey will be perilous."

"Surely not more perilous than staying here," Emelda insisted. "And you're stronger now, besides. Lynnea and Finneus were both only Masters, but their combined legacies must have doubled your strength."

Tyrius shook his head, a pained look in his eyes. "I was afraid to do more than receive the Transference from Lynnea. I'd be fifth tier now, if such rankings mattered anymore. I deeply fear, however, that you and I are the only mages left alive in the world."

"Don't forget Aidan," she reminded him, shuddering. Emelda had no idea how much her son had managed to amplify his strength in the Hall of the Watchers. Judging by the bridge of power she had witnessed him create, Aidan was easily as strong as any two or three Grand Masters combined. Melding light into such a solid state, even in minuscule amounts, was one of the most difficult acts any mage could perform. It strained the boundaries of Natural Law too far.

"Oh, I'm not forgetting him," Tyrius growled. "If it weren't for my Oath, I'd have thrown a lot more than a ripple of air his way." The look on her face made him moderate his tone. "I'm sorry, Emelda. I know he's your child."

"He is not the child I bore." Emelda's voice trembled. "The son I birthed is dead. Both of my sons are dead." She could feel the tears trying to come back again.

Below her in the street, she saw a fleeting glimmer of light. Startled, Emelda glanced back to Tyrius. The gray-haired Sentinel took a step back, staring down at the ruined and empty street.

"What is it?" Emelda gasped.

Tyrius didn't answer. Another flicker rippled across the ground below them, disappearing almost instantly. Immediately, Tyrius was in motion, sprinting inside the partially collapsed building. Emelda followed as quickly as she could around shattered blocks and chunks of plaster that had fallen from the ceiling. It was dark within. Without a thought, she produced a soft glow of magelight that pushed away the shadows.

"Don't!" Tyrius growled.

She let the magelight collapse back into darkness, silently berating herself. Any use of the field sent ripples out into the surrounding pattern that could be detected even at a distance. She had given them away by her own stupidity. The necrators would be coming.

"We must flee!" Tyrius took her by the arm.

He led her down a littered hallway and around a corner. There, they were forced to pull up short. Before them, the walls and ceiling had collapsed entirely, blocking any chance of escape in that direction. Half a wooden staircase swayed overhead, the lower half ripped clean away. Part of the ceiling dangled precariously, looking like it could break off and fall at any time.

Growling like a caged bear, Tyrius swung her around with a steel grip, forcing her back into the hallway. He started forward, Emelda running to keep up with him. At last he halted, wrenching open a jammed door and ushering her out into the merciful light of daybreak.

She glanced around anxiously. They were in a courtyard bordered on both sides by solid rock walls. The rear of the courtyard was contained by a cliff that climbed upward to the next terrace. They were trapped.

Beside her, the old Sentinel closed his eyes and uttered a protracted sigh. Then he turned away from her, fixing his narrow gaze on the wall to their left.

"Get down," he said. He grasped her by the shoulders and pushed her to the ground.

Emelda covered her head as the wall erupted in an explosion of stone that rained down all around, littering the courtyard. When she looked up again, she saw that Tyrius had razed half the wall, the edges black and smoldering around the rupture.

"Well, if that doesn't point out right where we are, then I might as well send up a signal beacon." As he turned back toward the building behind them, Tyrius added, "I don't think a beacon will be necessary."

Behind them, a shadow fell across the threshold of the doorway. Only, Emelda knew by the now-familiar sense of dread that it was no true shadow.

This time, she ran first. Toward the ruins of the wall, up and over the rubble, stumbling as her foot lodged between two blocks. Frantically, she tried to wrench her ankle free.

She fumbled through the terror in her mind, straining to hear the song of the magic field. But the necrator was too close, its dark influence too great. And it was gliding closer by the second. Emelda whimpered, tugging at her leg with both hands.

Then Tyrius was beside her, stooping down to pry at the stones with all his strength. One of the rocks shifted just a fraction. It was enough. Emelda jerked her foot clear and lurched to her feet as a lancing pain stabbed up her leg. She screamed.

Tyrius carried her, stumbling across another courtyard and into the building beyond as the necrators pursued. A flicker of light flowed behind them, writhing across the ground like a mass of glistening snakes.

Tyrius staggered, almost falling across the threshold of the next structure. He carried her up a winding staircase to the third level, only then pausing to set her down on the landing and catch his breath.

From below them came a strange scraping noise, like chains dragging on stone.

Emelda looked down at her ankle and choked back a groan. It was bleeding, her foot twisted at an unnatural angle. She couldn't heal it. She'd never learned and, besides, she didn't have the strength. But Tyrius pressed his hand against her foot, sending a wave of healing energy through her.

Emelda felt a sensation like a rush of cold water running up her leg. She watched her ankle straighten, the bone mending before her eyes. The pain vanished completely, as though it had never existed at all.

The scraping noises were louder, coming toward them up the stairs. Emelda pushed herself to her feet. Tyrius entwined his fingers with hers as he led her forward once more, up another two flights to a level high above the street. They followed a short hallway to an outside balcony, Tyrius leading her by the hand back out into the open air.

The balcony looked over the courtyard they had crossed five stories below. It jutted out from the building, extending to meet the mountain's stone face. An opening in the rail against the cliff led to a narrow stairway carved into the rock itself. The steps switchbacked up to the terrace above. Holding

Tyrius' hand, Emelda mounted the narrow, treacherous steps.

There was no handrail to grasp, nothing to prevent a fall if she slipped. Her vision swam. She glanced down at the courtyard, which was a mistake. The palms of her hands broke out in sweat, the soles of her feet tingling. Tyrius steadied her, squeezing her hand reassuringly as he led her up the granite face.

Emelda turned just in time to see a bolt of fire lancing toward them from the ground. She winced as it impacted with the cliff above them, sending chips of stone raining down on their heads. She felt Tyrius' hand like an iron vice as another flaming spear shot toward them. Her eyes had only time to widen before it exploded in her face.

There was no heat, no impact. Emelda reached up and touched the skin of her cheek, amazed she was still alive.

Tyrius lowered his hand, and the brilliant shield he'd conjured in front of them disappeared. Emelda could only stare at him in open wonder. She was a Chancellor and had never been trained for anything like this. She kept forgetting Tyrius was a Sentinel and had seen the face of war many times in his life.

Below in the courtyard, a lone figure emerged from under the balcony. Emelda gasped. It was a woman. She was staring up at them, dark hair stirred by a breeze, her gown rippling about her. She was flanked by an enormous demon-hound with eyes that gleamed an unearthly light. The woman raised her arm, palm upward, and a small white flame appeared to dance in her hand. She smiled as she gazed upon it.

Tyrius raised his hand but then dropped it again. He jerked Emelda toward the last rise of steps, shouting, *"Run!"*

The flickering flame rose from the woman's hand and hovered for a moment in the air. Then it began spinning. It spun faster, swelling to a brilliant white sphere.

It shot toward them.

Tyrius hauled Emelda off her feet and pulled himself over the cliff's edge, lifting her bodily after him. Emelda got her legs over just in time as the spinning globe slammed into the side of the mountain beneath them. The ground heaved, and the air around them became like molten fire. Emelda covered her head, shoving her face against the dirt and holding her breath.

Beside her, through the fiery din, she could hear Tyrius screaming.

The screams ended abruptly, as though cut off short. Emelda was too afraid to open her eyes, too scared to move. She was still holding the Sentinel's hand, but the grip that had once felt like iron was now limp.

Slowly, the world stopped trembling. Emelda drew a ragged breath, choking on dirt and ashes and the very heat of the air that filled her lungs. She opened her eyes but saw nothing. Her vision swam, the world a disturbing haze.

A slight tingling sensation stirred within her hand, the hand that yet clasped Tyrius' limp fingers. The tingling grew, became a throbbing pressure that climbed up her arm and invaded her chest, spreading out to every fiber of her body.

Emelda gasped as recognition flooded into her, closing her eyes as she wheezed a moaning sigh. The warmth that flooded into her body was like ecstasy, but the sorrow that filled her heart made it seem more like anguish. She felt the conduit close, the last of Tyrius' sweet legacy absorbed into her shuddering body.

She rolled over and screamed. The power that raged within her was terrifying. Before, it had been like a flickering candle flame, glowing gently in the back of her mind. Now it blazed like a roaring firestorm. Emelda caught hold of it, finding herself almost swept away by the torrent of energy that raged within. She jerked her mind back, shuddering and faint.

Reluctantly, she turned to look at the body at her side. Tyrius was lying in a patch of dirt blackened to ash. Emelda covered her mouth with a clenched fist, choking back a strangled sob that still managed to escape anyway.

Tyrius was very much dead, although his flesh was still mostly intact. But his gaping mouth was charred, the sockets in his face empty. The boiling juice of his eyes ran down his blistered cheeks. By the look of it, he had been seared from the inside-out, probably when he had drawn in a mouthful of molten air to make that last, shuddering scream.

Emelda turned her head and vomited noisily in the dirt. When she thought she was done, her stomach spasmed again, and again, until there was only bile left to bring up. Wiping her face with the back of her hand, she rose, trembling, to her feet. She turned and stumbled away from the grotesque corpse, not wanting to ever, ever see it again.

Like Gerald and their son, Tyrius was now dead because of the Oath. The Oath she had told them all to keep.

Emelda wept silently as she picked her way through the empty streets. It seemed there was no one left in the ruined city but herself—no one alive, at any rate. Aerysius was now a city of the dead. Where had they all gone—the residents, the servants of the Hall? She crept around the still forms of fallen bodies, and once she stepped on a hand half-buried in a pile of debris.

There were fires up above on the heights. Thick, choking smoke billowed into the air. Aerysius was silent, the city bathed in a haunting light. And above, the green pillar yet spired, its wraithlike glow consuming even the dawn.

The Temple of Death was not far; Tyrius had been right. And it was intact, which was more than she'd dared hope. But Emelda gravely feared it would be as silent and empty as the rest of the city. She could think of no reason for the priests to have remained behind when they could have easily evacuated by way of the Catacombs. If they were already gone, then there was no hope. She was now sixth tier, but all of her dreadful strength would not help her navigate the Catacombs. For that, she would need the help of a priest. Or a very brave and clever priestess.

The temple door was shut and bolted from the inside. Emelda pounded on the heavy wood with both fists, then stepped back to gaze up at the walls. The temple was far from the largest building in the city. The followers of Death were not many. Most people usually honored the goddess only when they had to.

No one came, so Emelda picked up a brick and used it to bang even harder. She shouted up at the windows, calling for anyone who might hear her pleas.

At last, the temple door cracked open. A face looked out, but in the shadow of the doorway, Emelda couldn't see well enough to make out features. When the door opened a little wider, she realized she was looking into a face hidden behind a sheer veil of white, the trademark of a priestess of Death. The eyes looking at her through that translucent fabric were wide and dark, gently untroubled.

"Sanctuary!" Emelda cried, almost throwing herself into the arms of the priestess. The woman received her, ushering her across the threshold and bolting the door behind them. Emelda could hardly see through the tears of gratitude clouding her vision.

The interior of the temple was dim, lit only by a few tapers on tall iron candlesticks. There were only two windows above the door that admitted little light. But the shrine at the far end of the room was brilliantly lit by the combined flames of hundreds of glowing votive candles.

Emelda blinked, not understanding how there could possibly be so many. Then she realized: each candle represented a soul lost in the catastrophe that had destroyed Aerysius. Those candles had probably saved her life. The priestess had lingered behind instead of fleeing to safety, probably to offer those hundreds of tiny prayers. It was a valiant effort. Emelda turned back to the priestess with a new appreciation for the woman.

"I claim the right of Sanctuary," she announced, fighting to keep her voice steady. "I request passage through the Catacombs of Death, by right of the Temple's agreement with the Hall. I am Prime Warden Emelda Lauchlin. I demand my right of passage."

The woman blinked at her through the diaphanous white veil. She was striking, with dark auburn hair that flowed down her back. Her eyes gleamed with the bright spark of intelligence.

"That would explain why your candle refused to light," the priestess said, the sound of her voice soft and resonate. Emelda immediately recognized the lilting accent of Chamsbrey on her tongue.

"I am Naia Seleni, First Daughter of the Goddess Isap," the young woman informed her. "Perhaps you should sit a moment before we attempt the shadows of Death's Passage. The journey is not easy. I recommend we wait a bit."

Emelda doubted they had time to wait. But, too exhausted to argue, she allowed the priestess to guide her to a bench in front of the shrine. Emelda waited there as the woman retreated into the shadows of the temple.

As she sat, she allowed herself to consider the altar and its flickering flames. Looking at them, she wondered about the death each candle represented. How many had been lit for mages she had known and worked with all her life? Emelda stared harder, seeing each candle individually, allowing her gaze to drift gradually down one of the lines. She must not think of them collectively, she realized. Each candle added its own, distinctive light to the dance of flame, and each deserved singular consideration.

The priestess returned, carrying a chalice in her hands, the white gown she wore flowing behind her as she moved. The woman handed Emelda the chalice and waited while she drank deeply. The priestess accepted the empty cup, gazing at her from behind the glossy sheen of her veil.

"Would you care to offer a votive candle? I lit as many as I could, but I fear there are thousands more my prayers have neglected."

Emelda nodded, feeling the grief rise up again inside. She would light two candles: one for Darien and one for Tyrius. There were many more she would like to include in her prayers, but she knew the list would probably take days and fill many such shrines. She did not have that kind of time.

So she accepted a candle from the priestess and took a striker into her hand. Kneeling down before the shrine, Emelda decided the first prayer should be for Tyrius, who had died trying to save her life.

She depressed the striker, and the wick of the candle flared instantly to life: a bright golden flame that wavered gently. Closing her eyes, Emelda whispered a soft, heartfelt prayer for the soul of her dear friend. Then she placed the votive candle on a shelf with the others, its single flame adding its light to the collective brilliance. A tear ran down Emelda's cheek as she withdrew her hand.

"Another?" the priestess offered.

Again, Emelda could only nod. She accepted Darien's candle, her fingers closing around the soft tallow. Her hand trembled as she depressed the striker. The first glowing spark missed the wick and floated to the floor, burning out long before it hit the stone. Emelda pursed her lips in concentration, desperately willing her hand to stop shaking. She squeezed the striker again.

This time the spark went right to the wick. A soft flame flared into being, glowing strongly. Then it immediately smoldered out.

Emelda sobbed in frustration. She tried again, but the candle refused to light. She started pumping the striker, producing spark after spark that rained down in a glowing shower to the stone floor of the shrine. She stopped only when she felt the woman's hand close around her own. Emelda looked up into the face behind the veil, her own eyes filled with tears.

"I don't understand," she cried, shaking her head. "Will the goddess not accept my prayers for my fallen son?"

The priestess looked down to regard the candle in her hand. "Try again."

Emelda squeezed the striker one last time. The spark wafted straight toward the wick of the small candle. The wick caught, the flame flickering only once before dying out again. The priestess nodded slightly, raising her gaze to look Emelda in the eye.

"The goddess accepts only prayers for the souls of the dead."

That meant nothing to Emelda. She shook her head again, weeping in frustration. In a voice quavering with suppressed grief, she whispered, "I don't understand."

The priestess' mouth turned upward in the faintest hint of a smile. In that comforting, resonate voice, she promised, "Your son's spirit yet lives."

Staring down at the unlit candle, Emelda almost choked in disbelief. She looked up and searched the priestess' face, but she didn't see any sign that the woman was toying with her.

"How is that possible?" she whispered. "I saw him fall."

The priestess gently removed the candle from her grasp and, taking her by the hand, guided Emelda away from the shrine.

"The goddess never lies," she said in a soothing voice. "Place your trust in her."

Just then, the door to the temple jolted as something outside battered hard against it. Emelda whirled toward the sound and, to her horror, saw the temple door straining against the bar that held it.

"They're coming!" the priestess gasped.

She took Emelda by the arm and hurried her toward a staircase that led down into a dim basement below the altar. On the wall ahead were three doorways that opened to utter darkness. Emelda knew exactly where those passages led, and the thought of going into one made her shiver.

"Do you know the strictures?" the priestess gasped.

"I do!"

The sound of the temple door breaking open spurred Emelda forward. She bolted into the nearest doorway.

"Not that one!" the priestess cried, too late.

As her feet crossed the threshold, Emelda felt an unnatural shadow slip over her. The world lurched as though suddenly unstable, then quickly righted itself. She closed her eyes, fighting off a moment of panic. When she opened them again, Emelda found herself…somewhere else.

She was no longer in the temple.

A long, rock-encrusted passage lay ahead of her, lit by the soft glow of swirling magelight. She turned to look behind her for the priestess. Through a smoky screen of fog, she could see the temple basement. But it was empty.

The woman wasn't there.

Filled with trepidation, Emelda turned in a full circle, glancing about frantically.

"Prime Warden!"

The voice of the priestess echoed as though from a great distance. There was an opening in the rock wall ahead. Another passage. Perhaps the priestess had entered the warrens through one of the other doors and was looking for her somewhere, wherever that passage led.

Emelda moved toward it, calling out, "Where are you?"

"Right here."

She turned around.

And froze.

The woman who had appeared behind her looked nothing like the priestess. She had platinum blonde hair and wore a chill, triumphant smile that was both beautiful and terrifying.

"You must be Prime Warden Emelda," she said, her smile deepening. "So nice to run into you."

Chapter Five
Sweet Lady Luck

Covendrey, The Rhen

Kyel Archer slouched, hands in his pockets, as he slogged with his head bowed through the muddy streets of Covendrey. His clothing was drenched, soaked through with rain, his hair plastered against his face. It had been storming for days with no sign of letting up. He'd almost forgotten what it felt like to be warm.

He missed the comfortable chair by his hearth back home. That chair had been lovingly shaped by his own hands. It fit him perfectly. He was not a craftsman by trade, though perhaps he should have been. He had a certain feel for wood. But he'd decided to keep his woodworking to a hobby, afraid of losing his love of the craft if he took to it for a living.

So he'd apprenticed himself to a merchant instead. He had a wagonload of trade goods to get all the way to Rothscard and back in a fortnight. In this weather, Kyel was skeptical he would be able to make that deadline.

The back door of the Dancing Boar Inn wasn't hard to find, even in the pouring rain. Kyel stamped the mud off his feet and let himself in. As he moved out of the rain into the comforting warmth of the inn's interior, he was surprised to find it nearly deserted. The Boar's common room was generally filled with patrons at any given time of day but, strangely, there were only two people sitting at a long table, another man squatting by the hearth, warming his hands over the flames.

Kyel knew everyone in Covendrey and recognized the men at the table as Aber Feldman and Dale Hodgens, the Boar's joint owners. The man by the fire was Traver Larsen, who ran a dye house on the other side of town. Kyel had grown up with Traver but knew Dale and Aber only socially.

He took another step, and a board beneath him groaned. The sound made all three men startle and turn toward him. Traver climbed to his feet, a slow grin forming on his wolfish face. He strode toward Kyel with his hand out, gesturing broadly.

"Well, look what the wind blew in!" he said with a laugh. "What are you doing, skulking around?"

"I came in the back way." Kyel directed his words to the two men sitting at the table. Both Dale and Aber stared at him with eyebrows raised, no doubt wondering if Traver's accusation of skulking had any grain of truth to it.

"Did I leave that damned door open again?" Aber said and rose from the bench, clunking his tankard down on the table.

"Next time use the front door," Dale admonished. "And don't just stand there, drippin' wet. Grab a towel and dry off next to that drunk of a friend of yours."

"You're drunk, Traver?" Kyel asked over his shoulder, heading to a neat stack of towels behind the counter.

"Cold sober," the man responded with a frown. "These good gentlemen won't even grant me a drop."

"And why should we, Larsen?" Dale asked. "You still haven't paid for all the crockery and chairs that were broken when you picked a fight with that fellow up from Southwark."

"Harlen Wood." Traver scowled, tossing his head against an unruly lock of hair that kept falling forward over his eyes. "He started the fight. I was just defending myself."

"Sure." Dale raised his tankard to his lips. "Just mind your manners, or you can find your way back out again. You know where the door is."

"Sure do," Traver said with a smirk that was almost a sneer. "You've thrown me out it enough times."

Kyel ran the towel over his face and scrubbed his hair with it. Sadly, there was nothing to do about his clothes. He tossed the towel into the rag bin then crossed the room to the river rock hearth, settling down by the fire next to Traver. The heat of the flames soaked quickly into his skin, a welcome relief.

"How are your boys?" he asked Traver, though he doubted the man had any idea.

"Oh, they're just fine. Getting to be real pains in the ass." He took a sip of water from the cup in his hand, his face skewing into a grimace. "How's your own get?"

"Just fine," Kyel muttered, the question provoking a sharp pang of homesickness. His son was little more than a baby. Kyel had never left home for so long. "I'm going to miss him," he sighed.

"Aye, I'll miss mine too."

Kyel glanced sideways at Traver. "Where are *you* going?"

Little bits and pieces of the conversation started tallying together in his mind, just like the long columns of numbers on the inventory sheets he worked with. What they added up to was certain trouble.

A broad grin broke out on Traver's face. He reached over and clapped Kyel on the shoulder. "Why, I'm going with you! I'm your driver. How's that for luck?"

Kyel reeled, feeling as though the bottom had just been yanked out of his stomach. What was the old man thinking, hiring *Traver* of all people? This run was too important for anything to go wrong. If Traver mucked it up…

He shook his head. "I don't understand. What about the dye house? What about Ellen and the boys?"

Traver waved his hand dismissively. "She gave me the boot weeks ago. I thought everyone in town knew."

The news made Kyel want to retch. The rest of the story totaled up, falling into place. So now Traver was looking for work, had no place to live, and no coin to pay for his habits. Somehow, he'd gotten snatched up by Kyel's own employer, who'd been looking for someone to make the Rothscard run.

And now Traver was his problem.

"I need a drink," Kyel said, standing up. He walked with shoulders slumped toward the back of the inn as images of drunken Traver disasters filled his mind.

Hunter's Home, The Rhen

The Great Northern Road looked more like a half-forgotten cart trail in the leagues between Dansbury and Hunter's Home. After almost a week of bumping along in the seat beside Traver in the wagon, Kyel still found himself wincing every time one of the wheels slipped into one of the ruts in the road. He couldn't help but wonder if Traver wasn't trying to bounce them around intentionally

Even still, they were making good time, despite the bad weather. Kyel slept under the wagon, afraid someone was going to plunder his goods in the night or assault them at swordpoint. There was rumor of deserters drifting down from the Front, which didn't instill Kyel with much reassurance. He almost wished he had hired a mercenary.

As the sun was starting to set, the wilderness gave way to farmland and pastures: a sure sign they must be approaching a town up ahead. They had left Dansbury three days before. There, they had stayed at a decent inn where Kyel had managed to get a good night's sleep between fits of Traver's snoring. Since then, they'd been sleeping under the wagon again.

Kyel's back longed for a bed. Almost every town they'd come across had offered some type of accommodations for travelers. The Great Northern Road was a major trade artery connecting many of the Rhen's kingdoms. Kyel just hoped the inn at Hunter's Home would be a civilized one and not like the seedy Scarlet Maiden in Weeping Springs or the Pig's Ear in Gentry.

The sun had already set by the time Traver drew the horses up in the inn's yard. Kyel jumped down and stretched his legs for the first time in hours. There were not many people about, just two men standing by the door of the inn and a stable boy crossing the yard with a bucket in hand. Kyel signaled the boy over, flipping him a coin for stabling the horses and locking the wagon up for the night. He waited for Traver to climb down then made his way toward the inn.

Two rough-looking men standing by the inn's door glared at him as Kyel gathered his things and crossed the yard. When he reached the door, the pair refused to move aside, forcing Kyel to turn sideways to brush past them. He looked down, unable to meet their stares. He'd run into other men just like them on the road and didn't like their type. Although unarmed, the two had the look of mercenaries, and not the kind looking for legitimate work.

The interior of the inn was musty and dark, redolent of smoke and liquor. Kyel crossed the great room toward a balding innkeeper who stood at a counter polishing crockery with a cotton towel. Kyel decided after a minute of waiting that the innkeeper either didn't see him or was ignoring him on purpose. He conspicuously cleared his throat to get the man's attention.

"What do you want?" The bald man didn't look up from his task.

"A room and a meal. And a place to lock my wagon up for the night, and board and feed for my horses."

The innkeeper raised his eyebrows as he set the crock he'd been polishing down on the counter, flipping his towel over his shoulder. Then he extended his hand, palm upward.

Kyel had to reach into his coin purse a few times before the man was finally satisfied. Then he turned to see where Traver had gotten himself off to. Kyel found him leaning against a wall by the door, staring longingly at a pair of men in the corner intent on a quiet game of cards. Kyel shook his head, starting toward him.

"Come on," he urged, tugging at Traver's sleeve. "I've got us a room for the night."

Traver glanced at him with a pleading expression. "Might I borrow some coin? I'll pay you back from my wages."

Kyel rolled his eyes and sighed. Traver had been behaving himself rather well the entire trip. It wasn't as if the Elk's Horn was a gambling den, and the two men in the corner seemed harmless enough. Reaching into his coin purse, Kyel pulled out a few coppers and dropped them into Traver's eager hand. The way the man's face lit up made Kyel shake his head.

"You have a problem," he told him as he clapped Traver on the arm.

"It's never a problem if you're winning," Traver grinned.

Turning, Kyel swung his pack over his shoulder and made his way toward the staircase. He didn't look back as he took the stairs up to the second floor. He was going to wash up and have supper. After that, he was going to bed.

He considered canceling Traver's meal but decided he'd better not. Traver was going to have to do an awful lot of winning. Kyel had only given him five coppers.

Traver grinned at the coppers in his hand as though they were gold pieces. Brushing a wayward lock of hair out of his eyes, he turned to assess the game in the corner. The men playing cards were probably regulars. Townsfolk, by the looks of them. The game they were playing was a quiet one. Too quiet, by Traver's standards. His coin probably wouldn't go very far with them, but he had to start somewhere.

He kissed the coppers in his hand, a little offering to his Lady of Luck, the goddess Dreia. Traver considered himself a special supplicant of hers, probably a favorite by now. She had blessed him many times before in the past—why not tonight? After all, he just wanted to take in enough winnings to buy himself a few rounds of drink. That shouldn't be too much to ask.

"Care if I join in?" he asked by way of introduction, hooking a chair over with his foot. He tossed a coin into the pot and plopped down, leaning forward with his head in his hands, elbows planted on the table.

That's how it started.

Three hours later, it was still going.

Lady Luck had never blessed him so well. He'd graduated from the corner table, moving up to a real game when a bawdy crowd of travelers wandered in. Since then, the Elk's Horn had turned into an entirely different sort of establishment. Word of his winning streak had gotten out, pulling people in from the street. Traver found himself the center of attention as a raucous crowd gathered around his table to watch him win hand after hand.

He'd had lost count of the number of pots he'd won in a row. He'd never even *heard* of a streak this hot. The cards in his hand were like a good woman. They knew when to stick, and they knew when to leave. People started buying him rounds. After the first few tankards, Traver stopped wondering who to thank. He just swished the ale around in his mouth, swallowed, and laid down another card.

He stared across the table at his current opponent, a merchant down from Rothscard who'd stopped in to buy a drink, then decided to try his luck. The cards in Traver's hand felt itchy, so he discarded the highest and decided to go low this time. That was the beauty of Knight's Cross, the game of the moment. Low cards stood as much of a chance as high, all depending upon how the hand was dealt. The merchant was dealing from three decks to prevent him from counting cards. Traver wasn't. But when he produced a perfect Cross for the second time in a row, the merchant folded and walked away.

Cheers went up all around the room. People clapped him on the back, while others beat on the tables. A woman leaned down to give him a kiss that started on the cheek but ended up with her falling into his lap with his tongue in her mouth. The kiss tasted like a salty twist of ale and wine, not unpleasant. Her breasts weren't bad either. Traver snaked a hand under her skirt to squeeze her thigh and was rewarded by a squeak of surprise. He winked at her and, settling her properly in his lap, looked around for another upstart who might want to try a challenge.

There didn't seem to be any takers.

But then one of the mercenaries he'd beaten earlier returned, probably wanting to win his coin back. Traver remembered the dirty, unshaven face well. The man had played a good game of cards. He must have managed to scrounge up more coin from somewhere.

The buxom girl in Traver's lap squirmed at the sight of the man. Traver draped a hand over her shoulder to steady her, although a certain part of him did appreciate her squirming.

He called a serving girl over with a wave of his hand, ordering another round. He patted the girl on the thigh then signaled his opponent to ante up.

Traver blinked, staring down at the gold piece the man pushed to the center of the table. He didn't have near enough to match that bet, even if he went all-in. He was going to have to walk.

Unless...

He lifted the girl by the hips and planted her firmly on the table. Standing, Traver excused himself and trudged across the room in the direction of the stairs.

He took the creaking staircase up to the inn's second floor. He knew which door was Kyel's as soon as he heard the snoring from the other side. He had those low, throaty sounds memorized. He opened the door and stooped to grope around in the darkness. As usual, Archer had stashed his coin purse under the bed.

Traver scooped up the purse and left. After all, he was riding the best winning streak of his life. That kind of luck just didn't happen every night. He swung the purse by its strap as he shuffled down the stairs and through the packed common room back to the table. Halfway there, he lost his balance and stumbled into a woman, jostling her drink. Ale spilled down the front of her dress, drizzling amber droplets down the gap of her cleavage.

The ringing slap that followed actually took him by surprise. Traver pressed a hand against his face. The woman had an arm like Harlen Wood. That one could try her hand at tavern brawling. She'd really be quite good at it.

He stumbled back toward the table, massaging his cheek and veering the whole way. It was almost time to call it a night. He was having a hard time focusing, and the sound of the room was becoming a muffled blur in his head. He hadn't bothered counting the number of rounds he'd put down, but he knew the total was up there. He just wanted to finish this one last hand then slip off to bed, preferably accompanied.

Traver almost sighed in relief when he saw the mercenary was still waiting for him at the table. The girl was gone, though, which was really too bad. He fell into his chair, thumbing the purse open enough to finger through the loose coins at the bottom. When he produced a fat gold piece, his rough-looking opponent raised an eyebrow in interest. Traver handed it over to the man, who put his teeth on it.

"A gold Silver Star," Traver boasted, slurring badly. "Can't go wrong with that."

The mercenary didn't reply. Come to think of it, he hadn't said anything all evening. But he did appear satisfied by the impressions his teeth made in the coin. He dealt, and Traver eagerly scooped his cards up off the table, trying to arrange them in his hand. He lost one in the process, groaning as it twirled downward to land on the table. He scooped it up as quickly as he could. Someone behind him laughed. Traver almost turned to say something, but then his eyes focused on the cards glaring up at him from his hand.

Another perfect Cross.

Traver threw his head back and howled, stamping his feet and throwing his cards down on the table. A cheer went up from the gathered crowd as he leaned forward to rake in his winnings. He couldn't believe it. He'd felt certain his Lady Luck had left him for another man.

He should have walked away then. But he didn't.

"How 'bout this," he slurred to his opponent. "Let's go another hand, and I'll give you a chance to win it back."

The sellsword shook his head. "Can't do it."

Traver screwed his face into a grimace. "Why not?"

"I got people I owe."

"You must have *something.*"

His opponent shrugged. "Just my horse."

Traver brightened. A horse was good. Archer could use a better horse. The nag he kept tied behind the wagon was a mean-tempered beast that was becoming nastier by the day. Traver put on his best game face, not wanting to appear too eager.

"Well, I'd have to see it," he allowed, trying his best to sound skeptical. He actually didn't care what the creature looked like, so long as it had four legs and a back to put a saddle on.

The mercenary looked over his shoulder and nodded at someone behind him. Traver's fingers itched for more cards to be dealt. He scooped his coins up from the table and downed the rest of his ale, waiting for the man to make his decision.

"Come on, then," his opponent said and scooted his chair back. "I don't have the bloody beast shoved down my pants, you know."

"Right." Traver stood up and caught himself on the table to keep from falling over.

He had to strain to keep the image of the man from becoming doubled as he followed him out of the inn and into the night. For some reason, his eyes kept trying to slide closed. How much ale had he put down? He knew his limit well, and he knew when he was well over it.

The mercenary led him into the dark stable. Traver scowled at the overwhelming stench of horse manure that assaulted his nose. Whoever the innkeeper was paying to muck out the stalls wasn't earning his keep. Soft nickers greeted them as they made their way down a dark aisle between rows of stalls. A soft nose brushed against Traver's arm, making him flinch.

The man opened the door to a stall, beckoning. Traver followed him in, stumbling over a pile of hay. It was dark inside, and his eyes hadn't adjusted yet. They weren't working well anyway.

He blinked, peering around at the shadows.

"Hey," he muttered, managing to slur even that one syllable. "I don't think there's a horse in here."

"He's a genius," said a voice from behind him.

Suddenly sober, Traver bent to reach for his boot knife. A steel-toed kick caught him in the side of the head before he could get his fingers around it.

Chapter Six
Dumb, Rotten Luck

Hunter's Home, The Rhen

The sound of the door banging open startled Kyel from sleep. Then hands were on him, hauling him out of bed and onto his feet. A group of men slammed him back against the wall, his head cracking against the wood. Someone twisted him around and snaked a muscled arm around his neck. He tried to struggle, but the man jerked his arm upward forcibly, holding it at an impossible angle.

Kyel groaned, feeling his tendons starting to give. He stopped moving, sagging as they bound his wrists behind his back with coarse rope. Then they wrestled him out the door. Kyel staggered down the hallway, two men guiding him firmly from behind.

When they reached the top of the stairs, he looked down to find the common room crowded with people. They were shouting and hollering, waving fists and brandishing weapons and tankards in the air. Kyel stared down at the crowd, his mind frozen by a numbing mixture of confusion and fear.

As he reached the bottom of the stairs, a young woman stepped forward and spat in his face. A blond-haired man took care of the spittle for him, tilting his tankard over Kyel's head and dumping the contents over him. He was propelled through the crowd as people screamed accusations in his face. He couldn't make out any of the words, didn't understand what they were shouting. It was all just a blurred, terrifying nightmare.

They hauled him out the door and into the night. The yard was full of people standing around, staring at another man who knelt in the dirt by the stable. A few men surrounded him holding lanterns and flaming torches, their faces glowing orange in the flickering light. Looking at the man kneeling on the ground, Kyel's confusion solidified into fury.

It was Traver.

Kyel felt his cheeks heat with a sudden flare of anger. What could the scoundrel have possibly done this time? By the looks of things, it must have been something far worse than just another rowdy tavern brawl.

Then he saw the body sprawled on the ground in the shadows of the yard.

The man holding him pushed him to his knees beside Traver. His companion looked even worse than usual, his head a bruised mess, his face caked with blood. He reeked a brutal combination of ale and horse manure. Traver's eyes were reddened and half-closed. Kyel couldn't tell if that was from the head injury or the drink, but it didn't matter. The facts were totaling themselves in his head. What they added up to was certain trouble.

"What did you *do?"* Kyel hissed at him.

Traver turned and regarded him with a dim expression, seeming to notice him for the first time. He grimaced and shook his head, looking baffled, as if it was all just dumb, rotten luck.

"I got jumped," Traver said. "But these lackwits who think they're the Emmery Deathwatch Guard keep saying I killed that man."

"What?" It was as bad as Kyel feared. Traver had stolen some coin from someone, gotten himself good and soused, then went and killed some poor fellow. "Oh, by the gods, Traver—"

A short but brawny fellow approached, waggling a finger at them. "Now, you just sit there quiet-like. Save your lip for the mayor. He's on his way, and when he gets here, you'll likely end up with your heads on a block."

"But I didn't *do* anything!" both Kyel and Traver exclaimed at the same time. Kyel turned his head and glared at his companion, who just shrugged sheepishly in his restraints.

"Well, I didn't."

They sat in silence after that, on their knees in the dirt of the yard. Kyel couldn't keep his gaze off the corpse sprawled only a few paces away. He thought he recognized the man, but it was hard to tell in the flickering light of the torches. The face had so much blood splattered all over it that the features were indeterminable.

He wondered if it was one of the men he'd seen in the yard when they'd first arrived. He hadn't liked the way they were staring at him. Kyel found himself wondering if Traver's story might have some grain of truth to it. It was possible they had seen the wagonload of goods and had marked Traver for an easy target.

Of course, that didn't explain how one of them had ended up dead.

Kyel made certain his voice was a dead whisper as he prodded his companion, "Why'd you get jumped? You don't have anything anyone would want to steal."

Traver hung his head. To Kyel, he looked like a mischievous boy who got caught by his mother. "I borrowed your coin purse."

"What?" Kyel couldn't believe it. He'd known that the man was a scoundrel—and a drunk, and a carouser, and a gambler—but stealing your own friend's coin was low. He wouldn't have thought even Traver's base morals were that appalling.

"It's a long story."

"I'll warrant it is! Everything with you is a long story. Your whole *life* is just one long, bloody tragedy."

"Actually, it might be a very short tragedy. Look."

Kyel looked. A small procession was headed their way up the street. The man who rode in front on a heavy draft horse still wore his nightclothes. Kyel took him for the town mayor. Behind him walked a mixed assortment of people, some holding torches, others wielding swords or farm implements.

He didn't like the looks of the man bringing up the rear. He was heavily bearded and carried the biggest half-moon axe Kyel had ever seen. The light of the torches reflected off the blade.

"Gods," Traver whispered beside him. "Wager that would smart a bit coming down."

Kyel couldn't take his eyes off that axe. He didn't understand. All he'd done was go to bed and, the next thing he knew, a group of townsmen wanted to take his head off. It wasn't fair. He thought of Amelia back at home and little baby Gil. He didn't want his son growing up without a father. He hung his head, wrenching his gaze away from the red glow of the half-moon blade.

Traver whispered, "You're a businessman, Archer. You talk us out of this."

Kyel let out a long, exasperated sigh. There was no hope. If only Traver truly would let him do the talking, there might be a chance. But Kyel knew there was no way the wretch beside him would keep his mouth shut.

The mayor dismounted a short distance away and tossed his horse's reins to one of his henchmen. He was a squat old man with salt-and-peppered whiskers on the sides of his face. He seemed like a good enough fellow, although anyone wearing his nightclothes couldn't seem too harmful. He leaned over the dead body, holding a spectacle up to one eye as another man handed him something that glinted in the torchlight.

Kyel frowned, staring at the object in the mayor's hand. "Isn't that your knife?"

Traver nodded. "What do you think our odds are? Three-to-one?"

"Is gambling all you ever think about?"

"Well, no, actually." Traver nodded in the direction of the headsman. "Right now, I'm thinking more about that axe. It doesn't look very sharp." He groaned. Tilting his head back, he worked his neck around stiffly. "Oh, gods, my head hurts."

Kyel turned back to the group of men still conversing over the body.

"We've scores of witnesses, Mayor," a man was saying. "Everyone saw the killer lose a heap of coin to this poor fellow. Not just coppers. Gold, mind you. Then everyone heard that bastard telling him to follow him to the stables. Seems he beat the poor chap senseless then knifed him real good. Then he passed out flat drunk. That's how we found him."

"Oh, is that the way of it?" Traver tossed his hair back from his face. "Then would you pray explain how I acquired this dent in my head? And if I knifed the 'poor chap' to get my coins back, then where are they?"

"We found this in the stable."

Kyel turned to see a tall and lanky man striding toward the mayor, carrying something in his hand. Kyel stared, trying to see what it was in the shadows of the yard. When the man stepped into the light, he almost groaned. It was his own coin purse. And, by the way the man was holding it, there was still a good amount of heft to it.

The mayor received the purse into his pudgy hands. He opened it, and Kyel could hear the sound of clinking coins as he sifted through the contents. The old man turned to Traver, shaking the purse as he walked toward him.

The mayor said, "So you're telling me there was a third party who knifed him, beat you senseless, and then didn't bother to abscond with the coin? That's a bit hard to swallow, don't you think?"

Traver shrugged. "That's the way of it."

"And what about me?" demanded Kyel. "I never left my room all night!"

The mayor looked over at the bearded fellow. The ugly brute stepped forward, gesturing toward Kyel with a wave of his hand. "We've two witnesses who say they saw him near the stable."

"I was sleeping!" Kyel shouted.

He was frustrated almost to the point of tears. He had no idea what had happened down in the stable. All he knew was that he had no part in any wrongdoing, and it should be perfectly obvious to anyone with half a brain.

He glanced across the yard, startled to find a mob pouring out the back door of the inn and moving in their direction. Kyel swallowed, looking again at the blade of the axe. His neck was starting to ache. He knew exactly where this was going.

"All right," the mayor grumbled, raising his hand to rub his balding head. "Give me a moment." He fingered Traver's boot knife, rotating it slowly. He glanced again at the corpse then held the small blade up to dangle in front of Traver's eyes. "Is this your knife?"

"Well, yes, but—"

Turning to Kyel, he hefted the coin purse. "And is this your money?"

"Yes, but—"

The mayor turned and walked away, by all appearances deep in thought. Kyel hoped he thought long and hard on it. The whole story didn't make any sense at all. But the mob gathered around them was growing impatient.

Kyel's stomach felt queasy. A town mayor was usually an elected official. The man would be thinking more about his endorsements than he would about true justice for the crime—which lowered their chances considerably. And, by the sound of the turbulent crowd, the people were demanding blood.

"I don't know, Halbert." One of the men who had ridden in with the mayor was shaking his head. "You can't execute two men on evidence this flimsy. Not a soul actually saw them do it."

The whole mob started shouting. Someone called out, "They murdered a man! Take their bleedin' heads off!"

There was a collective outcry of agreement. Some people shook their fists in the air as others began directing their wrath at the mayor. The poor man walked away, lumbering toward Kyel and Traver.

"Doesn't Rothscard send their convicts north to the Front?" the mayor asked one of his men.

"Aye, they do."

"Then we're in luck." He glanced back at his unruly constituents with a look of relief. "There's a group of Rothscard Bluecloaks in town. Perhaps they'll agree to take these two off our hands."

Kyel gaped. He shook his head and pleaded in a desperate voice, "I can't go to the Front! I've a wife and child at home! And a load of goods I'm supposed to haul out on the morrow!"

The mayor looked at him with pity in his eyes. His expression of sympathy seemed almost genuine. "Sorry, son. But if you really were in just the wrong place at the wrong time, then you're the unluckiest fellow I've ever met."

Kyel's head spun dizzily as the air in his lungs seemed to rush out all at once. "Damn you, Traver!"

Traver sighed. "Already am, Archer. Already am."

The bearded fellow chuckled, eyes sparkling with amusement in the glare of the torchlight.

"Your name's Archer?" he asked. "Hope you know how to use a bow."

Kyel glared at him vindictively.

Chapter Seven
The Bird Man

Vale of Amberlie, The Rhen

Darien was adrift in a sea of golden light that filtered downward in gentle rays. The light shimmered, shifting, and kept fading into darkness before coming back again. Hazy objects hovered overhead and all around. A soft breath of air stirred, making the shapes above him dance and spin. Gradually, the objects came into better focus. But even when he could make out the forms of the strange, fluttering shapes, they still didn't make any kind of sense. The whole image was surreal and utterly bizarre.

He found himself staring up at the forms of moving birds. Their wings were outstretched in the air overhead, though not in flight. Instead, the birds fluttered and spun on thin and almost transparent strings, dangling from a ceiling that sloped sharply overhead. There were dozens of them. Small sparrows and warblers, finches and jays. Hawks and eagles with great wingspans extended in a strange parody of flight. Above, mounted to a corner against the ceiling, a great horned owl regarded him somberly, eyes round and glassy, its expression perplexed.

Darien struggled to sit up, but the motion brought such a stunning pain in his head that he fell back again immediately. The light and the birds faded away, and it was a long time before they came back again.

When they did, he had no idea why they were still there. He had expected them to be gone, just another one of the strange dreams that had plagued his sleep. It took him a long time to come to the conclusion that this was no dream. It was just a very peculiar reality.

He was lying in a soft and comfortable bed. The birds continued spinning overhead, feathers stirring on a breeze admitted by an open window. Dim recollections were coming back to him, filling him more each minute with a tremendous sense of loss and foreboding. He remembered the disaster of the Hall, the column of light that pierced the night, his brother's cold, malevolent eyes. He remembered falling.

There was nothing after that until the birds.

He tried to sit up again, clenching his jaw against the pain and trying to fight back the queasiness in his stomach. He managed to get almost halfway up before the sound of a hoarse voice stopped him short.

"I wouldn't try that just yet."

He hadn't noticed the old man sitting on a stool in the corner of the room. The face was familiar, but Darien couldn't place it. He knew he had seen this man before, even recently, but couldn't remember where. The face that regarded him was quilted with wrinkles, age-stained and weathered. The nose was bird-like, resembling the beak of the golden eagle that dangled above his bed. The old man's puffy blue eyes were what made him realize that he was looking at the gatekeeper he had met the previous day in the Vale.

The old man stood stiffly, using his hands to push himself off the stool. With slow, shuffling steps, he moved toward the edge of the bed. He wheezed as he bent over, placing a hand on Darien's chest. He closed his eyes. As he did, Darien felt a rippling sensation pass through his body. The old man was another mage, and he was using his ability to probe his condition.

"The ways of healing are not well known to me," the old man said, removing his hand. "My specialties lie in other areas. I did what I could, but perhaps you can do a better job of it yourself when you are feeling a bit better."

Darien frowned as the import of the words sank in. Then his eyes widened. He'd forgotten that he was perfectly capable of healing himself now. He reached within and felt for the surge of the magic field inside. It was there, singing quietly in the back of his mind. Waiting to be used.

"Stop."

The urgency of the command made Darien force his mind back from the touch of the field. He opened his eyes, staring up at the old mage in confusion.

"Never attempt that again with a head injury," the man admonished, raising a finger. "You ought to know better, boy, especially this close to a vortex. But you're new, aren't you? Only yesterday, you passed my gate as an acolyte. Yet now I see a fresh set of markings on your wrist."

Darien lifted his hand and stared at the image of what looked like a heavy iron chain engraved into his flesh. The mark had not been there the previous day. The old man was right.

He had an identical emblem on his left wrist, which he'd acquired sixteen years before when he had spoken the Acolyte's Oath. Now, he bore a matching set of chains on both wrists, the symbol of a fully Bound mage. Darien rotated his arm, admiring the complexity of the pattern that wrapped all the way around his wrist, seamless and glimmering in the muted light.

"I suppose I should introduce myself," the old man said. "My apologies, but I'm unused to the ways of civilized manners anymore. My name is Edric Torrence, third-tier Master, if you must know."

Darien nodded weakly in acknowledgement. "Darien Lauchlin. Grand Master of the Fifth Tier." It felt incredibly odd to hear his lips utter his new title.

The old man blinked.

Such an elevated ranking was almost unheard of. Meiran was the only mage in all of Aerysius who would have been stronger than him. He had fallen in love with the only sixth-tier Grand Master in existence. But Meiran was dead. Along with all of the others.

"The city?" he whispered, though he really didn't want to hear the answer.

"Utterly destroyed."

Darien closed his eyes as a shiver passed over him. He had guessed that would be the case. His last memory of Aerysius was a shattered, desolate tomb. He wondered if his mother had managed to escape. The explosion of the bridge may have offered her a chance to get away.

"Are there other survivors?"

The old man shook his head. "As far as I know, my friend, you and I are the only mages left alive in the entire world. And you are indeed lucky to be alive. Every person in the Vale was turned out this morning, witnessing the destruction on the mountain. Your fall from the cliff was marked by many. Including myself, for which you are most fortunate. I slowed your descent as best I could."

Darien winced, hearing that. He remembered nothing of the fall. The last thing he remembered was thinking of Meiran as he stepped off the cliff. It was well beyond fortunate that Master Edric had happened to look up at just the right time.

"You have my thanks," he whispered.

"I was actually rather shocked at finding you still alive," the old mage went on. "A few townsmen helped me haul you up from the river bottom. One of them recognized you. Apparently, you grew up down here. Ah, bother, I'm rambling, aren't I? You must forgive me. I'm no longer used to the company of people. My work is a solitary thing."

Darien didn't know what to say. Whatever the mage's work was, it was certainly an odd branch of magic, judging by the dozens of dead and yet undecayed birds spinning in the air above his bed. Perhaps something to do with flight, though Darien knew that was an impossibility. The magic field could support accomplishments that were true wonders, but human flight was not one of them. Yet, it did make him think. It was no simple feat the old man had performed, slowing his fall the way he had. Darien wasn't sure he could duplicate it.

The sound of a shout made him turn his head in the direction of the window. Now that he was listening, he realized he'd been hearing a constant murmur of voices for some time.

"What is that?" He wanted to sit up and look out the window, but he knew better. He had no wish to repeat the same mistake.

Master Edric frowned, his jowls sagging. "It seems that rumor travels swiftly. Folk have been gathering throughout the day. They know that Aerysius has fallen and that some dire evil exists on the mountainside above. The villagers fear for their lives. Many have come here, looking for hope. Looking for you, my young friend. Apparently, they all expect you to save them."

The explanation made Darien ill. He closed his eyes, feeling the same frustration he had experienced all his life: wanting desperately to help, yet incapable of doing anything meaningful. What was ironic was, now, he finally *did* have the power to make a difference. Only, he had spoken a vow to never use it, at least not in any way that would prove effective. Darien stared down at the markings on his wrist, suddenly resenting them.

"You know as well as I that there's nothing I can do," he muttered.

"I know absolutely nothing." Edric gazed wistfully up at the feathered ornaments twirling gently above his head. "But for my birds. That's the one thing I do know."

Edric's words provoked a memory Darien had almost forgotten. Back when he was a boy living in the Vale, there'd been rumor of a crazy old man who lived somewhere deep in the grove. Some folk called him the Bird Man. He stared up at Edric with renewed interest.

The aged Master reached down and patted him on the shoulder. "Rest now," he instructed. "When you awaken, I'll round you up something to eat."

Darien nodded and closed his eyes. It didn't take him a moment to fall back to sleep.

His rest was plagued by a relentless series of nightmares that repeated over and over again, one only ending to make way for the beginning of another. In his dreams, Darien watched Meiran die a thousand different deaths, each with its own twisted and often brutal variation. Sometimes he was there with her, holding her in his arms as the Hall of the Watchers collapsed on top of them. Other times, he witnessed her death only as an observer, watching as his brother took her life a hundred different ways.

In one especially vivid dream, he looked on helplessly as Aidan used his own sword to slit Meiran's wrists and held a crystalline goblet to collect her spilling blood. In the vision, Aidan smiled as he tilted his head back to drink deeply from that terrible cup.

In other nightmares, he was falling. He fell endlessly, over and over. Sometimes he felt his body shatter as he collided against a wall of rock. Other times, there was no end to his fall. He plunged downward into shadow, and there was nothing in the world around him but infinite darkness. Sometimes Meiran was falling with him, the fabric of her gown rippling in the wind.

Darien awoke in a cold sweat, clamping his mouth shut to contain the scream he was feeling inside. The nightmare he'd awakened from had been the most terrible of all. In it, he had seen Meiran kneeling before the Lord of Chaos. She looked over her shoulder and smiled at him, her eyes empty pools of filthy green light.

Darien lay panting, sweat streaming down his face. The nightmares had been too real, too vivid. He lay there trembling, trying to slow the pace of his heart, staring upward at the twirling birds. He tried to clear his mind of the image of Meiran with the green light of hell shining in her eyes.

His breathing finally calmed as the terror of the dreams subsided. He glanced around, finding Edric sitting on his stool, eyes poring over a text of some type. Seeing him awake, the old man closed the book and rose to his feet. He shuffled toward the bed in a stiff, arthritic stride.

"How long?" Darien asked.

"Two days," the old man said. "I was growing a bit concerned."

Darien felt shocked by the amount of time that had passed. No wonder the nightmares had seemed endless. At least his head felt better, only throbbing mildly as he raised himself into a sitting position. The room spun for a moment then slowly steadied itself. He felt weak. Probably from three days without anything to eat. But he felt mostly well, maybe even well enough to stand.

The old man smiled. "You can try healing yourself

now."

Darien closed his eyes and took hold of the magic field, sending his thoughts probing deeply into his body. He quickly assessed the extent of his injuries, repairing everything amiss almost automatically. When he was done, he opened his eyes and moved his head, testing the feel of it. The pain was gone. The weakness, however, was still there. Hunger was not something that could be healed with magic.

"I have to admit, I'm envious," Edric said. "You could not imagine how difficult healing is for someone untrained to it."

Darien understood. As an acolyte, he had been allowed to choose the direction his studies would take. He had always aspired to be a Sentinel like his father. The charter of the order was to protect the people of the Rhen from the aggressions of the Enemy, all without the use of offensive techniques. He had spent many years studying under the guidance of skilled mentors. Knowledge of healing was a necessity on the field of battle, and one of the most difficult subjects to master.

Darien swung his legs over the edge of the bed, only then realizing he was naked. He looked around the small cottage and found his clothing piled on the floor, looking no better than tattered, filthy rags. Reaching down, he collected the formal robes his mother had given him and held them up. The black fabric was rigid with dried blood and crusted with grime. What had been a new and expensive garment now looked destroyed beyond repair.

Darien pictured how the robes had looked when he'd seen them new.

And, suddenly, they were.

In his hands, the garment had once again taken on a glossy black sheen, the cloth whole and unrent.

He slipped the robes on over his head then found his boots by the door, the same scuffed and dusty pair that had survived two years of soldiering in the Pass of Lor-Gamorth. Darien pulled them on and, as he did, his gaze was drawn to another object by the window.

His breath caught in his throat. He'd been holding the sword Meiran had given him when he'd stepped off the cliff. It could have fallen anywhere. The chance that it had ended up here, in this room, was nothing short of miraculous.

He took the black scabbard into his hand, raising it before his eyes with a feeling of reverence. The leather-wrapped hilt of the sword gleamed in the cool morning light. He ran his hand over it lovingly, his gaze drawn to the jeweled crossguard.

"We found that by your side," Edric said. "I recalled you carrying it, so I brought it along." What he left unspoken was the air of disapproval remarked by his tone.

Darien nodded, resting the sword back against the wall. "It was a gift," he explained in a voice gruff with sentiment. "It's the only thing I have left of the person who gave it to me. You have my gratitude for saving it."

He managed to turn away from the blade. As he did, he caught a fleeting look of sympathy in the old man's eyes.

"I'm going outside," he said. "Have a look around."

As he moved past Edric, the old man caught his arm.

"Wait."

The old mage let go and went to a chest against the wall. There, he bent over, carefully removing an odd assortment of birds from the top of the chest, setting them gently on the floor. He lifted the lid and rummaged through the contents, finally producing a folded black parcel Darien recognized. It was a mage's cloak, complete with the Silver Star embroidered on the back, the symbol of Aerysius.

The old man pressed the cloak into Darien's hands. "Here, put this on."

"But it's yours," Darien protested, shaking his head in confusion. Why was the man giving him his own cloak?

"I have no need of it any longer. You, on the other hand, must keep up appearances."

Darien put the cloak on, fastening it with a silver brooch Edric handed him. Then he opened the door and stepped out into the brilliant light of morning.

And froze, rooted by shock.

There were scores of people gathered in the clearing before the little cottage.

Darien fought the sudden impulse to flee back inside and shut the door on that sea of anxious faces. But Edric moved up behind him, blocking the doorway and any hope of retreat. Noticing him, the people in the crowd turned and started shouting, jostling each other out of their way.

"I don't understand," Darien muttered, appalled. "What do they want from me?"

"Hope," Edric said.

Dismayed, Darien glanced at the old Master.

"I…I can't," he protested. "There's nothing I can do for them. And why me? Why not you?"

Master Edric only chuckled, a mischievous glint in his eyes. "Why, I'm just the crazy old Bird Man who lives in the wilderness up 'yonder. But you, on the other hand, are the last surviving Sentinel of Aerysius."

"I'm not," Darien objected. "I never had a chance to take an order."

The old man just looked at him sideways and scoffed. "You are the son of Gerald Lauchlin. Of course you're a Sentinel. What else would you be?"

Darien shivered, thinking of Aidan. He, too, was a son of Gerald Lauchlin. But his brother was just about the furthest thing from a Sentinel Darien could imagine.

He realized the crowd had stopped stirring. Silence consumed the glade before the Bird Man's cottage. All eyes were fixed on him, regarding him with a mixture of wonder and fear. There was an almost palpable sense of expectation in the air.

Then it came to him: they were all waiting for him to speak.

Darien froze.

All he could do was stare from one face to the next. He recognized many. One of the faces he knew well was Corban Henley who, in his youth, had been a gangly boy prone to misadventure. He'd been the leader of the local band of mischiefs Darien had belonged to himself. But he hadn't laid eyes on Corban in over a decade. The man standing before him now was still tall, but his lanky frame had filled out remarkably. Unlike most of the people in the clearing, there was no trace of awe or anxiety in Corban's eyes.

"What will you do?" someone called from the back of the crowd.

Darien's nerves tensed. Everyone was looking at him as though they all expected him to call down lighting and save them from the terror in the sky. They had to know he couldn't do that. He was just one man—a man constrained by a vow to do no harm.

So, he did the only thing he could think of, the only thing that might make them understand. He pulled back his shirtsleeves, baring his wrists. He lifted his hands, the markings of the chains shimmering in the morning light.

"I've sworn the Oath of Harmony," he said in a raised voice. "There's nothing I can do against that." He glanced toward the thin pillar of light that shot straight up from the side of the mountain, visible even in the sunlight.

He'd hoped they would understand. But instead of accepting his words, the crowd in front of him devolved into chaos. People shouted curses at him. The cry of "Coward!" was raised by a group of men standing in the back.

Master Edric stepped forward, coming to his rescue.

"Now, wait a minute, all of you!" the old man bellowed.

The crowd went still as though stunned into silence. The only noise in the forest was the stir of air through the treetops.

Edric nodded, looking satisfied. He took a step back.

"Let the man speak."

Darien bowed his head, not wanting to confront the angry glares fixed solely on him. He could feel them pinning all their hopes and expectations on him and, for some reason, that made him angry. No matter what they thought, he was just one man.

He said just loud enough to be heard over the stirring of the crowd, "There's nothing I can do here. The battle was waged up on the mountainside, and it's over now. Aerysius is destroyed. I can't change that." He paused, taking a moment to gather himself. "But there's still a war going on in the North, and that's where I'll be headed. Perhaps, at the Front, I can make a difference."

His words were greeted by an uncomfortable silence. People exchanged glances, shifting uneasily.

One man called out, "Then you think the danger's passed?"

Darien shook his head. "If the Front fails to hold, there will be no place that's safe. If you wish to help fight this war, then you'll come with me. Otherwise, gather up your families and leave this place. The Vale of Amberlie is no longer safe."

"Why won't you protect us?" shouted a woman.

"That's your bleeding job, isn't it?" another man yelled.

"He's a bloody coward, that's what he is!"

"Stop it! All of you!"

Darien's gaze jerked to Corban Henley, who was making his way forward through the press of bodies in the crowd. "I've known Darien Lauchlin all my life. He's no coward." Corban stopped and looked at him. "You're going to the Front?"

Darien nodded. "I'm useless here. The Front is the only place I can make any difference."

Henley raised his voice to address the crowd. "What's wrong with you people? You're all standing here whining like a pack of helpless dogs. You all want something done, but instead of lifting a finger to help yourselves, you brand this man a coward because he won't do it all for you. Well, I see only one of him. And there sure as hell's a lot more of you." Looking at Darien, he said, "I'm no stranger to a blade. If you're going to the Front, then I'll come with you." He turned back to the crowd. "So, who's coming with us?"

No one spoke. Henley turned and spat on the ground. "Craven dogs."

A man stepped forward. "I'll go."

His voice was followed by a long gap of silence.

Then another man came forward, saying, "I don't have a family. I'll go with you."

Suddenly, the air was filled with offers of support. Darien let out a sigh. The critical moment had passed, thanks to Corban.

"I'll be heading out at first light," he told them. "I'll take any man who wants to come with me. The rest of you should go home and gather up your families. Leave everything behind. Make for Auberdale. That route would be your safest choice. We'll try to hold the North so that maybe, someday, you'll have a home to come back to."

There were no cheers; his words hadn't been meant to inspire. But the crowd dispersed, which was all Darien wanted to accomplish. Corban Henley gave him a nod as he turned away. Darien stood on the porch of the Bird Man's home and watched until the last stragglers disappeared into the forest.

"You need to work a bit on your delivery." Master Edric patted his shoulder then went back inside. Darien followed, having to duck under the outstretched form of a great heron hanging too low from the ceiling.

Once inside the cottage, Darien stopped. He stood gazing down at his wrist, rotating his arm.

"Don't stare at those chains too long," the Bird Man warned. "They'll begin to feel even heavier than they already are. Trust me. I know from experience."

Darien lowered his hand. "What will you do, Edric?"

"Me? I'm just an old man who loves his birds. I can't fight…the only thing I can do is fly." His voice trailed off. He stood gazing up at the birds slowly spinning on their strings.

The old Master shook his head sadly. "I know you think there's little you can do, but there, you're wrong. If you keep your wits about you, you'll find there are ways to win a battle without having to wash your hands in blood. Use your head. That's why I saved it for you. As for me…it's no good here anymore. My old friends have all flown away. Just listen."

Darien listened. Edric was right. Only the sound of silence greeted his ears. He hadn't noticed the complete absence of birdsong from the forest.

"Birds are smart." Edric smiled softly. "They always know when it's time to fly. As do I."

Darien wondered what Edric meant by that, but the aged Master didn't elaborate. Instead he left the cottage, closing the door behind him.

The Bird Man was used to waking frequently in the night to answer the urgings of a bladder that was just as old and tired as the rest of him. He crept out of bed, shuffling across the room under the spinning shadows of the birds that danced in the green light still piercing the sky above.

He knew what that light was. The gateway had filled his dreams, of late. Edric glanced at his birds, watching them dance in their endless pursuit of flight. He wanted to fly as well. He had always envied birds, envied them the freedom of their wings.

He relieved himself outside against the rough gray bark of a pine he had nurtured from a sapling. He turned to go back inside, but hesitated.

He wanted one last flight.

If anyone had actually been watching, all they would have seen was the form of an old man standing under the branches of a pine suddenly disappear into the shadows of the night. Their eyes would have entirely missed the small warbler that took wing from the place where the old man had just been standing.

The tiny bird fluttered, pumping upward and spiraling into the sky, its whistling queries the only sound in the still night air. The warbler fluttered across the disk of the rising moon, now diving, now soaring, finally backstroking to rest in the spot where it had first arisen.

If anyone had truly been watching, all they would have seen was a breathless old man shuffling out from under the shadow of an ancient pine, climbing stiffly back up the stairs to the door of his cottage.

Edric made his way back inside, but not to his own bed. Instead, he knelt beside the young man lying on a pallet on the floor. He waited, eyes studying the rhythmic rise and fall of the blankets, to make certain his young visitor was in the deepest stage of sleep.

Tenderly, he placed a trembling and rheumatic hand over Darien's chest, closing his tired old eyes. Above him, his silent friends whirled on a breeze, their feathers ruffling on outstretched wings.

The Bird Man filled his mind with the thrill of flight as he opened the conduit of Transference between them and offered up his ancient life.

Chapter Eight
Greystone Keep

Pass of Lor-Gamorth, The Front

Lightning streaked a sky filled with turbulent thunderheads, making the heavens blaze. As it faded, ice on the mountain peaks gleamed, a hellish afterglow soon devoured by consummate darkness. Winds ripped down from the mountain passes, brutally cold.

Kyel staggered as a gust of wind threatened to push him over, having to lean forward just to remain on his feet. The wind was so violent, it sucked the breath right out of his lungs. He'd lost the feeling in his hands a long time ago. His toes throbbed from the cold.

It should have been daylight.

When they'd started up into the Pass of Lor-Gamorth, the first hint of morning was warming the sky above the horizon. But as they'd climbed higher between the jagged black slopes, the light of day had slowly disintegrated.

Someone had warned him it would be like this. But no words could have prepared him for the horrifying reality of the Shadowspears. There was no sunlight, ever, in the mountains that bordered the Black Lands. There was only a death-dark sky filled with turbulent clouds that surged across the sky. The weather patterns here were an extension of the curse that had desecrated the lands to the north a thousand years ago, remaking them in hell's own image.

And Kyel knew he was walking straight toward those twisted lands, just one in a long file of exhausted men. He had known these men now for three weeks, the time it had taken them to journey from Rothscard across the grasslands of the North. They were convicts, one and all. Sentenced to death but delivered from that fate only to be conscripted into the war effort. It was still a death sentence, however commuted. There was no return from the Front. Everyone knew the only way out was to die.

Kyel had wept quietly every night the first week, facing the certainty that he would never see his wife or son ever again. He wasn't the only man who'd broken down. They all knew that every step of the long march carried them a little closer to the end.

Lightning flickered, and rolling thunder trembled the mountains. In that brief flash of light, Kyel made out the dark outline of a fortress built on a rocky outcrop. It was there for just an instant and then was gone, consumed by utter darkness.

The name Greystone Keep was legendary. The fortress at the edge of the Black Lands had existed for over five hundred years, holding the North against the incursions of the Enemy. Kyel had heard its name mentioned in stories, but had never imagined that he would actually see it with his own eyes.

As they climbed the slopes, the features of the keep became visible. A frayed banner whipped in the wind over a high turret, the only part of the fortress that looked intact. The crumbling walls were a lusterless gray, the stone infested with yellow growths of lichen. The ragged structure was supported by stone buttresses that appeared ineffective.

Kyel's legs were trembling by the time they reached the fortress. He followed the others through a large gate and into a circular room at the base of the tower. The wind ceased as soon as he crossed the threshold. Kyel sagged in relief. He felt weak and dizzy, his face stinging, his cheeks moistened by tears wrung from his eyes by the gale.

He wanted to stop there and rest. The air of the tower was warm, and he was exhausted. But the men who guarded them were merciless, forcing them forward through a doorway ahead.

The room they entered must have been the main hall of the keep at one time. But if there had ever been a ceiling, it had long since collapsed. The rear wall had also caved in, now just a heaping pile of rubble. There were no windows, only narrow slits that ringed the walls.

The guards ordered a halt, glaring at the prisoners with disdain. Kyel waited with a growing sense of unease as a soldier moved slowly down the line, unlocking their chains. Beside him, Traver leaned and almost fell over, earning a sharp look of reproach from the nearest guard.

Three men entered the room. They walked in crisp strides past the file of convicts, stopping halfway down the line. The man who stood in front had the look of a hardened soldier. He stood straight with his hands clasped behind his back, shoulders squared. He wore his long, graying hair tied back at the nape of his neck, his eyes cold and harsh like the black stone of the mountains. He turned to face them, running his gaze down the line.

"Welcome to the Front," he announced.

His voice resounded throughout the hall of the keep, echoing off the stark walls before falling off with a grim undertone of finality. There was a long pause as he surveyed the face of each man in line.

"Make no mistake, gentlemen. Every man of you is here to die. One and all, you've been convicted of crimes that warrant execution. That sentence yet stands—it has only been deferred. All of you will probably be dead in a year, much likely sooner. So, go ahead. Look around."

Kyel did as instructed, looking sideways at Traver, who returned his gaze with eyes widened by fear. Kyel glanced away, suddenly queasy, as he envisioned Traver lying dead on the black rocks of the pass.

"All those here are now your brothers," the soldier continued relentlessly. "How long you live and how well you die will depend exclusively on these men. So learn their faces well. They are all that stands between you and your grave.

"My name is Garret Proctor, Force Commander of the garrison here at Greystone Keep. The order that sends you to your death will come from my lips. I won't even think twice about it. There is no escape from the Front, so don't consider it. Every crack and crevice of these mountains is guarded by experienced sentries. If you are ever found even ten steps away from your post, you will be slain. No questions. No one will care that you just stepped away to take a piss."

Kyel swallowed. He vowed silently that he'd never so much as scratch without permission.

The commander swept his gaze down the line of terrified men. When his stare fell on the man to Kyel's left, his eyes narrowed. "There is one of you here that won't heed my warning. It happens every time, without fail. Someone always thinks they can escape and will try to make a break for it in the night. I can promise you this, gentlemen: at least one of you will be dead come morning.

"On my right is Captain Devlin Craig. Half of you will be under his command. Captain Craig has been charged with holding the bottom of the pass, and he has kept that charge for over three years. On my left is Captain Sutton Royce. Captain Royce is charged with the defenses of Greystone Keep."

Captain Royce stepped forward. He was a robust man wearing a chain mail tunic covered by a tattered gray cloak. His brown eyes were just as stern as the commander's, though decisively more brutal. His face was covered by a thick growth of beard a shade darker than his hair.

"Greystone Keep holds the Pass of Lor-Gamorth," he rumbled. "If it should ever fall, then we will lose the pass. If we lose the pass, then we lose the North. And if the North should ever fall, the Enemy will sweep southward until every last city, town, and village of the Rhen looks just like that."

He pointed toward the back of the hall, where the entire wall of the keep had crumbled and fallen away. At first, Kyel could see only darkness broken by occasional flashes of a queer, muted light. But then a strong fork of lightning illuminated the land far below and, for just an instant, he could see a large expanse of scorched earth that stretched as far as the eye could see.

Kyel gasped as he realized he was staring down at the Black Lands. What was more shocking was the fact that they were actually, consummately black. Nothing could live there in that shattered waste. Nothing…but the Enemy.

Royce continued. "These walls have stood for over five hundred years. As you can see, they have been breached many times, but they have always held. It is my duty to make certain they continue to hold, and I will not hesitate to sacrifice as many lives as it takes to see that they do."

"So." The force commander stepped forward. "I will leave you with these final words: fight well and die well. And always remember that you are all that protects your homeland from the fate that befell Caladorn, the kingdom to the north you've probably only ever heard of as the Black Lands. If this keep should ever fall, everything you know will be desecrated by the Enemy, and everything you love will be destroyed."

With that, he turned and let his long strides carry him out of the hall, his gray wool cloak flapping behind him in his wake. Kyel supposed he should have felt relieved as the commander disappeared through the doorway. But, somehow, he felt that his situation had not improved. He almost wished the grim man would come back again. Kyel did not like the malicious glint in the eyes of Captain Royce.

It was Captain Craig that stepped forward then, surveying the line of convicts with a look of distaste. His arms were heavily gauntleted, his straw-gold hair disarrayed about his bearded face. He stood with his hands clenched behind his back in a somewhat casual facsimile of the commander's polished stance, an enormous sword in his hands.

As he waited, groups of soldiers entered the room, hefting between them four large sacks. They carried the sacks to the far corners of the hall and there dumped out the contents gracelessly on the floor. The clatter of falling metal echoed off the crumbled walls, ringing through the keep.

The soldiers began spreading out what looked like garbage across the floor in front of the fires. It took Kyel a moment to realize he was looking at piles of weapons, probably scavenged from the bodies of dead soldiers who had fought and died with those selfsame weapons in their hands.

Devlin Craig smiled as he saw the expressions on the men before him. As though reading Kyel's own thoughts, he proclaimed, "You will now choose the weapon you will die holding. Whichever it is, be it sword, mace, bow, or spear, you shall eat with it, sleep with it, care for it like a child, and love it better than a wife. So, come forward. Choose your weapons well and then get back in line!"

Kyel walked toward the nearest assortment of arms. Unlike most of the boys he'd grown up with, he had never had the desire to wield a weapon. He watched Traver moving his hand over the collection, finally gripping the hilt of an enormous sword.

But Kyel had spent his entire adult life calculating totals and carving wood. He didn't think he would have the sheer brutality to drive such a blade home into living flesh. So he chose a longbow from the pile of scattered weapons, knowing well how the irony played on his surname. He didn't care; the smooth length of wood felt good as he closed his fingers around it.

He held the bow up, testing the weight of it in his hand. The wood looked to be cut from a single, long-grained stave of yew. There was no bowstring, just notches in the ends where a string could be anchored. The bow was slender and tapered, longer than he was tall.

The last man selected his weapon and filed back into line. Beside him, Traver was staring at the monstrous blade he had chosen, looking down at it with a perplexed expression on his face. If Traver had the strength to even swing that mass of steel, Kyel would be surprised.

They were divided then into groups, the men holding bows going to one corner of the hall while those holding swords and spears went their separate ways. Two soldiers walked toward Kyel's group of bowmen, their hands full of folded gray cloaks, which they threw on the floor. Kyel bent down, selecting one from the top of the pile.

They were then instructed to bed down right where they stood. There was to be no meal, no blanket. Just a rough wood floor and an open roof overhead. At least the fire behind him shed a little warmth.

Kyel donned the gray wool cloak and lay down, wrapping the cloak tightly around his body. As he lay there shivering, he found himself thinking of his family. He closed his eyes and tried to pretend it was Amelia there beside him instead of a longbow. He hoped, in his dreams, she would be.

The sound of shouts woke him from sleep. Kyel sat up and looked around. It was late; the fires had burned low. There was a commotion going on all around, soldiers rushing to scale ladders up to a narrow ledge that ran all around the tops of the walls. There, men were positioned at regular intervals, peering out through narrow slits. A few raised longbows, nocking arrows to bowstrings and sighting out through the gaps.

Commander Proctor strode into the hall, barking a demand for a report. He was met by Royce and Craig.

"A large party approaches from the south," Craig reported, nodding his head in the direction of the tower.

Above, a flaming arrow shot over the open roof of the keep. It was followed shortly by another. A signal, though Kyel didn't know what it meant.

As he turned in the direction of the shattered rear wall, his eyes fell on a prone form laid out on the floor behind them. The man's back was pierced with three long arrows with the same type of fletching as those used by the archers on the walls. Kyel remembered the commander's promise that one of them would be dead come morning. Apparently, he'd been right.

Above, a third fiery shaft blazed across the midnight sky. A shout rang out from the pass below. Both Royce and Craig moved to a long, horizontal slit, staring down into the darkness below as the commander took up position in the back of the room.

Over the sound of the wind, Kyel could hear the echo of approaching footsteps. Whatever force was coming, it was no few. The bowmen on the walls swiveled as one, their shafts now aimed at the door to the hall.

Garret Proctor stood regarding the doorway with narrowed eyes. Royce and Craig drew up in front of him, one man to either side.

The door to the tower room opened, and suddenly a crowd of men was spilling in through the doorway. It took Kyel a moment to realize that the men congregating at the front of the hall were no threat. They were not soldiers. If anything, they looked to be farmers. Exhausted farmers, though some did appear to be armed.

The men staggered in shivering, swaying on their feet, their eyes widening as they noticed the bowmen on the walls with shafts directed at their chests. But they kept coming, pouring in through the open doorway, at least seventy of them. Possibly over a hundred. As the last man entered the hall, Kyel drew in a gasp.

This was no farmer.

The man was young with dark hair that spilled past his shoulders. There was an alarming intensity in his eyes that made Kyel want to draw away from him. He was clothed entirely in black and carried a longsword on his back.

He strode confidently forward, crossing the room toward where Proctor stood with his officers. As the man passed by, Kyel saw that his cloak was embroidered with the image of an eight-pointed star. He recognized the symbol and knew what it meant: the man before him was a mage of Aerysius.

Silence filled the hall as the man drew up before the officers. Commander Proctor made no move, just stood regarding the mage in front of him with critical eyes.

Then a slow smile formed on Craig's lips. All at once, he stepped forward and clasped the man's arm with both hands. "Darien! I didn't think we'd ever see you again. And by the looks of it, you've brought us a kingly gift. Praise be to the gods, man!"

To Kyel's astonishment, the two men embraced as if old friends. Royce eased his blade back into its scabbard, stepping forward to shake the mage's hand. Garret Proctor nodded a curt greeting, his expression no longer quite so harsh.

Kyel's gaze was drawn to the sword carried by the mage. That was strange. Masters of Aerysius were forbidden to bear weapons. Perhaps the man was merely an acolyte who hadn't sworn his oaths yet. That might explain the presence of the blade.

"What news have you?" the Force Commander asked.

The mage's face grew serious. In a tone grim with finality, he pronounced, "The Well of Tears has been opened. Aerysius has fallen."

Garret Proctor took a step backward, looking rocked. Kyel's own mind reeled as it struggled to make sense of the horrific tidings. He swept his gaze across the room, looking from face to face, and saw that every man in the keep was shaken by the mage's statement. Even the most hardened soldiers stood with their mouths open, eyes wide and full of dismay.

If Aerysius had truly fallen, then everything was lost. The Sentinels were the last, strongest line of defense the Rhen had. Without the Sentinels, there was no hope. The Enemy would flood down upon the vulnerable nations unchecked. There would be no repeat of the Battle of Meridan, where defensive magic had turned the tides of war.

It only took Proctor a moment to recover somewhat, though he was still visibly shaken. The sound of his voice carried only a whisper of its former strength as he asked, "What is left?"

The mage in the black cloak of dead Aerysius bowed his head. "To my knowledge, I'm the only survivor."

The force commander drew in a breath and turned away. Kyel couldn't see his face. But he knew the depths of despair that had to be written there, the same as on the face of every man in the hall.

Garret Proctor took a faltering step away, and then another. He walked stiffly toward a wooden chair, one of the few pieces of furniture in the room. Without hesitation, he cast himself down upon it.

Captain Royce lay a hand in sympathy on the mage's shoulder. But then he, too, turned away and moved to stand behind his commander.

The mage looked out across the hall. Kyel shivered when those unsettling eyes fell on him. Their stares locked for just an instant, but the man turned away, striding over to stand at the force commander's side.

Garret Proctor reached out and grasped the mage's arm. He slid back the dark fabric of his shirtsleeve, exposing a marking Kyel knew well.

He'd been wrong. The man standing before him was no acolyte. He was a fully Bound Master of Aerysius.

Garret Proctor looked relieved at the sight of the legendary symbol.

"Which order did you take?" he asked.

"I chose the Order of Sentinels."

Proctor nodded slightly. Then, much more directly, he asked, "How strong are you?"

The mage dropped his gaze, bowing his head as though ashamed. There was a moment's pause. Then, softly, he answered, "I am a Grand Master of the Eighth Tier."

There was a shocked murmur from all around the room. Soldiers groped for the comfort of their weapons. Even Craig and Royce took a step back away from the man. Kyel's own mind spun as he recalled something he'd read in *The Mysteries of Aerysius* by the famous historian Cedric Cromm. It was one of the few books his father had owned, so Kyel had read it enough times to have the passage memorized:

> *A mage passed beyond the sixth tier would be a vile abomination, creating chaos beyond imaginings. No mind of man is capable of withstanding the vastness of such power and should soon be broken down.*

Kyel's stomach clenched in dread. The man standing in front of them clothed in black was an abomination. By the authoritative expert on the subject, this Darien was already condemned, destined to be consumed by the unthinkable amount of power within him. It was only a matter of time.

But Garret Proctor did not seem to understand the dire corollary. He stared up at the man with eyes full of brimming hope.

"We have a chance, then," he uttered in a whispered breath. "Yes. A chance."

Chapter Nine
The Last Sentinel

Pass of Lor-Gamorth, The Front

Darien slumped into a chair, taking in the circular room he found so familiar. Garret Proctor had made his home at the top of the tower of Greystone Keep for over fifteen years, yet in all that time, he had acquired few possessions. The dim chamber was as stark and barren as the man himself.

The only adornment was a large map that showed a rough image of the Shadowspears. The map ended at the northern extremity of the mountains. No one had ever managed to chart the Black Lands beyond the pass. No one who had made it back alive, at any rate.

There were a few pieces of furniture in the room: a small chest by the door and two decrepit chairs pushed up to a table that had been broken and mended so often that no two legs matched. The commander's bed was just a simple pallet, tucked up against the wall near the hearth.

Proctor took the chair opposite him as Royce fetched them earthenware cups. Miraculously, he produced a flagon of wine, hefting it proudly in his big hands before filling both cups. He placed one cup on the table before the commander and offered the other to Darien. The liquid inside was dark red, reminiscent of fresh blood. Darien swirled the wine around before tasting it, trying his best not to make a face.

"Don't you complain," Royce admonished. "That's all there is. A special present from the Queen of Emmery. You saw her latest shipment down in the hall. I'll wager she sent this wine along as a bribe to make sure we don't send that lot right back to her."

The Queen of Emmery was more gracious than other rulers. Infrequent shipments of prisoners and supplies was better than no reinforcements at all. Not a soul had been sent up from Auberdale in recent months, and Treshorne had stopped sending men to the pass years ago. The Southern nations had never aided Greystone Keep within living memory. Their kings had probably forgotten that the Front even existed. In the absence of a recent offensive, the nations of the Rhen had become complacent.

Proctor took a heavy drink from his cup. He closed his eyes as he swallowed the awful liquid, savoring it as though the wine were the most delicate vintage that had ever passed his lips.

"Tell me everything," he commanded.

Darien complied.

It was hard, reliving the memories. Harder still to see his own emotions mirrored in the eyes of the three men listening. When his words finally died, he felt emotionally exhausted. He sagged back in his chair, taking a long drink of the loathsome wine. After he swallowed that, he took another, tilting his head back and draining the cup.

For long moments, not a word was spoken.

Sutton Royce finally broke the silence. "Things haven't been much better here. Enemy soldiers are still massing in numbers unheard of. They're gathering just to the east, under the shadow of Orguleth. We've had raids almost nightly. They're probing us. Testing our fortifications and marking the locations of our sentries. Everything points toward a sizable offensive."

Darien nodded. The Enemy had been mobilizing even before he'd left the pass for Aerysius. His mother had known as well. That was the reason she had issued the summons, recalling every mage from the distant corners of the land. Aerysius had been gathering its might, preparing for open war. Bound as they were by the Mage's Oath, the Sentinels would have been meager defense against the size of the invasion that was surely coming.

And now he was the only mage left to wage that war.

Proctor must have been sensing the direction of his thoughts. The commander held Darien's eyes as he spoke with absolute conviction:

"You are the last surviving Sentinel of Aerysius. Your strength shall be our salvation."

Darien bowed his head, staring down at the empty cup in his hand. He set it down on the table, struggling with his emotions.

Garret Proctor had worked with the limitations of the Sentinels before, had calculated them into his tactics all throughout his long career. He had been at the Battle of Meridan. More than anyone, he should know better.

"I've spoken the Oath of Harmony," Darien reminded him, silently hoping the old soldier would understand.

It was Devlin Craig, his friend and brother in arms for two long years, who strode forward to challenge him on it. The huge man leaned forward with his hands on the edge of the table, staring across its length with a penetrating stare.

"I see you still carry your sword, Darien. Exactly what are your intentions? Are you going to keep your Oath? Or will you forsake it?"

Darien looked away, his eyes drawn toward the fire in the hearth. A log broke and rained sparks upward with a startling crack. He watched the them drift lazily, wafting on an updraft from the chimney.

"I thought to convince my mother to Unbind the Sentinels before Aerysius fell," he said, staring deeply into the fire so he wouldn't have to meet their eyes. "She refused me. I didn't understand at the time, but now I do."

He looked down at the symbol of the chain on his wrist, tracing it with a finger. "The Oath is all that separates me from the likes of Zavier Renquist and Byron Connel. Cyrus Krane, Arden Hannah…Myria Anassis. You must recognize those names. You know of whom I speak. It's a safeguard. An assurance that the power I wield does not corrupt me."

Garret Proctor waved a dismissive hand. "You speak of eight demons long dead and moldering in their graves. The fall of Bryn Calazar was a thousand years ago. You can't compare yourself to them."

The commander didn't understand. Just as Darien hadn't understood himself before he had been forced to decide between a cliff's sheer face or the shards of a broken vow.

He insisted, "The Oath is imperative, especially for me. Don't you understand? I *must* take it seriously. I am an *eighth-tier Sentinel.* There has never been a mage stronger than the sixth tier. Ever. In all of history. Do you understand why?"

Proctor's face was a study in grim resolve. "It doesn't matter. I've read Cromm's work. I can even quote you the very passage you're referring to. But that makes absolutely no difference to our present situation. Right here, right now, you can be a very effective weapon if you allow yourself to explore the full extent of your potential. Over time, you may even become a dangerous weapon. *But that is exactly what I need.*"

"I will not betray my Oath," Darien insisted.

Craig slammed his hand on the table, jolting Darien's cup. "Then why are you here? Tell me that! Aerysius is dead. Its traditions are dead! Why do you insist on holding to a vow you've always claimed you don't believe in?"

Darien started to push his chair back, but Proctor's raised hand kept him in his seat.

"There are other ways," Royce allowed. "The Sentinels who protected Meridan never broke Oath."

But Craig was having none of it. "Darien's father died at Meridan! And Lauchlin wasn't alone—twelve mages were lost within the first *hour* of battle!"

Proctor's eyes looked like smoldering, silvered coals. He said firmly, "We cannot use Darien the way the Sentinels were used at Meridan. If we put him in the thick of battle, he'll be a target for every Enemy spear in the Black Lands."

Darien had to nod in agreement. It was true. A

black cloak was a target on any field of battle, a trophy prized by the Enemy above any other.

In an effort to appease, he assured them, "I still have my sword. The Oath doesn't prevent me from using it, just tradition. And I can heal any wound I take almost instantly."

Royce lurched around the table and grabbed a fistful of Darien's shirt.

"Can you heal yourself when an axe takes your head off?" he growled. "Can you save yourself from the flames when you're beaten senseless? Your own father burned to death with those chains on his wrists! That's what the Enemy does to your kind. Is that how you wish to die? You're the last Sentinel left, Darien. You can't just throw your life away!"

"Or is that exactly what you mean to do?" Craig asked, his eyes filled with concern. "You've lost everything. Aerysius was destroyed by your own brother's hand. You've lost Meiran, and I know how dear she was to you. Tell me, Darien. Did you come back here just to die?"

Shaking in anger, Darien stood and firmly disengaged Royce's hand. The entire room reeled around him. Never in his life could he remember being so enraged at a friend. He clutched Royce's hand in a trembling fist as he glared his wrath into the man's face. Then he threw the soldier's arm away from him.

He growled between clenched teeth, *"I don't know what you expect from me."*

There was a long, gaping silence. Then:

"Stop."

The commander's word had the bite of an order. But neither Craig nor Royce backed down. Instead, they stood frozen in place, glaring.

Proctor said firmly, "Leave him be. He's been through enough."

There was a tense moment of hesitation before both soldiers finally relaxed. But Darien couldn't. He stood confronting the two men with shoulders tensed, quivering in fury.

Craig bowed his head, blowing out a heaving sigh. He took a moment to collect himself. Then he looked at Darien with sincere regret in his eyes.

"I'm sorry," he said, shaking his head. "And I'm sorry about Meiran. I'm sorry about everything. Gods, Darien." He turned and stalked away, a fist swiping out at the air in front of him.

Royce nodded. "Look. We're all tired. Let's get some sleep. We can hash this out in the morning." He looked over his shoulder and waited for Proctor to nod his permission before he left.

"You can bed down here in the tower," the commander said to Darien, rising from his chair.

Darien took a deep breath and then nodded. He turned out his bedroll along the wall next to the hearth. Proctor took to his own pallet, fully dressed, as was his custom. Darien placed his sword on the floor next to him and eased himself down beside it, pulling his cloak tight about him as he lay his head back and stared up into the shadows of the rafters above.

He closed his eyes. He could still hear the throbbing of his pulse in his ears, a constant and irritating rhythm that seemed louder than the shriek of the wind that hissed in through the arrow slits. He measured the pace of his breathing, trying to calm his racing heart.

He lay there a long time, but sleep didn't come. After an hour, he pushed himself to his feet and crept across the floor. Moving as quietly as he could, he started down the steps and let the winding stairs carry him around and down to the tower's base.

The keep's massive oak door stood closed and barred, so he turned away from it. He would have liked to have gone outside, to stand looking out at the tall crags of the Shadowspears, as he'd done so often in the past. But instead, he walked toward the soft glow of light coming in through the door to the hall.

He picked his way quietly around the scattered bodies of slumbering men to the far corner. There, he stopped beside a fire that had burned low, now only a glow of dying coals, nodding at the two sentries who tended it.

Darien let his gaze wander across the floor, moving from one sleeping face to the next until he found the one he was looking for. Then he moved forward and knelt beside the slumbering man with curly blond hair and the face of an innocent.

Darien stared deeply into the man's face, taking in every smooth feature, his gaze traveling to the hand clasped limply around a longbow. He had noticed the man earlier, and something about him had drawn his curiosity.

He reached down, lifting the flaccid hand away

from the smooth shaft of wood. He ran his fingers over the palm, tracing upward to stroke the pads of the fingertips. Beneath him, the young man stirred in his sleep, sensing the touch. Darien drew his hand away.

The skin he had felt was soft and smooth, but for a small buildup of callous at the base of the fingers. Those hands were used to the fine strokes of tools, not the steel grip of a weapon or the coarse handles of a plow. More intriguing was the small callous on the third finger of the right hand.

Darien turned his gaze to the bow at the man's side. It looked to be good wood. Gingerly, he drew it toward him, rising to his feet as he held the bow out before him, angling his gaze down the length of the shaft. There was no warp in the wood. It was an excellent bow, with a light draw weight, ideal for a beginner. He lowered it to his side, resting the bow on the floor like a staff. He turned, his foot scuffing against a metal hilt on the floor.

Darien raised his eyebrows as he took in the enormous bastard sword lying at the side of a slender man with tousled red hair. He appraised the man's delicate hands, scoffing silently. The man was a fool. He had selected a blade that was much too massive for him.

Darien picked the sword up off the floor and walked away.

Kyel awoke the next morning to find a full sheaf of arrows at his side, along with a new waxed bowstring. And Traver's sword had been replaced by another, this one much smaller and cleaner-looking. The blade was well-oiled, and someone had meticulously honed the dual cutting edges.

Traver had been irate. At least until he'd tested the edge of the blade with his thumb, wincing at the cut that appeared in his skin. After that, he stared down at his new weapon with growing appreciation.

It was still dark out, though the sun should have already risen. When he looked up through the open roof of the keep, Kyel saw the same black sky that had been there the night before, full of churning clouds and buffeting winds.

After a meager breakfast, they were assembled into lines and marched out to the practice yard. Fires lit all around the yard provided a good amount of light. A high wall on one side effectively blocked the wind. Kyel found himself separated from Traver and thrown in with a cluster of men holding longbows.

An old sergeant spent quite a bit of time modeling the proper grip to use and where to place the hand on the shaft. Kyel was already tired by the time he was finally allowed to nock an arrow to the bowstring. He gritted his teeth and pulled the bowstring back to his cheek. The action took every bit of strength he had.

He heard exclamations from the men up and down the line, which made him feel a little better. He trained his eyes down the arrow's shaft at the target, a man-size clump of hay with a circle painted on it. Exactly as he'd been instructed, he released his fingers as smoothly as he could manage.

The arrow flew wide of its mark. But that didn't matter. What mattered was what the bowstring did to his left wrist. Kyel yelped as the string slapped back against his skin, making him jump and almost drop his bow.

Behind him, he could hear the regular soldiers laughing. Kyel stared down at the red welt on his wrist in shock. That had really *hurt*. He glared back over his shoulder as he picked another arrow up off the ground.

This time, he held his wrist at more of an angle, away from the bowstring's recoil. Determined to get it right, he drew the waxed string back to his cheek. He took his time aiming, sighting down the shaft until the target slowly steadied. He was so afraid he was going to jerk at the last moment. With as much concentration as he could summon, he plucked his fingers away.

The bowstring hummed, and this time it didn't score his wrist. The shaft flew perfectly straight. It slapped into the clump of hay, hitting the mark just off-center. The farmer next to him laughed, grinning in approval. Another man clapped him on the back.

Kyel looked behind him, feeling no small amount of pride. He was the first man who had managed to hit the hay. The soldiers weren't laughing anymore. Feeling smug, Kyel almost said something. But then his eyes caught the shape of a dark form standing just to the right of the group of men.

Kyel's stomach lurched as he saw the look of

satisfaction in the Sentinel's eyes, right before the mage turned and stalked away.

Chapter Ten
Legacy

Pass of Lor-Gamorth, The Front

Kyel felt a tap on his shoulder and looked up to find Sergeant Ulric, the dour old bowmaster he had worked with in the practice yard, hovering over him. Ulric motioned for him to follow then turned and walked away without waiting to see if the command was being obeyed. Kyel set down the plate of charred meat he had been half-heartedly picking at. As soon as the plate touch the floor, it was snatched up by one of the soldiers seated next to him, who brought the blackened morsel up to his lips with a grunt of thanks.

Kyel rose and fell in behind Ulric. The man led him wordlessly through the crowded hall and into the circular chamber at the base of the tower. There, the old soldier halted and ran a critical gaze over him, starting at Kyel's boots and working his way up to his face. Evidently satisfied with what he saw, Ulric started up the tower stairs.

Kyel had no idea who had sent for him or why he was being singled out. He wondered if it had something to do with his progress in the practice yard, which was the only thing he could think of that might set him apart from the other members of his company. He didn't know what to expect at the top of that turret.

Or who.

The air was cold and damp, moving in through arrow slits that followed the curve of the stairs up into the shadows of the rafters high above. The dim lights of torches cast a flickering, eerie dance along the wall. Overhead, Kyel could hear the flutter of bird or bat wings beating against the rafters.

He followed Ulric with a growing sense of unease. The spiraling staircase led to a room at the top of the high turret that smelled strongly of wood smoke and dust. The first thing he noticed was a wide hearth in front of him that had two neatly made pallets to either side. A blazing fire seemed to be doing a fair job of warming the place, despite the cold air coming in through the arrow slits. The chamber was conspicuously lacking almost any kind of fixture or decoration.

Gazing at the hearth, Kyel almost missed the shadowy figure standing against the wall to his right.

The darkly clad Sentinel stood with his back to them. He was tracing a finger along a contour in the map, giving no sign that he was even aware of their presence. But suddenly he paused, his hand dropping to his side.

A shiver ran down Kyel's spine as the man turned, fixing him with the same look of quiet appraisal he had worn in the practice yard. The mage nodded, dismissing Ulric without a word.

Kyel shuddered as he realized he was alone in the tower with an eighth-tier Sentinel of Aerysius.

The man extended his hand in a welcoming gesture. Kyel sat down at the table, leaning his bow against the wall behind him. The mage remained standing, watching him for a long moment before speaking.

"I saw you down in the yard," he said. "Have you ever held a bow before?"

Kyel shook his head. "No. That was my first time."

The mage nodded slightly then slid into the seat opposite Kyel. "My name is Darien Lauchlin," he said, extending his hand.

Kyel shook his hand, surprised that the man hadn't offered his long and imposing title. "Kyel Archer of Covendrey Township."

To Kyel's astonishment, he found the man grinning at him.

"Archer the archer," Darien said. "Now *that* will go over well with the men."

His smile was so honest and reassuring that Kyel found himself grinning too. The irony of his surname hadn't been lost on the members of his unit. The others had taken turns ribbing him about it all day.

The mage let his smile slip, but his eyes remained mild. "Do you mind telling me what you did for a trade back in Covendrey?"

"I was apprenticed to a merchant," Kyel answered, remembering to add the honorific "Great Master" only as an afterthought. His nerves tensed, hoping the mage wouldn't take offense at his hesitation.

The Sentinel waved his hand. "My friends call me Darien."

Kyel was struck speechless. A Grand Master of Aerysius had just labeled him a friend, whether he had meant to or not.

Of course he meant to, Kyel berated himself. Mages never did anything that wasn't deliberate. He wondered what the man was after.

"A merchant's apprentice," Darien said thoughtfully. "That would make you good with numbers. And you know your letters as well, I take it?"

Kyel nodded, admitting, "My father was an acolyte of Aerysius, but only for a time. He taught me my letters."

Darien's eyes widen at his words. Slowly, the man stood up from his chair and paced away, head bowed and hands clasped behind his back. He paused beside the hearth, staring pensively into the flames.

"I noticed you last night when I arrived," he admitted. "I hope you don't mind, but I've had my eye on you throughout the day."

Kyel fingered his bow absently. He produced the waxed and expertly tied bowstring from his pocket as a thought occurred to him. "You left this for me. And you switched out Traver's sword. Why?"

"I did him a favor. The blade he'd picked was too much of a weapon for him. The sword I gave him will serve him better."

Summoning his courage, Kyel asked, "Why have you been watching me?"

The Sentinel looked at him. "Have you ever been tested for Consideration?"

Kyel felt stunned. No wonder the man kept staring at him that way. Darien was hoping to find an apprentice, probably someone to follow after him. Kyel knew the gift was transferred upon death from one mage to the next in an unbroken line of inheritance. But not just anyone could receive it. The ability was rare, and Kyel knew for a fact he didn't have it. Darien was going to be disappointed.

Kyel said, "I've been tested. Twice. I never passed."

"Yet your father did."

"Aye," Kyel admitted. "But he didn't last long as an acolyte. Only two years. I don't understand. Are you thinking I could have the ability?"

"I can see the potential in you, but I've no idea how strong it is. Some people take longer to develop an affinity. If you were tested again, you might pass this time. It's possible, at least. I'd like to try."

"It's too late." Kyel sighed and shook his head. "I have a family…I did, at least."

Darien dropped his gaze. To Kyel, it seemed he was struggling with something that was difficult for him, like a dark secret he was afraid, or even ashamed, of admitting. When he looked back up, his eyes had lost most of their intensity.

"You heard what I said last night. Aerysius has been destroyed. I'm the only Sentinel left alive. I can scarcely provide an adequate defense for this keep, let alone the entire Rhen." He paused, shifting uncomfortably. "And I've another problem. There is too much of the gift in me. No one was ever meant to take on this much. Eventually, it's going to be more than I can live with. I need someone to pass on my gift to so that the legacy of Aerysius doesn't die with me."

Kyel looked away. He hardly knew this man, but for some reason, he felt moved by Darien's plight. He truly wanted to help him, but he wasn't a mage. And, even if he were, Kyel didn't think he had it in him to give what the man was asking.

"Wouldn't it just kill me too?"

"Not necessarily. If I can find another with the ability, I can divide the conduit between you. It's been done before. Then there would be two of you. And if you both go out and find two others within your lifetime…"

Kyel nodded, seeing where he was going with that line of reasoning. Where there was now just one mage, in time there could be two…and then, eventually, as many as eight. But that's all there could ever be, no more.

Kyel frowned. "But all this hardly matters if I don't pass the test."

"That's right."

Kyel understood. He nodded slowly, drawing in a shuddering breath. He realized he was trembling as Darien stood and crossed the floor toward him. The mage lowered himself to a crouch in front of Kyel's chair, staring him keenly in the eye. Kyel cringed back, wanting to look away.

The last thing Kyel remembered was seeing the vast amount of grief that clouded the Sentinel's eyes.

And then the world around him dimmed to a distant point of light.

Garret Proctor looked out from the battlements at the top of Greystone's tower, Sutton Royce at his side. Softly, he asked, "Have you spoken with him again?"

The captain nodded, his hand clenching the baldric of the longsword strapped at his back. "He refuses to forsake the Oath. You know Darien. Once he's got his mind set, even a supreme act of the gods won't change his course."

It was Proctor's turn to nod. The man was just as stubborn as his father. It was that same arrogance that had gotten Gerald Lauchlin tied to a wooden stake.

Sometimes, in his nightmares, Proctor could still hear the sound of the man's dying screams.

Chapter Eleven
The Breaking Storm

Pass of Lor-Gamorth, The Front

The next two weeks went by in a blur of exhausting training sessions interspersed with tedious hours of boredom. Kyel found himself growing used to the routine, though he discovered he enjoyed the hours of practice with his bow far more than the time spent sitting around.

He remembered nothing of Darien Lauchlin's test. He only remembered wakening as if from sleep to find the mage backing away from him, head bowed. Kyel had felt horrible at the time. He knew how much the Sentinel had at stake.

"I'm sorry," he'd said.

But when Darien raised his head, his expression was one of wonder.

"No need to be," he said. "You passed the test."

The following days had gone by in a strange sort of haze. Darien had never approached him again, and Kyel made of point of trying to avoid him. Every day, he practiced with his bow until his arms were shaking.

Part of him still wanted to deny Darien's words. It all seemed so far from reality, it couldn't possibly be true. But when he left the practice yard, one look back at his target was enough to make him admit that perhaps the mage was right.

All of his arrows had hit the mark.

A vicious gust seized Darien's hair, playing it out behind him and tossing dark strands forward into his face. He felt ill at ease on the battlements at the top of Greystone's tower. He stood looking out through the opening of an embrasure, his hand resting on the wall.

Under the right conditions, he could sometimes see all the way down to the mouth of the pass, and even out across the distant wastes of the Black Lands beyond.

Tonight was such a night. The winds were violent, eliminating any chance that fog could gather to obscure the view. The Black Lands unfolded beneath him, revealed in their naked desecration, flowing out from the foothills like a dark sea to the gloom of the northern horizon.

He reached out from within to gain a sense of the swirling tides of the magic field. It felt different tonight, like slick rivulets of quicksilver draining off the slopes, rushing in unbridled currents toward the lowlands beyond. There was no good reason for the field to be surging so wild and unchecked.

Darien started thinking of the bad reasons. He felt certain there was a storm brewing. He could sense it in the air, just as he had the morning he'd arrived in the Vale. Only, this time, he didn't dismiss his intuition. He no longer had the luxury of mistrusting his own mind.

Turning away from the battlements, he climbed down the ladder back into the sheltered warmth of Proctor's quarters. He made his way over to the map on the wall, for the hundredth time tracing his finger over the faded markings. But still, nothing made sense.

Deep in thought, he tapped his finger absently on the yellowed chart, then traced a line across the map to the smudge that indicated the mouth of Lor-Gamorth. Then, slowly, he drew a line upward, about an inch, his finger pausing under the small letters that spelled the word *Orguleth.* As he figured the numbers in his mind, his finger traced out the path of his rough triangulation across a frayed fold in the map, out into the blank emptiness north of the mountain pass.

His hand paused then, the edge of his fingertip poised under the only mark in that entire void of uncharted area. It was an arrow, pointing toward the upper-right corner of the map. Underneath the arrow were inscribed the words *'To Bryn Calazar.'*

Darien's finger tapped twice on the arrow. Then he spun away from the map and made for the stairs, scooping up his sword. He took the steps two at a time to the tower's base.

Kyel Archer was not hard to find. He stood out like a beacon of flame amidst the dim glow of the men around him. Darien crossed the hall toward him, men scrambling to move out of his way. Reaching him, he took Kyel by the shoulder and turned him around with the pressure of his fingers.

"Stay clear of the battle," he warned, then strode away toward the collapsed north wall of the keep.

Ignoring the stares aimed at him, Darien mounted a ladder to the catwalk at the top of the wall. He paid careful attention to his footing as he worked his way down the narrow ledge; heights had been bothering him ever since his fall.

Royce saw him approaching and turned, a look of concern on his face.

"Look to the east," Darien said. "They'll be coming from Orguleth at dawn." He watched Royce's eyes widen in surprise. It was sooner than they'd been expecting.

"Our plan won't work, then," Royce shouted at his back as Darien was already moving away.

Darien looked back at him. "No, it won't. But I've a better idea."

Kyel watched the Sentinel's black cloak vanish through the door of the hall.

"Smells like trouble," remarked Traver, who had been occupying his time by honing his blade with a small whetstone. He held up the oiled sword, turning it slowly in the dim light. Apparently, he found a place he wasn't quite satisfied with. He lay the blade back down and started going at it again.

A ringing cry echoed from below on the cliffs. Then a volley of fire arrows hissed across the open roof. There was a clatter of boots as the regular soldiers took to the walls, followed by a panicked commotion as the recruits reached for their weapons.

A shout from the doorway returned order to the keep. The men turned to stare at Commander Proctor, who stood with feet apart and hands folded over the pommel of a sword planted blade-down in front of him. He was flanked by his captains. Darien stood next to him, a chain mail tunic gleaming under his cloak.

It was actually happening.

Kyel felt a surge of sudden panic. There was going to be a battle. And, judging by the number of fire arrows that had flared across the sky, it was going to be big.

Kyel glanced over his shoulder at Traver, who stood cradling his sword, his chest rising and falling in shallow, rapid breaths. His eyes were wide, though not in fear, Kyel realized. The look on Traver's face was one of anticipation, perhaps even excitement.

The officers conferred quietly. When Kyel looked up, he saw Darien shake his head in response to a question. Then the group broke apart as the regular soldiers moved out into the crowded hall, making their way through the spaces between clusters of recruits.

Sergeant Ulric wound his way through the hall, pointing out specific individuals and signaling them to follow him. When he came near Kyel's group, his finger waved in the air as he selected only a few of the men around him.

"You, you and…*you.*"

Ulric's bony finger was pointing right at Kyel's chest. Kyel's legs felt weak as he collected his bow and fell in with Ulric's small group of hand-picked archers.

He followed the sergeant toward the front of the hall. When he looked up, he noticed the mage's eyes upon him again. Darien was frowning, obviously displeased. The mage turned and muttered something to Craig, who looked at Kyel and nodded.

"Ulric," the captain called. The sergeant sprinted over to him. The three men conferred quietly for a minute. When Ulric returned, he wore a look of frustration on his face.

"You're coming with us," he told Kyel, as if there

had ever been a doubt. "But you're to stay clear of the fray and keep your head down. Orders from *above.*"

By 'above,' Kyel assumed he meant Darien. He nodded, feeling a little disappointed. It wasn't as though he wanted to go out there and risk his neck, but he also didn't like being singled out. He shifted his gaze to the floor, heat rising to his cheeks.

They stood there for minutes doing nothing as the commotion continued around them in the hall. Then there was another shout from below followed by another fiery round of arrows.

A man whispered beside him, "This one's going to be bloody."

Ulric gathered them up and then gave the order to move out. Kyel followed the other bowmen through the keep's tall door and out into the frigid bleakness of night.

———

Traver was grinning, amazed he'd even been picked. This was going to be big—maybe one for the history books—and he was actually going to have the chance to take part in it. His hand fingered the cold steel of his sword as he waited his turn in the line of recruits waiting to be armored. He could use a stiff drink about now, though the thrill that filled him was practically just as good. Maybe even better.

He was almost glad for his luck; the Front was where he was meant to be. Not running some wretched dye-house back in Covendrey or driving a wagon along a dusty road with the constant reek of horseflesh in his face. The thrill of impending battle was far more intoxicating than any of his frequent binges. His hand quivered on the hilt of his sword, eager with anticipation.

Two soldiers pulled a tunic of quilted armor over him, cinching it tight. A hand clapped him on the back, sending him forward. On his way to the door, someone thrust a pair of gauntlets at him. Another man passed him a breastplate and helped him strap it on.

As he followed the line of foot soldiers across the threshold of the keep, Traver closed his eyes, whispering a soft prayer to the goddess Dreia, his sweet Lady of Luck.

———

Darien pulled back sharply on the gelding's reins, feeling the dark warhorse beneath him quivering, almost as though the animal could sense the coming storm. He looked out over the edge of a steep escarpment, down into the murky shadows of a canyon almost at the base of the Shadowspears.

From that vantage point, he could see the deep ravines and narrow rivulets that fed into the mouth of the pass. Behind him, he could hear the nervous shuffle of the men spread out along the rim of the escarpment, overlooking the canyon below. To his left across a narrow gap, he could see Devlin Craig mounted on his silver warhorse. Craig nodded slightly.

It was the signal he'd been waiting for.

Darien closed his eyes and reached out with his mind. It was no small feat of concentration, summoning the eddies of power that churned at the mouth of the pass. He groped outward, measuring the energy and friction of the wind.

With the will of his mind, he dominated the air currents, doubling the wind back on itself. At the bottom of the canyon, dozens of violent whirlwinds burst upward, churning the black dust of the river bottom and splitting into double-twisters that finally slowed and exhausted themselves against the slopes. The anger of the wind was gradually spent, fading into the stillness of an unearthly calm.

Silence replaced the din of the gale.

Below in the canyon, nothing moved. It was as though the entire motion of the world had frozen in place, the pulse of reality halted to a standstill. The distant trickle of a running stream was the only indication that time still moved forward at all.

Darien glanced back and saw that the ranks of soldiers flanking him were entirely still. The restless stir of armor and weapons had ceased, the men now staring out into the utter quiet that had swallowed the pass.

He raised his hand, spreading his fingers over the crystalline-black calm.

A fog rose in the canyon, spreading out from the river bottom, groping up the black slopes of the surrounding bluffs. The canyon was gradually devoured by swirling gray mists that clung to the rocks, rendering the view of the approaches impossible.

Darien looked for the outline of Devlin Craig,

barely visible through the twisting tendrils of mist. Again, the captain nodded.

The sound of a distant thunder echoed up through the thick layers of fog. It seemed natural at first, like the rumble after a stab of lightning. But the noise was constant, growing. It increased in volume and proximity, swelling to a throbbing roar, escalating until it became clear there was nothing natural about it.

Darien glanced sideways at Craig. The captain was holding his hand in a fist above his head: the signal to hold. Darien could hear the ranks of the Enemy advancing under the cover of fog right below them.

The captain brought his arm down in a slashing motion.

Darien released his hold on the canyon. The fog abated instantly, revealing Enemy ranks spread out like dark waters across the river bottom. There were many more than he had expected. Cold fingers of dread traced upward from the small of his back, stealing down his arms to numb the touch of the reins in his fingers.

The gods had not listened to his prayers.

The advancing army below showed no trace of organization or discipline. But Darien knew better than to be fooled by the muddled appearance of those ranks. Somewhere in the choking desolation of the Black Lands, Chaos had transcended to devise an order of its own.

The ranks of archers behind him released their shafts with a throbbing hum of bowstrings. The first ranks of the Enemy dropped under the rain of gray-fletched arrows.

With a ferocious war cry, the black ranks of soldiers swept forward, storming up the side of the canyon under a hailing barrage of arrows. Armored forms dropped, littering the slope, to be consumed by the relentless flood that came behind, spilling over the lip of the canyon.

Craig drew his sword and spurred his mount forward. Volleys of arrows whistled over his head to drop in a deadly rain. To both sides, horse and infantry engaged with thundering force, pressing the Enemy back down the rise of the escarpment.

Darien grimaced as he saw a company of infantry rush forward, descending the slope in pursuit. He clenched his fist in frustration. The plan had been to hold the top of the slope, where they had the advantage, not follow the retreating Enemy back down into the gorge.

As he gazed out across that deadly sea, Darien felt the tension inside him ease, replaced by a numbing calm. He waited, watching as if through someone else's eyes as Craig ordered his horsemen over the slope to rescue the beleaguered foot soldiers.

The cavalry engaged the Enemy ranks. The sound of the battle resonated up the walls of the canyon, the ringing impacts of steel clanging against steel.

Darien opened his fist, sweeping his arm down to his side. With a cry that shook the air, hundreds of foot soldiers sprinted past him down the slope, feeding the frenzy of the battle. Beneath him, soldiers were flailing, rending, dying, breaking against the shield wall of the Enemy ranks.

He watched in frustration as his own men screamed and fell, their broken carcasses collecting in heaps upon the ground while he sat his horse out of range of the battle.

Darien looked to the north, toward the dark banks of a steep defile where he knew Kyel Archer was stationed. Sensing no threat to that position, he turned his attention back to the fight.

Traver brandished his sword as the first Enemy soldiers came crashing into the Greystone line of running infantry. He could feel his heart flailing wildly, the roar of blood in his ears dampening even the thunder of battle around him. Out of the corner of his eye, he saw the man beside him fall to his knees, a length of steel driven through his chest.

An Enemy swordsman kicked the man backward to free his blade. The eyes of the dying man glared up at Traver from the ground, a blood-washed hand clutching the gaping wound in his chest.

Traver tore his eyes away just in time to dodge a spear that hissed past him. At the same time, a sword slashed down from out of nowhere. He brought his own blade up just in time to block it, almost losing his grip when the jarring impact came.

He tried to recover, tried to get his sword back up as the Enemy blade swept around and came right back at his face. He dropped to the ground and thrust his own weapon up.

He felt the hilt wrenched out of his grasp as the Enemy warrior twisted above him. Something wet and soft splattered over his face. Traver brought his hand up to scoop whatever it was off, smearing it away. Rubbing what felt like slimy mud out of his eyes, he blinked and found himself staring down at the glistening wet ropes of entrails.

———

Devlin Craig wielded his sword like an extension of his arm as he wove through a sea of infantry, swinging his blade in great, hacking arcs. A rain of blood showered in his wake, bathing the flanks of his mount in a red, frothy sheen. Swatting a spear aside with a swipe of his blade, he continued the stroke downward to rip through the armor and bone of an Enemy swordsman.

———

Darien waited, the sounds of screaming horses and dying men assaulting his ears. The Enemy lines regrouped, the fragments of the Greystone troops wheeled and swept before them toward the mouth of the pass.

Darien sent his mind groping outward across the canyon, seizing a narrow wall of rock that sheltered the battlefield from a ravine on the other side. Wrenching the cliff, he watched the rock face tremble and then erupt with violence.

Scores of Greystone soldiers poured out through the gaping rent from the other side, taking up position where the cliff had just been. Archers knelt, firing volleys of arrows into the face of the Enemy charge. Bodies dropped to the canyon floor, showered with gray-fletched shafts.

The bowmen fell to the ground as ranks of cavalry leaped over their heads from the shadows of the ravine. Enemy soldiers turned and fled back toward Craig's charge of armored horse. As Darien watched, the Enemy ranks were cut down, wedged in a vice between two fronts of hurling death.

———

Kyel had been stationed with another bowman in a crevice far above the canyon. The sergeant had ordered him to wait there, keep his head down, and signal if he saw anything moving in the ravine below. But there had been nothing. And even if there had been, Kyel likely wouldn't have noticed.

His eyes were riveted on the clash of battle, watching in horrified fascination as magic and steel combined in a sinister combination that was brutally effective. Outnumbered and outmatched, the Greystone forces seemed to be prevailing against the crumbling Enemy resistance.

He was so fixated on the battle that he didn't notice the files of Enemy soldiers stealing up behind him in silence, far above on the ridge. He wasn't aware of their presence until a booming war cry issued from hundreds of throats.

———

Darien turned in his saddle, taken off guard by the appearance of a company of Enemy reinforcements across the canyon from him. Hundreds of armored men battered their swords against their shields and shook their spears.

Darien's breath caught as he realized Kyel Archer was stationed somewhere up on that slope, exactly in a position to be swept away by the Enemy charge.

Darien reached for the sword he carried strapped to his saddle. Sliding it from its scabbard, he brought the flat of the blade down against the dark hindquarters of his mount. The warhorse broke immediately into a gallop.

In a surge of wired muscle, the black beast gathered itself and took the edge of the escarpment in a powerful leap. The horse shuddered as its forelegs came down on the face of the slope, gaining momentum in long strides, descending the slope into the thick of battle and picking up speed as it went.

Darien raised his sword as the first Enemy soldier came at him.

He swept out with his blade, deflecting a war axe. More soldiers disengaged from the fighting, surging toward him, drawn by the sight of his cloak.

Darien's sword rose to meet them, brushing blades aside and shattering spears as the heavy warhorse pounded through the thick of the fight.

Using the heels of his boots and the flat of his blade, he urged the gelding across the canyon in the direction of the cliffs. The horse took the ford of the river at speed, its flanks glistening as it surged up the slope on the far side.

———

Kyel glanced up at the stream of black-mailed warriors descending upon him. The bowman he'd been stationed with was dead, an arrow embedded in his chest.

Kyel angled his bow upward, sighting down the length of a shaft at the armored bodies spilling down the slope. He loosed his round, nocked another arrow, and drew. He watched the arrow plunk uselessly off a black breastplate. Cursing, he swept his hand back for another.

Something wrenched him backward and up. He didn't know what was happening as a powerful arm encircled his chest and heaved him face-first over the withers of an enormous horse.

Kyel managed to haul his leg over the animal's neck as Darien mounted behind him, kicking the charger forward. The animal broke into a run, struggling to stay ahead of the oncoming Enemy line.

Turning, Kyel saw soldiers breaking away from the front ranks in pursuit. Behind them, archers angled their bows and released their shafts. A cloud of arrows took to the sky, arcing toward them.

The arrows exploded in a shower of sparks that drifted lazily toward the ground. Incredulous, Kyel turned his head enough to gape into the face of the mysterious Sentinel who had just saved his life.

Kyel could see nothing of the kind but troubled man who had tested him in the tower. The eyes that met his were like voids of frigid dispassion. He turned back around, clutching his bow and closing his eyes, and prayed with all his might.

———

Traver looked up into the helm of the Enemy soldier that stood over him, the thought suddenly occurring to him to wonder why he was even there. He didn't know anything about battles or wars, blood and death. His Lady Luck had been with him for a while, her loving hand guiding his steel.

But now his luck had just run out.

He watched helplessly from the ground as the blade above him started its fall.

———

Kyel knew they were going to die.

The thought didn't scare him all that much. It mostly made him sad. He tried to think of Amelia but couldn't summon her image to mind. The only thing he could see was the end of the ridge in front of them and the cliff that dropped off sharply over a bend in the ravine.

Darien pulled back on the reins, jerking his horse's head around. The gelding's legs almost slid out from under it as the animal skidded sideways.

The Sentinel raised his blade, holding it swept back at a threatening angle as he turned the horse directly into the face of the Enemy charge.

It would be only a matter of seconds, now. Kyel closed his eyes but could not close his ears. The thunder of the oncoming charge swelled, became deafening.

The horse beneath him wheeled and broke toward the edge of the cliff, nearly throwing him off. Kyel felt the destrier gather the last of its strength and kick off with its hind legs, propelling them over the edge, throwing its full weight forward into the air.

Then they were falling.

His scream was cut short as the warhorse landed in the middle of the air, staggered, then gathered itself and surged forward, stumbling ahead. Incredulous, Kyel glanced down at a bridge of solid shadow that had been melded beneath them, arching across the gap of the chasm.

The horse leaped off the end of that dark, impossible span, coming down hard on solid ground and turning as it drew up.

Behind them, the bridge seemed to melt away, the shadows draining back into the dark recesses of the gap.

The Enemy force halted on the other side of the chasm, bellowing their rage across the cliffs, shaking spears and rattling shields. A few archers loosed their shafts, which simply slowed to a stop in midair and dropped, falling straight down.

An abrupt silence filled the gorge.

Kyel frowned, wondering why the Enemy force had suddenly stopped moving. He turned, looking behind them. He opened his mouth to gasp.

Just as he did, the air was sucked right out of his lungs as a gale of wind swept past them with a shrieking hiss, plastering his shirt against his back.

For seconds, he couldn't breathe. The scream of the wind was the eeriest sound he'd ever heard in his life.

And then the world exploded.

Kyel threw himself from the horse as the air turned to fire. He covered his face with his hands as a vast firestorm crackled by overhead, spreading quickly over the rim of the gorge. He held his breath against the roiling inferno. But then he let it out slowly when he realized the flames produced no heat.

The firestorm swept across the gorge toward the ranks of the Enemy. The lines broke in chaos, collapsing in disorganized retreat. The wall of fire paused, then gushed down the cliff into the canyon below, sweeping toward the main host.

Kyel couldn't believe he was still alive. Glancing up, he saw Darien still mounted on the back of the dark warhorse, face frozen in a look of dangerous intensity.

———

Traver watched helplessly as the Enemy blade started its fall, mesmerized by the black steel that hissed toward his chest.

The sword never impacted.

Another blade swept up to meet it, turning aside the stroke that should have killed him. Traver rolled away as a red-bearded swordsman stepped in front of him, driving the Enemy soldier back in a barrage of furious blows.

Traver's ears rang from the fury of the attack. The bearded swordsman feinted low then cut upward. As the dark blade fell to the earth, the Greystone swordsman cleaved his opponent's head off.

Traver looked away from the ghastly head that had somehow managed to stay helmed. He took a step back, turning to stare wide-eyed into the face of the man who had saved him. It was one of the farmers who had arrived with the mage. Corban Henley was his name.

But he didn't have time to thank the man. Henley was already moving away, cutting a path back into the thick of the battle.

Traver looked at the slope ahead, and his mouth dropped open.

Hurling toward them was a fresh charge of Enemy reinforcements. Behind them swept a colossal firestorm driven by vicious winds of its own creation.

Traver closed his mouth, picked up his sword, and ran like hell the other way.

———

Devlin Craig pumped his straining horse with his spurs as he stole a glance back over his shoulder. What he saw was pure insanity. Enemy soldiers were fleeing an onrushing wall of flame, trampling the bodies of the fallen.

In the other direction, the Greystone ranks had reformed in a solid line along the edge of the canyon's wall. What was left couldn't possibly withstand the charging horde hurling toward them.

But then Craig glanced upward at the rim of the canyon. As he did, he almost lost his grip on the reins. There, lining the tops of the cliffs, were row upon row of foot soldiers and heavy horse, companies of bowmen and pikes. Banners rippled, even though there was no movement of air to stir them.

The charging Enemy soldiers saw it too. As one, the entire host wheeled, retreating toward the mouth of the pass. Greystone soldiers rallied as if in pursuit, screaming battle cries and shaking their weapons.

Before Craig's disbelieving eyes, the soldiers on the cliff walls seemed to ripple as one, flickered, then disappeared. His ears filled with ringing cries of victory.

Craig drew his horse up, glancing behind to see the firestorm swirling upward and collapsing in on itself, imploding into a brilliant ball high above the canyon.

In all his long years in the pass, that shining globe of fire was the closest thing to a sun Devlin Craig had ever seen.

For just a moment, the entire pass was lit as if it were high noon. Then the ball of fire exploded, showering the canyon with trails of sparks.

The cries of victory swelled, became a thunderous din.

Chapter Twelve
Grim Sense of Duty

Pass of Lor-Gamorth, The Front

Darien pressed his hand against the sweat-encrusted hair of his horse's neck, closing his eyes. He felt a shiver pass through the animal. The gelding staggered slightly then lowered itself to the ground, neck outstretched on the rocks as it lay down on its side. The black horse closed its eyes and nickered softly.

Kyel stared down at the animal with eyes full of concern. "Can't you heal it?" he asked.

"I already did." Darien lowered himself down beside the beast, running his hand over its wet and heaving side. "Now it only needs sleep to recover its strength."

Kyel nodded. Then his eyes widened. Reaching down, the young man fingered the torn black cloth of Darien's shirt, folding it back to expose a nasty-looking gash that had opened the top of his arm just below where the protective chains of ring mail ended.

"You're wounded," he gasped.

But Darien had already mended the injury before Kyel finished speaking. He stood up, trying not to look at the expression of wonder on the younger man's face. It made him feel uncomfortable.

Turning away, he started walking toward the bottom of the ravine, following the line of a dry stream bed back in the direction of the canyon. He could hear Kyel following him, the sound of his footsteps almost tentative.

"Where are you going?"

Darien didn't look back as he shrugged. He was too tired. The weight of the mail dragged at his shoulders. It was the same as it was with the horse. He could heal almost any injury with scarcely a thought. But there was nothing he could do to rid himself of the ache of exhaustion he felt down to his bones.

It was not just the battle that had taken the strength out of him. What he'd done that morning with his ability vastly outweighed any physical exhaustion he felt. As far as he knew, no mage in history had ever summoned the amount of raw power he had handled that morning without the aid of a Circle of Convergence. But it had taken its toll. As Darien trudged stiffly toward the canyon, he had to fight at each step just to stay on his feet.

Kyel must have noticed.

"We should rest a moment," he suggested.

But Darien forced himself to keep moving. He didn't have time to stop and rest. Not when he knew there were men up ahead dying.

Darien dreaded what waited for him in the canyon. It had always been the duty of the Sentinels after a battle to heal the injured. His duty, now.

He was not looking forward to it. It was hard enough, raising his hand and giving the order to send hundreds of men into battle. It would be much harder, looking into the eyes of those who had died by his command.

Darien remembered a time when he was a boy, when his father had come back from the Front and had stopped for a while in Amberlie to visit his sons before heading up the mountain. Darien remembered that visit well. His father had looked particularly haggard, and there had been a haunted look in his eyes. He had spoken of a battle, and of his grim duty afterward.

When his father had left, Darien remembered crying. Gerald Lauchlin had always been his hero. Darien had thought there was nothing that confident man couldn't handle with his usual, carefree tenacity. But his father had changed after that day. The shadows had never left his eyes. It was as though he'd taken a deep wound that all of his great strength could never heal.

Darien forced his feet to keep moving toward the mouth of the ravine. He tried not to think about what awaited him ahead. But at least he knew he didn't have to worry about his own eyes changing, shadowing, taking on the same haunted and battle-weary expression of his father.

He knew they already had.

He could see it in the face of every man that had the courage to meet his gaze. Even Craig and Royce, even Proctor. Even the young man following him now.

At last, they reached the place where the dry stream bed emptied into the canyon. There, Darien stopped, staring out across the carnage of the battlefield with growing dismay.

"Mother of the gods," Kyel whispered beside him.

Darien could only silently agree. He swept his gaze across the canyon floor, taking in the shocking sight of thousands of wasted human lives, literally piles of men fallen over each other, still limbs bent over fallen comrades, fingers limp and unmoving. Thin streams of blood flowed out from the heaps of Greystone corpses, running across the black soil in red rivers to mix with the blood of the Enemy.

He raised his right hand, staring down in contempt at the coldly glinting chain on his wrist. The piles of corpses were his fault. If it wasn't for his Oath, none of this would have happened. The fire he'd created could have burned hot more easily than cold. He could have immolated the Enemy ranks with a thought, melding flesh together with bone in a holocaust of will.

That was what Orien Oathbreaker had done. His one terrible act had driven the forces of the Enemy back into the Black Lands for over a hundred years. But Orien had also died a traitor's death, kneeling in shame to accept his punishment. Darien had always wondered why the man had surrendered himself so easily.

Now he understood. An Unbound mage was an abomination. That despised chain on his wrist was the only thing keeping him in check, saving him from himself. Corruption of the flesh was inevitable, a predestined fate meted out at the birth of every life. What Darien feared most was the corruption of his soul.

Sometimes, he could feel it already starting, an outgrowth of the vast amount of power he'd been forced to take in. The temptation to strip off that chain was growing harder to deny each day.

Especially now.

The sounds of the injured and dying accosted his ears. He forced himself to start forward, eyes scanning through the carnage for signs of movement, any trace of life. He quickly found an unconscious man with a gaping wound in his chest.

Bending over him, Darien placed his hand over the soldier's wound and closed his eyes. His head throbbed as he forced himself to grope through fatigue that was already almost unbearable. When Darien stood, he left behind a man slumbering in peaceful sleep, oblivious to the fact he had been scant moments from death.

Darien moved through piles of littered corpses, healing wounded as he went, working his way along the canyon wall while Kyel followed, trailing behind with his bow. The young man's expression was a mixture of horror, awe, and outright pity. Darien found himself consciously avoiding Kyel's gaze. He knew the pity was for himself, and he couldn't stand it. Shoulders shaking, he pushed himself up from the body of a man who his failing strength hadn't been able to save.

"Stop," Kyel begged. "You're exhausted. You need rest."

Darien shook his head, kneeling beside a man who lay groaning in agony, clutching his own dismembered arm as a steady pulse of blood pumped from the stump above his elbow.

There was nothing Darien could do about the arm. He willed the man into unconsciousness, his fingers gently loosening the soldier's grip on the gruesome appendage and casting it aside. He had to squeeze his eyes shut against the pain in his head as he staunched the flow of blood coming from the stump, forcing the flesh to fold and knit together over the white fragments of bone.

As he stood back up, a wave of dizziness made him stagger. He brought his hands up to his face, covering his eyes as he groped for balance. Kyel's hand caught his arm to steady him, an expression of concern clouding his face.

"Look." Kyel's voice was no longer pleading. "You can't keep this up. You can hardly stand on your feet."

Darien shrugged away from him. He could hear Kyel muttering under his breath, but he didn't care. He stumbled forward over torn limbs and shattered bodies, picking his way toward a motion on his left.

But as he knelt beside a dying soldier, he realized he'd made a mistake. He was staring down at the black helm of an Enemy swordsman. Darien started to push himself up, using his hand to wrench his weight off the ground.

As he did, a gloved hand snaked out and caught his arm, holding him down with an ironclad grip. He heard a low voice rattle in their vile tongue:

"We thought you dead, Battlemage. She'll be coming for you."

Darien ripped his arm away, staggering backward.

He could hear the man choking as he died. At least, it sounded like choking. Darien realized the soldier's death rattle was actually gurgling laughter. He could only stare in shock as the last breath wheezed from the gaping hole in the warrior's chest. After that, the man moved no more.

But that terrible laughter echoed on in his mind, along with the whispered promise: *She'll be coming for you.* He had no idea who *she* was, but the word sent a lance of dread stabbing through his heart.

He thought of the strange tides of the magic field, of the way the flows swirled and ebbed in ways completely different from normal. He thought of the map on the wall of Proctor's quarters, of his finger tapping the arrow that pointed toward the upper-right. The letters beneath the arrow that spelled out the words: *To Bryn Calazar.*

He thought of the gateway. What dark terrors had his brother unleashed? Closing his eyes, Darien drew in a trembling breath. There was only one kind of terror he could think of that went by the feminine pronoun 'she.' The mere thought was repulsive. Only, there was no other possible explanation.

Aidan had summoned the powers of the Netherworld to wield a deathblow to Aerysius. It made a terrifying kind of sense that his act had also liberated the Eight Servants of Xerys. And if either Myria Anassis or Arden Hannah were bending the lines of the magic field around Bryn Calazar, then he knew his life might very well be in grave danger.

The Eight had no chains on their wrists to Bind them, no Oath sworn to uphold. Only a dark compact with the Lord of Chaos. And if they were now aware of his presence, then the dead swordsman was probably right. *She* would be coming for him.

But there was nothing he could do about it.

Darien turned his back on the corpse and, stepping over the body of a decapitated bowman, looked for someone else, anyone else, whose life needed saving. He staggered forward, dropping down beside another man and forcing a flood of healing energy into his shattered frame. Then he went on to another, and another, until his head throbbed with the beat of every pulse and his vision blurred until he couldn't see.

Kyel Archer stumbled along beside him, holding him up and begging him to stop and rest. But his pleas fell on deaf ears. Darien forced himself to keep moving, keep healing, working across the canyon through jumbled piles of savaged bodies until he finally collapsed across the corpse of a Greystone soldier, overcome by sheer exhaustion.

That was how Devlin Craig found him.

Swearing an oath, the captain threw himself off his mount and trampled over the corpses of fallen comrades until he reached the young bowman who had flagged him down.

Dropping to his side, Craig glared his anger at him as he reached out and rolled Darien's unconscious body off the legs of a grisly cadaver. Craig pressed his ear against the mage's chest. Satisfied that his heart was still beating, he lashed out in anger at the boy.

"Why didn't you stop him?"

The young bowman opened his mouth, shaking his head. "I tried..."

Craig growled, heaving Darien's weight into his arms. He left the bowman there to fend for himself and heaved Darien over the back of his horse, swinging up behind him.

Kicking the stallion forward, he headed back up

the pass toward Greystone Keep. He was angry. Angry at Proctor for underestimating the strength of the Enemy. Angry at Darien for insisting on holding to an Oath that was going to get him killed. And angry at himself for ever riding away from his side.

———

Sutton Royce was furious.

"What were you *thinking,* leaving him alone?"

Craig hung his head. "I suppose I wasn't."

"You're damned right, you weren't!" Royce paced away, slapping a pair of black leather gloves against the palm of his hand with a shocking *crack*. He took a deep breath, striving for composure.

"Tell me again about the boy." It was the first time Proctor had spoken since the conversation began.

"His name is Kyel Archer. I don't know much about him, other than he picked up the bow incredibly quick. Darien asked me to position him away from the fight."

"Has he returned yet?"

"No." Craig shook his head. The last he'd seen of Archer, he'd been standing in a heap of stiffening corpses looking completely petrified.

"Send a rider down to fetch him."

As he strode out of the room to comply, Craig chanced a glance at the pallet where Darien lay sleeping. There had been no marks on his body; Craig had checked him over for wounds. But other than the rise and fall of his chest, the man hadn't stirred in hours.

He relayed Proctor's order to a sentry then returned to the command chamber. When he entered the room, he found Proctor and Royce bending over one of the maps on the table.

"These same tactics aren't going to work for us again," Royce was saying. "The Enemy wasn't expecting a Sentinel, and even when they found out, they didn't know for sure whether or not he was Bound. But next time they'll know for certain. They'll see right through Darien's illusions."

Proctor nodded thoughtfully. His face looked more haggard than usual. Craig couldn't blame him; it had been a long day for them all.

"I must speak with this Archer," Proctor said. "If I'm right, then he is the key." His eyes looked suddenly hardened, as though he'd all along been battling some internal struggle that had finally, brutally, been resolved. It must have been a tough one. Proctor's face had gone almost gray.

"What do you mean?" Royce probed with a frown.

Proctor looked up to meet his captain's gaze, but he hesitated before speaking. "I can think of only one reason for Darien's interest in this Kyel Archer. The boy must have the potential. It is the sole explanation that fits."

Craig's mouth fell open. *Of course.*

The commander went on in a voice devoid of emotion, "Darien won't survive another battle. He's too impotent with those chains on his wrists, and he's too damn obstinate to keep out of harm's way. Have no doubt—we *will* lose him.

"Which leaves us with only one question that we must answer for ourselves: is there any way we can somehow turn this situation to our advantage?

"This is the way I see it." His eyes shifted to Craig, his stare hardening even more. "If we are going to lose one mage because he refuses to forswear his Oath, then the gods may have just delivered us another not so Bound. Perhaps we should expedite the opportunity."

Craig stared at him long and hard. Then he turned and left the room, his vision darkened by anger. He'd known Garret Proctor nearly his entire adult life. Craig had never had a problem with Proctor's cruel strategies—when they were directed against the Enemy.

He'd just never thought to see them employed against a friend.

Proctor still had Craig's loyalty; he owed him that much. But the man had just lost every last shard of Devlin Craig's respect.

———

Kyel saw two horses coming toward him down a steep embankment. There was only one rider on a brown horse, holding the reins of a chestnut mare that ran beside him. Kyel expected the man to gallop right by and was surprised when both horses drew up, the helmed soldier dropping down to the ground next to him. Lifting his visor, the man looked at Kyel sidelong, passing his eyes over him as if confused about something.

"Kyel Archer?" The words carried a heavy undercurrent of doubt.

Kyel nodded, wondering how the man could possibly know his name. But then it dawned on him. *Of course. Lauchlin.* The mage seemed to be taking no chances with his new acolyte. If that's truly what he was. Kyel had never been given the opportunity to turn him down.

"I have orders to fetch you back to the keep." The soldier's eyes were skeptical. "The force commander wants a word with you."

Kyel's brow furrowed. *Proctor?* That was peculiar. A cold prickle of doubt itched his skin. He climbed up on the spare horse as the soldier threw him the reins. He hung his bow over his shoulder and followed the man up the narrow trail.

When they reached the steps of the keep, Kyel passed the reins back and jumped down. He didn't know where they kept the horses. He hadn't seen a stable. But, then, he also hadn't seen but a small fraction of the men gathered in the pass that morning. Their numbers had come as a shock, albeit a good one. Kyel suspected there were camps spread throughout the Pass of Lor-Gamorth.

At least, there *had* been. He wondered just how many could possibly be left. The piles of corpses he had wandered through following Darien on his grisly undertaking made Kyel fear their forces had been decimated.

Entering the keep, Kyel wasn't sure at first where to go. He decided to just follow orders and head up the tower on his own.

As he passed by the hall door, he ran into the intimidating form of Devlin Craig. The man's eyes were even more hostile than Kyel remembered. The captain glared at him with an expression of distaste, his mouth curled in a snarl.

Kyel couldn't quell the growing feeling of trepidation swelling in his chest. Something had changed, and he didn't like it at all. He had the feeling something had gone terribly wrong. As his feet approached the opening to the tower room, Kyel found himself holding his breath. He didn't know what he was going to find up there, but he didn't think he was going to like it.

He stepped over the threshold into the barren, circular chamber and paused. He felt Proctor's eyes fall on him: that hardened, ruthless gaze that unnerved him completely. Kyel did his best not to waver under the weight of that stare.

The commander said, "You are to stand down from future battles. Your place is now here. Return your bow to the armory and collect your things."

Kyel's eyes drifted to his bow, the golden wood he had become so comfortable with. Since his first night in the fortress, that bow had never left his side. He didn't want to give it back. And he didn't want to leave his fellows. Most of all, he didn't want to spend his days as the constant companion of the daunting old warrior who stood glaring at him.

"No. Please, no. I mean—what I mean is…" Kyel forced himself to take a deep breath. "Please, no, Force Commander. With all due respect."

He stood trembling as the man circled him slowly like a hawk, hands clasped behind his back, gray cloak swaying in his wake. As the target of that predator-like stare, Kyel felt exceptionally like a mouse hiding in an open field, waiting for the raptor to descend.

His eyes fell on a black, narrow hilt protruding from the belt at the commander's waist. He'd never noticed it before, but the knife looked viciously intimidating, even more so than the sword at the man's side.

"Your place is now here." Proctor's tone brooked no argument.

"Please, Force Commander. Just let me keep my bow." Now, why had he said that? The stick at his side was the least of his worries. Maybe what he wanted was a weapon to defend himself against the man.

He glanced to where Darien lay by the hearth, his face more peaceful than Kyel had ever seen it. He would not be stirring for a while, Kyel thought, remembering the exhausted black warhorse they had left behind in the canyon.

"You're an acolyte mage," Proctor said. "What use have you for a weapon?"

The man knew.

Kyel felt drenched in cold, petrifying fear. He groped deep down inside, desperately trying to summon the last scrap of courage he could find. He still wanted to keep that bow.

"What use has Darien for his sword?" Kyel challenged, then quickly added, "Force Commander."

The harsh angles of Proctor's face softened just a

bit. To Kyel, those stern blue eyes seemed to be almost smiling. A grim, satisfied smile that was more ominous than the man's outright glare.

"Keep the bow, then," he said softly, and strode past Kyel in the direction of the stairs.

"Wait," Kyel called after him.

Proctor stopped, turning slowly around.

"Tell me one thing," Kyel said. "Who are they? The Enemy?"

The force commander stared at him for a long moment without moving. Eventually, he said, "They were once the people of Caladorn. But they're not people anymore. They dwell in darkness and worship Xerys. For the last thousand years, they've made it their purpose to threaten us. To invade us. To destroy us. In the end, it doesn't matter who they are.

"That's why we just call them the Enemy. Because knowing what they call themselves isn't going to help us fight this war. We don't need to know anything about them. We just need to kill them."

With that, he turned and stalked down the stairs.

Chapter Thirteen
Two Vows

Pass of Lor-Gamorth, The Front

Kyel sat on a boulder protruding from an outcrop overlooking the Pass of Lor-Gamorth from the rear of the fortress. He'd wondered why no one had ever bothered to rebuild the keep's crumbled rear wall. Now he knew. There was nothing behind the structure but a small rock scarp and the sheer drop of a cliff. The mountainside was more of a defense than the rear wall of the keep had ever been. Incursion was impossible from that approach.

Kyel found it a good place to escape the stark chamber of Proctor's quarters. He didn't like being left alone with the force commander. Proctor reminded Kyel of a cleverly brilliant chess master who was ingenious enough to think six moves in advance, yet ruthless enough to sacrifice any given piece to gain an advantage. His eyes had taken on an emptiness just as barren as his chamber.

The sound of movement below startled Kyel from his thoughts. His hand dove for his bow, but he didn't nock an arrow to the string. The sentries were fewer in number, now, strung out at greater intervals along the length of the pass. But their eyes were now sharper than ever. No Enemy soldier could make it so far as the steps beneath Greystone Keep.

And he was right. The man who approached from below was no enemy. He might even be the only friend Kyel had left.

"It's a good view," Darien said, turning to glance over the lip of the outcrop. He didn't look like himself at all, wearing regular clothes, his hair falling in loose waves over his shoulders.

To Kyel, the different apparel seemed a drastic change. Darien looked shockingly less severe, shockingly *normal.* Even the chains on his wrists seemed to lose their emphasis.

He turned back toward Kyel, a smile on his face as he gestured at the boulder. "I see you found my rock."

"Your rock?" Kyel raised his eyebrows.

Darien nodded as he sat, bringing a knee up to his chest and leaning back. Kyel had to admit, he did look comfortable there.

"I come here often. It's a good place to sit, to think, if you've a mind to be alone."

Kyel winced. That was exactly what he'd been doing, though he didn't want to admit it.

"Have you given any more thought to my offer?" Darien asked.

Kyel opened his mouth but then closed it again, not knowing what to say. Other than his move to the top of the keep, there had been no mention of the test Darien had given him so many days ago. In fact, he hadn't brought it up once, not until now. Kyel had been starting to wonder if maybe the Sentinel had forgotten all about it.

Kyel shrugged. "I've been trying not to."

Darien seemed to accept his answer. He brought his hand up to the side of his face, stroking the stubble on his cheek as his eyes grew distant in thought. He sat there for a moment in silence as a breath of wind stirred his hair.

Summoning his courage, Kyel asked, "How was it for you when you became an acolyte?"

Darien's gaze remained inward as he replied, "It was different for me. Both my parents were mages.

Aerysius was in my blood. When I passed Consideration, it came as no shock."

Kyel nodded. "What was it like, growing up there?"

"I've no idea," Darien replied. "I wasn't raised there. I lived my entire childhood in the Vale. My brother and I were fostered out to a widow who lived down the mountain in Amberlie."

To Kyel, that seemed strange. From what he knew from his father, it was not uncommon for mages to have families, even large ones.

As if sensing his question, Darien explained, "My father was a Sentinel, so he wasn't around much to raise us. And my mother was elected Prime Warden shortly after I was born, so she never had the time."

Kyel's eyes widened. Throughout history, the Prime Wardens of Aerysius had always been the highest authority in the Rhen. Even kings and queens knelt at their feet, though to the rest of the world they remained somewhat a mystery.

In an attempt to lighten the mood, Kyel asked, "So you've a brother?"

The sudden change that came over Darien's face was not what Kyel had been expecting. In the second before he averted his eyes, Kyel got a glimpse of the same, haunting shadows he had seen the night Darien had tested him. *Of course,* he thought stupidly. Darien's brother was doubtlessly dead, killed in the tragedy that had befallen Aerysius.

"I'm sorry," Kyel said. "I ought to have thought."

Darien bowed his head, dark strands of hair falling forward to shroud his face. In a tone as dead as the heritage of his home, he explained, "It was my brother Aidan who opened the Well of Tears."

Kyel could only stare straight ahead, struck utterly speechless. Now he knew the impetus that fueled the storm that raged behind the Sentinel's eyes. Darien had lost everything he'd ever known and ever loved, all at the hands of his own brother. What could anyone say to that?

He whispered, "What are you going to do?"

Darien looked up, the expression on his face so intense that Kyel drew back involuntarily. He answered quietly, "I'm going to kill him."

Kyel stared at him hard for a minute. "What about your Oath?"

Darien just shrugged. An awkward silence followed. Then, from out of nowhere, he managed a smile. "Want to go for a ride?"

The suggestion had come from out of nowhere, and Kyel had no idea what Darien's purpose might be. He was getting the impression he might know the Sentinel for a hundred years and still never understand the man.

"That sounds good," he agreed.

Darien's smile reassured him. For once, even the shadows seemed gone from his eyes.

Kyel waited at the steps of the keep while Darien went off to make arrangements. When the mage returned, Kyel was dismayed to see he was once again wearing his cloak and had strung the harness of his sword over it. He found himself feeling a little disappointed. He'd enjoyed the scant moments he'd spent with Darien dressed in the clothes of a normal man. The cloak had a power of its own, and Kyel found it distancing.

They walked together down to a paddock hidden in a bottleneck canyon below the keep and selected their mounts under the watchful eyes of the sentries. Kyel chose a light riding horse, unlike the black beast that trotted up to Darien when he slipped through the fence.

The last time he'd seen the charger, the animal had been stretched out in the ravine, looking little better off than dead. But when Darien had the gelding saddled and swung himself over its back, the horse picked its legs up smartly and tossed its head, making immediately for the gate without any prompting from its rider. Kyel mounted his own horse and followed after.

The path they travelled wound around the mountainside, following the curve of the slope. After about two leagues, the trail narrowed and then disappeared. Looking back, Kyel could barely make out the tower of Greystone Keep, a shadowy silhouette against the pale flickers of light in the clouds. The wind was starting to pick up. He pulled his cloak more tightly about himself.

They rode up into a narrow ravine between two great legs of the mountain. The farther they went, the deeper the shadows settled around them. Kyel found himself growing a little unsettled by the intense quiet of the place.

Darien brought his horse to a stop and glanced up to inspect the ridges surrounding them. At last, seeming satisfied, he let his mount move slowly forward.

Kyel didn't like this place. He was starting to wonder why Darien had brought him there. Then a sudden, horrible feeling swept over him, like a terrible shiver of dread.

Kyel jerked back on the reins, eyes widening. He felt the skin on the back of his neck prickle. The feeling was like nothing he had ever experienced. It was as though something important had just been yanked away, as if a necessary and significant part of the world had been suddenly withdrawn. Only, he had no idea what had happened.

"You feel it," Darien said.

"Aye, I feel it. It's vile."

Kyel rubbed his arms, trying to scrub away the disturbing feeling. Darien didn't appear to be affected by the sensation. His gaze turned back to trace the folds of the mountain slopes. Without looking at him, he said flatly:

"Most men can't." He brought his hand up in a sweeping gesture, indicating the area around them. "This is a node. It's a place where the lines of the magic field come together in parallel direction but opposite in energy and cancel out. What you're feeling is the complete absence of the magic field in this place."

Kyel felt horrified as the impact of the mage's words sank in. "So, you're saying I've always been able to feel it, and this is what it's like when it's gone?"

Darien nodded. Kyel shivered; he didn't like it here and wanted to go back. But Darien urged his horse forward with the pressure of his legs, taking them deeper into the node. The feeling of dread intensified.

"You knew this was here," Kyel accused. "That's the reason why you brought me. You wanted me to feel this place." Suddenly, a new thought occurred to him, and the sensation of dread in his stomach took a nauseating, downward plunge. "You're powerless here."

Again Darien nodded, gaze sweeping upward to examine the slopes of the canyon. When he turned back, there was a small, sad smile on his face. "Like any other man."

Kyel reached for the comfort of his bow, caressing the soft wood. How could the mage just sit there on his horse, gripped in the terrible absence of the magic field, knowing how dangerous it was for him to even be in this place? But then he realized Darien was by no means as easy about it as he seemed. His gaze kept shifting back to the rocks as if scouring them. The shadows had once again returned to haunt his eyes.

"I want to go," Kyel urged. "This place is…foul."

Darien looked as though he agreed. Bringing his mount around, he turned it back in the direction they had come. As they started downward again, Kyel asked, "Why did you bring me here?"

"I think you know the answer. Consider it your first lesson."

Kyel had figured that. The mage had wanted him to get a taste of what he truly was. He'd never even known that he could sense the presence of the magic field, not until it had been utterly withdrawn. As they moved out from under the influence of the node, Kyel breathed a sigh of relief. The world felt abruptly…normal.

But now that he knew what it was and what it felt like, he could suddenly sense the magic field stirring, flowing around him like the currents of a river. There was nothing strange or foreign about the sensation. It was something he'd always known, all throughout his entire life. He had just simply never recognized it.

Darien stopped his horse and dismounted on the other side of the boundary. Kyel followed suit, letting his mount move away from him with its head to the ground, foraging for grass in the barren dirt. He followed as Darien wandered back in the direction of the node, then stood with his hand out, indicating that he wanted Kyel to walk back through the boundary one more time.

He didn't want to. But he did.

Again, Kyel felt that dreadful sensation of loss, as though part of the world had suddenly faded completely. This time, he was prepared for it, and the transition was not quite so shocking. It was as though there had been a quiet cadence in his mind, and now that rhythm was lost.

As he reemerged, he could feel the pulse coming back.

"Do you still deny your ability?"

Kyel cast a dispirited glance at the mage, wishing that he could. "No."

Darien had made his point all too well.

The Sentinel nodded, his expression enigmatic. He walked away a few paces toward the crest of the hill. His cloak played out behind him in the breeze as he stood gazing down at the pass, a black silhouette against the flickering sky.

Kyel found himself staring at the mage's profile, wondering if it would ever be possible for himself to cast such a similar, imposing portrait. He was a merchant by trade, a woodworker by choice, and now he was an archer in truth and not just in name. Where a mage's craft fit into that picture, Kyel could not begin to guess.

"I need an answer, Kyel."

Kyel rubbed his brow. He already knew what his answer was going to be, but it was not going to be easy, bringing that decision into reality by giving it a voice.

Darien was looking at him. Waiting.

He lowered his eyes. "All right, then. Yes."

Kyel kept his gaze lowered as he heard Darien's footsteps approaching. He was trembling, the bow in his hand quivering in his grip. The approaching footsteps stopped before him, and Kyel at last found the courage to look up.

"I need you to know what you're committing yourself to," Darien said. "You need to be certain of this decision. Your heart must be entirely in this, or I'm wasting my time."

Kyel found himself wanting more than anything to reject the man's offer. But he knew that was impossible. He had never been able to deny someone in need, and he couldn't think of another time in his life when he'd ever been needed more. He couldn't bring himself to look into Darien's eyes and tell the man no.

"I'm certain."

"Kyel." The way the Sentinel said his name made him shiver even harder. Holding his gaze firmly, Darien warned him, "You will not find me an easy master. There is a saying at the School of Arms in Auberdale I learned a long time ago: 'What hurts, teaches.' I find that applies to most lessons in life."

It was no more than Kyel had expected. His father had told him of the harsh burdens and constraints placed upon new acolytes. He didn't know if he would be up to Darien's demands, but he did know that he had it within himself to try.

"I understand," he said, forcing himself to look into the Sentinel's eyes.

Darien said, "I'm going to ask you to repeat the vow every acolyte of Aerysius swore before they were accepted into the Hall of the Watchers. The Hall doesn't exist anymore, but its ways are all I know."

When Kyel said nothing, Darien grasped his left wrist. His grip was firm, almost painful. Kyel could feel the circulation in his hand compromised by the pressure of it. As if in a dream, he found himself repeating every word the mage uttered, his lips moving slowly to form the syllables as their grim significance imprinted itself on his mind:

> *"I swear to exist only to serve the land and its people.*
> *With my life, if possible. If not, then by death."*

When he was finished, Darien removed his fingers from Kyel's wrist. Instantly, Kyel felt a flood of warmth moving back into his hand as the blood flow returned to it. He raised his arm, half expecting to find a red welt there from the pressure of the man's strong fingers.

But instead of a welt, Kyel found a glistening, metallic chain engraved into the flesh of his left wrist. He stared down at the ancient symbol, terrified by its implications.

Chapter Fourteen
Friends and Enemies

Pass of Lor-Gamorth, The Front

A shout from below woke Darien from sleep. He shot up out of his blankets and scooped up his sword. Taking the steps two at a time, he rushed down to the keep's main hall, where he found the men gathered around an injured scout who had been laid out on the floor. The man's chest was heaving for breath, his blood quickly spreading across the wood slats.

"The Enemy," he gasped. "Tens of thousands…"

Kyel flinched at the sound of Garret Proctor's fist smashing down on the oak table, jolting the entire piece of wood. But it was Sutton Royce who took up his argument for him, striding forward and raging into Darien's face:

"You have no choice!"

Darien glared back at him, fists clenched in rage. He growled at Royce, "What gives you the right—"

Proctor interrupted him. "He doesn't have the right. But I do."

Kyel had always thought the force commander was an imposing man with a daunting presence. But at the moment, he looked positively dangerous. The side of his face twitched as he rounded on Darien, lashing out at him in scathing tones, "Whatever else you might be, while you remain at my keep, you are subject to my authority."

"You have no authority over me," the Sentinel contradicted him coldly.

"You better believe I do."

Proctor glowered at him dangerously. "If I decide right now to have you dragged out to the yard and thrashed, there's not a damned thing you could do about it. Unless it's your intention to abuse your precious Oath?"

Darien stood regarding him silently for a moment then turned, stalking in the direction of the stairs. "Come, Kyel."

Kyel gathered his bow and shouldered his pack, then crossed the room to take his place at Darien's side.

Before Darien had a chance to take one step, Devlin Craig called out to stop him. "We number less than a thousand men!"

Darien glared back at him. "And I'm only *one man.* No one seems to understand that. Even if I did break my Oath, what do you expect me to do against *tens of thousands?"* To Proctor, he added, "You need an army, not a mage. Whatever happened to those birds you sent to Auberdale?"

The force commander's eyes narrowed even more than they already were. "Faukravar sends his regards, but regrets he has no men to spare us at this time."

"You're the only hope we have," Craig implored.

Darien hesitated only a moment. "Then there is no hope."

Darien's words still echoed in his ears as Kyel followed the Sentinel down the steps to the bottom of the tower. His emotions were so jumbled and confused that he didn't know which one dominated. He thought, perhaps, it was fear. He knew it ought to be.

Catching up to Darien, he asked, "Where are we going?"

Darien gestured with a nod of his head, off in the

direction of the slopes below the keep. "The last place they'll think to look for us: the node. Royce is a good tracker, but I should have a few hours of peace to sort this out." He took a deep breath. "Round up some supplies. I'll fetch the horses."

Kyel moved to comply, wishing that Darien would have picked any other place in the whole world.

Royce stood atop the battlements of Greystone's tower, stood atop the battlements of Greystone's tower, eyes tracking the two horses heading away from the keep, following the narrow trail that led to the river bottom. He kept his stare fixed on the black warhorse that walked in front, until it finally disappeared into the shadow of a ridge. He let his gaze drift heavenward. Above, thick clouds drifted across the sky, heavy with rain and sagging against the tall peaks of the Shadowspears.

Royce heard a soft rustling sound beside him as Garret Proctor shifted his weight. The commander's left hand was resting on an embrasure, his right hand fingering the hilt of the ebony knife he wore tucked in his belt. As Royce's gaze followed the path of the clouds, the force commander maintained a harsh scrutiny of the canyon below his fortress. Without looking up, he said in a half-whisper:

"You know what you have to do."

Royce bowed his head deeply.

Proctor's voice continued, cold and merciless as the mountains themselves. "Make certain the boy is touching him when he dies."

Rain began to fall. It came on slowly at first, just a damp, tentative mist that clung to Kyel's face and collected in glistening beads on the backs of his hands. Then light droplets started falling from the clouds, coming down erratically all around them. The raindrops grew heavier, fatter, until the clouds seemed to just open up and disgorge the weight of their water onto the thirsty flanks of the Shadowspears. A great rumble of thunder rolled expansively in the distance, dampened only by the whistle of the wind.

Eyes squinting, Kyel didn't know they were approaching the node until he felt the barrier come crashing down around him, stifling his perception of the magic field completely. The feeling was even worse, this time. He hadn't realized how much he'd come to depend on that comforting sense until he had started exercising it. When it was gone, the void it left behind was terrifying.

Confused and miserable, he slouched low in the saddle and tried not to think about it. He soon found even that impossible. The thirst of his mind for the telltale pulse of the field was like a gnawing hunger that only grew stronger and wouldn't subside.

Ahead through the rain, he could see the shadow of the black horse pull up. Kyel dismounted and walked to where Darien was unloading the packs he had tied behind his saddle. Soon even the absence of the magic field was forgotten. At the mage's direction, Kyel found himself pounding stakes into the ground with the blunt end of a rock as Darien unrolled a large square of oiled cloth.

In short order, they had a lean-to constructed and a small fire glowing beneath it. But though all he wished was to throw himself down beside the comfort of the fire and warm his shivering body, Kyel didn't get the chance. At the mage's direction, he found himself set to work preparing breakfast.

It was not much of a meal. Darien had only given him scant time to gather provisions before ushering him out of the keep. He'd grabbed a few small bags from the stores without looking to see what was inside. So Kyel found himself cooking up a meal of half-rotten turnips and a few strips of salted beef that looked as if the rats had been at it first.

When he served up the sick mixture, Darien ate without complaint, staring out across the dreary landscape, his eyes studiously introspective. Throughout the meal, he never uttered a word. His gaze was directed outward at the recesses of the ravine. Or perhaps inward, withdrawn somewhere into the frothing turmoil that haunted his mind. Whatever the case, Kyel was left feeling alone, even lonely.

In an attempt to draw him out in conversation, he asked, "Why is your Oath so important to you?"

Darien blinked, lowering his head as his gaze slipped downward in thought. To Kyel, he appeared to be struggling for just the right words. When he finally spoke, his voice was almost wistful.

"The only reason I'm alive now is because I stepped off a cliff. I had no idea that the fall wouldn't kill me. It was only by blind luck that I survived. There was another mage below in the Vale who saw me falling and saved my life."

He paused a moment, rotating his hands so that his palms faced upward, his eyes contemplating the gleaming duel chains. "Sometimes I feel like I'm still up there on that cliff, only dangling from the edge by my fingertips. I can choose to keep holding on, hoping that somehow everything will turn out all right. Or I can choose to let go. Only this time, if I decide to fall, I know there'll be no one around to stop me."

Kyel felt hopelessly out of his depth. Try as he might, he couldn't understand what the man was trying to say. "So, you're afraid if you give up your Oath, you'll die?"

"No." The Sentinel shook his head. "When I was up on that cliff, it wasn't death that scared me. What scared me most was the fall itself."

"I don't understand," Kyel whispered.

"I hope you never have to."

Kyel looked to him for further explanation, but there was none forthcoming. Darien's stare had once again retreated inward, the shadows now storming violently across his eyes.

The day lingered, the rains tapering on and off. Kyel sat with his arms wrapped around him, shivering in silence. The horses foraged across the black dirt, necks stretched down in search of food. But there was none to be had. No blade of grass broke through the soil. In a land where sunlight simply didn't exist, no seed could ever take root.

A sound from down below broke the uneasy silence of the ravine. Kyel leaned forward, listening. Beside him, Darien sat sharply up and reached for his sword. Kyel saw his movement and went for his bow, feeling a sudden stab of fear. He glanced around at the surrounding slopes, seeking, but finding nothing.

Then, echoing up from below, he heard the rattle of tack and the plodding of hoofbeats. He stood, bringing his bow up and nocking an arrow to the string. Horses were approaching. He trained the shaft of the arrow on the chest of the first horse, a target far larger than its rider. But as he narrowed his eyes in concentration, he found himself releasing the tension on the bowstring.

To his relief, Kyel recognized the form of Sutton Royce, flanked by a small number of mounted men. Darien had been right. Royce must be an excellent tracker, to have found them so quickly in the dark. The horses walked toward them up the slope, Royce out in front on his dark brown destrier.

Kyel lowered his bow as the captain and his entourage pulled up before them, perhaps twenty paces away from their makeshift camp. He felt heartened to see the man. Perhaps his presence meant there had been some resolution at the keep that would allow Darien to feel comfortable enough to return. Kyel longed for even the uneasy tension of Proctor's tower. At least the chamber was warm, and he could always escape if he had to.

Next to him, Darien let his blade slip fully back into its sheath. He stood still, watching warily as Royce climbed down from his horse.

"We need to talk, Darien," he said as he moved off to the side in the direction of a low hill to the north of their campsite.

Darien's eyes tracked Royce's gray cloak as he walked away with his back to them. Scabbard in hand, he moved out from under the lean-to and followed the soldier across the black soil toward the slope of the hill.

There, just out of earshot, the two men met and appeared to be speaking. Kyel had no idea what words were being exchanged. Darien seemed to be arguing heatedly, his expression irate, his motions brisk, though his voice was kept low enough that Kyel couldn't catch more than a few syllables. It was probably just a continuation of the argument in the tower, when Proctor had all but ordered Darien to forswear the Mage's Oath.

Darien turned sharply with a rippling length of his blue-black cloak, looking ready to stalk off and storm away. As he did, Royce's mailed fist came smashing down against the side of his head in a powerful strike that took him to the ground.

Kyel's mouth dropped open in disbelief. He grabbed for his bow but was immediately surrounded by Royce's men. They jumped down from their horses, caging him in with the bulk of their bodies, swords drawn and threatening. A man reached out and ripped the longbow right out of his fingers. Kyel started to fight for it, but the threat of a crossbow aimed at his face stopped him short. The grim soldier holding the weapon looked as if he had every intention of using it. The only thing Kyel could do was stand and watch the events unfolding on the hill, helpless to do anything.

Royce advanced, stalking toward Darien with his blade drawn and poised. His gaze was filled with cold fury, raging with a harrowing mixture of fire and ice. Kyel felt his eyes widen with a jarring slap of understanding.

Royce was acting under orders. He had to be. And, knowing the man those orders must have come from, Kyel feared the ruthless nature of their intent. Again, he thought of Proctor as a chess master, sitting in his dark tower day after day, brooding as his mind sifted through strategy in an attempt to find himself any desperate advantage within grasp.

Only, this time, Proctor was doing much more than sacrificing a mere pawn. Try as he might, Kyel couldn't think of any reason in the world *why*.

On the ground, Darien moved slowly, bringing an arm up to wipe a stream of blood from his eyes. Royce hovered over him, sword poised in the air. His lips moved, but Kyel couldn't hear his voice. In his hands, the blade of his sword trembled.

Royce bellowed, throwing his head back. The sound of his booming cry echoed off the walls of the ravine as he brought the sword up over his head in a double-fisted grip. The steel glinted white in a sudden flare of lightning. Then it was falling, streaking down.

Darien rolled out from under the blade as it cleaved deeply into the dirt. Somehow, he ended up on his feet, his own sword singing with a metallic ring as he drew his blade and flung the scabbard to the ground. He edged backward, holding the hilt with both hands as Royce advanced toward him.

Blood covered the side of Darien's face and ran down his neck. His eyes blazed with a molten fury that made even Royce's stare seem brittle in comparison.

The captain swept out with his blade, and Darien parried the strike. Then the mage advanced with a smooth series of cuts that made Royce's sword dance in the air to keep up with them. The soldier disengaged, swinging to the side as Darien dove after him, bringing his sword around to slice over his shoulder.

The blow was caught on the flat of Royce's blade. Steel shrieked as Darien's sword slid down the length of it.

They were both masters, Kyel realized, watching the graceful but deadly dance. Both men seemed equally matched, Darien's quick, confident movements making up for what he lacked of Royce's brutal strength.

They moved in a slow circle as their swords played in the air between them, first one man advancing and then the other, neither one losing an inch of ground. The soldiers surrounding Kyel were watching, also, attention riveted on the fight.

Royce pushed Darien away and thrust his sword out in a wicked undercut. But the mage dodged back, bringing his sword up to deflect the next hissing slice already coming at him.

Darien shifted into a two-handed grip as he pressed Royce backward down the hill with a quick succession of crisp, ringing blows. The captain was forced to retreat, his sword barely moving quick enough to deflect the attacks.

Royce's foot stumbled over a dent in the ground. He brought his blade up to shield his face as he fought to keep his balance.

But Darien didn't let up. He executed another precise sequence of attacks timed to exploit the opportunity and shatter Royce's defense. The captain was beaten steadily backward down the hill.

Darien lunged, letting his sword slide under the captain's blade. He caught Royce's crossguard with a twisting motion, then reached out with his hand and ripped the hilt out of his opponent's grasp.

Darien swept his blade back over his shoulder as Royce's sword fell from his hands. He stood there shaking, chest heaving, eyes burning with explosive rage.

A ringing peal of laughter echoed down from the ridge above them.

Thinking he was either dreaming or insane, Kyel glanced up the slope into the face of a pale and beautiful woman mounted on the back of a glistening white horse. Her platinum blonde hair spilled over her shoulders, stirring in the wind. The gown she wore was silver-blue silk, flowing luxuriously over the sides of her mount. Her youthful face was the picture of gentle innocence.

So in shock was he that Kyel almost didn't notice

the line of Enemy soldiers spread out on both sides of the woman's horse, lining the walls of the ravine. All were archers, and every bow had an arrow nocked and drawn tight against a black-helmed head.

The woman's melodic voice rang out over the mountain slopes like sparkling silver bells of laughter. "To think I rode all the way from Bryn Calazar just to kill a wayward mage. Imagine my surprise at finding his own friends already doing my work for me."

She smiled, a playful glimmer in her eyes.

Kyel watched the woman's horse descend the slope toward them. She wasn't wearing a black cloak, but Kyel didn't need to see one to know the woman was another mage. An Enemy mage, despite her honey-innocent looks. She slid down from her palfrey's back, stepping lightly as she crossed the ravine toward them. Her eyes were wide and crystalline blue. On her lips, she wore a childish grin.

Three Enemy soldiers advanced at her side, sweeping forward with blades held at the ready. Together, they pressed Royce away from where he stood frozen under the threat of drawn bowstrings.

Enemy soldiers poured down the slope, surrounding the group of soldiers who had come with Royce. Two came forward and caught Kyel by the arms, hauling him over to stand with the other captives.

The woman gathered her skirts as she drew up at Darien's side. She reached a slender hand up to touch his face, caressing a finger down the side of his cheek.

"So, you're the Battlemage I've heard so much about," she said in that bell-like voice. "Do you have any idea what we do to your kind?"

The smile on her face radiated a thrill of anticipation as her pale eyes glistened in delight.

———

Devlin Craig grimaced as he surveyed the sad collection of men going through the motions of practice in the yard. He had taken over their training for two days, and in that short amount of time had found himself growing more discouraged by the hour. After weeks of practice, the recruits had come a long way, but they were far too few, their talents still green and undeveloped. It took months to make a soldier, months these men simply didn't have. Not with the size of the Enemy host gathering on the other side of the two peaks to the north.

He stalked up to one of the recruits who was sweeping his practice sword around in a flowery dance of swirling arcs that looked impressive but were also grossly ineffective. Tearing the practice sword out of the man's hand, Craig hurled the wooden sword to the ground at his feet.

"If I wanted a dance master, I'd have sent to the Player's Guild," he growled, giving the recruit a sharp slap on the face. The frightened youth raised a hand to his cheek, mouth open wide.

"Get out of my sight," Craig growled, stepping forward menacingly and gesturing back toward the keep. "A few days of covering latrine pits might clear your head a bit. Now, *go!*"

The man whirled, ashen-faced in shame, and ran. Craig scowled, sweeping his gaze over the rest of the men who had paused in their practice to stare at him.

"Get back to work!" he bellowed, glaring as each man scrambled back into their stances.

Perhaps he'd been too hard on the boy, but Craig didn't care. He continued his survey of the men, strolling back down the line and examining each man's movements with a practiced eye.

Not one of them dared look up to meet his gaze as he walked by. They were all terrified of him, as well they should be. He was in a decisively bad mood.

———

The woman's breath stroked the skin of Darien's neck below his ear, the feel of it sending electric shivers down his nerves, spreading throughout his entire body. He turned his face away, refusing to look at her, as soft platinum curls brushed the side of his cheek. The scent of her filled his nostrils, a fresh yet subtle fragrance that reminded him of a field of blossoms. Her very presence exuded a frightening, seductive energy. She traced his lips with a soft caress.

"Do you know who I am?"

Darien shivered. There was only one person in the world she could possibly be, but that woman was a thousand years dead. He felt confident, though. She so perfectly matched the descriptions he'd read, it was uncanny. He decided to risk his guess.

"Arden Hannah."

The woman's eyes widened, a smile of appreciation blooming on her lips. "Oh, very good, my sweet. And you must be Darien Lauchlin, though I'm uncertain how that could possibly be. Your brother seemed quite convinced you were dead."

Darien's body stiffened. "How…?"

She pulled back enough to stare, smiling, into his face. Her hand moved to stroke the stubble on his cheek. She whispered in a low and breathless voice:

"You resemble your mother remarkably."

Darien flinched back from her touch. "You've never laid eyes on my mother."

The smile fell from her beautiful face, her lips pursing in an expression of profound sympathy. "But I have. I was staring right into her eyes the moment I killed her."

His vision reeled. Forgetting the threat of the bowmen, Darien staggered backward. His mind groped instantly for the field, but of course, there was nothing there. He cursed his own stupidity as his body shook in a furious mixture of revulsion and grief.

Arden smirked, her eyes wide and sparkling with amusement. She moved gracefully after him, the hem of her dress gliding across the black ground as she closed the distance between them. She was tall for a woman. As she drew up in front of him, her head came almost to the level of his eyes.

Darien clenched his jaw as she took his hand and pressed it into her own, running her soft fingers over his palm, stroking upward to trace the marks of the chain on his wrist. Closing his eyes, he suffered her touch as she leaned into him and whispered in his ear:

"Before you die, know this: a great host is gathering below Aerysius, waiting to sweep down through the Vale and flood into the North. A similar host is gathering here, in the shadows of Orguleth and Maidenclaw. In three weeks' time, when the sun rises between the Pointer Stones of Glen Farquist, those two forces will merge as one and topple the walls of Rothscard. This land you have sworn to protect will be desecrated, its people subjugated and destroyed."

As she spoke, a shuddering chill slithered over him, starting at his shoulders and working its way down the length of his arms, coiling in the pit of his stomach. He tried to pull away from her, but her arms wrapped around his back, drawing him close as she nestled her head against him, gazing into his eyes.

"But you won't need to worry about that," she soothed, smiling reassuringly. "Your worries end here today. My soldiers have brought plenty of wood. They know how much I delight in the sound of a man's dying screams."

Darien shoved her away from him forcefully, taking her by the shoulders and locking his arms to keep her at a distance. Arden stared at him as if wounded, her face darkening to a pout. But her eyes continued to gleam as she shrugged out of his hands and twisted away. She started to walk back in the direction she had come but then hesitated, turning back around as though she had forgotten something.

"By the way, your Meiran sends her love. I've seen her myself, kneeling at the feet of my Master in the Netherworld."

Darien collapsed to his knees as all the strength drained out of his body in a flood. He couldn't endure the vivid image that formed in his mind, provoked by the woman's malicious statement. It was the image from the dreams that plagued him almost every night, of Meiran staring up at him with the green light of hell in her eyes.

Above him, the sound of Arden's laughter echoed off the rock walls of the ravine.

The sound of hoofbeats made Craig turn. Frowning, he looked in confusion at the black warhorse loping up the trail toward him, empty stirrups bouncing at its sides. The Tarkendar halted in front of him, sides heaving, eyes rolling and showing the whites. Craig reached up and gathered the horse's reins, stepping back to let his gaze rove over the sweat-stained flanks of the gelding. There seemed nothing amiss with the animal, except for the alarming fact that it was absent its rider.

Instantly, Craig was in motion. Jumping on the horse's back, he wheeled the animal around and kicked his boots into its sides. Without hesitation, the warhorse broke into a gallop, angling back over the hill in the direction of the paddock.

Craig pulled the horse up next to the fence, his breath now coming in gasps from the grip of panic that seized him. He tore his eyes from horse to horse, dreading what he would find.

Just as he'd feared, Royce's dark stallion was absent from the herd.

"Darien," he whispered.

They had ripped the black cloak from his body, waving it in triumph like a captured banner. Then they had tied him to a stake. Darien hadn't even made an effort to struggle as he was bound tightly with sturdy rope. Then they had just left him there, lying on his side in the dirt.

He watched as Enemy soldiers hauled in armloads of wood, piling it in the center of the ravine. He didn't care. He was past the point of caring. The thought of the fire frightened him, numbing his body and chilling his mind. But that was all.

He feared the agony of the flames, but death itself would come as only a welcome release. He was tired of the nightmares. His passion for life had died with Meiran. Now, it seemed his very soul had been condemned to hell along with hers.

He watched as the logs of his pyre were mounded, dismissing the sight with acute indifference. His thoughts drifted to his father, wondering how that brave man had felt staring out at the same grisly scene. Darien found the thought strangely ironic yet comforting all the same. His mother had told him how alike he was to his father. Now, it seemed that parallel would be rendered complete.

Arden Hannah approached in a graceful sway of silk. Kneeling beside him, she whispered, "It's time. Are you ready to die?"

"I was ready a long time ago," he replied.

Black-armored soldiers stepped forward, seizing both ends of the stake. He was lifted and carried face-down toward the pile of wood in the center of the ravine. They laid him there beside it, angling the pole so that he had a clear, unobstructed view of what was coming.

As he watched, two more soldiers stepped forward, brandishing flaming torches that they threw onto the top of the pile. The dry kindling caught instantly, slithering ropes of flame racing over the thirsty fuel with a crackling, rushing hiss. Black smoke wafted upward, sparks drifting through the air like lazy snowflakes. The smell of it was chokingly thick. It stung his eyes as Darien tried to turn his face away from the intensity of the heat.

He felt soft fingers stroking the back of his head, running tenderly through his hair.

"Farewell, my sweet." Arden's delicate voice was barely audible over the crackling of the flames.

Then he was moving, the stake shifting as it was lifted upward into the air. He closed his eyes, holding his breath as the vicious heat of the smoke hit him square in the face.

He tried his best not to scream. He struggled desperately against his bonds as they braced the stake above the flames.

The heat was too much, too intense. He couldn't stand it, couldn't escape it. He felt his flesh starting to sear.

Darien writhed above the flames, howling in mindless agony.

Devlin Craig grimaced in dismay as he saw the column of smoke twisting upward in the distance, a black, roiling shadow against the flickering lights of the clouds. He knew instantly where the smoke was coming from and what its presence signified, realizing even before he veered his horse toward it that he was already too late.

He rode bareback, as did the rest of the men behind him. He hadn't wanted to waste the time it would take to saddle up and fetch his gear. He'd rounded up every man from the practice yard who could ride and put them on a horse.

But as he charged his gray stallion into the mouth of the ravine, he knew that his guess had been wrong. He'd feared Proctor had ordered Royce to slay Darien, trading the Sentinel's life for a new weapon, one potent enough to give him the slender chance he needed against the Enemy host.

Royce was Craig's friend, and Darien's, as well. But he was also a man enslaved by his commitment to duty. He would do anything Proctor asked of him, even if it meant sacrificing his soul along with the sum of his principles.

But the wafting column of smoke told Craig he'd been wrong. There was only one possible explanation for it. There simply wasn't enough wood in all the Shadowspears to kindle that kind of blaze. Only the Enemy could be responsible for such a fire, and there was only one reason they would have built it.

Craig resisted the impulse to close his eyes as his horse raced into the ravine. Darien Lauchlin had been the truest friend he'd ever had. Craig did not wish to look upon his burning remains.

The men behind him divided, spreading out, some angling their horses toward the slopes of the ridge, while those who remained formed a wedge behind him.

And then the fire was before him. He tried not to look at the charred body strapped to the stake, obscured by waves of heat coming off the blaze. Grimacing, Craig directed his mount toward the flames. He had no idea what the warhorse would do, presented with such a directive. But the gray stallion obeyed his command, charging faster as Enemy arrows whistled by him in the air.

The stallion bravely executed the maneuver taught to it by the horse masters of Southwark, reinforced by years of practice and training. The gray beast reared up as it dove into the fire, lashing out with its forelegs at the stake.

Craig dove off the horse, rolling away as he hit the ground. All around him, the sounds of fighting echoed through the ravine as his men engaged the Enemy. He forced himself into motion, blinking against the tears that stung his eyes. He ripped off his cloak and used it to beat the flames from Darien's body, then collapsed to the ground beside him, his ears assaulted by the screams of his dying horse.

Darien lay motionless, still tied to the smoldering stake. His clothes were nothing but ashes, his face blackened and blistered from the heat. Reaching for his knife, Craig sawed at the bonds with trembling hands.

He felt at Darien's neck for a pulse, detecting a flutter of heartbeat. But it was just one. That was all. Craig waited, but another didn't come. A tingling sensation stirred in the fingers of his hand, like a strange energy that seemed to want to slide up his wrist and into his arm. He almost withdrew his hand. But then he felt another flicker of pulse. The strange energy subsided, drawing back down into his fingertips.

Without thinking, Craig hefted the mage into his arms, stumbling as he surged forward with only one thought on his mind: he had to get Darien out of the node. He had no idea where the boundary was. Darien had only mentioned it to him once. Oblivious to the sounds of fighting around him, Craig staggered as fast as he could with the weight in his arms down the slope toward the mouth of the ravine. Once there, he collapsed in a heap over Darien's body.

He shook him as hard as he could, not caring that he touched scorched and blackened flesh. Charcoal-tatters of cloth came away with his hand. He raised a fist above his head, slamming it down into the mage's chest. Darien's head lolled to the side, blistered lips unmoving. Craig brought his fist down again with all his strength. Beneath him, the body jolted gruesomely.

He felt a hand on his shoulder and spun around, shocked to find himself staring up into the face of the boy mage. Kyel Archer knelt beside him, shaking his head, eyes glistening with tears.

"Stop," he pleaded. "Please. Let him go in peace."

Craig bowed his head, averting his eyes from Darien's ruined face. It was wrong. So wrong. He deserved a better death than this. Craig tried to think of a prayer he could say, something to ease his friend's tortured spirit out of life. His mind groped for words. None came.

But then he realized he couldn't do that. He couldn't sit back and let his best friend go without a fight. With a growl, Craig grabbed Darien by the shoulders, shaking him without mercy.

"Breathe!"

He brought his fist down again.

"Come on, you bastard, breathe! *Heal yourself, damn you!*"

Below him, Darien's blistered lips moved as if to draw breath, but instead produced only a choking gurgle. Then the mage shuddered.

It was almost like a wave that started at the top of his head, passing over his body to his feet. As Craig stared down incredulously, the charred flesh beneath him whitened, the burnt cloth rewove and mended. Darien's chest spasmed with a sharp intake of breath, his head arching backward, eyes opening to stare vacantly at the sky. His eyelids dropped as the breath was released, but his chest rose again, assuming its normal rhythm.

Devlin Craig sat back on his haunches, throwing his head back in relief. At his side, Kyel Archer stared down at the renewed body of the sleeping mage, mouth open wide in disbelief.

The sounds of the battle unwound behind them. Craig wasn't sure, but he thought he saw a fleeting glimpse of blue silk disappearing over the ridge.

Chapter Fifteen
No Price Too High

Pass of Lor-Gamorth, The Front

The dark tower of Greystone Keep rose above a bank of mist like a lone island encased by a gray and swirling sea. The fog broke against its stark walls like ocean swells upon a shoreline, white-capped breakers licking against the gray embattlements before receding back again like a tide. The dark banner at its peak for once hung limp for lack of wind enough to stir it.

Devlin Craig reached his hand down to soothe the brown warhorse beneath him that had once belonged to Royce. The animal was nervous, unused to the strange weight and scent of its new master. Royce had raised the stallion from a colt. he'd been the only man to ever ride it. But Royce was dead. Craig had buried him with his own hands and piled the rocks atop his grave.

Ahead of him, Darien pulled his horse up and dismounted, leading the black gelding forward by the reins. Craig followed suit, as did the remainder of the men behind him. Corban Henley drew up beside him, and together the two of them flanked the Sentinel down the path that led across a dip in the ground between ridges. The thick curtain of mist parted before them to reveal the steep stair that led to the fortress above on the cliffs.

Craig was worried about his friend. Darien had scarcely spoken a word since he'd awakened late the previous night. There was something different about him, a subtle yet significant change. Craig had noticed it immediately, almost from the first moment the mage had opened his eyes. It was as though the shadows that always seemed to move behind his eyes had solidified into a tangible obscurity.

Craig didn't know what that meant, but he knew he didn't like it. The Darien that had emerged from the flames was not the same man he'd known. An acute sense of dispassion had fallen over him, shrouding his emotions like a pall. Craig was starting to wonder if part of him really had died in that fire, the part that mattered most.

Ahead of him, Darien's muffled footsteps slowed, coming to a stop. Glancing up, Craig saw the reason. It looked as if half the keep had turned out to greet their solemn homecoming, lining the cliffs and the steps, the fortress walls and the high turret. Only, it was not a welcome reception.

To his dismay, Craig saw that every soldier had a weapon in hand, every shaft and blade trained on their approaching party. Their path was barred by none other than the force commander himself, standing with shoulders squared and feet apart in the middle of the opening to the stairs. Proctor's face was set in harsh lines of anger mingled with disgust.

Darien raised Royce's bared sword before him like an offering, cradling it in his open palms at a level with his chest. He left his horse behind, crossing the distance between himself and Proctor at a slow and deliberate pace. Craig stayed where he was, transfixed by the scene. Darien stopped before the imposing form of the force commander and, closing his hand around the hilt, wielded the sword in a backwards grip.

With a sudden surge of force, the Sentinel bent his knees and brought the blade around, driving it point-first into the ground at Proctor's feet. The sword quivered there as Darien removed his hands from the hilt.

The force commander stared down at the shivering blade. Darien brushed past him, his shoulder grazing Proctor's arm roughly as he moved by, the boy mage scurrying after him. Bowmen along the cliffs tracked his movements with their shafts, tracking him as he ascended the rock-hewn steps and entered the keep.

Craig found himself left confronting his superior officer. Garret Proctor brought his gaze up from Royce's quivering sword, fixing him with a look of molten fury.

"You betrayed my trust," Proctor accused.

Craig shook his head, feeling his anger mounting. "No. You betrayed mine. Royce is dead now because of it, and we came damned close to losing Lauchlin *and* Archer, both."

He frowned, sweeping his gaze over the man in front of him as if looking for a sign. "Do you even have a soul left, or did you sacrifice that too? Tell me, is there no price so high you're not willing to pay it?"

"No." Proctor's voice was cold as death. "The war we fight is the battle for existence itself. No price is too high, no sacrifice too great. I am willing to do anything it takes to survive. And I expect no less from any man who chooses to follow me."

Craig glared at him. Then he tossed his reins to Henley and followed Darien up the stairs. The archers slowly released the tension from their bowstrings, the soldiers lowering their blades.

He entered the fortress, the warmth flowing from the door of the hall a welcome relief. He yearned to go in and sit beside one of the hearths, to relax and ease the tension that gripped his shoulders like a vice. But instead, he let his feet take him up the winding stairs toward the top of the tower.

When he entered the circular chamber, he found Darien packing. The mage was squatting on the floor, tying up his bedroll. Kyel Archer stood behind him staring down at him with wide and fearful eyes. The Sentinel didn't look up as Craig walked toward him, but the boy glanced at him with a beseeching expression, as though begging him to do something, anything at all. He stopped a few feet away from Darien's back, watching him complete the knot he was working on with a sharp tug on the cord.

"You're leaving," Craig observed.

Darien just nodded, not pausing in what he was doing. Craig gazed down at him as the mage slapped his bedroll against his pack, securing it firmly with leather straps.

"Where will you go?"

Darien rose from the floor and, without looking at him, stalked across the room to the table and scooped up an old map.

"I'm going home," he said, still with his back to him.

Craig felt at a loss. He had no idea what to do. Darien couldn't be serious, but somehow Craig knew he was.

"Then I'll come with you."

"No." Darien shook his head. "This is my battle. You've your own war to fight."

With that, Darien slung his pack over his shoulder, gesturing for the boy to follow him. Craig moved forward, stopping him with a hand on his arm.

"Wait. Don't do this."

Darien finally brought his gaze up to regard him. "I don't have a choice."

He disengaged himself from Craig's grasp and started toward the opening of the stairs. But there he stopped, drawn up short by the form of a woman emerging from below, robed all in white with a sheer veil obscuring her features.

Craig's eyes widened in surprise. The woman seemed so utterly out of place against the stark confines of the chamber that her very presence seemed surreal. Distracted by her looks, he almost didn't realize the significance of the white veil and dress. When he did, the shock was like a blow in the face.

What was a priestess of Death doing here?

The woman swept her gaze across the faces of the three men in the chamber, her eyes finally coming to rest on Darien. She moved toward him, then swept to her knees at his feet, bowing forward and pressing her face against the floor. She remained there as the mage stared down at the top of her veiled head, frowning in consternation.

"Rise," he directed her finally.

Craig watched as the woman gracefully regained her feet, his mind spinning as he tried to make sense of the scene. It was not customary to abase oneself before any mage, even a Sentinel of Darien's status. Only the office of the Prime Warden had ever commanded such a humbling display of deference. He wondered what the woman was up to.

In a voice by no means gentle, Darien asked her, "What would the Temple of Death have of me?"

The woman dipped her head slightly, dark auburn curls spiraling out from under her veil. With an unruffled expression on her face, she stated formally, "Please allow me to introduce myself. My name is Naia Seleni, First Daughter of the Goddess Isap. I bear urgent tidings of your mother."

Darien glared at her, his jaw set in anger. "If you've come all the way here just to tell me she's dead, then you've wasted your time. I already know."

The woman blinked as if taken aback, her brow furrowing as she seemed to be reassessing the man before her. At last, she bowed her head. "I offer my most sincere condolences, Prime Warden."

"I am *not* Prime Warden," Darien corrected her. "Aerysius has fallen. The dead have no need of titles."

But the woman refused to yield. In a calm and yet adamant voice, she said, "You are the last surviving Master of Aerysius. Whether or not you acknowledge it, the office of the Prime Warden has fallen to you. And you are correct. The dead have no need of titles. However, the living still do."

Darien glared at her with a look that would have sent any other woman scurrying for the stairs. But the priestess held her ground and returned his gaze patiently.

"I have been sent to bring you back with me to the High Temple of Death at Glen Farquist, in the Valley of the Gods. There, your mother lies in state. The power of her gift has been transferred to a holding vessel and awaits you there to receive it."

Darien glowered at her. "Do you take me for a fool? A mage's legacy can be transferred only through physical contact."

The priestess gazed into his face through the screen of her veil. She said in a placid voice, "I apologize if I have distressed you. The vessel I am referring to is a relic of the Lyceum. It was placed in the keeping of Death's Priesthood before the fall of Bryn Calazar. I speak the truth, Prime Warden, this I swear."

"Don't call me that again."

The woman bowed her head, spreading her hands. "What would you have me call you, then?"

To Craig's surprise, the mage simply shrugged as though defeated. "Call me Darien, like everyone else."

"As you wish. Darien." The way she said it made it sound like a taunt. "But though you deny your right to your title, I must urge you to never forget from where the name itself was derived. The words 'Prime Warden' were chosen because they mean, literally, 'first guardian.' Aerysius is no more, but that does not mean your responsibilities ended upon the death of your home."

"What exactly are you insinuating?" Darien asked.

"I could not help but overhear your conversation on my way up the stairs. Tell me, Darien. Do you truly believe the First Guardian of the Rhen would best serve his duty by wasting his life in a futile quest for vengeance? If you return to Aerysius, you will die. You have no chance against your brother's strength, nor the power of the gateway. Would not your life be better spent in service to the Rhen?"

Darien's eyes narrowed, seething. "You presume too much. You came here to take me to my mother. I suggest we go before she rots." He stalked past her out of the chamber, the sounds of his heavy footfalls echoing up from below.

Craig did not want to believe what he'd just heard. Once again, he had the gnawing feeling that something had shifted in the man, as though the part of him that had any feeling had simply just given up and died. He turned his head to find Kyel Archer staring at him, a look of questioning disbelief on his face. The priestess was regarding the opening of the stairs warily, mouth open and eyebrows raised.

Kyel followed Darien down the stairs, pausing only long enough to retrieve his bow and pack. He didn't want to go with Darien, but his place was at his side now. He'd found himself growing nervous around the mage. He was starting to wonder if the man had finally broken. There was, after all, only so much a person could take.

Downstairs, he found Darien standing on the last step, confronting Garret Proctor. The mage's eyes were wide and wild, his hair falling in disarray. He stepped down onto the level of the floor, slowly circling the force commander with a glare of vicious contempt.

"Very soon, the Enemy will sweep down on you in numbers unimaginable." Darien leaned forward threateningly as he paced. *"You must fall back.* You'll have to harry them as much as you can and try to buy me time. I'll meet up with you at Orien's Finger at dawn on the morning of the Solstice. Draw the majority of their strength into the eye of the vortex, and I'll see to it you get your wish."

He started to turn away, but halted, stabbing a glare back at Proctor with hatred in his eyes. "I hope you're damn well satisfied. We're both going to burn in hell for this."

With that, he strode through the door of the hall as Proctor gazed after him in silence. Almost, Kyel thought there was the slightest hint of a smile on the commander's face.

Kyel moved as if through a haze into the hall, not really paying attention to anything but the panicked thoughts racing through his mind. So absorbed was he that he didn't notice Traver moving to intercept him.

"What's going on?" Traver asked, pulling him aside. Kyel looked at him in relief, comforted by the sight of his friend's familiar face.

"I think we're leaving."

Traver gawked. "You're going with *him?"*

He thumbed his hand over his shoulder in the direction of one of the hearths, where Darien was stuffing leavings from the evening meal into an oiled sack. Kyel hadn't told Traver about his commitment to the mage, fearing what his friend would say. Glumly, he reached down and folded back his shirtsleeve, exposing the markings on his wrist.

Traver's eyes went wide in alarm, his face paling. He grabbed Kyel's wrist, closing his fingers over the emblem, glancing quickly around as if making sure no one else had seen it.

He pulled Kyel after him by the wrist. Traver led him to a corner, where he pressed him back against the abrasive stone wall of the keep.

"What are you *thinking?"* he hissed. "That thing could get you killed!"

"Traver—"

But his friend continued right over him, "Look, if you were having problems, you should have come to me. I've lots of friends now that—"

Kyel shook his head. "Traver, it was my decision."

"Well, it sure was a bloody poor one!" the man shot back. "Perhaps it's not too late. Tell that darkmage you don't take well to responsibility. He'd have to believe you, because it's the plain truth. Tell him he'll have to find someone else."

"It's too late." Kyel shook his head miserably. "I've already spoken my first vow."

"Bloody hell, Archer! I always figured you were a little dense, but I didn't know you were downright stupid!"

Over Traver's shoulder, he saw Darien heading back toward the door of the hall. Kyel pressed his lips together, suddenly saddened. He didn't want to leave Traver behind. But the only other option was to talk Darien into bringing him along. He could only imagine how that would go over. Darien would put up with Traver for about as much time as it took the mage to toss him over the nearest cliff.

"Look, I have to go. Good luck to you, Traver. Try your best not to get killed, all right?"

"You're telling *me* not to get killed? With that damned thing on my wrist, I'd be a little more worried about my own hide! Do me a favor. If he tries to give you one of those bloody cloaks with the target on the back, just tell him black's not your color."

Kyel found himself grinning. "So long, Traver."

When he glanced back, he saw Traver slouching against the keep's cold wall, slowly shaking his head. Kyel left him there. He crossed the floor of the hall and, looking for Darien, walked out the gate into the cold, foggy night.

He strode down the stairs to where his horse was still saddled and waiting. Just as he drew up at the mage's side, Darien put his foot in the stirrup and swung himself over the back of his warhorse, sending it at a canter toward the path that led down and out of the pass. Kyel stared after the black gelding, not quite sure what to think.

Darien hadn't even looked at him, had just turned and ridden away. He felt wretchedly confused. Not knowing what else to do, he stood there by his horse and waited for the priestess.

It didn't take her long. The woman glided down the steps of the fortress with regal grace. She stopped beside him and regarded him with a questioning look. Her gaze slid slowly down his arm, and for a moment Kyel couldn't figure out what she was looking at. Her eyes widened as if she had just arrived at a startling revelation. When she looked up again, all trace of uncertainty had disappeared from her face.

It took him a moment to realize he'd forgotten to pull his sleeve back down after showing Traver the mark of the chain. Embarrassed, he tugged the fabric back over his hand. He was going to have to be more careful about that in the future. Traver was right. In the wrong places, that mark could get him killed. Even in the right places, it was not something he wanted generally known.

"Now, where did he run off to?" the woman muttered as she swung up onto the back of her mare.

Kyel nodded in the direction of the path.

"He certainly wastes no time," she muttered, kicking her mare forward.

They caught up to Darien about half a league down into the pass. He had slowed his horse to a walk and was riding with his head bowed. He didn't show any sign that he was aware of their presence until the woman's horse had drawn abreast of his own. Even then, he only glanced her way.

They rode in silence along the narrow path that carried them out of the mountains, winding along the steep slopes ever downward toward the Cerulean Plains. It was the same path Kyel had taken coming up, but he hardly remembered it. He hadn't been able to see much of anything and hadn't been in the mood to notice much, anyway.

But this was an entirely different journey. The wind was still, the lights of the clouds brighter. The sharp peaks of the Shadowspears thrust upward all around him, ranging away into the foggy distance. It was, he had to admit, the most beautiful night he had seen so far in the Pass of Lor-Gamorth.

The sound of Darien's voice actually startled him. "Where is the nearest entrance to the Catacombs?"

Kyel glanced toward the priestess, watching the frown that developed on her face beneath the obscurity of her veil. As if hesitant to answer, she took her time about forming a reply. "Death's Passage is no longer safe. Its secrets have been compromised. We must ride to Glen Farquist from here."

"Glen Farquist is a month's hard riding," Darien protested. "I can't afford that kind of time."

The priestess only shrugged, her motion disturbing the neat drape of her veil. "You must make the time. The Catacombs are not an option. They have become infested with dark creatures and fell shades. Also, the Eight are abroad and making use of them. Your own mother was murdered within."

Darien glowered. "The Enemy is preparing to mount the largest offensive we've seen in a thousand years. At Winter Solstice, two of their armies will sweep down through the North to merge at Orien's Finger. That's eighteen days from now."

The woman appeared startled. "How do you know this?"

"Arden Hannah told me."

The way he said it made it seem like the most natural thing in the world. But his statement made the priestess gasp. She yanked back on the reins, drawing her horse up. The look in her eyes was one of fear mixed with outright revulsion.

"You have actually spoken to one of the Eight?"

Darien nodded. "Right before she tried to kill me."

"You're quite a mystery, Darien Lauchlin," she said. "How exactly did you plan on returning to Aerysius to wreak vengeance upon your brother and still manage to make it to Orien's Finger by Solstice?"

Darien shrugged. "It's a week to Aerysius from here. And another week to Orien's Finger."

"And what do you intend to do once you arrive, Bound as you are?"

"I hadn't the faintest idea until tonight." A strange smile formed on Darien's lips, the first Kyel had seen since his argument with Proctor in the tower. "But we must make use of the Catacombs. It's our only chance of buying enough time."

The woman shook her head. "No. I forbid it."

"Then our journey ends here." To Kyel's astonishment, Darien brought his horse around and turned it back the way they'd come. The woman stared after him with an exasperated look.

"You would give up your own mother's rare and precious gift merely to have a chance at slaying your brother?"

"That's right. When the battle is joined in truth, I can't afford to have Aidan at my back."

Kyel frowned. Perhaps the man was not insane, after all. What he said did seem to make sense. A desperate kind of sense.

The priestess relented with a sigh. "You would have made a formidable priest of Death."

"What I really need to be is a formidable mage," Darien snapped.

"Have no doubt. You are." The woman didn't appear pleased by that. "The nearest entrance to the Catacombs is at a shrine off the Great Northern Road, southwest of Wolden. We can make it there by tomorrow if we ride straight through the night."

The horses plodded along, picking their way down the narrow trail. Kyel found it hard to stay afraid when such extraordinary changes were taking place all around him. It happened so slowly that, at first, he didn't notice the transition. But gradually, the clouds were loosening their hold on the sky, and the dawn was becoming brighter.

Plants started to appear on the sides of the mountain slopes: sparse at first, then becoming denser the further they went, until the hills around them began taking on a hue of astonishing green.

And then a wondrous thing happened. The clouds parted overhead, and a ray of luminous sunlight fell across Kyel's face, far brighter than he ever remembered. He brought his hand up to shield his eyes, blinking as he stared up into a blue morning sky.

The sun had never felt so warm or so welcome. Below, the verdant foothills of the Shadowspears spilled down into a grassland so rich and green and exceptionally bright that Kyel found himself wanting to cry with joy. It had been almost two months since he had seen blue sky, or even so much as a single green leaf. The breeze stirring toward them from the grassland was warm with the sweet, rich smell of autumn.

"The Cerulean Plains," Darien stated. He lifted his arm, pointing toward a branch of the mountains that marched southward to their right.

"Orien's Finger lies in that direction. There's a Circle of Convergence at its peak, where Grand Master Orien made his stand against the Enemy four hundred years ago. The plains are covered by an enormous vortex that begins just north of the town of Wolden, which means we'll be passing through the outer margin of it."

Darien's eyes settled on Kyel's, fixing him with a significant look. "Don't try to get a sense of the field from this point on. Not till I tell you to. Without training, the field lines in a vortex can cause you pain if you stroke them the wrong way."

Kyel had read enough to know what a vortex was and what it meant. It was like a hurricane of power, a place where the lines of the magic field swirled and converged. He felt a shudder of foreboding as he stared down at the grasslands, which suddenly seemed to have diminished in their beauty.

Before, when he had trekked up this way, a vortex had meant nothing to him. But now that he'd started exercising his mind to consciously sense the magic field, reaching out toward it was becoming second-nature. Still, he didn't understand. He was not a Master, so how could the vortex possibly harm him?

But if Darien sensed his question, he didn't say anything. With one last admonishing glance, the Sentinel sent his horse forward at a lope down the mountainside. Kyel's mount wanted to break after it, but he held it to a walk with a firm hand on the reins. He looked over at the priestess and saw that she was staring at him.

"You never told me your name," she said.

Kyel felt a flush of embarrassment. Beside her, he felt so insignificant that he really hadn't thought it mattered to her, one way or the other.

"I, uh. Kyel Archer, that is. That's my name."

Beneath her veil, the woman's lips drew upward in a smile. Kyel couldn't believe he'd just fumbled over his own name.

"It is an honor to make your acquaintance, Kyel Archer." The priestess was still grinning in amusement. "You may call me Naia, if it pleases you."

He wasn't sure if it did please him. For the second time since coming to Lor-Gamorth, a person with an imposing title had asked him to use their given name. The first time, he'd earned himself a chain on his wrist. But at least the mark Darien had placed there was out in the open, where he could stare at it and consider its implications. There were many types of chains.

But the priestess seemed to be regarding him casually, a wistful expression on her face. "Is he a hard master?"

Kyel found himself thinking that question over

for a minute, unsure of how to respond. The truth was, he really didn't know. His apprenticeship was only just beginning.

He shrugged, responding, "Darien is harder on himself than he is on anyone else."

Naia appeared to consider his words, glancing down at the place where Darien had drawn his horse up and was staring out across the plains.

Chapter Sixteen
Wolden

Wolden, The Rhen

Wolden was just as Darien remembered it: a large, ramshackle town that marked the end of the Great Northern Road. The very fact of its existence was something of a puzzle. Wolden had originally been established as a waypoint in the movement of supplies and soldiers to the Front, just an outpost of Greystone Keep. Yet, as trade to the pass had dwindled over the years, the town had continued to thrive and had even grown.

Other than Rothscard, Wolden was the most populated settlement in Emmery. And it was directly in the path an invading army would take, snug up against the foothills that climbed into the Pass of Lor-Gamorth.

Darien could not conscionably skirt the town without giving its people some type of warning. So he ignored the urgency that made him want to bypass the settlement.

The priestess was quick to figure out what he had in mind. She drew up beside him on her roan mare, adjusting her veil and saying in a lowered voice, "You must take great care in how you handle this. You'll not wish to create a panic."

Darien said, "I intend to find the mayor. I'll give him the information and let him figure out what he wants done about it."

The priestess nodded, though her eyes still looked troubled. He was starting to get the feeling he was in some odd sort of power struggle with the woman.

The trail they were following widened as they approached the town's north gate. Being situated so close to the Front, Wolden was fortified, ringed by a crenellated wall broken in places by guard towers. But Wolden had grown too big to be contained within the wall, and a good deal of the town had spread beyond it.

The first cottage they rode past looked dilapidated. A woman sat in a chair on the porch. Beside her was a basket of yarn and a small child that squatted next to it, intent on the basket's contents. The woman glanced up at the sound of their horses, a look of casual interest on her face. But then her expression crumbled, turning to a look of fear. She shot out of her chair, gathered the child into her arms, and bolted inside.

Darien frowned. What had prompted the woman to react that way? It was more than just the glimpse of his cloak. Most people of the Rhen were familiar enough with what that cloak represented not to be frightened whenever they saw one.

As they approached the gate, every person they came across seemed just as startled as the woman. They drew a broad variety of reactions, ranging from shock to dismay, even terror. Darien was used to people deferring to him, moving out of his way on the street, or staring at him when they thought he wasn't looking. But he had never experienced anything like this.

Even the guards stationed at the town gate gawked at them as they passed through, staring at him as though he were Zavier Renquist himself. They made no move to bar his way but edged away from him as far as they could. Darien turned to look over his shoulder, watching as a man with a crossbow abandoned his post and fled down a side street.

Darien cursed himself. He had been a fool not to consider the swift wings of rumor. No doubt word of Aerysius' fall must have preceded their arrival in Wolden. If the people of this town thought every last mage was dead, then he could imagine their shock at seeing him riding in with a priestess of Death.

Their party was quickly surrounded by mounted guardsmen. And even though their weapons were sheathed, Darien didn't like the looks in the eyes of the guards who ringed them. They were afraid. Frightened men could be desperate men. And he was powerless within the perimeter of Orien's Vortex.

A guard with graying hair approached them on his horse. He looked Darien up and down, dipping his chin in a stiff greeting. "Your pardon, Great Master, but the mayor would like a word with you. You are advised to come with us."

Darien ran his gaze over the tight circle of men, then nodded. The guard leaned forward and caught his reins. Immediately, two more guardsmen drew their mounts around to flank him. Another kicked his horse forward, insinuating his mount between Naia's and his own. Together, they led Darien's horse forward, encircling him like a hostile escort.

The mayor's house was not far from the gate. It was not a house at all, really, but rather a small palace. In the North, elected offices turned over about as often as Southern kingdoms changed dynasties. The mayor of Wolden had probably enjoyed his position for decades.

The guardsmen guided them through an iron gate to a path that wound through a garden of symmetrical flower beds. The whole affair reminded Darien of the Queen's palace in Rothscard, only on a miniature scale.

The guards ordered them to dismount before a flight of marble steps. Darien climbed down from his horse, studying the guards warily as he waited for the priestess and Kyel. His new acolyte looked a little unsure about what to do with his bow. Darien shook his head at him, indicating with his eyes that he ought to leave it behind with the horse. Kyel reached up and hung the bow from his saddle.

The guards led them up the steps and through a large door. A foyer spanned the entire front of the mansion, with a white staircase that curved upward to a balcony on the second floor. The room was elegantly furnished, every piece of furniture a work of fine craftsmanship. Letting his gaze wander, Darien discovered what looked like a priceless collection of oil paintings mounted high up on the walls. One in particular, a nude of a woman sitting alongside a bath, had the unmistakable broad strokes and bold contrasts of a Gabrizi. Darien swallowed, wondering how in the world he was going to convince the owner of this collection to leave it all behind.

They were led down a short hallway and into a snug room with a large table entirely too big for the space, leaving scant room for anything else. A man was already seated behind the table, his hands folded neatly on its polished surface. He made no move to stand, instead just gestured with his hand at two chairs across the table from him.

"Please, have a seat."

Darien paused before making a move toward one of the chairs, taking a quick survey of the man in front of him. He assumed it was the mayor he was looking at, although the man was younger than he had expected, with short brown hair and a plumpish face. He wore a simple tan jacket, though the cut looked well-tailored and expensive.

"Mayor Blake Pratson." The man nodded by way of introduction as Darien removed his sword and took the seat across from him.

By the rules of etiquette or even common courtesy, the mayor should have risen to greet his guests. Naia's presence alone should have been enough to demand it. But the mayor of Wolden just sat back in his chair and waited until Darien and Naia were seated, Kyel lingering awkwardly on his feet. The priestess looked furious, her dark eyes glaring through her veil. Kyel appeared to be making a conspicuous study of the wood of the tabletop.

Darien thought about demanding an explanation for the treatment they had received but decided against it. He needed this man's cooperation. Instead, he leaned forward, extending his arm toward the man across the table and supplied his name, leaving off his title. Pratson looked down at his offered hand with a look of disdain. At last, he reached out and clasped it in a tentative grip.

Darien said, "May I introduce First Daughter Naia Seleni of the Temple of Isap. And this is my acolyte, Kyel Archer."

He let go of the mayor's hand, noting the clammy feel of the man's skin. Like the guards, Blake

Pratson was afraid of him, which made no sense. As mayor of Wolden, the man should know that Darien was powerless here within the turbulence of the vortex. The entire town of Wolden was effectively mage-proof. Yet, if the feel of his hand betrayed his apprehension, the mayor's face was a study in unruffled self-assurance. Sitting back in his chair, Pratson folded his arms across his chest and regarded Darien with a skeptical expression.

"You'll have to forgive my shock, Master Lauchlin," he said. "You see, I've had word from the Queen of Emmery that Aerysius has been completely destroyed. Begging your pardon but, by all reports, you're supposed to be dead."

Darien nodded thoughtfully, thinking that, while such news might give the man pause, it still didn't explain Pratson's anxiety or the outright fear on the faces of so many of Wolden's citizens. There was something else going on here, but the man was being slow to let on about it.

"The report is accurate. To my knowledge, I'm the only survivor."

Outwardly, Pratson's face conveyed a look of polite interest. Only the slightest narrowing of his eyes gave away his doubts.

The priestess shifted in her seat, her fingers stroking the back of Darien's hand under the table in warning. Glancing up, he saw that another man had moved into the room behind him. He had come in so quietly that Darien hadn't noticed his presence. Which was alarming. His ear was trained to pick up on such noises. Either he had slipped in his vigilance, or this newcomer was not an ordinary guard.

Something about the man reminded him of the blademaster he had studied under in his youth. It wasn't a physical resemblance, more in the way the man held himself and the air of casual confidence he projected. Unless Darien missed his guess, the man was a Guild blademaster.

He found himself liking this situation less and less. Pratson was openly studying him now, analyzing his reaction. Darien could no longer pretend to ignore the insult of the guards. Striving to keep his voice as even as possible, he said to the mayor, "Why don't you tell me what this is all about."

Pratson shook his head. "First, you tell me what brings you to Wolden."

"As you wish," Darien allowed softly, folding his hands on the table. "I bear ill tidings from Greystone Keep."

He described the size of the Enemy host waiting on the other side of the pass while the man listened blandly. As he spoke, he had the growing feeling that not one word of his account was being taken seriously. Pratson just sat there, leaning back in his chair and looking almost bored. When he was finished, the mayor reached a hand up and rubbed his temple.

"Do you have a shred of proof that this army does, in fact, exist?"

The statement sent Naia bolt upright in her seat, hands gripping the edge of the table as she gasped in disbelief, "You dare question the word of a Sentinel?"

Pratson shrugged. "I fear I'm left with little choice." Turning to Darien, he said bluntly, "Your very presence here is a mystery to me. I find almost everything about you troubling. For one, I've always heard that mages were forbidden to bear weapons, and yet you come to me carrying steel at your back. What do you think, Broden? Is that sword just the fancy decoration it looks?"

"No." The tall guardsman shook his head. "He's had Guild training."

Darien's eyes narrowed as he turned to look at the man behind him. Broden hadn't been with the other guardsmen who had escorted them through town. In fact, Darien hadn't seen him at all, not until he had so silently entered the room.

"Broden's good," the mayor said with a wry grin. "Give him a few more minutes, and he could probably name the blademaster you studied under."

It was scarcely a secret anymore. "Nigel Swain was captain of Aerysius' guard. He taught me the art of the blade."

Broden nodded warily, sucking in a cheek. "I remember Swain." He glanced at Pratson. "He left the Guild for Aerysius some years ago, just as he says. You know him, too. He's captain of the Queen's guard now."

But the mayor still didn't appear convinced. Slowly, he said, "And then there's also the mystery of your name."

His words caught Darien by surprise. "What of it?"

"Everyone knows Emelda Lauchlin was Prime

Warden. Are you claiming to be a relation?"

"I am her son."

Pratson's eyes ticked toward Broden. Instantly, the man was in motion. Darien rose halfway out of his seat, hand reaching for his hilt. But he was taken by surprise, his reaction too slow. The cutting edge of Broden's sword was already frozen at his neck. Slowly, Darien retracted his hand, keeping his eyes fixed on Broden. Beside him, Naia was on her feet, glaring at Pratson in outrage.

The mayor explained, "In her note to me, Queen Romana mentioned that the downfall of Aerysius was brought about through the betrayal of the Prime Warden's own son."

Darien blinked in shock. That explained everything. They had mistaken him for Aidan. He felt a sickening nausea in his stomach at the thought of it. No wonder the people had stared at him that way on the street.

Beside him, the priestess addressed Pratson in a near-whisper of threat, "In most territories, it is considered a capital offense to detain a Master against his will."

But the mayor simply dismissed her words with a wave of his hand, smiling confidently. "The town of Wolden is well within the protective margins of Orien's Vortex. A black cloak means nothing here."

Naia looked down, her long veil brushing the surface of the table. Darien watched her from the corner of his eye, his gaze still locked on Broden. Slowly, the priestess raised her head, folding her hands neatly in front of her.

"What if we can offer the proof you require?"

Pratson shrugged. "Then, by all means, please do so."

Darien couldn't imagine what Naia was talking about. He listened to her as he stared into Broden's eyes, watching for any subtle change. Usually, where the eyes moved, the blade followed.

Naia explained in a patient, almost lecturing tone, "Prime Warden Emelda had two sons. It was Darien's brother Aidan who sacrificed his Oath of Harmony in order to bring about the destruction of his home. As you can imagine, if Darien had committed such an act, he would no longer bear the chains of the Oath upon his wrist."

Pratson pursed his lips, turning to Darien with eyebrows raised expectantly. Darien sighed, feeling disgusted. It always came back to his Oath. Always. Glaring at Broden as if daring him to strike, he raised both hands and shook back his sleeves, the material falling away to expose the hated markings there.

Darien shuddered as he looked at those twin chains. He found just the sight of them repulsive. He had to force himself to keep his arms raised as Pratson sidled out from behind the table, walking around Naia to take Darien's right arm into his hand. The mayor's palm was even clammier than before. Darien closed his eyes in loathing as the man raised his wrist up almost under his nose, inspecting the emblem closely.

He wanted to strangle Naia.

The mayor released his arm. As he did, Darien heard the guard's blade sliding back home into its scabbard.

"You have my most humble apologies," Pratson told him, drawing away. "And my most sincere condolences."

"Thank you," Darien muttered, falling heavily back into his seat. The priestess regained her own chair beside him, placing a comforting hand on his arm. When he looked over at her, he saw Naia's eyes were full of regret.

Pratson remained standing, bringing a hand up to rub his brow wearily. "One week, did you say?"

Darien nodded, feeling drained. "If that. Proctor has less than a thousand men under his command. It all depends on how well he can make use of tactics to slow them down."

The mayor looked as if he simply didn't understand. That, or he just flat-out refused to believe. "Surely, Greystone Keep can hold its own in a siege far longer than you give them credit for."

"There will be no siege," Darien insisted. "If Proctor allows himself to be surrounded, his entire force will be destroyed."

Pratson paced away toward the fireplace, raking a hand through his hair. With his back to Darien, he asked, "And if this Enemy host is not stopped in the pass, what makes you think our people will be safe even in Rothscard?"

"Your people will be far safer in a fortified city with its own standing army than they ever will be in Wolden."

The mayor nodded, turning back with a look of

resignation. His face was pale and glistening with a sheen of sweat. Shoving his hand into the pocket of his jacket, he retrieved a white kerchief, using it to dab at his forehead. "Then I suppose I ought to thank you, Master Lauchlin, for the warning. Is there anything further you require?"

On impulse, Darien pushed his chair back and rose from his seat. "I'd ask you to leave something behind for the soldiers passing through in your wake."

Pratson frowned at him. "What do you have in mind?"

"Anything you can think of that might be of use to a retreating army. Food. Remounts. Medicinals. Weapons, if you have any to spare. Arrows, especially, would be critical. An army on the run doesn't have time to stop and retrieve spent shafts."

"Greystone archers have always favored the longbow, have they not?"

Darien nodded.

Pratson raised his hands helplessly. "Out here on the plains, we've little use for them. I'm afraid I am simply not equipped to supply an army with arrows for bows we don't use."

But Darien was not about to let the man off that easily. "What sort of bows do you have?"

"The local nomads use horn bows to defend their grazing territories. I've supplied my own guardsmen with them."

Horn bows. As the mayor had suggested, arrows meant for the horn bow would be of no use to the Greystone archers. And yet...he had seen one of these horn bows on a guard at the gate. It was much smaller than the longbow yet had the look of an effective weapon.

Such a bow could be used from horseback. Longbows could not, at least not without enormous difficulty. The only chance of success Proctor had would be to strike and fall back, as fast as he could, as often as he could. If his bowmen were mounted and supplied with horn bows, their chances would be greatly improved.

Darien asked, "How many bows might you be able to lay your hands on in the span of a week?"

"While trying to organize an evacuation? You ask too much."

"What I'm asking for is the means of defending your homeland," Darien reminded him. "If you provide the Greystone archers with horn bows and remounts, they could make use of them to harry the Enemy and slow their advance."

Pratson stared at him with raised eyebrows. "I can try. But I make no promises."

"Do your best. For every Enemy soldier that falls along the way, that's one less to threaten the walls of Rothscard." He released his grip on the mayor's arm.

Pratson scowled at the floor. "Now I remember why I've never liked dealings with your kind. No good news ever comes on the wings of a black cloak."

He reached out and clasped Darien's hand in parting. Naia rose, gathering her white skirts and dipping her chin as she moved past Darien out the door. Kyel followed in her wake, looking a bit pale.

Darien almost smiled as he watched his young acolyte leave, thinking the meeting had been a good lesson for him. Then he frowned, remembering the next lesson he had planned. It was almost time to implement it.

Chapter Seventeen
Follow the Field

The Cerulean Plains, The Rhen

Wolden disappeared behind them, swallowed up by the rolling folds of the prairie. Kyel closed his eyes and slouched in his saddle, moving with the steady rhythm of his horse's gait. It felt good to feel the sun on his face. He tilted his head back, luxuriating in the warmth of the breeze that caressed his cheeks and ruffled his hair.

He paid little attention to where they were headed, happy just to watch the scenery go by. It wasn't until the priestess angled her horse off the road and guided it westward that Kyel began to wonder where they might be headed. Every once in a while, a small tree broke the monotony of the grass. Otherwise, the prairie was like a sprawling ocean, stretching out in infinite tides to the distant horizon.

"Where are we going?" Kyel asked, contemplating the enormity of the view that surrounded them. It made him feel extraordinarily small and insignificant, yet hale and fortunate at the same time.

Naia glanced back and smiled. "There is a shrine of the goddess a few leagues west of here," she said, her veil fluttering about her face.

Staring out into the vast emptiness before them, Kyel wondered aloud, "Why would anyone want to build a shrine all the way out here?"

The priestess slowed her mount, pulling back on the reins until she was riding abreast of him. "Death is a universal human experience, Kyel. It doesn't happen just in towns and cities. Also, the governorship of this province strictly forbade us from building a temple in Wolden."

Kyel found that strange. "Why?"

"Oh, for political reasons," Naia said as her mare twitched its tail into Kyel's leg.

"I fail to see how a temple has much to do with politics."

Darien glanced back over his shoulder and exchanged an amused grin with the priestess. Kyel frowned, feeling like the butt of some joke he didn't understand.

But when Darien turned his smile on him, Kyel realized there was nothing scornful about it. Rather, the mage's expression seemed almost fatherly. He said, "Once you become a bit more traveled, I think you'll find the temples have more authority than most people would guess."

Kyel nodded, thinking it strange a man only scant years older than himself could make him feel so much like a child. He figured it was because Darien's range of experiences was so vastly different from his own. Kyel had lived in the same remote township all his life, learning what he could about the world from what he could glean from the few books that passed his way.

Darien, on the other hand, had actually been to many of the places Kyel had only ever read about. More than that, a critical part of his training had been the study of the Rhen and its various peoples. It created a broad gap between the two of them, making Darien seem far older than he actually was.

Kyel realized he didn't even know the man's true age. When he'd first met Darien, he remembered thinking how young he looked for a full Master. Kyel frowned. That had only been two months ago. Yet, in those two months, the Sentinel seemed to have aged.

He thought back to the night Darien had tested

him, when the mage had shared his fear about the amount of raw power he'd taken in. Kyel couldn't help wondering if that had something to do with it. Darien no longer resembled the quiet, gentle man Kyel remembered meeting that night in the tower. There was nothing quiet or gentle about him any longer. Darien reminded him of a banked fire burning low, awaiting only the smallest draft of air to ignite.

The sun was starting to sink toward the horizon when Darien drew his horse up and announced it was time to make camp for the night.

Naia objected, "If we press on ahead, we could make it to the shrine before full dark. It's not much farther."

But Darien was already unloading his horse's saddlebags. "Not tonight. I've something for Kyel to do first."

Kyel waited for him to elaborate, but the man didn't say another word. Finished with unloading the last of his bags, Darien hobbled his horse and turned it loose to graze.

Kyel decided he'd better stop watching and offer to help. Soon, he found himself set to the task of wading through the tall grass in search of wood while Darien and the priestess finished setting up their campsite.

Finding enough wood for a fire in the middle of a prairie was not as easy as it seemed, Kyel soon discovered. He tromped through the grass over uneven footing, his boots sinking through the topsoil into burrows abandoned by whatever animal had originally dug them. He spread his hands out at his sides, letting the blades of grass trail against his palms as he moved through it.

At last, he found a small, dead tree hidden completely in the grass. He wouldn't have seen it if he hadn't tripped over it first. The wood was decayed and brittle, so it wasn't hard to snap off enough branches to make a few armloads of wood, which he hauled back to the campsite.

As soon as he had the wood brought in, he found himself set to clearing a space for the fire and then cooking supper, as well. After which, he got to clean everything up while the priestess lounged on a bed of grass and Darien occupied himself by sliding a whetstone along the edges of his blade in long, slow strokes.

By the time Kyel had cleaned out the last pan and stuffed it back into his pack, he'd had just about enough. He'd half a mind to tell Darien exactly where he could shove this whole acolyte business. It was starting to feel more like servitude than any apprenticeship he'd ever heard of.

He was just about to cast his tired body down beside the fire when the Sentinel finally sheathed his blade and rose to his feet. He walked away from the camp, beckoning for Kyel to follow.

Kyel didn't bother suppressing his groan as he trudged after him. Darien led him up the rise of a low hill, where he stopped and turned, waiting for Kyel to shuffle up the slope. The moon was rising over the mountains in the east, its disk a murky yellow-orange.

"It's time for your next lesson."

Kyel felt a shiver of dread caress his skin. There was something in Darien's tone he didn't like.

"The first step is learning how to sense the presence of the magic field," Darien said. "You managed that quickly. Let's see how well you do with the second step: learning how to read its strength and direction."

Kyel was taken aback, especially after Darien's warning to him earlier that day. "Can you do that? I thought you said this was a vortex."

Darien shook his head. "I can't. But for you, this vortex provides a great opportunity for learning."

"If you say so." Kyel still didn't like the sound of it. He also didn't like the way Darien seemed to be deliberately avoiding his gaze. Instead, he appeared to be looking out at the moonrise, as if studying it for some portent or sign.

Darien said, "You'll need to reach out from deep inside your mind and get a sense of the magnitude and direction of the field. In a vortex, the field lines run almost parallel and become compressed together till they overlap. It's called superposition. The strength of the field increases the further you go in.

"There's a trick about it. You'll have to ease your mind along the direction of the current. If you go against it, you'll know right off."

Kyel swallowed. "That doesn't sound very reassuring."

"It's not meant to be."

Kyel could only nod. Taking a deep breath, he did what Darien told him, opening his mind and tentatively reaching out toward the magic field. Immediately, he felt a stabbing jolt in his head that crackled down the fibers of his nerves like a slap of lightning.

With a cry, he brought his hands up and hugged his head. The pain was gone, but the memory of it still jolted through his body.

"That bloody *hurts!*"

Darien shook his head, folding his arms. "Then you went about it the wrong way. Try again."

Kyel brought his hands down and stared up at him incredulously. "You're not serious. I can't do that again!"

"You'll do it till you get it right. Now. Try again."

Kyel couldn't believe what he was hearing. Darien stared down at him, arms folded against his chest. There was no hint of sympathy or even compassion in his face. He just stood there, waiting expectantly.

Feeling at a complete loss, Kyel tried to do what the man wanted. This time, he used a slightly different approach, using the most delicate touch he could manage. He actually felt the field for an instant, a tremendous, wild energy that seized his control and wrenched it sharply away.

This time, the pain was exquisite.

Kyel screamed, doubling over. Clutching his head, he fell to the grass and flopped onto his back, gasping. The pain took longer to go away. His head throbbed with the pulse of every heartbeat, and his body shook in quivering spasms.

At last, the grip of the pressure in his head eased enough for him to relax back into the soft grass. He lay there, trembling, staring up at the stars as the Sentinel lowered himself down beside him and placed a steadying hand on his arm.

"Try again."

Kyel shook his head. He couldn't do that again. He blinked back tears as he stared up into Darien's face. *"Why are you doing this to me?"*

The look in Darien's eyes was as hard and desolate as the black slopes of the mountains behind them. He rose to his feet, turning his back. Then he walked away.

Kyel watched him go, feeling hurt and more than a little betrayed. He could still sense the weight of Darien's disappointment lingering in the air long after the man was gone.

He had no desire to return to their camp. He didn't want to get up. His joints ached, and it wasn't just from the ride. So he lay there in the soft and scratchy grass, looking up through the tall blades at the wash of stars above in the heavens. The stars were so many, their lights seemed to combine and run together.

He lay there for perhaps an hour. Maybe longer. He had no way to be sure. Around him, the night was cooling steadily, and the ground was growing hard. There was a rock digging into his back that he hadn't noticed before. Kyel sat up, yawning, and used his hands to push himself to his feet.

Looking around, he tried to remember the way back to their camp. The fire had burned out; he couldn't see the glow of the coals. But at last he made out the form of his horse grazing in the distance.

He trudged back down the slope of the hill toward the shadows of their campsite. But when he reached it, Kyel looked down in dismay.

Both Darien and the priestess were gone.

Kyel's pack and bedroll were still there next to the ashes of the fire that had been smothered with dirt. But Darien, the priestess, and their belongings had disappeared as surely as if the prairie had just opened up and swallowed them.

Angry, Kyel tossed himself down on his bedroll. Had Darien decided to abandon him, just because he hadn't been able to handle the test of the vortex? Or was it because he'd given up after only trying twice? Whatever the reason, it hardly mattered. He was alone.

Kyel's hand went to a foot-long piece of wood lying next to him on his blanket. He picked it up, wanting to throw something. He moved his arm back to toss it. Just as he did, he noticed words carved into the bark. Blinking, he held it up before his face, staring down at the letters that had been scratched there, then rubbed over with charcoal to darken them.

Follow the field.

Kyel almost choked on the sudden anger that flooded through him. He howled in rage as he threw the piece of wood with all his strength. His horse looked up from its grazing, snorting as if offended by his action.

He couldn't believe Darien was doing this to him. The man had said he wouldn't go easy on him, but this was downright cruel. He should just pile his things on his horse and ride back to Wolden. From there, he could follow the Great Northern Road all the way back to Covendrey, back to home. He'd been doing the man a favor when he'd agreed to accept Darien's offer. If this was the way he was going to be treated, it wasn't worth it.

He surged to his feet and went to his horse. The moon was full and bright, so it wasn't hard to see as he saddled the animal and loaded it up. He swung his leg over the horse's back and, with one last, contemptuous glance at the campsite, set his mount heading east, back across the prairie toward the road.

"You did it to yourself, Darien," he muttered.

He'd gone perhaps half a league before he pulled back on the reins. Cursing the mage silently, he wheeled the animal around and sent it at a gallop back to the campsite, where he climbed down and led the beast forward.

He had made the Sentinel a promise, and the mark it left on his wrist was a visible reminder that was going to haunt him to his grave. Kyel had never gone back on his word in his life. He wasn't about to start now.

He thought about just heading west, the direction the priestess had been leading them. Naia had said the shrine was only a short distance away. Maybe he could find it on his own, without having to open his mind to the fierce energy of the vortex.

Or maybe he would get turned around in the dark and find himself hopelessly lost. Grudgingly, he decided that strategy wasn't going to work.

Closing his eyes, he tried to brace himself for the pain. Then he groped outward with his mind.

The lightning-like strike in his head was immediate and intense. It almost took him to his knees. In his mind, he could hear Darien's voice coming back to torment him:

Try again.

"No," Kyel groaned, shaking his head even as he forced his will out again into the torrent of the field. This time, he actually got a sense of the direction of the current, right before the searing backlash of power drove into his mind like a molten dagger.

Sobbing outright, Kyel staggered forward, clenching the reins of his horse in one hand, his other hand clutched around the back of his head, gripping his hair in a fist. His vision was so streaked with tears that he could hardly see. He felt his way ahead with his feet, stumbling as he tripped over something in the grass.

He groped again for the field, taking just a tentative sample before flinching back away from it. He waited for the slap of pain. It took a moment to realize that it hadn't come. Startled, Kyel blinked the tears out of his eyes.

He'd done something different. Something right. Only, he wasn't sure what it was. He tried to remember, but it wasn't something he'd consciously thought about. He just hoped he could repeat it again when he had to.

But now he knew where he was going, at least.

The currents of the vortex were raging in a southwesterly direction, sweeping across the rolling swells of grass. It was a good thing he hadn't just started walking, hoping to blindly run into them. The flow of the field was slightly different from the direction they had taken in from the road. He would have ended up hopelessly lost.

Kyel put his foot in the stirrup and pulled himself into the saddle. He was too tired to walk, so he let the animal carry him over the open grassland, pausing after a while to check his bearing against the field lines. Again, he felt that sharp, searing jolt, though not as painful this time. So he refocused his mind and cringed in the saddle as he tried yet again.

This time it worked, and he knew now what he'd done differently. Instead of just casting his will out across the flow of the field, he had felt along it, going with the current instead of cutting across.

He almost laughed. It was so easy. He couldn't believe what he'd been putting himself through just to figure out this trick. He kicked his horse to a lope across the grass, not even bothering to draw back on the reins the next time he reached out and stroked the power of the vortex.

He rode for perhaps an hour, following the lines of magic as they bent gradually further toward the south. By the time the figures of two horses appeared on the horizon in front of him, Kyel had become adept enough at gauging the field that he no longer had to continue groping out to reach it. Instead, he just left his mind open to it, keeping it in a state of constant awareness.

When he reached them, Kyel saw that both Darien and the priestess were sound asleep, their horses grazing a short distance away. Kyel dismounted, making no effort to be quiet as he slung his pack down on the ground beside the sleeping figures and turned his horse loose to graze.

Darien didn't stir, even while Kyel rummaged through his pack and rolled out his bed. It made him so angry. While he'd been back there, all alone and sobbing in pain, Darien had been making himself a cozy little camp and falling blissfully asleep.

Kyel had almost come to think of the mage as a friend. How utterly foolish he had been.

When he woke, Kyel found the sun had risen well above the mountains. The camp was pretty much broken down around him. Darien was just fixing the last bag to his saddle.

Naia smiled a warm greeting Kyel's way as she broke off a bite of biscuit. He pushed himself up into a sitting position, rubbing the sleep out of his eyes.

His back was sore, his joints stiff, and he was still very tired. He'd had little sleep the previous night and none at all the night before. He felt as if he could have just gone on sleeping throughout the entire day.

Darien turned and, noticing him awake, started toward him. Kyel looked down, not trusting himself to keep the anger he felt from infecting his eyes. Darien stopped and knelt beside him in the grass.

"I'm not going to apologize for what I did," he said. "And I don't expect your forgiveness. You made it here. That's all that matters."

Kyel felt his stomach sink like a lead weight. The man had no remorse, harbored no feelings of guilt or shame. More and more, Darien was starting to remind him of Garret Proctor.

He seemed to be waiting for Kyel to say something. When he didn't, the mage stood and dusted off his clothes. As he started walking away, Kyel heard him mutter, "It took me half a year to learn what you did in two hours last night."

Kyel had a stinging retort ready on his lips but decided to leave it alone. Darien's mentor probably hadn't dumped him down in the middle of a vortex and left him all alone with a galling message to follow the field lines.

Chapter Eighteen
The Catacombs

The Cerulean Plains, The Rhen

They rode with their backs to the sunrise as the day grew warm around them. In the distance, a small structure rose from the sea of prairie. It looked so forlorn, only a square patch of brightness in a vast expanse of unrelieved green. Darien knew it must be the shrine. He'd seen others like it before, scattered in various places throughout the land. This one looked even smaller than most.

There were no paths leading to or from the shrine. The sea of grass just stopped at the threshold. Inside, marble tiles took over where the prairie ended.

They dismounted in front of the doorway and, to Darien's surprise, the priestess led her horse inside. Its hooves made a sharp clatter on the tiles, slipping a bit as they fought for purchase.

Darien had never much cared for the temples of Death, although this was the first time he'd actually been under the roof of a satellite shrine of the goddess. His mother had often compelled him to go with her to Aerysius' temple to offer prayers for the soul of his father. Those trips had always disturbed him, and he'd always left with the feeling that the Atrament must be a cold and dismal place.

The shrine was just like a temple, but on a much smaller scale, complete with all the typical trappings. Stationed at the far corners of the room, long tapers held by tall candlesticks burned with lively flames. Darien wondered who tended the shrine. Someone had to keep the tapers lit and sweep out the floor occasionally. But there was no one within, and certainly no space where anyone could possibly be living.

He led his horse into the shrine, bringing it up alongside the priestess' mare. The black gelding tossed its head as its hooves encountered the unfamiliar surface. The space inside was barely large enough to contain the three horses. The priestess walked forward to a ledge that supported three votive candles. She gazed down reverently at the tiny flames, then closed her eyes as if offering a prayer.

Darien felt drawn toward the candles himself. Each of those fragile lights represented a prayer for a departed soul. It had been a long time since he had offered such a prayer.

Compelled by a whim, he moved to stand beside Naia and picked up one of the candles from the ledge. The priestess' eyes followed the motion of his hand, but she said nothing as Darien held the small votive candle before him, contemplating it in silence.

He found a striker on the ledge. The flint was old, and it took him a few tries to create a spark. The wick of the candle flared up immediately, producing a strong, healthy glow as he set the candle down on the ledge with the others.

But then something happened that was entirely unexpected. The glowing yellow flame darkened as if a shadow had passed over it. The light dimmed, becoming pale. Then the candle's flame flared up brilliantly, as if seized by a sudden draft of wind, before turning a filthy shade of green.

Darien couldn't take his eyes from it, filled with horrified recognition. It was the same color as the pillar of energy he had seen in the sky above Aerysius. The putrid, ethereal glow of the Netherworld.

Naia hissed like a feral cat. Her hand swiped out,

knocking the candle off the shelf and casting it to the floor, where she stomped on it with her feet until it was reduced to nothing more than a crumbled pile of tallow.

The violence of her reaction appalled Darien almost as much as the sight of that terrible green flame. With one last kick of her slipper, Naia sent the whole pile scattering across the dark tiles of the floor.

Then she rounded on him, shrieking, *"How dare you* desecrate the altar of the goddess with that abomination! Whose spirit was that candle meant for? *How do you even know a soul so vile?"*

Darien took a step back away from her, struggling to control the sorrow that threatened to overwhelm him. But the priestess was relentless. She advanced on him, eyes flaring in anger and revulsion.

"Tell me who that candle was for!"

Darien twisted away from her. He hung his head, scrubbing his hands through his hair as he fought for the strength he needed to give voice to what had once been his most terrible fear, now twice confirmed.

He whispered, "Her name was Meiran Withersby."

"Who *is* that?" Naia demanded, her eyes narrowing in confusion. "It takes hideous acts to condemn a soul to the Netherworld!"

Darien couldn't bear to meet the priestess' eyes. Staring at the floor, he admitted, "She was the woman I loved. My brother killed her with my sword, then committed her soul to Xerys to unseal the Well of Tears."

Naia's mouth fell open, the anger draining away from her face to be replaced by a look of horrified disbelief. She shook her head, sagging visibly.

"Gods' mercy, Darien."

A terrible anger suffused him at her choice of words, eclipsing even the pain of his grief.

"The gods have no mercy." He spun away from her, footsteps echoing loudly as he crossed the floor of the shrine to the doorway.

There he stopped, staring out into the cool autumn sunlight, choking back the threat of tears. It was a truly beautiful day. He tried to take comfort in it but found he could not. There was only one thing he could think of that would ever bring him peace.

Darien closed his eyes, envisioning what it would feel like to drive his blade hilt-deep into his brother's chest.

He lingered there in the entrance, leaning against a marble column that supported the roof. Behind him, he could hear the priestess and Kyel conferring in voices too soft for him to make out the words. But he didn't need to hear to know what they must be saying.

At last, the murmured conversation ended. The sound of footsteps moved toward him across the tile. Darien turned as Kyel came to stand beside him. His young acolyte had been silently seething at him all morning, but now there was only a look of troubled kindness in his eyes.

"Naia says we need to go." Kyel reached up to place a tentative hand on his arm. "Are you all right?"

Darien nodded, swallowing. He closed his thoughts to his grief, walling it away in the back of his mind and sealing it there with the mortar of his will. He was surprised, actually, by Kyel's concern. After what he had put the young man through, Darien wouldn't have blamed him for holding fast to his resentment.

"Thank you," he whispered.

He turned and walked back into the shrine, away from the warm glow of morning. Inside, he found Naia occupied with lighting the tapers of a candelabra set into a niche in the wall. Darien looked on as the priestess moved to touch the wick of each taper with the glowing end of a slender wooden splint, working in no apparent order, until the last candle was lit. Then she reached out and extinguished the splint between her thumb and index finger.

Darien frowned, wondering what the purpose of the candle-lighting had been, watching as the woman moved back into the center of the room and took up the reins of her mare. She glanced toward him, a frown of concern on her face.

"The horses may not like this part," she warned.

Darien took her point. Moving to the head of his own horse, he grasped its bridle under the gelding's chin, staring down at the crumbled tallow that was all that remained of Meiran's candle.

It was such a simple thing, a votive candle. Simple, and yet amazingly profound. That was all he'd wanted: just one heartfelt prayer. Yet, even that was denied him. The remains of his good intentions were strewn across the floor under his feet like so much scattered dust.

He tried to avert his eyes from the sight, but it was impossible. His gaze kept slipping back to the remnants of the candle despite every effort of his will.

As he stared down at the crumbled tallow on the floor, he realized that it was vibrating, shimmying as the floor itself trembled beneath his feet.

Startled, Darien glanced up at the priestess. Her smile of reassurance calmed him, but he didn't like the way the floor seemed suddenly unstable. A terrible screeching groan, like the rake of metal against rusted metal, shrieked through the chamber.

Then the floor was moving, jolting downward.

His horse screamed, trying to rear, as Darien clung to its bridle and almost lost his footing. His stomach took a plunge as the floor lurched sharply out from under him and then settled, lowering almost smoothly. He glanced up, amazed, as the walls of the chamber seemed to stretch above them.

"If you wanted to scare me, it's working," Kyel said, staring upward with frightened eyes. All around them, the walls of the room seemed to be lengthening, the ledge where the candles yet glowed rising ever higher above their heads.

"Kyel, sense the field for me here," Darien said, feeling wretchedly ill at ease. The currents of the vortex were lethal to him, but he was only asking his acolyte to practice the same technique he'd learned the night before. He watched Kyel's face, pleased to see that the young man showed no sign of effort or fear of pain.

"It's not so intense," Kyel reported after a moment.

Darien took comfort in that. It meant he could soon take a sample of the field himself. Not just yet; he wasn't a fool. But he had been strangled for two days by the barrier he'd been forced to erect in his mind against the vortex. He was grateful to know that at least that strain was almost done with.

But the darkening of the chamber quickly quenched any relief he might have felt. The floor jolted again, coming to a rest as the light suddenly seemed to leech away as if sucked into the shadows of the walls. A crack appeared along the floor in front of them, yawning wider until it was an opening that shed a soft amber glow into the darkness.

Naia led her mare through the doorway, then waited for them to join her.

Darien led his own horse forward over the tiles. He found himself in a dim, cavernous hall. The source of the light came from huge urn-shaped braziers spaced at intervals along the walls. The ceiling was high, supported by massive stone columns that marched down the entire length of the room. The walls were carved in bas-relief, depicting various images from the Book of the Dead.

"What is this place?" Kyel wondered, openly gawking as he brought his horse forward into the space between columns.

"It is called the Inner Sanctum." Naia's voice echoed through the room. "Our temple has many holy mysteries, and halls such as this are one. Knowledge of its purpose is reserved only for initiates of Death's priesthood. Of course, should you wish to learn more, you could always join," she added with a smile.

"He's spoken for," Darien assured her.

Kyel winced, looking a bit pale, but nodded adamantly as his eyes continued to roam over the dark grandeur of the place.

They led their horses up the center aisle. The sounds of the animals' hooves echoed off the walls and ceiling, the noises magnified by the marble surfaces. As they approached the far end of the room, Darien noticed that there were two dark passages ahead, opening out of opposing walls. He could see nothing within, not even an inch beyond the openings. It was as if the dim light of the chamber just stopped at the thresholds, prevented from spreading further.

Naia stopped her horse and reached into her saddlebag, fishing out three silk scarves. She took one for herself, tossing the other two to Darien, who frowned down at them before handing one to Kyel.

The priestess took her scarf and began wrapping it around her mare's head, covering its eyes. Darien moved to his own mount and did the same, winding the fine material like a bandage around the Tarkendar's black face.

"These doorways mark the entrance to Death's Passage," Naia said as she watched him tying off the scarf.

When Kyel was done, she led them toward the black, gaping hole on the right. There, she drew up and turned toward them, a look of warning in her veiled eyes.

"Before we enter, know this: the Catacombs exist partly in the Atrament. There are many mysteries within, which you will doubtlessly find troubling. And there are dangers, as well. Especially now that Death's secret has been compromised. We must exercise great care yet proceed as quickly as we can. Fortunately, the way is not long.

"And I must warn you: the living are expressly forbidden to communicate with the dead. You *must* ignore any shade that tries to distract you. If you do not, then you will be guilty of breaking the Strictures of Death, and you will not be allowed to return again to the world of life."

She fixed her gaze on Darien. "I gravely fear what manner of shades you might draw to yourself."

Darien felt a spark of anger. "Meiran's not there, remember?"

But Naia shook her head, a regretful smile on her face. "I would love to meet your Meiran," she assured him softly, "but I was not referring to her. I was thinking, rather, of the troubling fact that nearly every person you've ever known has died. Remember the Stricture. No matter what you see, you mustn't interact with the dead in any way."

"I'll do my best."

Naia nodded and turned away toward the dark passage. She paused a moment, bowing her head in prayer, then stepped within. As she passed across the threshold, a shadow fell upon her. Her image flickered once and then was gone, lost completely in the darkness that moved to consume her horse as well.

"Are you sure you don't want to ride to Glen Farquist?" Kyel said as he stared at the dark passage ahead. He looked pale as he sucked in a deep breath and, holding it, stepped through the doorway.

Darien watched, fascinated, as his acolyte's image flickered before disappearing altogether, just as Naia's had. He was starting to get the sense that there was much more magic involved here than in just the trip down. Death's mysteries seemed to be fairly riddled with the workings of magecraft.

Which suggested a partnership that must have existed, at least at one time, between the priesthood of Isap and Aerysius itself. He could easily imagine such a trade-off. It would have been well worth the effort for the ancient Masters to assist in the construction of the Catacombs if, in exchange, they were allowed uninhibited access to them.

Shrugging off his thoughts, Darien whispered a soft word of comfort to his horse, then led the animal forward.

As he crossed the threshold of the doorway, it seemed as if the world wavered for an instant when the shadow fell over his eyes. He experienced a momentary surge of vertigo, as if the framework of reality had suddenly shifted. But then the shadow parted, and the motion of the world steadied. Blinking, he stepped out of the darkness into a dim stone corridor.

Death's Passage

The priestess and Kyel were there ahead, waiting for him. The corridor was more like a cave than a hallway, crudely hewn from granite rock. A soft light glowed along the walls and clung to the ceiling, a misty silver luminescence. Magelight, Darien realized, staring in open wonder. He had never seen its like outside of Aerysius itself.

"Welcome to the Catacombs," the priestess said in a lowered voice.

They walked forward, following the slope of the corridor, the horses picking their way carefully. The air was frigid, and there was a stale odor to the place. The churning magelight cast lurid shadows across the walls. A thick fog clung to the floor, stirred by their footsteps.

Darien didn't like the feel of the air. It seemed thin, almost stretched. Even sound seemed to carry differently through it. The plod of the horses' hooves sounded stifled and hesitant. There was a peculiar reverberation to the noise, like a muffled echo.

After a few hundred paces, the passage took a sharp turn and then opened up into an immense chamber. Darien let his eyes wander up the far wall and found himself having to crane his neck to get a glimpse of the ceiling high above.

This was no mere cavern. The chamber they were in could have engulfed the Hall of the Watchers several times over.

And the walls were not solid.

Darien studied them, attempting to figure out the architecture that lent the walls a honeycombed appearance. Then it dawned on him: the holes in the rock were vaults.

Thousands of them, each vault containing white-shrouded human remains.

The entire chamber was an enormous tomb. It even smelled like one. His nose was accosted with the commingled stench of myrrh and decay. In front of him, he heard Kyel make a gagging noise.

The priestess seemed completely unaffected. This was, after all, her profession. Darien found himself darkly speculating how many corpses Naia had washed and blessed before she had become so immune to the stench of death.

He gazed at the priestess, wondering what had possessed the woman to choose such a grim occupation in the first place. She was young, and elegantly lovely. Naia would have had suitors lined up at her door if she were a common maid. But, he had to admit, there was nothing common about her.

Naia carried herself with an air of confidence that was compelling, and her dark eyes behind her veil shone with intelligence and wisdom far beyond her age. He had to force himself to avert his gaze. Despite himself, he found the priestess intriguing. More intriguing than he would have liked.

His eyes lingered on her back as Naia led them into the middle of the vast chamber. They walked through the cavern, past rows of sarcophagi carved with the likenesses of the dead they contained. Darien found himself confronted by the marble faces of men, women, and even children.

"Who are these people?" Kyel asked, flinching back from the outstretched hand of a statue.

"Nobility, for the most part," Naia said. "Whoever can afford to pay for such treatment. Such a burial does not come without a price."

Darien found himself staring harder at the macabre faces, wondering if he might find one he recognized. They were moving through what amounted to a maze of marble, winding around statues and sarcophagi, even mausoleums with family names etched into their stony exteriors. Magelight glowed from the walls, pushing back the shadows only a fraction. The air grew even colder, the stench of decay more robust. Darien shivered, seeing his own breath turn to mist before his face.

"Stop," the priestess commanded.

She was staring at him with a frown of puzzlement on her face. Darien didn't like the look in her eyes.

"What is it?"

"You have an aura," she said, forming the words slowly.

Darien glanced down at himself. A faint green nimbus surrounded him. The glow was so pale, it was difficult to see. But the aura was there undeniably.

"What does it mean?" He spread his arms out and studied the unsettling hue that crept up his sleeves and surrounded his hands. He didn't like the color. It reminded him of Meiran's candle. A whispered breath of apprehension shivered down his spine. He looked at the priestess in alarm.

"I have no idea what it means," Naia said, her face slack with concern. "But I gravely fear the implications."

Darien stared at her, waiting for the priestess to elaborate. But she merely turned away and led her horse forward. Darien started after her, looking down at himself in trepidation, then followed the woman through the strange city of the dead.

As he passed by a statue of a girl with disquieting stone eyes, he thought he could hear the sound of distant laughter, soft, like the echo of a memory. He turned to study the statue, noticing the eyes had taken on a mischievous glint. Perhaps the expression had always been there. But he couldn't suppress the nagging feeling that, somehow, the statue's face had changed.

He started forward and heard the sound again, this time from behind. He turned to see a softly glowing shade, the hazy reflection of a small girl with a playful gleam in her eyes. The wight disappeared almost instantly. He backed away, filled with a mixture of wonder and sadness.

He found Naia watching him, a soft smile on her lips. "Death does not discriminate. It takes the very old and the very young, alike."

Darien nodded, glancing back again at the weathered granite statue. Strangely, he found himself mourning a child he'd never met and would never have the chance to come to know. But he found himself powerfully moved by the chance encounter with her shade.

The priestess led them into a marble mausoleum. It turned out to be the entrance to a passage that opened out of the floor, sloping downward. It was paved with glistening black marble, and the horses had to struggle to keep their footing. The air grew slightly warmer again, though the magelight barely sufficed to light their way. Darien thought of casting a misty light of his own, but decided against it, not fully trusting the magic field in this place.

The corridor leveled out, curving slightly. The passage ended at a bridge that spanned a drop of hundreds of feet over a slowly moving river of black water.

A chill breath of stale air stirred his cloak as Darien led his horse out onto the bridge. The walls of this chamber were vaults, just as the last had been. Only, this time, there seemed no end to their height, the ceiling lost somewhere deep in shadow. The dark waters below churned and bubbled, releasing a foul miasma like a festering swamp ripe with decay.

Stiffly, Darien asked, "How much longer?"

"The exit is not far."

They moved off the bridge and into a stone passage that cut between rows of sarcophagi. The scent of death was much stronger here, so much so that Darien had to hold his cloak up over his face.

From behind came a soft but nerve-grating noise, like the scraping of metal against stone. The noise slowly faded. But then it grew louder again, a shrill, raking sound, much closer this time.

"What is that?" Kyel demanded.

Darien spun around, eyes scanning the shadows of the passage behind them. He'd never heard anything like that in his life. Almost, it reminded him of the sound of dragging chains.

The noise faded and was gone.

Swallowing against a cold lump of dread, Darien decided it was time to try the magic field. He reached out with his mind and sampled the energy of the current, relieved to find it biddable. He opened his mind to the field, holding it at ready, just in case.

The noise was back. Louder. Right behind them.

Darien whirled, hand reaching for his sword. Slithering through the fog behind them swirled a glimmering mass of sparkling light. The glowing tendrils writhed toward them like a thousand squirming snakes.

Darien forced his mind back from the magic field, too late. The flickering threads angled toward him with sinister purpose.

"*Naia!*" he gasped, tugging on the reins of his horse.

The priestess glanced back, terror on her face. Then she was running, pulling her mare behind her as Kyel sprinted forward.

Darien's horse reared, breaking free and bolting away. With a curse, he started after it. Then he skidded to a stop, flinching back.

Out of a doorway appeared a creature that resembled a massive wolfhound, head lowered, eyes glowing green. It growled low in its throat, the crusted fur of its hackles rising. Darien backed away from the beast. His hand rose to his shoulder, baring his sword.

Behind him, one of the writhing tendrils of light groped toward him.

Darien threw himself sideways even as the demon-hound leaped for his throat. He spilled over the top of a sarcophagus, slipping to the ground on the other side. There, he lay on his back, panting, frantically looking for an escape.

The thanacryst appeared over the lid of the sarcophagus, snarling down at him. From its jowls dribbled fetid globules of slobber.

Darien rolled to his feet. He stumbled backward as the beast sprang after him. Whirling, he made for the shadow of a doorway. He slid around the corner, pressing his body close against the wall, his breath coming in shallow gasps.

From the other side of the doorway came a low, menacing growl.

Darien raised his blade, drawing it back and holding it there with trembling hands. He held his ground and waited for the beast to come.

The thanacryst's muzzle edged around the corner. The nose quivered, scenting the air. Its glowing eyes trained on him.

Darien brought the blade down with all his strength. The steel connected, but he didn't pause to see the results of the strike.

Spinning, he threw himself through a doorway.

A loud *thud* echoed behind him. Shocked, Darien stared at the marble door that had slid shut, cutting him off from the passage behind. He groped frantically at the smooth door, gripped in numbing shackles of fear. He backed away from it, blade held in a double-fisted grip.

He glanced around. He was standing in a broad corridor with passageways leading off at intervals to either side. His eyes swept from one doorway to the next, scouring the shadows beyond.

Hesitant, he edged forward. As he passed the first dark opening, another door slid closed with a resounding *thud.*

Darien stopped, staring at the door in disbelief.

He crept forward again, only to find his way immediately blocked by another closing door, this one cutting him off from the main passage, as another door swept open on his left.

Darien stared at the new opening warily. He was beginning to get the sense he was being herded, steered purposefully by some unseen hand. He didn't want to go in the direction that hand was leading. But there was no alternative. Every other way had been sealed.

Lowering his blade, he moved through the opening into another lightless corridor. There was no magelight here to see by, and he was reluctant to make his own. Another door slid closed beside him, then he found himself confronted by a solid wall ahead.

Darien sheathed his sword, using his palms to grope his way along the walls. He could see nothing except for the soft green aura that surrounded his hands. The terrible absence of light sharpened his fear. Anything could be stalking silently behind him. Anything.

The walls steered him into another passage just as dark and terrible as the last. He felt his way along, hands exploring. Up ahead, a soft light beckoned him forward.

Taking heart in the glow, Darien moved toward it. Another door slid closed, the sound a jarring *thud* that shuddered through his every nerve.

He stopped, glancing around at a chamber suffused with amber light. The room was completely empty, just four high walls climbing upward to a vaulted ceiling. Suspended by a chain high above hung an enormous wrought-iron chandelier that shed a muted, wavering light. Only, the glow did not come from the light of tapers. It came from six golden orbs that hovered above the chandelier itself.

Darien stood gazing up at the orbs, hands spread out at his sides. His eyes moved to the walls, desperately seeking a way out.

The light wavered, then slowly dimmed. Above him, the orbs began to rotate, their pale light fading out smoothly into darkness. Shadows lengthened, closing in and drawing over him.

An icy sweat broke out on his forehead. He edged backward, pressing his back against the cold marble door. Hardly daring to breathe, he gazed out into the blackness ahead.

Then, from out of the darkness, a faint azure glow appeared.

It seemed to bleed right out of the shadows, moving silently toward him. Darien gasped as he realized he was gazing upon the pale glimmer of a wight. Another appeared, this time on his right. Then another.

Soon there were dozens of shades ringing the walls of the chamber. The gleam of the wights illuminated the hall, casting back the shadows with their ethereal blue glow. More appeared behind, pushing the others forward.

With a terrified sense of awe, Darien found himself surrounded by shades, each hazy form vaguely familiar. His eyes leaped from face to face, startled recognition flooding into him.

They advanced slowly, emerging from the walls to creep silently toward him through the darkness. Darien wanted to draw back away from them, but there was nothing he could do. There were too many. The marble door at his back was hard and unyielding.

Terror in his heart, he stood his ground and faced the dead of fallen Aerysius.

They were all here, every Master and Grand Master he'd ever known. Tyrius Flynn, Grand Master Ezras, Lynnea, Finneus, Master Harrison. So many others. Scores of them, a host of familiar faces, as well as strangers he'd never met. They moved toward him, crowding him, gazing at him with unreadable expressions.

The shade of a man reached out an arm toward him. Startled, Darien found himself cringing away from the gnarled fingers of Edric Torrence, the strange Bird Man who had saved his life.

As Darien looked on, a lone wraith parted itself off from the host, moving toward him, stopping within reaching distance. Darien shook his head, knowing this was the one thing in the world he couldn't take. He wanted to turn away, wanted to deny the image that confronted him. But it was impossible. He could do nothing but helplessly stare at the face in front of him with features so achingly familiar.

His father looked just as Darien remembered him, the last time he ever saw him alive.

"My son," Gerald Lauchlin whispered. "You've come home."

A ghostly hand reached toward him.

Darien couldn't help himself. Impelled by nearly two decades of sorrow and remorse, he moved toward the comfort of his father's embrace.

Kyel clutched his horse's reins in a white-knuckled grip, his other hand shaking as he fought to control the wildly flailing beast that reared up over his head. The Tarkendar lashed out with its forelegs as Kyel jumped away from the animal's hooves.

"Get control of it!" Naia shouted.

"I can't!"

The priestess strode forward, raising a hand before her face. She reached out toward the black gelding's head, taking the horse firmly by the bridle. The animal settled back to four legs, its withers quivering and glistening with a slick sheen of sweat.

Kyel glanced back the way they had come. The corridor was dark and empty. There was no sign of the slithering lights. And there was also no sign of Darien. Realizing the mage was gone, Kyel jerked his gaze back to the priestess.

"We have to go back," Naia gasped.

Kyel knew she was right. He'd just assumed Darien was following them.

"You don't think…" he started to say but was unable to complete the thought.

The priestess blinked as if waking from a trance, eyes flicking toward him wide with fear. "We must hurry! Without my guidance, the halls will assume he is a wandering shade and seek to take his spirit back into their keeping."

Kyel frowned, troubled by her words. He didn't want to go back, afraid of what they might find.

Darien reached toward the glowing form of his father. He felt just as he had as a boy of eight, when he'd run bounding down the path from the widow's home in Amberlie Grove to greet his father returning from the war. The tall Sentinel in his black cloak had swept him up in his arms, spinning him around twice before clasping him against his chest in a strong embrace.

The joy of his father's homecoming had been tempered only by the look of resentment on Aidan's face when he discovered his little brother had beaten him, winning the race to be the first scooped up in their father's arms.

But Aidan wasn't here now, and the proud smile on the glimmering face before him was just as warm and genuine as Darien remembered it. He moved forward, filled with a numbing euphoria.

Another wight swept forward, reaching out to bar his way.

"Stop," commanded the shade of Grand Master Ezras, turning to glance back over his shoulder. "Gerald, don't touch him."

As Darien looked on in confusion, the smile drained from his father's face. The glimmering blue aura around him wavered. "He is my son. He has come home to us."

But the shade of Ezras was adamant. "No. He does not belong here. He is not destined for this place."

Ezras reached his ghostly hands out, clasping Darien's father by the shoulders and turning him gently but firmly away. Aghast, Darien watched as the glowing wraiths turned away from him as one, receding, departing back into the shadows of the walls from whence they came.

His father looked back to cast an imploring glance his way before he, too, faded and was gone. Complete darkness settled in, descending on the chamber like a moonless winter night. Darien took a step toward the center of the room, eyes groping desperately through the shadows.

"Father…"

He sank slowly to his knees, bowing his head in shame. There had been tears in his father's eyes. Never in life had he seen that proud man cry.

Kyel followed Naia down the passage, back toward

the chamber of vaults. The strange flickering creature didn't seem to be there. But neither was Darien. Except for its macabre stone furnishings, the wide corridor was empty.

The priestess stopped in an alley between two rows of sarcophagi, gaping around as if lost. Kyel felt a moment of panic, clinging fiercely to the reins of the two horses.

"What do we do?"

"There is only one place to look," she said. "The walls would take him for a lost spirit and direct him to the Hall of the Masters. Fortunately, the way is not far."

Kyel nodded. He followed the priestess back through the maze of stone monuments, winding her way through dark alleys toward a broad doorway. As he came around the corner, Kyel stopped as she knelt over a dark stain on the floor.

"What—?" he began, then noticed the trail of paw prints leading off down the corridor. The sight chilled him.

"Blood," Naia said softly, standing up.

"Darien?"

"No." The priestess shook her head. "Demon blood. A thanacryst, by the prints. We must hurry."

She led him onward, sliding open stone doors with a gesture of her hand. She led them into a passage far too narrow for the horses to walk side by side. Kyel had to tie the Tarkendar's reins to the saddle of his own mount, leading the horses single-file into the shadows ahead.

"This is it," Naia whispered. Her words echoed in the darkness.

The priestess' tone was tense with worry.

At last, another door slid open ahead of them. Kyel heard the sound of it, even if he couldn't see anything. There was the clop of hoofbeats as Naia's horse moved forward. He followed cautiously, a cold feeling of dread tingling his skin.

"Darien?" the priestess called.

The air was distinctly cooler here, and there was a slight draft. Kyel sensed they were entering some type of chamber.

Then he saw it: the soft glow of the aura that surrounded Darien's body.

The mage was sitting alone in the black emptiness, knees drawn up against his chest. Kyel gaped at the sight of him. He'd almost taken him for a shade. Darien's head was bowed, arms wrapped around his legs.

"Darien," Naia said again.

The Sentinel looked up, gazing at them with haunted eyes.

"We must go." Naia lowered herself at his side, placing a hand on his shoulder.

Darien nodded. He looked dazed. Naia took him by the arm, helping him to his feet and guiding him back toward the door. But as he approached the opening, Darien stopped and turned back.

"He said I don't belong here," he whispered. "He said I'm destined for another place. What did he mean?"

"You spoke with a shade?" the priestess gasped.

"No. He spoke to me. What did he mean?"

"I don't know," Naia whispered.

Kyel thought perhaps she did know. Darien seemed to accept her words, moving forward to claim his horse. He still looked shaken, more so than Kyel had ever seen him.

Naia led them back through the labyrinth of passages, stopping at a large, dark opening in the wall. There, she paused, her eyes once again fearful as she turned to look back over her shoulder.

"This is the exit to Glen Farquist." Her words carried a heavy undercurrent of fear. To Darien, she said, "This is where we find out if what you did broke the Strictures of Death. If everything is fine, you will arrive at a shrine in the High Temple."

"And if it's not?"

"Then you will find out what that shade you met was trying to tell you."

Darien nodded. Moving past her, he led his horse forward. He didn't hesitate as he stepped into the opening. His image flickered once then was gone, consumed by the shadows on the other side.

Chapter Nineteen
The Temple of Death

Glen Farquist, The Rhen

Kyel stepped out of Death's Passage into a sudden gush of brilliant light. He gazed around, trying to get his bearings. They were in a shrine made entirely of brown marble. Light streamed down in thick rays from the ceiling, washing over them.

Ahead, Darien turned to look at him. His mouth was slack, his eyes dark and weary. He looked dazed, but mercifully alive. Kyel led his horse forward to stand beside him. He found his gaze drawn past his master to the life-size statue of a woman situated in an alcove.

The marble face was serene, yet remarkably powerful. One of her long, elegant arms was swept back behind her, the other extended forward, palm upward with fingers slightly curled. It was as if she expected him to press an object into her waiting hand. The face seemed to be considering him with a pensive expression. He had the feeling he was being scrutinized by those daunting marble eyes.

Behind him, he heard a voice and turned. A young man had joined them in the chamber and was speaking quietly to Naia off to one side. The man was dressed in white robes with a white stole draped over his shoulders. He turned and regarded the entrance to Death's Passage uneasily, then took the reins of Naia's mare. He led the horse forward, walking toward Kyel.

"May I take your reins?" the young priest asked as he reached out and removed the scarf from the gelding's head. Kyel watched as the man tied all three horses together in line and then led them away.

When he was gone, Naia approached Darien. The mage still lingered at the base of the statue, gazing at the compelling marble figure. The priestess placed a hand on his shoulder.

"Who is she?" Darien asked, not taking his eyes from the statue.

"The Goddess of the Eternal Requiem."

At her response, Darien's study of the marble woman became much more intense. The priestess' mouth drew into the slightest frown. Kyel sensed something more had just passed between the two of them, something to do with the statue. The priestess did not seem to care for Darien's interest in it one bit.

"I'll show you to the guest rooms," she said, striding away a few paces before stopping to wait for them.

Darien shook his head wearily. "We've come all this way. I wish to see my mother now."

Naia's frown became a look of concern. "Perhaps it should wait until after you've had a chance to rest."

"I'm fine," Darien insisted. "I'd just like to see her, please."

The priestess nodded.

"I'll wait here," Kyel said, uncomfortable with the idea of viewing a dead woman he'd never met. Especially since this particular woman had been dead for some time now.

"I think you need to come too, Kyel," Naia said, glancing at Darien for confirmation. The mage nodded slightly.

Kyel didn't understand why. If it had been his own mother, he would have wanted to spend his last moments with her in private. But he did as they asked and followed the priestess through a doorway.

They climbed a flight of stairs to a wide corridor with windows on one side that looked out upon a large garden courtyard. Kyel was impressed. This particular temple was different from anything he had ever seen. He'd almost forgotten where he was, at Glen Farquist in the Valley of the Gods, where the largest and most magnificent temples existed, and where all the governing bodies of the various religious sects dwelt. This was the High Temple of Isap, a palace in its own right.

And it was spectacular. Looking across the courtyard, Kyel saw the main sanctuary, a majestic domed structure. Row upon row of stained glass windows graced its sides. Its tall dome was clad in bronze that had weathered to verdigris over time.

Kyel fixed his eyes on the sway of Darien's cloak. The mage was walking with his head lowered, shoulders slumped in weariness. Naia muttered something in his ear, earning herself a sharp glare of reproach. Kyel had never seen him look so haggard, as if all the recent events were just now catching up with him.

Naia bristled at his glare, dark eyes flashing even through her veil. Kyel wondered what she'd said. Darien's stride had shifted until he was almost stalking, fists clenched in anger. He didn't look at the woman again, keeping his gaze trained on the floor.

Under his breath, Kyel heard him mutter, "It's my right."

"I cannot bar you from the shrine, Darien," Naia said. "But I must urge you to reconsider and think very carefully about what I told you the night we met."

"And do what?" Darien asked. "Stand down and allow Aidan to admit a second Enemy host through the Vale?"

"There are other ways."

"No. Even if I could convince Faukravar to hand over his entire northern army, it would hardly be enough. This war will be won or lost by magic, not military strength."

"So instead, you intend to set yourself against your brother *and* the Enemy, alone?" Naia flung her arms out in exasperation. "I'm sorry, Darien, but as strong as you might be, you are only one man."

"Orien was just one man," the mage reminded her. "Yet he was able to turn back the entire Third Invasion by himself."

"Orien was a martyr."

"He was an *effective* martyr."

"The people of this land don't need another Orien," Naia snapped. "What they need is you, alive."

Darien stopped, turning to regard the priestess wearily. "I don't see any other way. And I don't believe you do, either. I appreciate your intentions, Naia. I truly do. But don't make this harder on me than it already is."

The priestess closed her eyes, drawing a deep, steadying breath. After a moment, she looked back up at him. "Very well. I'll leave it in the hands of the goddess. I just pray she finds your purpose unjustified."

"Unjustified?" echoed Darien, face flushed in anger. "Can you honestly think of one person in the last thousand years who's had better reason to kneel at that statue's feet than myself?"

"No, I honestly can't," the priestess replied. "That is exactly why your decision worries me so much."

The Sentinel looked as though he wanted to say something more. His hand rose from his side toward her. But then he let his arm drop and turned away, striding down the corridor as Naia stared after him with a stricken look on her face.

Kyel waited until the priestess moved to follow him before he fell in behind, confused by what he'd just witnessed. He had no idea what their words had meant, but the content didn't seem to matter all that much. More important had been the look in Darien's eyes right before he'd turned away.

The corridor ended at a door that opened into a transept of the main sanctuary. Naia swept open the door, admitting them into the hall. Kyel followed behind Darien, noting the way the mage so carefully avoided Naia's eyes as he brushed past her.

"This way," she said in a lowered voice, leading them across the white tiles of the transept.

Kyel found himself surprised by the simplicity of the sanctuary that seemed almost at odds with the temple's ornate exterior. The walls were faced with limestone blocks that glowed in the colored light that spilled through the stained-glass windows. The sanctuary was simply an enormous space decorated with nothing other than a wondrous kaleidoscope of dazzling light. The effect was stirring, like moving through a soothing, dream-like haze.

Naia led them to the center of the room, where the transept merged with the main hall. There, on a raised dais surrounded by layers of white roses, Emelda Lauchlin lay in repose.

Kyel stopped, feeling a sudden pang of trepidation. The Prime Warden lay in a shimmering blanket of light that filtered down from above. Her pale skin seemed to glow, suffused with a radiance that created an almost natural flush of life. She was covered by a transparent shroud set with thousands of tiny, shimmering crystals that scattered the light into glittering rainbows of color.

Kyel took a few steps closer as he gazed at the woman's body in wonder. The Prime Warden looked remarkably alive, even hale, as if in the embrace of a deep and gentle sleep.

And she was beautiful. Her hair was dark and rich, spilling down around her face in soft, gleaming strands. She looked no older than Darien, her face untroubled by the years. She looked so much like her son, it would have been impossible to mistake the relationship.

Darien moved forward into the wash of brilliant light and knelt at his mother's side.

Kyel resisted the urge to turn away, feeling his presence there an invasion on the fragile privacy of the moment.

But Darien wanted him there. So Kyel forced himself to watch as the mage leaned forward and pressed a tender kiss against his mother's forehead. Then he turned to Naia and asked softly, "How did she die?"

The priestess moved to stand beside Darien, placing a hand on his shoulder.

"A demon followed us into the Catacombs. Your mother was injured, and she died here a week later." Naia paused, allowing her gaze to slip down to the body of the Prime Warden. "I'm so sorry, Darien."

The mage nodded, looking thoughtful. He whispered, "Arden Hannah."

Naia's glance darted back to his face at the mention of that evil name. But she made no effort to either confirm or deny it. Instead, she squeezed his hand and rose gracefully from his side, leaving him there alone. She walked over to Kyel and took him by the arm, guiding him back toward a wall of the transept.

Kyel whispered, "She's been dead all this time? How…?"

Naia smiled sadly as she released his arm, stopping to lean with her back against the limestone wall. "The methods of preservation are another of our temple secrets. For funerals of state, it is customary that the deceased be available for public viewing anywhere from one to six months. The truth is, a body so preserved is protected for many, many years."

Kyel shook his head in wonder, marveling, "She seems alive."

"Thank you."

Kyel frowned. He started to say something, but the sound of another voice startled him. He turned to discover that a white-robed figure had drawn up silently beside him.

"The First Daughter's talents are sought after throughout the land," an old man wearing the stole of a priest of Death assured him. "In some circles, her work is considered an art form."

Kyel gaped at Naia, amazed. So the body of Darien's mother had been her work, every meticulous detail arranged by her own hands before she had departed on her journey to find Darien. Naia smiled with a trace of self-conscious pride at his reaction. Turning to the priest, she said:

"Your Eminence, may I present to you the acolyte, Kyel Archer. Kyel, this is His Eminence, the High Priest of Death, Luther Penthos."

Kyel gawked openly at the bald man who was smiling at him genially. Minus the white robes and the stole, Luther Penthos would look like someone's aged grandfather. His blue eyes were crystal-clear as he reached out a hand and clasped Kyel's arm in a warm gesture of greeting.

"It is a pleasure to meet you."

"Your Eminence," Kyel said. The man's grip on his forearm was strong. When he released it, Kyel had to resist the urge to rub his skin.

A motion behind the priest caught his eye, and he glanced up to find Darien walking over to join them. The mage looked even more haggard than before.

"Your Eminence, I would also like to present the new Prime Warden, Darien Lauchlin, Grand Master of the Fifth Tier."

"Eighth Tier," Kyel corrected her absently.

Naia visibly blanched as she turned to stare at Darien in shock. The high priest blinked, but his smile returned as he reached out and clasped Darien's arm.

The old man shook his head in wonder. "Eighth tier. I'm not certain if I've ever heard of such a ranking."

"It's not meant to exist," Darien confirmed darkly. "I fear I'd be considered something of an abomination."

"You don't look like an abomination to me. Although, I must say, you do look like a man who could use some rest."

"We all could," the Sentinel agreed.

"I should let you retire to the guest wing, then. But before I forget, I have something that is yours by rights."

The old man fished in a pocket of his robe, drawing out a wide, silver collar. It was attached to a medallion set with what looked like an enormous red jewel. The stone glowed a brilliant shade of crimson, the light coming from deep within its facets. It seemed to have a life of its own, pulsing like a heartbeat. The high priest pressed the medallion into Darien's hand, squeezing the mage's fingers closed around it.

"What's this?" Darien stared down at the gem's radiance, which moved over his palm like webs of light reflected off a pool of water.

Luther Penthos took a step back as if trying to distance himself from the object. "The medallion is called the Soulstone. It is a storage vessel that contains your mother's gift. For someone to accept the Transference, they must simply put it on. I must, however, caution you against its other aspects."

Darien fingered the medallion in his hand, studying it intensely. He traced his thumb over the gleaming band of the collar, then glanced up with an expression of concern.

"How is it that an object such as this came to be in the possession of the Temple of Death? Forgive me, Your Eminence, but Aerysius has always laid claim to such heirlooms of power."

Luther Penthos nodded sagely, crossing his arms over the white fabric of his stole. "A thousand years ago, this medallion was the property of the Lyceum of Bryn Calazar. It was placed into our keeping before the fall of Caladorn, with the one restriction that knowledge of its existence should never be allowed to pass to the mages of Aerysius.

"However, since Aerysius is no more, I have decided to place the Soulstone into your hands. I have never felt comfortable holding such a thing, even in my deepest vaults."

He went on, "You've spoken lightly of abomination today, Prime Warden, but that object you are holding is a true abomination, if ever there was one. I am more than glad to have it out of my possession than you could possibly know."

"Why is that?"

"Because it was with this very medallion that Zavier Renquist struck the first killing blow that precipitated the overthrow of the Lyceum. The Soulstone is far more than just a storage device, you see. When it is full with a mage's gift, the stone glows with an inner light, just as you see it now. But when it is empty, the stone is black and lifeless.

"If it is placed in that condition around the neck of a living mage, the gem has the effect of ripping the ability from that person. Such a death would be particularly cruel. So have great care with that medallion, Prime Warden. Should it fall into the wrong hands, it might be sorely used against you."

Darien stared down at the medallion in his hand. A play of emotions ranged over his face, as if a truly inspirational notion had just occurred to him. He raised the Soulstone to clutch it tightly against his chest. A wistful smile appeared on his lips, growing until it spread to touch his eyes.

"Thank you, Your Eminence," he breathed. There was no mistaking the ominous excitement in his voice.

The high priest didn't seem to miss it, either. The old man's face hardened into a frown, and he stabbed an anxious glance sideways at the priestess. Naia regarded Darien with a look of startled indignation. Kyel felt his own stomach wrench. He found it easy to follow the mage's train of thought. Darien wanted to use that medallion on his brother, and the desire for it was strong enough to make his eyes shimmer with the thrill of anticipation. The look on his face was frightening.

In a carefully controlled voice, Luther Penthos said, "You have my condolences on the passing of your mother. I knew Emelda Lauchlin well, just as

I also knew your esteemed father. And I can assure you, Prime Warden, that neither one of your parents would condone what is so obviously passing through your mind."

Darien blinked, torn away from his dark thoughts by the old man's blunt words. He shot the high priest a look of resentment, tightening his grip on the medallion until the hand that contained it was trembling.

"Before you presume to judge me, why don't you go stare for a while at the shades of my brethren in your Catacombs. While you're at it, go look upon the ruins of Aerysius and the unholy light of hell that corrupts the skies above it. Then, if you still can, come back and tell me the man responsible for those atrocities doesn't deserve to die a traitor's death in pain."

"He is your brother," Naia protested before the high priest could wave her into silence.

"The gods abhor fratricide, regardless of intent or reason," Luther Penthos said. "Such an act would condemn your soul to the Netherworld for all eternity."

Darien shrugged indifferently as he stuffed the medallion into a pocket of his cloak. "Then at least I'll be at peace."

Kyel heard Naia make a strangled sound as Darien strode away. Turning to the high priest, she explained rapidly, "He wants to offer himself before the Goddess of the Eternal Requiem. I tried to convince him otherwise, but he's obsessed with the notion."

Luther Penthos stared at Darien's back until the mage disappeared through the doorway.

"If you cannot dissuade him, then I'll try. But there is nothing we can do to stop him. It is forbidden to deny the petition of a supplicant."

Kyel moved forward, inserting himself between them as he turned to Naia.

"What are you saying? What exactly is he trying to do?"

The priestess looked up at him. "Darien intends to disavow his Oath of Harmony and commit himself instead to the Goddess of Death in an ancient rite called a Bloodquest."

Chapter Twenty
Goddess of the Eternal Requiem

Glen Farquist, The Rhen

The corridor was dark and silent, the echo of his boots the only sound, the azure glow at his feet the only source of light. There was no one in the halls but himself, no one to question him about where he was going and why. He had already made his decision. Now, all he wanted to do was get it over with.

Darien descended the stairs and pushed open the door of the shrine, letting the magelight spill ahead of him into the room. He fed the light with a trickle of power and looked on as it spread out toward the four corners of the room, illuminating the shrine in an otherworldly glow.

Darien turned his gaze to the nearest torch and watched it sputter into flame. He looked around the room. Fire erupted along the walls, each individual torch blazing to life in quick succession. Then he let go of the magelight, allowing it to recede into the shadows of the floor.

Pacing forward, Darien looked up into the marble face of the goddess. A shiver of apprehension stole down his back, inspired by the statue's serene but critical eyes. He stopped, his chest at a level with the goddess' outstretched hand.

Darien stared at the bent fingers as he contemplated the curious significance of the gesture. Then he dropped to his knees, bowing forward and pressing his hands against the cold stone of the floor. He closed his eyes, emptying his mind of all thoughts save one.

Sitting back, he raised his hand over his shoulder, his fingers closing around the hilt of his sword. He drew the blade slowly forth, wielding it before his face as he grasped the hilt in both hands. He lowered the weapon carefully, taking it by the flat of the blade.

"Goddess have mercy on me," Darien whispered as he stood. He offered the sword into the statue's outstretched hand. The hilt fit easily within the marble cradle of her palm, fixing itself perfectly in the clasp of her bent fingers. He stepped back, releasing his grip and staring in wonder at the sight of the goddess wielding his own sword, the point leveled at his racing heart.

A thin line of sweat streaked down his brow as he knelt on the floor, abasing himself before the statue. His breath came in gasps, heart pounding in his ears. Unbidden thoughts flooded his mind like a drowning river, churning images and twisted feelings of violence and tragedy, betrayal and grief.

Before the discerning eyes of the statue, Darien bared his innermost soul, ashamed by the bleakness of it.

He knelt there on the chill floor of the shrine, staring up into the face of the goddess as slow degrees of exhaustion stole over him. Sometime in the darkest hours of night, the torches winked out one by one.

When the last flame finally guttered and died, Darien did nothing to restore the loss of light. Instead, he lay back across the hard tiles. When sleep finally took him, his dreams were plagued by the shades that haunted the desolate vaults of the Catacombs, calling out to him across time and eternity. It was impossible to tell whether those pleas were cries for vengeance or urgent appeals to abandon his perilous course.

Drenched in a cold sweat, Darien writhed in his

sleep on the stone floor of the shrine, completely oblivious to the changes taking place above him in the darkness.

———

He awoke to bright, saturating light. Squinting, Darien pushed himself up off the floor, for a moment disoriented as he sat there blinking, trying to make sense of his surroundings. Dim memories of the night crept slowly back to him, and with them came a shiver of foreboding. He looked up at the statue, his eyes tracing the silken flow of the goddess' robes upward to her face. As he gazed up into her stone visage, a silver glint above her caught his eye.

It was his sword, held aloft by a slender arm that was now extended over the statue's head. The blade was poised in the air at a threatening angle. Darien froze, feeling a heart-numbing sense of dread. He brought a hand up to rub his eyes, an effort to deny what he saw. But when he looked back up, the blade was still there, wielded firmly in the goddess' stone grasp.

Darien pushed himself the rest of the way off the floor, rising stiffly to his feet. As he did, a soft rustling sound behind him made him turn. Startled, he saw Naia sitting behind him on a step. He wanted to turn away from her, anxious to avoid her grief-stricken face. But for some reason, he found he couldn't take his eyes off her.

Sitting there in her white gown, hunched over with her arms wrapped around herself, the priestess looked nothing more than a frail child, scared and alone. The look in her eyes was imploring. Part of him wanted to go to her and catch her up in his arms, to offer her what comfort he could.

But she was a priestess of Death, the white veil that stood between them an outward symbol of her vow of chastity.

And then there was Meiran, not yet even two months dead.

Darien bowed his head, ripping his gaze away from her and turning back to the statue of the goddess with fresh resolve. He took a step toward it.

"Don't."

The urgency in her voice stopped him, but he couldn't bring himself to look at her. Instead, he stood in the middle of the room as if frozen. He could feel her eyes on his back. Darien stared at the statue, praying for the goddess to give him the strength he needed to finish what he had started.

"Please don't do this."

Her words made it seem possible that he had a choice. It would be so easy just to turn and leave the shrine, to abandon his sword and simply walk away. The temptation was sweet. With one decisive act, he could preserve his integrity, his dignity, even the tattered remnants of his humanity.

But at what price? And who could he ask to pay it?

"I must," Darien said. He didn't know if the response was intended more for her, or rather for himself. There was scant conviction in his tone.

He heard the stir of her gown against the tile, the whisper of her slippered feet as they crossed the floor toward him. Her hand touched his cheek, directing his face toward hers with gentle pressure. He stared through her veil into her deep brown eyes, desiring nothing more than to drown himself in them and forget everything else in the world.

"No one's making you do this," she insisted. "No one has the right to expect this of you."

It took every shred of courage he had to turn away. "I don't have a choice."

"Have you even paused to consider the repercussions that might arise from this? Or the ethical considerations?"

"Of course I have." Darien backed away from her toward the statue. "This is war, Naia. I'll leave the question of ethics to the clerics of Om. Let them stew over it for the next hundred years. I don't have the time."

But she was relentless, moving forward until she had him cornered against the statue's base. "And what of you, Darien? Are you prepared to accept the personal costs?"

"What do you mean?" He frowned at her.

"Simply put, you don't seem like the sort of man capable of genocide. Yet, if you use your strength to turn back these armies, you will have the blood of thousands on your hands. And not all those deaths will be Enemy casualties, unless you intend to strike down each soldier individually, one by one. Are you certain you could live with that guilt?"

He bowed his head, knowing she was right. But he also knew it made no difference. This was the plate the gods had served him. Without meeting her eyes, he said, "I'm not certain of anything, at the moment. In truth, I've done my best to avoid thinking about the sort of questions you're asking."

"Then perhaps that means something, Darien. Perhaps you should give yourself more time to come to terms with this decision before rushing into a commitment that could destroy you."

"No." What she was asking was impossible. If he paused even a day, there was a chance he would lose his resolve. "I don't have time. If Arden Hannah's right, then both armies are already on the move. Everything else she told me has so far proven true. As we speak, men under Proctor's command are likely engaging the Enemy. Greystone Keep might have already fallen. I have but a fortnight to travel all the way to Orien's Finger, or Rothscard will be next. And then Auberdale.

"Don't you understand? I don't have the *right* to stand here debating ethics with you while the North falls around me. Once I thought I had that luxury, but I don't anymore. There are no simple answers to your questions. I could still be standing here struggling with them as the South falls, as well."

As he spoke, a change crept over Naia's face. The feverish intensity dissolved, replaced by an expression of uncertainty. And there was something else there as well, reflected back at him from the depths of her eyes. He wanted to deny it, but there was no mistaking the tender compassion in her gaze.

"Then I'm coming with you."

"*What?* Naia, you're a priestess. Your place is here, not on a field of battle. I don't understand what purpose you think you could even serve."

She shrugged as a sad smile formed on her lips. "Someone is going to need to keep you human."

Darien just stared at her. What did she think, that he was going to turn himself into the next Zavier Renquist? His mind reeled, suddenly plagued by doubt. That was exactly what he had been afraid of, all the times he'd argued so passionately about his Oath. But that had been before Royce's betrayal, before the fire. Before Arden Hannah had touched him, caressing his face the same way Naia just had. But Arden's touch had been poison, a slow-acting venom that was rotting his soul.

Naia said, "Take me with you. That is my one condition for helping you, if you insist on going through with this."

Darien sighed, shaking his head. "You'll do nothing but slow me down."

"And Kyel won't? I'm a far better rider than your acolyte."

"Kyel is not coming with me."

"You're turning him loose?" she gasped. "By the gods, Darien, the boy's not nearly ready!"

"I need him to do a few tasks for me. And he'll be much safer in Rothscard."

At that, Naia choked out an incredulous laugh. "You're sending that boy to the *Queen of Emmery?* Oh, I pity poor Kyel."

Darien couldn't help but smile. It had been one of the better notions he'd conceived late in the night. He had no doubt Kyel would find himself in over his head, but that was exactly the position he wanted him in. "It will be a good learning experience for him. A true lesson in diplomacy."

"You're a harsh master, Darien Lauchlin." Naia smiled.

"I try."

Her smile was so infectious he found himself grinning back. "So what do you think His Eminence will say about me stealing you away from him?"

Naia's gaze took on a positively devious glint. "I'm quite certain he won't stop me. Especially if I neglect to tell him I'm leaving."

"I hope Kyel isn't taking lessons in obedience from you." He let his smile fade, his thoughts returning to the issue at hand. Behind him, the goddess still stood with his sword held aloft in a warding stance. "So how do we do this?"

The priestess sighed, looking upward to the statue. "I need to make a few arrangements. Why don't you go clean up a bit, or the goddess still might find it in her heart to reject you."

Her words brought a vivid image to mind of the night of his Raising.

"What?" Naia sounded concerned.

Darien blinked, retreating from his thoughts. "Oh, it's nothing. This just reminds me a bit too much of the last rite I participated in. I only hope this one has a better outcome."

She stared at him with a look of incomprehension. "I hope so, too."

Frowning up at his sword firmly wielded in the goddess' hand, he asked, "If the gods abhor even the notion of fratricide, then why was my petition accepted?"

"It would seem, in this case, that an exception has been made."

Then she left him, departing in a shimmering sway of silk. Darien watched her go, following her movements with his eyes. When she was gone, he turned and glanced back up at his sword, seeking there for solace. But it was the wrong thing to do. The blade reminded him too much of Meiran.

As did Naia.

He found Kyel still asleep, wool blankets piled over him, his head resting on a mound of goose-down pillows. Darien sat on the edge of the bed, reaching his hand into the pocket of his cloak. He withdrew the silver medallion, running his fingers over the facets of the pulsating gem.

Kyel stirred, rubbing the sleep out of his eyes. He squinted upward, eyes fixing on the Soulstone in Darien's hand. His brow creased as he pushed himself upright.

"This is for you," Darien told him, offering the medallion to Kyel. The young man reached for it hesitantly, lifting it by the silver band of the collar. He held it, swaying, before his face.

"I want you to keep this on you at all times and never let it out of your sight. But don't put it around your neck just yet. You'll have to wait till I say the time is right. Do you understand?"

"Aye. I do." Kyel let his hand drop to the covers.

Darien studied the young man's face, trying to read his expression. So many of the plans Darien had made in the quiet darkness of the shrine depended on his young acolyte. He decided not to dilute his expectations; Kyel could only refuse him. And if he did, then it would be better to find out now, when he still had a chance to reformulate his strategy.

"I'll be leaving you for a time," Darien said as he studied Kyel's face intently. "While I'm gone, I have two favors to ask of you."

"You're sending me away."

The boy was perceptive. He was also not happy about the notion. Darien decided to admit the truth. Or, rather, a version of it. "In part. I can't risk us both. If something happens to me, I'll need you to carry on in my stead."

"I'm not certain I could do that." Kyel frowned up at him.

"Then let's hope you're not put in that position. But if you are, I trust you'll make whichever decisions are best."

Kyel nodded, looking sullen as he turned the medallion over in his fingers. "So where is it you're sending me?"

Darien stood up, reaching down to pluck the Soulstone out of Kyel's hands. He wanted the young man's full attention. Kyel finally looked up at him, silently fuming.

"First, I need you to ride to the Temple of Wisdom, which is just across the valley. Present yourself to the clerics there and tell them you represent the Prime Warden."

"I thought you didn't care for that title."

Darien shrugged. "It does seem to have its uses. In war, we must find whatever weapons we can, and use them however we can manage."

"So now you're going to war against the clerics of Om?"

Darien shook his head. "No. You are."

Kyel's look of shock was mildly satisfying.

He went on to explain, "I must find a way to seal the Well of Tears. I've no idea how to accomplish that. If anyone does know, it will be Om's clerics. Have them take you down to their vaults but insist they provide you with someone to help you with the research. If you don't, they'll just let you muck about down there till you die of old age having never found a single thing. It's one of their common ploys."

Kyel frowned up at him. "Why would they not wish to help me?"

"Because the clerics of Om are intensely jealous of their pearls of wisdom. Information is power, Kyel, and no one gives away power easily or freely."

Comprehension dawned in Kyel's eyes, yet doubt lingered there, as well. "You said you had two favors. What's the second?"

"You'll have only three days to search for information in the vaults. Then I'll need you to journey to Rothscard and meet with the Queen of Emmery. Again, tell her you are my representative, and I've given you full authority to treat with her."

"I suppose I can do that," Kyel responded skeptically. "But what exactly am I supposed to say to her?"

Darien allowed himself a smug grin. "You're to tell her that by order of the Prime Warden, she is to yield over command of her army to me. If she refuses, inform her politely that she's out of a throne."

Kyel's face drained to an ashen color. "You're not serious! You want me to threaten a *queen?!*"

"Believe me, Romana Norengail can use a good threat," Darien assured him. "If she attempts to argue—which she will—tell her *politely* that the new Prime Warden has forsworn his Oath of Harmony. That ought to convince her nicely. By the way, if she offers you wine, it would behoove you to refuse her. *Politely.*"

"Sometimes you scare me," Kyel muttered.

"Good. Perhaps if you emulate me, you can scare Romana out of her army. The Queen's general is a man named Blandford. Inform him he'll need to arrive at Orien's Finger by dawn on the morning of the Solstice, not an hour later. If he's late, then he needn't bother showing up at all. I'll meet him there if everything goes right."

"And if it doesn't?"

"Then you'd better learn how to command that army."

Darien let the door swing closed on Kyel's wide-eyed stare, smiling to himself as he strode down the hallway. The boy would do well. What he had said to Naia earlier was true. This would be an invaluable learning experience for him.

He found the door to his own room, where he had stuffed his pack the day before. It was still there, the bed undisturbed. A fresh pitcher of water had been left by the washstand, along with a tray of food that had sat there all night. Darien bypassed the tray, going instead to his pack and sliding out what was left of the sack of jerky he'd brought down with him from the pass.

He unfastened the silver brooch that held his cloak, drawing the dark fabric off his shoulders with one hand as he stuffed a strip of dried meat into his mouth. He went through the motions of chewing, not even tasting the food as he swallowed it, undressing at the same time. Darien pulled a fresh shirt and breeches out of his pack and put them on, dismayed by the fit. He was losing weight.

He walked to the looking glass that hung on the wall over the washstand, stunned by the image that gazed back at him. He scarcely recognized himself. He stared into the mirror, transfixed by his reflection as he reached up and drew his fingers over the dark stubble that covered his face, a face that looked ten years older than the last time he'd seen it. What amazed him most about the image that regarded him were the eyes. They were his father's eyes, exactingly recreated in his own face, complete in every detail, every haunted shadow. Darien shuddered, turning away from the mirror.

As he did, a wave of energy swept over him with violent, raking fingers. The reflection of his back in the looking glass wavered for a moment in a flare of indigo light that rose up from the floor to surround him. Tendrils of power crawled over him, groping at the fabric of his clothes, ripping through his hair, clawing at the skin of his face. The energy receded only slowly, drawing downward to the floor and then flickering out altogether.

Darien gazed somberly down at the garments he wore that suddenly fit his lean body perfectly. It was remarkable, what he could do with his power, without sparing scarcely a thought to the act. He didn't have to look back at the mirror behind him. The reflection would only confirm what he already knew. His face was clean-shaven, the grime and dust erased from his skin. Even his hair smelled clean as he raised his hands to draw it behind his shoulders, catching it up and tying it back. He went over to sit on the bed, finding his cloak where he'd tossed it down on top of the covers.

He couldn't put that cloak back on. At least, not as it was. Not if he was going to truly embrace the title Naia kept insisting he use. He would need the kind of authority that only the office of the Prime Warden could lend him if he was to accomplish the tasks he'd set out for himself.

As he looked down at the blue-black fabric of the cloak, Darien willed it to change. And it did. He stood up, drawing a cloak of gleaming white over his shoulders and fixing it in place. By all appearances, it could have been his mother's cloak, the defining emblem of the Prime Warden of Aerysius. The fabric felt strange. It felt heavier, although he knew his act had done nothing to the material but remove the pigment.

He passed the strap of his baldric across his shoulder. The leather scabbard hung empty at his back.

He opened the door and strode out into the hallway, determined to return to the shrine and reclaim his sword from the goddess' hand. He knew the price would be the chains on his wrists, but he was willing to pay it. The conviction that had held him to his Oath had been the first thing rotted away by the poison feel of Arden's touch.

He descended the stairs, working his way through the warren of halls and corridors to the shrine. White-robed priests and veiled priestesses glanced up with startled expressions before ducking their heads in deference to the cloak. Darien did nothing to acknowledge the looks, barely noticing the men and women that moved around him in the halls. His mind was intent on his purpose, to the point that everything else around him seemed irrelevant and remote.

Lost in thought, he almost didn't notice the high priest who stood in shadow, blocking the entrance to the shrine. Darien stopped in the middle of the stairs, one hand poised on the handrail. Luther Penthos regarded him with a careworn expression, eyes narrowing as they pondered the significance of the cloak.

"You must know I'm opposed to this," the old man said. "The goddess has made her choice, so there is nothing I can do to stop you. But nothing prevents me from stating my opinion. I believe you are making a disastrous mistake that will have far-reaching consequences. If you go through with this, know that you do so not only against my better judgment, but also against my will. From this moment forward, I will hold you in the utmost contempt."

Darien glared down at him. "Stand aside." Though spoken softly, his tone conveyed a dangerous insinuation of threat.

The high priest bowed his head. Darien swept down the stairs, brushing past him as he thrust open the door to the shrine. He stepped down the last tiled step into the brilliant light within, slamming the door shut behind him.

He let his eyes wander over the statue of the goddess as he fought to collect himself. His encounter with the old man had left him shaking.

A streak of white from the corner of his eye was the only warning he had as a sword swiped down in front of his face. Darien winced away from it, but a hand caught him by the hair, wrenching his head back sharply as the edge of the blade kissed the flesh of his throat. A strong jerk on his hair forced him to his knees as the blade followed his movement, its honed edge biting wickedly into his neck.

Darien stared up into the veiled face that hovered over him, appalled. The ruthless intent written in Naia's eyes was without compassion, her face terrifying in its authority. The woman he knew was gone, replaced by a sinister angel that threatened him with his own sword.

"There are three faces of the goddess," the priestess said. "The face of Mercy, the face of Sacrifice, and the face of Vengeance. They are three, as they also are one, each inseparable from the other. To gaze upon one is to gaze upon them all. To commit to one is to commit to all three. You have come here to pledge your life to the service of the goddess, to become her leveling hand of Vengeance. She has determined your cause just and worthy. Do you foreswear all prior oaths and dedicate your life to seek the blood of another?"

The press of the blade at his neck bit dangerously as Darien swallowed, his throat moving against it. "Aye, I do," he whispered.

Her hand coiled around in his hair, tightening its grip. "Hold out your hands."

He did as she asked. The sword swept down from his neck and parted the flesh of both wrists at the same time, laying open the skin across the twin markings of the chains. Blood welled from the deep gashes, beading to the floor in fat, crimson droplets. The priestess knelt beside him, setting his sword down on the floor and lifting a bronze chalice in its stead.

"You are now pledged to the service of the goddess, your duty consummated only when Aidan Lauchlin is destroyed, bereft of body and heart, mind and spirit." As she spoke, Naia took his right wrist in her hand, catching his blood in the chalice, and then lifted it to his lips.

"Come. You must now drink from hatred's bitter cup and taste of the blood you swear to mete."

She tilted the chalice, spilling the warm liquid into his mouth. Darien gagged, unable to bring himself to swallow.

"Drink!" the priestess hissed.

He squeezed his eyes shut as he forced himself to

gulp down the mouthful of blood. A spasm of nausea clenched his stomach, but the priestess had him by the hair again. She lifted the chalice again to his lips and forced the remainder of its contents down his throat.

Then she withdrew her hand. Darien collapsed forward, clutching his arms against his chest. Pain flared from the gashes in his wrists, as if a white-hot iron were being pressed into his flesh to cauterize the wounds.

He moaned, writhing with his head pressed against the floor, trembling in agony. Rolling onto his side, he brought his arms up in front of his face and gasped at the sight that confronted him.

The wounds were healed, though the pain was still there, still wretchedly intense. But where the chains had been was now only a set of fresh, angry scars. Darien sat up, consumed by a sudden, terrible feeling of loss.

"What have I done?" he whispered.

He couldn't stop trembling as the priestess wrapped her arms around him, drawing him close. He collapsed into Naia's embrace, clutching her against him desperately.

Chapter Twenty-One
Glen Farquist

Glen Farquist, The Rhen

Kyel set the breakfast tray down on the edge of the bed, staring at it wistfully. The scattered crumbs were all that remained of the second real meal he could remember eating in months. Had it only been that long? It somehow seemed like years. He tried picturing the face of his wife, but for some reason her image in his mind was vague and indistinct. Kyel finally gave up, feeling unsettled. He hadn't given thought to Amelia in days. And baby Gil. His son was two years old, now. Kyel had missed his birthday.

He looked out the window. Covendrey was not very far from here. Little more than a fortnight's travel. He was closer to home than he had been since the start of his journey.

Kyel lifted his arm, pushing back the fabric of his sleeve and staring down at the marking of the chain. He wished he could get rid of it, tear it right off his skin and simply go back to his family. He wished he'd never let Darien talk him into any of this.

But then, where would he be? Certainly, no closer to going home. He would still be back in the pass with an army coming down at him.

Sighing, Kyel turned and left the room. He knew he really didn't have time to waste, not if he was to accomplish any of the tasks set out for him.

He found the door to Darien's room open. But the mage was already gone, if he'd ever been there at all. The bed looked undisturbed, and there was an untouched tray of food sitting by it. Kyel frowned down at the tray, thinking of the two meals he'd eaten since arriving at the temple. Obviously, Darien hadn't been in his room all night.

And there was only one other place he would have gone.

Kyel felt saddened by the thought. He remembered asking Darien once why the Oath was so important to him. The mage had given him some vague story about falling off a cliff. Kyel hadn't understood a word of it at the time. Now he did.

I can choose to let go. But this time, I know if I decide to fall, there will be no one around to stop me. To Kyel, the meaning of those words now seemed as clear as a pane of glass looking out on a stormy sea.

Darien had chosen to take that fall.

Kyel knew there was a good reason why every Master of Aerysius was required to swear the Mage's Oath. The tradition had been instituted after the betrayal of the mages of Bryn Calazar, to prevent such a thing from ever happening again. The Oath of Harmony was a safeguard.

In his desire to seek revenge upon his brother, Darien was at great risk of becoming just like him. Kyel knew he had already seen it in him, the bitter poison of that hatred. It was spreading in him. Kyel feared it would eventually consume him, if it hadn't already.

"Excuse me…Kyel Archer?"

He turned to find the same young priest who had taken their horses the day before. The man was lingering in the doorway, holding a parcel wrapped in folds of white silk. He offered it to Kyel with a peculiar look on his face.

Kyel received the package uncertainly. As he did, he realized the priest was even younger than he'd previously thought, barely older than a boy.

"The First Daughter requested this be made for

you," the young man said.

Kyel stared down at the parcel in his hands. His fingers felt numb as he fumbled at the knotted strip of ribbon. When he had it undone, what the parting silk revealed made him wince.

Kyel lifted the black cloak up before his face, holding it with a feeling of revulsion mixed with reverence. The Silver Star seemed to glitter in the candlelight. Every stitch was perfectly even, tapering toward the eight points of the rays. Kyel stared at it, wondering how such careful embroidery could have been accomplished in just one night.

"My thanks." Kyel had the urge to take the cloak to his room and stuff it down as far as he could in his pack. But he knew he couldn't do that. Such an act would hardly be fit repayment for the gift. These people had been considerate hosts, and he owed it to them to show appreciation for their generosity.

So it was that Kyel found himself removing the tattered gray wool he had worn every day since his arrival in the pass and donned in its place the ill-omened badge of dead Aerysius.

From the doorway, the young priest said, "His Eminence requires a word with you."

Kyel turned to find the man looking at him with open wonder in his eyes.

"Just let me get my things." Kyel ducked his head, feeling self-conscious.

The new black cloak fluttered behind him as he walked back down the hall to his own room. There, he collected his longbow and shouldered his pack. He turned to leave. With a flare of panic, he suddenly remembered the Soulstone. The medallion was still lying on the stand beside the bed where Darien had set it. Relieved, he strode over and picked it up, stuffing the heirloom into the pocket of his new cloak.

Kyel followed the priest down the stairs and through a maze of hallways. He waited as the young man held a door open for him. He nodded his thanks then moved into a dimly lit study.

Luther Penthos was already there, seated at a desk that held three tidy stacks of parchment. The priest extended a hand, inviting him to take the seat opposite. Kyel removed his pack, setting it down awkwardly beside the chair along with his bow and quiver.

"Your Eminence," Kyel said.

The man scowled at the cloak. Then lifted his stare to confront Kyel.

"I want to know where your master is going. And why he took my daughter without my permission."

Kyel felt as if someone had just poured a goblet of cold water over his head. "Naia is your daughter? Your…*child*…?"

The old man nodded, his blue eyes narrowing dangerously. "And someday she may even be high priestess, unless your master corrupts her first."

"Darien would never touch your daughter."

But even as the words passed his lips, Kyel knew he had doubts. The interplay he'd witnessed between the two of them the day before made him wonder. For just a moment, Darien had looked like he'd been on the verge of embracing the priestess. Kyel had even felt comforted by the sight. It was a wonderful thing to see him display such a simple, tender emotion. But Darien also hadn't known what Kyel did now.

He had no idea what kind of fire he was playing with.

Leaning forward, the old man demanded, "Why else would Naia run off without even asking me? Without telling me where she was going? She left with *him!*"

He punctuated the last word with a jarring slap on the desk that made Kyel flinch.

He found himself wondering what Darien had done to merit such ire from the old man. There was more going on here than just Naia's disappearance. Something must have happened between the high priest and Darien that had set the man against him.

"I don't know what his plans are," Kyel admitted. "He didn't tell me. The only thing I know is that he'll be at Orien's Finger on the morning of the Solstice."

"Orien's Finger," Penthos echoed. His face went slack. "Are you quite certain?"

"Yes. Why? Whatever is the problem?"

The high priest leaned back in his chair as his eyes wandered up the wall behind Kyel. "In ancient times, there were eight Circles of Convergence. Two were lost to us when Caladorn fell. Three more have been either destroyed or lost through the years. There are only three circles remaining that we know of. One is on the Isle of Titherry. Another existed in Aerysius, but by all reports that circle now lies entombed beneath the ruins of the Hall of the Watchers. The only other Circle of Convergence in existence is on the summit of Orien's Finger."

Kyel wanted to kick himself for not seeing sooner what had been staring him in the face all this time. The numbers suddenly totaled themselves in his mind. The circle. The Soulstone. The Bloodquest. Naia. The cliff's edge. And, on top of it all, Darien had deliberately left him behind.

He'd wondered at the time if the mage hadn't simply devised those errands as a means of getting him out of the way. He'd figured Darien was planning something particularly dangerous. But now Kyel feared it was something much more sinister than he'd previously imagined.

Kyel whispered, "He said two Enemy armies are going to be merging there."

"So he intends to use Orien's Circle to turn them back." The priest's voice was chill, like a breath of air from a grave. "Your master is an eighth-tier Sentinel, and Orien's is a lesser circle. It was never designed to focus the vast amount of power he is capable of drawing."

Kyel groaned.

"Go," the high priest ordered. "If you ever see your master again, tell him that he's a contemptible fool. *And tell him I want my daughter back.*"

Kyel fled the high priest's study in a rush. Before he knew what was happening, he found himself being escorted out of the temple by two white-robed priests. As soon as he was outside, the reins of his horse were thrust into his hand and the temple door slammed shut behind him.

Kyel stood on the temple steps, slowly blinking in confusion. The chestnut gelding whinnied, shoving its muzzle into his chest. Kyel stroked its neck absently, looking back over his shoulder at the verdigris dome of the sanctuary. Everything was already starting to go wrong. And he hadn't even begun yet. He mounted his horse and kicked it forward, away from the temple out across the flat floor of the Valley of the Gods.

As he rode, Kyel marveled at the soft pastel hues of the desert around him. If Darien had wanted him to become better-traveled, then he was certainly getting his wish. The cliffs ahead were growing steadily larger, rising from the red soil of the valley floor. He thought he could make out something set in the sheer wall of rock ahead, like shadowy lines traced into the face of the cliff.

As the gelding approached the valley wall, Kyel felt compelled to draw back on the reins. The image ahead resolved into an enormous temple carved into the face of the cliff itself. Great stone pillars rose from a terrace, supporting an overhang that projected outward from the cliff.

The whole structure was bordered by two enormous images of bearded men engraved in bas-relief, their laureled heads encircled by halos of sunbeams. Kyel had seen such representations before.

He knew he had reached the High Temple of Wisdom.

The passage was narrow and dark, the ceiling so low that Kyel had to duck his head as he followed his hooded guide through a vast expanse of solid rock. The path ahead angled sharply downward. Kyel trailed his hands over the rough stone walls to either side.

The cleric was not the same man he'd met at the temple's entrance. He had waited by the door until a guide was summoned to lead him through the dark warren of tunnels within the cliff. From there, Kyel had been handed off from one guide to another, each leading him a little deeper into the labyrinth.

Kyel had thought the Temple of Wisdom looked massive from the outside, especially when he'd stood dwarfed beneath the carved rock pillars. But his journey through the dark passages had begun over an hour ago, and they had yet to reach their destination. The entire plateau must be hollow, to contain the enormity that was Om's temple.

The sloping passage seemed to go on forever, straight ahead and always down. The brown-robed cleric held a flaming torch that provided a globe of wavering light immediately surrounding them, but the passage both ahead and behind fell quickly into darkness. Kyel was starting to feel a slight sense of panic, as if the walls and ceiling were pressing in on him. He knew it was all in his mind, but he could not escape the feeling he was being buried alive.

It would have been some comfort if his guides had made any attempt at conversation. But he'd been passed along from one cleric to another without one word ever spoken.

The passage opened into a broad cavern dripping with natural embellishments. Their path wound through a maze of tawny spikes that hung from the ceiling and shot upward out of the floor. Kyel stood amazed, staring around at the jagged cave decorations. Their path led them through columns that erupted from the floor and past stony waterfalls frozen in time.

His guide led him through a dark opening in the wall ahead. Kyel stepped into yet another narrow passage even colder than the last. He wondered how far underground they had come, and how much farther they had yet to go.

They came to a place where the passage was cleaved by a broad corridor, then turned onto a main thoroughfare. Kyel found himself surrounded by scores of brown-robed clerics who passed by in silent swarms, as often as not laden with armloads of scrolls and manuscripts.

What was even stranger was the sound of this bustling underground boulevard. Other than the soft sounds of footsteps and the rustle of robes, the corridor was completely silent.

At the next intersection, Kyel was passed off to yet another guide, this one a young man with the cowl of his robe pulled up over his head. With only a gesture of his hand, the man directed Kyel down a narrow hallway that ended at a door.

That door was the first piece of wood Kyel had seen since entering the temple. His guide rapped once with his knuckles before opening it, then stood back to admit him into the room.

Kyel stopped as soon as his feet crossed the door's threshold.

Seated on an uncomfortable wooden stool was a man dressed in the clothes of a commoner. He looked to be roughly middle-aged and plump, with thinning brown hair parted over a high widow's peak. He wore a kindly expression in his red and watery eyes. There was even the hint of a smile on his lips as he nodded a cursory greeting.

But it was the man next to him who drew Kyel's attention. This man was very old, his white hair streaked with gray. A wiry beard groped down his chest, ending in a point. He sat with fingers steepled on the table in front of him.

Kyel squared his shoulders, thinking of how Darien would have conducted himself in a similar situation. *Emulate me,* the mage had said. But that was easier said than done. Kyel had nothing of Darien's innate self-assurance, though the black fabric of his cloak lent him a small amount of confidence.

"Your Eminence," Kyel said, bowing his head. He had no doubt in his mind that the old man was the High Priest of Wisdom. He felt a warm flush of satisfaction when the priest acknowledged him with the slightest nod.

Buoyed by this success, he took a step forward into the room. "My name is Kyel Archer. I'm an acolyte of the new Prime Warden, Darien Lauchlin."

The high priest raised his eyebrows and glanced at the man beside him, who returned his look with a frown. The two of them stared silently at one another for a long moment. Finally, the plainly clothed man leaned forward on his stool.

"Greetings, Acolyte Kyel. You must forgive him but, as all of Om's clerics, His Eminence has sworn a vow of silence."

That explained a lot, Kyel thought, while at the same time thinking how awkward such a vow would be, especially to men whose lives' work was the recording of information.

"My name is Cadmus," the man said. "I serve as the Voice of His Eminence. Why don't you have a seat?"

Kyel sat, shifting nervously. The two men looked as though they were mired in some sort of silent conversation, fixing their eyes on each other intently. After a few uncomfortable minutes, Cadmus turned back to him.

"His Eminence wishes to see your left wrist."

The unexpected request made Kyel wince. The chain was a private matter, not something he felt comfortable exposing to strangers. He felt deeply offended by the request.

But he found himself complying anyway. It was a small price to pay if he wanted access to their vaults. Lifting his left arm, Kyel pushed back his shirtsleeve. Exposed, the metallic marking on his wrist glimmered in the candlelight. Both men stared at the mark, stared at him, then turned back to each other, their eyes silently conferring as Kyel lowered his arm.

"His Eminence wishes to know how you came by such a marking."

Kyel didn't know what to say, or rather how much to say. Fumbling for words, he told them, "Darien—I mean the Prime Warden—he had me speak a vow…"

"Do you remember this vow?" pressed Cadmus, leaning forward.

"Aye." Kyel swallowed. "I do."

"Would you mind repeating it?"

Kyel took a deep breath, feeling a stir of tension as he recalled the words of the Acolyte's Oath. It wasn't difficult. They had been impressed deeply into his mind the day Darien had held his wrist and made him repeat them.

Even before he was finished, the clerics turned away, gazing at each other with shocked expressions. Kyel watched the silent conversation passing between the two as a play of emotions progressed over each man's face.

At last, Cadmus turned back to him. "His Eminence is confused," he said. "Darien Lauchlin died during the destruction that befell Aerysius. This fact is known and has been confirmed. His name has been added to the List."

Kyel wasn't sure what list the man was referring to. He assumed Cadmus meant some list of casualties, though the emphasis on the word made him wonder. But they didn't know everything, these clerics of Om. For the Temple of Wisdom, they'd certainly gotten some bad information.

"No." Kyel shook his head. "He's alive. I mean…"

Plainly, they didn't believe him. He closed his mouth, striving to think how he might convince them. He needed these clerics to believe that Darien was alive, was in fact Prime Warden, or he had no leverage to gain access to their information.

"You could ask the high priest at the Temple of Isap," Kyel suggested at last. It wasn't much, but it was the only proof he had to offer. "Darien was just there this morning."

The old man frowned at his words.

Cadmus said, "His Eminence wishes to know why your master was at the temple."

Kyel opened his mouth to tell them about Darien's mother but then decided against it. That line of conversation would inevitably lead to the Soulstone. Only, there was just one other explanation he could offer.

Forced to choose between the two accounts, Kyel chose the one he thought was the least damaging. It would scarcely be a secret much longer if Darien followed through with his plan.

"He swore a Bloodquest," Kyel admitted grudgingly.

The high priest's eyes widened, his cheeks flushing with color. He gestured angrily as he glared at Cadmus. Kyel wondered if he'd made a mistake. Whatever silent conversation was passing between the two men, it was hostile. They seemed to be arguing heatedly with their eyes. At last, Cadmus sat stiff on his stool, turning back to Kyel.

"His Eminence asks that you retire with him to his chambers, where he can speak with you at greater length."

"No."

Kyel was startled by the fierceness of his response. He hadn't meant it to come out that way. But he didn't have the time nor desire to be drawn into a lengthy explanation. He had too much work to do.

The Temple of Wisdom traded in knowledge, and that's what they were doing: pumping him for information. He'd already played into their manipulations and told them more than he ever should have. *Knowledge is power,* Darien had said. If that was true, then he had the upper hand. Kyel had been apprenticed to a merchant, and he damned well knew how to barter.

"That's not why I'm here," he said firmly. "I need access to your vaults. And I require someone to help me with my research."

After only the briefest pause, Cadmus asked, "His Eminence wishes to know what information it is you seek."

Kyel nodded. It was a fair trade, and necessary. If he wanted someone to help him with the research, then that someone would have to know the topic of his search eventually. He took a deep breath.

"I need to find a way to seal the Well of Tears."

Both men's eyes widened simultaneously, and they turned to stare harshly at each other. After long seconds, the high priest finally nodded.

"Your Prime Warden charts a highly dangerous course," Cadmus said, turning back to Kyel. "His Eminence agrees to allow you access to the vaults and will provide you with the assistance of a cleric to help you with your research during the hours of daylight. But in return, he requests that you join him in the evenings to share with him your story."

It was a fair trade, at least one that Kyel thought he could live with, if he watched himself and doled the facts out sparingly.

"That I can do," he said.

The high priest nodded.

"Very well." Cadmus stood up and offered Kyel his hand.

Kyel rose to his feet and took the plump man's hand in his own, feeling quite proud of himself as he sealed the agreement.

Chapter Twenty-Two
Fortress in the Eye of the Storm

Pass of Lor-Gamorth, The Front

Lightning traced the sky over Greystone Keep as a gust of wind ripped at the black pennant that clung tenuously to its staff at the top of the tower. The frayed banner crackled as a single fiery arrow arched above the stone walls of the fortress. Two more shafts whistled by overhead, followed by a volley. The pennant fluttered, wafting once more before it finally swayed to a rest.

Devlin Craig stared at the banner with a sense of foreboding confirmed by the hiss of the signal arrows arcing up from the bottom of the pass. He'd been expecting this for some time. But now that the threat was upon them, he couldn't help but feel that all the preparations they'd made in the past five days were merely an exercise in futility.

The reports coming in from Maidenclaw grew more dismal by the day, even by the hour. The most recent calculations placed the Enemy strength at somewhere around forty thousand, an estimate that was still growing.

His own men numbered less than one thousand.

Craig turned away from the battlements and strode toward the ladder, climbing down into the relative warmth of Proctor's chamber. Stamping his feet on the floor, Craig tried to work some feeling back into his legs. Autumn had faded sometime in the last week, and winter in the pass was always a harrowing affair. By the chill feel of the wind, Craig feared the first winter storm was already on its way.

At least there was some comfort in knowing he wouldn't have to spend another winter in the Pass of Lor-Gamorth.

For once, Proctor was not at his map. Instead, Craig found him staring out through the narrow opening of an arrow slit. The force commander had one hand raised, pressed against the wall by his face. The other hand fingered the hilt of the narrow dagger he always wore tucked into the belt at his waist. It was seldom visible, usually covered by the folds of his cloak.

Craig always found the sight of that dagger unsettling. It was called a misery knife, a traditional weapon worn by soldiers of the Enemy to give a final stroke of mercy to those fatally injured in battle. Proctor had received the dagger as a gift some years ago and had worn it at his side ever since. He even slept with it.

Craig walked stiffly across the circular chamber to stand behind his superior officer.

"It's happening," he said, and waited for the man to respond. But Proctor was silent, not showing any sign that he'd even heard.

Craig felt a stabbing slap of fury. After all the ruthless plots Garret Proctor had hatched, the man seemed suddenly indifferent, now that the end was at hand.

"If you hadn't driven Lauchlin away, we might've stood a chance," Craig accused. Then he stiffened, seeing the force commander's hand slide slowly down the ebony hilt of his knife, knuckles whitening as he gripped it.

"Is that what you think?"

Craig sensed that he was treading on very dangerous ground, but he continued all the same.

"Am I wrong?"

Proctor turned to fix him with an icy glare. He uttered in frigid, barren tones, "I did what had to be done. Before, we stood no chance. Not against a host this size."

Craig was still doubtful. "And you think we're better off now?"

Proctor raised an eyebrow as if challenging Craig to press him further. He appeared to be waiting, perhaps even patiently. But Craig knew better. He had an entirely different end in mind for himself than the blade of that wicked knife.

"I'm not accustomed to being questioned by the men under my command," Proctor snapped with narrowed eyes. "For over fifteen years, I've held the Front with little more than my nerve, my wits, and my audacity. I've never asked for accolades or even gratitude from the nations I protect, and I've never had either. The one thing I've ever demanded is the respect of my own men."

Craig lowered his eyes. Garret Proctor was arguably one of the best military strategists in all of history. Once, not even that long ago, Craig had felt an immeasurable swell of pride to have the privilege of soldiering under such a commander. He could remember nights when he would sit back at the table in awe, watching Proctor's eyes wandering over his map, struggling just to visualize the layered calculations and subtle inferences melding together within the man's head.

But his respect for Garret Proctor had been dealt a sobering blow. In his mind, the image of the man who had once been his hero was now irrevocably tarnished.

Into the interval left by Craig's silence, Proctor uttered, "Select a small contingent of volunteers to fire the keep and buy our escape with their lives. Then get every man you can on a horse."

Craig stared at him, stunned, unable to believe what he'd just heard. "You'll let them take the keep?"

"We fall back," Proctor confirmed, the threat in his eyes cautioning the captain not to question him again.

Craig took the warning to heart and turned away without another word. He left the command chamber, letting his boots carry him down the winding steps of the tower. He trudged into the open hall of the keep and crossed the floor in long strides.

Men who had already seen the signal arrows now drew forward to assemble by the shattered remains of the north wall, inferring the nature of the threat that confronted them from the look on his face. Silence fell over the hall as the soldiers gathered to hear him speak.

"We abandon the keep," Craig announced.

The reaction produced by his words was swift. Cries of protest rang from the walls as the men surged forward as one, shouting and brandishing fists, even weapons, in the air. Craig jumped onto a large pile of tumbled blocks, trying to elevate himself above the press of bodies. The upturned faces that glared at him were dangerous in their hostility.

"That's the order."

Craig stood and waited for silence. It came slowly, but eventually even the rustle of bodies ceased. When he was sure he had their full attention, he took a deep breath and summoned the courage to continue.

"I'm asking for volunteers: men who'll be willing to stay behind to offer resistance while the rest of us retreat down the pass. If you decide to remain, know that your death will buy the rest of us a fighting chance. I can promise you that your sacrifice will not go unremarked. Or unavenged."

The faces before him darkened, and he could almost feel their righteous skepticism. They knew well, just as he did, how hollow that promise was. The scouts who'd brought back reports from the mouth of the pass had not been ordered to silence. Every man in the keep knew the numbers of the Enemy host that confronted them.

The scornful faces before him reduced his words to the shameful collection of lies that they were. He knew he couldn't blame them if not a man stepped forward to volunteer.

They deserved better.

They deserved to know the truth: that every last one of them was going to die, and no good account would come from their ends. The vast strength of the Enemy would be like a raging tempest, and they would be simply swept away by that storm. But he couldn't bring himself to tell them that. In the end, it seemed, he was craven after all. Devlin Craig bowed his head and waited, but no one moved.

At last, a lone man stepped forward from the back of the crowd, winding his way through the press of bodies toward the front. Craig raised his eyebrows, frowning when he recognized Corban Henley's red-bearded face. The burly man had one hand clutched on the hilt of the sword that rode at his side, his face as impassive as a cold chunk of stone.

A murmur ran through the gathered men as they parted to let him pass. When he reached the front of the crowd, Henley stopped and simply stood. He didn't look at Craig, but stared beyond him, down into the blackness visible through the rift in the wall.

He was not the man Craig would have picked. Henley was a good soldier, far too good to be wasted in such a futile endeavor. But no one else was coming forward. Craig scanned the crowd, but their hostility was still almost palpable. Even Henley's example had not been enough to inspire, and it should have been.

Finally, another man drew forward. When Craig saw who it was, he almost gasped in disbelief. Traver Larsen had come to him as a scoundrel, an insubordinate rogue who Craig had felt certain wouldn't last a fortnight before getting himself killed, probably by his own comrades in arms. From the beginning, Craig had determined that the best use of the man would be to make a harsh example of him. But Larsen had never given him the opportunity.

Instead, the man had changed. From almost the moment he'd picked up a sword, Traver Larsen had transformed into one of the hardest-working recruits Craig had ever trained. And now he stood at Henley's side, just the two of them, alone.

But then the crowd shifted.

At first Craig didn't understand what was happening; the change was subtle. It took him a moment to realize that Henley and Larsen were no longer alone at the front of the crowd. The entire mass of men had moved forward collectively as one. He stared down at the group of soldiers, abashed by their courage.

Craig found himself in the grim position of having to choose his volunteers.

He limited his choice to a dozen, selecting mostly archers. He didn't pick either Henley or Larsen. He wanted both men by his side, not wasted on a hopeless venture.

When it was done, he looked up to find Garret Proctor standing in the doorway. The force commander stepped forward and addressed the hall in a booming voice:

"Take only what is necessary. We ride within the hour. *Now, MOVE!*"

Craig watched as men scurried in every direction. He lingered on the mound of blocks for another moment before turning away. As he scaled the ladder to the catwalk at the top of the walls, he could feel Proctor's eyes on him.

He paused and stared out through the opening of an arrow slit. At first, he thought he could see movement far below, somewhere down in the bottom of the pass. But it was just roiling ground fog, nothing more. The Enemy was not yet upon them.

He traced his hand over the stone blocks that rimmed the opening. These stark walls had stood for hundreds of years, protecting the nations of the Rhen. In his mind, he could hear Royce's voice as a distant, haunting refrain, that same speech the man had delivered to every batch of new recruits: *Greystone Keep holds the Pass of Lor-Gamorth. If it should ever fall, then we will lose the pass. If we lose the pass, then we lose the North. And if the North should ever fall, the Enemy will sweep southward like a storm.*

It had always been Royce's duty to hold the fortress. But Royce was dead, and now the walls he'd sworn to protect were simply being abandoned. In a way, Craig was glad his old friend was not alive to see this day. The fall of Greystone Keep would certainly have broken him.

Craig rode in silence beside his commander at the head of the long column that descended the dark cliffs, heading southward into the heart of the pass. Above and behind him, the fortress was visible as never before, aglow with the light of dozens of fires.

Proctor had turned Greystone Keep into a death trap. Nothing had been left behind for the Enemy. Nothing, with the exception of a half-dozen bowmen whose arrows hissed down from the high walls as the fortress burned beneath their feet.

Craig heard a distant crash and turned to see the roof of the tower caving in, consumed by the fierce glow of ravaging flames. Sparks shot upward, wafting high into the sky. He turned away from the sight, fixing his gaze on the black dirt of the path before him.

He almost brought his hands up to cover his ears as the sound of distant screams drifted toward him, carried by the still night air. The whistling hiss of arrows ceased, and a sad, eerie silence lingered over the remote crackling of flames.

Then another sound rose behind him, soft at first, then growing to a thunderous, echoing roar. Craig did cover his ears then, closing his eyes as well, against the deafening cry of victory pealed from thousands of Enemy throats.

Devlin Craig didn't have to look behind him to know that the fortress that had guarded the Pass of Lor-Gamorth for over five hundred years stood no more.

Chapter Twenty-Three
Unveiled

Northern Chamsbrey, The Rhen

Darien stared ahead at the sheer white train of Naia's veil, fascinated by the way it was played out at her side, rippled by the gentle current of a zephyr. He wondered at the veil's significance. It was reminiscent in some ways of a bridal scarf, a badge of goodness and purity. In other ways, it reminded him of his mother's funeral shroud, elegant even as it was isolating.

The veil fluttered upward, and for the briefest moment he had an unobscured view of her face. It was as if the clouds had parted, admitting a fragile, transitory ray of sunlight into his dark and winterish world. Then the skies closed again as the breeze ebbed, and the veil fell back into place. It had been but a chance gesture of the wind, nothing more. But to Darien, that brief glimpse of Naia's face had the magnitude of a sobering epiphany.

He realized that he loved her. And he damned himself for it.

They rode in silence into the bleak grayness that preceded the dawn, their horses climbing out of the desert into the green foothills of the mountains. The path they followed was the one that had led them out of the Valley of the Gods two days before, now rising into the rolling hills that marked the beginning of the Craghorns.

To the north, Darien could see the sharp peaks of snow-clad mountains in the distance, evocatively familiar. The sight of the Craghorns beckoned him, drawing him like a child intrigued by the candle's tempting flame. Aerysius was there, somewhere, high up on the vertical face of one of those white summits.

But instead of taking the northern fork, Darien turned his horse southward. He glanced over his shoulder for one last view of the mountains as he guided his mount toward the center of the path.

"You're going to Auberdale?" Naia gazed at him with a perplexed expression.

"I need Faukravar's northern army."

The confusion on her face turned to a look of comprehension. "So that's why you sent Kyel to Rothscard. To beg Romana for her army."

"Begging was not what I had in mind."

Naia pursed her lips thoughtfully. "I still fail to see how you plan to accomplish all that you intend to do in less than a fortnight. Travel alone will scarcely take us to Aerysius and back to Orien's Finger in that amount of time, and that doesn't include a stop in Auberdale."

"That's true," Darien agreed. "There's not enough time. Aidan will have to wait."

Naia looked concerned by his answer. Which confused him. That was the part of his plan he'd expected her to like most.

She said, "You told me you feared to have Aidan at your back. I wondered about that at the time. Your brother has done little but sit like a spider in his web ever since he gained control of Aerysius. Do you expect him to move against you now?"

Darien shook his head. "Aidan has not been idle, I assure you. For one, there are no passes above Aerysius to admit a force through that corridor. Aidan has been hard at work creating some sort of passage through the Craghorns. And the Eight are under his command, and they haven't been idle at all. Arden Hannah told me she came from Bryn

Calazar. That stinks of a union between Aidan and whatever dark terror governs the Enemy."

This time, the dawn of comprehension on her face was overshadowed by the worried lines of fear he'd been expecting.

"An alliance?" She looked appalled. "So all of this has been Aidan's scheme—to use the combined might of the Enemy and the Netherworld to conquer the Rhen for himself?"

"My family has always had an ambitious streak."

Naia shook her head. "To think, all of these horrors wrought by just one man. But you still didn't answer my question. What is the danger if you put off confronting your brother until after the battle?"

Darien shrugged. "Aidan commands Renquist. I'm going to have a hard enough time minding the Enemy without having to worry about being attacked by eight demons and their pets at the same time."

Naia's face went pale. "What will you do, Darien?"

"I'll have a few things on my side," he said, trying to reassure her with a smile he simply didn't feel. "I'll have two good-sized armies behind me. And Orien's Vortex will give me some protection. If he wants to take me, Renquist will need to move his mages in close, into the eye of the vortex itself. As I figure it, the battle will be won or lost depending on who gains Orien's Circle first. Whoever controls the vortex will control the field of battle."

"But, Darien, what if they're there already? The Eight? Even Aidan?"

Darien shook his head. "They're not expecting me. I'm certain Renquist thinks I'm dead, or at least Arden ought to. That's my greatest advantage: the element of surprise is on my side."

Naia looked as if she wanted to believe him, but her eyes beneath the veil were full of doubt. It was the best strategy he'd been able to come up with. Using Orien's Circle, at least he had a chance. But there were so many things that could still go wrong. His first big challenge lay just ahead over the hills.

And he couldn't afford to spend much time in Auberdale. Faukravar was known for stalling, miring his opponents in tangles of intrigue. The King of Chamsbrey had given Darien's mother headaches on more than one occasion, and Emelda had been a strong Prime Warden.

Darien didn't kid himself. He'd never had the patience for politics. In Auberdale, he was going to be very much out of his element.

———

They followed the road to the south for the remainder of the day. The landscape changed around them, the scattered trees thickening into a densely forested woodland. The sky gave way to a canopy clad in orange and burnished gold. Leaves rained down on the road as the branches stirred above them in the breeze. Winter was approaching swiftly. Already the air carried with it a sharp chill.

Naia had been silent for most of the day, her eyes either remote in thought or cast downward in a meditative study of the road. Darien thought he knew the reason. Her mood had turned after their conversation that morning. By the time the sunset arrived, he found himself missing her company.

He guided his horse off the road, looking for a place to set up camp for the night. They could have reached Auberdale easily by pressing on after dark. But Naia's silence bothered him, and it made him reluctant to enter the city with her in such a somber mood.

Determined to do something to cheer her up, he selected a spot on the rise of a hill, a patch of green grass in the midst of a stand of trees. The far side of the hill provided a sweeping view of the lowlands below, with the walls of Auberdale visible in the distance against the southern horizon.

To his disappointment, Naia seemed unaffected by the view, merely glancing once over the rim of the hill as she went routinely about the process of helping him set up the campsite. Darien felt dismayed, wondering what it would take to bring the smile back to her face.

When he saw her digging through her pack for the dried food stores they'd carried with them from Glen Farquist, it gave him an idea. Leaving her by the fire, he strode off alone into the thicket, eyes scanning the ground and the trees for any sign of movement.

It took him a little while of searching, but at last he found a hare. Yet, even as he did, he was unsure of quite what to do with it. If Kyel had been there, he would have borrowed his acolyte's bow to bring the animal down. But Kyel wasn't there, and all

Darien had was his sword. And his ability.

With the slightest wrench of his mind, the hare collapsed on the spot. There was no writhing or squirming. The animal simply dropped and was dead.

Darien felt himself shiver involuntarily as he walked toward the fallen hare. He knelt over it, staring bleakly down at the limp carcass. He had never before used his ability to take a life, even a small one. It was a new experience, and unsettling. What disturbed him most was how effortless the act had been. It had taken almost no thought whatsoever to transfer what he already knew from his study of healing and adapt it into a killing strike. He had taken the wondrous gift of life and had corrupted it into its converse: the ignoble gift of death.

As Darien grasped the limp animal by its hind legs, he felt wretchedly soiled. This was not the use his gift had ever been intended for. He thought of Grand Master Ezras, the mage who'd surrendered his life to pass on his ability to him. What he had just done seemed to slight that great man's noble sacrifice. Ezras had held fiercely to his Oath his entire life, even in the most dire of circumstances. The man would have gladly yielded his own life before slaying so much as a simple hare with the use of his gift.

Feeling sickened, Darien took out his knife and slit the animal's plump belly, scraping its guts out with trembling fingers. He skinned the carcass and drove it through with a branch sharpened into a spit, then knelt to wash up in the crisp water of a brook. By the time he returned to their campsite, his hands had finally stopped shaking.

Naia looked up as he sat down on the other side of the fire from her, bracing the spit hare at an angle over the flames. Her eyebrows raised in appreciation at the smell of cooking meat. Darien tried his best to smile, but his heart wasn't in it.

"Thank you," she said simply.

Darien just nodded. His entire motive for killing the hare had been to cheer her up. But now that his efforts seemed to have worked, at least a little bit, he found it was he who needed cheering. He leaned forward to turn the meat, but the motion was just a way of avoiding her eyes.

"What's wrong?"

She had seen through him anyway. It was an uncanny knack she had. No matter how well he tried to hide his feelings from her, she always knew them. Before her, every wall he threw up crumbled to sand and ashes. Darien leaned forward, folding his arms across his legs as he struggled to think of how to put his emotions to words.

"I've never killed anything with my gift before," he admitted finally. He felt ashamed. It had been only a stupid, tiny hare. Whether it had died in a trap or by the force of his mind shouldn't have mattered.

But it did.

The priestess seemed to sense it, too. A look of sympathy formed on her face. The expression made him angry. He didn't want her pity. Of all the range of emotions he wished he could elicit from her, that was the one thing he simply couldn't take. He stared down at the campfire's flickering flames as if drawn to them, mesmerized by the fire's orange-yellow glow.

"I care for you, Naia."

The look of stunned shock on her face hurt more than her pity. Darien pushed himself up, not knowing where he was going as he stumbled toward the edge of the hill. He stopped there, surrounded by the whispering branches of the forest. In the distance, he could see the lights of Auberdale, a dim glow on the dark line of the horizon.

He considered the lights, or tried to. But all he could think about was Naia. Why had he said that to her? He couldn't imagine what he'd been thinking. Without intending to, he'd been cruelly unfair to her. He hadn't even considered the decision he was forcing upon her, asking her to choose between his selfish desires and her life's work and ambitions. He had no right to put her in such a position. He was a fool.

He watched the lights twinkling below, wishing he could be anyone else in the entire world.

The crack of a twig snapping made him turn. She was standing not a foot away from him, her gaze intent upon his face. Darien squeezed his eyes shut against the torture of her presence.

As she moved into his arms, he grimaced against the anguish of knowing he was doing her a terrible wrong. At the same time, he felt such a thrill of exhilaration that everything else in the world seemed remote and trivial.

He drew her against him, pressing his face into

the silken softness of her veil. Her hands slid behind his back, stroking his hair as he closed his eyes and immersed himself in the tender compassion of her touch.

When she finally drew back, he found himself staring into her eyes, overwhelmed. His hand rose to the sleek transparency of her veil. With reverence, he lifted the fabric and drew it from her head. He let his arm fall to his side, still holding Naia's veil as he traced a finger over her cheek. When he felt her lips press against his, he could almost imagine what it felt like to be alive.

Auberdale, The Rhen

Godfrey Faukravar was the rightful King of Chamsbrey. But the man known infamously as the Vile Prince had earned his epithet long before the crown was ever placed upon his head. Faukravar was notorious for his brutal handling of the Crofter Rebellion, which had ended in the cold-blooded massacre of over three hundred commoners: men, women and children, alike. Another feather in Faukravar's cap was the War of Five Days, when he had used the combined might of both his armies to squash the small but embittered province of Glaster that had risen up against him. Godfrey Faukravar was renowned for both his cunning political intrigues and his ruthless nature, a potent combination.

Darien was not looking forward to meeting the man. In his opinion, the King of Chamsbrey was undeserving of the title. If he could be assured his action wouldn't spark a civil war, Darien would have considered removing the man bodily from the throne. But there were simply too many hounds lurking under the King's table, waiting to snap up the scraps their monarch threw at them from time to time. If a vacuity of power ever existed on the throne of Chamsbrey, every dog of the pack would fight tooth and claw over it.

Within, Darien heard the herald announce them:

"The First Daughter Naia Seleni, Priestess of Isap…and her escort."

Darien had not provided his name. He hadn't seen the necessity; the white cloak of the Prime Warden that fell down his back would be enough for Faukravar to identify him. If not, then the threat of his sword ought to give the man pause. Darien had donned a pair of leather gloves just for the occasion, to cover the glaring absence of the chains on his wrists.

He stepped forward, following the sweep of Naia's gown through the door to the throne room. His eyes moved over the priestess' slender figure as she walked before him. Naia seemed very much in her element. Having been on the receiving end of her political graces, Darien appreciated having her there. He watched as she dropped into an elegant curtsey before the throne.

Darien lifted his eyes to regard the King. He made no move to kneel. By rights, Faukravar should be the one on his knees. The white cloak worn by Darien outshone the splendor of any crown.

But the man on the throne appeared not to notice it. If he did, then he was certainly not ready to acknowledge the emblem of the Prime Warden that had inserted itself unannounced into his throne room.

The King of Chamsbrey was older than Darien had expected, a man somewhere in his late fifties. His silver hair was streaked with strands of faded brown, worn in perfect, shoulder-length curls under the golden circlet of the crown on his head. He was dressed in opulent layers of black and violet robes, with an ermine-trimmed cape covering the whole affair.

Faukravar stared unblinking into his eyes. When it became clear Darien had no intention of kneeling, the King's lips compressed to a narrow line. One of four men who surrounded the throne stepped forward, a hand resting on the pommel of the sword at his side.

"One is expected to bend knee in the presence of a King."

Darien kept his eyes trained on Faukravar. Behind him, he heard soft rustling sounds as the guards by the door tried to figure out what to do. A soft ringing noise scraped down his nerves as a blade was slowly bared. An uneasy tension spread through the room, growing as long moments dragged by. Darien simply waited and did nothing, while Naia remained frozen in the depths of her curtsey.

On the throne, the Vile Prince blinked.

"An interesting companionship," he said finally,

leaning back and raising a hand to finger his wiry goatee. "A white-cloaked mage, by all appearances, and a priestess of Death. Tell me, First Daughter, how might we be of service to the temple?"

Naia rose to glide forward with a swirl of her gown. "Thank you for the favor of this audience, Your Grace," she said in a clear and ringing voice. "But I am not here at the bequest of my temple. Instead, I have come to present to you the new Prime Warden, Darien Lauchlin."

The King glanced back at Darien, raising a skeptical eyebrow. *"Another* Lauchlin?" He sounded bored. "My, but that name does seem to be coming up rather often of late, and not always mentioned in the best of contexts. We are intrigued. But we are also mystified. By what right do you claim the office of Prime Warden?"

"I elected myself," Darien responded dryly.

Naia elaborated, "Darien Lauchlin is the son of Prime Warden Emelda."

The King's lips twitched into a smirk. "Aidan Lauchlin is also her son. Does that make him Prime Warden, as well?"

The silence that followed was broken by the sound of nervous chuckles. Darien waited.

At his side, Naia gestured expansively. "If I may, Your Grace? Aidan Lauchlin destroyed the Hall of the Watchers and ordered his own mother slain. Is that the kind of Prime Warden you would wish to replace her?"

Faukravar dismissed her argument with a wave of his hand. "It doesn't matter what we wish. The title itself is empty. Aerysius is fallen. A king without a nation is not a king. And the last soldier left standing is not a general."

Darien watched him a moment longer, then slowly shook his head. He'd known better than to let the man maneuver him into a corner, which was exactly what Faukravar was attempting to do. If he hadn't, in fact, already succeeded. Taking a step forward, he addressed the King in a carefully controlled voice:

"I'll not be questioned over my right to my title. Whether you like it or not, I'm the last mage left alive who hasn't sold his soul to Xerys."

By the look on Faukravar's face, the King couldn't have cared less if he had. "Then why *are* you here?"

"I came to ask you to lend me your northern army," Darien said, infusing all the confidence he could muster into his tone. "As we speak, two great Enemy hosts are swarming down from the Black Lands. They'll be close enough to threaten your walls in one month's time. If I hope to stand a chance of turning them back, I'll have need of your northern forces."

This time, the laughter that filled the chamber was much louder. Even Faukravar allowed himself a grin. "You expect me to just *give* you one of my armies? How incredibly impetuous."

Darien waited as the cold wash of anger drained slowly out of him, until there was only emptiness remaining in its place. Dredged up from the depths of the emotional void that consumed him, his tone was frigid.

"I need your army, Your Grace, and I'll not be leaving Chamsbrey without it. I thought to ask first, out of courtesy. You have until sunset tomorrow to make your decision."

"And should I refuse?" the King baited.

"Then I'll take it from you outright."

Gasps of indignation filled the chamber. All around the room, Darien could hear the shiver of a forest of steel being bared, the sounds of footsteps as the guards distanced themselves from the walls, preparing for a fight. He could have removed his gloves. That would have given them something to think about. But he didn't.

Instead, Darien turned and walked calmly toward the door, pausing only as two guards with swords bared stepped forward to block him.

He gazed at both men with the slightest dare of a smile on his lips, waiting for them to decide whether they were ready to die for their King.

It was Faukravar who decided for them, sparing their lives.

"Let him go."

"Well, he's certainly arrogant enough to be a Lauchlin."

Faukravar glanced sideways at Chadwick Cummings as the rest of his ministers snickered at the man's comment. The King himself sat clenching the arms of his throne, gripped in a cold rage provoked by the man who had just insulted his honor and his sovereignty. He couldn't recall ever being treated with such cavalier insolence.

"He's the very image of Emelda, in face as well as temperament," Clement Landry pronounced.

The King nodded, for once in full agreement with his Minister of State. He had met with the late Prime Warden on enough occasions to have recognized her looks glaring out at him from the face of her impudent son. It seemed the man had inherited a full measure of Emelda's overconfidence without a grain of her subtlety.

"Opinions?"

Cummings spoke first, his voice raised above the drone of the others. "His threat is empty, Sire. Even if he truly is a mage, he is Bound by the Oath of Harmony."

But Faukravar remained skeptical. There was something about the man that made him wonder. "Did any of you note the emblem of the chains?"

To his disappointment, all four of his ministers stood shaking their heads. He was furious at them, almost as furious as he was with himself for not thinking of the chains when the man was in front of him. He had allowed Lauchlin to unbalance him.

Lance Treaton, his Minister of the Treasury, bowed his head sadly. "I tried to mark them, my liege, but he was wearing gloves."

"I abhor riddles," the King grumbled.

"What of this Enemy host?" asked Landry. "Is there a reason to suspect it might actually exist?"

Cummings spoke up. "In his last letter, Garret Proctor mentioned he was facing a serious threat with a critical shortage of men and supplies."

"Proctor whines more than a tavern wench, and louder," proclaimed Treaton.

But the King was not troubled by Lauchlin's mention of the Enemy. It was the man's other threats, especially the veiled ones, that worried him more. "That doesn't concern me. To reach Auberdale, any force would have to cut all the way through Emmery and lay siege to Rothscard along the way. Let Romana deal with them, if such a host exists."

"What should we do about Lauchlin?"

"Nothing, until we know more about him." The King tapped his fingers on the armrest of his throne, frowning in thought. After a moment, he beckoned his guard captain forward.

As the man crossed the floor, Faukravar commanded him, "Find out where he's staying. I want men positioned around him at all times, watching every move he makes. I want to know whether or not he wears the marks of the chains. And find out more about that sword he carries, what significance it implies. Also, I want to know the nature of his relationship to that priestess."

"Maybe he's just fucking her," said Landry.

"Perhaps. If so, find out."

Cummings moved forward. "Your Grace, I must urge you to treat this mage with the utmost caution. He is, after all, the brother of the very man who brought Aerysius to its knees. It is conceivable they're in league. How else did this Darien manage to survive when all else fell?"

The King raised an eyebrow. "An interesting notion. Find out about that, too."

Another Lauchlin. He was already sick to death of the name.

Darien gazed down at Auberdale through the paned-glass window of the room he had taken at an inn. The size of the city never ceased to amaze him. It sprawled along the banks of the River Nerium, a mottled collection of disparate structures and haphazard streets ambling off in every direction. The dark towers of Glassenburgh Castle rose over the slow waters of the Nerium, the sharp teeth of its fortifications visible even at a distance.

Turning from the window, his gaze traveled across the floor to where Naia lay spread out across the covers of the room's only bed. He wanted nothing more than to collapse into bed with her and drown his troubles in her arms. But he couldn't do that.

Last night, it had taken every ounce of will he possessed to restrain himself when she'd crawled under his blanket. He'd fallen asleep with Naia in his arms, trying to ignore the desperate ache inspired by her closeness.

She looked up at him and smiled, her face unobscured by the fabric of her veil. Darien moved away from the window and sat down beside her on the bed. As he did, Naia touched the back of his hand, stroking his skin with her fingertips.

"You were magnificent today," she said. "I must admit, I had a few doubts."

He'd had more than just a few, going in. "No."

He shook his head. "You're the one who was magnificent. You must have been a courtier before you ever became a priestess."

She batted her hand at him with a look of feigned outrage. Darien tried to get up, but she caught him by the arm and drew him back down beside her.

He closed his eyes as her lips wandered over his cheek, trailing upward to his forehead. Again, he was filled with longing as he let his mouth explore the graceful curve of her neck. When he felt Naia's hands slip under his shirt, he wanted to groan.

But instead, he took her hands in his own and, removing them gently but firmly, rolled away from her onto his back. He stared up at the beams of the ceiling, fighting against a raging desire that made his breath ragged in his throat.

He wanted her, wanted all of her, with a need that was almost savage. The game they were playing was just too dangerous. Every time they touched, he found himself facing a losing battle. He felt besieged, his walls quickly caving in. Eventually, the struggle inside was going to defeat him. And when it did, Naia would be the one to suffer.

"What is it?"

She frowned down at him as she propped herself up with an elbow on the bed. Her auburn hair burned almost scarlet in the light streaming in from the window. It draped down to spread across the covers beside his face.

Darien shook his head. "I can't do this. It's not fair to you."

His words seemed to infuriate her. She rolled off the bed and wrenched herself up, stalking away from him as he watched in confusion.

"Perhaps you should have thought about that last night."

"I did, but…"

"But?" she spat, plucking her veil off the floor. "But then you led me to believe you have feelings for me, when it's obvious you don't."

Darien sat up and looked at her in amazement. "What would you have of me?"

Naia flung the veil at his face, but it only fluttered down to land softly beside him on the bed. "I want you to make up your mind, Darien. Do you really care for me as you say you do? Or are you just infatuated with the idea of me? You need to think about it. I can be your lover, or I can be a priestess, but I can't be both. You decide."

With that, she grabbed up her veil and stormed to where her gown lay folded on a chair, pulling it on over her shift.

And then she was gone, the door slamming shut in her wake.

Chapter Twenty-Four
The Pursuit of Wisdom

Glen Farquist, The Rhen

The vaults of Om's temple were not what Kyel had expected. He'd thought they would be like the libraries of Aerysius his father had often spoken of, well-lit rooms with shelf upon polished shelf of ordered manuscripts and well-tended documents. But the vaults of Wisdom were nothing like a library. They reminded Kyel more of Death's Catacombs.

The chambers where Om's clerics stored their vast accumulation of knowledge were a warren of man-made caves existing well below the level of the high priest's chambers. Indeed, they were so far beneath the earth Kyel could almost feel the weight of the soil overhead crushing down on him.

After three days of research, he still couldn't pretend to understand the system used by the clerics to catalog it all. Had he not managed to secure himself an assistant to help search for the references he needed, Kyel figured he could have spent years down there in the bowels of the earth without finding anything remotely related to his topic.

As it was, progress was tediously slow. The silent cleric assigned to him had found him a small table with an oil lamp as its sole adornment. Since then, the cleric simply came and went at long intervals, depositing odd assortments of manuscripts, maps, codices, and scrolls of parchment. By the third day, Kyel found himself encased by stacks of books he hadn't even had a chance to thumb through yet.

He had no idea how the man did it, but the brown-robed cleric was much quicker at locating information in the maze of vaults than Kyel was at searching through the man's findings. He was starting to grow desperate. As he stared down at the piles around him, he wondered if the priests weren't trying to throw him off his search by overwhelming him with information.

Most of which was completely useless. Kyel stared down at a dusty leather tome in dismay before carefully closing the ancient cover. After three days, it seemed he was no closer than when he'd first begun. Oh, he'd learned a lot of interesting facts he hadn't known before, but scarcely any of it pertained to the elusive subject of the Well of Tears. Kyel was beginning to consider himself an expert on the history and traditions of Aerysius and was even growing confident in other, darker, areas as well.

His hand moved to a copy of *The Mysteries of Aerysius,* which had been one of the first treasures the cleric had unearthed for him. Before now, that text had been his only source of written knowledge on the subject, and he had refused his assistant when the man had come to take it away. But Cromm's work, like almost everything else, yielded nothing pertinent.

In all his browsing, he'd found the Well of Tears mentioned only three times. The first instance had been almost as an aside, just a vague reference to its link with the gateway. It was mentioned again on a fragment of parchment. It told of how the Well of Tears had been opened once by a rogue mage, who had sought to augment his own strength with the power of the Netherworld. The Well had been successfully resealed that time only with the aid of Aerysius' Circle of Convergence. But then again, it had not been fully open.

The scrap was not very helpful. Kyel was starting to come to the conclusion that Darien had set him to the task of chasing his own tail.

He found the third mention of the Well of Tears in an account of the fall of the Lyceum of Bryn Calazar. The text referred to the subject of the Well frequently throughout its ancient pages. Kyel found himself scanning the book avidly, fascinated by its contents. He hadn't known that the evil which had consumed Caladorn had actually started in Aerysius itself—or, rather, beneath it. Apparently, in the cliffs that supported Aerysius, there was a network of passageways used by the founders of the city. But after hundreds of years, the network had fallen into disuse and was eventually abandoned.

It was discovered again some centuries later by the forbidden cult of Xerys. The followers of Chaos sequestered themselves down there in the dark, using the forgotten halls and chambers as places to convene secret meetings and dark masses, even ritual sacrifices. It was the malevolent priesthood of Xerys that created the Well of Tears in the first place.

According to the text, the gateway to the Netherworld had been established so that the powers of Chaos could be harnessed and used in the war against Caladorn. The Prime Warden of Aerysius, Cyrus Krane, had conspired with Zavier Renquist to establish a link with the Netherworld that would tilt the balance of power in favor of the darkmages. The Well was eventually resealed, but the damage had already been done.

In the end, Bryn Calazar fell and the rest of Caladorn was consumed by the Netherworld's taint. It was a war that had never really been won. The same battle was yet ongoing, the reason why Greystone Keep had been erected to defend the Pass of Lor-Gamorth from the Black Lands in the first place. Renquist had aspired to remake the world in hell's dark image, and the sinister machinations he had fostered in life had lived far beyond his span of mortal years.

The text was fascinating, and even though Kyel knew he shouldn't be spending his precious time reading it, he simply couldn't help himself. The book even contained a map of the vast cave network beneath Aerysius on a half-rotten page.

He wasn't able to resist the temptation. The page was already loose and falling out. So Kyel waited until he was sure the cleric would be away for some time.

Then he quickly pulled the map the rest of the way out, folded it up, and shoved it into the pocket of his cloak alongside the weight of the Soulstone. He felt awful after doing it, sorry to have desecrated the ancient text. Heart pounding, he kept glancing around to see if anyone had noticed his abuse of the book as he continued with his foraging.

By the dim light of the oil lamp, he scanned over the faded letters on a crumbling scroll of parchment, rolled it back up, then stuffed it into the pile collecting at his feet. He reached for the next book on the top of the pile and read the gilt title, *Diplomatic Etiquette.*

Kyel scowled down at the text, wondering what could have possibly been running through his assistant's mind when he'd pulled that one down from the shelf. Surely, there would be no mention of the Well of Tears in such a work. Still, Kyel found himself intrigued. He would have need of such knowledge for his meeting with the Queen of Emmery.

With a shrug, Kyel set the text aside, thinking he would take it with him to read later that night. The next book in the stack was a spectacularly illustrated manuscript with the title *Sieges and Scrimmages: A Compellation of Modern Warfare Tactics and Strategy.* Noticing the date on the cover, Kyel shook his head. The tactics described by the manuscript couldn't possibly be very modern. According to the date on the cover, the book was over three hundred years old.

He took a quick peek at some of the hand-rendered illustrations, then set the manuscript down at his side. Again, he had to wonder why the cleric would have brought him such a thing.

The man returned again, heaping another armload of books onto the top of the tall column already growing by his chair. Kyel nodded his thanks as he reached for the first book on top.

He almost dropped the thin text when he caught sight of the title. *The Family Lauchlin* was inscribed on the leather cover, the first cover he had seen unsullied by years of layered dust.

Kyel's mouth went dry as he flipped open the book and, thumbing past the first pages, considered the flowing script of the author's hand. To Kyel's amazement, he found that the first chapter was an encapsulated overview of Darien's family history.

> *Since the first recorded ~~mention~~ of a Lauchlin in the annals of Aerysius (circa 1266), the name has figured prominently in the histories and governance of the Assembly of the Hall. To date, Lauchlin has been the surname of ~~six~~ seven renowned Sentinels and ~~two~~ three Prime Wardens…*

Kyel skimmed the rest of the page, amazed, and flipped quickly to the back of the book. But, strangely, he discovered that almost half of the pages were blank. Thumbing forward again, he found the last entry at the end of the written portion of the text:

> **Darien Lauchlin, Grand Master** *(1718 – ~~1747~~): Mage of the Order of Sentinels*[?]*. Son of Grand Master Gerald Lauchlin and Prime Warden Emelda Clemley Lauchlin. Confirmed Acolyte in 1730 at 12 years of age. Mentored by Master Lynnea Nelle, Master Harrison Geary, Master Cedric Fisk, and Grand Master Roland Blentley. Commendations for Meritorious Achievement (6), Dedicated Service (9), and Distinguished Scholar (12). Demerits for Violating Curfew Restrictions (17), Insubordination (4), Willful Defiance (2), Unauthorized Research (3), Trespassing in Restricted Areas (3), and Gross Misconduct (1). Subject of Expulsion Inquiry (1745); suspended from active mentorship and exiled to Greystone Keep (1745–1747). Received fifth tier Transference from Grand Master Ezras Nordric in 1747 at 29 years of age. ~~A casualty of the destruction of Aerysius in 1747~~. The only known survivor of the destruction of Aerysius and self-declared Prime Warden. Foreswore the Oath of Harmony in 1747. Possible second Transference of third tier magnitude, source unknown; report unconfirmed. Father of Gerald Withersby (1746 – 1747).*

Shaken, Kyel read the last line again.

He closed the book's cover. Meiran had given Darien a son, and he didn't even know about it. And, Kyel silently swore to himself, he never would.

Not if he had anything to do with it.

It was going on early evening when he finally broke off his research with a feeling of failure and headed back up the long stairs to the living quarters. His brown-robed assistant led him back to his cell, where Kyel collapsed on the small, hard cot, thoroughly exhausted.

His time had run out, and he still had no idea how to go about sealing the Well of Tears. Darien had given him only three days. Even if it had been three months, Kyel doubted he could have come any closer.

It was almost time for supper, and His Eminence would be expecting him again. Kyel had promised the man three nights of his company, and this was to be their last meeting. Already, he had been forced to yield more information than he had originally planned on. The voiceless old man seemed to know when he was trying to be vague, and Cadmus was exceptionally talented at digging for details and prying facts out of him.

Brushing the lint off his black cloak, Kyel left his small cell and began the journey again, hopefully for the last time. Wandering through underground hallways and large subterranean avenues, he passed a large water clock, pausing as he looked up at it.

He was late.

He hastened past scores of clerics moving by him with distant expressions on their faces. It was a strange life these men led, living down in the dark with only the smell of dusty manuscripts to keep them company and no words ever heard. It seemed such a lonely existence. He couldn't imagine why anyone would want to commit themselves to such a way of life.

Kyel arrived at the door of the high priest's chambers. He found himself confronted by a beaming Cadmus, who beckoned him inside with a wave of his hand. The smell of supper made his mouth water as he crossed the foyer to the dining room.

There, he was amazed to find a bountiful feast spread out across the long table, with more courses than he could possibly eat. Kyel resisted the impulse to throw himself down in his chair and dive in. His stomach had been growling ever since he had made the decision to skip his midday meal and work through it instead.

But he hesitated, looking at the high priest seated at the head of the table. Suspicious, Kyel doubted the spread of food was simply a parting gift. He had worked in trade long enough to know when someone wanted something from him. Kyel took his seat across from His Eminence. As he did, he saw that Cadmus' smile suddenly seemed forced. What was going on that he didn't know about?

As Cadmus took the seat opposite him, Kyel sat back and waited nervously for his host to serve him the first course, as was the courtesy even in Covendrey. The old man took Kyel's plate and spooned on the helpings solicitously, even ceremoniously, before offering it back to him.

But as Kyel stared down at the food on his plate, he found himself losing his appetite. Even Cadmus had not spoken a word, and an uneasy silence lingered over the room in the absence of conversation.

"Do you mind telling me what's going on?" Kyel looked at Cadmus instead of the high priest. He regretted the words almost instantly, knowing he was overstepping the bounds of courtesy.

Cadmus shared a long, silent look with His Eminence, then set his fork down carefully across his plate. Standing up, he walked around the edge of the table, having to twist sideways to squeeze his portly frame around the corner of a bureau. From a drawer, he produced an elegantly bound text, which he held tucked against his chest so that Kyel couldn't see the title.

"We have something for you," Cadmus said as he moved back to his seat.

He handed the book across the table to Kyel. The black leather cover was imprinted with the words:

A Treatise on the Well of Tears
by
Master Devrim Remzi

Kyel felt his jaw drop as he folded back the dusty cover, trying not to crack the ancient binding. He quickly scanned the first few pages, realizing the text was exactly what he'd been searching for, exactly what he needed. He couldn't believe it. But instead of feeling appreciative, the text in his hand filled him with ire.

"You've known about this all along," he accused. "Why did you have me waste my time down there for three days?"

He closed the book with a snap that tossed a small cloud of dust up into his face, making his nose itch. The high priest and Cadmus looked at him silently, their expressions blank. What had they been doing, just feeding him rubbish while he could have been halfway to Emmery by now? Delaying him while they milked him for information at night?

"Was it truly a complete waste of your time?" asked Cadmus.

"Yes," Kyel insisted.

But then he thought about it. His research in the vaults had given him a much deeper perspective on the situation they faced, even some revelations.

"No," he admitted grudgingly.

The high priest nodded. At his motion, Cadmus reached into his shirt pocket and withdrew a folded piece of parchment, which he held up between two fingers. Kyel stared at it, at the words inscribed with heavy strokes of black ink: *His Eminence, the High Priest of Wisdom.*

Handing the letter across to Kyel, Cadmus informed him, "We received this note from your master shortly after your arrival."

Unfolding the crisp parchment, Kyel felt fury rising like angry heat to his cheeks. He traced his eyes over it, noting the careful script that seemed almost pressed with force into the page. A strange tingling sensation filled him the moment he started reading.

His Eminence, the High Priest of Wisdom,

Thank you for receiving my acolyte, Kyel Archer. Please provide him with a text which I require, A Treatise on the Well of Tears. If you would kindly allow my acolyte to borrow the original text, I will take great pains to assure that it is returned to you promptly. I regret that I must also beg a favor: please withhold knowledge of the text's existence from my acolyte until after he has spent three days' study in your vaults. I sent Kyel to you under the pretense that he is to be searching for information on the Well of Tears. However, it is my wish that he be provided with the following listed materials so as to progress further in his training. If you can think of any other resources that might be helpful to him, please include them in his course of study. I would be much appreciative, as Kyel does not have the benefit of Aerysius' libraries to broaden his knowledge. Thank you for your time and assistance.

Yours in the Pursuit of Wisdom,

Darien Lauchlin

Prime Warden of Aerysius
Distinguished Order of Sentinels
Grand Master of the Eighth Tier

Below the last line appeared to be an almost comprehensive listing of the books Kyel had been searching through for the past three days. *The Mysteries of Aerysius* was listed first, followed by *The Fall of Bryn Calazar.* The list of titles and authors continued even onto the back of the page. As he scanned down the rough columns, Kyel saw that he recognized most of the works.

But nowhere was there a mention of a book entitled *The Family Lauchlin.* That must have been an addition of the high priest's, probably falling under Darien's request for 'other resources that might be helpful.'

It had been helpful, all right. Kyel just wished he could get the name Gerald Withersby out of his head. It provoked too many images of his own son. He couldn't imagine the horror of seeing Gil's name and death date scrawled on such an entry.

"So this was all just some damned trick?" He crumbled Darien's letter in his hand, shoving it into his pocket. It was just as his trial with the vortex, one of Darien's callous lessons. Kyel was damned near fed up with them.

"You furthered your education, didn't you?" said Cadmus. "And you learned much more than if we had just given you a stack of books and asked you to sit and read. Knowledge is, after all, the First Pillar of Wisdom. Truly, your Prime Warden is as insightful as he is brash."

Insufferable is more like it, Kyel thought, fuming. Lifting *Treatise on the Well* in his hand, he stood up from the table and turned to the high priest.

"Thank you for your hospitality. I'll just be on my way."

But the old man shook his head.

Kyel sank back down in his chair. He set the text in his lap and held his head in his hands, propping his elbows on the table. Beneath him, his plate of food looked as cold as it was ever going to get.

"What is it you wish to discuss this time?" he asked dismally.

"His Eminence desires to know only one last detail before you leave our hospitality. He wishes to know, to what dark use does your master intend to put the Circle of Convergence on Orien's Finger?"

Chapter Twenty-Five Dangerous Audacity

Auberdale, The Rhen

"He's staying at an inn called the Four Quarrels in Southarbour, Sire. And it appears that Landry was right in his guess. They're sharing a room together, and a bed."

Faukravar nodded, absently stroking his goatee. He had figured as much. It was the only explanation that fit. Temple priestesses simply did not go flitting about in the company of vigorous young men, alone and unescorted.

"Excellent," the king said, feeling his mood lighten. "What else?"

Chadwick Cummings cleared his throat noisily. "I'm sorry, Sire, but he's kept to his room all day. Only the priestess has emerged. Apparently, they must have gotten into some sort of row; she left the inn this morning in quite a heat."

"I can't imagine, with his charm," the king muttered. The comment sparked a round of polite chortles from his entourage.

"Let me think!" He glared them all into silence. He still knew next to nothing about Lauchlin. He felt certain the man was who he claimed, but there were too many inconsistencies about him. The mage's sword bothered him the most.

"So we still don't know for certain whether or not this mage is tame. I don't like it. I don't like it at all." His grip intensified on the arms of his throne. Every puzzle had a solution, even this one. If he could just see it. Then he realized that the solution had already presented itself. A sinister smile formed on his lips.

"You had the priestess followed?"

"Of course, my liege."

The king nodded graciously. "Good. Have her escorted to the North Tower. Should diplomacy fail, we will use her as security."

Cummings stepped forward, a frown on his plump face. "Sire, do you truly think it's wise to provoke him?"

"Why not? He provoked me, didn't he? Let's just see if he can maintain his cloak of arrogance when he finds out we have his whore locked up in chains."

The shadows of the city were lengthening by the time Darien turned away from the window. He had been there often on and off throughout the day, staring out through the rippled glass at the busy streets below. He was growing weary of the constant bustle of people that moved beneath his window like a solemn and anonymous procession.

He had lost track of the number of white dresses he'd seen gliding by, yet none had brought Naia back to him. It was as if the priestess had been simply swept away by the tides of people flowing through the city streets. The hour was growing late, and he had no idea where she could possibly be.

If something had happened to her, it was his fault. Vaguely, he wondered if Naia's disappearance was some sort of punishment for his transgressions. Perhaps the vengeful goddess he'd sold his soul to was exacting atonement for his sins.

Darien realized now the magnitude of the injury he'd committed when he had chosen to lift Naia's veil. He hadn't thought the decision through. He had let his emotions rule him in a moment of vulnerability, and now he was paying the price.

At least he could give her the answer she wanted. He'd told Kyel once that sometimes it felt as though he were still falling from the cliff. He thought he had finally found someone to pull him back from the edge, another miracle like the Bird Man. He knew better, now.

What had happened last night had been the wrong place, the wrong time. The wrong person. He couldn't expect Naia to save him from the cliff's edge. He couldn't risk the real possibility he might pull her over with him.

He loved her too much for that.

Again, he was reminded of the ancient Bird Man who had saved his life. *Birds are smart*, the old man had said. *They always know when it's time to fly.*

It was Naia's time to fly. Perhaps she had flown already. If not, then he would somehow find the strength to open the door of the cage he had so selfishly placed around her. Then he would say goodbye, stand back, and watch her go.

A soft pattering noise tapped on the window. Looking up, he saw it was starting to rain. Once, he had loved the sound of the rain. He could remember many nights, lying awake late at night with Meiran in his arms, listening to the sound of the rain splattering against the window in her bedchamber.

Meiran was another woman he'd simply had no business being with. Why was he always drawn to the very things he shouldn't have? The only two women he had ever loved were forbidden him. Meiran was dead now, her soul condemned to hell because he had ignored tradition and chosen to take her anyway.

And now Naia was missing.

The parallel was too complete, too decisive. The more he thought about it, the more it filled him with dread.

Naia had left her pack, and her horse was still in the stable. She hadn't flown. Her coat was still folded neatly on the chair. Outside, there was a downpour. Naia would not be caught out in such weather without her coat. Even if she was furious with him, she was also sensible. She would have returned by now.

There was only one explanation left, and it made perfect sense. Darien cursed himself. He should have seen this coming. His mother had warned him about the King of Chamsbrey. And, if he were Faukravar, Darien figured he probably would have done the same.

The King had taken Naia to use as leverage against him. The only question that remained was what he was going to do about it.

It was really no question at all. One woman he loved had already been sacrificed simply because she'd made the mistake of loving him back. He would be damned if he was going to let that happen a second time.

Darien paused only long enough to test his blade before slapping the baldric on over his shoulder. He stuffed the white cloak into his pack and started to reach for his gloves. But he drew his hand back instead.

By taking Naia, the King had made an open declaration of war. And if Faukravar wanted a war, then that was exactly what he was going to get.

It was well past dark by the time he arrived back at Glassenburgh Castle. The rain had finally stopped, but his clothes were soaked through to the skin. It was bitterly cold. Darien shivered as he let go of the wall and dropped to the ground on the other side. It took only the slightest ripple of shadow to elude the watchful eyes of the guards as he walked toward the moat.

He gathered in the web of shadow that surrounded him and crossed the drawbridge. Once inside the bailey, he pressed himself against the wall and loosened the web. The shadows melted away, dissipating back into the night.

He removed his pack and sword, setting them down. Drawing out the white cloak, he pulled it on over his shoulders, fixing it in place. When he stepped away from the wall, his clothes were once more fully dry. He reached for the hilt of his sword, checking to make sure that the blade was loose in its scabbard. Then he stalked across the yard toward the castle's entrance.

This time, the guards saw him coming. That was the last thing they saw.

Drawing his blade, Darien sliced out with four quick, successive strokes. As he stepped through the castle's doorway, he left behind only dead men on the steps. He slammed his blade home, not bothering to wipe the wet sheen of blood from the steel.

Inside, he found the castle lit for an occasion, the sound of music and ringing laughter coming from a hall to his left. Darien followed the noise of distant applause as he strode down the empty hallway beneath a glowing spread of chandeliers. He moved as if in a dream, eyes loosely focused on the hallway ahead, the sounds of the castle muted and indistinct.

He turned a corner and vaguely noted the hazy shapes of people spilling in and out of a doorway as if moving through a mist. They were dressed formally, the women in long gowns of silk and velvet, the men in capes and embroidered vests.

Darien was hardly aware of the press of people around him as he inserted himself into the crowd. He didn't notice the frowns of the men who stepped back away from him. He couldn't feel the eyes of the women running over him as he moved through the doorway.

The fog that glazed his senses abruptly fell away, shattered by the sound of a woman's scream immediately followed by a ringing shriek of steel.

Someone had noticed the sword at his back. Or the star. Whichever. It made no difference.

The music stopped playing as people turned toward the sound of the commotion. All movement in the ballroom ceased as every face turned, fixing solely on him.

He had walked into a gala.

At the far end of the hall, a quartet of musicians slowly lowered their instruments as the motion of crossbows being raised drew his attention upward to the gallery.

Over the heads of the guests, he could see the King seated on a raised dais at the far end, flanked by his lackeys. Faukravar's eyes were dark and coldly seething.

The cruel look on the King's face washed away any doubt Darien had left. Provoked to a rage of fury, he stepped forward as the crowd parted before him, opening a clear path between himself and the King.

He trembled as he strode between the ranks of guests, the cold anger that filled him inflamed by the taunting promise in the King's malicious glare. He crossed the length of the room, ignoring the threat of the guards coming toward him. He didn't pause, even as the first man stepped forward to take him.

The crowd surged back as Darien slid his sword out and drew it downward, parting the flesh of the man all the way from his neck to his crotch.

He brought his sword around, sliding the steel under the next man's guard. He kicked the dead man off his blade, watching the body crumble to the floor. Darien stepped over the corpse as the mob surged back from him.

He closed on the dais as the rest of the guards fell back to protect their King.

The sound of wails and desperate weeping seemed strangely distant in his ears, as if the crowd behind him was very far away or in another world entirely.

Eyes only for Faukravar, Darien reached out with his mind and flung the guards away from him, throwing the men backward against the walls with a gust of solid air.

On the throne, the King glowered down at him as Darien sheathed his sword and mounted the steps to the dais.

He didn't slow his pace. Shaking in rage, Darien advanced on Faukravar and backhanded the man across the face.

The King's head whiplashed around as the golden circlet of his crown tumbled to the floor and rolled off the dais. Bracing his hand on the back of the throne, Darien clutched the man's collar and hauled him bodily out of his seat.

"Where is she?"

Dumping him back down, Darien simply waited. The King slowly brought a hand up and touched it to the red mark on his cheek, eyes glaring defiance.

"I thought it expedient to have her detained. If anything happens to me, your lover will suffer the same fate."

Darien shook his head. "No. I have neither the time nor the patience to play that game. Have Naia brought to me here, now, or I swear by the gods I'll kill you with a thought."

His words provoked a stir of movement in the gallery as the crossbows trained at his back adjusted their aim. Faukravar spared a glance at his recovering guards.

"Your threats grow just as tiring as they are empty. Since you've done no real harm here tonight except by the common steel of your blade, I must assume you've sworn the Oath of Harmony. There is nothing you can do to touch me with your power."

Darien scowled as he raked his sleeve back to expose the angry red scars on his right wrist. He held his arm up before Faukravar's face, watching the King's eyes slowly widen. He reached out from within, caressing the man's mind with the honed edge of his wrath.

A change came over the King's face. His cheeks went white, jaw clenching in pain. Trembling, his hands clutched the arms of the throne as he threw his head back, gasping a long and shuddering breath.

"Release her!" Darien commanded, wrenching Faukravar's mind.

The King slumped forward, moaning.

Darien waited as Faukravar recovered enough to draw himself up again. The defiance in his eyes was gone, replaced by a look of terror.

Faukravar raised a shaking hand, signaling his men.

Darien stood back, sweeping his eyes over the diminished crowd. Two men ran out even as more guards spilled into the back of the room. The guests who remained were few and seemed frozen in place, staring with looks of horror in their eyes.

He stood quietly, arms clasped behind his back, as long minutes dragged by. Gradually, the pulsing careen of his heart returned to normal, the rage that consumed him slowly dissipating.

He stabbed a glance over his shoulder at the King. "If she's suffered any harm, you truly will wish it was my brother here instead of me."

Faukravar lowered his eyes, either too frightened or too repulsed to meet his gaze.

Darien's breath caught as a small contingent of guards swarmed into the ballroom, Naia in their midst. The priestess' white dress was rumpled, her veil disarrayed. But Naia moved with a stately grace as she seemed to flow toward him through the parted crowd of onlookers.

Then she saw him.

A look of dismay formed on her face as she took in his blood-splattered clothes, saw the bodies of the fallen guards that impeded her path. The ashen face of the King, crownless, on his throne.

Naia stopped in her tracks, her skin paling to a shade just darker than her snowy gown. Darien felt his heart sicken as Naia's expression defeated him as surely as he had just defeated the King.

Darien slid the blood-stained cloak from his shoulders, shoving it back into his pack in a crumbled heap. He was exhausted, his head aching as he moved over to a bowl of water on the table. He dipped his hands into it and scrubbed them together violently, the water in the bowl turning a murky shade of red. He shook his hands dry, then walked back to where he'd slung his baldric over the back of a chair. As he reached for it, he felt Naia's hand on his arm.

"This morning, I asked you to make a decision."

It was the first time she'd spoken since they had left the castle. He drew the baldric on and lifted his pack over his shoulder.

He said, "In two days, I leave for Orien's Finger with the King's army. You won't be coming with me."

She blinked, staring up at him with an injured look. "Why not?"

There were too many reasons to name. He chose the one that mattered most. "In the past few months, I've lost everything I've ever cared for. You are the one thing I have left that matters to me at all. I don't think I could stand it if I lost you, too."

She raised her hand toward him, reaching up to stroke his face. Darien turned his head away from her touch, drawing back. Then, thinking better of it, he bent and pressed a kiss against her forehead, trailing his hand down the sheer fabric of her veil.

Solemnly, he whispered, "Goodbye, Naia. Fly free."

He moved out into the dim light of the hallway, shutting the door quietly behind him as he left.

Chapter Twenty-Six
Desperate Measures

Pass of Lor-Gamorth, The Front

The Pass of Lor-Gamorth was obscured by swells of fog that clung to the flanks of the Shadowspears. From his perch on a ridge overlooking the gorge, Traver could see nothing but the few men that shivered at his side, clustered together for warmth. It was as though the world more than ten paces away didn't exist. Even the light in the clouds seemed muted to a wraith-like glow.

With a trembling hand, Traver raised his limp waterskin to his lips, tilting his head back. When nothing came out, he shook the tanned goat's stomach next to his ear. All he heard was rattling ice. He tossed the waterskin down by his side.

He could feel Henley's body shivering, pressed up against him. The Valeman coughed, a wet and rasping noise that made Traver glance sideways at him in concern.

It was the third day since they had abandoned the keep. Traver wished they were out of the pass. Already, they could have been down from the mountains and out into the light and warmth of the plains below.

But Garret Proctor had ordered them to do anything they could to slow the Enemy advance. So that's what they were doing—or trying to do. Traver wondered how much longer they could keep it up. They had already lost a quarter of their number, as much to the relentless cold as to the whispering, black-fletched shafts that fell out of the sky.

Henley coughed again, and this time Traver could feel the Valeman's whole body spasm against him.

The sound of a birdcall drifted out of the stillness of the pass, a low and hollow-sounding *whooo-oo.* The noise made Traver start, his hand going to the hilt of his sword.

Men staggered to their feet, eyes darting as they scanned the haze of mist. Traver patted Henley on the back in a gesture of comfort as the Valeman pushed himself to his feet with a grimace. Trudging forward, Traver moved to stand at the edge of the ridge, looking down at the swirling ocean of fog that obscured the approaches.

Nothing happened for minutes. He started to hope that maybe the birdcall had been a mistake. The appalling silence that choked the Shadowspears remained undisturbed, as complete as the eternal night.

Then he heard it, softly at first, like the drone of a distant waterfall. As the sound built gradually, Traver could make out the deliberate cadence of it. The noise swelled, became a rumbling quake that shuddered the mountains as it drew ever nearer. Thousands of shod feet moved beneath them.

Henley's barked order spurred them into motion.

Traver crouched beside the pile of boulders at his side and shoved one forward with all his might. The rock's sharp surface raked against his numb fingers, but he felt no pain as the boulder rolled off the edge of the ridge, tumbling down into the line of advancing infantry below.

The sounds of commotion and screams echoed above the clamor of Enemy drums as a rain of stone hailed down all along the ridgeline. Bowstrings hummed, and a cloud of arrows parted the mist, arcing into the pass. Volley after volley hissed over the edge.

Traver gritted his teeth as the numbness in his

hands turned into a throbbing ache. But he kept moving, shoving stone after stone down the slope, while the rest of his company labored to do the same. Then another noise rose over the cries of death and panicked screams, drowning out even the sound of the war drums.

"Fall back!"

Traver ignored the command long enough to heave one last rock over the slope, then turned and sprinted away, just as a wave of black-armored warriors spilled over the ridge behind him.

He leaned forward, arms pumping at his sides as he tried to catch up to the men fleeing ahead of him. Whispering death hissed by all around as black-fletched arrows found their marks. In front of him, men were dropped in midstride, slumping forward with dark shafts bristling their backs. Traver sprinted for all he was worth.

It wasn't fast enough.

A lance stabbed downward, grazing the side of his cheek. Grabbing for his sword, Traver staggered as a warhorse wheeled back around in front of him. He could see the shadow of a face beneath the rider's helm. The lance dropped and angled at his chest, the dark warrior kicking his mount forward to charge again. Traver glanced desperately for any means of escape, but all he could see was the flooding tide of infantry behind him.

Turning back to the charging horse, he brought his sword up and swept it back over his shoulder. Then he brought the blade down with every last ounce of strength he possessed.

His arms shuddered from the impact as his sword sheared through the armor on the animal's neck. The horse went down, tumbling. One of its hooves clipped him in the leg and he fell with it, losing his grip on his sword. The blade flew from his grasp, spinning away as Traver fell to the dirt.

He started to get up, but for some reason his legs wouldn't work. He struggled, desperately clawing at the black earth with his hands, but his lower half simply wouldn't budge. With a frustrated scream, he wrenched his head back far enough to see the twisted form of the dead horse collapsed across his legs.

He did the only thing he could think of and squirmed up against the belly of the dead animal, tucking his head into the gap between the spread forelegs. Closing his eyes, he prayed to his sweet Lady Luck as the storm broke over him.

———

"We can't take another day of this," Craig warned, surveying their tattered campsite nestled in the cleft of a ravine. There were no fires, just a few scattered tents, and nothing but scores of men huddled together in tight clusters, shivering against the icy chill of the wind.

The force commander nodded, his cold eyes looking out at the campsite and seeing none of it. Instead, his eyes were loosely focused on something in the air right in front of him. There was nothing there; there never was. Ever since they'd abandoned the fortress, his gaze was drawn often to something Craig simply couldn't see. His eyes would wander, sometimes for minutes on end, tracing the empty air in front of his face.

"We go down tomorrow," Proctor announced.

Chapter Twenty-Seven
The Field of Tol-Ranier

The Field of Tol-Ranier, The Rhen

The first pale streaks of dawn were just beginning to gray the horizon as Darien looked down on the ancient battle site known as the Field of Tol-Ranier. There, the camp of the King's northern army lay spread out before him in orderly rows of black tents that stood out against the glistening white sheen of winter's first snowfall.

The sight of the encampment bothered him. It had been two days since he'd ordered Faukravar to prepare his army for the march, and yet it seemed that no measures had been taken to arrange for such an expedition. As Darien considered the silent encampment below, a slow anger filled him.

It was still very early. Yet, there should have been more movement than he could see among the tents. Soldiers should have been about stoking cook fires, honing their weapons, and preparing for the routines of the day. But instead, the encampment of Faukravar's army looked nearly deserted, just a token few men left behind to give the suggestion that there might be more.

He kicked his heels into the Tarkendar's sides, sending the horse forward down the hill at a springing trot. Darien reached down, feeling at his side for the comfort of the sword fixed to his saddle. He wrapped his fingers around it, the leather laced around the hilt rough and soothing to his skin.

He was glad he had lingered in the city as long as he had, shadowing Naia until she had finally slipped out in the falling snow, not knowing that her departure was remarked by a silent observer looking down from the city walls. Darien had feared Faukravar would move against her again, but now he knew why the King hadn't. The Vile Prince had been making other, more sinister, plans.

The camp ahead was a trap. He could sense it. A trap rigged to spring if he stepped his foot into it. But even with that knowledge, Darien felt no fear. There was little they could do if he was prepared.

And so he was. He had spent a lot of time in thought over the last two days, summoning the strength he would need to face the trials that awaited him in the days ahead. Laying new plans, altering old ones. Taking what he knew from his training and adapting it to new, more deadly, applications.

Naia's departure had helped, more than she could ever know. She had taken with her his heart, leaving him with only a festering wound in its place. Which was good. The emptiness that now filled him knew no compassion. Without compassion, there could be no pain, no mercy, no remorse.

With those feelings set aside, he was free to transform into what it was necessary he become: a weapon melded together with purpose. Tempered by Arden's fire, quenched by Naia's love. Forged on the anvil of Proctor's cruel cunning, dedicated in the font of Meiran's spilt blood.

There was nothing they could do to touch him. For the first time ever, he was truly Unbound.

The few men left behind in the encampment looked up as he rode through their midst. There was no surprise on their faces, no shock at the sight of his cloak. But there was fear.

Darien could almost smell it as he rode past them: a sickening, rank odor that disgusted him. He rode through the camp, past long lines of tents and doused fires. All the while, he was followed by the nauseating stench of their fear. He couldn't ignore it. He couldn't make it go away. It infected him.

Reaching out from within, Darien tasted the magic field. It was a delicate, throbbing pulse that flowed through him, following the contours of the surrounding landscape. It moved in a north-westerly direction, pointing like a compass arrow directly toward Orien's Vortex. The rhythm of the field was peaceful, like a slow and stately dance.

He kept his mind open to it as he directed the warhorse up a snow-covered hill, the animal's hooves making crunching noises in the loose white powder. At the summit, he drew back on the reins as the gelding sidestepped with a nervous snort.

Faukravar's army waited at the base of the slope in front of him. The soldiers were formed into divisions, with light cavalry in the front flanked by ranks of infantry, perhaps twelve thousand strong. Archers stood ready, bows raised skyward with arrows already nocked. And behind him, Darien could hear the empty encampment stirring.

The trap had sprung.

Glancing behind, he saw soldiers pouring out of the tents, hundreds of them, running through the snow with weapons drawn. At the same time, the archers in front of him released their bowstrings, hurling a thick cloud of arrows that seemed to choke the very sky. Darien watched the arrows arc upward, waited until they curved overhead and began their plunging descent. Smiling grimly, he drew deeply on the currents of the magic field.

The air around him shivered, then lashed out at the cloud of arrows like the crack of a thousand whips with a thousand angry tails. The arrows shattered, splinters of pulverized shafts drifting through the air. There was a sound almost like falling hail as broadheads rained down from the sky, splashing harmlessly to the snow.

Darien signaled his horse with the pressure of his legs. The gelding swept forward along the crest of the hill, moving quickly up to speed, sprinting with all its great heart to deliver him from the jaws of the closing vice.

On his right, the soldiers spilling from the encampment were almost on top of him. And on his left, a thundering wedge of cavalry was hurling up the hill.

The two jaws of the vise snapped closed behind him. The gelding reared on its hind legs, spinning around as a twisting rope of flame snaked across the ground, blooming instantly into a crackling wall of fire that thrust upward into the sky. Horses screamed, striving to break their momentum. The acute intensity of the heat forced the soldiers pursuing him to fall back.

Darien gazed upon his creation with a feeling of pride. The roar of the fire drowned out all other noise, waves of heat roiling in the air above licking tongues of flame. There was no smoke; nothing was burning. The fire fed itself, a creature of pure, voracious energy.

Darien compelled his horse toward it.

The gelding wanted to balk, so he wrapped its eyes in shadow and silenced the sound of the blaze in its ears. The heat did not touch them as they moved into the flames, but the wind of the fire did. It savaged his cloak and whipped his hair, rippling his horse's long mane. Engulfed by the flames and yet unconsumed, Darien leaned his head back and savored the rapturous wonder of the magic field surging like a torrent through his mind.

They passed through the heart of the fire and emerged again on the other side. Releasing his hold on his horse's senses, Darien let the blaze behind him slowly die. Ahead, the men of Faukravar's army stood as if dazed, weapons lowered, staring with mouths slackened.

No one moved to confront him as Darien directed his mount down the hill and out onto the Field of Tol-Ranier. Men stepped back as he moved past them. Their eyes followed him as he rode by, keeping his horse at a swaying trot right through the heart of Faukravar's army.

When at last he reached the small group of mounted officers on the far side of the field, he drew up beside the man wearing a general's insignia on his uniform. The soldier's face was ashen gray, his expression sagging. Darien regarded him for a long, silent moment. Then he informed him:

"You are relieved of your command."

The general blinked.

"Which one of you is his second?"

A young, aristocratic man with a contemptuous sneer nodded his head at him. "That would be me."

"You're relieved, as well."

The officer's stare glared hatred as his hand darted for his blade. Darien's eyes caught the motion. With a cry, the young officer retracted his hand, staring in horror at the glowing red hilt of his sword. Bringing his hand up, he gaped at the angry burns that covered his fingers.

Confident that there would be no further resistance, Darien backed his horse up until he could take in the small group of men together as a whole.

"The Enemy is advancing in numbers not seen since the fall of Caladorn," he said. "Which man of you has the courage to lead this army in a battle that will decide the fate of everything you know and everything you love?"

For a long moment, no one moved. Finally, a young man near the back looped the reins of his horse over the pommel of his saddle and dismounted. Walking forward, the young officer looked up at Darien with wide brown eyes that held no fear.

"I do, Prime Warden."

The young man dropped to his knees in the snow and leaned forward until his face was pressed up against the loose powder that covered the Field of Tol-Ranier. He remained there as his fellows stared down at him contemptuously.

"You may rise," Darien said. "What is your name?"

"Lieutenant Malcolm Wellingford, Prime Warden." The young officer stood up. He drew his sword and offered it to Darien hilt-first.

Darien received the sword, holding it up to inspect it. It was a common piece of steel, not elegant or ornamented in any way. The blade had seen much use, but it still held a keen edge. Extending it forward, he noted that the balance was good.

Darien nodded, handing the sword back. "This blade will serve me well. Do you swear on the honor of your house to follow wherever my lead should take you, deferring to whatever order I give immediately and without question?"

"I do so swear, Prime Warden."

Darien nodded solemnly. "General Wellingford, please issue the command to form ranks."

He waited as his new general darted back to recover his horse. Darien turned back to address the remaining officers:

"Any man not wholly committed to me should leave right now. Otherwise, if you choose to desert later, such an act will be considered treason. You shall be hunted down and slain without mercy."

He waited as the men before him exchanged nervous glances. Faukravar's former general turned his horse around with a quick jerk of the reins. He withdrew from the field, back stiff with injured pride, followed by three others.

The remaining officers stared after the departing men. But when they turned back to Darien, each man's expression was hardened with fresh resolve.

As the soldiers spread out across the field drew together and assembled, their officers dismounted and knelt silently in the snow. Darien accepted their oaths gravely. Then he rode out before the ranks of gathered men, and there drew up his mount. As he did, he sent his mind outward on the tides of air above the field, weaving shadows overhead to cover the face of the sun.

Night fell across the Field of Tol-Ranier, the daylight fading into darkness. An eerie stillness descended upon the plain as all motion ceased and all eyes were drawn toward him. Darien surveyed the soldiers before him, measuring the mettle of the men. Then he raised his voice to be heard above the compressed, silent tension.

"Greystone Keep has always held the Pass of Lor-Gamorth, and the pass has always held the North against the Enemy. But Greystone Keep has fallen. The North will soon fall also, unless we make a stand.

"We march to Orien's Finger, where we will be faced with two of the greatest Enemy hosts ever assembled. You do not go friendless and alone; the forces of Emmery will be with you.

"And I will be with you, as well. I am Prime Warden Darien Lauchlin, Grand Master of the Eighth Tier. I am the last surviving Sentinel of Aerysius, and I am also Unbound.

"We are all that stands between our homeland and the fate that befell Caladorn of old. Should we fail, then our lands will be desecrated, and our families enslaved by the Enemy. But if we succeed, then all of you will go to your graves knowing that it was by your courage alone that every last nation of the Rhen survives in the light and hope of the sun."

He released the gathered shadows and allowed the morning to dawn again, the sun emerging to glare brilliantly above in a clear morning sky. A thunderous cheer went up as the ranks before him collapsed. Discipline abandoned, the men swarmed forward around him like a breaking wave.

Darien closed his eyes and, smiling quietly, bowed his head.

He woke before the break of dawn to the sounds of the encampment already stirring. Darien dressed in the darkness, not even bothering with simple magelight. It had been hard to awaken. The air of the tent was cold, and his blankets warm. Sleep crusted his eyes, and he found himself terribly groggy.

It was still dark when he emerged and stood gazing out across the snowy field. Already, the men had most of the camp broken down. His own tent was one of the few still standing.

Darien opened his mind to the magic field. Ever since Naia had left, it was the only thing he seemed to take comfort in. He groped for it constantly, for no real reason other than the contentment it brought. Sometimes Darien fought with himself, knowing that the allure of the field was starting to become something of an obsession. But often he reached for it unconsciously, not even aware he was doing so until it was too late.

Arriving at the command tent, he found his young general busily poring over a list scrawled across a strip of parchment. At least the boy could read. That was more than he'd hoped for. He really didn't care, one way or the other. Darien hadn't accepted the young man's oath because he was in need of a strong commander. He had accepted Wellingford because he needed someone biddable.

Strolling up behind him, Darien looked over his shoulder and studied the first few lines of the list. "I see your King finally came through with the provisions I ordered."

Wellingford looked back at him, seeming a bit startled. Handing over the parchment, he said, "We received the wagons in the night. But His Grace only sent enough supplies to last us twelve days. That will do little more than get us there."

Darien nodded, scanning down the list appraisingly. "That's all I requested. We'll need to travel swift and light." Handing the list back, he started to turn away.

"But, Prime Warden, what are we going to do about supplies for the march home?"

Darien shrugged. "We'll just have to worry about that when the time comes."

The boy's brow wrinkled up. "You don't think we'll be coming home, do you?"

Darien didn't respond. Instead, he turned and strode away.

He walked over to the edge of the encampment, where he stood silently observing the last details being completed. In a short amount of time, the camp was entirely broken down, the men forming up in a long column for the march.

Movement on the ridge caught his eye. The King was riding toward them, surrounded by his knights, pennants fluttering from their lances. Faukravar himself was suited for battle, his thin frame covered with gleaming black plate. The King of Chamsbrey rode with his plumed helm in his hand.

Faukravar's party drew up, the King gazing down into Darien's eyes with rigid contempt. After a long moment, the man stated in a somber voice:

"Ever have the Kings of Auberdale ridden to war with the armies of Chamsbrey."

Darien nodded weary acceptance. There was little he could do about it. "As you like," he said, then added, "Just don't get in my way."

Chapter Twenty-Eight
Dreams

Pass of Lor-Gamorth, The Front

Traver awakened to a sharp, stabbing pain in his hand matched only by the throbbing ache in his head. He squinted up into the flickering lights of the clouds, wondering how he wasn't dead. The pain flared like a knife thrust. Traver recoiled his hand. As he did, he saw the beak of the scavenger bird that had mistaken his warm flesh for a piece of meat.

"Go away, damn you!"

The vulture spread its wings and hopped backward. Traver threw a small rock at the thing to get it gone. It flapped into the air a few feet before alighting back again, this time even nearer. Apparently, the thing didn't have the common decency to wait until he was dead.

Traver wanted to scream in frustration.

"All right," he said. "I'll tell you what. You go snack on somebody else for a while. Come back in a few days, and if I'm still here, you can have as much as you like. I won't even make a fuss about it."

When the bird bobbed its head, Traver took it for a sign of agreement. Turning his face away, he made one last attempt to pull his legs out from under the dead horse's carcass. But he couldn't get enough traction in the crumbled dirt. All he succeeded in doing was clawing sand into his face.

When he felt the bird's beak again, this time on his shoulder, he did scream.

"I told you to go find somebody else!"

"There isn't anyone else," responded a somber voice. "At least, no one else alive."

Startled, Traver craned his neck enough to take in the miracle of Corban Henley's face. He wanted to laugh. That thick red beard was such a beautiful sight. But instead, he found himself weeping.

"There, lad," Henley soothed, patting his shoulder. "It's good you like to hear the sound of your own voice so much. Otherwise, I never would have found you."

Traver beamed up at him. But then it occurred to him to wonder what Henley was still doing there. The skirmish was over, the rest of their fellows fled back to the camp in the canyon, or perhaps moved on by now.

As he stared at Henley's face, Traver thought he saw the answer. The big Valeman sitting beside him was scraped up, and there was a tightness around his eyes. Henley was in a lot of pain.

"What happened to you?" Traver asked.

Henley scowled, reaching down to pat his leg. "Broken. Snapped right clean. I guess neither one of us will be going anywhere."

Traver's cheerful mood took a plunge. "But, you can walk, right? You found me, didn't you?"

Henley shook his head. "I can hop a small distance, but that's as good as I can do. I'm sorry, lad, but I can't lift that carcass off you."

Traver grimaced. A snowflake fluttered down through the air to alight on his cheek. "So what are we going to do?"

"We go to sleep." Henley's voice was calm. "Maybe we'll dream a bit. If we're lucky, they'll even be good dreams."

Traver nodded. He could do that. It didn't sound so bad. He just wished it didn't have to be so awfully cold. He drew his cloak around himself as tightly as he could as another snowflake settled on his skin. At his side, he heard Henley coughing, a weak and rasping gurgle.

———

"Three feet of snow, or thereabouts," Craig grumbled, gazing out on the miraculous change that had transformed the Shadowspears overnight. No longer black, the sharp peaks above him glistened a deadly white. The men had scarcely enough blankets and cloaks for the summer months, and the onset of winter was like a harsh and bitter death grip.

The force commander had put the men to work as the blizzard broke over them, using their shields to pile the drifting snow up around their tents. Only eleven men had been lost during the night. It should have been much worse. The cover of snow around the tents created an insulating barrier. His own tent had been almost uncomfortably warm with twelve other men packed inside. In the middle of a raging snowstorm, Craig had woken up three times during the night dripping wet with sweat.

But now the camp was struck. His men stood shivering, their sockless feet crusted with ice that fell down into their boots. Craig staggered as he walked toward them, his own feet breaking through the treacherous surface, sinking down through the snow at every step.

He jerked his foot up with a rain of ice and grunted in dismay to find that his boot hadn't come up with it. Glaring down into the dim blue hole of the track he'd just made, Craig was forced to bend down and dig his hand around in the snow to retrieve his boot.

Behind him, Garret Proctor stared out vacantly across the white canyon, his cloak plastered against his back by the wind. As Craig inverted his boot to dump the snow out of it, he risked a quick glance back at the man.

"The path will have been sheltered in the night," Proctor said. "Get the men down to it, and you'll find the way ahead clear. Leave behind the dead and wounded."

Craig stared at him, appalled. "We can't leave living men behind for the Enemy—you know what they'll do to them!"

"Then don't leave any living men behind."

To Craig's horror, Proctor withdrew his dagger from its sheath and pressed it into his hand, squeezing his limp fingers tightly around it. Craig gazed down at the misery knife, sickened by the cruel feel of its narrow hilt in his palm.

———

Proctor was right, yet again. When they finally found the road in the narrow gap of the pass, it was covered with just a thin sprinkling of snow over a slick layer of ice. The high walls of the canyon had protected it from the storm.

Craig had done his duty with the dagger. It had been tempting to delegate that order, to hand the blade off to one of the men, as Proctor had handed the task to him. But it had to stop somewhere.

They left the dead behind in the ravine, dark and tattered shapes adrift in a calm white sea. Craig hadn't looked back as he turned his horse around and rode away, the beast lunging forward through the snowdrifts.

Somehow, they were still ahead of the advancing Enemy column. Craig could see where they were camped, just a few ridges behind in the twisting coils of the pass, their presence revealed by thin trails of smoke from their fires.

Proctor's mind had not been idle in the night. Somewhere in the dull haze the commander moved through, a tangled skein was unraveling.

At Craig's command, a single fire arrow shot into the sky. A roaring thunder echoed from high above on the cliffs behind them.

Kicking his horse forward at a gallop, Craig tried not to think about the dead men who had stayed behind to light those charges. He rode on as a mountain's weight of snow fell to choke the pass.

"Dig through that, you damned filth," he spat, jabbing his heels into his horse's sides.

———

Wolden, The Rhen

Wolden was deserted.

At least, it appeared that way to Craig's eyes as he rode at the head of the long column snaking down off the spine of the foothills. Proctor was with him, riding at his side on his dark and rugged stallion. The commander's eyes were narrowed and watering in the brilliance of a sun that, in over fifteen years, his face had seldom looked upon. The men trailing behind rode with their heads lowered, hunched forward in their saddles, their faces tightly drawn. The relative warmth of the afternoon did little to cheer their spirits; they had seen too many horrors.

When they reached the outskirts, it became clear Wolden was indeed abandoned. Not so much as a chicken foraged in the snow in front of the scattered, ramshackle huts. It was a bizarre and haunting sight, rendered even more distressing by the lingering silence that clung to the place. The squeak of an ancient windmill broke the tension of the quiet. Somewhere, a wooden gate squealed open on rusted hinges, pushed by a gust of wind.

"What's this?" he breathed, glaring at the gate that had startled him. To Proctor, he asked, "Is this your doing?"

"Not mine."

"Whose, then?"

Proctor didn't respond. Craig sat forward in his saddle, looking from house to house. Ahead, the lane widened as they approached the town wall. He could see the gate wide open before them. There was something else there, as well. A sign was posted beside the entrance.

Proctor dismounted and strode toward the gate. Craig followed him, glancing sideways at Proctor to find that his commander's eyes had become suddenly, piercingly intent. The old soldier tore the sign down from the wall and strode forward with it. Craig jogged after him through the gate and down a wide, snow-covered street, hurrying to catch up.

Wolden was just as quiet and vacant as its outskirts. Not a soul stirred on the street. The doors of the shops and houses stood shut, many of them barred with beams of wood that looked to have been just slapped up and nailed haphazardly to the frames. The town had been emptied in a hurry.

They turned at an intersection. There, Proctor came to a halt, eyes scanning the buildings that bordered the street. Craig glanced around to see what the man was looking for. The street was empty, except for a fine coating of ice powdered with snow. The only difference he could see was that many of the doors were standing open to the elements, not closed and boarded up like the rest.

Proctor strode toward the first open doorway. Craig pressed ahead of him, keeping one hand within easy reach of his hilt. The door stood slightly ajar, so Craig pushed it the rest of the way open with the toe of his boot as he moved into the room.

Dozens of unstrung bows lay spread across the floor, arranged in overlapping bundles along with bunches of arrows, hundreds of them.

Craig knelt and lifted a bow from the first pile by his feet, holding it up to inspect. The horn bow had a rustic look about it, though Craig could see that the workmanship was sound. He looked at the strange letters carved into the wood of the bow.

It was a poem. *Song of blood, song of heart.* Turning the bow around, he saw that the poem continued on the other side. *Fly true, true heart, die true.*

Craig found the simple lines powerfully stirring. He started to set the bow back down atop the pile, but hesitated. Instead, he drew it close, feeling an odd surge of sentiment toward the elegant weapon with its poignant verse.

"Horn bows," he muttered. Then he threw his head back and bellowed a whooping battle cry. *"Do you know what this means?"*

The force commander nodded, eyes once again staring fixedly ahead. "We'll hit them hard and break away fast. We will harry them all the way down the corridor."

Chapter Twenty-Nine
To Threaten a Queen

Rothscard, The Rhen

Kyel's last memory of Rothscard hadn't been a pleasant one. The last time he'd looked upon the walls of Emmery's capital, it had been in the company of a pack of condemned convicts and their guards. Then, Rothscard had seemed loathsome and dark, a stinking swelter of dirty people living in trash and filth.

But now, for some reason, the Rothscard he entered seemed altogether different. The stone of the city walls looked pure and white, the towers graceful and soaring. Vibrant banners billowed in the air from the tops of the turrets. The rolling band of hills that embraced the city looked like immaculate, emerald gems.

His horse took the last stretch of road at an eager lope, passing scattered groups of travelers. Kyel let the gelding have its head, waiting until they were almost at the walls before easing back to a trot as they reached the end of the road.

Rothscard's east gate was a tall arch cut into the wall between two fortified guard towers. Kyel guided his horse toward the middle of the passage. On either side of the gate stood groups of Rothscard Bluecloaks who seemed to be doing little of anything besides staring dully at the clusters of people moving through their gate.

As Kyel rode through, he heard one of the guards exclaim, "Isn't that a mage's cloak?"

To his chagrin, Kyel found himself the sudden focus of attention. The guards stared at him with wide eyes, necks craned at the sight of the Silver Star at his back. Kyel was reminded of the scene in Wolden, when the people there had made such a commotion over Darien's appearance. He hoped it wouldn't be like Wolden. Kyel didn't want that sort of trouble.

"Hold up there!" someone shouted.

Kyel sighed and pulled back on the reins, slouching in weariness. He shouldn't have worn the cloak. He should have taken it off, wadded it up, and thrown it away. Now, it was simply too late.

"That's the bloody Silver Star!"

Ringed by more than a dozen guardsmen, Kyel sat back in his saddle and raised his face to the sky. Why couldn't anything ever be easy? Why did every task always have to be so difficult? The gift of the cloak was going to turn out to be another one of Darien's damnable lessons. Just like the vortex or the Temple of Wisdom.

A guard reached up and, taking his horse's reins in his hand, said, "Pardon, Great Master. We're going to have to ask you to hold up for a minute."

"Fine," Kyel muttered, frowning as he realized what the man had just called him. They took him for a full Master, which he supposed was an easy mistake to make.

The guard turned to someone behind him. "Neville, go fetch the captain. Run along, now, lad!"

"What's the problem?" Kyel asked, watching the young Bluecloak dart off, disappearing in the turmoil of the crowd moving around them through the gate. He knew exactly what the problem was but wanted the satisfaction of hearing someone say it.

"Oh, no problem, Great Master," the man said, a wary look on his face. "Just that the likes of you'd be expecting an escort to the palace."

"Oh. Sure. That sounds good."

Hearing his response, the group of men ringed around him exchanged dubious glances. Kyel supposed he probably hadn't sounded very mage-like. He would have to try adopting a more confident air in the future, or no one was bound to believe him. Squaring his shoulders, he tried to strike a more assertive pose as he waited on his horse but found the attempt almost embarrassing. It was hard to look confident when there was a group of brawny men with swords ringed about.

Kyel waited uncomfortably as his horse stood there, swishing its tail at the flies. The guards stood silent, the crowd around them keeping their distance. He was drawing stares from the passersby, a mixture of looks that only made him feel more uncomfortable.

"Do you mind climbing down off that horse?"

Kyel flinched. He twisted around and found himself staring at a man who'd come up behind him and was now examining the longbow that hung from his saddle. The guard's interest in his bow made Kyel feel nervous, even protective. He didn't like the way the man was fingering it, his touch almost a lingering caress. But he did as he was asked, lowering himself to the ground on stiff legs.

The guard walked around his horse, a hand stroking the gelding's coarse winter coat. He was a tall and muscular man. He wore his chin-length hair parted in the middle. His face was exceptionally angular, his eyes stern and discerning. The man moved with an easy grace that reminded Kyel of a cat stalking a bird, precise and deliberate. It also reminded him of the way Darien moved. The similarity was almost uncanny.

"Mages are forbidden to carry weapons, are they not?"

Kyel didn't like the way the guard was standing so close to him, scant inches from his face. It was intimidating. He could feel the man's breath on his cheek.

Trying to meet the guard's eyes, Kyel nodded. "I'm no Master, if that's what you're thinking. I'm just an acolyte."

"What's your business in Rothscard?"

Kyel had rehearsed this line enough times, but actually saying it was a different thing entirely. "I'm here at the request of the Prime Warden. My business is with your Queen."

The guard smiled cagily and shook his head. "The Prime Warden's dead, son. I've seen her corpse myself. I was part of the Queen's entourage when Her Grace went to view it."

Feeling uncertain, Kyel couldn't help looking down. This was the part where it was going to get tricky. From his experience in Wolden and again in the Temple of Wisdom, he was going to be forced to do a lot of talking. Whenever his master's name was mentioned, there was always something to explain.

"There's a new Prime Warden. Darien Lauchlin."

The man's expression creased to an uncertain frown. It was not the reaction Kyel had been expecting. Warily, the guard said, "I've met Darien Lauchlin. Describe him."

Kyel had no idea what to say. "He's tall. Dark hair." He shrugged. That was the best he could do.

The guard tilted his head slightly, moving even closer to Kyel. "When I knew him, Darien was an acolyte, the same as yourself. But there was something different about him that set him apart, something he shared in common with you, actually. Can you tell me what that is?"

Kyel didn't have to think about it long. The man's fascination with his longbow brought the obvious answer to mind. "His sword," he said. "You know of it?"

A slow, arrogant smile bloomed on the guardsman's shadowy face. "Know of it? I'm the one who taught him how to use it." He extended his hand. "Nigel Swain, Captain of the City Guard. Formerly of Aerysius, and formerly of the Arms Guild."

Kyel found himself clasping the man's hand automatically, too stunned to think. "Kyel Archer," he mumbled, impressed by Swain's firm grasp. "I'm Darien's acolyte."

"So the boy thinks he's Prime Warden, now, does he?" Swain delivered a scoffing sigh that fanned his oily hair back from his face. "Aerysius must have fallen on his head. Come on, mount up. I'll get you to the palace. Ever been to Rothscard before?"

Kyel winced, quickly shaking his head. "I've only passed through."

The last time Kyel had visited Rothscard, he'd been in chains. That was scarcely something he wanted anyone to know, even if the man was a friend of Darien's. He wondered what the captain would think of him if he ever found out. It certainly wouldn't help with his current assignment as an ambassador to the Queen.

He waited for Swain to bring his horse around, a dark gray beast with a scruffy coat. The look in the animal's eye reminded Kyel of its owner.

He couldn't keep his eyes off Swain as they rode, noticing the way the man sat his horse, a reflection of his casually deliberate stride. Kyel was also having trouble dismissing the longsword slung at the man's back. It looked like a copy of Darien's. Or perhaps it was the other way around. Kyel felt almost in awe of the man. Swain had professed an association with the Arms Guild, so he was probably a blademaster.

They turned onto a broad, cobbled street lined with rows of houses stacked one against another. The city was already decorated for Winter's Eve, with bows and bells hung from almost every door, and ribbons wrapped around every lamp post. Even the bare limbs of the trees were bedecked with colored lanterns. The feel of the city made Kyel homesick.

And then Emmery Palace itself came into view. When he saw it, Kyel felt like he'd been there before. In a way, it was almost as though he had. The palace was practically the image of the mayor's home in Wolden, only on a far grander scale.

Swain had him dismount in front of a span of wide marble steps. Two liveried footmen came forward to take their horses, but Kyel was hesitant about handing his over. He reached for the smooth curve of his longbow, wondering if it would be possible to bring it inside. He didn't want to leave the bow there, attached to his saddle.

"Go ahead, bring it along. You may as well enjoy it while you still have the chance."

"What do you mean?" Kyel wondered with a frown.

"Well, once you become a Master, you can't very well have a longbow around, can you?" Swain said with a knowing grin.

But Kyel still felt confused. He knew it was traditional for mages not to carry weapons, but he figured that if Darien was going to prohibit him from keeping the bow, then his master would have done so long ago.

He said, "Darien still has his sword."

"He does, now, does he?" The captain's smile retreated from his face. "Maybe you'd better leave that bow behind, after all."

Kyel didn't like the fleeting look of concern that crossed the man's eyes. Swain had taught Darien the art of the blade, so why should it matter to him if the mage still carried it?

But Kyel thought he knew the answer. There was more to be had in learning a skill than the obvious result. Suddenly apprehensive, Kyel wondered what the man would think if he found out that Darien had gone much further than simply refusing to relinquish his weapon.

He didn't like the feeling he was getting in the pit of his stomach as he followed the captain up the steps. The man led him down a long hall to a circular foyer graced by an enormous vase. Rich tapestries hung from gilt staves, many having an antiquated look. Again, Kyel was reminded of the mayor of Wolden, of the man's obvious passion for art.

They found the Queen in her solarium, standing before a canvas with a paintbrush in her hand. It was not the image Kyel had been picturing, and neither was Romana herself. From Darien's description, he had envisioned the Queen of Emmery as pompous and aloof, a gilded monarch on an ivory throne. But the woman he found in her place defied his expectations. For one thing, she was far younger than he'd anticipated, perhaps even close to his own age.

And she was lovely, in a common sort of way that caught Kyel off-guard. Her gown was silk, but simple, lacking any fancy embroidery or jewels. She wore her dark brown hair in a loose twist that spilled fine curls down her neck, softening her appearance. As Romana turned toward the sound of their entrance, she paused with the paintbrush in her hand.

Nigel Swain swept into a low bow that Kyel tried his best to emulate.

"You may rise."

Her voice was a sweet soprano. Again, quite unexpected.

Swain said, "Your Grace, may I present Kyel Archer, acolyte of the new Prime Warden, Darien Lauchlin."

Romana's eyebrows shot up. Her gaze took in Kyel, lingering on his cloak, then swept back to

Swain with a questioning look. Carefully, she set the paintbrush down on the tray of the easel and walked across the room to a small mahogany desk. Rifling through the papers on it, she produced a letter. She held it up for Kyel's inspection, waggling the parchment in the air to draw his attention to it.

"I received this note from one of my most loyal subjects, Mayor Blake Pratson of Wolden. It has been often on my mind of late. In it, Mayor Pratson details a rather bizarre encounter he had with a mage, his acolyte, and a priestess of Death. He failed, however, to mention anything about this Darien Lauchlin aspiring to the office of the Prime Warden."

Kyel found himself taken aback. Thrown off by her appearance, he had almost forgotten that Romana was ruler of one of the largest and most prosperous nations of the Rhen. He couldn't let himself be fooled by the innocent appearance of her face. This was a woman to be reckoned with.

And she had opened their conversation with a direct attack on Darien's right to the title he had claimed. But Kyel had learned from his experience with the clerics of Om. It was just a tactic, a way of trying to put him on the defensive right from the start.

Not wanting to let her strategy succeed, he took a step forward and said, "Begging your pardon, Your Grace, but there was no one else to fill the position." A month ago, he would have never had the nerve to say such a thing to a queen, and certainly not in such a tone.

But Romana did not seem offended in the least. Rather, she actually looked a bit impressed. She went on, unruffled. "This letter addresses some issues I find quite troubling. I assume by your presence here that you were sent to enlighten me?"

Kyel took a deep breath, trying to remember the rest of the speech he had rehearsed all the long way from Glen Farquist. But as he opened his mouth to speak, his mind drew a complete blank. He would have to improvise.

"I really don't know what to tell you, other than what you already know from that letter," he said, with a hastily added, "Your Majesty." Then he summed up the situation with the two Enemy armies, including as many details as he knew.

"Darien believes they'll continue south to Rothscard if not stopped. He is aware that you have a standing army, and he asks that you yield over command of it to him."

There. It was out. Now there was nothing to do but wait for the tidal wave to break. Glancing sideways at Swain, he saw the man staring at him in astonishment. Romana herself looked stunned. Holding up her hand, the young Queen shook her head, closing her eyes.

"Allow me a moment to try to understand this. You are telling me that I should be expecting an imminent siege any day, and in the same breath asking me to give over my only means of defense?"

He'd known he was asking a lot. But the way she had just summarized his request made it sound downright ludicrous.

Swain stepped forward, inserting himself between Kyel and the Queen. "If I may?"

Romana nodded.

"I know Darien, or at least I used to," Swain said. "He's impudent, he's brash, he's stubborn as a goat, and he marches to no drummer's beat but his own. He's also one of the smartest men I've ever met in my life. I don't know what he has in mind, but I would urge you to hear his man out."

The Queen frowned. But with a graceful dip of her chin, she allowed, "You may continue."

"Thank you, Your Highness," Kyel said, feeling bolstered by Swain's unexpected support. "Darien didn't tell me all of his plans, but I think I've figured out some of it. He would never leave Rothscard defenseless. He plans to use the Circle of Convergence at Orien's Finger to turn back the Enemy."

"By himself?" Romana looked appalled at the very notion.

Kyel gulped. "Well, yes." He shrugged. "And your army."

The Queen whirled around, pacing back toward the window. "This is absurd! Who does he think he is, another Orien?"

Swain nodded, looking confident as he said, "I'm sure that's exactly what he's thinking."

Romana rounded on him with a furious look, demanding, "How do you know this man?"

He reached up and tapped the hilt of his sword. "I trained him in the art of the blade. He was an acolyte at the time, but I agreed to go along with it under his mother's nose. He studied under me for nine years. I probably know him better than he knows himself."

Romana looked aghast. "And what is your opinion of all this?"

The conviction drained from Swain's face. "My opinion?" he echoed, looking unsettled. Slowly, he shook his head. "All I can say is, I wouldn't want to be on the wrong side of Darien Lauchlin if he's got his back up against a wall. And if he never gave up his sword…"

His voice trailed off. His eyes shot up, fixing on Kyel. "He's broken Oath, hasn't he?"

Kyel found himself with no option. He admitted a grudging, "Aye."

The Queen of Emmery gasped. Her hand rose to her mouth as she turned back to Swain. "Then the man is just as rabid as his brother. And if the portrait you have just painted of him is accurate, then he is probably thrice as dangerous."

She seemed to be taking a moment to collect herself. Finally, she turned back to Kyel. "Take this answer back to your 'Prime Warden.' Tell him I have declined his request to yield command of my army. I may yet decide to send my forces northward, but if I do, it will not be to aid his cause—it shall be to hunt him down and destroy him."

Kyel just stared at her. He had expected argument. He had expected refusal. But it never occurred to him that the woman would actually threaten Darien's life.

"But, what of the Enemy?"

Romana merely shrugged. "Thank you for your concern, but these walls have survived sieges in the past. We will survive again; we always do. It is your own kind, young Kyel, that is endangered. Perhaps you should think about that and return to me again in the morning."

It was a dismissal. Kyel just stared at the young, seemingly innocent Queen for a long moment before turning to leave. He even started walking toward the door. But then he stopped, turning back to her.

"I'll come back in the morning, Your Grace. And when I do, I sincerely hope you've changed your mind. You see, my Prime Warden gave me another message for you: either hand over your army or hand over your crown. Because Darien's back *is* up against a wall. And believe me, he'll do anything it takes to protect your kingdom's future, even if that future doesn't include you in it."

Chapter Thirty
The Jenn

The Cerulean Plains, The Rhen

The dream ended, and there was only darkness. Terrible darkness. And cold. So bitterly cold. He couldn't stop shivering. Traver ached all over, but the worst of the agony was in his hands. He knew he was hot enough to be sweating, but for some reason all he could do was lie there wracked with violent chills that chattered his teeth and rattled his body to the bones. If only he could stop the shaking. It had awakened him from his dream.

He remembered the dream. He wanted desperately to go back there, become a part of that dream again. The dream was important, more important than any reality he could ever know. He had to see them again, to tell them, to warn them…

When he awoke again, the chills were gone, but the pain in his hand was terrible. Traver tried to open his eyes, but all he could see was darkness. He wanted to get a look at his hand, to find out what was wrong with it. His fingers throbbed, sending shooting pains lancing up his arms all the way to his shoulders.

Gradually, it was coming back to him. The dream, the pass. Corban Henley. He remembered falling asleep. At least, he thought he did. And he'd been right; it hadn't really been so bad. It was waking up that was terrible.

He made an effort to sit up. It wasn't much of one. He'd tried to use his hands to push himself up. He realized immediately what an awful mistake that was.

"Don't move," a female voice admonished him from the darkness.

Traver had no problem complying. He lay back, clenching his teeth as he waited for the stabbing pain to fade back to a dull, throbbing ache.

"Drink," the voice said, and he felt a cup pressed against his lips.

The water was cold, and it tasted wonderful. He hadn't realized how thirsty he'd been. Traver gulped it quickly, not caring that he wasn't getting all of it in his mouth. He felt the water running down his chin, dribbling down his neck. When the woman took the cup away, he felt disappointed.

"That's enough, for now," said her calm, easy voice.

"Who are you?" Traver asked, wishing there was light enough to see her face.

"My name is Kayna."

"Where am I?"

The voice hesitated. "You are in the tent of my husband."

He didn't like the sound of that. Especially since he was naked beneath the blankets. That's all he needed: some woman's husband coming home enraged at finding a naked man in his bed. Wouldn't that be just his luck? He could hardly defend himself the way he was. It occurred to him to wonder if maybe the woman's husband was responsible for saving his life.

"Where's Henley?" he asked, remembering the Valeman.

"I don't know who that is. You are the only one we found alive on the killing ground."

Her words brought a pang of remorse. It wasn't fair. Henley was one of the best men they had. He should have been the one to survive. Traver found himself wondering what kind of dreams the Vale-man was having. He hoped they were good dreams.

"You're lucky we found you." The woman's voice drifted through the darkness.

He asked, "What were you doing in the pass?"

"One of our herds strayed away a few nights back. We followed their tracks up into the Mountains of Shadow. When we found them, the beasts were already slain and slaughtered. But my husband found you instead."

"I suppose I owe him."

"You owe him your life. When he found you, you were almost frozen to death. The vultures had already been at your meat."

The thought was repulsive. Traver remembered the bird, the one that had mistaken him for a piece of carrion. "Am I whole?" he whispered, though he wasn't sure he wanted to know the answer.

There was a long pause. "Nearly. The frost and the birds got to your hands. We had to cut off two of your fingers."

"No." It couldn't be. He wouldn't have a chance of gripping a hilt with two fingers missing. In the space between horror and grief, he felt his anger rising.

"You had no right!" he raged at her. "I *need* my fingers, damn you!"

"Well, they're gone, so get used to it. Just be grateful for the eight you still have."

He'd gone back to sleep after that. It was not a peaceful sleep; the pain kept waking him. When he opened his eyes, he could see dim light coming in through a smoke hole in the roof. Kayna was gone. Looking around, Traver tried to figure out his bizarre circumstances.

When the woman had mentioned they were in a tent, he had taken it to mean some type of portable shelter. But this had the look of something more permanent. It was large, framed with wooden stakes and covered with tanned leather. Designs had been painted on the walls and over the flap that served as the door. There was a fire pit in the center, and the floor was covered in skins mounded into pallets. The tent even had its own peculiar smell, like a strange blend of spices mixed with smoke.

He thought about trying to sit up, but the idea was still daunting. His hands still hurt, but the texture of the pain was different, more of a stinging sensation. Hesitantly, he pulled his left hand out of the blankets and held it up. His whole hand was wrapped in strips of animal skin that had been soaked in water and then dried on stiff. The way the bandages were arranged, he had no idea what kind of damage was concealed beneath.

The flap of the tent parted, and a man stepped in. He moved across the space toward him, kneeling by Traver's side. The fellow was dressed in fur and tanned leather. He had long, greasy hair, and a beard that looked to have soaked up every drip of fat from his breakfast. And he *smelled.* The stranger fairly reeked of horse.

Without speaking a word, the man snatched up Traver's left hand and started peeling off strips of bandage. Traver closed his eyes, afraid to see what was under those hardened leather strips. With a crack, the entire casing fell away, and Traver found himself staring up at his naked, ruined hand.

The last two fingers of his left hand were gone. Only swollen, bloody tissue remained in their place. Traver just gaped at the ghastly wound. He still had his thumb and his first two fingers, which were the three best fingers to have. Traver couldn't stand it. He had to turn and look away. He felt ill, his stomach twisting.

"The wounds are healing nicely," the man said.

It sounded like a sick jest. Wanting to scream in frustration, Traver growled, "You had no right to cut off my fingers."

"Your fingers were already dead," the man said. "If I had left them on, the rest of you would be following."

It was small comfort. What was he going to do without the use of his hand? Certainly not soldiering.

"My name is Ranoch."

Traver looked up at him. The man had a kind face beneath the filth. In a way, Ranoch reminded him a little of Corban Henley. Just a darker, wilder version.

"Traver Larsen."

Looking around the tent, Traver couldn't help wondering what kind of people he had fallen in with. They were obviously nomads of some type, and from the looks of the skins, they were probably herdsmen. Staring at the fur of Ranoch's heavy winter robe, he couldn't resist asking, "You people are horse herders?"

Ranoch nodded, looking proud. "We are the Jenn."

The man reached down by his side and produced a plain earthenware cup, which he proffered in both hands. Traver stared at the cup suspiciously, wondering at the steam that was rising from it.

"What is it?"

"Hot mare's milk," Ranoch informed him solemnly.

"That's revolting." Traver grimaced, trying to turn his face away as the herdsman lifted the cup to his lips.

"Drink it. You need the strength."

Holding his breath, Traver opened his mouth. The milk was heavily spiced, and much sweeter than cow's milk. The fatty texture made him want to gag. Swallowing, he muttered bravely, "Not bad. It would do better with a chaser though."

Ranoch chuckled, tilting the cup again as Traver tried hard not to spit the foul liquid right back in his face. The second gulp went down worse than the first one. But the herdsman was insistent and made Traver drink the whole cup before putting it down.

"A crier came through our camp over a week ago," Ranoch said, leaning forward on his knees. "All men were asked to bring their bows and offer Horseright to the Callas Greathe. It is said that the Dakura are invading the plains. I was wondering if you knew anything about it, since you've fought them."

Traver stared at him blankly, hardly understanding a word. Slowly, he asked, "You mean the Enemy?"

Ranoch nodded. Traver struggled to sit up, using his elbows to shimmy himself forward. Ranoch caught him by the shoulders, easing him up the rest of the way. Traver felt suddenly faint, his body trembling with the effort. But it was a small victory, one he was proud of. He would have to get used to small victories.

"We've been trying our best to slow them down," he said. "The keep's fallen. There's just too many."

"Greystone Keep is lost?"

When Traver nodded, the man shook his head sadly.

"How did you know they were coming?" Traver asked. It didn't make sense. Proctor and the rest might be down from the pass by now, but that didn't leave enough time for word of their arrival to circulate around the plains.

Ranoch rubbed his eyes wearily. "I told you. A crier came through our camp."

"How did he know?"

The man shrugged. "There are two ways the cry can be taken up. It can come from the Tiborah, the spiritual leader of our people. Or a Sentinel might raise the cry, but that would indeed be rare."

Traver's eyes widened in understanding. "Lauchlin."

"What?" The herdsman stared at him in confusion.

"He's a Sentinel I know."

"You know a Sentinel?" Ranoch exclaimed.

"Aye, I do."

The herdsman shook his head, a look of newfound respect in his eyes. "I offer you my food, my fire, and my protection for as long as you wish," he said solemnly. "After you heal, if the Dakura have not yet blighted the plains, I would be honored to offer you Horseright."

Traver blinked at the man, thoroughly confused. "Sounds great," he muttered.

Chapter Thirty-One
Chains

Rothscard, The Rhen

His guest room at Emmery Palace was the most luxurious Kyel had ever seen. It was more than just a room; it was an entire suite. The sitting area had a warm fire already glowing in the hearth, with three plush chairs gathered around in an intimate setting. There was also a tiled washroom with a large marble tub. The bedchamber itself was draped in silk, the bed almost scandalously large.

It didn't take him long to discover a rope pull by the door that summoned a liveried servant. A boy arrived with a sharp knock and listened to Kyel's request for warm water with a bewildered expression on his face. But it was Kyel's turn to be confused when the boy strode into the room instead of going to fetch a bucket.

Perplexed, Kyel followed him to the washroom, where the boy leaned over the tub and threw a valve. A gush of water came out of a pipe that he hadn't even noticed, spilling out of the wall and into the tub. Amazed, Kyel put his fingers in the stream and was surprised to discover it already warm.

"How?" he gasped.

"The water comes from hot springs under the palace," the boy explained. "Don't drink the warm water. It tastes sort of funny. But the cold water comes from the river, and it's good to drink."

"I've never heard of such a thing."

The boy went to fetch towels down from a shelf. When he was gone, Kyel found himself neck-deep in the most soothing bath he'd ever experienced in his life. He lay with his head against the sloping back of the tub and scooted down until the water came up to his chin. Then he closed his eyes and relaxed, listening to the muffled thuds of his heartbeat.

He lay there until the water grew cold, then let some out and drew more fresh. Finding a brush, he scrubbed his body until he felt sure he had most of the grime off. When he was done, he dried off and shaved, then ran a comb through his wet hair.

He dug into his cloak pocket, bringing out *Treatise on the Well,* then crawled into the bed. It was the first chance he'd had to open the text since leaving Glen Farquist. He skimmed the first chapter, which was just another description of the creation of the Well. It wasn't until he got to the third chapter that he finally found something of interest.

Spread out across two pages was a diagram of the Well, drawn painstakingly in ink. The diagram showed the Well from two different perspectives. Kyel raised the book, flexing the spine back carefully as he studied the drawings. The Well of Tears looked just like any other well he had ever seen, with the singular exception of the odd markings that encircled its rim.

Turning the page, he saw the same markings expressed in a series, some circled and numbered. Unfortunately, there was no explanation as to what the numbers could mean.

Intrigued, Kyel flipped forward a few chapters and stopped when his eyes caught a glimpse of a heading that read, SEALING OF THE WELL. He read the entire passage, letting his eyes scan rapidly across the page with a growing uneasiness that increased with every word:

Resealing the Well requires two mages

> *working in cooperation. The Well itself must be manipulated in its chamber by de-activation of the rune sequence in reverse order. Concurrently, the Well must be sealed on the side of the Netherworld, which requires a Grand Master of no less than the fourth tier to enter the gateway. This is, by definition, a sacrifice, as any person entering the Netherworld would become there entrapped by the collapse of the gateway, condemned body and soul to the Netherworld for all eternity.*

"Merciful gods," Kyel whispered.

As soon as he said it, Darien's words came back to haunt him: *the gods have no mercy.* Kyel snapped the book shut and set it down. He didn't understand half of what he'd just read, but he understood enough.

It would take the two of them working together to seal the Well of Tears, and Kyel knew he wasn't remotely prepared to put the Soulstone around his neck yet. He might be in for years' more training before he would be ready to tackle something like the Well.

And then either Darien or himself would have to enter the gateway to become the sacrifice the Well of Tears demanded. Kyel knew he could never, ever summon enough courage to do that, knowing the repercussions. Sacrificing his life would be bad enough, but condemning his soul to hell on top of it? The very thought was horrendous, unspeakable. But how could he ask Darien to do it for him? The mage had already suffered enough. He deserved an eternity at peace.

But at least he'd be with Meiran.

As soon as the thought occurred to him, Kyel wanted to hit himself for even thinking it. He was being selfish, and cowardly on top of it. His mind was just groping for comfort, trying to reason its way out of the guilt he was already feeling. Thoroughly disgusted with himself, Kyel resolved not to think about it again. Maybe there was another way, maybe Darien could figure something out. Perhaps he was just getting himself worked up over nothing.

A knock at the door startled him from his thoughts.

Rising from the bed, Kyel crossed the room, expecting another servant as he cracked open the door. Instead, he was surprised to find himself looking into the face of Nigel Swain. Kyel let the door swing fully open, his heart skipping a beat as he took in a hallway full of blue-cloaked guards.

"Didn't anyone ever tell you never threaten a queen?" the captain asked.

As Swain moved into the room, Kyel found himself wondering why Darien had made it all sound so easy. He'd thought it was going to be just another one of his master's tests, this one a lesson in diplomacy. Well, if this was a test, then he'd just failed it.

Swain drew Kyel's hands behind his back and locked a set of iron chains around his wrists. It was only his second time in Rothscard, and both times he had found himself in chains.

Damn you, Darien.

The only thing he'd ever wanted was just to go home. Every day it seemed the chances of that happening were growing more dismal.

"What are you going to do to me?"

Swain directed him by the arm out into the hall.

"The Queen wishes to have a word with you."

"She had but to ask," Kyel grumbled.

He hadn't meant it as a jest, but his words inspired a cheerless smile on Swain's angular face. Guards fell in around them as Kyel was guided forward.

He was scared. Swain was right. He shouldn't have threatened Romana. He wondered what the punishment for something like that was. They'd already shipped him off to the Front once and, anyway, Greystone Keep had probably already fallen. The way things were starting to look now, the Front might even be right here in Rothscard in another week or so. Then they wouldn't have to ship him anywhere.

The thought almost made him want to laugh, though it would have been a bitter laugh indeed. Instead, he swallowed and tried not to stumble as they guided him down a flight of polished marble stairs. It was hard, walking down the steps with his arms chained behind his back. If he tripped, he wouldn't be able to bring his hands up to catch himself.

At the bottom of the stairs, Swain led him to a large white door. The chains on his wrists were starting to chafe, and the small gaps in the links kept pulling at his arm hairs. His shoulders ached from the way they had him trussed.

Kyel felt ill when he realized he was being taken to the Queen's formal audience hall. Romana sat on a raised throne at the far end of the room, and there was nothing commonplace about her now. She wore elegant blue layers of silk, embroidered and bejeweled. Her dark hair was arranged in a coif caught up by the Sapphire Crown of Emmery. She held a gold scepter in one hand. Romana was now the very image of a queen. Kyel found himself thinking that if she'd looked that way earlier, he would have never found the courage to say what he had.

Swain's grip on his arm forced him down into the bow that Kyel had forgotten to make. He resented the gesture. It was one thing, abasing himself before a pretty girl with a paintbrush in her hand. It was quite another when that same girl had transformed into the image of a glorious but wrathful monarch who had issued the order to have him restrained.

"Rise." Her clear soprano voice carried the commanding ring of authority.

Kyel obeyed, though there was little grace in his movement. The captain's grip remained painfully firm on his arm. Kyel waited nervously, wondering what sentence the Queen would pronounce. He thought Darien had greatly underestimated the woman's boldness. He waited, but the Queen said nothing. She seemed to be waiting for him, gazing down at him from her elevated throne with distaste in her wide blue eyes.

Not knowing what else to say, Kyel asked her, "Why did you have me placed in chains?"

Romana's eyebrows arched, as if she was surprised by his straightforward question. She moved her hand to the arm of her throne, brandishing the scepter as she replied:

"I had you placed in chains because I wished for you to experience what they feel like."

Kyel frowned, almost as disgusted as he was shocked by her answer. "I fear I don't take your point."

Swain's grip flexed on his arm, sending a shooting pain stabbing into his shoulder. Romana glared down at him, but her tone was even as she pressed, "Tell me, how do they feel?"

Kyel knew exactly what she was getting at, and he didn't appreciate it one bit. Shrugging, he told her, "Heavy. They chafe."

"And how do *you* feel, wearing them?"

"Vulnerable," he replied honestly. Her questions were becoming tedious. He wished the Queen would just make her point.

Romana gazed at him intently as she asked, "Can you tell me the purpose of chains?"

Angry now, Kyel growled, "I can think of several."

"Such as?"

"To constrain someone, to confine. To control."

"Exactly," Romana pronounced as if leveling a death sentence. "The mages of Aerysius chose to live their entire lives shackled to the confines of the Oath of Harmony. Even though the weight was heavy, and it chafed at times. Some of the most powerful men and women the world has ever known spent a lifetime feeling just as vulnerable and constrained as you do at this moment. And yet many sacrificed their lives to preserve that Oath; they felt it was that important." She paused. "What are your thoughts on this?"

Kyel could have answered that question the moment he'd walked in the door, without playing her infuriating game.

He told her in all honesty, "I am aware of its importance. I believe the Oath is a necessity."

The Queen of Emmery nodded. "What I require is your word that when you receive the Transference, you will swear the Oath of Harmony and uphold it throughout your entire life."

"You have my word."

The insult she was dealing him grated to the bone. Who did she think she was, to demand his word on something that should have never been any of her business in the first place? He wished Darien was there. The Sentinel would have been outraged by this little queen's temerity.

Romana looked supremely pleased with herself. "Very well. I would like you to know that I have reconsidered your entreaty. I have decided to send my army northward, after all."

Kyel was shocked. He hadn't expected this, not at all.

"I thank you, Your Highness," he said in a much calmer voice. He waited, but she said nothing further. "Now would you please take these chains off me?"

"No."

"What do you mean, *no?"* Kyel's face flushed hot with anger. "Why not?"

Romana raised her hands expansively. "Because you are my assurance."

"Assurance against what?"

The Queen sighed, setting her scepter down across her lap. "I have spent much time today contemplating a great many things. I have come to realize that, though desperate, this plan is probably the only chance of success we have. If your master wishes to play the part of Orien, then so be it. But he must agree to abide by the rest of Orien's script, right up to the very end."

At first, Kyel didn't take her meaning. Then, slowly, it dawned on him. She was talking about...

"No," he gasped, feeling utterly revolted and enraged. "I won't do it."

"Those are my terms." Romana leaned forward, gripping the arms of her throne. "If Darien Lauchlin uses the vortex, then he must follow Orien's example and kneel at your feet when the battle is done. You will keep your word and swear the Oath of Harmony the moment after you receive the Transference from him. Then that will be the end of this ghastly business."

"No," Kyel whispered, shaking his head. "There's more. He needs to help me close the gateway, seal the Well of Tears. And then there's Aidan—"

But Romana wasn't listening to him. Silencing him with a furious glint of her eyes, she uttered, "That is the purpose of legacy, is it not? When your master falls, you may take up his banner for him. But you will do so Bound."

Kyel tried to back away from her, but he was held fast by the steel grip of Swain's fingers. "You can't ask that of me. *I won't do it."*

"Then you will spend the rest of your life with *my* chains on your wrists." The Queen of Emmery turned to her captain and ordered, "Take this young man to a cell where he can think over his options carefully."

Swain hauled him around by the arm, wrenching Kyel's shoulder as he did. Stumbling, Kyel careened after him out of the throne room, head reeling in fear and revulsion. A contingent of guards fell in behind them as Kyel was compelled forward down the long halls of the palace and out into a dismal afternoon.

As he walked, Kyel tried to think of what he could do to get himself out of this. Romana's threat had scared him. It scared him even more because he thought he knew what Darien would do when he heard of it. Everything seemed to be pointing in one direction, and he could feel the numbers starting to total themselves together in his mind.

Darien would make Romana a counteroffer. He would insist on surviving long enough to reach Aidan and the gateway. With one decisive stroke he could fulfill his Bloodquest, seal the Well of Tears, and follow the example set by Orien that Romana demanded. And then, when it was over, all parties involved would be satisfied.

It was sick. It was also perfect.

Just like the rest of Darien's plans. As the cell door slammed shut behind him, Kyel realized with a gut-twisting wrench that this must have been his master's intent all along.

Sleep was impossible. And yet there was nothing else to do, so Kyel tried his hardest. But with his arms chained behind his back, there was no position that he could find that was comfortable. The hours dragged by as guards came and went, sometimes with prisoners and sometimes not. Sometimes they glared at him or whispered taunts. Often, they raked their swords along the metal bars of his cage as they strode by, a jarring sound that rattled his nerves.

It was hours before he finally had a visitor. And then, it wasn't who he'd been expecting. Appalled, Kyel watched as a blue-cloaked guard sifted through his iron ring of keys, throwing back the bolt of his cell door to admit a brawny, bald old man with the smell of the forge on his clothes. In his hand he carried a forger's hammer, wielding it upright like a club. An apprentice trailed behind him, lugging a small but heavy anvil into the cell, which he all but dumped down on the floor with a resounding *thud.*

Kyel stared at the anvil with a feeling of dread. Romana was carrying her point much too far if she was willing to drive it home with a blacksmith's hammer. To his disgust, three more guards surged into the cell in the wake of the forger's apprentice. Two came forward to restrain him while the third edged behind him and unlocked the chains on his wrists. Kyel's shoulders spasmed with relief the moment they were off. But the relief did not last long.

The guards wrenched him forward and down, one catching his head in a lock while another seized his arm and forced it down on top of the anvil, pinning it there with the full weight of his body. Kyel tried to struggle as he saw the blacksmith lifting his hammer over a fresh length of chain. But the guard who had him by the neck tightened his hold until there was nothing Kyel could do but watch and desperately pray that the blacksmith didn't miss his mark.

The hammer rose and fell with a sharp ring that made Kyel flinch. There was no pain, at least; the blacksmith's aim was true. In moments, the vile work was done.

As the guards released him, Kyel held his hands up before his face, staring down in revulsion at the lengths of chain wrapped around his wrists like a matching set of crude iron bracelets. The woman had gone too far. Much too far. He didn't care if she was a queen; Romana had no right.

The blacksmith looked back over his shoulder with sympathy in his eyes as he left. Kyel sank down on the cot, staring at the Queen's chains. There had to be something he could do. She couldn't get away with this. It was an insult, not just to him personally, but to every Master who had ever lived and died by the Mage's Oath.

If Aerysius still existed, Emmery's Queen would be bent over her knees for this, he felt certain. But Aerysius didn't exist anymore. And the man currently calling himself Prime Warden was not there to help him, even if he had the inclination to do so.

There was only one thing to be done about it—there simply was no other choice. He was fed up, and not just with Romana. Darien had known damned well from the beginning what he would be facing. Yet the mage had sent him anyway. This was all another one of his schemes, one of his twisted lessons. Perhaps he hadn't foreseen the chains, but Darien must have known how Romana would react. He had planned for it all along. It was just another stepping stone on his path to Aidan and the Well, to surrendering himself to Orien's fate.

Kyel had no intention of letting him go through with it. He was afraid of Darien's wrath, but someone had to save the man from himself.

Reaching into his pocket, Kyel pulled out the Soulstone and gazed deeply into its glimmering facets. It was terrible. And terrifying. The strange red light flickered and throbbed, pulsing like a living heartbeat. Knowing that he had no idea what he was getting into, Kyel spread open the silver bands of the collar and held the medallion up against his chest. It felt sinisterly cold.

His hands trembled as he brought the bands up around his neck, fumbling at the clasp with his fingers. At first, he didn't think it was going to work. The clasp seemed stiff and frozen. But then he heard a faint, metallic click.

As the stone's raging torrent gushed through his body and into his mind, Kyel squeezed his eyes shut and tried his best not to scream.

In the end, his best wasn't anywhere near good enough.

Chapter Thirty-Two
Fly True

The Cerulean Plains, The Rhen

The ancient copse of cypress trees stood stiff in the midst of a rolling expanse of white, their evergreen branches unmoving. The air was still, lacking even the suggestion of a breeze. Beneath the trees' gnarled limbs, an uneasy tension was brewing. It moved over the snow-fed ground like the probing fingers of an inquisitive hand.

The men could sense it. The horses did, as well. The animals worried at their bits, shifting and stomping uneasily. Craig's own mount stood trembling, eager for the charge. It was bred for the fight; the love of battle ran hot in its blood.

Craig kept a firm grip on the reins. He raised his other hand over his head, clenched in a tight fist. The tinkling of chain mail rattled under his cloak as the stallion beneath him danced in place. He waited, the eyes of twenty men behind him riveted on his fist.

In the distance, a single arrow arced upward into the sky, a red ribbon affixed to its shaft, fluttering in its wake. The arrow and ribbon reached the apex of their flight, curved, then plunged swiftly down toward the earth.

"NOW!" Craig bellowed, dropping his fist.

The horses broke into an all-out charge, emerging from beneath the cover of the trees. Craig's heels pumped his stallion's heaving sides, urging it faster. The warhorse swept forward with a great surge of speed, putting all of its heart and muscle into the race. Like the horse beneath him, Craig was eager for the fight.

Filled with the thrill of battle, he raised his horn bow as his mount crested the rise of a hill. He held the curve of the bow parallel to the ground and nocked an arrow to the string. The men behind him did the same.

Before them, the forces of the Enemy sprawled across the plains like a dark and dangerous sea. Craig kicked his mount faster, drawing the arrow back. Just as the black wall of Enemy ranks collapsed and broke toward him, he let the bowstring sing.

"Fly true," he whispered, quoting the verse inscribed on his bow.

Reaching to the quiver fixed to his saddle, he withdrew another shaft and launched it after the first, three more following. The air around him hummed with the hiss of arrows and screams of death.

Craig tugged at the reins, wheeling his horse around before a charging group of infantry that broke away from the main force. Enemy arrows whispered in his ear as they flew past him, finding purchase in the backs of his own men who fell, slouching sideways from the saddle. Craig leaned forward, pressing his face against his stallion's neck in an effort to make himself as small a target as possible.

He turned in the saddle and, raising his bow, sent a steady stream of arrows back in the direction of his pursuers. In front of him, he could see the green limbs of the cypress grove beckoning. Branches reached out for him, clawing at his helm and swiping at his cloak.

Behind, he heard the screams of outrage from hundreds of Enemy throats. They were quickly overpowered by the war cries issued from five hundred Greystone archers that ran out from under the cover of the trees.

Craig barked a laugh as he watched the Enemy fall, the air itself singing with the deadly whisper of shafts. The remaining Enemy soldiers struggled to retreat as Greystone soldiers charged forward with weapons drawn.

Craig watched from the edge of the skirmish as his men finished off the last few nodes of resistance. His leg throbbed fiercely. Looking down, he saw that an arrow had buried itself deep in the muscle, perhaps even to the bone. Swearing, he cursed his luck.

Soon, it was done. The swelling cries of triumph that rose from the battlefield drowned out even the stabbing ache in his thigh. Craig barked out a laugh as he gazed upon the fallen remains of black-armored bodies, hundreds of them. Once again, Proctor's tactics had worked.

The force commander himself came up beside him on his mount. Proctor's eyes were grimly pleased, until they fell on the black fletching that pierced Craig's leg. A frown of concern stiffened the hard planes of his face.

"Just a nick," Craig reassured him, grinning against the pain.

But then his expression fell. He recognized that distant look in his commander's eyes, noticed Proctor's hand absently stroking the hilt of the dagger at his side.

Grimly, Craig swallowed. Since their retreat from the pass, Proctor had been consistent with his policy that no living man should be left behind for the Enemy, while at the same time refusing to allow the wounded to impede their mobility. The commander's sinister knife had seen more use in the past week than ever since its forging.

Staring now at that ebony hilt, Craig realized the meaning of the stony look on Garret Proctor's face.

Chapter Thirty-Three
What Hurts, Teaches

Rothscard, The Rhen

His screams had brought the guards.

They had found him lying on his side, unconscious on the floor of his cell. Kyel remembered little of it, or of the frantic apothecary who'd been summoned to force a draught of some terrible liquid down his throat. He'd lain in his cot the rest of the night, shivering violently, fading in and out of sleep pierced through with disturbing and sometimes even shocking nightmares. The two times he'd managed to drag himself up enough to pass water into the foul bucket, he had barely managed the act. It reminded him of when he'd taken ill with Mountain Fever when he was a boy. His body felt the same: wracked and abused, and horribly weak.

Kyel had been utterly unprepared for the agony of Transference. He had never read anywhere or heard mention that it was supposed to be so excruciating. Somehow, he didn't think it was. Perhaps it was because he wasn't ready for it, or maybe it was because of the nature of the Soulstone itself. Kyel had never imagined so much pain could be compressed into such a short period of time.

Somehow, he'd managed to get the damn thing off his neck. He didn't even remember doing it, but he couldn't stand thinking about what might have happened if he'd left it hanging there. He remembered Luther Penthos' warning about how the stone, when black, had the effect of sucking the gift right back out again. The thought was particularly nauseating.

The stone was black now. The light had passed out of it, into himself, Kyel imagined. As he lay back in his cot staring up at the medallion, it was hard to believe that, only last night, the same stone had glowed with a dazzling inner radiance. It no longer even looked like a gemstone. Just a dull and lifeless clump of rock. It reminded him of some of the obsidian stones he had seen in the Pass of Lor-Gamorth.

He didn't like looking at it anymore. The sight of it filled him with a dread that made him think twice before shoving it back into his pocket. He wanted the thing as far away from him as possible, but there was nothing else to be done with it. Darien had called it an heirloom of power, and Kyel knew it was his responsibility to keep it safe. There couldn't be many such objects left in the world. Most had probably been lost in the destruction of Aerysius. For all Kyel knew, the Soulstone was the last of its kind, an obsolete relic of a dead civilization that existed now only in one man's memory.

No. Now there was yet another remnant of Aerysius' shattered legacy: himself.

Kyel stared somberly down at the iron chains on his wrists, contemplating them quietly in the dim light of the cell. He was a Master now, though Romana's chains did nothing to bind anything except his dignity. He had given his word to Emmery's Queen that he would swear the Oath of Harmony as soon as he came into his power, but Kyel didn't even know the words to say. Darien had never told him.

Which really was not a problem. At least, not yet. He had no idea how to use his newfound strength.

He could feel it moving within him, the vibrant power of Emelda Lauchlin's gift. It felt strange, being the recipient of an inheritance that wasn't his own. He might be a Master in name, but that was as far as it went. He didn't even know what tier he was, or what title he might someday come to use. Was he a Master or a Grand Master? He didn't know. He had no order to call his own and was trained to none. He had the cloak, the chain on his left wrist, and the beautiful quiescence of the magic field moving sweetly in the back of his mind. But that was all.

Sighing, Kyel sat up and rubbed his eyes. At least he was starting to feel somewhat normal again. His body was still a little weak, and the muscles in his legs kept cramping. But his head was clear, the fever-like symptoms gone.

He sat on his cot until a guard finally arrived with his breakfast and a ripe taunt on his lips. Kyel ate the scraps of bread in silence, gulping down the stale water with much more enthusiasm. He wasn't hungry. But he was beginning to grow bored.

For something to do, he lifted his hand and tried concentrating on the chain on his wrist. He had no idea what he was doing. He tried to imagine one of the links bending just enough to slide the thing off, attempting to visualize it in his mind. Nothing happened. He had known it wouldn't be that easy.

Yet, he couldn't resist the urge to explore his new talent. He had the feeling that he'd better learn its use, and quickly. He didn't have Darien there to show him, but he could almost hear the sound of the man's voice muttering in his mind. Just like they had in the vortex, the Sentinel's words kept echoing back at him like a refrain: *Try again.*

This whole business reminded him of the vortex. Then, all he'd needed to feel the current of the magic field was knowledge of the trick. It had taken him awhile to find the right technique, but once he had it down, the rest had been almost too easy. This had to be another trick. If only he could just discover it.

As he had in the vortex, Kyel reached out from within and felt the rhythm of the field, opening himself to it. That had to be the place to start. Otherwise, Darien wouldn't have bothered teaching him that skill. The mage had known what a short period of training he was likely to have and would have omitted any part of the normal lessons he didn't deem necessary.

Still, it didn't work. The chain remained fixed to his wrist, unaffected. Kyel squeezed his eyes shut, sighing in frustration.

Try again.

Biting his lip, he obeyed. Again, he reached out for the magic field, this time pulling at it instead of just groping along the currents. Instantly, a wondrous sensation swelled within him, a feeling of sweet contentment. Startled, Kyel released the field, looking up in amazement. He had done something right.

The chain was still there, the link yet unbent, but the feeling of bliss had been like no other he had ever experienced. It was a startling reaffirmation. He tried it again immediately, practicing the technique of filling his mind with the wonder of the field without another thought spared for the chains. That was all he did the remainder of the morning, until a voice startled him from his exercise.

"Good. You're not dead."

Kyel started, flinching back from the magic field as he turned to find Nigel Swain glaring at him through the bars of his cage. He sat up straight, suddenly afraid of what the man had seen. Hopefully, the wonder of the magic field had not been written on his face. Kyel rose to his feet, taking a few hesitant steps toward the man.

"So, do you mind telling me what all that ruckus was about yesterday?" Swain demanded, steel gray eyes peering through the oily strands of his hair.

Kyel lifted his hands, shrugging. "I had a nightmare."

"A nightmare." The captain shook his head. "I don't think so. Try again."

Try again. Kyel wanted to groan. He would have to come up with something much better. He had never been a good liar. It wasn't difficult to look as uncomfortable as he felt as he told Swain, "I was practicing something Darien taught me. It went wrong."

Those cold eyes just stared at him, making his flesh prickle. Softly, the captain said, "Acolytes are forbidden to practice without the guidance of a Master. At least, they were. Darien must have given you that directive."

"No," Kyel said. "He never told me any such thing. In truth, the last time he had me learn something, he dumped me down in the middle of a vortex and left me there to figure it out on my own."

"What?" Swain clutched the bars of his cage as Kyel took an involuntary step backward. "He's breaking you?"

"I don't know what that means."

"It means he's forsaken a lot more than his Oath," the captain snarled, eyes raging. "If Aerysius still existed and Darien was found to be using such methods, he'd be the subject of a Grand Inquiry."

Kyel shook his head, not knowing what to say.

"What I want to know is why," Swain demanded. "What's making him feel so pressured that he'd be compelled to go that far? I want an answer. And this time, it had better be a straight one."

Kyel felt like he was back in the Temple of Wisdom. Swain's threatening glare seemed all too much like the perceptive gaze of the high priest, taking the bare facts he admitted to and inferring much more than he ever intended.

"He's eighth-tier," Kyel found himself confessing. "If you don't know what that means—"

"I know damned well what it means!" With a growl, Swain wrenched himself away from the bars and swiped out at the air with a fist. "By the whoring mother of the gods, *why didn't you tell us this before?*"

"You know why I didn't!" Kyel shouted at him, appalled and scared by the man's reaction. "Your Queen already has it in for him. Darien's in enough trouble already without—"

"You stupid, ignorant boy. You don't even know what kind of man you've placed your trust in. Think about it! We're talking about an *eighth-tier* Grand Master who's foresworn his Oath, shouldered the weight of the world, and on top of it all, he's already lost everything! Plus, he's Sentinel-trained, which means he has every piece of knowledge he needs to corrupt what he's learned into something deadly wicked. You're apprenticed to a madman, Kyel. You'd better open your eyes before it's too late to do something about it and we have the next Zavier Renquist on our hands!"

Kyel's mouth dropped open. He stood there, shaking his head in denial. Swain unlocked the door to his cell, leading him out. Kyel went along complacently, staring at his boots as he walked, filled with a desperate sense of unease. Swain couldn't be right. Darien was a good, decent man. Sure, he had his moments and, sure, they seemed to be growing more frequent, but…

Kyel stepped out of the building into the glistening white sheen of fresh snow. Blinking, he forgot his train of thought as his eyes gazed upon the sight of what looked like every Rothscard Bluecloak that existed all assembled in front of the palace steps in neat, orderly files. And, before them all, the Queen of Emmery was seated in a sedan chair born on the shoulders of four enormous men, her golden scepter in hand, the Sapphire Crown on her lovely head.

Kyel couldn't believe his eyes. The scene looked like something out of legend. He waited with Swain as the ranks formed up behind the Queen's chair. A guard walked toward them leading two horses. One he recognized as his own. With a sigh of relief, he saw that his longbow was attached to his saddle. He had been worried that he'd never see it again.

The guard offered him the reins of his horse, but as Kyel stepped forward to take them, Swain jerked them out of his hand. The captain traipsed back to the saddle and snatched the bow from it, wielding it up before Kyel's face. With a look of contempt, he took it in both hands and brought the shaft down viciously over his knee, snapping the bow clean in half.

"No!" Kyel screamed. But it was already too late.

Mortified, he stared at the broken shards of his longbow in Swain's merciless hands. That single stave of wood had been his only friend, his constant companion, all through the long, dark months at Greystone Keep. It had been such a beautiful piece of wood, so elegantly simple, at the same time so comfortingly effective. Practicing with it had been the only thing he had taken pleasure in at the Front, and his developing skill had filled him with confidence and a blooming sense of pride. As he watched Swain throw the shards of the bow down like scraps of filth at his feet, Kyel felt like bending over to pick them up, wanting to run his fingers over the golden yew just one last time.

But he made himself stop. Deep down inside, he knew the captain was right. Mages were forbidden weapons, and there was a reason for it. Kyel couldn't help but tremble as he thought of Darien's sword. He wondered if things would have turned out differently if the Sentinel had cast the blade away as he should have or, better yet, never picked it up in the first place. He wondered if Darien would still have yielded his commitment to the Oath, or if he would have found the strength to rise above the temptation.

Kyel turned away from the sad remains of his bow. He was a mage now. Even if he hadn't sworn the Oath of Harmony, he would live it in his heart. In a way, he was glad Swain had done what he had. It made accepting the constraints of the Oath that much easier. Even if he didn't know them, not really.

When the captain approached with his horse, Swain lay a hand on Kyel's shoulder. His hard face held no sympathy. But there was another expression there, one that Kyel was thankful to find. When Swain placed the reins in his hand, he did so with a faint trace of understanding in his eyes.

"The hardest thing to learn about a weapon is knowing when it's time to give it up," the blademaster said.

"'What hurts, teaches,'" Kyel quoted, staring down at the reins in his hand.

Swain's brow creased. "That's the motto of the Arms Guild. Did you learn it from Darien?"

"Aye. He said it applies to most lessons in life."

Swain nodded, patting him on the shoulder. "Well, at least he remembers something I tried to teach him. Come on. We don't want to keep the entire army waiting."

Kyel glanced back over his shoulder at the ranks of men formed up behind their Queen. "That's not the army?"

Swain barked a laugh. "That's just the city guard, son. They go wherever the Queen goes, and right now she's coming to see us off. The real army is waiting outside the walls. Now, let's go, before the men get hostile."

Kyel nodded. He tried to resist taking one last glance back at his bow as he mounted up and rode away from it, but he just couldn't help himself. It was hard to part from it. But it was better this way.

And, in the end, he was even thankful.

Chapter Thirty-Four
Orien's Finger

The Cerulean Plains, The Rhen

He was vulnerable.

It was a loathsome, despicable feeling Darien had suffered for two and a half days. His very skin crawled as if infested with a thousand writhing maggots. No matter how many times he raked his ragged nails across the surface of his flesh, still the feeling persisted. His main source of solace was gone, the rapturous song of the magic field silenced in his head. That was the worst. Walled away from the raging torrent of Orien's Vortex, he could take no comfort in what had become his only source of solace.

The field's absence darkened his mood and fouled his temper. Those who dared come close enough to see the raging intensity that seethed in his eyes turned and shied away, often with great haste. The day before, he had almost taken Wellingford's head off for no greater crime than startling him.

Which was another problem entirely. The anxiety inspired by the field's absence was becoming too much of a distraction. He was starting to lose focus. A blundering fool like Wellingford should never have been able to catch him by surprise, even if the boy had sneaked up behind him intentionally. Within the turbulent fury of a vortex, such distraction could easily prove fatal. If the King even suspected he was so helpless, Faukravar would not hesitate to move against him. Fortunately, the King had never taken an interest in magic or mages, or the man would have schooled himself enough to know what a vortex meant for him.

And Faukravar was really the least of Darien's worries. If Renquist and his demons knew he was alive, then this would be the place they would try to take him. Not with the strength of their power; they were just as helpless within a vortex as he was. But their pets were as darkly potent within the torrent of a vortex as they were without.

If Arden Hannah suspected he'd survived her fire, he might find himself confronted with such a fate. But Darien didn't think she had any reason to believe he was still alive. By the time Craig's charge had driven her away, he'd been hanging over that blaze for minutes, slowly searing like meat on a spit.

What a surprise he had in store for her. Darien sincerely hoped Arden would be traveling with her army. He had read about Bryn Calazar's Battlemages lending their support in the theater of war. If Arden showed herself at Orien's Finger, Darien had prepared something special with her in mind. Like a solicitous suitor, he'd put a great deal of thought and effort into selecting the perfect little something, a gift personalized just for her. He hoped she would find it just as stunning as he thought she would. If she didn't, then he would just have to keep trying until he got it right.

He was glad now that he'd sent Naia back home. The coming battle was going to be terrible. It would be no place for a priestess and certainly no place for a lover. Darien couldn't guarantee her safety, just as he couldn't guarantee his own. But it was more than that. He was glad she wasn't there to see him, to see the black, festering place where he had once kept his heart. He'd noticed the look on her face in Auberdale, when she'd seen him covered in the blood his sword had so eagerly spilled. The sight of him had repulsed her, but she had quickly forgiven him.

Naia would not be so quick with her forgiveness if she could see him now. There was little blood on his hands yet, but he felt as though he had already bathed in a river of it. He might as well have. Over the course of the past week, he had rehearsed his part in the coming battle hundreds of times in his head. At first, he had quailed. But then he'd forced himself to go over it one small step at a time, visualizing every graphic image again and again in increasing detail, until at last he felt numb enough to actually go through with it.

Which was another reason for his foul temper. Already that day, he'd killed hundreds of his own men scores of times in his head. He made himself visualize each dying face, hear every scream of anguish. Each time, it got a little easier. And it was still early in the day.

He rode in the middle of the drawn-out column, eyes focused on the backs of the men ahead. He'd let Faukravar take the van, and not out of deference to Chamsbrey's King. Because of his vulnerability while within the vortex, Darien felt reassured only with a ring of armored men around him. He had even moved his tent. The first week of the march he'd pitched it out away from the encampment, prizing his solitude above all else. Already, too many eyes were growing too wary, fixing him with questions he had no intention of answering. But the last two nights they had spent within the vortex, and he had positioned his tent in the center of camp.

Still, he'd had a hard time getting to sleep. The crawling feeling of his skin bothered him, and his heart kept beating a thundering tempo in his chest, not wanting to slow its pace even for sleep. He lay there for hours staring up at the roof of his tent, feeling more isolated and alone than ever before in his life.

More than anything, he missed Naia. But he was glad she was gone. So very, very glad.

Up ahead, the sharp ridge of a mountain groped upward from the snow-covered plain. They had made good time. He could scarcely believe they had made it all the way from Auberdale to the Cerulean Plains in only eight days, even if it was according to his own plan. He'd calculated the pace of the march himself from scaled charts in the command tent. It was a harsh pace, yet the well-disciplined soldiers had handled it well.

Even Wellingford was proving true. The youth had a small but laudable charisma that went over well with the men. He was still far from a great commander, but the boy did seem effective at getting things done.

Darien saw him riding up now, his young general's horse working its way back from the front of the column. Wellingford's eyes scanned over the faces of the men, a frown of concentration on his face. When he spotted Darien, the frown intensified. Directing his horse into a gap between ranks, he turned his mount to ride beside him.

"The King is wondering why you're not inclined to accompany us," Wellingford said. He added, "I'm wondering also. It is not the Prime Warden's place to breathe the dust kicked up by an army of men and their horses. People are starting to ask questions."

"Let them ask," Darien growled, not willing to address the reasoning behind his choice of position. "But if anyone has the temerity to openly speak out, then send that man to me. I will not have my judgment questioned the day before the battle."

"But, Prime Warden, it would be wise to keep up appearances—"

"*What did I just say?* Now, go back and tell that pathetic wretch of a King that if he really desired my company, then he shouldn't have conspired to have me killed. *Go!* Or I'll make you my first example."

Wellingford paled. Darien watched him depart, silently seething. He didn't notice the gap that widened between himself and the men that marched at his side, or the looks of dismay in the eyes of the soldiers within hearing distance of his outburst. Instead, he summoned yet another image to mind, an image as grisly and appalling as it was comforting.

To the men around him, the new Prime Warden they had sworn to follow seemed to be riding in a kind of trance. He sat slumped on his horse with eyes closed and arms slack as his face, gloved fingers maintaining only a flaccid grip on the reins. His long, unbound hair stirred in a breeze, playing forward into his face, unnoticed. Once in a while, he would give a slight flinch, as if in the throes of a bad dream. Perhaps he really was asleep and dreaming.

Or perhaps, more likely, he was mad.

It was late afternoon when they had their first glimpse of Orien's Finger. It rose slowly up from behind a jagged ridge, a narrow column of dark gray rock. Its surface was strangely textured, cracked and age-worn, with lighter patches of lichen speckling its sides. About a quarter of the way from the top, a wide, diagonal crack had the appearance of running all the way through the stone. The summit looked in danger of slipping off at any time, given but a chance breath of air, or even a whim.

To Darien, the crag had the ominous portent of destiny. It looked much as he had imagined. Subtly different: taller, darker. Eminently more sinister. The shadow it cast fell across the horseshoe-shaped valley behind it, the angle of the shadow bending across the smooth face of the surrounding cliffs, where its tip touched a carved, numeric rune. Orien's Finger was an enormous natural sundial, and the ancients had taken advantage of it. Only, Darien had no idea how that sundial was meant to be read.

Darien left the center of the column and sent his horse toward the edge. From there, he kicked the animal forward at a lope, his pulse quickening as he closed the distance between himself and the slender pillar of rock. He rode past the head of the column, right up to the King's entourage and beyond.

At the base of the dark tower, he came to a halt and climbed down from the saddle. Confident that he stood within the eye of the vortex itself, Darien opened his mind and groped for the magic field like a blind man tantalized with the promise of sight.

It was rapturous. Darien gasped, collapsing to his knees in consummate relief as he immersed himself in the field's soothing intensity. Here in the eye, where the lines converged together, the sweet savor of the field was like no other.

Darien filled himself with it, saturating his body completely. He drew on the field, soaking it in, like a man dying of thirst trying to drown himself in a pool of water. He pulled in more, until agony blended with ecstasy. The sweet song in his head became an anguished scream.

Reluctantly, Darien released his hold on the wild energies, letting the power drain out of him and slip away. He held just a little back to hoard jealously, unable to distance himself from the field completely. His head ached, and his body trembled with weak spasms, but he paid them both no mind. Wondrously complete again, he rose, shaking, to his feet.

And saw an army of men gaping at him in dismay. Faukravar was staring with eyes wide and full of disgust, his face a pallid shade of gray. At his side, Wellingford looked crestfallen and bitterly ashamed.

Darien turned his back on them. What had they seen? Something they never should have. What had he looked like, there in the cold shadow of the spire, writhing in the field's anguished ecstasy? Probably mad.

He should have never succumbed to the temptation of the magic field. Now, he had much to atone for. From the looks on their faces the damage was extensive, and there was simply not enough time to fully repair it. Solstice was only a dawn away. In his moment of weakness, he had just lost the respect of every last man that followed him.

Worse, they probably thought him dangerously insane.

Ignoring the fatigue that yet lingered from his struggle with the field, Darien turned and forced himself to face his men. They must see him as strong. If he played this right, he might be able to convince them that he was some kind of troubled martyr, casting himself in Orien's image. It was not a persona he would wish to emulate if he had a choice. He didn't see himself as even approaching the nobility of Orien's legend. He was creating an altogether different legend for himself, one trenched in infamy.

But if the men needed to see him as Orien, then he would have to play the role.

Taking his horse by the reins, Darien led the gelding back toward the column, testing the field as he went. Later, he would need to make certain he knew where the eye of the vortex ended, and the cyclone of power began. But for now, he was satisfied with the feeling of contentment brought to him by the eye, the calm within the storm.

He stopped in front of Faukravar. Pretending that he didn't notice the disgusted look on the King's face, Darien dredged forth a somber smile.

"It's a good day," he told the King. "Tomorrow will see the dawn of a better one. The banners of

Chamsbrey shall wave triumphant over the field."

To Wellingford, he ordered, "Set up camp on the south side of the ridge. No fires. The smoke will give away our presence. Use up as many rations as it takes to make certain every man has a good meal."

"Aye, Prime Warden," his general responded. His face looked perhaps a bit less pale, but he was still gazing at Darien with an expression of doubt.

Darien thought of the character of Orien they so desperately needed for him to imitate. With that in mind, he decided to elaborate with a little added mystery.

"I'll be up there." He nodded his head in the direction of the crag. "Allow no one to disturb me. I'll need to prepare myself, and I must do so alone."

Darien dropped the reins of his horse as he turned away, noting in satisfaction that the looks on their faces had once again changed. His strategy had worked, it seemed. The doubt and dismay were gone, absent even from Faukravar's eyes. Instead, he left them staring at his back, eyes wide in wonderment.

Darien hid a grimace as he walked away, feeling disgusted by the lie. He felt shamed that he'd brought himself to stoop so low, forced to win back their trust with a vulgar display. But if that was what it took to win the battle ahead, it was just another sin to add to the long list of them he was already accruing.

He wouldn't need the closing of the gateway to condemn his soul to hell. He was getting there just fine on his own.

Stone steps wrapped around the face of the dark column, a narrow and winding stair. It had broken and collapsed in many places. In other spots, the steps had been worn down to nothing more than a ramp. Darien took his time, picking his way carefully. It wouldn't do if he slipped and fell to his death on the eve before the battle. And eve it was. Already, the sun was beginning to slip behind the snow-clad mountains in the west. Tomorrow was Solstice, the shortest day of the year.

Darien kept his eyes averted from the edge. Once, heights had never bothered him. Now they did. The memory of his fall from Aerysius was kept fresh in his mind by the constant nightmares that plagued him almost every night. As he moved up the treacherous steps, he kept one hand braced against the rock face at his side, the other extended in front of him.

He slipped once, his fingers raking over the stone until they caught on a crack in the rocks, the only thing that saved him. Trembling, Darien pressed forward on legs that seemed suddenly less stable.

Before his fall, he could have skipped up this path. He had the balance taught to him by a blademaster, but it did him little good when his vision reeled, and his knees turned to jelly. He tried to will the path ahead to stabilize, but he could do nothing about the sweat that glazed his palms and ran trickling into his eyes.

More than once he came to a place where the steps had crumbled away completely. There, he was forced to gather his courage before making a staggering step across the break. Fortunately, it was never more than just a few feet. He tripped attempting the last gap, roughening his palms on the stone. But he drew himself up, feeling the bite of a cold breeze inspired by the height.

He was almost there, hundreds of feet above the horseshoe-shaped valley. It was getting dark. Darien shivered as he staggered up the last few steps, hands groping at the rock wall for stability. The stairs made a quick turn then leveled out.

Darien paused, closing his eyes and bracing himself. Then he stepped cautiously out over the snow-traced markings of the Circle of Convergence. He crossed the circle, stirring the slight dusting of snow that covered one of the lines with the toe of his boot. Walking across to the far side, Darien stepped off and moved toward the cliff's harrowing edge. There, he drew up, still yet paces away, but unable to move another step.

The view was awe-inspiring. And it was also terrifying. The sun had set completely, its light only the palest gray on the horizon. The snow-covered plains swept out away from him, glowing in the soft light of the rising moon. Above, the stars were strung across the heavens like innumerable glittering crystals. Their myriad glows were cast in red reflection below, slightly to the north, where the campfires of the Enemy seemed to outnumber even the light of the stars.

A breeze reached out, whipping his hair and

chasing his cloak. The feel of it was brisk and chill, stimulating. Slowly, he lowered himself to the flat summit of the crag, pulling his legs up to his chest and wrapping his arms around them.

Once, as a boy, he had tried counting the stars. He'd given up not long into the endeavor after reaching several hundred in just a trace amount of sky. The remainder of the heavens lay yet unnumbered above him. He had come to realize that such a task would probably take him the rest of his life.

This time he was determined to number them all, no matter how long the chore would take. It was imperative he know their total. Darien stared down at the red-orange lights below that twinkled brighter than the stars and started counting.

He knew Wellingford was behind him. He'd heard the scraping of his travel-worn boots crest the summit. The boy hadn't startled him this time, which was good. Darien hadn't moved from where he'd been sitting, gazing down at the fires below. He'd finished counting some time ago but was unwilling to leave his perch.

Staring out across the plains, his thoughts had drifted to Naia. He'd let the hours wear away, quietly savoring the image of her in his mind. It was very late, or perhaps very early; he wasn't sure. Whichever the case, Wellingford had no business being there. The boy should have been asleep hours ago.

His new general said, "I know you wanted to be left alone, but you did give the order that every man must have a good meal."

"So I did." Darien turned to glance over his shoulder.

Wellingford approached cautiously, a small sack in his hand. Remembering his own trouble with the broken and nerve-wracking stair, Darien found himself looking at Wellingford with new respect.

The young man seemed hesitant. Darien took the sack and, opening it, discovered that it was filled with dried meat, slices of bread, and even some cheese. Wellingford produced a waterskin and handed that to him, as well. Darien accepted it with a muttered word of thanks.

The boy stared out at the flickering lights, his cloak stirring behind him. Softly, he whispered, "Is that the Enemy?"

"Aye." He watched as Wellingford stepped forward, stopping right at the edge of the cliff. Just seeing him there made Darien shudder. Wellingford didn't seem bothered by heights in the least. He stood motionless, gazing outward across the plains, one foot slightly ahead of the other.

"Mother of the gods," he whispered.

Looking up at him, Darien asked, "Have you been taught how to estimate an army's strength by counting campfires?"

Wellingford turned back around, taking a step away from the cliff's edge. "Yes, but...there's too many. It would take all night."

"Not all night." Darien shook his head. "Judging from the lights, I estimate their numbers at somewhere near fifty-two thousand."

The boy swept a hand back through his hair, shaking his head as his eyes glistened in the moonlight. "I never thought there would be so many," he said, lowering himself to sit at Darien's side.

"There were more, once. I can only assume that the men under Garret Proctor's command have put their courage and their horn bows to good use."

Wellingford just stared at him blankly.

Darien raised his hand, pointing toward the dark swell of a ridgeline. "Look there." He indicated a patch of starless sky hanging inches beneath the moon, slightly above the rolling hills that sloped upward into the Craghorns.

"I see nothing."

"The stars above the ridge," Darien specified.

"There are none." Wellingford shook his head in puzzlement. "I don't understand. What could be obscuring them?"

"Smoke. From campfires."

The boy drew in a sharp gasp of breath. "The second army," he whispered. When Darien nodded, Wellingford's face seemed on the verge of collapse. He had that crestfallen look again, although this time it made his face seem older instead of younger.

"Do we really stand a chance? The forces from Emmery you promised us never arrived."

"I won't be expecting them till the morrow." Darien stared hard at Wellingford's face. The boy needed reassurance, needed it desperately. "Why don't we go over strategy? I was thinking to wait, but seeing that you're here..."

"That would be good," Wellingford said eagerly, leaning back with his gloved hands in the snow. His fingers sank deeply into the icy powder with a crunching noise, exposing a wide, man-made crack in the stone below. Perplexed, he brushed away the snow with his fingers to reveal a curving line.

"What's this?"

"You're sitting on a focus line of the Circle of Convergence."

Wellingford stared down at it, frowning. "I'm afraid I don't understand."

"You don't want to," Darien assured him. "Just listen, do your part, and leave the rest to me."

Chapter Thirty-Five
Black Solstice

The Cerulean Plains, The Rhen

"Time to get up."

Kyel groaned, wondering what hour it could possibly be. Squinting into the darkness, he made out the form of Nigel Swain, a mere shadow against the other shadows within the tent. Outside, it appeared to be ink black through the open flap, and cold. Terribly cold. Why hadn't Swain closed the flap when he'd entered? Probably a tactic to get him up and moving faster.

Then he remembered: Solstice. Dawn. Today. Feeling suddenly wide awake, Kyel threw his blankets back and shot up from the covers.

"What time is it?"

"Too damn early," came Swain's acidic growl. "Come on, I brought you some of that fodder they're serving in place of food."

Kyel shook his head even though he knew the man probably couldn't see him in the darkness. The thought of eating curdled gruel within scant moments of waking was frankly nauseating. Besides, his bladder was so full it ached. He dragged himself up from his pallet, moving toward the opening. "I need to go out for a minute."

He was stopped by the captain's warning growl. "Better be *just* a minute."

Kyel nodded, taking the man's point. He had spent the entire first day of the march making frequent trips into the bushes before he was finally able to bend one single link of his chains. Then, it had taken him another day and a half of side trips to close the same link back up again. He'd practiced opening and closing the link at every chance he found, until the presence of the vortex had given him other things to think about. That was all the practice he'd had. And it was all he was going to get.

That was precisely what Swain was grumbling about. After the first two days of Kyel's prolonged excursions afield, the captain had caught on that he was up to something, though he never figured out what. But after that, Kyel had found his movements strictly watched. If he didn't make it back quickly enough, Swain made certain he missed his next meal.

He made his water then returned to the tent, the first light of dawn still absent from the sky. The moon was setting, though, which meant sunrise couldn't be that long in following.

The captain met him outside, waiting for him. As Kyel strode up, he could feel Swain's eyes looking him over, lingering a moment on the chains. Kyel pretended he didn't notice.

"How long will it take us to get there?" he asked. They couldn't be that far away. Most of the camp still had to be broken down, and he'd told Blandford that Darien was expecting them by sunrise.

Swain transferred his bowl to his left hand, wiping his mouth with his sleeve. Pointing, he said, "See that ridge?" He indicated a jagged patch of blackness against the slightly grayer sky. "Orien's Finger is about two more ridges north of it. We'll be there about an hour after sunrise, so that's about a two-hour march."

Kyel felt stunned. Betrayed. "But Darien told us to be there *at* sunrise!" He rounded on Swain. "We can't arrive an hour after the fighting starts—it might be too late!"

The captain just shrugged. "Blandford wants the

Enemy bloodied a bit before we engage."

Kyel couldn't believe what he was hearing. What did they expect Darien to do, take on both armies by himself? Or was that exactly what they intended? Feeling a sudden, searing anger, Kyel took a threatening step toward the captain.

"This has been your plan all along, hasn't it?" he accused. "You intend to just bide your time while he wears himself down, then sweep in when he's no longer a threat to you."

Looking at the coldly gleaming hilt of Swain's sword, Kyel felt his rage swell to scalding. "That's why you're here," he realized. "You're captain of the *city* guard. You don't even belong with the army! Romana just sent you along because Darien trusts you—you're the one who trained him. That's it, isn't it? You're here to kill him!"

Swain looked at him sideways, a dangerous glint in his eyes. Then he took a step back and, tossing aside the flap of the tent, ducked inside. Kyel wanted to scream in rage. Not bothering to bite back the curse on his lips, he followed Swain into the tent. He wasn't going to let him get away, not without an explanation.

In the darkness of the tent, he saw the captain's shadow as only a blur. Then hands were on him, restraining him from behind. He felt the warm brush of Swain's breath at the back of his neck as the captain warned, "Don't press me further."

But Kyel couldn't help himself. "I don't understand you. You must have been his friend. How can you do this?"

The hands eased their pressure on him gradually. Kyel turned around, peering intently into the shadows of the man's angular face. Swain's eyes glared at him with a dangerous intensity, his chest heaving with every drawn breath.

"I knew a *boy* named Darien Lauchlin, once," he said. "But that was a long time ago. The man up there on that mountain, now…I don't know him anymore. I don't want to know him. And if you had any brains in your head, you wouldn't want to, either."

Sunrise.

Darien had spent the hours after moonset pacing the circumference of the circle, stirring the dusted snow off with his boots and with the power of his mind. He dared not use too much. There were creatures that could sense such stirrings of the field. But a trickle here and a tad bit there gradually revealed the deeply hewn lines that ran inward from the margin of the circle, forming an exactingly rendered copy of the star he wore on his back, only many times larger.

Two stars, one offset against the other. He knew the pattern of the circle was not a star at all. At least, not by intention. The rays were a focus that directed the lines of power in the eye of the vortex, merging them together in one place, one single point in space at the circle's center. That was the power of the Circle of Convergence. All the energy of the vortex could be gathered here. The rays of the star functioned like lenses to bend the lines of the magic field together and filter them, rendering that tremendous well of power safe to use.

But like glass lenses, each circle had its flaws, its little imperfections. Even minuscule faults had an impact on its ability to focus the surrounding vortex. Orien's was a lesser circle, which meant its flaws were more problematic than the greater circle that had existed in Aerysius, now buried beneath the rubble of the Hall. Darien was not sure what impact those flaws would have on the circle's use. Only time would tell. All he could see from his cursory study was that Orien's Circle was still functional after its long sleep of over four hundred years. All he had to do now was awaken it.

Gazing down from the rim of the crag, he could see the gray sky in the east giving way to vivid hues of gold and vermillion. Sunrise had always been his favorite time of day. The colors of the sky seemed more saturated than they did at sunset, especially when there was just a splattering of clouds on the horizon, as there was today.

But there was no joy to be had in this sunrise, this dawn, this day. Darien ignored the timorous beauty of the wakening sky as if it didn't exist. To him, nothing existed in the world except for the vast black wedge approaching from the north, that and the Circle of Convergence beneath his feet. It was almost time.

This dawn, this day, this purpose.

Steeling himself, he walked to the tip of the nearest ray and drew upon the potent rapture of the magic field, a wonder far more stirring than any daybreak. He felt the power moving through him, a bliss unlike any other. The magic field had never felt this way, not until lately. Not until he had clothed his heart in ashes and cloaked his soul in apathy. But now it seemed the tranquil stirring of the field was the only thing keeping him going, the only thing keeping him alive.

Beneath his boots, the ancient stone-carved lines began to glow with a silvery light that ran like quicksilver down the length of the ray to the circle's focal point. Unnoticed, the first rays of the sun broke above the white rolling plains in the east.

———

His back to the sunrise, Garret Proctor contemplated the advancing army before him. He had worn their numbers down considerably. But it had hardly made a difference.

So many dead. All for the trust he had placed in one man. One man who he still had no guarantee would come through for them.

He sat his horse and waited. His new captain, a man by the name of Wade Tarpen, was at his side. Tarpen had Craig's horse and Craig's gear, but none of the other man's spirit. Proctor grimaced as he looked to the east, toward the sunrise, despising the wait.

Today, he knew, he was going to die. He doubted Lauchlin had even known it at the time, but the mage had sentenced them all to death with a few simple words uttered at the base of the tower at Greystone Keep.

Draw the majority of their strength into the eye of the vortex, and I'll see to it you get your wish.

Proctor wondered if Lauchlin had realized at the time the hone of the blade he'd let fall that day. Because there was only one way to draw both Enemy hosts deep enough into the eye of the vortex for Darien's purpose to succeed.

He had missed the break of dawn. It had been over fifteen years since his face had last gazed upon the rising sun. Garret Proctor savored the warmth of daybreak, knowing there would never be another. Death was always cold, just as the grave was always dark and stale. He knew; he had buried enough friends to be certain.

———

Darien heard someone approaching up the steps. It could have been Wellingford, but he knew it wasn't. It might have been any number of people, but he already had a very good idea who it would be. He recognized the sound of her footsteps even before she came into view. It was a noise firmly ingrained on his mind. The sound of her slippered feet moved often through his nightmares.

He turned to face her as Arden Hannah came into view, picking her way over the last treacherous step to emerge at the glowing summit of the crag. Her creatures must have sensed the ripples in the field he'd created by awakening the circle.

Dark forms swept out from behind her, gliding past her to line the edge of the rim, six in all. Necrators. Darien had begun to feel the effects of their approach minutes before. He had known they were drawing nearer when the song of the magic field had started to fade in his head. It was almost gone now. Almost, but not quite. He could still feel the pulse of it dimly, like the tremulous echo of a dying heartbeat.

He wasn't there yet. There must be something further he needed to do.

Arden stood regarding him with sparkling eyes, resplendent in an intriguing mixture of blue silks and silver chain mail. Slowly, a smile bloomed on her lips. It was a triumphant smile, and its radiance swept upward to gleam in her eyes.

There was a low growl. Darien's eyes were drawn behind her, to the beast that glared at him with glowing green eyes. The thanacryst was black and large with matted fur. It had a rabid look. Its mouth was open and panting, a wide and cavernous hole that drooled thick saliva to the stone. Revolted, Darien felt an instinctual impulse to draw away from it.

"You're so full of surprises, my dear."

Her voice was like silver droplets of moonlight. She took a step toward him, placing a slippered foot inside the margin of the glowing circle. Tilting her head slightly, her eyes narrowed as she considered him.

"Oh, my, but you've changed. When we first met, you were just a little sweetling. My fire must have scorched your soul." Gazing into his eyes, she said in a voice full of conviction, "Look at you. You're positively glorious."

Darien shuddered, the silken tone of her voice eliciting memories he had struggled to forget.

Behind her, the thanacryst uttered a low, guttural growl of yearning. Its nose quivered as it sensed the proximity of its prey. Arden placed a hand on its head, soothing it with the liquid texture of her voice.

"Easy, my pet. Not yet."

Turning back to Darien, she brought a hand up. Her fingertips stroked the pale flesh of her neck.

"Come to me," she commanded. "There is nothing in the world so erotic as two mages united, naked bodies and unrestrained power intertwined. I can give you a little taste of what it would be like, if you were mine."

Standing there on the margin of the circle, offering herself up to him like a sacrifice, her seductive energies took hold of him with an influence that was overwhelming. This time, Darien allowed it. He did nothing to resist the electric tension that shuddered down his nerves. It was almost like the longing ache he felt for Naia, though shockingly more feral. It filled him with a desperate urgency he had no inclination to ignore.

His eyes took in the shape of her figure, the sleek curves of the chain mail draped over her hips. He found the sight of her as enticing as it was repulsive. But, strangely, the dichotomy just added to her attraction.

He needed to take her. And he needed to enjoy every hungry second of it.

Moving forward, he kept his gaze fixed on Arden's as he reached up and grasped the platinum locks of her hair. Consumed with untamed rage, he scoured his lips over the silken crease of her neck, the intensity of his assault driving a gasp from her lips.

He reached his hand up and released his cloak. Drawing it from his shoulders, he spread it out over the glowing lines of the circle's rays with the star facing downward, pressed against its larger counterpart.

He pulled his shirt off over his head and drew her toward him, dragging her down with him to the ground. Her power flowed over him, through him, the electric intensity of her gift searing like wildfire through his mind.

Conscience forsaken, Darien gave her everything she asked for, everything he had, everything he was. Most important, he gave Arden exactly what she wanted from him most.

There on the flattened summit of Orien's crag, Darien surrendered to Arden Hannah all that remained of his tortured soul.

———

His raised fist a silhouette against the red disk of the rising sun, Garret Proctor himself bellowed the command to send his men forward to their deaths. He kicked his boots into the flanks of his horse, drawing the cold length of steel he had not wielded in battle since Meridan. The hilt felt good in his gloved hand, the balance of the sword excellent. He had never favored a fight from horseback, but a man had to eat from the plate the gods served him, even if the fare was cold and bitter.

With a grim smile on his face, Garret Proctor swept his blade downward, sheering through the end of an Enemy spear. Pressing his mount forward with his legs, he raised his shield and warded off the attack of a mace as he wheeled his horse around, charging back out of the thick of the fight.

———

Darien rolled over to lie gasping on his back, staring upward into the sky. He felt Arden's hand caress his chest, heard the silken texture of her voice as she whispered in his ear, "I think I'll make you my pet. Yes. For a little while, at least."

Darien closed his eyes, the sound of his pulse ringing in his ears, the song of the magic field a sudden, rapturous symphony in his head. Reaching up, he took her hand in his.

The raging current he sent through her took Arden by surprise. Twisting in agony, her mouth drew into a rictus as she screamed, blue lightnings of power clawing into her flesh. Darien watched in fascination as her pale skin glazed and then crisped, cracking to ooze boiling fluid that ran like tears down her face.

He let the crackling energies die with the sound of her screams. Leaning over her, he smiled in satisfaction.

"The necrators…"

Startled by her voice, Darien drew back. Somehow, she was still alive. But not for long; the sound of her breath was but a gurgle in her throat.

"They have no power over you."

"Because my heart is black," she whispered as she died.

Darien nodded, staring down at her charred corpse. He felt no sympathy for her whatsoever, absolutely no remorse. The only thing he felt was a satisfying sense of vindication.

"So is mine, now," he assured her.

He rose to face the ring of necrators who stood regarding him with acute disinterest. They had no reason to challenge him. If they looked deeply into his heart, the only thing they would find was an ally.

———

Proctor raised his sword to block the blade that cleaved down at him as his stallion reared and attacked the Enemy with its hooves and teeth. He clung to his shield, warding off blow after blow from one soldier as another worked furiously to get his blade inside his guard. He parried the thrusts, then changed through to a downward cut that took his opponent in the neck. The man crumbled as Proctor swung his sword around to ward off a glancing slice from the opposite direction.

He spun his horse away, angling the destrier back toward the charging horde.

———

Darien gazed down from the rim of the summit, his boots scant inches from the edge. He was no longer troubled by the reeling vertigo he had experienced earlier. Many things he had been afraid of before had ceased to be a problem. Arden's thanacryst sat on its haunches at his side, nose quivering as it scented the wind, drooling an awful fluid that slicked its dark fur and dripped, viscous, to the stone. The necrators at his back remained silently at their stations. He paid them no mind. They would linger there until he deigned to send them away. He was their master, now.

Darien gazed down, considering the view below with calm indifference. To the north, he could see the wedge of the first host, dispersed now as they rushed to harry what was left of Proctor's men. To the west, he could see the van of the second host emerging from behind the ridge. There was still no trace of Emmery's support, but now he doubted he would need it. Orien's Circle glowed behind him, pulsing to the cadence of the magic field.

He waited, watching as below him, men of Proctor's command were swept under by a breaking tide of death.

He waited and did nothing.

Reaching down, he ran his fingers over the coarse fur of the thanacryst's head. The beast had been anxious, ever since he had dumped its mistress' corpse off the edge of the cliff. He soothed it with quiet, whispered words, hand ruffling the slathered fur of its neck.

———

Garret Proctor felt the arrow take him in the chest, piercing through his armor even as his sword smashed through the visor of an Enemy pikeman. Gritting his teeth, he brought his blade up again. Hacking his way out of a thicket of shields and swords, he sent his mount at a gallop across the snow-covered plain. Ahead, he could see the tall spire of Orien's Finger like an ancient and decrepit pillar thrusting upward into the sky.

All he had to do was reach the pillar's base. After that, his final duty would be consummated.

———

The thanacryst growled. He thought perhaps it might be hungry. Patting its head, Darien took one last look down at the flagging chase below, then turned away from the edge. Under the silent watch of the necrators, he strode calmly to the center of the circle, taking his place at the focal point of the glimmering lines of the star.

It was time.

Darien closed his eyes, shrouding his mind in concentration as he felt the Circle of Convergence through his feet. The lines of power pulsed once, harkening to his call. Gathering the energies of the focus, Darien summoned the strength of the magic field, offering himself as a conduit for the vast intensity of the vortex.

The battle below forgotten, he opened up his mind. The surge of power flooded into him, filling him, consuming him utterly.

The lines of Orien's Circle glowed, glimmering, increasing to a white brilliance unequalled even by the sun. A breeze stirred, playing with the strands of his hair. The wind swelled, became a vibrant gust of air that moved along the perimeter of the circle, slowly rotating. Almost stately, the spinning column of air grew, groping upward into the sky as the new-found morning began to darken.

The thanacryst threw back its head and howled. The necrators looked silently on, their dark forms unaffected by the first strains of the grand resonance forming around them, groping upward to choke the sky.

Chapter Thirty-Six
Grand Resonance

The Cerulean Plains, The Rhen

Garret Proctor fought the reins of his horse, wincing as his arm grazed the arrow in his chest. The entire front of his padded gambeson was stained a dark burgundy sheen. Fighting had enlarged the wound, and the battle-rage that quickened his heart only served to pump the blood out faster. He had seen such wounds before and knew it was mortal.

Grasping the arrow, he snapped off the protruding end of the shaft and flung it away. The pain was fierce, almost incapacitating. His vision swam, and for a moment the pillar of rock before him wavered and grew dim. Looking down, he could see his lifeblood now coming in spurts timed to the rhythm of his heartbeat.

Orien's Finger reared sharply overhead, jutting upward into the sky. As his horse took the hill at the base of the crag, Proctor drew back on the reins and wheeled his mount around. Behind him, what was left of the men under his command were embroiled in a desperate race. There were so few left. Two more fell from their horses even as he watched. The writhing mass of both Enemy armies flooded behind them, churning like an ocean at the place where two swift currents meet.

The hurling onslaught slowed to a halt. His back to the rock face of Orien's Finger, Proctor brandished his sword over his head as the men that were left formed up at his side. Before them, the front ranks of the Enemy pierced the air with a resonating cry.

The cry was taken up like a wave through the ranks, sweeping out from the crag like a deafening riptide. The clamor rose even further as the second host joined in, over fifty thousand fresh voices adding their thunder to the din.

And then every voice suddenly silenced in unison as all eyes were drawn upward to the sky.

From horizon to horizon, the dawn went abruptly, alarmingly gray. Proctor saw a shadow slip across the face of the sun, rendering its disk pale and colorless, like a face taken by the pallor of death. The new white sun glowed like an ill omen in the sky, its veiled face emitting little warmth and little light. The day turned rapidly, sinisterly cold. The air seemed almost to congeal, became stiff and still.

A dreadful calm descended on the plains, silent and impassive. Even the dark ranks of the Enemy stood motionless, like a frozen black sea. His own men glanced around fearfully, faces as pale as the dim sun overhead.

Garret Proctor did not need to look up. He knew what was coming. Instead he closed his eyes, fondly remembering the few friends he had known in life and praying the gods would forgive his sins.

The sky grew dark as the sun paled to a ghostly hue. Staring up at it, Malcolm Wellingford knew his face only reflected the ghastly shade. The summit of Orien's Finger could be seen looming high above the ridge behind them, encased in a circulating mass of black clouds that expanded even as it rotated, groping out across the sky.

"The signal," Wellingford whispered to himself through the fear that gripped his heart. The turmoil above surpassed anything his nightmares had ever conceived. He had been expecting something big, perhaps even terrible, but nothing as darkly *evil* as the sickness above that infected the sky.

The boy still in him wanted to turn his horse and flee, gallop away as fast and as far as he could. But the new-found man within him knew he had a duty to perform. A duty that, at all cost, had to proceed.

General Wellingford drew his sword, striving to keep the point of the blade steady as he held it skyward over his head. Raising his voice, he addressed his men:

"Ring them in to the line, push them up against the pillar as close as you can! They'll try to run but accord them no escape! We have but one chance at this. There'll not be another. *Do not fall back!*

"Now, *FORWARD!*"

With a downward slash, he leveled his sword in the air. The blade did not waver in his hand, so unlike the heart that faltered in his chest. He was but a boy, but he was also a man with a homeland to defend.

He held his breath as twelve thousand men rushed out from behind the cover of the ridge, the sound of their charge shaking the very ground and trembling the air around him.

As Swain had promised, they were exactly an hour late. Kyel had fidgeted in the saddle the entire ride, terrified of what awaited them up ahead. He strained for a view of Orien's Finger, but the sight of it was still blocked by a range of hills that stretched out in front of them to the north. What he did see ahead was disconcerting.

"What is that?" He pointed at a dark patch in the distance that was almost hidden from sight by a small grove of trees.

Swain squinted, a frown of concentration on his face. A look of surprise dawned in his eyes. He whispered, "It looks to me like a bunch of fools. Something tells me you held back a few bits of Darien's plan."

"I told you what I knew," Kyel said defensively. "He's the one who didn't share everything with me."

Swain looked skeptical. "So you're telling me you had no idea an army from Chamsbrey was going to be meeting us here?"

Kyel shook his head, wondering what on earth Chamsbrey's presence could mean. He didn't wonder long. Looking up into a sky suddenly dark and gray, he saw with dread that the sun had gone a pasty shade of white.

And then the crag came into view. At its summit was a spiraling mass of black clouds. Appallingly unnatural, they spread outward like a rotating saucer that was rapidly increasing in size. Kyel stared up at it, horrified.

At his side, Nigel Swain drew up his mount. "Not dangerous, you say?"

Kyel barely heard him. He gaped at that writhing mass with acute disbelief. That couldn't be Darien. It couldn't be. The thing in the sky was *evil*. There was no other word for it. And the sun...whatever had been done to the sun was repulsive. Something malevolent was taking place ahead, something both hideous and terrifying.

"What is it?" he whispered.

Beside him, Swain never took his eyes off the abomination in the sky. "I have no idea."

Kyel pulled his horse up, transfixed by the view ahead. In the distance, he could see Orien's Finger with its black, swirling crown. At its base was almost the mirror image of what was taking place above in the sky.

The dark mass of the Enemy host was ringed by a thin line of infantry desperately fighting a pitched battle to hold their line. The scene was as heartrending as it was appalling. The army from Chamsbrey had no chance. Their numbers were like a child's dike of sand trying to hold back the rising flood of a river.

In the sky above, the black clouds rumbled. A low, resonating thunder built gradually until Kyel could feel it in his chest. The sound of it swelled, unrelenting.

His horse reared, almost throwing him off, and still the echoing thunder rose. Kyel jumped down and grabbed his mount by the bridle, holding it with one hand as he tried to cover his ears. The rumble became a deafening vibration.

And then the entire world went black. Looking up, Kyel saw that the racing clouds had utterly consumed the sky. They swirled overhead, raging. The only light to be seen was at the summit of Orien's Finger. There, a white brilliance gleamed from out of the darkness, pulsating with thrumming vibrations that shook the air and trembled the very foundations of the earth.

Kyel's horse reared again, knocking him to the ground. The gelding bolted, galloping away, but he hardly noticed. His eyes were fixed on that pulsing beacon of light.

An explosion of orange-yellow flame shot upward from the summit, blazed there for a span of seconds, and then turned and swept back down upon itself. It poured over the sides of the crag, spilling like a ferocious, glowing waterfall to rush outward in an expanding cloud that whipped across the plains. There was a brief, blinding flare of light. Kyel screamed, throwing his hands up before his face.

Then it vanished, as if stopped by an invisible and impregnable wall. The noise of it hit, a terrible, air-splitting thunder like the sound of all the heavens collapsing straight into hell. Then the sound was gone, dying almost as abruptly as it came. A warm wind like a summer breeze drifted toward them from the crag, billowing great clouds of dust up high into the air.

Kyel watched from the ground, mouth gaping, unable to believe what his eyes had just seen, what his ears had just heard.

It had taken seconds. Only seconds. Nothing could have survived that.

At the summit, the white light faded to a dim afterglow, then died away completely. Overhead, the sky was still encased in darkness, though the clouds seemed to be slowing. Below on the plain, nothing moved. An appalling stillness had taken hold of the morning.

Kyel looked out into the darkness, his mind numb, his heart heavy with tears.

Darien opened his eyes to find the demon-hound nuzzling its head against his face, whimpering. His vision blurred, and for a moment there seemed to be two beasts leaning over him. The images wavered, gradually blending into one. The thanacryst crouched at his side, its forelegs sprawled across his chest. Doglike, it reached its head out and slathered the side of his face with its black and oozing tongue. The smell of the creature was foul, like moldering death.

The sky was not as dark as it had been. The unnatural night had given way to an overcast sky. The clouds above were drizzling, a gentle sprinkle that was warm and comforting.

"Move," Darien told the beast, patting his hand on the stone by his side. The thanacryst whined a complaint but shifted its weight off his chest. It lay down beside him, its muzzle between its paws, looking dejected.

Darien rolled onto his side then pushed himself up weakly. He was sitting near the edge of the summit, though he didn't remember getting there. Before him, the circle was quiescent. Sadly, he realized it would never again awaken. Orien's Circle was ruined. The stone itself seemed to have liquefied and run, then cooled once more in rippling pools of slag. The star itself was grotesquely distorted. The lights of its rays would never shine again. The abusive torrent of power he had subjected it to had destroyed the circle completely.

It was a waste, one of a great many wastes that had come from this day.

He tried to push himself to his feet but found he lacked the strength for it. So instead Darien leaned back, resting his head against the thanacryst's heaving side. He gazed upward at the gray, overcast sky and let the rain drizzle down on his face. Dimly, he could see the dark shadows of the necrators still present at their stations around the summit's rim, silent guardians watching over him sightlessly. He found their presence strangely comforting.

He closed his eyes and let his mind wander toward sleep. But almost as soon as it came, his rest was disturbed by a fragile sound from below. Sitting back up, he stared warily at the place where the stairs met the summit's rim. Behind him, the thanacryst uttered a low growl.

Darien did nothing; there was nothing he could do. If it was one of Renquist's darkmages, then they would have him. The bone-weary exhaustion that filled him prevented him from touching the field. He had a suspicion of whom it might be, and he wasn't prepared for that challenge, either.

But he was wrong. To his horror, it was Naia's veiled face that crested the rim.

She froze as she took in the vision of the necrators and the thanacryst at his back. Face pale, she looked at him, slowly shaking her head. She was the last person in the world he wanted to see. He had wanted Naia to remember him the way he was. Not like this.

She crept forward, gaze wandering over the melted circle at her feet. Then she stopped, eyes drawn to the necrator that glided forward to confront her. Darien frowned, not understanding the demon's sudden motion. Naia's presence should not have provoked it; she was no mage.

"Visea," he whispered, and watched as all six shadows melted downward, disappearing into the stone.

She pressed forward again, crossing the ruined circle to stand before him, eyes on the thanacryst that stood growling from deep within its throat. Darien put a hand on the beast, stilling it. Then he looked down, not wanting her to see the shadows that he knew consumed his eyes.

She knelt beside him, reaching out a hand to touch his face. He shrank away from her touch, wincing as if in pain. Her hand found his hair instead, running through it soothingly.

He closed his eyes, wishing to the gods he was dead. If he were dead, she wouldn't have to see him this way. Better that she gaze upon his corpse than be witness to the decayed corruption that had become of his soul.

"Easy," she whispered, trailing a hand down his cheek.

He suffered her touch. A week ago, he had longed for it. But Naia's hand was pure and wholesome, and it had no business touching such a filthy thing as his face.

"I'm here," she whispered. "I won't leave you again."

But that wasn't what he wanted. He needed her to leave, right now, before it was too late.

"Can you stand?" she asked. "We must go down from here. It's not safe."

He couldn't understand why. The Enemy was no longer a threat. Or, at least, they shouldn't be. Darien felt confused. His senses were jumbled, and he was feeling even fainter now than he had before, as if Naia's soft touch had sapped away the last vestige of his strength.

She stood up and pulled him to his feet. Darien staggered as the world seemed to lurch, but he managed to remain standing with Naia's support. He had to lean on her heavily as she guided him across the destroyed circle to the stairs.

He could hear the sound of the thanacryst's paws padding along behind, dutifully following its new master.

———

Kyel walked at Swain's side over the blackened ground. The blast from the circle had created an almost perfect ring of devastation that extended out about a league from Orien's Finger, where it suddenly just stopped. After that, the plains continued off to the horizon, untouched.

Kyel didn't understand it. But apparently, someone else had. The remains of Chamsbrey's army were wandering in dazed shock on the other side of the boundary, not daring to set foot within the ring of scorched earth. Someone had known where that boundary would be and had positioned most of the soldiers on the other side of it during the battle, saving their lives.

But the Enemy hosts had not been so lucky. Kyel picked his way around what remained of the two armies, now reduced to twisted lumps of melted armor. There would be no graves dug here; there was nothing left to bury. Not even bones had survived the tremendous heat of the blast. The black soil that crunched beneath his feet glittered where it had been melted into glass.

The sight was appalling. Swain walked in silence, face constricted in a grisly scowl. Kyel didn't know how to feel. In a way, he was almost as dazed as Chamsbrey's soldiers. A victory had taken place here today, though it had more the feel of a bitter defeat.

War had been waged, but what kind of war? There was no honor in what had happened here, only cold inhumanity. His homeland was safe, but at what cost? A price had been paid, and it was more than the sum of the souls that had been taken so brutally out of life.

Orien's Finger loomed overhead, its sides scorched black, its summit appearing dangerously offset. A crack had widened near the summit, and the stone itself had slipped forward. The entire top of the pillar seemed in danger of toppling at any moment. Kyel shivered, almost hoping to see it go.

They reached the base of the column, feet still

crunching on glass that looked like dried and cracked pools of mud. Kyel stared down at one such puddle, wondering how hot the sand must have been to melt like that. It was beyond imagining.

A hand on his arm made him look up.

Swain had stopped, fingers reflexively going for the hilt of his sword, though he didn't draw the blade. Kyel looked ahead to the base of the crag.

Naia sat at the opening of a narrow stair carved into the side of the cliff, Darien's head resting on her lap. His eyes were closed as if in sleep. Naia's hand stroked gently through his hair. Behind them, a hideous beast sat on its haunches, panting. It looked almost like a dog—a dog exhumed from the grave. It drooled long strings of saliva that dripped to the stone.

Kyel felt stunned by fear. He wasn't sure what provoked it—whether it was inspired by the repulsive beast or the sight of Darien lying cradled in Naia's lap. Kyel couldn't tell whether he was dead or asleep, and he wasn't sure which would scare him more. This was the man responsible for the atrocity that had turned even the very sand to glass, and the fell beast that lingered above him only affirmed Kyel's fear.

Swain started forward and Kyel followed, stopping as the captain knelt at Naia's side. The priestess looked up at him through her veil, an unspoken question on her face. As Swain moved a hand to Darien's arm, the mage opened his eyes.

Kyel turned away. He couldn't bear to look at him. The shadows that had once wandered across the Sentinel's eyes had since utterly consumed them. Darien's face was a mask of pain.

"I thought you'd come," he whispered, staring up at Swain. The words didn't even sound like his own. The beast above him whimpered, edging closer. Naia encircled him in her arms, looking fiercely protective.

"Then you know why I'm here," Swain muttered softly.

Darien nodded.

"I can't leave you Unbound," the blademaster said, sitting down next to him on the step below. "You're too dangerous now."

Darien shook his head. "There are some things I have to do first."

Swain drew back, a considering look on his face. Almost kindly, he assured him, "Kyel is perfectly capable. He's come along well. You've done what you had to do, now leave the rest to him."

Naia stared at Swain with a contemptuous look in her eyes. Darien grimaced, pushing himself up with effort. He squeezed his eyes shut as he leaned on the step above to stabilize himself. Kyel wanted to go to him, but something held him back.

"It takes two mages working together to seal the Well of Tears," Darien said. "Kyel can't do it alone."

The captain shrugged indifferently. "Then leave the damn thing open. Come on. You knew the price before you started any of this. Don't try to wheedle out of it now."

Darien glared at him. "You know me better than that."

"I don't know you at all anymore."

Darien brought a weary hand up to rub his face. "Aidan must be stopped. He's using the Well of Tears to coordinate the Eight with the strength of the Enemy. If you leave him be, everything I've done here today won't matter. They'll just keep coming."

"I don't know," Swain muttered, looking around at the charred earth that surrounded them. "If you're asking me to choose between you and your brother, I'd have to pick Aidan. From what I'm seeing, he's the lesser of two evils."

"Do you think I enjoyed this?" Darien demanded, eyes narrowing.

"I don't know, Darien. Did you?"

Behind them, the beast growled, standing up. The hair on the back of its neck raised, its mouth open and cavernous. Darien put a hand out. The creature sat back down, closing its mouth with a snap.

Swain sighed, shaking his head. "Look, Darien, I'm not here to argue with you. Either Transfer your gift to Kyel, or I'll be forced to end this myself. You're the son of Gerald and Emelda Lauchlin. Honor their memory and die with some dignity."

Naia gasped, and even Kyel felt his anger rising. Staring down at the iron chains on his wrists, he remembered the resolution he had made, back in Romana's cell. The reason he had put the Soulstone on in the first place. He wasn't supposed to be letting this happen.

"You can't touch me," Darien said, spreading his

hands. The sleeves of his faded shirt fell back, revealing a set of fresh pink scars that encircled both his wrists where the marks of his Oath had once been. Kyel found the sight of them appalling, and not just because of their appearance.

Swain sneered down, unconvinced. "Look at you. You're wiped out. You couldn't even think of touching the field in your condition."

Darien raised his eyes to Kyel. "Show him."

"Show him what?" Kyel frowned.

Darien's eyes hardened. "You know damn well what I mean."

Kyel thought he did. Only, it took him completely aback that Darien already knew about it. Still, he found himself holding his breath as he reached out with his mind and did the only thing he knew how to do with his ability: he bent a link on each chain.

The iron bracelets slid off his arms, falling to the dirt with a clinking noise. Swain stared down at the chains, stunned. Kyel just hoped it would be enough.

In front of him, Darien pushed himself up, rising to his feet. He still looked unstable, but the dark shadows in his eyes compensated for any weakness his stance implied.

Glaring down at Swain, the mage said, "You can take your chances against two of us, Unbound. Or you can listen to my offer."

Still gazing at the chains, the blademaster said, "I'm listening."

"Come with me to Aerysius. Let me finish what I've started. After that, you can do whatever you desire with me. You have my word. I'll do nothing to resist."

Nigel Swain appeared to be thinking, his eyes considering the beast behind Darien. "I don't know if I trust your word."

"Do you trust mine?" Kyel asked him, stepping forward.

The captain turned to regard him. "You came to me claiming to be an acolyte. That doesn't do much for my trust."

"I was." Reaching into the pocket of his cloak, he withdrew the Soulstone, letting it swing by one of the heavy silver bands. "The stone contained his mother's gift," he admitted. "I put it on and received the Transference in the cell."

He took a deep breath, wondering how far he dared go. Glancing at Naia with a look of apology, he turned back to Swain.

"Darien will no longer be a threat if we close the gateway. The Well of Tears demands a sacrifice in order to seal it. He's known about it all along. It's always been his intent to offer himself."

Naia surged up, demanding, "Is this true?"

Darien nodded, turning to fix Swain with a look of rigid contempt. "When the gateway collapses, my soul will be trapped in the Netherworld. Is that end dignified enough for you?"

Kyel looked down. He had seen this coming all along. He had been hoping Darien had found another way. But there was no other way. Swain was right; one look at the hideous beast confirmed it. Darien had planned this well. He had known from the beginning about the Well and had known the price of giving up his Oath. He had devised a perfect strategy to pay both tabs with a single coin.

Swain never took his eyes from the creature as he grated, "I guess it'll have to do. You've already damned yourself anyway."

Naia's hand shot up and slapped him on the face.

The captain stared at her for a long moment then turned and strode away. Kyel glanced after him, wondering what Swain was going to do. But the sound of Naia's voice made him turn back around.

"Darien, *no,*" she pleaded, reaching out for him.

But the mage jerked his arm out of her grasp. "You should never have come back."

Darien took a lurching step down the stairs, followed by another. Not knowing what else to do, Kyel rushed forward to support him, glancing back at Naia in sympathy. He helped Darien down the last few steps as the priestess stared at his back, looking just as devastated as the surrounding landscape.

They hadn't gone far when the sound of Darien's voice halted him. "Give me the Soulstone."

Kyel looked at him, taken aback. But nevertheless, he drew the medallion from his pocket and handed it over. Darien clutched the stone tightly, holding it against his chest for a moment before dropping his hand. His body trembled with the strain of just staying upright.

Darien reached up and removed Kyel's hand from his arm. "Now, repeat each word I say, exactly as I say it: 'I swear to live in harmony with all of creation.'"

Kyel gulped, realizing his master's intent. Numbly, his lips moved, uttering the phrases of the Oath of Harmony:

I swear to live in harmony with all of creation,
To use my gift with temperance and wisdom;
Always to heal and never to harm,
Or my life will be righteously forfeit.

When he heard the sound of his own voice trail at last into silence, Kyel looked down at his right arm, reveling in the beauty of the shimmering chain that had appeared, graven into his skin by the conviction of his words.

Chapter Thirty-Seven
A Deeper Look

The Cerulean Plains, The Rhen

Kyel pulled back the flap of the tent and ducked as he entered. It was dim, though still bright enough to see by the ambient light. Once inside, he was able to stand upright, letting the flap swing back into place.

Naia turned to look up at him, her veil rendered almost opaque in the poor lighting. She was kneeling on the floor, fingers resting on Darien's hand. The mage was curled at her side in a bundle of covers, for all appearances deep in sleep. A sleep that had lasted for three days.

In all that time, the priestess had never left Darien's side. Kyel had come often to look in, making sure she didn't need anything. Each time he did, he was reminded again of Luther Penthos, the High Priest of Death. Naia's father. Kyel had almost confronted her about it. But then he'd thought better of it.

Her presence stirred his hopes. If anything could possibly save Darien from himself, it was Naia's willing love. From Kyel's perspective, the priestess was the last, best chance Darien had of salvaging his soul before he died.

"How is he?" he asked.

"The same." The priestess sighed. "He still hasn't awakened."

Kyel could tell by the sound of her voice that she was worried. Naia was fiercely protective of him, especially when Swain was around. Whenever the captain came to glance in, Kyel could almost see the priestess' hackles raise. It was a reflection of the way that strange beast looked whenever Kyel came too near it.

"The sleep's normal," Kyel assured her for what seemed like the hundredth time. "He did the same thing the last time he wore himself out."

From its place at Darien's feet, the hideous creature stirred from sleep, awakening with a wide, cavernous yawn. Kyel found the thing revolting. Like Naia, the beast hadn't moved from the vigil it kept at Darien's side. Whenever Kyel came near it, the thing uttered a low growl, its nose wetly quivering. Kyel felt certain the creature would have attacked by now, if it wasn't for Darien's presence holding it at bay.

"What is it?" he asked, giving voice to the question that had echoed so often in his mind.

"A thanacryst."

Kyel glanced at Naia in surprise. She had never mentioned knowing anything about it, and he wondered where she had come by the knowledge. The thing made his skin crawl, especially the way it was always studying him with yearning interest.

"It doesn't like me," he muttered, staring at it.

The priestess nodded, her face pensive. "I think it's hungry. It senses food."

Kyel didn't like the sound of that. He had the feeling there was something inside him the beast desperately wanted to feast upon. The creature turned away, laying its head across Darien's legs with a desolate whimper.

The mage stirred, groaning and tossing in his sleep. Naia's hand moved to fix the blanket that had slipped down. As if comforted by her touch, Darien's face immediately relaxed. Almost, Kyel thought he could see the man he remembered from Greystone Keep.

———

Naia's veiled face was the first thing Darien saw when he opened his eyes. He had been drifting in and out of sleep, each time coming a bit closer to full wakefulness. It was difficult. His body resisted even the most fundamental impulse to stir from the heavy weight of the covers and the soft pallet beneath him. He stretched, for a moment basking in the soothing warmth of Naia's tender smile.

And then he saw the thanacryst. And remembered.

Her smile was anathema, as poisonous to him as deadly nightshade. If he succumbed to it, he would lose every advantage he had gained by consummating his sins between Arden's legs. Then he would be prey once more for the necrators. Even the thanacryst would turn on him to slake its ravenous thirst for the life force of a mage. He would lose the only opportunity he had to prevail against his brother. No. Love was a luxury his impoverished heart could not afford.

He could barely stand to look at Naia after what had passed between Arden and himself. There had been no love in the act, but there had been passion. Desperate passion. It was a requirement. If he hadn't enjoyed the moment to its fullest, then his ploy would have failed utterly. The necrators would have probed his heart and found him still wanting. He would have never regained his perception of the magic field and, in all likelihood, he would be dead by now. That, or on his way to Bryn Calazar in chains. Nevertheless, the guilt plagued him fiercely. He could never expect Naia to understand or to forgive him. Darien doubted he could ever bring himself to ask. He didn't want to.

He had to find a way to make her leave. Her very presence was a corruption, a temptation he knew he didn't have the strength to fight. The part he had left to play was going to be difficult enough. If she stayed, he doubted he could go through with it at all.

"I thought you'd be gone by now," he said. He didn't have to work hard at instilling the cold dispassion that came through in his voice. It was there naturally now, a brittle outgrowth of his twisted soul.

"I'm not leaving you again," she assured him, ignoring the cruelness of his tone. "You need me by your side."

He seemed to recall her saying something similar once before, though he couldn't remember when. Grimly, he shook his head. "This is no place for you."

But Naia just smiled down at him, a poisonous, rapturous look. Taking his hand, she said, "In Auberdale, I asked you to make a decision that was not yours to make. I didn't realize it at the time, but it was my decision all along."

"Naia, that makes no difference—"

"It does," she insisted firmly, her voice ringing out above his own. "I told you I can either be a priestess or your lover, and I've made up my mind."

"No," Darien growled, jerking his hand back and sitting up. "I've made up *my* mind. I don't want you here. Go home."

"Darien—"

"Go home, Naia," he raged coldly, feeling frustrated and lost. "I want you to leave. *Just go.*"

"No."

Her eyes trail down to the thanacryst at his feet. The creature noticed her attention, growling softly as it rolled over on its side in a submissive posture.

Holding fast to her quiet smile, she told him, "I've sat here for three days looking down at this wretched beast. People come and go. It ignores everyone. Yet, strangely, it doesn't seem to like me. It's appalling, really, the way it keeps sniffing me, almost as if it's hungry."

"Perhaps it is," Darien said, staring at the thing.

"It doesn't seem to like Kyel, either. Every time he comes here to look in on you, that creature stares at him and growls dreadfully."

Darien frowned as the meaning of her words slowly sank in.

The priestess continued, "I found myself starting to wonder, isn't it odd that the beast ignores the presence of every other person, with the exception of Kyel and myself? And then I began wondering, what in the world could Kyel and I possibly share in common?"

Any feeling Darien had left was drained away by the time she had finished speaking. He stared at her, his mind and heart utterly bereft. It was impossible. And yet…it also made sense.

"Look at me," he commanded.

Naia did. Her dark eyes were wide and clear

through the fabric of her veil, those eyes that before had consumed his dreams, his hopes and desires. He must believe they held nothing for him now. Naia's eyes were perfect in every way, wide and glinting with the fierce spark of intelligence he found so compelling. Compassion was there, too. Her gaze was suffused with it, along with a caring tenderness that made him ache. But if there was anything else in her eyes, the translucent fabric that hung between them obscured it from his sight.

"Without the veil," he commanded.

What he asked was tantamount to ordering Naia to strip naked there in front of him. Before, it had been a wondrous gift she had shared with him willingly. Now, with all that had transpired, asking her to remove her veil felt like a transgression.

As if to torture him, Naia smiled tenderly as she lifted both hands and drew the fabric back from her face. He found himself confronted by the unconstrained radiance of her gaze, unable to look away. It was wondrous, mesmerizing. Her face held an irresistible solace, an unconditional promise of hope and commitment.

Naia's dark eyes promised him everything he'd ever wanted and more. He could never have any of it.

"Put it back," he whispered.

She obeyed, lowering the veil back into place. As she did, it seemed as if the last light faded quietly from his world. He looked down, squeezing his eyes shut against the pain. Her presence was torture enough. He never should have allowed this. He couldn't stand it.

"I have the potential, don't I?" Her words stirred across the bleakness of his heart.

It took him a moment to answer her. "I never saw it before."

But it was there, undeniably. He didn't even need to test her to be certain. There could be no mistaking it.

"Perhaps you didn't want to see it," Naia said. "Or perhaps you weren't looking deep enough."

But he already knew why he'd never noticed it there before. Her veil obscured the shine of the potential in her eyes. And the two times he had seen her face in its absence, his mind had been on other things. Near her, he was blinded to even the blatantly obvious. Her presence befuddled his senses, fouled his edge. Another potent reason why she had to go.

"This changes nothing," he said.

"Yes, it does. Kyel is no longer your acolyte. You need someone who can inherit your gift."

There, she was wrong. The power within him was a monstrous legacy too potent for any one mage. He would never condemn her to such a fate. It would be too much for her, even as brightly as she burned. He could never do that to her, even if he had a choice. Which he didn't.

"I'm sorry, Naia, but my gift dies with me."

Her face paled, her expression faltering. With a look of desperation, she fiercely shook her head. "I won't accept that. You always find a way."

He whispered, "Not this time."

"You're not even going to try, are you?".

He wasn't. There was no point. "You heard Swain. Mages were never meant to exist Unbound. Look at me. I'm living proof of the reason for the Oath."

"There has to be a way," she insisted. "Can't you just say the words again?"

"Once forsaken, thc Oath can never be reaffirmed."

Naia's brow creased in frustration, her eyes wet and glistening. "So you're just giving up?"

Her grief only served to provoke him. This was exactly why she had to leave. Now. Before the sight of her tears softened his heart. He told her in a tone devoid of mercy:

"Now do you understand why you have to go? We have no chance, you and me. No future. *Look at that thing.*" He nodded at the thanacryst. "That is my soul, Naia. Do you know how I came by that creature? I killed its former mistress—right after I lay with her."

He ignored her sharp gasp and pressed on. "I don't deserve you, and you sure as hell deserve better than me. Now, take your things and get out. *Leave.*"

She was sobbing. Her shoulders were shaking, her hands pressed against her face over the fabric of her veil. Darien watched, unmoved. She could spill every last tear in her body, but it was better this way. Much better.

Still, she didn't go.

In the end, it was he who left the tent, the

thanacryst jogging dutifully behind in his wake.

Kyel was bored. There was nothing to do in the encampment, at least nothing for a mage. The soldiers seemed busy enough, scurrying here and there about their duties. The camp of Faukravar's army had an entirely different feel to it than Emmery's. It was easy to tell a Chamsbrey soldier without looking at the uniform. They all seemed to be going through the motions of their various labors in a daze, their efforts halfhearted. There were far fewer men wearing black and violet uniforms than blue and white. What Chamsbrey did have was a disproportionate supply of tents. Counting tents, Kyel had figured that Faukravar's army was now roughly half the size it had been before the morning of Black Solstice.

That's what they were calling it now. He'd heard the words often throughout both camps. It seemed apt. Black for the clouds that had darkened the sky, black for the charred earth beneath Orien's summit. Black for the lives that had been so cruelly ripped out of life, both friend and Enemy alike. And black for the atrocious means used to attain such a one-sided victory.

He knew what to call it now, the awesome and horrendous undertaking Darien had performed alone on the summit of the crag. According to the priestess, Darien had created a grand resonance, something conceived of in theory but never before employed. Not even Orien himself had worked such appalling devastation. Darien's desperate act on the summit had far surpassed even the most notorious feat of Aerysius' most infamous Grand Master. Orien couldn't have even accomplished such an act; he'd been only fifth tier.

Only.

The sound of raised voices startled Kyel out of his thoughts, and he hurried forward out of curiosity. As he moved past rows of tents, men noticed his cloak and stepped away from him with looks of fear. Kyel didn't blame them. What they had seen on Black Solstice had given them more than enough reason to fear the sight of a mage.

Rounding a group of tents, Kyel saw the cause of the commotion. To his surprise, he recognized Nigel Swain standing beside General Blandford in what looked like a heated argument with the King of Chamsbrey.

The King was seething, face red and eyes scalding. One white-gloved hand was fingering the pommel of the sword he wore at his hip, the other twisting one of the points of his goatee.

"Who do you think you are, to presume to gainsay me?" the King growled.

Swain stood in a fighting stance, his body at an angle to the King. He said, "There's another army headed this way, and I'm not about to let you just pack up your toys and leave."

Kyel frowned, walking closer. Swain's words shocked him, the vehemence in them nearly as outrageous as the news of another army. If the captain wasn't careful, he was going to wind up with his head on a block.

"How dare you," spat Faukravar, face turning an even deeper shade of red. "General Blandford, I want this man scourged!"

Blandford looked at the King dully, lifting one of his long-whiskered eyebrows. "I'm sorry, Your Grace, but my Lady Queen would be most put out if I consented to scourge her fiancé."

Kyel stopped in his tracks. Looking at Nigel Swain, he felt like hitting himself over the head for not seeing it before. Romana had all but deferred to the captain, back at the palace in Rothscard. And Swain had been passionate in his devotion to her.

Faukravar's face melted through several shades of red into pasty white. "What?"

"That's right." Swain grinned smugly.

Faukravar's gloved hand dropped from his goatee as he struggled to compose himself. He said, "It would seem that Romana has even worse taste in men than she does in wine."

Swain shook his head. "My Queen has excellent taste in wine. She just has better sense than to waste a good vintage on a coward like you."

Gasps issued from the small crowd of onlookers as Faukravar's face turned a glaring purple. Tugging the glove from his hand, he threw it down in the snow between them, visibly trembling in outrage. Swain stared down at the white glove, eyes coolly considering.

It was time to intervene, Kyel decided. Surging forward, he bent down and retrieved the King's glove, holding it up and offering it back to him. Faukravar's eyes took in the glove then moved to linger on Kyel's black cloak. His face looked ready to burst from the amount of blood that engorged it.

"I'd take it, if I were you," Kyel urged him, indicating the glove in his outstretched hand. "Unless you have a champion eager to duel a Guild blademaster."

Faukravar stared at the glove, stared at Swain, then glared at Kyel. His lips curled, revealing a set of chipped and yellowed teeth that had the look of worn daggers. He snatched the glove out of Kyel's hand and stalked off, followed by a small group of lackeys, muttering something about "contemptible mages" under his breath. When he was gone, Kyel turned back to face a still-grinning Nigel Swain.

"What's this about another army?" he demanded.

The grin disappeared from the captain's face. "Thirty thousand, coming from the Gap of Amberlie. They'll be here by evening." He sighed, blowing a greasy lock of hair back from his mouth. "It seems Darien was right, after all. They'll just keep coming."

"Rider approaching!"

Kyel turned at the sound of the outcry, glancing across the blackened terrain. He saw the exhausted horse before he saw the rider, recognizing the man from the color of his cloak. It was the first gray cloak he had seen south of the Pass of Lor-Gamorth. The rider was from Greystone Keep, and by the looks of it, badly injured.

Kyel ran toward him, Swain following at his heels as he captured the spent horse by its bridle. The soldier was already sliding out of his saddle when the captain caught him up in his arms, easing the man to the ground.

Kyel leaned over him, placing a hand on his chest and desperately trying to probe the man with his mind, the way he had seen Darien do before. An image came to him, fleeting and unintelligible. But his eyes saw enough to tell that the man was dying. His face already wore a pale mask of death, the shirt beneath his mail vest saturated with blood.

"Archer?" the soldier muttered weakly, looking perplexed.

Kyel frowned, staring down at the man, trying to see under the caked blood and grime that splattered his face. He thought he might recognize him but couldn't be certain. It didn't matter anyway. His own name was the last word the soldier would ever utter.

Kyel grimaced as Swain bent down to close the dead man's eyes. If only he knew enough of his gift to do something useful with it, he might have been able to save him. Darien could have done it. But Darien wasn't there.

"What's this?" Swain whispered.

Looking down, Kyel saw what the captain referred to. The dead man's hand clasped a piece of rolled parchment that was stained brown with dried blood. Swain had to fight the man's death grip to retrieve it. Unrolling the scroll, he scanned the page harshly before shaking his head and crushing it into Kyel's fist.

"Here," he grunted. "I can't read."

Kyel found himself staring at the captain in mute disbelief. If he was going to be a royal consort, Kyel figured the man had better learn how to read. Turning to the wadded scroll, he uncrumpled it, smoothing it against the palm of his hand. Letting his eyes trace over the neat, embellished script, he felt his heart lurch to a halt in his chest. He had to start reading the note all over again, taking it from the top. The last line he scanned at least five times before he finally believed it.

"Well?" Swain pressed. "What does it say?"

Kyel felt too stunned to speak. His hand violently clenched the parchment, wadding it up into a ball in his fist.

"It's a summons," he said finally. "Darien's presence is requested at a parley tonight under flag of truce. It's signed 'Zavier Renquist.'"

Darien backed away from the crowd of onlookers that lingered over the body of Wade Tarpen, a soldier from Greystone Keep he'd known from the two years he'd spent there. He had arrived too late to save the man. Intent on the corpse, no one paid him any mind. No one noticed as he quickly bent to retrieve a wadded ball of parchment off the ground and then silently slip away.

Without his cloak, he was harder to recognize, and few people did. They were used to marking him by the white emblem of the prime warden. But the cloak was gone now. After the transgression he had committed on its fabric, he hadn't been able to put that cloak back on. Instead he had wrapped it around Arden's body and sent it over the cliff with her vile remains.

He was clothed only in his black breeches and a shirt that he'd borrowed from one of the empty tents, his baldric tossed over it. The shirt was part of an officer's uniform, the insignia of Chamsbrey embroidered on the breast, bars of rank stitched onto the shoulders. The fabric wasn't nearly warm enough. He shivered as he strode toward the place where he'd bid the thanacryst wait.

The creature was still there, stationed in the exact spot he'd left it in front of an abandoned tent. The beast loped over to him, froths of spittle flying from its jowls. Its green eyes glinted banefully as it stared up at him, looking expectant.

"Ceise," Darien whispered, spreading his fingers at his side.

The thanacryst obeyed, falling in to heel beside him as he walked toward the margin of the camp. With the beast at his side, Darien no longer had the luxury of anonymity. Men stared, first at the thanacryst and then at him, with expressions of fear and repugnance.

The mood of the men toward him had altogether changed. It was easy to see why; Chamsbrey's army had been decimated. From what he could judge, there were perhaps a little over half the number of soldiers as had left with him from Tol-Ranier. Still, it was better than he had anticipated. Wellingford had heeded him well and had managed to keep a good number of his men out of the eye of the vortex. The boy had turned out to be a decent commander.

He trudged by a group of soldiers lingering around a fire. Darien felt their eyes upon him, heard the quiet, whispered words uttered behind his back. He could almost smell their hatred and fear. They blamed him. They were lucky to be alive to blame him. If he'd held back even a fraction, they would all be dead. He almost felt like turning to confront them, their reproach kindling a simmering fury.

As if sensing his mood, the thanacryst growled. Darien dropped his hand to steady it, feeling the beast's wet tongue licking the tips of his fingers. As he moved out of earshot of the group, he heard one of the soldiers mutter the word "darkmage" under his breath.

So that's what they thought of him, did they? Darien felt his bile rising as his temper cooled to an arctic chill. He groped for the solace of the magic field, tugging at it sharply with the full force of his mind. He took in too much, too quickly. The excess energy bled off his body in crackling blue tongues that drew stares from everyone nearby. Soldiers gaped at him, backing away. Darien paid them no heed, suffused with the soothing ecstasy of the field.

Comforted, he released it slowly.

He turned and stared out into the blackened ground that spread before him. The amount of devastation was overwhelming, beyond anything he had expected. Everything within the eye of the vortex had been reduced to char and ashes. The land itself seemed tortured.

Orien's Finger was blackened. The stone had a glassy, molten appearance. The summit looked dangerously detached, shoved to the side and leaning precariously atop its dark pedestal. He had been lucky that it hadn't given way completely.

The crunch of boots told him Wellingford was approaching. Darien had the distinctive sound of the boy's footsteps memorized. He was vaguely surprised that anyone would have the temerity to seek him out. He pretended not to notice the young man's approach, letting his general come to stand at his side unacknowledged.

"Prime Warden." Wellingford's voice was hesitant. "I didn't know you were recovered. Are you sure you're well enough to be about?"

Darien felt a mild stir of resentment that anyone would care about his health. Hadn't the boy looked out on the devastation that surrounded him? Hadn't he seen with his own eyes the injury that had been dealt here? And the dead; could he not hear the silent screams of the tortured dead that lingered in the air? So much horror could never occur in a place without leaving a lasting imprint behind. A thousand years from now, the grief of those who had died here might still be heard, a telltale whisper on the wind.

"How many total casualties?" Darien asked, wanting a number he could use to scourge his soul.

"Estimates are over a hundred thousand," Wellingford replied after a moment's hesitation. "Six thousand of our own."

Darien stared out across the blackened land, searing the numbers into his mind. "Have there been any survivors from Greystone Keep?"

"Only three, Prime Warden. All infantrymen."

Darin bowed his head, overcome. Devlin Craig had been the staunchest, most loyal friend he'd ever known. And though he still held some resentment toward Garret Proctor, Darien understood him better now. Neither man had deserved so cruel an end. Craig especially; the captain had risked his own life to save him from Arden's fire, only to be immolated by his own.

"What is the situation with this third army?" he asked in a deadened voice.

"Our scouts have reported thirty thousand on the march, coming by way of the Gap of Amberlie."

Darien nodded. His brother's work, again. "There's a darkmage with them," he informed Wellingford. "At least one. You'll need to meet them outside the eye or be faced with a magical assault."

"Where will you be?" his young general asked, looking at him anxiously.

Darien raised his hand, pointing toward the slopes of the Craghorns, his eyes seeking out the summit of the highest peak. The one surrounded by a faint green nimbus that was barely visible through a veil of white haze.

"I'll be up there. If I can seal the Well of Tears in time, it ought to neutralize their darkmage."

Wellingford looked at him in mute incomprehension, but Darien didn't explain. Instead, he said, "We'll meet tonight in the command tent to discuss strategy. Come with your officers at the turn of Third Watch. I want the officers from Emmery there as well."

"Aye, Prime Warden." Wellingford sounded doubtful. As well he should.

Darien turned his stare back to the devastated earth, imprinting its scorched features on his mind. He asked, "Have you ever seen the Black Lands, Wellingford?"

"No. I haven't."

"Well, now you can say you have."

He found Kyel and Swain together, sitting by a fire in front of a blue tent. Neither man saw him approaching. Swain looked occupied with honing his blade, while Kyel seemed to be contenting himself with picking lint off his black cloak. The cloak suited him, Darien decided. It made him appear taller, stronger. More confident. Or perhaps it wasn't the cloak at all.

The boy he had met at Greystone Keep had grown. He wasn't a boy anymore, Darien realized sadly. His innocence had been the price of those chains. It was a shame. Kyel's innocence was something Darien had always admired and even envied.

Swain glanced up and scowled. The noise of the whetstone became a shrill scrape, grinding down the length of his blade. The sound made Darien's neck prickle. He understood the threat.

"I'd like to speak with Kyel. Alone," he added, glaring at Swain.

The man shrugged, slamming his blade home in its scabbard as he rose to leave. He kicked out at the thanacryst as he stalked past, but the beast didn't seem to mind. Its attention was riveted on Kyel, its ears laid back and hackles raised.

"Theanoch!" Darien snapped at it. The thanacryst whined, slobbering furiously.

Kyel frowned up at him. His hands fell away from his cloak, the markings on his wrists gleaming metallically in the sunlight. Darien stared down at them, his interest captivated. He had found another thing about Kyel to envy.

"You're awake." Kyel sounded surprised, but not necessarily pleased.

Darien gestured toward the tent behind him, hoping that the pain he felt didn't show on his face. The young man had every right to hate him, just the same as everyone else. But it hurt, all the same.

"It's time for your last lesson," Darien said, avoiding his eyes as he moved past him into the tent.

Inside, he waited for Kyel. He wished things could have been different. In a different world, Kyel might have been his friend. In a different world, he could have married Naia, even raised a family. In a different world, his hands would not be stained in a river of blood, wiped dry on a bed of ashes. His conscience would be clean. He could be the man he'd always wanted to be, was meant to be. Not this.

But there was no other world, no easy escape. Darien staggered as he lowered himself to the ground, reaching out his hand to steady himself. Kyel stared down at him in concern. The thanacryst in the doorway sounded as if it were purring.

"You're not well," Kyel observed.

Darien ignored him, gesturing at the ground. "Have a seat."

"Darien, you need to listen to me—"

"Sit down."

Kyel obeyed, but his expression was anything but compliant. When he was settled, Darien considered him a moment before saying, "You put on the Soulstone against my command."

Kyel shrugged. "You knew all along I was going to do it."

It was true. Nevertheless, he couldn't let the slip in obedience go unmentioned. Kyel was no longer his acolyte, technically, but he was still far from being ready to assume the mantle of a full Master. There was little Darien could do for him now. The remainder would be up to Kyel himself. He could choose to make himself as great as he wanted or settle for much less. It all depended on how much effort he was willing to invest.

"I figured Romana would leave you little choice," Darien admitted.

Kyel scowled and shook his head. "I'm so tired of your games. That's all I've had, ever since I agreed to become your acolyte. I don't know the first thing about using my gift. All you've ever done is set hurdles in my path, then sit back and watch me go over them. The vortex, the Temple of Wisdom, Romana…all just more of your games. I'm tired of them. I don't wish to play anymore."

Darien sighed. "Whether you agree with my methods or not, you've learned from them."

"*What?* What have I learned?"

"For one thing, you would have never stood up to me like this a month ago. And I wager you gave Romana quite a headache."

Kyel glared at him. Slowly, his anger seemed to fade, and he dropped his stare to the ground.

"I was in awe of you," he said. "When we first met, back at Greystone Keep. You were everything I wanted to be. You seemed to know so much, you were so confident, so committed to what you believed in. But now…I don't know if it's losing your Oath, or the Bloodquest, or if your gift's just eating you up inside. Perhaps it's everything. But you're not the same anymore. I think you're sick, Darien. The truth is, you scare me."

Darien nodded, reflecting on Kyel's words. More gently, he said, "Then learn from my example. Always hold to what you believe in, fix your sight on what's most important, and you'll do fine. Everything else doesn't matter at all." With a quiet smile, he added, "I wish I could have done so many things differently. Now, it's too late."

"But it's not too late," Kyel insisted. "Forget about Aidan. Leave the Well of Tears open, like Swain said. Just go someplace quiet and marry Naia. Settle down in a village and make a life for yourself. Give yourself a chance to heal."

The idea was tempting. But he shook his head. "No. We're leaving for Aerysius on the morrow."

"You're making a mistake."

"It won't be my first." He left the implied corollary unsaid. "Now. I came to tell you one last thing. You can do almost anything you want with your gift, within reason. There is a natural order that governs everything. Even magic obeys it. If you know how something works, then you know how to manipulate it. But you must be utterly committed to the task. Never mire yourself in doubt.

"And you need to broaden your knowledge. When this is over, set yourself to the task of study. Learn everything you can about everything there is. Only then will you truly earn those chains."

Chapter Thirty-Eight
An Unexpected Offer

The Cerulean Plains, The Rhen

The evening was clear and furtively still as Darien directed his horse across the threshold of the vortex. Nose to the ground, the thanacryst loped along at his side, its enormous paws making deep tracks in the snow.

Darien felt reassured by its vile presence. The beast was small comfort, but its strange devotion was the only protection he retained. Under the torrent of the vortex, the solace of the magic field was once again denied him. Into the night he rode alone, unarmed, and utterly powerless. It was a despicable feeling, but necessary. All weapons were proscribed by the ancient conventions of parley.

In his right hand, Darien clutched a white banner improvised from a torn bedsheet. The strip of cloth was much longer than it was broad, and he carried it draped over his hand, its frayed edges trailing almost to the ground. The banner was large enough to be seen from a distance. Darien could only hope that any sentries ahead would see it before loosing their shafts.

His life now depended exclusively on the honor of a demon.

He rode in thoughtful silence, reflecting on his decision to obey the crumpled summons in his pocket. He'd convinced himself the parley was a necessary risk. He needed to look Zavier Renquist in the face and take the measure of his enemy. But now that he was fully committed, Darien realized he had been prompted by an underlying motivation much more reckless in nature: he was fascinated by the man.

In legend, Zavier Renquist had been the greatest Prime Warden the Lyceum had ever produced, vastly potent and passionately committed to duty. Renquist's treason had been as unexpected as it was devastating. Meeting the man face to face, Darien thought perhaps he could gain some insight into what had driven the most esteemed Prime Warden in all of history to become the most reviled.

And it burned, the desire to know what the man wanted of him.

Ahead, there was movement in the snow. Darien slowed his horse, raising the banner to be certain it was duly marked. Squinting, he made out the forms of four riders approaching, their armor as dark as the mounts they sat astride. As they drew nearer, he saw that the men wore full battle plate, tassels swaying from the tips of their spears. If he were in any other place, and these were any other soldiers, he would have taken their strange presence for an honor guard.

He could hear the jingle of their tack as they approached. Darien waited, the white cloth held in his outstretched hand. The thanacryst stood by his side in the snow, head cocked and ears erect. Its grisly tail began to wag, hesitant at first, then eagerly.

"Theanoch," Darien hissed at it. The creature obeyed instantly, whining as great globs of slobber dripped from its mouth.

One of the soldiers reined his mount around, backing the horse up and drawing abreast of him. Darien peered into the grate of the helm, trying to make out the dim features of the face beneath. He raised the banner in his hand, offering it out across the distance between them. The Enemy soldier lifted a chain-gloved hand and accepted the fragile badge of truce.

"Demas tur narghul, nan ledro." Darien said. *I have come, as agreed.*

The soldier tipped his dark helm approvingly. *"Nan ledro.* Come. Follow."

The man jerked the reins out of Darien's hand, riding forward with them held high enough to clear the Tarkendar's head. The others closed in around him, encircling him tightly as the first soldier led his gelding forward through the snow.

He sat straight in the saddle, wondering about the significance implied by the tight formation the soldiers were assuming. He had come willingly enough. They had no reason to fear he would try to bolt. It was almost as though the men were arranged defensively, forming a living shield around him.

Darien wondered what they felt he needed protection from. Perhaps the discipline of the Enemy was faltering, if Renquist feared betrayal from within his own ranks. Of course, Darien had to consider, he was personally responsible for the slaughter of a hundred thousand of their fellows. That could breed resentment despite any amount of discipline, in any army. Renquist was probably just being prudent.

Darien found himself missing the comfort of the magic field with a desperate sense of urgency. And he missed his sword, the familiar weight of the baldric on his shoulder. Even with his guard, Darien felt more vulnerable than since he'd entered the vortex. He couldn't stop his eyes from wandering over the snow, alert for sign of treachery. The soldiers that surrounded him rode in silence, but he noted that all four men were examining the surrounding terrain just as avidly as he was.

Behind him, the thanacryst whined. Darien had forgotten it was there, faithfully jogging along on the heels of his mount. Every so often it paused, scenting the air, and uttered an eager growl.

They crossed a long, crescent-shaped fold in the land where a frozen stream ran its course. They followed the streambed until a dark object came into view. It was a pavilion, Darien realized, erected in a solitary location at the summit of a snow-draped knoll. Darien took heart in the sight. He'd feared he was being led into the thick of the Enemy encampment. But he also felt a wary sense of apprehension. It seemed Renquist was taking no chances.

They led his horse up the hill to the front of the pavilion, where the soldiers that ringed him halted together as one. Darien dismounted as two figures emerged from the tent. They were the first men of the Enemy he had ever seen unhelmed, with the sole exception of the dead. Both wore long robes of the same indigo blue, an insignia embroidered on the breast. Darien frowned, trying to make out the features of the emblem, but his view was blocked by a soldier who stepped in front of him.

"This way." The man gestured with his hand.

As Darien moved toward the entrance of the tent, he managed a glance at the two robed men guarding the doorway. The insignia on their chests glared at him, igniting a spark of outrage as he recognized it.

It was the Silver Star, or something so similar that it made little difference. Darien felt a cold rage in his chest. The two men were mages. That they would dare emblazon themselves with the star of fallen Aerysius took him beyond ire, well past contempt.

One of the two, a dark-haired man with a cruel scar on his face, glared at him fiercely. Darien almost missed the significance of the white cloak draped over his robe, the cloak of a Prime Warden. Darien stopped, staring at the man in patent astonishment. There was only one person it could possibly be: Cyrus Krane, ancient Prime Warden of Aerysius, now one of Renquist's fell companions.

His guards stopped short of the tent's entrance. The two mages stepped forward, Krane's eyes coldly examining him, scouring up his body from his boots, lingering on Darien's eyes. He didn't appear to like what he saw.

In contrast, the red-haired man was wearing an almost amiable expression on his face. For some reason, he reminded Darien of Corban Henley, and it was more than just the color of his beard. The man had Henley's way about him, a cool and deliberate air. He nodded slightly, a look of intrigue in his eyes.

"Byron Connel," he gave his name without preamble. "This is Cyrus Krane. Come inside. We've been expecting you."

He turned, sweeping back a flap of fabric and holding it open for Darien as he ducked to enter. Krane fell in behind them, the hem of his cloak rustling over the snow-covered ground. The warm air that hit his face made Darien feel almost relieved.

Within, the interior was dark, lit only by softly glowing lanterns set about on a floor covered with lavish rugs. Otherwise, the tent was empty. There was no furniture and, more disturbing, no one waiting within.

Darien paused, his frown deepening as he felt a sudden stab of panic. He had expected to find Renquist inside the tent. Casting a sidelong glare at Connel, he turned to find that Krane had halted, bodily blocking the only exit.

"Is this how you honor a badge of truce?" Darien demanded, taking a step back away from the two demons. He should have been more afraid. But the anger he felt overshadowed even his fear.

"Be at ease," issued a low voice from behind him.

Darien spun toward the sound. There had been no one there. But suddenly, inexplicably, there was. Zavier Renquist stood and moved toward him, emerging from the shadows of a corner.

Darien stared, too frozen to draw breath. He felt Renquist's stare moving over him. He found himself unable to do anything but stand and be measured, feeling that his every nuance was being probed and exposed.

Renquist paced slowly forward, hands clasped behind his back. He was tall and exceptionally broad of shoulder, his figure imposing. He wore his long, brown hair pulled back from his face, gathered in a braid at the crown of his head. The white cloak of a Prime Warden hung down his back. He had the look of a raptor, one poised in the air with claws and wings extended.

Shoulders relaxing, he said at last, "You're not remotely what I was expecting. Come. Have a seat." He extended his hand, indicating the rugs thrown over the ground as he lowered himself down upon them, cross-legged.

Darien struggled to collect himself as he sat across from him. Renquist had caught him off-guard. He had obeyed the summons thinking it an opportunity to evaluate the nature of this legendary man, but instead had become himself the object of scrutiny. Darien tried to swallow the rigid lump that was rising in his throat, threatening to claw its way out. Now that it was too late, he realized he had made a serious error in judgment.

He should never have come.

Trying his best to maintain his composure, Darien leaned forward and stared unblinking into the ancient demon's eyes. What he saw there was harrowing. Renquist's eyes were sinister pools of shadow that perfectly mirrored his own.

"What were you expecting?" he asked.

"A twisted and pathetic wretch like your brother. But you're nothing like him, I see."

Darien hesitated before stating, "No. We are nothing alike."

Renquist's eyes bored into him, probing. It was as though he were considering Darien with sinister intent and was only too pleased at what he was finding. He leaned back, knitting his fingers together, his elbows resting on his knees.

"The truth is, I find myself rather fascinated by you," Renquist admitted. "You are the first mage in all of history to ever successfully employ a grand resonance. And it seems you have bested one of my own. I take it that is Arden's thanacryst?"

Darien followed his stare, finding the beast curled up behind him in a corner of the tent. He gave a slight nod, wondering what Renquist had to be implying from his possession of the creature.

To his astonishment, the ancient Prime Warden's smile broadened. "I thought I recognized it. An unusual pet, for one such as yourself."

Darien shrugged. "It seems to like me well enough."

"So it seems," uttered Renquist. "Though I must caution you: thanacrysts have a tendency to turn when you least expect it. They make unreliable pets, at best."

"I'll take my chances."

Renquist nodded, looking down at his hands. "I brought you here to make a proposition. My army is twice the strength of your own. I still have six mages at my disposal, along with some unusual pets of my own. Orien's Circle has been reduced to a lump of slag by your abuse of it. I was up there myself this morning. I've seen it. You are left with very few options."

Darien shook his head. "If that were the case, then you wouldn't have bothered with this parley."

The demon's stare was beginning to unsettle him. Darien could feel himself becoming unnerved, cold beads of perspiration collecting on his brow.

Renquist raised a hand. "What I propose is this: I will withdraw my forces back into the Black Lands and agree to refrain from hostility for a period of two years. All I ask is that you agree to my terms."

Darien asked suspiciously, "What are your terms?"

"You. I want you to surrender yourself to me."

Darien glared at him contemptuously. He had seen this coming. It made perfect sense. If he was taken out of the equation, then Renquist could afford those two years to sit back, bide his time, and replenish his armies. He would not want to risk another Black Solstice.

"I'm no fool. My father was murdered in your fires, and Arden already gave me a taste of your flames. I have no desire to repeat the experience."

But Renquist only smiled. "It is not my intent to kill you. You have impressed me, and that is no easy thing to do." He paused for a moment, his gaze slipping to the side as if in thought. Then his eyes snapped back to lock on Darien's with rigid intensity.

"What I propose is this: I want you to accompany me back to Bryn Calazar as my apprentice. I seem to be down a mage, and our number has ever been Eight. You would make a formidable *nach'tier.*"

Darien blinked, taken completely aback. *Nach'tier* was an ancient term for darkmage. Renquist was offering him Arden's place at his side. He would make a demon of him, a minion of Chaos such as himself. Darien was utterly unprepared for the suggestion. The very notion made his skin crawl. Yet, at the same time, it was almost flattering.

Behind him, the thanacryst purred.

"No."

It was only a moment's hesitation, but Renquist hadn't missed it. Black eyes gleaming, he seemed to be savoring the gloating smile on his lips. "Why not? You are almost there already. I can sense it in you. It would take only the lightest brush of a finger to push you over the edge."

His words were like a whispered omen of damnation. Darien felt them slithering over his skin like the cold coils of a serpent. He couldn't deny the truth of those words, which made it all the more critical that he deny them urgently.

But there was no conviction in his tone as Darien mumbled softly, "I'm nothing like you."

He felt dazed, the cold sweat on his brow now running in icy rivulets down his face. The dim lighting of the tent seemed suddenly darker, the air cold and atrociously stale. The sound of his own shivering breath hissed like a gale in his ears.

The smile on Renquist's face was almost fatherly. "We have so much in common, you and I. A thousand years ago, I sold my soul for a price that, to this day, I've never regretted paying. Tell me, Darien. What is your price?"

Darien squeezed his eyes shut as he fought to gather his scattered thoughts, whispering, "You could never afford it."

"Can't I?" Renquist challenged ominously. "Then let me sweeten my offer. In addition to the withdrawal of my forces, my Master has agreed to relinquish the spirit of Meiran Withersby, reuniting her soul and body, and returning her to life. It is within His power. What do you say? Commit your soul to Xerys. With one simple word, you would save thousands of soldiers under your command and give them a chance to live to fight another day. And you would be saving the mother of your only child from an eternity of despair and pain."

Renquist's words hit with the force of a deathblow.

It was impossible. Meiran would have found some way to get word to him. But he had been at the Front two long years, where news was scarce. Only two birds had arrived from Aerysius the entire time he had been there, both from his mother's private coops.

Darien whispered, "I have no child."

"That's not what your brother told me."

"Aidan's lying." He silently pleaded it was so, even as he knew it was too much to hope for.

"You have a son, Darien," Renquist insisted. "His name is Gerald, after your father."

"No...it can't be."

Even as he said the words, he realized he was wrong. Aidan was simply not creative enough to come up with something so clever. His brother had a knack for taking the ideas of others and corrupting them to fit his own particular needs. But actually devising something so perfectly cruel? It was as beyond him as the stars.

Aidan would have known that he would never accept Renquist's offer for any advantage to himself. But this was about Meiran. For months, he had dreamed of her, sometimes falling, sometimes screaming, sometimes writhing in tortured agony. At other times, she was simply smiling at him, the green light of hell shining in her eyes. She had meant everything to him. She had been the singular passion of his life.

And, together, they had made a son.

Aidan had chosen the one leverage he knew Darien could never endure. He had passed along the information knowing it was exactly the fatal brush Renquist would need to send him hurling over the edge.

But Darien had already taken that step himself. At the cliff's edge in Aerysius, he had looked his brother in the eye and denied him then.

Somehow, Darien found the strength to stand. Staggering, he backed away, shaking his head. As he moved to duck under the low opening of the tent, he heard Renquist's voice behind him:

"I'll leave the offer open. Should you decide to change your mind, you'll know where to find me."

Chapter Thirty-Nine
The Edge

The Cerulean Plains, The Rhen

Kyel was tired of waiting. And he was growing increasingly apprehensive as the long minutes dragged by. Everyone was, especially Swain. The blademaster had a look on his face like curdled death, his oily hair stringing forward into his eyes. The interior of the command tent seemed almost charged with the compressed tension in the air. Even Wellingford was pacing, every so often slapping a pair of white gloves against his thigh with a resounding *crack.*

"We're here to discuss strategy," Blandford said finally. "Let's get on with it."

Wellingford shook his head. "We can't hold this meeting without the Prime Warden. We need his input. He told me there is a darkmage with the approaching army, and only he knows how to counter them."

Swain grimaced at Wellingford's use of Darien's self-proclaimed title. But that was nothing compared to the fury that sprang to his eyes at the mention of the word 'darkmage.'

Fixing his glare on Kyel, Swain demanded, *"You told him about Renquist's summons?"*

At the mention of that name, the tent fell abruptly silent. Kyel glanced around to find every man there standing with faces paled in astonishment. Wellingford stood shaking his head, lips moving soundlessly. Even Blandford's usual composure was shattered. Emmery's general slouched with mouth slack and eyes glazed as if poleaxed.

"No!" Kyel gasped. "I tossed it away!"

"Where by all the graceless gods did you toss it?"

Kyel's mind spun furiously. He didn't know what he'd done with the note. He remembered crumbling it up in his hand, but after that…

"I don't know," he admitted. "I can't remember."

Swain's oath was lost in the clamor that exploded in the tent. Everyone was shouting, bandying words like "Renquist" and "darkmage" in panicked voices. Things were deteriorating rapidly, Kyel realized, taking in the faces of the officers around him. Someone was going to have to get the men back under control.

He was about to raise his hands to get their attention when the commotion suddenly silenced. Every man in the room stood rigid, attention rapt on something behind him. Kyel turned to look over his shoulder and froze, taking in the form of a man who had appeared behind them in the tent's entrance.

It was Darien. But not the Darien he knew.

The mage's face was ghostly white, eyes squinting and bloodshot. He stood as if wracked, arms clutched across his chest, shivering. His black hair was spilled over his face, but nothing could hide the look of tortured devastation written there. His eyes were dull and blank, absent even a trace of the presence that was his signature. He looked well past grief, well beyond torment. To Kyel, he looked like a man utterly destroyed.

Swain surged toward him first, grabbing Darien by the arm and swinging him around, maneuvering him out of the tent. Kyel followed, only dimly noticing Wellingford stepping in behind to block the exit. Outside, he followed as Swain dragged Darien into a space between tents. There, the captain seized him violently by the shoulders.

Kyel ran toward them, fearing that Swain was

going to start tearing into him by the look on his face. But as Kyel stopped behind him, he realized Swain's strong grip was the only thing keeping Darien standing. His knees were slack, his body wilting like a droughted stem.

Swain gripped Darien's face, demanding, *"What did he do to you?"*

Darien didn't respond. He just stood staring dimly into Swain's eyes, sweat trickling down his brow. Kyel looked on as the captain increased the pressure of his fingers, squeezing them mercilessly into Darien's skin.

"By the whoring mother of the gods—*what did he want?"*

With a growl that sounded like an injured wolf, Darien broke away from him, twisting his face out of the blademaster's grasp. He bent over, hands on his knees, glaring up at Swain through the sweat-plastered strands of his hair. His eyes were red pools of scalding hatred.

"He wants me."

It took Kyel a moment to understand Darien's whispered words. His voice was so low and broken it was almost unintelligible.

Swain demanded, "What terms did he offer?"

The Sentinel ignored him.

"His terms, Darien!"

Without looking at him, the mage drew himself up and uttered flatly, "He offered to withdraw."

"What else?"

Darien looked at him, eyes imploring. To Kyel's horror, he saw the mage's eyes were filled with tears that spilled freely down his cheeks. The sight struck Kyel with alarm. In the entire time he had known him, through every trial and every sorrow, he had never once seen Darien break down.

"He told me I have a son...and he told me he could bring Meiran back."

Swain spun away from him with an oath.

Renquist had found the one thing certain to tear Darien apart, the one temptation his nature would never allow him to refuse. Yet, somehow, he had. Somehow, Darien had scraped up just enough strength to refuse him and walk away from that meeting.

But, Kyel realized with dismay, Renquist may have achieved his goal, nonetheless. Darien would never be able to bear the guilt that decision had cost him. One look at his anguished face made it clear the mage believed he'd damned Meiran all over again, just as surely as if he'd thrown her into the pit himself.

And the part about his son...Kyel groaned. What was worse, Darien thinking he had a son somewhere that he could have chosen to bring a mother home to? Or the closure of knowing the boy was dead?

If it were his own child, Kyel decided, he would rather know the truth.

"You don't have a son, Darien," he said softly.

"What?" The Sentinel stared at him in bleary confusion.

Kyel shook his head, fighting back tears of his own. "The boy's dead. I'm sorry."

"How do you know?"

"They had a book about your family in the Temple of Wisdom. I read it."

Face constricted in grief, Darien collapsed to his knees. Kyel looked away, glancing to Swain for help.

The captain shook his head. He said in a voice impassively calm, "This is sick, Darien. I'm going to end it right here. Kneel."

He drew his sword with a shivering scrape of steel and brought it back over his shoulder. The oiled blade gleamed in the moonlight as he adjusted his grip.

Darien just stared at that glistening length of steel as though it was the one thing he desired most in the entire world. His face relaxed, and for a moment he looked calm, almost relieved. But then, firmly, he shook his head.

"No. That sword you're holding would be a *mercy*. But I have to finish what I started. There's no one else left to do it."

Swain's blade held fast. He regarded Darien with a level stare that Kyel found impossible to read. There was no trace left in his eyes of the hostile contempt that had been there whenever he had so much as glanced at his former student. Nor was there the barest hint of compassion, or even clemency. But the blade faltered. Swain took a step back and dropped his sword to his side, nodding his head.

"All right," he allowed, sheathing his blade. "We leave for Aerysius at first light. Come on, Kyel."

Kyel followed him as Swain turned and strode

away. He couldn't help chancing a glance behind, which revealed Darien kneeling with his head thrown back as if gazing up at the sky. Fine ripples of blue energy coruscated over his body, bleeding off into the night. It was a sad and eerie sight, one Kyel didn't think he would ever forget. He turned away, leaving Darien alone to silently shed his grief.

He wandered back to the command tent, where he found Swain shooing the collected officers out the back, sending them off without a word of explanation. Wellingford was the last to leave, following the others with a look of intense concern.

"He's gone," Swain said when they were alone. He tossed himself down in one of the scattered chairs, bringing a hand up to his brow. "Renquist pushed him too far."

"I don't think he'll make it to Aerysius," Kyel said softly, thinking of the strange blue light he had seen welling from the mage's body like lifeblood from his soul.

"I should have ended it back there. This is just cruelty, now. And what if he changes his mind?" Swain sighed, shaking his head. "Can you think of anything that can hold him together, just long enough to get him up the mountain?"

Kyel didn't hesitate with his answer. "Naia."

Swain grimaced. "Go ask her."

He found Naia alone a short distance from the camp, knelt in prayer before a small statue of her goddess. Two small votive candles flickered in the blackened soil just in front of the cloth the priestess had spread over the ground. Sensing his presence, Naia straightened, turning. She didn't appear surprised.

Kyel felt profoundly sorry for her. He walked toward her, hands clasped together in front of him, and knelt at her side.

"We're leaving for Aerysius on the morrow," he said.

The priestess looked down, her eyes trailing back toward the statue. It was hard to tell through her veil, but Kyel thought perhaps she'd been crying.

"I want you to come with us," he said. "Darien needs you."

"Did he send you?"

"No." Kyel shook his head. Something must have happened between them. Darien had probably treated her wrongly, the same way he seemed to be treating everyone. Kyel didn't want to hurt her worse than she already had been. But there didn't seem any way around it.

He drew a deep breath and said, "He met with Zavier Renquist tonight."

"What? Why?"

"I don't know. But Renquist really got to him, Naia. I don't think he'll make it to Aerysius without you."

Bowing her head, Naia said, "I don't think I'm the answer, Kyel. I'm not important to him."

"Is that what he told you?"

The priestess nodded, pressing her lips together tightly. Kyel didn't know what else to do, so he reached out and took her into his arms, lending her what small comfort he could. Naia accepted his gesture, laying her head on his shoulder and closing her eyes.

"I've seen the way he looks at you," Kyel said. "He's just trying to push you away because he doesn't want to see you hurt."

"I wish I could believe that." Naia pulled back from his embrace.

He didn't want to, but he had to tell her. "Renquist offered to bring Meiran back. He told Darien she gave him a son. The child's dead, Naia."

She gasped, bringing a hand up to her mouth. "How can he stand it?"

Kyel sadly shook his head. "I don't think he can anymore. That's why he needs you. Without you, I'm afraid we'll lose him."

Naia bowed her head against her chest and sighed weakly. "I'll come."

"Thank you," Kyel whispered, standing up. As he moved away from her, he glanced back to see Naia knelt once again in prayer. The small, wavering lights of her candles had died, drowned out by the melted tallow. The same tallow that, when solid, had once kept the delicate flames alive.

Kyel couldn't sleep. It was getting on toward morning, anyway, so he rolled out of his blankets and dressed. He occupied his time before sunup by leafing through the text he had brought back with him from Om's temple, *Treatise on the Well.* After all he'd gone through to acquire it, Darien had never once asked for it.

Kyel read and reread the passage about sealing the Well. But he found he understood it no better now than he had back in Emmery Palace. The book said something about 'deactivation of the rune sequence,' which made no sense to him. He didn't know what a rune was, how it was activated, or what it would take to deactivate the thing.

And, besides, he found he couldn't concentrate on that part. His eyes kept jumping down to the bottom of the page, to the last sentence that described the sealing of the gateway.

Kyel finally closed the book with a sigh. It was useless. And it was also time to leave.

He scooped up a bowl of millet gruel on the way to the command tent, throwing back his head and trying to hold his breath as he swallowed it down. The clumps stuck in his throat, making him gag. He couldn't finish it.

Not knowing what else to do with the bowl, he handed it off to a soldier who sat alone at a campfire looking hungry. The man took one look at his cloak, another at the bowl in his hands, then tossed it on the ground.

Kyel tried not to let the soldier's display of resentment get his temper up. It was galling, though, the way these men were always staring at him. Before Aerysius' fall, a black cloak had commanded immediate respect wherever it was seen. Now a mage's cloak seemed more like a badge of iniquity. Somehow, when this was over, he was going to have to work at changing that.

Kyel arrived at the command tent to find Swain already there, waiting beside his horse. The captain didn't look like he'd gotten much sleep, either. Kyel greeted him sullenly.

"Is she coming?" Swain asked.

Kyel nodded. At least, he hoped Naia hadn't changed her mind. He shivered. It was a bitterly cold morning, and the wind was coming up. Freshly fallen snow covered most of the blackened ground, except in places where men had trampled through it, reducing the fine white powder to ashen-gray sludge. The sky was still overcast, the sun only a pale glow. Looking up, Kyel wondered if it might not snow again before the day was through. That would be just their luck, to get mired in a blizzard.

He heard footsteps behind him and turned to see Darien approaching. The mage looked a little better than he had the previous night, but there was still a pall of gloom lingering about him. He was dressed all in black with his hair tied back for once, the hilt of his sword protruding over his shoulder. Somehow, he had found himself a new black cloak to wear, though Kyel doubted there would be a Silver Star on the back of it.

His attention was drawn to the thanacryst that followed at the Sentinel's heels. The creature jogged along with its tongue hanging out, drooling avidly. Kyel averted his eyes in disgust.

Darien stopped in front of Swain, slouching, his eyes downcast. That wasn't like him at all. Just yesterday, he had been trudging around the camp shooting glares at Swain. Now it seemed he couldn't look the captain in the eyes.

Swain put his hands on his hips. "Just out of curiosity, have you thought about how we're going to get up there?"

Darien nodded, hand tensing on the leather strap of the baldric slung across his chest. "We'll need to go through the Gap of Amberlie. After that, there's only one way up the mountain. We climb."

The blademaster appeared exceptionally unconvinced. "That's a three-thousand-foot cliff, Darien."

The mage shrugged. "We'll take the stairs."

Swain cast a glaring stab of doubt at him. "I was captain of the guard there for nine years. I don't remember any stairs."

"Do you recall the system of passages beneath the city?"

The captain nodded.

"Aidan showed them to me. We used to go down there sometimes when we were both still acolytes. We got along occasionally, if you can imagine it. There's a stair that goes all the way down inside the mountain and comes out somewhere at the base. Aidan told me about it. He used it all the time."

"So you don't know where this stair comes out?"

"No. But I'll know it when I see it. It's the only way."

With a surge of excitement, Kyel threw his pack down on the ground and started rifling through the contents, his fingers at last closing around the leather cover of *Treatise on the Well.* Righting himself, he flipped the book open to the page he'd marked with a folded piece of parchment that had completely slipped his mind.

"Here." He stuffed the paper into Darien's hand.

As Darien looked down at it, Kyel thrust the text at him, as well. "And here's this book you wanted so badly. You never even asked me for it."

Darien refused the book with a shake of his head, gazing down at the map in his hand. "I have no need of it," he grumbled absently. "You're the one who'll be sealing the Well, not me. Wait. Where did you come by this?"

Kyel felt a surge of resentment. "I found it in a text down in the vaults. I was *supposed* to be researching ways to help us, remember?"

Darien ignored him, eyes poring over the map in his hands. He whispered, "This is *exactly* what I need."

Kyel nodded, feeling smug as Darien continued his fervent examination of the map. The mage stood there for minutes, just staring down at it, eyes scouring the page. Then, at last, he let his hands drop, fingering the parchment as he turned to glance behind them with a bewildered expression.

In a voice just as slack and stunned as his face, he said, "The entrance is on this side of the mountains. It's just behind Orien's Finger."

Kyel glanced up at the blackened rock pillar, his face doing an unintentional imitation of Darien's. "It couldn't be." His gaze darted to the line of the Craghorns jutting away into the distance. "The Vale's yet leagues from here. Isn't that Aerysius over there?"

He pointed at a bank of clouds that hung against a jagged line of tall peaks. To his eyes, the gray gloom of the thunderheads seemed to be tinged distinctly, unnaturally green. Seeing Darien's slight nod, Kyel stared even harder at the summit beneath the cloudbank. It was leagues to the north, beyond even the Gap of Amberlie.

"We'll place our trust in your map," Darien muttered, a strange expression on his face as he folded the paper back up, running his fingers along the crease.

Kyel wondered what thought had occurred to him. Before he could ask, he was distracted by the sound of an approaching horse. He looked up to see Naia leading her small roan mare across the field toward them.

The priestess was dressed for travel, a coat thrown over her white gown. She wore a new veil he had never seen, one that glimmered with hundreds of tiny crystals worked into the fabric. She smiled as she saw them. But her expression wilted as her eyes sought Darien.

The mage turned to Swain with a look of fury. To Kyel, he seemed ready to reach for the blade at his back.

"No."

If Kyel hadn't heard it, he would never have believed it possible that one simple word could be infused with such resentment. Darien took a threatening step toward the captain, looking like a wolf moving in for the kill. Kyel could see Swain's hand drawing slowly toward his sword as the air around Darien fairly crackled with blue energies.

The captain stated firmly, "That's the condition. Either she comes, or we're not doing this at all."

Kyel backed away a step as the strange energies that writhed over Darien's body condensed into a brilliant aura that completely enveloped him. With a cry, Kyel threw his hands up to cover his eyes from the intensity of the light. The air itself seemed disturbed, a whistling wind that ripped at his hair and tormented his cloak.

"Darien," Naia called over the sound of the wind, "Is this truly your wish?"

The brilliant light collapsed into glowing filaments that wavered for a moment in the air before burning out completely. Where the light had just been, now only the Sentinel remained. He stood with his head bowed, eyes focused dimly at the ground between his boots.

"Damn you, Swain."

Without looking up, he moved away toward the horse pickets, shoulders slouched and feet scraping the ground with every step. When he was gone, the captain let out a slow, lingering breath.

"That was close."

Chapter Forty
Absolution

The Cerulean Plains, The Rhen

Darien let the black warhorse pick its own path toward the west. Ahead, Orien's Finger looked nothing more than a cracked and blackened log dug up from the ashes of an abandoned fire pit. Its summit had slipped even further off its charred pedestal than he remembered and had twisted slightly askew. Someday soon, the entire mass of broken rock was going to come crumbling down.

Darien looked toward the green glow above dead Aerysius. He tried to dredge up a picture in his mind of that terrible pillar of light, but the image was dim and bleary. It had been months since he'd last seen it, stabbing into the foundations of the ruined city like a spike through the heart.

Then, the sight of the gateway had terrified him. But now he was almost eager to view that dreadful column of power again, anxious for the promise of release the gateway could afford him. He gazed ahead toward the bank of storm clouds that hung over the jagged mountain peaks, a look of distant yearning in his eyes.

He was finally going home.

The sound of hoofbeats made him aware that a horse was drawing up alongside his. Not in the mood for conversation, Darien turned to glare at whoever had the temerity to invade the one, small moment of privacy he had claimed for himself. Expecting either Kyel or Swain, he was surprised to find himself glaring at Naia instead. His anger diffused instantly. Feeling ashamed, he glanced away.

"Can we talk?"

Out of the corner of his eye, he could see her peering at him through the sheer fabric that covered her face.

"I don't know what there is to talk about," he muttered in reply.

"Stop it."

The ferocity of her words took him aback. He almost pulled his horse up as he turned to look at her. Naia's dark eyes were filled with resentment, her cheeks red with ire that could be seen even through the mist of glittering crystals before her face.

"Stop trying to intentionally hurt me," she told him. "It's unkind. And it's not getting you anywhere."

As always, she had seen right through his walls as if they were made of glass. To her, his defenses were as thin as the translucent drape of fabric she always wore. She was becoming expert at tearing right through them, rendering him naked and exposed.

He didn't know what to say to her. He rode in silence, trying to ignore her presence. It was impossible. He longed for her, missing her company more now that she was here, riding at his side, than when he had thought her leagues away in Glen Farquist. He let his gaze trail back to the light of the gateway in the clouds above Aerysius, thirsting for the comfort of its promise.

Softly, she said, "I know what you're trying to do. You think that by distancing me, you can protect me. But you're wrong. You have a lot of audacity if you think you are responsible for my feelings. You are not. You have no right to treat me this way. What you're doing is cruel. And it hurts."

She was right, of course. She had looked into his soul and seen for herself the bleakness that was there. Why wasn't she riding away? She was still there, still at his side. And she was waiting for a response, he realized.

He had no idea what to tell her that wouldn't hurt her more.

"Talk to me," Naia insisted. "You owe me at least the truth."

He didn't know what version of the truth she wanted to hear.

"Do you care for me, Darien?"

He whispered softly, "Aye."

"Look at me."

It was hard. Naia's eyes were more beautiful than ever, burning with a fierce compassion he hadn't earned and would never deserve.

"I love you. And I forgive you," she said.

It was the last thing in the world he wanted to hear. Kicking his heels into the Tarkendar's sides, Darien sent the warhorse forward at a gallop.

Kyel's eyes followed the sight of the black gelding racing ahead, feeling a fresh swell of resentment. He regretted asking Naia to come. He should have left her behind with her votive candles and her goddess. Her presence didn't seem to be making a bit of difference anyway. Rather, it seemed to be having the opposite effect. Naia's company seemed to be instilling in Darien an even deeper melancholy.

The ruined crag towered over them, its shadow obscured by the gloom that still hung overhead in the sky. Looking ahead, he saw Darien's horse disappearing behind the dark column of stone.

When Kyel's own mount finally trotted around the circumference of the pillar, he found Darien sitting cross-legged in the snow, staring upward at the shattered summit. The hideous creature he'd adopted sat beside him. Kyel felt like uttering a choice word from Swain's extensive vocabulary of curses. Had Darien done nothing in the time he'd been there? Dismounting, Kyel scowled as he led his horse up behind him, further embittered by the fact that his arrival went completely unacknowledged. Darien still sat there, staring up at the sky, eyes dark and distant.

"Well?" Kyel demanded.

He glanced around at the curving walls of the small valley, finding nothing but burnt and ruined stone. If there had ever been a stair, it was gone now. The full force of the grand resonance had hit this area the hardest of all. Still, the mage just sat staring up at the dilapidated pillar, unblinking.

Kyel wanted to throttle him.

But then Darien stood up and lifted his hands as if trying to hold some enormous weight. Kyel felt a sudden surge of fear as he realized what the Sentinel was readying himself to do. He turned to find Naia and Swain approaching on their horses.

"Go back!" he yelled.

The captain frowned at him for the briefest moment then followed Darien's gaze upward to the summit of the crag. Eyes widening, he leaned over and grabbed the reins from Naia's hand, swinging both horses around and sprinting away.

The entire summit of Orien's Finger shuddered, rock and debris raining down. Kyel threw his arms up to cover his head as, with a horrible, grating noise, the broken mass of stone twisted on its pedestal, righting itself. The summit shifted forward, grinding as it slid slowly back into place. Kyel looked up, dropping his arms as he realized that not so much as a grain of dust had touched him.

Darien was not yet finished with his work. He was still staring upward, concentration bent on the column overhead. He extended the first two fingers of his left hand, angling them upward toward the restored cap of stone. White light burned, hissing, along the crack in the rock face. The stone melted from within, running outward from the crack and reforming again whole.

When it was done, Darien lowered his hand. Kyel stared in wonder, realizing he hadn't even broken a sweat. How many tons of rock had Darien shifted, using nothing more than the force of his mind? And he made it look so effortless. Kyel couldn't even think about performing such a feat himself. It was inconceivable. As he stared up at the intact pillar of stone, he found himself wondering why Darien had performed the task at all.

When he asked, the mage just shrugged, replying, "I needed to know the time."

Kyel stared at him blankly as Darien sat back down in the snow and stared out across the canyon.

That's all he did for another hour. Only, this time, the mage's attention was focused at the cliff walls behind. Kyel stared at them until he had their every feature seared into his mind, but he saw nothing to warrant such scrutiny. So he paced, growing increasingly impatient, as Naia and Swain stood silently looking on.

It was getting frustrating, and every time he asked Darien what he was doing, the Sentinel would only reply, "Just wait."

At last, Darien stood back up from the ground. His pants were soaked through from the snow, but he went through the motions of dusting them off anyway. The thanacryst bounded to his side, jumping up and pawing at his shirt. Darien whispered something to it that Kyel didn't catch, and the thing lowered itself to its haunches and sat there, panting like a dog. To his disgust, Darien reached out and ran a hand fondly through its wet, matted fur in praise.

"What now?" Kyel demanded.

"Just wait." Darien turned away and stared up into the sky.

A gust of wind rose from behind him. It increased in strength until it blew over the valley with the force of a gale. Above, the gray clouds moved quickly by overhead, increasing their speed until it seemed they crossed the sky at an impossible rate. Gradually, a break formed between the thunderheads to reveal blue sky between.

Kyel stared in amazement at the golden beams of sunlight that slanted down from the gap in the clouds, even as the air around him remained dark and chill. He was almost afraid; the whole scene reminded him too much of Black Solstice. But then he realized the darkness that encased them didn't come from some dread power blotting out the daylight. It was the shadow cast by Orien's Finger, revealed only now by the dramatic appearance of the sun.

The wind stopped. Overhead, the clouds ceased their motion as Darien turned and walked toward the blistered cliffs, following the dark shadow cast by the crag. He paced up the exact center of the broad line drawn across the ground, stopping only when he came to the blackened wall of rock. There, he muttered something under his breath that Kyel couldn't hear.

But something heard him.

Above his head, the outline of a marking glowed from the seared rock of the cliff face, glistening with a golden light. The rock ahead of them dissolved, a dark opening appearing in its place. In the dim light beneath the shadow of Orien's Finger, Kyel could just make out the beginning of stairs angling upward into the cliff.

"I'll be damned," Swain muttered, staring ahead.

Darien glared at him.

The Craghorns, The Rhen

They had to leave the horses behind. Darien had a hard time turning away from the Tarkendar. Craig had given him that horse. Watching the black gelding wander away with its nose to the wind, he felt almost as if he was giving up the last part of his old friend that still remained. But there was no other choice, so he shouldered the weight of his pack and, collecting Naia's without asking, turned toward the darkness of the opening he'd created.

As soon as the sole of his boot found the first step, he knew something about it was peculiar. The step didn't seem formed of solid rock, but rather of a strange, spongy material. It was almost like stepping off the ground onto a cloud. When he reached the fourth step, he was hit by an intense revelation.

"Kyel." He whirled around, searching desperately back through the opening. But he could see no trace of his former acolyte, or any of the others. He waited. Presently, Naia came through. Then Swain. It was strange. The opaqueness of the opening reminded him of the entrance to the Catacombs. It might have been the same, peculiar spell. Kyel appeared, looking past him into the darkness beyond.

"Shield yourself," Darien warned, appalled he hadn't thought of it sooner. He had almost made a lethal mistake that could have killed them. "The stair is spelled."

"Like the Catacombs?" Naia asked.

Darien nodded. "In the Catacombs, time and distance have no meaning. I feel the same principle at work here. I wouldn't be surprised if we reach the level of the Well far sooner than we'd thought.

"But," he said to Kyel with a look of dire warning, "that means we'll be walking into Orien's Vortex at any time. And then the vortex that surrounds Aerysius. We won't know when one ends and the other begins. No magelight," he added with a sigh.

"You want us to climb in the dark?" Swain asked. "That's insane."

Darien shook his head. "It shouldn't be long. It makes sense. Acolytes had a very strict curfew. Aidan said he followed this stair all the way down to the bottom and back. Aidan was a model acolyte. He was never caught out past curfew."

"It's a bad idea," Swain grumbled.

Darien looked down at him, almost finding it within himself to smile. In the years since he'd seen him last, he had missed Swain's abrasive temperament. The captain was one of the few constants he knew he could depend on. Swain could always be counted on to say what he meant and do what he believed. His personality was as economically efficient as his signature style with the blade: he never embellished, and he never sought to soften a blow.

He was glad Swain was with him. He was glad to have them all. Sweeping his gaze around at his companions, Darien realized that, unwittingly, he had surrounded himself with every friend he had that was still alive. He wished Craig could have been there, and even Proctor. Even Royce. So many others, all gone on ahead of him. Looking now at the friends that remained, Darien realized how grateful he was to have them there.

Feeling better than he had in a long time, Darien turned and started up the dark flight of stairs. And, as he cut himself off from the solace of the magic field, he found that he didn't need it so desperately, after all.

Kyel groaned, trying to keep his concentration focused on the next step ahead of him. They had been climbing ever upward in darkness for what seemed like hours. The journey was grueling, made even worse by the fear of falling Kyel felt at each step.

He was at the rear of the party. There was no one to catch him if he fell. The blackness that surrounded them was consummate, as if he'd been rendered completely blind. He could see nothing, not even the fingers of his own hand.

He groped forward tentatively, probing the step ahead with the toe of his foot before transferring his weight to it. He dared not take more than one step at a time. If not for the intermittent sounds of voices, he wouldn't have known any of the others were still with him.

As the long minutes dragged on, the fear that he was being left behind grew stronger. He started humming, the sound of his own voice making up a little for what he lacked of his perception of sight. And he hoped the sound would alert the others if he started trailing too far behind.

More than once, he bumped into Swain's back as the captain came to a lurching stop in front of him. Naia was having trouble with her dress and had to keep pausing to collect it out from under her feet. After several halts, Kyel heard Swain mutter something under his breath, followed by the distinctive sound of ripping fabric. There were no more dress problems after that, though Kyel wondered about the results of Swain's hasty tailoring job.

His legs ached, not used to so rigorous and prolonged a climb. He was afraid his calves were going to start cramping. At least the stair was not as steep as it could have been, and the steps were decently wide.

At last, they came to a narrow corridor where Darien called a halt. When Kyel moved to sit down, he found himself squatting in a puddle of water. Or something like water. In the darkness, it could have been anything.

"Can we not have a light yet?" he asked, sick of the gloom and anxious to find out the nature of the substance he had just stuck his hands in.

Darien's answer was long in coming. "We must be at the bottom of the cave system by now. I'll wager it's safe enough to risk it."

And then, miraculously, a hazy blue light bloomed from out of the ground that instantly revealed the forms of his companions. Kyel sighed, feeling relieved to be out of the darkness.

Darien consulted the map while they rested, a diffuse orb of magelight casting its glow above the page. The thanacryst sat dutifully by his side, its eyes glowing in the darkness. When it was time to go, Darien folded the map and shoved it back into his pack, staring ahead at the narrow passage before him. The magelight ran forward over the wet ground, following the motion of his eyes.

Fascinated, Kyel tried to form a glowing ribbon of his own. A faint golden tendril appeared briefly before winking out. It was the best he could do. He didn't think he could manage anything bigger.

Maybe with practice, but not yet.

Darien said, "The Well of Tears is up three levels."

"Great. So how do we get there?" asked Swain.

Darien pointed down the corridor in front of them. "We take this straight ahead. We'll come to a series of rooms. One has a winding stair that will take us up to the level of the Well."

"Doesn't sound too bad," the captain muttered, staring ahead with his hands on his hips. "We'll have this done and over with by nightfall."

But Darien shook his head. "No. We should wait till dark, on the chance Aidan is using the caves. He pushed himself up from the wet floor. "We'll stop for a rest in one of the rooms up ahead."

That sounded good to Kyel. He could use a rest after that climb. They moved forward again, following Darien's glowing mist down the corridor. As Kyel walked, his feet splashed through dark puddles.

The cave seemed saturated with water. It dripped from the ceiling and ran, oozing, down the walls. The roof overhead was covered in creamy bumps that collected water on their ends until a full droplet was formed, then released it to splash down to the puddles below.

After only minutes, the corridor opened into a good-sized chamber. Unlike the passage they had just emerged from, the room had more of a man-made appearance, or at least it had been man-altered. There, Darien and Swain spread out, each taking a doorway, the captain moving cautiously ahead with his steel bared. Kyel waited with Naia as the priestess stared at the doorway Darien had disappeared through. At last, both men returned through completely different passages.

"It's clear," Swain announced.

Darien nodded his agreement.

They settled down together in a dry corner of the room. Kyel broke into his pack, rummaging through it for a bite to eat. All he had managed to pack was stale bread, so stale bread was what he had. Darien produced an apple that looked only a few days too old. He handed it to Naia, who smiled her thanks.

After the short and meager dinner, Kyel decided he'd better ask Darien the questions that remained unanswered. Removing *Treatise on the Well* from his pack, he opened it to the page he'd been fretting over.

"I still don't understand what I'm supposed to do," Kyel said, moving over to sit beside him. "It says to deactivate the rune sequence in reverse order. How do I do that?"

"What's the order?"

Kyel had no idea. Flipping to the runes listed a few pages back, he handed the book to Darien. "Here. Have a look."

Darien stared at the page for a moment, increasing the intensity of magelight that surrounded him. "This isn't the true sequence. It's a cipher."

Kyel frowned, not understanding him. He watched as Darien bent over the book, tracing the line of markings with a finger. *"Metha, calebra, noctua…benthos…"*

He paused, brow wrinkled in concentration. His finger moved back again to the beginning of the line, squinting down at the page. Then he sat back, eyes narrowed, his gaze lowered in thought.

Above him in the air, a faint blue line sprang into being. Kyel scooted back, startled at the line's sudden appearance in front of him. Twisted branches grew out from the line, until Kyel realized he was staring at one of the strange characters from the page. The rune moved, circulating upward, as a different character appeared where the first had just been.

Soon, the air was filled with glowing runes that formed a circle that hovered, floating above them. Naia and Swain both crept forward, staring in fascination. Slowly, the runes moved to form a line that crossed the length of the chamber. Kyel recognized the order of the characters. It was the sequence from the book.

But then the runes began rearranging themselves. The first one slid upward and to the right, settling into the space between two others that moved over to make room. Then another character near the end of the line slid all the way across the chamber to the beginning of the sequence.

As Kyel stared in awe, the glowing blue figures began moving, sliding in and out of sequence, spiraling up from their positions and dropping back into new ones. He glanced at Darien and saw the mage's eyes rapidly sliding back and forth, tracking the motion of the runes.

And then all movement abruptly stopped.

Kyel let out a breath as he stared at the glimmering chain of characters that hung above them in the air. He almost flinched when the entire line suddenly condensed, shrinking and falling at the same time, rotating once as they fell onto the open text in Darien's hand. Kyel heard a faint, sizzling noise as the markings scorched themselves into the page.

"Here's the reverse sequence," Darien said, handing Kyel the book as if nothing had happened. Kyel could only stare at the fresh markings that had inscribed themselves across a previously blank portion of the page as Darien went on, "Progress left to right, just as you would reading. Begin with this one, *dacros*." He indicated the first rune of the sequence. "*Ledros* will be on the far side of the rim. Work counterclockwise around the Well, following this progression."

Kyel looked back up at him, dumbfounded. "What do I do? How do I deactivate the runes?"

Darien scowled. "They were activated with Meiran's blood. You must purify each rune, one by one, in that order."

"How do I do that?"

Darien looked down at the markings scorched into the page, a solemn and resolved expression on his face. "Fire should work best," he answered in a voice strangely gruff. "Burn them clean."

Kyel swallowed. Then he nodded. "I'll try."

Darien's shook his head. "No. There can't be any halfway with this. You know fire. You know how it's made. Your doubt is the only thing holding you back. You'd better start believing in yourself. Otherwise, all of this is for naught."

Swain broke in, "What exactly do we do if this doesn't work?"

Darien turned toward him, eyes adamant. "Then there's nothing you *can* do. Renquist wins. He's a demon—he's *dead*. When he died, his gift was Transferred to another mage or lost to the air. His power over the magic field comes only through his link with the Netherworld, through the Well of Tears. The only way to stop him is to seal the Well. That's the only thing that will cut him off from his power."

Swain nodded, sucking at his cheek. "So if this doesn't work, then we're left facing that Enemy host down there as well as Renquist at full strength."

"And six more just like him," Darien reminded him. "You won't have a chance." He turned back to Kyel. "Do you understand, now, how much of this depends on you? Once I walk into that gateway, I won't be able to help you anymore. You'll be completely on your own."

Kyel dropped his gaze to the floor, feeling suddenly shamed. At last he nodded, unable to look Darien in the eyes.

"I understand," he whispered softly.

Darien stared down at the scars on his wrists. He sat with his back against one of the rough walls, listening to the steady sound of Kyel's breathing. The others had chosen to try to get some sleep. They hadn't had much the previous night.

Darien had offered to stand watch. There were too many things on his mind, too many emotions churning inside his head. And he didn't want to face the dreams he knew would come. He'd had enough of them.

The sound of Naia stirring broke him away from his thoughts. Lowering his hands, he looked up and saw her moving toward him. Swain had done a number on her gown. It came to only knee-length now, with frayed threads hanging off where the captain had ripped it. Darien appreciated the look. Naia had beautiful legs. He found it hard to shift his gaze away from them.

"I can't sleep," she complained, sliding down the wall to sit at his side.

"You ought to go back and try," he said.

But Naia shook her head, leaning back against the rough wall and looking at him through the fabric of her veil. "No. I want to be with you."

Her eyes held his own, capturing him. Slowly, he reached his hand up and drew the glittering fabric off her face.

"You are beautiful," he said, gazing into her eyes. "Thank you for everything. I should have told you that before." He looked back down at his wrists, feeling suddenly very sad. "You should try to get some sleep," he whispered.

The feel of her lips on his made him forget the scars, forget what could not be. For one, brief moment, he closed his eyes and forgot everything but her. He reached up and pulled her into him, holding her close.

Chapter Forty-One
The Well of Tears

The Craghorns, The Rhen

"It's time to go."

Kyel hadn't realized he'd fallen asleep. Stretching, he sat up and stared around the dim chamber that glimmered in the quiet tendrils of Darien's magelight. The others looked like they were already prepared to set out again. Swain walked toward one of the exits, his pack swung over his shoulder.

Darien had burdened himself with the weight of both his own pack and Naia's. They were standing together in the middle of the chamber, Darien's hand clasped around her slender fingers. For once, Naia was without her veil. Kyel couldn't help but stare openly at her face, feeling moved. He was glad for them. But also very sad. Stuffing his blanket into his own pack, he pushed himself up off the ground.

"It's not far," Darien said as he led Naia toward one of the doorways.

Kyel fell in behind them, limping on legs that ached even worse than they had before. Swain followed, drawing his blade.

The magelight lit their way, trailing ahead as Darien led them through a series of adjoining chambers, each one just as dark and empty as the last. After minutes, they came to the stair Darien had told them about. Kyel followed him up the rough stone steps that wound around into blackness.

The stairwell almost reminded him of the tower of Greystone Keep, but infinitely darker. It smelled of old mold and wet rock. Water dribbled under his feet, running over each step in thin streams before trickling down to the one below it. The water spilled over the side of the first landing they came to, falling like a thin waterfall to the floor below.

"Stop," he heard Darien's voice echo in front of him.

Kyel stood motionless, staring up into the pale glow cast by the magelight. The Sentinel groped along the wall with his hand. Kyel heard a faint clicking sound that emanated from deep within the wall.

"What was that?" he asked.

"A trap." Darien pointed out a small circle recessed into the wall. "Thanks to that map you found, I knew to look for it. Otherwise, we'd all be dead."

Kyel stared at the small but lethal circle, shivering. "Are there more?"

"Two more up ahead before the chamber of the Well."

"How do you know there aren't others? Ones not marked on the map?"

The mage shrugged as he started forward again. "I don't."

Kyel kept his gaze angled at the wall from that point on. But Darien didn't stop again until they reached the third landing on the stair. There, he did another quick inspection of the wall, this time beckoning Kyel forward to point out the circle he found before depressing it.

"You're going to need to remember where these are for when you come back this way."

Kyel nodded, swallowing, as Darien pressed his finger against the circle. Again, there was a faint click. Then Darien moved on, clasping Naia's hand as he led her beside him through an opening.

Kyel followed, glancing both ways as he stepped into a long and narrow corridor. The passage ran perfectly straight, angling slightly upward. Ahead, Kyel could see a faint green glow. Darien paused, disarming yet another trap, then moved forward toward the source of the light.

"We're nearly there," he announced grimly.

The passage brightened gradually as they drew ever closer to that strange and sickly glow, until

Darien was able to release his magelight altogether. They turned a corner, moving cautiously toward a doorway that flared with a brilliant spill of light.

Kyel followed him toward the opening with an unfolding sense of fear. He didn't like the look of the light, was repulsed by its unnatural hue. He stopped within the stone frame of the doorway, holding a hand up before his face to shield his eyes against the glare coming from a column of terrifying brilliance at the far end of the chamber.

He stared at it with a mingled sense of awe and horror, eyes taking in the surging energies that swept upward from the column's base, from a ring of stone that rose from the floor. Beyond it, he could make out the black silhouette of what appeared to be a stone table or altar with sinister-looking chains. His eyes went back to the circle of stone, then looked to Darien for the confirmation he was dreading.

"Is it…?"

"The Well of Tears," the Sentinel affirmed.

Kyel stared, transfixed by the writhing light stabbing upward from the Well. The air of the chamber crackled with energy. A low humming sound echoed off the walls, intermittently disturbed by a sharp hissing noise. The air was permeated with the pungent scent of decay.

Kyel let his eyes trail down the terrible pillar of light to the rough stone of the Well itself. There, along the rim, he could see the glowing runes. It came almost as a shock when he realized he could actually read them. The first rune glared out at him with a piercing brilliance that seemed to want to inscribe itself into the backs of his eyes: *dacros*.

Mesmerized, Kyel moved forward, his boots sloshing through dark puddles of water collected on the floor. He wasn't aware of the others behind him, knew nothing but the glaring markings that looked like claw marks raked into the stone of the Well's rim. He knelt beside the character of *dacros*, his hand reaching out until he could almost touch the luminous marking with the tips of his fingers. He traced the rune's outline in the air above it, lips moving silently to form the syllables of its name.

"You know what to do," he heard Darien's voice from behind him. Looking up, Kyel found the Sentinel standing over him. "Remember—believe in yourself. Be steadfast, and do not doubt."

As Kyel looked up at him, Darien nodded slightly, confidently, then turned away. Suddenly dismayed, Kyel realized that it was Darien's way of saying goodbye. Kyel didn't want him to go, didn't want to be left without the comforting scaffold of his presence.

Kyel watched Darien cross the chamber away from him, his heart sinking as he realized he would never see him again. He suddenly realized that in the entire time he'd known him, Darien had shown only confidence in him. Through every test he had prepared, every trial, Darien had never doubted him once. Kyel understood then what he hadn't been able to understand before: that the mage had been his friend all along, and he had just never realized it.

Darien stopped beside Naia, turning to regard her with a softened expression on his face. "Stay here," he said. Reverently, he traced his fingers down her cheek.

"Darien—" she began.

He shook his head, silencing whatever it was she had started to say.

To Swain, he uttered, "Take care of them."

The captain nodded. "I will."

The thanacryst padding at his side, Darien strode out through the chamber's dark opening, disappearing into the shadows on the other side. Kyel stared after him into the darkness beyond, profoundly saddened.

He turned back to the Well. He had a part to play, and he couldn't falter. He owed it to Darien not to fail.

First, he needed to locate the rune progression. Then he could wait, giving Darien the time he needed to accomplish his part of the task before them.

Lifting his fingers back to the rune, Kyel muttered, *"Dacros."* Moving around the rim, he located the next marking in the sequence. *"Ledros."* He found he didn't need to refer back to the text to remember the pattern. The sequence was already established in his mind. With growing confidence, he hunted down the next vile marking. *"Noctua."*

Darien moved through the darkness of the caves, a pale azure glow of magelight revealing the path before his feet. If he remembered correctly, somewhere up ahead was another trap. This one, he intended to trigger. He needed to draw Aidan's attention to him. He didn't have time to go hunting through the rubble of Aerysius to find his brother.

Somewhere deep below, Kyel would be preparing to start his work on the Well of Tears. There wasn't much time. He would have to find Aidan before Kyel finished his task. Otherwise, his brother would be alerted to the threat to the gateway. Swain was an accomplished blademaster, possibly the best, but he was no match against a mage. And, Bound and inexperienced as he was, Kyel would be all but defenseless.

The corridor he moved through was narrow and dark, its walls wet and covered with spongy secretions from the rock. The magelight groped along just ahead of his feet, lighting his way. He tried not to let his thoughts wander back to his companions at the Well, but they kept slipping back that way despite his efforts. It had been hard to leave them. But what awaited him ahead, he had to face alone. Where he was going, his friends could not follow.

The magelight revealed the shadows of an intersection just ahead. There, Darien paused. His eyes scanned the walls to either side as the magelight traveled up the stone, following the motion of his gaze. He found a small circle in the wall that depicted the nature of the trap: the button was inscribed with a small pictogram.

The marking was so worn by the constant trickle of water and the passage of years that it was almost indiscernible. It took him a moment to interpret the symbol. Thankfully, it was just the type of device he needed. Any movement through the intersection would trigger it, unless the circle was depressed.

This time, Darien stayed his hand, walking purposely into the trap.

He hadn't known what to expect. An alarm of some kind, a screeching wail or distant tolling of a bell. But there was nothing. No evidence the device had even been triggered. It was possible the mechanism had failed after so many years of disuse and neglect. Possible, but he doubted it. Aidan would have made certain his defenses were well maintained. His brother had always been one to err on the side of caution, if not downright paranoia.

With a sense of conviction, Darien knew his presence had been made known. All he had to do now was wait.

Waiting was never easy.

He roamed forward, pacing slowly, casting the magelight ahead and brightening its intensity. He would give them a luminous trail to follow, so there would be no guessing his location. Already, he felt too pressed for time. Not daring to move far from the trap he'd sprung, Darien stopped, bending over to pet the thanacryst. The beast whined, its tail beating against the wet stone as Darien passed his fingers through its fur. However dreadful, the beast was a faithful companion. Its eyes gleamed in the darkness, wide and eager.

Abruptly, the motion of the tail stopped. The thanacryst lifted its head, nostrils quivering as it scented the air.

Darien straightened, alerted by the sudden change that had come over the demon-hound. He closed his eyes and listened but heard nothing. No distant echo of footsteps, no rush of armored bodies. Of course, whatever might be coming may not tread on legs and feet. He opened his eyes, scanning the narrow path ahead.

The necrators that rose up from the floor all around him came as no surprise. Darien merely regarded them, releasing the magelight and letting complete darkness settle in. He felt no trace of the awful dread their presence had once inspired. The rhythm of the magic field continued on in his mind, uninterrupted.

They were no threat to him. He had rendered himself immune to their influence. His meeting with Renquist had taken him beyond the point of return. Now even the indiscretion of his feelings for Naia was not enough to lessen the sickness in his heart. Darien smiled, knowing he was now free to feel anything he wished. There was no going back, not anymore. Not ever.

The necrators had not been a surprise. But the sight of Cyrus Krane striding toward him gave Darien a shock. He had not expected the darkmage, and the significance of Krane's presence was alarming.

The demon drew up before him, his gaze lingering on the thanacryst that stood at Darien's side, purring and drooling profusely at the same time. Krane's stare roved upward as a smile came to his lips, distorting the dreadful scar on his face into a jigsaw pattern that made his appearance seem even harsher than it was already. His eyes were satisfied, perhaps even gloating.

"We had a feeling you might try something like this," he stated. "My Master will be well-pleased."

Darien refused to be intimidated. The advice he had given Kyel held true, especially now. He had to remain steadfast. To doubt was to die. He held no white banner in his hand this time.

"Which master are you referring to?" he taunted. "Aidan or Renquist?"

"I have but one Master," was Krane's terse reply. "Now, so do you."

Darien made no effort to resist as the necrators pressed in around him, surrounding him with their shadowy forms. Krane turned away, striding back down the long corridor the way he had come as the necrators moved to follow him, gliding like shadows over the ground. Darien allowed himself to be herded forward, moving in the wake of Krane's flowing robes.

Strange, how Krane felt comfortable enough to walk with his back to him, as if he considered him no threat at all. Perhaps the demon felt confident enough that the necrators had eliminated any possibility of his resistance. Or, perhaps, he really did pose no threat to the ancient darkmage, which was a thought altogether more disturbing.

The corridor wandered upward, turning back on itself as they approached the surface. There, a narrow stair was carved into the rock, curving as it rose. Krane mounted the steps first, his magelight a crimson mist pouring up the stairs. Darien followed, walking within the confines of his shadowy guard. After what seemed like minutes, the stair opened up, emerging at the base of the ruined city.

As he stepped out of the darkness of the warren, Darien realized he was once again finally home. Only, Aerysius was no longer as he remembered it.

There were no structures, no crumbled ruins, no traces of the devastation he remembered from that dreadful night. There, on the cliff face high above the Vale, the slate had been wiped completely clean. Except for the soaring arches that rose like a forlorn and obsolete monument over the snow-covered square, only empty terraces remained. The ruins were gone, scoured away. The arches were all that remained, and the terrible column of light striking upward into the heavens.

Darien craned his neck, gazing up at the towering pillar of the gateway. The sight of it filled him with a mixture of dread and anticipation. The glowing spear of light inspired nothing of the terror he'd experienced the night it had first appeared. He understood its purpose better now. He had internalized it, making it his own. With that strange sense of ownership, he allowed Krane to guide him toward it, out into what had once been the ornately tiled square. Now just a flat expanse of snow and rock.

Looking around, he realized there was nothing left for him here. This desolate mountain face no longer held even the memory of his home.

"Darien?"

So transfixed was he by the barren foundations of the city, he had almost missed the small, dark figure kneeling in the snow only a few steps away.

Like Aerysius, his brother was nothing as Darien remembered. Indeed, his face was more of a devastated wasteland than the city he had brought to ruin. Aidan was gaunt, the flesh sagging on his pale face, eyes but dark hollows above the sharp ridges of his cheekbones. His hair had gone completely gray, almost white, and had receded dramatically. He knelt on the ground, arms bound behind his back by bonds of red light that twined about his arms in a grim parody of the scars hidden beneath Darien's own sleeves.

Darien froze, forgetting the presence of even Krane. He wanted to look away but found it impossible to do anything but stare at the sad, twisted man that had been the object of his hatred for so long. Almost, Darien thought he could feel sorry for him. Almost. But then he reminded himself of Meiran, of the Hall of the Watchers, of the mother he had lost. That was just the beginning of the long, blood-written list he wanted to hold this man accountable for.

"They want to remake you," Aidan rasped, staring up at him with wide, startled eyes. "Why did you come?"

Confused, Darien felt a terrible, growing sense of dismay. Aidan was insane. It was written on his face, gaped out from his reddened, tortured eyes. The realization came as a startling shock. Darien could feel the hatred he had nurtured so carefully for so very long simply dissolve. In its place, he felt only an emergent sense of pity.

Turning to Krane, Darien silently implored the man for an explanation.

"He drained too many before the Hall of the Watchers fell," the demon stated, glaring down at Aidan as if he were some abject and broken tool to be discarded. "There is only so much power the human mind can endure."

Not knowing what to feel, Darien gazed down on his brother somberly. Slowly, he moved toward him. As he lowered himself to kneel at his side, Aidan shrank back, turning his face away. But not before Darien caught a glimpse of the tears that streaked his ruined cheeks.

Peering intently, Darien searched the man before him, trying to find something left within him to hate. But he found nothing. Just a pathetic, miserable creature that cowered from his presence. Darien found himself instead searching his own heart, wondering if he had it within himself to deliver the justice he had sworn in blood to mete.

Sighing, Darien reached out with his mind and unmade the bonds that constrained Aidan's wrists. His brother sagged visibly, chin falling against his chest, eyes staring vacantly at the ground. Tears fell from his cheeks, dribbling to the snow.

Wretchedly, he whispered, "Forgive me."

Darien almost wished he could. The sight of his brother's tears brought back memories of their boyhood together. For once, not all of those memories seemed so terribly bad. There had been times when he'd enjoyed Aidan's company. Not often. But times. For a long period of his life, his brother had been the only connection he'd had with his family. He had never been fond of Aidan as a person. But, once, Darien had loved him as a brother, the only brother he'd ever had.

"Take my hands," Darien whispered. "Let's be done with this."

"What are you going to do?"

Darien shook his head. "I can't forgive you, Aidan. Mercy is all I have left to offer you."

Behind him, he heard the soft footsteps and shivering robes of Cyrus Krane.

"Yes," the demon hissed at his back. "Take his life. That is the first step."

"The first step of what?" Darien turned to glare up at him, resenting the intrusion.

"Your new life as one of us." Krane smiled down at him: a gloating, sinister grin.

Darien shook his head, feeling suddenly uncertain. "I declined Renquist's offer."

"You were under the protection of truce last night. Not so, now."

With a shiver of dismay, Darien realized Krane was right. Aerysius was a snare, with his brother set out as bait. After their meeting, Renquist had anticipated he would come here. It was a trap, and he had fumbled blindly into it.

Darien rose from his brother's side. "I'll never be one of you."

"But you already are." The confidence in Krane's tone made Darien take a step back, consumed by a cold numbness that eclipsed his every perception.

"What do you mean?"

"The thanacryst." Krane nodded at the creature. "Such a beast cleaves only to a soul already damned. You are a Servant of Xerys. You have surrendered yourself to Him freely. You belong to Him, now."

"No."

He refused to believe it could be that heinously simple.

But Krane seemed very certain it was. He dismissed Darien's denial with a curt wave of his hand. "You already made your choice. There is no going back. Now, go. Do your duty by your brother. I wish to depart this vile place."

Darien glanced up at the gateway. The beacon throbbed, beckoning, its slithering ropes of energy calling out to him with a promise of hope and release. There was no chance he could reach it. Krane stood before him, physically barring his path.

There was only one thing to do. Dropping back to Aidan's side, Darien reached out and took his brother's hands in his own. As their fingers touched, Darien felt a pulling sensation from deep within, a strange and distant tingling. Startled, he realized that his brother was establishing a conduit between them, locking them together in a treacherous link. Reviled, he tried to pull back.

But Aidan clenched his hands, a look of hungry desperation in his eyes. Darien fought as the pulling became a tearing ache that grew into a tangible pain. The pain swelled, increasing to a wrenching agony. Darien threw his head back, gritting his teeth and clutching his brother's hands as he fought to turn the conduit back around.

A lightning spear resolved from the sky and stabbed into Aidan. Darien felt the conduit slam closed with a force that hurled him backward.

He rolled onto his side, looking up to see Aidan writhing on the ground, red energies crackling as they clawed over his body. The sounds of his shrieks were terrible, and they seemed to go on and on. Finally, Aidan collapsed back to lie in the snow, his tortured body limp and still.

Darien looked away, horrified. Cyrus Krane moved toward him and, to his amazement, reached down and offered him his hand. Darien accepted it, allowing the ancient darkmage to help him to his feet. His legs trembled as he walked over to where Aidan lay motionless on his back. Darien bent down over the body of his brother, laying his head against his chest to listen for a heartbeat. Unbelievably, he heard a faint stirring, weak and irregular, but undeniably there.

"I don't understand. He summoned you. I thought you were required to obey him."

Krane shook his head. "Only until the initial purpose of our summoning was fulfilled. Since then, we've been under our own recognizance."

Darien looked back down at his dying brother, not quite certain how to feel. Aidan had been responsible for the tragedy of Aerysius, but everything that had happened since had been Renquist's doing all along. All this time, Aidan had been merely the demon's pawn, nothing more.

Feeling strangely weak, Darien struggled back to his feet. He was unable to take his eyes off his brother, watching the shuddering rise and fall of his chest.

"Come, now," Krane commanded, extending his hand with a welcoming invitation on his lips. "Renquist is expecting us down the mountain."

Darien shook his head, the demon's cool assurance distilling a cold anger within him. "I'm not going anywhere with you."

Krane only shrugged. "I'll compel you if you leave me no choice. But I must warn you: our Master exacts harsh punishments from his Servants. And you must also think of Meiran. Her soul will be made to suffer along with yours."

Darien gaped at him, appalled, feeling his anger chill to a frozen sea of contempt. He couldn't accept that. Not Meiran. Too many souls had already paid the price for his decisions. Meiran was innocent and had already suffered far more than she ever deserved. Looking at Krane, he narrowed his eyes and coldly shook his head.

"Your master can go to hell."

He reached out from within, summoning the fatal potency of his rage. A shaft of fire bloomed from his hand, hurling viciously at Krane. The demon seemed to shrug slightly as a wall of red light appeared in front of him, neatly absorbing the lance of flame. Krane smiled, black eyes gleaming with sinister promise as he reached his hand upward to the sky.

Darien dodged, but he wasn't quick enough. A writhing net of living energy fell, draping over him and tugging him to the ground.

The searing fibers of the net burned, scorching his skin with blistering heat as he struggled to free himself. Through the web of glistening light, he could see Krane's robe trailing toward him over the ground, through his groans he could hear the demon's malevolent voice:

"Is it your wish to spend an eternity in such pain?"

The net lifted, dissolving into threads that slithered away into the air. Darien lay on his back, shuddering as he healed the burns the ghastly thing had made. He struggled to sit up, but no sooner had he accomplished the motion then a series of rings appeared around him, constricting. The rings tightened inexorably, compressing his ribs a little more with each breath.

Soon, even breathing became impossible. Frantic, Darien reached deep inside the mage. He clasped his mind around the demon's heart, envisioning it shuddering to a standstill in his chest.

But, as he groped for that blackened and twisted organ, he discovered to his horror that Krane's heart was already dead.

With a laugh, the ancient Prime Warden threw out his hand. The rings fell away as a ferocious blast of air hit Darien full in the face. He sagged to the ground, feeling the sharp stab of a sword thrust take him between the ribs.

He looked down to see blood welling over the hand he held clutched against his side. He could hear Krane's laughter, almost drowned out by a clamorous ringing in his ears. He groped within, trying to get enough sense of the wound to heal it. As he did, he felt a shooting lance of pain descend like an axe through the middle of his head.

Abruptly, the magic field was gone. He couldn't even sense it.

Darien looked up and saw Krane moving toward him as if through a fog, a dim silhouette backlit against the brilliant light of the gateway directly behind him. The demon seemed to be moving impossibly slow as he knelt at his side, smiling that baneful grin, fingers roving over him scant inches above his body.

"Your first lesson, my acolyte," Cyrus Krane pronounced. "Never seek to defy your masters again."

He pressed his hands to Darien's chest, wielding vicious, searing agony. Darien convulsed, the noise of Krane's harsh laughter drowned out by the sound of his own screams.

———

Kyel figured he had waited long enough. It was time.

He moved back to the first rune in the sequence and raised his hand. Behind him, he could feel Naia leaning over him, looking on over his shoulder. Her presence made him suddenly self-conscious, and he clenched his hand into a fist. He couldn't doubt. He had to believe. He knew fire, knew how to summon it from flint. All he needed to do was transfer that knowledge to the air.

Raising his finger to the glowing rune, he muttered its name and willed the air above it to warm. At first, there was nothing. Then, slowly, he could feel the heat. But it wasn't enough. He steeled his mind in concentration, consuming his thoughts with a determined, singular intent. A fine dagger of flame flared toward the rune, hissing as it came in contact with it. Kyel almost fell backward into Naia in alarm, staring up at the rim of the Well to see the unholy light of *dacros* suddenly dim and fade out.

"That's it," Naia whispered. "You can do this."

Kyel nodded. He moved around the Well, swiftly finding *ledros*. Kneeling beside the vile mark, he quickly conjured the tiny knife of flame. Within seconds, the next rune turned a dull, lifeless black.

He repeated the task, working counterclockwise in the sequence Darien had given him, wandering in circles around the Well of Tears until, at last, he found himself kneeling before the pale light of the final marking. Raising his hand, Kyel seared the last vestige of Meiran's blood from the dark stone of the rim.

The column of light shivered, white energies crackling through it. Kyel stared up at it, terrified, as the gateway seemed to throb, its form suddenly unstable.

The Well of Tears was sealed, at least in this world. But the awful energies of the gateway still shivered, throbbing in the air like a dilapidated pedestal on the verge of collapse.

"The rest is up to Darien, now," he whispered.

———

The gateway shivered, pierced through by white streaks of energy that shrieked violently upward. The whole pillar throbbed, shuddering fiercely.

Cyrus Krane turned toward it, an expression of horror on his face. On the ground beneath him, Darien squinted up, admiring the beauty of the white streaks that tarnished the vile perfection of the green column of light. He smiled a small, sad grin. Then he drew in a long, wheezing breath that sent a lancing pain from his ribs.

"Crenoch!" he shouted.

The demon-hound obeyed, springing up from the ground in a great leap, catching Krane in the chest with its paws and shoving him backward with the force of its weight.

Krane staggered, arms pinwheeling, as the thanacryst's huge mouth closed on his throat. Together, beast and demon tumbled into the gateway, disappearing in a brilliant flash of light.

The smile slowly faded from Darien's lips. The pulse of the magic field was still nothing more than a faded memory in his head.

He struggled to roll onto his side, shaking and weak from Krane's vicious assault. Clenching his jaw, he pushed himself up and crawled painfully toward his brother.

Aidan still lay where he'd fallen. Reaching his side, Darien collapsed on top of him, laying his head on his brother's chest. Surprisingly, there was still a heartbeat in that ruined body.

Darien grasped Aidan's limp form in his arms, clutching him tight as he struggled to rise. His body trembled, refusing the effort he was asking of it.

Darien groaned. He heaved himself onto his

knees, then rose, locking his arms around Aiden's middle. His legs shook as he took a lurching step backward, dragging his brother after him.

"Darien…"

He looked down, surprised to find Aidan's blue eyes cracked open.

"It hurts…"

Darien gazed down into his brother's wretched face and assured him, "It'll be over soon."

He took another step backward toward the pillar of light. The pain in his side was like a fiery brand that flared with every motion of his body.

"I'm scared," Aidan whispered in a weak, trembling voice.

Darien took a last, long look up at the towering pillar as he whispered, "Me too."

Gripping Aidan under the arms, he crossed into the ethereal light.

The Gateway

At first, he saw only mist. A hazy green bleakness that unfolded before him, expanding outward in swirling clouds of vapor. Beyond the mist, there was darkness. This place had the feeling of closeness, as if there were walls all around he simply couldn't see. This couldn't be the Netherworld, Darien decided. Somehow, he must still be within the gateway.

And he was alone. His brother had gone on ahead of him.

Darien collapsed to his knees, raising his hands before his face. Appalled, he took in the sight of the aura that surrounded his fingers and emanated from his skin. It was the same awful glow he remembered from the Catacombs. The aura was brighter, now, writhing up his arms, very visible against the darkness and the mist.

This time, he knew exactly what it meant.

Dropping his hands, he raised his voice and called out into the bleakness, "I accept your offer. Now, make good on your end."

The mist around him continued to swirl, unaffected by his words. Scowling, Darien realized what he had to do. Somehow, he'd known it all along. He closed his eyes in dread and forced himself to utter the same infamous phrases spoken by Zavier Renquist a thousand years before:

I commit my soul to Chaos. From this day forth,
I will be the obedient servant of Xerys.
I will serve faithfully all the days of my life…
and may not even death itself release me.

His voice trailed off into silence. Still, the haze that enveloped him yet lingered, swirling. Darien wondered if he had been heard at all, or if his proffered oath had been rejected entirely. Only silence surrounded him. Only silence and the mist.

But then, a soft light spawned before him, a pale and wondrous glow that confronted the mist and turned back the darkness. To Darien, it was the most beautiful sight he'd ever seen.

Mesmerized, he crawled toward the radiant promise of that glow. Before his eyes, the light assumed definition, solidifying into the image that for months had haunted his waking memories and his dreams. He reached out toward it, his trembling fingers tracing the soft profile of the face that glowed before him like the first light of a rising moon.

Meiran lay beside him on the ground, dark waves of her hair spread out at her side. The gown she wore was stained and tattered, her eyes closed as if sleeping. But then, as he watched, those lovely eyes fluttered open.

For a moment she stared up at him vacantly, as if waking from the depths of the deepest slumber. Dim confusion nettled her features. Then, slowly, her expression changed. Meiran's lips parted, dark eyes widening.

She was even more beautiful than he remembered. She was gazing up at him with such a look of joy it wrung his heart. Clutching her against him, Darien held her close in his trembling arms. He closed his eyes and kissed her, his nostrils filled with the sweet fragrance of her hair.

With effort, he forced himself to draw back away. He took her face in his hands, cupping her cheeks, as he told her gently, "I need you to be strong for me."

The joy in her eyes collapsed, replaced by a look of shadowy confusion. Darien shook his head, grimacing through the sorrow in his heart. He wished he had time to explain. He wished he had time to hold her longer in his arms.

Shaking, he brought the Soulstone up, encircling

the bands of the collar around his neck as his fingers fumbled at the clasp.

"As soon as I'm dead, get this off me."

The look of confusion on Meiran's face dissolved into terror.

He let the clasp of the necklace snap closed.

The onslaught of pain was instant and terrible. Darien fell back against the ground, shuddering in agony as the talisman around his neck stirred awake with a deep inner glow.

Meiran held him in her arms as his soul was ripped out of life. Her beautiful face was the last thing Darien saw as he died. It was all he wanted to see. It was enough.

Chapter Forty-Two
Wiped Clean

The Craghorns, The Rhen

The chamber shuddered, the whole world lurching under Kyel's feet.

"Quick, get the cover on!" Naia screamed.

Swain was already bent over the enormous circular slab of stone, heaving against it with all his might. Kyel saw the captain didn't have near the strength it would take to budge it.

"Stand back," he commanded. He raised his hand as Swain released the cover and backed away. It was just a push, that's all. He could not doubt.

The cover of the Well of Tears rose silently from the wet floor, dripping liquid filth as it hovered, sliding stately through the air, at last lowering to a gentle rest on the rim.

Then there was only darkness. Kyel tried to see through the emptiness that surrounded him, but all he saw was the red afterglow of the gateway. Confused and scared, it took him a moment to realize what had just happened.

The Well of Tears, finally, had been fully sealed from both sides.

"He did it." Swain's voice echoed through the darkness.

As if from somewhere very distant, he heard the soft sound of Naia weeping. The noise made Kyel's heart feel heavy with sorrow. Moving toward it, he groped through the darkness until his fingers found the silken texture of her gown. He folded his arms around her, pulling her close and wishing there was something further he could do.

But there wasn't. So he stood there, holding her, as long minutes dragged by. Through the darkness, her voice whispered, pleading, "I want to go up there."

He couldn't say no, even though he wanted to. He knew it was the wrong thing to do.

Kyel produced a soft, misty glow around his feet. The magelight drifted out away from him, coursing in glimmering tendrils of burnished yellow-gold. He had read that every mage produced their own signature color. This was his, and Kyel stared down at it with a sense of pride.

In its pale warmth, Naia's face looked very young and incredibly fragile. Taking her by the hand, he let the golden magelight spill before them as he guided her out of the chamber. He didn't turn back. He had no desire for a last glimpse of the Well.

Instead, he followed the long corridor, eyes scanning the walls for the tiny circles that indicated the presence of the magical traps Darien had pointed out to him. He found only one and disarmed it with a click. Letting the ribbons of magelight spill before them, he moved ahead, leading his two companions up a wide, curving stair.

At the top of the steps was an opening that revealed a gray expanse of sky. Overhead, storm clouds were gathering. Kyel mounted the last few steps with growing unease.

He didn't know what to expect at the top of that stair and wasn't sure if he wanted to see it. He had never known Aerysius, but he harbored a long-established and cherished image of what he thought it must have looked like. Wanting to hold onto that vision, he was hesitant to see the reality that confronted him over the top of the steps.

What he found surprised him. There was no city at all. Only empty terraces on a high mountain face, barren rock covered by a thin layer of snow. And, to his amazement, it was snowing still. Soft white flakes drifted down from the sky, alighting on his shoulders and clinging to his face. Kyel moved out into the white haze, Naia at his side.

It was hard to see anything through the falling snow and swirling mist. He could make out the shadow of a tall and thin arch, but there was virtually no other trace that people had ever lived in this place. The wide terrace he stood on could have been a natural indentation in the cliff. Perhaps, one day, it would go back to nature, be reclaimed by the mountain face that had nurtured it for so long.

Aerysius was truly gone. Except for the soaring arch, not a vestige of the city remained. There was no trace of the gateway. The sky above the mountain had been released from the grip of that unholy light.

Kyel stared straight ahead into the falling snow, feeling Naia's fingers tighten around his own. He wished he hadn't brought her. There was nothing for them there, nothing but hurt. It was time to go.

Swain placed a comforting hand on Naia's shoulder. "We should leave, now."

The priestess nodded, bowing her head.

Kyel moved to turn away from the stark and lonely terrace. As he did, his eyes caught a motion ahead in the drifting snow.

He peered through the mist, seeing what looked like a shadow moving toward them through the obscurity of the haze. He hesitated, a muddled turmoil of hope and fear choking his heart. Eyes fixed on the shadow ahead, he watched it resolve into the features of a woman.

Kyel felt Naia's fingers trembling in his hand, heard the sound of her moan as she threw her head back. Then she broke away from him, stumbling forward through the snowdrifts. Kyel started after her as the strange woman staggered forward. He reached her just in time to catch her before she fell.

"Who is she?" Kyel all but whispered.

Swain knelt beside him and brushed matted strands of dark hair from the woman's face. Her skin was ashen pale, her body shivering violently in Naia's arms. Tears ran down her cheeks, falling from her chin to land softly in the snow. She gazed up at Swain with a look of uncertainty.

"Captain?" she muttered.

Nigel Swain nodded, his face sad and solemn. "Hello, Meiran."

Kyel gasped, filled with sudden understanding. Renquist had delivered on the promise he had made to Darien.

A glimmer of light in Meiran's hand captured his attention. She raised her trembling hand from her side, offering out the necklace clasped in her fingers. Kyel felt an urgent flair of grief when his hand closed around the glowing medallion.

He held the Soulstone up before his face, marveling at its myriad facets. The gem pulsated with a radiant inner life, brighter than he remembered it being ever before. A sad sense of finality rushed over his body like a wash of cold water. This was legacy he was holding. Now more than ever before, he fully understood what that meant.

But this legacy was not his own. Wordlessly, he offered the medallion to Naia. She received it from him timorously, her expression a mixture of sorrow and awe. She held the medallion in her open palm, fingers trailing over the gem's smooth texture.

"He left this for me," she whispered.

Kyel nodded, though he knew she was partially wrong. The power in the Soulstone was an inheritance that would have to be shared. The heritage of Aerysius was in that stone, the power it contained too great for just one person. Looking back down at Meiran, his eyes confirmed what his heart had already guessed.

There were no chains on Meiran's wrists.

It was then that Kyel fully understood the nature of the gift. Deep within the gem's glowing facets moved the same inner power that had moved through Darien. It was a part of him that would be with both women always, would never grow old and fade, never sicken or falter.

Kyel wrapped his arms around both of them as he bowed his head, thoroughly overcome.

The Cerulean Plains, The Rhen

Traver watched the wild man on his buckskin horse galloping away, smiling a crooked grin of thanks after him. It had been downright decent of the herdsman to ride with him all this way. Reaching down with the three remaining fingers of his left hand, he ruffled the mane of the horse Ranoch had given him. It was a tough beast, although an ugly and temperamental one. Ranoch had given him the pick of his herd, and Traver had chosen the piebald. He liked the stallion's one, glaring blue eye.

He rode bareback; the Jenn didn't see the need for saddles or tack. The horse was guided by a simple rope, using pressure to guide its movements instead of a bit. Traver was beginning to consider himself a decent rider after all the time he'd spent on the piebald's naked back.

Ahead, he could see the encampment of two armies, and he thought he recognized the blue colors of Rothscard. He didn't want to get involved with *those* again. He'd had enough of Rothscard Bluecloaks to last a few lifetimes.

There had been a third army that had concerned him more, the black armor of its warriors standing out as a deadly barrier between himself and the forces of his countrymen. But that army was heading in disorganized retreat back toward the Gap of Amberlie. Traver watched them go, wondering what had prompted them to leave. There was no sign a battle had been fought, nor even a skirmish. Something strange was going on down there.

He kicked the piebald to a gallop, leaning forward as they raced over the snowy fields. Ahead, he saw a thin tendril of smoke and, drawing back on the ropes that served for reins, decided to go investigate. The smoke was coming from a small fire built under the bare branches of a tree.

Squinting, Traver made out the form of a man leaning up against the tree trunk, appearing quite asleep. But as Traver came nearer, the man's eyes shot open. The man reached for the black hilt of a knife at his belt.

Traver almost went for his sword. But then he remembered he'd lost it. He had lost more than just the blade. He'd lost the ability of ever wielding a weapon again. At least the man on the ground looked like he'd changed his mind about attacking him. He sat up straight, head cocked to the side, a look of disbelief on his face.

At the same moment Traver recognized him, Devlin Craig said wonderingly, "Larsen?"

Traver threw back his head, laughing as he slid down from the back of his horse. "What are you doing here?"

Craig scowled, pointing to his leg. Traver grimaced as he saw the bandage wrapped tightly around the man's thigh. It was ironic, actually. He raised his hands, wiggling the fingers he had left.

Craig cracked a grin, chuckling and shaking his head. "We're two fine soldiers, aren't we?"

Traver laughed and clapped him on the shoulder as he knelt at his old captain's side. Nodding in the direction of the departing Enemy army, he asked, "What's happening down there?"

"I don't know." Craig shrugged, picking up a fallen branch and pointing with it. "They've been sitting down there for two days, then this morning they just packed up and began withdrawing."

Traver frowned. "I wonder what happened."

With a grimace, Craig leaned his weight on the branch, using it to help push himself to his feet. Limping a step forward, he offered, "Let's go down there and find out. I'm starving."

Traver moved toward him and helped support the man's weight, wondering how, with only eight fingers, he was ever going to get Craig's big bulk onto his one-eyed horse.

Darien's story continues in 'Darklands'...
...but will he be the same?

Darklands

BOOK TWO

Khazahar Desert
Tokashi Palace
Qul
The Ghost Waste
Malikar
BRYN CALAZAR
Ishara
Desert of Maridur
Greystone Keep
Wolden
Cerulean Plains
AERYSIUS
Glen Farquist
Orien's Finger
Auberdale
Rothscard
THE Rhen
Isle of Titherry
Meridan
Southwark
THE Southern Continent
c. 1749 DCE

Chapter One
Infernal Commission

Aerysius, The Rhen

The old man wandered the dark corridor toward his death, the girl trailing after him.

The girl's right hand clutched a thin-bladed knife, the sort of knife once used by hunters of the clans to scrape the flesh of beasts away from bone. But the girl had encountered no such beasts in her nineteen years of existence. The knife in her hand wasn't meant for the flesh of animals. It thirsted for the blood of the old man.

Azár glared ahead at her master's life-weary gait with a scowl of derision on her face. Zamir was selfish, and his selfishness had imperiled all the clans. He should have made this last journey months ago, back when his death might have actually counted for something. Now, too late, Zamir's belated gesture of sacrifice was just as wretched and irrelevant as the old man himself.

"Here." Zamir grimaced, bringing a trembling, rheumatic hand up to trail down the weeping surface of the stone passage. In the darkness, his damp and gnarled fingers resembled the tangled roots of trees. Azár's gaze lingered on them, apathetic, her hand compressing the hilt of the knife in her palm.

She waited, staring dully, and said nothing.

Azár watched in silence as her master shambled forward through the nebulous tendrils of magelight that churned at his feet. Her eyes remained fixed on the scraps of colorless fabric that clung to his emaciated back. She made no move to follow him into the shadowy chamber beyond, not until his voice called out from the darkness to rebuke her. Azár forced herself to move forward through the doorway.

She stopped, mouth agape. Her hand on the blade fell limply to her side as she gazed at the bleak images that confronted her. To one side of the chamber was a dark stone altar set with four ancient, rusted chains. To the other side of the room stood an ominous ring of man-carved stone.

Azár watched with morbid curiosity as Zamir sat himself down upon the worn surface of the altar that rose from stagnant pools of water collected on the floor. He lay himself back, adjusting his position, folding his arms across his chest. His age-leathered face gazed upward into the shadows, eyes fiercely introspective.

"Recite the forward sequence," he instructed her in a gravelly voice.

Azár's gaze swept across the room in the direction of the well.

The Well of Tears appeared exactly as she'd expected, exactly as she'd feared. It was made of staggered granite blocks stacked as high as her waist. Carved all around the rim were runes at once both sinister and familiar, sad vestiges of a lost heritage one thousand years dead. The runes themselves seemed to beckon, compelling her to approach.

Azár scowled at the markings, resenting them. It was because of the runes that they were here, such a far and dangerous distance away from anywhere they were supposed to be. The runes were a key that unlocked a door, a door between worlds. Azár had spent the past two years preparing for this journey. Even so, she felt horrendously anxious. This was a path she had never desired for herself, would never wish upon anyone.

"*Sistru, qurzi, calebra, ghein, vimru...*" Her voice faltered. Azár cleared her throat, edging cautiously forward as she continued reciting from memory the order of the ancient cypher. "*Ranu, benthos, metha, zhein, noctua...ledros. Dacros.*"

She dropped to a crouch beside the Well of Tears as her voice trailed off into a festering silence. She lifted a finger to trace over the first of the sacred markings to confront her: *dacros*. The final rune of the sequence. Ancient symbol of Xerys, God of Chaos and Lord of the Netherworld.

"You make me proud," uttered the old man from behind her. "What will be is better than what is gone."

Azár didn't turn back around to look at him. Instead, she remained squatting in a tarry pool of stagnant water with her hand raised before her face. Her eyes considered the rune that seemed to glare out at her like a brand seared into the Well's stony hide. Azár slowly lowered her hand and cast a wordless glance back over her shoulder.

Zamir yet lay on his back on the stone altar, arms folded across his chest. His tired eyes stared upward at the ceiling or perhaps straight ahead into eternity. He made no further effort to instruct her. There was no need.

Azár rose to her feet and stalked back across the chamber. From the woven belt at her waist, she produced a small pewter cup, which she set down on the rough surface of the altar rock at her master's side.

Face utterly impassive, Azár took Zamir's arm into her hand. Wielding the thin-bladed knife, she drew a deep slit into his skin all the way from his elbow to his wrist. Azár stared down at the blood that welled from the gaping incision. As she watched, the dark fluid coursed over her fingers and ran, dribbling, over her hand. Gradually, she became aware of the sound of the old man's voice muttering the phrases of the *dhumma*, the prayer that is spoken with the last breath before dying.

Azár studied Zamir's face, gazing with curiosity into the old man's dimming eyes. She set the knife down and centered the pewter cup beneath the running trickle of blood to better collect the spilt offering. The vessel filled quickly to the brim. Azár gazed down into his face as his lifeblood drained out of him.

The girl said nothing. She stood there, holding her master's hand, watching as the last light faded quietly from his eyes. As it did, Azár felt the warm stirring of power that grew within her fingertips. Her eyes went wide, her breath catching in her lungs.

The swelling warmth of the Transference swept up her hand into her arm, spreading outward through her chest, raging like a firestorm through her veins. The power coursed through her, filling her, penetrating every fiber of her being.

Then, abruptly, Azár felt the conduit slam closed.

She cried out, cringing back away from the emptied husk of the old man. Her eyes bright with alarm, she took a staggering step away, her breath coming in sharp and panicked gasps. Her gaze darted wildly around the dark chamber, her brain struggling to make sense of the confused perceptions that assaulted it. Tears wrung from her eyes by the violence of the Transference streaked her face, dribbling from her chin. Her whole body was shaking, weakened from the deluge of powerful energies.

Panting, Azár summoned a faint glow of magelight. A shimmering mist was inspired into being, roiling tendrils exploring the wet floor around her feet. The magelight pierced the shadows of the chamber, driving them back against the recesses of the walls. By the light of her own newfound power, Azár's eyes were drawn once again toward the Well of Tears. She glared at the portal, despising it utterly.

Steeling herself, Azár reached for the life-warm pewter cup at her side. Taking it into her hand, she made her way across the chamber. She knelt beside the Well, holding the cup of her master's blood with trembling hands. She dipped a shaking finger into the cup and then raised it up before her face. Turning her finger slowly, she observed the wet sheen of blood in the soft tendrils of magelight. Azár leaned forward and applied Zamir's spent lifeblood to the first rune of the sequence. The blood absorbed quickly into the porous stone as if sucked inside.

Before her eyes, the ancient rune *sistru* awakened from sleep and began to glow with a green, ethereal light. Azár moved around to the far side of the Well, to the next marking of the sequence. She brought that rune, too, to life. Then she moved on to the next. Calm and deliberate, Azár took her time, working meticulously all around the rim until, at last, all of the ancient markings glowed with their own inner light.

When Azár was finished, she stood up and backed away. She regarded her work, satisfied. The gateway was unlocked in this world. But someone else would have to open it from the other side.

Azár rose and used her nascent powers to slide the cover off the Well of Tears. The thick granite slab lifted of its own volition and glided smoothly aside. It hovered for a moment in the air, as if suspended from invisible strings, before lowering the rest of the way to the floor.

Azár turned back toward her master. Zamir had one last journey to make. The Well of Tears demanded a sacrifice, and the old man's soul would be the final gesture that would unseal the gateway.

Zamir had been frail, but the dead weight of his corpse was still too much for Azár's slight build to manage. So she closed her eyes, aligning her thoughts with the rhythmic pulse of the magic field, allowing the power of her mind to supplement the strength of her flesh. Azár lifted Zamir's body up over the Well's rim, giving him a shove.

With the slightest scraping noise, the corpse slipped into the gaping shaft and tumbled downward into darkness.

Azár turned away. It would take some time for Zamir's spirit to complete the final task he had set for himself. There was still yet time to ascend the long flights of steps to the level of the surface. She would have to hurry; her part was still far from complete.

Azár sent her magelight roaming forward, her feet following its glowing trail out of the chamber and into the dark passage beyond. She knew exactly which direction to turn; her master had made certain she would not falter in her task. The corridor she traversed was part of a larger warren of passageways that infested the mountainside below what had once been proud Aerysius, city of the mages. Now just a sad and desolate foundation that stood forlorn three thousand feet above the Vale of Amberlie.

Following the map she had committed to memory, Azár let her feet carry her up a narrow stair, moving through a glowing trail of magelight that spilled ahead of her. Her eyes rejoiced in the texture of the light, awed by the magelight's warm, summery glow. It was her own creation, her very first. A lifegiving thing of wonder and graceful beauty.

Azár sent her mind out, sampling the pulse and rhythm of the magic field in this place. It was soothing and vibrant. It was hers, now, to command as she pleased. She could feel Zamir's power stirring within her, a wondrous and potent legacy.

She emerged at last from the depths of the mountain into a cool, clear night. She gazed out upon the terrace that stretched before her, captivated by the stark austerity of Aerysius' bare foundations. Azár gazed upward into the sky, tilting her head back as an abrupt gust of wind seized her long, dark braid.

Before her, violent energies shot toward the sky, penetrating the dome of the heavens with a violence that was alarming. Lightning licked down to assault that awful spire, raining trails of sparks across the sky.

Confronted with such a daunting vision, Azár felt her courage falter. She lowered her gaze, biting her lip. She concentrated on the sound of her breath, willing her mind to focus. When she opened her eyes again, she regarded the gateway with newfound resolve.

Azár's breath caught in her throat.

From out of the dazzling brilliance of the column, dark figures were emerging. Stirred by the sight of them, Azár's heart quickened its pace. She stood her ground with fists balled against her sides, feet apart, back rigid. Shivering with excitement, Azár looked on as the first man-shaped silhouettes drew forth from the glaring wash of light to converge on her position.

The man who approached first was easily identified by the spiked weapon he bore: Byron Connel, ancient Warden of Battlemages, wielder of the legendary talisman Thar'gon. To his right strode an elegant woman in a flowing white gown, dark of hair as well as skin. A demon-hound with menacing green eyes stalked at her side. Azár had heard enough tales of the Eight to recognize Myria Anassis, ancient Querer of the Lyceum.

Another woman with loose chestnut hair approached Azár. She strolled alongside a man just as handsomely sinister as the woman was deceptively beautiful: Sareen Qadir and Nashir Arman. The pair approached gracefully. The woman's eyes seemed to glisten, a smile of excitement growing on her lips.

So distracted was she by the pair that Azár almost didn't notice the two men approaching from the opposite direction. She turned, startled to find herself confronted by the imposing forms of Zavier Renquist and Cyrus Krane. The two ancient Prime Wardens drew up together before her, the white cloaks of their office billowing behind them, stirred by gusts of wind displaced by the gateway. Cyrus Krane regarded Azár with a sneer rendered all the more cruel by the jagged red scar that bisected his face. His dark eyes were murky pools of unveiled threat.

Zavier Renquist paused before her, arms behind his back, gazing down upon Azár with an expression of somber esteem. His dark hair was pulled back from his face, gathered into a thick braid at the top of his head. He gazed at her expectantly, as if calmly waiting for her to speak first. Had he been any other man in the world, Azár might have considered it.

Appearing satisfied, Zavier Renquist lifted his chin and addressed Azár in a deep and resonant voice:

"Our Master extends to you His gratitude. In you, Xerys is well-pleased. He commits to you the services of the Eight and His army of the night until the initial purpose of our summoning is fulfilled. So, my child, it is time to speak your desires. What shall be your command?"

Azár swallowed, unable to look away from the mesmerizing shadows that simmered in Zavier Renquist's eyes. She held his gaze with her own as she summoned a fragile voice, praying her words would not falter and betray her fear.

"I command you to save my people." Azár channeled every scrap of assertiveness she could muster into her tone. She squared her shoulders, lifting her chin. Her fists were still clenched tightly at her sides. "Deliver us from the darkness. Raise us up from the ashes. Return to us our birthright—this is my command!"

Zavier Renquist stood there regarding her for a prolonged, searching minute. It was impossible to read his expression; the ancient demon's face was altogether blank, without any hint or trace of emotion. He stared deeply into Azár's eyes as if scrutinizing her worth, contemplating the fabric of her soul, weighing the mettle of her character. At last, apparently satisfied, he gave a terse nod.

"Then it shall be as you command," he said, shifting his weight over his feet. His indigo robes swayed with his motion. He turned to cast a predatory stare across at Cyrus Krane then turned again toward Azár. Very formally, he spread his hands and assured her:

"Malikar's deliverance is long overdue. And this time, there will be nothing in this world that can deter us from our goal. Allow me to introduce to you the man whose responsibility it shall be to reclaim the light and heritage that was lost so long ago when Caladorn fell into darkness."

He gestured with his hand, indicating a man who had drawn up silently behind the others and now stood with hands clasped in front of him, head bowed against his chest. As Azár's attention focused on him, the man glanced up through matted strands of long, black hair that had fallen forward over his face. His yellow-green eyes locked on hers with an intensity that was frightening.

Azár felt herself taken sharply aback; she had no idea who this man was. He fit none of the descriptions she had ever heard spoken of the Eight. The look in his eyes chilled her very soul.

She frowned in consternation, her brow nettling. "I don't understand," Azár whispered. "What has become of our mistress? Who is this man? How is it that he alone is expected to accomplish what all Eight of you could not achieve before?"

Zavier Renquist clasped his fingers together in front of him: a gesture of patience. "Your mistress failed. Her soul has been consigned to Oblivion." He fixed Azár with a flat, significant stare. He extended his hand, indicating to Azár the stranger across from her with the haunted eyes. "This is the man who bested your mistress in combat and has replaced her at my side. He has assumed all of Arden Hannah's rights, privileges, and obligations."

Azár fixed this newcomer with an incredulous stare, shaking her head in confounded dismay. "Who *is* he?"

Zavier Renquist explained, "Darien Lauchlin is the lone Sentinel who laid waste to Malikar's legions at the base of Xerys' Pedestal."

Azár's mouth dropped open. She had not been present at the massacre, but she had heard of the atrocities committed by Aerysius' Last Sentinel, his final act of desperation. Thousands of brave warriors had not returned from that campaign, their bodies reduced to charred ash scattered on the wind. Azár shivered as she regarded the disquieting man before her, coming to the slow conclusion that Zavier Renquist had to be telling the truth about him. It was the only explanation for the depths of torment in those harrowing eyes.

"This is impossible!" Azár managed at last. "The man you speak of is dead!"

"As am I," the Prime Warden reminded her with a shrug and a smile. Spreading his hands, he went on to explain, "Darien Lauchlin committed his soul to the service of Xerys. He is now one with us in purpose. He has assumed all rights, responsibilities, and covenants of the Servant he replaces. So Darien is, in every respect, the overlord your people have been so long awaiting. Your request is his singular purpose to fulfill."

Azár turned her head and spat upon the ground. Whirling away, she exclaimed in anger, "I will not suffer the company of this man! He is not even a man—he is a demon, a monster!"

"Perhaps." The ancient Prime Warden raised his eyebrows. He did not appear affronted in the least by Azár's accusation. "But I would strongly advise you to reconsider and think very carefully before declining Darien's assistance. Because, considering the nature of your demands, it sounds like a monster is exactly what you need."

Azár gazed at him with dread in her eyes, knowing deep down in her gut that Renquist's assessment was probably accurate. She sighed, giving in, heart heavy with dismay.

"Go with her," Zavier Renquist commanded his newest Servant in a voice suffused with arrogance and ice. "You heard her demands. Go forth and fulfill them."

The dark-haired demon nodded slightly. "I will do my best, Prime Warden." His voice sounded terse, strained. He strode forward.

"Stop."

Renquist's sharp command halted him in his tracks. As Azár looked on in fascination, Darien Lauchlin turned back around with weary patience in his eyes.

Zavier Renquist promised him, "Your best isn't going to be good enough. Instead of your best, *I demand your worst.* You must let go of your past and embrace your destiny. Unchain your inner demons. Conquer your own ghosts just as you once conquered my armies. Transcend the constraints you have used to shackle your conscience and experience firsthand what true freedom feels like."

Darien Lauchlin nodded, dark strands of hair swaying forward into his face. "It shall be as you ask, Prime Warden."

"It had better be. For your sake. And for hers."

Azár stared long and hard at the two men, her brow furrowed in consternation. Renquist's threat had not been directed toward herself. She let her gaze linger on the man trudging toward her, a demon-hound jogging behind in his wake. Frowning, she wondered which woman's life Zavier Renquist had just threatened. And why that woman's life mattered so much to this tormented monster of a man.

Chapter Two
Message from the Past

Rothscard, The Rhen

Kyel Archer gazed up at the corrugated towers of Emmery Palace with a growing feeling of trepidation gnawing at his already soured stomach. He'd never liked Rothscard, and today's visit was certainly no exception. Kyel's every experience of the city had been riddled with misfortune in some significant way. The first time he'd passed through Rothscard, Kyel had found himself falsely accused of murder, chained, and swept away to the Front as a conscript to fight in the war. His second visit to the city had ended with him in chains of a very different nature, though the experience had been no less demeaning. Kyel couldn't help but wonder if this visit would prove just as treacherous. This time, the matching pair of chains he wore on his wrists were of his own creation, forged by his own convictions. But that did little to ease the burden of their weight, or to render their harsh constraints less difficult to bear.

Kyel gazed up at the ramparts of the palace with a whimsical expression, one thumb stroking the new growth of beard he wore on his face. As the coach drew up before an elegant fountain in the courtyard, Kyel cast a quick glance at Naia, seated across from him on a leather bench. The smile of reassurance she gifted him helped a little. It gave Kyel enough strength to conjure up a fleeting smile of his own.

Naia appeared exceptionally in her element, he realized, completely at ease. The former priestess seemed more radiant than usual, her dark auburn hair gathered in a bun. Her face, once kept concealed by the white veil of Death, was almost shocking in its beauty. In the past two years, Kyel had grown more accustomed to the sight of Naia's naked face, though he had never been able to take it entirely for granted. The absence of the veil remained conspicuous.

Their coach drew to a halt with a sudden jolt. Kyel swallowed against a hard lump in his throat, surveying the tall towers of the palace through the window.

He could hear Meiran's voice beside him, muttering in her usual, no-nonsense alto, "Breathe, Kyel. You look like you're going to be ill."

"I'm still not sure that I won't be."

There was a sharp clank as someone outside threw open the door of the coach. Kyel stared for a moment at the door's leather skin, then let his gaze drop to the boots of the footman awaiting them.

Kyel took his time about climbing down out of the coach; it had been hours since he'd last had a chance to stretch his legs. Fortunately, the footman had positioned a small stool just under the carriage, making the drop down to the ground far less of an undertaking. Kyel took a few unsteady steps, gazing around as his hands went to straighten the thick black cloak that hung from his shoulders.

Naia alighted gently at his side, followed immediately by Meiran, who strode forward between the two of them. The white cloak of her office flowed gracefully down her back, swaying with each movement of her body, the embroidered Silver Star glistening in the sunlight.

Kyel fell in behind her, Naia at his side, the uniformed guards of Emmery Palace forming ranks behind their small entourage. Kyel had to rush to keep up with Meiran's long strides; she hadn't bothered to wait for an escort. Instead, she set her own course up the white marble steps as dignitaries rushed forward to intercept her.

"Thank you, Prime Warden, for your swift response to our invitation." The first breathless minister fell in beside Meiran, matching her stride for stride. He wore an opulent ensemble, sporting a plumed hat and a cape.

"Of course." Meiran didn't favor the man with so much as a glance. She kept her gaze fixed straight ahead as she strode swiftly into the depths of the palace, forcing the man to take hurried strides to keep up. "It's never a problem. Without the support of Emmery's Crown, our time in exile would be much less comfortable. Queen Romana has been a most generous benefactor."

The minister smiled with an accommodating nod. He brought a folded kerchief up to dab at his brow as he continued to keep pace with Meiran's long strides. "My Lady Queen thanks you for making such haste. Her Majesty is anxious to hear your opinion on a certain, most urgent matter, and is wondering—"

Meiran cut him off in mid-sentence, snapping, "If your Lady Queen is so anxious for my opinion, then why isn't she here to greet us personally?" Meiran raised her eyebrows in speculation as she finally turned to regard the man laboring beside her. Kyel allowed himself an amused grin as he watched the interaction. He could hardly imagine anyone more suited for the office of Prime Warden than Meiran Withersby.

Blotting at the sheen of perspiration on his brow, the minister looked troubled. "My apologies, Prime Warden, but Queen Romana requests that you convene with her in the Blue Room."

"So, I've been relegated to the Blue Room, now, have I?" Meiran sounded irritated. Following behind her, Kyel couldn't get a good look at her face. But he had no trouble imagining the characteristic scowl she must be wearing. "Has Romana become skittish of magefolk again, or is this 'urgent matter' really that desperate?"

The minister led her around a corner and into a long corridor lined with painted wood panels. "I'm afraid I couldn't begin to speculate, Prime Warden," he murmured in placating tones.

Meiran harrumphed. "No, I don't suppose you're capable. Ah. Here we are."

She drew up before a wide set of double doors as Kyel almost stumbled into her back. He shot a small, knowing grin in Naia's direction, who returned the expression in kind. They waited, Kyel glancing around as liveried servants threw open the paneled doors, exposing the bright interior of the chamber.

Meiran swept forward into the room, quickly crossing the patterned rugs. There, in the center of the room, she drew herself up formally and simply waited. Her cloak swung from her thin frame, which was covered by a sumptuous gown of pristine white. Her rich brown hair was gathered behind her head in an elegant twist. Her gaze moved over the interior of the chamber in critical assessment. She drew herself up, shoulders squared and head held regally. Her very presence was suffused with authority.

"The Prime Warden of Aerysius, Meiran Withersby," the voice of the minister announced belatedly.

Kyel's eyes shot in the direction of the man, catching just a glimpse of him as the doors swung closed, shuddering as they latched. A long, tense silence followed. With a wrench of nausea, Kyel forced himself to look Romana Norengail in the eye.

Emmery's Queen had matured in the two years since he'd last seen her. Romana was no longer the disarming young girl he'd first met in her solarium. She seemed even more regal now, as though years and experience had somehow consecrated her right to her throne. She wore the Sapphire Crown of Emmery on her head, her shoulders draped in winter ermine. Her lovely face was both patient and serene.

At her side, seated in a chair not quite as tall or elaborately carved, was Nigel Swain, Romana's husband. Kyel's stomach physically squirmed at the sight of the prince consort. Even after all this time, Kyel was still not sure how he felt about the man. Swain had conspired to murder Darien Lauchlin and had manipulated Kyel into helping him. The underhanded way he'd gone about it still galled. Swain was a harsh man, uncompromising in his character. But his loyalty to Romana was flawless.

Confronted with the presence of the Prime Warden, both Romana and Swain stood and, taking a step forward in unison, dropped to their knees upon the rugs spread before them on the floor.

"Arise," Meiran directed them with a curt wave of her hand. Without any further attempt at ceremony, she seated herself in one of the chairs arranged before them, Kyel taking the seat to her right as Naia claimed the one beside him.

"Tea?" a butler inquired, indicating a wheeled cart that held an elegant silver service.

"Yes, that would be lovely." Meiran's hands moved to smooth the fabric of her gown.

The butler thrust an elegant cup and saucer into Kyel's hands. Yes, he wanted cream. No, he didn't care for any honey. No wafers, thank you very much. He brought the teacup to his lips, holding the saucer in his left hand as he managed a sip. The tea was fragrant with chamomile and very hot. He lowered the cup back down, resting it against his leg.

Queen Romana made a majestic but half-hearted attempt at a smile. "Prime Warden, let me first begin by saying—"

"Please." Meiran cut her off, lowering her own teacup from her lips. "Let us dispense with formalities. We're all very tired from the journey. So, just tell me: what has happened?"

The smile vanished from the lips of Emmery's Queen. Her gaze wandered toward her husband. Kyel studied the two of them, trying to find meaning in the silent conversation that passed between them in the span of a single heartbeat. Turning back to Meiran, Queen Romana said in a troubled voice:

"A green spire of light has been reported in the skies above Aerysius."

Kyel sputtered as he choked on a swallow of tea. Coughing, he leaned forward over his legs and set the cup and saucer down on the floor beside his chair.

"Has this report been confirmed?" Meiran sat as if frozen, her cup paused halfway to her lips.

Nigel Swain nodded. His gray-streaked hair swayed forward into his face. "The gateway is very visible, especially at night. It can be seen for miles in all directions."

"It's been only two years," Naia whispered at Kyel's side. The despair in her voice was painful to hear. "How could this be happening already? Who could have opened it? Who *would* have?"

Meiran cast a withering glance in Naia's direction. She took a deep breath, appearing to be collecting herself, then uttered with a scowl, "It doesn't matter. What's done is done. No matter how it was accomplished, we now must deal with the consequences."

Kyel squirmed in his chair, his thoughts pulled in a hundred separate directions at once. He found himself transported back in time, back to a dark room in a damp cavern in the heart of an ancient mountain. Where a granite well encircled with glowing, sinister markings awaited him. It had been his job to seal those runes, to burn them clean of the blood that fed them life.

Apparently, his work had been undone.

"Have there been…other types of reports?" he said to no one in particular.

Queen Romana answered his question. "Not yet. But we must assume that the Eight walk the earth again. We need to consider the possibility that war might soon be upon us."

"They are no longer Eight," Naia corrected her. "Darien destroyed Arden Hannah. Their number has been reduced to seven."

The Prime Warden shrugged dismissively. "One less darkmage won't make a bit of difference. There's only three of us, each fettered by the Oath of Harmony. Kyel is the closest thing we have to a Sentinel."

Swain leaned forward, elbows resting on his knees. "Which order did Naia take?"

Meiran responded, "I've been training Naia as a Querer."

Swain leaned back in his chair, eyes narrowing. "So. We've got one half-trained Sentinel and one half-trained Querer. And a Prime Warden we can't risk letting anywhere near a field of battle. Those are our assets. Against seven Unbound demons. Including Byron Connel, one of the greatest military minds the world has ever known."

Naia's gaze lifted to confront him. In a voice thick with the lilt of Chamsbrey, she asked Swain, "Perhaps now you can appreciate Darien's quandary?" The resentment in her tone was scathing.

Nigel Swain shook his head. "No. I don't. Because here we are again two years later, in the same situation as before. All Darien did was buy us time. Nothing more."

Naia glared at him, her lips compressed with

bitterness. "No," she growled in a voice low and defiant. "Darien's sacrifice was not in vain. I will not believe that. I cannot believe that."

Swain leaned forward, capturing her eyes with a cold, unfeeling stare. "It doesn't matter what you believe; the portal's open again. They'll be coming. And this time, Darien's not here to save or damn us."

Kyel found himself gazing down absently at the chain on his right wrist, rotating his arm so that the markings shimmered in the light. "We must reseal the Well of Tears," he said. "That will cut them off from their source of power." He didn't dare voice his next thought: that one of their own number would have to volunteer to be the next sacrifice demanded by the gateway. It had to be a Grand Master. Naia was only third tier; she ranked too low to be an option. That left only Meiran and himself.

Meiran was fingering the necklace she always wore around her neck. It was a habit she had, something she tended to do whenever something troubled her. The necklace had a silver pendant that looked to be made of one sinuous, intertwined strand that wove around about itself without beginning or end. The symbol was called an eternity knot. Darien had given her that necklace the day he'd left Aerysius for Greystone Keep. The same day Meiran had presented him with the sword he could never bring himself to part with.

"No," Meiran sighed at last, still fingering the fragile pendant on its chain. "They'll be expecting us to move against the Well. This time, they'll be guarding it much more carefully. The Well of Tears will have to remain open, at least for now."

Romana leaned forward, her hands squeezing the arms of her chair. "What, then?"

Meiran dropped her hand, looking up into the face of Emmery's Queen. "I've spent the past two years rallying the southern kingdoms in support of our cause. It's time for those monarchies to do more than just offer lip service. On the morrow, I will pronounce a formal declaration of war. Let's see how many battalions the South will be willing to muster."

Looking at Swain, she asked, "What's the status of Greystone Keep and Ironguard Pass?"

Nigel Swain shrugged. "Fortifications are well underway, though neither keep is combat-ready."

Kyel frowned. "Has Force Commander Craig been notified of this?"

"I sent a bird to him before I sent for you."

A liveried servant entered the room, swiftly circling the small ring of chairs and leaning over to whisper in Swain's ear. The man's voice was much too low for Kyel to hear. But he could see Swain's reaction. The prince's eyes widened reflexively, his body stiffening in his chair.

"Wait here," he growled as he rose to his feet. He crossed the room in three cat-like strides and was already out the door before Kyel could wonder what had happened. He kept his gaze focused on the doorway, frowning after the man.

Naia was still talking, going on as though she hadn't noticed Swain's abrupt disappearance. "We should talk about making use of the temples. I could travel to the Valley of the Gods and speak with my father. It's not far."

"That's not a bad idea," Meiran muttered, looking at the doorway rather than at Naia. "Do me a favor and bring it up again later."

A loud noise echoed from outside. The sound of many running footsteps rang clearly from the hallway. Kyel started, surging to his feet just as a cluster of blue-cloaked guardsmen spilled into the room, sweeping forward around the chairs to converge on their Queen.

Romana was on her feet in an instant, eyes wide with alarm, as the guardsmen encircled her, forming a protective ring. Meiran and Naia were forced to back away to make room for the swarm of armored bodies. Kyel found himself reaching for the magic field, holding it ready.

"Naia, retire with the Queen."

Kyel whirled at the sound of Swain's voice calling out from the doorway. He clutched the scabbard of a longsword. He was flanked by two more guards with bars of rank upon their sleeves.

Kyel stepped forward, inserting himself between Meiran and Swain, shielding the Prime Warden with his own body. He had no idea what was happening, had no clear evidence whether the guards were security or threat. He only knew that Meiran's life had to be protected at all cost. And he was the only thing close to a Sentinel they had.

Turning to the prince, Kyel demanded, "What happened? What's going on?"

Eyes only for his Queen, Swain responded, "Two of Renquist's demons just showed up on our doorstep." To his guardsmen he instructed, "Escort the Queen and Master Naia to the Residence."

Naia opened her mouth as if to argue as guards moved in close, pressing her backward with their bodies. She turned to Meiran with a questioning look in her eyes. The Prime Warden nodded, bestowing her assent, eyes glazed with worry.

"Protect the Queen," she said.

Naia dropped a formal curtsy before turning away. The guards immediately surrounded her, directing her along with Romana toward a door on the opposite wall. Within seconds, both women were gone. The room was swiftly emptied. Kyel turned back to Swain.

"Now what, exactly, is going on?"

Swain explained as he donned his sword, "My men detained two darkmages at the palace gates. They carry a badge of truce. They say they desire parley with the Prime Warden."

Face aghast, Meiran strode toward him. "Who are they? Did they give their names?"

The prince only shrugged, adjusting the strap of the baldric that crossed his chest. "I have no idea who they are. I didn't care to ask. I had them escorted across the grounds to the citadel. I didn't want them under the same roof as the Queen."

The Prime Warden stopped, lifting a pair of perfectly arched eyebrows. "You had them detained? Under a badge of *truce*?"

Swain grimaced. "Give me a little credit, Meiran. It wasn't that kind of escort."

Kyel frowned, not liking the situation one bit. He stared down at the markings of the chain on his wrist, gazing at it as cold prickles of dread needled his skin. There was little he could do against two darkmages. Strong as he was, there was only so much he could manage within the confines of his Oath of Harmony.

Never to harm.

The words he had spoken to Darien beneath Orien's Finger echoed in his memory, chilling him just as thoroughly as they had the moment he'd uttered them. He had never doubted his decision to take that Oath, had never questioned it, not even once.

Never, until now.

Meiran was already moving toward the door. "Very well. Kyel, you're with me."

Kyel had to move quickly to catch up. Swain swept ahead of them with a glare, two guards bringing up the rear. He moved with the casual grace of a blademaster, a stride that reminded Kyel of the way a cat stalks a bird. There was no attempt at conversation as they continued down the long, paneled corridors of the palace. It became apparent that every door was warded, guards stationed at intervals all up and down the length of the hallways. There were many more than he remembered.

They followed their escort out of the palace and across the grounds. Kyel kept pace at Meiran's side, his black cloak rippling behind him as he moved, the Silver Star of Aerysius glistening at his back. They moved through a maze of garden walkways bordered by boxwood hedges. At the far side of the inner ward was the citadel, a sprawling building surrounded with what looked like an entire company of Bluecloaks. Kyel had been inside the citadel once before. It had been there, in that prison, that Kyel had received the Transference through the Soulstone.

They paused at the entrance to a circular chamber ringed by guards. There, Swain bid them halt as he strode toward an officer, pausing to confer quietly with the man. Kyel gazed around, taking in the martial look of the place, the combined scents of oiled metal and aged leather.

Swain nodded and took a step back. The officer barked an order. The guards that ringed the chamber turned and strode together toward the door, clearing the room. The door was shut, the bar thrown.

The three of them were alone.

Meiran turned to Swain, expectantly cocking an eyebrow. The prince motioned with his head in the direction of a door, at the same time reaching up to remove the sword from his back, leaning both sword and scabbard up against the wall. Meiran nodded, eyes narrowing as she considered the doorway. Then she started toward it.

Kyel fell in behind her, drawing in more of the magic field until the song of it swelled inside his head and the energy bled from his body in a visible, golden nimbus that surrounded him. Whatever happened, he wanted to be ready.

At the door, Meiran hesitated. She reached out and clenched the handle and, closing her eyes as if uttering a prayer, pulled the door open.

As they moved through the doorway, Kyel's eyes immediately widened in dismay. He pulled harder on the magic field, sending a spill of magelight forward into the shadowy corridor ahead.

He hadn't known what to expect. Certainly, not this.

He halted in mid-stride, confronted by the most beautiful woman he'd ever seen. She stood waiting in the center of the dark hallway, poised, a congenial smile on her face, chestnut hair spilling down her back. She wore an indigo robe with the image of the Silver Star embroidered on the breast. Kyel frowned at the sight of it, his eyes roving over the woman with blatant curiosity. She didn't look evil; there was no amount of malevolence in her eyes. In her upraised hand, she held a white drape of torn fabric: the badge of truce Swain had spoken of.

Beside the woman stood a man with dark, unkempt hair that curled about his collar. He appeared very thin, even gaunt. He was wearing a long black coat that covered a knee-length tunic. He held a black felt hat in front of his chest. There was a quiet sadness about his eyes that Kyel found intriguing. He couldn't help but wonder the reason for it.

Meiran raised her hand, stopping a short distance away from their visitors. She stood there, considering the man and woman before her. She merely regarded them, her eyes narrowed and pensive. Kyel realized that Meiran had produced a glowing shield around her own body, a blue nimbus barely visible against the shadows.

She demanded in a firm voice, "What are your names?"

The woman brought a hand up to her chest. "I am Sareen Qadir." She spoke in a voice thick with a rich and melodic accent. "This is my partner, Quinlan Reis. You must be Prime Warden Meiran Withersby."

Meiran nodded, her face devoid of all emotion. "I am," she responded flatly. "But help me clarify something. You both claim to be Servants of Xerys. So why is it that history has no record of your names?"

A good question, Kyel thought. He gazed expectantly at the two darkmages before him, realizing for the first time that he was staring at two people one thousand years dead.

The chestnut-haired woman offered Meiran an indulgent smile. "Trust me when I say that many things have become lost since our time in this world came to an end. Our names, unfortunately, were not the greatest casualties of Bryn Calazar's fall."

At her side, the man replaced his hat back on his head, adjusting the brim low over his eyes. Gazing at Meiran, he told her, "I once heard that Prime Warden Sephana Clemley had my name expunged from the record books. It's my guess she didn't want my reputation to tarnish my brother's good name."

Meiran frowned at his words, gazing at the man with kindled interest in her eyes. "And who was your brother?"

"Braden Reis," the darkmage responded without hesitation.

Kyel's mouth dropped open.

"Your brother was the *First Sentinel*?" Meiran gasped, obviously just as shocked as Kyel. She made a searching gesture with her hands. "And yet...you're a Servant of Xerys. Explain."

The darkmage sucked in a cheek, issuing a slight shrug. "It seemed like the right decision at the time I made it. Of course, in retrospect, I often find myself wondering why I didn't do things rather differently."

Kyel couldn't help but stare at the man. He was fascinated by the two of them. He found himself far more intrigued than afraid, even though he knew that defied common sense.

"Why are you here?" Meiran asked.

The woman spread her hands. "We are here to deliver a message to you from Prime Warden Zavier Renquist."

Kyel shivered at the very mention of that terrible name. He needed no further reminders that these two mages were very dangerous, indeed. He had been wrong to lower his guard. Kyel chanced a glance over his shoulder at Swain, finding the prince looking none too pleased and very much on edge. His sword arm twitched at his side, seeming to hunger for the hilt of his blade.

Meiran bowed her head for a moment. When she brought her eyes up again, her gaze was rigid. "Very well. Deliver your message and then be gone from this place."

The woman named Sareen nodded formally, giving no indication that she had taken any offense to Meiran's terse command. She said, "Prime Warden Renquist has no desire for a war between our two nations at this time. Instead, what he proposes is an alliance. I have been sent to guide you north with me to Bryn Calazar, where Zavier Renquist desires to meet with you to negotiate the terms of a treaty that will be forged between our two peoples. I am to accompany you, Prime Warden, as your protector and guardian through the Black Lands. I have been instructed to leave Quin behind as assurance for your safe return."

Kyel realized that he had stopped breathing long before the woman had stopped talking. Meiran couldn't accept such an offer. It was much too dangerous.

"And what if I refuse to come with you?" Meiran wondered. Kyel stared at Sareen, very interested in hearing what her response would be.

"I would advise against it," the chestnut-haired beauty shrugged, casting her eyes downward and to the side. "That would leave our Prime Warden with little recourse but to act."

Meiran stared at her unblinking. At last she said, "I will think on it. Is there anything else?"

"Yes."

It was Quinlan Reis who stepped forward, offering out a scroll of parchment toward Meiran in his hand. "I bear another message for you. This one is from Darien Lauchlin."

Kyel stiffened at the mention of that name.

He took a step back away from the offered scroll. Meiran remained where she was. She stared down at the parchment as if it were a venomous snake, the color draining slowly from her face. Her blue eyes were wide with revulsion. Long moments ticked by. She stood staring at the scroll in the darkmage's hand, refusing to accept it.

"I don't understand," she whispered at last. "Darien Lauchlin is dead."

"As am I," Quinlan Reis reminded her, gazing deeply into her eyes. "Like myself, Darien is now a Servant of Xerys."

Kyel gaped at the darkmage, paralyzed by revulsion and dismay. His eyes darted to Meiran. He wanted to go to her, but he couldn't bring himself to move. He remained rooted where he was, heart frozen in dread.

"Darien is one of the Eight?" Meiran gasped in a voice full of despair. She shook her head, gazing down at the scroll as her face collapsed into grief. But then she clenched her jaw, brittle strength returning to her eyes. She shook her head firmly. "No. I don't believe you. Darien would never do such a thing. *You are lying.*"

Quinlan Reis just shrugged, hand still extended toward her in the air. "He wasn't left with much of a choice, I'm afraid. It was the only way he could secure the release of your own soul from the Netherworld."

Kyel closed his eyes, bowing his head. There was little doubt left in his mind; he knew the demon before him was telling the truth. He had to be.

Meiran's whisper was barely audible. "My soul…? *That was the price?*"

Quinlan Reis nodded. "I'm sorry if these tidings bring you grief. I know how much you meant to him. Here. Take it."

He pressed the scroll into Meiran's hand, squeezing her fingers closed around it. Then he stepped back. His eyes seemed even more saddened than they had before.

"Excuse me," Meiran gasped.

She turned and fled the room, leaving Kyel and Swain alone with the two unlikely emissaries. Kyel turned back to regard the darkmages who stood before him, waiting.

He felt completely at a loss.

He had no idea what to do.

Chapter Three
Demon

Aerysius, The Rhen

Darien awoke to the lambent orange glow of flickering torchlight distorting the shadows on the stone walls. The fact that he was even awake and alert in this world at all was strange enough, a sensation that was half-remembered, like a dream. The ruddy hue of the crackling flames seemed surreal, saturated with a bright intensity of color. A vibrant contrast to the monochromatic palette of the Netherworld. The flames of the torches seemed animated, intense, *alive*. They writhed in a vivacious dance, fueled by a breeze that stirred from the depths of the warrens.

He was awake and alert in this world, the same world that, somewhere, Meiran also occupied. Darien's first thought was that he wanted to go to her. He wanted that very badly. He wanted to tell her how grateful he was that she had been there with him at the end.

Meiran's presence at his side had kept the fear of death at bay. Her soothing touch had been the last thing Darien felt as death rose to claim him, catching him up and bearing him away, downward into darkness.

But the darkness had not been eternal.

On the other side, there *had* been light. An unholy light. A sickening pallor, the color of pestilence, of corruption, of decay. Within that cold and brittle light, Darien's soul had been received with delight by his new Master.

He'd had much to atone for.

Darien sat up, shivering, filled with a terrible sense of dread. He drew his knees up against his chest and leaned back against the rough stone wall. He sat there for a long time, letting the chill horror of the memories slowly recede. All across the underground chamber, the other members of their party were beginning to stir. It would be morning soon. Almost time to depart.

He glanced down at the clothes he was wearing, the same tattered outfit he had worn to his death. He was dressed all in black: black breeches, a frayed linen shirt, the same black cloak he'd taken from an abandoned tent in the Chamsbrey encampment below Orien's Finger. There was no Silver Star embroidered on the back; as far as Darien was concerned, he'd lost the right to wear that emblem. He wore only a simple, plain wool cloak, something an officer might sport. Not a mage's cloak. He was a Sentinel of Aerysius no longer.

On the ground beside him lay the sword that Meiran had given him. It rested in its worn leather scabbard, the rubies set into the hilt glimmering like crystalline droplets of blood. His hand went to the sword, sliding it possessively nearer. It was the only thing he had left of her, the only thing he was likely to ever have.

Darien figured the letter he'd written should be enough to destroy any lingering feelings Meiran might still have for him.

He turned toward the sound of approaching footsteps. His hand closed reflexively around the hilt of his sword. But when Darien saw the face of the man who approached, he released his grip. Common steel could not defend him against such a monster.

Nashir Arman dropped into a crouch at Darien's

side. His face was angular and chiseled, his stare intense and penetrating. Darien froze under the severe inspection of those eyes, dropping his own stare to the ground. In the Netherworld, Nashir had been assigned the role of Dariēn's tormentor. The demon took great pleasure in delivering pain. And he was very good at it.

Nashir stared at Darien with an ice-dead gaze. "You took the life of my woman," he said in a low and threatening tone, soft enough so that the others couldn't hear. "I promise you this: before you leave this world again, I'll see to it that you pay."

Darien kept his eyes lowered, focusing his own gaze on the floor. He knew by now not to try to look Nashir in the eye. The pain simply wasn't worth it.

The darkmage leaned forward, staring him in the face. "Perhaps I'll take the life of your woman. Flesh for flesh. Blood for blood. Pain for pain."

Darien glared his hatred at Nashir. It was the only thing he could do, the only defense he had against the sinister demon. He couldn't even sense the magic field, thanks to Cyrus Krane. The man had severed his connection with the field, and that damper was still in place.

"Stop provoking him, Nashir."

Byron Connel drew up behind Nashir, Myria Anassis at his side. Connel wore the indigo robes of the Lyceum of Bryn Calazar, the talisman Thar'gon swaying from a leather strap affixed to his belt. Darien was relieved the two of them had come to his defense, but not surprised. Connel seemed a man of character, patient and even-tempered. Myria was a stalwart intellectual, kind and sincere.

Nashir acknowledged Connel with a stiff nod of his chin. He rose to his feet, his eyes still intently focused on Darien. He turned and stalked away, but not without casting a significant glare back over his shoulder. Darien kept his eyes trained on Nashir, not trusting him at all.

Byron Connel knelt at Darien's side. "Never lower your guard around Nashir Arman," the Battlemage cautioned. "He can be...unprincipled. And unpredictable."

"I know." Darien's attention was still focused on Nashir's retreating back.

"Do you?" inquired Myria, hovering over them with arms crossed in front of her. "I don't know if you appreciate how dangerous he can be."

Darien allowed his gaze to wander upward. Gazing into Myria's face, he assured her, "I can be dangerous, too."

Myria Anassis shook her head, her long, dark hair swaying like a curtain to her waist. "No. Not like him. You have a conscience. A creature like Nashir does not."

Byron Connel adjusted his posture, draping an arm over one knee. "Compared to Nashir, you're like a child, Darien. He was trained as a weapon from birth. He's well-schooled in both offensive magic and tactics, and he's had a thousand years to hone those skills. Your training as a Sentinel was grossly deficient. You wouldn't last a minute against him."

"Then teach me," Darien challenged.

Connel grinned, shaking his head. He cast an amused glance up at Myria. "Sorry, but I can't do that. My duties lie elsewhere, unfortunately. Just remember to watch your back." He reached out, clapping Darien on the shoulder as he rose to take his leave.

Myria regarded Darien with a look of sympathy. "I'm sorry. I wish I could be of more help to you."

Darien found himself intrigued. "Why?"

She paused in the action of turning away. She gave a slight shrug. "Because you remind me of someone I once knew."

"Who?"

The look on Myria's face made it obvious she had not expected either question. "Just a man," she responded after a moment's hesitation. "A man who's been dead for a thousand years."

Darien considered her answer carefully. "Did you love him?"

Myria blinked. Then she frowned. "No. But I did admire him." Still frowning, she turned and strolled away.

Darien allowed his gaze to follow the pale texture of her gown that seemed to flare like fire in the torchlight. Like Byron Connel, Myria defied the concept of darkmage he had nurtured so carefully for so very long. He had thought they would prove to be all just like Nashir Arman and Arden Hannah. Sadistic and power-hungry. Potently cruel, like Cyrus Krane. But there seemed to be more than one type of demon. Apparently, there were many shades and gradations of evil. He wondered where on that continuum his own soul would rank.

At his side, the thanacryst made a noise that sounded almost like purring. Darien moved his hand to its neck, ruffling the course and matted fur. He had been surprised to find out that the demon-hound had once belonged to Nashir. He had offered to return it, but Nashir had wanted nothing to do with his former pet. Darien was grateful; in all the world, the thanacryst was the only friend he seemed to have left.

He gazed across the chamber at the others going about the business of breaking down their small encampment. His eyes found Azár, the Enemy mage whose action of unsealing the Well of Tears had undone everything Darien had given his life for. Azár was awake and rummaging through her pack. She'd made her bed on the far side of the chamber, as far away from him as she could possibly manage. It was very obvious to Darien that he wasn't the savior Azár had been anticipating.

She glanced up and, for the briefest instant, their gaze met. Her eyes narrowed in anger before darting quickly away. Azár was ferocious despite her small size. She was thin and delicate, with ink-black hair that hung in a thick braid all the way down her back. She had a proud and slender nose, smooth bronze skin, and wide, almond-shaped eyes that liked to gleam at him with hatred.

Darien pushed himself up off the ground and strode away from her toward the doorway. As he walked, he shrugged the baldric of his sword on over his shoulder, letting the scabbard fall down across his back. They were still within the warrens beneath Aerysius, in a chamber somewhere in the levels beneath the Well of Tears. The Servants had used these rooms as a kind of headquarters during their last campaign. There were still plenty of supplies left over from that time: dried food stores, blankets, even weapons. They had lingered there for the past two days: provisioning, formulating plans.

Darien followed the damp passage ahead toward a narrow rise of stairs, the demon-hound padding along at his side. He wanted to go up that long flight of steps. He desired one last view of the mountainside before he had to leave, just one last glimpse of the foundations of dead Aerysius.

But it was not meant to be.

The sound of his name stopped him short. Darien turned, glancing behind down the passageway in the direction he had come from. Zavier Renquist was standing there, lingering in the doorway, face stern and expectant. Darien moved immediately to retrace his steps. Of one thing he was completely certain: Zavier Renquist was a hundred times more dangerous than Nashir could ever be.

As Darien drew up before him, he ducked his head in silent deference. The ancient Prime Warden reached out and draped an arm over Darien's shoulders, pulling him in familiarly close. "Let us take our leave," he uttered in a deep baritone voice. With gentle pressure, he steered Darien back toward the deep bowels of the warrens. Glowing tendrils of magelight appeared at their feet, swirling to illuminate the path ahead. Darien's shoulders tensed at the feel of Renquist's hand on his back directing him forward.

"I thought you'd be interested to know that Quin and Sareen arrived safely in Rothscard," the Prime Warden said. "Hopefully, all will go well with their embassy. The letter you prepared should help. In the meantime, the hour has come for us to depart and be about our separate responsibilities."

His stomach clenched at the thought of the letter Renquist had compelled him to write. Darien had spilled his soul out in ink onto that parchment, knowing how imperative it was that Meiran believed him. If she didn't, the consequences were too terrible to consider.

Renquist continued, "Myria told me about Nashir. Be at ease. I've spoken with him."

Darien nodded his gratitude, his thoughts still on Meiran. He wondered what she must be thinking of him now, after reading that letter. The very thought of her reaction to his news made him feel physically ill with shame.

It didn't really matter what Meiran thought of him. In the scheme of things, that was of little consequence. All that mattered was that she believed him. Meiran could despise him for all eternity, so long as her anger kept her and the others alive.

"I want you to know that I have the highest expectations of you, Darien," Renquist said as they strode side by side down the dark corridor, glowing mist swirling beneath their feet. "Of all my chosen Servants, you are by far the most powerful and also the most decisive. You don't shy away from the hard decisions, the kind that keep most men awake at night. You are intelligent, resourceful, and uninhibited. Once you have been properly trained, you will be the greatest Battlemage our world has ever known."

Darien muttered, "If you say so, Prime Warden."

Zavier Renquist stopped, taking Darien by the shoulders and turning him to face him. Darien forced himself to look the Prime Warden directly in the eye. It took every scrap of nerve he possessed to confront Renquist's indomitable stare.

"I realize this is not easy for you," the ancient darkmage confided in a gentler tone. "You made the right decision, Darien. You made the choice that was in the best interest of both our peoples. I think, finally, you're beginning to understand just how imperative our work is here. I have every faith and confidence in your ability to succeed where others have failed."

Darien couldn't help it. He dropped his gaze to the floor under the weight of Renquist's expectations. "Thank you, Prime Warden."

Renquist patted him on the arm. "You'll do just fine. Now. I'm going to remove your field damper. When I do, you'll have a choice to make."

Darien nodded, still staring at the floor. He understood. Renquist was going to give him back the magic field. When he did, there would be nothing preventing him from lashing out with his ability. But Renquist knew he presented little danger; Darien already had a deep appreciation for the consequences of such a betrayal.

Nashir had taught him that lesson very well.

The Prime Warden's eyes narrowed slightly, his face going rigid in concentration. Then the magic field came flooding headlong into Darien's mind like a river overwhelming a dam. He closed his eyes and reeled with the thrill of it, savoring the sweet ecstasy he had gone so long without. Darien took a deep breath, cherishing the feeling of comfort and sentiment the magic field inspired in his mind. Then he opened his eyes, conjuring a mist of his own.

Wondrously, his own magelight appeared at their feet, a shimmering blue glow that mingled with the turbulent vapor Renquist had already summoned.

"I don't understand," he whispered, reveling in the splendor of the cobalt mist, the signature color of the legacy he had surrendered at death. "The Soulstone took my gift. It drained everything from me."

Renquist informed him flatly, "You don't need the gift anymore. You're not alive."

Darien glanced up from the ground, confused and suddenly uncertain. "If I'm not alive, then what am I?"

Renquist allowed him a sad and fleeting smile, the kind of smile a father might bestow upon a young, wayward son. "You have been remade and brought back into being for a time," explained the ancient darkmage. "You are clothed in your own flesh only by the will of Xerys. Through the Onslaught, you have access to the magic field. But only for a time."

Darien shook his head, spreading his hands out before him. "I don't understand. I breathe. I hunger. *I feel.*"

The Prime Warden dismissed his arguments with a shrug. "You are not alive, Darien, and you would do well to never forget that. You are a Servant of Xerys. A demon. Your soul has given up any chance or hope of salvation. When this brief flirtation with life is over, the best you can hope for is a return to our Master's dominion. But, should Xerys ever become displeased with the quality of your service, He will exile your spirit into Oblivion. Your soul will be unmade, and you will simply cease to exist. It will be as though you had never been born. There's no coming back from such a banishment."

Darien considered this information, mulling it over, at last nodding his acceptance. He speculated, "Is that what happened to Arden?"

Renquist nodded. "Yes. That is exactly what happened to Arden." He started down the passage, compelling Darien forward with a hand on his shoulder.

"What did Arden do to earn such displeasure from our Master?"

"She failed," Renquist responded simply.

Darien understood. Failure was something their Master had little tolerance for. He was quiet for a long time as he contemplated the idea. He arrived at the conclusion that such a harsh penalty for failure was not as frightening as it first seemed; at least there was another option besides an eternity spent in hell. It was some small comfort knowing that. Darien pondered the notion as he followed

Renquist down a flight of long, twisting steps that seemed to descend forever into blackness.

"Release the magic field," Renquist commanded. "From here, we walk together in darkness."

Darien understood the request. They were descending the long staircase buried deep within the heart of the mountain, the same one he had travelled with Kyel, Swain, and Naia two years before. Somewhere along that stair they would run into the vortex that surrounded Aerysius. He would need to shield his mind from it; the magic field would be inaccessible for a time.

He was reluctant to release the field's soothing energies. But he did, allowing them to ebb and drain away. Complete darkness stole in around them. Darien could see nothing, not even the stairs beneath his feet. The pressure of Renquist's hand on his arm compelled him forward. Together, side by side, they descended the stairs in consummate blackness.

"What other duties shall you have for me?" Darien wondered into the darkness. He could hear the sound of the thanacryst's paws padding after them, keeping pace at a distance.

"Nothing for now," Renquist's voice responded. "You have enough on your plate. Attend to Azár and her people. That's sufficient, for now. We'll be using the transfer portal beneath Orien's Finger. It will take us to Bryn Calazar. From there, Azár will lead you westward to the ancestral lands of her people."

A cold breeze stirred up from the depths, playing with Darien's cloak. He shivered. The air wasn't fresh; the scent was stale, as if it had remained pooled within the mountain for a very long time.

They traveled together in silence down long flights of stairs broken every so often by the occasional landing. The journey took hours. The stairs led them ever downward, deeper into the mountain's cold and clammy heart. They paused occasionally to rest in the thick blackness amidst the shadows. Neither man spoke; the descent was taxing, demanding a good deal of concentration.

Eventually, they reached the bottom of the steps. The stairs leveled off, arriving at a rock wall that marked the entrance to the warrens.

"Qurfin," Renquist whispered. A door appeared like a growing crack in the rock wall ahead, yawning open with a silvery glow.

They stepped out of the mountainside into a pale gray morning. Darien was surprised to find that the other members of their party had already arrived ahead of them. Then he remembered: the stair within the mountain was like the Catacombs, a place where time and distance had little consistency. The other members of their party could have started out much later in the day and yet still arrived at the bottom of the mountain ahead of them.

He looked to the east, where dawn warmed the horizon beyond the dark frame of the valley walls. The tall pedestal of Orien's Finger loomed ominously in the center of a horseshoe-shaped canyon. The ground at their feet was blackened, as well as the surrounding cliffs. There was no trace of green, not even a single blade of grass. The entire canyon was charred and scorched. Darien bowed his head, knowing this was his own doing. His intention had been to protect this land. Instead, he had defiled it.

As if sensing the direction of his thoughts, Azár turned to gaze at him with accusation in her eyes. Just looking at her rattled Darien's nerves. She hated him, with good reason. The damage he'd inflicted upon the rocks of this canyon was trivial compared to the horrors he'd wrought against Azár's own people. Thousands of lives torn instantly asunder. Charred remains, blackened to ash. Scattered about the ground and tossed by the wind.

"Azár," Renquist called out. "Take Darien ahead to the transfer portal. Meet up with us in Bryn Calazar."

The girl nodded, still glaring at Darien with hostile contempt in her eyes. Then, shouldering her cloth pack, she turned and stalked away, crossing the black canyon floor toward the jutting tower of rock.

Flustered, Darien watched her go.

"What are you waiting for?" Byron Connel chided mildly, drawing up at Darien's side. He nodded his head in the direction of Azár. "Better go after her before she leaves you behind."

Darien grimaced. He hooked his hand around the leather baldric that crossed his chest and trudged after Azár. He trailed her around the wide base of the rock pillar until, mercifully, she drew to a halt on the far side. There, she stopped with her back to him and moved no further.

Darien approached her cautiously. She was

standing stock-still, facing the orange disk of the rising sun. Darien paused, gazing at her with a questioning look.

Azár was staring straight ahead, her mouth slack, eyes wide with startled amazement. Her lips quivered. She was trembling all over, he realized, her whole body shaking. Darien took a hesitant step toward her, then another.

"You've never seen the sun before," he surmised in wonder.

Azár tensed, her mouth snapping shut at the sound of his voice. She shot a smoldering glare his way. Then she shook her head, looking ashamed.

Darien chanced another step in her direction. "It can't hurt you," he assured her, trying to guess the cause of her reaction.

She glared at him with searing hatred in her eyes. He could almost visualize the anger bleeding off her skin to saturate the air between them. But then, suddenly, Azár's expression faltered.

"What if it falls?" she whispered.

Darien was mildly shocked by the question. "What makes you think it will fall?"

"They say that is what happened to my homeland," Azár explained without looking at him. "They say that the sun fell from the sky and charred the ground."

Darien frowned, knowing for a fact that was not what happened. He'd met the man responsible for Caladorn's demise. The sun was innocent of any such wrongdoing. A gust of wind seized his hair, whipping it forward into his face. Darien reached up, pushing it back out of his eyes.

"I don't think that's going to happen here," he said.

Azár fixed him with a cold, lingering stare. "Why not?"

"Because I won't let it happen."

Her gaze trailed slowly up the length of his body. Her lips curled in distaste, as if she despised everything she saw. "You are a very arrogant man," she said at last. "And you are also a hypocrite."

"Why am I a hypocrite?" Darien demanded, baiting her intentionally. This was the most he'd ever heard her speak. He was intrigued. He wanted to know more about this woman, this mage of the Enemy.

Azár gestured around them with a wave of her hand, eyes wide and incredulous. "Look around. The ground is charred, just as black as the soil of my own country. You did this. You desecrated your own homeland. You murdered a *hundred thousand* of my people!"

Darien nodded, knowing this had to be the source of her hatred. "There was a hundred thousand of them and only one of me. I did what I had to do."

Azár seemed repulsed by his response. "You immolated an entire generation of warriors!"

Darien could only shrug, accepting full responsibility. "I swore an oath to defend my land and my people."

Now it was Azár's turn to take a step forward, her presence looming with hostility despite her size. Arms crossed in front of her chest, she sneered at him, "And now you've sworn another oath to defend *my* land and *my* people!"

Darien closed his mouth, having no idea how to respond to that. He dropped his gaze to the demon-hound, sitting on its haunches against the dark and ruined earth.

"You *are* a hypocrite," Azár accused. "What are you going to do if you have to protect my homeland at the expense of your own?"

Darien could only glare at her in sullen silence. He had no answer to that. She had very quickly isolated and exposed his greatest weakness, his gravest fear. His naked vulnerability. She stood there before him, arms crossed, eyebrows raised expectantly. Awaiting his response.

"So much talk," she mocked him, "and now you have absolutely nothing to say! Why am I burdened with you? You are not a man to be trusted!"

Darien seethed at her in anger, his eyes scalding pools of resentment. He took a last step forward, closing the gap between them, and raised a finger before her face.

"I'm not a man," he reminded her in a voice hoarse with caustic fury. "And you'd do very well not to trust me. I've broken every promise I ever made."

With that, he turned and trudged away, back toward Orien's pedestal. The thanacryst remained behind, growling at Azár, teeth bared.

"*Theanoch*," Darien called back at it. With a yelp, the demon-dog sprang after him, bounding to catch up.

Chapter Four
Deal with a Devil

Rothscard, The Rhen

Kyel raised his hand to knock on the door. He clenched his fist instead, lowering it back down again to his side. He scowled, staring down at his hand as he contemplated the wisdom behind his intended act. He was having second thoughts, maybe even third or fourth thoughts. He took a deep breath, holding the air in his lungs for a long moment before letting it back out again. Then he raised his fist with firmer resolve.

He knocked twice upon the wood. Then he waited. He could hear the soft sound of footsteps approaching from the other side. A sharp, metallic click as the bolt inside was thrown. The sound of the door creaking open.

Meiran's pale and grief-weathered face confronted him in the doorway. Just one look in her eyes told Kyel that all his fears had been justified. He grimaced, shaking his head. He hated being right.

"I'm so sorry, Meiran," was all he could bring himself to say.

She collapsed against him, her whole body quaking. Kyel wrapped his arms around her as she hugged him back, clinging to him fiercely. He felt the warm moisture of her tears against his neck. Her back shook as she cried against his shoulder, shedding her sorrow into the black wool of his cloak.

Eventually, the tears subsided. Meiran withdrew, pulling away and swiping angrily at her eyes with a sleeve. She wandered back into the depths of the dimly lit quarters. Kyel lingered behind a moment before following, pushing the door closed behind him. He glanced around, taking in the dark features of the guest room.

Meiran stood beside a painted writing desk, composing herself. Her hand was on her necklace again, fingering the interlaced pendant on its silver chain, her eyes gazing off into nothing. She was wearing a white wide-sleeved gown, her dark hair falling in loose waves down her back. She looked vulnerable, like a lost and frightened child.

"Are you all right?" Kyel asked softly.

She shook her head, eyes haunted by misery. "No, Kyel. I'm not all right."

She gestured helplessly at a curled page on the writing desk: Darien's letter, given to her by the darkmage Quinlan Reis. Kyel recognized the bold, flowing script from across the room. Meiran scooped the parchment up into her hand, rolling it back up before offering it out toward him.

"Go ahead. Read it."

Kyel swallowed as he accepted the letter. He stared down at the scroll in trepidation, loath to unfurl it and view the message it contained. As if denial could make the whole situation somehow evaporate. Kyel had many reasons for not wanting to read that letter, but they all really boiled down to one simple thing: Darien Lauchlin had been his friend. That was the way Kyel wished to remember him.

As he unrolled the scroll, Kyel's fingers were already shaking.

My Dearest Meiran,

I have no idea how to tell you this, so I suppose I'll just come right out and say it: before I died, I committed my soul to

Chaos. I have taken Arden Hannah's place at Zavier Renquist's side. I am a Servant of Xerys.

Kyel had to stop, squeezing his eyes shut against a pang of horror. He glanced up at Meiran with sorrow in his eyes, a look that mirrored her own. He forced himself to continue reading, a terrible feeling of dread gnawing at his heart.

I know how atrocious this must sound to you, the most grievous of all betrayals. I understand. I don't expect your forgiveness. But, I beg you, please hear me out. I am still myself; nothing inside me has changed except for my perspective. I have gained a depth of understanding that was unavailable to me before.

Please believe me, Meiran, when I say there is another side to this story. There are many facts we were ignorant of, things omitted from the histories. Maybe our ancestors didn't know the whole story. Or perhaps they suppressed the knowledge on purpose. I don't wish to speculate; I'm not here to judge. I am only here to bear witness.

By now, you must have heard that Zavier Renquist desires to negotiate the terms of a treaty. I urge you to consider his offer carefully. You can trust Quin. Please accept whatever proposal he brings you.

I do love you, Meiran. I know that you will probably no longer bear any love for me, especially after reading these words. I am sorry for that. I want you to know that what I did—the decisions I made—none of that was your fault. I did what I felt I had to do. If I made one mistake, it was not realizing that the Well of Tears could be reopened again so quickly. I never imagined that we would end up in the same war but on two different sides. Had I known that, I still don't think it would have changed anything. I can honestly say that I have no regrets.

All My Love,

Darien

Kyel lowered the letter, letting the scroll roll itself back up in his hand. He stood there silent for a minute, frozen in place, unable to do anything but gaze woodenly down at the floor in front of his feet. The tiles were cold and polished, reflecting the wavering light of the tapers ensconced around the room. Kyel gazed at their shimmering gold reflection as his mind scrambled for clarity in a roiling cauldron of conflicting emotions.

"I was afraid of something like this," he whispered at last. He moved forward, setting the scroll back down on the writing desk.

Meiran made no comment. She stood with her hands clasped in front of her, dark waves of hair falling about her shoulders. She looked very young, completely bereft of her characteristic fortitude.

"Do you believe him?" Kyel asked, his eyes searching her face.

Meiran blinked, bringing her arms up to hug herself.

"It doesn't matter what I believe," she muttered. "This letter can bear no weight on my decision."

Kyel nodded. "What are you going to do?" he asked. "Have you decided?"

Meiran flashed him a look of resentment. "I'm certainly not going to give Renquist what he wants." Color bloomed on her cheeks as Meiran quickly recovered herself. Kyel understood why Darien had so loved this woman. Though no older than himself, Meiran had more grit and tenacity than anyone Kyel had ever met.

"What does Renquist want?"

"It's obvious what he wants," Meiran snapped, pacing away. "He wants *me*. What I don't understand is why."

"He wanted Darien, too," Kyel reminded her ominously. He ran his hand along the surface of the writing desk, eyes lingering on the scroll.

"And he got Darien, didn't he?"

Kyel swallowed. "Aye. Apparently, he did."

That settled it, then. Kyel rounded on her, eyes full of galvanized resolve. "You can't treat with him, Meiran. It's too dangerous. I saw Darien after his parley with Renquist. It destroyed him. He couldn't live with himself after that."

"Because that's how Zavier Renquist operates," declared a voice from behind them.

Kyel whirled, reaching immediately for the magic field. He had a shield thrown up in front of them before he could think.

Hands clasped behind his back, Quinlan Reis strolled forward into the sitting room, nodding his approval toward Kyel. He paused, shutting the door quietly behind him. Then he continued talking as if nothing at all was out of sorts:

"He discovers what matters to you most. That's what he uses as leverage against you. He takes something you love and twists it into a knife to slide between your ribs."

He reached up and scooped his black felt hat off his head. Holding it against his chest, the darkmage remarked to Kyel, "You have absolutely no idea what you're doing, do you?"

Eyes ablaze with ire, Meiran advanced on him, waving a finger. "You don't have permission to be here! *Get out now.*"

Eyes only for Kyel, Quinlan Reis smiled and assured her with calm disregard, "I'm not here in an official capacity."

Meiran pointed at the door. "You have three seconds to get out."

"Or what? You'll frown at me? I'm sorry, but those chains on your wrists aren't very intimidating."

Meiran drew herself up, hands going to her sides. Very formally, she addressed him, "You disregard a badge of truce. Have you abandoned all honor?"

The hat-wielding darkmage scowled. "I never had any honor when I was alive, so why would I suddenly come into it after death? I don't think inheritance works in that direction." He turned back to Kyel with a derisive glare. "You can drop that shield now. If I came here to kill you, you'd already be dead."

Kyel ignored him, maintaining the glowing shield that was their only protection from the demon. Quinlan Reis waited, scrutinizing him derisively. When it became obvious that Kyel had no intention of doing as he bid, the man simply shrugged, replacing his hat back on his head.

"I came to make you an offer." He glanced at Meiran out of the corner of his eye.

"I don't make deals with demons," she promised, indignant.

Quinlan Reis glowered at her. "Wait until you've heard my offer, Prime Warden. You may rethink your policy."

Meiran stared at him for a long, searching moment. A soft and fleeting expression passed across her face, unreadable. She appeared to be groping with her feelings. At last, she calmly turned to Kyel. "Leave us, please."

Kyel's throat went dry. He glanced up at Meiran in alarm. "Prime Warden?"

Meiran nodded, her face full of conviction. She raised her hand, pointing toward the door.

"Go."

Kyel blinked, staring back and forth between Meiran and the darkmage. She was serious, he realized. With a pang of dread, he released his hold on his golden shield, letting its pale glow dissipate into the surrounding air. Kyel glared hard and long at Quinlan Reis. Then, against his better judgement, Kyel did the only thing he could do.

He followed his Prime Warden's command, exiting the guest room and leaving Meiran alone with a Servant of Xerys.

Kyel's head was spinning in a daze of confusion by the time he reached the ground floor of the palace. His body had broken out into a cold sweat, his emotions on the cusp of panic. He had no idea why Meiran had dismissed him from the room. In the face of grave danger, she had sent him away. Just as Darien had done before Black Solstice.

Kyel ran down the long corridor, shouting at the first stationed guardsman he could find. "The Prime Warden's in danger! Summon the captain! Summon the prince! *Now!*" He bellowed the last word, prompting the man into action.

The guard dashed off with a look of mortified panic on his face. Kyel remained behind, battling the urgent compulsion to run back up the stairs. He settled on pacing back and forth across the long hall, addled by fear and nervous energy. He kept glancing back up the stairs, resisting the impulse to storm up there and invite the demon to a duel.

But he knew better. He was no match for Quinlan Reis. Or Meiran's ire.

More than that; his Oath of Harmony wouldn't allow it.

It was long minutes before Nigel Swain finally

arrived, flanked by a small contingent of guardsmen. The prince consort was carrying a longsword in his hand, his face tense with focused aggression.

"What the hell's all the ruckus?" Swain demanded, drawing up in front of Kyel. The guards behind him had their weapons drawn, shields at ready.

"The Prime Warden's in danger!" Kyel said. "One of the darkmages slipped in past the guards! He has her cornered up there!" He pointed up the stairs in the direction of the guest rooms.

Swain's gaze followed Kyel's motion. "So, there's only one up there? *Where's the other one?"*

"I don't know!"

Swain turned to his men. "Fall back to the Residence and protect the Queen! *You*," he growled at the man nearest him, "gather reinforcements and meet me upstairs!"

Kyel turned and started toward the steps.

"Where do you think you're going?"

He stopped and turned back around. "I'm coming with you."

Swain shook his head, strands of chin-length hair swinging forward into his face. "You're going to stay the hell away from there. You're not trained for this."

Kyel glared at him. "Neither are you."

The two men stared at each other across the empty hallway. Kyel waited, eyebrows raised, hands spread wide in question. Nigel Swain at last issued a stiff nod. He strode forward, passing up Kyel in three large strides.

Kyel reached within for the magic field, holding it at ready in the back of his mind. When they arrived at the second-floor hallway, he was surprised to see the door to Meiran's room already ajar. He remembered closing it when he'd left. Swain brought a hand up. He pointed at the door and made a quick series of gestures. Kyel just stared at him, unable to fathom what the man was trying to communicate.

"You call yourself a Sentinel?" Swain growled under his breath.

"*What*?" Kyel mouthed silently.

"Just get behind me. *And try not to hurt yourself."*

A group of guardsmen spilled past them over the top of the stairs in a rush of armored bodies. They fanned out across the hallway, weapons drawn.

Swain held up his fist. He extended a finger, pointing forward. The guards swept past him on both sides, storming into the guest room. Kyel moved behind them, cloaking them all in a glowing shield of light.

"*Meiran*!" Kyel shouted, gaze darting frantically around the room. Except for the milling clot of blue-cloaked guards, the sitting room was empty.

Heart thundering, Kyel charged toward the bedchamber. That room, too, was unoccupied. He swung back around, dropping the magic field like a hot brick.

"They're not here," he gasped in confusion. He wandered forward, eyes fumbling over the room as he groped through a barrage of desperate feelings he simply didn't understand. He glanced at the painted writing desk. Darien's letter was gone.

"Which one was it?" Swain demanded.

"Which one what?"

"The man or the woman—which one was in here?"

Kyel wrenched his gaze up off the surface of the writing desk. "The man."

Swain was already moving toward the door. *"Come on."*

"Where are we going?" Kyel called after him.

"To find the woman!"

Kyel's eyes widened in alarm. He followed Swain and his men back down the stairs and out into the night. The palace grounds were abuzz with frantic guards and liveried servants running every which direction. They crossed the inner ward to the citadel, where they joined a throng of men already gathered at the tower's entrance.

A shout from the guard captain opened up a path before them. Sheathing his sword, Nigel Swain strode between his men into the tower's base. There, under the vaulted roof, he drew up sharply with a whispered oath. Kyel stopped behind him, staring down in shock at the body sprawled across the stone floor in front of them.

Sareen Qadir lay face-down, chestnut hair fanned out like a gilded halo around her head. Blood was leaking from a wound somewhere underneath her, running along the crevices between the floor tiles like irrigation through a field.

"It's her," Kyel gasped, kneeling down at her side. He placed his hand on the woman's back, closing his eyes in concentration. The image that came to him was definitive: there was nothing left to heal.

"She's dead," Kyel pronounced, staring down at a

woman who, by his reckoning, had cheated death at least twice already. He didn't trust it.

The look on Swain's face could have curdled milk. The prince leaned forward and ran his hands over the corpse, searching through the garments. He combed through the pockets, pried open Sareen's clenched fingers. He dug beneath her fingernails. He rolled her over, expertly probing even the lining of her robes.

"Nothing," Swain grumbled, standing up. He swiped a hand back through his hair, eyes roving upward toward the ceiling.

"Handle that," he ordered the guard captain, pointing down at the corpse.

The man gazed down at the carcass, face skewed with uncertainty. "How…do you want it handled, Your Grace?"

Swain worked his lips against clenched teeth. "Burn it."

Hearing that, Kyel anxiously shook his head. "No. We need Naia."

Swain nodded thoughtfully, running his tongue over his lips. "Then go get her."

Chapter Five
City of the Damned

Orien's Finger, The Rhen

Darien swung around, glaring back over his shoulder at Azár. At his side, the demon-dog yipped at him, cocking its head. He ran his hand through its coarse fur as he stared back at Azár in annoyance. She was still standing in the same place, arms crossed over her chest, the orange sun rising at her back.

She chortled a derisive laugh in his direction. "You have no idea where you're going, do you?"

Darien closed his eyes, groping within to find the peace and patience he would need to weather this woman's scorn. He drew in a deep breath, letting it back out again slowly. When he opened his eyes, he saw that Azár was strutting toward him across the blackened ground. She brought a hand up to fend off wisps of dark hair that had escaped her braid.

He waited, stroking the thanacryst as she approached. Azár drew up in front of him, dark eyes mocking him in silence as she stared up into his face. She was a tiny thing; the top of her head reached no more than the center of his chest. She narrowed her eyes. Then she turned her head and spat upon the ground.

Darien glanced down to consider the wet stain of her spittle upon the blackened rocks. He wondered if Azár was even aware that her action had just desecrated what amounted to the mass gravesite of her countrymen. He doubted that she had even considered it.

"Would you show me where the transfer portal is, please?" Darien asked in as kindly a tone as he could muster.

He waited as she continued to glare up at him, hands on her hips. His gaze fell to the dagger she wore at her belt. The ebony hilt reminded him of the knife once carried by Garret Proctor, yet another man whose grave Azár's action had just defiled.

For the first time, Darien took notice of the garments she was wearing. Azár's clothing was of ash-dark cotton, thickly layered for warmth. There was absolutely no leather or hide anywhere on her body; even her sandals and belt were woven from what looked like coarse fibers of reed. She wore a thick shawl tied around her shoulders. There were many holes and tears in the fabric. Darien took note of these subtle inconsistencies. She was of the mage class of her society. Yet, Azár dressed as an indigent.

She was still staring up at him, unblinking.

"I know I'm not what you expected," Darien said. "I'm sorry. What do you want me to do? Do you want me to leave?"

"I want you to die." She was gazing steadily upwards into his face.

"I did that already," he said flatly.

"A thousand deaths are not enough for you. The transfer portal is this way."

She moved away from him, feet crunching over the rocks and molten glass scattered everywhere across the ground. Darien tracked her motion with his eyes, watching her as she approached the charred rock wall of Orien's Finger. There, she muttered something under her breath. A Word of Command, he surmised. The fractured basalt rock of the pedestal seemed to shimmer, wavering for a moment. Then it disappeared altogether, revealing a gaping entrance cut into the side of the cliff itself.

Fascinated, Darien moved to follow her as she disappeared within. He conjured up a mist of magelight as he entered the dark chamber at the base of the pedestal, sending its glow spreading forward into the room.

He allowed his eyes to roam upward as he stood in the threshold of the doorway. The dark walls and tall ceiling glimmered with the sheen of thousands of tiny crystals that sparkled in the magelight. He watched as Azár moved forward into the center of the chamber, toward a tall, cross-vaulted arch. The arch was made of ruddy-colored marble that looked particularly out of place.

"I'd no idea this was here," Darien muttered.

"That's because you are ignorant."

Darien shook his head, bringing a hand up to rub his eyes. "I'm still in hell," he whispered under his breath.

Azár glanced back over her shoulder with a smirk. "Come. Take my hand."

Darien raised his eyebrows in surprise as he crossed the chamber toward her. He contemplated her offered hand for a long moment before accepting it. Her olive skin was smooth and silken, like none other he had ever felt before. He couldn't help himself; he ran his thumb across the back of her hand, noting the complete absence of lines. It was the softest hand he'd ever held.

"How old are you, Azár?" he wondered in awe.

She glared up at him, looking ready to snatch her hand back out of his grasp. "Empty your mind," she said, anger roiling under her tone.

Darien closed his eyes and did as she commanded. She pulled him forward with her under the arch. He followed, letting go of the magelight and allowing the chamber's natural darkness to settle in around them. He felt the transition as his feet stepped onto the marble foundation of the arch.

Then the whole chamber jolted and seemed suddenly to shift.

Bryn Calazar, The Black Lands

Darien staggered and almost fell, catching himself on the marble pillar of the portal itself. He turned in a confused circle, taking in the new surroundings that confronted them.

He was in a different room, somewhere completely dissimilar to the one he had just been standing in only moments before. This room was large and brightly lit by braziers and flaming torches. They were not alone. Darien's hand reached reflexively for his blade.

The cold prick of steel at his throat stopped his motion. Darien lowered his hand slowly, spreading his arms out at his sides. He could hear the thanacryst growl.

Azár stepped in front of him with a satisfied smirk.

"Peace," she said at last. "He's no threat."

The sword retracted. Darien reached up to rub at the spot where the blade had scored his neck. His thumb came away with a slight stain of blood. Azár frowned, studying the cut with cold and critical eyes.

"So, a demon can bleed," she commented.

Darien wiped the blood off onto his shirtsleeve, turning around to confront the man who had assailed him. He found himself staring up into the black-helmed face of an Enemy soldier wearing full battle plate. And the man was not alone. The room was ringed with them, at least a dozen plate-mailed guards. Darien felt a shiver of chill creep over him at the sight. The last time he had been surrounded by such men had been at his ill-fated parley with Zavier Renquist.

Azár motioned him forward away from the transfer portal. As he walked, Darien let his gaze rove over the room. Startled, he noticed that there were many of the cross-vaulted arches arranged in concentric rings. A few of the columns had collapsed, now only heaps of spilled rubble. He stared in wonder at the sight, understanding immediately the significance of what he was looking at. Each of the archways must be a portal to somewhere else, a transit system the ancients had once used. There had been nothing like it in Aerysius; such industry had been lost long ago.

There was a blinding flash of light. Blinking against the glare, Darien saw that Byron Connel and Nashir Arman had joined them in the chamber. With two more brilliant flashes, the rest of their party emerged. Zavier Renquist appeared last in a glimmering pool of light, striding behind the white-cloaked form of Cyrus Krane. He moved forward toward the center of the room as, all around him, plate-mailed bodies lowered to abase themselves upon the ground at the Prime Warden's feet.

"You may rise," Renquist commanded. "I must speak with the grand vizier. Bring him to me at once."

There was a stir as two sentries ran out of the room to comply. Darien stood still, bringing a hand up to dab at his neck. The guards that ringed the room yet lingered at their stations with weapons drawn, blades held at ready across their chests, shields at their backs.

After minutes, the sound of marching feet echoed from above. A large retinue spilled down a flight of curving stairs: more plate-mailed bodies followed by men dressed in fine cloth. At the rear of the procession strode a bearded man dressed in embroidered robes and a tanned leather vest, a tall hat upon his head. The newcomers knelt before Renquist immediately upon their arrival in the chamber. Even the man in silk and leather dropped to his knees, pressing his forehead against the floor.

"Arise," the ancient Prime Warden greeted his servant.

The large man regained his feet, sweeping forward to embrace Renquist warmly, as one brother to another.

"Thank the gods you have returned! Honor and glory to you, Prime Warden." His voice was deep and throaty, with a thick accent that sounded nothing like Renquist's own. Darien realized the difference must be the result of the centuries that separated the two men.

Zavier Renquist smiled, returning the vizier's embrace. "Peace and blessings, Vizier Sarik. It is only through the sacrifice of the Asyaadi Lightweaver that our return to Malikar has been achieved. It is to him the honor and glory is owed."

The nobleman turned to regard Azár. "Peace to you, Lightweaver. I am Sarik Uthmar, Grand Vizier of the city-state of Bryn Calazar. I offer congratulations upon your ascendance."

To Darien's amazement, Azár looked down, lowering her gaze before the vizier. The young woman seemed humble, a state altogether out of character.

"Very kind of you, Vizier," she whispered, her voice full of humility.

Zavier Renquist stepped forward, draping his hand over the nobleman's broad shoulders as he pulled the man close. "Vizier Sarik. Perhaps you can help us with a difficult situation." He motioned to Darien, urging him forward.

Darien complied with a wary glance at the nearest guard. He strode across the room toward the two men, drawing to a halt before the Prime Warden.

Renquist indicated him with his hand. "Vizier Sarik, I present to you Darien Lauchlin of Amberlie, Aerysius' Last Sentinel. He is the newest of our Master's faithful Servants."

The bearded man's eyes narrowed at first, then widened slowly. "Prime Warden…are you saying this man is the self-same abomination who rained fiery death upon Malikar's legions?"

"The same."

Darien found it almost impossible to maintain eye contact with the man as the vizier leaned forward to peer directly into his face. The intensity of his stare was alarming, burning with the righteous fire of a zealot. Darien couldn't manage it. He dropped his gaze to his feet.

"Ash'zeri!" the man exclaimed under his breath. "Prime Warden, you have vanquished Malikar's greatest enemy and delivered him to our cause! There are no words to adequately express the greatness of your works!"

To Darien's dismay, the man's hands were suddenly upon him, taking him roughly by the shoulders. To his men, the vizier cried, "Light the braziers of the ziggurat and call forth the citizens of Bryn Calazar! This is a wonder that must be witnessed by all!"

The vizier turned to Renquist, lowering his voice to explain, "We must take great care in how we handle this, Prime Warden. The legend of Aerysius' Last Sentinel is steeped in horrors and atrocity. The people will demand his lifeblood to fuel our fires. We must bring him before the citizens of Bryn Calazar as a captured slave is brought before the master of the house. Even then, we risk revolt if we do not compensate blood for blood."

Darien stared hard at Renquist, his brow furrowed in concern. He mistrusted this bearded zealot. He was gravely troubled by the man's words.

"Very well." Zavier Renquist turned to face Darien, his face devoid of all expression. "I command you to bear what comes with shame and humility."

Darien understood. He lowered his eyes, a sinking

feeling settling deeply into his gut. He swallowed against the sudden dryness in his throat.

"Aye, Prime Warden."

The vizier stepped forward, pointing down. "Kneel," he commanded.

Darien obeyed, dropping to his knees on the floor. He glanced at the demon-hound that suddenly stood growling with hackles raised, eyes glowing a menacing green.

"Theanoch!" he commanded it. The hound fell down on its belly with a whine, head between its paws.

Vizier Sarik gazed down at Darien from under his tall red hat. He was fat; his bearded cheeks were ripe, his lips puffy and puckered like a fish. Nevertheless, he was strong. He brought his arm back, forming his hand into a fist. With a grunt, he struck Darien across the face with all the strength and weight of his body.

Darien's head whiplashed around as blood sprayed from the force of the blow. Reeling, he almost fell over. He was caught and held upright by Azár's firm grasp on his shoulders. The vizier hit him again, this time from the other side. Darien leaned forward, spitting blood onto the ground in a thick stream that dribbled from his chin.

The vizier leaned forward, hovering close over Darien's head. In a deathly calm voice, he explained, "That is for the blood of Malikar's sons and daughters you spilled upon the ground. Strip to your waist."

Darien had no choice but to comply. He shrugged out of the baldric, laying his longsword down on the floor at his side. With trembling hands, he removed his black cloak and stripped his shirt off over his head. Those, he let fall to the ground around him.

"Bind him," the vizier ordered his men.

Darien did not resist as two mailed bodies swept forward, one holding him securely as the other tied his wrists together in front of him with a woven cord.

"Let his blood flow," the vizier whispered.

Darien closed his eyes and cringed as the blows began to fall. One man beat him with a coiled rope, the other with a gauntleted fist. Another man joined in, kicking him several times in the ribs. Darien fell to the floor, drawing his knees up to his chest.

"Enough!"

The soldiers withdrew. Darien rolled onto his back, chest heaving, his whole body shaking and wet, glistening with a slick sheen of blood and sweat. A sharp pain stabbed at his side with every drawn breath.

"Stand, Darien Lauchlin, last of the fallen Sentinels," the vizier commanded.

He could do nothing but obey. Trembling, Darien rose unsteadily to his knees and then, staggering, to his feet. Blood ran from wounds on his back, arms, and head. His lip was split, his left eye throbbing. He caught a glimpse of Nashir's satisfied smirk. Darien glared at the darkmage with smoldering hatred in his eyes.

The vizier stood in front of Darien, placing his enormous hands on Darien's shoulders. Then, leaning forward, he pressed a kiss against first Darien's right cheek and then his left.

"That is for the grace and mercy Xerys has shown you," he said, drawing back. To the guards, he commanded, "Collar him as a slave is collared."

An armored man came forward and wrapped a supple cord around his neck, tying it with a slipknot attached to a length of rope. This he offered to the vizier.

Sarik shook his head. With a finger, he indicated Azár. The black-helmed guardsman strode over to the girl and placed Darien's lead into her hand. Azár accepted the rope gravely, allowing her gaze to travel up its length toward the collar, her eyes progressing upward to Darien's face. He expected her to sneer at him again as she had before. To Azár's credit, she did not.

Darien lowered his head. His eye was already beginning to swell. He could have healed it in a heartbeat. He dared not.

Vizier Sarik informed him, "You will be presented to the citizens of Bryn Calazar as one who is utterly vanquished, defeated in body as well as spirit. You must submit yourself before the populace in shame. This is necessary. You can show no amount of pride or resistance. Do you understand what is expected of you?"

Darien could only nod, still staring at the ground. His mouth was once again filling with blood. This time he swallowed it, gritting his teeth against the taste. He noticed Azár studying him closely. He felt discomfited by her cold, unfeeling eyes.

"Whenever you are ready, Prime Warden," the vizier announced.

"By all means. Lead the way."

Renquist's words were spoken with dispassionate authority. He stooped to retrieve Darien's sword from off the ground. He held the scabbard up in his hands, clutching the weapon in front of him. He turned it slightly, allowing the rubies to catch the fire of the torchlight. Then, followed by the others, the ancient Prime Warden strode out of the chamber.

Darien was made to follow at the rear of their small procession, Azár leading him by the rope. She did not tug at his collar. Instead, she commanded him forward with the cold authority of her eyes. Darien followed her lead; he had no choice. The thanacryst trailed behind, nose to the ground, tail tucked between its legs.

Black-armored guards fell in behind. He was led out of the chamber of portals into a rock-encrusted hallway that seemed to stretch a very long distance ahead. Darien limped forward, favoring his right leg. His side pained him with each breath. He despised what they were doing, even as he understood the necessity. This was still part of his atonement, just like the other tortures he'd already been forced to endure. He would bear this one, as well.

After minutes of walking, they emerged from a cliff side into the thick darkness of night. There, they paused on a high terrace overlooking the city of Bryn Calazar. The smell of the night air assaulted Darien's nostrils. It had a hideous odor, thick and acrid, like black smoke from a forge. Darien tried to catch a glimpse of the city below through the press of bodies that surrounded him. He could see nothing. He moved forward, pulling the leash taught as he leaned over the edge of a crumbling balustrade.

The view below was chilling.

Darkness encased the city, but it was not the natural darkness of night. It was like the blackness that consumed the Shadowspears and the Pass of Lor-Gamorth. The ancient curse that had blackened the skies above Caladorn so long ago. Overhead, a cold and angry wind propelled a thick bank of cloud-cover across the sky, tumbling and churning like the foaming froth of an ocean. Sheet lightning flickered from deep within that roiling mass. With a shiver of dismay, Darien realized he was gazing out across the corrupted heart of the Black Lands. And it was more thoroughly despoiled than he had ever imagined.

Sprawling outward to the distant horizon, the city of Bryn Calazar was revealed before him in all its tortured desecration. Thick plumes of smoke billowed over the city, fed by fires that seemed to burn everywhere. The smoke had a foul and oily taste to it, thick and bitter. The structures resembled distorted honeycombs, built of successive layers, one atop the other, dark walls haphazardly thrown up at odd angles. The roads were paved with tar and lined by great, snakelike clusters of pipes that twined and coiled about the twisted heart of the city. The heavens wept hot tears of ash that drifted softly to the ground, wafting from the skies like despoiled snow.

Darien stared open-mouthed at the sight, struggling to come to terms with the terrible *wrongness* of it. There was nothing left; all trace of nature had been either corrupted or consumed. This was not civilization, he realized.

This was hell.

A tug on his leash pulled Darien away from the edge of the terrace. Still, he couldn't tear his eyes away from the vision of the repulsive city below. He stared down the side of the cliff, out across the dark waters of an ocean that seemed to bleed thick streaks of oil from its tides. In the harbor, iron-clad ships rode at their moors.

Eyes wide, he turned in horror to Azár.

"Maybe, now, you understand," she snarled, twisting the length of his leash once about her hand. With a sharp tug, she jerked him forward after her as the others started moving.

Darien struggled to keep up with her brisk strides, gasping at the pain that flared in his side with every step. The road they traveled led down and off the hillside, out into the tar-paved streets of the city. There, the citizens of Bryn Calazar had gathered to line the boulevard ahead.

At the sight of their approaching party, a tremendous cry was raised from the assembled masses. People came running, flooding in from the side-streets, jostling and vying for a better view of their Prime Warden's entourage. For the first time in his life, Darien had an unobstructed view of the inhabitants of the Black Lands. A people who, before, he had only known collectively as the Enemy.

They were people, just as he had always known they'd be. He had seen their dead, questioned their prisoners. Azár was the first Enemy that Darien had actually ever spoken with except under condition of duress.

Before him, bobbing and shoving like a roiling mass that bristled with thin arms and bulbous knees, was a population of starving, indigent, and yet jubilant people. They were clothed in filthy rags darkened by years of soil and ash. Most wore scarves tied over their mouths and noses, exposing only their eyes. Eyes that peered out through skin obscured by soot and grime. They were screaming, bellowing, waving weapons or brandishing oil-soaked torches in the air.

On the left, a fight broke out over a coveted viewing spot. The instigator was quickly put down with a sword through his chest. Two other men surged forward, ostensibly to avenge the loser, but ended up suffering the same fate. Their bodies were left lying in the street, trampled over by the crowds that just kept gushing in from outlying districts.

Black-armored bodies with weapons drawn and shields raised rushed forward to contain the surging masses. The throng was pushed back, clearing a path for the Prime Warden's party to pass. The crowds cheered, the sound an explosive thunder as their entourage gained the level of the street.

Darien tripped, almost falling as he struggled to keep up with Azár's ruthless pace. The pain in his side was worsening, and his wounds ached from the salty sweat that streaked his body. His left eye was now thoroughly swollen shut. He staggered, Azár jerking him forward with a tug on his lead.

Something grazed the back of his head. Another object hit him hard between the shoulder blades. Darien whirled, sweat spraying from his forehead, to find that a group of men were picking apart the street to gather rocks to assault him with.

Their party turned, mounting a long flight of stairs that rose above the level of the city. The steps led up a tall, terraced structure to what looked like a temple far above. The ramp of stairs was lined with copper braziers that lit their path, spewing choking, caustic smoke and sparks into the air. Darien ducked as a rock streaked by, nearly hitting him in the head.

They rose ever upward above the city, the stairs a relentless, unbroken rise to the top of the terraced structure. Upon gaining the summit, their party came to a halt beneath the portico of a marble temple. There, Zavier Renquist and his Servants assembled together in a single line. The two Prime Wardens, Renquist and Cyrus Krane, stood at the center. Byron Connel and Nashir Arman stood together to Renquist's right. Myria Anassis took her place to the left of Cyrus Krane. Before them lingered Azár, still holding tight to Darien's leash, and Vizier Sarik, standing before them all with arms raised over his head.

Gradually, the crowds quieted. Silence descended upon the city as the grand vizier stepped forward to announce:

"People of Bryn Calazar, by the grace of Xerys, His Chosen Servants have been restored to us once again! *Ishil'zeri!*"

To Darien's amazement, the entire gathered population dropped to the ground as one, abasing themselves before the ancient darkmages. They remained on their knees for seconds. Then, together as one, the masses rose collectively again to their feet.

Darien stared with a mixture of awe and dismay at the sight, having no reference at all in which to frame it.

"Citizens of Bryn Calazar, Prime Warden Zavier Renquist presents to you his prisoner, his manslave, his spoil of war." The vizier raised his hand, indicating Darien. "Before you stands the defiled Last Sentinel of Aerysius, Darien Lauchlin of Amberlie, vanquished by Prime Warden Renquist's own hand!"

There was a tremendous outcry from the crowd below as the mob surged against the restraint of the guards. People brandished torches and weapons. Spears were hurled into the sky, landing far below on the long rise of steps. Darien could almost feel the scalding hatred of the populace that was directed toward him. He stepped back, face slack with dismay.

The vizier told him, "Turn and abase yourself before the people."

Darien didn't hesitate. He went instantly to his knees, bending over until his forehead touched the ground. He could hear the timbre of the crowd instantly change as the result of his action. Once again, the voice of the masses rose in exuberant jubilation. People blew horns, beat weapons against shields, stomped at the ground with their feet. The thunder of their outcry was deafening.

The vizier had to shout to be heard over the cacophony:

"Now abase yourself before your Prime Warden!"

Darien obeyed. He rose first to his knees and then to his feet, staring down with trepidation at the raucous crowd. Then he turned and faced Zavier Renquist. Once again, he dropped to his knees and bent forward until his long hair was spread out on the ground beside his face.

The sound of the crowd climaxed, the furor terrifying.

Darien remained in that position, trembling, sweat mingled with blood dribbling off his chin.

"Rise," the Prime Warden commanded.

Darien obeyed, heaving his weight up off the ground despite the stabbing pain in his ribs. He gazed into Zavier Renquist's face with his one good eye. He was surprised to find that there was no trace of malice in the Prime Warden's expression.

Darien saw that Zavier Renquist was still holding his own sword. His hand moved to close around the hilt, drawing the blade forth from its scabbard. The ancient darkmage held Darien's sword aloft over his head, rotating it slightly, allowing the steel to catch the light of the braziers' flames.

Then he lowered it until the blade was level with Darien's heart. Face expressionless, he drew a slice across his chest.

Renquist turned the sword in his hand, bathing the flat of the blade in the blood that welled from the cut. He turned the sword around, liberally wetting the other side. Then he brought the weapon up next to his face, caressing the melded folds of steel with his hand, using his palm to ritually wash the blade with the blood of its master.

Accepting the scabbard back from Connel, Zavier Renquist resheathed the purified steel. To the vizier, he gave a slight nod.

Vizier Sarik stepped forward and stoically removed the rope and collar from around Darien's neck, unbinding his hands. There was a quiet rustle behind him. Suddenly, a mass of fabric was being lowered over his shoulders, pulled down over his body. Someone drew the cloth over his breeches, arranging it about his feet. Darien spread his hands, gazing down at his new garments with an acute feeling of trepidation.

They had vested him in the formal indigo robes of the Lyceum of Bryn Calazar, the Silver Star emblazoned over his heart.

The taste of bile rose in his throat. Darien choked, swallowing against it.

Zavier Renquist offered out his hand. The expression on his face was merciful. "Please. Take your place at my side."

He gestured to his right.

Darien looked down once again at his chest, at the emblem of the Silver Star, at the small stain of his own blood that was quickly spreading across the fabric. Then he glanced up into the Prime Warden's expectant face. He looked to Nashir, at the malevolent sneer on the man's lips.

In a dim haze of confusion and pain, Darien Lauchlin moved forward and fell into line beside Nashir, assuming his place in the line of Servants. Below, in the streets, the crowd erupted into a thunderous din.

Vizier Sarik strode forward, hands in the air, waving the pandemonium into silence. It took a moment. But, slowly, an ominous quiet stole over the city of Bryn Calazar. Into that gaping space the vizier proclaimed:

"Let it be known throughout the lands that Darien Lauchlin of Amberlie, the Last Sentinel of Aerysius, has sworn allegiance to Xerys, God of Chaos and Lord of the Netherworld! His service has been accepted by Prime Warden Renquist and the Citizens of Bryn Calazar! Let the people of the Rhen tremble and despair, for their savior has returned to become their subjugator!"

Chapter Six
Enemy or Ally

Rothscard, The Rhen

Kyel stared down into the reposed face of Sareen Qadir. Her flesh had not yet taken on the cold pallor of death. Instead, her face was still a warm bronze, an alluring combination taken together with the dark sheen of her hair. The only woman Kyel had ever seen who might be capable of rivaling her in beauty had been Arden Hannah, the seductive darkmage Darien had slain at Orien's Finger. But while Arden's allure had been diminished by her cruelty, any evil kept locked within Sareen's heart had never had a chance to reveal itself. Her beauty remained untainted by the corruption within.

Kyel didn't trust it.

Naia had lain her out upon a table, composing Sareen's limbs and arranging her robes about her body. The fatal wound to her chest had been tended and wrapped to prevent seepage. Naia was still lingering over the corpse, making small adjustments here and there, like an artist obsessing over the perfection of her craft. Naia had once been in the business of ministering to the dead, and it seemed that she had forgotten little of her art. She tended to Sareen with all the care she would have shown a sister.

"Has there been any word?" Naia asked.

Kyel shook his head, still gazing warily at the corpse. "Nothing." He wished he had better news to report. "There's no trace of either of them."

Naia muttered, "I pray to the gods that she's safe."

Kyel gestured down at the body. "What of her?"

"Oh, she's very much dead," Naia assured him, plucking a fiber of lint off Sareen's indigo robe. "I suspect it's probably not the first time."

She reached down and took a folded sheet of linen into her hands. Carefully unfurling the cloth over the body, she drew it up to cover the whole of the corpse. The shroud was thin and did a rather poor job of concealing what lay beneath. Sareen's outline was still very visible in silhouette.

It was strange how such evil could be concealed behind such a pleasing façade. It was a shame, really. The woman hadn't *seemed* all that bad. Not like the man who had accompanied her. Quinlan Reis had projected an inherent aura of cunning and threat that had chilled Kyel's blood. He had sensed no such menace coming from Sareen.

"What do we do with her?" he wondered.

Naia responded, "Prince Nigel is correct. We need to burn this corpse."

"Why burn it?"

Naia glanced up at him, her hand going to correct the drape of the shroud over Sareen's face. "Do you know why the Enemy always executed our mages by ritual immolation?"

Kyel frowned, disturbed by Naia's mention of the practice. He had been witness to one such gruesome act. When Arden Hannah had tried to burn Darien alive. "I suppose I really hadn't thought about it."

"Well, there are two reasons. First, so that the mage's gift could not be Transferred upon death to another. But there was more to it than just that. It was also to make certain their soul could never be reunited with their body."

"So, there's some chance that this woman could actually come back to life?"

"She is a Servant of Xerys," Naia reminded him.

"That dark god wields enough power to part the veil of death. I'd rather not take the chance."

Kyel nodded, reaching up to scratch the growth of beard on his face.

"Unless…" Naia whispered.

Kyel glanced up at her. "Unless what?"

She turned toward him, eyes suddenly bright with intensity. "If Quinlan Reis is responsible for Meiran's disappearance, then this woman is likely dead because she tried to stop him. Sareen was sent to bring Meiran to meet with Renquist. What if Reis abducted Meiran to foil that plan?"

Kyel raised his hands. "Why would he do that?"

"I don't know. But Sareen is dead, and Meiran is missing. I doubt that's coincidence."

Kyel warily considered the draped body. "That still doesn't make Sareen our ally."

"Perhaps not. But there's a good chance she knows what happened to Meiran. And she may be willing to help us get her back."

"For all we know, Meiran could have left of her own accord," Kyel argued.

"Without getting word to us? What is the chance of that?"

Kyel turned to confront her. "My point is this: we know *nothing*. All we have is conjecture. The one thing we *do* know for certain is that this woman is extremely dangerous. If she comes back to life and decides to murder us, there's precious little we could do to stop her." He swallowed, his throat suddenly tight with sorrow. "And besides. There's a good chance Meiran's not coming back. Quinlan Reis probably killed her, too."

"But we don't *know.*" Glancing at the corpse, Naia whispered, "What if we could bring her back?"

"Bring her back?" he echoed, incredulous. "And what happens if we do manage to 'bring her back?' How could we guarantee our safety? She's Unbound, Naia! And we are not."

"We could take her to the Catacombs," Naia pressed. "Her body will not decay, and there are plenty of spots where the magic field is highly unstable. We would have to obtain permission, of course. I'd have to ask my father…"

Kyel shot her a questioning glare. "I thought you weren't on speaking terms. Has he ever forgiven you?"

Naia's father was the High Priest of Death. Naia had once been a priestess, her father's own chosen successor. But that was before she'd abandoned her duties for Darien...before she'd inherited his legacy of power.

"I never gave my father the *opportunity* to forgive me," Naia admitted, her gaze cast downward at the floor. Kyel nodded, understanding. He had been confronted once by Luther Penthos himself. The man could be quite intimidating.

"All right, then," he decided. "What do we do?"

"You stay with her," Naia said, starting toward the doorway. "I'll head to the Temple of Death and inform them there's a cadaver in need of attention."

She brought her hands up, drawing the cowl of her cloak over her head.

Kyel stared after Naia even after she was gone from the doorway.

Then he pulled up a chair, spinning it around and straddling the seat with his arms draped over the back, cradling his chin. He sat there, gazing down at the contours of the body beneath the drape.

He still didn't trust it.

It seemed to take Naia an awful long time to return. Kyel wasn't certain how many hours it was since she'd left. He had dozed off over the back of the chair, losing all track of time. He hadn't gotten any sleep the night before, and the exhaustion had caught up with him. He startled awake at the sound of the door opening, blearily rubbing his eyes.

Naia entered the room, drawing back her cowl. Behind her followed a man dressed all in white robes with a stole draped over his shoulders. His fine, pale hair hung in limp strands to the middle of his back. He drew behind him a long cart with a curved wooden handle. The man leaned the handle up against the doorframe, leaving the cart behind in the hall.

Naia gestured with her hand. "Brother Carol, please allow me to introduce Kyel Archer of the Order of Sentinels. Grand Master Kyel, this is Brother Carol Desmond of the Temple of Death."

The pale priest of Death strode forward with a loathsome smile, clasping Kyel's offered hand. "Such an honor, Great Master." The touch of his eyes seemed tentative, as if not wishing to linger on Kyel's face. Instead, his attention was drawn rapidly downward to the corpse. He studied the outline of Sareen's body under the shroud with professional detachment.

"Thank you for coming, Brother Carol," Kyel responded, releasing the man's clammy hand.

"My condolences on your loss," the priest muttered. He reached down and drew the shroud back to reveal Sareen's face. He stood over her, his face devoid of expression. After a moment, he replaced the shroud, reverently smoothing the fabric's drape.

Naia said, "Condolences are unnecessary, Brother. This woman was no friend of ours."

The man seemed taken aback. "Pardon, but where is the deceased's next of kin?"

Naia shook her head. "She doesn't have any next of kin. Look, Brother. This is not your typical corpse. I apologize, but I am really not at liberty to explain. I need to beg a favor of you on a highly delicate matter. I need these remains transported to the High Temple in Glen Farquist. The Grand Master and I will be accompanying you through the Catacombs. We must seek the advice of my father."

The priest of Death appeared exceptionally concerned by this revelation. He gazed at Naia with a look of confusion, slender fingers cupping his chin. "I'm sorry, Great Lady, but what you ask is…irregular, to say the least."

Naia clasped her hands, squaring her shoulders formally. "Believe me, Brother Carol. This corpse merits such irregularities. Now, pray, don't push me further. As representatives of the Hall, I demand our right of passage through the Catacombs."

Hearing her words, the young priest's face hardened. "Such a demand can only be issued by the Prime Warden herself."

Naia's stare wandered as if internally grasping at straws. Somehow, her eyes ended up on Kyel. "The Prime Warden would ask you herself, were she here. Unfortunately, she's taken a leave of absence. Grand Master Kyel is acting in her stead."

Kyel shot Naia a look of alarm. "Now, hold on just one moment! We haven't discussed this!"

The pale priest blurted out, "Has something happened to the Prime Warden?"

Naia raised her hand, drawing in a long-suffering breath. "Brother Carol. Please. Help us get this corpse to Glen Farquist. As you can probably tell, our need is quite dire."

Brother Carol looked even paler now than he had upon arrival. His face was grimly set, thin lips pressed together in consternation. "Yes. Yes, of course. Please, if you will excuse me, I must make a few ministrations before the body can be transported."

But Naia shook her head. "Hold off on any ministrations, Brother. This corpse must be left pristine."

The man's frown deepened considerably. "That is…inadvisable. But it will be as you say, Great Lady."

He moved toward the door and grasped the handle of the cart he had left there, pulling it forward into the room. Kyel realized immediately what the contraption was: a wheeled bier, crafted of wood with the purpose of transporting the dead to the temple.

Brother Carol cautioned, "We'll have to handle her carefully. She must be kept as level as possible. I'll need your help."

Kyel felt a pang of queasiness in his gut. The sudden thought of body fluids made his stomach twist into knots. He stepped forward, regardless.

"Thank you, Great Master," the priest muttered. "I'll take the head if you take the legs."

Kyel swallowed, feeling suddenly rather ill.

Chapter Seven
Daffodils in Winter

Emmery, The Rhen

Meiran Withersby glanced over at the silent darkmage who rode at her side and felt suddenly very afraid. She wasn't afraid for herself. She had given up long ago on the delusion that her life would ever be peaceful or fulfilling. Everything important to her had already been cut away, severed and cast down the Well of Tears. The man riding next to her on his shaggy horse was just another reminder of how desolate her life had actually become.

The sun was at their backs, filtering down through a dense, white blanket of haze. Meiran loosened the coarsely woven shawl she wore over her shoulders. She had purchased the shawl from a peddler on their way out of the city. Her white cloak of office she'd left in the guest room back at the palace. In the thick winter garments of a peasant, Meiran knew that few would be able to recognize her. Only the chains on her wrists might identify her, and only then to a very observant eye.

"So where, exactly, are you taking me?" she asked of her silent companion. Quinlan Reis hadn't spoken so much as a word since they'd left the city gates. Meiran reached down and patted the neck of the brown mare she was riding. The horse snorted and twitched its hide beneath her touch as if shaking off flies.

"I'm taking you to Malikar. What you know as the Black Lands," the somber darkmage answered without looking at her.

Meiran peered over at him skeptically. "Then aren't we heading in the wrong direction?"

"We're not riding all the way to the Khazahar, Prime Warden. Especially not in this intolerable contraption." The man gestured down, indicating the leather saddle beneath him with a grimace of distaste. "Believe me, I've endured enough torments already. I'd rather not have to suffer any more."

Meiran raised her eyebrows. So, either the man wasn't familiar with horses or was more practiced at riding bareback. She suspected the former. Although, in the case of Quinlan Reis, anything was possible.

She gazed openly into his chiseled, almost skeletal face. Meiran couldn't help herself; she found the darkmage fascinating. For one thing, Quinlan Reis was from a time and place that no longer existed in the world. His skin was olive, darker in pigment than any person Meiran had ever met. His features were distinctly different, foreign, and yet somehow vaguely familiar. He might have been rather handsome if he weren't so terribly gaunt.

"Then, where *are* we riding?" she demanded.

The man shrugged. "We're riding to the nearest transfer portal. From there we'll transfer north to the Black Lands. After that, we'll have to walk a fair distance to get to where we're going. I'm afraid we can't take the horses."

Meiran was intrigued. "What is a transfer portal?"

The man's eyes snapped wide open, clearly astounded by her question. "Why, Prime Warden, how is it possible that you're so thoroughly unenlightened?" Shaking his head, he flashed her a scornful grin. "Upon second thought, perhaps I shouldn't be all that surprised. I'm likely the reason you're so grossly ill-informed."

Meiran opened her mouth to respond but closed it again quickly. His reaction shocked her. On the surface, Quinlan Reis seemed nothing more than a sardonic, self-absorbed ass. But there was far more to it than that, Meiran was starting to realize. She was beginning to wonder just how far Quin's egotism went. And what flaws it had been cultivated to mask.

"Was that supposed to be some kind of answer? Or are you trying to be purposely evasive?"

The darkmage managed to smile through a sneer. "In my time, there was an entire transit portal system. Unfortunately, I destroyed the Portal Chamber beneath Aerysius, which, actually, does explain your ignorance. Without that hub, most of the Rhen's satellite portals would have stopped working."

Meiran raised her eyebrows, absorbing this new information in silence. She was uncertain which she found more intriguing: the existence of a lost technology that surpassed any wonder she'd ever heard of, or the knowledge that her newfound companion was the person responsible for its loss.

She demanded, "Where is this portal?"

Quinlan nodded ahead of them, gazing down the empty path. "A few hours' ride to the west of here."

Meiran stared at him hard, speculating on the scale of destruction this man had wrought in his lifetime. "Tell me," she pressed. "What made you choose to become a Servant of Xerys?"

Quinlan Reis frowned, twin lines etching themselves deeply across the bridge of his nose. He lifted his hat and stroked his hand back through his hair. "My brother and I sought to defy Renquist," he answered, replacing his hat and adjusting the brim. "We were captured. Things didn't go so very well, as you can probably imagine. Renquist can be...persuasive...when he wants to be. My brother refused him and was put to death. Suffice it to say that I lacked that kind of courage."

"I'm very sorry," Meiran said. "About your brother, I mean."

The darkmage scowled. "There's nothing for you to feel sorry about. Braden died a thousand years ago. As much as it pains me to admit it, I can't remember what he even looked like." His scowl deepened, the shadows sculpting his gaunt face.

"What was he like?"

He drew in a slow breath, his mouth screwed into a grimace. "Braden was a man of integrity. Not like me." He shook his head sadly. "I've never had one scrap of honor."

She gazed at him for a long moment, waiting to see if there was any more insight forthcoming. But Quinlan Reis bowed his head, slouching in the saddle as his gaze drifted downward to the ground.

Meiran's mind wandered back to the events of the previous evening. When she had stood in her guest room in Emmery Palace, attempting to gauge this same man's character.

As soon as the door had closed, Meiran spun back around to confront the darkmage.

"You've got one minute. Start talking."

Quinlan Reis responded with a gushing torrent of words. "Darien sent me. Well, Renquist sent me—but I'm really here for Darien. He needs you to—"

"You have fifty seconds. Start making sense."

"I'm trying! It's complicated." He was starting to look angry. Frustrated.

"Forty-five seconds."

He threw up his hands. "My people—you know them as the Enemy—they're all going to die unless you can help us escape the Black Lands."

"Why is that?" Meiran demanded.

"Because the magic field is going to reverse in polarity. We tried to stop it before, but all we really did was put it off for a thousand years. When the Reversal finally does happen, every person living north of the Shadowspears is going to die."

Meiran scowled. "Thirty seconds. Why?"

"The light is going to go out," he growled. "Without light, there will be no crops. Without crops, there will be no food. Everyone in Malikar is going to starve to death if we can't escape the darkness."

Meiran contemplated his words. "What does Renquist want?"

"He wants to deliver his people, Meiran. That's all. Renquist is leading a nation of refugees who, for a thousand years, have wanted nothing more than to simply escape the Black Lands."

But that wasn't true. Quinlan Reis was lying, at least about this.

"They've never come to us as refugees," Meiran argued. "Always, they have come as invaders. As conquerors. Never once have your people ever laid down their arms and thrown themselves on our mercy."

He sighed. "Well…there's a catch."

"What's the catch?"

"Xerys is the catch. If we come, the Dark God comes with us. It's part of the covenant we made a thousand years ago. If we use the Hellpower to stabilize the magic field, then we must remain His servants. We can be subject to no laws but His own."

"I see," Meiran muttered. "Thank you, Quinlan, for your honesty. What does Darien have to say about all this?"

"Darien has a lot to say, actually. But he wants to say it to you himself. In person. Not through me. Will you come with me and hear him out?"

Meiran shook her head, not trusting this man at all. "I'll think on it."

"Unfortunately, you don't have time to think on it. We have to go. Now. Without telling anyone where we're going. You can trust me, Meiran. I'll take you to Darien."

"Why?" she demanded. "Why do we have to leave here with such urgency? Why can't this wait till the morrow?"

"Because I just killed Sareen."

Meiran gasped, her eyes growing wide.

Relentless, Quinlan Reis continued, "Renquist wanted to use you to guarantee Darien's allegiance. Sareen was part of that plan. But when Renquist finds out what I've done, he's going to come looking for us. We can't tell anyone where we're going. If they know, they'll be made to talk. It'll go worse for them. And worse for us."

Meiran was reeling. If he spoke the truth, then they were all in terrible danger.

"I don't trust you," she whispered.

"You don't have to trust me," he asserted. "Trust Darien. You read his note. If you don't come with me then you'll all be executed. They'll show you no mercy, Meiran. Renquist's legions will march over the Rhen, conquering and subjugating everyone in their path. Darien and I won't be able to do a damned thing to stop any of it."

Meiran didn't trust Quinlan Reis at all. But she did trust Darien. She couldn't help it, even though he had given her every reason in the world not to. Meiran existed in a state of flux, caught somewhere between abhorrence and guilt. Hating him while blaming herself. It was a horrendous place to be.

"I can't just leave!" she exclaimed. "I have to tell Kyel and Naia. I have to warn them. If what you say is true, then their lives are in grave danger!"

"They can know nothing!" he insisted with a feverish heat in his eyes.

Trembling, Meiran scooped up Darien's letter into her hand. She bent to retrieve her pack off the floor, shoving the scroll inside. She moved to the wardrobe, stuffing her white cloak deep within.

"Gods damn you both!" she swore at Quinlan Reis as she stalked toward the door.

The darkmage glared at her with a wounded expression. "Well, isn't that just original."

They rode in silence for a very long time. Meiran occupied herself by keeping track of the vegetation that grew on either side of the rutted roadway. The valley was aglow with an unseasonal supply of yellow daffodils. Meiran frowned at the sight of the cheerful blossoms dancing on the breeze, hundreds of them. The sight brought back a half-remembered saying from her youth: 'Daffodils in winter herald misery in spring.' Considering their present set of circumstances, Meiran found the sight of the joyful flowers full of ominous portent.

She turned and inquired of her companion, "So, tell me, Quinlan. If you've never had any honor, then why does Darien trust you?"

The acerbic darkmage took the reins of his horse together in his left hand. With his other hand, he reached down and brought a water skin up to his lips, taking a long, thirsty sip. He wiped his mouth on his sleeve before answering her.

"There's an old proverb," he explained. "I suppose it's now an ancient proverb. Translated, it would go something like this: 'I and my brother against my cousin. My cousin and I against the world.'"

Meiran contemplated his words carefully, trying to get a sense of their meaning.

Noticing her struggle, Quinlan elaborated, "I grew up in a tribal society. In Caladorn, loyalty was always kinship-based. Immediate family comes first, then extended family. Then clan."

Meiran nodded slowly. "I think I understand. But what does that have to do with Darien's trust in you?"

Quin shot a sad smile in her direction. "Because Darien's mother was born Emelda Clemley, daughter of Lester Clemley. She descends in a direct line from Prime Warden Sephana Clemley and my own brother, Braden Reis. So that makes Darien and I very distant kin. In truth, he's the closest thing to family I have left in the entire world."

Meiran gaped at Quinlan Reis in shock. "You're serious, aren't you?" she whispered, not sure whether she should be feeling more awed or appalled.

"I'm afraid so," he muttered. "I am sworn to the service of Xerys. But, after that, my loyalty is to Darien. Even ahead of Renquist."

Meiran stared back down at the worn road, her eyes wandering to the nearest clump of daffodils. The bright yellow flowers bobbed their heads in the breeze. Meiran considered them joylessly. The sight filled her only with melancholy.

They travelled in silence for the remainder of the day. At sunset, they arrived at a place where the road curved around a sharp rock spur that ambled up into the high country toward the Craghorns. There, they turned their horses off the road. It was already getting dark, the sun shedding its last light over the ridge in front of them. Quinlan nodded ahead with his chin.

"The transfer portal is up this way."

With that, he climbed down off his mount. He staggered as his shoe caught in the stirrup. While he struggled to free it, Quinlan's gelding continued walking forward. He reached out and took the horse by the bridle, forcing its head around and pulling the animal firmly to a halt against his chest. The gelding stamped its hoof in protest as Quin managed to reclaim his foot.

"Whoever invented such a contraption obviously knew nothing of horsemanship," he muttered testily, claiming his pack and sword from the saddle. He turned back to Meiran, face expectant. "Are you coming, Prime Warden? It's starting to get dark. Better say your farewells to the sun while you still can. You won't be seeing it again for a long time."

He loosened the horse's girth strap and lifted the saddle off its back. He removed the blanket, stroking the beast's damp fur with the palm of his hand. Then he slipped the bridle over the horse's ears and off its head. With a slap on the rump, he set the animal free. The shaggy horse sprinted forward, head and tail carried high.

Meiran reached the ground with much more grace and set immediately about the task of liberating her own mount. She glanced back at Quinlan as she uncinched the saddle's girth.

"What do we do if this transfer portal doesn't work?" she asked.

"It will work," he assured her, adjusting his hat. "It's one of the portals tied in with the Bryn Calazar hub." He shouldered his pack and fixed his sword's scabbard to his belt.

Meiran turned her horse loose and watched the mare trot away. Standing there with her pack, she glanced sideways at Quinlan Reis. For the first time, she noticed the intricate artistry of the belt he wore at his waist. It had a large golden buckle that was worked into the image of a horse bent over backwards. It was a beautiful piece that had the look of something from antiquity.

"Your belt," she stated, nodding toward it. "What type of craftsmanship is it?"

Quinlan glanced down at the buckle, running his hand across the body of the golden stallion. "Omeyan," he answered. "My family's clan. This was my brother's warbelt."

Meiran admired the belt, noticing the small collection of implements and sacks that hung from the worked leather. "It's beautiful," she told him sincerely. Her eyes went to the weapon that hung at his side.

"Your sword. Show me?"

Quinlan shrugged, drawing the curved blade from its scabbard and offering it up to Meiran with both hands. She didn't accept it. Instead, she examined the blade as he held it up in front of her. Reaching out, she touched the thin scimitar with her hand, letting her fingers trace the carved elegance of the sword's ivory hilt.

"It's a masterwork," she commented. "I've never seen anything like it before."

"Nor shall you ever again," Quinlan Reis smiled. "Zanikar is the only one of its kind."

Meiran nodded in appreciation. "Where did you come by such a weapon?"

"I forged it."

Meiran blinked. She crossed her arms over her chest. "*You* forged it? Quinlan Reis, are you an Arcanist?"

"I was," Quinlan responded as he slid Zanikar back into its scabbard. "A long time ago. Not anymore."

"What are you now?" Meiran whispered, almost afraid to hear his response.

"Now?" Quinlan shrugged, looking down at the

ground at his feet. "Now I'm just a demon. The only thing I create anymore is pain."

Chapter Eight
Ignoble Protector

Bryn Calazar, The Black Lands

Darien sat on the edge of the bed and gazed blearily around at the stark confines of the guest room they had provided him. The walls were made of baked mud bricks, as black as the scorched earth they had been molded from. There were no wood furnishings anywhere, not even a door. The bed itself was little more than a straw-stuffed sack covered by a thin blanket with a pillow thrown on top. A granite stand set against one of the walls supported a beaten copper wash-bowl and ewer. There were no rugs or carpets, no tapestries of any kind. A clay oil lamp rested on the floor in a corner. It produced a softly glowing flame, the only source of light in the room. The indigo robes they had given him lay in a wad on the floor where he'd thrown them down.

Darien stood, pushing himself up slowly with a grimace of pain, and wandered over to the wash-stand. There, he leaned over, gripping the edge of the cold stone surface with his hands, stretching out the aching muscles of his back. His hands and arms were caked with dried layers of blood.

At least there was water in the ewer. Darien poured it into the copper bowl and dipped his hands in, scrubbing them together vigorously. He continued the motion up his scarred wrists, cupping his hand to scoop the water onto the backs of his arms. He worked the crusted blood into a lather, smearing it around more than actually washing it off.

"May I come in?"

Darien started, flinching at the sound of the voice. Since there was no door, the bedchamber was defined only by a curtain made of strands of beads that hung across the room's entrance. Through that thin drape, he could make out the serene features of Myria Anassis.

Darien glanced down at himself. He stood clothed only in blood and bruises from the waist up. His arms were dripping fouled water onto the dark bricks of the floor. He was in no shape to receive company.

There was a soft tinkle as Myria's hand parted the drape of beads enough to peer inside. From the corner of the room, the thanacryst growled.

"*Theanoch,*" Darien commanded it, wiping his hands on the wool of his breeches. The beast went immediately silent, resting its jowls on its paws.

"I hope it's not a bad time?" Myria asked, pushing toward him through the veil of beads. She had changed clothes, he noticed. She was now wearing a simple but elegant shift woven of raw linen. Her raven hair hung in lustrous waves down her back, all the way to her slender waist.

Myria drew toward him, a look of concern in her eyes. "I wasn't sure whether you had knowledge of mending." She reached her hand toward the side of his face.

Darien winced at the feel of her touch. "I know how to heal. I just didn't know if it was permitted." He reached up to where her fingers had so lightly brushed his swollen cheek.

Myria scowled. "Of course it's permitted. That business down there was all for show. The populace wanted blood. You gave them a taste of it. Now, sit down." Her tone was suddenly all business-like. She gestured briskly toward the bed.

Darien obeyed even though he was very capable

of tending to himself. He sat down on the edge of the stuffed mattress, gazing up into her wide, dark eyes. Myria moved toward him and, bending over, cupped his face with her soft hands. She closed her eyes in concentration.

He could feel the probe she sent through him to ascertain the nature of his injuries. The feel of her power was warm and comforting. Darien closed his eyes, steadying himself for what he knew was about to come next. He gasped when the violent surge of energies hit. At first he fought against it, his mind on the edge of panic from the sudden force of raw power she applied. The healing washed over him like a wave breaking on a shoreline. The pain was erased completely, swept clean away, replaced by a soothing flush of contentment.

He couldn't fight it any longer. Darien fell back against the mattress, his mind drifting away, born on peaceful tides of slumber.

———

When he awoke, Myria was still there, still keeping watch over him. She sat on the side of the bed, her face tranquil in the wavering lantern light. Darien reached up and rubbed his eyes. Disoriented, he glanced down. His body was still unclothed, but remarkably whole and clean. The only marks left were old white scars, along with the gruesome markings the Oath had left behind on his wrists. Those would never be healed. They would remain with him always, a constant reminder of the betrayal he had committed.

"You slept a long time," Myria remarked, peering down at him with a smile. "I didn't realize you were that injured. Those men were brutes. Here. I brought you some food."

She stood up from the bed and knelt down, lifting a round serving platter up off the floor. On it were arranged three metal bowls and a copper cup. She slid the platter onto the mattress beside him.

Darien glanced up as the smell of hot food imme diately captivated his interest. He squirmed into a reclining position on the bed, gazing down at the platter. All of the small bowls were only partially filled, one with rice, another with a thin red broth. The largest bowl contained a small amount of what looked like vegetable stew.

"My thanks," he muttered. The healing sleep had left him ravenous. He picked up the bowl of rice first, holding it in his left hand as he spooned the grains into his mouth with his fingers.

"I apologize there is no meat," Myria informed him as he dined, settling back down on her knees. "In Malikar, it is forbidden to eat the flesh of animals."

Darien didn't mind. The spices in the broth consumed his senses. He drank it down thirstily, throwing his head back and draining the small bowl. When he lifted the stew to his lips, he opened his eyes and realized that Myria was still gazing at him.

Suddenly self-conscious, Darien lowered the bowl, replacing it on the serving platter. He wiped his mouth with the back of his hand. Her eyes still lingered on him, a quiet smile on her lips. He didn't understand why she was even still there.

Darien shifted uncomfortably. "Is there…something more you need from me?"

Myria's face brightened at his question. Her eyes sought his. "There is," she admitted with a shrug. "I think you know why I'm here. You're a desirable man, Darien. We have some time before dinner."

He blinked, taken completely aback by her candor. Never in his life had he ever heard a woman speak so forwardly. He didn't know what to say. Discomfited, he dropped his gaze to the bed.

"I'm sorry." He shook his head in confused wonder. "I can't help you with that."

Myria reached up, stroking the side of his face with her hand. Her fingers found a stray lock of hair and brushed it aside. She gazed deeply into his eyes with a wistful expression. "Why not? Do you not find me pleasing?"

Darien couldn't help the half-smile that slipped to his lips as he mused where women like Myria might have been when he was younger. Her dark brown skin was smooth and flawless, her lips plump and perfectly shaped. She was an attractive, elegant woman. And intelligent, perhaps her most compelling feature.

"You're pleasing enough," he admitted in all honesty. "But my heart belongs to another. I'm afraid it wouldn't be fair to either of you. Or to me, for that matter."

Myria sat back, retracting her hand. She canted her head slightly to the side, her eyes dark and penetrating. "Have you given any consideration to her heart?"

Darien frowned, not taking her meaning. "What are you saying?"

"Meiran isn't going to want you any more, Darien."

Her words were just as brutal as they were honest. They hurt more than the wounds she had healed on him. With a grunt, he shoved himself up off the bed. *"You can't know that."*

Hands on his hips, Darien stalked away across the room toward the wash basin. The thanacryst tracked him with its eyes, a low growl lingering in its throat as it sensed the tension in the air.

Behind him, Myria rose to her feet. To his back, she stated, "Then let me ask you something. Doesn't Meiran deserve a man she can spend eternity with? Or, at the very least, a lifetime?"

Her words halted Darien in his tracks. He clenched his hands into fists until his nails bit into the flesh of his palms. He closed his eyes as the cruelty of her remark sank home, thrusting like a knifepoint into his chest.

"Get out."

He didn't look at her again, but he could feel her leaving. The tinkling sound of the beads told him that she had paused in the doorway. Her voice, sad and calm, filtered back toward him.

"Someone had to point that out to you, Darien. I'm just sorry it had to be me." The strings of painted beads made fragile music as she withdrew. "I'll be here if you change your mind. Don't forget to come down for dinner."

When she was gone, he set the platter on the floor and threw himself back down on the mattress, staring miserably up at the ceiling. Gradually, the rate of his breathing finally slowed. His pulse was still a loud drumming in his ears. Try as he might, he couldn't get her cold logic out of his brain.

She was right.

That's why it hurt so much.

The demon-hound stood up and yawned expansively, thrusting its hindquarters up in the air and stretching out its front legs. Then it turned and jumped up onto the mattress behind him. With a desolate whine, the beast nudged its great head between Darien's shoulder blades as it curled up against his back.

Darien lay there on his side, staring off into nothing. Eventually, he fell back to sleep.

The sound of clinking beads awoke him. Darien sat up, hand going behind him to steady the growling hound. He was almost relieved when he looked up into Byron Connel's face. In all the Black Lands, the red-bearded darkmage was the closest thing he had to an ally.

The man stood over him, arms crossed over his chest. "Renquist is looking for you. You were supposed to come down for dinner. I told him you were probably still sitting up here sulking."

Darien raised his eyebrows. "Oh, is that what I've been doing?"

Connel smirked. "That's what it looks like to me. Anyway, collect your things. You're leaving."

Darien pushed himself up off the bed. The demon-hound jumped down onto the floor beside him. "Leaving for where?"

"The Khazahar," Connel informed him.

Darien frowned as he bent over to retrieve his blue robes from off the ground. "Where is Azár?"

"She's with the Prime Warden. I suggest you join them."

Darien pulled the indigo robes on over his head. He spread his hands out, shaking the sleeves down over his arms. The garments felt foreign and altogether unfamiliar. Heavy. He still wasn't sure exactly what emotion wearing them evoked.

He reached for his longsword, drawing the baldric on over his head. Seeing it, Connel took a step toward him, reaching up to admire the hilt.

"That's one hell of a weapon," he remarked.

Darien glanced down at the silver morning star that hung from a leather strap at Connel's waist. "So is that," he said appreciatively. "May I hold it?"

Byron Connel chortled, his eyes glistening with mirth. "Only over my dead body."

Darien glanced at him sideways. "I didn't mean to offend."

The ancient Battlemage shrugged. "No offense taken." He reached down to his waist, untying the weapon and offering it haft-first to Darien. "Here. Take it."

Darien frowned, sensing that something wasn't right. He reached out, his fingers closing around the weapon's leather-wrapped haft as Connel released his hold.

The morning star fell through his grip with the weight of ten iron anvils. It impacted with the floor with a loud *thump*.

Darien glanced up at Connel with startled eyes. The Battlemage chuckled. "Go ahead. Pick it up."

Darien already knew that he couldn't. But he bent over and tried, anyway. Just as he suspected, the weapon refused to be shifted by his hand. It held fast to the floor, unyielding even as he exerted all his strength against it.

"Thar'gon is an artifact," Byron Connel explained. "It can be wielded only by the hand of the Warden of Battlemages."

Darien righted himself, gazing down at the silver morning star on the floor. "But the Lyceum doesn't exist anymore."

"Nevertheless." Connel scooped the talisman up easily into his big hand. He held it up before him, wielding it like a club. "If I should ever fall, Thar'gon will pass to Nashir. After that," he shrugged. "Then I suppose it would pass to you. If we can ever get you properly trained, you'll be the only other Battlemage amongst our number."

He reached out, clapping Darien on the back. Then he tied the weapon to his belt. "Let's go. You already missed dinner. It's never a good idea to keep the Prime Warden waiting."

Darien followed him through narrow corridors lined with dark bricks that seemed erratically placed. The floor was coarse and uneven. It was hard to walk without tripping. Wall-mounted oil lamps supplied enough dim light to see by.

Connel led him deep into to the dark bowels of the ziggurat. It was cool but not cold within; the mud bricks did an excellent job of regulating the temperature of the air. They passed through a drape of beads into a long room lined with many-colored tapestries and colorful drapes of cloth that hung down the walls from the ceiling.

Darien stopped, gazing around as his eyes adjusted to the brightness of the chamber. The entire room was richly aglow with the light of hundreds of lanterns, each of a different shape, size, and workmanship. The wash of color was almost jarring after the dim austerity his senses had become accustomed to.

It was obvious that a banquet had been served. Bowls of every size were arranged on wide platters scattered across the rugs, surrounded by brightly embroidered cushions and tall pitchers of drink. Very little was left, Darien realized. Servants moved silently on the fringes of the room, clearing away the remnants of the feast. Of their own party, only Myria, Renquist and Azár remained. The others had already departed.

Upon seeing his arrival, Myria stood and approached. Darien's stomach tightened as she drew near. She leaned forward, her lips softly brushing first his right cheek then his left.

"Go in peace," she whispered softly in his ear. Her hand caressed his. Then she turned and left.

When she was gone, Darien continued to stare into the space she had just occupied, vexed by conflicting emotions. He had nothing against Myria; the more he thought about it, the more he realized she was absolutely correct. But neither was he attracted to her. Her cruel words had quenched any spark of desire he otherwise might have felt.

"Nur a'nach," the Prime Warden uttered in greeting. "Please. Come join us." With a sweep of his hand, he indicated a spread of embroidered cushions in front of him. Azár yet remained seated at his side.

Darien frowned, puzzled by his master's greeting. "Dark's grace?" he said, his mind groping through his knowledge of the language for the correct interpretation.

"Evening's grace," Zavier Renquist corrected him. "That would be the literal translation. It simply means, 'good evening.'"

"Peace," Byron Connel whispered as he turned to go. He squeezed Darien's arm in warm reassurance before departing.

Darien gestured with his hand, stationing the demon-dog at the chamber's entrance. Then he approached the Prime Warden and sat down upon a cushion on the floor across from him. He gazed down at the nearest platter of food, eyes wandering over the wide assortment of dishes that remained. One in particular attracted his attention. It was a plate of grilled meat served with herbs over a bed of grain.

"I thought flesh was forbidden," he said.

Renquist cast him a stare weighted with ominous significance. "Nothing is forbidden me."

Darien nodded, silently absorbing the import of the man's assertion. He gazed straight ahead at the plate of meat.

"Go ahead," Renquist offered. "Have some. I will arrange for more if you find it to your taste."

Darien shook his head. "Thank you, no, Prime Warden. I ate earlier."

Zavier Renquist leaned forward, eyes raking over Darien's face and down the robes that covered his body. His dark eyes narrowed. At last, he nodded slightly, seeming satisfied.

"Myria tended you well," he said. "Do you resent me, Darien, for consenting to have you beaten?"

Resent him? No. Darien did not resent him. It had not been Renquist's intent to do him lasting harm. It had been his own actions that had brought about the necessity. Darien understood that, now, and accepted it. It had taken him a long time spent in contemplation and suffering to achieve that level of acceptance. The demons that haunted the Netherworld dealt harsh but practical lessons. They had little patience with justification or intent.

"I don't resent you," Darien assured him quietly. "I understand why it was necessary."

Zavier Renquist nodded. "I was very proud of you today. You displayed the appropriate amount of restraint and humility. Even the vizier commented on how naturally you complete our Circle of Eight. He sees in you the same thing I do."

"What is that, Prime Warden?"

"A man capable of making even the hardest decisions. I can trust you to always make the right choice, no matter what it costs you."

Feeling a flush of humility, Darien glanced downward at the floor. Instantly, the Prime Warden's hand shot out across the platter between them and caught his chin. Renquist's eyes were suddenly wide as if enraged, his jaw set in anger. With the pressure of his fingers, he forced Darien's head back up, capturing his stare with the shadowed intensity of his gaze.

"Never lower your eyes, Darien." His voice was soft but full of fire. "Never. Not even to me. It is considered a sign of weakness."

His fingers tightened, becoming painful. Darien said nothing, holding the Prime Warden's stare with his own unwavering gaze. Renquist released him, sitting back and returning his attention to his plate.

He plucked a date up into his hand, plunging it into his mouth and sucking the flesh off the pit.

"Do you know what your name means in Venthic?"

Darien swallowed, unnerved by the man's unpredictable temperament. "I'm told it means 'Protector.'"

"That's right. You are a protector of *my* people, now. Apparently, that's what you were born to be."

Darien considered Renquist's words. He knew why his mother and father had chosen his name; it was because of his birth order. His elder brother, Aidan, had been slated to follow their mother's path toward political gains. Darien, being the second-born son, had been intended to follow their father's example and become a Sentinel. Hence the name: Darien. Protector. He swallowed, awash in the miserable knowledge that, even though he had lived up to the name his parents had given him, he had also thoroughly disgraced his family's legacy of honor.

"I don't believe fate is predetermined," he said at last.

Zavier Renquist shrugged. "Fate is simply the result of our actions. There are always consequences to the choices we make. Those consequences define our destiny."

He set the pit of the date he was chewing down on the side of his plate. "So. Darien. Your chance has come. Are you willing to embrace the destiny you have created for yourself?"

Darien nodded. "Aye, Prime Warden."

Renquist turned to the slight woman beside him, who had so far been listening in silence to their conversation. "Lightweaver Azár, you speak for all of the Khazahar. Will you accept this man's offer of protection? Will you allow Darien Lauchlin of Amberlie to assume domination over the hinterlands?"

Azár's eyes shot toward Darien, considering him with a contemptuous scowl. "If there is no other choice, Prime Warden."

Renquist worked his lips, sucking them together. "There is not. Not for the purposes you have defined. Darien is by far the strongest mage at our disposal. And, because of his unique training, he is also the most versatile. There is not one amongst our number more suited to your needs."

Azár looked as though she would rather throw her support behind anyone else in the world. Her eyes full of disdain, she said, "The Khazahar will have to decide for itself if it is to accept this man's protection, Prime Warden. I will lead him westward to my village. From there, he can work to gain the support of the Tanisars."

"Very well," Renquist allowed, at last seeming satisfied. He looked at Darien, then, standing up.

Following the Prime Warden's lead, Darien rose and moved to stand before him. Renquist took his hands into his own, considering him quietly with a long and searching gaze.

"Darien Lauchlin, I proclaim you Overlord of the Khazahar. Go in peace. Live up to the name your parents saw fit to bestow upon you. Become the protector our people have so long awaited and so rightfully deserve."

He turned to the woman beside him, taking both of her hands together into one of his own, joining the three of them together in bond. "Lightweaver Azár, you must strive to forgive the past and put aside your preconceptions. What is gone is dead. Your new overlord knows nothing of his people nor of the challenges he will face. Take him by the hand. He will be in dire need of your support."

Azár's eyes did not falter as she looked at him. "I understand, Prime Warden. On my head and my eyes, this man will have my support."

"Call him by his name."

The woman blinked, her face suddenly uncertain. She frowned, shifting her weight over her feet. "His name, Prime Warden?"

"His name. I have yet to hear you actually speak it."

Azár blinked. Her lips parted slightly. "You will have my support, Darien Lauchlin of Amberlie."

Darien stood appraising her, distrusting the sudden change. She continued staring at the ground, showing him only the top of her head and the long strands of dark hair that escaped her thick braid.

"Call me Darien," he said. It was not a request.

"Darien," Azár repeated. "You will have my support."

Darien nodded, satisfied. "Then you shall have mine."

Renquist released both their hands. "Go in peace with the grace and blessings of the gods."

He turned toward Azár and kissed her on the cheek. Then he took Darien and drew him into a rigid embrace, locking his arms around him and resting his nose against his face. "Go in peace."

Darien closed his eyes, made anxious by Renquist's close proximity. When the Prime Warden withdrew, he had to fight to keep his gaze off the floor. He turned and strode out of the room, Azár following behind him. He pushed the tinkling drape of beads aside, moving out into the corridor. At his whistle, the demon-dog sprinted after him.

"Darien."

He stopped, shocked that Azár had actually used his name again, and so soon. He turned toward her.

"You murdered my sister in your fire," she informed him coldly. "You took her soul. That is why I hate you. I thought you should know."

Chapter Nine
Ties that Bind

Glen Farquist, The Rhen

Naia gazed up into the carved face of the Goddess of the Eternal Requiem, seeking for solace but finding none. The statue's stone eyes appeared harsh and judgmental. As well they should be; Naia had betrayed the goddess she'd once served. She had sacrificed her vows and veil in favor of the chains she now wore on her wrists and the mage's power that burned in her veins. All for a man who had betrayed his own purpose and had striven at every step to push her further away.

"Are you all right?" she heard Kyel ask.

Naia blinked, unable to tear her eyes from the critical visage of the goddess above her. "I'm not," she admitted, her voice breaking with emotion. "What if all this is really my own fault? I helped Darien vow his Bloodquest, right here in this very shrine. I struck the chains from his wrists with my own hands. I set his feet down this path and I held him up when he couldn't walk it alone."

"None of this is your fault," Kyel said, putting a comforting hand on her shoulder. "Naia. It's not."

She managed to wrench her gaze away from the statue, compelled by the insistence in his voice. She turned toward him. Kyel's face was careworn, his eyes full of concern.

"You didn't make Darien's choices for him," Kyel said. "All you did was follow him down that road."

"I didn't see where his path was leading him," she said. "I should have tried harder to stop him."

"He wouldn't have listened to you. You did all you could do. You did your best."

She looked up again into the face of the statue, silently imploring her goddess for forgiveness. Maybe if she hadn't betrayed her vows, none of this would have happened. Maybe this was all some sort of punishment for her own transgressions.

"I need to speak with my father," she whispered.

Kyel nodded, looking as though he understood. "I'm going to go across the valley. I'll be back later tonight, or perhaps tomorrow."

Naia reached out and caught his arm. "Good luck," she said, pressing a kiss against his cheek.

Kyel nodded, pulling back. She listened to the sound of his footsteps as he strode away, leaving her alone at the feet of the marble statue.

Naia placed her hand on the rough oaken door, feeling the coarse grain of the wood through her fingers. Curling her hand into a fist, she knocked twice. From the other side, she could hear the sound of approaching footsteps. Then the door swung open, revealing the form of an old man she almost didn't recognize.

"Father?"

Naia gasped, bringing her hand up to cover her mouth. Tears filled her eyes. She did nothing to wipe them away. She stood there in the doorway, silently willing the old man in front of her to show some sign of recognition. At last, he did. Luther Penthos' lips parted as he sucked in a sharp gasp of air. He took his daughter into his arms, hugging her against his chest.

Naia couldn't believe how fragile her father had become. She could feel his sharp bones through the rich fabric of his vestments. He quivered in her arms, his bony fingers rubbing her back. Her father's frailty made Naia cry even harder. She kissed his forehead, clinging to him as her shoulders shook with shame and grief.

"Stand back and let me look at you," he whispered, cupping her face with his hands.

Naia obeyed, wiping her eyes. She backed away from his embrace, doing her best to smile at him through her tears.

When his eyes had finally had their fill of her, he nodded slightly. "I've missed you. Why didn't you come sooner?"

Naia shrugged, spreading her hands to reveal the matching set of chains on both wrists. "I didn't know how to tell you," she admitted. "I was so afraid I'd broken your heart."

"No, my child. You could never break my heart," he assured her, stepping back and inviting her within.

Naia moved inside, brushing past him as she walked across the small room to his desk. There, she took a seat in one of the chairs. She brought out a kerchief to dab at her eyes. Her father moved behind her, setting his hands on her shoulders and squeezing her gently before edging past. He sat himself down in his own chair across the desk from her, leaning back and folding his hands in his lap.

"You are just as beautiful a mage as you ever were a priestess," Luther Penthos commented.

Naia smiled her gratitude, clutching her kerchief in her hands as she brought it down from her face. "Thank you."

Her father looked very different. Older. Thinner. Careworn by years and grief. But he was still very much in command of his faculties, she could tell. He was, every inch, a High Priest.

"So, tell me. Which order did you take? What tier are you?"

"I am a Querer, Father. But only third tier."

His smile was warm and proud. "That is nothing to be ashamed of. My daughter has become a powerful mage."

Naia blotted away tears of joy that clouded her eyes at the sound of his acceptance. "To be honest, the Prime Warden hasn't had much time to devote to my training."

Her father looked down at the surface of his desk, his smile retreating. "That's unfortunate." There was a long gap of silence. At last he spoke, his voice sad and serious. "Why did you abandon me, Naia? Why did you leave me for *him?*"

"Because I believed in him, Father."

That was the simple truth. She could have elaborated. She could have told him all the things that had gone through her mind on the day she'd left Glen Farquist with Darien. She could have talked about how much she had come to admire the man in the short amount of time she had spent with him. She could have spoken of how lost and alone he had seemed, how defiant and courageous. Darien's plight had tugged at her heartstrings. She had not been able to stand aside and watch him destroy himself.

"Did you love him?"

Naia's throat clenched in grief. "Yes," she admitted with a grimace. "I did...and I still do."

"I don't understand." Luther Penthos frowned, leaning forward. "Naia, what are you trying to tell me?"

She drew in a deep breath, dreading to confess the depth of her anguish. "Before he died, Darien swore his soul to Xerys. He's become a demon, Father, just like Renquist. And the Well of Tears is open once again. I'm scared, Father. I'm scared because..." Her voice trailed off. Naia swallowed, summoning enough courage to continue. "I'm scared because I'm still in love with him. *I'm in love with a demon.*"

There. It was out. She looked up into her father's pale face and saw his expression.

He'd been wrong.

She still had the power to break his heart.

Kyel followed the brown-robed cleric through the maze of underground passages that made up the Temple of Wisdom beneath the Valley of the Gods. Scores of clerics moved about them; the broad corridor was a busy thoroughfare that cut right through the center of the temple. No one paid Kyel any mind; they had become used to his frequent visits. He had been using Om's temple as a retreat, a place where he could meditate in quiet and practice the countless exercises Meiran was always giving him. He found the temple quiet and soothing, very much to his liking. Within the last year, Kyel had frequented the temple so often that he'd almost started thinking of his quarters there as home.

The cleric before him drew up, gesturing at a door in front of them. He then turned and walked away, leaving Kyel on his own. With only the slightest moment of hesitation, Kyel reached out and turned the knob. The door swung inward, revealing the room beyond.

"Papa!"

Kyel was almost knocked over backwards by the force of the small body that collided with his own. He scooped his son up into his arms, clutching him tight against his chest. He attacked the plump cheeks with the wiry growth of his new beard.

"No, Papa, no!"

Gil kicked and giggled in his arms as Kyel laughed, overwhelmed with joy at the feel of him. At last he relented, letting the child squirm away. But it was only seconds before Gil was back, begging for his attention.

"More, Papa, *more!*"

Kyel laughed, grabbing him up and tickling him under the arms as Gil squealed and bucked to get away. Kyel set him down, motioning for him to stay.

"I've got something for you," Kyel said, squatting down and reaching his hand into the deep pocket of his cloak. He pulled out a small sack, offering it out to the boy. Gil gasped at the sight of it, his blue eyes going wide and round.

"What is it, Papa?"

"It's a birthday surprise," Kyel told him. "You didn't think I'd forget your birthday, did you? Go ahead. Open it."

Gil undid the cord that held the sack closed, his four-year-old fingers working clumsily at the knot. He shook the sack, letting the contents spill out into his hand. He gasped, staring down wondrously at the painted object in his palm.

"A toy!" he exclaimed, turning the red piece of wood over in his hands. He unwound the string that was looped around it.

"It's a top," said Kyel, ruffling Gil's hair with his hand. "Give it here. I'll show you how it works."

He wound the string around the top's axis and, setting the wooden toy down on the floor, gave the string a solid tug. The red top flew suddenly into motion, scooting away from them toward the center of the floor. Gil squealed, clapping his hands in delight as the top danced around in slowly compressing spirals until it finally came to a rest on its side.

The boy ran forward, catching it up in his hands.

"Don't forget to wind the string!"

Kyel tossed the wadded string over to him. It fell to the floor as Gil laughed, his reactions not quite fast enough to catch it. Kyel smiled as his son ducked out into the corridor to play with his new toy.

The smile fell from his lips at the sight of Cadmus. The layman stood up from his chair, ambling toward him with his hands clasped in front of him. He wore the simple clothes of a commoner, a tan vest over a stained wool shirt.

"How's he been?" Kyel asked, his voice full of concern.

Cadmus shrugged. His thinning brown hair was parted too far over on the side, giving him an almost comical appearance. "He's been missing his father. And he's been missing his mum."

Kyel's gaze dropped to the floor at the mention of Amelia.

His stomach soured as he remembered the day of his homecoming. He had knocked at the door of his own home and waited for his wife to answer. He wasn't sure why he'd even bothered to knock; it was his own door, after all.

But he'd wanted to surprise her.

Only, the face that confronted him through the cracked doorway had not belonged to Amelia.

"Kyel…?"

His father swept Kyel into a long, crushing embrace. When he finally let go, his father took him inside and broke the news to his son.

Kyel had been gone from home for an awfully long time.

While he was away, his family had received word from Rothscard of his fate. They were told that Kyel had been found guilty of murder. That he and Traver had been tried, convicted and condemned.

Kyel's wife had mourned him for dead.

And then Amelia had done the only sensible thing she could do: she married another man.

Kyel blamed himself, not her. He'd never been able to forgive himself for not being there, not being at her side. For putting her through that. By the time he'd arrived home, Amelia and her new husband were already expecting a child of their own. There was very little Kyel could do at that point.

He'd shaken the man's hand and bid Amelia goodbye. He'd collected up his son. And then he'd left Covendrey forever.

"His Eminence requires a word with you."

Kyel blinked at the sound of Cadmus' voice. He glanced up bleakly at the man, roused from his dark reverie. His Eminence was always requiring a word with him. Every time Kyel visited the temple, the High Priest of Om was always eager for a chat.

"I figured." Kyel sighed.

Cadmus' stare went blank for a long moment, his eyes wandering up and to the side. At last his focus solidified. "His Eminence wishes to know if you have come here to discuss the unsealing of the Well of Tears?"

Kyel was used to this form of communication; it didn't surprise him any longer. What shocked him was that Om's clerics had already guessed the nature of his visit. He still didn't know how they came by much of their information.

"We don't know who did it," he admitted. "All we know is that it's been opened. Renquist and his darkmages are loose upon the world again. And Darien Lauchlin is with them."

Cadmus' stare drifted away. He was gone a long time, his mind focused elsewhere. Then:

"This is very ill tidings, indeed. His Eminence extends to you his sympathy. Your master was a courageous man with noble intentions. It's a tragedy that he did not show better restraint."

Kyel couldn't agree more. "Already, Renquist has moved against us. Quinlan Reis and Sareen Qadir came to Rothscard to treat with the Prime Warden. We found Sareen murdered. The other one—Reis—disappeared along with Meiran. We fear she's been taken. Or worse."

Cadmus showed no visible reaction to the news. Instead, his eyes glassed over. This time, he was gone for a very long while. When he finally came back, his face was grimly set.

"It is lamentable that you are even aware of those names, Grand Master Kyel," Cadmus said at last. "That the Prime Warden might be at the mercy of a monster such as Quinlan Reis is truly harrowing."

"You know of him?" Kyel was surprised.

Cadmus nodded. "We know only what has been recorded, which is very little. But what we do know is enough cause for grave concern. Quinlan Reis is perhaps the most dangerous man in all of history."

Kyel frowned. "If Reis is so dangerous, then how is it that no one's ever heard of him?"

It took a long moment for Cadmus to answer. "His name was purposefully expunged from the annals of Aerysius. It was not, however, excluded from the texts of Om's temple."

Kyel nodded, remembering the darkmage mentioning something about that. "What can you tell me about him?"

Cadmus closed his eyes, appearing to concentrate. He stood there for minutes, face slack, arms dangling at his sides. When he opened his eyes again, his expression was very bleak. "Quinlan Reis was the brother of Braden Reis, the First Sentinel. From what our historians have managed to reconstruct, it was Quinlan's betrayal that resulted in his own brother's execution. He was also personally responsible for the Desecration of Caladorn. The man was noted in his lifetime to have few moral scruples. According to one text, he was actually a trained assassin. A mage-hunter. If Quinlan Reis truly has kidnapped the Prime Warden, then her life is in grave danger."

"That's what we're afraid of," Kyel said, feeling dismal. "We've taken the body of Sareen Qadir to the Temple of Death. We're hoping that there might be some way she can be brought back to life, so we can glean some information from her."

Hearing that, Cadmus winced. He closed his eyes for a time. "That is a very reckless endeavor," he said at last. "His Eminence would strongly advise you against such action. The corpse of Sareen Qadir must be speedily put to the torch." There was a pause. "I hope you understand...the same holds true for your former master, should the opportunity arise."

Kyel blinked. "Darien...he was more than just my master. He was also my friend. I don't think I could do that."

A delighted squeal from outside in the corridor assured Kyel that his son was still enjoying his new toy. He turned toward the doorway, suddenly very grateful he had found such a distracting gift.

"Some time spent in our vaults would do you great benefit, Grand Master Kyel," Cadmus offered stiffly.

Kyel shook his head. "Thank you, but I've got to be going."

"You really ought to consider making the time, if you deem it reasonable to try negotiating with a darkmage. Even a dead one."

"Then what would you suggest?" Kyel demanded. "How do we go about finding the Prime Warden?"

"You are advised to abandon that effort," Cadmus said, reaching out and patting him on the shoulder. "Let Meiran find you. Or count her name among the lost. If she is truly in thrall to Quinlan Reis, then there are only two possible outcomes. Neither one is very hopeful."

Kyel sighed wearily. Casting a beleaguered glance around the small room, he discovered an empty chair and wandered over to it, plopping his weight down dismally.

"Does His Eminence think Renquist will invade again?"

It took only a moment for the man to answer. "His Eminence would rather not venture to guess. Of course, if Zavier Renquist does have your master as an ally, that puts us at a distinct disadvantage."

"Why?"

"Because, in life, Darien Lauchlin had intimate knowledge of the Rhen's defenses. As a Sentinel, he was very well-versed in all of our military assets as well as the limitations of those assets. He fought alongside many of our greatest commanders. He knows how they think."

"That's true," Kyel agreed reluctantly. "Do we even stand a chance?"

Cadmus' eyes drifted to the side. "His Eminence says we must focus our efforts on neutralizing their darkmages."

"How do we go about doing that?"

"That will take a great deal of planning and careful coordination." Cadmus walked forward, pulling up a chair of his own. He sat down on it next to Kyel. "But it's possible. It can be done. His Eminence thinks we should begin with your former master. He will be the easiest to target, as he still has ties that bind his heart."

Kyel frowned, not liking the sound of that. From the corridor, he could hear Gil clapping in delight.

He was suddenly reminded of Darien's own son, who had died before his father had ever had a chance to come to know him. The thought made his heart sink.

Naia gazed over the desk at her father, whose face looked no better to her than stretched leather mounted over a thin scaffold of bone.

"We will need the help of the temples, Father," she said. "It's the only way we'll have the strength to make a stand."

Her father shook his head. "The temples are forbidden from interfering in this conflict."

But she dismissed his argument with a wave of her hand. "This isn't a border dispute between two rival nations. This is something far more insidious. The temples themselves are directly threatened by Xerys' legions."

"It doesn't matter," Luther Penthos insisted. "Still, we must respect and honor our covenants."

"Those covenants were made with two Assemblies that no longer exist. The Lyceum was destroyed a thousand years ago. And now Aerysius itself has fallen."

"And yet the temples still remain."

"That will not be the case if the Enemy is allowed to run roughshod over us. The temples will not be spared. Just as they weren't spared when Caladorn fell."

"No." Her father shook his head. "We cannot actively participate in this dispute."

Naia was beginning to feel exasperated. "Father, without the might of the temples behind us, all is lost. There aren't enough mages to bolster our military. Kyel is our only Sentinel. I'm strong, Father. But I'm untrained. I'm begging you. Kyel and I can't do it alone."

Her father sat back in his chair. For a long while, he didn't speak. He appeared to be ruminating on her words. At length, he said, "I will convene a Conclave so that you may present your case before the Great Temples of Glen Farquist. That is the best I can do."

Hearing his words, Naia surged out of her seat with a sudden rush of joy. She rounded his desk, throwing her arms around him. "Thank you,

Father!"

He brought his hand up to pat her back. She pressed her cheek against his head, holding him tight before releasing him.

"Thank you," Naia said again as she returned to settle back into her seat. "You know I wouldn't be asking this if it wasn't absolutely imperative."

"What you ask has never been considered since the Great Schism," her father reminded her sternly. He leaned forward, folding his hands atop his desk. "I need to warn you: you are a Master, now. But before that, you were a priestess. And not just any priestess; you were the First Daughter, my own chosen successor. You have much more knowledge of temple secrets than any mage has any right to know. The amalgamation of those two knowledge bases can be a very dangerous combination. You would do well to forget everything you ever learned during your time here."

Naia knew exactly what he was saying and why he was saying it. She understood completely. Nevertheless, she knew it would be impossible to follow his advice. "I can't, Father. The Temple of Death is just as much a part of me as the gift I inherited from Darien. I can't simply forget everything I learned."

Her father closed his eyes, bowing his head.

"So, the gift that moves within you did, in fact, come from *him.*"

"Yes," Naia admitted.

Her father sighed, shaking his head. "It yet astounds me that one man could have possibly wrought so much damage in such a short period of time. It pains me that you had to inherit such a corrupted legacy."

His words, though well-intentioned, provoked Naia's ire. She responded defensively, "Darien was a very courageous and passionate man, unmatched in his commitment to duty. The Rhen has never known a greater champion."

Luther Penthos sat back in his chair, gazing at his daughter with sadness in his eyes. Ominously, he uttered, "And now the Rhen has never faced a fiercer adversary."

Naia threw back her head, knowing he was right. Fresh tears filled her eyes. In a small voice, she whispered, "That's why we need the help of the temples, Father."

The High Priest of Death nodded his understanding.

"I'll see what I can do."

Chapter Ten
The Caravansary

Bryn Calazar, The Black Lands

Darien gazed out across the writhing horde of citizens gathered at the base of the ziggurat, the sight making his stomach sour. The throng was tumultuous, surging against the efforts of guardsmen in full battle plate who labored to hold back the churning masses. He'd hoped the crowd would have dispersed since that morning, when the rabid hatred of the entire populace had been directed against him.

But there was an entirely different tenor in the air this evening, as if the atmosphere of the city had inverted with the change of tide. The crowd seemed impelled by a fanatical zeal. At the sight of Darien and Azár emerging from the temple at the top of the ziggurat, there was a loud outcry from the roiling masses below. Bodies surged wildly, clamoring toward the long ramp of steps. The armed guards managed to contain the multitudes, but only just barely. The mob seemed fomented to a rage.

A harsh gust of wind kicked up, bitingly cold and scented with the salt of the ocean. It rippled Darien's blue robes and whipped his hair into his face. He started down the long ramp of steps, Azár stalking silently at his side. The demon-hound followed behind them both, unholy eyes gleaming like twin green embers in the shadows. Braziers lined the stairway, defying the darkness with wavering orange glows. The din of the crowd swelled as the two of them neared the level of the street. People surged against the line of guards, shouting and brandishing torches, even weapons, in the air.

Guards spilled forward, forming a shield wall around them while pressing the crowd back away from their path. Darien and Azár moved forward in the midst of the ring of guards out into the crowded street. The throng opened up to receive them, reluctantly giving way before their passage. Darien tried to see past the wall of armored bodies that surrounded him, but it was impossible to glimpse much of anything. His efforts frustrated, he instead focused his attention on Azár. He was still more than a little numbed by the confession she had made about her sister.

At least he understood, now, why she hated him. He knew very well how it felt to lose someone you loved.

Their party finally managed to break out of the throng. The guards fanned out, sweeping back to flank them on either side. The streets ahead were dark and sparsely populated. Only shadows moved against the walls that lined the roadside.

Thick smoke billowed across the avenue, drifting like noxious plumes of miasma. Darien inhaled a burning chestful of harsh fumes that made his eyes water. "How do you breathe this air?" he complained to Azár. "It's thick enough to scald the lungs!"

Azár's eyes ticked toward him. "The smoke is from hearth fires. There is nothing to be done about it."

Darien scowled at the taste of the oily film that coated the inside of his throat. He had never breathed anything so noxious in his life. "What sort of fuel are you using?"

"Coal cakes are used for cooking and heating," Azár said with a shrug. "The coal does not burn cleanly."

Darien gaped at her, incredulous. *"Coal?* Why not use wood?"

"Wood is very precious in Malikar," Azár explained. Her words were terse; there was very little patience left in her voice. "Wood cannot be wasted or used for burning."

Darien's eyes widened in understanding as he followed her line of reasoning to its logical end. "I take it there aren't many forests in the Black Lands."

Azár nodded, squinting her contempt at him. "It takes much light and time to grow a tree. Look up at the sky. What do you see?"

Darien glanced up at the swirling mass of cloud-cover that choked the heavens above. He realized that he really had no idea if it was even day or night; there was absolutely no distinction between the two in this hellish land. It was just like the Pass of Lor-Gamorth, just like the skies above Greystone Keep. The glowing luminescence in the clouds was the only source of light in a vast wasteland of shadow. Beneath those dark skies, no plant could ever grow.

Azar cast a smug grin. "I think, perhaps, you begin to understand."

Darien nodded, still gazing upward at the clouds in mute consternation. He *was* beginning to understand. His mind was just starting to grapple with the logistics of providing for an entire population clutched in the grip of yearlong darkness. Softly, he asked, "How do you feed your people, Azár?"

She looked at him with an arrogant sneer on her face. "Wait until we are outside of the vortex that surrounds Bryn Calazar. There, I will show you."

At last, they reached their destination: a wide portal cut out of a mud-brick wall on the side of the boulevard. The opening was broad and encased by a tall horseshoe arch set in stone. Azár walked through the entrance, her dark braid writhing like a snake in the wind. Darien followed, shooting one last glance up at the hostile cloudscape. The demon-dog came along behind, stalking with its nose to the ground.

On the other side of the portal, Darien paused. They were in some type of dim courtyard bordered on all sides by a honeycomb of niche-like openings. The courtyard was not empty; it teemed with people and flickering torches. Darien followed in Azár's wake as she wound through the press of bodies. The buzz of conversation was an incessant drone. A few people shot curious glances their way, eyes widening when they took in the sight of the thanacryst. A few stepped away to let them pass. One man, noticing the emblem of the Silver Star on Darien's chest, bowed and backed quickly out of their path.

Azár led him toward a circle of men gathered before a fountain in the center of the yard. The men were laughing and carrying on; no one paid them any mind as they drew up in their midst. Darien stood patiently beside Azár, watching in curiosity as the men bantered playfully back and forth in their native tongue. He couldn't make out much of what was being said. It was Venthic, but of a dialect that he was utterly unfamiliar with.

Azár strutted forward, angling toward a tall, bearded man who stood slouching against a wall. The man had a subtle air of authority about him. It was something intangible, but immediately apparent. Maybe it was in the way the other men deferred to him, giving him extra space and grinning at his every comment. Or perhaps it was the careless grace of his posture.

Azár walked right up to the slouching man and launched into what appeared to be a fluid bout of negotiation. Darien hung back, watching as her body language conveyed her intentions just as much as her words, which were beyond his level of comprehension. He waited, one hand clutching the leather strap of the baldric that crossed his chest. His gaze roamed from face to face around the group of surrounding men.

Azár at last turned away, glancing back at Darien with concern in her eyes. "This man—his name is Haleem—he is the caravan master. He asks that you remove his wife's consumption. In exchange, he is willing to offer us a place in his caravan and on his barge, as well as food and water for the journey. You do have knowledge of healing?"

Darien glanced at the man, considering the offer. Haleem was grinning broadly in his own direction as the other men around him continued their bantering. Darien wasn't sure he liked the look of him. The man's smile did not come close to touching his eyes.

Grudgingly, he nodded. "Tell him I'd be honored to look in on his wife."

Azár translated his words to the grinning Haleem, whose thin smile only broadened. He took Azár's hand in his own and, bending forward at the waist, pressed a kiss against her fingers. He then pushed his weight off the wall and strode forward until he was standing before Darien, offering his hand. Haleem's handshake was firm, and he did not release it immediately. Instead, he stood holding Darien's hand as the smile crept back to his face.

"Ranu kadreesh, nach'tier," he uttered in a deep and melodic voice.

The salutation was one that Darien understood. *May you know peace, darkmage.* The man's use of his Venthic title made Darien's skin crawl.

"Akadreesh iranu," he responded stiffly, gazing stone-faced at the caravan master.

The man finally released his hand, taking him instead by the arm. Darien allowed himself to be guided back through the throng of men. Haleem led him through the opening of a dark niche built into the opposite wall. There, on the floor all around, were stacked man-high piles of provisions. Haleem led him toward the back of the niche, to a narrow doorway at the far end. At the opening, Haleem paused, shaking the shoes from his feet.

"You will need to remove your shoes," Azár's voice commanded from behind.

Darien obeyed, bending over to slide the worn leather boots from his feet. Haleem took him once again by the arm, urging him forward through the narrow entrance into the interior of the building.

Darien ducked through a woven curtain, finding himself in a narrow room with walls that squeezed oppressively close. He could scarcely see; the dim glow of a single oil lamp did a poor job of dispelling the shadows. He could make out the forms of bodies huddled together on the floor against the opposite wall. There was a rustle of fabric. Someone coughed, the sound wet and rasping.

Darien conjured a mist of blue magelight at his feet. One of the women gave a piercing shriek, the whole cluster of bodies writhing back away from him toward the wall.

Haleem raised his hands, a rapid string of words spilling from his mouth. Darien waited, cautiously assessing the faces of the women huddled before him. He thought he could tell which one was Haleem's wife. She was young but sickly, her skin moist with perspiration.

Raising his hands, Darien took a step toward her. "Tell her I'll have to touch her," he cautioned Azár. He waited for his words to be translated. The sick woman before him gave a slight nod.

Darien lowered himself to the ground before her, crouching as he took the woman's hand into his own. He brought her fingers up to his mouth, kissing them the same way he had seen Haleem kiss Azár's hand. The woman seemed shocked by his gesture, her eyes shooting up to find her husband.

"It is not appropriate to kiss the hand of a woman," Azár corrected him sternly. "It is she who must kiss your hand."

Darien frowned. "But Haleem—"

"I am a Lightweaver," Azár snapped. "My status is much greater than that of a caravan master."

Darien understood. He turned back to Haleem's wife. "What is your name?" he asked, seeking to put her more at ease. *"Ismir'och?"*

"Esvir."

"Esvir," Darien repeated, testing the feel of the name on his tongue. He looked deeply into the young woman's eyes, surprised by what he found there. "I'll need to see inside you, Esvir." He glanced up at Azár, pausing for her to translate. "You'll sense something...a stirring. It won't hurt."

He took Esvir's hand and rubbed her soft skin in reassurance as he waited for Azár to finish communicating his intentions. The young woman nodded, inviting him to proceed. Darien leaned forward, cupping her pale face in his hands and closing his eyes. It didn't take a moment to probe her condition, to sense the extent of the corruption in her damaged tissues.

Dairen inhaled a deep breath. Then he sent a gush of healing energies flooding through Esvir's body, repairing the injury that had been done to her airways and burning the corruption from her blood. The woman stiffened, her eyes rolling back in their sockets. She swooned, falling forward against his chest.

"Ishil'zeri!" Haleem cried out, catching his unconscious wife in his arms.

Darien kept his hands on Esvir until he was certain that the poisons had been driven completely from her frail body. He kept a measure of the beat of her pulse, the steady rhythm of her chest. Through his fingertips, he could sense her vitality renewing. At last, Darien opened his eyes and removed his hands.

"She'll sleep," he informed Azár. "When she awakens, she'll be hungry. Tell Haleem she must have all the food she can eat."

"Sukrien," Haleem muttered, cradling his sleeping wife against his chest.

Darien nodded, standing up. Without another word, he left the dark room, brushing the curtain aside as he passed through the doorway. He replaced his boots and strode back outside to the courtyard. There, he glanced up at the sky, feeling the weariness of the healing sink deeply into his bones. He heard the sound of Azár's soft footsteps dashing up behind him.

"That woman," Darien said softly without looking at her. "Esvir. She has the potential. Do you need an apprentice, Azár?"

"No. I will not take an apprentice. I will be the last of my kind."

Darien scowled, not understanding what she meant. "Why? Why would you be the last, Azár?"

"Because, one way or another, Malikar will not be needing another generation of Lightweavers."

Darien spread his hands, turning to face her. His eyes sought her own. "Perhaps. Perhaps not. But surely another use could be found for the gift that lives inside you. There aren't many mages left in all the world."

Azár glared at him for a long, silent moment, hating him with her eyes. "Find a place to sleep," she said at last. She turned and stalked away. His words halted her.

"I'm sorry about your sister, Azár. I'd take it back if I could."

She whirled back around, her thick braid undulating like a whip. She snarled as she promised him, "Someday you, too, will lose someone you love. On that day, I will smile as you weep."

She grinned then, a joyous expression that brightened her entire face. It touched her eyes, plumped out her cheeks. The delight that filled her eyes chilled Darien's heart. He had seen such a look once before in a woman's eyes. A woman he had been forced to murder.

"There's no joy in hatred, Azár," he cautioned her. "Find something else to do with your anger. You don't want to end up like me."

Azár's mouth opened as if she had a retort ready to let fly. But then she turned away, instead. She stalked back toward the fountain, braid swaying with her gait.

Darien spent the night huddled up in a niche-like compartment off the central courtyard of the caravansary with the thanacryst curled up against his side. The wind howled most of the night, making sleep all but impossible. By morning, he was stiff and exhausted, his joints aching from the cold.

The morning brought no dawn, only more of the same dark expanse of cloudcover. Perhaps the sky was a little brighter than it had been at night; it was hard to say. The wind was still up, bitingly cold and brutally fierce. Darien left the shelter of the niche and sought the comfort of a fire. The smell of burning coal was dreadful, but the warmth was necessary. He stood, huddling in the indigo robes they had given him, warming his hands as the acrid smoke wrung tears from his eyes.

"My wife is well this morning."

Darien turned, startled to find Haleem standing beside him.

"You are welcome to my food, my fire, and my protection," the caravan master told him solemnly. This time, the warmth of his smile touched his eyes.

Darien considered him. "I didn't think you spoke Rhenic."

"He doesn't."

Darien turned to find that Azár had come up silently behind them.

"He asked me for the words," she clarified. "He wanted to tell you himself how thankful he is. Here. This is for you from Haleem and his wife."

She offered a woven satchel out to him. Darien accepted it, opening the flap and taking a look inside. It was filled with gear. He realized he would have to sit down and take his time if he wanted to go through all of it.

"This bag is called a *sufan,"* Azár said.

Darien nodded in gratitude and sat down on the ground. He upended the *sufan*, spilling its contents into the lap of his robe. He ran his hand through it all, stirring the assortment of items around. He picked up the first thing that caught his eyes: a curving knife, about as long as his hand. There was also a ceramic pipe. Darien turned the pipe over in his hands, wondering at it. Such an object was hardly a necessity. There was also a flint and striker, a char-cloth, a pair of tweezers and a small blade. A patterned scarf was folded neatly into a small square, along with various assorted objects.

"You have my thanks," he muttered, replacing the items back into the *sufan.*

"There is also this." Azár handed him a waterskin that hung from a long hemp cord. "The Khazahar can be a thirsty place."

"Again, thank you," Darien said, glancing up gratefully at Haleem. "*Sukrien.*"

The man bowed, bringing a hand up to his chest, and backed away.

"Haleem says it is not a good day to travel," Azár informed him, watching his movements out of the corner of her eye as she stared at the brazier's dancing flames. "We will stay here today and head out tomorrow, instead."

Darien didn't like the sound of that. "Why's today not a good day to travel?"

Azár shrugged. "It is the fourth day of the month. The fourth day is never a good day to travel."

Darien looked up at her, carefully studying her face. The young woman appeared quite serious. He stood up, dusting off his long blue robes. "So, is the fifth day of the month any better for travelling?"

"It is better," Azár confirmed.

Darien broke into a grin. "Then, I suppose we ought to wait till the morrow."

The next morning, Haleem at last gave his consent to move out. Darien was impressed at the speed with which his group of laborers assembled in the courtyard, swiftly filing into lines that stretched all the way down the middle of the yard and out of the gate into the open street. Many men had equipped themselves with travois loaded with bags of provisions. Others pulled two-wheeled carts constructed of woven rattan and reinforced by metal bars. There were no animals; manpower alone would be exerted to transport Haleem's supplies to the river.

Darien had changed out of the robes they had given him in favor of the far more practical black shirt and breeches he was used to. He folded the robes of the Lyceum carefully and stored them in the bottom of a large pack Azár had purchased for him. Over his shirt, he donned a set of black metal spaulders, another gift from the Lightweaver. She had supplied herself with a similar pack, just the same as every other member of the caravan. The large packs were filled with all of the personal provisions each person would need for their own sustenance along the journey.

"Why are there no beasts of burden?" Darien wondered aloud. "Just one pair of oxen would make all the difference in the world."

Azár motioned upward at the sky. "Do you have any idea how much light it takes to feed just one ox? Haleem is a prosperous merchant, but even one such as he has never seen the amount of wealth it would require to sustain such a beast."

Darien shook his head, unable to comprehend how such a society could have possibly managed to continue for so long without collapse. They had no animals, no wood. No leather, no meat. And yet, in some respects, the Enemy's civilization seemed more advanced than the Rhen. What they had learned to accomplish with coal and oil was unsurpassed by any technology he had ever seen.

There was a shout from the rear of the yard, and then the long line of men began to move out. Darien and Azár fell in behind a throng of women. The wives were laboring just as hard as their men, pulling behind them wheeled carts filled with coal bricks and cooking supplies. They wore long, dark dresses covered by coarsely woven shawls. Darien noticed that Haleem's wife was there, walking in their midst. Esvir seemed completely hale, casting a thankful smile in his direction before turning to mind the cart she pulled behind her.

The smoke that blanketed the city was thick, made worse by the dust kicked up by so many wheels and feet. As they started out, Darien quickly found himself reduced to fits of coughing. He glanced beside him at Azár, wondering how the woman could stand it. He saw that she was in the process of wrapping a scarf around her head, tying it in place to cover her mouth and nose.

"You have one in your sufan," Azár reminded him. Her voice sounded almost as if she were smiling, but it was impossible to tell. Darien reached down and fished his own scarf out of the satchel Haleem had given him, shaking out the folds. He tried to wrap it around his head, first one way and then the other. Despite his efforts, he couldn't manage to make it stay in place.

"That is completely wrong," Azár scolded, observing his struggle. "Fold it first into a triangle, then wrap it over your head. Leave one side longer than the other," she instructed. "You bring it around your face and then up behind your head."

The whole while she was speaking, she was wrapping the fabric around him, finally securing it with a harsh tug. Darien could see only her eyes, the rest of her face hidden beneath the patterned cloth. The look emphasized the shine of the gift in her eyes.

They followed the long line of people down the street. Their group passed through the city gates and out into the vast expanse of black nothingness beyond. Darien paused to consider the sprawling wastes that lay ahead of them, league upon league of black, frozen terrain that stretched in every direction to the cloud-choked horizons. Above them, the heavens churned and flickered with the light of electrical storms that teemed deep within the cloudbank. Far to the west, a diffuse white glow could be seen. A breeze kicked up, flinging smoke toward them from Bryn Calazar.

Azár said, "We will follow this road until we reach the village of Ibri. There, the river is deep enough for boats. In Ibri, there will be a barge waiting to take us up the river. We will be entering the vortex that surrounds Bryn Calazar. Shut your mind away from it."

Darien frowned, immediately throwing up a shield to protect himself. A vortex was like a cyclone of power, a place where the lines of the magic field converged. The fury of a vortex was overwhelming, lethal to any mage. Darien had no idea how far out the Bryn Calazar vortex extended. He only knew that while they were within the grasp of those energies, he would be forced to keep his mind shielded from it. He would be vulnerable, a state he detested.

The absence of the magic field reminded him of when Arden Hannah had cornered him in a node, a place where the field lines cancelled out. Arden had tied him to a stake, hanging him out to roast over a searing fire. He would have died on that stake had it not been for Devlin Craig. Cut off from the magic field, all he could do was writhe and scream as his flesh was broiled off his bones. He'd been utterly powerless, completely at Arden's sick mercy.

That's why he so despised the shield he was forced to throw up to protect his mind from Bryn Calazar's vortex. It cut him off from the comfort of the field. The knowledge made his skin crawl, sending shivers of dread down his spine. He could almost feel the heat of Arden's flames licking at his flesh.

"What is it?" Azár pressed, staring intently into his eyes.

Darien shook his head, adjusting the scarf over his face.

"Something is bothering you. What is it?"

"It's nothing." He clenched his hands into fists, squeezing his fingers until his knuckles went white. He could feel the raging torrent of power already clawing at his skin.

"How big is this vortex?" he grumbled. "How long till we're out of it?"

"Two days."

A surge of panic seized Darien's throat, choking him. He winced, recoiling with dread. He gasped for air, but still couldn't get enough breath to fill his lungs. Reaching up, he ripped the scarf away from his face. He bent forward, hands on his knees, panting as his vision swam with sudden vertigo.

"Something happened to you in a vortex," Azár guessed, dark eyes widening. "Take hold of your nerves!"

Two days.

"What happened in the vortex, Darien?"

Two.

Days.

"Tell me what happened!"

Darien closed his eyes, bringing his hands up to cover his ears as he struggled to conquer his panic.

"It wasn't a vortex," he admitted. "It was a node."

"What happened?" Azár's eyes were bright with excitement.

"Arden Hannah," he gasped, squeezing his eyes shut against the pain of the memory. "She tried to immolate me."

Azár glared at him. "Good," she said at last. "I hope you screamed until your lungs blistered."

Darien opened his eyes, gaping up at her in revulsion. He'd forgotten all about Azár's sister. The satisfaction in her eyes was appalling to witness.

"Why do you hate me so much?" he gasped,

jerking back away from her. *"You're sick."*

"And you're a murderous demon. What is there not to hate?"

All Darien could do was stare at her, unable to think of a suitable retort. Azár stood before him with arms crossed, eyebrows raised. There was a low growl from behind him. Darien realized that the demon-dog had become alerted to his mood. He spread his fingers wide, motioning for the beast to desist.

"Keep your distance," he warned Azár, striding away from her. He didn't trust the woman in a vortex.

"Darien!" she called after him. "The moment you died—what was the last thing you were thinking?"

He turned and glared back at her over his shoulder, incredulous that she would dare ask such a thing. *"That's none of your gods-damned business."*

As he stalked away, he caught a brief glimpse of the smile in her eyes.

Chapter Eleven
Ishara

Ishara, The Black Lands

Meiran spilled forward, her body slapping hard against stone. She glanced around fearfully, startled by the absolute darkness that encased her. There was no light at all. She could see nothing, not even the outline of Quin's body at her side. And it was freezing. The ground beneath her legs felt like ice, sucking the warmth right out of her body through her skin.

Quin's features resolved beside her in a wash of wine-colored magelight. Its churning glow spread outward across the ground away from his feet. Meiran gasped, her eyes scanning quickly over the walls of the small cavern. The room they were in was like a grotto carved out of black volcanic rock of a rough and porous texture. The ceiling was high, tapering to a point far above the portal's cross-vaulted arch.

"Welcome to Malikar, Prime Warden."

Meiran turned to Quinlan Reis. "Malikar. Where did that name come from?"

"Well, they couldn't very well call it Caladorn anymore, now, could they? Not after the Onslaught wiped it off the map. Malikar literally means 'Cursed Lands.' That's where you are, my dear. Everything around you is cursed. The sky. The air. The rocks, the people. Even the gods here are cursed."

Meiran stared at him. Cautiously, she opened her mind and formed a tentative link between herself and the unsuspecting darkmage. Through that thin sliver of connection, she could sense Quinlan Reis' mood. A profound sadness filled him as he spoke, the same sorrow that lent a life-weary texture to his voice. And there was something else there, as well. Something she hadn't expected to find at all.

Guilt.

Guilt infested this man like maggots in an old, rotten corpse.

Meiran raised her eyebrows in surprise. There was little doubt in her mind that Quinlan Reis had a lot to do with Caladorn's transformation into Malikar. It was obvious that he felt responsible for the curse that had befallen his homeland. Which made sense, she supposed; the man was a Servant of Xerys. Meiran wondered just how direct a part he had played in that tragedy.

"Why is it all cursed, Quin?" Meiran pressed, abandoning formality. "Tell me."

His eyes narrowed as she stared at him, but he said nothing. Instead, Quin Reis walked toward the volcanic rock that formed the cavern's thick wall. With a phrase muttered beneath his breath and a casual flip of his hand, the rock before him seemed to dissipate, dissolving into gaping space. In place of the wall, there was now a doorway into cold, black emptiness.

Into that dim and murky space Quinlan Reis strode ahead, reaching up to secure his hat against a fierce gale of wind.

Meiran stole after him, the wall of rock solidifying behind her as she exited the chamber. The moment she stepped foot out of the protection of the hillside, the wind seized her hair, whipping it forward into her eyes and tossing it about her face. She brought her hands up, trying to constrain it as she called out to Quin. But either the darkmage didn't hear or didn't care. He walked on ahead into the wind, holding his hat against his head, black longcoat billowing.

Meiran turned, glancing behind. Beyond the small volcanic hill that housed the portal chamber arose an exceptionally tall peak, its crown frosted white with snow. The ice blazed as a strobe of lightning zigzagged down from a thick cloudbank overhead. Below and slightly to the right was another mountain, swaybacked, its ridgelines distinctive and familiar. Meiran knew the names of those two peaks, even if she had only seen them in sketches and read their descriptions in text: Orguleth and Maidenclaw. Infamous landmarks that marked the gateway to the Black Lands. As far as she was aware, no person from the Rhen had ever managed to view those two peaks from this angle. No one who'd lived to tell about it, anyway.

Meiran was shocked to discover just how black the Black Lands really were. From one horizon to the other stretched a flat plain of barren darkness. The sky was draped with sinister stormclouds, just as dark as the earth they eclipsed. Meiran's eyes went wide, her jaw going slack at the sight of forked streaks of lightning jabbing down in every direction from the sky.

"Mother of the gods," she whispered.

Ahead, Quin Reis stopped to smirk. "What did you expect, Prime Warden? It's called the Black Lands for a reason."

Meiran blinked at him, still groping with the magnitude of devastation that surrounded her. She whispered, "Where are we going?"

Quin gestured ahead with a finger. "To the north."

"How far to the north?"

"Far enough to get to know each other a little better." He made a sweeping gesture with his hand. "After you, darling."

A harsh gust of wind whipped at her dress as Meiran strode past him into the night. The air was chill and miserable, reeking of sulphur and ash. Ahead of them, glowing magma spilled down the steep sides of a cinder cone in slow-creeping rivulets.

"Where are we?" she asked, staring around at the frozen, sterile wastes that stretched expansively to the far horizons.

"Skara," Quin responded. "Well, it used to be called Skara. Now they call it Ishara, but it's the same damn place. The town's up ahead. We can hold up there for the night before moving on in the morning."

"There are actually towns here? With people?" Meiran was surprised.

Quin fixed her with a stunned expression. He shook his head slowly in amazement. "Yes, Prime Warden. There are towns here. With people, even. What were you expecting? A race of savage hordes wandering the open wastes, feeding off the remains of their own dead?"

Meiran sighed. "I'm sorry, Quinlan. A thousand years of warfare does tend to breed a seed or two of resentment."

The darkmage cracked a loathsome grin. "A seed or two, I could understand. But you act as though we're not too far removed from animals. I can assure you, we're far beyond that. A thousand years of darkness is a brutal penance, but it does make for a resilient population. Anyone unworthy of survival has no chance to endure. In the Black Lands, only the strongest and most resourceful survive. The weak and ill-equipped have long since perished. You know, Prime Warden, I do think the people of Malikar may surprise you more than you think."

There was very little talking after that; the ice-chill gale sapped Meiran's strength, leeching it right out of her. They trudged on against the wind into the endless shadows of the hostile wastes. To the left, the cinder cone belched a thick spew of bright orange magma. A glowing river of lava meandered toward their path, spanned by a narrow arch of volcanic rock. Meiran followed Quin up and over that treacherous bridge.

After perhaps an hour of walking, a diffuse white glow appeared on the northern horizon. Quin angled toward it, holding his hat with his hand. The wind still labored against their progress, struggling to impede their every step. Meiran walked leaning forward, her arms hugging her chest. Her fingers were numb, her body shivering violently.

"What is that?" she called to Quin, indicating the bright horizon with a nod.

"The lightfields of Ishara," Quin informed her.

Meiran did not press him to elaborate. He didn't look as though he cared to and, besides, she didn't have the energy. Up ahead a creaking vertical windmill spun violently around its axis in the gusting wind. It was missing more than a few steel blades, like a smile that lacked enough teeth to sustain it.

"Ah. We must be getting close to civilization," her darkmage companion muttered.

Meiran's gaze lingered on the windmill as they passed, wondering where the people were who tended the mechanism. She didn't have long to wonder. Within minutes, a tall wall appeared ahead of their path, built of massive stones. At the sight of it, Quin pulled up, turning back to her with a worried expression on his face.

"That's Ishara. In just a few minutes, we'll be walking through the town gate. From this point on, I want you to keep your mouth shut and let me do all the talking. Some people still speak Rhenic here, or, rather, a version of it. But your accent would take a fair amount of explaining. Especially if someone gets a glimpse of those chains on your wrists. If anyone sees those, you'll be lucky if you don't end up skewered in a bonfire. Do you understand, Prime Warden? From here on out, you're mute."

Meiran nodded. She had no desire to be identified. She pulled the long sleeves of her gown down lower over her hands, making certain the marks of the chains on her wrists were well and truly covered.

"What is my name going to be?"

Quinlan Reis glanced at her sideways. "What?"

"My name," she insisted. "You can't call me Meiran Withersby."

He shrugged. "You can still be Meiran. It's a common enough name, even here."

"Meiran what?"

"There's no family names here. We use different conventions." He frowned. But then he smiled, amusement glimmering in his eyes. "We'll tell everyone you're my wife. It's the best way to avoid uncomfortable questions."

Meiran's mouth fell open as shocked anger kindled in her eyes. But Quin held up his hand, halting her protest.

"Listen, darling. Try not to get too excited; you're really not my type. I prefer my women more...affable." He supplied a wry grin. "It's just the best way to keep attention off of you and onto me. As my wife, you'll be all but invisible. But if I bring an available young woman into a border town like Ishara, I'll be fighting every man to the death. I very much doubt you'd want that kind of attention. Am I correct, Prime Warden?"

"No," Meiran was forced to admit. "I don't."

Quin shot her a sardonic grin. "Good. Then we're in agreement. Let's go, *my dear.*"

To her horror, Quin caught her by the hand, pulling her in familiarly close. He kept his eyes off her, at least. Arm in arm, they strolled toward Ishara's fortified outer wall, toward a wide opening that appeared to serve as the town gate.

There, Meiran found herself confronted by the first man of the Enemy she had ever seen.

A stationed guardsman stood to the side of the entrance, surveying their approach. Like Quin, his skin was olive, his dark hair thick and lustrous. A long nose, thin and proudly arched, lent dignity to his face. The guard was dressed in a thick gray tunic over a lean and muscular frame. He wore an iron breastplate and carried a spear in one hand, a round shield at his back. The guard glared at them as they approached, the expression on his face openly hostile.

Quin walked right up to the man, holding his hat against the wind. *"Ranu kadreesh,"* he shouted loud enough to be heard over the gale. As the guard glowered at him in silence, Quin launched into a harsh-sounding string of words that Meiran had no hope of comprehending.

By the time Quin was finished speaking, the guardsman was on his belly on the ground in front of Quin, folded over his knees in the dirt. The darkmage waved his hand in the air over the man's head in a gesture that looked something like a benediction or blessing.

He turned back with a smile, inquiring of Meiran, "Well, then. Shall we, my dear?"

He took her again by the arm, guiding Meiran through the gate and leaving the guardsman lowered in the dirt.

Meiran started to speak but was instantly halted by a shake of Quin's head. Turning, she caught sight of scattered villagers scurrying through the dark and narrow streets. The town stank of coal smoke, mud, and human waste. Some people carried baskets that dangled from yokes worn over their shoulders or pushed carts loaded with goods. There was smoke everywhere. No one looked as though they'd had much to eat in a very long time.

Meiran glanced down and saw that Quin was

walking in a pool of magelight that swirled about the ground at his feet. Those who were moving toward them stopped, often mid-stride, when they saw that glowing mist. Men and women bowed forward before backing deferentially away, clearing a path for them. It was obvious they had a good understanding of Quin's nature and were certain of his status in their society. Taking Meiran's hand in his, the darkmage led her toward the center of town. Quin's glowing mist roamed ahead of them like vaporous wisps of dark-red flame.

"The magelight marks me as a Servant of Xerys," he explained under his breath. "Their Lightweavers don't have the energy to waste on such indulgence. Nor can they produce anything close to this saturation of color."

Meiran frowned, not fully understanding what Quin was trying to say. Up ahead, she noticed a large group of people gathered at the base of a terraced structure. Meiran glanced at Quin with a questioning look.

"The Temple of Xerys," he informed her.

Meiran's eyes widened. They walked toward the temple, striding through the glow of Quin's magelight. The people in the back of the crowd took notice of them first, drawing back out of their way. The crowd seemed to ripple as it opened up before them, folding back to clear a path ahead of them to the temple steps.

Meiran glanced over at Quin, noticing that the darkmage did not seem surprised by the crowd's reaction. Instead, he seemed indifferent to it. She opened a thin link between them, gauging his emotions. To her surprise, she found that Quinlan Reis was a compressed bundle of nerves. She never would have guessed that just by looking at his face. His hand guided her firmly forward at his side as he mounted the temple steps.

Meiran allowed her gaze to wander toward the gray-columned portico at the top of the highest terrace. There, at the summit of the steps, knelt a trembling and shirtless youth. Tears streaked the boy's cheeks. Above him a dark-robed man was wielding a long, reed-shaped cane. Meiran gasped, glancing sharply at Quin.

"Don't speak," he growled under his breath.

Meiran glared at him, eyes full of ire. By the vexed expression on his face, Quin took her meaning. He worked his lips in frustration as they drew up before the cowering boy.

"Who is responsible for this child?" Quin demanded, glancing around. He repeated the statement in his own language. A dark-robed man stepped forward, hefting a long cane in his hand.

Meiran knelt down and reached out her hand, resting it gently on the boy's quivering shoulder as she examined the raised welts on his back. Above her, Quin erupted into a furious dialogue with the boy's tormentor. Meiran closed her eyes, establishing a link between herself and the child. What she sensed filled her with fury.

"No!" Quin shouted at her, too late.

The boy's wounds were already healed. His eyes rolled back in his head and he fell forward against Meiran's chest, soundly asleep. She caught him up, enfolding him protectively in her arms as the shouting above her turned abruptly hostile. The next thing she knew, Quin was tugging at her arm, trying to get her to follow after him. She fought back, wrestling with him for control of her own hand.

"We need to go, *wife,"* he rebuked her acidly.

Meiran couldn't bring herself to leave the child behind. She refused to budge, clutching the boy fiercely against her chest.

"He's a criminal," Quin insisted. "He stole coin from the temple coffers!"

The boy's protruding ribs and sunken cheeks were explanation enough for Meiran. She glared at Quin, refusing him with her eyes.

Realizing his quandary, Quinlan Reis licked his lips, scowling in frustration. Behind him, two priests of Xerys were approaching. They turned and barked at their companions in their guttural language. All of the men gathered on the temple steps withdrew to the side, appearing to confer. Quin remained, standing protectively over Meiran, feet spread apart in the semblance of a fighting stance.

At last, the small node of men seemed to reach some kind of agreement. They broke apart, the oldest priest striding toward Quin, head bowed in deference. Staring at the ground, he mumbled something to the darkmage. A short conversation ensued. Meiran listened hard, trying her best to pick out as many words as she could.

At last, Quin Reis seemed satisfied. "We've reached an accord," he told her softly. "You can relax, now."

She glared up at him, skeptical.

"The temple priests are displeased," he explained. "Although the boy's punishment was delivered, your healing interfered with the impact of the lesson. I have managed to convince them to accept compensation in lieu of punishing the child further for his crime."

Meiran stared up at him, eyes questioning.

He elaborated, "The priests initially wanted you to bear the penalty for the boy's crime of theft. I explained to them that, as my wife, there was no chance in hell that I'd be allowing that. So they have asked me to bear the child's punishment in your stead."

Meiran gaped up at him, jaw dropping.

"I have decided to accept their offer. It is a matter of *sharaq*, what we call honor. All I ask is that you stay here, keep your mouth shut, and *don't intervene.*"

Stunned, Meiran watched as Quin promptly removed his hat, thrusting it into her keeping. Then he reached up and wriggled out of his black longcoat and cotton tunic. He folded both garments primly and set them aside on the ground. Startled, Meiran gazed up at the man's naked torso, appalled by the sight. Quinlan Reis was emaciated, his angular bones jutting against his tight and sallow skin.

"You don't have to stare," he admonished her, turning away. "Even here, amongst us uncivilized barbarians, it's considered quite rude."

He lowered himself to his knees in the place the boy had occupied at the top of the temple steps. To Meiran's horror, the eldest priest stepped forward, wielding a thin rattan cane that was longer than his arm. He lifted the cane up high in the air, bringing it down forcefully across the darkmage's back with a shocking *crack*.

Quin winced, jaw clenching in pain.

Meiran brought her hand up, covering her mouth in revulsion as she reflexively squeezed the unconscious boy tighter against her chest.

The cane was brought down again, scoring another mark. And another. The cane rose and fell several more times, cracking sharply each time it scored another welt across Quin's bare flesh. He suffered in silence, eyes squeezed shut, fists clenched against his sides. Meiran counted: ten lashes were delivered in all. The last one left Quin bowed forward over his knees. The robed priest handed the cane off to a man behind him, at last nodding in satisfaction before stepping away.

Meiran was shaking by the time it was done, horrified by the shocking brutality she had just been forced to witness. She remained where she was, cradling the unconscious boy against her, as the crowd at the base of the steps slowly began to disperse. Minutes crept by. At last, she realized that the priests had retreated. They were finally alone on the temple steps.

"Are you all right?" she whispered to Quin.

He nodded, eyes squeezed closed. He hadn't moved from the spot where they'd left him. His back was crisscrossed with raised welts. A couple of the stripes had parted his skin, penetrating into the deep tissue beneath. The priests had not gone easy on him, despite his status. Perhaps they had been even harsher on him because of it.

"Can you walk?" she asked.

Again, Quin just nodded. He opened his damp eyes, pushing himself up off the ground slowly with both hands, grimacing as he straightened his back. He squared his shoulders. Then he indicated his hat in Meiran's hands.

Meiran lay the boy down gently and rose, offering the darkmage back his hat. She concentrated, opening a link to him. Probing Quin, she sensed his condition. He was in a good deal of pain, but there was surprisingly no resentment within him.

"Does Darien know you're a sensitive?"

Meiran blinked, gazing in shock into Quin's eyes. "How did you know?" she whispered.

The darkmage scowled. Or perhaps it was a grin. With Quin, it was often hard to tell the difference. "I was in love with a sensitive, once. A long time ago. There's a certain look she used to get on her face whenever she read me. You get the same look. Does Darien know?"

"He knows," Meiran admitted, keeping her voice low.

"And he doesn't mind? My, but that's rare. Most people would have a big problem with it."

Meiran gazed at him levelly. "Did you ever mind?"

Quin shook his head. "With Amani? Never. I was always glad that she could tell what I was feeling; I had nothing to hide from her. I always enjoyed having her in my head, all the way up to the day she died. But that day…no. It was no good." His voice trailed off as he shook his head.

"What happened?" Meiran prodded softly.

Quin lowered his chin until his eyes were lost under the shadows of his hat. "The day Amani died was the first day I ever drank. I drank until I pissed myself, hoping that would stop her from reading me. I didn't want her feeling my emotions. She had enough to deal with already."

He turned away. With his hat in his hand, he gestured at the sleeping boy. "Somewhere that child has parents. Maybe we can talk them into giving us a meal and a place to sleep."

"Wait. Let me heal you," Meiran insisted.

"No, darling. I'll be wearing these stripes for another day or two. At least until we're out of this gods-forsaken town." His face became stern. "But just so we're clear on this: next time, Prime Warden, you can pay the price for your own decisions. I've already got enough on my tab."

They remained at the temple entrance until the boy's father finally arrived, sprinting up the steps, confused and belligerent. Meiran couldn't understand anything the man was shouting at Quin, only that he was fierce and hostile, the brunt of his anger directed at the darkmage. He scooped his son up in his arms, tossing the boy over his shoulder like a sack and, still shouting curses behind him, carried the flailing body of his child down and off the temple steps.

"Well, that's gratitude if I ever saw it," the darkmage seethed, watching the pair disappear into the streets. "Rub *my* nose in the sand, will you?" He turned his head to the side and spat.

Meiran could only shake her head. "These people are awful," she muttered quietly. "They're barbarians."

"No, Prime Warden. They're not barbarians. They're just desperate," Quin corrected her, staring off into the shadowed distance. "A brutal country makes for brutal people. They've endured so much for so very long." He sighed, adjusting his hat. "Come on, let's get going."

"Going where?"

Quin gritted his teeth as he bent over to retrieve his clothing from off the ground. Then he turned and trudged away from her, his gait stiff as he wandered toward the entrance to the temple. "The priests offered us a place to stay for the night. Since that child's father wasn't inclined to shelter us, I figure we should take the clerics up on their offer of hospitality."

Meiran tensed at the idea, not liking it one bit. She had no desire to spend an evening in a house of Quin's dark god. "Is there another option?"

Quin shook his head. "Not if you want to eat."

He strode back toward the temple, carrying his coat and tunic wadded against his side. A thin line of blood leaked from one of the welts raised on his back. Meiran followed him, a gust of wind fanning the strands of her long brown hair.

Within was a narrow corridor lit by blazing torches ensconced upon the walls. The passage angled sharply downward, curving. It was chill within, but not nearly as cold as the ground outside. The air was moist, thick with smoke and the stench of oil and decay. Meiran walked with her eyes on Quin's wounds, silently counting his protruding ribs. In life, Quinlan Reis had not been a healthy man. In death, he hadn't fared much better.

That last thought made her stop. For a moment, Meiran stood frozen between strides, her weight balanced over her feet. For some reason, it hit her. Just then. Quinlan Reis was not alive. Even though he stood there bleeding before her, he was not a living human being.

"Everything all right, darling?"

He had paused to turn back and stare at her, eyebrows raised expectantly.

Meiran gaped at him, appalled. "Are you truly dead, Quin?"

His face turned into a troubled mask of confusion. Slowly, understanding grew in his dark eyes. "Oh, I am very dead, I assure you." he told her gently. "Reunited with my body, but only just temporarily. I'm afraid it's not a permanent condition. But then again, life is never a permanent condition, now, is it?"

"No. It's not," Meiran whispered. She swallowed. "So, tell me, Quin. What is the difference?"

He stared at her flatly. "Are you asking me what it means to be a demon?"

Meiran nodded.

Quinlan reached up and scratched his chin. He moved toward her until he was gazing down into her face. His expression was very solemn and very tired. "It means that this is all there is," he said softly. "This is all that's left for me. No more."

Meiran frowned up at him. "I don't understand."

"Well, let's take you, for example. You've got your life to live, Prime Warden. Maybe you'll make a difference and maybe you won't. Maybe you'll be happy. Maybe you won't. It really doesn't matter. Because when you die, no matter what, you get to move on to a better place. A place where you can be with the people you love and who love you. You will know happiness and peace.

"But for me, this is it. This is as good as it gets." He spread his arms, turning slowly around, displaying the angry stripes that crossed his back. "I have nothing to look forward to. This is my moment of glory. My chance to prove myself. Either I make a difference now or my entire existence has been for absolutely nothing. Because if the Well of Tears is ever sealed again, I won't be coming back. I'll be trapped in hell forever—and hell is not a happy place to be. In truth, I wouldn't wish it on anyone."

Meiran found herself staring at the ground by the time he had finished speaking. She had drawn a link with him and had been reading his emotions the entire time. She knew that Quin Reis was telling the truth. She could feel the weight of his weary despair.

At last, she finally understood the price Darien had paid to bring her back. He had given up far more than just his life; he had sacrificed his every last hope of peace.

"There must be something you can do," she protested, feeling a hot stab of grief tightening her chest. "There must be some way you can redeem yourself."

Quin quirked his mouth, shrugging slightly. "There is. But I would have to accomplish something profound enough to tip the balance of my soul."

Meiran considered his words. "You don't seem so very evil," she argued. "Such an act might be possible."

"Oh, I'm evil enough, have no doubt," the darkmage assured her.

Through her link with him, Meiran could sense the truth of his words. As unbelievable as it seemed, Quinlan Reis spoke nothing but fact.

"How can that be?" she asked. "I don't sense that kind of evil in you."

"There is nothing *but* evil left in me, darling. Don't you understand?" He leaned forward until his face was only scant inches from her own. An angry desperation seethed in his eyes. "I betrayed the woman I loved. I betrayed my own brother. I betrayed the Lyceum, my clansmen, my entire nation. I even betrayed my own gods! There is literally no one alive in this world today whose life hasn't been impacted by my choices. Don't you get it? *I* caused the Desecration. *Me!* No one else. All of this horror that you see all around you: the darkness, the starvation, the suffering, the wars, the death — *it's all my own damn fault!*"

Meiran stared up at him, too horrified to speak. For long seconds, all she could do was gape. "How can that be?" she demanded, face twisted in disgust. "You didn't create the Well of Tears."

Quin Reis pulled back from her and spun away. He reached up, settling the brim of his hat lower on his head, adjusting it down until his eyes were lost in shadow.

"You're right," he agreed. "I didn't create the Well of Tears. But I swear by all the gods, I'm going to be the one who destroys it."

Chapter Twelve
The Black Lands

The Ghost Waste, The Black Lands

Darien stared out across the bow of the vessel that carried them, smoking and sputtering, against the river's swift current. The terrain on both sides of the watercourse was dark and undulating, blacker than the pit of hell and twice as deadly. It was as if they were adrift in a tempestuous sea of shadowy dunes that rolled like the swells of an ocean, broken only by the occasional rock that seemed to bob like flotsam in the rolling darkscape.

The boat they had boarded in Ibri was contrary to anything in Darien's personal experience. Instead of sails, the barge was powered by steam. River water was heated in an iron boiler and then condensed, its energy directed through long, corkscrewing shafts that drove two paddle wheels on opposite sides of the vessel. The barge was flat and long, big enough to hold every person in Haleem's caravan, along with the assortment of goods they carried. The craft was fitted with two large stacks that belched forth dense plumes of smoke into the air. The going was tedious, painfully slow.

"They call this the Ghost Waste."

Darien nodded in silent acknowledgement. He hadn't been able to bring himself to speak to Azár in two days. The anxiety provoked by the absence of the magic field taxed his patience; he didn't trust himself to speak. Funny; ever since he had made a purposeful decision to ignore the woman, Azár seemed hell-bent on conversation.

"They call it the Ghost Waste because the Spirits of the Wild roam this desert," Azár elaborated. She was leaning on her elbows over the rail beside him.

Darien didn't reply. Instead, he focused his attention on the deck just under his feet and did his best to ignore her. The loss of the magic field made his skin crawl. Even after two days, he hadn't been able to rid himself of the feeling of infestation, like a host of parasites burrowing just beneath the surface of his skin. For the twentieth time that hour, he scratched at the same red spot on the back of his arm. It didn't help. No matter what he did, he couldn't be rid of the feeling that there were insects crawling over him.

"It is said that the Spirits of the Wild are the shades of all the animals that once roamed these wastes," Azár went on. "I cannot tell you if that is accurate. All I know is that they wander endlessly and hunger endlessly. They are very dangerous and must be avoided at all cost."

Again, Darien could only bring himself to nod. She was speaking in answer to a question he'd never asked. He raked his nails over the back of his hand then brought his arm up to scrub the acrid sting of smoke out of his eyes.

The desert was cold and clear. Despite the darkness, it was just as parched as any desert he'd ever looked upon. Azár insisted that the Ghost Waste had once been a rich and fertile grassland. But that was before the Desecration. Now, with no plants to hold down the topsoil, wind had eroded the steppe into a denuded expanse of black sand drifts. The thin line of the River Nym followed a meandering course along the bases of the dunes, progressing ever westward.

Darien glanced up and blinked, frowning intensely.

"Is that *magelight?*"

Ahead, in the distance, the horizon was bathed in a diffuse warm glow, like a blanketing, ethereal haze.

"Those are the lightfields of Bryn Calazar," Azár said, drawing herself up straight. "When we reach the lightfields, we will then be outside of the power vortex. There, you can feel safe again."

Darien glared at her. His foul mood had as much to do with this woman's contempt for him as it had with the vortex. He grimaced, regretting ever speaking to Azár at all. He lowered his hand back to his side, taking comfort in the thanacryst's presence. He scratched the demon-hound on the back of the neck, running his hand up and over an ear. The beast leaned its head back, nuzzling Darien's thigh in gratitude for the attention.

The boat glided onward, following the course of the river as it snaked its way around the gravelly base of an eroded drumlin. A breeze came up, pungent with the smell of coal-soot. The glow on the horizon grew ever-brighter as they neared, like a golden aurora washing the sky in sparkling tides of light.

And then he saw the impossible: vibrant, living fields of green.

The black plains ahead miraculously yielded to sprawling acres of verdant farmland, extending outward away from them as far as the eye could see.

Darien moved forward, his hand fiercely gripping the steel rail of the barge. His mouth gaped in disbelief. Under the sinuous ribbons of magelight grew enough food to sustain all of Bryn Calazar. Perhaps all of Malikar.

"Lightfields," he whispered. "You use magelight to grow your crops. How can that be? Plants require such a broad range of colors. How can you produce enough magelight to cover enough of the sun's spectrum?"

Azár smiled with pride. "Many legacies were brought together long ago to produce the most effective blend of light."

Darien regarded her in wonder. That explained the golden brilliance of the magelight that mirrored the light of the Rhen's living sun. It was a mixture, the combination of many magical lineages. Because that's how sunlight worked; it wasn't like paint, where blending all of the colors together on a palette would only yield black. Sunlight was the result of mixing together every color of the rainbow at once.

Such an undertaking, though…such a tragedy. Blending enough magical legacies to produce this character of light must have required rivers of mage-blood.

"Gods' mercy," Darien whispered, voice gruff with horror. "How many deaths did that take?"

"Not as many as you would think," Azár assured him, looking both proud and dreadful at the same time. "There were not many mages left after the Desecration; all those trapped within the Lyceum were killed. So, it took a lot of time. Many generations. Many years of starvation, until we could begin to approach the quality of light that was necessary."

"You're a Lightweaver," Darien spat almost accusingly. "How many combined lineages are inside you? What tier do you rank?"

Azár shrugged. "The number of lineages doesn't matter. There is no record of that. But I can tell you that I am second tier."

"Second tier?"

"Yes. Second tier."

Darien spread his hands, indicating the wide swath of magelight that rippled across the sky above them. "How can you come close to managing something as vast as all this if you are only second tier?"

Azár lifted her chin, her eyes hostile and seething. "Because this is what we are trained to do. It is *all* that we do. When we arrive back at my village, I will weave the light. That is *all* I will do, every day of my life, until my death. Then someone else will weave the light after me."

At last, Darien finally understood. He understood completely.

He lowered his eyes, too appalled to gaze any longer at the verdant fields that lined the riverway. He understood the tremendous sacrifice it took to grow those fields, of the lives of the mages who sustained them.

He walked back toward the stern of the boat, leaving both Lightweaver and thanacryst behind. Soft golden rays streamed down from the sky, dappling his shoulders and warming the skin of his face. Even the cool breeze moving across the bow couldn't suppress that glowing warmth. Darien closed his eyes. He spread his hands beneath the coruscating ribbons, savoring the warm texture of the magelight. For just a moment, he felt almost content.

The Khazahar Desert, The Black Lands

They were a week out from Bryn Calazar's lightfields. The sky had grown dark once again, the clouds stretching high overhead, hostile and angry, ever-brooding. A queer green light emanated from deep within their depths, fluttering spastically like a failing heartbeat.

Darien hadn't spoken to Azár again. He stood now at the bow of the steam vessel, feet apart, cloak drawn out behind him on the wind. He gazed out across the still, black waters and dark expanse of terrain. The hardpan of the desert bristled with a forest of vertical pipes that were shoved hither and thither like great spikes driven fast into the ground. Every so often one would give a great, fat belch of flames. More pipes sprawled across the soil, twisting like iron snakes.

He didn't know what manner of hell the pipes brought forth from the ground. He only knew that the sight and stench of such industry caused a thick lump of dread to catch in his throat like a ball of half-chewed food. He swallowed against that lump, forcing it down into his stomach. There, it sat like a brick, eating at his middle.

The sound of shouts came from behind them. Darien turned. Men were running toward the side of the craft, carrying thick coils of rope over their shoulders that they cast out over the railing of the steamer.

They were putting into shore.

"This is as far as the river will take us. After this, the water becomes too shallow. Get your pack. We walk from here."

Darien flinched at the sound of Azár's voice. It was the first time she had spoken since the lightfields. He complied without a word, striding over to where he had left his pack, picking it up and shrugging it on over his shoulders. He straightened his back under the weight of it, then looked expectantly at Azár.

Haleem's people disembarked first, dragging their possessions along after them in a drawn-out, single-file train. Darien and Azár fell in toward the end of the line, the demon-hound trotting dutifully after.

A paved road led away from the way station, cutting through the black center of the desert. It was lined with rocks and human bones and all manner of debris. On either side of the road, the barren waste appeared exceptionally sinister and foreboding. The blackened sand shifted and shimmered with tiny flecks of mica that sparkled like stars in the brief flashes of cloud light.

Azár smiled and asked, "How long are you going to remain sulking?"

Darien ignored the woman. He concentrated on the path under his feet, on the clank of items that shifted in his pack at every stride. On the crunch of gravel just under his boots.

"There is much you need to learn. Like this. Do you even know what this means?"

She was gesturing at a formation of long, flat stones stacked purposefully one atop the other, arranged into a knee-high projection along the side of the path.

Darien shrugged. He didn't know or care about the purpose of the rocks.

"It is a marker." Azár fumed at him with turbulent eyes. "It says, 'Water is this way.' Another could say, 'A village lies this way.' Things like that."

Darien stopped. He wandered over to the column of arranged stones and considered it for a moment. He thought about knocking the damn thing over with his boot. The notion was tempting. Instead, he scowled at Azár, glaring at her through a dark lock of hair that had fallen forward into his face.

"You need to decide how you feel about me," he said flatly.

Azár narrowed her eyes, lifting her chin in defiance. "What do you mean?"

"You can't keep doing this. Either you forgive me or you don't. Either you despise me or you don't. You can't have it both ways. So, which will it be?"

Azár's lips compressed together into a thin line. Resentment smoldered in her dark eyes. She didn't answer him.

He waited, staring at her as members of Haleem's caravan ambled by, considering the pair of them with kindly smiles and warm curiosity. Behind him, the thanacryst growled softly.

At last, Darien nodded.

"All right, then. You've made your choice."

He turned and started walking away. Her voice stopped him.

"I chose nothing!"

He didn't turn around. "Aye, you did."

"I did not!"

"You *did,"* he insisted, casting a weary glance back over his shoulder. "You've made your decision, Azár. Now, leave me be."

A gust of wind came up, raking at his cloak. He turned his face in the direction of the wind, gazing out into the darkness that encased the sky.

The expression on his face collapsed.

"What is that?"

Azár whirled, startled eyes lurching in the direction of his gaze. Her mouth fell open.

"That is death!" she shrieked over the sudden howl of the wind. "We must find shelter! *Run!"*

She scrambled forward and caught Darien by the arm, yanking him after her as she careened off the road. People were panicking, fleeing, dropping their burdens in the dirt and dodging off the path in every direction. Darien glanced back at the surging mass that loomed like a thick black curtain across the center of the desert, obscuring all evidence of the horizon.

The day grew suddenly, impossibly, darker.

A tidal wave of sand was hurling toward them, a churning wall that reached high into the sky and loomed ominously, threatening to consume everything in its path. Ahead of the storm, forked tongues of lightning stabbed downward at the ground, strobing across the desert.

Darien gripped the straps of his pack, fighting against the wind to keep up with Azár as she dragged him forward off the road toward a crumbling, eroded embankment. He had to fight at every step against the brutality of the wind.

The wall of sand was right behind them, spanning the desert's broad length, reaching the way station and the river. The wind scooped the steam barge right up out of the water and tossed it high into the air like a child's toy. It landed bow-first, speared like a skewer into the desert.

Darien yanked his arm out of Azár's hold, turning back to face the violent assault of the storm.

"What are you doing?" Azár screamed at him, jerking frantically at his arm. "This is *sakeem!* A man-killer! We must find shelter!"

Darien gazed at the scattered provisions left haphazardly where they lay. Far down the trail, two women struggled toward them, one tugging with both hands on an iron cart handle while the other pushed from behind. One wheel of the cart had become mired in a rut.

Darien took a step forward, closing his eyes, and sampled the currents of the magic field. He sent his mind out across tides of air, testing his will against the fury of the storm. It was far worse than he'd thought, a severe disturbance in the air that encompassed much more of the atmosphere than he'd thought. Against such a force, he found his own strength seriously wanting.

Darien opened his eyes, feeling numb.

"I can't do this alone," he admitted.

Azár gazed at him with wide, terrified eyes. She brought her hand up to draw her scarf across her face, fixing it in place against the fine grains of sand that pebbled them with scouring fury.

"This thing cannot be done," she insisted. "Please! It is *sakeem!* It will eat your flesh and throw away your bones!"

Darien shook his head, offering his hand. "Feel through me. I'll show you what to do."

Azár backed away as if repulsed. "What you ask…"

Darien waited silently, palm extended. After a moment's hesitation, Azár finally swallowed and took his hand. He closed his fingers around hers, locking his grip firmly around her own. He closed his eyes. He could hear the howl of the storm, feel the sting of the sand biting his face. He could sense the torrent of charged energies carried toward them by the gale. The wall of needling death was almost on top of them.

Darien filled his mind with a startling, amber calm.

Once again, he sent his thoughts out across the air, groping at the violent reaches of the sky. He grappled mentally with the force of the wind, struggling to quell its sinister fury. Overhead, lightning flared and thunder exploded as the clouds retaliated with violence against his meddling.

Balls of hail rained down from the sky, pelting the ground all around them.

Darien clutched Azár's hand, imploring her silently. Her fingers trembled in his grasp.

All that he had was not enough. Nowhere close to enough.

But then Darien realized: without knowing it, he'd been holding back. The magic field was not the only resource he was capable of tapping. Despite his reservations, Darien realized that he could no longer afford the luxury of denying the darker aspects of his nature.

He had died and been remade.

He was no longer a man. He was a demon.

A demon with a confused but sinister purpose.

For the very first time, Darien Lauchlin opened his mind to the power of hell and drew on the cold fury of the Onslaught, letting it ravage his brain with velvet claws.

He gasped, falling to his knees, tormented by rapturous waves of bliss unlike anything he'd ever experienced.

Compared to the seductive violence of the Onslaught, the magic field was impotent, insignificant.

He was no longer aware of Azár at his side.

He struggled to his feet, panting, drowning, writhing in wondrous, frantic ecstasy. Above, the wall of billowing dust shuddered backward, collapsing in upon itself as if repulsed by the infernal assault that was being delivered.

Lightning flared and thunder clashed. Hail pelted the ground with vicious abandon, the roar of it almost deafening.

"What is that? *What are you doing?*"

Darien opened his eyes and peered at Azár in dazzled confusion. Submerged in the violent bliss of the Onslaught, he had a hard time even recognizing her. It took him a long, bleary moment to focus on her face. She was considering him, studying his features. Then something in her expression subtly changed. Inside, something clicked. Somehow, she understood what was happening.

Azár's eyes widened with excitement. She threw her head back with a whoop of elation.

"Ishil'zeri!" she exclaimed through her laughter. "You are magnificent! You are *my* Sentinel, now!"

Darien shot her a look of gaping dismay.

Above, the heavens flared as the clouds slammed back together, showering zigzag trails of sparks across the sky. Darien trained his attention upwards, focusing his mind on the approaching storm. The billowing wall of dust crumbled backward as if repulsed, collapsing. The wind reversed in direction, driven back the other way.

Darien could feel the moment when Azár added her own strength to the battle that raged above them in the sky. With delicate skill, she tamed the unruly currents of air, pacifying what was left of the storm's resistance.

A thick blanket of calm settled in around them, the wind stilling to a quiet breeze. Sand rained straight down from the sky, the failing updrafts no longer capable of sustaining it.

Azár was only second tier. But she was far more skilled than Darien in the ways of light and air and sky. Together, hand in hand, they quelled the storm's fury. The breeze ebbed, disappearing entirely. Eventually, the roar of thunder became a fragile, half-remembered whisper on the wind.

In the stark calm that settled, Darien finally relaxed enough to release the Hellpower and let it drain out of him. He fell to his knees, overcome by a jarring wash of dizziness. He felt suddenly, desperately weak. Azár's grip on his hand steadied him enough so that he didn't fall over on his face. Propping himself upright with a hand thrust down into the sand, he struggled to catch his breath, panting, his pulse echoing in his ears.

Azár ripped the scarf away from her face, revealing cheeks flushed pink with excitement. "I've made my choice," she announced proudly into the darkness. "I choose you."

Darien peered up at her, shoulders heaving as he gasped for breath through a ball of dust that choked his throat. "How can you say that?" he whispered in a gravelly voice, gagging a bit on the words. "What's changed?"

She cracked a grin, reaching out to brush away the sand that still clung to his face.

"Everything has changed," she assured him. "The Prime Warden said to trust you. I did not believe him, but now I do."

"Why?" Darien demanded, frowning in exasperation. "What changed your mind?"

"Because I have seen the power that Xerys has placed within you. It is pure. It is beautiful! There can be no going back for you. I understand that, now. You are His Eternal Servant, and I am your Lightweaver. I will follow wherever it is you lead, for you will deliver my people from the darkness just as you promised."

Darien gazed at her, mouth slack. He shook his

head, patently confused.

That night, they camped by the side of the river. There were no tents; tents were too bulky and heavy to be transported across the wastes. Instead, Haleem's people camped under the clouds, building fires of coal bricks.

Darien ate alone off to the side, well away from the smoke of the cookfires and the constant stares of the people in the camp. He sat leaning back against a boulder, cupping a bowl in both hands. The thin stew was heavily spiced. He took his time about eating it, savoring the blend of flavors in his mouth, the heat of the stew warming his belly.

He glanced up at the sound of approaching footsteps. It was Haleem, his wife at his side. Behind the two of them stretched a long line of people. Darien set the bowl down and rose awkwardly, dusting off his pants and shaking the dirt from his cloak. Haleem's expression was enigmatic; Darien couldn't guess the man's purpose.

The caravan master stopped in front of him as the others surrounded him, their bodies pressing in closely. Darien gazed from face to face, alarmed by their proximity. The presence of so many people seemed like an oppressive weight bearing down on him, making him feel like he couldn't get enough air to breathe. He brought his arm up, wiping his mouth with a sleeve.

Azár appeared, stepping out from the crowd of people to stand on Haleem's right. Her hair was freshly plaited, her skin washed. She appeared completely unaffected by her part in the struggle against the storm. There was no trace of fatigue in her eyes. She was wearing a new shawl wrapped around her shoulders, a rich ochre fabric, frayed at the edges.

Without speaking, Haleem raised his hands, offering out a folded garment.

Uncertainly, Darien accepted the offered parcel from Haleem. He held the fabric up in front of him, shaking out the folds. It was a rectangular piece of black woven cloth, heavily embroidered with gold thread in an interlaced design. Two gold cords with thick tassels hung from either end.

"My thanks," he told Haleem sincerely. He gazed down at the splendid garment, having never seen anything like it before. He couldn't figure out how it was meant to be worn. "It's beautiful. But it's not necessary."

Azár moved to stand beside him. "Haleem is very grateful to you for protecting both his people and his investment."

Darien shrugged. "He doesn't need to thank me."

Azár muttered a rapid burst of speech under her breath, translating Darien's words with more than a few additions of her own. Then she plucked the garment out of his hands and moved behind him, reaching around to wind the fabric around his hips.

"It is meant to be worn this way. The tassels should hang to the left. It can be worn either over pants or by itself. It is a very fine gift."

She tied the cords, tugging the knot twice to make certain it would hold. Then, with a curt toss of her head, she stepped back, appraising him.

Darien ran his hand over the fine embroidery, continuing the motion downward to finger one of the cords. "My thanks. *Sukrien,* Haleem. I'm honored."

Haleem nodded stiffly, apparently satisfied. He brought his hand up to his chest, bowing his head. Then he turned and walked back toward the camp. As he left, another man approached, muttering something and smiling as he laid one hand on Darien's shoulder, his other hand on Azár. Yet another man moved forward and repeated the gesture before turning to follow Haleem. As Darien stood still, every person in the caravan came forward and laid their hands on the two mages in an expression of gratitude before turning back toward the camp. Eventually, the last woman turned and limped away into the darkness.

Darien was left standing alone with Azár. He stood as if in a daze, gazing in wonder at the retreating backs of the people whose lives they had saved. He was thankful for their gratitude, but even more thankful to be left alone. The closeness of so many bodies wore on his nerves.

"Did that trouble you?" Azár asked, considering him.

Darien shook his head as he brushed his palm over the new wrap Haleem had given him. "No. I just wasn't expecting it."

Azár nodded. She gazed at him with a searching look. "May I stay and speak with you for a moment?"

"Of course."

She dropped to the ground, sitting cross-legged, and motioned with her hand for him to sit down at her side. Darien hesitated, not wanting to soil Haleem's gift. He dropped to a crouch.

Azár made a clicking sound with her tongue. "Sit," she admonished him. "It was made to be worn and used. What, are you never going to sit or sleep?"

Darien couldn't help the small, fragile grin that slipped to his lips. She had a point. Carefully, he settled all the way down into the dirt, leaning back against the boulder he'd claimed previously.

Azár nodded in approval. "Tomorrow, I'll take you to my village. I would like to talk to you about the people you will meet. They are a good people. A hard people, full of pride, full of stone. But I must warn you: they will not like you."

That came as no surprise. "Because of Black Solstice?" he assumed.

Azár shook her head. "It is much more than that. You are a Sentinel of Aerysius. The warriors of my clan once followed a man who called himself a Sentinel. We followed him to our deaths. He lied to us, betrayed us, and then he abandoned us. In all the history of the Khazahar, there has never been a man so reviled."

"You speak of Braden Reis," Darien guessed.

Azár lifted a finger. "That name is never to be spoken. We speak only of his treachery. Because of this man, the people of the clans will have no trust for you at all. In truth, some may even try to kill you on sight."

"Then they'll try," Darien shrugged dismissively, spreading his hands. "There's little I can do about it."

And, indeed, there wasn't. He could defend himself if he had to, even without resorting to magic. He had been trained by a Guild blademaster; the sword that rode at his back was just as lethal as his mind. But he hoped it wouldn't come to that. Any defense he could offer would only solidify their distrust in him.

Azár was staring at him sideways, surveying him critically, her gaze harsh and full of doubt. "How do you intend to save my people, Darien?"

He hadn't anticipated that question. He was caught completely off-guard. Darien raised his eyebrows, spreading his hands and shaking his head. "I've no idea," he admitted.

Azár tilted her head to the side, her eyes narrowing. "If there is no other option, are you willing to lead my people south to invade the Rhen?"

Darien bowed his head, breathing out a heavy chestful of air. He sat there for a long while, wrestling within himself for the answer to her question. It was not the first time he had weighed this option. He had struggled with it before, many times. Just as always, the very notion made him shudder in dread.

He knew very well it might have to come to that.

As always, he found himself arriving at the same, terrible conclusion: it was not an option he could rule out.

"I'm hoping I won't have to," he whispered, staring at the ground.

Azár scooted forward until she was sitting right next to him. She gazed up piercingly into his face.

"You would, wouldn't you?" she pressed. She peered deeply into his eyes without blinking.

Darien said nothing, troubled by her directness. And her proximity. Azár's stare hardened, her lips compressing.

Somehow, somewhere in his eyes, she found her answer.

"You would," she gasped. "How is that possible? You gave your life in defense of the Rhen. Now you are willing to lead Malikar's legions against it? What changed?"

Everything, Darien realized. Everything was different, everything had changed.

Nothing could ever be the same again.

Ever since he'd started looking at the world through the eyes of a dead man.

Darien groped for the right words, struggling to find a way to describe the conflict within himself. "I didn't know the whole truth back then," he fumbled, desperate to gain her understanding. "I didn't know anything about Malikar, what the conditions are like here. I didn't know there were so many of you in such terrible need. I was always taught to just think of you as the Enemy…as if you weren't even human. Maybe animals or savages. Demons, perhaps. We were told you were evil, that you sought only to conquer, to enslave. To destroy."

He swallowed, looking down, unable to meet her gaze. "But I know better, now. Your people are not conquerors, Azár. And you're certainly not demons—you're not even the Enemy. *We are.*"

Those last two words he spat with contempt. Without looking at her. His troubled eyes wandered to the side, regarding the severe darkscape before them in angry doubt. A shadow stirred within him, settling deep into his bones, chilling his brittle soul.

He knew he was a traitor. In heart, now, as well as deed. Azár had been right; he could never go back to what he was before.

That man was dead. The part that mattered, anyway.

He had been dead a long time.

"*I'm* the demon," he whispered, gazing off into the distance. "Not you."

Chapter Thirteen
The Conclave

Glen Farquist, The Rhen

Kyel felt like a quivering mass of abraded nerves. He paced relentlessly up and down the floor of the vestibule, fingers interlaced behind his back. When he reached the far end of the chamber, he turned on heel and doubled back. He finally drew up in front of Naia with an exasperated sigh.

"Are you sure I look all right?" he said as he tugged at his shirt collar with a finger.

"Stop fretting. You look like a Sentinel."

He adjusted his posture, squaring his shoulders. "Do I look official?"

"Very official." She paused, frowning. "Except for that."

She reached out and smoothed the collar of his shirt. "That's better. Now you look official."

Kyel groaned and ran his hands through his hair. "This is bloody killing me. Why can't they just get on with it?"

Naia plucked a bit of lint from his cloak. "Be patient. There's certain protocol that must be followed. Think of it as a series of steps. Each step must happen in a particular order with a great deal of pomp and ritual. They certainly won't rush the process simply because we're the first mages who've had the audacity to grace their doorstep in five hundred years."

"Well, it's unnerving."

They had been left in the vestibule of the Chapel of Nimrue. Naia's father had told them to remain there while he presented their request to the Conclave. Then he'd withdrawn, the great mahogany doors shut and locked from within, the tumblers echoing as they fell into place.

That had been hours ago.

There was a ringing, metallic noise, and then one of the tall doors was thrust suddenly open.

Kyel sucked in a sharp breath, heady with panic. He wasn't ready for this; politics had never been his strong suit. And yet, somehow, he was supposed to convince the most ancient governing body in the world to act in a way completely contradictory to its charter.

"The Conclave is ready to receive you now," a servant in bright livery announced, beckoning them forward with a red-gloved hand.

Kyel shot a glance at Naia, hoping against hope that she'd take the initiative and enter ahead of him. Just as he'd feared, she merely looked at him expectantly.

"You're the Grand Master. Not me," she reminded him.

Kyel wanted to growl. Instead, he bit his lip and followed the guard through the chapel door. *Emulate me,* Darien had once told him long ago. But every time he tried to imitate his former master's confidence, he failed miserably; he simply didn't have it in him.

But it was the only model he had. So Kyel shifted his stride, aiming for the same arrogant grace Darien managed so naturally. He felt like a fool. He clamped his jaw and clutched his hands into fists, doing his best to keep the anxiety he felt from reaching his eyes.

He stopped in the center of the chapel under the vault of the dome, Naia at his side. A straight line of six wooden thrones occupied by the various leaders of the Holy Temples stretched before him. Behind the great thrones sat rows of assistants, both lay clergy and fully ordained priests and priestesses.

Naia's father, the High Priest of Death, rose from his throne. He wore pristine white vestments with a silken stole draped over his shoulders. He seemed older than Kyel remembered, but he still had the same fire in his eyes that Kyel recalled very well.

Luther Penthos raised his hand, indicating the two mages before him. "I present to this great body Grand Master Kyel Archer of the Distinguished Order of Sentinels. And Master Naia Seleni of the Distinguished Order of Querers."

Kyel nodded, acknowledging the introduction, just as Naia had instructed him to do.

"Thank you, Your Eminence," he responded tightly. To the others, he said, "And thank you for receiving us. It is a great honor that you do us."

He glanced down the line of thrones, noting that the temple monarchs were studying him with looks of intense mistrust.

"Grand Master Kyel, Master Naia," Luther Penthos continued, "as you know, I am the Vicar of Isap, Goddess of Death. Beginning on my right, may I present to you the Vicar of Om, God of Wisdom."

Kyel issued a brief nod in the old man's direction; he was very familiar with the bronze-robed and silent cleric.

"The Vicar of Athera, Goddess of Magic."

Kyel glanced toward an elderly woman in a purple brocade gown. The priestess regarded him with arched eyebrows, her gaze critical.

"The Vicar of Enana, Goddess of the Hearth."

This was a stout woman who wore her hair in a tight bun at the crown of her head. The woman regarded Kyel with an expression of distaste as she nodded formally in his direction.

"The Vicar of Zephia, Goddess of the Winds."

Another man, younger, with a muscular frame. His long hair was gathered back from his face. He wore a dark beard and an even darker glower. He disregarded Kyel, looking away as if unaware of his own introduction.

"The Vicar of Alt, God of the Wilds."

This man was large and impressive, with a mass of tangled beard that fell almost to his waist. He wore a belted tunic of forest green. He gave a grunt, staring at Kyel without blinking.

"And, lastly, the Vicar of Dreia, Goddess of the Vine."

Kyel flinched at the assault of color that confronted him. The High Priestess of Dreia peered at him with a sullen look through a cascade of honey-colored hair that draped over one of her eyes. She was garbed in an alarming shade of red, reclining sideways on her throne, a glass of blood-red wine held aslant between her fingers.

There were six temples accounted for, Kyel realized. The Temples of Grief and Chaos had no representation at the Conclave, for which he was grateful. Suddenly uncertain, Kyel glanced sideways at Naia for reassurance. She nodded without looking at him, her face confident as she gazed ahead at the temple monarchs.

Kyel cleared his throat, summoning the last scraps of confidence he had left. "Greetings, Your Eminences. Thank you for allowing us to present our petition before this great council. It is my understanding that this is the first time in over five hundred years that a mage of Aerysius has been allowed to address this body. I take that as a sign that the temples appreciate the gravity of the threat we all face."

As his words trailed off, Kyel's gaze slid to Naia. To his relief, he found her looking at him with a mixture of pride and appreciation in her eyes. He took that for a good sign, feeling his self-confidence bolstered.

The Vicar of the Wind raised his eyes from his lap to glare at Kyel. "Believe me, this council has a very *deep* appreciation for the gravity of this situation, which has been—yet again—forced upon us by the mage class. Which is the only reason the two of you are even here, I should point out."

Mutters of agreement echoed from all around the chapel, accompanied by a general bobbing of heads. The Vicar of Dreia tossed back a sip of wine with a grimace. Kyel glanced again at Naia, who nodded.

"Your Eminence," Kyel said, addressing Naia's father. "We accept that our predecessors are responsible for the inception of the Well of Tears in the first place. For that, we have never sought to avoid accountability. But please also understand that the Masters of Aerysius have born singular responsibility for the containment of that evil. So much of our blood has been spilt toward that end that there are only three mages left in the entire world."

Cadmus, who served as the Voice of Wisdom, raised a finger. "That is untrue."

Kyel hesitated with a frown. He was unsure whether he should feel more confused or more affronted. He felt both in equal portions.

Cadmus clarified, "His Eminence wishes me to remind you that there are yet seven darkmages walking abroad in the world. His Eminence would also like to inform you, if you are not aware already, that the Enemy has mages of their own. Mages who have never been constrained by the Oath of Harmony."

Kyel felt his heart sink at hearing that news. He hadn't considered such a possibility. Not for the first time, he wondered how the Temple of Wisdom came by their troves of knowledge.

"I was…unaware of that, Your Eminence," Kyel admitted. "That news is…deeply troubling."

"Members of the Council, if I may?"

Kyel glanced sideways at Naia. She had taken a step forward, her hands clasped in front of her.

"You may," her father allowed.

Naia's smile was all-encompassing. Even the Vicar of Winds looked up to gaze with interest.

"The Grand Master and I understand your reservations," she announced in sparkling clear tones, eyes bright with purpose. "However, you must realize that all of the points you just mentioned only serve to bolster our argument."

"And what, exactly, is the nature of the petition you bring before this Conclave?" demanded the Vicar of Magic.

Naia motioned for Kyel to continue. He moved forward to stand beside her.

"As you are all aware, the Well of Tears has been unsealed. We will strive to close it, but that can only be accomplished by the sacrifice of a Grand Master." Kyel lowered his eyes and drew a long, quavering breath, swallowing the dread that clenched his throat. "I volunteer."

There was a hollow silence in the chapel. Kyel kept his gaze trained on the floor, unable to meet their stares. He was aware of Naia looking at him in stunned horror.

The priestess in the blood-red dress chortled in his direction. "A very noble gesture, Grand Master Kyel. I will be sure to offer a toast if you actually manage to work up the nerve to match your bravado. But what I don't understand is why your decision to commit suicide must be ratified by this council?"

Kyel felt a flush of anger at the insult. "It doesn't, obviously," he said. "We came here today to beg the temple leadership to help us bolster the defenses of the Rhen. The last time the Well was open, Darien Lauchlin broke Oath to turn back the invasion of the Enemy. As it turns out, that solution was only temporary."

"What solution?" demanded the feral-looking Vicar of the Wilds. "That was no solution at all—for now we have a demon of Darien Lauchlin's abilities to contend with!"

Naia raised her voice. "Which is exactly why we need the help of the temples so desperately! Kyel and I do not have the strength to defend the nations of the Rhen by ourselves. There are only two of us and, besides, we are both Bound by the Oath of Harmony. I know there is great might in the assets entrusted to the temples by our ancestors. They were placed into your keeping as a safeguard, as a balance against the mage class. To prevent the Assemblies from becoming too powerful and despotic. I say it's time that the temples use those assets for their intended purpose: to defeat Renquist's darkmages before they destroy everything in this world we hold dear."

Kyel took up her point, "We ask this of you, not for ourselves, but for the people of the Rhen. Without the might of the temples, our combined military strength will not suffice. Naia and I will be of little help. We can't defend against something like this."

Cadmus raised a finger. "Grand Master Kyel. His Eminence is wondering what you will do if you are ever confronted by your former master?"

Kyel considered the question. It almost felt like a kind of test. He had no idea how they wanted him to answer.

"I suppose I would try to negotiate with him," he managed.

"*Negotiate* with him?"

"What else would you have me do? I am Bound. And Darien is not." It was the plain truth, even if it wasn't what they wanted to hear.

"Darien Lauchlin has sworn his soul to Xerys," the Vicar of Magic grumbled. "Do you honestly believe such a demon would pause to chat before slaying you outright?"

Kyel could only bow his head. "I think he might. Surely, something of the man must still remain. I'd have to try—I can't kill him. Against a darkmage, my words are the only weapons I possess."

But Naia's father shook his head. "There, you are wrong. Your Oath prevents you from striking out against him. But nothing prevents us. Working together, we should be able to bring Lauchlin down. We can bring them all down, eventually, one by one."

All around the chapel, the other clerics and their assistants were nodding, the room filling with whispered conversation. Luther Penthos turned back to Kyel. "That *is* what you're asking, is it not? Our assistance in defeating these demons and their armies? We have the right to ask: would either of you feel conflicted by such a plan?"

Kyel did feel conflicted. But he knew better than to admit it. "That is indeed what we're asking, Your Eminence. And, no. I would feel no conflict."

"And what about you, Master Naia?"

Kyel glanced at the woman beside him. Naia was staring at the ground, her hands clasped in front of her.

"Of course I would feel conflicted," she said honestly, her eyes wandering upward. "How could I not? But I have to agree, it's the right thing to do."

"Do you truly believe that?" her father pressed.

"*Yes.* Darien would have rather died than raise a hand against the Rhen. It might be that he is nothing more than a mindless shell, completely unaware of his own actions. But I suspect that's not the case. Much more likely, he's being compelled to act against his nature. If that's the case, then I cannot imagine the depths of his torment. I would not wish for him to exist in such misery."

Her father nodded, his expression softening. "Very well. Please excuse us while we deliberate."

Naia nodded. "Thank you."

Kyel took her by the arm, maneuvering her back toward the chapel's entrance. The double doors slammed closed behind them, the ancient locks clicking into place, sealing the chamber tight from within. They were alone once again in the vestibule.

Kyel sagged, scrubbing his face with his hands. "That went bloody terrible!" he gasped. "I'm not cut out for this sort of thing."

Beside him, Naia appeared wilted. Her serene air of confidence had melted clean away. She looked pale, her eyes sorrowful and downcast.

"It could have gone better."

He could tell by the sound of her voice how dispirited she was. He grumbled, "I don't even know what I'm doing in there! Why can't you do more of the talking? You're the one who's good at this sort of thing!"

Naia finally looked up at him. "Because you outrank me," she reminded him. "You are a sixth-tier Sentinel. You must learn to speak from a position of authority."

Kyel threw up his hands, barking a bitter laugh. "What authority? I can hardly call myself a Sentinel—what a joke!"

Naia's jaw clenched in anger. "You are Grand Master Kyel Archer of the Distinguished Order of Sentinels, the most powerful mage left in the world who hasn't sold his soul to Xerys. That is the man you are. *And that is the man we need you to be.*"

Kyel shook his head. "I don't know if I can be that man. I honestly don't think I've got it in me."

"You do. You just need time. And experience." She narrowed her eyes at him. "What were you thinking, volunteering your life to seal the gateway?"

He'd forgotten all about that. Kyel paced away, rubbing the back of his neck. "Well, that should be obvious. There's no other choice, is there?"

"Why not Meiran?"

Kyel shot her an exasperated look. "How could I ask that of her? She's already made that trip once."

Naia sagged, looking defeated. "I understand," she murmured softly, But her eyes said otherwise.

The lock on the chapel doors clicked, and the massive doors swayed inward. A liveried guard appeared, beckoning them within. Kyel closed his eyes, gathering his courage. He drew in a long breath. Then he opened his eyes and offered Naia his arm. Together, they entered the chapel and walked forward to stand before the awaiting members of the Conclave.

"Grand Master Kyel Archer. Master Naia Seleni. We appreciate your patience."

Kyel straightened his posture as he strove to

project the most authority he could muster. Despite his best effort, the clerics on their thrones surveyed them both with acute indifference. Even Naia's own father appeared to be looking at them through a murky pool of contempt.

At last, Luther Penthos rose to his feet. His voice resonated off the polished walls. "It is the decision of this Conclave to grant your petition…with one provision."

"What provision?" Kyel asked.

The Vicar of Magic rose to stand beside Naia's father. She explained in a crackly voice, "We agree that it has become necessary to commit the might of the temples to the defense of the Rhen. However, such a decision breaks with our covenants and puts in jeopardy many of our traditions. To offset our risk, this council demands that you surrender the governing authority vested in the office of the Prime Warden. Going forward, you will submit to the decisions made by this body."

Kyel stiffened, feeling the warmth drain from his face. His vision swam, his flesh going numb. For a moment, he couldn't react, not even in anger. He stood there gaping, breath stuck in his throat.

"What kind of offer is that?" he finally managed to gasp, still reeling from the sting of the insult. "The temples were created to balance the mage class, not dismantle it!"

But Naia's father differed. "The mage class has already been effectively dismantled. You've admitted as much yourself."

Naia spread her hands, face pale and eyes wide. "How could you even suggest such a thing? I know your intent, Father. This is no way of going about it!"

Kyel turned to her. "What is their intent?"

Eyes only for her father, Naia explained, "The temples and Aerysius have a very long history of vying for political advantage. The Conclave is exploiting our desperation to secure a position of dominance."

Luther Penthos shook his head, eyes cold and detached. "There's more to it than that. This council has access to knowledge that has, since the time of the Great Schism, been withheld from the mages of Aerysius."

Kyel demanded, "What knowledge? And why was it withheld?"

"We can tell you nothing more than what you already know. But be assured that this is the only way we can feel comfortable enough to move forward."

The grandmotherly Vicar of Magic crossed her arms across her chest. "Please consider this our final offer, Grand Master Kyel. If you reject it, then you'll leave us no choice but to align the Rhen's kingdoms against you. Which won't take much convincing; Darien Lauchlin seeded fear and distrust everywhere he went. The entire kingdom of Chamsbrey wants nothing more to do with you. Even Emmery, your greatest ally, has only suffered your presence because of Meiran's unfaltering diplomacy."

Kyel closed his eyes, his anger drowning in desperation.

Naia said, "The office of the Prime Warden has existed intact for thousands of years. Kyel and I will not be the ones to concede its authority."

Her father gave a slight, dismissive shrug. "The office is already vacant and obsolete. You would be conceding nothing."

"He's right, Naia."

Kyel was startled by the sound of his own voice. He hadn't meant to say that out loud. But he had. And Naia had heard him. She turned to gape at him in shock.

"What are you saying?" she gasped.

Kyel explained, "Aerysius is gone; there's only just the two of us. By ourselves, we can accomplish nothing. We *are* obsolete."

It hurt to admit it. But there was no use denying it, either. Before Aerysius fell, the combined might of the Sentinels had mattered for something. Even if they couldn't inflict harm with their gift, they could still protect, and what they couldn't protect, they could heal.

But the Sentinels were gone. Now there was only him.

And Kyel felt certain that, on a field of battle, he would be far more of a liability than an asset.

A strange sense of calm unfurled within his chest. He turned back to Naia's father. "Neither of us has the authority to enter into negotiations that might result in limitations to the office of the Prime Warden."

The Vicar of Magic waved a liver-spotted hand. "Then produce Meiran Withersby so we can negotiate with her."

"We don't know where she is."

The woman sat gazing at him down the length of her nose as she tugged at the bottom of her shirt. "You two *children* may as well admit it: Meiran Withersby is lost. Name her as such and be done with it. Grand Master Kyel, Master Naia. The patience of this council is not without end. One of you must volunteer to act as Prime Warden in Meiran's place."

Naia shook her head. "We will not."

"I will." Kyel took a step forward.

Naia's hand shot up, catching him by the sleeve. "Don't do this."

"I'm sorry, Naia. I have to." Kyel felt saddened as he turned away from her. He knew what she had to be feeling. He felt it, too. To the Conclave, he announced, "I am willing to speak on the Prime Warden's behalf."

The Vicar of Magic nodded. She clasped her hands together, eyebrows raised in anticipation. "Very well. Then as acting Prime Warden, we formally ask that you surrender to this body all rights, powers, and authority vested in the office of the Prime Warden. In exchange, this council formally pledges its support in the theater of war in the defense of the Rhen. Do we have your agreement, Kyel Archer, Acting Prime Warden of Aerysius?"

"You have my agreement."

To Kyel, the words didn't sound like his own. He heard them as though from a distance. As if they were just words floating toward him on the air. Words without substance or meaning. They settled in on him gradually, bearing down slowly on his shoulders, until he felt almost crushed under the sheer weight of them.

It was getting very difficult to breathe.

"Thank you, Acting Prime Warden Kyel."

The voice seemed disembodied, echoing from very far away.

"Don't thank me," Kyel gasped, staggering under the enormity of his own defeat. "Just help the Rhen. Help our people."

There was no mistaking the gloating triumph in the voice of the High Priestess as she commanded them, "Leave. Your business here is done."

Chapter Fourteen
Sharaq

Qul, The Black Lands

Darien wrenched his eyes from the ground, recalling Renquist's admonition against lowering his gaze. He looked Haleem directly in the eye as he brought his hand up to his chest, bowing solemnly. Above them, stormclouds roiled. Fat, round drops of rain began streaking haphazardly toward the ground, hitting the soil in random patterns. The rain made little difference; Darien's hair was already wet, plastered against the sides of his face. The sand at his feet smelled like wet, muddied ash.

"You have my thanks," he told Haleem. Darien lowered his hand, fingering the golden tassels of the embroidered wrap the man had given him.

Haleem took him by the arm, drawing him into a brotherly embrace. Darien winced as he felt the man's face brush the skin of his cheek. He was unaccustomed to such intimacy. The people of Malikar were used to far less personal distance than he was comfortable surrendering. Their constant closeness made Darien feel besieged, setting his already-frayed nerves on edge.

Haleem drew back, folding his hands and turning away. Darien was left staring after the man, trembling ever so slightly. He turned to find himself confronted by Azár, who stood gazing at him with a look of concern. The glare he shot her made her stare even harder.

"You don't like people, do you?" she said.

"No. I don't."

The rain was letting up. They stood at the head of a trail that wandered around the perimeter of a rock escarpment. A knee-high stack of flattened rocks marked the trail's entrance.

Darien took up the handle of one of the two carts Haleem had left for them. It was filled with bags of provisions, mostly salt and bricks of coal. He started down the trail, pulling the cart behind him, the thanacryst jogging behind.

The trail led them around the escarpment into a narrow box canyon bordered by tall cliffs. Darien didn't like the feel of the magic field in this place; it made his skin crawl. He wondered if they weren't close to another vortex. The field's energies were stronger here, more charismatic. There was a certain *pull*, urging him toward the back of the canyon.

After a short distance, the narrow corridor opened up into a gaping bowl surrounded on all sides by a tumbling array of blackened cliffs. A village had been erected in the center of the basin, a haphazard collection of jagged buildings and high, crumbling walls. The light of many lanterns spilled toward them through the darkness, emanating from balconies and windows, glowing from gaps and recesses in the cliffs above. The sound of distant laughter drifted toward them on the air.

Darien paused, taking it all in, feeling apprehension settle deeply into his bones.

Azár drew up beside him with her cart. "This is Qul, my home. My village." There was an uncharacteristic softness to her expression. "It is the home of the Jenn Asyaadi. They are my people."

Darien's eyes scanned over the layers of buildings separated by narrow paths between them. A thin gap cut into the outer wall marked the village entrance. He started toward it, dragging the wagon behind him. The hound padded after, head and ears alert. Its eyes glowed a sinister green.

The smell of coal smoke was heavy on the air, but not nearly as thick as it had been in Bryn Calazar. And there were other odors, as well, some pleasant. As they passed through the arch into a narrow walkway, the aroma of cooking made Darien's mouth water. There was also the smell of fragrant incense lingering on the air.

A man stepped out from one of the houses into the shadows of the alley in front of them.

Darien spread his fingers, signaling the demonhound.

The man noticed them as he turned. He stopped and stared, as if trying to make out features in the darkness. He stood there frozen, blocking their path.

Darien's hand drew slowly toward his sword's hilt.

"Fareen!" Azár called out.

Hearing her voice, the man strode forward. He was thick and burly, clothed in coarse linen covered by a padded overcoat. He had the same dark skin as Azár, his hair worn drawn back behind his head. He wore a pair of knives tucked into his belt, as well as a long, curving sword. His dark eyes were startled and concerned, raking over every inch of Azár.

When his gaze fell on the ebony-hilted dagger at her side, the man's eyes widened in recognition. He bent forward, taking Azár by the hand and pressing her fingers against his lips. He muttered something under his breath that Darien didn't catch.

Azár smiled. "This man is Fareen son of Mohsen. He is my cousin." To Fareen, she said, "This man is Darien Lauchlin of Amberlie. He is here at the command of Prime Warden Renquist."

The man recoiled, his face twisting in anger. His hand went to grip the hilt of his sword.

Azár reacted, positioning herself between Darien and Fareen. Her arm shot up, staying Fareen's hand. "Darien has submitted to the will of Xerys!"

The man turned his head and spat upon the ground. He jerked his chin up, glowering as he bared threatening inches of his blade.

"Then deliver him to Xerys! Why did you bring him here?" He spoke perfect, though accented, Rhenic. He reached out as if intending to force the small woman from his path.

But Azár danced away, springing back to Darien's side. "Darien Lauchlin has been named Overlord of the Khazahar! He is *nach'tier!*"

A broad smile grew on Fareen's face, genuine humor filling his eyes. He scoffed as he slid his blade back into its scabbard. Then his expression chilled to ice. "Your hands are stained with the blood of the clans," he said to Darien. "You may be *nach'tier*, but you are not welcome in our village."

Darien nodded his head back in the direction they'd just come from. "What about over there?"

Fareen squinted, frowning as if he didn't understand the question.

"Over there," Darien specified. "The cliffs across from the gate. Is that part of your village?"

Fareen's expression remained troubled. "No…"

"Then that's where I'll make my camp." He turned and strode back toward the gate. He left the wagonload of goods behind for Azár and the people of Qul; he had no need of them. Thanacryst at his side, he walked back out through the narrow gate and crossed the dirt path to a pile of large boulders.

There, in a wide crevice between two curving legs of tumbled rocks, he rifled through his pack, finding a few morsels of flatbread and a small sack of coal. He grabbed his waterskin, throwing his head back and taking large gulps of the brackish water it contained. Then he threw himself down in the sand and began to go about the business of setting up his campsite. He found a flat rock and used it to hollow out a fire pit in the ground, laying out his blanket next to it.

"What are you doing?"

Darien glanced up into Azár's bewildered face. "Avoiding problems," he responded.

She lowered herself down onto a rock across the fire pit from him. Her face was set in grim lines of frustration.

"This avoids nothing," she said, leaning forward over her knees. Her long braid swayed over her shoulder. "You want my advice? You must eat him for lunch before he eats you for dinner."

"Are you suggesting I should murder your cousin in cold blood? That doesn't sound very honorable."

Azár scoffed. "So now you decide to worry about honor? Don't. The wicked live longer."

"I know."

She was staring at him in consternation, the smile half-frozen on her lips. She rose to her feet, flipping her long shawl back over her shoulder. "I am going to my home," she informed him. "You are welcome to come with me. If you decide to stay here, take mind: Fareen and his kin will most likely come for you in the night. You have no guest-right in this place."

Darien tilted his head to the side, studying her profile. "Why are you telling me this, Azár? Isn't your first obligation to your kin?"

"Normally, yes. But you are Overlord of the Khazahar, and I am your Lightweaver. It is my duty to help protect your life." With that, she left, walking back toward her village.

Darien woke to the sound of footsteps approaching in the night. Quiet. Stalking. He rolled over to free up his sword arm, lying still for a moment and listening, hoping the noises would retreat.

Of course, they didn't. He was never that lucky.

"Go home, Fareen," he grumbled into the night. He was exhausted; all he wanted was sleep. But his ears told him that Fareen wasn't alone. Azár's cousin had brought company. Which was problematic; Darien didn't want to kill even one man. He certainly didn't want to kill four. He pried his body up off the ground with an elbow, peering into the darkness beyond the rocks.

"It's late. Go back to bed," he called at the approaching figures. The glint of light reflecting off a drawn blade commanded his attention.

"We'll sleep when you're dead."

Darien recognized Fareen's accented Rhenic. He sighed, reluctantly scooping his sword up in his hand as he rose to his feet. He didn't bare the blade. Instead, he held it down at his side, trying to appear as nonthreatening as possible. The shadows in front of him stopped, still paces away. He couldn't make out the men's faces in the darkness.

Darien reached out with his mind and tugged at the magic field. He summoned a glowing pool of magelight at his feet, feeding it with a trickle of power until the groping mist grew and spread.

Calmly, he uttered, "You've heard what I did to Malikar's legions. What do you suppose I could do to the four of you?"

One of the shadows in front of him took a step backward. Another wavered, shifting uncertainly. Fareen's face was revealed in the blue glow of the magelight. He didn't look intimidated. If anything, Darien's display of power seemed to only solidify the man's resolve. He nodded once, lifting his chin.

"You won't use your magic on us," Fareen announced. "There is no *sharaq* in such killing."

Sharaq. An ancient word for honor, or honor code. Darien understood the concept; he'd learned about it in his training, though he had no idea how the system actually worked in practice. Besides, the knowledge Darien had was a thousand years outdated.

Much had changed.

But he knew enough to guess he'd have to gain *sharaq* of his own if he hoped to stand a chance with these people. He couldn't risk losing even a drop of it. Reluctantly, Darien released his hold on the magic field, letting the glowing mist dissipate around his feet. He felt a sensation of loss as the energies drained away, diffusing into the air. The shadows returned to settle in around him, seeming thicker now than they had moments before. Slowly, he drew the scabbard down the length of his blade and flung it aside. He kept the tip of his sword lowered, swept back.

He said, "There's four of you and only one of me. How much *sharaq's* in those odds?"

Fareen scoffed as he raised his own blade, a long scimitar. "You are a Sentinel of Aerysius. Whoever spills your blood will receive great reward."

Darien trailed the tip of his own blade forward across the ground. He left his guard lowered, presenting Fareen an enticing target. "All right, then. Here I am. Come get your reward."

Two of Fareen's men fanned out to either side. The third rushed in, sweeping his blade downward. Darien moved as if to parry, but allowed the blow to knock his blade aside. He twisted his sword, slicing his opponent in the neck.

The next man was already advancing.

Darien stepped back out of range, drawing his sword back with both hands. He blocked a diagonal slice, letting his blade slide down the length of the man's steel. He stepped forward, pinning the man's sword against his chest. Then he struck out with his foot, taking his opponent in the knee.

Darien sliced downward, gutting the man as he fell.

He jerked back, spinning just in time to parry a strike coming at him from behind. He twisted, catching the attacking blade on his cross-guard. Darien pivoted his sword under the other man's blade. His opponent fell with an agonized scream.

Darien whirled to confront Fareen. He swept his blade back over his shoulder in a two-handed grip, winding his arms.

The big clansman made no move to attack. He was frozen in a defensive posture with his sword raised straight out in front of him. His face had lost all trace of its former confidence.

Darien advanced, thrusting forward. Fareen recovered himself enough to block, catching Darien's sword on the flat of his blade. Darien tested the pressure of Fareen's steel. He fanned his sword to the right, disengaging.

Fareen stumbled backward, losing his footing. He brought his sword up, thrusting out in an attempt to keep Darien at a distance. Darien shoved the attacking blade aside and dove in close, trapping Fareen's sword against his arm. He brought the hilt of his own blade up, bashing the man's face with the pommel of his hilt. He smacked him again. And again, flaying back the skin of his cheek.

Fareen's sword fell from his grip as Darien swept out with his foot, kicking his legs out from under him. He caught him by the hair as the clansman fell, holding him upright over his knees with his sword against the man's exposed throat.

Looking up, Darien realized that they were no longer alone. At least half the village had turned out and stood arrayed before him, weapons brandished and ready to attack. Darien swallowed, realizing the gravity of his predicament. He couldn't fight them all off. Not without magic. Not and retain any amount of *sharaq*.

He froze with the honed edge of his blade poised against Fareen's larynx. His eyes wandered over the agitated crowd, searching, at last finding Azár. She was weaving through the press of bodies toward him. Seeing him, she met his gaze and drew her index finger across her own neck.

Darien took her meaning.

He closed his eyes, sucking at the magic field as if sucking in life. He pulled until the field saturated him, filling him to capacity, until gleaming blue ribbons of energy bled off his body in distorted waves. The crowd drew back away from him, aghast, brandishing their weapons defensively. Men cried out, some falling to their knees. Others turned and fled. Some just stood there, mouths agape. Women pulled their children in close.

Fareen struggled against Darien's hold, his neck straining away from the pressure of the blade. Darien tightened his grip. He raised his voice to address the crowd:

"Whether you like it or not, Zavier Renquist named me Overlord of this region." He swept his gaze across the gathered mob, glaring at each face in turn. "Tonight this man betrayed my authority and led three of my own warriors against me. I sentence Fareen son of Mohsen to death."

He didn't hesitate. He drew the honed edge of his blade across Fareen's exposed neck. He held the man back against his legs and watched him bleed out, observing Fareen's face go from defiant to slack in the span of heartbeats. Darien released him. The body slumped forward over its knees, bowing into the spreading pool of blood.

Darien lowered his sword back down to his side. His body was trembling in a mixture of rage, revulsion, and chaotic energies. He raised his voice, scolding the people of Qul with the fury of his wrath:

"The rest of you'd better get it through your heads: I was sent here by *Zavier Renquist himself*, who saw fit to place the welfare of the clans *in my hands!* You are all welcome to my food, my fires, and my protection. I'll do everything in my power to further the interests of the Asyaadi, as well as the other clans of the Khazahar. But the one thing I will not suffer is stupidity. And I'll not waste my time crossing steel with the next man who seeks my blood. I'll just drop him where he stands."

He turned and bent over, scooping his sword's scabbard up in his hand. Then he stalked off into the night, leaving the villagers behind to deal with their dead.

Darien walked alone the rest of the night. He had no idea when morning finally arrived; in a land without sunlight, day and night had little meaning. His shadow confronted him at every turn, cast by the muddled light that emanated from deep within the clouds above. But there was no trace of dawn's awakening when it came.

Darien wandered toward the glow of Qul's lightfields, attracted by the radiance. He hadn't made a conscious decision to go there, but then again, he hadn't made a conscious decision not to. So he followed where his feet led him. He found himself strolling the edge of the lightfields, gazing out across the manicured landscape in wonder.

Ahead, row upon row, were tilled, orderly stripes of cropland that extended all the way to the jagged edge of a ridge of mountains to the north. An impressive system of irrigation ditches fed the farmland with water. There was vegetation of every sort, orchards and berries, date palms and greens. Golden trails of magelight ribboned the sky, as bright as he remembered the sun. For minutes, all he could do was stare. Then he stepped a foot across the thin boundary that separated shadow from light.

He stood there for a moment, spreading his left hand beneath the dappled texture of magelight, half his body basking in warm radiance, the other half still lingering in the chill darkness of the waste. He turned his head, gazing harder into the verdant distance. A butterfly fluttered by right in front of him, lofting in random dips and arcs above the fields. Bees ranged from flower to flower, the sound of their myriad wings creating a low and consistent hum.

Darien stood still, mouth open, reveling in the serene beauty of the fields. He wanted to wander further in, to trail his fingers over the wispy strands of grain. But something held him back. He swallowed his desire, turning instead away from the light. He stepped back across the boundary, back into shadow. Immediately, he felt an alarming sense of loss. He bowed his head, gazing at the ground.

On the trail back to the village, he encountered Azár. He drew up, considering the woman in silence. He had killed her cousin; yet another member of Azár's family had died by his hand. Darien didn't know what to say.

"Nur a'yiid," Azár uttered. *Morning's grace.*

Darien nodded. *"Nur a'yiid,"* he responded. He shifted his weight over his feet, staring down at his hands. They were still stained with Fareen's blood, he realized. The thought hadn't occurred to him to wash it off.

"Why did you have me kill Fareen?" he asked without looking at her. "He was your kin. And he was disarmed. Why not show him mercy?"

The woman was gazing up at him with the strangest expression on her face. He couldn't place it. The look in her eyes ranged somewhere between doubt, care, and concern.

"Because mercy is a sign of weakness," Azár told him. "You cannot afford to be seen as weak."

Darien shrugged. "They'll resent me, now."

"Maybe some will resent you, but you have won their respect. You gained much *sharaq* last night."

Darien spread his hands. "Where is it? I don't see it."

Azár moved a step closer to him. She had plaited her hair since the last time he'd seen her. She was also wearing a new ochre vest. It suited her complexion.

"Has anyone else challenged you?" she asked.

"No."

"You see? Had you spared Fareen, every man of this village would be seeking your blood. And perhaps some of the women."

Darien had to admit she was probably right. Wanting to change the subject, he gestured back toward the lightfields. "I was just admiring your work. What can you tell me of it?"

Azár smiled. It was a beautiful smile that brightened her whole face just as much as her magelight brightened the darkness.

"I will come here every day to weave the light," she explained, taking Darien by the arm. She turned him back around to face the lightfields. With her hand still on him, she strolled forward, guiding him alongside her. "The light can last for a week, sometimes more, before it begins to fade. I must weave new light where the old light has gone out. It takes much concentration and effort. I can only do this for so long before I must rest. Right now, there is much catching up to do. While my master was gone, the Lightweaver from another clan came and tried to help. But we were gone for too long, and it was too much for her to light both Qul's fields and her own. Already, we have lost more than half the harvest."

Darien looked to Azár with concern. "So your village will be short on food?"

"Not just Qul. Many villages are served by these fields." Azár released his arm, nodding her chin.

"Look there."

Darien allowed his eyes to follow in the direction she indicated. There, across the fields, was a large patch of darkness. Now that he saw it and knew what to look for, he realized there were many other such patches.

He asked, "What can I do to help you?"

She appeared grateful for his concern. But she shook her head sadly. "There is nothing you can do. Even with all the power of the Netherworld, you cannot weave the full spectrum of magelight."

There was a long span of silence between them as Darien stared at the ground. Without looking at her, he muttered, "I'm sorry I killed your cousin, Azár. And I'm sorry I killed your sister."

There was another long gap of silence. Finally, Azár responded, "I never liked Fareen. But I am sorry that my sister was fated to die by your hand. She would have liked you, I think."

The bodies had been removed by the time Darien returned to his makeshift camp. But not the blood. The blood remained, staining the ground. Darien threw himself down on the opposite side of the fire pit he'd shoveled out of the dirt. His pack and blanket were still there, he realized with relief. His possessions appeared untouched. He wondered at that.

But he didn't wonder long. A low growl reminded him why no one would dare ransack his things. He'd forgotten all about the thanacryst.

"Narghul," he whispered, patting the ground at his side.

The demon-dog trotted out from the rock it had been lurking behind, green eyes glowering in the darkness. The beast settled down at Darien's side, nuzzling its big head into his armpit. The creature purred.

Darien reached up, running his hand through the hound's thick and matted fur. He was rewarded by a slobbering lick on the cheek.

"That's enough," he scolded the thing, scrubbing the wetness off his face with his sleeve. He snapped his fingers and pointed, ordering the demon-hound away. The creature slinked away a few feet then turned back toward him.

"Go," Darien chided it.

The beast trotted away, disappearing into the darkness.

When it was gone, Darien rummaged deep in his pack, hoping to find some of the dried food stores he'd brought with him from Haleem's caravan. There wasn't much left; he hadn't anticipated living in a ditch upon his arrival in Qul. All his search produced was a single piece of hard and moldering flatbread. Darien held the bread up before his face and picked at the areas of discoloration, peeling off the mold and flicking it away. He turned the bread over, examining the other side. Tearing off a bite, he stuffed it in his mouth and started the arduous process of chewing.

He lived in the ditch between the rocks for over a week. Every dark morning Darien watched a steady stream of villagers filing out of Qul's gate, headed toward the lightfields. Every evening they returned, weary and shambling. After the first day, Darien decided to follow the group of laborers, hoping to lend a hand. But Azár saw him and shook her head, gesturing him away. Darien took that as a sign his help was not wanted.

So he stayed away. He spent his time exploring the shadowed landscape around Qul. He took long walks: sometimes down to the river, sometimes into the hills above the lightfields. Mostly, he just lingered about his camp. The time passed slowly, a relentless cycle of darkness followed by night. Fortunately, Azár took enough pity on him to spare a loaf of bread and a few sacks of dried fruit.

Darien waited, hoping for a break. None came. Azár seemed to be avoiding him, either by design or by circumstance. The villagers ignored him, often pretending as if they didn't see him, as if he didn't exist. Like an unwanted ghost lingering on the frayed margins of their dark and threadbare world.

After finishing a meager breakfast, Darien fished the pipe Haleem had given him out of his *sufan*, holding it up in his hands. He turned it over, admiring the workmanship. He had never smoked a pipe before; it was just not something that was done. The pipe sparked Darien's curiosity. Rummaging deeper into the satchel, he found a small supply of tobacco. He withdrew a pinch of leaf, wadding it up and stuffing it into the bowl.

He lit the contents of the pipe and took a long

draw off the stem. Immediately, his eyes filled with water and he wheezed, his lungs burning. He coughed, sputtering.

From far away came the sound of distant screams.

Darien lurched to his feet, dropping the pipe and scooping up his sword. Without a second thought, he sprinted down the path toward the lightfields. When the cliffs opened up, he stopped, trying to get a sense of the cause of the commotion. More screams drifted toward him from out of the darkness. The glow of the lightfields on the horizon was an ominous red-orange.

He ran down the dirt path toward the fields. By the time he got there, it was already too late. Darien staggered to a stop, taking in the scene of devastation that confronted him.

Everywhere he looked, the lightfields were ablaze. Fires seared the earth, consuming everything in their path. Flames leaped high into the sky, engulfing the dry orchards and rows of light-starved grain. Hot ashes rained down, drifting all around him.

Darien just stood there, groping through shock. It took him a moment to gather himself enough to react. He bared his blade and, heart pounding, tried to summon enough courage to confront the flames.

"Azár!"

He started toward the fire, but fear got the better of him. Darien stopped, grimacing, his blade sagging in his grip.

A barrage of unwanted images flooded his mind, one after another in relentless succession. A crackling pyre. An inferno of his own creation, swifter than the wind and hotter than the sun. The torments of the Netherworld, searing his flesh and scalding his soul.

Shaken, Darien closed his eyes, shuddering as he strove to master his emotions. He called upon the fury of the Onslaught, hoping the Hellpower's wrath might cauterize his fear. Calm instantly settled over him, soothing the rage of his brittle nerves.

When Darien opened his eyes, the images were gone. So was the fear. His fear of the flames had been replaced by a white-cold sense of purpose. Darien used the Onslaught to quell the heat of the blaze in front of him. Then he stepped across the boundary, transitioning from a world of shadow into a world of fire and smoldering ash. Sword in hand, he trudged forward under the lambent glow of licking flames, smothering the blaze before him as he went.

"Azár!"

He could hear the sound of shouts ahead of him. He sprinted forward, dousing the flames to either side. He swept his gaze across the field, extinguishing the hot spots. Steam rose from the charred mat of scorched vegetation on the ground.

Motion ahead caught his attention. Darien drew up, bringing his sword back up over his shoulder. A man was riding toward him on a horse, a moving silhouette against a writhing background of flames. Darien held his ground, waiting for the rider to approach.

It wasn't until horse and rider were almost on top of him that the man's features were revealed by the lambent glow of the inferno.

Nashir Arman pulled back on his stallion's reins. The horse snorted and crabstepped, eyes rolling as it fought for the bit. The darkmage smiled down at Darien, a cold and gloating smirk.

Darien drew harder on the Onslaught, numbed by its fury. Even the sight of Nashir wasn't enough to unsettle the liquid calm that dampened his emotions. Darien raised his voice, challenging him over the roar of the fire:

"What do you want, Nashir?"

The demon regarded him. "I want your tears. But I'll settle for your blood."

Darien's blade wavered in his hands. He'd forgotten all about Nashir's promise of vendetta for Arden's death.

He brought his blade down to level, daring the man with his eyes. "Then come get it."

The demon barked a laugh, giving the reins of his horse a sharp tug to settle the dancing stallion beneath him. "It's not that easy." Nashir nodded his head toward the smoldering fields. "You seem good at putting out fires. That's good. Where you're going, you'll have need of that skill."

With a cry, he kicked his horse to a gallop, racing away across the burning plain.

Chapter Fifteen
The Double-Edged Sword

The Khazahar Desert, The Black Lands

Meiran staggered down a gritty, brittle hill that kept giving way beneath her feet. Quin moved much more skillfully, half-sliding, half-jogging all the way to the bottom of the slope. Sheet lightning flared across the sky, creating a momentary illusion of sunlight that cast Meiran's shadow out ahead of her. For a split second, Meiran caught a glimpse of Quin's eyes under the brim of his hat as he glanced back in her direction.

They made camp for the night in the open. There was no fire; they didn't need one and, besides, there was no fuel to burn. The evening meal consisted of hard sweetbread and dried fruit, the same as every meal. After dinner, Meiran took a brush to her hair, starting at the ends and working upward. She watched Quin out of the corner of her eye as she moved the brush down the sable length of her hair.

The darkmage was sitting with his knees pulled up against his chest. He closed his eyes and summoned a pale green light that raked over the flesh of his face and roved, groping, over the fabric of his clothes. When he released the light, his skin was freshly shaven, his clothing unsoiled. Even his hair looked clean.

"Why do you rely on the Hellpower?" Meiran asked, working her brush a little further up the lock of hair she was holding. "Wouldn't it be less dangerous to use the magic field?"

At the sound of her voice, Quin twitched his eyebrows. "It keeps me cold," he stated in his usual clipped and melodic drawl.

Meiran kept the brush moving through her hair. The tone of her voice was conversational. "Why the need to feel cold?"

Quin looked at her. "Because I'm a demon. Can you imagine the nightmares that await me every time I close my eyes?"

Meiran lowered her hairbrush in her hand. Using her fingers, she smoothed the long strands down over her shoulders. She cast him a skeptical look. "So, that's how you live with yourself? You numb your emotions with the Onslaught?"

Quin frowned slightly. Then he gave a casual shrug. "I used to drink in order to tolerate my own existence. I had to give all that up. There simply isn't enough wine to sustain the enormity of delusion it takes to preserve my sanity."

Meiran chuckled. "I can imagine. So, instead of drowning your guilt in wine, you immerse yourself in evil. How, exactly, do you justify that?"

The darkmage stared at her flatly. He was leaning over his bent knees, arms draped around them. "When we're drowning, we all have the tendency to grasp at whatever desperate straws are available."

Meiran supposed that made sense. Not the kind of sense she was used to. Darkmage kind of sense. She was getting accustomed to Quinlan Reis. She even felt that she understood him a little bit, at least most of the time. The man was fueled entirely by guilt, grief and apathy. There was no pride left within him at all. Just a false sense of ego he wore like a bandage over his heart.

"I want to hear more about this sensitive you say you loved. What was her name? Amani?"

"Yes. Amani."

The texture of Quin's voice was coarse. Meiran could tell that she'd broached a subject he would much rather avoid.

"Tell me more about Amani."

Quin slouched back, propping his weight on his elbows. He glared at her sideways, focusing on her with one disgruntled eye. "What do you want to know? She was my brother's wife."

"Keep going," Meiran ran her fingers through her hair.

"Amani was the daughter of Prime Warden Renquist," he said.

Meiran's mouth formed a wide *'O'*. She hadn't expected that. She leaned forward, motioning for him to continue.

"My brother and I both pursued her. But I think Amani was always fonder of me. She said I made her laugh, if you can believe it." His lips flirted with a weak attempt at a smile that disappeared just as quickly as it came. "But Braden was like a son to Renquist. The son he'd never had. Everyone expected Braden to follow after him as Prime Warden. So, it really came as no shock when Amani was promised to my brother instead of me."

Meiran nodded, commiserating. "I'm sorry, Quinlan. I can't imagine how that would hurt."

Quin glowered. "I loved my brother very much. But I was also very jealous of him. Braden was the man I always wanted to be. I just didn't know how. He always did everything *right*, never anything halfway. I don't have that kind of patience. Never did."

He glanced down, hiding the emotion in his eyes under the brim of his hat. "Braden's marriage to Amani was just more fuel for my jealousy. That's when I really started hating him. Well, hate is a strong word. I *resented* Braden very much. And then, when I found out that he didn't love her, well…that made me *very* bitter."

Meiran frowned. There was something distorted about the portrait Quin was painting of his brother. It just didn't seem to match the descriptions she'd heard of First Sentinel Braden Reis. From what Meiran had learned—and from what she could glean from Quin—Braden had been almost a paragon of righteousness. A marriage of convenience to advance his career just didn't seem to fit.

"Why did Braden marry Amani if he didn't love her?" she wondered.

Quin shrugged. "Oh, everything went fine until the day Braden found out that Amani was a sensitive. And even then, I think he still would have treasured her with all his heart—if it hadn't been for her father. You see, Braden didn't exactly see eye to eye with the Prime Warden on every issue. Renquist can be an exceptionally callous man, as I'm sure you can believe. I don't know what my brother was plotting but, whatever it was, he didn't want Renquist finding out. He distanced himself from Amani. I think he was afraid."

"Afraid of what?"

"Afraid that his loyalties might be questioned."

"Were they?"

"Perhaps. Amani's death might have actually saved Braden's life. Who knows? After that, Renquist sent him away to Aerysius as an ambassador. I think he suspected that Braden was a threat. I think Renquist wanted my brother very far away from him, yet still within reach."

His voice trailed off. "I'm tired. I'm going to get some sleep. If you want to hear more, you'll have to ask me about it again some other time. Goodnight, Meiran."

With that, he lay on his back, sliding his hat down over his eyes. Meiran sat there gazing across at him for a little while, reflecting on their conversation. Despite herself, she found Quinlan Reis fascinating. He was a darkmage, yes. A Servant of Xerys. But he just didn't seem very evil. Complex, yes. Flawed, most certainly. But evil? She just didn't see it.

Against her better judgement, Quinlan Reis gave her hope.

Perhaps not all demons were as awful as she'd feared.

The next morning didn't dawn. It *darkened.*

Meiran awoke to a world blanketed in thick gray mist that had settled all around like a still and imposing ocean. She could see nothing through that haze, not even Quin. The fog had the effect of dampening all of her senses, not just sight. The world was rendered silent and drab, as if all trace of vitality had been sucked right out of it. It didn't even feel like the world she knew. It reminded her of what the Netherworld had seemed like.

She could hear Quin, even if she couldn't see him. He was rummaging around in his pack. Tentatively, Meiran reached out and probed his feelings, taking the measure of his emotions. But Quinlan Reis had wrapped himself in the chill detachment of the Onslaught; she could sense nothing through the link.

They ate a tasteless, meager breakfast by the wan glow of Quin's magelight. He didn't speak; he hadn't said anything since settling down to sleep. Meiran didn't bother to press him; she could sense his gloom. It was as cold and murky as the fog that encased them. She knew better than to try to draw him out when he was like that. He could clam up tighter than an oyster in its shell, and all the prying in the world wouldn't make him open up until he was ready.

After breakfast, they collected their things and shouldered their packs. Meiran followed as Quin resumed his interminable trek ever northward. At least she assumed they were still on course; the fog was disorienting. For all she knew, they could have doubled back on their path.

It was hours before the haze began to lift. And even then, the mist continued to roam in thick, slow-moving patches. Quin's magelight was like a diffuse, red glow. The silence was explicit, isolating. Meiran walked forward, hugging herself for warmth. Each step she took filled her with a deepening sense of foreboding.

The fog opened up into a flat plain of crisp, cold darkness. In the distance, there was light. Meiran couldn't help herself. She hastened her pace toward the glow, drawn toward it as if by compulsion. She caught up to Quin, drawing past him.

His hand shot out, pulling her back.

"Something's not right."

Meiran frowned.

"Stay here," he commanded, adjusting his hat. He stared at her until she finally nodded, relenting.

Then he stalked off without her. Meiran stayed where she was, letting a wandering cloud of mist envelope her. She strained her ears after the crunching sound of his footsteps.

From the distance came the sound of frantic screams.

Meiran shivered as a wave of panic washed over her. She thought about going after him. Instead, she stayed where she was, dropping to her knees in the dirt. She used the fog to her advantage, trying to make herself as inconspicuous as possible.

The sound of screams grew louder, rising to a shrill, blood-curdling climax. Then there was silence. Followed by another noise: the sound of distant keening.

Whatever had happened, it was over. And it was terrible.

Trembling, Meiran knelt on the grainy black dirt, her senses groping through the fog in despair.

"I need your help."

Meiran flinched, jerking to her feet. Whirling, she found Quin standing right beside her. His face was pale.

She gasped, "What is it? What's happened?"

Quin licked his dry lips. His expression was slack.

"There's been a raid on a village up ahead. Evidently, there's a new warlord in the region making his presence felt. His soldiers came demanding tribute. But the good people of Deryah had nothing left to give. So instead of taking food, the warlord's soldiers took their share of blood. I need your help; you're better at healing than I am."

Meiran started after him, running just to keep up as Quin jogged back toward a patch of light. Lightfields. It wasn't long until Meiran saw the small group of villagers clustered together on the edge of the fields.

The ground was littered with scattered bodies.

Meiran gasped, her hand coming up to cover her mouth.

Many of the corpses had been savagely skinned. Ribs had been separated from the spinal column and pulled out, one by one, sticking up through the flesh, giving the appearance of flayed wings. Some of the victims were just children.

Meiran gagged at the sight, clutching her stomach as the taste of acid rose to her throat. All around, she could hear the sound of moaning and weeping along with tortured, anguished groans.

"They're still alive," she gasped with a sob.

"Some of them," Quin confirmed. "I can't do it all myself. There's too much damage."

Meiran was already in motion, throwing herself toward the first victim at her feet. Trembling, she placed her hands on the man's shoulders, the only place on his body not covered in blood and exposed tissue. She closed her eyes and grappled with the magic field in desperation. Tears leaked down her face; she could feel the man's suffering as if it were her own.

Meiran threw back her head, screaming in anguish as she forced a torrent of healing energies into him. The bones moved, popping back under the skin. Muscle rewove over the ghastly wounds and exposed openings. Flesh squirmed back into place. The pain of the healing was almost incapacitating.

Meiran turned her head to the side and vomited. Then she vomited again. She stood up, wiping her mouth, and forced herself to stagger toward the next victim.

This one was beyond saving.

With a cry, Meiran flung herself toward the next grizzly, tortured soul.

It was a child.

Meiran wept as she laid her hands upon the girl, her fingers shaking so hard she could hardly cup the blood-splattered face. When the pain hit, it almost took her to the ground. Crying out, Meiran screamed until she was hoarse, furiously working to reweave flesh and bone back together. When she was done, she rolled over onto her side. She couldn't get up.

"That's enough!"

Sobbing, Meiran looked up into Quin's contorted face. The darkmage's eyes were moist and reddened.

"You're a sensitive!" he gasped. "Sensitives aren't meant to be healers! You feel everything they feel!"

"It's what I do," Meiran protested, shaking, fighting against the pressure of his hands. There were still many others left to care for. "I'm a Querer! *It's my job.*"

He shook his head, aghast. "Why would they train a sensitive as a Querer? It's inhuman!"

She brought her hand up to her face, scrubbing the tears from her eyes. As she did, her sleeve fell back.

Behind her, a woman screamed. Then everything happened at once.

Meiran whirled as Quin flinched back, his eyes widening in alarm. The woman was pointing at Meiran's arm, screaming at the top of her voice. Meiran looked down and saw the exposed chain on her wrist. She jerked her sleeve back down to cover it, too late.

The woman fell silent. Her eyes glassed over. She slumped sideways and collapsed to the ground.

People surged toward them, shouting, shoving each other out of the way.

Suddenly, Meiran was being hauled to her feet. Quin jumped in front of her, inserting himself between Meiran and the small but enraged mob that confronted them. He started yelling at the top of his voice in his native tongue. The way he ran the words together, Meiran couldn't understand a single thing that he said.

But the villagers understood. They drew back, settling into a mournful, quiet mass. One by one, they turned away, moving back toward the flayed corpses of their loved ones. Meiran was left standing there trembling, alone with Quin. She took his hand and led him back in the direction they had come, shaking in rage and shame.

"You killed that woman," she accused him under her breath. *"Why would you do such a thing?"*

Quin stopped walking, turning to stare at her. His eyes were reddened and intense. "I didn't exactly have a choice, now did I? Unless you'd rather be put to the torch?"

Meiran's lips contorted into a grimace. "That woman did nothing wrong!" she cried out in despair.

Quin raised a finger in front of her face, leaning forward. "Make no mistake, Prime Warden: this was your fault. Now, pray, *never let it happen again.*"

Meiran gaped at him as Quin turned his back on her. She stood there in the darkness, shaking her head, sobbing in muted grief. She could feel the cold rage of his anger through her link with him.

He was right. The woman's death was her fault. Quin had done exactly what his nature demanded: he had acted decisively to neutralize a threat.

Meiran whispered, "Promise me something, Quin."

He was still standing with his back to her, hands on his hips. His shoulders rose and fell with every sharp, ragged breath. *"What?"*

More firmly, Meiran told him, "Never kill for my sake ever again."

He turned to glare at her over his shoulder, gaze narrowed and contemptuous. "I beg your pardon?"

Meiran turned fully toward him, lifting her chin. "I mean it. I swore an Oath of Harmony. 'Always to heal and never to harm.'"

Quin's lips curled in disdain. "I think I've heard it."

Meiran swallowed, unable to tell if he was being

sarcastic or serious. She took a tentative step toward him. "I mean it, Quin. If you kill another person because of me, it will be because I allowed you to. It would be the same as if I'd killed that person myself."

Quin gaped at her. He turned fully around to face her, his hand shooting up to sweep his hat off his head. "Please tell me you don't believe that drivel!"

"I do," Meiran stated adamantly. "Never kill for me again. Even if it means my death."

Quin stared at her hard for a moment, saying nothing. At last, he replaced his hat squarely back atop his head. "Let's make certain I understand this," he said at last. "You want me to escort you through the most dangerous and inhospitable territory in the entire world, where every person you meet—every man, woman and child—is your sworn blood enemy…but you don't want me to lift a finger in your defense?"

"That's right."

He stared at her very long and very hard. "Very well, Madam." He tipped his hat in her direction. "I hope that both you and your swelled sense of righteousness enjoy a glorious death together."

With that, he turned and strode away.

Meiran couldn't believe it. Was he actually going to abandon her there?

"What are you doing?" she called after him, trotting forward.

"What does it look like I'm doing? I'm leaving." He didn't turn to look at her.

Meiran shook her head, throwing her hands up in frustration. *"Why?* I need you!"

Quin whirled around with a snarl. The wind kicked up, billowing his longcoat out away from his legs as he strode back toward her. "You don't need me, Prime Warden. What you need is someone stupid enough to dignify your martyrdom. Trust me, any audience will suffice. But it won't be me."

Meiran stared at him, her mouth open, limbs trembling. Her eyes pleaded with him to change his mind. She could feel him, feel the enormity of his anger. He was suffused with it, and with the chill fury of the Onslaught.

"Quin. You go too far."

"No, Prime Warden. *You* go too far," he growled. "If you want to bind your own hands behind your back with those chains on your wrists, then go right ahead. Feel free. But no one—and I do mean *no one*—is going to bind me! I was there when my brother devised that wretched Oath you flaunt so zealously. It was the last thing Braden ever said—*right before they killed him."*

Meiran gaped at Quin in startled confusion. She hadn't known that the Mage's Oath had been conceived of by his brother. It made sense. But it still didn't change anything.

Tightly, she stated, "Then it sounds like Braden died with a great deal of honor and dignity."

The flood of rage that washed from Quin into Meiran was so forceful that it made her gasp.

"My brother died screaming in agony!" Quin raged. He stalked away a few paces, fists balled at his sides. He kicked out at something on the ground.

At last he turned back to Meiran with a look of desperation in his eyes. He licked his lips, his face a mask of grief. "Don't you understand? The Oath doesn't protect you from becoming someone like me! Generations of mages existed before Braden ever came up with it! If you don't want to end up like me, then just *don't end up like me!* You don't need some irrational and aesthetic Oath to keep you from doing something that's entirely against your own nature to begin with!"

Meiran shook her head. Tears leaked unbidden from her eyes. She didn't believe him. Quinlan Reis was a darkmage. How could he possibly understand?

"You can't convince me that the Oath of Harmony is worthless," she said gruffly. "Darien is a perfect example. Look what happened to him!"

"Don't talk to me about Darien!" Quin snarled. "You weren't there. The truth is, you really don't know a damn thing about him."

Meiran was shocked. *"How can you say that?"*

"Darien swore the Oath," Quin reminded her. "It didn't help him."

His anger was contagious. It was infecting Meiran, now. She could feel it burning at her from within, scorching her heart. Quin was wrong; that's all there was to it. He was a darkmage, a Servant of Xerys. How could he understand? His life and death were lived in complete opposition to everything the Mage's Oath stood for.

"Darien forswore his Oath," Meiran reminded him in a voice suffused with anger. "That's why he became a darkmage."

Quin barked a bitter laugh. "Sorry, darling, but you're getting it backwards. Darien was already a darkmage. That's *why* he broke Oath."

His words stung like a slap because she knew he had to be right. Her anger dissolved into anguish.

"That's not true!"

Quin strode right up to her, planting his feet just inches from her own. The brim of his hat pressed against the flesh of her brow. "Tell me something, because I've been curious about it." He peered intently into her eyes. "Whatever possessed you to give your mage-lover a sword as a fare-thee-well gift? Why a weapon of all things, out of everything else in the entire world you could have possibly given him? Why not a nice warm cloak or a new pair of boots?"

Meiran's face twisted in grief. Tears filled her eyes, blurring her vision. She pulled back away from him, bringing her hands up to cover her face. "You have no idea how often I've regretted that decision," she whispered, her voice shaking. "It was such a stupid thing to do. I acted on impulse!"

"But why?"

How could she explain? She had been so young then, so foolish. In the thrall of a man whose child she carried in her womb. She hadn't had the courage to tell Darien she was pregnant, to send him off like that, possibly to his death. So she'd kept it a secret.

Instead of telling Darien that he was going to be a father, she had given him a sword, instead. Then she had kissed him and sent him off to war. That was the last she had ever seen of him, until the moment he had appeared before her in the gateway. The moment of his death.

"When I gave him that sword, Darien was only just an acolyte," Meiran said. "Weapons were not yet forbidden him. And he'd trained so hard for so many years. Darien always had a passion for the art of the blade…and he was going into battle. So many men we sent to the Front never came back. I chose the gift that I thought would have the most meaning. I didn't think what kind of meaning it would have. I didn't think it through."

Quin's gaze had been softening the whole while she spoke. He stared at her with conviction in his eyes. "You chose the gift that suited him best, Meiran. That's why you did it. Darien was born to be a Battlemage. I think, even then, you understood his nature."

"I've regretted it every day," she insisted. "Giving him that sword…I may as well have been giving him my blessing to strip those chains off his wrists."

Quin shook his head. "You acknowledged the warrior within him. I can think of no greater gift."

Meiran strangled back a sob. "I damned him, Quin. *I damned his soul.*"

"No. You didn't. Darien damned himself." He reached out, touching the marking of the chain on her wrist. "So…am I leaving? Or staying?"

"Stay." She bowed her head. "Please don't leave."

His hand lingered on her wrist. He rotated her arm just a bit, causing the silvery luster to gleam in the light of the clouds. He glanced back up at her, eyes solemn. "Don't ever use those chains to justify weakness, Meiran. I guarantee you, that's not what Braden intended. And, besides, you're the Prime Warden of Aerysius. There's too much riding on your strength."

Chapter Sixteen
Oathbreaker

Qul, The Black Lands

Darien scooped Azár up in his arms, her head lolling against his shoulder. Her eyes were closed. She looked like she might have been sleeping, except for the blood that drained from her scalp, staining the side of her face. Darien reached within, probing her with his mind. What he found was comforting. The head wound was only superficial. There would be no lasting damage.

He used his power to heal her, anyway, and removed all trace of blood and grime.

He carried her, unconscious, all the way back to the village. But he had no idea which house was hers. So he took her instead to his own camp, laying her out upon his blankets. He settled back against a rock, determined to watch over her while she slept.

Sometime during the night Darien fell asleep at her side, his body stretched out beside hers in the dirt. When he awoke the next morning, Azár was gone.

Another week went by. Every day, Darien wandered out into the lightfields to help the people of Qul with the replanting. This time, no one objected. He worked all day, every day, very hard. He rarely saw Azár. And when he did, she usually avoided him. He didn't understand why. It was almost as though her old resentment had returned.

The fields were tilled entirely by hand; there were no oxen or horses available to turn the soil. Just hand-ploughs. He tried a few ways to use magic to lessen the chore. But it turned out to be more taxing than just resorting to muscle. He finally gave up and put his back into the labor. All the while keeping an eye out for Nashir.

But the darkmage didn't return.

Every night, Darien retired exhausted to his makeshift camp, taking comfort in the thanacryst's company. Every morning, he found a hot meal awaiting him, arranged on mats set out around the fire pit. The people of Qul had not yet accepted him, but they had at least begun providing for his needs. The households took turns every day preparing him food. He was grateful; it was a step forward, at least.

That night, Darien cast his tired body down beside the bowls of food and tore into the meal with more urgency than usual. He used his fingers and pieces of griddled bread to scoop the soups and stews into his mouth. He dipped and chewed, hardly tasting the mixture of spices. He was weak, his unwashed fingers shaking as he ate. His body longed for meat, but there was none to be had. His bones ached, either from lack of flesh in his diet or sunlight on his skin. Perhaps a combination of both.

After dinner, Darien leaned back against the demon-hound and stared up into the hostile sky. For some reason, his mood was even more melancholy than usual. His hand scratched absently at the thanacryst's neck as his eyes scanned the flickering lights in the sky above. His mind sought for images in the clouds he could recognize. He found none. Instead, all he found was conflict.

A hand shaking him by the shoulder startled Darien awake. He flinched, reaching for his sword. His arm was captured in a firm grip before he could get his fingers around it.

Darien struggled, opening his eyes to gape up into the face of the last person in the world he expected to see. His breath caught, his heart lurching in his chest. He sat bolt upright. He could feel the blood draining out of his face.

"Is she…? *Did you bring her…?"*

Quin nodded once, eyes lost somewhere in the shadows beneath his hat. "Of course. I told you I would, didn't I?"

Darien sprang to his feet, shrugging his sword's leather baldric on over his shoulder. Beside him, the thanacryst snarled. The beast's hackles were raised, its fierce green eyes glaring at Quin. That surprised Darien; he'd never seen the demon-hound respond so aggressively to another Servant.

"Theanoch!" Darien ordered. The hound gave one last snarl and then sat back down on its haunches. It looked up, gazing intently into its master's face.

Darien was breathing in gasps, his heart floundering. Whether in anticipation or fear, he had no idea. Not that it mattered; Meiran was here, somewhere close by, almost within reach. He couldn't stand it. His entire body quivered with a mixture of anticipation and panic.

"Take me to her."

Quin raised his hand, a small, reassuring smile on his lips. "Relax. You're living proof that love is the elevation of the irrational over reason. We have time. Meiran's not going anywhere."

Darien paced away, scrubbing his hands back through his hair. He leaned forward, taking slow, deep breaths, trying to calm the relentless fury of his pulse. He couldn't relax. Every nerve in his body was raw and frayed.

"What's she like, Quin? Tell me she doesn't hate me."

Quinlan Reis raised his eyebrows. "Of course she doesn't hate you. You're the love of her life, the sad, unfortunate fool. I'm just not certain she's quite up to trusting you as yet. You've both been through a lot. She might need some time to adjust."

Darien just nodded, eyes sliding sideways as he groped to sort through his scattered feelings. He paced away, trying in vain to gather up his thoughts. His heart was still racing, tumbling along at a furious pace. His mind spun in circles.

"I need to see her. *Please."*

Quin pursed his lips, shaking his head. "Not like that. I mean, look at you! You look like something I just dug out of the ground."

Vexed, Darien raked his fingers through his hair, ripping through the snarls. He dove into his pack, rummaging around, finally drawing out a leather cord. He gathered up his long hair, tying it back. Then he took a long gulp of water, swishing it around in his mouth before spitting it out again, sliding his tongue over his teeth. He spread his hands wide with an exaggerated, questioning motion.

Quin shook his head sadly. "It's not good. But I suppose it'll do; you're actually not too awful-looking for a dead man. Shall we, then? I'm actually rather anxious to see how all of this is going to play out."

He turned and strolled away toward the bottleneck canyon. Darien jogged after him, turning back and commanding the thanacryst to stay with a gesture of his hand. The last thing he needed was the demon-dog following after him; Meiran already had enough changes to get used to without the sight of that.

"Did you run into any trouble?" Darien asked, nervously worrying at the wrinkles in his shirt. He tried to smooth them out with his fingers, dusting off a smear of mud on his sleeve.

Quin pursed his lips. "Not any more than one would expect. All in all, I'd say the journey was rather unexceptional. How about yourself? You seem rather worse for wear. Or is there some reason why you're camped in a ditch rather than ruling the hinterlands?"

"You knew?" Darien was surprised. Quin had left long before Renquist had revealed many of his plans.

Quin smiled. "It wasn't hard to guess Renquist's intentions for you. The Khazahar was Braden's and my own ancestral home. As it was, Arden Hannah inherited Braden's lands and legacy. Upon Arden's death, as her successor, the Khazahar has fallen to you. Guard her well." He tipped his hat in Darien's direction.

The narrow path they were following took a sharp turn, switchbacking up into the rocky cliffs above the village. Darien's stomach was tying itself into knots. He could hardly manage to follow the winding trail. He kept glancing up fervently, hoping for a glimpse of Meiran.

"What lands were you promised?" he asked, though he really didn't feel in the mood for conversation. His feet ached to go faster. He wished Quin would hurry and pick up the pace.

The darkmage chuckled. "You're not going to like it. If Renquist's plans ever come to fruition, then Rothscard will be my capital."

Darien gaped at Quin's back. "You were promised the Kingdom of Emmery? That's your territory?" He hadn't known they'd already carved up the Rhen to dispense with as they pleased. The thought brought with it a flare of outrage.

Quin nodded. Then he stopped, gesturing toward the cliff beside them. "She's in there."

Darien turned, noticing for the first time that what he'd thought was just a recess in the rock was actually the entrance to a cave. Suddenly, he felt very lightheaded. He brought his hand up to steady himself against the cliff face. He turned to Quin with a look of uncertainty.

"Go on in," the darkmage prompted. "Take your time. I'll be right here."

Darien nodded, swallowing. "My thanks," he whispered. His eyes sought Quin's face for reassurance. Then he turned and slipped inside the cave.

Darkness encased him. It was colder inside, and silent. Darien conjured a glowing blue mist that groped ahead of him, illuminating his path. The passage was longer than he'd expected, angling sharply back into the rock. It wasn't a man-carved passage, but rather seemed to have been eroded by running water. He pressed his hand against the rough, chill wall and frowned. The rock was light-colored sandstone. It was the first natural-looking stone he had seen since entering the Black Lands.

Darien followed along the low passage, having to walk slightly bent forward, stooping to avoid hitting his head. His magelight spilled ahead of him, leading him forward with an iridescent trail. The passage opened up a bit, allowing him to walk fully upright. Darien slowed his steps, pausing to calm his ragged breathing. His mouth and throat felt terribly dry.

The passage swung to the right. Then it opened up into a room-sized chamber. Darien paused, one hand resting on the rock wall beside his face.

She was right there in front of him.

He couldn't move. He couldn't breathe. He stood there stunned, unable to even blink. His eyes raked over every inch of her, taking in the sable luster of her hair, the perfection of her face. Her gaze was a siren song, and he was helpless.

Darien moved toward her, catching Meiran in his arms as she buried her face against his chest. He held her close, rocking her gently back and forth. He inhaled deeply, breathing in the silken scent of her hair, relishing the familiar fit of her body against his.

Then his lips were on hers, desperate and insistent, making up for lost time. Meiran gasped, her hands sliding down his shoulders. In his arms, he could feel her body stiffen. He sensed the hesitation in her kiss.

His lips stopped moving. Darien drew slowly back, searching her face.

Meiran's skin was flushed, her eyes full of compassion and regret. Her lips quivered, her whole body trembling. Looking in her eyes, Darien felt a gut-twisting wrench of loss. He drew her closer and buried his face in her hair. Closing his eyes, he walled the world away and just held her there.

"Darien."

It was the same, sad voice that haunted his dreams.

He wasn't ready to let her go.

"Darien…I have something to tell you…"

He grimaced, knowing their one, fragile moment was over. He knew another would likely never come. Darien strangled back a curse, resenting the hell out of fate. He squeezed his eyes shut, unable to bring himself to look at her.

He turned his back and wiped away his sorrow on his shirtsleeve. Somehow, he managed to compose himself, collecting what was left of his strangled feelings. He stood there with his back to Meiran, unable to turn around. He didn't want her to see the raw emotion written on his face.

He felt her hand against his. Her fingers laced softly through his own.

He let her lead him by the hand toward a woven rug spread out in the center of the chamber. Stiffly, he lowered himself to sit beside her, his fingers still entwined with hers.

He tried not to stare, but he just couldn't help

himself. It was impossible to look anywhere else.

"I'm sorry," he managed feebly. "It's just..." he shook his head, his voice trailing off.

Meiran placed her other hand on top of his, caressing him softly. Her fingers wandered up his arm, pushing back his sleeve. Revealing the scars hidden there.

Her hand froze.

"Why?"

There was so much hurt in that one, simple word.

Darien felt a surge of shame. He leaned forward, his eyes imploring. "Meiran. I need you to trust me."

Tears fell from her eyes. "I don't think I can," she whispered.

He had to find a way to make her believe him. There was so much riding on this moment. Far more than just his own blackened heart.

"Look at me," Darien insisted. He took her by the chin, directing her gaze upward and into his own. "I died for you, Meiran. And I'd do it all over again. Right now, in a heartbeat."

"Don't."

She struggled to pull away. Darien refused her. He moved his hand behind her head, leaning into her. He stroked his fingers softly through her hair. "I need you to hear me out."

She was crying, her arms wrapped tightly around herself. She sagged against him, her body shuddering with the force of her sobs. "Your words are poison," she moaned into his chest as he hugged her against him. *"Why did I come?"*

Darien pressed his cheek against her, closing his eyes. Gruffly, he whispered, "I've always believed in you, Meiran. Now I need you to believe in me. I know it's hard. Here. I'll make it easier for you."

He released her and drew away. She gazed up at him with wide, bewildered eyes as he staggered to his feet. Darien felt his courage start to slip as he took a step back away from her. He felt a sudden, tangible fear. He had visualized this moment, rehearsed it over and over in his head. He'd thought he had the strength to go through with it. But now that the moment was upon him, Darien wasn't sure that he could.

But there was really no choice. If he stood any chance of gaining her trust, he could hold absolutely nothing back.

Darien closed his eyes and opened his heart and mind to the Onslaught. He let it fill him, bathing his soul in euphoric filth and vile ecstasy. He could feel hell's energies violating him, exciting him. He let the Onslaught sear away the cloak of vitality that covered him, exposing the depths of corruption that consumed both his spirit and his flesh.

Darien raised his hands, spreading his fingers. The skin appeared grayed, sagging. Desiccated. He reached down and lifted his shirt, exposing first his stomach and then his chest. Before Meiran's eyes, he turned slowly around, revealing the full extent of his ruin. Every tortured scar of hell's abuse of him, the decayed corruption of the grave. Before the woman he loved, he bared both his body and his soul, drowning in black depths of shame.

Turning back to face her, Darien lowered his shirt and tore his eyes up off the ground. He released hell's spent energies, shuddering as the Onslaught slipped away from him. Slowly, the chill of death receded as warmth returned to flood his veins. Darien glanced down at his hands.

His flesh was whole again, unbroken. Remade.

His aching spirit yet faltered.

Meiran's face remained fixed. She gaped up at him, gagging slightly, trembling in revulsion. She staggered to her feet.

In a dismal voice, Darien said, "Now you've seen me for what I really am. I'm a demon. A monster."

"So all this,"—she gestured savagely—"is just *illusion?"*

He nodded sadly. "I'm dead, Meiran. I've been dead a long time."

She was crying again. Darien let her. He bowed his head, sagging, his shoulders trembling in shame.

"You're not real!" she raged at him. *"I felt you die!"*

"I'm sorry," he whispered, knowing exactly what he'd put her through.

He took a step toward her, holding her gaze with his own. When she didn't retreat, he took another hesitant step. "I still love you, Meiran. Death can't change that." He reached up and stroked the side of her face. "You've come all this way. Would you please listen to what I have to say?"

"I'll try," she whispered. Her hand rose, wiping her tears.

Darien nodded. He lowered himself back down to the rug that had been spread over the floor of the cave. He waited for her to join him. She sat, not as close as before, hands folded in her lap. Her face was yet very pale, her body still quivering. He felt terrible for her.

Darien said, "I'm going to tell you a story. One I don't think you've heard before."

"Is it about Quin?"

Darien nodded. "And his brother. And me…and even you."

She relented, nodding her permission. He took a deep breath before beginning.

"A thousand years ago, a mage of the Lyceum discovered that the magic field reverses in polarity from time to time. I gather it's just something that happens periodically, every once in a great while. It was due to happen again. Had the Reversal been allowed to proceed, everything ever crafted by magic, along with every mage, would have been destroyed.

"The two Prime Wardens, Cyrus Krane and Zavier Renquist, decided to set aside their differences and collaborate in an attempt to stop it from happening. They forged a secret alliance with the Priesthood of Xerys. They created the Well of Tears in order to gain access to the Onslaught. They needed a power source that could stabilize the magic field at the moment of collapse. Together, they made a covenant with the God of Chaos; that's how the union of the Eight Servants came to be."

"And now you're one of them," Meiran stated with a glare of reproach.

"Aye. And now I'm one of them." He drew in a deep breath to calm his nerves. "Please, Meiran. I need you to listen."

He waited. When she said nothing further, he continued, "Quin and his brother Braden tried to stop them. They believed that the destruction of all things magic would be better than living in a world where Xerys held sway. Quin and Braden failed. The magic field was stabilized, at least for the most part. The Rhen survived intact, while Caladorn was savaged by Quin's mishandling of the Onslaught. But the Well of Tears was sealed, which betrayed the Servants' part of the covenant. The reign of Xerys never came to be."

"Thank the gods," Meiran whispered.

"Don't thank the gods just yet," Darien warned ominously. "We've yet to deal with the full consequences of the fallout. The Servants' covenant was breached, and Xerys was not pleased. And I'm afraid it was all just a temporary fix, anyway. The magic field is ready to depolarize again. And this time, we don't have enough Circles of Convergence left to stabilize it."

Darien leaned forward, taking her hand. Remarkably, she didn't try to pull away.

"Meiran, in just a few months, every mage, including yourself, is going to die. Everything ever created by magic will be lost from this world. All of the works of the temples. The infrastructure of the kingdoms. All of our stores of amassed knowledge—it will all be gone. You, Kyel, Naia…" His voice trailed off. He closed his eyes, summoning the nerve to continue. "There's absolutely nothing we can do to stop it."

The expression on Meiran's face did not change. Very quietly, she whispered, "Then whatever will be, will be."

The courage and determination in Meiran's voice broke his heart. It reminded him again of all the reasons he'd fallen in love with her in the first place.

"I wish it were that simple, Meiran. It's not." His soul was very saddened, very weary. "The people of Malikar, what you know as the Black Lands, depend on magic for survival. I know you've seen it. Without magic, there can be no lightfields. They'll have no way of obtaining food. They'll all die unless you allow them passage into the Rhen."

Meiran wrenched back, snatching her hand out of his grasp. She surged to her feet. *"You're asking me to open up our borders to the Enemy?"*

Darien rose after her. "I am, Meiran. They're not the Enemy. They've lived in a world of darkness for a thousand years. All they've ever wanted was escape into the light."

She backed away from him, circling the rug to put some distance between Darien and herself. She glared at him with the hurt of betrayal in her eyes. Everything about her body language branded him a traitor.

"That's not the whole truth, and you know it," Meiran accused, raising her voice. "They've never come as refugees! They've always come as conquerors, seeking blood and vengeance. Your own father was immolated in their fires! How can you stand there advocating for them? They're savages—brutal and uncivilized, hostile and despicable! Since I've been here, I've seen nothing to convince me otherwise!"

Darien clenched his jaw in anger and desperation. "If you don't let them in, you'll be sentencing them all to death."

"Then so be it," Meiran dismissed him with a wave of her hand. "I am the Prime Warden of Aerysius. My first duty is to the Rhen—not the Black Lands! You should know; you swore the same vows I did, *Darien Oathbreaker.*"

He sucked in a sharp gasp, feeling slapped in the face by more than just the sting of the insult. "You can't be serious, Meiran. They're people! Many are just children!"

He could tell by the set of her jaw just how serious she was. Her face was utterly dispassionate, thoroughly resolved. She stood up straight, composing herself like a queen.

"I'll think on it, Darien. It's not that simple, as you said."

"No, it's not simple," he agreed softly. "But it is what's *right.*"

"So now I have a darkmage lecturing me on my moral duty?" The sarcasm in her voice bit deep.

Darien glared at her in wounded outrage. "If it comes down to it, aye." He started to walk away. But he couldn't help turning back to her, eyes full of hurt. "So, is that all I am to you now? Just a darkmage? Nothing more?"

Meiran scowled, her face hardening. "You're a Servant of Xerys, Darien. What did you expect?"

He nodded thoughtfully. What had he expected? Not this. He lowered his eyes, staring at the ground. His hand fingered the gold tassel that hung from his waist. "We're not all evil, Meiran. We're not despicable. We're just *desperate.*"

Meiran took a few steps away from him then paused, looking back. "I'm sorry, Darien. I need you to go, now." She raised her chin, brushing her hair back away from her face. "You've given me much to think about. Now give me time to consider your petition."

To his dismay, he realized she was no longer the woman he remembered. Before his eyes, Meiran had transformed into the image of the Prime Warden, armoring herself in grace and formality. It stood like a shield between them, shutting him out. There was nothing more he could do.

Darien drew himself up and offered a stiff and proper bow in her direction. "May I return on the morrow?"

"Yes."

He nodded and turned to leave. But something stopped him. He glanced back in her direction. "Please. Do me one favor before I go?"

Meiran considered a moment before nodding.

Darien clasped his hands in front of him, offering her a gesture of supplication. "Please, Meiran. I need to know what happened to our son."

The fortified composure she had managed to gather around herself collapsed like sand. Meiran's hand came up to her face as her mouth contorted into a grimace. She choked back a strangled sob.

"I didn't want to tell you!" she gasped, her eyes glistening. "You were leaving for Greystone Keep. You had enough to worry about!"

Darien moved forward until he was standing right in front of her. He reached out, placing a soothing hand on her arm. "I understand why you didn't tell me. But I do need to know what happened."

Meiran gazed up at him with large, moist eyes. "I had to hide the pregnancy from your mother. I gave birth in the Vale and gave the babe up to be fostered. It was the only recourse I had. I named him Gerald in honor of your father."

"Thank you for that," Darien whispered. His voice was very gruff.

"I visited from time to time. He was a very happy babe. He had your hair. And my eyes. He had the sweetest cheeks…" Her voice broke. She turned away, bringing her hands up to cover her face.

Darien swallowed against the pain. "What happened, Meiran?"

She shook her head, dropping her hands. "I didn't know what happened for a long time. Not until last year. I went looking for the family just as soon as I could. They were hard to find; there's no one left any longer in the Vale. After Aerysius fell, all the villagers fled. I finally caught up with the family in Auberdale."

Darien closed his eyes, dreading to hear what he knew was coming next. He steeled his heart against it.

"Go on."

"Our son died, Darien." Her voice broke. Fresh tears spilled down her cheeks. "He took ill…his lungs filled with water. Darien…I'm sorry…"

He blinked, feeling only cold, bleak emptiness. His vision blurred. He couldn't bring himself to look at her. He felt her soft touch on his shoulder. He took a step away, pulling back out of range.

Meiran pressed on, "The day Aerysius fell, Gerald's foster mother tried getting him up the mountain for help. She told me about an acolyte who aided her, a man with black hair who wore a sword at his back. It was you, Darien…wasn't it?"

He couldn't respond. The entire world had stopped.

"It must have been," Meiran insisted miserably. "It was the same day you returned home from Greystone Keep."

Darien's entire body was trembling. He couldn't see through the tears that collected in his eyes, tears he was too numb to shed. A hard knot pressed against his throat like a garrote, tightening, strangling him in grief.

"I held my son," he muttered raggedly.

He blinked, eyes finally shedding their heavy weight of tears.

"I held my son."

He turned and strode away, bringing a hand up to his mouth. He could hear Meiran's voice behind him, calling out his name.

He ignored her and just kept walking.

Chapter Seventeen
The Demons We Love

Qul, The Black Lands

Quin lingered outside the cave long after Darien had stormed past him. One look at the man's face was enough to warn Quin against trying to go after him. He didn't feel in any particular need of self-abuse. Neither did he have a desire to go inside and confront Meiran; he could practically sense the wake of destruction Darien had left behind. There was probably little he could do to better the situation. Not without getting his head bit off, at any rate. So he sat down on the narrow path with his back up against the rough cliff face. He bided his time, picking up a small rock and tapping out a rhythm with it against another, larger, stone at his side.

Time crept slowly by. Below in the shadows, the village of Qul was beginning to awaken. There was movement in and about the dwellings as people stirred from their beds and went about their morning routines. Women stoked cook fires on the flat rooftops of the houses and began preparing the morning bread. Below, children swept out the courtyards and ran to haul water from the village well. The foul odor of coal soot soon permeated the air, comingling with the aroma of roasting dough and fragrant spices. There were few people out and about in the streets; it was still far too early.

From his vantage, Quin had a very good view of the small camp Darien had made for himself in a ditch at the bottom of the ridge opposite. The campsite was empty; Darien hadn't returned to it. Above, on the stony cliffs, he could see a brief flicker of light. Quin peered intently into the shadows, wondering what could have possibly caused it. It had been there for just a second then was gone, almost like the eyeshine of an animal. But there were very few animals in all of the Black Lands. The flicker was gone and didn't come back again. The cliffs across from him yielded no answers, only shadows.

"Oh, hell," Quin groaned finally, rubbing his tired neck. His legs were sore from sitting so long, confined to the narrow ledge. He stood up, stretching out the aching muscles of his thighs. He stamped his feet until the feeling returned to them. Then, with weary reluctance, he stooped and entered the cave.

"I'm coming in," he called out, figuring he'd better give Meiran some type of warning. In a much quieter voice, he added, "whether you want me here or not."

He walked forward stiffly, taking his time, letting his magelight wander ahead to chase the gloom of the passage away. He listened, hearing nothing. The cave was quiet and austere, infinitely still.

When he came to the room-like chamber, Quin drew up and lingered in the doorway, his magelight collected in a glowing pool directly beneath his feet. Meiran glanced up at him from where she sat on the rug, lit by sinuous strands of mist she'd gathered around herself like a glowing azure sigil. In that cold, wavering light, Meiran looked very pale and very fragile. He could tell she'd been crying.

Quin moved forward hesitantly, lowering himself beside her on the rug. Meiran said nothing, but the look in her eyes was one of unspoken reproach. Quin frowned, skewing his lips as his eyes surveyed the terrain of her face.

"I take it that didn't go so very well."

Meiran shook her head, eyebrows knitting together in a frown. "Why didn't you tell me?"

"Tell you what, my dear?" Quin reached up, removing his hat from his head and resting it upside down in his lap.

"That he'd be so *different.*"

"Is he?" Quin shrugged dismissively. "I really wouldn't know, now would I?"

He'd never known Darien Lauchlin in life. While Darien had been busy immolating Malikar's legions at Orien's Finger, Renquist had stationed Quin deliberately far away. He'd spent the entire war mired in Bryn Calazar, tasked with the impossible goal of resurrecting the Lyceum's lost Circle of Convergence. Not once had he come face to face with the man he now considered his closest relative.

Quin had only met Darien for the first time in the dark reaches of the Netherworld. Not the best place to get to know someone but, then again, not the worst place, either, if you wanted to truly judge the colors of a soul.

What had struck Quin most about him was how much Darien reminded him of Braden. He was just a more turbulent version of the man. Despite the gap of generations that separated them, much of his brother's character and mannerisms had endured in his bloodline. Quin could see Braden in the way Darien carried himself, the way he moved. That look of dangerous intensity that came so naturally to his eyes. The decisive, cool logic he employed. Like his ancestor, Darien was born to be a warrior. What he lacked was Braden's sense of grace and serenity.

"In some ways, he hasn't changed at all," Meiran remarked. "That's the hardest part. But the words coming out of his mouth…" She shook her head. "Darien was always an idealist. It's like he's abandoned every principle he ever had. I don't understand what could have changed him so much."

Quin scratched at the unkempt whiskers on his cheek. "Is what he's asking really so unreasonable? I mean, it seems entirely within the scope of your Oath of Harmony. Or does 'Always to heal and never to harm' only apply to citizens of the Rhen?"

Meiran shot a contemptuous glare in his direction. "Spoken like a true darkmage, Quinlan. Is your tongue just as poisoned as Darien's?"

Quin couldn't help the flicker of smile that jumped instantly to his lips. "You have but to taste to find out."

"Ugh," Meiran groaned, grimacing as if in pain. She raised a hand as if to fend him off. "You're just as tactless as you are wretched."

This time, Quin didn't try to suppress the grin he felt. "Why, Prime Warden, you do bring out the best in me."

Darien didn't return to camp. Instead he wandered into the cold and dismal waste, the demon-dog trotting behind. He walked with his head thrown back, staring up at the hostile sky. Strobes of lightning flickered deep within the clouds' murky depths. The sky's unrest mirrored the turmoil in his heart. It was oddly comforting to know he wasn't alone.

Above, lightning flared in a shower of sparkling wrath, followed by a swell of thunder. Darien stopped walking, gazing up through the afterglow left behind in his vision. He shook his head, grimacing against his anger.

He fell to his knees, throwing his head back, and wept. His shoulders quaked. He clenched his fists until his nails bit the skin of his palms. But the pain didn't help. It was insignificant next to the ache of knowing how far he'd fallen. He blamed Meiran, hating her for rejecting him after all he'd done. He blamed fate, blamed the gods. Hated them all, hated everything. Most of all, he hated himself.

Somehow, it seemed vastly appropriate when rain began to fall. A needling rain, driven by an icy wind, relentless and without mercy. Darien didn't try to escape it. Instead, he spread his arms out at his sides. He tilted his head back, letting the rain wash over his face. A soothing comfort settled in, his grief overshadowed by purpose, despair replaced by a sense of trajectory.

He rose and walked back in the direction he had come, making his way back toward his camp as the downpour subsided. Once there, he dug down deep in his pack, finding the clean, dry robes Renquist had provided him. Darien withdrew the folded garments, holding them out reverently in his hands. For the first time, he fully appreciated the significance of the robes. They were far more than just a gift; they were a symbol. A symbol he could no longer afford to ignore.

He reached up and removed the brooch that held his cloak in place, letting the wet fabric fall off his shoulders. He shrugged out of his shirt, wadding it up and throwing it down in the dirt at his feet. Then he pulled the indigo robes on over his head. He trailed his fingertips over the delicate, embroidered star. So much like the emblem of dead Aerysius he had once worn at his back.

That had been a lifetime ago, a different life.

He wasn't that man anymore.

Darien returned the next day to the cave.

He didn't feel the same anxiety he'd felt before. Those feelings had been washed away, replaced by the calm clarity of resolve. He didn't hesitate as he ducked inside and followed the low passage toward the back. He paused at the entrance of the room-size chamber, collecting himself as he regarded Meiran in silence.

She was standing next to Quin, garbed in an azure pool of magelight. Darien recognized the color; it was his own legacy, passed down to Meiran through the Soulstone. Only, she had come by it legitimately. The magelight Darien wove was like a lingering reflex, only made possible by the Onslaught.

When Meiran noticed him, Darien dropped to his knees, bending forward in the formal gesture of obeisance demanded by the office of the Prime Warden. He maintained that position, forehead pressed against the floor, palms beside his face. His mind was focused, his heart free of tension. It beat a deliberate cadence in his chest.

"You may rise." Her voice was rich and clear.

Darien regained his feet with a blademaster's grace. He reached up and drew the strap of his baldric over his shoulder, setting sword and scabbard aside. Then he turned back to Meiran with a questioning look.

Her anxiety was visible on her face. It was obvious she could sense the change in him, and it was profound enough to give her pause. She glanced sideways at Quin before finally nodding wary permission.

Darien approached Meiran carefully, one hand behind his back, the other held clenched at his side. When he stood in front of her, he took her hand and brought it up to his lips, pressing a kiss against her fingers in the manner of the clans.

"Nur a'yiid," he said. *Morning's grace.* He released her hand, drawing himself up to his full height. "Thank you for receiving me."

Meiran gazed up at him with grave concern in her eyes. She swept her gaze over him, taking in the significance of his new garments. Her eyes lingered on the emblem on his chest. After long seconds, she asked him simply:

"Why?"

There were so many subtle layers of meaning woven into the various textures of that word. He didn't know which Meiran wanted addressed. Darien stood looking at her for a moment, allowing himself one last opportunity to enjoy the sight of her. Finally, he spread his hands. "These are the formal robes of the Lyceum of Bryn Calazar. They were presented to me by Prime Warden Zavier Renquist."

"I know what they are," Meiran snapped. "What I asked was, why?"

Darien nodded, now understanding her meaning. "I decided it was important that there be no misunderstandings between us. I want you to be absolutely certain of who I am and what I stand for. And why I'm asking what I am."

The look on Meiran's face didn't falter. "So, you've finally picked sides, is that what you're telling me? I take it by your choice of attire that you didn't pick my side. Yesterday I branded you an Oathbreaker. I suppose 'turncoat' would be more appropriate."

"Call me what you like," Darien shrugged. The barb of her insult failed to find purchase in his feelings. "Just so you're aware, Zavier Renquist proclaimed me overlord of this region. But I want to be perfectly honest with you, Meiran. I don't have Renquist's permission to treat with you. Any agreement we make, I'll take back to him with my full support and recommendation. But I can't guarantee anything. That's the best I can offer at this time."

Meiran nodded. "Then it will have to do. Please, have a seat. You'll have my response."

He followed her gracefully to the floor, Quin lowering himself to his knees at his side. Darien sat cross-legged with his elbows draped over his thighs, hands clasped together in front of him.

Meiran wore her hair up in a knot of elaborate braids. She looked every inch a Prime Warden, despite her ragged attire. Meiran, too, had armored herself for combat in her own subtle way.

She gazed into his eyes, her expression fortified by her calm inner strength. "I thought about what you said. Here is my decision: I can't assume the risk of opening up our borders to the Enemy and letting your hordes pour unchecked into the Rhen. For all I know, you could be lying. Your entire story might be just a ploy to slip your legions past our defenses."

"I speak the truth, Meiran. You of all people would know if I were lying."

"I know you *think* you're telling the truth," Meiran contradicted. "But what if you're the one who's been lied to? Have you even considered that possibility?"

Darien shook his head. "No one is lying, Meiran. Although you've no idea how much I wish we were. Look. There must be some compromise we can negotiate. What if we offer to disarm? Leave our armor and armaments behind? Then we would be entirely at your mercy. That should give you some reassurance."

Meiran shook her head. "No. You would still have seven Unbound mages to bolster your armies."

Darien nodded, understanding her reservations. He didn't know what he could offer that might alleviate the threat posed by even one Unbound darkmage. He took a moment, thinking. At last he offered warily:

"Quin and I could surrender to you. You could use our lives as assurance against the others."

But Meiran wasn't having it. "No. Renquist could just sacrifice the both of you to cut his losses."

Darien scowled in frustration. "If you won't compromise at all, you'll give us no choice but to invade."

"What if there's another way?"

Darien glanced at her sideways, eyes narrowed in suspicion. "What are you talking about?"

Meiran raised her chin. "What if there's a way to lift the curse over the Black Lands?"

Darien looked at Quin. The darkmage shrugged. Apparently he, too, had no idea what Meiran was talking about. Quin cleared his throat, sitting up a little straighter. "And how, my dear, do you propose going about doing that?"

"I don't know," Meiran admitted. "But I think it's worth looking into. Don't you?" she added, turning back to Darien.

He shifted his posture, uncertain what to think. It almost seemed like a false trail meant to deter him from his purpose. But that wasn't a tactic Meiran would use. He argued, "If there was a way to remove the curse, surely in a thousand years, someone would have come up with it already."

Beside him, Quin fidgeted. "Not necessarily…"

Darien's eyes probed him sharply. "What are your thoughts?"

"Well, my first question would be, what's causing the curse to begin with? I mean, it's obviously not a curse; there has to be some rational explanation for it. So, what kind of force is holding the cloudcover over Malikar and darkening the sun? It's not the Onslaught, because the clouds persist even when the Well of Tears is sealed."

He was right. Some other force was maintaining the cloud cover in place.

"Then what is it?"

Quin shrugged. "I don't know…it's almost as if the Onslaught enclosed Caladorn in some sort of bubble, trapping in the clouds and keeping out the light. I'm not saying that's what it is, but it's as good an analogy as any. So…what if we could pop that bubble?"

"How do you propose doing that?"

Quin rose to his feet. He paced away a few steps then started circling the rug as he spoke, gesturing with his hands. "The Arcanists of Aerysius were always a pathetic lot compared with those of the Lyceum. When Bryn Calazar was destroyed, many of the most powerful artifacts ever created were lost to humanity. But an even greater loss was the knowledge of how to create those artifacts in the first place. I don't mean to brag but, in my own time, I was considered the foremost talent of my order. If there's ever been a mage capable of challenging the curse over the Black Lands, well…that mage is me." He stopped pacing and spread his hands.

"All right," Darien allowed. "What would you need?"

"First, I'll need access to Athera's Crescent. And for that I'll need a living Harbinger or Querer."

Athera's Crescent. Darien had forgotten all about that ancient relic. Just the mention of it filled him with hope. Not only for Quin's purpose, but it was also possible they might find one or more living mages educated enough to help their cause. He was thrilled with the idea, except for one part.

"So, you'll be needing Meiran to go with you."

Quin glanced back at him and nodded.

Athera's Crescent was an artifact so significant and complex that an entire order of mages had been dedicated to its study: the Order of Harbingers. There were no Harbingers left alive in the entire world, at least none that he was aware of. The next best thing would be a Querer such as Meiran. It had always been the Order of Querers who roamed the land, making themselves available for Query, or petition, by the populace. Most Queries involved healing. But Querers had to be prepared for almost anything, which was why they studied bits and pieces of the lore of every order. Of their number, Meiran alone would have the most knowledge of Athera's Crescent.

Darien turned toward her. "It's up to you. Are you willing to support him?"

"I think it's the only option we have," she responded with calm certainty.

Darien drew in a long, slow breath. He took a moment to deliberate. At last, he said, "I can give you four months. But after that…we'll be coming. Whether we're invited or not."

Meiran rose from the ground. "Four months," she agreed. She didn't sound very happy about it.

Darien followed her to her feet.

Meiran said, "Quin, would you mind waiting outside? I'd like to speak with Darien alone."

Hearing that request, Darien felt his stomach tighten. The cloak of dispassion he'd adopted slipped just a fraction, like a crack in the armor of his soul. He knew what was coming; it was inevitable. He'd thought he was prepared to hear it. But he was not, he realized sadly.

"Of course," Quin muttered. He fumbled for his hat. Then he turned and slouched away into the shadows of the passage.

Darien found himself alone with Meiran. He glanced down, staring at his worn leather boots. "You don't have to say it."

"Yes, I do."

"Then make it quick." He glanced off to the side, focusing his stare behind her on the wall of the cave. He couldn't bring himself to look at her.

Meiran gazed up at him, her arms held crossed against her chest. Her eyes were full of sadness and resolve.

"You were once my greatest love and the father of my child. But that was before you betrayed everything we ever stood for. Now…you've gone somewhere I can't follow, Darien. I will always love the man that you were. But I can no longer love the man you've become."

"You mean the monster I've become."

He pivoted and stalked away, pausing only to snatch up his sword and scabbard. Then he left her, striding briskly out of the cave.

Meiran lingered alone in the chamber a long time after he was gone. She stood there, head bowed, heart heavy with sorrow. She didn't cry, which surprised her. Not only did she feel the full measure of her own guilt and grief, but she also felt Darien's, a heavy weight that pressed against her chest. Because of their link, she felt his pain just as tangibly as she felt her own. She barely noticed when Quin slipped silently back into the room. He held his hat in his hands, eyes downcast.

"I'm terribly sorry," he offered awkwardly, moving toward her across the floor. "It's always hardest to cast aside those demons we love." He paused, looking patently uncomfortable. "Which leads me to wonder…are you still coming with me? Or have you decided to forgo the pleasure of my own disreputable company?"

Meiran regarded him silently, probing his intentions with her mind. Quinlan Reis did not seem to be hiding anything. His emotions were straightforward and reasonable.

Meiran reached down and scooped up her pack, striding toward the entrance to the cave. "Where exactly are we going?"

"Back to Ishara to use the transfer portal there," Quin answered as he shouldered his own pack. "Hopefully, we can transfer directly to the Isle of Titherry. If not, gods help us, we'll have to find another way. Which will probably involve a ship."

Meiran peered at him. "Don't tell me you're afraid of water?"

"Water? Of course not." Quin shook his head.

"But I do become atrociously seasick."

Meiran cast a blue swath of gleaming magelight across the floor, making her way out of the cave. Once outside, she found the world encased by mist. Thick, billowing fog roved slowly over the ground, shutting out the rest of the world.

"How convenient," Quin muttered. "Maybe he didn't want a long goodbye."

Meiran glanced at him. It was possible the mist had been conjured, but unlikely. Darien simply wasn't the type to cower beneath a fogbank. She let her magelight wander forward, illuminating their path down the face of the cliff. "Goodbyes have already been spoken."

Quin followed behind her down the path, complaining, "Well, *I* didn't get a chance to say goodbye."

"Stop brooding."

"I hate to say this, but I'm having a hard time being silent."

"Then speak your mind," Meiran snapped.

The darkmage gestured with his hands as he talked and walked. "Now, I'm usually not one to judge, but looking at your situation from my lowly and contemptuous perspective, it just seems…well…"

"Well, what?"

"Well, it just seems to me as though you're being rather hypocritical."

"Hypocritical?" she echoed, turning back to him with a look of amazement. "How so?"

"Well, by all appearances, you just set aside a man who loves you more than anything just because his soul is damned. A situation, I'd like to point out, he got himself into because of you."

Meiran stopped walking, feeling a sudden heat of anger flush her cheeks. She turned back to glare her resentment at him. "That's not fair. I never asked Darien to do what he did. Committing his soul to Chaos was his decision, not mine. I would have never asked that of him."

Quin spread his hands. "That's all very well, but that doesn't change the fact that he did it for you. How does it feel, Prime Warden, to break the heart of the same man who damned his own soul to rescue yours?"

His words were like a slap in the face. She reeled from the sting of the insult. "That's a disgusting oversimplification, and you know it."

"But it's the truth. If you find it either simple or disgusting, then I'm sorry. The truth is often exactly what we don't want to hear."

Meiran ran her eyes over him with a contemptuous look. "You really are his creature, aren't you?"

"Actually, Prime Warden, right now I'm doing *you* the favor."

"How so?"

Quin set his hat back on his head. He adjusted the brim carefully until his eyes were half-hidden beneath it. "I'm trying to talk you out of a decision that you'll likely regret for the rest of your life. However short that life may be. Why, just think of—"

There was a loud *crack* followed by a thick splatter of blood. Quin's eyes rolled back in his head as he collapsed to the ground. Before Meiran could react, his body slipped sideways, falling over the side of the embankment.

Meiran threw herself down against the trail, bringing her hands up to ward her head even as she summoned a glowing shield around her body. Her eyes groped through the murky darkness, but the fog was like an insulating curtain, cutting her off from the rest of the world.

"Quin!" she screamed into the shadowy ravine where his body had disappeared.

Two dark forms emerged from out of the mist directly in front of her. Meiran scrambled away from them, surrounding herself in a protective aura of blue energies. Terror chilled her heart. There was very little she could do to protect herself. She was no Sentinel, trained in the subtle gradations somewhere between attack and defense.

A large, bearded man reached out to catch her by the arm. She whirled away from him—into a third man standing right behind her. The grisly warrior surged forward, wrapping his arms around her and pulling her tight against him. She could smell the rank odor of his armor.

Immediately, Meiran lashed out with the force of her mind, shoving him off her with a whiplash draft of air. At the same time, she threw up a shield, blocking the strike of the other man's blade. She shoved him forcefully away, hurling him back against the rocks. The man with the sword lost his footing, teetering on the edge of the cliff as he groped desperately for balance.

Meiran gasped, feeling a sudden rush of panic. She couldn't let him go over. She couldn't let her magic be the cause of any man's death.

Meiran reached out and caught her attacker by the hand, wrenching him toward her and away from the cliff's edge. She fell backwards onto the path, the man she had saved falling on top of her with the full weight of his body. She struggled, trying to wriggle herself out from under him.

The man raised the hilt of his sword and brought it down hard, driving the pommel with force into her temple. The world flared briefly, brilliantly red.

Then everything went black.

Chapter Eighteen
Parting the Veil

Glen Farquist, The Rhen

Kyel gazed up into the face of the Goddess of the Eternal Requiem. The marble statue seemed to be condemning him with its sightless gaze. Her arm was outstretched toward him, perfect in every detail, every ripple of muscle and fabric. The hand was open, inviting.

Kyel considered the gesture. He brought his own hand up and caressed the cold stone fingers. "I can't imagine what it was like for him."

Naia's face darkened. *"It was awful."*

Kyel nodded, looking down. He had figured as much. The Oath of Harmony had meant everything to Darien. He glanced back up at the statue, finding its empty gaze terrifying. All of the atrocities Darien had committed had been set into motion in this room, with the knowledge and blessing of this very goddess. Perhaps that's where the blame should rightfully be laid: at the feet of this cold, inhuman effigy.

"Are you sure you want to go ahead with this?"

Naia's voice interrupted his thoughts. He forced his attention back to her. "What choice do we have left?" That was the point; they didn't have any. Especially after their meeting with the Conclave had so thoroughly tied his hands. "What are we going to do if she strikes out against us?"

"We can retreat through that portal." Naia pointed in the direction of the far corner, to a slender arch that appeared to open into a curtain of shadow.

Kyel didn't like the looks of that passage. He took a step toward it. "What's in there? Where does it lead?"

"It leads to the Hall of the Masters," Naia informed him. "It's warded. The spirit of one so damned as Sareen could never survive more than a few steps beyond the portal's entrance. Her soul would begin to unravel the moment she walked in."

"I suppose it's as good a plan as any." Kyel brought a hand up to scratch his beard. "The Conclave certainly hasn't left us too many options. Without Meiran, we're little more than their puppets. So when do we start?"

Naia glanced sideways at him. "In just a few minutes. I want to conduct a test first."

"Test? What kind of test?"

She was moving toward a ledge filled with small votive candles. A few were already glowing with soft, wavering flames. "I want to make certain we're not wasting our time."

She stooped down, lifting a small candle. With her other hand, she grasped a metal striker. She closed her eyes, her lips moving in silent prayer. Then she paused, hesitating for just a moment before depressing the striker.

The candle's wick flared instantly to life with a warm, vivacious flame. Naia smiled as she gazed down at the fragile light in her hand. Shielding it from the air, she bent forward and placed the glowing candle beside the others on the shrine. Then she moved to select another.

Naia lifted the next votive candle up in front of her. Once again, she closed her eyes as she prayed, then depressed the striker. The wick caught instantly. Another warm glow erupted in the cup of

Naia's hand.

But then something altogether different happened. A shadow passed over the candle's flame. The dance of light sputtered, glooming. It changed, turning a putrid shade of green. Naia's eyes shot up, fixing on Kyel.

"Sareen's soul is still in the keeping of her master." Naia clenched her fist, crushing both candle and flame. She worked her fingers together, crumbling the tallow. She opened her hand and spilled out the remains.

"What are you doing, Naia?"

Kyel spun toward the shrine's entrance, his heart lurching at the sound of Luther Penthos' voice. He found the old man standing at the top of the steps, one hand on the shrine's great oaken door. His face was pinched into a frown of concern.

"Father," Naia gasped, sweeping toward him.

The High Priest of Death lingered in the doorway. He was staring back and forth between Kyel and Naia with cold conjecture in his eyes.

Naia moved up the stairs, her black cloak billowing out behind her. When she reached her father, she drew up and embraced him. The old man made no attempt to return the gesture.

"I'm lighting votive candles, Father," Naia explained, releasing him. She glanced back at Kyel.

"Votive candles? For whom?" Naia's father looked profoundly skeptical.

Naia shrugged, retreating down the stairs. She walked with her hands clasped in front of her, a tranquil smile on her lips. She appeared unbothered by her father's abrupt appearance.

"The first is for Mother." She stood before the shrine, indicating the first glowing candle on the ledge. It still gleamed with a wavering dance of light.

"The second is for Sareen Qadir. To make certain that her soul is yet confined to the Netherworld."

She dropped her hand, pointing downward at the scattered tallow on the floor. She nudged at a cake of it with her foot.

Her father nodded slightly. "That is wise, I suppose. What of the third?"

"The third," Naia echoed. Reaching down, she took an unlit votive candle into her hand and grasped a metal striker. "The third candle is for Meiran Withersby. To make certain she's still alive."

"And does she live?"

Holding the candle up before her, Naia muttered another brief, unspoken prayer and depressed the striker's mechanism. Another spark flared into being, wafting directly toward the candle's wick. The spark missed, arcing downward to the floor. Naia repeated the motion, producing another spark. This, too, had no effect.

"I conclude that the Prime Warden is most likely still alive." She set the items in her hands down upon the ledge of the shrine.

Luther Penthos seemed accepting of the news. A thin smile spread on his lips. A proud smile. There was still a trace of sadness in his eyes, though, enough for Kyel to detect. No matter how impressed the priest might be with his daughter, he still regretted losing her.

"That's good news." Naia's father leaned forward, pressing a kiss against her forehead. "Continue with your prayers, my dear. Just please keep me informed of any changes."

"I will, Father."

Nodding, the High Priest of Death released his daughter and turned back toward the stairs. As soon as his foot reached the first step, he stopped and turned toward Kyel.

"And are you here to offer prayers, as well, Grand Master Kyel?"

Kyel shook his head. "No, Your Eminence. I'm not."

"Please remember that the Conclave is awaiting your answer. Are you still considering their request?"

"I am," Kyel answered stiffly.

Naia shot Kyel a questioning look as her father took his leave. She waited until the old man was well out the door before striding across the shrine.

"What is this about the Conclave?"

"It's nothing," Kyel grumbled. He wished Naia hadn't been made privy to that particular exchange. He intentionally hadn't told her; Naia was upset with him enough already.

"Don't be evasive," she admonished. Her eyes glimmered with impatience. "Out with it. What's going on?"

Kyel sighed, outmatched by her stubbornness. He ran a hand through his beard. "The Conclave wishes to address my training as a Sentinel. They feel that I haven't progressed as far as they think I should have."

"You can't be serious! The audacity—!"

Kyel cut her off. "We're beholden to the Conclave now, Naia, not the other way around. At any rate, I have a feeling they're going to want me to make a change. I'm not sure what kind. I suppose I'll be finding out."

Naia raised a finger, eyes gleaming with outrage. "Don't let them control you, Kyel. You may have yielded some authority to them, but that doesn't change the fact that you're still your own man."

"Not anymore," Kyel said. "Not unless we can get Meiran back. The truth is, I'm inclined to agree with them. I learned more in the few months I spent with Darien than I have over the past two years."

Naia looked troubled by his statement. "We both know Darien was much too hard on you."

Kyel hadn't shared his feelings with Naia on the matter. At least, not recently. Not since his feelings had changed. "Darien knew exactly how much time he'd have with me. And he also knew it wouldn't be enough."

Naia's frown deepened, but she nodded anyway. She gazed up at Kyel with turbulent eyes. "So, you've forgiven him?"

Kyel had to think a moment before answering that question. Like everything else, it was complicated. "For the way he treated me? Aye." Kyel's gaze hardened, his jaw tightening. "But not for what he did to you." He looked down. "For that, I'll never forgive him."

Naia reached up and patted his arm with a valiant attempt at a smile. "It's getting late. We need to start."

She turned away, striding across the floor toward the entrance to Death's Passage. "Bar the door."

Kyel followed her directive, moving quickly up the stairs and bringing the wooden beam down across the doorway, preventing anyone from accessing the chamber while they worked. He joined Naia at the base of the steps.

"Do you still remember the Stricture?"

Kyel nodded. "No talking to the dead."

"No *interacting* with the dead," she corrected him. She reached up, physically turning his face toward hers until he was looking into her eyes. "Not in any way."

Kyel nodded. He understood. She smiled, patting his cheek. Naia took his hand, guiding him forward. As they moved across the portal's threshold into Death's Passage, the world flickered. Kyel stumbled, feeling suddenly unstable on his feet. He could feel the small hairs on the back of his neck standing upright. No matter how many times he entered, he never grew accustomed to the Catacombs.

The light was different, surreal. Low-lying fog swirled around their feet, retreating from their footsteps. The air seemed different: thin, stretched. There was a distinctive odor to the place, like the smell of an old tomb.

The wheeled bier they had lain Sareen upon was still resting where they'd left it, pushed back into a dark recess of the passage. They hadn't moved her since arriving in Glen Farquist. The corpse lay draped with its thin shroud, features only visible in silhouette.

Naia moved to the handle of the cart, motioning Kyel toward the rear.

He gave a good push, putting his back into it. At first the wheels didn't want to give. With another shove, the cart lurched forward, Naia tugging at the long wooden handle. The wheels creaked, the cart shuddering. Kyel pushed as, together, they escorted Sareen's bier out of the Catacombs and back to the shrine.

Reality shivered as they crossed back over the threshold into the world of life. This time, Kyel was ready for the transition. He pushed on the cart, keeping his feet moving until they were on the other side of the room. He was grateful for the return of the shrine's golden light and for the scent of uncorrupted air.

Naia set the cart's handle down on the floor and moved to Sareen's side. She peered down at the corpse's shrouded form, her expression soft and reflective. Kyel took up position on the other side of the bier, watching as Naia lifted the edge of the fabric and folded it back, turning it down to expose the face beneath.

The corpse still looked fresh.

Kyel was mildly shocked. Sareen had been dead for almost a month, and nothing had been done to preserve her body. Nevertheless, the corpse looked as though only hours had passed since the heart had stopped beating. Thus was the nature of the Catacombs: beyond the Veil of Death, time and distance had little meaning. But it was one thing to acknowledge such power, quite another to actually experience its effects.

"She's beautiful," he commented in wonder.

Naia raised her eyebrows. "She's dangerous," she corrected him.

Kyel nodded. He had no trouble remembering Arden Hannah and the evils that woman was capable of despite her feral allure. He tore his eyes away from Sareen's perfect face.

"How do we do this?"

Naia crossed her arms in front of her, suddenly pragmatic. "We need to heal her body. Give her spirit a place to return to."

Kyel frowned. "How do you heal death?"

"Death cannot be healed. All we can do is try to heal the flesh itself. I can't part the Veil of Death. Only the goddess can do that…or Xerys, if he is so inclined."

That did bother Kyel. The lines of his forehead creased. "So, now we're aiding Xerys?"

"We are *not* aiding Xerys," Naia insisted with a toss of her head. "We are simply helping Xerys help us."

Kyel didn't like the sound of that. He took a moment, muddling her logic in his mind. "There's a distinction?"

Somehow, he doubted that there was.

"We have to begin before my father returns," Naia changed the subject. She offered one hand out to Kyel. The other, she placed on Sareen's chest. "I'm going to probe her. Come. I want you to feel her through me."

Kyel reached over the corpse, accepting Naia's offered hand. He closed his eyes, opening himself up to the magic field. Immediately, he felt the warmth of the currents moving through him, through Naia, penetrating Sareen's lifeless body. The image that was returned painted a dismal picture of the cadaver's state. The body was lifeless, breathless, its fluids clotted and pooled, collected in the depths of the cavities. Every muscle was lax, devoid of tension. Deep within, there was only a constant, echoing stillness. There was nothing at all that spoke of life or vitality.

Worse, the body had deteriorated more than he'd expected, far more than it appeared on the surface. Through Naia's probe, Kyel could feel the breakdown of tissues, the collapse of capillaries, the destruction of nerves and fibers and connections.

Kyel looked up, feeling the retreat of hope.

"Did you get a sense of what we're dealing with?" Naia asked.

Kyel gazed down at the corpse. "I think so. There's nothing to be done, is there?"

To his surprise, Naia shook her head. She was animated, vibrant. It took Kyel a moment of disorientation to realize that she was very much in her element. This was death itself they faced, and to Naia, death was no adversary. Far from it; it was her area of specialty.

"There are two types of damage we'll be working through," Naia lectured, pacing away. "There's the wound that was the cause of death. Then there's the natural changes that occur as soon as the heart stops beating. Both types of damage will need to be overcome."

"I'll heal the wound," Kyel offered. Out of everything he had sensed through Naia's probe, that seemed by far the simplest task they would be performing. "You're more familiar with the other…things. The changes."

Naia smiled, pacing back toward the bier. She reached out her hand and caressed a lock of hair back from Sareen's face. "It's not going to be that straightforward. We'll need to go about this systematically if we're going to have any chance at all." She turned, pacing away again. "First, we must reverse any decomposition that's already begun. Then we can start worrying about other things: stability of the veins, fluid distribution, things like that. We'll save the biggest challenges for last."

"Which are…?" To Kyel, it all sounded quite impossible.

"Healing the brain enough to carry out basic functions. Maintaining body temperature, pulse, respiration. We'll have to watch her closely for a while to make certain the organs function properly."

Kyel shook his head, staggered by the enormity of the task ahead of them. "I wouldn't have thought of any of that. Are you certain this is even possible?"

"I'm not," Naia admitted, almost physically deflating. "As far as I'm aware, this has never been attempted before. At least, not for centuries."

She squeezed his hand. Kyel cast a doubtful look her way.

"The wound itself is going to be one of the last things we worry about," Naia continued. She placed her hand over Sareen's chest, where the ghastly rent had been sewn together and bandaged.

"And then…what?" Kyel demanded, gesturing with his hands. "Do we just wait and see if she wakes up?"

"That's all we can really do," Naia confirmed with a shrug. She was gazing down into Sareen's face with a whimsical expression. She fussed with another wayward curl, smoothing it back.

"Are you ready?" she asked softly.

Kyel knew he was not. Nowhere near ready, not for any of this. For anything *like* this. The vicars of the temples were right: he needed to intensify his studies. Quickly, while there was still yet time.

"Let's get started."

Naia nodded, gripping his hand in reassurance. She positioned herself over the corpse, a look of determination in her eyes. "This is what we'll do: I'll initiate the healing. The more I heal, the more other things are going to start falling apart. Your job is going to be more about damage control than anything else."

"I don't understand."

"You will. Right now the system is in balance," Naia indicated the body. "The moment I start healing, things are going to go out of balance very quickly. I'll make the changes. You stabilize."

Kyel swallowed, for the first time feeling tangible fear. He wasn't sure why; they couldn't make this corpse any more dead than it was already.

"Very well. Here I go." Naia placed her hand on Sareen's forehead, closing her eyes.

He wasn't ready. But Naia started anyway.

Kyel could feel her tug powerfully on the magic field, sending waves of healing out away from her fingers, spreading throughout the cadaver. He could feel it almost personally, as if he were doing the work himself. He could visualize exactly what Naia was attempting very clearly in his mind. Through the link they shared, he watched the slow changes she was making unfold.

She started with the tissues, reversing the process of decomposition, adding structure where structure had already broken down. She moved on next to the capillaries, restoring collapsed and disintegrated vessels, driving fluids back into the system.

Almost immediately, Kyel felt things starting to go wrong, just as she'd warned. Freshly repaired tissues, reawakening, screamed for blood, gasping for air. Sareen's body seemed to be dying again just as quickly as Naia was resurrecting it. Kyel scrambled, doing what he could, which amounted to frenetic scurrying, a continuous propping up of what was already falling back apart. Sweat broke out on his forehead as he concentrated, forcing himself to work faster, trying to keep up with the momentum of the healing. He strove to anticipate what was going to go wrong next, to get ahead of it.

Naia moved on to the congealed blood, thinning the clots, redistributing the fluids throughout the tissues. Saturating it with air. Kyel couldn't keep track of all she was attempting—it was too much, all at once. He could hardly keep up with his own struggle. It was all he could do to prioritize, react, and contain.

Gradually, he realized something was happening. What Naia was doing was having some type of effect. He paused just long enough to probe the corpse.

And was shocked by what he found.

The body was no longer still, silent and cold. Organs were stirring, reawakening. Heat bloomed in the depths of the body's core. Within her chest, Sareen's heart quivered for the first time in weeks, eager in its desire to start beating.

"Now, Kyel. The wound!"

Kyel reacted, mending the torn tissues, repairing damaged membranes, shoring up the rent walls of organs. Beneath his fingers, Sareen's body shuddered. Her heart spasmed, lurching back to life. Blood, long stalled, rushed to fill waiting ventricles, coursing through long-emptied veins.

With a gasp, Sareen's lungs filled with their first breath of air since death.

Kyel looked up, startled, his eyes wide, mouth hanging aghast. His stare met Naia's, equally alarmed, equally frightened. Through his hands, he felt the body draw another, shuddering breath.

"What do we do now?" Kyel whispered, feeling a sharp pang of excitement mingled with a terrible sense of foreboding.

Naia looked down at Sareen's face, her eyes set in grim determination.

"Now, we wait. The rest is up to Xerys."

Chapter Nineteen
Transgressions

Qul, The Black Lands

Darien flinched at the sound of a distant, startled scream. An icy sweat broke out all over his body, prickling his flesh. He gazed out into the roving fog, eyes scouring the shadows. A shiver traced down his spine, caressing the small of his back like the lightest brush of fingertips. He ran forward two brisk strides then stopped.

He brought his hand up and whistled, a piercing sound that cleaved right through the mist.

Then he waited, the speed of his thoughts far outpacing the speed of his pulse. He stared with dread into the murky haze, disoriented, unsure which direction he was even facing. After moments, he heard a swift, pattering sound. A moving shadow burst through the blanket of fog, careening toward him and hurling into his legs, almost knocking him over. The demon-dog yipped as it pressed its muzzle into Darien's hand, tail thrumming against his thigh. A slobbering wet tongue slicked the palm of his hand. The smell of the beast was like mold and old decay.

"Find Meiran," he commanded the thing.

He didn't expect the beast to understand or obey. It was more an act of desperation than anything else. But the thanacryst shot immediately away, sprinting off again into the tumbling mist. Then it stopped, glancing back toward him, green eyes beckoning from out of the darkness. Darien followed after as the creature ranged forward, nose to the earth, intent on its purpose. It covered the dark ground in a broad searching pattern. Every so often it would turn and sprint back to Darien's side then turn and bound away.

This continued for minutes. Then, suddenly, the demon-hound abruptly froze in its tracks. Its tail went stiff, swept back straight as a stick, one forepaw lifted slightly off the ground. Then it darted off across the plain, following a straight trajectory across the rugged terrain.

Darien lost sight of the beast quickly in the fog. He did his best to run after it, hoping the hound didn't veer very much from its course. He eventually slowed to a walk and then finally stopped. There was no sign of the creature. He almost turned back. But then a distant baying sound urged him forward.

He jogged toward the noise. He found the thanacryst by following the sound of its guttural growls. The beast appeared to be worrying at something on the ground, making frantic, slobbering noises. Darien drew up, alarmed by the sight of the hound gnawing on a man's outstretched arm.

"Theanoch!" Darien gasped, using his fists to batter the creature away.

The demon-dog yelped and scampered off before turning back to him with a snarl, feet planted wide in the dirt. Its teeth barred, the beast lowered its head and glared at Darien with menacing eyes.

Darien ignored the thing, throwing himself down beside where Quin lay face-down in the dirt. Blood welled from puncture marks all along his arm and from a wound in the back of his head. Darien closed his eyes and drew quickly on the magic field, probing the man's condition. Satisfied that he had a good sense of his injuries, he turned Quin over, cradling him in his arms.

Darien squeezed his eyes tightly shut and set his mind about the task of repairing the damage Quin had sustained. He worked quickly, almost automatically. The magic field was by now like a treasured old friend, familiar and comfortable. Darien heard a low groan as Quin's body flinched. The darkmage relaxed, fully surrendering to the peaceful bliss of healing sleep. Darien waited until the sound of Quin's breathing was even and deep before squirming out from underneath him. He lay the sleeping form down gently in the dirt, slowly backing away.

Only then did he notice that the thanacryst had disappeared into the night.

Darien glanced around, frowning, wondering where the demon-dog had disappeared to. He hadn't liked the way the thing had growled at him. At the very least, it was enough to give him pause.

The fog was starting to break up. The sky had returned to its usual, sinister cloudscape. Thunder echoed as lightning forked in the distance. Drops of rain started falling erratically to the dirt. Darien paced away, whistling. But the beast did not return. His loathsome companion had abandoned him, it seemed.

And Meiran was gone, as well.

Another flicker of lightning sliced across the sky. Darien frowned, wrestling with indecision. He couldn't leave Quin lying prone in the dirt with a storm breaking over him. The slight depression where he lay could easily flood if enough water drained off the hillside.

But there was no trace of Meiran. She, too, could be lying injured in the storm.

Darien turned and glanced back toward the village. The town of Qul lay sprawled behind him, its dark walls lit by oil lamps and coal-fed fires. If he could carry Quin into the town, the people there might take care of him.

Or they might kill him, just the same.

Movement in the darkness caught his attention. Villagers were beginning to emerge, men and women moving through the shadows down the path that led away from the town toward the lightfields. The sight fed Darien with hope. He sprinted toward the road, eyes scanning desperately over the faces of the people emerging from the town's gate. The people of Qul paid him little mind, just strode past him with gazes lowered respectfully, keeping their distance. A few looked startled at the sight of the blue robes he wore, a look of wonder filling their face before they lowered their eyes.

Apparently, some people still recognized what those ancient robes once signified.

"Ranu kadreesh, nach'tier," one man muttered as he passed by, right hand pressed against his chest. Darien brought his own hand up reflexively, returning the greeting. He frowned in puzzlement.

But then he saw Azár's face coming toward him through the crowd. She looked up, eyes widening at the sight of him. She forged a path toward him through the press of people.

"What are you doing here?" Azár hissed, her face seeming to pale at the sight of him. Her eyes scoured the robes he wore, obviously troubled. "Have you decided to claim our village as your own?"

Darien frowned at her for a moment, at first not taking her meaning. He shook his head in confusion. "No. No, it's not that..."

He rubbed his eyes, shivering as he desperately tried to collect his thoughts enough to communicate his need. "I have a friend. Another Servant. He's been injured. I need you to watch over him for me."

A look of confusion pinched Azár's face. She pursed her lips, brow crinkling. "I didn't know you had any friends among the Servants. Except for Myria Anassis." Her tone sounded almost accusing.

Darien scowled. "It's not Myria. It's Quinlan Reis."

The rain was coming down harder. Fat droplets wet his face, drizzled down his cheeks.

Azár canted her head, staring up at him. "Quinlan Reis was not with us in Bryn Calazar. His name is...*malaaq."* Darien had never heard that word before. But its meaning wasn't too hard to figure out. Like Malikar: blackened. Cursed.

Darien reached up to rub the back of his neck. He shifted his weight over his feet. "I knew him from before. From somewhere else."

"You met this man in hell," Azár concluded dourly. "What sort of friendship can be spawned in the Netherworld, Darien Lauchlin? It can't be very good."

"You'd be surprised." Darien stared past her to avoid her eyes. "Look, there's someone else who's gone missing. I need you to watch over Quin. Get him some help from the village. Don't leave his side, not for a moment."

Azár stared up at him, mutely searching his face. At last she nodded, seeming a bit saddened by what she saw. "This person you seek must be very important to you," she said at last. "Go, then. I'll watch your friend."

The Khazahar Desert, The Black Lands

The road was long. And dark.

Darkness fell like cloth torn from the long drape of sky. It bled like running dye trailing downward to the ground, seeping into the depths of rock and soil. Meiran regarded the ink-black sky through the tattered fabric of the scarf she wore tied over her face. The scarf kept away the scouring dust flung at her by the wind. The fabric was a kindness, one of the only two she'd been allotted on the journey. In her right hand she clutched the other: a thin string from which dangled a small sack of water. They had not allowed her any food. Meiran understood why. She was not a guest of the soldiers who accompanied her; she was their captive. Her life was not by any means guaranteed.

Meiran glanced sideways at the man who walked beside her. He was tall and heavily muscled, with dark bronze skin and a meticulously groomed beard. Like the other soldiers in the column, he was dressed in a long blue tunic. He wore a curved sword and dagger tucked into the gold sash that encircled his waist.

The soldiers marched with the practiced silence that comes only with years of hard-earned discipline. The man leading Meiran with a hand on her arm kept her moving at a merciless pace. There was no slowing between halts, no matter how much her lungs and legs burned. If she stumbled, they dragged her forward until she got her feet beneath her again. The stone-faced warrior never glanced her way, never offered any words of assurance. His vision remained fixed on the back of the man ahead of him, one hand on her arm, the other on the hilt of his weapon.

There was nothing she could do to resist; they had taken her into a vortex. She had been forced to seal her mind off from the magic field, protecting herself from the surging currents that surrounded her.

Meiran loosened the scarf over her face and brought the water sack up to her lips. She tilted her head back and tried to shake the last few drops free from the sides of the container. There was barely enough to wet her tongue. She glanced at the silent man striding next to her, but he refused to look at her. Meiran drew the scarf back into place, letting her arm fall to her side.

She stumbled ahead, icy gusts of wind pushing at her from behind, rippling the skirt of her dress about her legs. Her mouth was horribly dry, her whole body weak and faltering. Meiran staggered, the iron-forged grip of her guard the only thing keeping her upright, keeping her in line.

They walked for hours through the darkness, through the cold and brutal wind. A mountain range grew upward from the ground in the distance, cutting like jagged teeth from the flat desert. The summits were encased with snow that shimmered with an eerie phosphorescence. The peaks rose before them, higher and higher, until they seemed to loom overhead, spiking upward to stab the clouds.

The road they travelled took a turn at the edge of a lake that lapped against the foothills. Here, there was no wind. The water of the lake was black and smooth, like polished obsidian glass. Meiran gazed down into the inky water, not liking the look of it.

Her escort led her across a stone bridge built over a narrow arm of the lake, to the walls of an imposing fortress carved into the mountainside. Conical towers and jagged fortifications marked where the walls of the mountain gave way before the labors of men. Narrow windows winked from random heights among the towers, lights flickering like a sky full of stars.

The entrance to the fortress was a high, vaulted arch guarded by an enormous raised portcullis. Meiran staggered forward through the opening, compelled by her guardian's iron grip. Once inside the outer gate, the soldiers assembled silently into two ranks, arrayed out to either side. Meiran sagged over her feet, lightheaded and shaking. She was grateful they had arrived *somewhere*. The long march across the desert was finally at an end.

But she was still within the raging torrent of the vortex. She knew better than to lift her hopes too high.

The air around them was cold.

The dark fortress was enormous and daunting in

every dreadful way. The courtyard bustled with silent efficiency. Meiran's hand snatched the shawl from off her head and wound it instead about her arms and shoulders for warmth. Her exhausted trembling became shivering, her muscles reacting violently to the chill. All around the edge of the courtyard, flaming braziers provided light and heat for stationed sentries. But the warmth of the flames didn't travel very far.

A group of officers approached from the other side of the courtyard, plumed helms carried at their sides. Their uniforms were much more elaborate the than men Meiran had travelled with. The soldiers on either side of her remained standing stiff and straight, not twitching so much as a muscle. Their absolute stillness was both impressive and frightening.

The officers stopped in a line in front of her not an arm's length away. Meiran kept her gaze focused on the man positioned right in front of her. Like most of the other soldiers, this man wore a short beard expertly groomed to accentuate the angle of his jaw. His eyebrows were thick, his eyes black and penetrating. He stared at her with a face devoid of expression. After a moment, he issued a slight nod.

The two soldiers to either side of Meiran caught her up by the arms and dragged her forward, staggering, around the line of officers. She tried to keep up with their long strides, but her legs wouldn't work fast enough. She was too tired, too weak, too exhausted. They half-dragged, half-carried her toward a portal on the other side of the courtyard. At first, she struggled. But struggling took more energy than she had. Meiran collapsed, only to be scooped up in a rock-iron embrace.

———

Darien gazed up pensively at the sky. Then he lowered his eyes back down to the ground, at the gray-flecked sand beneath his boots. His eyes darted back upward before he swung his body around, heading back in the direction he'd just come from. His skin itched, crawling with the feel of infestation produced by the vortex that surrounded him. He'd walled his mind away from it going in, and had kept that barrier in place for half a day as his boots crunched on brittle clots of sand, every step harder to bear than the last. He had gone as far into the vortex as he could stand. He couldn't bring himself to take another step.

Gusts of wind drove clouds racing toward him. The same wind whipped at his face, fed his eyes with dust. He walked stooped forward into the wind, letting it beat against his brow and ripple his robes out behind him.

His eyes found the tracks he had followed into the vortex.

They had passed this way. A group of twelve men who marched in disciplined formation. Darien's eyes flicked across the ground, retracing the prints back again in the direction of Qul. The signs of Meiran's passage in their midst were obvious. Every so often she'd taken a lurching step to the side, breaking the even tracks of the files. She was alive, at least. That was some comfort. Darien trudged forward into the hellish wind, eyes narrowed against the chaffing dust.

You've gone somewhere I can't follow.

Meiran's words seemed to linger, tormenting him on the wind. They dripped with the bitter poison of irony. Meiran had gone somewhere Darien couldn't follow. He couldn't bring himself to, not without more assurance than just the sword at his back.

He trudged on, shoulders sagging and back bent under a heavy burden of guilt. He walked for hours until, at last, he staggered into the rock-strewn ravine by the village. The wind had died down; the night was still. The town of Qul was aglow with the light of dozens of lanterns and cook fires.

Azár and Quin were gone. Instead, in their place, lingered a tattered old man with leathery skin and a toothless grin, face pitted by years and disease. He sat leaning against a large rock, his skeletal hands encircling the protruding burls of his knees. His beard was like a thick mass of cobwebs that engulfed his neck, hanging low over his chest.

"Darien Nach'tier. Azár ni Suam asked me to wait here for you. I will show you to her home."

Darien drew up, considering the unlikely fellow before him with a mixture of gratitude and confusion. There was something peculiar about this stranger who stared blatantly past him. It took Darien a moment to realize that the fellow must be blind. He moved forward, helping him gain his feet.

He took the old man by the arm. The fabric of his tunic was coarse, no better than a shredded, brittle rag. The man reached up and laid a wrinkled hand on Darien's face. The hand roved slowly over his cheeks, exploring his nose and the angle of his jaw, the corners of his mouth. The stubble of his chin.

"Lead me into town." The man waved in the vague direction of the gate.

Darien couldn't help but stare into the man's face as he walked. He wondered who this new companion was. Was he a relation of Azár's? Or just someone convenient she had found to keep watch?

They entered the town through the thin opening in the wall. Darien allowed his guide to lead him down a slender path between the town wall and a mud-brick dwelling two stories high. The blind fellow seemed to know exactly where he was going, leading him forward with sure, unfaltering steps. He didn't seem to need much help to find his way; it was almost as though his feet had the path before him memorized.

"You are married?" the old fellow inquired. He spoke Rhenic very well. Darien wondered where he'd learned it.

He shook his head, glancing into the opening of an alley. "No. I never had the chance."

The old man patted his arm. "The chance will find you. It is better to be married."

Darien arched an eyebrow, the thought occurring to him that maybe his new companion wasn't aware of who he was. Didn't he know he walked beside a dead man clothed in borrowed flesh? What woman would let herself be shackled to such a monster?

Not Meiran. The one person in the world he thought might understand had rejected him utterly.

Darien scowled, the expression looking more like a grimace. "Love is for the living. The dead can only regret."

The old man nodded, but it wasn't a nod of agreement. He was bobbing his head as he ruminated on the words.

"You can do better than regret," the blind man said at last. "You can atone."

Darien realized the old man was probably right. He had been given a rare and precious gift, an opportunity to put to right some of the wrongs he had committed in life. Not often was a soul given such a second chance. He had absolutely no idea what to do with it, or where to even begin.

Darien felt a tug on his arm and realized he'd stopped walking. He allowed the blind old man to guide him forward again, deeper into the shadowy heart of Qul. A thick blanket of darkness cloaked the village, the stench of coal soot heavy in the air. The unpaved path beneath his feet was wet and oozing with wastewater from the dwellings. He saw no trace of litter anywhere on the ground, no sign of insects or vermin. The streets were narrow and murky, oddly canted in places. They smelled of damp soil and mildew.

There were very few people about, mostly older women and young children who wandered the streets in small groups, thick robes swaying from their slight frames, fringed shawls draped from their shoulders. Some bore earthenware pots on their heads, others carried baskets in their arms. They took note of Darien with darting glances filled with curiosity and dismay.

The old man patted his shoulder, steering him through an opening in the wall. They entered an alley, so narrow that he could reach out and trail both hands along the walls of the houses to either side. The smell of mold was pervasive, the walls slimy to the touch. Darien hesitated.

"This way." The blind man urged him onward.

His companion guided him to the entrance of a dwelling halfway down the alley. There was no door. Strings of dark beads and threaded scraps of pottery hung like a curtain across the entrance. The old man swept a hand out, parting the odd drape with a tinkling clatter. He motioned Darien within.

He started inside, but paused, turning back around as he realized that his companion wasn't following.

"Aren't you coming?"

The old man grinned and pressed a hand against his breast. Still grinning, he turned and ambled off down the path, trailing a hand along the bricks. Darien frowned and turned away, letting the curtain of trinkets fall closed behind him. He walked forward into a shadowy courtyard. Ahead, he could hear the faint trickle of water. A fountain, perhaps. No one was about; the courtyard stood empty. His eyes scanned ahead, noting the openings of rooms to either side. Grilled windows looked down from the second story, some lit, some not.

Darien walked toward a gentle wash of light coming from the nearest doorway, his hand sweeping back a thick drape of cloth. He paused, looking in. His hand lingered by his side, holding the cotton drape at bay as he stood there motionless in the room's entrance.

Azár's face glanced up at him from where she was seated on a thin ledge that ran the length of the far wall. At her feet, Quin lay sleeping in a bed of padded matting covered by a thin blanket. His mouth was open, snoring lightly. Azár regarded Darien with a questioning stare before rising to greet him.

Seeing his face, she said, "I'm very sorry, Darien."

He nodded his head in gratitude. "I couldn't find her," he admitted gruffly. "It's my fault. I should have seen this coming."

Azar regained her seat, motioning her hand to the mats laid over the ledge at her side. "Sit. Rest."

He moved toward her, casting his tired body down next to her. He leaned back against the wall, stretching his muscles with a sigh. Glancing miserably around the room, he took in the barren chamber. There were no decorations, no furniture. Diverse pottery was scattered on the floor along the fringes of the room: various jugs and jars, plates and bowls. A few bunches of herbs hung upside-down from the ceiling, ostensibly to dry. A bronze lantern pierced through with hundreds of holes cast the room in an eerie, dappled light.

"How's Quin?" he asked, looking down at the slumbering figure.

Azár spread her fingers in a vague gesture. "He sleeps the healing sleep. He has not yet awakened. I'm thinking, though, soon. He has slept a long time."

Darien nodded, staring down at Quin's peaceful form. Odd, to think he was gazing into the face of the very man responsible for all this tragedy in the first place. Once, Darien had found it expedient to hate Quin. That hadn't lasted long. Despite his tarnished past and unfaltering penchant for misfortune, Quinlan Reis meant well. He was every inch an idealist, just a failed and broken one.

Azár lifted a pitcher from a tray on the ledge and poured Darien a cup of water. He accepted the cup from her hand, considering her face silently. Azár seemed older, somehow. She no longer had the look of a wild and furious child. Her rough edges had softened somewhat; her eyes had lost much of their accusation.

She said, "Tell me what happened."

He threw his head back and drained all the water in one swallow, his throat dry and aching from grit and thirst. He held the cup up for her as Azár refilled it, her eyes locked on his own.

Darien broke away from her stare, fidgeting and uncomfortable. He raised the cup to his mouth and took another drink. Lowering his hand, he looked down into the shadows of the cup.

"When I died, I used an artifact to preserve the legacy that was inside me. So that it wouldn't be lost from the world. It was too much power for me; too much for any one person. It was slowly driving me mad."

He drained the rest of the water, wiping his face on his arm. He leaned forward, setting the empty cup down on the mat by his side. His eyes wandered away, gazing off into the shadows of the room. Not at her.

"The legacy in the artifact was split between two people. Both were women I had loved. At different times. For different reasons. One of them, Meiran, became Prime Warden after me. When you brought us back from the Netherworld, Renquist took an interest in her. He sent Quin to bring Meiran to Bryn Calazar."

Darien indicated the slumbering darkmage with a nod. "Renquist intended to leverage Meiran the way he'd leveraged me. He can be very...persuasive." Darien scowled, swallowing his anger. "And very cruel. I wasn't about to stand for that. Quin owed me a favor, so I had him bring Meiran to me, instead."

Azár's eyes widened. Her posture stiffened, her hand dropping to her side. "You defied the Prime Warden?"

Darien sucked in a cheek. "Not explicitly."

Azár glanced sideways in thought. Even in the dim lighting of the room, the look of alarm on her face was easy to discern.

"This is very serious, Darien Lauchlin. What you have done...it could be considered treason."

"Perhaps." Darien dismissed her concern with a shrug. "But right now I'm not worried about Renquist. He's not responsible for any of this. But I know who is: Nashir Arman, the same man who put your lightfields to the torch. All of this is his own personal vendetta. He has a grudge against me."

Azár frowned, twin creases etching the skin between her eyebrows. "Why? What did you do to earn this man's wrath?"

Darien stared down at his hands in his lap. One of the sleeves of his robe had slid back, revealing the puckered red scar on his wrist. He answered Azár without looking at her, his voice gravelly and barren.

"I seduced Nashir's woman…and then I killed her."

He sat there for a long moment staring down at the awful scar. The lingering silence that filled the room was almost like a third participant in the conversation, its very presence obvious and awkward. It was a long time before he heard Azár's guarded whisper:

"You have very cold nerves, Darien Lauchlin."

He looked up at her, eyes full of spite. "I acted out of desperation, Azár, but that's beside the point. Nashir wants blood for blood, and now he's taken Meiran. I tracked his men as far as I dared into the vortex to the north. I couldn't risk going further in."

She threw her hands up. "Then there's nothing to be done. The only thing in that direction is Tokashi Palace. If this man Nashir has assumed control of the fortress, then he'll have legions of Tanisars under his command. I am sorry, Darien, but this woman you seek is already lost."

"Meiran's not lost," he insisted, rising from the ledge and moving over to kneel at Quin's side. He lay a hand on his chest, probing the man's condition. The sense of health that was returned to him eased his mind.

He stood back up and turned to Azár. "I'll get her back," he said.

Azár rose from her seat, moving to stand right in front of him. The top of her head came no higher than his chest; she had to look up to glare him in the eye. "You said there were two women that you loved. What became of the other?"

Darien frowned, realizing that since Meiran had returned, he had not even once given thought to Naia. Guilt seeped into him, cold and bitter. Of all the sins he'd committed in life, his transgressions against Naia were the ones that shamed him most. No amount of apology could ever suffice. He'd used Naia terribly and then cast her aside. He had robbed her of all she was. For him, she had abandoned her vocation, her identity, all of her aspirations. And then he'd taken his own life, leaving her selfishly behind.

Darien shook his head, staring emphatically into Azár's dark eyes. "It'd be better for Naia if she thought I was still in hell."

Azár seemed to accept his response. She backed away with a saddened expression on her face. "I've been here too long. I must go tend the lightfields."

He nodded, gazing down at his boots.

Azár reached up, draping her shawl over her head like the cowl of a cloak. "Stay here, Darien Lauchlin. Don't go north to Tokashi. Only death awaits you there."

Darien grinned mirthlessly. "Death and I have an understanding." More seriously, he added, "I won't abandon Meiran."

Azár paused. "Do what you will, then. What will be is already written." She frowned, her eyes dropping to his side. "That knife you carry…may I have it?"

The question took him by surprise. Darien fished the knife Haleem had given him out of the satchel he wore at his side. Frowning in consternation, he extended it hilt-first toward Azár, searching her face as she plucked the weapon from his hand.

"I thought you already had a blade."

Azár shrugged, holding Darien's knife up before her face as she slid the hilt from its sheath. She rotated it slightly, admiring her new possession before tucking it back away. "I can always use another. It's a good blade and, besides, you won't be needing it any longer. The shroud has no pockets."

She turned and left.

Chapter Twenty
Tokashi Palace

Tokashi Palace, The Black Lands

When Meiran woke, she was lying on her back in a cold, lightless room. The stone beneath her was frigid, and the chill penetrated deep into her body, making her bones ache. She groaned, rolling onto her side before sitting up and wrapping her arms around herself for warmth.

She stared at the iron grate that served as the door. It was old, covered in rust. In the cold and silence, her mind began to drift. Would she die in this room? Perhaps. She had no idea whether Quin was still alive, or if Darien even knew she was missing. She shivered harder as cold and despair seeped further into her bones.

From somewhere outside came a loud, metallic *clang*. She heard the sound of footsteps. Someone was coming. Meiran hugged her knees against her chest, gaping through the bars of the iron grate. There was only darkness on the other side. The sound of footsteps stopped. She let her gaze wander upward.

A man appeared on the other side of the grate.

Meiran scrambled back against the far wall. The man stood still, staring at her with an impassive gaze. He was beardless and rippled with muscle, garbed in a long white tunic and formal coat. His face betrayed no hint of his intentions.

The man unlocked the grate, letting it swing open. He took a step into the room and paused. Crossing his arms over his chest, he stood motionless, black eyes considering her in silence. He said nothing, just stared, as cold seconds crept by.

He prompted her forward with a sideways jerk of his head.

Trembling, Meiran got up from the ground. She walked three lurching steps toward him, her legs shaky and weak. The dark man grabbed her by the arm, guiding her firmly out into the corridor. Meiran went along without struggle. They were well within the vortex, and the chiseled muscles of her guard brooked no argument.

She followed him into a wide corridor lit by the melancholy glow of hanging lanterns. The man guided her through an open doorway. There, her feet transitioned onto marble tiles. Meiran stumbled, her eyes drawn upward to the walls. Her mouth hung slack.

The hallway they entered was tiled from floor to ceiling in elegant, changing patterns. The designs scrolled around the walls, sometimes blue, sometimes red. Elaborate gilt metalwork wove in and out through the figures. Gold inlay wrapped around the columns that supported the vaulted roof, more gold than Meiran had ever seen in any one place.

Whoever controlled this fortress commanded enormous wealth.

And enormous power.

They passed other people in the hallway, mostly servants carrying trays and pitchers. Kitchen or serving staff, perhaps. Meiran had no idea where her escort was leading her, but it became apparent that they were heading deep within the living quarters of the fortress.

Her silent companion stopped in front of a large, gilded door. He paused there, seeming to take a moment to collect himself, straightening his posture, adjusting the collar of his tunic. Then he opened the door and guided Meiran inside.

A room-length wooden table was the focal point of a long chamber lined with dazzling wall tiles. The ceiling was painted blue, sprinkled with golden stars. Liveried servants stood like human statues, stationed at intervals along the walls. The table was empty, the chairs unoccupied.

A jerk on her arm pulled Meiran to a halt. She turned to glance up at him and found the man staring straight ahead at a golden screen at the far end of the chamber. She followed his gaze, her eyes drawn toward a motion on the other side.

A voice proclaimed, "Nashir Arman, Overlord of the Khazahar, Xerys' Shadow on Earth."

The screen slid back, admitting a man into the chamber. He was tall and dark of complexion, his eyes full of malice and shadow. Just the sight of Nashir Arman made Meiran's stomach spasm. She took an involuntary step back against her captor's chest.

Nashir fixed his gaze on Meiran as he took his place at the table's center, his eyes moving slowly over her. His angular face was rigid, devoid of all emotion. For just a moment, their gaze met. Meiran felt her stomach lurch; there was no trace of a soul left in Nashir's shadowed eyes. If there had ever been any humanity there at all, it had long since eroded.

Nashir Arman was far more demon than man.

Meiran swallowed, rocked by waves of revulsion that made her feel physically ill. Servants swept forward, helping Nashir settle in at the table, removing his overcoat and arranging his fine robes. A boy brought a silver bowl of water, placing it down on the table before him. Nashir dipped both hands into the bowl and brought them up to wipe over his face.

Movement on the other side of the table attracted Meiran's attention. She gazed in interest as a woman entered the room through the screen. Nashir's lips drew immediately into a smile at the sight of this newest arrival.

He raised his hand, beckoning the woman to join him at his side. She strolled into the room with a casual grace, her eyes flicking upward to alight on Meiran's face before shying away. She wore a brilliant green gown encrusted with jewels, the fabric swirling gracefully as she claimed a seat beside Nashir.

The demon made a gesture with his hand, inviting Meiran to take the chair opposite him. As she took a seat at the great table, none of the servants came forward to attend her, remaining at their stations along the walls. She stared down at the dinner service set out in front of her. The plate was jade-green celadon worked with a honeycomb motif. It was empty.

Nashir Arman smiled cordially. "Welcome to Tokashi Palace, Meiran Withersby."

A line of servants filed into the room, carrying an assortment of trays and bowls, which they arranged in an elegant spread in front of Nashir and his guest. Meanwhile, other servants came forward to wordlessly remove Meiran's utensils and plate. The hospitality of a meal, then, would not be extended. Meiran felt a little of her courage slip, afraid of what that might signify.

She watched as Nashir and his lady helped themselves to the steaming platters of food. It was a sumptuous variety: breads and pickles, vegetables and grains. As Meiran sat there looking on, Nashir tore off a piece of bread, which he used to dip into a bowl. He talked as he chewed, staring down into his plate.

"The last I remember of you, you were kneeling at the feet of my Master's throne. I see that both your life and gift have been restored to you." His eyes rose to meet hers. "I am wondering…how was this accomplished?"

Meiran glared into Nashir's soulless eyes, watching him take another bite. He gazed at her expectantly, chewing slowly as he awaited her response. The woman at his side cast Meiran a condescending smile as she bit into a plump grape.

"I inherited Darien's legacy through the Soulstone," Meiran said. It was hardly a secret, and there was nothing to be gained by holding that information back.

Nashir's thick eyebrows flicked upward in curiosity. "Impressive. All eight tiers?"

Meiran didn't respond. She dropped her gaze to the table.

Nashir's smile faltered. "Not all eight, then. The legacy was split." He shared a glance with his woman as he scooped a morsel of eggplant into his mouth. "Who did you share this legacy with, I wonder?"

Meiran ignored the question, still staring down at

the wood of the table before her. Her stomach growled. The smell of the food made her mouth water.

The woman leaned close to Nashir and whispered something in his ear. An affectionate smile flitted across his lips as he patted her hand. It was evident that he genuinely cared for her.

Nashir smiled proudly as he took his lady by the hand and said with a gracious smile, "I would like to introduce to you my newest apprentice, Katarya Safiye. Katarya has the potential. Alas, she lacks a living master to Transfer the gift into her. Perhaps Katarya can receive the legacy that gleams so brightly within you?" He reached up to stroke the woman's chin, smiling deeply into her eyes.

Katarya flashed Meiran a grin full of mischief.

Nashir plunged his hands into the fingerbowl beside his plate, wiping his skin dry on a cloth. He stood and moved behind his lady's chair, placing both hands upon her shoulders. He gazed across the table at Meiran. In a voice colored by a rich, melodic accent, he explained:

"I am the sovereign of a hungry, naked, and wretched people. It is my desire to deliver them from this state. With Katarya at my side, I intend to lead the people of Malikar out of these cold, forsaken wastes. Together, we will conquer the nations of the Rhen. We will force your monarchs to bow their heads and bend knee before us. We will show them that we are the iron race, and they will know what it is to hunger and despair."

Meiran raised her eyebrows, directing her gaze at Nashir. "Your own Prime Warden declared Darien Lauchlin overlord of this region. You are not the sovereign of these lands you pretend to hold."

The demon glowered, drawing himself up and placing a hand on the sheath of a bone knife he wore tucked into the sash at his waist. "I was born a thousand years ago on these very slopes, the son of a warlord who was the son of an overlord. My mother's grandfather was Khoresh Kateem, the most glorious and ruthless conqueror in all of history. Kateem's empire stretched from sunrise to sunset, from ocean to ocean. I was born to rule these lands. The Khazahar is mine by birthright."

Meiran chose to ignore the danger in his eyes. She stared at him unblinking. "And, yet, your Prime Warden saw fit to invest another with these lands. That must be so humiliating."

She had meant to bait him into a rage, forcing him to lose composure and face. Her words, however, had exactly the opposite effect. Instead of exploding in fury, Nashir Arman said nothing. He regained his seat, taking Katarya by the hand. To Meiran, Nashir's self-possession was even more frightening than his outright anger would have been. This, she decided, was a very dangerous man.

"A ghost cannot rule," he said finally, sitting back and taking a large goblet into his hand. "I will drink Lauchlin's blood from his skull and feed my fires with his flesh." He brought the goblet to his lips and took a swallow of its contents.

Meiran stared at him flatly. She knew how unwise it would be to provoke him further. But she also understood how unwise it would be not to.

"And how do you intend to do that?" she taunted with a toss of her chin. "Darien Lauchlin is far more powerful than you will ever be."

Her words somehow brought a smile to Nashir's face. He chuckled, a hand going to caress Katarya's cheek. "Did you hear that, my shining moon?"

He turned back to Meiran with a look of contempt. "I was trained by the greatest masters of the most ancient school of magic this world has ever known during the most enlightened period of human history. What is a fallen Sentinel of a shattered race compared to me? In this vortex, I alone have the advantage."

"Darien isn't fool enough to be lured into a vortex." Her words carried little conviction. Even as she spoke, Meiran knew she was probably wrong.

Nashir made a dismissive gesture with his hand. "He was lured into damnation for you, Meiran. My guess is Darien will chance a mere vortex."

"He won't," Meiran maintained. She spared a glance at Katarya. More softly, she added, "I am nothing to him any longer."

Nashir Arman appeared to contemplate her words. He stared deeply into Meiran's face as he raised the goblet to his lips.

"My eyes and intuition tell me otherwise," he said at last. He set the goblet down on the table. He extended his hand out toward Meiran, palm upward, across the table.

"Remove your necklace."

"No." Meiran's hand went possessively to the

silver pendant at her neck. Not once had she ever taken it off.

Nashir's eyes flicked to the servant behind her. Before Meiran could react, an iron-clad arm slipped around her chest, bracing her back against the chair. She gasped as the silver chain was ripped away. She glared hatred at Nashir as the burly guardsman released her, necklace in hand.

"Have that delivered to Darien Lauchlin in Qul," Nashir commanded.

The guard bowed gracefully, stepping back. He handed the necklace to a page, who fled out of the room.

Meiran stared across the table at Nashir, appalled, her mind filled with confusion and resentment. "Why would you risk the wrath of your own Prime Warden to murder another Servant?" It was irrational; it made no sense.

"Zavier Renquist doesn't care what we do, just as long as there are Eight of us ready when the time comes. It makes no difference to him who those Eight are. My Katarya will make a fine Servant once she inherits the legacy of power trapped within you. I will enjoy watching you die," he added with a cold smile. The woman beside him leaned forward, planting a kiss on his cheek.

For the first time since entering the fortress, Meiran felt truly afraid. Her fear wasn't for herself. She reached down, pushing back her sleeves and baring the sparkling dual chains that were there. "Then here it is," she taunted, her eyes daring Nashir to act. "Let her come take it."

The darkmage cracked an amused half-grin. "Patience, little warrior. It is not yet time. For the death I have imagined for you, we require the proper setting. And the proper audience."

Chapter Twenty-One
Tangled Eternity

Qul, The Black Lands

Darien awoke, blinking his eyes to gaze upward at a ceiling steeped in shadow. It was dismally cold in the mud-brick room. There was only one source of light: a clay oil lamp perched on a shelf that cast a pale, wavering glow with its miniscule flame. It did little to drive back the darkness.

He lay on his back on a thin mat covered by his cloak, still wearing the robes Renquist had given him. His body was shivering despite the thick layers of fabric. The cold in the floor seeped upward through the mat, leeching into his skin. In a land that had long ago forgotten the warmth of the sun, ice and darkness ruled the seasons.

A movement on his right caught his attention. Darien rolled over, surprised to find Quin already awake. He brought his hands up to his face, rubbing his eyes. He rose to a sitting position and squinted at Quin, his vision blurry.

The darkmage was sitting with his back against a wall, eyes hidden by the brim of his hat. His attempt at a smile was a wan and mirthless endeavor.

"You're here and Meiran's not," Quin observed. "Does this mean I've fallen pathetically short of heroism yet again?"

Darien shook his head. "You were ambushed. You didn't have a chance."

"I'm sorry," Quin muttered, staring down at his arm as he tugged at a shirtsleeve. "Some people are just unfit to be heroes; they either try too hard or lack the necessary skillset. I fall into the latter category."

"There's nothing you could have done." Darien threw off his cloak and rose to his feet, stretching out his legs. His muscles were stiff and aching from the cold and the damp. He limped across the room to a tall water jug with a narrow neck, kneeling down beside it. He poured some water into a bowl, which he raised in both hands to his lips, drinking thirstily. When he'd had his fill, he cupped his hands and splashed chill water over his face.

"So, do I get to find out what happened?" Quin prodded, peering at Darien. He'd pushed his hat back so that it lay across his forehead at a slant. Quin's extreme age was apparent in his eyes. He had a defeated look about him, as if his soul were weary of the years. Darien understood. It was indeed possible for a soul to outlive its allotment of joy. His own tolerance for life had deteriorated well before his death.

He set the bowl down, moving back across the room. "Nashir must have found out about Meiran. He's figured out a way to get the revenge he's always threatened. He's established himself in a fortress to the north of here. That's where they took her."

Quin arched an eyebrow, sucking in a cheek. "So, if I may ask…what are you still doing here?"

"Nashir's fortress is protected by a vortex. I didn't dare go too far in."

Quin sat up straight, his face going tight with concern. "He's taken over Tokashi Palace? That was meant to be your stronghold, you know."

Darien shrugged. "No, I didn't know. Renquist never mentioned it. In truth, he never mentioned a lot of things."

Quin leaned his head back against the wall, gaze angled upward at the ceiling. "Tokashi Palace has been the bastion of power in the Khazahar for over four hundred years. I'm sure Renquist intended you to claim Tokashi as your base. But if Nashir got there first...he must be greatly emboldened to move against you so overtly. It's not like him, to take such a risk." He chuckled, sneering wryly. "I've got to hand it to you, Darien. More than any other person I've ever met, you really do know how to piss someone off."

Darien closed his eyes, shaking his head at Quin's graceless quip. He was right, of course, which didn't help.

"This is one honey of a pickle," Quin remarked.

"Aye, I guess it is." Darien brought a hand up to rub his temple. "I suppose I can't just walk in there and rescue her, can I?"

"No." All trace of humor fled Quin's face. "No, you cannot." The weariness came back to shadow his eyes. "There's really not much you can do. Not if Nashir's already established himself."

"It's a vortex," Darien grumbled. "That means there's a Circle of Convergence in there somewhere. Is there a chance I can reach it without being discovered?"

Quin shook his head. "I destroyed it."

Darien gaped at him. "*How?*"

Quin scooped his hat off his head, tossing it down in his lap. He ran a hand back through his hair, sighing heavily. "Tokashi Palace is built over the remains of an ancient fortress called Vintgar. Vintgar was..." His voice trailed off. He shook his head. "I don't know that I have the words to describe it."

He seemed to be struggling to gather his thoughts. "The ice caverns of Vintgar were the source of the River Nym. Vintgar's Circle of Convergence was tucked away deep in the bottom of the caverns, far below where Tokashi Palace exists today. That was my circle to protect. I was assigned to guard it on the night of the Reversal." He paused then, letting a long gap of silence stretch between them.

In the two years Darien had known him, through all of hell's tribulations, Quin had never once broached the subject of what had happened that night, so long ago. How it had all gone so terribly wrong. Except in fleeting moments of self-deprecation, Quin refused to talk about it.

"What happened?" Darien urged softly.

Quin took a deep breath. "I stabilized the magic field. But then I dropped the circle before tying it off. Braden..." His voice cracked. He brought a hand up to cradle his brow. "I thought that if I left right then, maybe I could get back before they executed my brother. I thought there still might be a chance I could save him." He shook his head. "I was wrong. Braden was already dead by the time I got there. And, in my folly, I left the vortex exposed to the Onslaught. Everything got out of hand before anyone realized what was happening.

"The air itself caught fire, the ground beneath seared to ash. The inferno swept across Caladorn, destroying everything in its path. It was as though all the fires of hell had risen up to consume the very earth." Quin spread his hands helplessly before dropping them back down again to his sides. He sat there, biting his lip, slowly shaking his head.

Darien stared at the ground with no words to offer into the heavy silence that followed.

Quinlan Reis looked up at him, fixing him with an ancient, desolate stare. "Vintgar was reduced to rubble. The River Nym jumped its course and flooded the ice caverns. The Circle of Convergence lies now lost somewhere beneath the waters of the lake that formed. It won't be of any use to you."

Darien nodded. He had heard of Caladorn's lost Circles of Convergence. He had read about the destruction of the Lyceum's Greater Circle, but he had never known where the other had been located or what had become of it. That Quin had a part in the circle's destruction did not surprise him in the least. Disaster seemed to follow Quin like a second shadow.

"Darien Lauchlin Nach'tier."

He glanced up at the sound of his name. Two men he didn't recognize stood in the open doorway. He rose immediately to his feet as Quin did the same.

"I'm Darien Lauchlin," he acknowledged warily, stepping forward.

One of the men had the appearance of a villager. The other did not. That one was a uniformed soldier, probably an officer, spectacularly arrayed in a blue and gold waistcoat. A long sash was tied about his hips, to which was affixed an array of various knives and implements.

The soldier nodded curtly. He was carrying a plumed hat tucked in the crook of his arm. Very formally, he effected a perfect bow, folding forward at the waist. Then he strode forward with measured stride, halting before Darien. He fell immediately to his knees, then bent forward until his face touched the cold bricks of the floor.

Darien stood frowning down at the prostrated man, his eyes flicking back to the villager still standing in the doorway.

"Rise," he muttered.

The man obeyed, bringing himself to his knees, but not to his feet. Keeping his gaze fixed on the ground between Darien's boots, he held a small silver box up before his face, proffering it with both hands.

"I, the Chamberlain of Armorers, Sayeed son of Alborz, have been sent on behalf of the Madashar Overlord Nashir Arman, Xerys' Shadow on Earth, to present to you this token."

Darien glared at the offered parcel, distrusting it. Very slowly, he extended his hand. But, instead of accepting the silver box, he curled his fingers into a fist and retracted his hand.

"Open it," he commanded.

Still with eyes lowered to the ground, the officer obeyed. He removed the lid from the small box and offered its small treasure up toward Darien in the palm of his hand.

Darien's face did not change. His expression didn't reflect the blunt thrust of anger that tore up through his middle, stabbing him first in the chest and then again in the stomach. He accepted the thin silver chain with an air of reverence, holding it laced between the fingers of his hand. Unable to breathe through the suffocating dread that filled his chest, he raised the pendant up before his eyes.

He didn't look again at the soldier on the ground. His eyes remained fixed on the pendant that hung swaying from his hand, turning, white globs of light running like quicksilver across its interlaced design.

The shadows in the room thickened visibly. The chill in the air crystallized as the chamber darkened.

Darien continued staring at the pendant as if mesmerized, his eyes tracking its motion. At his feet, the soldier began rocking back and forth, moaning, face contorted in a rictus of pain. The floor around him turned dark with spreading ice.

"Go."

Somehow, the trembling soldier managed to regain his feet with some semblance of grace. Cloaked by the dignity vested by years of discipline, he bowed stiffly and backed away. He turned and hurried out of the room. He was followed closely by the villager, who glanced back once with a look of horror in his eyes.

When they were gone, Quin shook his head and whistled softly.

"You really are a devil," he commented, striding forward from his position against the wall. "I suppose you've never heard the phrase, 'spare the messenger?'"

"I spared him."

Darien lowered the pendant, caressing it with the pad of his thumb.

"Narrowly," Quin scoffed. "For a moment there, it could have gone either way." Then, more gently, he asked, "What are you going to do?"

Darien's eyes locked with Quin's. "What are my options?"

"I don't know that you have any options. Nashir might be hellspawn, but he's wicked-cunning."

"It's a vortex," Darien argued. "He'll be at just as much of a disadvantage as I. What assets does he have?"

Quin quirked his face into a withered grimace. "He'll have warriors at his disposal. Tanisars: highly trained infantry. They've been preparing for hundreds of years, waiting for the day a Battlemage will return to lead them forth into glorious conquest. I'm sure Renquist meant them to be yours."

"And now they're Nashir's," Darien observed. The trap had a failsafe.

He frowned, slipping Meiran's pendant into a pocket.

"You can't win this," Quin assured him with a look of regret. "You have to let her go. I'm sorry, but there's no other choice you can make."

Darien sighed, gazing dismally down at the floor. Contemplating his options. His heart felt heavy, like a thick iron weight. He'd made a commitment to Azár and to the people of Qul to help them. He couldn't honor that commitment if he threw his second chance at life away. All for a woman who didn't love him back.

"There's always a choice," he said. "Some choices are just harder to make than others."

"You're starting to sound just like my brother," Quin grumbled, clearly irritated. "Don't. Don't fool yourself, Darien. You're no hero."

Darien flashed him a resentful look. "I never claimed to be."

His eyes fell on the sword at Quin's side. A thought occurred to him, jolting him right out of his melancholy. "Your sword—it's an artifact. Do you have any others? Something that might work within a vortex?"

Quin frowned, his face going quite serious. "Nothing that'll do you much good," he said thoughtfully. But he walked over to where his pack lay against the wall of the room and bent over. Scooping it up in his hand, he began rifling through the contents. Eventually, he withdrew a small copper cube, held it up before his face, then grimly shook his head. Replacing it back in the pack, he withdrew another item, what looked like some sort of scepter that ended in a carved wolf's head. This, too, disappeared back into the bag. With a sigh, he lowered the pack, setting it back down on the floor.

His eyes suddenly froze. Slowly, his hand moved to his side, coming to rest on the hilt of his sword. Quin's frown became deeper, much more serious. He stood there, one hand on the hilt of his ancient blade, staring at the wall in front of him.

"What?" Darien finally prompted him.

Quin turned toward him, a mischievous glint in his eyes. "My sword's a dampener."

Darien just stared at him, perplexed. "What good's that? Nashir can't use the magic field in a vortex."

Quin flashed him a wry, crooked grin. "It's not for Nashir. I'm going to use it on you."

Darien froze, at last understanding. Dampened, his mind would be protected from the fury of the vortex. But he'd still have access to the Onslaught. His mind reeled, filling with a euphoric sense of optimism.

"Have you ever used the Hellpower?" Quin asked. He was gazing down at his fingers, worrying at a hangnail.

"Aye."

"Then you know what it's like."

"A bit. Not much," Darien admitted. "For me, it's mostly just a way of reaching through to the magic field. I've used it, but…I really don't know much about how it works."

Quin brought his finger up to his mouth, biting off the torn nail. "There are some things you're going to need to know, then." He motioned with his hand toward the mats set out on the floor. He waited for Darien to settle cross-legged on one before following him down to the ground.

He flicked the shard of nail across the room, his eyes following its trajectory. "You can't use the Onslaught the same way you use the magic field. It has different rules. It's a bending of Natural Order, but it's tricky. Every use increases Chaos, increases disorder."

"So healing's out," Darien surmised.

Quin nodded. "By definition, healing is the restoration of order to a body that's injured or out of balance. Directly in conflict with the nature of the Onslaught. And then there's the issue of habituation."

Darien glanced up at him. "What's habituation?"

"The more you work with the Hellpower, the more you come to rely on it. Cyrus Krane's a perfect example of someone who didn't back off in time." Quin shrugged dismissively. "Just be careful. Don't ever let yourself get to the point where you feel like you *have* to use it. Don't become enslaved by it."

Darien nodded, fully appreciating the danger. Toward the end, he'd come to rely too much on the magic field. He had used it as a tourniquet to bind his pain. Thinking back, he realized what a mistake that had been. Immersing his mind in the field had distanced him too much from his feelings.

"Your best chance is to try to win the Tanisars over to your cause," Quin said. "It may be possible. By now, they must surely have some inkling that Nashir isn't the overlord that was promised. If you can appeal to the Zakai, their senior officers, you might be able to convince them to help you overthrow Nashir."

Darien doubted that. "Why would the Tanisars follow me?"

Quin cast him a withering scowl. "Darien, your reputation precedes you; your notoriety is just as legendary as your arrogance. You've already proven yourself a formidable adversary. Now, you just need to prove yourself a worthy ally. The Zakai won't just follow you out of the kindness of their hearts; you'll need to persuade them. Offer them something Nashir can never give them."

Darien spread his hands wide, shrugging

hopelessly. "What could I possibly offer them that they don't have already?"

There was a heartbeat's moment of silence.

"Hope."

"Hope?" Darien echoed dubiously.

"Yes. Hope."

Quin lowered his chin until the brim of his hat overshadowed his eyes.

Chapter Twenty-Two
The Lion's Maw

Tokashi Palace, The Black Lands

Quin tipped his hat down further on his head as he gazed out across a hellish scene. Overhead, dark clouds raced across the sky. Below, the black waters of a lake stretched silently away from the hillside where he stood. The ground was white with recent snow, save only for the serpentine line of the road that followed the edge of the shoreline, meandering toward a narrow bridge that spanned the calm waters.

In this very place, a thousand years ago, the Black Lands had arisen from the ashes of dying Caladorn. Right here, where the headwaters of the Nym had sprung from caves of ice. This vale, once overshadowed by the hallowed gates of ancient Vintgar, now covered by the still, black waters below.

The lake was as old as Malikar itself. Its obsidian-flat surface obscured more than just Vintgar's fabled gates. The lake's deep, dark waters obscured the past. They buried secrets. They drowned the truth in their quagmire depths. Somewhere deep inside, Vintgar's Circle of Convergence yet slumbered. Quiescent, but aware. Lurking beneath. It was down there, somewhere.

Right where Quin had abandoned it a thousand years before.

He heard a crunching noise. He raised his head to note that Darien had come up to stand alongside him. The mage was still dressed in the indigo robes of the Lyceum, the same style Quin's brother had once been so fond of. Quin frowned, not liking it. The robes didn't suit Darien at all. They fit him well enough, but there was something about the look that seemed unsettling, even misleading. It took Quin a moment to put a finger on it.

Darien just wasn't Braden. No matter how much he wanted him to be.

Quin sighed, returning his attention back to the lake below. "Are you certain you don't want me coming with you?"

"I'm going alone."

Quin licked his lips, considering. "Then I'll wait for you back in Qul."

A ball of lightning flared briefly across the sky.

"Don't wait too long."

Quin nodded slowly. He turned to consider Darien's face. The man looked haggard. Drawn. Quin could hardly blame him.

"Are you ready, then?"

"Aye."

Darien reached down, hiking up his robe. He drew the fabric up, exposing his chest, shrugging the garment off over his head. He held it in a ball at his side, clothed only in the trousers he'd had on underneath.

Quin let his eyes trail over Darien's bare torso, observing every mark on him. The grotesque scars on his wrists, the etched white lines that striped his chest. Two small, V-shaped depressions where blades had pierced his skin. Quin considered the flesh before him critically, eventually deciding on a spot. The right arm; that would do best.

Darien was left-handed, just as Braden had been.

Decisively, Quin drew Zanikar from its scabbard. He raised the blade, setting the honed cutting edge against the meat of Darien's upper arm and, without hesitation, drew the sword swiftly down.

Darien didn't flinch. He stood with his eyes

trained on the lake. Blood welled from the slice, running in thin red lines down his arm to his hand, thick droplets pitter-pattering to the ground. The warm blood made a random pattern in the snow at his feet.

Quin reached down and drew a rag from his war-belt, using the cloth to wipe Zanikar's blade clean. He sheathed the sword, then turned to consider Darien's new injury.

"I'll bandage that," he offered.

Darien stood still, allowing Quin to tie the cloth around his arm like a tourniquet. "Keep it clean," Quin advised.

Darien reached up, groping at his brow with his fingers. He looked suddenly upset. "Are you certain it worked? Is there any way to tell?"

Quin shrugged. "It just needs a healthy taste of blood. The binding does the rest. You've been dampened before; you know how it works."

"I suppose I'll just have to trust it." He grimaced as he drew the robes back on over his head.

Quin felt offended at the remark. Zanikar was his own creation, a masterwork exceeding every other artifact he'd ever fashioned. It was the only dampening sword in existence. To have its reliability questioned was downright insulting.

"You really do go to pieces in a vortex," Quin grumbled. "Are you sure you can hold yourself together? I'd hate to think what would happen if you started coming apart in front of Nashir."

"I'll manage," Darien muttered. He extended his hand across the space between them.

Quin considered the offered hand. He'd already forgiven Darien, but that forgiveness came at the price of other emotions. The plan they'd devised was by no means foolproof. Quin understood that this could very well be their last handshake.

He clasped Darien's arm with both hands, pulling him in close. It was a brotherly gesture, one from a different time, a different place.

"Darius dreoch," he whispered on impulse. The ancient, formal greeting of the clans. *May you offer protection,* was the loose translation. Quin used the phrase out of context on purpose; he did it to avoid saying goodbye.

He gazed with respect at the man before him with matted black hair and a hide full of scars. Darien had a wild, unkempt look about him, like the men of the horse clans Quin had been born to. Darien was not Braden; he never would be. But, then again, he didn't have to be.

"All right, then," Quin muttered.

Darien waited until he'd gained the road before turning back for one last glimpse of Quin. But the darkmage was already gone, obscured somewhere in the shadows of the desert. Darien wasn't surprised. He wouldn't have lingered, either. Not if he had a choice.

He turned his stare back to the still waters of the lake, setting his feet down the muddy path. The lake was black, devoid of life. There was no algae encrusting the rocks along the shoreline, no rippling movement of fish beneath the quiet surface. The lake was cold and still as death. The water wasn't murky, but crystalline-black.

He strode down the silent length of road, lost in troubled thought. His eyes stared with lazy focus at the sharp mountain peaks ahead and the looming fortress at their base. From this distance, Tokashi Palace seemed oppressive and sinister, like an upthrust shield made entirely of sharpened spikes. Dozens of conical turrets of varying heights were carved as if in bas-relief from the mountainside, like an enormous palisade. The tallest were quite spectacular, looming hundreds of feet above the valley and the lake. An enormous, gaping arch formed the river's channel where it emerged from beneath the mountain, tall and broad enough to maneuver a ship through under full sail.

Darien reached the bridge that spanned a narrowing of the lake. The bridge itself was a testimony to the industry of the people who dwelt in this place. It was made from enormous blocks of hewn basalt, jigsawed together without mortar or gaps. Gods only knew how deep the bridge's piers extended, deep down into the lake's gloomy depths.

He glanced back at the fortifications above, feeling a stab of trepidation. He was surprised they'd let him come this far, alone on the road. He'd marked their sentries a long time ago. He knew they were watching. They were waiting, staying their hand. They wanted him to come to them, not the other way around.

A bank of fog rolled in from across the lake,

encasing the bridge in a murky haze. A queer, eerie silence settled in with the fog.

And cold. A frigid chill stung his cheeks and clawed beneath the cloth layers of his robes. Darien didn't like it. He didn't trust the fog, any more than he trusted the cold.

And the silence; that was the most unnerving of all. It was as though, one by one, all his senses were being purposefully deprived.

A shiver of foreboding crept across his flesh, followed by an urgent stab of panic. Darien's mind screamed for the comfort of the magic field. But there was nothing to reach for. That sense, too, had been stripped away.

Darien gained the other side of the bridge and stopped as his feet encountered soil.

Ahead, a line of soldiers barred his path. All wore uniforms of royal blue with long sashes of gold. One of the men stepped forward ahead of the others, striding toward him. Darien recognized the soldier; it was the same man who had brought him Meiran's necklace. The same man he'd almost killed.

Darien held his ground as the officer stopped in front of him. This time, the soldier did not fall to the ground in a gesture of deference. Instead, his hand rested on the hilt of his sword. He stared at Darien for a long time without expression. At last, he remarked:

"He said you would come. I did not believe him. I told him no man would ever be so foolish."

He made a sharp gesture with his hand. The men waiting behind him jogged forward, surrounding Darien with their bodies. He didn't struggle as they restrained his hands behind his back, searching him roughly for weapons. Finding none, two men took Darien by the arms, the rest fanning out around him. The officer moved forward until his face was uncomfortably close.

Darien gazed into the soldier's hardened stare, taking the man's measure. This was an officer who was comfortable with his command, steady and well-disciplined. There was no trace of fear in his eyes.

Calmly, the man asked, "I must know. Why did you come?"

Darien allowed himself a slight, wistful grin. "Because of a woman," he responded in all honesty.

The man in front of him raised his eyebrows. "Well, then. That does explain it." With a troubled frown, he wondered, "You are Aerysius' Last Sentinel. How is it that you are also *nach'tier?*"

"I'm no longer a Sentinel," Darien corrected him.

"It has been said that the Prime Warden himself chose you to rule the Khazahar."

"Aye. He did."

The man gazed at him, eyes narrowing. "Then why is it you enter Tokashi Palace in chains?"

Darien shrugged. "Because chains have never defined me."

He spoke figuratively, doubting the officer would be informed enough to take his meaning. To his surprise, the man nodded as if he understood the reference perfectly well.

"I am Sayeed son of Alborz, in case you've forgotten," the soldier said. He motioned to another man who stood slightly behind him. "And this is Iskender, first son of my brother."

Darien nodded a curt greeting. To Sayeed, he asked, "If you know Nashir is not the overlord that was promised, why do the Tanisars follow him?"

"Nashir Arman is the first Battlemage to ever walk the halls of Tokashi Palace. From birth until death, the Tanisars are sworn to follow whatever Battlemage is brought forth to lead us. It is our greatest honor, our most sacred duty."

"Wouldn't it be a greater honor to serve a commander who's actually ever won a battle?"

Sayeed son of Alborz fixed Darien with a flat stare. In a voice as cold as the surrounding air, he stated, "Your achievements are well-known to us, Darien Nach'tier. It is unfortunate that you chose to champion the wrong cause."

There was no disguising the resentment held barely in check beneath his disciplined composure. Darien sighed, realizing that Quin had been wrong about these men. There would be no winning over the Zakai. The officers that led the Tanisar corps had a very good idea of who he was. And they knew very well the enormity of atrocities he was capable of committing. They wanted nothing to do with him. Darien sighed, his hopes quietly shattering.

"I was a Sentinel of Aerysius before I ever swore allegiance to Xerys," he informed Sayeed. "I served my duty to the Rhen. I served it as best I could, even unto death. Through the will of Xerys, my soul has been remade. I serve a higher purpose, now. Your duty and mine no longer conflict."

Sayeed regarded him without a trace of compassion in his eyes. At last, he nodded curtly.

"Come. Let us enter your palace, Darien Nach'tier, last of the fallen Sentinels."

The men to either side prodded Darien roughly forward. He stumbled, staggering in their embrace.

They guided him under the high archway where the lake was born from the mountainside, down into a warren of passageways lit by flickering torchlight. It was dark and frigid, every corridor unadorned and monotonous. What was most remarkable about the fortress, Darien discovered, was the startling absence of sound. Many soldiers strode the long passageways, lined the walls of the hallways and courtyards. Not one word was ever spoken. The posted sentries stood as immobile as chiseled stone. The deeper they walked into the gaping quiet, the more conspicuous the silence loomed.

His guards guided Darien down into the depths of the fortress, to levels far below, where the cold, moist air was even more oppressive. The silence followed them even there. They stopped outside an iron door and waited while one of the men flipped through a ring full of keys, finally finding the one to throw the lock. The door shivered open on its hinges.

Darien flinched at the wall of ice-chill air that gushed out at them from the other side of the doorway. Goosebumps rose instantly to prickle his flesh. His guards forced him forward, his feet slipping on ice. It took him a moment to realize that the entire corridor was carved from the body of an enormous glacier. Darien gaped at the sight even as he shivered from the intensity of the cold. He had never seen the like. The walls of the glacier were black and sleek and transparent. An odd blue light shimmered down through its crystalline depths. The air was appallingly crisp, sucking thc warmth right out of him. Even the thick robes he wore did little to contain his body heat.

His guards stopped beside another iron door, this one recessed into the wall of ice. Another man came forward to unlock it, throwing the door open. Darien gazed with dread into the narrow opening that was revealed. All he could see on the other side was darkness.

They shoved him toward the doorway.

"Wait."

He was jerked roughly back.

Sayeed stepped forward and grabbed him by the hair. He glared into his face. Then he shoved him head-first into the wall with all his strength. Darien reeled, slumping to the floor even as the soldiers hauled him back to his feet. They held him there against the wall as other men accosted him, slapping his face, shredding the blue fabric of his robes.

When they had him mostly naked and bloodied, Sayeed at last relented. He gripped Darien by the throat, pressing him back against the wall. The strength of his grip made it impossible to breathe. Darien's throat worked against the man's rigid fingers, to no avail.

"Tell me one last thing," Sayeed Zakai demanded in a patient voice. "If you did take rule of the Khazahar, what could you offer us that Nashir Arman cannot?"

Darien returned Sayeed's stare with a glare of his own. The man released his grip enough to let him speak.

"If you follow me, I'll give you back the sun," Darien said roughly.

Sayeed scoffed. An amused smile spread on his lips. He released his hold on Darien's neck and backed away. He turned, nodding in the direction of the doorway.

The men hauled Darien into the cell, throwing him to the floor. He scrambled, slipping on the ice. He managed to rise to his knees. A man came forward and doused him over the head with a bucket of frigid water.

Darien cried out and lurched back from the chill shock of it. The water soaked his hair, running down his naked torso.

He fell to the hard ice as his body shook in terrible spasms of chill. The soldiers took turns dousing him with more water, soaking his trousers and his legs. Another pail was upended directly over his face.

At last, the sounds of the guards finally retreated. The hinges of the door shrieked closed. But the door's motion was interrupted. Into the darkness, Darien heard Sayeed's voice echo calmly:

"I hope you find the sun, Darien Nach'tier. Before you freeze to death."

The iron door was pulled the rest of the way closed, encasing him in shadow. Only the wan blue light of the glacier filtered down through the ice.

Darien curled up in a ball, shivering violently, alone with only his anger and his misery to keep him company. Reflexively, he reached out with his mind for the comfort of the magic field.

But the magic field wasn't there; its song was just a faded memory.

Desperate, Darien groped instead for the Onslaught.

Like a fickle lover, the Hellpower fled from his touch.

A terrible fear clenched his gut. Too late, Darien realized the folly of his mistake. In surrendering himself to Nashir, he had placed his own desires and concerns above the interests of his Master. And that was something Xerys would never tolerate.

Despair settled deeply into his bones along with the throbbing ache of chill. Both the Zakai and the Onslaught had rejected him. He'd been wrong to put so much faith in Quin.

Darien lay alone in the darkness, sprawled across the ice, shivering from the cold and shuddering with despair.

Azái had been right. He should never have come.

Meiran's stomach growled. She stared across the table at the elegant platters of food arranged before the beautiful Katarya, Nashir's new apprentice. The smell of the various dishes was enough to make Meiran's mouth water. They'd given her nothing to eat. Just water. Nothing more.

She watched Katarya eat, noting how well-mannered and elegant the woman was. Katarya plucked at her food daintily, taking small, delicate bites. She tore off tiny pieces of bread and took her time about chewing. Everything she did, every motion she made, seemed artfully practiced and executed. She was clothed in the finest silks and draped with gold and jewels. Her hair was curled and meticulously arranged. Her lips had just the faintest dash of color. Everything about Katarya was an elaborate pretense designed to both allure and obscure at the same time.

Katarya noticed Meiran's stare and smiled gently in her direction.

"The *bostalek* is scrumptious," she announced conversationally, indicating a particularly strong-scented dish. "The *mustaq* could have simmered longer, I'm afraid."

Meiran stared at her woodenly.

The woman's smile deepened. "What types of dishes do they prepare in the Rhen? Tell me, what are your favorites? I've always wondered what Southern food tastes like."

Meiran continued to gaze at the woman, lips pressed firmly together. She refused to be baited. She could sense the waves of amusement emanating from Katarya, and it galled her. She refused to be this woman's plaything.

A uniformed officer swept into the room, holding open the door. He was followed closely by Nashir. Katarya immediately rose to her feet and lowered her head to her chest, clasping her hands together in front of her. Her eyes glanced up beneath her long lashes, casting a hostile glare at Meiran, who made no attempt to rise.

Nashir approached the table and extended his hand, waiting as Katarya pressed a kiss against his fingers. A fond smile grew on his lips at the sight of her.

"My rose," he greeted Katarya as he seated himself at her side. "How is our guest?"

"Quiet," Katarya scoffed, fixing Meiran with a glare of disdain. "I try to make conversation, but she will not speak. She thinks she resists."

Nashir chuckled mildly. His hand went to clasp his apprentice's fingers, his thumb caressing Katarya's olive skin. He gifted Meiran with an indulgent smile. "So, our little warrior stages a protest?"

Meiran turned away from him in disgust. She fixed her eyes on the door opposite.

"It doesn't matter," Nashir assured her. "In the end, we will all get what we desire."

"What exactly do you think I desire?" Meiran spat, turning to glare her disdain at him. Nashir was demon to the core. It was his nature; there was something broken inside him. No matter how hard she tried, she couldn't get a sense of his emotions. It was as if they simply didn't exist. She was beginning to think he didn't have any.

Very patiently, Nashir explained, "Soon, you will long for death. You will wish for it more than anything you have ever wished for in your life."

His promise, spoken with such sinister assurance, sent a shiver of dread through Meiran's body. Somehow, she understood that his words were much more than mere threat. They had the ominous ring of prophecy.

"Why would I wish for death?" she asked softly.

Nashir was no longer smiling. He still held Katarya's hand in his own, stroking her skin gently. Gazing into Meiran's eyes, he explained, "Because with death comes the slow peace of the grave. It is a kindness, a gentle mercy. One that I will surely never know."

Meiran felt a hard knot of anger balling up inside. "You speak as though you're immortal. Are you?"

"No," Nashir corrected her firmly. "Xerys does not grant eternal life; what He grants instead is eternal servitude. In return, my Master demands unfaltering allegiance."

Meiran raised her eyebrows, surprised by his candid admission. "Do you regret your pledge to Xerys, then?"

"Not at all. I have no reason to regret my decision. Not yet. A thousand years in hell is a long time. However, it is but an eyeblink when compared to the wide span of eternity. You are very fortunate, little warrior. Your fight is almost over. Mine is only beginning."

Meiran lowered her gaze to the table's surface as she contemplated his words. So, Nashir Arman was not entirely happy with his circumstance. Which might explain why he had the temerity to defy Renquist's commands.

"What about Oblivion?" she found herself wondering.

"Ah, sweet Oblivion. The last refuge of the soul." Nashir smiled. His fingers froze, no longer caressing Katarya's hand.

Meiran pressed, "Wouldn't Oblivion be preferable to an eternity spent in hell?"

Nashir shook his head. He raised Katarya's hand to his lips, favoring it with a tender kiss.

"I am not yet so very desperate," he confided, gazing overtly into Katarya's eyes. "It is said that when a soul enters Oblivion, the spirit unravels like a thread pulled from a woven shirt. Oblivion is the negation of existence, the cessation of eternity. There is nothing after that."

He let go of Katarya's hand and reached for a bowl of crushed salt. He scooped up a large pinch into his hand, rubbing his fingers together to dispense the salt in a line across the table before him. "Everything that a person is, all that they ever were…all erased in a heartbeat." He leaned forward and blew across the line of salt, scattering the tiny crystals across the table's surface. "Like dust flung by the wind."

A gracious smile returned to his lips. "May your soul never be scattered by Oblivion. It is a gentle peace that you go to, little warrior. In the Atrament, you will know the companionship of all you have ever loved. You will never be alone or sad or afraid."

"That's not true," Meiran insisted, goading him on purpose. "Darien won't be there."

"No," Nashir agreed. "Darien will never be there. Like myself, the Atrament is denied him. But before you die, you can do your lover one last kindness."

"What is that?" Meiran shivered with an acute sense of foreboding.

"You can offer Darien the mercy of Oblivion."

"Why would I do that?" Meiran whispered.

"Because if Darien Lauchlin can be convinced to deny our Master, then his soul will be unmade. He will be spared an eternity of hell's torments."

Meiran's eyes widened in dismay. So that was Nashir's intention. He meant to use her as his weapon against Darien. Anger suffused her at the very notion; she could feel the heat of it scald her cheeks.

"I won't do it," she told him firmly. "I won't break my Oath of Harmony."

Nashir raised an eyebrow. "Would it truly betray your Oath to lead a damned spirit out of hell? Surely, it would not. Think of the favor you would be doing the man who gave up his life to deliver your own soul from such torment. And there is also this: there would be one less demon for your armies to face when the time comes for battle."

Meiran gaped at him, growing more horrified with every word. A chill panic suffused her, starting in her cheeks and descending to her core. Her emotions screamed in anger and outrage, appalled by the very notion of what he was suggesting.

And yet, the rational part of Meiran's brain was still groping to find fault in Nashir's logic.

Try as she might, Meiran could find no argument

to refute him.

Because, appallingly, he was right.

Meiran's mouth went dry as she realized Nashir had left her no moral recourse.

She was still gaping down at the table when Nashir pushed his chair back and rose to his feet. He motioned with his hand toward the door. "Come. I have something to show you."

Thoroughly numb, Meiran made no attempt to refuse him. She followed in a daze, around the end of the table and out of the room, into a wide, torch-lit hallway. Nashir strolled at her side, one arm draped across her shoulders, compelling her forward. She had no choice but to go along with him. She was too weakened by hunger, too shackled by fear. Too appalled by her own sense of helplessness.

The walk was long and unremarkable, broken only by the occasional flight of stairs. Nashir spoke not a word, but strode silently at her side. They were trailed by a small group of Zakai, Nashir's personal escort, though Meiran scarcely noticed them. Her thoughts were focused inward on her own mind. Exploring paths of possibility, differing avenues of choice. Until all possibilities eventually fused into none.

She drew up, realizing that Nashir had stopped walking.

Meiran gazed around, blinking and confused, finding herself in a dark corridor made entirely of ice. Nashir stood at her side. His hand squeezed her shoulder, drawing her close against him.

It was horrifically cold.

Nashir made a motion to one of his officers. The man came forward and immediately offered up his own overcoat. Nashir draped it himself about Meiran's shoulders, delicately adjusting the fabric. When he was satisfied, he gave a stiff nod.

"Come, see what I have found."

Two soldiers sprang forward and unlocked an iron door recessed into the wall of the passage. Meiran held her breath, dreading what she might find on the other side. The door shivered open. Frigid air poured forth from the gaping opening.

Meiran gazed ahead into the darkness within, seeing nothing.

Nashir reached out, grasping a torch from the opposite wall. He held it up in front of him and thrust it forward through the doorway.

Meiran gasped in dismay.

Darien lay on the floor of a cell made completely of ice. He was drenched with water, his flesh pale. He was curled into a ball on the ice.

"He presented himself to us just as I said he would," Nashir stated. His tone was smug.

Meiran felt the warmth of tears gathering in her eyes. "What have you done to him?"

"No more than he deserves." Nashir's hand wrapped once more about her shoulders. He guided Meiran forward into the cell of ice. "I'm not fool enough to destroy another Servant by my own hands. But I can make him suffer. And so I have."

Meiran gazed down into Darien's pale face. She whispered, "What exactly do you want from me?"

"Convince him. Convince him to deny our Master and embrace Oblivion. It would be better for you. And better for him. You don't really think Aerysius' Last Sentinel ever wished to spend his afterlife fighting to destroy everything he ever loved? Of course not. Darien just needs to be made aware of his options. And he needs to exercise them."

Meiran looked up at Nashir in despair, marveling at the man's sadistic cunning.

"How does one become so evil?" she whispered, horrified.

"I am not evil," he disagreed. "I am merely a Servant of a cruel but effective god. All I desire is salvation for my own people, just as you desire salvation for your lover. Do as I suggest, and all of our interests will be served."

Nashir knelt to the floor. He placed a hand on Darien's forehead. Frowning, he rose and strode out of the cell. Once outside, he turned to face two of his Zakai.

"Fools. My order was to keep him alive and suffering. Instead, I find him near death and almost beyond the reach of pain. You failed entirely at your task. Go. Both of you. Provide blankets to the prisoners then present yourselves to the headsman."

Meiran flinched at the audacity of such a command. She whirled around just in time to see both condemned officers bow deeply in acknowledgement, just before the door swung closed with a jarring *clank*, eclipsing them in darkness. The only light was a wan blue glow shimmering through the surrounding ice.

Meiran squeezed her eyes shut, blinking back

tears. She brought her hands up to cover her face. She wanted to be strong, but it was too hard. She felt so helpless.

She didn't want to become the instrument of a monster.

Meiran lowered herself down to the frigid ground, wrapping her arms around Darien's body. His skin felt horribly cold, his hair crusted with ice. She wormed her arms beneath his torso and heaved him up into her lap, hugging him tight.

The cell door creaked open just a crack.

A growing sliver of light revealed the silhouette of a man. One of the officers had actually troubled himself to find blankets on his way to the headsman's block. Meiran peered up, distraught, into the condemned man's bearded face. He handed her the blankets in silence, bowed low, then departed with grace.

Cold blue darkness returned at the *thud* of the closing door.

Meiran lay down alongside Darien and drew the blankets around them both, pulling him close to share her body heat. She closed her eyes and wrapped her arms around the man she had once loved, contenting herself with the feel of him. She was determined not to cry, so she didn't. She held him tight, wishing that the little time they had left together could last a bit longer. But she was too exhausted, the cold too depleting.

Far sooner than she'd intended, Meiran fell asleep.

Chapter Twenty-Three
Death's Doorstep

Glen Farquist, The Rhen

Naia awoke to an eerie, unsettling feeling that brushed down her back like the soft blur of spider's legs scurrying over her skin. She blinked her eyes, opening them just a crack. White, diffuse light filtered down from holes set high above in the ceiling, giving the marble statue above her the glowing appearance of warmth. The vacant eyes of the goddess stared down at her.

A shadowy motion on the other side of the shrine captured Naia's attention. She lay still, closing her eyes, pretending to be asleep. She slowed her breath, willing her fingers to relax. She focused on the slow, shallow rhythm of her breath as the sound of soft footsteps approached across the tiles. Fear wrapped around her spine, groped with chill tendrils through the pit of her stomach.

The rustle of fabric, soft, against the floor beside her. The brush of a finger, tracing her cheek.

Naia fought the urge to scream. She breathed in…then out. In. Out.

A hand, resting with gentle pressure against the fabric of her bodice. Fingers softly circling her stomach.

The touch sent shivers throughout her body, charged, like an electrical storm.

The rustle of fabric stirred again. The sound of soft, slippered feet moved cautiously away.

A gush of profound relief flooded Naia's mind, paralyzing. Her breath hitched in her chest. The sound of the footsteps paused. Then they continued, retreating across the chamber.

Naia cracked one eye open, just a sliver, and gazed across the shrine in the direction of the bier. The wooden cart was empty. The shroud had slipped to the floor, where it lay in a sprawled rumple of fabric.

Naia turned her head ever so slightly, glancing over to where Kyel lay sleeping. A woman was bending over him. A woman in a dark robe, chestnut hair spilling down her back.

Sareen.

Naia clamped her mouth shut against a scream, both eyes opening wide. She squeezed them shut again quickly before the woman glanced her way. She fought to relax the tense muscles of her face.

In. Out.

She peered out from beneath the long lashes of her eyes. She could see Sareen's graceful form, a golden silhouette against the warm wash of light, settling down beside Kyel on the floor. He lay curled on his side, head resting on his hand, his cloak enveloping him like a blanket. Sareen set a hand lightly on his back. She tilted her head, tracing her fingers over the soft embroidery of the star on Kyel's cloak. She continued the motion, sliding her hand down the length of his arm, caressing his hand.

Kyel flinched awake.

As Naia watched through cracked lids, he scrambled back away. The woman before him stayed her ground, raising her hand in a gesture of reassurance.

"There's no need to be afraid," she whispered. "I suspect I owe you both a great deal of gratitude for returning my life to me."

Naia blinked at the sound of Sareen's voice, elegant and tender-soft, with an accent that was at once both exotic and sophisticated. She watched as the darkmage bent forward, laying a comforting hand on Kyel's arm. The expression on her face spoke of wonder and exhilaration.

Kyel gaped up at her, aghast, muscles flexed as if ready to bolt. His face was a medley of dismay, fear, and fascination.

"It was Naia that healed you," he finally managed.

Naia winced internally, hearing that. She didn't trust the enticing darkmage, who seemed to be trapping Kyel under the spell of her allure. He looked utterly baffled, captivated.

Sareen smiled down at him. Reaching out, she stroked her fingers over Kyel's bearded cheek. "But you helped, didn't you?"

"I did," Kyel admitted, gazing wide-eyed up into her face.

Sareen's smile broadened, her eyes sparkling. Leaning forward, she pressed a tender kiss against Kyel's brow. "Thank you so much. I owe you my life."

Naia felt an appalling chill slither over her body. Things were getting quickly out of hand. She didn't know what to do. Sareen's placid voice drifted toward her across the chamber:

"So…why?"

"Why what?" Kyel whispered, licking his lips. He struggled to sit up, resting his weight on his elbows. He gazed up into Sareen's eyes as if transfixed by what he saw there. Naia clenched her fists in consternation.

"Why did the two of you conspire to return the breath of life to one such as I?" Sareen traced her fingers down the sides of his face, first one cheek, then the other. She smiled, a tender, caring expression.

"We need your help," Kyel croaked, wriggling away from her.

"Truly?" Sareen scooted after him.

This had gone on long enough. Naia could no longer pretend to feign sleep. She sat bolt upright.

"Be very careful, Kyel," she warned.

"Kyel?" Sareen glanced back over her shoulder at Naia, flashing her a smile of gratitude. Then she turned back to the subject of her attentions. "That's an intriguing name." She reached out, taking his hand. She brought it up to her lips, kissing it.

Then she rose gracefully to her feet. Her body swayed as she paced across the shrine, dropping to her knees in front of Naia. She canted her head to the side, smiling coyly.

"So, here's the gentle beauty who woke me from my grave." There was a hungering desire in Sareen's voice that also simmered in her eyes. More for herself, Naia realized, then for Kyel. "I owe a special thanks to you." Sareen's smile seemed genuine, as did her admiration. "That took quite a bit of talent; I've never heard of anyone healing through death before in all of history. What order are you trained to, dear?"

"You owe me nothing." Naia edged back away from her. Her eyes shot a stabbing glare at Kyel: a warning.

"Your name is Naia?"

There was no denying the interest of attraction in that voice. Sareen maintained her beguiling smile, her face smooth as butter cream.

Naia knew better than to answer. The woman was already armed with too much information about them already. She gazed defiantly at Sareen.

The darkmage smiled. "It's just a name. A very beautiful name. Nothing to be afraid of." She leaned forward, her lips brushing against Naia's ear. "Do you know my name?"

Naia shivered. Unbidden, the words slipped past her lips. "Sareen Qadir."

The woman's smile brightened. She straightened, taking a step back away. She moved to the center of the room, where she could stand and consider both Naia and Kyel together without turning.

"Now, tell me. What do the two of you need so desperately that you're willing to wake the dead?"

Naia glanced to Kyel, her eyes capturing his gaze and holding it. Fear needled her spine. Gathering her courage, Naia rose to her feet and stood facing the alluring darkmage. Kyel followed suit, edging closer to her until he was standing at her side.

"We want to know where Quinlan Reis took Meiran Withersby," Naia announced. She gazed at Sareen expectantly, hoping that her fear didn't show outright on her face.

Sareen spread her hands. "Well, that's a difficult question for me to answer. Being that Quinlan Reis was responsible for my own particular…condition."

"Why would another Servant try to murder you?" Naia asked.

"I have no idea. I could only speculate."

Naia narrowed her eyes. "Then speculate."

Sareen turned away to face the Goddess of the Eternal Requiem. She stared up into the statue's cold face. With her back still to them, she said softly:

"I imagine he was probably trying to avenge his brother's death."

Naia frowned. "You killed his brother?"

"Not directly, no." Sareen glanced back over her shoulder. "But I was involved."

Naia considered the explanation. It was possible Sareen was telling the truth; she most likely was. Only, Naia doubted it was the only explanation, or even the correct one.

"Where would Quinlan Reis have taken Meiran?" she pressed.

The woman turned back toward her, clasping her hands. "I honestly don't know. If he has turned completely away from Xerys, then his soul is forfeit. Perhaps he took your Prime Warden ahead to Bryn Calazar to give the appearance that he's still doing the work of our Master even as he plotted against me."

Naia clenched her jaw in frustration. This was going nowhere. This woman did not have the knowledge they sought. Either that or she was a subtle and convincing liar. The truth probably lay somewhere in between.

Naia asked, "What does Renquist want with Meiran?"

"Control," Sareen responded immediately.

Naia blanched, feeling her stomach sink. "What do you mean?"

The woman's smile returned, this time almost gloating. She strode forward until she was standing right in front of Naia, gazing down into her eyes. "I'm sorry, darling, but I do believe it's my turn." She trailed a finger down Naia's cheek. "If you want me to keep speaking, you must answer a question or two of mine."

Naia stared resentfully into Sareen's face, shuddering from the touch even as she fought the impulse to blurt out an affirmative. She regretted healing Sareen. She had vastly underestimated this demon's sophistication. Sareen was working on her mind, seducing Naia's will and intentions. Bending them subtly in the directions she wanted. Naia could feel Sareen's power working, helpless to do anything about it.

"I will answer two questions," Naia allowed. It was the most resistance she could manage. She swallowed, unable to break eye contact.

Sareen asked, "Where did you learn to heal as you did? To turn back the clock on death? The most talented healers of my own time couldn't have managed it. How is it possible that you were able to accomplish what has never before been achieved?"

Naia felt a sharp pang of fear. This, she knew, was very dangerous territory. But before she could stop herself, she was already answering.

"Before I became a mage, I was a priestess of Death."

Sareen's eyes widened with a look of astonishment. "That explains a great deal," she said, pacing away. "In my time, neither the Lyceum nor the temples would have ever countenanced such a dangerous union of knowledge. Yet, what a wonderful resource!"

Sareen paused, blinking.

She whirled back around, fixing her stare on Kyel. "And do you have any such special talents?"

Kyel immediately shook his head. "No."

"None at all?"

"Nothing," Kyel admitted with a shrug.

Sareen frowned, her eyes darkening. "That's too bad. I'm really very sorry, Kyel."

Her eyes filled with sincere regret.

"No!" Naia screamed, throwing herself forward. A strong slap of air brushed her easily aside, throwing her to the ground.

Kyel dropped to his knees, eyes bulging, mouth agape as he struggled for breath. His hands groped frantically at his chest.

"Kyel! By the goddess! No!"

Sareen turned to Naia with an expression of genuine remorse. "I'm sorry, little one." Her voice was full of sympathy. "He's just not valuable like you."

Kyel fell forward to the ground, limbs flailing helplessly. His chest seized, lurching for air.

With a scream of rage, Naia closed her eyes and lashed out at Sareen. It wasn't planned, wasn't thought out. She used the knowledge gleaned from years of working with the dying and the dead. She didn't think of the consequences. She just acted.

Naia reached deep into Sareen's body and silenced the beating heart she had so recently brought back to life.

There was no gasping, no struggle. Sareen's

expression went slack. She crumbled face-first to the floor, her hair shrouding her face.

Sobbing, Naia threw herself down on the floor beside Kyel. He was breathing again, his eyes watering as he gasped for air. Naia hugged him fiercely. She brought her right hand up to wipe away her tears—

—and saw the hideous red scar that twisted around her wrist in the place where the chain-like marking had been just seconds before.

Naia screamed. She scrambled backward, staggering to her feet. She grasped her wrist with her other hand, clutching it against her chest. She screamed again and kept screaming, over and over. Her panicked shrieks filled the room, echoing off the walls of the shrine. She collapsed to her knees as her wails faded into violent, wracking sobs.

A thunderous clatter echoed through the shrine. The great oaken door jolted as it was assaulted with force from the other side. Naia couldn't move. She hugged her arm against her chest, sobbing wretchedly. On her knees, she wobbled over next to Kyel. He was unconscious, but mercifully still breathing.

An echoing *crash* resounded through the shrine as the door gave way. Priests in white vestments rushed forward into the room, spilling down the stairs. Striding through their midst was Luther Penthos, rushing through them toward his daughter.

He swept Naia up into his arms, hugging her close against him. Then he pulled back, cupping her tear-stained face in his hands. His frightened gaze probed her eyes. He must have seen something there. His jaw fell slack as he stared at Naia's wrist.

His face collapsed in despair.

And then he reacted. Clutching her by the arm, Naia's father dragged her forward across the room. Before she could protest, he forced her across the threshold of the portal into the otherness of the Catacombs. The light shivered, shifted. His grip on her wrist was violent and painful.

Naia fought for her hand back, wrenching her arm free of her father's grasp.

He swung toward her, looming in his anger, more formidable than Naia had ever seen him. No longer was Luther Penthos a fragile old man. He was the Vicar of Death, the incarnation of his office, in all its fearsome majesty.

"Use the Catacombs to flee the Rhen!" Naia's father ordered her. "Flee the Rhen and never come back! Do you understand? Don't tell me where you're going. *I don't ever want to know.*"

Naia stared at him through tear-filled eyes, grimacing through her terror. *"What? Why?"*

Luther Penthos raised a hand as if to strike her across the face. But he clenched his fist, instead, eyes turbulent with sorrow and wrath.

"You broke Oath, Naia! By rule of law, your life is now forfeit!"

"Father, *I didn't mean to—!*"

He shook his head, eyes chilling in their fury. *"It doesn't matter!* The only thing that matters now is time. You must hurry! They'll be looking for you. Don't leave a trail for them to follow."

Tears streamed down her face as Naia shook her head in protest. *"No, Father!"*

He wrapped his arms around her, forcing her against his chest in a last, violent embrace. "I can't protect you, Naia. But neither will I be party to my own daughter's execution. *Now, go!*"

She walked away a few steps, burying her face in her hands, sobbing wretchedly. She stopped and turned back. *"Father, no! Please!"*

Luther Penthos waved her away, his glare terrible and uncompromising.

"Go, Naia. Go now and never come back. *Never.*"

Sobbing, Naia stumbled forward into the Catacombs, clutching her ruined wrist against her chest.

Chapter Twenty-Four
Chaos

Tokashi Palace, The Black Lands

Meiran felt warm, secure. Shrouded in comfort. As if everything wrong in the world had been suddenly made right. For the first time in years, she awoke to feelings of security and contentment. No longer was there that aching, throbbing place inside. That emptiness was now full. It abounded with warmth, gratitude, and compassion. They were not her own feelings.

They were Darien's.

Once, Meiran had awakened each morning saturated with the comfort of Darien's presence in her mind. She could feel him throughout the day, always there, always with her. She had never been alone. It was almost as if she wore him around with her, deep within her heart. She always knew what he was feeling, whether he was excited or melancholy, frustrated or confused, angry or desperate. Even after he'd left Aerysius for Greystone Keep. The connection between them had grown so strong she could still sense it, despite the distance. Though weak, the link between them had comforted her quietly from afar.

When Darien died, Meiran had felt that link shatter. One moment he was there with her. The next, he was gone. She was left with only a hollow, empty ache.

But now, somehow, he was back with her again. Filling her mind with feelings of warmth and a sense of solace. She could feel the heat of his body pressed up against hers, the peaceful rhythm of his heart. His fingers stroked her hair back away from her face, his touch soothing.

Meiran opened her eyes even though she didn't want to.

Darien was lying beside her. Propped on one elbow, gazing down into her face with a soft expression in his eyes. His skin was flushed from the warmth of the blankets.

"Are you all right?" His voice was low and hoarse.

Meiran nodded, feeling the urgency of his concern for her.

"I'm fine," she whispered. "Are you?"

"Better," he answered. He was smiling at her wistfully, fingers still absently stroking her hair.

"What?"

"I was just thinking of the day I fell in love with you."

She raised her eyebrows. "You can actually remember which day that was?"

Darien nodded. "It was the day of your Raising."

"Why that day?"

"It was supposed to be *my* Raising. Remember?"

She did remember. The legacy she'd inherited had come from Neria Terrant, Grand Master of the Sixth Tier, one of the most powerful mages in the history of Aerysius. The Sentinels had put forth Darien as their candidate to receive Neria's legacy. Since he had the backing of the Sentinels, Darien was an easy selection. But Grand Master Neria overrode the decision. She reconvened the Assembly, staunchly and publicly refusing Darien as her successor.

The result was a political skirmish between orders as both Sentinels and Querers set themselves at each other's throats. In the end, Meiran was chosen to be the recipient of Aerysius' most powerful magical lineage. Darien left the Assembly humiliated, still years away from another chance.

"They were awful to you," Meiran whispered. "Especially Grand Master Neria."

Darien's fingers continued their slow stroking of her hair. His eyes grew distant, a quiet smile forming on his lips. "I remember. She called me a 'cavalier delinquent.' She told me my greatest attribute was that I probably wouldn't survive long enough to do much damage."

"At least you proved her wrong."

Darien's smile turned devilish. "I did. She grossly underestimated the amount of damage I was capable of."

Meiran was taken aback by Darien's self-deprecating wit. It was so utterly out of character. It was something the old Darien would have said. The man who'd gone away to Greystone Keep, never to return.

He continued, "At any rate, that's why I fell in love with you. You were there for me when no one else was. And you didn't have to be; you really didn't know me well at all. But you went out of your way to walk me back to the Acolyte's Residence. Along the way, you told me something I'll never forget."

"What was that?"

"You said I needed to start ignoring everyone else's expectations and start living up to my own. It's the best advice anyone's ever given me." More softly, he added, "I just wish I'd have followed it."

Meiran stared up into Darien's face. His expression was pensive, his gaze remote. His eyes were focused somewhere far away, perhaps at the shadows, perhaps somewhere in the past. There was a quiet serenity to his features she hadn't seen in years.

"You were more deserving of that legacy than I was," he said. "You're a remarkable woman, Meiran. You've always had my admiration. And my heart. You still do."

His fingers caressed her brow, smoothing the strands of hair back away from her face.

Hearing his words, feeling the warmth of emotion that flooded into her through the link, Meiran felt a drowning ache of sorrow. She pulled away from him, sitting up in the cold darkness of the cell. Darien looked at her with eyes full of anxious uncertainty. The link didn't work both ways; he couldn't sense the layers of guilt and dread she was feeling. But he could see them implied on her face.

Meiran explained as levelly as she could, "Nashir intends my gift for his lover, a woman named Katarya. He wants me to convince you to deny Xerys and follow me to the grave."

Darien sat up. His eyes widened slightly, but his expression never changed. He looked her directly in the eye, his stare unfaltering. "I'll follow you anywhere you ask, Meiran. But you're not going to the grave just yet. I won't let that happen."

Meiran lowered her eyes. She took a deep breath. "What if there's nothing you can do about it?"

"I'll find a way." There was absolutely no trace of doubt in his voice.

"Darien…what if you can't?" Meiran insisted. She peered into his face, her voice firm. "If you don't, if something happens to me…then I want you to abandon Xerys."

A troubled sadness filled his eyes. He set his jaw, stubbornly shaking his head. "You've no idea what you're asking."

"I *do,"* Meiran said, leaning forward. "I know you, Darien. And I know that this…*existence*…it's not what you ever would have wanted. It goes against everything you always stood for, everything you love and believe in."

"It doesn't, though. That's what you have to understand."

"Then *help me understand!"* Meiran insisted, waves of frustration bleeding into her voice. "Because, right now, I don't."

Darien nodded. Meiran could sense the tension in him as he struggled to gather his thoughts. She could feel how exasperated he was, how desperate to gain her understanding.

He explained, "When I was a Sentinel, I was sworn to defend the Rhen. Now…I'm pledged to a higher purpose. I serve Chaos. The entire magic field is born of Chaos. That's what I protect. That's what I serve. It's bigger than the Rhen. Bigger than Malikar. Bigger than us all.

"It's my duty to bring the people of Malikar out of darkness. They've endured here too long, and for no good reason other than our own inability to find fault within ourselves. And, after that, I've another obligation: I have to make damn certain that something like this can never happen again. *That* is my duty. That's why I'm here."

Softly, he added, "I'm sorry, Meiran. This isn't my

life to live any longer. I gave that up." He lowered his chin, staring up at her through tousled strands of hair.

"How would you define Chaos?" His words were little more than a whisper.

Meiran shrugged, not knowing how to respond. Frowning, she uttered the first words that came to mind. "Disorder, mayhem…evil."

Darien nodded. "That's why you're confused. You can't simply chalk everything up to disorder and mayhem. Good and evil. Those notions are entirely too simplistic."

Defiant, she lifted her chin. "What's *your* definition, then?"

He looked away. His expression was remote. "It's not what you'd think," he said. "It's hard to explain. I don't know that I can."

"Try."

Darien scowled as if daunted by the task. He took a moment before speaking, as if carefully framing his answer.

"Things happen the way they do because they're set in motion by our actions. And then, from there, they tend to follow a certain trajectory. Every decision we make has consequences. Tremendous consequences, so many that we have no way of foreseeing them all or anticipating what direction they'll take us in. Everything that happens, happens as a result of our own actions, our own decisions.

"That's what Chaos is," he said, leaning forward. "It's the sum of the consequences of every decision we've ever made coming back to haunt us in the end."

Meiran stared at Darien with profound sadness in her eyes, her heart quietly breaking.

They'd remade so much more than just his flesh. They'd reimagined everything about him that had once defined who he was. They had harnessed Darien's boundless passion for duty, turned it against him, corrupting it to their cause. Transmuted his guilt into a collar to constrain him. They had taken the pureness of his soul and worn it down into a soiled, gritty thing that justified ends with means.

She understood him better, now.

She also understood she couldn't leave him like this.

This was the man who had saved her when her soul had been past any hope of salvaging. Meiran took a deep breath, closing her eyes against remorse. She took his hands in hers.

"This is not your responsibility, Darien," she said, gazing into the shadows of his face. "It's not your fight any longer. That's what death is for. It releases us from our obligations, relieves us of the burdens life places on us. Only in death are we truly free." She added in a whisper, "If you deny Xerys, you can have that kind of freedom, Darien."

"You want me dead," he said dully, eyes flat and leaden.

"You're already dead." It was such a cruel thing to say. Nevertheless, it had to be spoken. "Now…I just want you safe. I want you someplace they can't hurt you anymore."

He turned away. "In my entire life, there's been only one person capable of hurting me. Thank you for the pain." The cold way he said it, combined with the raw depth of hurt flooding into her through the link, acted on her like a kick in the gut.

She couldn't hold back the tears. They spilled down her cheeks like rain. She brought her hands up and wept silently into her palms, face hot with scalding shame. Her shoulders shook with the quiet force of her guilt. All the while she could feel the heat of Darien's anger condensing, cooling, as the link between them faltered. To her dismay, she realized he was walling his emotions away, shutting her out.

The cell door creaked. Then it shuddered open.

"No!" Meiran shrieked, panicking at the sight of the thin strip of light that suddenly appeared, widening into the span of a doorway. She scooted back away from it until her back was pressed up against the chill wall of the cell. Her fingers clawed at the ice for traction.

At the sight of the first guard that entered, Meiran shouted, *"No! Please! I need more time—!"*

A group of men streamed into the chamber, surrounding them. They went for Darien first. They threw him down onto his stomach as one man knelt on top of him with a knee pressed into his back. They bound his arms behind him with a set of iron manacles. Then they grappled him to his feet, maneuvering him out of the cell.

The remaining guards spun Meiran around against the wall, holding her pinioned against the ice. One man forced her arm up over her head, holding her wrist with a crushing grip as he brought the other arm up, as well. They lashed her wrists together over her head, tugging fiercely on the rope. They shoved her backward. Hands grabbed her, forcing her through the doorway and down to the ground of the passage outside.

She fell to her knees beside Darien, who was crouching with his arms shackled behind his back. In front of him stood a man Meiran instantly recognized.

It was one of the Zakai officers Nashir had ordered to the headsman. Apparently, the man had chosen to ignore the command. He leaned forward, stooping down until he was almost at eye level with Darien. His brow was broken out in beads of perspiration despite the icy chill of the air. His expression was rigid, intense. His dark eyes simmered with brutality.

"You said you can give us back the sun. Tell me how."

Darien glared up at the man through wet strands of hair. She could feel the scorch of his anger even through the faltering link. Meiran heard every breath he sucked into his chest, the sounds sharpened by the intensity of his wrath.

"There's two options," Darien said through gritted teeth, looking up at him with an unwavering gaze. "First, I'll try to break the curse over the Black Lands. If that fails, then I'll escort your people southward into the Rhen. With the strength of my power and my knowledge of their command structure, their armies won't stand a chance."

Meiran gaped at Darien, her eyes widening in disbelief. Horror seeped into every crevice of her being, her stomach clenching into a hard burl of knots. Even after everything Darien had said back in the cell, the way he'd argued so passionately about Chaos, Meiran was still shocked. She would have never believed him capable of embracing such treachery.

He never even looked at her.

He crouched on the floor, gazing up into the bearded face of the Enemy officer, calmly awaiting a response. No emotions came back to her through the link. No remorse, no regret, no anger, no shame. Nothing. He was completely empty.

More men spilled into the corridor around them. One leaned forward and whispered something into the officer's ear. The bearded man nodded, righting himself. He glared imperiously down at Darien, hands on his hips.

"He sends for you," the officer announced, stepping back. "If you can defeat Nashir Arman, then you will have the support of the Tanisars." He turned and strode briskly away down the corridor.

Hands gripped Meiran by the arms, hauling her onto her feet. She resisted, thrashing frantically, struggling to break free.

"Don't!" she screamed back at Darien as they dragged her brutally down the corridor away from him. *"Don't give them what they want! Please! Don't do it! Don't let them destroy you!"*

Chapter Twenty-Five
Blood for Blood

Tokashi Palace, The Black Lands

He could still hear the shrill sounds of Meiran's screams echoing down the passage: frantic, pleading, hysterical. There was a sharp, scuffling commotion. Then silence. An eerie calm descended on the passage, clinging to the walls.

Darien knelt with his knees drawn up against his chest, wrists crossed behind his back, restrained there by cold iron manacles. He was naked from the waist up, his body trembling more from horror than from cold. He stared down in misery at the blue-ice floor of the cave beneath his feet as waves of shock, revulsion and despair broke over his body in rapid succession, one after another. He clenched his jaw until it shook, biting his lip against the despair trying to claw its way up from his insides.

They were going to kill Meiran.

Meiran, the woman he loved. The woman who wanted him dead.

That thought bore down on him like a cruel iron weight, crushing and brutal. He swayed over his feet, the muscles of his calves burning from the stress position they had him in. Someone slipped an arm around his neck, restraining him. Another guard shoved a filthy rag into his mouth, feeding it in all the way back past his teeth. He gagged and struggled, retching against the rough, dry taste of the rag.

They shoved a woven sack over his head, tying it with a cord around his neck. Not enough to choke him. Just enough to hold it in place.

With the rag in his mouth, the sack over his face, Darien labored just to breathe.

Panic seized him. He flailed against the unyielding grip of the guards. They threw him down hard against the ice, restraining him there with the weight of their bodies as he fought and squirmed, bucking and kicking. At last he went limp for lack of air and will to fight. Darien slumped against the ice, struggling just to draw breath, gasping at stale air and rotten fabric.

"Are you done?" someone above him growled. The sound of the voice was muffled by the sack.

He couldn't respond.

They lifted his dead weight, hauling him forward. His heart surged, the sound of his pulse a careening thunder in his ears. He couldn't walk, so he let them drag him down the corridor. He felt consciousness slowly leaking out of him.

The sounds around him were muffled, distant, disorienting. He could see only darkness. His mind groped through a haze, desperately fumbling to cope with his situation. There was nothing he could cling to; his senses were deprived, the magic field just a memory. The fickle Hellpower had betrayed him, fleeing from his touch. There was nothing for his mind to latch onto. They had rendered him utterly helpless.

The guards halted, propping him upright with the force of their bodies. There was the sound of chains. Someone jerked his arms upward behind his back until his shoulders screamed in anguish. They held him there, securing his wrists above his head. Darien clenched his teeth against the pain, feeling the tendons of his shoulders starting to give. Behind, he could hear a sharp, metallic *clank*. Then another, much more ghastly sound.

The noise of gears going *click, click, click*...

His body began to stretch as his weight was lifted off his feet. Pain like molten fire seared down his arms and into his shoulders, radiating across his chest. He could feel the joints of his shoulders starting to give. There was a dull popping sound.

Darien howled against the rag.

He could still touch the ground with the tips of his toes. They left him there, dangling, twisting at the end of the chains, the tissues of his shoulders slowly separating. Darien groaned, gasping through clenched teeth, biting on the wadded fabric stuffed in his mouth. It didn't help. The pain was acute, relentless. It worsened by the second.

He could see nothing. Hear nothing except the sound of his own muffled groans and the sharp hiss of breath wheezing through his nostrils.

A disembodied hand rested softly against the skin of his back. It caressed him, the way a rider strokes the muscles of a horse. The sensation raised goosebumps on his flesh. A sense of appalling dread clenched his throat, terrorizing him from the inside.

He fought for every strangled breath, his consciousness reeling.

A deep, familiar voice addressed him from the darkness:

"I told you I'd have my revenge. 'Flesh for flesh. Blood for blood.' That's been the unwritten law of the Khazahar for thousands of years. It's still the law today."

The hand on his back moved, stroking downward across his naked flesh. Darien shuddered against the awful feel of it. That deep, emotionless voice resonated in the stifling darkness:

"Your greatest mistake was taking Arden away from me. Your last mistake was thinking that you might actually get away with it. What hubris you must have."

The hand lifted, moving away. There was a shudder in the chains restraining him.

Click…click…click…

Darien screamed into the rag as both of his feet lifted completely off the floor. The hand was back, this time resting against the back of his head. It clenched the material of the sack in a fist, drawing the suffocating fabric tight against his face.

Instead of sucking in air, his nostrils sucked only dust-filled cloth. His lungs spasmed, burning.

Darien thrashed, making the pain even worse. His arms were going numb, but his shoulders seared with fire. Spent, his body went limp. He sagged in his chains as the world faded little by little. Nashir's voice murmured something in his ear. Darien didn't have enough presence of mind left to make out the words.

The hand released its tension on the fabric. He drew in a desperate gasp of air through his nostrils. Head throbbing, he labored for breath, sucking fabric against his face.

"Does that hurt?" Nashir's voice echoed through the darkness of his horror. "Trust me. This is nothing compared to what I'm about to do to your Meiran."

Darien growled. He groped for the Onslaught like a drowning man scrambling for a length of rope. But the Hellpower was like a sadistic taunt, dangling just within reach before jerking back away.

From across the room came a frantic, muffled sound.

Meiran.

She was in there with him. Somewhere in the chamber. Panic seized him. Reflexively, Darien fumbled again for the Onslaught. Of course, it wasn't there. His body spasmed, shaking all over, his muscles quivering in terror and agony.

"Quiet, now," Nashir's voice whispered. "Listen. Can you hear it? More softly. Yes. There it is."

Darien listened, even though he didn't want to. Inside, he was silently sobbing. He couldn't hear anything. The sack muffled most of the noise in the room. All he could hear was the shuddering sounds of his own ragged breath.

From across the chamber, there came the softest whimpering sound. Then a startled, muffled shriek.

They were torturing her.

Darien howled and twisted, writhing against the manacles that held him up. The pain was ghastly. His shoulders were coming apart, the iron shackles sawing at the flesh of his hands. He bucked, fighting against them.

Another gruesome shriek filled his ears.

Darien collapsed in his traces, feeling the warm wetness of blood running down his arms, dripping to the floor. His mind groped in vain for the Onslaught.

"Katarya is very skilled with a knife," observed Nashir's patient voice.

Meiran screamed again, the sound curdling Darien's nerves. The sack prevented him from seeing what they were doing to her. All he could do was listen and imagine.

His imagination was a powerful thing. A powerful, toxic, vindictive thing.

"You do have a choice, of course," Nashir whispered, his voice very low. "Deny our Master and cast your soul into Oblivion. If you do this, I promise you, she will feel no further pain."

The offer brought some small shred of hope. Darien's thoughts went sadly to Azár. He'd promised Azár he would help her people. He'd had every intention of following through with that promise. But not at this price. This price was far too high.

Meiran screamed again, a horrifying shriek that trailed off into wracking sobs. Darien couldn't stand it any longer. Beneath the sack, he could only envision what they were doing to her. In his mind, he saw the strips of flesh being peeled away from her body, curling like apple rind. The exposed, bloody tissues revealed beneath.

Nashir's voice uttered softly, "I wonder how many days it will take to break you? How many screams? You *will* break…the only question is how much you will let her suffer before you do."

Darien drew in a gasping breath, letting it out again in a long, shuddering sob. His entire body shook in violent spasms. Nashir was right. Better to let go now, before Meiran suffered any further. Much better than to wait.

Maybe, in Oblivion, his soul would finally know peace.

Isn't that what Meiran had promised?

Only in death are we truly free. That's what she'd told him.

Anger suffused him at the thought. Anger at Meiran. Meiran, who'd rejected him, despite all he'd suffered to get her back. His death alone hadn't been good enough for her. Now she wanted his very soul torn to ash.

He would give her what she wanted. It would be the last damned thing he ever gave her.

One last time, Darien groped for the Onslaught. This time, the Hellpower responded. It rushed into him, filling him. It gushed through him with the violence of a flood, the fury of a maelstrom. It was as terrible as it was beguiling. It entranced him, bewitched him. Bewildered and comforted him. Darien shivered, not in pain, but with the violent throes of brutal ecstasy.

He turned his wrath on the iron shackles that held him up. A strange sensation gripped his wrists, like focused rays of sunlight. He could feel a warm wetness slick his skin as the iron melted and ran like searing, molten wax down the length of his arms.

Darien dropped to the ground, falling forward on his face. He tried to push himself up, but his arms didn't work. He thrashed on the floor, somehow managing to squirm his head out of the sack. Vision assaulted him, confronting him with a macabre and gruesome scene.

Nashir's face, pale, gaped down at him full of horror. Stunned guards ringed the walls of the chamber, a room made all out of jagged rocks, twisted hooks and dangling, rusted chains. Across the room lay Meiran, sprawled, strapped down by thick ropes. Her left arm was stripped of its tissues, completely denuded. He couldn't see her face.

Beside her stood a woman wielding a long and gruesome knife. She stood frozen, gaping at Darien as if staring into the face of death, eyes full of revulsion and dismay.

The room was aglow with a terrible green light. Darien couldn't tell where the light was coming from. It seemed to be seeping from every crevice all at once, shining through the mortars of the bricks, leaking from the shadows.

He surged to his feet, glancing desperately to Meiran. Then he looked back to Nashir. Hatred filled his eyes to boiling. He lifted his hands up, forcing his unwilling arms to move just enough to embrace the darkmage like a brother.

"Impossib—"

Nashir drew in a sharp, pitiful gasp. Then he blinked. A single drop of blood leaked from the corner of his eye, ran dribbling down his cheek. Blood trickled from his nose, foamed at the corner of his mouth. He staggered backward as strangled, frothing noises rasped deep within his chest.

Darien stood still, locked in place, watching the grisly scene unfold with acute dispassion. Before him, Nashir lurched, moving awkwardly like a wooden puppet. He collapsed to his knees, bloody froth gurgling from his nostrils.

Darien knelt beside him, placing his hands on the

dying man's face. There was an awful, crackling noise. Then a smell like grilling meat. Nashir Arman moaned hoarsely, inhumanly. The sound didn't come from his ruined lungs; it came from the depths of his blackened soul.

The sound faded out into an airy, whispering hiss that sizzled with misery.

Satisfied, Darien rose from the ground and turned away.

He glanced back. There was no corpse. Only a dark stain on the floor where Nashir had fallen, as if his flesh had been seared into the stone. But it was more than that. It wasn't a stain; it was a shadow. A living shadow that coalesced and rose, solidifying as it drew upward from the ground. A shadow that took on a distinctive man-like shape, one that Darien immediately recognized.

It was a necrator.

His very first.

The woman behind him issued a hysterical, horrified scream. She launched herself at Darien with the knife. He reacted without thinking, trying to bring his hands up to ward her off. But his arms didn't work fast enough. He dodged back, a second too late. The blade took him in the gut, sinking deep under his ribs all the way to the hilt.

The guards swept suddenly into motion. They descended from the walls, weapons drawn. One caught Darien, hauling him back away. Another confronted the girl, dispatching her with a sword thrust through the throat.

Darien gazed down at the woman's body in shocked dismay, clutching his middle as the guard lowered him to the floor. He dropped the knife and glanced down at his hand, seeing the dark stain that coated it.

He looked to the necrator that seemed to be floating in the exact center of the chamber, a sinister observer rooted in silence and shadow. Awaiting his command.

Darien was too shocked to command anything. He could only gaze down at his hand, at the amount of blood, and speculate. One of the soldiers knelt beside him and began tending to his injury, using his own garments to bind and bandage the wound.

Darien stared up into the man's face, addled with confusion.

He nodded at Meiran.

"Help her first," he whispered gruffly. He didn't know how the men would react, whether they would listen to him or not. To his gratitude, they did. Two rose immediately and strode around the periphery of the room toward Meiran, covering her with their own coats as they worked to undo the bonds that held her in place.

He turned to the guardsman who still lingered over him. "I have to get out of the vortex. Where's Sayeed?"

The man shook his head without reply, as if he didn't understand.

"Get him," Darien commanded.

The soldier nodded once and rose without a word.

Chapter Twenty-Six
Never to Harm

Tokashi Palace, The Black Lands

Meiran trembled as she struggled into a warm kaftan held out for her by one of the soldiers. The man stood with eyes lowered respectfully to the floor, waiting for her to robe. Her fingers shook so violently that she could hardly work the coat's fastenings. Her arm blazed with fire from where the flesh had been peeled away. The guard had bandaged up her wounds with his own sash, which helped ease the pain just a little. But the damage was severe; Katarya had managed to strip off every inch of flesh from the underside of Meiran's forearm, all the way up to the mark of the chain on her wrist.

She let her eyes roam across the floor, over to where a living shadow hovered in the exact center of the chamber. Just the presence of the necrator filled Meiran with a harrowing sense of dread. She had once been touched by one of hell's dark minions; she knew the horrors they could inflict. This one seemed even more sinister, somehow. This shade had not been raised from the flesh of innocents. If necrators had souls, this one's was hopelessly damned.

Meiran backed away from it as far as she could go, pressing her back up against the rough wall of the chamber. She edged around the periphery, never taking her eyes off the ghastly thing. To her horror, the necrator responded to her movement. It rotated slowly, tracking her motion. An appalling sense of dread chilled Meiran's blood.

She used her fingers to grope along the wall, at last dropping down to her hands and knees. Keeping her eyes on the necrator, she scooted the rest of the way across the floor, clutching her bandaged arm against her chest.

She knelt at Darien's side, shaking, trembling with revulsion and dread. The evil shade hovered above them just an arm's length away, blacker than the deepest abyss, smooth like glass and utterly featureless. It had no eyes, but she didn't doubt it could sense. She could feel its hunger, its lust for life. Its soulless, yearning desire for her death.

She gazed down at Darien helplessly. He lay on the floor, a strip of cloth binding his middle. Blood had already begun seeping through the bandages. The wound's drainage was dark, almost black. Seeing that, Meiran felt numb.

She could do nothing for him in the vortex.

She bowed her head, trying hard not to grieve, even though she knew it was better this way. One glance back at the necrator confirmed what she already knew: Darien was far too dangerous to live.

Sounds in the corridor made her turn. Two Enemy officers staggered forward into the room. They stopped in the doorway, gazing around the chamber with wide and startled eyes, taking in the sight of the necrator and the scene of carnage that confronted them. To their credit, it took the men only seconds to recover.

One soldier dropped to Meiran's side, while the other moved off to check on the dead woman. She recognized the man beside her: it was the officer who'd been ordered to the headsman. She didn't know his name, but he seemed like someone in a position of authority. The man knelt over Darien, shaking him gently.

"Can you walk?"

To Meiran's astonishment, Darien nodded. "I think so."

With the man's aid, Darien rose unstably to his feet. The soldiers moved forward and helped support his weight. Darien clutched his middle with one hand, taking a step forward. He winced in pain.

"What's the quickest way out of here?"

The bearded officer frowned, considering. "We should make use of the boats."

"The boats?" Meiran echoed, surprised. She hadn't seen any boats, not since arriving in the Black Lands.

The Zakai officer nodded. "Yes. The river is the fastest way."

"What's your name?" Meiran demanded.

The officer glanced back her way. "I am Sayeed."

"Thank you, Sayeed."

They left the chamber, the two soldiers supporting Darien between them. Meiran followed after them, glancing back one last time down the passage. The necrator was not following, she realized with a profound sense of relief. She walked behind, watching with a grim sense of inevitability as Darien limped ahead of her. She took note of the dark trail of blood that marked his passage.

The soldiers might get Darien to the boats, Meiran decided, but they weren't doing him any kindness. Not with that injury. The best thing they could do would be to find a quiet place where he could rest.

"Don't press so hard," Sayeed admonished. "You'll just bleed more."

Darien nodded, grimacing. The pain was getting worse. Meiran could feel it through the link. Darien limped forward, sweat dribbling down his brow, wetting his hair despite the cold. Only force of will and the strength of the officers kept him on his feet.

Meiran walked with her eyes lowered, focused on the pitter-patter trail of blood she followed along the ground. She was beginning to grow more and more uncomfortable with what they were doing. It was just as futile as it was cruel.

As they turned a corner, the bearded officer announced, "We're almost there."

Meiran sighed regretfully. She didn't want Darien on a boat. She wanted him here, where she had some control.

The corridor opened up into a natural cavern formed by the passage of water. Meiran breathed in the humidity of the air, staring in wonder at the dark waters that stretched out before them. Lashed to their moors, small wooden boats bobbed up and down on the current.

The two soldiers helped Darien toward the nearest vessel. Sayeed jumped onto the boat first, steadying it as they helped Darien climb in. They laid him out on the bottom of the boat then turned and beckoned for Meiran.

Hesitant, she accepted Sayeed's offered hand, the other man steadying her as her legs spanned the gap between the dock and the bobbing vessel. She dropped immediately down to the boards, trying to position herself as close as she could to the craft's center of gravity. The small boat rocked treacherously, threatening to spill them over.

Sayeed seated himself on a cross plank and took up the oars, signaling the other man to cast them off.

His companion stooped over, unwound the coils, then threw the rope back into the boat. As they drifted out into the river, Sayeed slid the oars into the rowlocks and dipped the blades into the water. He leaned back and, with deep and graceful strokes, began rowing.

Meiran shivered in the chill breeze that gusted out of the depths of the ice caverns. She scooted herself around, repositioning her body against the gunwale. Darien lay curled on his side on the floor of the boat, arms hugging his middle. He was shivering. Looking down at him, Meiran felt a knot of sadness in her throat. She reached down and felt his skin with her fingers. It was cold and damp, like the flesh of a cadaver.

"Give me your jacket," she said. The officer obeyed immediately, releasing the oars and struggling out of his coat. Meiran used it like a blanket to cover Darien, tucking it in around him as much as she could.

She glanced upward as they emerged from the cavern, noticing great stalactites that spiked down from the ceiling. They gave the cave's mouth the appearance of a monster grimacing with sharpened teeth. Sayeed put his back into the oars, propelling their little craft across the glass surface of the lake. The waters parted before them easily, their vessel making good headway.

Meiran's hand moved to Darien's head, stroking his hair. She took his hand in hers.

"How long until we're out of the vortex?" she asked.

Sayeed answered without faltering at the oars. "Difficult to say. An hour, maybe two."

Meiran didn't think Darien had an hour left in him. She smoothed back a lock of hair from his face. He was resting comfortably, at least. Not as cold anymore. The wound didn't throb so very badly.

He mumbled something she couldn't make out.

She bent down to hear him better.

"Water."

Through the link, she could feel his terrible thirst. Even if she had water, Meiran knew better than to give him any. She felt saddened by her decision to withhold such a simple comfort. Saddened, but resolute.

"I can't, Darien. I'm sorry."

He didn't ask again. He closed his eyes and faded into restless sleep.

She held his hand as the lake narrowed into a river around them. Here, the waters didn't seem quite as black. The wind wasn't as chill. Overhead, churning clouds clogged the vast expanse of sky.

They rowed with a strong current that swept them speedily along, racing the angry clouds above. Sayeed's face was streaked with sweat, his body glistening with perspiration. In the muted light of the clouds, his features seemed jagged, almost surreal.

They followed the river for minutes, perhaps an hour. Black cliffs rose around them, forming a steep gorge. The night was silent, save for the constant drone of the river.

"Are we out yet?"

It took Meiran a moment to comprehend Darien's words; they were mumbled under his breath. And his breath was very weak. It took another moment to realize what he was trying to ask.

"No, Darien. Not yet." She caressed his hand tenderly.

With her mind walled away, she had no way of actually sensing the presence of the vortex. But she knew it was still there, still mercilessly compressing the currents of the magic field around them. She didn't dare open her mind to it; the backlash would kill her in a heartbeat.

And it really didn't matter. She had no intention of healing him, anyway.

Meiran stared down at her wrist, at the emblem of the chain that shimmered coldly in the cloud light. *Never to harm.*

She couldn't end Darien's life. But there was nothing in the Oath of Harmony that obligated her to preserve it. Meiran searched deeply within herself, realizing she had the strength to let him go.

She caressed his hand, running her fingers over his skin. He responded to her touch, his fingers trailing once over hers.

He was quiet after that. So was the river. It wound like a graceful ribbon down through the center of the gorge. The only sound in the darkness was the constant creak of the oars, the gentle lapping of water against the hull of the boat. Sayeed had fallen into a steady pattern with his rowing. The boat rocked them gently.

Minutes passed. Another hour, perhaps. The whole while, Darien was very still. Meiran was starting to wonder if he hadn't already slipped away, left her behind without her knowing.

With cold apprehension, she lifted the coat.

His bandages were soaked in blood. There was so much of it. The blood dripped thickly, pooling on the boards on the bottom of the boat. Meiran lowered the coat, tucking it back into place. She gazed up at the sky, studying the clouds.

More minutes passed. The oars creaked. The river rocked them in its arms.

Meiran frowned, recognizing one of the hills across the river. They must not be too far away from Qul. She hadn't realized they'd come so far so quickly.

"Are we out yet?"

The sound of Darien's voice unsettled her. Meiran flinched. She didn't want to answer. Yet, she couldn't bring herself to lie to him.

"Yes," she whispered. "We're out."

His eyelids fluttered open. He gazed up at her with the same gold-green eyes she'd fallen in love with. His face was haggard, pale. Exhausted.

"Will you…release the damper on me?"

His lips barely moved. He was gazing up into her face.

Meiran ran her fingers through his hair. "No, Darien. I'm not going to do that." Her voice broke. She hadn't wanted it to come to this. She'd prayed he'd be gone by now.

Darien frowned. A look of vague confusion clouded his face. "Heal me...please?"

Meiran shook her head. She clenched her jaw against the sorrow that wrenched her heart. "No."

His eyes widened with understanding. Then they darkened with hurt. He turned his face away, closing his eyes. For just a moment she could feel the depths of his pain, so intense that it almost made her retch. Right before he walled her out completely.

Meiran looked up and found herself staring into Sayeed's outraged glare. His expression was treacherous.

"If he dies, I'll kill you."

It was plain, simple fact. Not even a threat.

Meiran nodded. She could accept that; it was a price she was willing to pay. She looked back down at Darien. With her hand, she caressed the side of his face.

He didn't respond. He was unconscious again.

Meiran lowered herself down and curled up on the boards at his side. She pulled him close, weeping quietly into his hair. His flesh was pale. Moist. Already cold.

Qul, The Black Lands

"Madam, I cannot!" Quin insisted, waving his hands feverishly in the air. "I couldn't possibly take another bite of food from your family's plate!"

Across the low table from him, his hostess smiled graciously and gestured again at the platter she'd set down in front of him.

"You must eat! I insist!"

Quin chuckled, smiling around at the group of young women seated around him on pillows, all gathered around Uma Abada's table. They'd come under the pretenses of helping Uma prepare dinner for a special guest. But, curiously enough, not a single one of Uma's young visitors had lifted a finger or lent a hand to assist the hostess. They had piled into Uma's house, showering Quin with questions and responding to his answers with choruses of giggles.

Quin spread his hands helplessly. "I really can't eat another morsel. See? I'm stuffed!" He pointed at his stomach which, of course, didn't help prove his point at all. His frame was just as thin now as before he'd started the meal.

A fresh eruption of laughter chorused all around the room, followed by a sibilant flurry of whispers.

This was too much for Uma Abada. She threw her hands up in the air, exclaiming, "You must not like the food!" She began reaching for the platter to take it away.

"No!" Quin gasped, catching her arm. "The food is delicious! Truly! I've never tasted anything so exquisite! Please, I'd be grateful to have another plate?"

To Uma's never-ending gratitude, Quin scooped himself another serving, quickly shoving a large bite into his mouth.

"Scrumptious!" he announced around the mouthful.

The women that surrounded him burst into rippling laughter. Quin grinned despite himself. It had been a very long time since he'd been the center of anyone's attention.

A tinkling clatter of beads signaled someone's entry into the dwelling. Quin glanced up just as the girls' laughter extinguished like a doused candle flame. He took one look at Azár's face and swallowed his food whole. It went down hard.

"Quinlan Nach'tier!" Azár cried, her voice fraught with panic. "Please, come quickly!"

"Sorry!" Quin gulped at Uma and the girls as he sprang to his feet, in his rush knocking over the wash water that was offered. He dashed after Azár, but the woman was already gone, disappearing through the doorway. He paused only long enough to retrieve his shoes.

Quin ran after her into the darkness, onto the narrow streets of Qul. He staggered forward five or six steps and then pulled up short, realizing he had no idea which direction the girl had even gone.

"Quinlan!"

She was standing a block away, beckoning him furiously. Holding his hat, Quin sprinted after her. He followed her out of town and out into the open night, down the path that led away from the village. She didn't pause to let him catch up. Azár ran ahead at full speed, gradually outdistancing him.

Down by the bank of the river, she finally turned

back, gesturing for him to hurry. Quin sprinted forward, at last seeing the cause for her concern.

A man lay on the beach by the river, another man stooped over him. Azár threw herself down beside them both, motioning frantically for Quin.

"He's near death!" she cried. "Can you heal? For I cannot!"

Quin gasped when he realized who it was that Azár wanted him to heal. He knelt down on his knees beside Darien, fear taking him in the chest like a sword thrust.

"Damn."

Closing his eyes, he placed a hand on Darien to gain a better sense of the extent of his injuries. His fear immediately collapsed into panic. He didn't dare wait another second.

Bracing himself, Quin reached within and pulled at the magic field as if grasping for life, drawing it in with all the force of his mind, focusing with every fiber of his concentration. He threw everything he had into Darien, all of his training, all of his skill, all of his effort and experience, uncertain if all he had would even be enough.

With a gasp, Quin shrank back, blood draining from his face. He reeled, almost passing out. He steadied himself with a hand thrust in the dirt, his other hand clasped against his forehead. He sat there, rocking himself, slowly shaking his head. It took him a long time to finally pull himself back together.

Leaning forward, he probed Darien one more time. He was sleeping deeply, mercifully still alive.

Quin closed his eyes, sighing in relief. He opened them just in time to see the other man fall to his knees, prostrating himself fully prone in the dirt.

Still a little dizzy, Quin had to use both arms to wrench his body up off the ground. He gazed down at the prostrated figure, absently chewing his lip.

"Get up," he chided the man. "Who are you? Can you tell me what happened?"

The bearded man regained his feet in one elegant, fluid motion. He effected a perfect bow, one hand pressed against his heart. "I am Sayeed son of Alborz, Chamberlain of Armorers," he stated proudly. Indicating Darien, he said, "This man was gravely injured. I brought him out of the vortex to you."

Quin chewed on that information, wishing the soldier would elaborate just a tad. It was only then that he recognized him: the officer from Tokashi who'd delivered Meiran's necklace. The man was Zakai to the core: direct, succinct, and thoroughly uninformative. "Where's Meiran?" he demanded. "Is she with you?"

"The woman is still in the boat," Sayeed gestured toward the craft. "She would not help. He asked, but she refused."

Quin's eyebrows shot up. "Refused?" he echoed, exchanging a wide-eyed look with Azár.

The soldier nodded. "Yes. She refused to help him even though he begged."

At that news, Quin hung his head, heaving out a long, exasperated sigh. If Meiran had refused to help Darien despite the ghastly nature of his injuries, it spoke volumes of her character. She had committed herself to his death, despite the depth of her feelings for him. It was a deplorable act, both selfish and selfless at the same time. In all his life, Quin had only known one other person capable of making such a decision.

Sagging, he removed his hat from his head and turned to Sayeed with a weary expression on his face. "Can the two of you get him back to the village?"

"Will he live?" the officer seemed surprised.

"Yes, but…he'll be sleeping for a couple of days." Quin bounced his hat against his thigh a few times, absently collecting his thoughts. Meiran was his responsibility, even more than Darien. He needed to make sure she would be all right.

The officer appeared to be considering. "I will take him back to Tokashi," Sayeed decided finally. "He will be protected there. It is where he belongs."

Quin frowned. "He has the support of the Tanisars, then?"

Sayeed solemnly spread his hands. "Darien Lauchlin is the overlord that was promised. He has the full support of the Tanisar corps."

Quin nodded, reserving judgement. He glanced to Azár, who was likewise staring at Sayeed with a shocked expression on her face.

"And do you have the authority to speak for all the Zakai?" Quin pressed. He needed to know Sayeed's claim was legitimate, and not some rogue faction of the Tanisars throwing their support behind Darien in an attempt at a coup.

The soldier bowed low. "I, Sayeed son of Alborz,

have the authority to speak for all the Zakai and the whole of the Tanisar corps."

That was good enough for Quin. He turned immediately to Azár. The look of shock on her face only supported his decision. "Go with them," he directed her. "I'll take Meiran back to Qul."

Azár stared up at him with a mixture of disbelief and outright fear. "I'm a Lightweaver!" she gasped. "I can't just abandon my lightfields!"

Quin waved his hand in a dismissive gesture. Replacing the hat on his head, he reminded her, "Tokashi Palace must have Lightweavers aplenty. Send one of them back here to replace you."

Azár licked her lips, indecision knitting her brow. She glanced back up at Quin. "I do not have that kind of authority."

Quin shrugged, casually pointing a finger down at Darien. "He does."

Azár looked lost. Her brow furrowed even more. She seemed to be grappling with some enormous internal struggle. At last, something seemed to yield inside her. Nodding, she clenched her hands into balls at her sides. "I will go to Tokashi Palace," she said at last.

Sayeed nodded with a look somewhere split between gratitude, respect, and downright doubt. Quin wasn't quite sure how it was possible for one human face to manage so many emotions all at once. The soldier could convey in one look what it would take a scribe a page or more to fill.

"Let's get Meiran," Quin grumbled.

He left Darien lying on the shoreline and walked to the boat to check on the Prime Warden. He found her fast asleep, curled up in the bowels of the vessel, cuddled up in a kaftan stained dark with blood. Gore streaked her face, her hands, her skin. The bottom of the boat was coated with sticky filth. Quin felt an instant pang of fear. All that blood couldn't be Darien's.

Then he saw the bandage on Meiran's arm.

He reached out and probed her with his mind, getting a sense of her condition. She wasn't good. She had been starved for days on top of the torture she'd obviously been subjected to. Her skin was hot to the touch; the wound on her arm had already started to fester.

Quin mended her just as he'd mended Darien, then gathered her sleeping body up into his arms. He rested her head against his shoulder, staring down at Meiran's peaceful face. He tried to feel angry with her, but realized that he couldn't do it. He didn't agree with Meiran's actions. But he understood her, all the same. He understood her all too well.

"What are you going to do with her?" Azár asked, wandering over to gaze at Meiran as if she were something of a curiosity.

"I'll take her back to Qul. She's my responsibility. From there…" he shrugged. "Who knows?"

"I could run my sword through her," suggested Sayeed.

Quin barked a laugh, casting the man a sideways smirk. "Trust me, I've been tempted. Unfortunately, that wouldn't go over very well with your new overlord."

He knelt down, laying Meiran out on the black sand of the riverbank. Then he went to help Sayeed and Azár load Darien into the boat. When they had him in, Sayeed immediately sat down and took up the oars as Quin waded out into the water, pushing the boat and casting them off. He gave a good, hard shove that sent the little craft floating quickly away. Quin gazed at Azár, watching the distance between them slowly widen, standing in water up to his hips. He remained there as Sayeed dipped the oars into the river, pushing back, turning the boat into the current.

"Keep him safe," Quin called after them.

The little craft pulled slowly away even as a cloud of fog rolled in around them, cloaking them in mist. Quin turned and waded back toward the shoreline. But before he could gain the bank, a sudden splash made him turn.

His mouth dropped open. Darien's hound had thrown itself into the river and was paddling dutifully after its master. He watched the beast overtake the boat, bobbing furiously and pawing at the side of the craft. Sayeed stopped rowing, clearly perplexed.

Between the soldier and Azár, they somehow managed to get the demon-dog over the side and into the boat. The beast shook the water from its fur and, circling several times, finally positioned itself at the bow of the craft as if determined to keep watch. It's hellish-green eyes gleamed from out of the darkness.

"Now, that's quite a sight," Quin muttered, shaking his head.

Chapter Twenty-Seven
Hard Choices

Qul, The Black Lands

Meiran awakened to a pale amber glow. The flickering light of a lantern cast murky shadows on the walls, bizarre patterns of dappled light mixed with shadow. She was warm and comfortable. She stretched languidly, feeling the stiffness leech slowly from her bones. She felt content.

A sudden pang of emptiness jarred her fully awake. Meiran sat up, blinking as she gazed in surprise around a room that was altogether unfamiliar.

Quin's skeletal face was the first thing she saw. He was sitting, leaning against the far wall of the room with one leg drawn up against his chest, the other stretched out in front of him. He regarded her with a hard, callous stare. He was chewing on something that hung dangling from his mouth. Some type of root, it looked like.

"Where's Darien?" Meiran asked, her stomach in knots.

Quin's stare was like cold, unfeeling lead. "Alive. No thanks to you."

Meiran swallowed, feeling the grief inside tighten into a ball at the base of her throat. That was not the news she'd been expecting to hear. Not good news at all. She lifted her eyes reluctantly back to Quin. Yet another darkmage who was too dangerous to live.

"You healed him."

Quin plucked the root he was gnawing out of his mouth, gesturing with it in the air. "Well, I wasn't going to just sit back and watch him die. Like you were planning to do."

"I did everything I could to save him," Meiran said defensively. She *had* been trying to save Darien. In her own way. The only way she could.

Quinlan Reis sneered at her in mocking contempt. "What exactly were you trying to save him from? *Life?"*

Meiran grimaced, utterly resenting his cruel sarcasm. "I was trying to save Darien from hell," she informed him, not expecting him to understand.

"Darling, you bring new meaning to the phrase 'damned if you do, damned if you don't.'"

Meiran glared at him. "It's nothing to joke about, Quin. The man I loved has become a demon. A *true* demon. One who channels the powers of hell, raises necrators from the dead, and wants to rally the legions of Chaos against his own homeland. *My* homeland."

Quin sneered, gesturing in the air with the half-chewed root. "That's because the 'legions of Chaos' are going to starve to death if they stay here too much longer. Are you really so coldblooded that you'd condemn an entire nation to death? Honestly, Meiran, you're the one who's starting to sound more demonic."

The look on his face was haughty and insolent. He was a contemptible creature, just as wretched as Darien. Perhaps more so.

"There's hard choices to be made," Meiran said. "On *both* sides. I'm not denying it. Compromises will have to be made. But Darien's way—your way—it's not the answer. The Rhen will never submit to the rule of Xerys."

Quin popped the root back into his mouth and sprang instantly to his feet. Dusting off his long, black coat with the palms of his hands, he strode toward the door, making a sweeping gesture toward it.

"Well, then," he announced. "We'd better get started. Shall we?"

Meiran gawked up at him. "Started?"

Quin cracked a broad grin. "Titherry, remember? To find Athera's Crescent? Ending the curse over the Black Lands sounds like it just might be the only recourse we have left. If you're still willing to make the journey with me, that is."

Meiran glared at him suspiciously. So, the darkmage still wanted to go through with it. She'd thought he'd forgotten all about the bargain they'd struck with Darien. Well, she'd since had a change of heart. She'd had enough.

"I'm not going anywhere with you," Meiran told him coldly. "In fact, I'm going home."

Quin gazed at her levelly. Reaching up, he plucked the root out from between his teeth and flicked it away. She couldn't see his eyes under the shadow of his hat. But she could see the set of his jawline. He stuffed his hands into the pockets of his coat, facing her with feet spread apart.

"I wouldn't advise that, Prime Warden. If we don't find an end to the curse, you'll leave Renquist no choice but to invade."

Meiran glared up at him, her face set in anger. "I don't care. I've seen enough. You're just like Darien. They've manipulated you, Quin. They've manipulated your mind. I didn't know you in life, so I can't look at you the way I can look at Darien. I can't tell you exactly how much you've changed and how corrupt you've become. But I do know this: at one time, you were the brother of Braden Reis. You must have had some sense of honor. Just look at how far you've fallen. I'm sorry, Quin. I can't trust you."

With that, she stood up. Looking down at her arm, she rotated it to confirm it was indeed very well mended. Not even a scar remained. She was grateful for that. But not grateful enough to stay.

"I'm going home," she said. "I'll find my own way from here. Please don't follow me."

She started to turn away, but Quin's voice stopped her.

"Wait."

Meiran turned back around. She looked at him sadly. Somewhere deep inside that emaciated husk of a body there was a soul, a soul that once might have been worthwhile. Perhaps Quin was irredeemable. Perhaps not. It didn't matter; he wasn't her problem any longer.

Quinlan Reis moved toward her, pausing right in front of her. He gazed down plaintively into her face. The silence between them was long, echoing. The lantern on the floor revealed his eyes, no longer hidden beneath the shadow of his hat. His expression was full of regret.

Meiran tilted her head back, peering up silently into his face, exploring every coarse feature. With effort, she could almost visualize the man he used to be. The man he was no longer.

Quin brought his hand up from out of his pocket and pressed something against her palm, closing her fingers around it. His dark eyes never left her own. He didn't say a word. He squeezed her hand once, almost tenderly, then let go. With a sigh, he stepped back away.

Meiran looked down, opening her fist. Her throat constricted when she saw what it was that Quin had placed in her hand: the necklace given to her by Darien. The sight of it dredged up far more emotions than Meiran felt capable of dealing with at the moment. She swallowed most of them, deciding to nurse the anger for just a bit longer.

Glancing back at Quin, she held his gaze as she turned her open palm upside down, letting the silver necklace spill from her hand, falling to the floor at her feet. She didn't look down. She stood holding Quin's gaze with a steadfast glare of defiant resolve.

She turned and left.

With a tinkling clatter of beads, Meiran walked out into the crisp, cold darkness of night. She closed her eyes, breathing in the foul stench of coal smoke and ash. Overhead, turbulent clouds raced across the vast expanse of sky, lights flickering deep within their depths.

This was the Black Lands.

Not her lands.

She owed these people nothing.

Darkrise

BOOK THREE

Khazahar Desert
Tokashi Palace
Qul
The Ghost Waste
Malikar
BRYN CALAZAR
Ishara
Desert of Maridur
Greystone Keep
Wolden
Cerulean Plains
AERYSIUS
Glen Farquist
Orien's Finger
Auberdale
Rothscard
THE Rhen
Isle of Titherry
Meridan
Southwark
THE Southern Continent
c. 1749 DCE

Chapter One
Darkening Dawn

Pass of Lor-Gamorth, The Front

There's a kind of promise the dark makes. Kyel Archer thought he remembered it well enough.

He stared up at the ink-black slopes of the Shadowspears, at the ghostly lights that flickered in the clouds. His memories of this place were vivid with shadow. The darkness whispered at him from the gullies and ridges, echoed off the high mountain passes. Unfurled before him in the storm-tossed sky. Its vast emptiness raked dread into his heart, feeding his soul with trepidation.

The dark that encased the Shadowspears promised only a legacy of sorrow. After a thousand years of conflict, that was all it had to give.

He glanced at the gray-cloaked sentries warding the long stair ahead. It was not the same stair he remembered, just as Greystone Keep wasn't the same fortress. It had evolved. The Pass of Lor-Gamorth had changed a great deal in the past two years.

Below, he could make out the ruins of the old keep, now just a shattered and scorched foundation. The new stronghold lay farther up the ridge, perched high on the cliff. The new keep made better use of the natural defenses of the slopes, half-built and half-carved out of the mountainside itself.

The steps to the keep were narrow, zig-zagging up the ridge. Kyel felt short of breath before their party was even halfway up; he wasn't used to the elevation. Or the exercise. At his side, a weary Cadmus panted and gasped, grappling his considerable weight up the treacherous stair. Kyel felt sorry for the cleric. Cadmus hadn't journeyed a step outside the Valley of the Gods in decades.

It took their party long minutes to gain the entrance of the fortress: a narrow arch formed from hewn granite that opened into darkness. A tunnel leading straight back into the heart of the mountain itself.

Kyel stopped to catch his breath, craning his neck to glance up. Far overhead, a high curtain wall skirted the summit of the ridge. There were no stairs that could be seen; the keep's entrance must be buried somewhere deep within the rock. Kyel was impressed. Whoever had designed this new stronghold had intended it to be impregnable.

He continued onward with Cadmus at his side, a small group of uniformed soldiers treading behind them. The Conclave had seen fit to provide him with five Guild blademasters to form his personal retinue, as deadly an honor guard as a man could wish for. Unfortunately, the swordsmen were a necessity.

Kyel was, after all, the last surviving mage left in all the Rhen.

He'd sworn a vow to serve his land and his people. He'd sworn another vow never to inflict harm upon a living thing. Those two oaths, each contradictory, nagged at Kyel every moment of every day. He could feel the oppression of their conflicting doctrine dragging him down, like iron counterweights dangling from his wrists.

Within the tunnel, the dark descended with its promise of sorrow. Vibrant torchlight labored in vain to constrain the shadows, forming orange pools of flickering light. The flames did little more than illuminate the path beneath their feet. Kyel walked with his head bowed, hands clasped in front of him.

The tunnel ended at a portcullis. They waited as soldiers labored to raise the iron grate, heaving on long chains suspended from a mechanism overhead. On the other side, a stairway veered upward, angling steeply.

"Avoid the wood. Walk only on stone," cautioned a Greystone sentry.

Kyel nodded his understanding. Behind them, the portcullis lowered with the clattering whirl of chains racing through systems of pulleys. The stairs were made of steps arranged in alternating patterns of wood and stone. Kyel obeyed the sentry's instructions, avoiding the boards and stepping only on the granite-hewn stairs. He didn't know for certain what would happen if he missed a step, but it wasn't difficult to imagine. Kyel had no wish to plummet to his death.

The stairs emerged into a wide courtyard surrounded by crenelated towers and soaring palisades. The keep itself loomed before them, its imposing stone ending abruptly in a jagged array of blocks. The main fortress was left unfinished, Kyel realized with dismay.

"Bloody hell," he muttered under his breath, staring at the structure. It reminded him too much of the old Greystone Keep, with its crumbling rear wall and caved-in roof. The sight of the incomplete stronghold made his stomach clench in apprehension.

"Great Master."

He turned to face the soldier who acted as his guide. The young man carried a hornbow slung across his back, a quiver strapped to his leg. Probably a conscript, Kyel presumed.

"This way."

He motioned the young soldier forward, falling in behind. His gray-cloaked escort led them across the bailey to the castle's upper ward. From there, they proceeded through a series of hallways to a rather unremarkable door on the second floor of the tower. The soldier he followed knocked twice.

The door opened immediately.

"Your men will need to wait outside," the soldier said.

Kyel nodded, signaling his guards. Then, gathering his courage, he stepped into the room.

The first thing he saw was Traver's narrow face, now covered by a wiry growth of whiskers. No longer lanky, Traver had the hardened body of an infantryman. Kyel's mouth dropped open; he almost didn't recognize his old friend. Before he knew what was happening, Traver crossed the room in two large strides and scooped Kyel up in his arms, hefting him off his feet.

"You damnable fool!" Traver exclaimed, giving Kyel one last squeeze before setting him down again. "You've no idea how worried I've been!" He grinned wryly, a shaggy lock of auburn hair falling into his face. He flipped it back with a toss of his head.

"I'm fine, Traver. Really." Kyel made a half-hearted attempt at a smile. It was difficult. He was glad to see his old friend. But the sight of Traver was accompanied by a pang of sadness. He felt suddenly homesick. "How've you been?"

"Well enough." Traver grinned and raised his left hand, wiggling the three fingers he had left. "Except for this. But I rather think I'm better with half a hand than most men are with a whole one. Forces me to use my head."

The other man in the room shifted his weight conspicuously over his feet. Kyel turned toward the imposing form of Devlin Craig. Craig's straw-gold hair was pulled back from his face, which was covered in what looked like a week's growth of stubble. He wore a quilted gambeson that hung to his knees, an enormous sword strapped across his back. Kyel extended his hand, smiling at his former commanding officer.

"Force Commander Craig."

"Archer." Craig nodded curtly. His gaze travelled over Kyel, lingering for a moment on the black cloak that fell from his shoulders. His face conveyed a look of profound skepticism. He took a step forward and accepted Kyel's handshake with a firm, double-fisted clasp.

"Thanks for coming. We've got a problem." His voice was low and gruff. Kyel could see the tension in his eyes.

"I know."

Craig shook his head. "No. I don't think you do."

Kyel frowned, uncertain what the soldier was alluding to.

"Come with me." Craig tossed his head, already

moving past him.

Kyel fell in behind, following Craig's burly form as the man strode through the doorway, moving toward a flight of stairs. Kyel mounted the steps after him, jogging to keep up. He walked beside the commander up a spiraling staircase that ascended into the reaches of the unfinished tower.

He trailed his hand along the wall as he climbed, at once taken back in time to the old Greystone Keep of his memory. The old fortress had a very similar stair that had led to Garret Proctor's quarters at the top. This new tower preserved much of the same character, down to the arrow slits that followed the rising curve. Only, this tower ended halfway up. Kyel gasped as he realized he was standing on the last stair with one foot already lifted off. One more step would have sent him over.

Kyel flailed his arms, groping to catch himself on the unfinished wall at his side. Craig's hand shot out and caught him by the scruff of his cloak, clenching a fistful of fabric. He jerked him roughly backward. Kyel dropped to his knees as the world surged beneath him.

"Watch your step."

He rose, trying to catch his balance and his breath. Then, leaning over, he looked down over the unfinished portion of the wall. The view below was harrowing.

Kyel's vision swam as his stomach dropped right out of him. His palms broke into a sweat, toes curling in his boots. His eyes traced down the length of the tower, past the curtain wall and parapets, all the way down the side of the mountain. Before him rolled the sprawling black peaks of the Shadowspears stabbing out of a murky bank of fog. If it weren't for the fog, he might have been able to see all the way down to the bottom of the pass. Perhaps all the way out into the Black Lands themselves.

"Look."

Craig raised his arm, pointing out across the foggy sea below. Kyel tried to make out what the commander was trying to indicate, but there was nothing to see. Just thick, blanketing mist that extended like an ocean to the distant horizon.

Then the mist parted.

Kyel saw what the fog had been obscuring. Black, sinister forms arranged in geometric patterns extended across the dark plain ahead, no natural design. Fires glowed in the distance: thousands, perhaps tens of thousands. So many. Strangest of all, a set of dark, parallel lines, curving away toward the north.

"Mother of the gods," Kyel whispered. "What is all that?"

"That," Craig responded, lowering his hand, "is the Sixth Invasion. So far, they're eighty thousand strong, with more arriving each day."

Kyel's jaw sagged as he looked out across the fog. Below, cold fingers of mist trailed together to conceal the staging army. He turned away from the site, not wanting to see more. He looked down at the stone in front of his boots, instead. His heart beat furiously, tumbling within his chest. His nerves were cold. Numb. He felt unable to conjure an emotion.

This is what Darien must have felt like.

Kyel swallowed, slowly shaking his head as he worked his fingers together. He dug into the skin of his hand with a nail, finding the pain somewhat helpful. It gave him something else to focus on. Not that distraction was the answer. It wasn't. There was no answer to the size of the army gathering beneath the fog below.

"What do you expect of me?" Kyel asked, his words trembling under his breath. "What do you think I can do against that?"

Craig stared at him, his face impassive. Then he reached out and snatched Kyel's wrist. The burly man raked back his white cotton shirtsleeve, exposing the intricate markings of the chain engraved into Kyel's wrist. The mark of the Oath of Harmony.

"By my best guess, you've got less than a month to figure it out."

Craig dropped Kyel's arm with a final glare and stormed away, his long strides carrying him quickly down the steps. Kyel rushed after him to catch up. He was too stunned to protest and too appalled to think clearly. At the bottom of the steps, he almost ran headlong into Craig's back.

The force commander turned toward him with a harsh expression, considering him wordlessly, as if he were sizing up a piece of meat. Kyel could do nothing but stare right back. He knew fear was etched into his face, but there was nothing he could do about it. He didn't bother to try to hide it. He knew he had every right to be afraid.

Devlin Craig scowled and brought a hand up to rub his eyes. When he looked back again at Kyel, his expression was softer but even more unsettling. It spoke volumes of regret.

"I'm sorry, Archer. I wouldn't be doing this if I had any other choice. But I don't. I promised myself years ago that I'd never do to you what Proctor did to Darien. But when all's said and done, it comes down to this: you're just another asset. No more, no less. Like all the rest of us here. And with the size of that army down there, I'm going to have to exploit every asset I can get my hands on."

Kyel's throat tightened, hearing that. Now he knew how Darien must have felt, staring down at such a similar scene. Knowing that all he could give would never be enough. Knowing that he was defeated even before he began. And knowing that every man in the keep would be looking to him, seeing him as their one desperate chance to even the odds.

Kyel's shoulders slumped. He felt vaguely sick to his stomach. But he forced himself to gather his courage and look the commander straight in the eyes. "I'll do all that I can. Anything you ask. Anything in my power. *But I will not break Oath.* That is where I draw the line. Do we have an understanding?"

Devlin Craig's eyes wandered over Kyel's face for a long, silent moment. At last, he nodded. "I won't ask that of you. You have my word: that is the one thing I won't do."

Kyel stared back hard, searching the commander's face. There was nothing in Craig's gaze that gave him reason to doubt the man's sincerity. Devlin Craig had remained loyal to Darien's commitment to his Oath, standing by his decision even in the face of calamity.

"Now. There's something else you need to see." Craig turned on heel, beckoning Kyel to his side. The young mage had to move quickly, working hard to keep pace with the man's long strides. Craig spoke without looking at him as they crossed Greystone's bailey past roving groups of cloaked men.

"Two days ago, one of our patrols stumbled across a woman who escaped the Enemy. She's not one of theirs…She's one of ours. She's the only person ever to walk back out of the Black Lands after walking into them. I'd like to get some information out of her. The only problem is, there's not much of her left. I'm hoping you can help. At least heal her up enough to answer a few questions."

Healing wasn't Kyel's strong suit. Especially if this woman was as badly injured as Craig made her out to be. "I'll see what I can do."

He followed Craig toward a long building that looked like a barracks. Craig led him to one of the wooden doors and, nodding at the man who guarded it, stood back as the door swung open. The ceiling inside was low; Kyel had to duck as he entered. Inside, he groped through the dense shadows. When his gaze fell on the form of a woman on the floor, he froze.

She was lying on her side, her hands clenched before her face. Her fingers were contorted, wrapped in stained rags that seeped blood and pus through the fibers. Kyel could smell the stench of her wounds. It turned his stomach: a putrid, sick-sweet odor.

"She's rotting," he whispered, looking at Craig.

The commander nodded. "Aye. I'll get some of my men to carry her out of the node. I want you to see what you can do with her."

Kyel doubted he could do anything. On the floor, the woman moaned and thrashed. He didn't have any idea what to do about this kind of injury. He'd never dealt with anything so severe on his own. Kneeling, he reached out to lift the fabric that obscured her face.

He flinched back with a gasp.

Kyel tried hard not to wretch. Beside him, Craig dropped to one knee, laying a steadying hand on his shoulder. "What is it?"

Kyel's tongue didn't want to work. He brought a hand up to his mouth, choking on horror.

"Gods' mercy," he whispered. *"It's Meiran."*

Chapter Two
In Darkness, There is Light

The Khazahar Desert, The Black Lands

Soft ribbons of magelight filtered down from the sky, unfurling in gentle, amber strands. Warm rays fell on Darien's skin, delivering comfort like a summer day. A breeze stirred, moving the tall grass of the pasture, rustling the leaves overhead. The entire world was awash with roiling swirls of orange and gold.

He sat beside Azár under the sprawling branches of an oak, one knee drawn up against his chest. His attention was captivated by a chestnut horse that loped in slow circles, roaming the confines of its enclosure. The stallion tossed its head and bucked, muscles rippling beneath its coat. With a snort, the animal bolted in the opposite direction, turning only when it reached the fence line. It moved in easy circles around the pen, the sound of its hoofbeats marking time to the wind. Darien watched, enthralled by such display of power tempered by grace.

A soft breeze chased his hair. If he closed his eyes, he could imagine that he was someplace far away. If he tried very hard, he could almost imagine he was home.

To the woman sitting beside him, he asked, "What would you do if you woke up one morning and realized that everything you believed was all just a lie? That everything you thought was right was actually wrong? Would you think you'd gone insane?"

The question had been rhetorical; he was surprised when she answered.

"I'd thank the gods for opening my eyes."

Her words came from a startling perspective. Darien turned to look at her as if seeing her for the first time. What he saw surprised him. When he looked into Azár's face, he saw beauty. Wild, untamed grace like the kind on display in the paddock before them. Despite the golden warmth of the magelight, Darien felt abruptly cold.

"I don't know what to believe anymore," he confessed.

Azár scooted toward him and brought a hand up to touch his face. She leaned forward, staring into his eyes. "Then believe in me."

Darien bowed his head. The cold settled further into his bones, became a disturbing sensation. It took him a moment to recognize it as fear. It numbed him. Paralyzed him. The feel of her touch was too much, too soon. Too raw. He didn't want anything to do with it.

He felt her soft lips against his, questioning.

The fear welled into panic. He broke off the kiss, wrenching his face away. "I can't do this."

"Then don't." Azár shrugged, pulling away.

Darien collapsed back against the tree, dazing up at the silhouette of oak leaves twirling against a background of golden light. Confusion nettled him, a violent storm of conflicting emotions.

"I am your Lightweaver," Azár said. "That is all I need to be."

He considered her face, marveling at her pride. Azár had remained by his side after Meiran's betrayal. She'd tended him when he was at his most vulnerable, helped him find his way back to himself. In so many ways, she'd proven her loyalty. In all the world, she was the one person he knew he could trust.

He should be able to feel something for her.

Anything. Conjure some scrap of emotion. But he couldn't.

The fear subsided. It was replaced by anger: anger at Meiran. He hadn't deserved what Meiran had done to him. She'd robbed him of everything he had, all that he was, everything he had ever been. Left him hollow and ugly inside.

"You should marry me," Azár said.

Her words knocked the wind out of him.

He couldn't move. He felt dizzy. Stricken. He went stiff, gazing unblinking into her face. She looked wild, beautiful. Terrifying.

"Why?" he gasped. He couldn't understand. "Why would you wish to marry a demon?"

She scoffed. "You were not always a demon. Once, you were a man."

"I'm not that man anymore." He scowled. "The truth is, I don't know what I am."

She raised her chin, defiant. "I know what you are, Darien Lauchlin; it was I who summoned you…and now you must do as I ask. That is the rule, is it not?" Her smile was mischievous.

But Darien shook his head. "You only get one request. One. And you've used it up already. I'm pledged to deliver your people. That's the end of it."

Azár raised her eyebrows, a confident smirk on her face. "And how are you going to deliver my people if they refuse to follow you?"

Darien frowned, suddenly concerned. He didn't know where she was heading with this. It was a new direction. Azár could be unpredictable, but she was always honest.

"I have the Tanisar corps behind me," he reminded her.

Azár shrugged, standing, and paced away a few steps. Then she turned back to face him. The cotton skirt she was wearing rippled around her knees. "You will need more than just the Tanisars. You must have the support of all the tribes of the Khazahar. But they will never follow you—not without blood ties to the clans. If you marry me, then my clan would claim your blood as their blood. It has been done before."

At last, Darien understood what she was trying to do. She was trying to help him achieve the goals she'd set out for him. Azár had sought to motivate him emotionally. But when that failed, she'd resorted to winning him over with logic.

He stood up, shaking his head. "I can't give you what you want, Azár."

She chortled at his words. Her eyes traced over him, moving down his body. All the way to his feet.

"Always so arrogant. What makes you think you have any idea what I want?"

Darien could only guess. The woman never ceased to confound him; every time he thought he had her figured out, she delighted in proving him wrong. It was a favorite game of hers.

He said, "I assume you'd want a husband who has the capacity to love you back?"

Azár spread her hands. "Love is not important. What I desire is a husband I can trust. And I trust you."

Darien stared into her eyes, probing her intent. He had to make certain she felt as little for him as he did for her. In Azár's brown eyes, he found only sincerity.

"I'll think on it," he said at last.

She smiled, pausing as she turned away. "Think on it well. The future of the Khazahar rides on your decision. We need you to be more than just a Sentinel. We need you to be an overlord."

Darien sent his horse away from the lightfields at a trot, guiding the red stallion with the pressure of his legs. He gave a quick glance back over his shoulder, wanting one last sight of Azár. But the darkness fell like a shroud around him, cutting off all sight of her. He turned back to the road ahead, concentrating on the rhythmic sound of hoofbeats.

Sayeed rode at his side on a mare that was the same delicate breed as Darien's own mount. Both horses were of similar color, without one mark of white despoiling their red coats. Darien rode without a saddle, just a richly embroidered blanket beneath him. Blue tassels swayed from his horse's bridle, which jingled with the sound of tinkling beads.

Sayeed said, "Your Lightweaver does not seem happy."

Darien shrugged. "She wants to marry me." He didn't know why. It was all so confusing. He reached a hand up and rubbed the back of his neck, avoiding Sayeed's look of speculation.

The Zakai officer grunted, a small grin forming on his lips. "May you have more luck with this woman than you had with the last."

Darien clamped his lips closed to hold back the retort he wanted to let fly. The old anger flared. He closed his eyes against images of Meiran. Meiran, the mother of his child. The woman who'd wanted him dead. His chest still tightened every time he thought about her.

"I am sorry," Sayeed said. "I didn't mean to offend."

"You didn't offend."

Darien rode in silence, listening to the hypnotic rhythm of hoofbeats. He cleared his mind, throwing a shield up between himself and the violent energies of the vortex that closed over them. It was a long ride back to Tokashi Palace from the lightfields. Already, he missed the golden warmth of Azár's magelight. And he missed her company, he had to admit.

Sayeed said, "I am indeed sorry. May the gods bless your union, and may the both of you know happiness."

Darien glared at him. "I haven't decided yet."

A long gap of silence passed with only the constant jingle of tack. Darien felt foolish; he hadn't meant to snap at the officer. Like Azár, Sayeed had been nothing but loyal. He was Darien's staunchest supporter, his closest friend. He deserved better treatment.

"She says the tribes of the Khazahar will not follow me," Darien said. "Not without blood ties to the clans. Is she right?"

Sitting up straighter on his horse, Sayeed appeared to be considering. At last he shrugged. "Your Lightweaver is correct. The Tanisars are bound by oath and duty to follow you. But the tribes care only about blood-bond."

"What is blood-bond?" Darien had never heard of the term. Whatever it was, it sounded ominous.

Sayeed explained, "All the kinfolk of a tribe share the same common blood. It flows through all their veins, every last person. 'The blood of the son is the blood of the father,' it is said. Blood-bond is what binds a people together in obligation and duty."

Darien considered Sayeed's words, his mind mulling over the ramifications. The concept was altogether foreign to him. The politics of the Rhen had nothing to do with blood or kinship. Alliances and feudal allegiance went much further in inspiring loyalty. And though Sayeed's concept of blood-bond explained a lot, it still didn't account for everything. A marriage to Azár might bind him by blood to a single tribe, but he failed to see how that would advance his cause much. The other tribes would have no obligation to follow him.

"I don't understand. The prime warden proclaimed me Overlord of the Khazahar. Shouldn't that be enough?"

Sayeed spread his hands. "Zavier Renquist pronounced you overlord, but that title is all but empty unless you can unite the Khazahar behind you."

Darien frowned. "Would the tribes follow a man of foreign blood?"

"No."

He rode in silence, ruminating on the information. Overhead, sinister clouds raced across the ever-black sky. In the distance, the jagged spikes of a mountain range stood backlit by flickering cloudlight. It was damn cold. The kind of cold that seeped under the skin, burrowing all the way to the bone. It seemed years since he'd last felt sunlight on his skin.

A thought occurred to him. "One of my ancestors was Omeyan. Could I claim that as my clan?"

Sayeed flashed him a startled look. "There are no Omeyans left in all the world. The Omeyan Jenn perished during the time of Desecration."

Darien shrugged; it was just a thought. "It's a distant relation," he admitted.

"Very distant." Sayeed maintained a stiff look of concern. "And yet…if you can prove your lineage…" His face brightened. "Can you name all of your ancestors, all the way back to this ancient Omeyan?"

Darien thought about it. At last he nodded. "Aye. I think I can. The lineage of my family is well-known to me."

Indeed, he had been made to memorize his entire pedigree, both his father's side and his mother's. Both bloodlines figured prominently in the history of Aerysius. His father's line had produced several prime wardens and many famous Sentinels. His mother's ancestors had been just as esteemed, her line extending back even further into the records.

"You must write down your family's lineage and present it to the elders. Only then might your claim be considered." Sayeed looked at Darien with a pensive expression. "Never has a perished tribe been restored to us. I truly hope this thing can be done. It would be a great blessing to all the clans. When we arrive back at the palace, I will make arrangements."

"I'd be grateful." Darien smiled his appreciation. He'd come to lean heavily on Sayeed in the months since his arrival at Tokashi Palace. He'd let the man into his confidence, closer than anyone.

Anyone but Azár.

They rode in silence across the darkness of the wastes, clouds surging toward them from the bleak horizon. Hours passed with only the clip-clop of hoofbeats to mark the slow passage of time. Eventually a long lake appeared in front of them, its water's dark and opaque. Darien gazed into the lake's black depths. Somewhere down there, beneath the waters, lay the ruins of ancient Vintgar and the Circle of Convergence it contained, now drowned beneath the lake.

They crossed a long bridge, arriving finally at an enormous fortress pressed up against the hillside. Tokashi Palace was like a continuation of the mountain itself, towers spiking like teeth into the air, looming over the dark valley and the lake. The lights from hundreds of windows made the fortress gleam like a night sky full of stars. The two men rode through the arching gate into the courtyard, drawing their horses up as soldiers bowed and backed away, pressing their bodies up against the walls.

Darien acknowledged the Tanisars with a stiff nod as he dismounted. He swept his gaze around the courtyard, wary. Even after all the months he'd spent at the palace, the behavior of these people still made him tense. The soldiers stood still like statues along the walls, unflinching. Even the servants seemed frozen in their positions, heads bowed, hands clasped. There was no sound in the courtyard, not even the rustle of fabric. It was the totality of silence that unsettled him most.

Darien looked around, sweeping his gaze over dozens of men who had sworn to serve him with their lives. Or with their deaths. He took note of their conduct with solemn respect. He had never known a better fighting force. Certainly, nothing in the Rhen could equal the discipline of the Tanisars.

He set out across the courtyard with Sayeed, leading his mount into the depths of the fortress. Servants bowed and backed away from his approach, lowering their gaze respectfully. Darien walked past each of them without acknowledgement. He was used to the treatment now. At first, just walking the corridors had been difficult for him. He had never felt so self-conscious. It was surprising what one could grow accustomed to.

Looking ahead, he saw a small group of officials clustered in front of the entrance to the Residence, awaiting his arrival. They formed a small clot outside the grilled gate that separated his living space from the rest of the fortress. The men turned toward him, forming a line and bowing in unison.

"Blessings upon you, Darien Nach'tier, if I could have just a moment of your time?"

"*Ranu kadreesh,* Lord, five minutes is all I need!"

"Overlord, I have just one question!"

"Back away!" Sayeed bellowed, startling the horses.

The officials bowed and scrambled aside to clear a path to the doorway. Fear radiated from their bodies, so sharp he could almost smell it. They hated him; he could see it in their eyes. But they were too terrified to do anything about it.

"I'll meet with all of you after *domadh,*" Darien assured them, raising his hand.

The doors to the Residence swept open before them. Darien led his stallion into the corridor beyond, Sayeed following with his own mount as the grilled doors were bolted behind.

Inside the Residence, the character of the fortress changed drastically. They moved through a wide hallway illuminated by gilt lanterns. The walls and floor were tiled in sprawling geometric patterns of red and blue, broken by draped folds of colored cloth. Scalloped columns lined the passage, wrapped with scrolling inlay. Darien moved under the warm light of countless lanterns, pausing at the first wide doorway they came to. There, he offered his horse to a servant waiting at the entrance.

The boy took the stallion's reins, conspicuously avoiding eye contact. Another took the reins of Sayeed's mount. Darien waited for the Zakai officer to retrieve their packs and then turned toward his own bedchamber, just across the corridor from the stable.

He lingered as Sayeed opened the door and entered first, taking his time about inspecting the interior of the room. Only when the officer gave a nod did Darien enter behind him. The chamber was large, an enormous canopied bed the focal point of the room. There was also a hearth recessed into an alcove on the far wall. Only a few items of furniture were scattered about: two wooden chairs and a small writing desk. Silken fabric hung from the walls and the bed's canopy, echoing the colorful patterns of the rugs.

From the corner of the room emerged a living shadow that approached with gleaming eyes. Darien smiled, moving forward to greet his pet. He'd left the demon-hound behind intentionally; the horses didn't care for the scent of damnation. He ran his hand through the beast's thick fur, tugging one ear affectionately. The thanacryst purred at the attention, managing to seem both dreadful and content.

"Will that be all, Lord?" Sayeed still lingered in the doorway, his face expectant.

Darien turned toward him with a nod. "That's all, Sayeed. Thank you for your company."

The officer bowed and backed away, pulling the door closed behind him.

Darien stared at the door for a long moment before turning away. He gave the thanacryst one last scratch, then moved to the writing desk in the corner. He slouched down into the chair, drawing in a deep breath. He smelled of horse. It was a scent he was rather fond of. It mingled nostalgically with the fragrant incense that permeated the chamber.

With a whimsical smile, Darien picked up an *elam* from the desk, a writing instrument made from a hollow reed, its tip carved to a tapering point. He held the *elam* in his left hand, pausing a moment in reflection. Then he unstoppered a pot of ink that smelled of soot, giving it a quick stir before dipping the tip of the *elam*.

At the top of a page, he inscribed his own name in bold calligraphy. Below, he wrote the names of both his mother and his father. Upon second thought, he crossed out his father's name. He was descended from the Omeyans on his mother's side; his father's lineage was not important in this context. Under his mother's name he wrote out his maternal grandfather's name and title. He kept scribing, one name after another, moving slowly down the parchment as the tapers on the desk burned lower. About halfway through the list he paused, using a blade to sharpen the dulling tip of the *elam*.

Minutes passed. At last, Darien finally scribed the last name of his lineage:

Braden son of Marthax,
Omeyan Clan of the Dur ul-Jenn

Darien gazed at his ancestor's name for a long moment. Then he set the *elam* down on the writing desk, stoppering the ink pot.

He rose then, strolling toward an ornate chest pushed up against the wall. There, he knelt and lifted the lid. He stared into the depths of the chest for a moment before finally removing the first item that caught his eye. Holding it up, Darien felt his face burn with anger as he gazed down at the silver pendant that had once been Meiran's. He squeezed his fingers closed around it. Reluctantly, Darien placed the necklace back in the chest. Then he withdrew the other items left behind by Quinlan Reis.

He stood up, holding the Omeyan warbelt in one hand and a scroll of parchment in the other. Quin had left both items behind in Qul. Darien unrolled the scroll, his eyes scanning quickly over the page.

This belt is yours by rights. It belonged to your ancestor, Braden son of Marthax, Warlord of the Omeyan Clan of the Dur ul-Jenn. It is the last of its kind in the world, just as you and I are the last of our kind. Wear it with pride in memory of my brother.

-Quin

Darien stared down at the worn leather in his hands, his eyes roving over the golden buckle that depicted the image of a horse bent backwards at an impossible angle. The belt itself was decorated with many hooks and thongs, from which an assortment of implements could be hung.

Before, he had lacked the conviction to put it on.

Now, Darien lowered the scroll and drew the belt around his waist, fastening it securely with the gold buckle. He stared down at himself, at the black wrap he wore about his hips tied with gold tassels. The warbelt complemented the wrap, adding a martial quality to the ensemble. Rubbing the weeks' worth of stubble on his chin, Darien wondered if any of his old friends would recognize him if they saw him. He didn't think he looked much like a man of the Rhen any longer. He'd been away too long.

His eyes found the demon-hound slumbering in a corner by the hearth. He made his way to the bed, fingers working at the buttons of his shirt. He let the soft fabric fall to the floor and sat down on the edge of the bed, leaning forward.

The thanacryst startled awake, raising its head. A low, menacing growl rumbled deep in its throat. The hound's green eyes narrowed to slits, its attention rapt upon the door.

Darien looked up, his body stiffening.

There was no knock. The door burst open, admitting Sayeed. Darien opened his mouth, but then he saw the look on the officer's face.

"Sorry to disturb you, Lord," the man blurted, his face pale. He lowered his head to stare intensely at the ground. "You have a visitor..."

Before Darien could react, another man strode into the bedchamber.

Darien froze. He'd been expecting this for some time. He was just surprised it had taken them so long. His eyes locked on Sayeed's. "You may go."

The officer bowed formally before backing out of the room. He pulled the door closed behind him.

Darien raised his eyes to Byron Connel. With his hand, he indicated the nearest chair. "Please. Have a seat."

But the ancient Battlemage shook his head. Connel's face was as hard as chiseled stone. "I didn't come for conversation. I'm here to formally charge you with the murder of Nashir Arman."

Chapter Three
An Orlian Knot

Ishara, The Black Lands

Quinlan Reis scowled as he stalked toward the town center of Ishara. The air was damnably cold, made worse by a penetrating mist that clung close to the ground. It had rained earlier, and the streets oozed with muck. Quin trudged through mud that stuck to the bottom of his shoes, making suctioning noises as he walked. Every scrap of clothing he wore was soaked through. He shivered and rubbed his hands together for warmth, which didn't do much good; his gloves were just as saturated as the rest of him.

He was miserable. For some reason, luck just never seemed to be on his side. It avoided him completely, like a discarded lover. He'd thought that swearing his soul to the God of Chaos would have improved his lot. Occult intervention or something of the sort. But no; even Xerys had no patience for him, it seemed. He'd used the transfer portal system to journey as far south as Meridan in the Rhen. But that was as far as the crippled system went. Without the Aerysius hub, it was impossible to transfer directly to the Isle of Titherry. Which left Quin with only two options: abandon his quest or hire a ship.

He wasn't about to hire a ship. So he'd given up.

Quin had returned to the Black Lands to bide his time. He had no plans for going forward. His strategy was recklessly simple: avoid Renquist. He didn't wish to be taken to task for the murder of Sareen, even though he knew he had it coming. Other than making himself as inconspicuous as possible, he had nothing on his plate. Which surprisingly left him with a scarcity of options.

Up ahead, the sounds of commotion came from the square around Ishara's temple. Quin's first inclination was to turn down the next alley and disappear into the shadows of the night; his last visit to the temple had left visible scars. But curiosity got the better of him. Instead of doing the sensible thing, Quin set his feet in the direction of the town's ziggurat.

The streets of Ishara were deserted. Ramshackle households bordered the avenues, surrounded by mud brick walls. Clouds of soot belched from stone chimneys, thickening the air with oily grit. Quin reached into his pocket and pulled out a scarf, holding it over his mouth to make it easier to breathe. He despised the filth that polluted the air, even though he knew the burning of coal was necessary. After all, it had been his own actions that had created the situation.

What he found at the center of town was a now-familiar sight: scores of people surrounding the base of the temple, waving and shouting, jostling each other as they vied for a better view. Some held flaming torches; others brandished weapons in the air. It was a scene of civil chaos and disorder that seemed to be the hallmark of the Black Lands. Just the same as the last time he'd passed through this wretched town—a town all the gods, save one, had abandoned.

A few people on the margin of the crowd turned to mark Quin's passage. Seeing the red mist that trailed at his feet, the eyes of the villagers widened in recognition. Their jostling ceased, their gazes lowering to the ground. A few men fell to their knees, bowing low at Quin's approach. It was like a wave that passed through the crowd, starting at the back and rippling toward the front, leaving only a lingering silence in its wake. A path opened up before him as the crowd drew back, yielding an approach to the temple steps.

Most of Ishara's citizens already knew his face. But even more familiar was the color of his magelight. No one moved to confront him as Quinlan Reis mounted the ramp of steps that led to the topmost terrace of the ziggurat. Above, a group of men dressed in crimson robes waited to receive him. The square was motionless; the frothing turmoil had stilled.

As he crested the top of the steps, anxiety spread like a toxin through Quin's body, awakening every nerve. He tried to shrug it off. Maybe it was just the memory of the beating he'd taken at the hands of these same men, when he'd entered Ishara with Meiran. But it seemed to be more than just that. Something much more pressing.

For some reason he couldn't explain, Quin felt a haunting sense of urgency.

He paused to consider the crowd of men gathered at the top of the terrace. He let his gaze sweep over them, lingering on each face in turn. The men in red cloth were priests of Xerys. They were assembled in two tight clusters on either side of the stairs. It seemed they had amassed quite an impressive stack of coal bricks in the center of a raised platform. Sprigs of herbs and flowers had been laid over the pile the coal, along with the branches of fruit trees. As though the priests had assembled the makings of a spectacular feast.

Only, it wasn't an animal they were preparing to roast.

Quin's eyes fell upon the focus of the priests' attentions, his throat going tight.

This wasn't a feast. It was a cremation.

Before the mounded stack of coal lay the body of a dead woman. At least he assumed she was dead, judging by the amount of blood still leaking from the carcass. The strange thing was, it all looked so very *recent.* As if she'd been beaten to death right there, at the top of the temple steps. She hadn't died somewhere else, her body dragged here for a funeral pyre. Blood was everywhere, splattered across the gray stone of the temple.

Quin's stomach clenched in anger. He took a step forward, his eyes falling on the dead woman's outstretched arm. The skin of the arm was papery white, a bright contrast to the puddles of blood pooled on the stone.

Then Quin saw the scars on that pale wrist. And he knew.

Not a cremation. An immolation.

The woman wasn't dead.

He tugged hard at the Onslaught, filling his gaunt body with all the power of hell he could muster, all the vile energy he could withstand. A terrible green light suffused his flesh, surrounding his body like an insidious aura. The priests of Xerys backed away, eyes filled with awe and fear. Quin trudged forward, glowering at them from beneath the shadow of his hat.

"I'll take it from here." He spoke softly, dangerously. It was a tone he hadn't used in years.

The priests did not argue.

Quin knelt down beside the bloodied form of the woman. He lay a hand on her forehead and closed his eyes. Anger flowed into him along with knowledge. The young woman at his feet had been beaten within an inch of her life. The priests had cruelly left her that narrow inch. They were going to use it to feed her soul to their vengeful god. Which was, of course, his own vengeful god. Quin didn't stop to consider the ramifications of that fact. He just acted.

He flooded the woman's body with healing energies, working quickly but efficiently to repair the damage she had sustained. Then he lifted her dead weight into his arms. The temple priests made no attempt to deny him. They knew better.

Carrying the unconscious woman, Quin turned and made his way down the long flight of steps. When he reached the level of the street, the parted crowd drew back from him even further, looks of fear on the face of every person gathered in the square.

Quin said nothing as he strode back through Ishara's empty streets, the unconscious woman in his arms. He kept walking until he reached the town gate. Even then, he didn't stop. He walked straight out into the thick nothingness of the waste. He didn't look back. He didn't pause. He just kept walking.

The woman slept for two days.

Quin had built a campsite beside the hill that housed Ishara's transfer portal, tucked away in a deep recess in the cliffside. There, he'd built a small fire, just enough to take the edge off the chill. He would have preferred to camp inside the portal chamber itself, but he didn't dare take the risk. He still didn't know if Renquist had figured out his involvement in Sareen's death. Quin reckoned it was probably a good bet he had.

He hunkered down beside the fire, rubbing his hands together. He shot a glance at the woman sleeping next to him against the cliff face. She was hardly old enough to be called a woman. And cleaned up, she was rather quite lovely. She slept with her lips parted, infinite volumes of dark auburn hair surrounding her face. Quin leaned forward, reaching out to adjust the blanket he'd thrown over her.

She moaned, tossing a bit in her sleep.

Quin's eyes fell on the scar on the woman's wrist. Her right wrist. He stared hard at that cherry-red marking, unable to take his eyes off it. It was dreadful, distinctive in its pattern. He'd seen such scars before. And he knew well what they signified. It was hard, but he finally managed to look away.

Only to find her staring up at him, wide awake.

The woman's eyes were fierce and bright with fear. She thrashed, scooting away from him as far as the rock behind her would allow. She sat there in a tight ball, hands raised defensively as if trying to ward him off.

Quin shot up a hand. "Relax. You're safe. I won't hurt you…I think."

The woman glared at him, eyes full of spite and accusation. "Who are you?"

Her voice was melodic and rich, thickly accented. Moving deliberately slow, Quin removed his hat. Tucking it against his chest, he said, "Grand Master Quinlan Reis of the Order of Arcanists, at your service. I deduce you must be Naia."

Her eyes narrowed. "How do you know my name?"

Quin smiled wanly. "Process of elimination. There are not so many mages left in the Rhen. You're not Kyel, obviously. And you're not Meiran—thank all the gods!"

Her eyes narrowed even more. "What did you do to Meiran?"

Quin chortled, thrusting his hat back atop his head. "*Do* to her? Why, absolutely nothing that she didn't agree to in advance. On the contrary; despite my rather blemished reputation, I can make for rousing company. Really. It's true, so you don't have to look at me like that. You just might hurt my feelings."

Naia sat up, glaring her ire at him. "I have no desire for your wretched company, and I couldn't care less about your feelings. Take me to Darien Lauchlin. *Immediately.*"

Quin couldn't help but laugh. "I'm sorry, darling, but Darien isn't in the mood for any more visits from former sweethearts. He only narrowly survived the last one."

The expression on Naia's face transformed, her ire replaced by a look of concern. "What happened?"

Quin shrugged, thinking the answer should be obvious. "Meiran did her damnedest to send his soul back to the netherworld. Fortunately for Darien, I deigned to intervene."

The woman's eyes widened. She had beautiful eyes. They were wide and dark, radiant with the spark of the gift within her.

Quin said, "As you can imagine, after that, I won't be letting you anywhere near him."

Naia fixed him with a look of disdain. "Then what are you going to do to me?"

"That depends." Quin picked up a thin metal rod, using it to prod at the graying coals of the fire. "By the look of your arm, I gather you've been forced to make some rather difficult choices lately. Dare I ask?"

The woman looked away. She folded her arms, refusing to answer.

Quin cracked a grin. "I seem to have the same effect on every woman I meet. They all end up speechless and appalled."

Naia's eyes widened in shock before they narrowed to smoldering, slivered coals.

"I killed Sareen," she growled, leaning back against the rock wall.

"No. *I* killed Sareen," Quin differed astutely.

"I killed her again."

Quin frowned in consternation. He couldn't believe the woman was actually arguing with him over this. She was turning out to be nearly as infuriating as Meiran. He was starting to get a feel for the kind of woman Darien was drawn to. Come to think of it, the man really did seem to have a penchant for abuse.

Quin reached up to scratch the side of his face. "This is turning into quite the Orlian knot. Perhaps we should start over. I killed Sareen the night I left Rothscard with Meiran."

He waited for Naia to supply her part in the tale. When it became obvious that she wasn't going to, he raised his hand in a beckoning gesture. "It's your turn. That's the way this works, you see. I talk. Then you talk. We take turns."

Naia scowled in distaste. But at last she favored him with an explanation. "Kyel and I found Sareen dead. We wished to question her. We wanted to find out where you had taken Meiran. So we did what we could to preserve her body and then later brought her back to life. She tried to kill Kyel…and so I acted. Without thinking, obviously."

Quin stared at her for a moment with eyebrows raised, mouth hanging slack. He waited for her to elaborate. When she didn't, he reached up and rubbed his tired eyes.

"You do realize that nothing you're saying makes any type of reasonable sense?"

"I *am* making reasonable sense!" Naia snapped. "You're just too *unreasonable* to understand it!"

Quin smiled acidly. "So…it seems you're not as shy and timid as you would lead me to believe. Which is fine; I can fight fire with fire. I *am* a demon, you know." Seeing her expression, he continued in a blander tone, "Perhaps we should back up a bit. Retrace our steps. First, what in the world could possess you to want to question a dead woman?"

Naia wriggled into a more comfortable position, scooting forward to warm her hands over the fire. She glanced up at him through a lock of spiraling hair, obviously still ruffled. "We had no idea what happened to Meiran. All we knew was that you'd taken her. We thought Sareen might have that information. And we had reason to suspect she would be willing to help us…Since you were the cause of her death, after all."

"And you just spontaneously decided to reanimate a corpse?" Quin supplied a weak grin. "And how, may I ask, did you accomplish this?"

Naia didn't answer. She sat staring down at her hands, warming her fingers over the flames as though she hadn't heard him.

"So, it's to be the silent treatment?" Quin sighed, resigned. "I seem to receive that from most women I encounter. I don't have the faintest notion why." He sagged back with a yawn. "All right, then. Let's change the subject. Assuming that you did somehow manage to wake the dead, what did Sareen have to say?"

Naia glanced at him. "She told me you killed her. And she said I was valuable…and that Kyel was not."

Quin sucked in a cheek. "How uniquely disturbing. I fear I'm starting to believe you. So, Sareen tried to kill Kyel, and you killed Sareen, which voided your Oath of Harmony…And then you somehow ended up here beside a pile of coal bricks. But that still doesn't explain how you fled the Rhen."

Naia looked down again at the fire without answering. Which was really too bad; out of all the questions he'd asked her, that was the one Quin wanted answered most. He sighed and tossed his hat down in his lap.

"Well, my dear, it seems I have no choice but to lay it all out for you. Let me tell you a bit about my situation. And what you can do to help." Leaning forward, he made sure his eyes captured her attention. "If I don't find a way to end this darkness, there's going to be a war. And not just any war. A war unlike anything we've ever seen in all of history. The land will run with rivers of blood and the fallen will outnumber the living."

He waited, watching her eyes as the information seeped through her skin.

He continued, "I need to journey to the Isle of Titherry to use Athera's Crescent. You came along at just the right time, you see. I could really use your help…Especially if your talents are as exceptional as they seem."

She glared back at him through thick lashes. A hand came up, fingering a crease in her blue gown. She asked, "What makes you think I'd want to help you?"

"Because I believe I've found a way to lift the

curse over the Black Lands, which would stop this war before it starts." Quin's smile waxed exultant. He offered his hand to Naia, open and inviting. "Care to help?"

Chapter Four
The Darkness Within

Tokashi Palace, The Black Lands

Byron Connel asked, "Do you deny killing Nashir?"

Darien took a deep breath. "No."

There was no use denying it. Another Servant had died by his hand. It wouldn't do any good to lie about it. He didn't want to give Connel any reason to doubt his word; there were far more pressing things he needed to keep hidden.

The Battlemage shifted his weight over his feet, his expression grave. The indigo robe he wore swayed with his motion. "Very well. Do you have anything to say in your defense?"

Darien said, "He moved against me. I was left with no choice."

Connel took a menacing step toward him, eyes full of skepticism. He set his gloved hand on the leather-wrapped haft of his weapon, a silver morning star that was a powerful talisman. "How did he move against you?"

"He tortured me. He wanted me to deny our Master." Darien's voice was matter-of-fact. He made no attempt to elaborate; there was no reason to.

Connel's expression remained doubtful. "Why would Nashir do that?"

Darien shrugged. His hand went to the buckle of the warbelt at his waist, his fingers tracing over the raised image of the horse. "Revenge. He intended to banish my soul for killing Arden."

Connel's grip on Thar'gon's haft relaxed slightly. His frown remained dangerous. He ran his hand back through a thick mane of red hair. "What did you do with Nashir's corpse?"

"I disposed of it."

"How? Where did you dispose of it?"

"Come. I'll take you to him." Darien extended his hand toward the chamber's entrance. He waited, eyes fixed on Connel's glare.

At last, the Battlemage relented and strode to the door. Darien fell in at his side, matching his pace. He led the big man into the hallway, turning in the direction of the stable. Sayeed was there, lingering along the side of the hallway. He stood rigid as stone, staring straight ahead into nothing.

Connel made no attempt at conversation as Darien led him into the stairwell that accessed Tokashi's warren of subterranean dungeons. Spiraling steps took them downward, away from the warmth of the Residence, into the frozen heart of the glacier that consumed the lower levels of the fortress. The air grew colder the further they went. The walls of the stairwell darkened, became moist with condensation. A pool of chill air greeted them as they reached the bottom of the steps.

There, Darien opened a large metal door that led into the bowels of the dungeon. A gush of frigid air rushed past them, along with a wash of eerie blue light. Darien stepped into the ice-carved passage then turned back, waiting for Connel. The Battlemage looked around, planting the palm of his hand against the slick wall of ice.

"He kept me here," Darien explained as he strode forward into the depths of the ice warren. "They locked me up and kept me near death. Then they dragged me there."

Darien pointed, indicating an iron door straight ahead at the end of the hall. He made no move toward it. He had no desire to look within; he didn't wish to confront the nightmares that door unlocked. His memories of the chamber beyond were riddled with holes. Some things he remembered luridly well, like the feel of the dust-filled rag in his mouth and the ghastly sounds of Meiran's screams. The clicking noise of the mechanism. Other things he couldn't remember at all. He had no recollection of how he'd come by the gut wound that had almost killed him. He had no idea how he'd survived.

He stepped aside and waited for Byron Connel to work the latch. The Battlemage regarded him with a long, searching gaze. Then, one hand on his weapon, he opened the door and stepped into the dark chamber within. He walked forward a few paces then stopped, stark-still.

Darien followed grudgingly. He moved to the side, standing with his back against the jagged rock wall. Above, rusted chains and hooks dangled from the ceiling. Mechanical devices with winches and gears, cogs and screws, had been placed all around the edge of the room. A long, narrow table equipped with leather straps stood on the far end of the chamber, its surface stained dark with blood. The scene was gruesome, appalling. Darien's gaze avoided all of it, remaining instead on the one object in the room that overshadowed all the rest.

A living nightmare hovered in the center of the chamber, rotating slowly, its silhouette form orienting toward them.

Darien stared at the necrator, repulsed by his own reaction to the thing. He should be frozen in fear, terrified beyond capacity to act.

Instead, Darien felt nothing.

This monster was his own creation. He had willed it into existence from the scorched fabric of Nashir's soul, granting it life by feeding it death. Only, he had no recollection of doing so.

Connel turned to look back at him. His mouth hung slack. Revulsion and disbelief glassed his eyes. "You did this?"

"Aye." Darien nodded once. He stared fixedly at the necrator. He didn't trust it. Even though he was well beyond the creature's influence, he loathed it utterly.

"Can you command it?"

The question took Darien by surprise; he hadn't thought of that. "I don't know," he admitted.

"Try."

Darien looked down at the floor. To where a dark brown stain mottled the stone near his feet.

"Visea," he whispered.

Immediately, the necrator in front of him melted into the ground. It was gone, as if absorbed by the porous stone. Byron Connel turned to gape at him, his expression full of dismay. His hand clutched his spiked weapon tight against his chest.

"Bring it back," he whispered.

Darien closed his eyes and willed the necrator back into existence. When he looked up again, the shadow was back, hovering, crystalline-black and sinister. Silently awaiting his command.

Connel stared long and hard at the abomination. Finally, he dropped his chin to his chest, shoulders sagging. "What you have done..." He sighed heavily. "If I didn't know Nashir so well, your soul would be halfway to hell right now. But fortunately for you, I did know Nashir. I know what he was capable of. And now I know what you're capable of."

He glared at Darien significantly.

Darien nodded, internalizing the threat.

Connel dropped his hand, strapping Thar'gon back to his belt. He was trembling in either rage or fear; Darien couldn't tell which. The look on Connel's face was impossible to read.

The Battlemage said, "You're absolved of the murder of Nashir Arman. But make no mistake: I will never turn my back on you. Ever." Connel glanced at the necrator. "Get rid of it."

Darien obeyed, watching as the malevolent shadow melted away. He turned, walking back through the doorway. In the corridor outside, he waited for Connel to emerge. The door closed behind them with an echoing *thud.*

Byron Connel said nothing the entire long climb back up to the level of the palace. As they moved out of the cold stairwell, he stopped beside a servant standing to one side, rigid enough to appear painted on the wall.

"Bring wine," Connel ordered. "And plenty of it."

The servant bowed, backing away, then hurried off in the direction of the kitchens.

Darien led Connel back to his own chamber, offering the man a cushion by the hearth. He sat down across from him, eyes darting to the thanacryst across the room. The demon-dog was curled up in the corner by the door, staring at them with disinterest.

The servant returned with a decanter of wine and cups arranged on a silver tray, which he set down on the floor between them. Without uttering a word, the man bowed and backed out of the room, closing the door in his wake.

Darien waited for Connel to serve himself before pouring his own cup of wine. He raised the cup to his lips, breathing in the sweet scent of the grapes. Then he threw his head back, draining half the cup in one swallow. The wine was harsher than it smelled. It burned his throat going down.

"Quin and Sareen have vanished." Connel set his cup down on the floor at his side. His eyes locked on Darien. "Do you have any knowledge of their whereabouts?"

Darien took another swallow, finishing the remainder of the wine in his cup. He wiped his mouth dry on his shirtsleeve. He answered truthfully, "I've no idea where they could be."

He'd had no word from Quin. Darien assumed the man must be halfway to Titherry by now, but he had no way of knowing for certain. In this case, he was grateful for his ignorance.

"We have reason to suspect the temples are aligning against us," Connel said as Darien poured himself more wine. "The disappearance of two of our own is disconcerting. And now with Nashir…"

His voice trailed off. He took a heavy sip from his cup. "We're down to only five of our former number." Connel regarded Darien with a frank expression. "I'll be relying on you as a Battlemage. You're my second-in-command, now."

Darien looked away, gazing intently into the fire. The oversized hearth burned bricks of coal instead of logs. The coals glowed orange, silvering at the edges. The smell was acrid, mingling with the floral scent of incense that permeated the room. It was not a pleasant combination.

Connel grumbled, "We're running out of mages, and we're running out of time. The southern population centers are already mobilizing. Renquist wants the entire Khazahar ready to deploy within a week."

Darien glanced up. "A week isn't enough time to prepare an invasion."

"This isn't an invasion," Connel corrected him. "It's an evacuation. We're emptying all the Black Lands." He downed the remainder of his wine and set the empty cup on the floor, holding Darien's gaze the entire time. Watching his reaction to the news.

Darien shook his head, unable to contain his surprise. Everything was happening so much quicker than he'd expected. Which complicated his plans. He'd hoped that Quin would find a way to break the curse, to release Malikar's skies from the grip of darkness. Evacuating the entire population into the Rhen was a nightmare situation that Darien hoped they could avoid. He still had faith in Quin.

He insisted, "I need more time."

"Time is the one thing you don't have. Travel alone to the staging area will take you a minimum of three weeks."

Darien felt hampered at every turn. He needed a way out, a change of direction. A jarring thought occurred to him. "Isn't there a transfer portal nearby?"

"Under the lake." Connel poured himself a fresh cup of wine. "How deep can you swim?"

Darien scowled, not appreciating the sarcasm. He lowered his cup, leaning back against the wall beside the hearth. The warmth of the fire felt good despite the noxious smell of coal. He could feel the effects of the alcohol on his mind, smoothing his tattered nerves. He felt suddenly weary.

Connel leaned forward and clapped Darien on the shoulder. Then he climbed to his feet. "I'll have your man find me a room with a bed in it. Report to me after *thalath*. We'll begin your education."

Darien followed Connel to his feet. The Battlemage extended his hand, palm outstretched. Darien accepted the gesture, noting the hesitance in Connel's grip. There was a void of trust there he'd have to work hard to bridge.

Connel turned away. But instead of making his way to the door, he wandered instead toward the writing desk in the corner of the room. Darien stiffened, remembering the catalogue of his ancestry he'd left there in plain view. The list that ended with the name Braden Reis.

He did not want Connel to discover his relationship to Quin Reis.

The red-haired mage picked up the parchment from the desk, raising it up before his face. His eyes scanned over the long list of names, starting from the top. But he broke off not even halfway down, his eyes flicking back to Darien.

"What's this?"

"My family lineage," Darien answered stiffly. It was hard to keep the anxiety out of his voice.

Connel set the parchment back down on the desk. "What inspired you to write this all out?"

Darien shrugged. "Sometimes I fear I'm starting to lose myself." That, at least, was sincerest truth.

Connel nodded. He strode toward the door, clapping Darien on the back as he passed by. "You can't lose something you never had, Darien. Get some sleep."

He strode out the door, shutting it behind him as he left.

Darien sank down on the edge of the bed. He leaned forward, cupping his head in his hands. His stomach felt ill. He could feel the effects of the alcohol draining out of him like blood leaking from his veins. The warmth of the wine was replaced by stone-cold fear.

The next time he saw Connel was early afternoon.

The Battlemage had assembled a small party of Tanisars, men who would normally follow only Darien's command. But in the shadow of Connel's presence, it seemed he'd been outranked. They rode out from the palace on the few mounts they had. Past the dark lake, beyond the denuded foothills to the south. Out from under the oppressive energies of the vortex that swirled around Tokashi Palace.

Connel didn't speak a word to Darien the entire ride. The Battlemage remained encased in the cold grip of silence, his intractable stare scouring the landscape. Sayeed trailed behind on his own mount, a quiver of spears hanging from his shoulder. His mare dragged an empty travois that raked a trail behind them that looked like dual claw marks in the sand.

Darien wondered about the travois, speculating why it was necessary. He almost asked. But then he stopped himself, reckoning that he probably didn't want to know the answer. He didn't know where they were riding or what to expect; Connel wouldn't tell him. But by the long looks on the faces of the men, he had a feeling it wasn't going to be pleasant.

Connel angled his horse off the road, guiding his courser down a path that led to an opening in the cliff wall just ahead. At first it seemed just an indentation in the rock. But to Darien's surprise, it turned out to be the entrance to a slender canyon that parted the cliff face.

Connel reined in and climbed down from his horse. Darien followed him to the ground, leading his mount forward to examine the opening. The walls to either side had been carved in bas-relief. Twin images depicting winged horses with hawk-like faces stood like a pair of ancient sentries on either side. The gate they created was daunting, striking in every detail. Running his hand over one of the sentinels, Darien could feel every rippling muscle, the barbs of the feathers that decorated the wings.

They led the horses on foot through the opening between the stone guardians. The walls of the crevice beyond were tall and steep, smooth like fire-polished glass. The path they tread had been a streambed; now dry. The water had eroded the rocks, forming the narrow passage. Darien could make out different layers of sediment, some ruddy, others more golden in hue. The splendor of the cliffs had been diminished by the Desecration but not permanently undone.

"What is this place?"

Connel glanced back at him but said nothing.

It was Sayeed who answered. "This is an ancient place that is held to be sacred by all the tribes of the Khazahar. There is a spring hidden deep within that seeps water blessed by the gods. It is said that drinking from this well cleanses the heart of all fear. Men come here to drink their fear before going into battle. It is tradition."

Darien nodded even as he dismissed the man's claim. The culture of superstition ran deep in Malikar's bloodlines.

The canyon curved sharply then ran straight ahead for some distance. Looking ahead, Darien saw that soldiers had been stationed every so often at intervals along the passage. Each man stood alone beside a small campfire.

Connel stopped and handed the reins of his horse to a soldier. With a gesture, he instructed Darien to do the same. As Sayeed relieved him of his horse, Darien saw a trace of sadness in the man's dark eyes.

"May the gods lend you courage, my friend," Sayeed whispered. "Drink your fear."

Darien turned to Byron Connel in alarm. "What is this? What's going on?"

Connel untied the spiked silver weapon from his belt, wielding it like a club. His red-bearded face was full of arrogance and ice.

"It is called the Rakkah," he said. "The final test of a Battlemage. You are well-schooled in defensive tactics, but that's only half the equation. Now you need to learn how to kill. Above all else, you must fortify your resolve."

He motioned ahead at the line of men stretched out along the walls of the canyon.

Darien felt ice-cold dismay as understanding hit him in the face.

"You want me to kill *all these men?*"

The Battlemage nodded. "I need you combat-effective."

Darien paced away a few steps, eyes studying the first man in the long, drawn-out line. The man was a soldier, a Tanisar by the uniform. He stood at attention beside his small fire, face untroubled by emotion. He had the look of a man resigned to duty and fate.

Darien spun away, feeling sickened. "Who are they?" he demanded. "What have these men done to deserve death?"

Byron Connel moved to stand in front of him. He was taller than Darien, his face set in harsh, uncompromising lines. "They are Tanisars. Soldiers who volunteered for this duty. Men who desire only to serve you."

That explanation sickened Darien even more. His throat clenched in revulsion. "Why would they volunteer for this?"

"Because I asked them to. There is much *sharaq* in such a death. They know they lay down their lives to help prepare the greatest weapon Malikar has ever known. The selfsame weapon that will deliver their families from the curse of darkness."

Darien shook his head, backing away from Connel. "I'm not a weapon," he whispered.

The Battlemage narrowed his eyes. "After today, you will be. You will be the most fearsome weapon our world has ever known. Never before has there existed an eighth-tier Battlemage trained in offensive tactics and capable of wielding the power of the Onslaught. After today, you will be indomitable. No mortal force will be able to stop us."

Darien shuddered, sickened with disgust. "I will not murder these men."

"Yes, you will," Connel said gruffly. "This is the Rakkah. The final trial of an apprentice Battlemage. You must pass the Rakkah to earn admittance into our order. The price of failure is death. There is no going back. There's no halfway. The Rakkah has already begun."

"I won't do it." Darien turned his back on Connel and began stalking away.

The hand of the gods reached down from the sky and slapped him off his feet, hurling him hard against the face of the cliff. Darien slumped to the ground, where he lay stunned, gazing up at the ink-black sky, slowly blinking. The taste of blood filled his mouth. His vision went from white to red.

Connel reached down and hauled him to his feet. He wielded his spiked talisman in his right hand, bracing Darien upright with his left. Darien staggered, reeling. He couldn't seem to focus on the man's face. Pulling at the magic field, he struggled to heal his injuries. The world went dark, and he wilted to the ground.

Pain flared inside, tearing him wide awake.

"Be warned," Connel growled into Darien's face, leaning over him menacingly. "The next blow will be a killing strike." He motioned to the first man behind him. *"Stand up!* You bring dishonor to Sinan."

Darien rolled over, pushing himself weakly to his knees.

"Who's Sinan?" he asked, still half-dazed by the talisman's magical strike. He staggered to his feet, taking a limping step ahead. He brought a hand up to his face, smearing a trail of blood that trickled from his nostril.

"Sinan is the soldier whose duty it is to teach you the *hijaz* attack."

Darien glanced at the young Tanisar by his lonely campfire. "I don't understand. How can that boy teach me anything?"

"Ask him."

Darien didn't want to ask. He swallowed against a knot of despair in his throat, feeling the last of his resistance crumbling away. He knew when he was beaten. There was no use in putting up a fight; with Thar'gon in his hand, Connel was far too powerful.

Heart pounding in his chest, Darien walked toward the first man in line.

He regarded the soldier before him: a young man with dark, shoulder-length hair and a prominent nose. There was no trace of struggle nor sadness in the soldier's eyes; only a calm, determined strength. The man dipped his head in greeting.

"Lord, I am Sinan son of Semal. It is my honor to teach you the attack known as *hijaz*. It is a very complex attack to master, I am told, so you must pay very careful attention."

Darien blinked, gazing deeply into Sinan's dark eyes. The young man was rattling off a prepared statement, something he'd been made to memorize. It had the distinctive formula of a ritualized speech.

"The *hijaz*, if performed correctly, will cause the body of a victim to explode. This is a very effective tactic for spreading fear to demoralize your enemy. Darien Nach'tier, please allow me the honor of teaching you the *hijaz* attack."

Darien swallowed, his mouth filling with the sour taste of acid. He brought his hands up, gripping the man's shoulders. "Your name is Sinan son of Semal?"

The soldier nodded. "It is, Lord."

Darien closed his eyes, clenching his teeth against the ache of horror.

"I don't want you to teach me this, Sinan."

The young man regarded him with an expression akin to sympathy. "I am sorry, Lord. It is my duty."

Darien released Sinan's shoulders, glaring his hatred back at Connel.

"Don't make me do this."

The Battlemage stepped forward, taking Darien's hand in his. "Feel through me."

There was absolutely no emotion in his voice. Darien could feel his hand shaking in Connel's grip. His whole arm trembled. He closed his eyes, opening himself to Connel's link. Instantly, he felt inside of Sinan. He could feel the pressure of the young man's blood as if feeling his own veins. It pulsed and throbbed, swelling in volume with every heartbeat.

"Please. *Don't.*"

He could feel what Connel was doing with his mind. Increasing the pressure of the blood against Sinan's arteries, at the same time applying a counterpressure that kept the system in balance. He could hear Sinan groaning as the pain became unbearable.

"Do you feel it?" Connel asked.

Darien grimaced. He felt it. It was awful. He could feel Sinan's blood on the verge of boiling. The soldier in front of him collapsed to his knees, throwing his head back as he moaned in tortured anguish.

"Do you feel it?"

Darien nodded, clenching his teeth. *"Aye."*

"Then finish it."

"I can't," Darien gasped, shaking in revulsion.

Byron Connel leaned forward and growled in his face, "Don't let him suffer!"

Darien stroked Sinan's body with his mind. He released the counterpressure Connel had applied to contain the man's raging blood.

Sinan exploded in a showering rain of gore.

Darien shielded his face with his hands. He stood there shaking, hands trembling over his face, unable to bring himself to open his eyes. He felt Connel's hand on his neck, grabbing him by the fabric of his shirt, hauling him forward. Darien's stomach wrenched. He swallowed against the taste of vomit in his mouth.

Connel's harsh grip jerked him to a halt.

"Lord, I am Alton son of Orhan."

Darien opened his eyes. He stood in front of the next soldier in the line. This man was slightly older than Sinan had been, slightly taller. A fine mist of blood covered one side of his face. His forehead had broken out in a sheen of perspiration despite the chill of the air.

Darien stared at Alton son of Orhan.

"It is my honor to teach you the attack known as *nebiza*. If performed correctly, the *nebiza* causes the nerves of your opponent to quit functioning. This is a very effective tactic for stopping the hearts of many warriors at once. Darien Nach'tier, please allow me the honor of teaching you the *nebiza* attack."

Darien groped for strength, his breath shuddering in his throat. He stepped forward, gripping Alton's shoulders with his hands.

"Your name is Alton son of Orhan?" He wanted to make sure he had it right.

Sinan son of Semal. Alton son of Orhan.

He would remember those names. He swore right then and there he would never forget them.

"It is, Lord."

Darien bowed his head. "You honor me, Alton."

"The honor is mine, Lord."

Darien pulled back, glaring at Byron Connel. The Battlemage took his hand. Again, Darien found his consciousness fed through Connel into the soldier standing in front of him. He could feel the man's nerves at work, regulating the pace of Alton's heartbeat. A subtle change in those impulses could stop that instantly.

"Do you feel it?" Connel whispered.

"Aye."

"Then finish it."

Darien sagged, groaning. He didn't want to kill Alton son of Orhan. He admired the gentle depths in the man's dark eyes.

"Forgive me."

With a wrench of Darien's mind, Alton's heart seized in his chest, his body crumbling to the blackened earth. Darien stared down at him, drowning in self-loathing.

Connel guided him forward to the next man in line.

"Lord, I am Devrim son of Enver. It is my honor to teach you the attack known as *ruhk*. If performed correctly, the *ruhk* will cause the flesh of your opponent to catch fire. This is a very effective tactic for causing a terrible, excruciating death. Darien Nach'tier, please allow me the honor of teaching you the *ruhk* attack."

Darien leaned forward, gripping the man's shoulders in his hands. He stared into the depths of the young man's eyes.

"Your name is Devrim son of Enver?"

"It is, Lord."

Sinan son of Semal. Alton son of Orhan. Devrim son of Enver.

"You honor me, Devrim."

"The honor is mine, Lord."

Darien offered his hand to Byron Connel. Instantly, he was transported deep inside Devrim, feeling the warmth of the young man's core. He could feel the source of that heat. He understood how to change it. Such a subtle difference. But if done in every tissue of the body altogether at once...

"Do you feel it?"

"Aye."

"Then finish it."

Darien squeezed his eyes shut, trembling as Devrim burned. The soldier's screams were appalling. They went on for a very long time.

He felt Connel's hand on his back. He walked forward, swallowing his emotions, stoppering them up inside. He raked his shirtsleeve across his eyes, wiping away his humanity.

Darien approached the next man in line.

"Lord, I am Serkan son of Arsil..."

Chapter Five
A Sentinel's Duty

Pass of Lor-Gamorth, The Front

Kyel staggered as the magic field surged back into his mind. The relief was so intense that it wrenched a gasp from his lips. He swayed over his feet, relishing the field's sweet comfort. He stood there for a moment savoring the pulse, a feeling of contentment unlike any other. The magic field had been denied him ever since his arrival at Greystone Keep. The fortress had been constructed within the protective confines of a node. He understood the necessity, but the field's absence ate at Kyel every second he was away from it.

His hands tightened reflexively on the wrapped bundle he lugged in his arms. A crackling noise issued from beneath the layers of cloth, a sound no human body should ever make. He took one last step just to make certain the field was at full strength. Then he lowered Meiran to the dirt as Traver wrestled with her legs. Gusts of wind whipped at their backs, cold and punishing. Traver righted himself and took a step back, staggering. He held his hand up in front of him, flexing the three fingers he had left. Then he grimaced, wincing back and covering his mouth with his cloak.

"Gods' mercy, she stinks!"

Kyel nodded, his eyes watering as he held a cloth up over his own face. His stomach lurched, threatening to spill its contents into the dirt at his feet. "It's the rot."

They'd shrouded Meiran in thick folds of cloth, which covered the raised blisters that oozed gore over her blackened flesh. But there was nothing they could do about the stench. It was terrible, much worse than the smell of decay. Whatever disease had hold of her, it was consuming her entirely.

"Is there anything you can do?" Traver was pale, his eyes watering. He looked a bit green. The captain had handled enough corpses in his career that he should be used to the stench of decay. Maybe it was different when the victim was still alive.

Kyel looked back up the hill in the direction of the keep. The path they'd taken down the ridge was empty; no one had followed them. Kyel felt relieved—he was glad to be free of Cadmus and the retinue of guards that followed him everywhere he went. Thanks to Traver, they'd managed to slip out of the fortress unaccompanied.

He turned his attention back to Meiran. "I don't know if I can cure this," he admitted, dropping to a crouch at her side. She looked asleep. But Kyel knew better; it wasn't sleep that was taking her. The way he figured it, Meiran didn't have much time left.

He swallowed the lump in his throat and went right to work. Using his knife, Kyel sawed through the cloth wrappings to expose the blackened flesh beneath. He drew back away from the smell that spilled out. Meiran's bloated form was barely recognizable as human. Viscous fluids streamed from cracks and large blisters in her flesh. Her limbs were deformed, fingers and toes withered and rotten. Kyel fought the urge to retch, clamping his teeth together.

"What happened to her?" Traver gasped.

"I don't know. And I don't have time to speculate. Do me a favor and just stand back."

A flare of lightning stabbed the mountainside nearby, followed by a deafening peal of thunder.

For a split-second, the Pass of Lor-Gamorth lit up bright as day. Then the darkness came crashing back down on top of them. A gust of wind tore at Kyel's cloak, rippling it out behind him.

Kyel set his hands on Meiran's shoulders, holding his breath against the stench. As his fingers caressed her skin, something inside made a crunching noise. His stomach twisted. He closed his eyes and reached within, grappling with the power that sustained him. The magic field flooded into him, coursing through his hands into Meiran's corrupt tissues. He reached inside her, probing the full extent of her ruin.

"Oh, gods," he gasped, pulling back. Vomit surged into his mouth. He swallowed it back down again. Steeling himself, Kyel sent a desperate flood of healing energies into Meiran's failing body. It didn't go very far; it was like pounding a fist against a stone wall. He drew back with a cry of frustration.

"What is it?" Traver called over the rising wind.

Kyel was unable to answer. He was too horrified. He stood there numb, shaking his head as precious seconds ticked by.

"She's more dead than alive…" he finally managed to whisper. "I can't…" He gaped at Traver, shrugging helplessly. Another bolt of lightning splintered the air.

Kyel glanced around, at last recognizing where they were. It was the same spot where, two years before, Devlin Craig had saved Darien's life after Arden Hannah had tried to roast him over a bonfire. Craig had carried Darien out of the node and dumped him down in this same place. He'd worked on him until Darien drew breath again.

Craig hadn't given up on Darien.

Kyel knew he couldn't give up on Meiran.

Closing his eyes, Kyel knelt and placed his hands on her rotting flesh, using the magic field to probe deep inside her. He needed to make sense of the damage, at least get an idea of where to begin. It was like healing a corpse; most of her was already more dead than alive. He seared the toxins from her blood first, then set about burning away corrupted flesh. Beneath his fingers, new skin wove together, tightening, squirming into place. He invaded her core, restoring blood to organs starved for air. The whole process took only minutes, but to Kyel it seemed like hours. The infected flesh sloughed away, revealing fresh pink skin underneath.

Meiran lurched, drawing in a sharp gasp. Her chest heaved, her back arching. Then she collapsed in a fit of coughing before going limp again. Kyel put his ear to her chest, listening to the faint sound of her heartbeat.

"Is she healed?" Traver shouted over the wind.

Kyel pulled back, watching the rhythm of Meiran's chest, not trusting it.

"She's alive," he said in wonder, only half-believing himself.

Devlin Craig picked up a roasted fowl and held it up to his mouth, tearing off a long strip of meat. He chewed noisily then swallowed, chasing it down with a swig of mead. "Did she say anything at all?"

Kyel shook his head, gazing down at the blackened hen on his own plate. The cooks had done a number on the small bird. It reminded him too much of what Meiran's skin had looked like. He didn't think he could eat it. He nudged the plate away a fraction, taking a sip from his cup, instead.

"No." He shook his head. "She hasn't awakened yet. Where exactly did you find her?"

Craig tore off another strip of charred meat with his teeth. He chewed with his mouth open, smacking the food around noisily. "Sentries found her lying in the riverbed. She'd been peppered with arrows and left for dead."

Kyel tugged at a bird wing, twisting it between his thumb and forefinger. The joint separated, coming apart. He picked it up and sucked the flesh off the bone, closing his eyes as he tasted the fatty juices. Despite being charred, the hen wasn't as bad as it looked. It was far better fare than he'd been treated to during his last stay at Greystone Keep. Apparently, the Southern kingdoms now took the Enemy threat more seriously.

"That's not like them, is it?" he mused as he chewed. "To leave a mage just lying about on the ground like that? I mean, why didn't they burn her like all the others?"

"Don't know." Craig plucked a bone out from between his teeth and tossed it down on the board. "Maybe they didn't know she was a mage."

Kyel wondered at that. The chains on Meiran's wrists were conspicuous. But perhaps they hadn't been evident with all the rot.

Craig wiped his mouth on the padded sleeve of his gambeson. "How is she?"

"She'll be unconscious for a few days, I suspect. We won't know for sure until she wakes up. The arrows were poisoned. I did my best, but there's no way of knowing if I got it all. If I didn't, the rot will set right in again."

Craig tossed the bird carcass down on his plate, fixing Kyel with a smoldering glare. His wheat-colored hair fell in disarray about his shoulders, his beard matted with greasy juices. He looked a lot older than Kyel remembered.

Craig nodded at the charred hen on Kyel's plate. "You about done with that? There's some reports I'd like you to take a look at."

Kyel hesitated, seeing the commander's expression. There was something there that he didn't like. He pushed his plate back. He felt suddenly on edge. "What kinds of reports?"

Craig stood up from the table, casting down the napkin he hadn't used. "The Enemy's been redistributing forces along their perimeter. They're splitting their assets."

Kyel glanced up at the man's looming hulk. He dabbed at his mouth with his own napkin before setting it down. His mind fumbled with the information. "I don't know what that means," he admitted finally, a little embarrassed. "Am I supposed to?"

"Aye. You're supposed to." Craig planted his big hands firmly on his hips, glowering down at him. "The problem is, you don't. It's high time you learn to actually *be* a Sentinel instead of just strutting around calling yourself one."

Kyel blinked, the sting of the insult coloring his cheeks.

Craig turned away and walked back across the room to another table with maps and charts layered over its surface. A larger map hung from the wall, a replica of the one that had been mounted in the tower of the old keep. Kyel felt drawn to the map, feeling suddenly sentimental. He reached up, running a hand over the vellum's soft texture.

Craig rapped his knuckles on the table to get his attention.

"Look, Archer. There's some things we need to get settled between us. There's going to be a battle here in a matter of weeks, possibly days. I'm supposed to be able to rely on you. But I can't. As far as I'm concerned, you only know enough to be dangerous."

Hearing that, Kyel hung his head. He knew he wasn't the Sentinel that Darien had intended him to be. But he'd been trying his hardest to make himself more effective. In the past few months, he'd spent every spare moment with a book in his hands. But learning was proving to be all but impossible without a master to guide him. "I can give you my best," he said. "That's all I can do."

"It's not enough," Craig snapped. "You're the only Sentinel we have. And I need you to do your gods-damned duty. What do you know of siege warfare?"

Kyel stared hard at the floor. "Not enough."

"Then welcome to your first day of training." Craig planted two fingers squarely on one of the maps laid out on the table. "This is their primary staging area, right here, at the base of Orguleth." He punctuated each syllable with a tap of his fingers. "They're well-entrenched and sustained by robust supply lines. More forces arrive by the hour. Soon they're going to reach a point where they'll have to either disband or advance. They can't just sit there forever.

"The way I see it, they'll deploy an advance force consisting mostly of foot soldiers…"

Kyel stared at the map as the man's words droned on into meaningless noise. He tried to pay attention. But all he could focus on was the image in his head of the mounded piles of corpses he'd been forced to walk through after his last battle in the pass. Kyel remembered it well, the wails and moans of the fallen, the stiffening limbs, the spreading rivulets of blood. The smell of the aftermath. He'd witnessed the personal hell Darien had gone through trying to heal the injured. That battle had changed him; after that, his eyes had remained forever haunted. Darien had never recovered from that day.

Kyel bowed his head in resignation. He didn't want that kind of future for himself.

He didn't think he could handle it.

When he went to bed that night, Kyel's sleep was fitful. He snapped awake drenched in sweat, consumed by a terrible sense of foreboding. He sat bolt upright, throwing off the covers. Gazing blearily into the darkness of his quarters, he tried to make sense of the shadows. He scanned the corners of the room, his heart and mind racing.

He remembered having a nightmare. Only, this nightmare had felt real.

Kyel rolled out of bed and reached for a ceramic jug set out by his bedside. He brought the jug up to his lips, gulping a mouthful of stale water as sweat trickled down his face. An eerie feeling of apprehension slid down his spine as he set the water jug back down.

A shadow lurched toward him from the corner.

Kyel flinched back, bringing his hands up and gasping, "Who's there?"

The shadow fell across him. Kyel sagged in relief, breathing an audible sigh. For a moment, he couldn't move, just stood staring into the familiar face revealed by a streak of light slanting in from the window. It took him a moment to compose himself enough to smile.

"Meiran," he whispered. "Thank the gods."

The woman nodded. Then she collapsed into his arms, sobbing wretchedly as she clung to his shoulders.

Chapter Six
The Whim of the Gods

Tokashi Palace, The Black Lands

Darien let the blood-soaked wrap fall from his hips, stepping naked into the gray-tiled bath. The air was warm and heavy with humidity. He moved forward through a thick mist of steam, feeling heat radiating up into his feet through the tiles of the floor.

Blood leaked from his body at every step, pattering in dark droplets that mixed with beads of water already on the ground. It ran in crimson streams toward the drains.

He reached the far wall and groped at a gilt handle protruding from the surface. Immediately, a shower of warm water flowed from a spout set high above, falling in soothing droplets about his shoulders. Darien leaned forward, resting his forehead against the tile, arms pressed against the wall. He closed his eyes and let the warm water course over his skin. He could feel the crusted blood softening, releasing from his body. Gently washing away.

None of the blood was his own.

Sinan son of Semal. Alton son of Orhan. Devrim son of Enver. Serkan son of Arsil…

His lips moved without words, forming names without sound, a droning litany in his head. Darien kept his eyes squeezed closed, head bowed under the steady stream of the water. The blood of innocents ran in streams across the floor, collecting in shallow puddles around the drains.

The walls of the bath wept garish streaks of red.

He stayed there for minutes in the water, shivering despite the warmth of the steam.

At last, he turned around. Darien pressed his back against the tiles and let his body slide down the wall to the floor. He leaned forward, cradling his head against his knees.

He sat there for a long time, grimly contemplating death.

It wouldn't take much to rend his tattered soul and scatter what was left of him on the winds of Oblivion. Just three simple words:

I deny Xerys.

If he could say it in his mind, then he could say it out loud. It shouldn't be very difficult.

Sinan son of Semal, Alton son of Orhan…

Darien clutched his head, shoulders trembling. He gripped his fingers into fists.

"I…deny…"

The words collapsed, his intent imploding in his mouth. He lacked the conviction to say the words that would end him. He threw his head back, letting the water from the spout drizzle miserably over his face. It felt almost like rain. But bitter, like hot, salted tears.

Eventually, Darien wandered out of the bath. He bent down and picked up the black wrap he'd discarded earlier, holding the stiffened fabric in his hand. With just one thought it was clean and unsoiled, supple, as if no stain had ever corrupted it. He wound the fabric around his hips, knotting it in place.

With a knock, the chamber door shuddered open.

Sayeed appeared, his face rigid with concern. He held a bottle of wine in one hand, a cup in the other.

"Better bring more," Darien muttered. He trudged forward, relieving Sayeed of the bottle but not the cup. He unstoppered the wine and took a long pull from the bottle. The Zakai officer bowed and left. Darien settled down onto a cushion, leaning back against the wall. He knocked another mouthful back then upended the bottle, draining its contents down his throat. He set the spent container down on the floor then stared vacantly into the fire dancing in the hearth.

Darien was relieved when Sayeed returned quickly.

He hoped that, with enough wine, he could work up the nerve to cast his soul to the winds.

———

Darien awoke on the floor in a jumbled collection of bottles, his head throbbing in time to every heartbeat. He lay on his side, staring at a blurry, overturned bottle in front of his face. His fingers twitched. With a scowl, he wrenched himself upright, his vision fading before sharpening.

The door to his bedchamber boomed three times, jolting on its hinges. Someone outside was growing impatient. The insistent knocks had woken him from his stupor.

He shoved himself to his feet, staggering across the floor. Darien opened the chamber door and stood there regarding Byron Connel in silent contempt. He stepped back enough to admit the darkmage into his quarters.

Connel paused, shaking his head at the array of bottles scattered about the room.

"I hope it was worth it."

Darien ignored him. He walked away, casting his graceless body back down on the mat. He focused his stare on the wall behind Connel, his fingers caressing a soft tassel that hung at his side.

Connel dropped to a crouch in front of him. Hands on his knees, he peered intently into Darien's face.

"Yesterday, I forged you into a weapon. I neglected to explain how much that would cost you. You see, weapons don't feel. They don't wrestle with indecision or grope for understanding. They have but one purpose: they simply kill. They don't regret. They never hesitate. And they're never to blame for what they do."

Darien's stare remained fixed on the wall as Connel's words crawled under his skin, worming their way into his brain. He understood very well what the man was trying to say. He had an acute appreciation of what he'd become. And all that he'd lost.

Connel reached out and clapped Darien on the shoulder. Then he pushed himself erect. "I'm leaving. Rally the Tanisars. I'll expect you at the staging area in one month's time." He stared down at Darien for a moment, awaiting a response. When none was forthcoming, the Battlemage simply shrugged.

"May you know the peace and blessings of the gods."

With that, he turned toward the door.

"Who's to blame?"

Connel stopped. He turned back around.

Darien finally looked up at him, resentment seething in his eyes. "You said a weapon is never to blame. If not the weapon, then who?"

The Battlemage reached into a pocket of his robe and withdrew a folded pair of gloves. He worked his hand into one, flexing his fingers to stretch the fabric. "No man has the authority or power to determine another man's fate. All lives are lived at the mercy and whim of the gods. They alone are to blame."

He turned away, tugging the other glove on over his wrist.

Darien lowered his stare back to the hearth. "Then damn all the gods. And damn you, too."

Connel nodded. "Take care, Darien," he said as he left.

———

Darien waited only long enough to be certain the man was well and truly gone. Then he scooped up his sword and shirt and thrust open the chamber door. He strode across the empty hallway and tugged open the door of the stable. There, the strong scent of horse filled his nostrils.

From the other side of the dim room came a welcoming nicker.

Darien moved forward, his hand reaching up to stroke his stallion's soft neck. It didn't take him a minute to slip a bridle on over the horse's head and laid a blanket over its back. Thrusting open the stable door, he led the animal into the hallway.

He mounted swiftly and rode at a trot through the corridors of the palace, the echoing sounds of hoofbeats ringing off the walls. Tanisars and servants scattered out of his way, dodging back to let him pass. Darien rode out the gate into the night, urging the stallion forward at a gallop.

———

He found Azár in the lightfields. She looked up at his approach, confusion pinching her face.

"Darien?"

He dropped his horse's reins, trudging stiffly toward her through the grass of the meadow. Azár held her ground, face frozen in concern as her eyes tracked his motion. Her stare delved into him, searching. Her mouth twisted in compassion.

"Come here," she whispered.

Darien crushed her against his chest. His lips moved over her, desperate, scouring her face. His shaking hands groped behind her back.

He lifted Azár in his arms then bent to spread her out on the grass. He collapsed on top of her, the strength of his need rendering every motion frantic. His lips found hers, furious, ravaging. He slid his hands under her shirt, forcing back the thick fabric and exposing the soft flesh of her middle. His hips bore down against hers.

He was desperate.

Desperate to feel something beautiful again.

He parted her legs with a knee, fumbling with the drawstring of his trousers.

"Stop." It was the faintest, saddest sound.

Darien froze.

"Please," Azár whispered. *"Stop touching me."*

Panic infused her voice, so much that it made him sick.

Darien rolled off her, sitting up. He clutched his head in his hands, his body quivering.

"Look at me."

Azár wrenched Darien's face toward her. He kept his eyes lowered; he was too ashamed to look at her.

"If you ever touch me like that again, I'll kill you."

He forced a nod. Then he lurched to his feet and staggered away.

Chapter Seven
The Semantics of Servitude

Ishara, The Black Lands

Quin hovered over the kettle, bringing the spoon up to his lips for a taste. The fragrance of the stew filled his nostrils with warmth, bringing a whimsical smile to his lips. The sweet blend of seasonings tingled on his tongue, transporting him back in time with a nostalgic flood of aching sentiments. The smell reminded him of home. Not any recent home, but the Bryn Calazar he remembered. The city had been filled which such rich flavors, sweet fragrances and incense.

Now, all lost.

Lost in time. But not in memory.

The smile slipped from Quin's face. The taste of his cooking was another unsubtle reminder of his damnation.

"What is it?"

"Mujaz." Quin's voice was hollow with melancholy. "A stew made from dried fruits and seasonings." Noticing the dubious expression on her face, he added, "You eat it."

He dipped the spoon into the kettle then offered it across to her. Naia stared at the spoon for a moment, finally guiding it into her mouth. She closed her eyes as if savoring the taste. Then she crinkled her nose, wincing as if in pain.

"Strong," she complained. "What do you do, carry spices around in your pockets?"

"In fact, I do." Quin reached into his pack, extracting a rolled satchel that he opened in front of her. One by one, he began pulling out an assortment of small cloth sacks tied with drawstrings, laying them out on the ground between them. "In Malikar, spices are rare and highly prized. They are used in place of currency."

Naia reached out and grasped one of the small sacks in her hand. She brought it up to her nose, sniffing. "This is familiar."

"Cumin," Quin said. "It aids digestion."

She looked up at him with interest in her eyes. "How do you know which spice it is?"

He pointed a finger, indicating the color of the braided drawstring. "Each spice is associated with a particular pattern of braid. It's an ancient system that's survived since before my time."

Naia set the small sack down and picked up another, giving it a whiff. "Cinnamon. This is used in the preparation of bodies for funeral. I would never have imagined seasoning food with it."

"Cinnamon has extraordinary value." Quin plucked the sack out of her hand. "It's used to prevent food from spoiling, but it also has medicinal properties. It can treat festering wounds."

Naia frowned. "Don't your mages tend to the injured?"

"No." Quin raked the packets toward him and stuffed them back into the woven satchel. "If there's one thing in Malikar more precious than spice, it's mage-power. Next to light, that's the most limited resource."

Naia nodded, seeming to understand.

Quin served up a bowl of stew for her, thrusting it into her hands. "Enjoy your *mujaz*. Tonight, we feast like royalty."

She lifted the bowl with both hands and tasted the mixture, making a face.

Quin plunked the spoon back into the pot. Under his breath, he muttered, "I sometimes forget how much you people eschew anything that stimulates the senses or even reason."

Naia stared at him over the brim of her bowl. "What is that supposed to mean?"

"Nothing, really." Quin shrugged, serving himself a portion. "Just that you Southern folk seem to lead a very drab existence devoid of any substance. Now, eat your stew or go hungry."

He raised his bowl to his lips, drinking the sweet nostalgia delivered by the taste.

Looking defiant, Naia raised her own bowl and ate without further complaint.

When the meal was finished, Naia sat in silence while Quin went about the business of cleaning up their little camp. He could feel her eyes on him, tracking his every motion as he scrubbed out the cook pot with blackened sand and added coal to the fire. At first, he tried to ignore her looks. When the work was finished, he relaxed back against the cliff wall and tried using the brim of his hat as a shield against her stare. He focused his eyes and thoughts on the flickering of the campfire. It didn't help; he could still feel her there.

At last, when he could stand the attention no longer, he pushed back the brim of his hat, demanding, "*What?*"

The infernal woman continued to glare at him. "You lied to me."

Quin frowned, not understanding at first. It took him a moment to figure out what she was getting at. Even then, he disagreed. "No. I didn't."

"You told me you knew how to lift the curse over the Black Lands." Her eyes lingered on his face, accusing. "That was a lie."

He wondered what had given him away. Quin scowled, not wanting to be cornered into elaborating. "I told you I'd found *a way* to lift the curse. I didn't say that I knew *exactly* how to go about it."

Naia raised her eyebrows, scoffing at his explanation. "Semantics. Be more specific."

Quin grimaced, bringing a hand up to scratch his chin. "I can't."

"Why not?"

He sat upright, pulling his knees up against his chest and sweeping the hat off his head. This was exactly the conversation he'd been hoping to avoid. "All right, if you insist. But first, we must talk about the ground rules I have to live by." He took a deep breath, sorting through his thoughts. Trying to figure out how much to tell her. And how much to keep hidden.

"First of all, I'm a Servant of Xerys," he said finally. "That means I'm compelled to act with my Master's objectives always in mind. The moment my own interests lead me astray, I risk losing my Master's support. If I stray too far from my path then, why, my soul will be erased"—he snapped his fingers—"like that. Unmade and consigned to Oblivion. Understand? I walk a very treacherous and narrow path.

"My Master's purpose is to protect the magic field. Which can't happen if what I suspect about the curse is correct. So…I really can't divulge any information that would jeopardize my mission. That would conflict with my nature, and I'd find myself unmade rather rapidly and painfully."

The woman gazed at him with a healthy dose of skepticism. "So you can't tell me anything? Isn't that rather convenient?"

"Actually, I find it rather *in*convenient," Quin countered. "Believe me, I'd love to avoid the verbal sparring and skip right to the part where we agree to help each other. All I can tell you is this: if there is a way to lift the curse—which I believe there is—we can find it by using Athera's Crescent. And then, after the magic field is stabilized…why, then, my services will no longer be required by my Master. And I'll be at liberty to act."

"After this Reversal of the magic field you keep insisting is coming," Naia elaborated. Her eyes grew cold. "After we're all dead, you mean."

"Yes." Quin nodded. "After *you're* dead, rather. I'm already dead—which, in this case, works out serendipitously."

At least she'd listened to him when he'd told her about the Reversal. Unlike Meiran, Naia seemed to have a good appreciation for the threat it posed. Not just to magekind, but to all the rest of the world. He studied the woman's face, watching the flickering expressions that played across it.

When her eyes met his again, the icy fire was gone. "I believe you," Naia said finally. "Darien trusts you, so that tells me a lot. I suppose I'll have to trust you also. In all honesty, you've given me no reason not to."

Quin blinked. He had anticipated much more of

a fight. This was almost too easy.

To his shock, a small smile brightened Naia's face. "I understand why you killed Sareen," she said. "You're not like her at all."

"No," Quin agreed with a wry smile of his own. "I'm not. Not that Sareen was entirely bad. Our objectives were just…incompatible. It was my intent to reunite Meiran and Darien simply because it was the right thing to do. Sareen wanted to use Meiran to control him. I believe you'll find, if you ever get a chance to meet the other Servants, that not all demons are evil. We're all just damned. There is a distinction, you know."

"I believe that I see it," Naia whispered. She dropped her gaze to the ground, looking suddenly saddened. Quin thought he could guess the reason why.

He adjusted his posture, slouching further down against the rock and draping an elbow over one knee. So far, Naia was proving to be a much more reasonable companion than Meiran had. Of course, the scar on her wrist spoke volumes for her character. As far as Quin was concerned, that ugly, puckered welt was far more virtuous than Meiran's unbroken chain. It was a bold declaration of freedom.

He pushed his hat back, cocking his head. "I need to know how you escaped the Rhen," he said in as gentle a tone as he could muster. "We're going to have to travel to the Isle of Titherry, and we don't have time to take a ship. If you've found a transfer portal south of Rothscard, then I need to know about it."

Naia stared at him hard, brow knitting in confusion. "Transfer portal? What is that?"

Quin managed a smirk. "Not a transfer portal, then. Look, darling, why don't you just tell me how you got here?"

Naia's face turned toward the fire, her eyes distant in thought. Her hand came up to tuck a lock of soft auburn hair behind her ear. She glanced away. And then her gaze snapped back to him.

"I came to the Black Lands through the Catacombs of Death," she admitted.

Quin blinked. And blinked again. Never in a thousand years would he have thought to use Death's Catacombs for that purpose.

"Truly?" He sat fully erect, his interest piqued. "Well, don't stop there. Pray continue…"

Chapter Eight
Come the Monster

The Khazahar Desert, The Black Lands

Darien staggered away from the lightfields and wandered alone into the dark turmoil of the waste. He lumbered northward, following the snaking line of the river. He wasn't particularly aware of where he was going. He didn't care. His feet carried him forward, so the rest of him followed. His thoughts swam across his vision like the swirling colors in the clouds.

He didn't understand. Didn't try to understand. Didn't care. Nothing mattered.

I am a monster.

The image of Sinan exploding in a showering mist of blood made him flinch.

From his memories, an avalanche of fire poured forth to vaporize armies.

Naia stared at him through her veil, hurt collecting in her eyes.

Azár's firm legs spread out beneath him in the grass.

Darien brought his hands up to cover his face as his feet stumbled over rocks. All around him, the wild flux of the magic field surged with fury. The vicious energies sawed at his head, raked at his brain. The violence of the field became uncomfortable. He ignored it for as long as he could. Until the pain demanded his attention.

Darien stopped, blinking dumbly at the river that had appeared in front of him. He turned slowly where he stood, eyes taking in the landmarks all around him. He could feel his stomach loosening as he realized where he was. And what he'd almost done.

He'd stumbled into a vortex without shielding himself from it.

He slammed up a barrier in his mind to protect him from the wailing torrent of energy. Trembling in dismay, he continued on toward the river. He walked with no particular destination in mind. Away from the lightfields. Away from Azár. Away from his past. He could feel the vortex raging against his shield, suffocating in its fury. He didn't care.

Let it rage.

The river beside him became a whitewater. And then a blackwater.

Darien stopped, gazing out at a solid wall of rock that bent the river in its course. He looked up. And up, craning his neck. The wall of debris stretched across the great expanse of the gorge. It blocked the passage of the river, diverting it from its channel. He could see where the canyon ahead forked. Another riverbed, long dry, veered away to the west, into the vast expanse of shadowlands beyond.

Darien's mind snapped suddenly into focus.

The wall of rock was the source of the black lake that lapped at Tokashi's gates. It must have fallen from the mountainside, damming the gorge and redirecting the river from its path. If he could move the rubble, then the lake behind it would drain…which would uncover the transfer portal lost beneath it.

Only, such an act was impossible beneath the fury of the vortex.

Darien paced forward, eyes scanning the massive wall of debris in front of him. The entire side of the mountain had collapsed into the canyon. The obstruction stood hundreds of feet high, an enormous dam made of black earth and chunks of stone.

When he had attacked Nashir in the dungeon, Darien had drawn on the power of the Onslaught within the same vortex. The difference was, his mind had been protected by the dampening effect of Quin's sword, which was a powerful magical talisman. But here, his mind wouldn't be protected. One slip, and the raw fury of the vortex would end him instantly.

Perhaps he could keep his mind shielded while drawing on the Onslaught. It might be possible. It might also send his soul screaming back to hell.

Darien stared down into the gorge, contemplating the rocky dam, weighing his options. Long minutes wore by. A breeze came up, ruffling his hair. A cold sweat broke out all over his body. At last he made his decision.

He had nothing better to waste his death on.

He searched the canyon around him and found a trail that cut up along the wall of rock. Seeking higher ground, Darien took the trail up the rock face of the cliff. As he walked, he allowed his mind to wander, unfocused and adrift. Eventually he reached a plateau that overlooked the canyon and the lake. It was much cooler at that altitude. Overhead, clouds raced in dark streaks across the sky. Lightning flickered in the east, jagged forks stabbing down at the desert.

His skin crawled; he could sense the hostility of the vortex that surrounded him.

Darien tilted his head back, closing his eyes, and spread his arms out at his sides. He fixed his attention inward, at the shield he'd thrown up to block his mind from the vortex. He focused on that shield, reinforcing it with every effort of will he could muster. Then, dividing his attention, he opened a window to the Onslaught. Darien grimaced, feeling the strain of concentration. It felt as though his mind were being pulled in two different directions at once.

At first there was nothing. Then, ever so slowly, the Onslaught began leaking into him. When it started, it was just a trickle; not enough to do anything with. Darien willed himself to relax, to open up. Tried to open one part of himself wider while keeping another part walled off. Clenching his jaw, he reached out and took hold of the Hellpower, drawing it greedily from its source.

Scorching fire lanced into him, searing down every nerve of his body.

Darien screamed and fell to the rocks. He lay there moaning, writhing, gasping for breath through bubbling froth in his throat. His sight went black and then red as his eyes filled with tears of blood.

Mercifully, the pain didn't last long.

Darien's mind was swiftly overcome.

When he awoke, Naia was somehow sitting at his side, her dark eyes obscured by the sheer fabric of her veil. She reached down and tenderly stroked his face, her touch a soothing grace. Darien relaxed a little, savoring the feel of her. He couldn't remember why she was there.

"What is my name?"

Naia...

But that wasn't right. He struggled, wrestling for clarity through a fog of pain.

"Azár..."

The image of her face receded into darkness. Then someone was shaking him. The pain in his head exploded into agony, threatening to drag him back under.

"No!" Azár gasped. "Stay awake!"

She smeared the blood from his eyes, her fingers trailing down to cup his head. Darien drew in a deep, choking breath that rattled in his throat. It wasn't enough. Azár wrapped her arms around him, leveraging him up until he was staring into her face. Her forehead touched his, her hair swaying forward to veil them both.

She was panting, eyes wide and full of panic. "Were you attacked?"

Darien struggled to remember. All he could do was lay there gulping mouthfuls of gurgling air. Every muscle ached. His head felt like it had been smashed with an iron maul.

"No..." he finally whispered. "Not attacked. I tried to use the Onslaught..."

Azár's mouth fell open, her face aghast. "Why? Why would you try to destroy yourself?"

Was that what he'd intended? Darien struggled, unable to recollect his purpose. The fog in his brain weighed down at him, dragged him back toward unconsciousness.

"What does it matter?" He let his eyelids slide closed. The pain eased. He was drifting away.

A ringing slap startled him awake. He cried out, cringing as Azár clawed at his hair, wrenching him up off the ground.

"Listen to me!" she raged, spittle flying from her lips. "Until my people are free, *I do not release you from your duty!* I didn't raise you from hell just to have you die a coward's death! Take hold of your nerves!"

Her anger cleaved right through the fog that shrouded his mind. Darien struggled, fighting to sit up. He only got halfway there before a surge of nausea made him fall flat on his back again. He stared up at Azár, blinking miserably.

"I was trying to drain the lake," he explained. "Underneath, there's a transfer portal. I need it."

"Why?" she demanded, leaning over him. "Why must you risk death to find this thing?"

Darien sat up, swallowing back nausea. "Because we could transfer our people directly to the staging area. It would save hundreds of lives that might be lost travelling across the desert. And we can use it as a supply line, so we won't need a baggage train to cross the waste."

He looked up into her face. To his surprise, she seemed more shocked than appalled.

She said, "You exposed your mind to the vortex. How is that possible? You should be dead."

Darien brought a hand up to rub his temple. Even his scalp was sore to the touch. "I'm a demon," he reminded Azár. "I used the Onslaught, not the magic field. Like I did with Nashir."

Azár folded her arms across her chest, looking defiant. "With Nashir, your mind was protected. You were dampened by your friend's talisman. This is different, Darien Lauchlin. How can you justify such a risk?"

Trembling, he used his arms to leverage himself off the ground, struggling to gain his feet. He staggered and had to catch himself on Azár's outstretched hand. The horizon veered sharply before stabilizing again. Darien put his hand out, trying to halt the motion of the world in front of him.

He said, "If I can shield my mind while drawing on the Onslaught, I'll have an advantage no other mage in the world has ever had. No one would be expecting that. It almost worked…"

"You nearly sent your soul back to hell!" Azár snapped, anger infecting her tone.

"But I didn't." He turned away from her, glancing back toward the canyon. He took a step toward it. Then another.

She stalked after him, as if incensed by his resolve. "You want to try this thing again?!"

"Yes."

He paused next to the cliff's edge, motioning toward the dense wall of rock that spanned the gorge.

"That used to be the side of the mountain." He indicated the dark slopes across from them. Jagged ridgelines stabbed at the sky, piercing the ocean of clouds that swarmed overhead.

"It must have collapsed and blocked the river. If I can shift some of the rubble, even just a fraction, the weight of the water behind it should clear the rest." He nodded his head. "That's the old river bed. If I can force the water back into its proper course, the lake will drain itself."

Azár stood at his side with her hands on her hips. "You think to move all those rocks? There are too many. What you propose is impossible."

Suddenly dizzy, Darien dropped to a crouch. He closed his eyes and brought his hands up to his brow. His head throbbed in time to his pulse. "I'm eighth tier," he said wearily. "Such an act is not beyond me."

"Eighth tier…?" Azár stared down at him, looking dumb-founded.

"Aye."

She lowered herself down by his side, her face softening into a look of pity. She reached a hand out, setting it on his shoulder. "Why did you never tell me this before?"

Darien shrugged, lowering his hands. He kept his eyes averted. "I don't like to speak of it."

For a long moment, she gazed at him in silence. Finally, she whispered, "No wonder you were such a monster. You were mad."

He turned to look at her, wondering if she might be right. He sat back, propping himself with one arm. The cold breeze felt good on his damp skin. His eyes lingered on Azár's, exploring the depths of forgiveness there.

He licked his lips, trying to work up the nerve to apologize. "I want to talk to you about what happened—"

"Don't."

Darien nodded, glancing away. He drew in a deep sigh. "I *am* a monster, Azár. But you have my word:

I'll never touch you again."

Her lip curled, drawing up like a dog's. "I don't want your promises." Her tone seethed with sadness and ice.

Darien felt defeated. His shoulders sagged, his body slouching. Not for the first time, he found himself questioning the necessity of his own existence. He was sick of this world, sick of his sad and sorry place in it. Each day seemed to reduce him to new depths of shame. He was weary of it all.

He asked, "What kind of reassurance can I give you?"

"I already told you."

He knew what she meant. She was talking about marriage again. Darien bowed his head; he couldn't give her what she wanted. In truth, he was surprise she still wanted him at all. Resigned, he pushed himself to his feet.

"Stay here."

He limped toward the edge of the cliff, reeling like a drunken man. He stood there, swaying, as the world rippled in front of his vision. He hated heights, hated cliffs. This one didn't bother him as much as others. Probably because he didn't care an ymore whether he lived or died. Still, he could feel his feet start to itch. The palms of his hands grew clammy.

He closed his eyes and groped within. Keeping his mind closed against the vortex, he called on the Onslaught and let the Hellpower trickle in. This time, he let it fill him gradually, not seeking to hurry it. He could feel it dribbling through his pores, saturating him slowly. He stood there on the edge of the cliff, swaying, soaking it all in. Eventually, he was full. He could hold no more.

Darien opened his eyes.

The world was darker and tinged with green. His head and body no longer hurt. The wind no longer blew. Azár no longer existed or even mattered.

There was only the cliff in front of him and the rubble-wall of rock.

His eyes found the biggest boulder, one positioned like a keystone in the center of the massive wall of earth. He narrowed his eyes and focused his concentration on it. He felt the rock start to *shift.*

The boulder disappeared. Its sudden absence produced a small avalanche of debris that rained down into the depths of the gorge. Darien found another rock and *shifted* it, as well. The boulder was gone, leaving a large hole in the space where it had just been. The rubble around it gave way, filling in the gap.

Darien removed another great chunk of mountain. This time, a shudder ran through the entire dam. Rocks poured down into the gorge. A thin spray of water shot out from a crack, followed by another further up.

Darien directed his focus at the base of the obstruction, at a large swath of mounded rubble. He concentrated, his brow furrowing. The canyon itself started to vibrate. Then the whole world shuddered. There was a loud popping sound. More water sprayed out in shooting cones, bursting in quick succession all across the face of the dam. Rocks and rubble poured down into the gorge below.

There was a terrible, grinding sound. And then a deafening roar.

The entire dam gave way, consumed by a deluge of water. Rocks shot upward, flung high into the air in impossible trajectories. Water gushed through a narrow fissure that quickly widened, spilling out across the canyon before sloshing over the edge of the cliff.

A violent tremor knocked Darien off his feet. He rolled onto his knees, scrambling back away from the cliff's edge. Suddenly Azár was there beside him, shrieking his name and gripping him under the arms. She struggled to drag him backward as the roar of the flood drowned out everything else in the world. The ground jolted and buckled beneath them, threatening collapse.

Darien regained his feet, lurching as Azár dragged him forward. Behind them, the cliff gave away completely.

Azár screamed something, but Darien couldn't hear her over the roar of the deluge. She took his hand, pulling him forward. They climbed the rise of a hill then stopped, turning to look back.

The water of the lake had consumed the dam, obliterating any last trace of the obstruction. The River Nym raged into the canyon, rushing to reclaim its long-abandoned course. The lake drained quickly, its waters subsiding to reveal embankments of chalky gray. The roar of the water continued, relentless, the air dampened by spray.

"What you have done…!"

Darien could barely hear her voice over the surging roar of water. He released the Onslaught, allowing it to drain out of him. As he did, the world brightened just a bit. Still, the dim green of the netherworld lingered like an afterglow.

Azár gaped at him with a look of outright wonder mixed with revulsion.

Darien backed away from her, feeling soiled. He turned and walked to the top of the hill, brooding as he stared down at the receding lake. Across the valley, two soaring structures appeared, striking upward from the lake's churning surface. They had the look of something from antiquity, statues perhaps. Once finely wrought, now eroded and decayed.

"What are they?" he wondered aloud.

"They are the gates of ancient Vintgar," Azár answered, her voice barely audible over the raging thunder of the flood. "Darien Lauchlin…you have achieved the impossible. You have freed the past."

Darien looked at her, unable to feel even a small sense of accomplishment. Perhaps he had freed some small part of Malikar's history. But that act, in and of itself, was meaningless. Because Malikar's future was still very much uncertain.

Chapter Nine
A Single Blade

Pass of Lor-Gamorth, The Front

Kyel watched Meiran sipping tea at the table in Devlin Craig's quarters. She held the teacup in both hands, her slender fingers pyramided to support it. Her face was still pale and gaunt. A little grayish, especially under the eyes. She looked unwell. But at least she wasn't dead.

For that, Kyel was grateful…but also mystified.

Craig sat down on the bench beside Kyel, setting his cup down on the gouged and splintered table. Kyel's eyes went to the cup, noticing the steam rising off of it. The smell of coffee made his mouth water. He looked down at his own cup, filled with the same weak tea Meiran was drinking. He took a sip, trying not to make a face.

"The arrows were dipped in toxin," Meiran explained wearily. The cup in her hands trembled ever so slightly. "I healed the wounds, but I couldn't clear the poison from my blood. It worked too fast. I was out within seconds." She brought her teacup to her lips, closing her eyes as her hands trembled.

That explained why Kyel hadn't found any wounds on her, just rotting tissue. He thought it odd, though, that the toxin itself hadn't killed her. She'd gotten lucky. More than lucky.

Craig grunted. "That's why they left you for dead."

Meiran leaned forward, her hair swaying into her face. She pushed it back absently. "I still can't believe you healed me," she said to Kyel with a flat expression on her face. "You never had a talent for it. You must have come a long way since I left."

"Naia helped," Kyel admitted, feeling a sharp pang of sorrow.

Meiran said nothing, but took another sip of her tea. She hadn't reacted when he'd told her about Naia and Sareen. And about the Conclave. He really didn't know how Meiran was taking it all, whether she was angry or sad or anything in between. Come to think of it, she'd shown barely any emotion at all since she'd first woken up and cried her eyes dry against his shoulder. She was like a cloth that had been wrung out, all the substance within her drained.

"What can you tell us about the Servants?" Craig pressed. He leaned forward, the rickety bench shifting and groaning beneath his weight.

Meiran looked up, gazing at him through dark strands of hair. "There's a lot more depth to them than I ever expected. They're far more human than I ever thought they would be. So much more…but also so much less."

She stared down at the table as if studying the furrows in the wood. Her fingernails scratched at a nick on the surface. "I always thought they'd be nothing but soulless demons. Pure, perfect evil. But they're not. They're different. In a way, they are even more sinister.

"Quinlan Reis is a textbook example," she went on, her voice strengthening. "He seems utterly normal: polite, conversational. Sophisticated. His heart seems to be in the right place, at least on the surface. But deep inside, he's desperately flawed. I watched him strike out and kill an innocent woman without sparing her a second thought or a moment's regret. It was like watching him squash an insect."

Devlin Craig leaned forward, crossing his arms, his face deadly serious. "What about Darien? Is it the same with him?"

Meiran took another sip, her cup trembling in her fingers. Kyel's eyes followed the motion of her hand as she set it back down again. He could tell the question bothered her deeply.

"I'm afraid so." Her voice was stiff. Unemotional. "On the surface, he seems perfectly normal. He's the same man I remember. His personality hasn't changed one bit."

Her eyes shot up, locking on Craig. "But they've corrupted him in *significant* ways. He's entirely committed to their cause; he's very passionate about it. But he still holds a deep love for me and for the Rhen. He's conflicted. It's actually quite painful to watch. He doesn't understand. He doesn't see what he's become."

"And what exactly has he become?" Craig gazed at her steadily.

'Evil.'" Meiran's voice hissed through the shadows. "Darien wields the powers of hell. He raised a necrator from the dead right in front of me. He's planning to lead the legions of the Black Lands in an invasion of the Rhen. He believes it's all justified. The truth is, he terrifies me."

Kyel frowned, struggling to understand how any of that could be possible. "Well, they've obviously done something to him," he said. "But maybe he's still salvageable. Maybe we could help him, do something to help bring him back."

"He's beyond saving, Kyel. Believe me, I tried." Meiran shook her head wearily.

Craig's face was set in deep lines of concern. He leaned back on the bench, the legs creaking under his weight. "What's his rationale?"

Meiran took another sip of tea. The cup clinked against its saucer as she set it back down again. "He told me some vague story about the end of all magic. He says the Enemy depends on magic to grow their food in the absence of sunlight. He says they'll all die if they don't escape."

To Kyel, Darien's concerns sounded legitimate. It would certainly explain the way he was acting. It would be dangerous to dismiss such an apocalyptic warning. He asked, "What if it's true?"

Craig waved his hand in a dismissive gesture. "It doesn't matter if it's true. It wouldn't change our position. We still can't let them in."

Kyel planted his cup on the table, glancing up. "Why not? This changes everything. Don't you understand? If Darien's right, then they're not invaders—they're refugees."

Craig cast a long-suffering glance Meiran's way.

The prime warden brought her hands up, closing her eyes and massaging her temples. "We can't just admit a million hostiles into our midst," she explained to Kyel in overly patient tones. "Our responsibility is to our own people. We vowed to keep them safe. And that is exactly what we are going to do."

Kyel felt abashed. That was indeed the gist of the Acolyte's Oath: 'To serve the land and its people.' Of course, it didn't actually specify *which* land and *which* people he was supposed to be serving. Somehow, he doubted that oath had been devised to justify genocide.

He stood up from the table, feeling flustered. He paced away, letting the cup he was holding warm his hands. He chewed on his lip as he tried to sort out his feelings. It just didn't sound right. In his gut, he knew that Craig and Meiran were making the wrong decision.

"We can't just sentence an entire society to death by starvation," Kyel said at last. "We need to put a lot more thought into this. There must be some sort of compromise we can reach."

Meiran looked up at him with pity in her eyes. "Kyel, sometimes deciding what *not* to do is more important than deciding what *to* do. And, in this case, the answer is obvious. We must think about our own citizens who depend on us for protection. The people of the Black Lands chose to worship Xerys. They brought this fate upon themselves. I've seen them—they're savages. Barbaric. We cannot risk bringing such creatures into our midst. Look at me."

He looked at her, even though he didn't want to.

She said, "If we let them in, and then later find out we've been wrong about them, then it will be too late. They have the numbers and the magepower to overwhelm the kingdoms. Our only hope is stopping them here in the pass."

Kyel knew better than to argue. He knew she was right…but she was also dead wrong. He turned away, breathing out a protracted sigh. He'd almost forgotten the way Meiran made him feel. She treated him like an ignorant child. He'd put up with it for two years.

"I'm very tired," she whispered, standing up from the table. "I'd like to go back now."

"I'll take you back," Kyel offered.

"No. You stay. I can find my own way."

She pulled the cowl of her cloak up over her head. It was thick gray wool, the kind worn by the soldiers of the keep. Not the white cloak of a prime warden. Meiran left her teacup behind, steadying herself in the doorway as she left the room. The door closed softly behind her.

Kyel settled into a chair opposite Craig. "What do you think?"

"It's a lot to take in." The commander took a stiff gulp of his drink, scowling as he plunked the cup back down on the table.

Kyel regarded him for a moment. Craig had always been a reasonable man. He decided to level with him. "Look. Darien was my friend. And he was your friend, too. I think we should trust him enough to talk to him, at least. We should hear his side of the story."

"No." Craig shook his head. "Darien *was* my friend. But I can't let that get in the way of my duty. And neither can you."

"Duty," Kyel echoed sourly, clutching his cup in both hands. "What if Darien's right? What if they really are just refugees? I don't care what Meiran says. If that's the case, then we can't just turn them away."

"They're not just refugees."

"How can you be sure?"

Craig looked at him hard. Then he pushed himself up from the table. "Come with me. I'll show you who they really are."

Kyel sprang up after him as the big man turned and crossed the room, jerking his cloak from a peg by the door and tossing it on. Kyel scrambled after him, following the commander out of the tower and into the keep's inner ward.

Outside, the courtyard was dark, the odor of wood smoke thickening the air. Fires lit all around the ward provided enough light in which to see. Gray-cloaked soldiers collected beside the flames, going about their business: repairing armor, fletching arrows, sharpening weapons. The whole fortress had a mechanized feel of well-oiled efficiency that Kyel could appreciate.

Craig led him through a portal to a spiraling staircase that wound down, corkscrewing, into the guts of the mountainside. The stairs were steep, lit only by the occasional torch that fluttered weakly in the currents of air that rose from the depths. Kyel stopped to listen. It was quiet; there didn't seem to be anyone else about.

A low wailing sound drifted up from the darkness below.

Kyel's eyes shot to Craig. "What is that?"

The big warrior didn't answer. His nostrils flared with each drawn breath.

Guttural sounds of pain rolled toward them up the stairs. Craig led him downward in the direction of the noise as the air cooled around them. The torches flickered, the light inconsistent, casting long, wavering shadows. Another piercing cry echoed from below, louder this time. The anguish in it made Kyel's stomach twist into knots.

At last the stairs ended in a subbasement that had been turned into an impromptu dungeon. Metal cages lined the walls, the straw-strewn floor stained with blood. Everywhere he looked were chains and iron implements, along with a range of sinister devices. On one side of the room a large bronze kettle steamed over an open fire. The air had a thick odor to it, like the smell of a kitchen: full of wood smoke and burning grease. It almost smelled like roasting pork.

Walking forward, Kyel made out the shapes of three men. One was already dead, stretched out on a low table. It looked like he'd been hacked to death, that or hacked up after death—Kyel couldn't tell which. Another man, this one a white-haired soldier, was tending to a prisoner stretched out across the wall, this one still alive. The man was naked, brown arms and legs held spread-eagled by fetters attached to the wall. He moaned and thrashed, writhing in the bonds that held him.

Kyel stopped walking as it occurred to him what he was looking at. His eyes bounced from the cauldron to the dead man to the splayed prisoner in chains. It took him only a moment to put it all together.

"Gods' mercy…" Kyel whispered, the horror he felt seeping into his voice. He held his stomach, feeling like he was going to be sick.

The old soldier lifted a long-handled ladle from

the kettle and raised it over the prisoner's naked body. The man started screaming, struggling frantically against his restraints. The soldier tilted the ladle slowly, dribbling a thin stream of liquid over the man's naked chest as the captive howled in agony. The old man set the ladle down and, using a fingernail, started picking at the flesh that bubbled up.

Kyel gagged and covered his mouth, the prisoner's shrieks echoing in his ears.

Craig walked over to the kettle and dipped the ladle into it. He gave it a good stir, then brought it up to his face, sniffing at the contents.

"Rendering lard?" he asked, grinning as he set the ladle back down in the pot.

"Not a lot of lard on this crop," the grim old-timer remarked. "Seems they get thinner by the batch. Must not be a lot of food left in the Black Lands."

Craig beckoned Kyel forward, but he didn't want to move. He remained rooted in place, too appalled to twitch a muscle. He couldn't stop staring at the poor captive, now hyperventilating and hanging slack in his chains, chest and shoulders a gory mess.

"Come on," Craig insisted, eyes commanding.

Grudgingly, Kyel moved toward him, keeping a good distance from the cauldron of boiling human lard. His eyes lingered on the captive's face, studying the man's bearded features with curiosity. He'd never seen a living man of the Enemy.

The prisoner's face twisted when he noticed Kyel approaching. His eyes widened in recognition, his struggles becoming frantic. He pumped his wrists against the manacles that held him until blood slicked his arms.

"You're torturing him." Kyel whirled on Craig, turning away from the grotesque display. He couldn't understand why the prisoner was more terrified by the sight of him than he'd been when his own flesh was being peeled away.

"Of course we're torturing him," Craig snapped, his face ruddy. "That's how we get information." He turned to the grizzled soldier who was standing by with ladle in hand. "Has he said anything else?"

"No, Sir. Nothing intelligible."

Craig's arm whipped out and caught the Enemy prisoner by the hair, wrenching his neck back against the wall. The man grunted, squeezing his eyes shut as slobber dribbled down his chin.

"What's your name?" Craig growled into his ear.

"Firat," the prisoner gasped. He cracked his lids open, eyes darting sideways at Kyel.

"Just Firat?"

"Firat son of Cozcun." The man's reddened eyes locked on Kyel and didn't budge. He was panting, chest and shoulders heaving as he tried to wriggle his head away from Craig. But the commander tightened his grip and pressed Firat back with the full bulk of his weight.

Craig leaned into him as if ready to plant a kiss on Firat's gasping mouth.

"Why are your forces massing?"

The man grimaced, twisting his face away. But Craig caught him beneath the chin, pinning his head back against the wall. *"Why?* We've made no acts of aggression!"

The prisoner said nothing, just groaned and squirmed. Craig wrenched him by the chin, turning his face toward Kyel.

"Do you know who this is?"

The man cowered, flinching away.

"Tell me, Firat, what would your people do if we let you into the Rhen? Would you lay down your arms and surrender?"

The man growled, eyes burning with furious zeal. From somewhere inside, he'd managed to conjure a last, desperate flare of resistance. He twisted his head out of Craig's grasp and rained spittle into the commander's face. Craig didn't flinch, just blinked the offensive fluid out of his eyes. He stepped back, crossing his gauntleted arms.

"We will arrive as conquerors!" Firat cried, lurching against the rusted chains that held him. "We will put your sons to the sword and enslave your daughters! Your cities will burn to ash, and your rivers will run with blood!"

Craig reached out and smacked the man's head against the wall. Firat went limp, thick blood running in globs from his nose. He slumped in his traces, blinking dumbly like a bludgeoned animal.

Craig turned back to Kyel. "As you can see, Firat is pretty specific about their intentions for us. Doesn't sound like they plan on negotiating." He wiped his eyes with the sleeve of his gambeson before turning back to his captive. "When are they coming?"

The man said nothing. He stared at Craig dully,

eyes glassy and unfocused. He opened his swollen mouth, letting out a low moan.

Craig nodded toward Kyel. "This is Kyel Archer, Sixth Tier Sentinel of Aerysius. He has some questions for you."

The prisoner's face contorted in terror. *"No! No—please! I'll tell you what you wish—!"*

Craig grasped Firat behind the head and jerked him forward as far as his restraints would allow. He leaned forward until he was brow-to-brow with him. "I want to know when you're coming. I want to know who commands your armies. And I want to know numbers."

The prisoner thrashed against the granite strength of Craig's arm. Panic filled his eyes, rendering them wide and luminous. Sweat streaked his face and torso, along with the congealing juices of his butchered friend. "I will tell you! Just get him away!"

Craig cast a sidelong grin at Kyel. "The Grand Master will remain here until I'm satisfied with your answers. *Now answer my questions!"*

Firat shuddered. Eyes only for Kyel, he gasped, "We're waiting until all of the tribes can be gathered. A few more weeks..."

"All of your armies?" Craig demanded.

"Yes. Everyone. All must leave..."

"Everyone? You mean every man, woman, and child of the Black Lands?"

Firat nodded, then turned to glare at Craig. "Yes! Yes, everyone! Everyone must leave!"

Craig's hand squeezed a fistful of the man's hair, eliciting a scream. Kyel stood stunned, looking on in revulsion. He wanted to intervene. But he couldn't do anything but watch, transfixed by Craig's brutality.

"Who's in charge of your armies?" Craig demanded, grabbing Firat's flayed and blistered shoulders. *"Who?"*

The prisoner let out a strangled moan, clenching his fists in pain. "Byron Connel leads the legions of Bryn Calazar...and there is a new overlord, another Battlemage. He's rallying the legions of the Khazahar..."

"Do you know his name, this new Battlemage?"

Firat glanced fretfully at Kyel.

"His name, Firat!" Craig bellowed.

The man grimaced, glaring fiercely. "I do not know his name. But it is said he was once a Sentinel."

With a growl, Craig released him. Firat moaned a ragged gasp then sagged in his restraints.

Craig straightened and stood back, wiping his soiled hands on his gambeson. He nodded at the old-timer. "See what else you can get out of him. I think he looks hungry." He glanced down. "I don't think he needs his ball sack anymore. Why don't you fry it up and feed it to him."

"Aye, Force Commander."

As Firat began to scream, Craig's big hand grabbed Kyel by the nape of his cloak and swung him around, propelling him toward the door. Kyel lurched across the chamber, gagging as he passed the cauldron of boiling human fat. Firat's screams followed them out, all the way into the stairwell.

Back on the steps, Kyel jerked away from Craig, whirling to confront him. His heart pounded in his chest, his face heated by outrage. He felt like he was going to throw up, was actually surprised that he hadn't yet.

Firat's shrieks gurgled with agony before collapsing into muffled, strangled sobs.

"You all right?"

Kyel glanced up at Devlin Craig, eyes brimming with hatred. He shook his head as he righted himself, leaning with one elbow against the cold stone wall. "No, I'm not all right. That was despicable."

Craig just looked at him. "This is war, Archer. We do what we have to. Get used to it."

Kyel clenched his hands into fists, taking a step back away from him. His face burned with pent-up rage. He realized that he hated Devlin Craig. Hated him more than he'd ever hated anyone in his life. "He told you what you wanted to know. So why are you still torturing him?"

Craig shrugged. "Trust me, Firat's got a lot more stories to tell. Sheb will get them out of him."

Kyel just stared at the man hard and long, groping to understand how a person could be so callous. He'd been a Greystone soldier once himself. He remembered war being brutal. But this wasn't war—at least, it didn't have to be.

"What you're doing isn't right," Kyel maintained. "You should kill him cleanly."

Craig shook his head. "No. Information saves lives. That's the plain and simple truth. And the life of just one of my men is worth every second of

Firat's pain. Do you have any idea what they do to our own captives?"

Kyel nodded, remembering the rumors. He could feel Craig's eyes boring into him, piercing through the shadows of the stairwell. He felt suddenly deflated. "I've heard."

Craig pressed on, "Every man here is under orders to never leave a living man behind for the Enemy. There's good reason for that. I'd do the same for you. I hope you'd do the same for me."

Kyel shook his head, spreading his arms in a gesture of futility. "I can't use my power to take a life…"

"But you can use your hands."

"I…" Kyel tried, but couldn't finish. He wasn't sure where the commander was going with this. All he knew was that he wasn't going to like it. He studied Craig's face resentfully.

"Here." The soldier stepped forward, plucking a knife from his belt and planting its hilt squarely in Kyel's outstretched palm.

Kyel flinched, almost dropping the weapon. But for some reason, he clung onto it. It was a long, thin-bladed dagger with an ebony hilt. It looked familiar, but he wasn't sure where he'd seen it before. He stared down at the weapon, face aghast in silent denial.

"I can't carry a blade," he said.

"Yes, you can. Your Oath doesn't prevent you from using a weapon. Only tradition."

He knew Craig was right; that's how Darien had justified keeping his sword. Only, Kyel had a lot of respect for the slippery slope Darien had thrown himself down. It had all started with a single blade…a blade he'd refused to give up.

"It's called a mercy knife." Craig nodded at the wicked-thin dagger in Kyel's hand. "Look, there's no easy way of putting this, so I'll just state it plainly. You don't want to be taken alive. Remember what they did to Darien? For you, it'd be a whole lot worse."

Kyel swallowed, squeezing his palm around the hilt of the dagger. It felt like an iron weight in his hand. He remembered watching Enemy soldiers hoisting Darien over a flaming pyre. He remembered the sounds of his screams.

"I don't understand," Kyel said. "Why would it be worse for me…?"

Craig placed a steadying hand on Kyel's shoulder. "Because with Darien, they were pressed for time. But they wouldn't be with you. Their mages can heal you while you burn. They can keep you alive for hours, perhaps days. I want you to think about that. Really think about it." He paused, giving Kyel a moment to do just that.

Kyel did. The numbness in his hands and feet spread up his arms, chilling his insides. In the dim silence of the stairwell, his own thundering pulse rumbled like thunder in his ears.

"Right here." Craig reached up, drawing two fingers across his neck under his left ear. "And here." He repeated the motion on the other side. "You'll bleed out in seconds. You'll go right into shock; it won't even hurt."

Firat's last, agonized scream echoed atrociously through the stairwell.

"Keep that dagger close," Craig whispered.

Chapter Ten
Vintgar

Tokashi Palace, The Black Lands

"Your petition was denied."

Darien paused in the action of pulling on a worn leather boot. He glanced up at Sayeed. "Why?"

The Zakai officer took a step toward the bed Darien was sitting on. He held his hat tucked in the crook of his arm. The expression on his bearded face was dour.

"The Omeyan Clan perished," he explained in a voice devoid of emotion. "You are allowed to claim the blood of your ancestors, but that claim alone does not suffice. You have no men of your own bloodline who will follow you."

Darien tugged the boot on over his heel then stood up from the bed. He reached for a linen shirt and wormed his arms into the sleeves. Then he wrapped the warbelt around his hips, fixing it in place.

"I have the Tanisars."

"The Tanisars are not blood of your blood."

Darien nodded. He fastened on his cloak with a silver brooch then reached up to tie back his hair.

"What are my options?"

Sayeed shifted his weight over his feet, screwing his face into a thoughtful grimace. He stood there for some time while Darien waited, gazing at him steadily. In the corner, the demon-dog scratched at an itch, its foot hammering on the floor. The coal-fire in the hearth crackled and popped.

"You should accept your Lightweaver's offer of marriage," Sayeed said. "Then you would have the Jenn Asyaadi behind you. The Asyaadi have great respect among the tribes. Their blood is very ancient, and they have long controlled the Khazahar's trade routes."

Darien stood frozen, staring at the fire in the hearth. It cast an oily light that blurred across the walls of the bedchamber. At last he blinked as if waking from a trance. "Marriage is not an option."

Sayeed looked patently uncomfortable. A host of conflicted emotions ranged over his face, settling finally into a look of grave concern. He took another step forward, shifting his hat to his other hand. "May I speak frankly?"

"Of course."

Sayeed's tongue traced over his lips. He seemed to be searching for the right words. Or perhaps he already knew the words he wanted to say, but was reluctant to utter them.

"What your woman did to you was cruel," he said at last. "But it was also deserved."

Darien frowned. He hadn't expected to hear that. Neither did he agree; he had done nothing to deserve such treatment from Meiran. He'd given everything for her. All he'd ever wanted in return was a trace amount of understanding. Or compassion.

She'd given him neither.

Sayeed went on, "You betrayed every cause you ever championed. Including hers."

Darien felt as though he were a straw man with a straw soul, and the stuffing inside him had just been ripped out and thrown asunder. For it was true; Sayeed had a point. He had abandoned Meiran's cause and taken up another.

"But it's not your fault," the officer continued quickly. "You were ignorant. Your eyes were closed. And now that they are open, you cannot help but see things differently." He paused, his expression quite serious. "It is said that a wound that bleeds inwardly is the most dangerous of all. You have such a wound, Darien Nach'tier. I see you struggle with it. I fear what will happen if you don't find a cure."

He walked forward and placed a hand on Darien's arm. "Take my advice: forgive the woman who betrayed you, knowing that you also betrayed her. Then marry your Lightweaver."

Darien sidestepped Sayeed and retreated across the chamber. He couldn't help it. He was just as repelled by the man's proximity as he was by his advice. He didn't like to be touched.

Sayeed withdrew, understanding in his eyes. By now, the man was more than aware of Darien's peculiar idiosyncrasies. The people of Malikar needed much less personal space than he was accustomed to. It had taken Darien some time, but at last he'd convinced Sayeed of his need for distance.

"Are you ready?"

"Aye." Darien scooped up his sword from where it hung by his bedside, drawing the baldric on over his shoulder. It was the sword Meiran had given him. More than once, he'd come very close to throwing it in the lake. But each time he'd stopped himself just shy of committing the act. He couldn't bring himself to give the blade up; it was too much a part of him.

"Are you sure you want to do this?" Sayeed said as he cast open the door. "The caverns are still wet and very treacherous. We should send an expeditionary party down first."

"I'll risk it," Darien said. When he moved toward the door, the demon dog rose and made as if to follow him. But Darien raised his hand. The awful beast circled its cushion once then lay back down again. It stared up at him with its muzzle between its paws, looking dejected.

Once out in the corridor, Darien was surprised to find Azár there waiting for him. She stood beside his door next to the retinue of Zakai that followed him everywhere. Darien shot an accusatory look at Sayeed, who just shrugged in reply.

Raising his eyebrows, Darien asked, "Aren't the krill in need of your magelight?"

Azár had assumed the duties of a palace Lightweaver, so every few days she rotated in from the lightfields to tend to the true riches of Tokashi: the krill ponds beneath the fortress, beneath even the swirling energies of Tokashi's vortex. Deep down in the depths of the ice warrens existed enormous salt pools teeming with krill that could only be supported by a constant input of magelight. The krill were harvested and used in place of meat to feed the Tanisar corps. They were also exported for their weight in riches, which accounted for the enormous wealth the Tanisars had amassed.

Seeing Darien's irritation, Azár smirked, managing to look both arrogant and innocent.

"The ponds can go hours without light," she assured him, gazing defiantly into his face. She wore a single red ribbon draped across her brow that wound down through the length of her braid. A small stone dangled in the center of her forehead. Darien had seen the style before on some of the serving women. It lent a softness to her features he wasn't used to.

He asked, "Is there something you need?"

"I came to speak with you."

Darien indicated his retinue of Zakai. "We're on our way down to the chasm. I can speak with you upon our return."

Azár smiled as she shrugged. "I will go with you. We can speak along the way."

Darien felt the heat of frustration rise to his cheeks. He glared at Azár. Then he glared at Sayeed.

"As you like," he muttered, then turned and strode away down the corridor.

His men fell in behind, hurrying to catch up. He didn't turn to see whether or not Azár was following; he knew that she would. Sayeed hastened to match his pace, face stern, hand resting on the sword hilt at his waist. When their group reached the stairs, Darien relented and let the senior Zakai move ahead of him, the rest lingering behind. He followed after, Azár silently fuming as she fell in at his side.

The men lit torches, passing around a flaming rag soaked in lamp oil. They descended the staircase, the air becoming chill and moist as they moved farther into the subterranean glacier. Darien could see his breath like a fog before his face. He shivered in a way that had nothing to do with the cold; the chill of the air provoked memories he'd rather leave forgotten. They continued downward until the ice eventually gave way to rough, dark stone.

The stone below the glacier was weeping, the steps covered with oozing mud that leaked water in small, gushing streams. They had arrived at a level of the warrens that had been submerged by the lake only days before.

The going was slow, the path murky and uneven. Darien struggled through spongy silt pebbled with rocks, slogging along after Sayeed and his men. The walls bled mud and slime down their surfaces. Water ran down the stairs, eroding the deposits of silt. Soon they were walking through what amounted to a rushing stream fed by frigid water from the glacier.

Ahead, the officers drew up and stood consulting in whispering echoes. Darien moved forward through the press of bodies, interested to find out what they'd discovered.

"What is it?"

Sayeed pointed at a small, circular indentation in the wall. Darien's eyebrows shot up at the sight of a small button. It had a glyph carved on it, one he knew well. Beads of sweat broke out across his brow despite the chill.

"Everyone, move back," he warned.

When the soldiers had yielded him room, he reached down and depressed the ancient switch. There was the slightest clicking noise followed by the sound of a mechanism moving somewhere within the wall. For a moment, he held his breath. When nothing happened, Darien sighed, feeling a heady surge of relief.

"That trap would have killed the lot of you," he said. "I'll lead the way from here."

"Darien."

Turning, he saw that Azár had come up silently beside him. She had drawn her shawl up over her head, her arms wrapped tightly around herself for warmth.

"You should let me go first." Her tone was much softer than he was used to hearing from her. "Most of the Lyceum's knowledge was lost. But not all. What remains has been passed down to me. I have experience with this type of device."

That surprised him. He hadn't known any of the Lyceum's vast troves of knowledge had been retained by the mages who were the descendants of that culture. As long as he'd known her, Azár had professed only ignorance of even the most basic knowledge of magecraft. He hoped she knew what she was doing.

But he deferred to her with a wave of his hand, motioning her to go first.

Azár walked forward with an almost regal grace, parting the group of Zakai who stood in front of them. Darien watched her for a moment, admiring the confidence she projected. Then he moved forward, following closely on her heels.

Azár led them down the mud-encrusted stairs, pausing every so often to depress some of the trigger switches, ignoring others. Some appeared to be nonfunctioning. Others would have resulted in deadly consequences if they'd been tripped. As Darien walked, he studied Azár carefully. He took note of the way she moved, trailing her fingers along the wall at her side. The deliberate placement of her feet among the rubble with never a misplaced stride.

She led them deeper into the warrens, shadows and silt collecting under their feet. The cold was relentless, clawing its way through his wet garments. Darien began to shiver despite his thick cloak.

Azár paused to disarm the next device they encountered. There was a small click in the wall. Then she turned to look back at Darien, eyes glinting with excitement. "Do you feel that? We must be nearing the eye of the vortex."

Darien didn't feel anything; with his mind walled away, he had no sense whatsoever of the magic field. Azár must have a rare talent to sense the field's currents while shielded. He hoped she was right; he was anxious to find out if all the risk he had taken to drain the lake was worth it.

The silt-slick stairs they trudged down eventually ended in a tunnel encased by mud. Water had collected on the floor, forming deep pools. Up ahead, a blue-green light filtered in through an opening in the rock. Darien squinted, wondering where that gush of cool light could be coming from.

Azár started forward, feet slogging through water and oozing muck. The claustrophobic space they were in opened up into a vast cavern, the path they were treading leading toward an arching stone bridge that spanned a gaping chasm. Chill air wafted up from far below, carrying a fresh riverine scent.

Darien moved quickly past Azár, out onto the arching span of the bridge. A wind seized his hair, rippling his cloak. Turquoise light streamed upward, saturating the cavern in a scintillating dance of color. The chasm was enormous, both continuing upward and cutting down into the depths. Darien walked to the edge of the bridge, to a low wall that was chipped away in places. He leaned over, staring down, seeking the source of the light.

Far below, the River Nym cut its way through the bottom of the chasm, its waters swift and turbulent. The glow that filled the cavern emanated from the river itself, filtering up through the air, reflecting off the water-polished rock. A breeze delivered the scent of the river, wild and fresh and teeming with life. Darien felt exultant. He'd never seen anything so beautiful in his life.

He turned to find Azár standing behind him, basking in a pool of summery magelight.

"The eye of the vortex," he breathed. "The river flows through the source."

"No." Azár's eyes were fixed on the Nym's swift currents. "The river is the source."

Darien frowned, suddenly troubled. That's not how the magic field worked. "Come on, let's get down there. I'll show you. At the center of the eye will be a Circle of Convergence. That's what we'll find. That river's just a river. Nothing more."

"It's beautiful," she whispered, gazing down into the turquoise wash of light.

So was she, Darien had to admit. He muttered, "Aye."

Azár took a step back away from the edge then turned and crossed the bridge to the other side. Darien followed her, anticipation speeding his stride. On the other side of the gorge, the path became encased by rock. Another mud-ruined stair took them downward. Water dripped from the ceiling, splashing on his head and wetting his hair. His feet sloshed through puddles of oozing mud.

They came to a point where the ceiling had partially collapsed. Large boulders and debris filled the narrow passage, blocking their path. Darien and Azár lingered behind as Sayeed's men labored to clear away the rubble. They formed a human chain, handing rocks and debris from one man to another, depositing them along the cave walls.

Feeling idle, Darien turned to Azár. "You said you wanted to speak with me?"

Her face darkened. "Later. Now isn't the time for it." She turned and moved to the opposite end of the passage, leaving him feeling awkward and alone.

When the path was clear, their small party forged ahead again. They came to a place where many corridors branched off their path, lightless, boring into the depths of the rock that surrounded them. Darien wondered where the passages led; the ancient fortress of Vintgar surrounded them, but there was no sign yet of its former grandeur, only of its decay.

The deeper they went, the more the tunnel became clogged with filth and debris. Eventually they came to another place where the ceiling had collapsed entirely. Sayeed's men strained against the wall of rock without success; it seemed as if the weight of the entire mountain bore down upon it.

Darien watched the men labor, nettled by frustration. At last, he'd had enough.

"Stand back," he ordered. Then he opened his mind to the Onslaught. The corridor darkened then flared a sinister shade of green. Darien was aware that his entire body blazed with an unnatural glow, exuding the Hellpower from his pores.

He concentrated, willing the debris to be gone. Nothing happened, so he concentrated harder. Suddenly, he felt the entire obstruction *shift*, just as he had *shifted* the boulders of the dam. The mountain above them rumbled, provoked by his meddling. The floor shook as pebbles rained down from the ceiling. The blockage ahead had disappeared completely, revealing a tiled mosaic that gleamed up at them from the floor.

Darien let go of the Onslaught and walked toward the spot where the rocks had just been, eyes fixated on the floor. He knelt down, running his hand across the vibrant tiles. They formed an elaborate pattern of wine and gold. It reminded him of an ornate tapestry, somehow preserved in ceramic and time.

"Is that…what this place once looked like?" Azar whispered, stroking a tile.

Darien looked up at her. "It would seem."

He regained his feet, still marveling at the mosaic beneath his feet. Only then did he realize the stares that were aimed at him, the gaping disbelief on the faces of Sayeed's men. He spread his hands. "This is your heritage," he told them. "Perhaps someday Vintgar can be restored. But not today."

He motioned Azár to go ahead then followed after her, gazing down at his feet as he crossed the intricate web of tiles. They marched along another mud-strewn passage decorated in crumbling rock and oozing slime. The noise of the river was much louder now. The sound of its rushing current echoed through the darkness from somewhere close by. They came to another passage, one that sloped downward into black depths of shadow.

Reluctant to use magelight, Darien let the green glow of the netherworld light their path. The sloping corridor they followed led to the bottom of the caverns, opening into a wide space that bordered the gorge. They stood in a many-vaulted chamber lit by the river's vaporous glow. Ruined archways and crumbling corridors led off in all directions.

"Here," Darien said, closing his eyes. He tore down the barriers that protected his mind from the vortex and let the magic field come gushing in. He gasped, reveling in the sweet perfection of the field lines that converged in this place, here in the eye of the vortex. He sucked in the power, basking in euphoric bliss. When he opened his eyes, he saw that Azár's face had taken on a smile of elation.

He couldn't help himself; he sighed in relief, glad just to feel whole again. But the contentment he felt was short-lived. A feeling of cold purpose stole over him, reminding him of his business here. Darien turned back to his men, beckoning them forward.

"Stay close. The Circle of Convergence is this way," he said, and started off across the filth-covered chamber, splashing through puddles on the floor. He felt his way with his mind, following the smooth currents of energy.

He found Vintgar's Circle of Convergence in an adjoining chamber, on the other side of a collapsed archway. Darien stopped in the entrance to the hall, glancing around at the slime-encrusted walls, and taking in the shattered ceiling. A solid bank of mud encased the floor. They would have to dig down through layers of silt and fallen rock to unearth Vintgar's Circle.

Still, even through the layers of mud that covered it, he should be able to sense something of the Circle below. But that wasn't the case. The Circle of Convergence lay buried mere inches beneath his feet, but he could feel no connection to it at all.

It was not slumbering beneath all that mud.

It was dead.

He was sure of it. Darien bowed his head, letting the tragedy of the loss settle in. He needed the Circle, needed it desperately. He'd hoped to use it to disrupt the curse that infected the skies. Now that chance was gone. Gone forever.

"There's nothing here," he said at last, sorrow heavy in his voice. "Nothing for us, at least."

Azár nodded, a look of understanding in her eyes. Sayeed and his men started back toward the entrance of the hall, faces grim. Perhaps they sensed his mood. Or saw the burden of loss in his eyes. It didn't matter; they knew something had gone terribly wrong.

Darien allowed the light of the river to guide their way through the system of littered corridors. Even here, in the heart of ancient Vintgar, there was nothing of the past left to find. No furniture or artifacts had managed to survive. Everything was encased by mud or weathered away. The fortress of Vintgar had drowned under the Nym's displaced waters a thousand years ago. Nothing of its former grandeur remained.

"Lord, over here," one of the men called from behind.

Darien turned, starting toward the officer who beckoned him from the opening of a passage. He stopped in a doorway, his feet rooted to the floor.

He couldn't move. His eyes were locked on the center of a shattered room, where a pristine cross-vaulted arch rose majestically from the mud and slime. It glowed with a soft amber light that was both eerie and comforting. The arch appeared as though neither time nor floodwaters had dared touch it. Darien moved toward the artifact, drawn as if compelled. He stopped inches away, reaching out to run a hand down the rose-colored pillar. He could almost feel the charged power that surged within it.

"What do we do?" Azár asked, drawing up at his side. She was staring in awe at the transfer portal, an expression of wonder on her face.

Darien extended his hand in invitation. "We go through."

She looked at him with surprise in her eyes then eyed the portal skeptically. "What if it's broken?"

"Then I suppose we'll find out. But I don't think it is." Darien was sure of it; he could feel the stirring of power in the artifact. The lines of the magic field warped around it then disappeared smoothly within.

Azár nodded, taking his hand.

Sayeed moved quickly, inserting himself in front of them. "No! Lord, let me go first. It is my life that should be risked; not yours."

Darien's first impulse was to deny him. But he found himself relenting. As mages, both he and Azár were irreplaceable. Sayeed was not, as much as Darien hated to admit it. There were many Zakai who would be willing and honored to take his place.

"Very well," Darien said and stepped back, letting go of Azár's hand.

"Thank you, Lord, for this honor." Sayeed bowed stiffly then moved into the center of the portal, positioning himself between the pillars that supported the cross-vaulted arch. He turned back around, his face set in lines of determination.

"What do I do?" he asked.

"Close your eyes," Darien advised. "Empty your mind and let the portal do the rest."

Sayeed nodded, closed his eyes, then took a step back, adjusting his position under the arch. There was a brief, brilliant gush of light. And then he was gone.

Darien moved quickly around the transfer portal. He hoped he wouldn't find Sayeed's body slathered across the rocks behind it. He had no idea what the portal would do if not configured correctly. Suddenly, he was very glad Sayeed had volunteered. He could kick himself for almost risking Azár's life. Despite the cold, he began to sweat. The man should be back by now.

"What is he doing?" Azár grumbled.

"I don't know." Darien placed his hand on the stone of the portal without actually stepping inside. He closed his eyes and felt deep within the artifact. There was no resonance, no distortion of the energies that moved within it. Nothing seemed amiss.

A strong flash of light startled him, making him flinch back. Sayeed staggered out of the brilliant glare, face pale and covered in sweat. He bent forward, hands on his knees, catching his breath.

Darien felt more excited than concerned. "Where does it go?"

Sayeed drew himself up, still panting, his expression dour. "The portal leads to Bryn Calazar. Lord, your presence is requested immediately."

Darien felt his excitement wither. "By whom?"

Sayeed swallowed, managing to look even paler than he had before. "By Prime Warden Zavier Renquist."

Darien nodded somberly. After Byron Connel's visit, he had every reason to fear the wrath of the prime warden. He should have seen this coming.

"Wait here," he told Azár, and moved stiffly toward the portal.

She shook her head, inserting herself ahead of him. "If you go, then I go also." She offered out her hand.

Darien stopped, staring for a moment at her soft fingers. He glanced back up at her face, at the stubborn set of her jaw. At the firm resolve in her eyes. He knew better than to argue.

"As you like," he said, and took her hand in his.

Chapter Eleven
Blood Bond

Bryn Calazar, The Black Lands

Darien released Azár's hand and stepped away from the transfer portal, moving out of a blinding wash of light. He found himself in a vaulted chamber filled with many similar arches. He recognized the space immediately: the portal chamber in Bryn Calazar. All around him, black-mailed bodies fell to their knees then bent forward to the floor. Darien gazed at the sight, awed and shaken. This was an entirely different reception than he had experienced before.

"Arise," he said.

At his word, the mailed bodies returned to their feet, coming forward to form a tight cluster about him. His gaze leaped from helm to helm, the sight intimidating. This had once been the only image he had of a people he'd known only as the Enemy. Now he understood there were real people behind those helms: fathers, brothers, husbands, sons. He wished he could see their faces.

"Remove your helms," he ordered.

When they did, he realized that he'd been wrong. Darien stared in shock at the stern faces of the guards that surrounded him. More than a few were female. He hadn't expected that. He looked from face to face, making eye contact with each man and woman in the chamber. At last, he nodded, more than a little shaken.

How many women had he killed at Orien's Finger? He would never know the numbers. He knew it shouldn't matter. But it did. He sensed Azár moving to stand beside him as the guards replaced their helms.

A white-bearded man wearing the robes of a priest of Xerys appeared at the top of the steps. "Darien Nach'tier," he said in a raspy voice. "Your presence is requested."

Darien did his best not to cringe at the sound of the old man's voice. The words felt like a noose slipping around his neck. He could almost feel it tightening. He said to Azár, "You should wait here."

"Where you go, I go." Her tone brooked no argument.

Darien didn't want her accompanying him to this meeting with Renquist. He couldn't guarantee it would have a good ending. But he relented, knowing better not to protest. After all, it was his life, not hers, at risk.

The guards parted to let them pass as they made their way toward the stairs. The priest in crimson robes greeted them with a nod, saying nothing as he led them up the steps. The man's face was skeletal, his eyes sunken in their sockets. He shuffled as he walked, one leg obviously weaker than the other. They emerged from the stairs into a large, domed room with a Circle of Convergence set into the floor.

Darien halted, at once stunned and dismayed at the sight. It was larger than Aerysius' Greater Circle had been. Alas, this one was quiet. Staring harder at the patterns on the floor, he realized that the lines of power had been irrevocably warped. It wept, leaking magical energies like a sieve. Another Circle, lost to time.

Only, this loss was staggering.

He tore his eyes away from the distorted artifact that seemed to bleed power from its pores. Instead, he fixed his stare on the back of the red-robed priest who walked ahead of them. He followed the old man across the floor and into a hallway beyond. With a bow and a flourish of robes, the priest stepped aside, gesturing toward a wooden door.

Darien paused, considering the door. He was hesitant to open it; it was the only wooden door he had encountered in all the Black Lands, made of solid oak and bound by iron bands. He understood the vast wealth and power conveyed by that single fixture. He feared that door, feared what might await him on the other side of it.

He grasped the cold handle and depressed the latch. The door creaked open a fraction on its own. He pulled it the rest of the way, exposing a dim chamber within. Darien drew back and raised his hand, signaling Azár to let him enter first. He paused, collecting his nerves. Then he stepped forward into the room.

At the sight of Zavier Renquist, he dropped to his knees and bowed forward, pressing his head against the rugs as, beside him, Azár did the same. Closing his eyes, Darien engaged his other senses. Fragrant incense thickened the air, masking the odor of coal soot. There was the rustle of fabric from across the room. A soft, trickling noise. Then silence. Silence and agarwood and soft woven carpets. The combination provoked a nauseating wave of fear.

For a moment, he felt transported back to the tent where Renquist had manipulated him into submission. Or into hell; there really wasn't much difference. It all had the same unnerving feel.

"Arise and be heard."

That resonant voice chilled his blood to ice. It was distinctive, and singularly disturbing. Darien rose from the position of prostration, regaining his feet.

Resplendent in robes of deepest indigo, Zavier Renquist stood to greet them both. *"Sulimu kadreesh,"* he uttered, moving to clasp Darien in a close embrace.

"Akadreesh issulim." Darien shuddered at the proximity of the man. He didn't like anyone that close to him. Especially someone with the amount of power he sensed in Renquist. He'd never known another mage who commanded such strength and authority. By comparison, Darien felt like a mere pawn to be moved at will.

The prime warden released him and turned to Azár, who bent forward to kiss the hem of his robe. He extended his hand, inviting them to sit beside him on embroidered cushions arranged in an intimate circle upon the floor.

A serving boy came forward, carrying a bronze pot with an elongated spout. He produced a cup and poured a small amount of brown liquid into it. This, he handed to Renquist, who received the beverage without thanks. Azár was served next. The third cup went to Darien. He knew that the cups were poured in that order intentionally; Renquist was making certain that Darien was aware of his place.

He knew better than to decline the offer of drink; he valued his life. The odor of coffee filled his nostrils. He took a taste, finding the bitter flavor to his liking.

"Tell me," Renquist said, setting his cup down at his side, "how is your health?"

"I've been well, Prime Warden." Darien took another sip, savoring the taste. The coffee was strong but not overpowering. It was also very hot; the cup felt wonderful in his hands after the chill of Vintgar's ice warren.

Renquist nodded. "I hear you returned the River Nym to its proper course. That was no small feat. Tell me, Darien. How did you accomplish such a miracle?"

Darien winced internally at Renquist's choice of words. It was no miracle. His actions had been stupidly reckless. That or attempted suicide; he wasn't sure which.

"I found a way to use the Onslaught while shielding my mind from the vortex." He didn't bother to elaborate. He just hoped Renquist would let it go at that. He waited, gazing down into his cup at the patterned swirls of cream.

The prime warden seemed to accept his answer. Raising his own cup, he said, "And what is the state of Vintgar's Circle of Convergence?"

Darien thought of Bryn Calazar's dead Circle, feeling a pang of loss. "I'm sorry, Prime Warden. Vintgar's Circle was destroyed beyond repair."

"Perhaps. I will have it examined by someone more competent."

Darien paused in the action of raising his drink to his lips, shaken by the insult. He set the cup back down, a growing unease tightening his gut. The chamber seemed colder than it had just moments before.

Renquist continued, "You have fulfilled many of the tasks set out for you. In that respect, I am pleased. But there is still the matter of Nashir…" His voice trailed off into a festering silence.

Darien drew in a deep breath, fighting to steady his already rattled nerves. "I assume you've heard from Byron Connel."

"Yes. A message did arrive." The prime warden took a sip of his drink. "I was greatly troubled by the news. You shouldn't have been able to best Nashir; he had superior training and a thousand years more experience than you. I must admit…I can't help but find myself impressed." His eyes locked with Darien's. "I hear you raised a necrator. That is a rare talent. We may need you to produce more."

"I don't know what I did," Darien said quickly. "I don't think I could repeat it." He didn't remember much of the torture or its aftermath. It was not something he wanted to remember; he'd done his best to forget.

"You will try," Renquist directed. It was not a request.

"Aye, Prime Warden." Darien drained the last of his coffee, an attempt to hide the sickened look on his face. The cup was replenished as soon as he set it down.

"Lightweaver Azár." Renquist turned to the woman. "Are you satisfied with Darien's progress?"

Azár shot Darien a nervous glance. "I am, Prime Warden. He has proven a worthy ally. He has gathered many fine warriors behind him."

"And yet…" Renquist's gaze slid back to Darien. "I hear you are having difficulty uniting the tribes?"

Darien had to nod; there was no use trying to hide it. Renquist must have anticipated the challenges he would face. "I rule the Khazahar in name alone. I've the support of the Tanisars. But I've failed to gain the support of the tribes."

"Because of your blood."

"Aye. Because of my blood." It was hardly a secret.

The prime warden's stare drifted downward to Darien's waist. To the golden buckle of the warbelt fastened there. The prime warden's stare lingered on the buckle. "What an interesting piece of workmanship," he said finally. "Omeyan, unless I miss my guess?"

Darien closed his eyes, feeling the last of his hopes slip through his fingers. The room felt suddenly, oppressively cold. Perhaps Renquist had seen the warbelt on Quin. Or even on Braden Reis a thousand years before; whichever. It didn't matter. His own possession of the belt was inexplicable. And incriminating.

The game was up.

Renquist leaned forward, capturing his gaze. Very softly, he said, "Do you have something you wish to tell me, Darien?"

Cold beads of perspiration broke out on his brow. Immediately, Darien was transported back in time to the pavilion below Orien's Finger, to his first meeting with Renquist. When the demon had broken him with nothing more than the simple, crushing truth.

A trickle of sweat dribbled down his face, dropping to the floor. He wet his lips with his tongue. "Quinlan Reis left me this warbelt along with a note. He claims it belonged to one of my ancestors."

The gap of silence that followed his words seemed to drag on forever before finally wearing out. With the silence came the creeping feel of danger. Darien knew he was being judged. He also knew he may not survive the judgement. He was well aware of the price of betrayal.

"When was the last time you saw Quinlan Reis?"

There was no use being evasive. "I saw him when he brought Meiran to me in Qul."

Another gaping silence. Darien counted the seconds with the ebb and flow of his breath. Another drop of sweat leaked down his face.

"And where is Quinlan Reis now?"

"I sent him on to Athera's Crescent."

Another pause. Another drop of sweat. Darien kept his eyes focused on the bronze cup in Renquist's hand.

"Toward what end?"

"To find a way to resolve the curse over the Black Lands."

He shifted his weight. His fingertips twitched.

"And where is Sareen Qadir?"

Darien's breath froze in his throat. He hadn't thought of Sareen.

"I don't know. I never saw her."

The warmth of the air seemed to bleed right out of the room.

"And where is Meiran now?"

"I don't know."

His breath turned to mist before his face.

"Darien."

He squeezed his eyes shut, unable to look the demon in the face.

"Do not lie to me, Darien. If you lie to me…I will know."

Which had to mean Renquist was a Sensitive…and he'd been reading Darien's emotions all along. The information clicked into place like the last piece of a wood knot. Darien froze, unable to breathe.

He sat in a room with the most dangerous creature in all the world's history. There was a reason why Renquist had gained that reputation. Darien struggled to find his nerve under the weight of realization. The man could sense anything he felt.

"I'll say this one more time." The prime warden's voice sliced through the air like the edge of a blade. "Where is Meiran now?"

Darien took a deep breath. "She sided with Nashir against me. If it wasn't for Quin, they'd have gotten their way. Meiran bolted after that. I've no idea where she went."

Renquist absorbed this information in silence. At last, he motioned for his drink to be replenished. Raising his cup, he commanded, "Return immediately to Tokashi Palace. Find a way to win the allegiance of the tribes. I want every last human transferred out of the Khazahar by the end of the week." His eyes filled with shadow and malice. "Now. You are going to stand up and walk out that door. *While you still have the ability.*"

Darien didn't hesitate. He swept to his feet, managing a stiff bow.

"Prime Warden," he breathed as he turned to leave. Before he reached the door, he heard Renquist utter:

"Lightweaver Azár. Please remain."

Darien pulled the door closed behind him. The corridor outside was empty. He leaned his back against the wall, closing his eyes as he struggled to control his pulse. His arms trembled at his sides.

He knew exactly how close he'd come.

He waited, staring at the floor, for an infinite period of time.

At last, the door to the chamber opened and Azár rejoined him in the hallway. She glanced at him with an expression that suggested everything but said nothing.

They traced their steps back the way they had come. Azár walked at his side, conspicuous in her silence. Back across the cold Circle of Convergence that writhed and wept like a dying thing. Down the stairs, into the chamber filled with portals and black-mailed bodies.

Azár gave him her hand. There was a brief flash and Bryn Calazar was gone.

Somehow, he was still alive.

Darien stepped out of the portal and turned to Azár, knowing he'd been left without a choice.

"Please join me for dinner tonight," he said.

She turned and studied his face. At last, she consented with a nod.

Darien buckled the Omeyan warbelt about his waist. Then he turned to face Sayeed. "Is there anything else I'll need?"

The Zakai officer frowned, face squirming through several layers of thought. He slowly shook his head. "Not at this time. All will be negotiated after." He took a step forward, fixing the lay of Darien's robe. He handed him an embroidered vest.

Darien pulled it on, avoiding the looking glass next to the bed. He already knew what the image would tell him: that he looked nothing like the man he remembered. His hair had grown longer, worn tied back in a single braid. The green robe and vest were unlike any style he'd ever considered wearing in the Rhen. Indeed, he could have never afforded such luxury. Other than his complexion, he looked every inch Malikari.

It felt like he'd left the Rhen behind completely. It didn't even feel a part of him anymore.

"Let's go."

Sayeed bowed and swept the door open. Darien strode out into a cluster of Zakai, who moved quickly to surround him. They accompanied him to the dining hall where, mercifully, he was allowed to enter alone.

A long wooden table awaited him there. He took a seat at the table's center, a footman moving forward to assist him. The servant's attentions made Darien uncomfortable; he still wasn't used to such treatment. It went against every grain of self-sufficiency he'd been trained to rely on.

"My thanks," he muttered as another servant set a fingerbowl down in front of him.

He sloshed his fingers around in the water, scooping some up in his palm to wipe over his face. He blotted his cheeks dry on an offered cloth. The bowl was removed, a celadon plate set before him in its place.

Then he waited.

A servant came to pour tea.

Another brought arak.

Darien took his time about draining them both.

He stared at the table, at the walls, at the blue-painted ceiling. He considered the workmanship of the beaten copper bowls in the center of the table. He studied the table's hardwood grain. He was about to stand up and leave when Azár entered, clothed in a gown with flowing sleeves, her hair wrapped in ribbons.

He'd never seen her in a gown. He almost forgot to stand.

"Thank you for coming," Darien said, rising awkwardly.

Azár looked at him sideways. Her expression was just as fierce as it had ever been. He motioned for her to take the seat opposite him as maids rushed to settle her in. She suffered their attentions much more gracefully than he had.

After the meal was served, Darien dismissed the servants with a wave of his hand.

They ate in silence. The kitchen staff had prepared a rich stew made from krill harvested from the ponds below the palace. Darien ate hungrily, relishing the taste. His body, starved for meat, had learned to crave the dish. It was seasoned with spice hot enough to make him break out in a sweat.

The silence became uncomfortable. Darien was conscious of every clink of silverware, of the sound of his own teeth working in his mouth. He tried to think of something to say, something to ease the tension in the room. But he couldn't force one word past his lips. He couldn't think of anything to say that would not betray his intentions.

Abruptly, Azár pushed back her plate, sitting up straight in her seat. "I'm not hungry."

She was glaring at him, he realized. He supposed he'd been an inconsiderate host. Darien swallowed the food in his mouth, bringing his napkin up to wipe his face. Moving purposefully, he pushed back his own plate. Azár's eyes were intense, probing, daring. Still, he couldn't speak. He just gazed back at her.

"Why did you invite me here?" she asked.

Darien sighed, knowing he couldn't put off his purpose any longer. He folded his napkin on the table, taking his time about it, using the space to summon his nerve.

"I don't know how to say this. So I'll just say it," he said, gazing down at his plate. "I don't wish to marry. It doesn't have anything to do with you. There's nothing wrong with you. It's just that…I lived my life already. Understand? There's nothing left of me to offer a woman. I'm empty."

He glanced up, searching her face. He expected to find it full of hurt and resentment. But Azár's expression hadn't changed. She sat motionless in her chair, eyebrows raised. Waiting for him to continue.

He cleared his throat, scooting forward in his seat. "So I'll not lie to you and tell you that I'm proposing marriage out of love. I'm not. I'm asking for your hand because it's the only option left to me." His gaze shot down to the table, fixing on a knot in the wood. He didn't want to look at her. He was too ashamed by his own audacity.

To his surprise, she didn't walk out. Instead, she leaned forward and took his hand. "I am not a woman of the Rhen. I understand what you are saying, and I'm not offended. Marriage is not about love. It is about commitment. Love comes and goes many times throughout the lifetimes of two people. It is the commitment that remains. If you wish to commit to me, Darien Nach'tier, then I will commit to you, as well."

He looked up to study her face. To his surprise, her expression had lost all of its ferocity. He was confused; he didn't understand. She should despise him for what he had said.

For some reason, she didn't.

He asked, "Are you certain?"

"Yes. I am certain." There was absolutely no doubt in her eyes. He couldn't understand it.

"You know what I am…and you've no problem with it?" He held her gaze firmly, looking for any trace of reluctance but finding none.

Her voice was adamant. "You are a demon. I

know this…*and I don't care.*"

Darien couldn't fathom her reaction. It made no sense. "Why not?"

She shrugged and squeezed his hand. He stared down at her fingers, creamy brown, soft and delicate.

Azár said, "You made many wrong decisions in your past. For this, you are damned. But there is much *sharaq* in you. I have seen it. I will honor you as my husband. And I know you will honor me as your wife."

Darien found the nerve to look her in the eye. "Then I ask you formally: Azár ni Asu'am, will you marry me?"

"I will."

Uncomfortably, he squirmed in his seat. "Then I'll have the clerks prepare the marriage contract. I understand I need to provide you with a bride-gift. Feel free to write into the contract whatever it is you desire. If I have it, it will be yours."

She nodded, her eyes sliding to the side. "How soon will you want the contract signed?"

"As soon as possible." This was not about love. This was about war. He needed the legions of the Khazahar, and he needed them yesterday. Azár was only a means to an end, and she knew it.

Still, her thumb stroked his skin. Her fingers squeezed his. Then she released his hand and stood up.

"I will go prepare," she said and left the room.

Darien sat staring at the door, staring at her plate, staring at his hand, long after Azár had left. He tried to label his emotions, but found that he couldn't. The truth was, he had no idea what he was feeling. Or what he was supposed to be feeling.

Certainly not this.

Chapter Twelve
Of Sorrow and Ash

Ishara, The Black Lands

The prevailing wind blowing down from the Sagros Mountains was razor-sharp and gnawed at the bone like a pack of dogs. Naia shook her head in frustration at its power, pushing all of her weight against the brute force of it. The sting of the wind wrung tears from her eyes, sucked the breath right out of her lungs. Her fingers throbbed even in her thick cotton gloves. She held her cloak closed against her chest, clutching it tight. She had tried pulling her cowl forward to warm her head, but the fiendish wind just yanked it back off again. After a few attempts, she'd given up.

Battered and exhausted, Naia staggered to a stop.

She felt a hand on her back. The demon at her side was attempting to reassure her. It wasn't working.

"Come on!" Quinlan Reis shouted in her ear, tugging on her arm. "…a little further! We have to…" His voice faded out, suffocated by the hellish wind.

Naia didn't need to hear him to understand his point. They had to find shelter. The wind was just as wet as it was chill. It sucked the heat and energy out of her body, leaving her shivering and staggering.

She glanced at the sky, awestruck by the clouds that raced across the dark expanse, flickering and flaring with light. The clouds moved at an impossible speed, surging toward them from the vast horizon that loomed larger than the world. A ball of lightning silhouetted the jagged mountains in the distance. They looked like the black-toothed jaw of some predatory beast.

Another stab of lightning revealed a tall, cone-shaped peak just ahead, its flanks charred, its summit oozing rivers of blood.

Not blood, she realized. Lava.

Stooped and shaking, Naia followed Quinlan Reis in the direction of the volcano. They made camp in the lee of an ancient lava flow and prepared to wait out the wind. Naia sat in the dirt, hugging herself as her teeth clattered and her flesh shivered. Her companion dug out a fire pit and lit a small pile of coals. The heat of the flames was more than comforting; it was life-saving. Naia held her hands over the coal-fire as waves of exhaustion stole over her. The wind howled overhead, wailing like a wounded thing.

As her companion set about the business of cooking their meal, Naia curled up into a tight ball. She wrapped her cloak snugly around herself and fell asleep.

"Time to eat."

Naia opened her eyes, feeling rested and warm. She sat up, rubbing the crusted sleep from her eyes. For a moment she sat there considering Quinlan's profile in the flames. The flickering light of the coal-fire created a harsh rendering of his features, the flesh of his face shadowed and sunken under sharp cheekbones. His expression spoke volumes about nothing.

He leaned forward, offering out a piece of stale bread. Naia blinked in distaste.

"You missed dinner," he explained. "This is breakfast. Better eat this time."

Naia accepted the bread and took a bite, worrying it around in her mouth. She supposed she should be grateful. She swallowed the pasty lump, chasing it down with a sip of water that tasted like dirt. Unable to help it, she made a face.

The darkmage noticed her and smirked. "My apologies. Malikar has a sad lack of mountain springs. It's deplorable, I know. My fault, of course. Just like everything."

Naia forced a smile, unamused. She was becoming accustomed to the man's self-deprecating wit. It was quickly becoming just as stale as the bread in her hand. "The water is fine, Quinlan."

"Call me Quin."

He rose and shouldered his pack. Then he stomped out the fire, kicking dirt over it with his feet. Not that it mattered; there wasn't anything nearby to burn. The wastelands of Malikar were a sterile rockscape. There wasn't a trace of detritus in the soil. Even the riverbeds were far more sand than clay.

Naia pushed herself to her feet, grateful that the wind had died down. The hardpan that stretched before her was crystalline-calm. The clouds moved across the sky with far less urgency. Their shadows striped the desert below in ever-alternating patterns of black and gray. The expanse before them wavered, surreal.

"Well, we're almost there, at least," Quin said as he trekked off.

Naia followed a short distance after him. It wasn't long before they came to the end of the lava flow and skirted a tumbled array of sharp rocks before turning northward. A flat plain stretched ahead of them, broken by strange geometric patterns. Naia stopped, staring at the view, her mind groping to find an explanation for the unnatural terrain.

"What is it?" she asked.

Quinlan Reis turned back to her, swiping a sleeve across his brow. "What's left of Skara. An ancient city that was destroyed in the Desecration."

Naia's eyes scanned the ground ahead of them, at last recognizing the geometric shapes for crumbled walls and jagged ruins. There was not much left, really, only the footprints of what must have been a vast metropolis. The ruins stretched across the flat expanse to the distant foothills ahead. Not too far away, the remains of an ancient statue stuck out of the dark soil of the desert. It had once been a marble sculpture of a rearing horse, now forlorn and obsolete. Half the horse's head had crumbled away.

"How did an entire city perish?" Naia wondered out loud, feeling disturbed by the amount of death that must have occurred here. Her eyes scanned the ruins, her mind estimating casualties.

The demon beside her nodded at the large, conical peak leaking lava and belching great plumes of smoke. "The side of the mountain blew out. This entire region was consumed by mud and hot ash."

Naia shook her head, envisioning all the dead that had been left unattended. Left to rot, covered in debris. The image was sickening.

"How awful," she whispered. "I can't imagine what their deaths must have been like."

"Quick. They broiled where they stood."

Naia shot a glance at him, shocked by his indifference. The expression on the man's face was unreadable. She took a step away from him, suddenly uncomfortable.

"Why are we here?" she asked.

Quinlan Reis gestured to the rubble spread before them. "Because the people of Malikar have all turned away from the old gods. You won't find a temple of Death intact anywhere in the Black Lands. Except here."

Naia looked at the patterned terrain and then back at her companion. She frowned, not understanding what he was talking about. "How? This isn't even a ruin. Everything's been leveled down to the bare foundations."

Quin offered the same, sardonic grin he liked to wear so much. "Why don't you look again, darling." With that, he turned and walked away, over to a large, flat slab of stone poking out of the black wasteland. He jumped onto it and walked across to the exact center of the slab. There, he found an opening. With his foot, he scooted a wedge of sand over the edge, watching as it rained down into the space below.

Naia hadn't the faintest idea what the man was trying to demonstrate. Then it occurred to her. She sprinted toward him.

"Are you saying this is a roof?"

Quinlan Reis smiled. "So it would appear."

Immediately, the entire ruin took on entirely different dimensions. Once again, Naia's eyes wandered over the symmetrical patterns of the rubble. Only, this time, she didn't see bare foundations. She saw rooftops. Ancient Skara lay yet before them, intact, but submerged beneath the ground.

Her mind reeled in wonder. The possibilities…

"So the entire city lies beneath us?" she gasped as she scrambled up next to him on the stone rooftop.

The darkmage flashed her a grin. "By all accounts."

Naia turned slowly, her eyes tracing the lines of the buried city. "But how do we know which of these rooftops is the Temple of Death? There are far too many to just start digging down and looking into all of them."

Quinlan crouched, snatching off his hat and holding it over his knees. He looked up at her, his face suddenly weary. "As it happens, I lived in Skara for a time. I once knew my way around the city quite well."

There was a heavy weight of sadness in his voice. Someone he'd known had lived here, Naia surmised. Someone he'd cared for deeply. She almost felt empathy for the man. Then she remembered who he was. And what he was.

"So you know where the temple is?"

He nodded. "The Temple of Death in Skara was one of the great wonders of the ancient world. I could never forget it. No matter how much I'd like to." He bowed his head, looking a bit deflated. "It was in the civic center across from the palace. It shouldn't be hard to find."

With that, he rose and set his hat on his head. He walked to the edge of the slab and jumped down. Turning back, he offered out his hand. Naia accepted it, exploring the lines of Quinlan's face with her eyes.

She let him lead her up what must have been a broad avenue, now a wide road paved in ash and bordered by stone walls. A low rumble echoed in the distance, like the earth groaning under its own weight. She had no idea whether the sound came from thunder or the guts of the volcano. She glanced sideways at Quinlan. The darkmage didn't seem to notice or to care. He was walking with his gaze focused on the street ahead. He wore a melancholy expression, not seeming the least bit interested in the wonders buried beneath their feet.

"Who lived here?" Naia asked, attempting to draw him out in conversation.

He shot an irritated glance her way. Then he scowled. "It doesn't matter. She's dead." But his expression softened, and at last he relented. "There was a girl. We were both apprenticed to the same master who brought us here for study. The geology of the region is…unparalleled. And so was the metallurgy. We studied together and became quite close. But she ended up marrying someone else."

"What was her name?" Naia asked.

"Amani." The way he said it proved he loved her.

Naia bowed her head in commiseration. She could feel the pang of his grief. "I'm sorry. It always hurts when the person you love loves someone else more."

Quinlan Reis stopped walking. He turned around, anger and hurt infecting his eyes. Naia stopped too, wondering what she'd said that could have been so wrong.

"This is a completely different situation," he growled, making a futile sweep in the air with his hand. "It's not like you and Meiran; Darien didn't have to choose between the two of you. Amani didn't *choose* to be the wife of my brother—*he chose her*. And neither she nor I had any gods-damned say in the matter. There wasn't anything we could do."

Naia just looked at him. His words stung like a spear-thrust, hitting her in the heart.

"What are you saying?" she said, her voice quavering. "Did Darien choose Meiran over me?"

Quin looked flabbergasted. For a moment he just stared at her. Then he spread his hands broadly and shook his head. "What do you mean, choose? There was no choice to be made! He never even *mentioned* you."

Naia froze. She stood there looking at him stupidly, her mouth hanging slack. The hurt clenched her throat, heated her cheeks.

"I'm sorry," the darkmage said. "That was rude."

"No." Naia blinked the tears from her eyes. "Don't apologize. I needed to hear that." She tried to swallow the feelings back down where they came from. It hurt. Gods, it hurt. But she had other things to think about. Darien was the least of her problems. Apparently, he wasn't even her problem anymore.

"Quinlan," she began, but he cut her off.

"I told you. Call me Quin."

She nodded, swiping at the stubborn tears that refused to go away. "Quin. I'm sorry about what happened between you and Amani. You're right; it is an entirely different situation. You and your lover were torn apart. Darien and I…No. What am I saying? There never *was* a 'Darien and I.' I was just a fool."

She turned and took a step away—

—and tripped as a gaping hole loomed right in front of her feet.

Naia cried out, pinwheeling her arms and arching her back away from it. For an eternity, she teetered there on the edge. Then the hole reached up and sucked her in. She was falling.

A hand caught her cloak, jerking her back. Naia fell on her rear in the dirt and scrambled away from the edge.

Quin leaned forward, squinting as he peered into the dark opening in the ground. He knelt and picked up a rock that was lying half-buried in the sand. He held the rock over the shaft and dropped it in. There was a long delay before Naia heard the sound of the rock hitting stone. Quin straightened, adjusting his hat.

"Careful." He offered Naia a hand. "That would have been quite a drop."

Still shaking, Naia allowed the darkmage to pull her to her feet. She leaned over the hole as far as she dared, trembling fingers grasping Quin's hand. Down below, she could see only blackness.

"It's probably the interior of a building." Quin leaned in close to dust her off. His palms moved briskly over her shoulders and down her back. "You nearly fell through the roof. Which isn't the most practical of all entrances."

Naia was too shaken to appreciate his humor.

"Here." Quin patted her arm in reassurance. "Just hang onto me and watch your step."

He guided her wide of the cavity. Naia glanced behind, distrusting it, worried that it might collapse and widen toward them. Her suspicion extended to the entire street, not trusting any of it. Any step she took could end in disaster. They could break through the fragile crust of a rooftop and fall to their deaths without warning.

She let Quin guide her down an ash-paved boulevard lined with the tops of block walls. The rooftops of ruins peeked out of the ground to either side, some taller than others. Some of the jutting masonry looked like it had been used recently to shelter travelers. There were no people about, though. No one lived in Skara. No one alive, at any rate.

They walked past fragmented ruins to the center of the sprawling maze. There, they came to what appeared to be a lake of gray powder. It was encircled by enormous slabs of stone thrust out of the ground at odd angles. Quin drew up in the center of the flat circle, turning slowly as his eyes scanned the wedge-shaped marble that surrounded them. With a grunt and a nod, he started toward a broad slab that sloped upward out of the dust.

He paused with one foot lifted on the rooftop where it rose from the sand. "This is it."

Naia looked up at the enormous structure that slanted away from them, hundreds of feet long and just as wide. It appeared seamless, as if formed from one singular chunk of marble. Which implied that it was wrought by magic. She had never seen anything of the like since leaving Aerysius.

"How do we get in?" she asked, despairing. The temple doors had to be several stories below the level of the roof; it would be impossible to dig through that amount of dirt.

Quin shrugged his pack off, setting it down on the ground. Then, squatting beside it, he proceeded to rummage through the contents. At last he produced a palm-sized copper cube with strange markings on every facet. He hefted it in his hand, appearing to study the object critically. Then he glanced sideways up at her, nodding in the direction of the ruins across the street.

"Go wait for me on the other side of that wall. Oh, and you might want to cover your head."

Naia frowned at him, wondering what the strange object could be. Something dangerous, if he wanted her that far away from it.

"What is it?"

The darkmage grinned. "Something extremely useful, under the circumstances."

Naia considered the innocent-looking cube and shrugged. If Quin thought something that small could move that much dirt, she wouldn't argue. But she was still curious; was it an artifact? Or something more sinister?

She turned and walked across the street, taking refuge on the other side of the block wall. Squatting, she gazed down at the silken dirt beneath her feet.

Naia ran her fingers through it, making parallel furrows in the dust. The sand was light and soft, like fine powder. It shimmered with miniscule crystals, like twinkling stars in a matte-black sky. She lifted her hands and noticed the tiny minerals clinging to the fibers of her gloves. She rotated her hands, watching them glisten.

"Get down!"

Naia covered her head as Quin's body slammed into the ground beside her. Then a resonant *THOOMB!* sent a plume of dust straight up into the air, raining down on their heads like pelting hail. The clatter of pebbles bouncing off stone went on for several seconds before finally letting up.

Naia dropped her hands from her head and gaped at Quin, who gaped back at her. He took a peek over the top of the wall.

"Shall we go assess the damage?"

Naia could only nod as she stood up, finger-combing the dust out of her hair. The street was no longer smooth, but littered with chunks of marble and scattered debris. A crater had appeared next to the sprawling slab that was the roof of the Temple of Death. The hole was significantly deeper than Naia had imagined it would be. Quin's little cube had done a lot more damage than she'd anticipated.

But it was still just a crater; nothing more. The explosion hadn't managed to even crack the temple's exterior.

Quin fidgeted, chewing his lip in obvious frustration. He raked a sleeve across his brow. Then he made a vague gesture back the way they had come.

"One more time," he said. "And this time, *get down!"*

Naia didn't need to be told twice. As Quin jumped inside the crater with another cube in his hand, she ran back across the street and took up position behind the eroded wall. Only, this time, she lay with her body flush up against the stone, on her stomach in the dirt. She closed her eyes tight, knowing what was coming.

There was the sound of running footsteps. Then another *THOOMB!*—even louder this time. She heard Quin's body landing somewhere behind her, followed by the clattering noise of raining pebbles. Eventually, the torrent tapered off. For a moment, the ruined city was as silent as the dead it contained.

Naia rolled over and found Quin on his back, staring up at the sky. His face was covered in dust, blood dribbling from a cut over one eye. He blinked, and the air over him seemed to ripple. The blood and grime immediately disappeared. He rolled over and sprang to his feet.

"Are you all right?" Naia gasped.

"I'm dead." The darkmage shrugged as he bent over to dust his pants off. "So I suppose that makes me, by definition, not quite all right. Let's just say that I'm about as right as I'm ever going to get."

Naia folded her arms, glowering at his failed attempt at sarcasm although small part of her appreciated it. The world they walked through was dark enough.

"Well, now." He turned and strode back across the street. "Let's see if that made a dent."

Naia followed, noticing that the crater was now twice as wide as it had been before. Quin jumped down into the newly formed pit. Naia paused, looking down. The cavity was much deeper than it looked. And this time, the explosion had ripped a gash in the temple wall, scoring a larger hole out of what must have been a window.

Quin grinned up at her, beckoning her to join him.

Naia slid down the crumbling slope, catching his hand to steady herself. She paused to dump the pebbles out of her shoes, then straightened to examine the wall. Quin dropped to a crouch, running his hand over the marble façade of the temple. A bright glowing orb erupted beside her face. Naia flinched away from it before realizing that it was just a globe of magelight. She caught herself on Quin's shoulder, almost knocking him over.

"A bit jumpy, aren't we?"

"The word you're looking for is fearful," Naia corrected him. "And yes, I am. Mostly of you."

The darkmage cracked a grin. "Excellent. Then you won't try arguing with my next idea."

She stared at him then stared at the gaping hole. Her eyes widened slowly, and she started shaking her head.

"No."

"Yes."

Chapter Thirteen
Perfectly Damaged

Tokashi Palace, The Black Lands

Darien extended his arms out to his sides, holding the position awkwardly as Sayeed buttoned the sleeves of the black tunic they'd had tailored to fit him. The garment was unlike anything he'd ever felt before, stiff and heavily embroidered. Looped buttons ran from the high collar all the way down to the hem. Sayeed finished with his sleeves then strapped the Omeyan warbelt around his waist. Over the belt he wrapped a golden sash, through which he hung a long, curved dagger in a tasseled scabbard.

Sayeed retrieved a matching sword, bowing low as he held it up, presenting the blade. He bared a few inches of steel, exposing a single edge with three deep grooves. The hilt was wrapped in bronze wire and set with semiprecious stones that matched the stones on the scabbard. It was a handsome weapon that looked ornamental. But it bore the scars of battle. This blade had seen war.

"This is the sword carried by Khoresh Kateem in the battle of Harmudi," Sayeed stated, sliding the elegant scimitar fully back before slipping it through the sash at Darien's waist.

He arranged a scarf over Darien's shoulders, saying, "First will be the ceremony. Afterward, there is the reception. It is then that the warlords of the Khazahar will declare their support for you."

Darien nodded, tugging at his collar, which was buttoned up so high he could scarcely breathe. He could feel his throat fighting against it every time he tried to swallow.

The Zakai officer drew away, considering his appearance gravely. He issued a stiff nod of satisfaction. "Have I answered all your questions?"

"Aye."

Sayeed took Darien by the shoulders and pulled him close, pressing a kiss against his forehead. Darien suffered the touch, not liking it, but was too surprised to object. Sayeed bowed and stepped back, opening the chamber doors.

Setting his hand on the hilt of the scimitar, Darien strode out into the hall. There, a retinue of Zakai awaited them dressed in formal uniforms. Today they were far more than just his personal escort. Today, the Zakai stood in place of the family he no longer possessed.

Sayeed fell in at his side as they left the residential wing.

Darien was shocked to find the usually silent halls of Tokashi Palace teeming with people. At the sight of their party, a cry went up from the gathered onlookers. Drums and pipes began to play as shrill trilling noises rang off the walls. The crowd surged forward, people scrambling to reach out and touch him as he passed.

Sayeed had warned him about the custom. Something about luck, though Darien didn't understand it. He bowed his head as a wash of panic overcame him. The world lurched, suddenly unstable. He couldn't stand the proximity of so many faces, the feel of their hands on him. He closed his eyes and tried to trust Sayeed to guide him through the crowd. Fingers brushed his face, pawed at his clothes, slid over his hair. The noise of the crowd and the blare of instruments overwhelmed his senses.

"Are you well?" Sayeed whispered in his ear.

Darien nodded, swallowing his panic.

At last, they broke out of the thick of the crowd as his entourage led him onto a bridge that spanned the chasm above the river. There, Darien felt comfortable enough to open his eyes and look down. It was much cooler here, the air fed with chill from the ice caverns below. The bridge arched upward toward a canopy that had been erected for the occasion.

Great crowds gathered to line both sides of the river's chasm. Darien drew to a stop under the colorful fabric of the canopy, his eyes falling on the priest who awaited him in crimson robes.

A priest of Xerys.

He shouldn't have been surprised, but for some reason he was. Despite his reservations, Darien moved ahead of his retinue and strode forward to shake the cleric's hand. The gaunt and dark-haired man said nothing, looking confused by the gesture.

A loud, ululating noise erupted from all around the cavern, coming from every direction at once. Darien glanced down and saw the crowd parting like a wave. A lone figure emerged from the thick press of bodies, veiled in red, a red sash tied around her waist. Women in colorful robes guided her forward through glistening tendrils of magelight that gleamed like daybreak, escorting her onto the bridge.

Darien felt his mouth go dry as he watched Azár's procession. His grip on the sword hilt grew intense. He tried to get a glimpse of her face beneath the veil, but the thick red lace obscured her features. She came to a halt on the far side of the canopy, the priest of Xerys between them.

The priest turned away to light the flame of a single taper on an altar behind him. He then raised a pitcher and waited for Azár to present her hands. He poured a thin stream of water onto Azár's open palms, then did the same for Darien.

The solemn man took Darien's hands and led him forward until he was standing in front of his bride, a woman whose face he couldn't see, whose heart he didn't know. With the priest's guidance, he took her hand in his.

Skin so soft.

He traced his thumb over the back of her hand.

Words were spoken, but he wasn't listening. The contract was signed, first by his bride and then by himself. More words passed him by. The whole while, he was gazing down at Azár's hand, studying every fine detail of it.

An explosion of noise echoed through the cavern, swelling to a deafening thunder. Shaken, Darien at first didn't understand the reason for it. Only when Sayeed nudged him forward did he realize it was time to kiss his bride. Reaching up, he drew Azár's veil back over her head, revealing her face.

His breath clotted in his throat.

This was not the fierce woman he thought he was marrying. A soft beauty stared back at him with nervous eyes, unbound hair flowing down her back. Her red-stained lips trembled. Darien hesitated, unsure of himself. Then he leaned forward, kissing his bride on the forehead, just as Sayeed had instructed him to do.

The noise in the cavern crescendoed to a climax. Drums clattered and bagpipes skirled. Trills of celebration echoed off the walls of the ice chasm. Through it all, Azár somehow managed to smile. He found it comforting. Taking his bride by the arm, he led her down and off the bridge, following his retinue of Zakai.

The thunder of celebration followed them all the way to the Grand Hall of the palace, already teeming with color and noise and wondrous smells of food. Darien took a seat beside Azár in cushioned chairs on a raised dais. Men and women flooded in, dressed in regional costumes and bearing gifts.

One by one, the men of the clans stood and came forward. They mounted the stairs to the dais, where they fell to their knees before Darien and his bride. One by one, the warlords knelt and kissed the hem of Darien's robe, pledging their fealty. One by one, he accepted their allegiance with a nod. His fingers still clutched the hand of his Asyaadi bride who looked on but said nothing. After the last man rose from off the floor, the drums thundered back to life and the feasting began in earnest.

"It is time, Lord," Sayeed whispered in his ear.

Darien stood, Azár rising at his side as the guests rushed forward to link hands, forming a long tunnel to the door. Darien ducked, still holding Azár's hand as they moved beneath the span of arms, swords, and spears. The thunder of applause vibrated the walls even as the doors of the hall swung closed behind them. The guests returned to continue their celebration as the newlyweds retired to their wedding night.

Darien turned to Azár as uniformed Zakai swarmed around them in the hallway. "Are you well?" he asked her.

She nodded, uncharacteristically demure, flashing him a fragile smile.

He held her hand the whole way as the officers escorted them back to the Residence. Mercifully, they let him enter his own chambers alone with his bride. As the door closed behind them, the soldiers outside gave a loud, whooping shout.

Darien closed his eyes and sighed, thankful just to be alone.

Almost alone.

Obviously, he was not.

His nerves snapped tight like over-tuned harp strings.

There was a rustle of silk as Azár moved to stand in front of him. He felt her hand touch his cheek. He resisted the urge to draw away. Her fingertips stroked the whiskers of his face, tracing his jawline. Then her lips were on his, the slightest pressure of a kiss.

It was too much. He winced, taking a step back.

"You don't like to be touched," she said. It was not an observation. More like an acknowledgment of a boundary.

"No," he admitted. "Not anymore."

She reached out and took his hand in hers. "My poor husband," she whispered. Her kohl-darkened eyes slipped to the floor. "You are just as damaged as I."

He frowned in concern, his thoughts faltering. "What do you mean?"

Her gaze fixed on the ground, she informed him, "My master used me every day. Sometimes more than once a day. He hurt me badly. In many different ways."

Darien's nerves turned to water, then to ice. Then to fire. Anger consumed him until he burned and shook with rage. But there was nowhere to direct his wrath; Azár's abuser was already dead. Already right where he needed to be: burning in the depths of hell.

Where Darien's wrath would find him eventually.

His bride continued, "I told you I was not looking for love. Above all else, I need a man I can trust not to hurt me. I am sorry, my husband. That is why I chose you."

Darien shook his head, his mind grappling with this newfound reality. "I don't understand," he whispered, drawing back. "You're the one who kissed me. You said you wanted me…"

"I'm sorry. It was just a test. I had to know how you would react."

"But that time in the lightfields—"

"You made a promise to me. And you kept it. You and I are a perfect match, don't you see? You desire sex but are unwilling to risk your heart. I desire love but am unwilling to share my body. Together, we will learn from each other. We will conquer our fears. In the meantime, feel free to indulge in concubines." She placed a hand on his chest. "Just save your heart for me. Someday, I will come to collect it."

As Darien stood in shock, she turned and moved away, wandering deeper into their shared quarters. She glanced around, appraising the dim space.

"We will need another bed," she muttered.

Chapter Fourteen
The Goddess of Mercy

Skara, The Black Lands

"We're going down there." Quin gestured into the gaping blackness of the hole that the explosion had created in the side of the building.

Naia could feel her face paling, draining of its color. She leaned over to peer into the jagged crack in the temple's wall. Her gaze traveled only as far as the glow of Quin's magelight would allow. From what she knew of Death's temples, she could tell the hall below was part of the Inner Sanctum, a network of chambers secreted away from the public eye, where many of the temple's holiest rites were performed. Imposing columns, many stories tall, marched up the length of the room on both sides. A series of wrought-iron chandeliers were suspended from the ceiling, hung at intervals one after another until they disappeared into shadow.

Naia's palms tingled as she gazed down at the floor many stories below. Unless they could fly, they could never get down to it.

"It's too far…" she began, staring at the black circlets of the chandeliers that formed what looked like an aerial skipping path.

"I think we can drop from here down onto the top of that column." Quin nodded down at the ledge created by the flared lip of the column below, where it met with the lintel of the wall. The column was a lot closer to them than the ground, but still quite a fall. And a narrow target to aim for. Naia couldn't believe he was even suggesting it.

"Not without breaking bones," she disagreed. The tingling in her palms swelled to needling pinpricks.

"So what if we do break some bones? We can heal them."

Quin's wry tone was entirely too jovial for Naia's liking. She spared him a sharp glare of reproach, growling, "What if we break our necks?"

The darkmage shrugged. "Don't land on your neck." He added a belated grin.

The expression didn't help. Naia frowned as she examined the narrow ledge below them. She wasn't sure it could support their weight. But she didn't see any other way down to the floor, either. She looked around for another path down the wall, but didn't see any other option.

Naia sighed. "Say we do manage to make it down there without falling off. Then what?" She stared at Quin fiercely, challenging him to come up with a solution.

He complied. "I think I can sway that chandelier over. Then all we have to do is jump on."

Naia looked down at the light fixture. It was an enormous, black iron circlet bedecked with dozens of tapers. It hung suspended from the ceiling by a lengthy chain. Naia was uncertain whether the chain would break beneath their weight. Especially considering it had been hanging there for a thousand years.

"I don't believe I can do that." Her voice trembled in her throat. The pinpricks in her palms had devolved into cold, clammy numbness. She felt terribly dizzy.

Quin grinned and patted her on the shoulder. "It will be an adventure, but I think you can manage it. You seem nimble enough."

How could the infernal man be so optimistic?

There was a very real chance both of them would fall to their deaths. Well, perhaps not both of them. Naia had to remind herself that Quin Reis was already dead. Which might explain his casual cheer in the face of near-certain disaster.

She said through clenched teeth, "Assuming our weight doesn't snap the chain right out of the ceiling, where do we go from there?"

Quin spread his hands as if the answer should be obvious. "Then we sway it over to the next chandelier. And then the next. And the next, all the way down the line."

Naia stared into the darkness that encased the far end of the hall. The glow of Quin's magelight didn't penetrate far enough to disrupt the shadows at that end. There could be anything down there. Or nothing.

"And what then?" Naia asked, still gaping into the dark.

The darkmage issued an exaggerated shrug. "We'll figure it out when we get there."

Naia arched an eyebrow. "You're not serious."

"I'm always serious. I seldom get taken seriously, but that's a topic for another conversation."

Naia shook her head, settling back against the side of the building. "I…I can't. Do. That. No." Her head-shaking became emphatic.

Quin patted her back and grinned. "Of course you can. There's nothing stopping you."

"Just common sense!"

"Overrated. Never got me out of trouble."

"Then what did?"

He appeared to consider that for a moment before admitting, "Usually murdering somebody."

Naia scoffed. "And that's supposed to make me feel comforted?"

"No. But you did ask." He reached up, adjusting his hat. There was a fiendish sparkle in his eye. "It's either this or we walk all the way back to Bryn Calazar and hire a ship. By the time we actually make it to Titherry, the war will be over, and you'll be dead. Then I suppose I can just retire to hell and rot for all eternity."

Naia sighed, glancing once more at the shadows. "Fine. Do you want to go first, or shall I?"

"Oh, I think I should go first," he said, standing up. He shrugged out of the straps of his leather pack, handing it down to her. "Here. Would you mind hanging onto this? You can toss it down to me later."

Naia accepted the pack, throwing it on over her shoulder next to her own. Before she could come to terms with the fact that they were actually going forward with this ludicrous plan, Quin was already seated on the edge of the hole. He hoisted his legs over then dropped down, clinging to the blocks with his hands. His head shot up from the other side like a gopher popping out of a hole.

"Kiss for luck?"

Before Naia could gasp her disapproval, he let go and disappeared.

There was a short span of silence. Followed by an echoing wail of pain.

Naia surged forward, leaning over the break in the wall to search the shadows below. Quin had landed on the ledge. He was tossing about like a turtle on its back, holding one knee against his chest, face twisted in pain. She could tell the moment he healed the injury, watching him sag visibly in relief. He sighed and collapsed back against the stone.

"Are you all right?" Naia called down to him.

"Never better." His voice wasn't as cheerful as before. He rolled into a sitting position then pushed himself erect, back flush against the wall. At least the ledge was wider than it had looked. Smiling up at her, Quin raised his arms. "My pack, if you please?"

Naia held it out over the wall, letting the pack sway over him before letting it go. Her aim was a little off. Still, Quin managed to snatch it out of the air with one hand.

Naia realized it was her turn to jump down to the ledge. Suddenly, she felt very pale and very clammy, and more than a little queasy. The world seemed off-kilter, the ground unstable. Her heart kicked up its pace, sprinting in her chest. She didn't care for heights. She cared even less for drops.

Swallowing, Naia paused to gather her dignity and her courage. She lifted her skirt and settled down on the crack in the wall, swinging her legs over. She made the mistake of looking down.

The floor of the temple was very far below. And the ledge was exceptionally small. Quin stood directly beneath her, holding his hands up as if preparing to catch her. Naia wasn't sure that was a good idea; she was likely to fall off and take him with her.

"A little to the left," he called up.

She scooted over. She could see him just between her feet.

"There! Now just kick off."

Just kick off, she thought. As if it were that easy.

It was.

She flung herself forward before indecision could stop her. The edge of the column came rushing up, and she smacked hard, face-down against the stone.

The next thing she knew, she was staring up, blinking, into Quin's grinning face. He was absent his hat, which was peculiar. A darkmage needed a dark hat, she figured, and thought he looked rather diminished without one. His curly hair hung tousled about his shoulders, lending him a feral appearance that seemed entirely out of character.

"Where's your hat?" she muttered. Her voice sounded weak and bleary. She didn't understand why.

"In my pack. How do you feel?"

She gazed down the length of her body. She was lying stretched out on the marble top of the column, her head pillowed in Quin's lap. It was dim and cold, the air thick with mildew and humidity. It smelled like rain.

"I feel…alive," she said. "You deserve a good kick. You almost got us killed!"

"But I didn't." The darkmage smiled. "And we're right where we need to be. See?" He gestured around at the expansive emptiness that surrounded them.

Naia sat up and gazed at the shadows of the hall, its walls and arcades awash in the glow of Quin's magelight that trailed like a red mist down the length of the hall. The far end of the chamber was no longer lost to shadow. There, two great statues of the goddess sat on enormous thrones, a thin waterfall spilling between them. Naia recognized the statues: the aspects of Mercy and Sacrifice, two faces of the goddess she knew well.

The floor of the hall was still so very far below. She had no idea how they were going to get down to it. Magelight erupted from the ancient rings of the chandeliers, drenching the hall in a greasy, blood-red light.

"Are you ready for the next hurdle?"

Quin climbed to his feet, shaking the dust off his pants. Without waiting for her answer, he reached out a hand toward the nearest chandelier. With a groan of protest, it bent toward him on its chain as if drawn by a magnet. The edge of the iron circlet came close to their stone perch…but not all the way. There was still a sizeable gap between the column and the fixture. They would have to jump. And it was a jump up, not down.

"Oh, no…" Naia gazed at the chandelier open-mouthed. "You're not thinking…" Of course he was. She shook her head, not bothering to complete the sentence. It was no use.

She stared harder at the chandelier, studying its structure in an attempt to understand how either of them could ever scale it. The fixture was composed of two iron rings that held candle cups, a smaller ring at the top, and a much wider ring below. Both rings were reinforced by iron crossbars. The chandelier was mounted to the ceiling by a long chain that hooked onto the smaller ring. Four more chains came down to stabilize the larger circlet on the bottom.

Quin looked at her with a reckless glint in his eyes.

"No, don't—!"

Without a word, he drew back against the wall and took a running leap. He caught the iron ring by his fingertips, the whole fixture lurching under his weight. Tapers rained down, tumbling to the floor stories below. The magelight flickered, dimming, on the verge of going out.

"Quin!" Naia screamed.

The chandelier recoiled, swaying away from the column as Quin scrambled to pull himself up over the rim. At last he hooked one leg over, clinging to the bar as the fixture swung in great arcs like the bob of a pendulum. He got another leg over, pulling himself upright. Below, the floor of the hall seemed to lurk hungrily.

To Naia's horror, Quin wasn't satisfied with his perch. He grasped one of the stabilizing chains and pulled himself to a standing position on the iron crossbar, reaching out toward her with his other hand. The chandelier swayed back toward the ledge and then stuck there, frozen at the extreme of its arc.

"Come on!" The look in Quin's eyes was just as insistent as his voice.

Naia knew there was no argument; she couldn't remain on the ledge forever. Neither could she retreat back up the wall. She wiped the sweat off her palms onto the bodice of her gown. Just to be sure, she wiped her palms again. Then, just as Quin had done, she took two steps back and pressed her body flat up against the wall. Naia stood there for a moment, breathing in shallow, rapid gasps, as the world spun around her. She took a failed step forward and stopped. She backed up again. Sagging, she groped for resolve.

"You won't fall. Just jump. I'll catch you."

Naia wished she could trust him. But he was a demon, and she couldn't.

She squeezed her eyes closed then opened them again. She glared fiercely at Quin. She wished he still had that stupid grin on his face, but he'd lost it somewhere along the way. Clenching her hands into fists, she ran and leaped from the top of the column. She plunged right past Quin's outstretched fingers and started screaming as she fell.

Her body jerked upward, as if snapped back by a rope. Quin's strong grip caught her wrist. She was hauled upward into his arms as she gasped and trembled in terror and disbelief.

"How did you do that?" she gulped.

"Darien fell from Aerysius and lived," he responded with a shrug. "If I knew for a fact I could do it again, I'd tell you to jump off and I'd float you right to the floor. Unfortunately, I'm not sure I could repeat it."

The chandelier swayed steadily to and fro. The chain groaned and creaked. Below them, the floor contorted in an unsteady motion.

Naia asked, "You don't know what you did?"

Quin shook his head. "No idea. Just happy as a daisy that it worked."

"A lark."

"What?" He looked confused.

"The phrase is, 'happy as a lark.'"

Quin gazed at her and smiled. "Well, I'm happy as a lark, then." His smile went back to where it came from. "I'm going to go first. Wait until I'm across, then follow behind me. Do what I do."

Naia shook her head. "No. Let me go first. If you fall, I don't want to be trapped up here."

He frowned as if unsure about that plan, but ended up nodding. "Fair enough. Drop down and hang from that bar, then go hand-over-hand."

She gathered her courage then did as he suggested, sitting down on the crossbar that supported the chandelier's outer ring. The bar wasn't very thick; she could get her hands around it. Which was good; the ring that held the candle cups was much thicker, and she doubted she could keep a good grip on it. She dropped down, her legs kicking as she swung from the bar.

Hand-over-hand, she made her way slowly down the length of the bar toward the outside edge as the fixture dipped lower, tilting beneath her weight. When she reached the outer ring, she stopped and looked back at Quin.

The chandelier righted itself. It began to sway, gently at first, picking up speed as it went. Then it paused and swung back the other direction. It stopped at the apex of its arc, the iron ring frozen above the next chandelier in line. The gap was too much. Terrified, Naia glanced back at Quin.

The next chandelier swung toward her until it rested up against the ring of the fixture she was riding. Naia breathed a sigh of relief and swung from one giant ring to the next. But as she grabbed on, the whole contraption lurched beneath her weight. Quin righted it, but not before it sent her heart leaping into her throat.

Naia sucked in a deep breath as the chandelier tilted back to level. Her hands were slick with sweat. She pulled them off one by one, wiping her palms dry on her gown. She made the mistake of looking down. The floor swam in shadow far below her dangling feet. She broke out in a sweat all over again.

Naia bit her lip in concentration and started forward again, hand-over-hand down the bar as the fixture tilted.

This time, the transition was easier. Quin had anticipated the weight redistribution. Naia paused, wiping her hands. She healed the blisters that were forming on her fingers and palms. Then, little by little, she edged along the bar and onto the next fixture. And the next. And the next. Six chandeliers in all.

Until she reached the far wall. And had no idea what to do next.

There was nowhere to go. Naia clung to the bar still stories above the floor. The only thing beneath her was the statue of Mercy seated upon her marble throne. But it was too much of a drop; even if she did make it, Naia felt sure she'd roll right off.

She glanced back at Quin in desperation.

"Just close your eyes and let go!" he shouted, still standing on the first chandelier. His voice rang off the walls, his face bathed in crimson magelight that made him look even more demonic than he was. "Either you'll make it, or you won't!"

"That's not very reassuring!"

"Don't think about it! Just let go!"

She sucked in a breath and gasped out a prayer. "Merciful goddess!"

She screamed as she fell. The slap of her body against stone knocked the scream right out of her. Then she was falling again.

Something jerked her to a stop. She hung in the air, her feet swinging beneath her.

Her head throbbed, and her stomach recoiled in a surge of nausea. She tried to concentrate, healing herself as best she could. Her vision went dim. A profound sense of weariness dragged her downward. She swung gently in the air, like a bird riding a tree branch on a breezy day.

"Wake up!" That was Quin shouting.

Naia dragged herself back to consciousness, blinking awake. She clawed her mind back into focus. Was she still hanging in the air?

"Open your eyes and look at me!" His voice sounded much closer than before.

Naia looked up and saw him hanging overhead from the fixture right above her. He was clutching the outer circlet with both hands, looking down at her with his chin against his chest. His feet dangled uselessly, the toes of his boots pointed at the floor. The chandelier swung in a slow circle, the frame that held the candles wrenched at an unnatural angle.

Naia saw Quin's precarious situation and felt a swift jolt of fear. Then she saw what was holding her own body up, suspended in the air. The fear turned to a wave of panic that broke over her, ripping a scream from her throat.

The strap of her pack had somehow hooked on to the statue's upraised hand, caught on one delicate thumb. She hung suspended, still far above the floor. The hand of the goddess had saved her life. The hand of Mercy. The coincidence felt like a gut-punch. Guilt filled her face with heat that overwhelmed even her fear. She had abandoned her goddess two years before. Yet her goddess had not abandoned her.

She squirmed, kicking, until she managed to slide out of the straps that held her pack. She fell and hit the floor.

Naia rolled over on her side, scrunching her knees up to her chin. She rocked there back and forth, trembling and sobbing in relief and regret. She was barely aware when her pack lifted on its own, rising from the statue's hand to settle softly by her side.

"Naia!" Quin called down. He was still hanging from the acutely tilted fixture, taking turns flexing the fingers of first one hand then the next.

Naia staggered to her feet, craning her neck to look up at him. He looked pathetic up there, legs kicking as the contraption swayed and creaked, the chain groaning in a fatigued voice. She glanced from Quin to the statues of the aspects, at the water streaming thinly to a pool at the base of the thrones. The sound of the fall was a muted, sibilant drone.

Above, the chandelier Quin dangled from lurched and began to sway. Her eyes went wide as she saw what he was attempting. He was causing it to swing far enough to time his drop over the head of the nearest statue.

"Don't!" she shrieked up at him. If he missed, he'd drop all the way to the floor. The chandelier swayed all the way to the far wall with a contemptuous creak. It slowed with a grating noise, then swung back toward her again.

With a shout, Quin let go.

He dropped right onto the goddess' head, slapped hard, then slid down her front. His body tumbled past her outstretched hand, landing face-down in her lap. Naia rushed forward, plunging into the pool, splashing as she surged toward the statue's feet. She could see Quin's legs hanging over the marble knees. He didn't appear to be moving.

"Quin!" she called up at him.

A foot twitched. There came a low groan. Then:

"Why do I always end up in the laps of stone-cold women who won't spread their legs?"

Naia gasped, more in dismay than relief. Her hand flew to her mouth. "You dare blaspheme the goddess in her sacred hall?!"

Above her, the feet disappeared and Quin's face poked out, grinning down. "Doesn't feel very sacred. More like haunted and abandoned."

Hanging on to the statue's knees, he swung his

legs over then dropped. He landed in the reflecting pool, staggering to catch his balance. He bent over, panting and swaying. Naia waded toward him, catching hold of his shoulders.

"Do you want me to heal you?"

He shook his head. "No. I've got it."

He closed his eyes, screwing his face into a grimace. A wave of energy passed over him, and he caught his breath. He wavered over his feet then straightened, hands going up to tug at his rumpled coat. He plunged his hand into his pack and retrieved his hat. He took his time about adjusting it. At last seeming satisfied, he spread his arms out at his sides.

"See? All just a grand adventure."

Naia looked at him. "I'm beginning to understand why you're dead."

Chapter Fifteen
The Beautiful Dead

Skara, The Black Lands

Naia slipped her pack on over her shoulders and waded through the shallow, murky pool in the direction of the waterfall. The spray was chill, the mist dampening the dusty air of the sanctum. The water poured from an opening high up on the wall between the two stone statues of the goddess. It plunged in a thin, veil-like stream between the hewn thrones. She couldn't tell if the feature had been created by man or by time. She supposed it didn't matter.

She turned and stared back toward the anterior of the hall. By the diffuse red glow of Quin's magelight, she could make out the tall doors that led to the temple's sanctuary. From her years of study and worship, she knew that was not the direction they needed to go. They would need to find a way deeper into the heart of the temple, where the most sacred of all mysteries was contained. There was no obvious exit from the sanctum, but that didn't surprise her. The Catacombs were one of Death's most closely held secrets.

She looked back toward the statues of the goddess, feeling certain. "We must go through the waterfall." It wasn't a guess; she just knew.

Quin glanced up, a look of surprise on his face. The spray of the mist collected on his face in a dewy sheen. Almost reverently, he removed his hat.

Hiking her skirt up over her knees, Naia splashed forward through the frigid pool. She closed her eyes as she moved into the waterfall, clamping her jaw as the chill of the water washed over her head, wetting her hair and awakening every nerve in her body. Shaking and drenched, she stepped out on the other side and opened her eyes.

Darkness confronted her.

Teeth chattering, she cast a trail of magelight ahead, a brilliant azure glow that flowed like mist to illuminate a filthy corridor ahead. She heard the sound of splashing behind her and then Quin appeared at her side, soaked and shivering, hugging his hat against his chest. He looked at the magelight and stiffened, his eyes flashing back to her.

"I keep forgetting you inherited Darien's legacy," he said, looking suddenly somber. "What tier are you?"

"Third," Naia replied through chattering teeth. "Meiran inherited the other five."

"That's too bad," Quin said, voice brittle with scorn. "She doesn't deserve them."

Naia found herself silently agreeing. Quin had told her about Meiran's betrayal of Darien. She didn't hate the woman for it, but the contempt she felt was only a moment's reflection short of hate. Of course, she couldn't claim that she was more worthy of the legacy. By the ancient laws of Aerysius, she had forfeited her right to it when she'd forfeited her Oath. No matter how much she regretted that decision, it was something she could never take back.

Naia returned her attention to the corridor ahead. The ceiling had crumbled, creating a debris field at their feet. Tall, rusted candlesticks lay scattered across the floor at haphazard angles. A thick layer of ash coated everything. Naia trailed her fingers over the relentless gray of the wall, revealing the colorful design of the tile beneath. The corridor must have been beautiful at one time.

She lifted her wet skirt and stepped over the first tumbled candlestick, picking her way carefully across the mangled floor. At the far end of the passage were three imposing openings that led off in scattered directions: one to the left, one to the right, and another leading straight ahead. There were no doors; doors were unnecessary. No light could enter the passages beyond, and no shadow dared cross the thresholds. It was as if there was an indomitable barrier separating the light of the world from the velvet darkness beyond.

Naia stopped, turning back to her companion. "Quin. Look at me."

He did. His face was streaked with water that dribbled from his hair. His ancient eyes spoke of weariness and sorrow, wisdom and regret. Naia shivered harder, taken aback for a moment by the layers of depth in his eyes. He really was a demon, she realized. She would have to remember that…especially where they were going.

"On the other side of these openings is the Catacombs," she said with a fierceness that surprised her. "I must warn you: the living are forbidden to communicate with the dead."

A mirthless smile shadowed Quin's face. "I deduce that doesn't apply to me."

He was most likely correct. But she had no idea how to deal with Quin's peculiar circumstances, or how he might be affected by the Strictures. He was not alive, but nor was he a shade. He existed somewhere apart, a despoiled soul denied all hope of the Atrament.

Naia frowned. "Perhaps. But for you, there may be other dangers."

Quin folded his arms. "Such as…?"

"There are places within Death's Passage that are sacred to the goddess. A soul such as yours will be forbidden to trespass. Entering such a shrine would shred the fabric of your soul." There were few such shrines, but they did exist. And they were difficult to avoid, if they came across one.

Quin scowled reflectively. "I'd like to avoid any amount of soul-shredding if I possibly can."

Naia looked at him in sympathy. "I'm sorry. Some aspects of the Catacombs exist more in the Atrament than they do in this world. And, as you know, your soul is incompatible with the Atrament."

He chortled. "'Incompatible.' That's a diplomatic way of putting it."

Naia squeezed his arm, as if by pressure she could impart an appreciation of the danger he faced. "Speak to no one. Touch nothing. Go nowhere unless I say it's safe. Do you understand, Quinlan?"

Holding his hat in his hands, he executed a formal bow. "Madam, you have my word I'll behave. As much as I can, at any rate."

Somehow, Naia doubted that. Nevertheless, she nodded before turning back to the darker-than-black openings before them. Quin's sarcasm was quickly forgotten as she put her mind to the problem of selecting which path they should take.

Atrament, Oblivion, Netherworld.
Mercy, Sacrifice, Vengeance

"Skara's temple," she murmured, her brain working to decipher the code. "Which face of the goddess was displayed at the pinnacle of the dome?"

Quin appeared to be wrestling with an unpleasant memory. "The ugly one," he said finally. That would be the aspect of Sacrifice.

They would choose the Oblivion portal.

Not that the portal actually led to Oblivion, just as the portal on the right didn't lead to the netherworld. It was a mnemonic, a device used for aiding memory. The Catacombs existed apart from distance and time, though travel through them still took time and covered distance. The paradox was one of the temple's holy mysteries. She was determined to select the shortest route to their destination, even if it wasn't the straightest.

Her hand clenching Quin's wet sleeve, she guided him toward the looming entrance directly ahead. She could see nothing but perfect darkness on the other side of the doorway. No path. No light. It was like the world ended right there in front of them. She stepped across the threshold.

Death's Passage

The world wavered a bit around her then steadied. She was no longer in the gray corridor conquered by years and volcanic ash. Instead they had arrived in a mist-filled tunnel hewn from solid rock. Beside her, Quin sucked in a sharp, rattled breath.

She turned toward him. And winced when she

saw him.

He positively glowed with a brilliant aura of sickening light. He was staring down at himself, rotating his arms slowly, a look of concern in his eyes. Naia knew immediately what the queer, putrid light represented. She'd seen such an aura before, on Darien. But it hadn't been anywhere near this vivid. Compared to the green brilliance surrounding Quin, Darien's aura had been a mere foreshadowing.

Quin's damnation was undeniable.

He raised a glowing hand before his face and said, "Well, this is certainly disconcerting."

Naia wished she had better tidings to offer. But she was used to being the bearer of ill news. "It is not an optimistic sign," she said, mustering all the tact and evasion of an anointed priestess of Death.

Quin dropped his hand, appearing resigned. "I don't suppose it is. Apparently, the goddess is well-aware of my transgressions."

Naia looked at him in sympathy. There was no glossing over the truth. "It means your soul is not destined for the Atrament," she told him directly. "It is destined for hell."

He shrugged, forcing a smile. "Hardly anything I wasn't aware of before." He raised his hands, using the aura to illuminate the wall next to the opening of a passage leading off. "Comes in rather handy, actually. Look here."

Naia peered around him and saw a set of markings etched into the wall. Quin leaned closer, examining them with keen interest. "Well now, I wonder what that means."

Naia took him by the arm, turning him away from the inscription. "It means you need to keep out," she said firmly. "That passage leads to a warded hall, and you're not welcome there. You could walk in there. But you'd never walk back out again."

"Interesting." Quin ran a hand back through his hair then set his wet hat on his head. "What's so important that it needs warding?"

There were some secrets a demon like Quin Reis should not know. Perhaps this was one of them. Or perhaps this was something he really should know. Naia decided on the latter. With a sigh, she informed him, "That passage leads to the Hall of the Masters. It is a shrine dedicated to the souls of mages who have passed on to the Atrament."

"I see. And since I'm damned…"

"You don't belong there, Quin. I'm sorry." She said it as gently as she could. Even so, it sounded harsh to her ears. "If you were to walk in there, you might make it halfway to the center of the room. Then the wards would be activated. The last thing you would see would be a brilliant flare of light as your soul incurred the wrath of the goddess…and then nothing. Forever."

Quin stared apathetically at the passage. "Doesn't sound entirely bad. I can certainly think of worse. I'm destined for worse, come to think of it."

"It would not be painful," Naia agreed. "But it would be very final."

Quin dismissed the assessment with a wave. "Anything's better than an eternity spent in hell. Perhaps it's an option I should remember for later."

Naia could only gaze at him, agreeing with him quietly in her heart. He didn't seem that awful of a person. She couldn't wish an eternity of suffering upon his soul, no matter what sins he had committed.

"Let's go," she prompted gently.

He turned and walked beside her down the dim corridor, soft mist swirling out of their path like a writhing mass of snakes. The air was sharply cold but not humid here. It had a stale, dry quality that smelled of dust and old decay. Naia scarcely noticed. She was used to the atmosphere of the place. She had spent years of her life within these passages. If anything, the odor was slightly nostalgic.

She led Quin out of the tunnel and into a vast chamber honeycombed with vaults that contained the remains of the dead. The walls stretched higher than she could see, until they disappeared, lost in distance and shadow. A cold breeze sweet with the stench of rot rustled her skirt. There was magelight here, glowing in the recesses of the vaults. She could make out the shrouded corpses in the lowest levels.

Quin made a face at the ripe odor, craning his neck to look up into the endless heights of the surrounding walls. Naia took him by the hand, leading him forward. They walked into what looked like a small city or a maze, past mausoleums and ancient sarcophagi, monuments and statues with faces of the deceased. They were on a street of sorts in a city of the dead. The stench of decomposition grew stronger, almost overwhelming. Quin covered his nose with the collar of his coat. He looked back at

Naia with a look of apology.

She couldn't blame him. She remembered how it had been for her, so long ago. When she had first begun ministering to the dead. Before she'd become accustomed to the culture of decay.

They walked onto a bridge that spanned a river of what looked like black water. It wasn't water, Naia knew. But she wasn't about to tell Quin that. Not all cadavers ended up in the vaults. Not every corpse was worth the space. Or the effort. The black liquid below took care of the rest.

They reached the end of the bridge and exited the cavern, passing under a horseshoe arch decorated with iron filigree. The ever-present mist tumbled forward ahead of them, creating an illuminated path that split just ahead. One fork led to the next vast room of vaults. The other veered away toward chambers she was eager to avoid.

Quin stopped at the fork, looking at a side passage with speculation in his eyes. Naia didn't wait for him, knowing that was not a path he should tread. She walked quickly toward the curving passage ahead, calling back to him over her shoulder, "Hurry, it's this direction. We still have a long way to go."

She'd taken several steps before she realized he wasn't following. She stopped, turning to glance back with a feeling of trepidation. She could see the glow of his body clearly through the fog, moving toward the open doors.

"Quin," she called, starting after him. Her shrill voice rang strangely in the darkness, as if muffled or half-muted.

He paid no attention. She wasn't sure that he heard.

Naia hurried toward him, catching him by the shoulder and forcing him to turn around. "What are you doing?" she demanded. He had no business going past that door. She knew what was there; she could taste the danger like metal on her tongue.

Quin didn't answer. Instead, he shrugged out of her grasp and strode into the dim chamber, following an illuminated path of mist. Naia trailed behind him, unsure of what to do. He seemed determined to ignore her.

"Quin, stop. Please trust me. You don't want to go in there."

The hall they entered was empty, save for one columned structure at the far end: a mausoleum made of glistening white marble with veins of gold. The glowing mist led straight toward it like a signal beacon. Quin lurched toward the mausoleum as if compelled. He only stopped when he encountered the iron grate that guarded the entrance to the tomb.

He gripped the wrought iron bars and gave the grate a sharp tug. When it didn't give, he started wrenching at it, rattling the bars as if trying to rip them off their hinges. When the grate still refused to budge, he whirled back toward her, eyes burning with fury and frustration.

"How do you open this?"

"Why?" Naia demanded. "You don't understand what you're doing. Why do you want in there?"

"Because of that!" He pointed above the tomb's entrance, to a triangular slab of marble held up by fluted columns, where the word REIS was etched into the stone. Naia stared at the letters then stared at Quin, feeling deflated.

He looked at her with self-hating desperation in his eyes. "How do I open it?"

Sighing, she yielded to his need, though it went against her better judgment. She reached out and took hold of the grate, pressing the release mechanism on the back. With a throaty groan that sounded like a death rattle, the grate swung outward. Quin stood for a moment with his hand lingering on the marble of the doorway, staring into the dim shadows beyond. His face was stern and haunted. Solemn but resolute.

Naia felt a twinge of apprehension in her chest as she watched him take an echoing step inside, crossing onto the marble tiles of the floor. She moved to follow him, magelight trailing in beneath her feet. There wasn't much space within; it was a small room just big enough for two people, white marble walls to either side. Halfway up the wall in front of her, an anchored vase held a single white rose. She pressed her hand against the cool face of the marble, running her fingers over the etched words:

SEPHANA CLEMLEY
PRIME WARDEN OF AERYSIUS

The rose blossom looked perfectly fresh, as if it had been placed there just that morning. Naia reached out, touching the marble on the opposite wall. There, in letters carved boldly into the polished surface:

BRADEN REIS
FIRST OF THE SENTINELS

Reading that name, she felt a lump rise to her throat. She turned to look at Quin, wondering what he must be feeling. She knew from previous conversations with him that he had never come to terms with his brother's death. She supposed it might be good for him to confront his feelings about it. Grief had a purpose, after all. It was the first step of forgiveness, of letting go.

Quin stood next to her wrapped in his glowing aura of corrupted light, hat in hand, head bowed solemnly. The other hand rested against the wall of his brother's tomb. He was leaning on it heavily, staring downward at the ground. He stood there silently, reverently, alone with his loss.

At last he looked up and asked, "Is there a way to open it?"

Naia frowned, profoundly disturbed by the request. Opening tombs was something that simply wasn't done. It went far beyond disrespect, to a place that bordered on blasphemy. "Why would you want to open it?" she whispered, appalled.

"I want to see him." Quin's gaze was hard, his face resolved. He wasn't asking her permission.

Naia wasn't sure what to do. He was obviously distraught. She set a hand on his arm, seeking to comfort him. Or at least deter him. "Quin. Your brother has been dead for a thousand years."

He shook his head. "I don't care. I want to see him."

She had dealt with grief before; it was something she was used to. She had trained most of her life to deal with the circumstances surrounding death. Not just the care of the departed, but also tending to the wounds of loved ones left behind. But this went far beyond grief; she could see it in his eyes. This was something different. It wasn't grief. It was guilt.

She resorted to appealing to his morals. "It's not right to disturb the peace of the dead. It's disrespectful. And undignified."

Quin shot her a hostile glare. "Is that why you chose to wake Sareen? Because disturbing the dead is undignified? Don't patronize me—just tell me how to open it."

He turned and felt along the marble wall, at last locating one of the release mechanisms that would, if depressed, unlock his brother's crypt. Naia reached out and caught his hand.

"Please. Braden earned his rest."

But Quin was apparently disinterested in his brother's rest. He was drowning in guilt and shame. Quin's gaze seared through the filthy green aura that framed his face, a white-eyed look of wildness and reproach.

"Just tell me how to open this gods-damned box!"

Naia realized there was no use trying to dissuade him. She didn't understand his need but, then again, she didn't have to. Perhaps this would help him put the past in perspective. More likely, it would leave a permanent scar, like ripping open an old wound. She just hoped it didn't fester.

Naia reached up and turned his face toward her. Gazing into his eyes, she said very carefully, "Quin. I need you to understand something before we open this. It's important. I'm sure the temple worked very hard to insure your brother was well-preserved. But a thousand years is an awfully long time. He may not look anything like you remember."

He grimaced, growling through clenched teeth, "That's the problem—I can't remember! I don't remember what Braden looked like, and I promised I'd never forget! I gave him my word…" He swallowed, looking feeble.

Adamant, Naia shook her head. "This isn't the answer, Quin. I don't think your brother would want you to see him like this."

He jerked back from her. "Listen to me plainly: *I don't care.* Open it. Now."

Naia sighed, collecting herself. "If you insist." She leaned forward, depressing the twin mechanisms recessed on either side of the wall. There was the slightest clicking sound. Then the marble face of the crypt parted at the seams. Naia twisted the device, creating handles to slip her fingers through. She pulled, putting her back into it; the marble face was heavier than it looked. It folded down, the drawer of the crypt sliding effortlessly out of the wall.

Inside the drawer lay a body covered by a thin shroud.

Naia's breath caught in her throat. She knew who

lay beneath that delicate fabric. The legend of Braden Reis overshadowed the accomplishments of any other mage in all of history. He was not only the founder of the Order of Sentinels; he was the one man who had stood opposed to Zavier Renquist.

She glanced at Quin, feeling terrible for him. And terrible for his brother. This was not the choice she would have favored for either of them. Or for the temple she had once held allegiance to.

She feared what lay beneath that cotton shroud.

Quin stared at the covered remains, his face fixed in a scowl of infinite sorrow. Solemnly, he reached down and fingered the fabric of the shroud. He whispered, "I want to see him."

Naia closed her eyes, a nervous wave of tension passing over her. She let out a lingering sigh. Then she took hold of the shroud's soft fabric and drew it back.

At her side, Quin made a quiet gasping sound.

She already knew what her action had uncovered. She didn't have to look. She drew the fabric lower, folding it down. She smoothed it out with her hand. Only then did Naia open her eyes to gaze upon the remains.

Braden Reis was garbed in the indigo robes of the Lyceum, his hands folded neatly over his chest. Naia stared down at him for a long moment, afraid to move. Afraid to say anything. She was too frozen by dismay.

Quin whispered, "I don't understand…"

Naia did. The remains of Quin's brother had not been preserved. Instead, Braden Reis had been frozen in time. His flesh had been placed here scant minutes after death, probably before the body had even cooled. Here within the spelled wonder of the Catacombs, time had not been allowed to touch his flesh to work its ills. Whoever had tended his remains had done well by him. He was perfect in every way: the flush of life still touched his cheeks. His hands looked supple, the skin smooth and plump. He was a handsome man, far more so than his brother. There was a strength about him that even death could not deny.

Quin shook his head, drawing in a shuddering breath. "How is this possible?"

Feeling terrible for him, Naia took him by the hand. She said in a lowered voice, "The Temple has many holy mysteries. This is one. I'm sorry, but I'm not at liberty to elaborate."

Quin's eyes widened. Then they narrowed. "You knew!" he accused. "You knew he'd be like this! That's why you didn't want me to see him!"

Naia struggled to maintain her composure. It was difficult; there was so much she wanted to tell him. And so much she could not. "Quin. It's time. We've disturbed your brother's peace long enough."

"No." He shook his head, drawing back from her. "Wait. You can bring him back! Like you did to Sareen! You can bring him back, can't you?" His eyes were wide, glinting in desperation.

But Naia was already shaking her head, fending off the idea by waving her hands in front of him. "No! Quin, I can't bring him back."

"Why not?"

Because it was forbidden.

"I could heal his body," Naia confessed, avoiding his eyes. Instead she stared down into the face of his dead brother. "Maybe with prayer and supplication, we could convince the goddess to part the Veil of Death. But Braden was a mage, not a demon like Sareen. I have no way to heal the loss of his legacy. You know as well as I: once a person inherits the gift, it becomes inseparable from their life-force. We would be healing him just to watch him die all over again. I'm sorry, Quinlan. I truly am. You must say goodbye to your brother now. I'm going to wait outside."

She squeezed his arm then turned to slip past him. As she did, something in the drawer caught her eye. Something tucked beneath the shroud, only one silver glint visible to the eye. She knew instantly what it was. While Quin was focused on his brother's face, Naia scooped the silver necklace up in her hand and fled the mausoleum, head bowed, shoulders shaking, hands clasped in front of her. She ran forward through the glowing spill of mist without aim or direction. She didn't have a destination in mind; she just wanted to get away. She couldn't escape the image of Braden Reis. It followed her even as she fled.

Naia chanced a glance back over her shoulder, then paused and opened her hand. She held up the object she had stolen from the crypt: a silver medallion with a dull, black stone of many facets that hung from two silver bands. Just the sight of the Soulstone made her sick. She thrust it deeply into the pocket of her cloak, then turned to wait for Quin.

It was a reckoning long overdue; she sincerely hoped he'd found what he sought so desperately.

She had the troubled feeling that he hadn't.

Chapter Sixteen
Lessons in Patience

Pass of Lor-Gamorth, The Front

The wind howled under the door, fanning the candle's fragile flame. The shadows in the room flickered, first growing bolder then shrinking. The wind gusted again with a howl that sounded like the shriek of a dying animal. The candle's flame blazed to life, flaring for a split-second before dying.

Kyel stared at the cooling wick, willing the tiny flame back to life. It sprang up with a jubilant glow, as if excited to be reborn.

Kyel pushed away the text he'd been studying and grumbled, "I don't understand this passage at all. It says, 'a net preponderance of shadow is required to offset a net preponderance of light.' How is that bloody possible? Isn't shadow just the absence of light?"

"Let me see it." Meiran extended her hand without looking at him, engrossed in the scroll she'd been reading.

Kyel shoved the book toward her and watched as she turned to settle over it, one elbow on the table, palm supporting her head. Her eyes scanned slowly over the scrawled writing. Finally, she shook her head, shoving the text back in his direction. "I'm not a Sentinel. I know very little about the nature of light. What I do know is this: we don't have much time. So if you come across pages like this that you find yourself struggling with, just skip over them and move on to something else."

From the other end of the room, Cadmus cleared his throat. "Pardon, Prime Warden, but do you mind if I take a look at it?"

Meiran didn't glance up at him. "Go ahead."

Kyel got up and walked the book over to Cadmus, who donned a pair of spectacles then hunched over to read the passage. He pressed a finger to the page, trailing it beneath the lines of text as he read. When he was done, he looked up to consider Kyel over the frames of his lenses. "Well, it seems obvious to me. This type of shield forms from a web that absorbs or reflects weaponized light. Shadow, in this context, is merely referring to the web's capacity for absorption. Look, it says so right here." He tapped his finger on the page.

"Right." Kyel took the text back, snapping it closed without looking at it. "I'm sick and tired of energy transformations—they make my brain want to bleed!"

Cadmus shook his head. "You keep forgetting Nerid's Second Law."

Kyel tossed the book down on the table, throwing himself down in his seat. "Damn Nerid's Laws! If I want something to disappear, I'll bloody well make it disappear!"

"I've had enough." Meiran set the scroll she was reading down at her side, staring from face to face. "From both of you. Brother Cadmus, if you insist on continuing to interfere with Kyel's education, then have the grace to do so away from my presence. Kyel, patience is a skill that continues to elude you. I hear from the forgers that weaving mail is an excellent way to acquire patience. Go spend the rest of the day in the smithy."

Kyel gaped at her. "You're not serious?" There was a war coming. How could Meiran want him wasting his time when there was still so much to learn?

"I am. Consider this a demerit." Her tone brooked no argument. She picked the scroll back up, unrolling it in her hands.

Kyel stared back and forth between Meiran and Cadmus, blinking slowly. Then he whirled in disgust and careened through the door, slamming it behind him. He strode out of the tower into the inner ward, his black cloak billowing in the wind of his wake. He crossed the ward in a hurry, hot with anger. He was aware of the stares of the men on him, tracking his every motion. Everywhere he went, it was always the same.

A soldier guarding the cistern muttered the word "darkmage" and spat on the ground. Normally, Kyel would have ignored the insult. This time he stopped, spinning back toward the man. He grabbed the soldier by the collar and slammed him back against the wall.

"What's your name?" he demanded, not caring that half the yard had stopped to stare at him.

The bald soldier smirked, eyes laughing and daring him. "Go ahead. Do it. Show everyone what you're made of. It ain't gonna shock nobody."

"This is horse piss," Kyel gasped, leaning into the man's face. "I haven't done anything to you!"

"You're the Oathbreaker's little cunt. I was at Orien's Finger. I know what you mages really are."

"I am *not* Darien Lauchlin," Kyel growled. He released the man, forcing his sleeve back past his elbow and holding it up in front of him. "See? I've still got the chains of my Oath. I've never used my power to strike a man, and I never will."

The soldier scoffed, staring at the markings on Kyel's arm with a look of revulsion. "We'll see about that. We'll see what you do when the first spear comes at you and you piss your pants. 'Cause none of us here's gonna have your back. Most of us lost brothers or fathers at Orien's Finger. On the battlefield, you'll be on your own." He looked up into Kyel's face and sneered, chuckling softly. "You're gonna burn, boy. I and my mates, we're gonna watch."

Kyel stared at him, feeling the heat of anger scalding his cheeks. He didn't say anything; he was too shocked to respond. Instead he drew back, turned, and stalked away. He kept his stare fixed on the ground, knowing for certain that the eyes of every soldier in the courtyard were pinned on the embroidered star on his back.

Meiran stood up from her chair, crossed the room, then took the seat across the table from the temple watchdog who had managed to embed himself like a tick in their midst. His interference was starting to wear. She'd had just about enough.

The man looked up at her, a kindly smile on his face. He had gentle eyes, but his nose was bulbous and red with broken veins that extended onto his sagging cheeks. He was either too stupid or too smart to take her seriously. She suspected the latter.

Removing his spectacles with one hand, Cadmus rubbed his eyes and said to her, "I understand your frustration with my involvement, Prime Warden. But what we really need is a functional Sentinel, not soldiers with gaps in their mail coats."

"You and I must talk." Meiran leaned toward him with her elbows on the table. "I need the help of the temples, which is the only reason you're not straddling an ass back to Glen Farquist. You and I both know that the little 'agreement' you pulled over on Kyel means absolutely nothing. There *is* no more Aerysius; the office of prime warden was decapitated the day Emelda Lauchlin died. You have no authority whatsoever over Kyel or myself. I've only suffered your presence so far because I might be able to gain something by it."

The kindly smile didn't slip from his lips. Cadmus was simply sitting there, staring, blinking. He wore the same expression a parent would while patiently waiting a child to finish a tirade.

Meiran ignored him and went on, "You, on the other hand, have everything to lose. When the Reversal of the magic field happens, every one of your temple mysteries will become undone. Then everyone will know the truth: that your gods are made of tin, and your miracles are manufactured. What will you do when the only true power in the world comes from a hole in the ground and is wielded by demons hell-bent on destroying you?"

Cadmus' expression didn't crack. If anything, his smile broadened. "We need each other, Prime Warden," he said finally. "Our 'manufactured miracles,' as you call them, are the only chance you have of stopping Xerys' armies. You and Kyel are both crippled by your Oath and too self-righteous to acknowledge it. Without the aid of the temples, the Rhen will most assuredly fall."

His eyes took on a look of sympathy. "It pains me to say this, but I'm sure you already know: both you and Kyel are already dead. Your corpses just haven't finished twitching yet. When all is said and done, what kind of legacy do you wish to leave behind? If you cooperate with the temples, at least some small remnant of civilization will remain. If you don't…then the world will belong entirely to Xerys, to be forever remade in *His* image. I don't think you'd want that."

It was like someone had just drenched her with a bucket of ice-cold fury. Meiran felt physically numbed by the shock of it. For moments, she could do nothing more than just sit there, glaring at him contemptuously, hoping that somehow the violence in her eyes approached the wrath she felt inside.

"Why do we need your help?" she asked in a whispered hiss.

Cadmus shrugged and spread his hands, the patient smile returning to his pudgy face. "Because we are not Bound. And we have the power to bring them down."

Her wrath condensed, sharpening into threat. "Then I hope you have a plan."

His smile was oily and triumphant. "Don't worry, Prime Warden. We do."

Kyel dropped another circular piece of wire onto the anvil. He picked up a blacksmith's hammer and, taking careful aim, started pounding the wire ring. It took about ten solid hits before it was perfectly flat, the ends overlapping. He picked it up and threw the flattened ring into a bucket full of other flattened rings, just one among hundreds.

Another thirty thousand of those, and they may have enough for a mail shirt. Of course, that was all Kyel knew how to do. An actual blacksmith would have to do the punching and riveting and link the chains into the right pattern.

He picked up yet another circlet of precut wire. Ten or twelve solid hits on the anvil, and another flattened ring went into the bucket with a *clink*. He thrust his fingers into the can and picked up another wire.

"What the hell are you doing?"

Kyel turned to find Traver gawking at him from the doorway. He went ahead and pounded the next ring flat before plunking it in the bucket. "Hammering chain."

Traver strolled over, face distorted by an expression of incredulity. "What the bloody hell for? We've got blacksmiths to do that!"

Kyel shrugged, pounding out another ring. "I'm supposed to be learning patience." He tossed the finished ring into the bucket.

"And are you?"

Kyel turned toward him, massaging his right arm. "No." He sighed wearily.

He cast a dispirited glance at Traver, motioning to the bucket of flattened rings. Traver plunged his fingers in and picked up a handful. He nudged them around in his palm before tipping his hand and allowing them to spill back out.

"Doing that all day would make me desperately *im*patient," Traver said, running a hand through his hair. Then he grabbed Kyel by the arm, firmly steering him toward the door.

"Come along. Day's done already; you may as well come back tomorrow. How 'bout you join me for a drink?"

Kyel tossed the hammer down then followed the captain into the chill night air of the ward. The lights of bonfires danced from the corners of the yard, sparks zipping through the air like glowing fireflies. Halfway across the courtyard, he became aware of the stares he was collecting. Which brought back the memory of the soldier he'd confronted.

Kyel glared at the first sentry they came to, a bearded man guarding the tower's entrance. "What are you looking at?"

The soldier glared back at him, jaw clenched tight in a scowl of disgust.

Traver stepped forward, scant inches from the man's face. "He asked you a question, soldier. I think you'd better answer him."

The guard's hard eyes focused on Kyel. "I'm lookin' at a dead man, Captain." He spat on the ground, the glob landing between Kyel's feet.

Traver threw both hands out and slammed the man back against the wall. Kyel caught hold of him, pulling him back. "It's fine, Traver! Leave him be!"

"It's not fine!" Traver ducked out of Kyel's grasp and shot forward, grabbing the soldier by a fistful of hair and bringing a fist back to throw a punch. The man didn't fight, but neither did he cower. He received the blow willingly, his head cracking back against the wall. He leaned forward, spitting out a tooth along with a drooling string of blood.

Traver gave him a last, good shove. "Report your ass to latrine duty!"

"Aye, Captain." The man saluted and strode briskly away, leaving his bloody tooth behind on the ground. Traver glared after him, looking fit to kill.

"It's not his fault." Kyel sighed, staring down at the tooth.

"What do you mean? You're the last damn Sentinel we have! You're the only thing between us and those demons out there—so they'd better start respecting that cloak on your back."

Kyel shook his head. "Respect has to be earned. I haven't done anything to earn it."

Traver nodded slowly. Then he turned, clapping Kyel on the back. "Come on. Let's get some mead in you." He guided Kyel into the tower, up to his own quarters on the third floor. There, he pulled Kyel up a chair and rummaged around in a wooden chest, pulling out a sack of mead. He poured them each a cup, brandishing his own in the air before throwing his head back and chugging it down.

"So how'd you make captain with only half a hand?" Kyel asked him, taking a sip of mead. He made a face. It was wretchedly strong, and he wasn't used to the taste of fermented honey.

"Well, I had seniority," Traver shrugged. "And it wasn't like I could go back to being a foot soldier. So Craig stuck me in the armory and helped me work myself up."

"So you have Royce's old job?" Kyel asked, trying another sip. This one went down harder than the last. He smacked his lips together, running his sleeve across his mouth.

Traver shook his head. "Nothing all that grand; I'm in charge of requisitions." He drained his cup and poured more. "So tell me…you've been getting a lot of that kind of treatment?"

Kyel took a heavy gulp and made a face as it went down. "It's not their fault. Ever since Orien's Finger, there's just no trust for mages. People fear what they don't understand."

"Aerysius wasn't destroyed that long ago," Traver pointed out. He dropped down on his cot, sliding his boots off and throwing them in the corner. "People should still remember what the Sentinels stood for."

They should, Kyel supposed. But they didn't. "All they remember is Darien," he said regretfully. "He didn't make it very easy for people to trust him."

"No. He sure didn't." Traver knocked back another swallow.

"I need to change that before the battle," Kyel said. For some reason, the mead was starting to taste a whole lot better. It was calming his nerves, making it easier to think, even as the magic field tapered off. What the soldier in the yard had said to him had shaken him up more than he'd realized. He needed the men to have his back. He had to be able to trust the soldiers defending him. But in order for that to happen, they'd have to trust him. It seemed like a paradox.

"Aye, you're going to need to work on that," Traver agreed. "You can't lead men who see you as a threat." He glanced sidelong at Kyel. "How long's it been since you've played a game of cards?"

Kyel couldn't help the grin that slipped to his face. "Too long, actually."

Traver immediately set his cup down and produced a pack from his pocket. His hands went to work shuffling, expertly sending the cards dancing between his fingers. His skills had improved considerably, Kyel realized, especially considering he was short two fingers. Traver sent the cards into a showering cascade then offered the pack for Kyel to split.

"All right. What do you got to bet?"

Kyel split the deck, then groped at his pockets, finding only a few coppers, a small rock, and a tiny ball of lint. Traver snatched up the rock, holding it in his palm with an expression of delight on his face.

"Isn't this the same damn rock you used to carry around?"

Kyel had to chuckle. "It is. I picked it up on the practice yard two years ago. It's my lucky rock. Although I'm not sure its luck has been working lately." The piece of white quartz had stood out at him from all the black rocks of the pass. He'd picked it up to remind himself of what hope looked like. He'd carried it with him ever since.

Traver tossed the stone back to him. "You need to keep that. Don't be gambling with it."

"So what, if you win it from me? You might need

the luck more than I do."

"Oh, no!" Traver shook his head. "I wouldn't take your damn luck for all the gold in Chamsbrey. But I will take those coppers off you, so you'd better ante up."

———

"Are you sure?"

Devlin Craig let his hand fall to his side, still clutching the report. The old soldier named Kelbs gave a slight shrug. His face was as hard and cratered and cold as a winter in the pass. He had a no-nonsense way about him that suffered no stupidity.

"Those are the best estimates we've got, Commander."

Craig squeezed his hand, crumpling the strip of parchment. "Gods be damned."

"Don't blame the gods, Commander," Kelbs advised in a practiced monotone. "Blame our own damned lack of foresight. We should have seen this coming."

"You mean *I* should have seen this coming," Craig growled.

He trudged over to the table with its collection of maps strewn across it. He leaned over, planting both hands on the table. He examined the array of implements already spread out across the surface and took a deep breath. Then he started moving rocks and broadheads, repositioning them.

"They're draining all the Black Lands," he decided finally. "They're sending everything they've got against us."

To the two officers still lingering by the door, he said, "Send messengers to generals Blandford and Horthall. I want the Northern armies pitched at our rear. And I want men up on those ridges tomorrow, planting powder kegs and laying out charges. If they want to take the pass, we'll let them. But we'll make it their graveyard."

To the old sergeant, he directed, "Prioritize supply. We need provisions. And arrows—as many arrows as you can get. There shouldn't be one goose with a feather on its wings anywhere between here and Rothscard."

"Aye, Commander. How long do you think we have?"

Craig took one last glance at the maps, feeling fate kick him in the ass. "Not long enough."

Chapter Seventeen
Blood Feud

Tokashi Palace, The Black Lands

Darien awoke to soft rustling noises coming from the other side of the room. He cracked his eyes open just enough to gaze across the dim bedchamber. He could make out his wife's silhouette illuminated by the wan glow of an oil lamp. She was kneeling in the corner, rummaging around in the small chest he kept there. Darien watched her closely, not sure how he felt about the situation. He kept some very private tokens in that chest. She had no business going near it.

He sat up.

His movement caught her attention. Seeing him awake, Azár turned and smiled, making her way toward the bed. She knelt next to him. Her hair spilled freely down her back, unconstrained. Her eyes were wide and dark like a sea after sunset.

"It is time to wake, my husband," she said. "I was just finishing packing. I hope you don't mind, but I put a few of my own things in your chest."

"I don't mind," he responded, settling back into the deep pillows of the bed. That explained her invasion of his privacy, he supposed, although he still didn't like it. He rubbed his eyes, wishing she'd go away. He was naked beneath the blankets and feeling the usual morning urgency. The proximity of her soft skin wasn't helping the situation.

"I need my clothes," he grumbled.

She handed him his trousers. He struggled into them beneath the covers then walked stiffly into the adjoining bath. Bracing himself with a hand against the wall, he had to lean forward to angle his stream into the keyhole-shaped opening in the floor. When he returned to the bedchamber, Azár was still there, now sitting in the chair by the writing desk. He didn't understand why she remained; in the days since their wedding, she'd made a steady practice of avoiding him.

He found a fresh shirt and pulled it on, covering it with his new black cloak: a present from his wife. He bent over, pulling his boots on by the straps. She watched him the whole while, eyes tracking his every motion.

"Are you packed?" he asked her, more to break the tension than anything else.

"I am."

She had brought few belongings with her to the palace. Most of her physical wealth she carried on her person in the form of jewelry he'd given her as part of her bride-gift. But all the jewels in the world were worthless in comparison to the true wealth that Azár was rich in: the character and quality of her magelight. That was a princely treasure, worth more than any riches.

There was a knock at the door and Sayeed entered alone, bowing gracefully. He looked a little puzzled at finding Azár and Darien in the same room together. He'd been conspicuously restrained ever since the second bed had been hauled in and Darien's ghastly hound evicted to the stable.

Sayeed said, "Word has come from Bryn Calazar that the Kajiri portal is now available to us. We have only four days to empty the Khazahar of all its people."

Four days. That wasn't much time.

Thankfully, the tribes were gathered in the valley below; they'd been trickling in little by little since before the wedding feast. Still, the journey down into the ice caverns was difficult. It would also take time to move that many people through two transfer portals. First, a journey to Bryn Calazar, the hub that connected all the portals in the Black Lands. Then another transfer to Kajiri Flats, where Malikar's armies were staging. They would have to be precise about the logistics, or the evacuation could quickly degrade into disaster.

"Get the first twenty battalions through the portal," Darien said, buckling his warbelt. "Then the baggage. Then the civilians. Have the rest of the battalions bring up the rear."

Sayeed bowed his way out the door as a young girl entered with a breakfast tray. Darien helped himself to a piece of flatbread, absently offering a bowl of fruit to Azár. He tore off a bite, then set himself to the task of packing up the ink pots and parchment on the writing desk.

"You are quiet this morning," Azár said. "Why?"

Darien shrugged. "I'm bringing war against my own homeland. I still have friends there." He stooped to tuck the papers in his hand into the chest, checking the stoppers on the inkwells.

Azár finished chewing, her eyes studying him intensely. She asked, "And how does that make you feel?"

He turned to look at her. "It makes me feel sick." His voice carried more venom than he'd intended. He strove to modify his tone. "I don't understand why any of this is necessary. I'm still hoping that more reasonable minds will prevail."

She raised her eyebrows, plucking another plump grape off its stem. "More reasonable minds than Meiran?"

"That's what I meant." He put the ink pots into the chest and closed the lid.

She asked, "Do you still think it's possible to negotiate with them?"

"I don't know. I aim to try." He slid into the chair opposite her, one arm resting on the desk. Looking at her suspiciously, he probed, "And what about you? You're about to leave everything you've ever known behind. How does that make you feel?"

She shrugged dismissively, her face bland. "There is nothing that holds me here. I have seen the face of the sun. I've felt the warmth of it on my skin. I want to feel the sun again."

Darien understood. It was no more than she deserved. He said, "I'll give you the sun, Azár, if it's within my power."

Her kohl-lined eyes stared at him suspiciously. But then a dazzling smile dawned on her face, glowing brighter than any sun that he remembered.

"Then I know I will see it," she said. "Because there is nothing that is outside of your power."

He grimaced, finding the statement ironic.

"What?" she asked.

"That's just a lot of faith. I hope I can live up to it." He scooted his chair back, standing up. "Are you ready? We've a long road ahead of us."

She set the fruit down on her plate. Then she rose, drawing her scarf up over her head. It was bright turquoise, a color that complemented her skin tone perfectly.

Darien took one last look around the chamber, wondering if he'd miss it. He thought he would. It was the most luxurious quarters he'd ever had. He doubted he'd ever find better. He wasn't sure how much longer he even had left in this world. Not very much, he was afraid. It felt like time was speeding up, winding tighter like a spring about to snap.

He offered his arm to Azár, his innocent wife who was just as doomed as he was. He tried not to think about it, shoving the thought aside. He would save that worry for another time. It didn't matter, really. The Reversal was coming, and there wasn't a damned thing anyone could do about it. Especially not him.

Together, they walked away from the Residence enveloped by a cluster of Zakai. Two horses were led toward them, their hoofs *clop-clopping* on the tiles. Alongside his red stallion trotted the demon-hound, its nose to the floor, eyes like glowing green coals. At the sight of its master, the beast cocked its ears forward, its throat emitting a low purr. Or perhaps it was a growl; he really couldn't tell. The beast had been relegated to the stable ever since the wedding, much to the horses' dismay.

Darien helped Azár onto the mare that was part of her bride-gift, then waited as an officer held his own stirrup for him to mount. The Zakai led the horses forward by their tasseled bridles, the sounds of their hoofbeats echoing off the walls.

As the doors to the Residence closed behind them for the last time, Darien couldn't help but wonder if the sounds of their passage would be the last to ever ring in Tokashi's magnificent halls. They were leaving the Black Lands, possibly forever. Unless he could find a way to clear the curse over the skies, there would never be a reason to return.

Kajiri Flats, The Front

The horses didn't like the transfer portals.

Darien's stallion reared and nearly bolted, while Azár's mount put its head down and bucked like an unbroken colt. After the first transfer to Bryn Calazar, both horses balked, refusing to enter the second portal. Only after their heads had been wrapped in cloth did they relent and allow themselves to be led under the cross-vaulted arch.

There was an intense flash. And then Darien found himself stepping out onto the black dirt of a floodplain he'd only ever looked down upon from the pass above. Directly ahead loomed a familiar peak: the Spire of Orguleth. He'd only ever seen it from the other side. The peak on the left must be Maidenclaw, though it looked nothing maiden-like from this direction.

He unwrapped his horse's head and looked around with a growing mixture of wonder and dismay. He'd never seen so many tents. They stretched out toward the vast horizons in every direction, arranged in perfect rows. Each tent had a lantern that hung before it on a pole. Thousands of tents. Thousands of lanterns. Thousands upon thousands of men and women.

The dark plain that swallowed them resembled a night sky full of stars. Above, the clouds roiled as the clouds ever did, racing and crackling with uneasy energies deep within their depths. His horse snorted, bobbing its head and stamping a hoof.

A group of Tanisars moved forward, speaking in hushed voices to Sayeed. The Zakai officer turned to Darien, translating, "Our camp is to the south, Lord. Your tent has been made ready. However, your presence is requested in the command pavilion."

Darien nodded. "Please have my wife escorted to our tent."

"It will be as you say." The man bowed.

Azár glanced at Darien but said nothing; it was impossible to read her eyes. She gazed at him with absolute trust and didn't bother saying goodbye. Darien watched Sayeed's men swarm protectively around her, leading her mount away. He was grateful for the Zakai; a woman of Azár's beauty had no business in a military encampment.

That was his first thought. Then he remembered the women who served in Bryn Calazar's legions and was reminded of his wife's ferocious nature. Perhaps a military encampment was exactly where Azár was intended to be.

Sayeed led his horse forward as soldiers emerged from the tents to watch their small procession through the camp. It didn't take Darien long to realize that it was not a warm reception. Many of the men and women that lined their path looked at him with hatred in their eyes, some spitting on the ground as he passed. No one spoke a word; the camp was eerily quiet. But the anger of the soldiers didn't need a voice.

Sayeed looked at him and explained, "These are the legions of Maridur. Their numbers were decimated in the last invasion. They will have no love for you."

Darien nodded without saying a word. All along their route, men and women spat and turned their backs to him. He could almost smell the stench of their hatred. It sapped the energy from him, making him feel drained and weary. He understood their anger and contempt; he had killed thousands of their comrades. Their anger was justified.

At last they reached the command tent, a purple pavilion supported by many poles. It was the size of a small house, with flaps tied back to serve as the opening to a dim interior. Their party drew up in front of it. Darien left his stallion with Sayeed and started walking forward.

"Darien Nach'tier!"

He turned just in time to see a spear hurling toward him. It gored him right through, pinning him fast to a tent post.

He gaped in shock at the trembling shaft sticking out of him. The world was darkening quickly, like heated paper charring at the edges. His mind groped frantically for the magic field as his vision faded. He drew in the field as hard as he could, throwing it mindlessly at the pain. Then he started screaming as his flesh began to burn.

The last thing Darien saw was Sayeed standing in

front of him, scimitar held high in a warding stance. Then he relaxed into darkness.

He was surprised that he woke at all.

Darien opened his eyes to find a familiar face staring down at him.

"Well, here we are again," said an equally familiar voice.

"And where is that?" he whispered hoarsely.

He was groggy, to the point that he couldn't make heads or tails of his surroundings. The woman leaning over him had dark brown skin and sleek ebony hair. She was elegant in an unusual way, beautiful without meaning to be.

He blinked a couple times, fumbling through hazy bleariness to remember her name. The woman placed a hand on his chest, closing her eyes. He could feel a faint stirring of power deep inside. She was another mage, and she was probing him, he realized.

"You are in my tent," she explained, smiling at him with her eyes. "I had your men bring you here so I could watch you while you recovered." Her smile slipped a bit. "You seem to have a hard time keeping yourself alive."

Her name finally came to him: Myria Anassis. He was surprised to see her there. He'd thought she was in Bryn Calazar with Renquist. With effort, he squirmed into a sitting position. "What happened?"

"As you can imagine, not all of Malikar's soldiers think highly of you. One man in particular decided that vengeance was more important than his own life. He lost his entire family at Orien's Finger. All five of his brothers. Do you understand the concept of blood feud?"

He did. Darien realized that he'd been a fool; he should have expected such an attack. "Thank you for saving me," he murmured.

Myria scoffed, trailing a hand down her waist-length hair. "You saved yourself. You burned the spear to ash and cauterized the wound. You were lucky; we couldn't have gotten to you in time."

He reached up, rubbing the place where the shaft had penetrated. There wasn't even a scar left. Myria had done a masterful job with the healing. He gazed at her in speculation, remembering the time she had healed him in Bryn Calazar, right after his arrival in the Black Lands. Then, she had propositioned him for sex. He'd rejected her at the time. The look in her eyes made him regret that decision.

She stood up. "Do you feel up to walking? Warden Connel would like a word with you. Well, more than a word. Frankly, I think he's quite pissed."

He still felt groggy, but figured he was up for a walk if he had to be. Darien pushed himself up off the pallet, rising stiffly. He looked down at his body, realizing he wasn't wearing much.

"Here's your trousers," Myria said, and tossed them to him. Her eyes lingered on his chest.

He caught the trousers and drew them on, lacing them up the front. Then he donned the tunic she handed him.

"And here's this." Myria offered him a chain hauberk. "Orders. You're not to go anywhere without at least a mail shirt. And I'm told you're to be fitted for a set of field plate."

Darien stared at the ring mail before accepting it with a shrug. He pulled it on over his head, tugging it down his chest. It was well-made, and not as heavy as it looked. He girded his belt over it then pulled on his boots, snatching his swords up off the ground.

"I hear you wed."

Darien glanced over his shoulder as he shoved the scimitar through his belt. "I did."

"Congratulations." Myria smiled in a friendly way, handing him his long sword. "I also hear the marriage remains unconsummated."

Darien paused in the action of shouldering his baldric. For a second he stood frozen. Then he straightened, turning away from her. "I suppose I'll have to speak to my men."

"Rumor flies swifter than the arrow," she assured him. "Don't blame your men, Darien. Blame your wife."

He turned to look back at her, searching her face.

"Don't worry," she commiserated, trailing a hand down the tent post that stood between them. "I understand a marriage of necessity. I had one of those myself once." She leaned forward, long hair swaying over her shoulders. "The offer I made is still open. If you ever get bored, well…you know where to find me."

Her words took him off-guard. Hadn't she just been congratulating him on his marriage? He stared at Myria, wondering what kind of city ancient Bryn Calazar must have been like. Obviously very different from Aerysius. She saw the look on his face and grinned, obviously happy to have unsettled him.

"Come on." She turned, beckoning for him to follow. "I'll show you to the command tent."

As soon as they stepped outside, Darien found himself confronted by two rows of Zakai who fell immediately to their knees. Sayeed walked toward him, head bowed, and fell to the black dirt at his feet. There was a small commotion as soldiers from the surrounding tents moved in closer to watch. Soon, Darien found himself surrounded by armed and spiteful men ringing him dangerously.

He was already grateful for the mail shirt.

His eyes scanned the crowd warily, at last coming to rest on a man who knelt behind the row of officers, his wrists and ankles bound. The man bled from his nose and an abrasion over his eye.

Head bowed, Sayeed offered Darien the hilt of his own sword. "I failed you, Lord. Please take my life."

Darien ignored him and walked instead to the prisoner bound on the ground. He recognized him now. It was the man who'd assaulted him with the spear.

He knelt in front of him. The warrior's dark eyes regarded him with fierce abhorrence before he tried to turn his face away. Darien reached out and caught his chin, denying him. He forced the man to look him in the eye.

"I understand I killed your brothers," he said.

The prisoner made a snarling noise and showered him with a rain of spittle. Darien wiped his face dry on his shirt sleeve. Then he leaned closer, as if daring the man to do it again.

"I understand anger," he said softly. "I understand vengeance. That's why you have to die."

Darien rose, summoning the magic field. He turned his back as the screams began. He strode toward Sayeed. He could hear the prisoner thrashing on the ground behind him, howls turning to shrieks as the anguish became unbearable. Darien paused, focusing his stare at the ground, listening to the gruesome sounds of death by implosion. The rhythm of the convulsions went on and on, finally expiring with a popping noise. When Darien turned to look back, what was left of the body was still twitching spastically.

The remaining soldiers had drawn back away from him a fair distance. He glared his anger at the gathered crowd, raising his voice. "Anyone else feel the need to settle a score? Let's get this over with *now.*"

Apparently, no one did.

When not a soul came forward to challenge him, he turned his wrath on the kneeling Zakai. "You failed me once. Never fail me again. *Now, get up.*"

He tugged at the magic field until energy clawed like blue flames over his body. The men sprang back away, fear wild in their eyes. Darien trudged forward, his very presence boring a hole right through the center of the crowd.

Myria followed, her face smug as she jogged forward. "You're creating a scene," she whispered when she caught up. "That mail shirt won't stop everything they can hurl at you."

"I don't care."

He stopped, scanning the dark plain ahead for sight of the pavilion, changing his course toward it. Seeing the hostile energies leaking out of him, soldiers moved back, scrambling out of his way. Darien let a wash of azure magelight erupt from the ground in front of him, trailing forward to light and clear his path. People saw it as a sign, backing away with their palms held up in a gesture against evil.

Darien released the magic field as he stopped before the pavilion. He ducked as he entered, thrusting back the tent flap. The interior was dark and dappled with ruddy light. The scent of agarwood did a poor job of masking the stench of sweat and coal smoke. The tent was larger than it had looked from the outside, with multiple rooms cordoned off by hanging fabric, the floor carpeted by ornate rugs. To one side, a group of people were arguing heatedly over a table dominated by an oversized map. Darien couldn't help but stare at the two women among their number who seemed even more vocal in their military opinions than either of the men. One was pounding a fist on the map to elucidate her point.

"This way."

Myria pulled back the fabric of a partition and guided him into another, dimmer area. Darien ducked as he went in, straightening to find himself staring at Byron Connel. The Warden of Battlemages reclined on a long sofa positioned up against a wall of the tent. He leaned forward, setting a waterpipe down on the rug as he beckoned Darien to come forward.

Darien stiffened, wanting nothing more to do with the man. Memories of their last encounter still haunted his nightmares.

"There you are," the Battlemage said, standing up. He clasped Darien in a mercifully quick embrace then turned to kiss Myria on the cheek.

"I'll leave the two of you alone," she said, smiling at Darien as she turned away. Her hand trailed down his back.

Connel chuckled. "You had him long enough. It's my turn." He sat back down on the sofa and lifted the pipe, putting the mouthpiece to his lips. He waved his hand, indicating the seat across from him made from a bale of hay wrapped in cloth. Darien sat heavily, eyeing Myria through a gap in the partition.

Connel said, "I hear you've been trying to get yourself killed before the fighting starts."

Darien couldn't help but grin. "That wasn't my intention, actually."

"Yes, well, intentions are always worth their weight in gold, aren't they?" Connel took a heavy draw on the pipe.

Darien shrugged. "I suppose they are."

Connel set the pipe down, his face going grim. "Welcome to the Front, Darien. Here's the situation: about half the population of Malikar wants you dead for what you did at Orien's Finger. The other half would rather see you tortured slowly over a long period of time. Which is unfortunate, because they're the ones tasked with keeping you alive on a battlefield. So you're already at a disadvantage."

Darien sighed. "I never figured it would be easy."

Connel narrowed his eyes. "It's not going to be. You'll be a target everywhere you go."

He passed him the waterpipe. Darien accepted it, drawing the smoke into his lungs. The tobacco went down smoothly, with a strong taste of fruitwood. It was decadent, unlike anything he'd ever experienced in the Rhen.

"So what do you suggest I do?"

Connel appeared to be pondering the question as he accepted the pipe back. He sat with his face screwed into a frown for a long moment, hand resting on his bearded chin. At last, he said, "We'll have to find a way to prove your loyalty very publicly."

Darien wasn't sure he liked the sound of that. His thoughts went to his ordeal in Bryn Calazar, when he'd been paraded like a beaten slave through the streets of the city.

"And how are we going to do that?"

"I don't know. I'll come up with something." Connel glanced back at him. "In the meantime, make yourself at home. Just be careful. We'll be settled here for about another week as the last of the stragglers find their way to us. Then we'll be heading south."

South. Into the Rhen.

Darien felt the strangled chill of that thought settle into him, penetrating deep into his bones. He'd known when he'd come here that war was on the imminent horizon. But sitting at the Front in a command tent made it seem that much more of a reality. Quietly, he asked, "Any plans for negotiation?"

Connel shrugged. "There's plans. Of course, you'd be a part of any negotiations that take place."

Darien wasn't certain if that was a good idea. After his last interaction with Meiran, he didn't think he was capable of talking anymore. He asked, "What's the status of Greystone Keep?"

"It's been rebuilt."

"In only *two years?*" It seemed inconceivable. The monarchies of the Rhen had ceased to support Greystone's defenses in previous years. Apparently, the last invasion had shaken them up enough to make them reevaluate their priorities.

Connel said, "They allocated the resources and dug in."

Darien was having a hard time envisioning it. The logistics seemed impossible. Whoever had coordinated that effort already had his respect, and then some. "Who's their new force commander?"

"A man named Devlin Craig."

Darien shot up straight in his seat. "Craig?" Hope flared like a beacon in the darkness. But it was brief. Devlin Craig had been his friend, but that had been under different circumstances. Like Meiran, Craig would be opposed to him now. He'd see him as a traitor.

"You know him?" asked Connel.

"Aye. I know him."

"Will he work with us?"

Darien shook his head, breathing out a heavy sigh. His eyes gazed at the waterpipe. "I don't think so.

Although he might be willing to talk." If he could just get Craig to sit down at a table and hear him out…but no. He'd been unable to convince Meiran. What chance would he have with a man who'd forged a career defending the pass from the Enemy?

Connel leaned forward. "That's all for now. Go get some rest. You look like you need it. Oh, and congratulations on your nuptials."

Darien was taken aback that Connel already knew of his marriage to Azár. "My thanks," he muttered awkwardly, rising to his feet.

He swept the cloth partition aside, emerging into the main area of the command tent. The argument over the maps had wound down. The tent was quiet, filled with a slight haze of smoke that snaked through the slanted light from the lanterns. He turned toward the entrance but stopped as he spotted Myria seated on a cushion in the corner. She noticed him and rose, gliding over to stand in front of him.

"Leaving already?"

Darien nodded, feeling weary. "It's been a long day."

A mischievous grin sprang to her face. "We could make it a long night. I've got wine."

He blinked, shocked by her forwardness. He stared at her hard, taking her all in. Her smooth, dark skin, the sweet curve of her hips, the long drape of her hair. He had to admit, he found the offer enticing. The playfulness in her eyes sealed the deal.

"I suppose I could use a drink," he decided.

Myria's grin was triumphant. "Let's go out the back way," she urged. She scooped a conical helmet off the floor and handed it to him. "Here. Put this on."

Darien tugged the helm down over his head, figuring it wouldn't look too out of place in the context of their surroundings. He understood her intentions: the helm had a wide nose guard that would render him anonymous. He followed as Myria took him by the hand, guiding him out of the pavilion and into the darkness.

She led him across the bustling encampment that was oddly quiet for the amount of activity going on. None of the soldiers they passed paid him any mind; the helm did its job. The eyes of the men slipped right over him, past him, beyond him. They looked but didn't see; he was invisible.

In all his adult life, Darien couldn't remember one single day when he hadn't been the object of every stare. To be so completely inconspicuous was a bizarre feeling. A freeing feeling. No one noticed. No one cared.

Myria pushed back the cloth drape of her tent.

She made her way over to the far wall while he lingered in the entrance, struggling to remove his various armor and armaments, making a small pile of his things in the corner. She returned to present him with a cup of wine, which Darien accepted gladly. He stared down at the blood-red liquid in his hand. Then he raised the cup to his lips and let the wine slide down his throat. It did little to quench his thirst. He grimaced, handing it back.

Myria set the cup aside and drew him in for a kiss.

Darien stiffened, pulling back. "No."

"No?"

He shook his head. That wasn't what he wanted, not why he was here. He didn't want to be touched like that.

Myria peered at him until understanding dawned in her eyes. For a moment, she looked almost wary.

"No," she agreed.

Her fingers slipped to the blue sash at her waist, tugging at the knot. Her gown fell open, exposing long inches of firm, smooth skin. Darien stared, his eyes sucked into the gap between fabric and held there fast. Her hand stroked across his chest then altered its course, skimming downward.

She sank to her knees on the rugs in front of him, gazing upward into his eyes. Her slim brown fingers worked at the drawstring of his trousers, taking their time.

The lanterns dimmed around them, wavering, then went out.

There was no light or love in the act that followed.

Chapter Eighteen
Isle of Winter

Isle of Titherry, The Rhen

Naia winced and squinted as brilliant light clawed away the darkness of the Catacombs. The screech of metal grinding against rusted metal shuddered down her nerves, making her clench her teeth as the doors of the shrine peeled open in front of them. They stood in a shard of garish blue light that widened with the yawning of the doors.

"I do believe we're underdressed for the occasion," Quin remarked, and started buttoning his coat.

Naia held her cloak closed against the searing chill that invaded the shrine's outer door. "What's the occasion?" she asked, shivering.

"Winter." Quin didn't appear particularly happy about it.

"What were you expecting?"

"Not winter." Quin jumped down off the marble foundation of the shrine, turning back to offer Naia a hand.

She landed in the snow and staggered a few steps, making crunching noises with her boots. She glanced around at a world clad all in white, pristine and radiant. The ground was covered in freshly fallen snow, the trees frosted with ice that shimmered beneath a cold sun. The air was crisp and deadly cold.

Naia's breath made a misty cloud before her face. She glanced at Quin in alarm.

"Have you ever been here before? Is this normal for this time of year?"

"No," he responded, glancing around with a concerned expression. "Only Harbingers were ever allowed here, even in my day. The entire island was off-limits."

Naia said, "I've never met a Harbinger before."

"Then you're not alone. No one but Harbingers meet other Harbingers. They've always been a secretive lot."

Snow frosted the landscape, unmarred by bird or animal tracks. A powdery field ranged away from them to the rolling mountains in the distance. A crystalline woodland bordered the foothills. Except for the small shrine behind them, there was little trace that civilization had ever existed here.

Naia listened to the great silence that surrounded them. "Where do we go?"

Quin didn't seem to know the answer to that. He stood with his hands on his hips, glancing nervously about. He worked his lips against his teeth.

"Athera's Crescent is somewhere high in the mountains. That's all I know."

His tone was dismal. Perhaps he was still grieving for his brother. Or perhaps their situation was far more dire than she'd feared. Naia stared at him, wondering if there was something he wasn't telling her.

She asked, "How much food do we have?"

"It's not food I'm concerned about." He turned slowly as he surveyed the stark landscape around them. "Something's not right. Don't you feel it?"

She did. Something was *off*. That's the best word she could think of to describe it. Like a bite of food that had just turned; that's what the world was like here. Not fresh. But not tainted, either. Just *off*.

"I think so," she whispered. "Do you see a road?"

"No." Quin shook his head. "But I bet it's over

there."

He gestured across the snow-fed meadow to an archway half-buried in the distance. Naia agreed; the arch looked like a gateway to something.

"Let's go."

She started across the meadow, her feet crunching through the top layer of snow. Quin came along at her side, arms wrapped around himself, looking thoroughly miserable.

A wind kicked up, chilling them all the more. The sky didn't seem quite as bright as it had just a minute before. Naia couldn't see the sun through the gray haze that closed in over them, but she had the feeling that the day was winding down. Night would soon be following. Which was a daunting prospect, considering how cold it was already.

"We need to find shelter," she complained.

Quin nodded but didn't say anything. He seemed focused on where he was walking. They trudged on through murky grayness that smothered like a blanket. They found a straight path that ran along the edge of a wood that seemed grown from crystal.

Up ahead, there was an orb of diffuse, golden light.

"What's that?" Naia asked.

"Looks like a lamp." Quin frowned at the pallid glow that filtered toward them through the haze.

"What's a lamp doing all the way out here?"

He shrugged noncommittally as Naia tried to make sense of it. They were both shivering, and the cold was only getting colder. Naia's toes and fingers were already numb. They would have to find shelter soon.

They arrived at the base of a lamppost that stuck out of the snow. Its presence there was bizarre; utterly out of place. There was nothing else around. Nevertheless, it glowed with a defiant flame, its glass murky.

"Someone had to light it," she said.

"Not necessarily."

She didn't like the expression on Quin's face. He was considering the lamppost with a look of anxious dread. Whatever it was that was *off* about this place was sinister enough to frighten even a darkmage. Which made Naia doubly afraid.

She glanced back at the crystalline wood then turned back to the path ahead.

Then she turned and looked again.

"Is that…?"

She raised a trembling finger, pointing at a shadow set amidst the ice-frosted trees.

"A cottage," Quin agreed. He took a reluctant step toward it.

"Maybe whoever lives there will put us up for the night," Naia said hopefully, starting after him.

"And maybe they appreciate their solitude." Quin caught her arm, forcing her to stop.

Naia looked at him, torn. "Are we going to find out? Or shall we just stand here until we freeze to death?"

"I suggest a more cautious approach. Why don't you wait here while I go check it out?"

"No." Naia shook her head. "We go together. We're stronger together than we are apart."

Quin gave her an appraising look. "Are we? You freed yourself from the chain on your wrist. But did you also cast aside the indoctrination? In other words, are you comfortable killing someone if that's what it takes to survive?"

Naia looked at him through the mist of her breath. He was staring at her, face implacable, arms folded in front of him. Waiting for an answer.

"If that's what it takes," she agreed finally. She'd taken a life once already. And she knew she could do so again, if the situation called for it.

Quin seemed mollified. "Good. But I'm still going first. Count to twenty then follow me. At the first sign of any trouble, don't wait. Just run."

Naia nodded as a creeping white fog stole over them. Quin turned and walked into the thickening mist and was quickly shrouded from sight. The fog swallowed him whole, just as it gobbled up the rest of the world. Naia could see nothing but ubiquitous, unrelieved white. She heard his footsteps moving away from her, the sounds seeming more distant than they should.

She waited in the wan yellow glow of lamplight, counting, "One. Two. Three…" The lamp itself made the slightest hissing noise, almost inaudible, like the final gasp from a dying throat.

On twenty, Naia started after him. Her feet crunched on crispy snow that yielded beneath her weight, the noise strangely muffled by the fog. She couldn't see the cottage up ahead, so she walked to where she imagined it would be. When the wooden planks of steps appeared in front of her, she felt relieved.

Across a porch made of roughly hewn boards, the cottage door was cracked open already. Naia pushed it open the rest of the way and slipped within. The interior was musty and dark. It had a dusty, abandoned feel. The floorboards creaked beneath her weight. The chill of winter lingered even here inside the cabin. The cold was relentless, going on forever.

Naia glanced around and saw Quin standing in a liquid pool of magelight. There was no one else in the one-room hovel. Only a bed and a table with a bench. A cupboard stuffed with plates and bowls was shoved into a corner. But no people.

A lantern sat on the table, uncorrupted by rust. Quin lit the wick with the power of his mind. By its faltering glow, he started rifling through the cupboard. He stooped down, leaning far into the cabinet as Naia approached behind, surveying the goings-on.

"Is there food?"

"A little," he said, shutting the doors and rising to his feet. He turned around, scanning the stark confines of the room. "Not much. Unless it's stored somewhere else." He walked over to the bed and picked up what looked like a nightshirt, holding it up in front of his face. The covers had been tidied, a patterned coverlet folded neatly at the foot. Naia ran a hand over the linen sheets. The straw of the mattress was fresh, not mildewed.

"Whoever lived here left in a hurry. They left everything behind." He tossed the nightshirt down in the corner.

"How long ago?" Naia asked. The cottage looked like it was dozing, waiting for its family to return home. Plates and cups were set out on the table beneath a thin layer of dust.

Quin took his glove off and ran his finger along the surface of a shelf beside the bed. He held it up before his face, rubbing the dust off with his thumb.

"A couple years, I'd say."

A spot of color caught Naia's attention. Bending down, she retrieved a comb from off the floor. It was made of bone and painted red. Long blonde hairs wove between the teeth.

"I wonder what happened," she whispered, setting the comb down on the table.

Quin moved behind the bed, inspecting the far corner. There, he hunkered down, prodding at something on the floor. With a grunt, he wedged open a door built right into the floorboards, exposing a flight of rickety steps leading down beneath the cottage.

Naia moved quickly to his side, bending over to see where the steps led.

"What do you see?" Quin asked.

"A root cellar, I think," she said, taking a step down.

"Stop. Let me go first," he insisted, moving around the opening in the floor. "I'm far more dark and rotten than anything that could possibly be lurking down there."

Naia didn't argue. She withdrew, letting him go ahead down the steps, following right behind. The stairs creaked and grumbled under her weight. Quin's magelight erupted into view like hot magma spilling down. He stepped off the last stair onto the straw-strewn floor of the cellar. Drawing to a halt, he raised his hand.

It was the look on his face, more than the gesture, that stopped her short. Naia turned slowly in the direction he was looking, toward the far wall of the cellar.

Two corpses sat frozen in the corner.

Naia gasped. Not because they were dead; that didn't bother her. What bothered her was *how* they had died. The agony frozen on their faces was horrific.

Naia moved past Quin, her mind already working. She knew that muscles relaxed upon death. Sometimes rigor mortis would produce facial expressions that were disturbing, but that was transient. Nothing like this. These people had died in agony and had frozen that way. The terror of their final moments was perfectly captured, perfectly preserved, never-ending.

A man and a woman, curled up in the corner, clutched tight in each other's arms. The man's hand was raised before his face, as if warding something off. His other arm cradled the woman against his chest. Her mouth looked stretched, her scream silent and eternal.

There were chains on both their wrists.

Naia turned away, filled with a bone-numbing sadness. She was used to the dead. There were times she preferred them to the living. But this was not such a case. Something awful had occurred here.

Something hideous.

"What happened to them?" Quin asked, bending down to take a closer look at the dead man's face. His magelight cast his shadow on the wall, long and distorted in the blood-red light.

"Hard to say," Naia whispered. "I will need to examine them."

With his help, they laid the stiffened cadavers out on the cellar's earthen floor. She knelt over them, first the man, then the woman. Unbuttoning shirts, probing tissues with her mind and fingertips. There was no physical damage that she could find; all their vital organs were intact, just frozen.

Only their brains had melted.

Melted was the right word for it, she felt certain. It was as if their heads had been heated until everything inside had turned to liquid.

She tried pushing the man's up-thrust arm back down to his side, but it refused to budge. She knew some tricks that would tame an uncooperative limb, but she was hesitant to use them. These corpses were not destined for the hereafter. She left the arm as it was and stood up, dusting off her skirt.

She said, "I can only guess it was some type of regional surge of the magic field. What's strange is, the decomposition is not nearly as progressed as it should be. It's as if they've been frozen here since death."

"Maybe they have been," Quin said.

Naia frowned. "That doesn't make any sense. They must have died years ago. They would have thawed out over the summers."

"Unless summer never came." Quin rubbed the back of his neck, his gaunt face shadowed in thought.

Naia gazed at him, mouth open. "Are you saying the winter never lifted?"

"Look around." Quin spread his hands. "It's supposed to be the middle of spring. I don't see any signs of it. No thaw. No birds. No animals. It's still the depths of winter here."

Naia had to agree. Even here, this far to the south, spring should have taken hold by now. But the trees were still clad in white, the snow still fresh upon the ground. He was right; spring had never come to the island.

"How is that possible?"

Quin shrugged. "I don't know. How is it possible that Malikar has no sunlight?"

"That's different, though."

"Not if they're related."

Naia supposed she'd have to give some thought to that. As Quin moved off into a corner of the cellar, she turned back to the corpses on the ground. She wished she could do something about the faces. She supposed she could. Kneeling down beside them, she rested her palm against the ghastly face of the woman. She reached out with her mind and massaged the tissues into submission. She closed their eyes, eased their gaping jaws, smoothed dead lips over teeth. With a little effort of will, she returned the man's outstretched arm back to his side.

Then she left them to each other.

Quin rose from the corner of the cellar, arms laden with roots. From somewhere, he managed to work up a half-hearted grin. "At least these tubers are still good."

Naia nodded without speaking.

"I'm in the mood for curried yams," he called over his shoulder. "What about you?"

The meal was enjoyable, despite Naia's reservations. The tubers, like the corpses, hadn't gone to everlasting rot. She was even starting to grow accustomed to Quin's peculiar style of cooking. The spices he used were good at disguising ingredients that had lasted long past their time.

After supper, Quin grew quiet, his face going solemn. He raked out the ashes in the hearth and built a fire without a word. Naia stretched out, basking in warmth and savoring the scent of wood smoke. Quin sat at the table, gazing at the lantern's glass chimney, hands clasped on the splintery wood. She thought she knew what was troubling him. It was troubling her, too.

Naia got up from the floor and moved to sit beside him on the bench. When he turned to look at her, she said, "I'm sorry about your brother. I can't imagine what you must feel. I wish I could do more."

Quin bowed his head.

"Braden's dead," he said simply. "Just like we'll all be soon." He shrugged. "He actually has it better than the rest of us. He'll never have to face the repercussions of what he brought about. I suppose I spared him that."

"*You* spared him?"

Quin nodded, grimacing. The lines around his eyes looked like furrows in a droughted field. "The artifact they used to execute him was my own creation. A medallion I called the Soulstone. I didn't create it with that purpose in mind…but nevertheless…" He rose from the table and crossed the floor toward the hearth. He settled down there next to the fire, kicking off his shoes.

"You can have the bed," he said, then said no more.

Naia reached into the pocket of her cloak, fingering the medallion on its silver band. Her mind and heart spun slowly in dizzying circles.

Naia awoke to the sound of shifting dirt.

She pushed the covers off, scrambling into her shoes and fastening her cloak. She paused long enough to look around the empty cabin. There was no sign of Quin. Only a constant scraping coming from outside. She moved to the door and, opening it, walked out into a heavy white mist that clung like sorrow over the woodland. The silence of the forest was expansive. Another grating noise came from behind her.

She turned to find Quin standing over two dark graves that looked to have been ripped right out of the snow, patting at a mound of wet earth with the blade of a shovel. He wiped his brow and looked up at her, thrusting the shovel into the ground.

Naia moved to stand beside him, staring down at the freshly turned soil. The two graves made her feel almost heartbroken. But the sight of Quin disturbed her more. He had arisen well before dawn to care for the deceased. She had neglected her duty, so he'd done her work for her. Apparently, the demon had managed to scrounge up more compassion for the dead than she'd been able to herself.

He turned toward her with eyes darkened by remorse. He even had the courtesy to remove his hat. "You're the priestess. Why don't you say some words?"

Naia bowed her head, thinking herself unqualified. Nevertheless, she closed her eyes and raised her hands, palms spread as if beseeching. "May these souls know the peace and blessings of the goddess." It was a simple prayer said over simple graves. She opened her eyes and gazed down at the black scars in the snow.

"That's it?" Quin said. "I was expecting something a bit more profound."

Already moving away, Naia said, "I'm not a priestess anymore. And, even if I were, my temple would never condone planting the dead in the ground. There is no prayer for such a burial."

The darkmage looked perplexed. He tugged on his hat and wrenched the shovel out of the ground. "Why bother with the Catacombs? I've never understood that. My people always just covered our dead in a pile of dirt. Then they used the occasion as an excuse to drink and fuck."

"That sounds like a pagan custom," she said dismissively, ignoring his language. Such a practice sounded blasphemous. "Such burials were never endorsed by the temple, not even a thousand years ago. The Catacombs are necessary because we believe in the resurrection of the dead at the end of times. It is our temple's sacred duty to preserve the remains of those who are worthy."

That got his attention. "What resurrection? How?"

Naia shrugged, knowing that she'd said too much already. "It is one of the most holy mysteries. The Book of the Dead says only that we must prepare. It does not specify why."

Quin's lips curled into a sneer. "Sounds like a load of mystic horseshit to me."

Naia frowned at him. "Just because it hasn't happened yet doesn't mean it's not going to."

"Well, let's hope it doesn't happen today. We have a very long road ahead of us." He snatched the shovel up and pitched it away from him. It speared into the snow, quivering at an angle.

They returned to the cottage and salvaged what they could. Blankets and warmer clothes were high on Naia's list. She found a wool coat that had once belonged to the dead woman. Quin provisioned himself with a scarf and mittens, along with fur-lined boots only slightly too big for his feet. They filled their packs with provisions from the cupboards and the root cellar.

Then they started out toward the mountains, which seemed to loom much larger than they had the previous day. They walked a straight path, keeping the ice-clad forest to their right. The fog eventually burned off, the sky turning a fierce azure blue, but the sun burned cold. The isle clung tenaciously to its winter cloak, refusing to yield.

A breeze blew through the branches overhead, which swayed and crackled, showering ice crystals all around. Naia glanced at Quin. He shook the ice off his hat and squared his shoulders under his pack. A gray fog rolled in.

They walked for hours in a world silenced by gloom and powdered by white. Eventually, they reached another forlorn lamppost surrounded by a yellowed glow of light. Naia reached out, running her hand down its frozen surface, wondering at its murky glow.

"Please say it's not just me who finds this curious?" she said to Quin. "We're on an island where everything is either frozen or dead. So who's left to employ a lamplighter?"

Quin gazed up at the mysterious fixture. He raised a gloved hand to his face, rubbing his eyes wearily. "Well, now that you mention it, yes, it is curious. But I'm not gullible enough to believe that these lamps are tended by anything other than magic."

With that, the lamp guttered and went out. Then it sprang back to life.

"They're artifacts," he explained. "No tending required. They sense the gloom and react accordingly. It's magelight. Not lamplight."

Naia saw it now, the subtle difference in the quality of the light. He was right; the lamp was artificial, manufactured. He was further correct in labeling her gullible. She felt chagrinned.

"This lamppost is here for a reason," Quin said. "It's a marker. I think we should turn this way."

He scraped at the snow with his boot, exposing a path that wandered away in the direction of the mountains. Naia hadn't realized they'd walked all the way across the valley and were now so near the foothills. Towering cliffs rose before them in granite majesty, cloaked in frost and crowned by fog.

They started down a path through a grove of white-barked trees that grew in perfect rows, casting long shadows at odd angles across the snow. At last they came to a wall of precipitous cliffs. The trail they followed led toward a split in the rock face, more like a deep crack than anything else. A narrow stair led up into the crack, continuing upward hundreds of steps before disappearing in the fog.

Another lamppost marked the entrance to the jagged stair.

Quin looked at Naia and gestured at the marker. "It appears we're supposed to climb."

And climb they did. The stairs were steep and unforgiving, rising with the mountainside as the walls of the crack narrowed overhead, becoming more like a chimney. The smell of wet rock and mold lingered heavy in the air. Naia let Quin toil ahead of her, his back bent under the weight of his pack. She placed her feet carefully, nervous about her footing. The stairs were, in places, slick with ice.

Naia slipped and caught herself with her hands. Fortunately, she didn't tumble down the mountainside. In a short span of time, the stairs were proving themselves the enemy she'd feared. Her knees ached, her lungs burned, and her back strained under the weight she carried. Still, the stairs continued relentlessly.

Ahead of her, Quin stopped and cast his pack down at his side. He planted his rear on the step ahead of her. He was breathing hard, his face flushed and beaded with sweat.

"Time to eat," he announced.

They ate right there on the steps. Above, a frozen waterfall glistened in the shadows, made of thousands of slender icicles. When they finally started moving again, the stair seemed somehow more precipitous. More fog drew over them, darker and colder than the last.

"How much longer, do you think?" Naia asked, shivering.

"I don't know." Quin sighed, gazing upward with a hand on his hat.

The stairs eventually had an end. They came at last to a place where the crack in the mountain twisted around then finally wore itself out. They had reached the top of the monolith. Ahead was a sprawling display of rolling white peaks that tumbled into the distance. An imposing castle loomed before them on the crest of a hill, rich walls reflecting the sun's rays. Light spilled from dozens of windows with a promise of welcome and warmth.

Naia felt a surge of relief upon sensing the end of their journey. She rushed toward the castle's drawbridge, but was jerked immediately to a halt by Quin. She whirled around, trying to pry her arm out of his iron grasp.

"Stop!" he rasped, his face sterner than she'd ever seen it. "Something's wrong. This isn't right!"

He wrenched her back behind him.

"What is it?" Naia peered around him at the castle, not seeing any reason to be afraid. Then, slowly, she understood what he meant. Her jaw dropped. She stared up the limestone walls in shock.

Unlike everything else around them, the castle was not caught in the perpetual throes of winter. It stood in a bright patch of sunlight, banners rippling in the air, its walls shining and pristine. As if winter's grip had never touched it.

"It's new…" Naia gasped.

"The castle is very old," corrected a low voice from behind them.

Naia whirled to confront a woman who looked like no other person she'd ever met in her life. A woman of skin surpassingly dark, her lips painted with a golden sheen. A series of white dots arched across her brow. She wore a blue turban with a large stone set in the middle of her forehead.

"My name is Tsula, daughter of Mundi," she said in a thickly accented voice. "Master of the Third Tier of the Lyceum of Bryn Calazar."

Quin winced, staring at the woman with an expression of incredulity. "That's not possible," he gasped. "The Lyceum was destroyed a thousand years ago. Even if everything here's frozen in time, it hasn't been frozen that long."

The woman turned and considered Quin with dead-cold eyes. "I am not frozen, Grand Master Quinlan Reis. I am, most fortunately, *thawed.*"

Chapter Nineteen
A Man of Wrath

Kajiri Flats, The Front

Darien rose and dressed in the musky warmth of Myria's tent. He pulled the mail coat on over his clothes and hung his small arsenal of weapons from his belt. The hauberk was heavy to wear, dragging at his shoulders. He felt sluggish beneath all that chain. He worked his arms back and forth, getting used to the feel of it. He glanced back over his shoulder.

Myria lay where he'd left her, the steady sounds of her breathing whispering through the quiet. The dark drape of her hair spilled like a waterfall over the covers. One of her slender fingers twitched in her sleep. He didn't bother waking her. He had nothing to say.

Tugging the helm down over his head, he left the tent, stepping out into darkness. He trudged through the camp past clusters of men going on about the business of warfare: stoking cookfires, sharpening weapons, fletching arrows with dried willow leaves. No one paid him any mind; there was no reason for them to.

He found his way to the command tent, looking for Sayeed. The encampment was enormous, like a vast, sprawling city, and he had no idea how to navigate it. He didn't even know where to find his own tent or his wife.

His *wife*. Just the word in his head made his lips twist into a scowl. He felt affection for Azár, but that was all. He admired her; she was clever and independent. She had summoned him from the dead, but that was the extent of her power over him. It was too bad; Meiran had cauterized his capacity to feel.

He thought of Arden and Meiran, two women with voracious appetites for causing pain.

And then there was Myria, who sated his lust without requiring intimacy. She'd been accommodating to his particular needs, which was all he could ask. He'd done his best not to leave her wanting.

He found Sayeed and his retinue of Zakai resting in the lee of the command tent. They didn't see him coming, or at least didn't recognize him. A couple of officers glanced up casually, taking note of his passage, before glancing away. It was Sayeed who finally identified him, frowning at Darien's warbelt until recognition finally dawned on his face. His look of surprise was quickly replaced by a look of fury.

He surged to his feet, every movement sharpened by anger.

"Where have you been?"

The other Zakai followed him to their feet, confusion rampant on their faces. Darien removed the helm and slipped past Sayeed into the tent. The officer followed him in, lowering his voice as he whispered:

"How are we supposed to keep you safe if you elude our protection?"

Darien turned to fix the man with a sidelong glare, not liking his tone. "I had my reasons."

But Sayeed refused to be intimidated. He drew himself up, one hand on the hilt of his sword, returning Darien's glare right back at him. "I do not care what you do—or who you do it with—as long as it does not compromise your safety. But I must insist, *Lord,* in the future, that you trust our protection. And our discretion."

Darien shook his head, frustrated and furious. "Just get me to my tent."

But a voice from behind him stopped him short. "That didn't take very long. Myria must be losing her touch."

He turned to find Byron Connel standing in the gap between partitions. Darien felt his blood sour to vinegar in his veins. The man clapped him on the arm, amusement brightening his eyes. "I've got a favor to ask of you."

Darien wasn't in the mood for favors. "What is it?"

Connel laid a hand on his shoulder, steering him back into the dim interior of the tent. "I need you to scribe a note for me."

"What kind of note?"

"An invitation. To your old friends."

Darien's eyes narrowed, but he forced himself to keep walking anyway.

The note didn't take long to write. But it took a lot out of him, a lot more than he'd ever thought it would. Considering whose hands that scroll would eventually end up, Darien was starting to feel more and more like a traitor. It wasn't a feeling he was comfortable with.

He'd seen this day coming; from the very beginning, it had been inevitable. But that didn't mean he had to feel good about his part in it, or good about himself. He knew exactly what he was, had no delusions about it. He was not a man of honor. He was a man of wrath.

He indulged himself in a brooding melancholy as Sayeed and his men led him back through the encampment. He said nothing the entire way. Neither was a word spoken to him; the officers were still angry at him for slipping away. As he walked, Darien took careful note of the camp's landmarks, taking a survey of banners and numbers. It was quite an assortment of people they'd gathered, most not even regular military. A mixture of men and women, city folk and common villagers. There were small, dirty children running about the camp, laboring at chores just as hard as the adults. It was a sight unlike anything he'd ever seen before. A hard sight.

What surprised him most was the odor of the place. It didn't smell like any encampment he'd ever been in; there was no reek of filth or human waste. Wherever they'd dug the latrine pits, they were well away from the heart of the camp and well-tended. The efficiency and discipline of these people never ceased to impress him.

Sayeed led him to a large tent raised slightly apart from the rest of the camp, flying the blood-red standards of the Tanisar corps. Darien removed his boots and stepped within, glancing around the dim interior. The space looked comfortable, even opulent, lit by hanging lanterns and oil lamps, the floor carpeted, the walls paneled with cloth. There was even furniture: a low table surrounded by seats and, behind a half-drawn partition, an over-stuffed bed. The posts of the tent were wrapped in spiraling ribbons, creating a chaotic splendor of color.

He moved further into the space, drawn toward the bed's promise of comfort. In the dim light of the lanterns, Darien undressed and crawled beneath the covers. He extinguished the lanterns with a thought and closed his eyes, letting complete darkness settle in.

A rustling sound made him start.

The mattress shifted as Azár lay down alongside him, her body naked and pressing close against his.

Darien froze, unsure of what to do. Never once had he ever shared a bed with his wife, nor anything more than just a kiss. Her hand stroked his shoulder, sliding down his arm. He closed his eyes and suffered the feel of it.

"I lay with Myria," he said.

The hand stopped moving.

"Good."

That wasn't the answer he'd been expecting. On the floor, magelight bloomed and spread in glowing azure pools, running over the carpets like a blazing stream. Darien rolled over, taking in Azár's face in the writhing blue light. He gazed at her steadily, contemplating her non-expression, feeling dread sink deep into his heart.

He sighed. "I think you need your own tent."

"No." She shook her head. "That is not the answer."

"Then what is?"

She gazed at him with that same, indifferent stare that yielded nothing.

"We must build trust between the two of us," she said at last. "We are alike, you and I. We have both been hurt, and are both afraid of pain. But we will be needing each other very much, very soon. And we do not have much time."

She was right. About all of it. Only, he had no idea where to begin. "So, what do you propose?"

Her stare ticked upward toward the patterned roof of the tent. Her soft fingertips brushed his skin.

"Kiss me, Darien."

A cold weight gripped his chest. He couldn't move.

So she kissed him, instead. Slowly at first, her fingertips tracing the whiskered line of his jaw. He closed his eyes, his muscles going tense. The kiss became deeper, more adamant. Her hair fell forward, filling his nostrils with the fresh scent of her. He could feel her soft skin pressed against his.

She pulled back. "Is this affecting you?"

"Aye," he admitted. "But probably not in the way you'd like." His body was stirring, awakening, very aware of her presence and disposition. He was reminded of Myria's practiced touch.

Azár gazed down at him, her disappointment evident. He couldn't blame her; she deserved more. Far more.

"Hold me." Resigned, she collapsed against him.

He couldn't deny her. He wrapped his arms around her and drew her close. She lay there cradled against his chest, staring straight ahead into nothing. She felt so small, so fragile in his arms. He wondered how she could possibly survive the firestorm that was surely coming.

Then he remembered that she wouldn't.

The Reversal was coming. And there was nothing he could do to stop it.

Something inside Darien clicked. Deep down inside, that realization brought about a subtle but significant change.

He held her tighter.

He pressed a kiss against her hair then closed his eyes, letting the magelight fade softly into darkness.

Chapter Twenty
Rabid

Pass of Lor-Gamorth, The Front

Raindrops splattered the stone pavement as thunder rumbled overhead. The musty smell of rain and wet masonry lay heavy on the air. It was cold. Kyel rubbed his aching fingers, trying to work some heat back into them. The continual darkness was already miserable enough; the damp weather made it intolerable. Rain soaked his cloak, streamed down his face. He paid little heed to the groups of roving soldiers that patrolled the fortress, backs stooped, necks bent under the oppressive weight of the endless gloom. It was stretching too long. It was starting to wear on all of them.

He looked to Cadmus and Meiran, who were standing by his side. He caught just a glimpse of Meiran's face beneath the shadows of her cowl. She looked pale. To Kyel, she'd seemed frail of late. Perhaps he'd done of poor job of burning the poisons from her system. Or perhaps it was something else, the threat of war taking its toll. He didn't know. She was quiet, quieter than she'd ever been. She barely spoke to him of late, and when she did, her tone was usually biting.

A stab of lightning glared white off the stones of the tower as a rumble of thunder rattled his bones. Kyel ducked through the tower's entrance, waiting for Meiran, then made his way in silence as he blinked away the after-glow. By the time they reached Craig's quarters, only a few motes still danced across his vision. That strike had been close. He could still smell the sharp stench of charged air.

Meiran reached up and rapped hard on the force commander's door. The door clanked and then groaned, shivering open. Kyel moved in and glanced around, noticing the table in the far corner with its scattered maps and haphazard trinkets. A melted candle with pearls of wax leaking down its sides provided meager light.

Commander Craig beckoned them in, shutting the door behind them.

"What is it?" Meiran asked, drawing back her cowl as she moved deeper into the room.

Craig raised his hand, offering out a scroll. Kyel saw that the wax seal had already been broken. "Our presence is requested at a parley tomorrow," Craig said. "It's signed by Darien."

Meiran took the scroll from his hand, unfurling it slowly, as if wary it would bite. Her eyes scanned over the page, her expression darkening. "It's his signature," she confirmed, handing it back.

"I know." Craig tossed the summons down on the table, peering deeply into Meiran's face. "Are you sure you're up for this?"

Meiran locked eyes on him. Her pale, smooth features tightened like a compressed spring. "Yes. Whatever it takes." Her voice was dull like lead.

"No second thoughts?"

"None."

Kyel glanced back and forth between the two of them, an unsettling feeling of trepidation creeping under his skin. He didn't like where this was going, what this was coming to. He was starting to wonder if they would even give Darien a chance to negotiate.

Craig cast a piercing look at Cadmus. "What about your part?"

The cleric squared his shoulders, clasping his pudgy hands in front of him. "I've summoned a priest to assist us. He should be arriving sometime in the night."

Kyel frowned. A priest? What need had they of a priest? Surely they could use a blessing, but this seemed extreme. Unless they were preparing for annihilation. Even then, a clerical blessing wouldn't matter much. But Craig just nodded, distilling this new information with a glower. He turned to Kyel.

"I want you with us tomorrow," he said. "You know him best."

Kyel shook his head, moving away from Craig toward the wall. He turned around, leaning with his back up against the uneven stones, crossing his arms. "That would be Meiran, not me. I don't know him at all anymore."

Craig disagreed. "You were there with him at the end. You watched him turn."

"Meiran met with him," Kyel argued. "Of all of us, she knows him best—"

"That's not the same," Meiran insisted, moving forward. She clasped Kyel's hand, gazing intently into his eyes. "He only showed me what he *wanted* me to see. But you actually know him, Kyel, the way he is now. Better than any of us."

Kyel supposed she might be right. He drew in a deep breath and let it out slowly with a shrug. "I suppose I could…"

Craig nodded. "Report to the armory. Get yourself fitted with some gear. You're the only Sentinel we have, and we'll be needing you alive."

Kyel started across the floor but paused and glanced back. He saw that neither Meiran nor Cadmus were following him toward the door. They stood paused by the map table, watching him go. Seeing the looks on their faces, he had a strangling feeling. Like he was being purposefully sent away.

Darien had sent him away, too. To protect him.

This didn't feel anything like that.

He could still feel their eyes on his back as he pulled the door closed behind him.

He walked across the courtyard to the armory, where he procured a padded gambeson. The armorers had him try it on right there in front of them to make sure it fit. He left the armory and found his way to his own quarters, ignoring the pointed stares that followed him everywhere he went.

That night, he had a hard time sleeping. The rain rattled the roof above his bed, splattering and clawing at the window. The door leaked something fierce; cold air whistled under it as the wind ripped and howled through the corridors outside. The small fire in the hearth fed little warmth into the place. The wind chased the heat away as quickly as it was made.

Kyel tossed and turned on his straw-stuffed mattress. All night long, his dreams eluded him. He finally fell asleep sometime very late, or perhaps very early; he couldn't tell. He woke up cold and sad and more than a little bit afraid.

He sat up on the edge of the bed, running his hands through his hair. Perspiration beaded on his brow even though he sat shivering. He raked at the sweat with his cloak, shaking his head to clear his thoughts. It didn't make sense. He didn't understand what he was feeling. Or whether he should trust it.

The pavilion had been raised on the rise of a low hill, against the backdrop of Orguleth's bell-shaped dome. Kyel checked his horse, drawing back on the reins. The gelding snorted and stamped, nervous about being so far from home. At his side, Craig sat astride a brown destrier, a white cloth held in his chain-gloved hand. Meiran rode alongside the priest summoned by Cadmus. The priest had been introduced to Kyel as Brother Desco, a quiet and oily man whose stare tended to linger in one spot far longer than was appropriate. He'd arrived late in the night with a supply caravan up from Wolden. Kyel wasn't even certain which temple Brother Desco was ordained to. He'd taken an instant dislike to the man.

Ahead, armored figures emerged from the pavilion.

Kyel remained on his horse as a group of mailed soldiers approached their position. They all wore helms, so he couldn't make out faces. It took him a moment to realize that the approaching party carried no weapons. Craig raised his arm, holding up the white fabric in his hand for all to see. The Enemy soldiers halted in front of them, helmed faces regarding them. Then their ranks opened, parting fluidly.

A lone man moved forward through the tight press of armor and bodies.

Kyel felt his face go slack as he recognized who it was. Cold ice encaged his heart, numbing his limbs until all he could do was sit his horse and stare.

Darien Lauchlin strode toward them with a dangerous grace, his face cold and terrifying. He was garbed all in black, in a style as foreign as his features. He was surrounded by the same cloak of confidence Kyel remembered so well.

Darien's gaze locked on Meiran and stuck there.

Kyel swallowed, unable to move. Unable to react. He shot a sidelong glance at Craig, seeking reassurance. But the look on the commander's face was anything but reassuring. Kyel reached within, latching on to the magic field. He drew at it slowly, taking comfort in its feel.

Darien stopped in front of them, his eyes moving from Meiran to Kyel to Craig.

"Thank you for coming," he said.

His voice was not harsh. The familiar sound of it startled Kyel from his thoughts, sent his head roiling in a turbulent mixture of emotions. It took him instantly back. Back to his pledge to Darien in the pass, back to his trial in the vortex, back to the sinister chamber that housed the Well of Tears. He remembered the master who had never doubted him, not even once. Darien had always trusted him, even when he couldn't trust himself.

He stared hard at the demon standing before him, and felt afraid.

Darien Lauchlin turned to Craig. "I have nothing to say to Meiran. I'll speak with you and Kyel alone. No one else." He cast a significant glare at the priest, who favored him with a slight nod, as if from one adversary to another.

Craig sat frozen on his horse, arm still holding the long strip of white cloth. At last, he gave the slightest nod. "Very well."

He draped the banner over his saddle and swung down from his horse's back. He turned to Meiran and the priest as Kyel followed him to the ground. "Wait here. This won't take long."

Kyel wasn't sure he believed that. Looking at that dark pavilion, he rather thought it had been erected for a purpose far more substantial than a minutes-long dialogue. He considered the small retinue of black-mailed guards, uncertain that he trusted them.

Then he looked at Darien, not certain he trusted him, either.

A bleak feeling crawled under Kyel's skin. This could be a trap, he realized. By the look on Craig's face, he could tell the commander had arrived at that thought ahead of him.

Darien turned, gesturing for them to follow as he showed them his back and strode toward the tent. Kyel followed him through the guard of plate-mailed bodies, his eyes trained on the sway of Darien's cloak. The mage's hair was longer, the cloak different, the whiskers on his face overgrown. But there was no mistaking that graceful confidence the man projected with every stride. It was Darien's signature.

He held open the flap of the tent, allowing them to enter. Once inside, Kyel stood still, letting his eyes adjust to the dimness of the interior. The pavilion was lit by a subtle amber light, the glow of lanterns set about on a floor draped with rugs. There were a few cushions thrown down for them to sit on; that was all. Save for the shadows, the tent was empty.

Darien sat cross-legged in the center of the room, resting his arms upon his knees. Kyel took one of the cushions across from him, seating himself awkwardly. Craig sat down beside him, adjusting and readjusting his posture several times. He looked patently uncomfortable.

At last, Darien nodded at Kyel. "It's good to see you. How have you been?"

His voice was rich and warm, exactly as Kyel remembered it.

"As well as can be expected," he managed, unsure of what to say. He didn't trust the man in front of him. Darien didn't look like a demon, like the monster Meiran had described. But neither did he look like himself. He had changed. Calmer, steadier, more focused. Much more sure of himself. Yet, the shadows Kyel remembered still haunted his eyes.

"I'm thirsty," Craig said. "What have you got to drink?"

Darien spread his hands. The thick sleeves of his robe fell back to reveal a tangle of red scars on his wrists. Kyel remembered them well. The sight of them made him want to retch.

"I'm sorry," Darien said. "Among my people, it's considered inappropriate to share cups with our enemies."

Devlin Craig scoffed. "*Your people.* Are you serious?"

Darien's expression didn't change. He remained impassive, staring at Craig levelly. "I am very serious. This is the path I've chosen. These are my people now."

Craig scowled. He thrust a hand into his pocket and produced a metal flask. Removing the stopper, he took a healthy drink from it. He took his time about stoppering it back up again, setting it down carefully.

"What the hell are you doing?" he asked. "I see you sitting there with my own eyes, and I still can't believe it."

Darien stared at him for a lingering moment. Then he said very quietly, "I assume Meiran's told you about the Reversal of the magic field that is coming."

"That you *say* is coming, aye. She did." Craig's face conveyed his doubts. Kyel still wasn't sure whether or not he believed it.

"It *is* coming," Darien insisted. "And when it does come, every person living north of the Shadowspears is going to starve unless you let us in. I can't let that happen. Condemning an entire nation to death goes against every fiber of my conscience."

"You swore your soul to Xerys. Apparently that didn't go against the fibers of your conscience."

Darien only shrugged, casually dismissing the insult. "I did what I had to do. You've got Meiran back because of it. I have no regrets."

"Well, I have plenty. Starting with saving your life."

Darien glanced down, seeming to be taking a moment to collect himself. When he looked back up again, his face was full of resolve. "I asked you here because both of you were once my friends. I'm hoping that together we can forge a peace between our two nations before this escalates into something awful. I'm here to save lives, as many lives as I can. I don't want to spill one drop of blood that I don't have to."

Craig's eyes turned as hard as tempered steel. "I don't mind spilling blood."

The comment took Kyel aback. He didn't know why the man was acting so unreasonably. He figured they should hear what Darien had come all this way to offer. Especially with so much at stake.

"There are over a million people in the Black Lands," Darien said evenly. "That's an awful lot of blood to have on your hands."

Craig just shrugged. "It won't be on my hands. We didn't blacken the skies over Caladorn. It was Renquist and the rest of your kind who chose to dance with the devil instead of doing the right thing. Renquist sold his people out. Why don't you go talk to him about blood."

"Renquist was trying to save civilization as we know it," Darien said. "Both our societies depend on a magical infrastructure that's still in place today. Our entire way of life is threatened by the Reversal. Someday soon, the world you wake to is going to be very different than the one you know today. And then it will be your problem to deal with."

Kyel thought about that, wondering if he was right. He'd seen it, the magical infrastructure Darien was referring to. The hot water in Rothscard's pipes, the city lanterns that looked so much like captive magelight. Aqueducts that shuttled water uphill. The way Cadmus could communicate with the High Priest even at a distance. The troves of knowledge in Om's libraries, the vast warren of the Catacombs. That was just the beginning, he knew. He envisioned a sprawling network of magically enhanced technologies that were so taken for granted that most people weren't even aware of their existence.

"It sounds like we're going to have a lot of work on our hands," Craig said. "The last thing we'll need's a million more mouths to feed."

Darien leaned forward, his eyes intense. "Food isn't going to be the problem. The Rhen has enough arable land to go around. Cities like Rothscard and Auberdale are going to be the hardest hit when the infrastructure collapses. What you're going to need is a larger labor pool. We can provide that."

Craig sneered. "How do we know this Reversal's even real? That this isn't just some ploy to slip your forces past our defenses?"

Warily, Darien said, "My offer to Meiran still stands."

"And what offer is that?"

"I said I'd surrender myself to you as a guarantee of trust."

For the first time since the beginning of the conversation, Darien looked less than arrogant. He licked his lips, fidgeting with a flap of leather on his belt.

Craig glowered. "You want to bring a million people through my pass. It's going to take a hell of a lot more than that to gain my trust. If what you say is true, then you're running out of options. I'd say it's time to start discussing the terms of your unconditional surrender."

Darien's eyes hardened. He looked suddenly very much like a demon. "Believe me: we are far from out of options. Our legions outnumber your own, and our Battlemages can stop your hearts and level your walls. And then there's the very simple fact that every member of our population will fight to the death *because that's all they've got left.*"

Craig stared at him, unblinking.

When he didn't respond, Darien went on, "We don't want a war. All we want is to survive."

"At our expense," snapped Craig. He blew out a sigh, glancing at Kyel. Kyel didn't know what to say. He understood the very real danger in Darien's threats. He also understood the underlying plea for help. He wasn't sure Craig did.

"All right, Darien. Let's talk terms." The commander planted a finger on the rugs in front of him. "You want more than just safe passage. You want land and homes and the means of making ends meet. And all that's going to have to come from somewhere—so *where?* I don't know of any farmers eager to hand over their harvests to—."

Darien cut him off. "We need passage, Craig. Sooner. Not later. Before the light goes out and famine decides our fate for us. There's something you have to understand. We're coming, and there's nothing you can do to stop us. Either you let us in willingly, or we'll march right over your bones."

Craig took a slow sip from his flask. Then he stoppered it and set the container down at his side. "These are my terms. You want to end this without a fight? Then we demand nothing less than your unconditional surrender. You disarm and leave your armor and armaments behind. You submit yourselves to our rule of law. Every mage, commander, and senior officer becomes our prisoners of war. We'll let the rest of your population through the pass one fraction at a time. If there's any sign of treachery, we'll slit all your throats and seal the pass."

The more he talked, the darker Darien's expression became. He was shaking his head long before Craig came to the end of his demands. "You can't have every mage," he said. "Our Lightweavers are useless on a battlefield, and they're all condemned, besides. They'll not spend the rest of their lives in a Greystone dungeon. You can have me and Myria. But that's all."

"There's Eight Servants, Darien. You're offering us only two. That's not near enough."

Darien glared defiantly at Craig. "I told you. We're coming, one way or another. I offered myself and Myria as a token of trust. This is the last offer I make before I walk out of this tent and tell half a million men to burn you to the ground and grind your bones to dust."

Craig's eyes studied Darien's face without blinking. He reached for his flask and drained the last of its contents down his gullet. He set the container down hard, as if emphasizing a point.

He rose to his feet. "Tomorrow evening in the canyon," he said abruptly as Kyel and Darien rose after him. "You will formally surrender your arms, colors, and hostages. If I get one whiff of treachery, the deal's off."

Darien stared at him long and hard before finally nodding. He extended his hand.

Craig sealed the agreement with a handshake.

"I want to speak with Kyel," Darien said. "Alone."

Craig nodded his permission and ducked out of the tent.

Kyel turned to face his former master, finding the harshness gone from Darien's face. Suddenly, he looked just like the man Kyel used to know. For a moment, he was caught off-guard. He didn't know what to say.

Darien took a step toward him, real concern on his face. "Tell me truly. How've you been?"

Kyel almost answered him with the truth, but stopped himself short. The truth was unpleasant, and Darien already knew it anyway.

So he spread his hands in exasperation, demanding, "That's all you've got to say?"

Darien sighed, shaking his head. "What else can I say? I can't say I'm sorry, because I'm not. I can't say I wish things were different, because no amount of wishing will ever change anything. You'll be dead soon. And I'll be the one who killed you. That's a fact."

Kyel could see the pain of guilt in his eyes. This was not a monster, Kyel realized. Darien might be a demon, but he was not demonic.

"I'm the one who put on the Soulstone," Kyel reminded him. "You didn't force me to do it."

Something about what he said had an effect on Darien. A gloom settled over him. Reaching out, he placed a hand on Kyel's shoulder. "For whatever it's worth, I'm very proud of you," he said sincerely. Then he pulled back, looking away.

"Are you evil, Darien?"

The man paused. He glanced back at Kyel wearily. "My actions speak for themselves. I most certainly am evil. But my people are not. Don't confuse that distinction. The people of Malikar are not the Enemy."

"Then who is?"

Darien stared at him, eyes pleading. Pleading for what, Kyel couldn't fathom.

"*We're* the enemy," Darien said at last. "You, me, Meiran, Naia…us mages, with all our contemptible power. It's our power that makes us weak. It gnaws at us. Robs us of the strength of our humanity. Deep down inside, we're all just children playing with fire, thinking we can control it. Thinking we can contain it. We can't.

"I am sorry about one thing," he said as he turned away. "I'm sorry that I ever dragged you into any of this."

He left through the back of the pavilion, leaving Kyel feeling confused and melancholy. He hadn't realized how much he'd missed his former master. And now he felt even more conflicted than before. He understood Darien. He understood him better than he understood Craig.

He left the tent and made his way toward the horses picketed outside, his black cloak fluttering behind him. He kept his gaze lowered to the ground, refusing to look at Meiran even though he could feel her eyes on him. When he reached his horse, he released it from the tether and swung his leg up over the saddle. Then he kicked the beast forward, following on the heels of Craig's mount. The captain didn't stop until they were well away on the other side of the ridge. There, he drew up, swinging around.

"You're right," Craig said to Meiran. "They twisted him. They twisted him good. He's gone rabid."

Meiran nodded in agreement, her eyes filled with sorrow and understanding.

"What do we do?" Kyel asked.

Craig glanced down, his face darkening. "There's only one thing to be done with a rabid animal. We have to put him down."

Kyel looked away, feeling his gut wrench.

"You did good back there," Craig continued, nodding at Kyel. "It was the look on your face that gained his trust more than anything."

Kyel's eyes shot up, his heart staggering as he realized what the man was saying without actually saying it. He realized he'd been used.

From the back of his horse, Brother Desco cracked a festering grin.

Chapter Twenty-One
Harbinger of Destiny

Isle of Titherry, The Rhen

Quin awoke, shivering violently.

His eyelids snapped open to blue-black nothingness. It was cold. The kind of cold that seeped into the flesh, prickling like a thousand icy needles. He didn't know where the cold came from, only that it consumed him. He couldn't feel his hands, his feet, his fingers—like they didn't even belong to him. He wasn't in charge of them anymore. Someone else was shaking them, shaking *him*. He could feel his whole body trembling as if some invisible stranger were trying to jostle him awake.

"W-w-waa…do you w-want?"

The effort of forcing the words past his frozen lips was almost beyond him. His jaw was clattering so hard he almost couldn't understand himself. He bit his tongue trying to fight out the last syllable.

"You know what I want."

He recognized that voice. He'd heard it before. Many times, come to think of it. This wasn't the first time she'd been here. He'd denied her before, countless times. Countless denials. Before slipping back into numb nothingness. But something was different this time. There was an urgency in her voice that hadn't been there before, all the other times. He wondered why it was there now.

"I…c-can't…help you…"

His words stumbled over his shuddering jaw as his teeth tried to clatter their way into his brain. He blinked several times, finally succeeding in clearing his vision enough to make out the woman standing over him, staring down. Her face was stern, her cat-like eyes dazzlingly black, as deep and vibrant as the shadows that surrounded her. Her skin glistened with what looked like golden dewdrops.

She stared at him, her gaze implacable. "I was frozen in this very room for a thousand years. I know what it's like. I won't let it happen to me again."

She waved her hand, and at once ice crystals formed and started groping up his legs, spreading upward from the frozen floor. They entwined about his calves, twisting like a thorn bush as they crept over his knees and groped at his thighs. Quin didn't want them going any further. His mind strained for the magic field, for the Hellpower, for anything he could use to fend them off.

There was nothing but the cold and the spreading tendrils of ice.

He glanced to the side and was appalled at what he saw. There, leaning against the wall beside him, was Naia. Her face was white, her long lashes frozen closed. Her hair, iced over and plastered to her face. Her hands, clawed into stiffened knots in front of her.

She was frozen solid. Like the mages in the cabin.

"N-naia…" he moaned.

The woman above him had no mercy. She said, "When the Reversal hits, she would die anyway. It is better this way."

"No…"

"There is nothing in the world that will prevent it. She will die no matter what you choose. On the other hand, there are many lives that will be saved if you choose to assist me."

He believed her. He didn't know why, but he did. His teeth chattered harder. The ice inside of him clawed deeper, threatening his heart. The frozen vines twined about his hips, his groin, constricting.

"I'll h-help you…"

There was a crackling sound as the creeping ice receded back down his legs. The frozen tendrils didn't melt; they un*grew*, writhing and unbranching until they were once again part of the glassy floor. Quin gasped in pain as hot blood gushed back into his legs. The warmth spread throughout his torso, into his shoulders and arms, flushing his cheeks. Pain followed like scalding water boiling his blood.

He gaped up at the woman's staring face, marveling as he felt his body come back awake. His shivering stopped, his muscles relaxing. He looked over to where Naia sat rigid, just as pale and frozen as before. The thaw hadn't reached her.

"Come," the woman commanded, extending a two-toned hand with long, tapering fingers.

Quin gazed at that hand, blinking at the memories it evoked. It had been a very long time since he'd seen a person with skin that color.

The sight of that beautiful hand made him want to weep.

He reached up and clenched her fingers.

"Do you swear?" she demanded.

"I swear."

"Very well." She pulled him ungracefully to his feet.

He turned immediately back for Naia. In two steps he was by her side, kneeling down, taking her clenched fingers in his hands. They were rock-solid. Ice crystals shimmered in her frozen hair. She was alive in there, somewhere. He could feel it. She wasn't dead. But he had no way of reaching her. Quin cupped her cold face with his hands. Her skin was stiff but soft. Frozen, just like the rest of her. He stroked her cheek with a finger.

"Let her be." The harsh voice behind him stopped him short. "Trust me; it is better this way."

Anger like red heat suffused his vision, clenching his throat. He glared back up at the woman as if trying to sear her with rage. She remained indifferent, her stare penetrating. Drowning in hopelessness, Quin leaned down and pressed a kiss against Naia's cold forehead.

Then he rose to his feet and moved away. He was shaking again, and this time not from cold. Naia was a lovely woman, and this was a cruel mistake. He swallowed a hard lump of anger in his throat as the door to the cold room swung shut behind him, sealing her in. The lock clicked, making him flinch. He cast a glare of reproach at his stern companion.

The mysterious woman awaited him in the corridor, appraising him with an indomitable gaze. Her dark face shimmered with gold, some type of powder, he suspected. She turned her back on him and preceded him down the hallway. He followed her up a rise of flagstone steps into a sprawling room that dominated the entire bottom floor of the castle. It was warm, even summery. Radiant light streamed in through windows set high above.

Quin glanced over the room, which was filled with rugs and furniture arranged in intimate clusters. Hundreds of people could have easily filled this hall and never felt pinched for space. Many hearths girthed the chamber, promising warmth and comfort to prospective visitors. It was a space designed for the specific purpose of bringing many people together.

Eerily, they were alone.

The unoccupied chamber resounded with emptiness. It stank of dust and abandonment. Even the light coming in from the windows seemed bereft of energy. Quin paused, arching an eyebrow as his eyes scanned the hall.

"Obviously, not all is as it should be," his guide answered his unspoken question. "Come."

She started forward past clusters of chairs and couches, striding over to a door recessed in the far wall. She pulled it open, ushering him within.

He moved through a tinkling clatter of beads that hung in the doorway, parting them with his hand. He stepped into a dim, confined space that screamed color from every wall. Quin stood still, staring around, letting his eyes wander over the variety of tapestries and decorative items laid out on shelves or dangling from the ceiling. Some of the patterned textures he recognized. He turned back to the woman in front of him, finally understanding.

"You're from Aeridor," he observed.

"I am. Aeridor as it was a thousand years ago."

She smoothed her silken robes and settled into a chair, beckoning for him to take the one opposite. He did, running his hand over the woven texture of the chair's fabric that echoed the colorful patterns of his memories. It occurred to him that no other room like this probably existed anywhere in the entire world. It was a saddening thought.

"What was your name again?"

"I am Tsula daughter of Mundi," she reminded him.

"Why are you here, Tsula?" He shifted nervously in the chair, reaching up to adjust his hat. The room was warm, and he could feel prickles of sweat breaking out on his forehead.

The woman folded her hands in her lap and stared at him flatly. "I am here because I have no choice. As are you."

His gaze wandered over the cluttered, claustrophobic space. Tsula's bed was tucked into a corner, piled high with blankets. Tables littered with knickknacks defined the small space. Chests and slender cabinets of polished wood, candles and oil lamps, aglow with wavering flames. And a fragile scent lingered in the air, putting him at ease.

"You're a Harbinger?" he asked.

"Yes."

"And just how old are you?"

"As old as you are, Quinlan Reis. Like you, I was born before the Desecration."

Reaching to the table at her side, she removed the lid from a woven basket and produced a loaf of bread. She broke off a piece, setting it on a plate. This, she offered to Quin.

He didn't have to think twice. He snatched the plate from her hand, stuffing his cheeks full. There was no oil to dip the bread in; it was dry. But even still, it was one of the best things he'd ever tasted in his life. He was literally starving, he realized. When the bread was gone, he licked his finger and dabbed up every crumb on the plate before setting it aside.

He glanced up to find Tsula watching him.

"That was delectable," he said at last. "Your baking staff should be commended."

He looked around, wondering what other food could be stored in the room's various baskets.

"We are alone in the castle."

"So it seems. Forgive me for my prying ways, but…where does your food come from?"

"The food comes from the cold rooms down below. When I am hungry, I simply thaw, cook, and eat." She rose and picked up Quin's plate, clearing it away to a basket by the door. Quin stared after it, wishing she'd offer him more. But instead, Tsula returned to her chair.

From the small table at her side, she picked up a pair of jaw-like tongs and used them to hold a small clump of charcoal over a candle's flame. The charcoal eventually grayed, the smell of it filling the air. Tsula set the smoldering lump in a small copper brazier that looked very much like a wine goblet. On top of the charcoal she placed chips of wood. They began curling and smoldering with a rich odor that quickly filled the room.

"I'm sure you have many questions," she said, setting the tongs down and turning back to Quin. "You may ask."

"Why, how very gracious of you."

Quin closed his eyes and breathed in deeply, his emotions stirred by the vivid odor. Flickers of reveries traced his closed eyelids, along with the profound sentiments that accompanied them. A sharp pang of loss stabbed his chest, making him stiffen in his seat.

"It's been a thousand years since I last smelled the scent of agarwood," he said at last. "It evokes such powerful memories. Some beautiful. Some despicable. It leaves me feeling…quite conflicted."

"Good," Tsula said. "Conflicted is exactly the state you should be in."

Quin opened his eyes and looked over to her. At her side, the smoke from the small brazier drifted upward in a thin trail toward the ceiling. Tsula stared back at him without expression.

"What do you want from me?" Quin asked.

"I am going to ask for your help in bringing about the end of the only world you've ever known."

She said it as easily as if asking him to carry water for her. She reached for a tea pot beside her chair and poured two cups, one for him and one for herself.

Quin accepted the cup and brought it to his lips, never taking his eyes off her.

He said, "Pardon me if I seem skeptical, but the last time someone asked me to help bring about the end of the world, things didn't work out so very well."

"That is because you were only halfway committed to your cause."

He cocked an eyebrow. "Oh, is that why Caladorn ended in darkness and ash? And all this time, I've been thinking it was because I helped open a gateway to hell."

Tsula set her tea down and raised her hand. "Hear

me out. Let me tell you my story."

"By all means." Quin took a long, loud slurp of tea, watching her reaction over the cup's brim. But Tsula didn't react. Instead, she simply waited for him to set his cup down before continuing.

"A thousand years ago, I was the Warden of Harbingers. When the Reversal came, I was here in this castle, operating Athera's Crescent at the very moment the magic field reversed itself over the isle. That's how I came to be frozen."

"I don't understand," Quin admitted. The field hadn't fully reversed. And, if it had, Tsula would have been dead, not simply frozen.

"Of course you don't understand," she snapped. "Athera's Crescent is the largest and most sophisticated artifact ever to exist in the history of the world. You would need to know something about its workings to understand anything I have to say."

Quin grimaced. "I *am* an Arcanist, you know. I do know some things."

"But you are not a Harbinger," she pointed out.

"No. Not a Harbinger." He rolled his eyes and gestured with a flourish. "By all means. Proceed."

She nodded. "Athera's Crescent is like a bowl, collecting rivers of information from every corner of the world." She cupped her hands in demonstration. "Any use of the field—any disturbance anywhere in the world—sends echoes throughout the entire magic field like ripples in a pond. These variations are collected and analyzed here by Harbingers. Or at least they were—before every last Harbinger was killed."

"How were they killed?" Quin took a loud slurp of tea.

"Athera's Crescent requires a tremendous amount of power in order to operate. It harvests this power by siphoning field energy away from specific locations across the world. Places you know of as vortexes. The power of a vortex is harvested by its Circle of Convergence and then delivered here through a series of conduits."

Quin frowned. That was new information. He'd never heard anything like it before, and it was jarring that he hadn't. "So…you are saying that Athera's Crescent is the reason why every vortex in the world exists?"

If that were true, he couldn't fathom why he hadn't learned of it long ago. Perhaps it was some secret of the Order of Harbingers; every order had them. But a secret of that magnitude…

Tsula nodded. "That's right. A vortex is simply a whirlpool created by harvesting a magical reservoir. When the Lyceum's Circle of Convergence was destroyed, that cut off a significant supply of power to the Crescent. Fortunately, there was enough power coming in from the other vortexes to sustain it. At least, there was…until Aerysius fell."

"What happened then?" his voice was a mere whisper.

"When Aerysius was destroyed, its conduit was severed. After that, there simply wasn't enough power to sustain the Crescent. The Harbingers did everything they could to try to redirect power back to it. They even resorted to tampering with the vortex here on Titherry, altering it so that it sucked the heat right out of the air, converting it into flux. Their plan didn't work. All they succeeded in doing was destroying themselves in the process. It was too much, all at once. It created a surge that killed every last mage on the isle."

Quin nodded, thinking of the frozen corpses they had discovered in the root cellar. "So that explains the cold. But that doesn't explain you. Why is it that you thawed out while everything else froze solid?"

Tsula lifted the tongs and used them to flick some of the blackened ashes off the charcoal. She then added fresh chips of agarwood.

"I was frozen by magic," she explained. "When the power failed, so did my containment."

That made sense. Quin breathed in the heady odor of incense, the smoke becoming quite thick in the small chamber. "Well, that's fortunate. At least there is one surviving Harbinger left in the world."

"No, Quinlan Reis. That is most *un*fortunate," Tsula corrected him.

Quin frowned. "And why is that?"

"Because it has become my duty to rid the world of magic."

He blinked as her words sank in. He folded his hands in his lap. His eyes traveled from her face to the swirling tendrils of smoke that rose from the burner.

"Well, I do hope you've got something stronger to drink around here," he muttered finally, setting the tea aside.

Tsula stared at him with those eyes that only

accused and never forgave. She rose and made her way toward a cupboard set against the wall. From within, she produced a golden flask. With a glance at Quin, she poured the liquor into a cup, then began adding water from a pitcher. He raised his hand quickly.

"Stop."

She righted the pitcher, handing the cup to Quin. He gazed down at the milky color of the arak, contemplating it for a moment.

"Here's to apocalypse," he murmured. Then he tilted his head back and tossed it down. The liquor burned his throat, the strong spices awakening his senses. When it hit his belly, it lit a warmth that shot excitement through every nerve. It had been a long time since he'd taken a drink.

He offered the cup back to Tsula, motioning for more. She refilled it with a scowl, this time without any attempt to dilute it. Quin savored the taste. He closed his eyes, swirling it about on his tongue before swallowing it down.

"You have no idea how good this feels," he said. Then he drained the rest, setting the cup upside down on the small table at his side. "No, thank you," he said when Tsula went to refill it.

"So why do you feel the need to end all magic?" he asked, still with his eyes closed. "Isn't that sort of like biting the hand that feeds you?"

"Not when that hand is responsible for the oppression of half the world's population," the woman said, settling back into her chair.

"And by oppression, you mean…?"

"I speak of the curse that blackens both Caladorn and Aeridor. I have seen it through the mirror of Athera's Crescent. I've seen what it's done. To your people…and to mine."

"I wasn't aware that the curse had affected Aeridor."

"Aeridor was consumed by darkness. But unlike Caladorn, we had no mages to provide us with light. No lightfields. My people starved to death long ago, trapped on a continent with no light and no means of escape."

Quin hung his head. His memories of Aeridor were dim. Palaces sprouting from jungle, covered in flowering vines. Fountains and reflecting pools, manicured gardens and acres of lawn where exotic creatures roamed and grazed.

Lost to darkness because of him.

His mouth went dry. The effects of the arak evaporated from his mind. The once-fragrant incense now smoldered, reduced to char and ash.

"That's why I came here," he muttered. "To find a way to break the curse. There must be a way to do it."

The woman stared at him with those merciless eyes. Hands clasped in her lap, she told him, "Athera's Crescent must be brought back fully online. Then, we will search for that way together."

Quin nodded. It wasn't a nod of agreement. More like resignation. "What do you need?"

Tsula sat forward, her eyes claiming him entirely. "I need an Arcanist. Someone with the skills and knowledge that were lost a thousand years ago when the Lyceum burned to the ground. In short…I need you."

"What do you need me to do?"

"I need you to repair the conduits that were severed when Aerysius fell to dust and rubble."

Quin reached down and fingered the stoneware cup. He didn't turn it over. He just let the pads of his fingers trail over its cold smoothness. His gaze wandered to Tsula's hands, hands that looked so familiar. Amani had been born in Aeridor. Her mother had been a prominent mage from the Empire. Amani had favored her mother in both looks and grace. Quin stared at Tsula's lovely hands with bittersweet sorrow.

"I'll need my tools," he said finally. "And I'll need Naia."

"Why do you need the girl?"

"Moral support." Quin picked up the empty cup, turning it back over.

"No."

"Why not?" Leaning forward, he plucked the pitcher off the table and poured the undiluted liquor into his cup. Keeping his eyes fixed on hers, he took a long, savoring gulp.

The look on the woman's face was contemptuous. "Because. The world needs you to perform this service. A service which, if successful, will kill every last mage that still exists, including the girl. I can't risk having your emotions conflicted."

Quin cocked a cynical eyebrow. "Didn't you say conflicted was exactly the state I should be in?"

Tsula's eyes hardened to stone. "I misspoke."

"Why should I help you at all?" Quin tossed back more of the potent liquor. "Call me deranged, but I happen to like the world exactly the way it is. Mages and all."

The smoldering glare she leveled at him was venomous. But with the liquor to fortify his courage, Quin didn't heed the warning in her eyes.

"Because," Tsula snapped as she rose from her chair. "Destroying the magic field is the only way to free the skies over Caladorn. And over Aeridor. This is your duty, Quinlan Reis. You brought about the curse because of your inability to face the consequences of your actions. For a thousand years, the world has suffered those consequences for you. No longer. You are the last Arcanist this world knows, and I am the last Harbinger. Together, the two of us will endeavor to repair that which you tore asunder."

Quin stared up at her as he drained the last of his cup.

"Not without Naia."

Chapter Twenty-Two
Surrender

Pass of Lor-Gamorth, The Front

Darien stood looking up at the dark and jagged ridgeline. A light breeze ruffled his hair and chilled his skin. The gloom of the stark landscape seemed more oppressive than it had just moments before. He glanced at the clouds, frowning at the faint traces of light that flickered there. He was tired of darkness, tired of the constant melancholy that filled his soul.

He wanted to see the sun again. Even if it was just one last time.

The crunch of Connel's boots alerted him to the man's presence at his back. He didn't turn around, just stood gazing upward at the devastation in the sky.

"You did well," the darkmage remarked. "I know how hard that had to be for you."

Darien nodded. It had been hard, much harder than he'd expected. He wasn't sure which had been worse: having to look in Meiran's eyes or admitting to Kyel his shame. In a way, he was responsible for them both. Craig, too. Their friendships were casualties of his own self-destruction.

"I don't trust the commander," Connel said.

Darien nodded. He didn't, either; he knew better. Devlin Craig had been a disciple of Garret Proctor, just as Darien had been himself. Craig knew how to wrest opportunity from desperation.

"He knows exactly what he's doing," Connel went on. "The new keep's positioned in the center of a node."

"I know. I'm the one who told him about it." Darien's eyes followed the craggy slopes of the Shadowspears. Somewhere up there, lost in the choking mass of cloudcover, was the new keep, a fortress his eyes had never once looked upon. Built right over the spot where Arden Hannah had tried to burn him at the stake. Where Devlin Craig had saved his life from the flames.

He breathed a sigh. "But the node actually works to our advantage. Craig's mages will be impotent, but we'll still have access to the Onslaught. They won't be expecting that."

"If you use the Onslaught, that will void the truce you just negotiated."

Darien looked at him. "If I use the Onslaught, they'll have voided it already."

The man nodded thoughtfully then started walking back toward the pavilion. Darien fell in step with him, matching his pace.

Connel said, "I wish you hadn't surrendered our officers. We can't afford that kind of loss."

"We won't have to." Darien ducked as he parted the flap of the tent. "Order every senior officer to find an infantryman with their same height and build. Have them trade uniforms and weapons."

A look of appreciation grew on Connel's face. "You're good at this."

"That's why I defeated your armies."

"No." Connel shook his head. His smile disappeared. "You defeated me because I overestimated you. I assumed that just because you were a Sentinel, that you wouldn't be morally depraved. I was wrong. You're willing to sink to depths that I'd never imagine."

Darien stared at him, returning glare for glare. Then he turned and stalked out of the tent.

Kajiri Flats, The Front

Darien took his time about riding back to camp. He wasn't in a hurry. His mood was just as bleak as the horizon. He let his horse pick out its own trail, head lowered, foraging fruitlessly in the barren soil. It was late in the day when he finally rode into the outskirts of the encampment, helm pulled down to hide his face. He thought about paying a visit to Myria but reconsidered. He made for his own tent, instead.

He tossed the reins of his horse to a foot soldier and moved into the tent, tugging off his helm. He unfastened the brooch that held his cloak, letting the heavy garment fall from his body.

Azár burst through the tent's partition, nearly startling him off his feet.

His wife's face was red with anger. She held her hands clawed into fists, her eyes narrowed like slivered coals. He'd never seen her so enraged. The hostility on her face made him take a step back in retreat.

"There is talk that my husband intends to abandon our cause and return to the side of our adversaries! Is this true?"

Darien was surprised that word of the parley could have reached the camp ahead of him. He'd been hoping to break the news to Azár himself. What bothered him most was the distorted version of his agreement that had gotten back to her ears. It made him fear what the men under his command must think.

"It's not true," he answered coolly. He walked past her toward a jug of wine set out on a table. He didn't bother with a cup. He upended the jug and let the cool liquid spill into his mouth, drinking it down in thirsty gulps.

"Then tell me, what is the truth?"

Darien set the jug back down. He lowered his gaze to the table's surface. It wasn't made of wood. Something like slate. He poked his fingernail into a crack, musing at the texture. Without looking at her, he explained, "I volunteered to become their hostage—Myria and myself, actually. To guarantee we'll honor the terms of the truce I struck with their commander. It was the only way they'd agree to let us enter the pass uncontested."

Her eyes widened. "They will kill you," she whispered.

"No." He shook his head. "That would violate the terms of the agreement." He raised the jug and took another gulp of wine. Then another. The magic field wavered for just a second. He set the jug back down with a heavy *clunk*.

Azár moved toward him. She wore a blood-red shirt with flowing sleeves, her hair collected in a single braid. She looked just as fierce as the first day he'd met her. She reached up and took his face in her hands, gazing piercingly into his eyes.

"My people have a saying: 'Be a thousand times more wary of your friends than of your enemies.' This is because your friends know best how to harm you."

To Darien, the proverb sounded wise. He couldn't argue with the logic. "I'll be wary," he said to assure her.

Azár's gaze lingered on his face. Finally, she drew back, whirling away. She snatched the jug off the table and poured herself a cup. Then she lay back on one of the sofas arranged along the tent's perimeter, stretching out her legs.

"I am concerned for you," she said, glancing up at him. "When do you intend to surrender to these people?"

"On the morrow." He placed his hand around the handle of the jug but didn't lift it. Instead, he traced his fingers along its cool, engraved surface. The copper jug commanded his attention. It was far easier to look at than his wife's anxious face.

"So, we have only tonight, then." Regret cooled her tone.

He nodded, still engrossed in the textured handle.

"Have you managed to find any feelings for me yet?"

His eyes shot up. She was staring at him expectantly, he saw. Waiting for him to reply. "I feel something," he forced himself to admit. "I'm not sure how deep it goes."

"But you do feel something?"

He nodded, not certain what his own feelings even were. Grief, sorrow, guilt...one of those, or more likely a combination. Nothing good. Certainly not what she wanted.

Azár sat up, setting the wine cup down by her side. Her eyes drilled into him, as if trying to bore a hole right through his skin. She rose to her feet and stalked toward him, her stare wandering downward, taking in all of him. She circled slowly, her fingers trailing over his shirt. Darien tensed, her touch sending electric shivers through his skin.

She came to a halt in front of him.

"My husband is a handsome man," she said at last. She reached up and pulled at the thong that held his hair, allowing the dark strands to spill down his back.

She leaned in, studying his expression. Then she said firmly, "You will do as I say and only as I say. You will stop if I say stop."

He nodded, understanding the need. "Aye. I will."

"Kiss me."

He closed his eyes and complied. He brushed his lips against hers, not quite a kiss. Then he drew back, frowning deeply.

"Lower your guard," she whispered.

He realized that she wasn't asking any more of him than she was willing to give of herself. Somehow, that made things easier. He brought a hand up to her face, caressing her soft skin. Then he gathered her in and kissed her hungrily.

The sunless morning came too soon.

Darien wasn't ready for it.

He rolled out of bed, leaving Azár slumbering with her lips parted slightly, the expression on her face for once tranquil. He found his clothes and pulled them on. But then he took them right back off again. Instead, he went to his chest and rummaged around, producing the same pair of black breeches and cotton shirt he'd worn on the day he'd died. It somehow seemed fitting. He'd abandoned the Rhen and his former life wearing those clothes. It seemed appropriate that he should return in them. He donned his cloak and broke his fast with a piece of bread and a handful of dates.

The whole while he chewed, he stared at Azár's sleeping face, contemplating her broodingly. It wasn't that he regretted the act they had shared; he didn't. But it did complicate matters. It made what he had to do that much more difficult. It was one thing, walking into uncertainty, when he'd felt his wife was cold and distant. It was completely different, knowing that he left someone behind who genuinely cared for him.

He would have to make provisions, he realized, for the chance he didn't return. Overnight, Azár's security had become a new priority, one he hadn't taken into his calculations before.

He frowned, studying her soft beauty as he munched down the last bits of bread and washed it down with a glass of wine. Then he rose, wiping his mouth, and bent down before the bed. He leaned over and kissed Azár on the cheek. She didn't stir. He could hear the peace in her soft breath. He could see it written on her face. It made him glad.

Straightening, he donned his boots and made his way out of the tent. As he emerged, the thanacryst rose to its feet with an enormous yawn. It stretched, first its front legs, then the rear, then stood staring at him with expectant, sinister eyes.

Darien raised his hand, signaling the demon-hound to remain. He didn't know what the thing would do when the camp moved on. The beast seemed to not mind Azár. He hoped it would follow her. So far, it hadn't shown any inclination to use her as a food source.

Darien frowned, suddenly worried. He'd never questioned the wisdom of keeping the creature. It had always proved a loyal companion. Now he found himself doubting his own judgement.

"Stay here," he told it, knowing full well it probably wouldn't obey. He decided to try anyway. "Protect Azár." The thing continued to gaze at him. He turned away. The hound settled back down again into the dirt, its nose between its massive paws.

Darien trudged away toward the heart of the camp, aware of the sound of footsteps jogging to catch up with him. He turned to find himself flanked by Sayeed and his nephew Iskender, a clot of Zakai hurrying in their wake. He noticed that Sayeed and his nephew had traded uniforms. He was glad to see that his commands were being heeded, especially by his own men.

"Lord, I must tell you that I am opposed to this plan," Sayeed growled in a voice lowered so that none of the other men could hear.

"Your opinion is noted," Darien said. He had no intention of getting sucked into an argument. He walked over to where the horses were picketed and, stooping, pulled at the knot to free his own.

"I don't think you understand. They cannot be trusted —"

"Sayeed," Darien said, laying a hand on the man's

arm. "I want you to keep my wife safe. Stand by her side, no matter what. Don't come looking for me."

"Lord—"

"No matter what," Darien insisted. "Be in the vanguard when they open up the pass. Get her through as quickly as you can."

Sayeed looked ready to argue. But instead, he effected a stiff and formal bow.

"Yes, Lord."

Darien considered this man who had stood at his side through so many battles. Not physical battles. But the inner kind that mattered more and hurt harder. He finally realized the depth of his appreciation for him.

"Don't call me 'Lord,'" Darien corrected him on impulse. "Call me 'Brother.'"

Sayeed looked stunned. He stood there for a moment with his face going slack, the color draining from his copper skin. "My Lord…"

Darien shook his head. Sayeed was the one man Darien knew he could trust. He had grown tired of the formal distance demanded by the Tanisars' rigid code of honor. Damn formality. What he needed was a friend, not another subordinate.

"Go in peace, Brother," he stated gruffly.

Sayeed swept forward and clasped him in a rigid embrace, nearly pulling him off his feet. He kissed Darien on both cheeks. Darien returned the gesture as best he could, trying not to seem as awkward as he felt.

"May the peace of the gods be with you," Sayeed said, patting his back. Then he pulled away, collecting himself.

Darien climbed onto the back of his horse as Iskender mounted the spare. Zakai trotting along at their sides, they rode through the camp as onlookers came running to line their path. War drums thundered, men stood shaking spears and swords at the sight of their approach.

To Darien's surprise, the hatred of the men for him seemed to have cooled overnight. A fiery outcry swelled from the heart of the encampment. They rode through dirt streets lined by howling warriors, finally reaching a large crowd gathered in the assembly area in front of the command tent.

There, Darien dismounted, leading his horse to where Byron Connel stood at Myria's side, ranks of uniformed officers gathered behind them. Darien surveyed the assemblage, taking a moment to realize what he was looking at. These were the men the officers had traded roles with, gathered now to accompany him into the pass. Darien's gaze swept over their faces. Not a man looked as though he didn't belong. The officers had chosen their replacements well.

He drew up in front of Connel and Myria, the Battlemage nodding a terse greeting. Myria regarded him with an expression of amusement. She was wearing a short, brightly patterned tunic over trousers, a broad shawl draped over one shoulder.

"So, here's the man who sealed my fate with a handshake," she said.

Darien knew he owed her an apology, or, at the very least, some reassurance. "If everything goes as planned, we'll be guests of the commander for a week." It was an attempt to sooth her nerves.

It didn't work.

Myria cocked a perfectly arched eyebrow in his direction, looking skeptical. "And how often do things go as you plan, Darien?"

He couldn't help but smile. "Not often," he admitted.

Myria nodded, her face smug. "And what happens when they don't?"

"Then I improvise." He gestured toward the mountains. "They built Greystone Keep within a node. Their mages won't have access to the magic field. But we'll still be able to use the Onslaught."

"We can't heal ourselves with the Onslaught."

"Then we'd best not get injured."

Sincere doubt shadowed her expression. He couldn't blame her. Darien turned to Connel, nodding his head in the direction of the gathered men. "Is this everyone?"

"It is," Connel said, stepping forward. "Volunteers, one and all. Their lives are in your hands. Better pray your friend doesn't see fit to double-cross you."

Darien couldn't guarantee it. If Devlin Craig was bent on treachery, then there was precious little he could do to prevent it.

Connel clapped his shoulder. "Go in peace."

Darien returned the gesture then climbed astride his horse. The stallion danced sideways with a nervous snort and a jingle of tack. Darien gathered the tasseled reins in his hands, bringing the animal back under control.

Iskender jumped lithely down from the mare and held the stirrup for Myria. She mounted gracefully, clucking her horse forward while Sayeed's nephew joined the group of foot soldiers.

Byron Connel gave a nod.

The low, throaty moan of a war horn rose over the field, sliding up dismally through the octaves. At the sound of it, the men started forward, marching to a syncopated meter tapped out on a single drum.

Darien urged his horse forward at a walk, Myria at his side, as over a thousand men formed up in a great column behind him. He turned his horse toward Orguleth, toward the Pass of Lor-Gamorth, his eyes taking in the flanks of the Shadowspears. Roiling cloudcover obscured the tops of the mountains. The flickering lights in the clouds beckoned him onward.

The horn cry rose again, the sound more ominous than before. The drum tapped out its fatalistic cadence.

Darien glanced back at Connel to find that the man had already turned and was walking away, hands clasped behind his back. Myria rode to his left, head bowed. Two standard bearers trailed at their sides, one holding the red emblem of the Tanisars, the other the green field of Bryn Calazar's legions.

They marched forward, toward destiny or death. He didn't know which. One path led to sunlight, the other to eternal darkness.

Darien stared up at the mountains, feeling a terrible sense of foreboding.

———

It took hours to march the distance between the staging grounds and the alluvial fan that formed the wide mouth of the pass. By the time they started up into the canyon, it was already late in the day. The soldiers walked with their backs straight, showing no signs of fatigue. The drum continued tapping out its relentless beat.

At the mouth of the canyon, Darien pulled back on the reins and raised a hand, commanding a halt. Behind him, silence reigned over the columns behind him as the men stopped and stood motionless in perfect ranks. A slight breeze chased his cloak and ruffled his stallion's mane.

Ahead, the fog that shrouded the pass parted just enough that he could make out the dark outlines of palisades. Fog and shadows obscured the air, but at last he saw the strength of Craig's army. His scouts had already warned him about the numbers.

Still, it was an intimidating sight to behold. Ahead, an army numbering in the tens of thousands stood guarding the wide bottom of the pass, lining the walls of the canyon, continuing up the slopes.

Beneath him, Darien's horse stamped nervously. A strong odor on the air made his eyes widen: the scent of wood smoke. Orange fires glowed from behind the fortifications, following the path of the river up as it snaked into the Shadowspears. In all his time in the Black Lands, Darien had never once smelled the odor of burning wood. The smell conjured an intense wave of anxiety sharpened by a sense of dread.

Movement ahead caught his attention.

A group of riders had broken away from the main host and was approaching his position. Darien kept a tight rein on his horse, letting the party approach. There were about twenty men, all mounted. Two rode in the fore, the others following in a single, spread-out file. Every man held a hornbow at his side.

Devlin Craig stopped his horse yet fifty paces away, Meiran drawing up next to him on a silver gelding. Craig's men came up behind, forming a line as if taking up position to advance.

Holding Craig's eyes warily, Darien dismounted. He glanced at Myria, nodding for her to follow suit. Then he turned, signaling his men to stay back.

Darien and Myria walked side by side toward the awaiting Greystone entourage, leading their horses behind them. It was a long, sobering walk across the canyon floor, painful in many ways. Darien could feel the eyes of his men lingering on his back, as well as the suspicious glare of Devlin Craig. Meiran's bitter stare tracked his every movement.

It had been right here, in this very canyon, where the Enemy had dealt a deathblow to Greystone's infantry under Darien's command. That defeat had been counted as a victory, even though the graves had outnumbered the living. Now Darien returned to the same site, the same defeat.

Only, this time, he was the Enemy.

His gaze wandered over the faces ahead of him.

There was a sadness in Meiran's eyes that he hadn't expected to see. The look on her face, on Kyel's face, made everything that much more difficult.

He halted as soldiers jogged forward to relieve them of their horses.

He turned to Craig. Darien stood for a moment, staring into the eyes of his old friend, searching there for some trace of compassion. There was none.

He said formally, "Force Commander Devlin Craig. I present to you myself, Grand Master Myria Anassis, and the commanding officers of the combined legions of Malikar. We are here to surrender unconditionally and throw ourselves upon your mercy."

Before Craig could respond, Darien reached up and drew the leather baldric off his shoulder, offering out his scabbarded sword. Devlin Craig accepted the blade solemnly then handed the weapon to the officers at his side. Meiran's eyes left Darien to follow the retreat of the sword that had once been her gift to him.

When it was done, Craig nodded. "Tell your men to ground their arms."

Darien called back over his shoulder, "Ground arms!"

Behind him, the first line of men stepped forward and dropped their arms and armor down on the black dirt of the canyon floor. They then turned as one and were ushered away toward the canyon wall by Greystone soldiers. There, they were made to kneel, hands on their heads. The next rank of men stepped forward and did the same, dropping their arms and shields in a growing mass of weaponry. Then the next rank, until row after row of kneeling men collected along the canyon's walls.

Darien watched until the last of his men knelt at the mercy of Craig's soldiers. Gray-cloaked sentries walked up and down the lines, binding wrists, patting down bodies. The entire process of surrender would take some time; it was only just beginning.

In front of him, Craig plunged a fist into a pocket, producing two small vials of liquid. He moved forward, holding the vials in his hand. One he handed to Myria. The other he offered to Darien.

"Drink."

Darien received the vial warily, holding it up and noting the small amount of dark liquid it contained. "What's this?"

"It'll put you out," Craig answered.

Darien nodded, understanding. He felt a sinking feeling in his gut. He glanced back up at Craig. "Will I wake?"

"You'll wake."

It didn't sound like a lie. That didn't mean it wasn't. He felt drenched in fear; his plan hadn't accounted for this. Darien lifted the vial and drained the contents in one swallow. The mixture had a bitter taste. It made his mouth go instantly dry.

He dropped the vial on the ground.

He could feel it hit his stomach. A warmth ignited in his belly, spreading quickly to his limbs. His skin felt suddenly cold. The magic field quivered, then drained completely away.

At his side, he heard Myria groan. She wavered, staggering. He reached out to grasp her.

His arm was captured by a soldier who pinned him from behind. The man shouted something at him, but in his confusion, he couldn't make out the words. Another man slapped Darien in the face. He swayed, blinking, perspiration streaming from his forehead.

A skeletal man clad in gray robes stepped forward, peering into his face. A priest, Darien realized. He gaped into the man's face, his confusion rampant. What need had they for a priest? The man smiled odiously. Then he took Darien's hands one at a time, snapping something around his wrists.

He looked down, seeing heavy black manacles with strange markings that flickered and began to glow.

Darien's eyes went wide as he felt the Hellpower die inside him. Panicking, he fought against the manacles' power. But it was no good; his mind was ebbing, drifting away. He sank to his knees. The world faded even as he fought its fading. It didn't matter. In the end, the drug won out.

The last sound he heard was Myria's weeping.

Chapter Twenty-Three
Fatally Flawed

Isle of Titherry, The Rhen

Quin knelt down beside Naia's frozen form. She was covered with a thick coating of frost, her hair brittle with ice. Her fingers remained clenched like gnarled stone in front of her face. He placed a hand on her arm. Cold. Damn cold; so cold it hurt. He shot a glare up at Tsula.

"Move back," she warned, then struck out with the raw force of her power.

There was a sizzling sound, and steam rose from the floor, from the walls, from Naia herself. It made the air of the room hot and moist. Immediately, Naia relaxed and toppled over, spilling limply across the floor of the ice cellar.

Quin lunged to catch her, but not in time. Naia's head hit the ground with a hollow *thunk*. He scooped her up, cradling her head against his chest. Her skin was still gray, but brightening even as he looked at her. He patted her cheek a few times lightly, then harder. He stopped only when he felt her body spasm and quiver.

Naia's face twisted into a gruesome expression. Then her eyes burst wide open, deep black and unfocused. She sat up rigid.

"Watch out!" she screamed.

Quin hugged her close, not knowing what else to do. He ran his hand through her wet hair as her body trembled against his chest. She was sobbing, he realized. He wasn't sure if it was from shock, pain, or terror. Or a twisted combination of all three. He touched her cool hand, seeking to reassure her.

"Look at me," he said.

She did, tilting her head back enough to peer feverishly into his eyes. Her cheeks were splotchy red, her pupils large and round, staring through him instead of at him.

"What? Where?"

He could barely make out the words through the force of her chattering teeth. He released her hand, cupping her face as he glared up at Tsula.

"You're going to be fine," he assured Naia. His eyes shot hatred at the woman towering over him with arms crossed, face a mask of brutal calm.

"So cold!" Naia's jaw trembled against his chest.

Quin struggled out of his coat. Still clutching her against him, he wrapped her in the fabric, tucking it tightly around her body. He took her hands into his own and rubbed them briskly.

"Bring her along," the Harbinger commanded, backing out of the room.

Naia still trembled in his arms, her eyes staring dimly up at him. Quin wasn't even sure if she knew who he was. She wasn't up to walking, that was for certain. So he scooped her up, lifting her shuddering body off the ground.

There was a metallic clink as something fell out of her clothes. He looked down. And just about dropped her.

There, on the ground by his feet, lay the Soulstone medallion. Quin stared down at it, blinking dumbly, as his brain slowly registered its presence there in the cellar. It had fallen out of Naia's pocket. The stone was dull and black, like a faceted lump of damnation. Quin found himself holding his breath. To him, that sinister stone was the most terrifying thing in all the world.

He knelt, supporting Naia's weight on his knee,

then stooped to snatch the medallion off the ground and replaced it in Naia's pocket.

"Bring her this way," Tsula said.

He followed the woman down the corridor and up a flight of stairs. Naia's weight was slight; there wasn't much to the woman. Her body still trembled from the cold, but not near as violently. When he looked down at her face, she was gazing up at him with dim awareness in her eyes.

Tsula led them down a long corridor lit by yellow magelight. Many doors lined the hallway. She picked one, seemingly at random, indicating they should enter with a jerk of her head.

"She can remain here."

Quin ducked past her into what looked like some sort of living quarters. He bent to deposit Naia in a chair as he scanned the room for blankets. He found a bed shoved up against a wall, piled high with covers. He picked them up in a bundle, surprised to find that the blankets had a freshly laundered smell. He layered them over Naia.

"Let's get you warm," he said.

Then he looked up, noticing Tsula lingering in the doorway, watching him without expression. He stood and flung the door closed. Her hand shot out and stopped it, jolting the door back open. She stared at him blandly.

"Come to me in the morning," she commanded. "I'll show you where to begin your work."

With a chilling stare, she pulled the door soundly closed behind her as she left.

"Who is she?"

Quin turned back to Naia, pausing to tuck a corner of the blanket in beneath her chin. Her skin still felt cool to the touch. He answered, "I think she's the best chance we have."

Naia's head inclined toward the door. "Do you mind elaborating?"

"Actually, I do mind," Quin said. "Right now, all I care about is getting you warm."

Quin rose and glanced around the room, taking in their surroundings. They were in some sort of guest room, it seemed. There was a bed and a chair, along with a small writing desk in the corner. Against the far wall was a wood-burning stove with an iron crock set atop it. Curious, Quin strode over to the stove and took in the ancient-looking kettle.

"I'll be damned," he muttered, dipping his finger into the fine sand that filled the inside of the kettle. He leaned over and opened the door of the stove, happy to find it filled with a good supply of tinder. With a thought, he conjured up a flame. The stove sprang to life, instantly warming the cool air of the room. And the sand in the kettle.

Quin searched the room's interior until he found a small copper cup with a long handle. To his delight, there was a pitcher already filled with water and a coffee grinder. He wasted no time, grinding up coffee and pouring the grounds straight into the copper pot. As an afterthought, he reached into his pocket and added a pinch of spice. He then thrust the pot into the heated sand.

Naia sat up, watching him closely as Quin waited for the coffee to come to a boil. When it did, he spooned some of the froth into two cups and returned the pot back to the sand. When it was done, he divided the rest of the coffee between the cups, handing one to Naia.

"Drink," he commanded her.

Naia lifted the small cup to her lips and immediately made a face. "Ah! That's strong!"

"But it's warm," Quin insisted. "Drink it." He scooped his own cup into his hand, plopping down on the bed. He closed his eyes and took a sip, savoring the taste.

He glanced up at Naia with a grin. "You like it, don't you?"

She took another sip, at last returning his smile. "I suppose I'm getting used to your spices."

"Life is never bland when I'm around." He saluted her with his cup, then took another taste. Like the smell of Tsula's incense, the flavor of the spiced coffee took his mind back in time.

Naia asked, "What happened, Quin? Who is that woman?"

"Tsula's a Harbinger," he responded with a shrug. "She says she's been frozen here since my time. She wants me to fix Athera's Crescent for her."

"But…?"

"She wants to destroy the magic field."

Naia's face filled with concern. "Can that be done?"

"Apparently so." Quin took another sip of his coffee.

"How are we going to stop her?" Naia's face was quite serious. The coffee in her hand went untouched.

That was a good question, indeed. Quin had no idea what the answer could be. "I'm not certain that we want to stop her. It's possible it's the only way to break the curse."

Naia leaned forward, pulling the covers up around her. Her hair was still wet, falling in wavy ringlets around her face. In the poor lighting of the room, it looked almost black.

"What are you going to do?"

"I'm going to repair the Crescent," Quin decided. "And then I'll use it."

"What can I do to help?"

"You can keep me alive."

She frowned. "What do you mean?"

Quin set his cup down on a table beside the bed. He scooted back, leaning up against the wall. "My profession can be exceptionally hazardous," he explained. "That's why there were never many Arcanists in the world. The better you are, the higher your risk. The good ones always ended up dead, usually sooner rather than later. Challenging projects are always risky. Especially something like Athera's Crescent; none of the mages who built it survived the process."

Naia looked down, her expression grim. She took a slow sip of her coffee. Lowering her cup, she said without looking at him, "Thank you, Quin. This is very good."

"Just one of the many services I provide," he said with a wan smile. "You should get some sleep. I'll see you in the morning."

He rose from the bed and started toward the door. But a thought tugged at his mind, forcing him to turn back around. He extended his hand toward Naia. "Give me the Soulstone."

The startled look on her face was satisfying to see. "Why do you want it?"

"Because I made it," he snapped. He wiggled his fingers. "Now, give it here."

Naia's mouth dropped open. *"You…?"*

Quin nodded, quirking a brow and flexing his fingers.

She gave a long, protracted sigh, then fished the medallion out of her pocket and handed it over to him. He closed his fingers around the dark stone, squeezing it tightly. Then, with a curt nod, he left the room, closing the door behind him.

Once in the hallway, he clutched the Soulstone against his chest. The corridor was lined with rough-hewn doors, the same as the one behind him. He didn't know where else to go, so he tried the door across from Naia's, finding it unlocked. It opened into another guest room much the same as the one he'd left. It took only a glance and a second of concentration before every candle and lantern in the room was ablaze, the room's woodfire stove awake and radiating heat.

Quin sank down in a chair at the writing desk, tossing the Soulstone down on the desk's smooth surface. In the light of the room, the medallion didn't look like a stone at all, but more like a dull chunk of coal. The silver bands of the collar were far more lustrous, glowing a liquid white in the candlelight. He spread the collar out on the surface of the desk, positioning the medallion upside-down.

Quin reached up and slipped his hat off his head, tossing it aside. He stared down at the Soulstone medallion, then gave a dispirited sigh. The last time he'd seen the artifact, it was lying beside the corpse of his dead brother. The Soulstone had been used to kill Braden. And Amani; Renquist had issued the order to execute his own daughter. Not to mention Darien, who'd been coerced into fastening the medallion around his own neck.

Three torturous deaths. All his own fault. When he'd created the Soulstone, Quin had overlooked the flaw that prevented the smooth transfer of power through the well-stone. He hadn't realized that one of the crystals was misaligned, creating resistance, but not enough to nullify the artifact. Instead, the Soulstone's victims were subjected to agonizing deaths, tortured as long as they had the strength and will to fight.

Quin stared down at the dull black stone, despising it utterly. So much suffering. All because he'd rushed the job and had the arrogance to think that his work didn't need double-checking. He resisted the urge to throw the damn thing against the wall. But he knew the Soulstone couldn't be destroyed like that. Besides, it offered him a singular opportunity that he desperately needed.

It had been a thousand years since he'd last engineered anything. His skills needed honing.

"Ah, hell," he muttered, running a hand back through the sweat-slick curls of his hair.

He reached into his pack and withdrew a tool roll. With delicate regard, Quin rolled it out on the desk in front of him, eyes scanning over the many implements of his craft that he'd collected throughout his lifetime. They were old, just like him. Some were much older. Small hammers and delicate probing instruments, wedges and corkscrewing drill bits, all with intricately worked handles, some bone, some wood or even ivory. Some were ancient. Some he'd made himself. Each separate tool was tucked into its own little sleeve in the leather roll.

He ran his hands over the tools reverently. It had been a very long time, indeed. Reaching into the rightmost pocket, he wriggled out a pair of wire spectacles with a swing lens loupe. He put them on, the vision of his right eye immediately blurring. He pushed the lens back and lifted the Soulstone up in front of his face. He clicked down a different lens, nudging it into place. One of the stone's dark facets popped into detail. He clicked down another lens, squinting as his eye adjusted to the depth of field.

At first, he could make out nothing. He moved the stone in and out until at last the individual crystals were revealed to him. He scanned the latticework: backward, forward, moving in and out through the layers. At last, he saw it: the one cuboidal crystal that was aligned different from all the others in the pattern.

He'd found the flaw.

He had never viewed it before. Not with his own eyes. He'd known it was there, but had never had the opportunity to see for himself that tiny imperfection. It seemed so innocent: one subtle, almost undetectable, crystal.

It had inflicted so much damage, so much pain.

Quin fumbled with the tool roll, extracting a copper probe. He held it up to the dark surface of the Soulstone and, focusing his concentration, willed the probe to sink inside. He watched it descend through the lattice of crystals as they bobbed out of the way of the moving tip. Until the probe was nudged up against the single crystal that was misaligned.

With the slightest dribble of magic, Quin focused all his will into that one crystal through the instrument in his hand. He watched it slowly rotate into position, sliding into place. He held his breath. When the crystal settled fully into the pattern, he let out a protracted sigh.

The flaw was fixed. Only, the crystal above had been pushed out of alignment.

Quin scooted his spectacles up and rubbed his eyes. He knew it wouldn't be that simple. Nothing was. Propping his elbow on the desk, he squinted harder and sank the probe back into the stone to reconfigure the next crystal in the pattern, pushing it back into position. Which knocked aside the next crystal above it.

A bead of sweat dripped from his forehead, dropping onto the desk. Quin wiped his face with his sleeve. Then he forced his mind to concentrate as he gazed into the deep black depths of the Soulstone, pushing the next crystal back into place. And the next. And the next, as the hours sped by and the nighttime waned…

Quin jolted awake at the sound of a piercing scream.

"What?!" he shouted, dropping the instrument he was holding as he jerked his head up off the desk. He stared blearily into Naia's ghost-pale face. Her eyes were wide, her mouth gaping at him in horror.

He wiped the slobber from the corner of his mouth, righting himself in his seat. His eyes scanned over the room, desperately seeking the source of the threat. But there was just Naia and himself. They were alone.

He frowned up at her with a vacuous look on his face.

"You're…alive…?" she gasped, taking a step toward him.

Quin frowned even harder. "Well, not precisely alive, but I take it that's not your point. By the way…why do you ask?"

She shook her head slowly, her hair swaying into her face. She pointed to the desk. Glancing down, he saw the Soulstone. And almost screamed himself.

The medallion was glowing red, full of a lively, scintillating light.

Full of a mage's gift.

"Who…?" Naia gasped. Then her face wrinkled in a look of disgust. *"Did you kill Tsula?"*

"No!"

"Then who?"

Quin ignored the question, scooping the

Soulstone up in his hand. He donned the wire spectacles, flipping quickly through the lenses, staring deep into the perfect latticework of glowing crystals. Somehow, it was fully charged. Each crystal vibrated with radiant energy.

"Then why is it glowing? What's filling it?" Naia demanded

"The air," Quin gasped, not quite believing it himself. It wasn't possible…but it was the only explanation. It couldn't have sucked the gift out of him. He was not a living mage. He had no gift left in him.

"How?" Naia pressed.

"I don't know." Quin shook his head. "I was working on it last night. Just tinkering. I was trying to fix the flaw. I must have done something…"

He squinted harder, staring into the glowing depths of the jewel, at the charged crystals pulsating with life. There was no sign of the flaw. Every crystal was perfectly aligned. He'd made certain of that before falling asleep.

"I wonder…" he whispered. Removing the spectacles, he set them down on the desktop. Then, before he could change his mind, he wrapped the silver bands of the collar around his neck. With a click, the clasp snapped closed.

"No!" Naia lurched forward.

The stunning power that surged into him took his breath away. Quin's muscles locked rigid, his back arching in the chair as a gush of energy flooded through every fiber of his being. It was like a lightning strike that hit every nerve, a torrent of colors and sounds and feelings. The power was exhilarating, thrilling him completely.

The flow of energy stopped, his body going limp. He sat back in the chair, panting, sweating, every muscle quivering. He could still fill it, the stirring of power that moved within, pulsating quietly in the back of his mind. Greater and more fulfilling than ever he remembered. And it hadn't hurt one bit.

"What did you do…?" Naia gasped.

Quin reached up behind his neck, opening the silver clasp. The Soulstone, now dark, slid down his chest into his lap. He fingered it, nudging the medallion slightly. He looked up at Naia. Then he closed his eyes.

With his mind, he tugged at the magic field. Not through the Onslaught. This time, he touched it directly. He let it seep into him, feeling its soothing cadence, the rhythmic pulse of power he had known all his life. He did the simplest thing he could think of: he willed a mist of magelight into being.

The sound of Naia's gasp told him that his attempt had been successful. When he opened his eyes, he was surrounded by a mist of glaring white light. Quin flinched, pushing his seat back. He rose to stand, argent strands of mist weaving between his feet. He gaped down at it, unable to explain the nature of the color. Before, his signature had been dark red, the hue of spilled blood. The color of the legacy he'd inherited from his predecessor.

But this…

He looked down at the Soulstone in his hand as the explanation became clear to him. The gift inside him now wasn't the same legacy he'd inherited from his master. It wasn't even a legacy, not something handed down. It was the beginning of something *new.* Staring down at the Soulstone, Quin gave a mirthless laugh.

"What is it? What happened?" Naia demanded, confusion paling her face.

"I have the gift in me again," Quin said with a euphoric grin. "I feel it inside me. Ha! *Do you know what this means?"*

"No. I don't." She shook her head.

Quin whirled toward her, clutching the medallion against his chest. "It means I don't need the Hellpower anymore! I can reach through to the magic field *on my own!"* His eyes widened as the implications sank in. "Naia…*I'm alive."*

Chapter Twenty-Four Cruel Choices

Pass of Lor-Gamorth, The Front

Kyel stared at the long line of prisoners being escorted into the practice yard below Greystone Keep. There, the captured men were lined up in rows and made to kneel, their hands secured behind their backs. Crackling bonfires blazed at the edges of the yard, casting a contortionist's dance of light across the faces of the captives.

Kyel couldn't help but stare, disturbed by the silence the warriors observed, even in the face of defeat. No one spoke a word. Their faces were grim and stern, staring straight ahead. Their expressions never wavered, even as more gray-cloaked soldiers poured into the yard.

At an order from a captain, one of the prisoners was dragged forward and forced to his knees in front of a wooden block. There were many blocks along the wall of the practice yard, Kyel realized. They'd appeared there overnight without him realizing.

A Greystone soldier came forward, hoisting a massive sword.

"What's this?" Kyel gasped to Meiran. "This isn't part of the agreement!"

The prime warden cast a troubled stare his way. "The agreement has been modified."

The burly soldier brought the weapon around, laying the blade across the prisoner's neck. He adjusted his grip. Then he lifted the sword up and brought it swiftly down. The corpse slumped sideways to the ground. The executioner kicked the severed head away.

No one moved. Not one man made so much as a sound. The prisoners knelt in perfect lines across the yard, heads held high, backs straight. Four more men were dragged forward to their deaths.

Kyel turned away from the gruesome scene. There were a thousand captives. Did they intend to behead them all? He heard the dull *thud* of a sword striking off another head. Then another.

"Why are you doing this?" he demanded.

Meiran's face was sad but resolute. She was still pale, dark circles lingering beneath her eyes. He suspected they arose from lack of sleep over the decisions she'd been forced to make. Decisions he'd not been party to. He understood why. He would never have condoned any of this.

"We can't take any chances," she said evenly. She held her hands clasped in front of her, taking in the grisly scene. She flinched slightly as another sword reaped its harvest of blood.

Kyel couldn't watch; he kept his back to it all. *"Why?"* he demanded. "They surrendered. They came willingly!"

Her eyes shot toward him. "*Why* did they come willingly? Have you asked yourself that? Why would they surrender? Why take such a chance? Because they had a plan, that's why—a plan that we foiled."

Another thump, this one followed by an agonized scream. One of the headsmen had missed his mark. Kyel closed his eyes against the impulse to turn and take in the carnage. Another dull *thud* ended the victim's pain.

"So you're just going to kill them all?" Kyel spun away from her, casting a frantic glance back down the rows of prisoners awaiting their turns to die. No one begged for mercy or wailed against their fortune. It was the eeriest sight he'd ever seen, these soldiers patiently awaiting calamity, watching their own impending fate enacted over and over before their eyes.

Then he thought of the people of the Black Lands whose very existence depended on this broken treaty. Kyel's stomach soured, his joints stiffening. His heart staggered under the weight of guilt. He'd been a fool. He should have seen this coming.

"What about Darien?" he whispered, though he thought he already knew the answer. One look in Meiran's eyes confirmed it.

"He's too dangerous."

He couldn't keep the shock off his face. Meiran saw it and offered him a look of sympathy.

"I'm sorry, Kyel. It pains me, too."

He looked at her as if she were a stranger, unable to understand how she could so betray a man she had once loved. A man who had sacrificed his soul to save her own. It went beyond dishonor. Kyel peered into her eyes, trying to get a sense of the emotions living there. Meiran's eyes reflected the flames of the bonfires. But there was sadness there, as well. She had not made this decision lightly. But neither did she regret it.

"They are demons, Kyel," she reminded him. "We're just sending them back to where they came from. That's all. They don't belong here."

The logic of her words was lost on him. He wanted no part of it. "So this was all just a trap from the beginning?" He waved his arm in the direction of the prisoners being slaughtered behind him. "What about the rest of their people? What about the children?"

"They're the Enemy," Meiran pronounced.

Kyel stared at her, horrified. How could she justify any of this? He couldn't believe she could be so callous, that any of them could. It went against every principle of honor he'd ever been taught. "How can you…? *We gave them our word!*"

Meiran looked at him in pity. "Kyel. You're the last Sentinel we have left. What do you suppose our chances were before this? We had no choice."

"No," he disagreed. "We *did* have a choice—but you just made the wrong one!"

With that, he turned and stormed away, leaving Meiran to reap the fruits of her deception.

———

Darien's body shivered, but not from cold. His arms trembled violently, quaking the chains that held them. He couldn't help it. It was an effect of the drug they'd given him. His eyes stared blearily into the shadows, making very little out of nothing. Another harsh chill wracked his muscles. He clenched his fists against the awful feel of it.

"I'm sorry…"

He recognized the voice that whispered toward him through the darkness. It spoke to him from the past, from out of his memory. The sound of that voice was comforting. He struggled to force his eyes open, but his lids were heavy and kept sliding closed again. Blinking, he fought to put a face with the voice. But the features were blurry, unrefined. He couldn't keep focus. Behind, a torch dripped buttery light into the shadows. He heard another soft noise echoing toward him from the darkness, like the sound of distant weeping.

He squinted, peering, his body quaking in shuddering spasms. He squinted harder, willing the features in front of him to resolve. They finally squirmed into a blurry image of Kyel Archer's distorted face. His former acolyte sat in a chair beside him, hands clutched together in his lap. The look in Kyel's eyes spoke volumes of shame.

"What?" Darien shivered through clenched teeth. They had him tied down to a table of some kind. He was in a dungeon. The infernal manacles the priest had placed on him still encircled his wrists, cutting him off from the Onslaught.

Cutting him off from hope.

"They're going to burn you," Kyel said, his face pale.

Anger gripped Darien. He'd suspected treachery, but nothing this decisive. His mind leapt immediately to the men he'd brought with him.

Kyel went on, "I tried talking them out of it. They won't listen."

"What about the treaty?" Darien whispered hoarsely, struggling in vain against the arcane shackles that held the Onslaught in check. He pumped his wrists against them until his flesh tore open.

"There's no treaty. It was all just a trap. I didn't know—" Kyel's voice lurched. "I didn't know. I'm sorry…"

Darien's mind struggled to grapple with the implications. The men he'd surrendered, the armies that followed in their wake. The clans. His people…his wife. Nothing was safe. Everything was in jeopardy. And his one asset, the Onslaught, was denied him. He trembled harder.

"My men—"

Kyel shook his head. "All dead. Every last one of them."

Darien squeezed his eyes shut against the fury brought on by that knowledge. He wrenched against the manacles until blood flowed freely down his hands. He had to get out, had to warn them—

"Kyel. I need you to help me—"

"I can't." Kyel shook his head, eyes filling with regret.

Darien gasped for breath, shuddering as he fought against the death grip of the iron bands. *"Just get these damned things off me!"*

"I can't. I'm sorry, Darien. I have to go now."

He wanted to scream. Thousands of lives depended on him. Tens of thousands. If he could just get out of the dungeon—

"Kyel…"

"I'm sorry." His former acolyte rose from his chair and, reaching down, patted Darien's arm.

Darien locked eyes with him, capturing him and holding him there. "You can stop this! Kyel, you can stop it!"

Kyel shook his head. "I can't."

"You swore an oath to defend this land *and its people!*"

"That's what I'm doing."

"It's not!" Darien shouted, choking on desperation. "You're the last of us, Kyel! You can't pick sides—you don't have that luxury! These are *people!* People of this land who *need* you! Who are going to *die* without you! Think, Kyel! *You've got to be stronger than those chains!"*

Kyel glanced down at the emblems on his wrists. He took a deep, lingering, breath. He seemed to be struggling with his conscience. When he looked back up again, his eyes were moist. "I'm sorry, Darien. I wish I could help you." He turned and left, his long strides carrying him swiftly out of the room.

Darien sagged in his restraints. The last of his hope faded with the sound of Kyel's footsteps. He would get no clemency from Devlin Craig.

"Myria!" he yelled at the ceiling, wondering if she was even still alive.

"I'm here, Darien." Her voice sounded just as dismal as his own.

He craned his head to the side, looking back over his shoulder. They had her in an iron cage across the room from him. She stood watching him, gripping the bars. She caught his eyes and shared a look that told him everything there was to say. Darien looked away, grimacing. He could do nothing for her. He'd condemned them both.

Silence lingered in the dungeon. Silence and shadow. For a long time, he lay there, just listening. The flickering flames of the torches snaked their dance, holding back the darkness by only a fraction. Eventually, the drug cleared enough from his system that his body stopped shivering. He lay there in the darkness, listening to the quiet sounds made by Myria in her cage. It sounded to him as if she'd accepted her fate, just as he had. There was nothing else either of them could do.

He heard the echoing sounds of footsteps approaching from the corridor outside.

Darien stared across the room into the blackness of the doorway. Craig entered the dungeon followed by the priest. They paused in the doorway as Myria fled to the other side of her cage, pressing her body back against the iron bars. The sight of Devlin Craig made Darien stiffen. His bloodied hands clenched into fists. He seethed with feelings he didn't understand: a fierce mixture of hatred and sorrow, desperation and fury, all churning together in a quagmire of emotion.

Craig glanced at the priest. "I want a word with him, first."

"Of course." The oily haired man flashed a wan smile, stepping to the side.

Darien finally recognized the unfamiliar gray robes: this was a priest of Deshari, the Goddess of Grief. The people of the Rhen considered Xerys evil. But in Darien's opinion, the goddess Deshari was far more deserving of their terror. Deshari's adherents embraced pain, yearned for heartache and trauma. They viewed agony as a catalyst of transformation.

It was a despicable cult. Their practices went beyond the immoral, and for no clear benefit to society. He considered Deshari far worse than Xerys, the same way a murderer was different from an executioner. At least his own dark god seemed justified for the evils He perpetrated. For the worshippers of Deshari, evil was both ends and means.

The gray-robed priest peered at him, an eager smile on his lips. In his eyes lingered a promise of pain.

Craig started forward, glancing at Myria as he rounded the corner of her cage. He strode up to the table Darien was strapped to, pausing to linger at his side. Seeing the look on his old friend's face spiked Darien's rage.

"Spare my people, Craig." It took everything he had just to get the words out. To swallow his anger and embrace humility. There was nothing else to do.

Devlin Craig gazed down at him with eyes that contained a mixture of disgust and pity. He shook his head in obvious confusion. "They're not your people, Darien."

He could tell by Craig's face that he didn't understand. He thought him unbalanced, perhaps even insane.

"They *are*," Darien insisted. "I wasn't born to them. But that doesn't make it any different. Please. Listen to me. They're good people. They're not the Enemy you think they are. They don't deserve this —"

But Craig cut him off, already shaking his head before Darien was finished. "It's not for me to decide. I'm just a soldier. I do what I'm told. And right now, I've been told to carry out your execution."

Darien sagged in his bonds, overcome by a feeling of hopelessness. He had failed before, many times in his life. But this was different. The stakes were too high.

"I'm sorry." Craig looked as though he was sincere. "I don't have a choice." He looked to the side, avoiding Darien's eyes. "So I'll let you decide. Do you want us to kill you first? Spare you the pain of watching her burn?" He nodded back over his shoulder at Myria's cage. "Or would you rather spare her?"

It was a cruel choice. Darien clenched his fists in rage. *"Gods damn you,"* he growled.

"I'm sure they will. Who first, Darien?"

No amount of begging would change Craig's mind. Darien realized that he only had one choice left to make. He closed his eyes and made it. He decided to spare Myria.

"Her first."

"All right." Craig nodded at the priest, who had been watching the exchange.

A sick smile formed on the man's lips. He reached long, bony fingers into the deep pocket of his robe, withdrawing a flask that contained a clear liquid. He turned to Myria, who stood clutching the bars of her cage.

The priest said something under his breath that Darien couldn't hear. Then he doused Myria thoroughly with the liquid from the flask. She lurched backward with a cry, fleeing to the corner of her cage as the priest backed away, laying down a trail of liquid all the way to the center of the room.

Myria stood clutching herself, shaking, her hair and clothes dripping. She began to hyperventilate, her breath coming in sharp, choking gasps.

Darien could only stare in horror, too sickened to react.

The priest walked over to the wall and fetched a torch down from its holder. Seeing the flame, Myria's sharp gasps turned to shrieks. She brought her hands up in terror, covering her face.

The priest lowered the torch to the ground. A trail of flame sprang into being, racing across the floor toward the cage. The flames leaped onto Myria, engulfing her instantly. Her screams filled the room as she staggered, ablaze. She fell to her knees, writhing and shrieking as the flames enveloped her completely.

Darien stared, transfixed by the shocking horror of the scene. Myria's flesh turned black then started to gray. She burned for minutes, her screams finally coming to a pitiful end. Still, the crackling of the flames persisted. The awful smell of roasting flesh thickened the air of the dungeon. Soon, Myria was reduced to a charred, featureless lump that sizzled and smoked.

Darien trembled in revulsion, praying that she was finally beyond pain.

There was a long gap of silence in the chamber, broken only by the sound of his own shuddering breath.

Craig laid a hand on Darien's arm. "You were once my friend," he said. "I hope your soul finds peace."

Darien looked up at him, unable to respond.

Craig walked away, his long cloak swaying in his wake. He strode to the center of the room, head bowed, as the priest of Deshari moved forward.

The repugnant man fussed over Darien, making sure his bonds were secure, all the while staring at him with a ghastly eagerness in his eyes. Darien cringed away from the man, repulsed. The priest produced another flask and held it over him.

He uttered, "May the flames redefine you. This is your moment of pause before your soul breaks wide open. I want you to know…I envy you this opportunity. Relax. Embrace your transformation."

Darien shivered, appalled by the man's hungering gaze, the anxious yearning to see him burn. He closed his eyes as the priest upended the vial over him, drenching his face and hair, dousing his clothes. Then the man backed away, laying down a trail of accelerant across the floor.

Darien gagged at the reek of lamp oil, the fumes burning his throat and wringing water from his eyes. His heart lurched as the panic set in. He fought against his restraints, lashing his fists against the manacles, not caring if he broke every bone in his hands. His mind flailed desperately for the Onslaught, to no avail.

The priest of Deshari grabbed another torch down off the wall, its flame crackling in a stir of air as he walked back toward the center of the room. Darien's eyes followed the torch's flame, his body trembling in misery.

Devlin Craig looked away.

The priest stopped in the center of the room and slowly lowered the torch toward the trail of accelerant.

Something struck him from behind.

The priest was hurled off his feet, the torch tumbling from his grasp. His body slapped hard against the floor and lay there, a gray-fletched shaft protruding from his back.

The torch rolled across the floor toward the trail of oil.

Devlin Craig sprang toward the door, drawing his blade. Another arrow drove deep into his neck. He reached up, fumbling at the shaft as his knees buckled under him. He slumped to the ground, dropping his sword.

Kyel Archer lowered the longbow in his hands. He cast the weapon on the ground, a look of revulsion on his face. His eyes snapped back and forth between the priest and Devlin Craig, who lay thrashing about on the floor, pawing at the arrow embedded in his neck as he fought for breath.

Kyel ran forward, kicking the torch away. He knelt beside the body of the priest and searched frantically through the man's robes, at last springing back up with a ring of keys in his hands.

Darien almost wept at the site of him. Kyel was filthy and ragged, trembling as he crammed the keys one at a time into the manacles. The arcane restraints fell away, releasing the gushing torrent of the Onslaught. Darien groaned as he felt it rage into him, filling his mind with terrible ecstasy.

Kyel ripped off the rest of the restraints. Darien sat up, weak and almost too shaky to stand. He had to brace himself against Kyel to get his feet under him. He took a lurching step forward. The smell of lamp oil was strong on his skin, wetting his hair and saturating his clothes. The fumes choked his throat. He seared it away with the taint of the Onslaught.

Kneeling, he dropped to Craig's side and lifted his old friend up off the floor. Craig was still alive, wheezing and gurgling, his hand worrying at the shaft buried deep in his throat. There was little blood; it hadn't pierced the artery. Craig's panicked eyes scoured Darien's face, his mouth open and gasping.

Darien couldn't heal him.

"Close your eyes," he said.

Craig complied.

He died instantly, going limp as blood streamed from his nostrils. His shuddering stopped, his suffering ended. Darien felt no pity for him. He laid Craig out across the floor and rose, turning back to Kyel.

"What did you do to him?" Kyel whispered.

"I gave him mercy." Darien stepped over the corpse, moving toward the door.

"How…?"

"With the Hellpower."

Darien stopped in the doorway, extending his hand. Kyel stared at him wide-eyed, his mouth hanging slack.

"Come with me, Kyel."

"No." The young mage shook his head, taking a step back away. Darien could see the disgust on his face.

He pressed, "I need your help. I don't know the way out of here."

"I can't," Kyel gasped, edging backward another step. His eyes drifted to the corpses on the floor then flicked back to Darien's face.

Darien took a step after him, holding his gaze steady, his hand still outstretched. "You know we're in the right. That's why you did what you did. Come with me. I need you. *We* need you."

But Kyel shook his head. "I can't. These are *my* people. And I'm their Sentinel."

Hearing that, Darien went cold. He didn't want to kill Kyel. But he also couldn't leave such a threat behind. He closed his eyes, summoning resolve.

Darien reached within. The Hellpower was there: morbidly euphoric, darkly vibrant, beckoning. He gathered it in and probed deep inside Kyel, finding the nerves that drove his heart.

"You're going to kill me," Kyel realized.

Sinan son of Semal. Alton son of Orhan. Devrim son of Enver…

He opened his eyes.

"No," Darien whispered. He pointed at the cage where Myria's corpse lay charcoaled on the floor. *"Get in."*

Kyel looked like he was going to be sick. But he obeyed. With fumbling hands, he found the right key and unlocked the door. He straddled the grotesque remains and locked the cage door behind him.

"Throw me the keys."

Kyel did, tossing them down on the floor. They slid across the stones, coming to a rest beside Craig's body. Kyel retreated to the far end of the cage, where he dropped to a crouch, covering his face with his hands.

The cold gleam of metal attracted Darien's attention. He moved toward it, realizing they'd piled his things in a corner against the wall. He shouldered his blade's leather harness and fastened his cloak. Then he turned, eyes sweeping over the carnage in the chamber.

"Narghul," he whispered, his blood turning to liquid ice.

Two necrators rose from pools of shadow, twining upward from the floor.

Darien stared at the pair of lethal shades, grimly satisfied. He turned and strode from the chamber, his dark servants gliding behind in his wake.

Chapter Twenty-Five
Hapselon's Amulet

Isle of Titherry, The Rhen

A glance down at the Soulstone revealed what he'd already suspected. The dull black stone stirred with a fleck of radiance deep inside where the flaw had been. Quin held it up between them, dangling it in front of Naia's face. The cold necklace swayed in front of her, the bands of the collar catching the light, while the stone sucked it in like a black maw of darkness.

Except for that one rose-colored fleck.

"Look," Quin said. "It's charging again. It's drawing a new legacy right out of the air."

She leaned forward, peering deeply into the stone. Slowly, Naia's eyes widened. "How is it doing that?"

"Because that's where all legacies go when mages die without a successor…And it's where they all came from in the first place."

"I don't understand."

Quin shot her a quizzical look.

Naia took a step back then sat down on the bed. She crossed her arms in front of her chest. "I'm afraid there is a tremendous gap in my knowledge. Please remember I never received a formal education."

Quin lowered the Soulstone, dropping it down on the desk. He sank into his own seat, splaying his legs in a sloppy posture. "You've never read the *Praymayana?*"

When she shook her head, Quin nodded slowly. He was aware Naia had only spent two years in training, and in those two years had learned little more than the essentials. She was ignorant of all the foundational knowledge that a mage's training was typically built on. She knew what she was doing—generally—but had absolutely no idea why things worked or how they worked. It boggled his mind that she could be even half as effective as she was.

He took a steadying breath, summoning the magelight he'd created. It gathered around him, dancing in misty filaments. The soothing surge of the power within him raised goosebumps on his flesh. He closed his eyes, savoring the sweet bliss.

"I feel whole…" he whispered with a smile. It had been so long. Awash in the magic field, he could fill it moving through him of its own accord, without any external prompting.

"The *Praymayana* is an epic poem that dates back thousands of years before my time," he began, opening his eyes. "It chronicles the adventures of an ancient sage named Hapselon who thought he could climb to the top of the world and steal the fire of Om, thereby becoming a god himself. Unfortunately, due to his hubris, Hapselon neglected to realize that Om's fire would engulf him rather than granting him the godly powers he desired. As he lay dying, the goddess Isap took pity on him and healed his wounds. But Hapselon tricked her. As soon as he was healed, Hapselon took Isap captive and threatened to throw her off the top of the world unless Om granted him the powers of a god.

"So Om granted his wish. He placed upon Hapselon's neck an amulet that caused the magic field to feed Hapselon with so much power that the sage went mad. He was cursed, you see. His mortal mind couldn't handle the power of the gods. Hapselon ran raving down from the top of the world, reduced to a mindless lunatic. Everyone he touched was infected with the power of the amulet and received a small portion of godly power. In the end, after spreading the gift to thousands of people, Hapselon was diminished to just an empty husk, a withered and pathetic creature, drained of the power the gods had granted him. He finally died, passing from this world into Isap's domain, his soul to be tormented throughout eternity. His punishment was to watch generations of mages born and die, enjoying and then passing on the gift that should have been his, and his alone."

Naia nodded slightly. "What a tragic story. Like so many holy mysteries, its inception is most likely rooted in the truth."

"Perhaps." Quin shrugged. "I doubt there was ever any man named Hapselon and, even if there was, he certainly never climbed to the top of the world. But I do believe that some artifact like Hapselon's amulet did indeed exist, and that the gifts of the first mages were absorbed by it from the magic field itself. That myth was what inspired me to create this." He reached out and fingered the Soulstone, running his fingers across its dull black surface.

A voice spoke at them from the door. "You're awake. Good."

Quin startled, jerking his hand back away from the talisman. He turned to find Tsula standing behind them in the doorway, gazing at them with her arms crossed. Like always, her expression was devoid of emotion.

"There is food for you in the kitchens," she informed them. "After you break your fast, I'll show you where to gain access to the conduits." With that she turned and departed, the sounds of her footsteps fading down the hallway.

Naia turned to Quin. "Do you trust her?"

He lifted his hat and raked a hand back through his hair. "No."

"Why not?"

"Because she was going to leave you frozen." He shrugged. "Regardless of her objectives, that's going too far. If I had a copper to wager, I'd wager she's afraid of you."

"But why?" Naia leaned forward, her hair spilling over her shoulders like a wash of molten bronze.

"I have no idea," Quin admitted. It was indeed quite a mystery. He wished he could unravel that tangled skein, but had no idea where to begin. He stood up. "Well, let's hope this breakfast isn't poisoned. Shall we?" He motioned toward the door.

Naia nodded, stepping into the hallway. He pocketed the Soulstone and followed her out. Taking her by the arm, he directed her down the corridor, away from the sprawl of the castle's living quarters. He had no idea where the kitchens were situated; Tsula hadn't given him a tour. But he had a good idea where they should be, somewhere around or beneath the castle's great hall.

They found their way down a flight of stairs. At the bottom, the steps opened up on a sunny courtyard lined with a series of kitchen stalls. There were many, enough to provide food service for the entire castle. All empty, of course. All deserted. No smoke rose from the chimneys. The hearths were cold.

"Not much in the way of options," Quin complained as they strode through the courtyard. He glanced up, noticing that it was a pleasant, sun-filled day. At least, it was on the castle grounds. He had no doubt the rest of the isle was still gripped in the cold embrace of winter. He could hear the sound of bird-song in the distance, the rustle of wind through the branches of trees. The warmth of daylight felt good on his shoulders.

"Where's the food?" Naia wondered.

Quin guided her toward one of the kitchen stalls. It looked unused, though not unclean. In fact, there was no dirt anywhere. He ran a finger over the surface of a carving board. No dust. He frowned at that; Tsula had been frozen in time, but not the rest of the castle. Supposedly. He was beginning to wonder at that. So far, he'd seen no servants. So who dusted the counters? Who swept out the floors?

"This makes no sense," he said.

"Look." Naia pointed across the kitchen to another counter. There, arranged neatly in baskets, were pieces of flatbread and large rounds of cheese. There was even a basket of fruit. Quin and Naia exchanged glances.

"Was that there before?" Naia asked as she walked over and lifted an apple in her hand.

"I hadn't noticed it," Quin said.

Naia inspected the apple, turning it slowly, then bit into it with a loud crunch. She chewed cautiously. "Good."

That's all Quin needed. He helped himself to the bread, tearing off a large bite and cramming it into his mouth. Then he grabbed up a few slices along with some cheese, balancing a couple of apples in the crook of his arm. Jumping up to sit on the counter, he eagerly stuffed food into his mouth as fast as he could chew it. It had been a while since he'd eaten a hearty meal.

Naia hopped up beside him. She sat there eating hungrily, swinging her legs and looking around, gazing at the oven, the hanging kettles, the clean-swept floor. Anything but him. Quin watched her out of the corner of his eye.

The silence between them resounded.

Quin tore off a strip of bread and said, "Do you mind if I ask you a question?"

Naia looked at him. "Not at all."

Quin tore the bread in half, popping a bite in his mouth. "Do you still have feelings for Darien?"

The sound of her chewing stopped. Her legs paused in their swinging. Naia sat beside him perfectly still as the awkwardness between them turned into tension. Quin closed his eyes, cursing himself, already regretting the question.

"Why do you ask?" she said.

Quin swallowed the lump of bread in his mouth. It didn't go down very well. "Just curious," he muttered.

Naia shrugged. Then she took a bite of cheese. "I haven't really thought about it." Her legs resumed their swaying motion as the silence settled back between them. Apparently, she considered the subject dropped.

But Quin didn't want to drop it. He decided to press the issue. "He doesn't love you, you know." This time, he turned to look at her and didn't look away. He watched the emotions range over her face.

"Yes. I know."

He nodded. He tore off another strip of bread and started chewing. He gazed at the floor, at a little chip in the tiles. A breeze came up, pushing a leaf into the kitchen stall, scooting it across the floor toward them. It was an oak leaf. He realized he hadn't seen any oaks in a while.

"I didn't mean to offend," he murmured into the gaping silence that stretched between them.

"Then what did you mean?" Her voice was blunt with irritation. Her legs had stopped swinging again.

"I…" He shrugged. "I suppose I just don't want to see you hurt."

Naia jumped down from the counter. She turned to face him. "My feelings are my own," she told him in a firm voice. "I've known for a long time that Darien doesn't love me. Nevertheless, I chose to care for him. It was my choice. I felt very strongly he was in the right, so I followed him, and I was there for him…even when it hurt. But he doesn't need me anymore."

Quin stared into her sad, dark eyes and could only nod.

"And that's fine with me," Naia went on. "I spent a large part of my life being what other people needed me to be. My father needed me to be a priestess, his successor. So that's what I became. I never paused to ask myself if it was what I wanted. I made my father very proud; that's all that mattered to me. But then I found a person who needed me more. So I left my father and went with Darien…and I became what he needed me to be."

Quin gazed at her, watching her face as she worked her way through all the emotions bubbling to the surface. He felt sorry for her. "Naia," he said. "I think the important question is…what do *you* want?"

She raised her chin. She put her hand out, pushing back her sleeve to reveal the red scars where the marks of her Oath had once been. "I have failed at literally everything I have ever attempted," she said. Tears streaked down her cheeks.

Quin reached out and caught her arm, wrapping his fingers around the markings on her wrist. "No," he insisted, leaning forward. "You've only failed at trying to be something you weren't meant to be. So tell me. Who is Naia? What does she want?"

"I don't know…" her voice faded away, her eyes filling with hurt.

Quin released his grip on her arm, tucking her sleeve back down to cover the welts. Then he leaned in close. "Look at me."

She did.

Staring into Naia's dark eyes, Quin told her, "You need to decide who you are and what you stand for. Until you do, you aren't much good to anybody. That's why you've always failed." He sat back, his eyes becoming quite serious. "But I can't let you fail this time. This is too important. I need your help, Naia."

She gazed at him with incomprehension in her

eyes. He reached out, stroking a wayward strand of hair away from her face. "I need you to help me destroy the curse over the Black Lands. And you won't be able to do that without a strong sense of self. Somehow, in the very near future, you're going to have to figure out who you really are."

Chapter Twenty-Six
Feast of Souls

Pass of Lor-Gamorth, The Front

Darien left the dungeon behind, following the flights of stairs upward. He couldn't get the awful stench of charred Myria out of his nostrils. He couldn't get the look in Kyel's eyes out of his head; he was infected by both. He braced his hand against the wall and vomited, spilling his guts onto the stairs. Then he wiped his mouth and kept going.

At the top of the stairs, he staggered through a doorway into the open courtyard of the keep. He cast a bleary glance around. He felt overwhelmed. He wasn't sure what to focus on; he couldn't separate what was important from what was not. Scores of soldiers swarmed the yard in a flurry of activity. Darien drew back against the wall, stepping into shadow. He stood there panting, fighting to catch his breath.

He was vaguely aware of the gray-cloaked man who noticed him. The soldier went immediately for his sword, crying an alarm. It was too much at once; the man was just a blur. Frantic, Darien pulled at the Onslaught and sent it hurling out of him like a terrible spear of damnation.

The soldier howled a cry of mortal anguish, his muscles locked rigid. He collapsed forward, flesh smoldering and popping as he died. The necrators swept in to swarm the corpse, feasting off the soul.

Darien stared at the gruesome sight, quietly satisfied. The confusion that had addled him fell away, leaving only a calm sense of clarity.

Another soldier attacked. Darien drew his blade and blocked the first strike. He pulled his arms up, swinging the pommel out, and took the man down with the short edge of his blade. The necrators wasted no time.

He lowered the sword and backed away, stumbling over the first corpse. Shouts rang out from all across the ward. An arrow streaked down from the fortress, lodging in the dirt next to him. Darien glanced at the half-built tower and saw that Greystone archers were taking up positions at the arrow slits.

He tried summoning a shield to defend himself, but it didn't work. The Onslaught couldn't be used like that; it was strictly an offensive weapon. He could do nothing to protect himself from injury. All it would take was one well-placed arrow to bring him down.

With that thought in mind, Darien recalled the necrators and sprinted back toward the palisade. More soldiers ran forward to meet him, forming a line of spears and interlocked shields, blocking the only exit from the yard. Darien stood for a moment in indecision.

He took a step back.

Then he lashed out at them savagely.

The wall of soldiers collapsed, melting into a vile-smelling mass that steamed and gurgled in the chill night air. The necrators glided eagerly forward. Darien gripped his stomach, unable to tear his eyes away from the sight. He stood frozen, hit with the sudden awareness of what he was capable of. Figuring out how far he was willing to take it.

A dark thought occurred to him, sicker than all the ones he'd already had.

"Narghul," he whispered.

More sinister shades rose from the hummock of

melted flesh. As Darien sheathed his blade and fled through the portal, eight necrators drifted after him. *It takes twenty deaths to raise a necrator,* he'd heard once. He'd already done it with far less.

Outside the ward, he encountered more stairs. But as soon as his foot touched the first step, the wood broke beneath him. He fell through, catching himself with his hands as his legs dangled under him. He glanced down at the forest of sharpened stakes that awaited him below.

Darien grimaced, using all his strength to pull his body up through the broken cage of the stair. He rolled sideways, extracting his legs. Pushing himself to his feet, he eyeballed the trap warily. He saw that the stairs followed a particular pattern: alternating wood and stone. It was exactly the sort of device Devlin Craig would have devised. He cursed himself for not noticing the pattern immediately. He'd almost paid for his distraction with his life. He started down again, stepping over the wood and walking only on stone, his demonic companions gliding smoothly behind.

The stairs ended at a raised portcullis that marked the entrance to a long tunnel lit by torchlight. Darien grabbed a torch off the wall, holding it as he strode through the darkness. Eerie shadows swarmed around him, none more sinister than the shades trailing at his back. When he reached the end of the tunnel, he flung the torch to the ground. It continued to burn, its flame rippling in a gust of wind blowing up the mountainside. The savage wind caught his cloak, billowing it out.

Two guards saw him and started forward, spears leveled at his chest. They died horribly, the price for their vigilance. While the necrators feasted, Darien brought down a third man, who dropped and slid to a stop in front of him. Another two fell where they stood, their corpses smoldering.

Darien glanced down at himself to find his body saturated with the Onslaught. It leaked out of him like a green aura, just like the one he remembered from the Catacombs. But he knew better what it meant now. The aura wasn't a symptom of his damnation. It was a mark of grace, a flaring symbol of his god's vengeful wrath.

A soldier running up the steps stopped in his tracks and stood staring at Darien, his sword arm wilting. He turned and fled. One of the necrators glided after the man, overtaking him swiftly. The soldier writhed on the ground, shrieking as his soul was devoured.

Darien stepped over the corpse and started toward the stairs that led down the face of the mountain. Below, he could see a serpentine trail of lights snaking through the bottom of the pass. It could only be one thing: the hosts of Malikar escaping the Black Lands through the canyon. He stared at the long, drawn-out column as cold fear clutched his heart.

Craig's treaty had been a trap. Not just for him, but for them all. He realized then how thoroughly he'd been betrayed.

A war horn sounded from behind him in the fortress. The cry was answered by another, somewhere in the faint distance across the pass.

Darien drew up, his hand reaching reflexively for his blade. He waited, listening, panting for air. A glacial stillness gripped the pass. There was silence. Then another horn brayed across the black distance.

There was a low, deep-throated rumble.

A series of explosions burst out of the side of the mountain opposite him, disgorging thick clouds of hurling debris. The ridgelines buckled, fracturing. Then they gave way completely. Avalanches of snow and tumbling rock collapsed into the pass with a deafening roar that shook the air.

The thunder ended and silence reigned, the entire profile of the mountainscape forever changed. Thick clouds of dust rose from the bottom of the pass, choking off his view of the devastation.

Darien froze, panting, numbed by raw emotion. He gaped slack-jawed down into the bottom of the pass, searching the rubble for signs of survivors. Visions of fallen Aerysius filled his mind. At first it was all he could see. He chased the images away and concentrated on the tragedy below. Clouds of dust rose from the gaping maw of the canyon, bathing the mountainside in gray.

The entire world was gray.

Everything that mattered to him had been down there.

He stood blinking, the ache of loss slowly settling in. He hadn't loved his wife as he should have. He'd taken her for granted. And now she was gone.

Darien sheathed his sword. He staggered down the hillside, slipping and stumbling, until he burst through the invisible barrier that marked the edge of the node. He fell to his knees, rocked by the sudden presence of the magic field.

He threw his head back, gasping for breath as the magic field slammed into him, pulsing like a living thing. The necrators hovered as he knelt there, drowning in the field's soothing bliss. He sucked it all in, every drop he could stand, until his body bled with energy and his soul cried in pain.

Shaking, he heaved himself up from the ground, fighting to stand on legs that were desperately weak. He started down the hill again, stumbling down the stairs until he reached the main trail that descended into the canyon. If there were more soldiers about, he didn't see them. Perhaps they had fled. Perhaps he had killed them already. He didn't care. The world was gray and Azár was dead.

In the bottom of the pass, the dust was still settling. He couldn't tell if anything moved down there. There was nothing to see. In the riverbed below, there was nothing but silence. And a long, echoing sense of horror. He followed the trail down, hope leaching away a little more with every step. He knew it would take him at least an hour to follow the trail down off the mountain. And he feared what he would find.

The sound of hoofbeats behind him made him turn. A group of riders were approaching from the direction of the keep. Even from a distance, Darien could tell they were heavily armored. He stopped and gathered the magic field around him until blue energies crackled over his body.

More hoofbeats approached from the opposite direction.

He turned, sensing the danger.

Darien tugged at the magic field, summoning a pool of magelight at his feet. The approaching riders drew up in front of him, reining their horses in. From behind, an equal number blocked his retreat. Most held hornbows trained on him. A few men bared swords. Some leveled crossbows at his chest. Horses whinnied and tossed their heads, eyes rolling nervously.

Darien stood his ground, assessing the situation. He sought the eyes of the men, gauging their resolve. His gaze leaped from face to face, grimly studying each. He didn't make a move for the hilt of his sword. He knew he didn't need it.

"Ride away," he warned.

No one moved.

Darien turned and started walking in the direction he'd been heading, keeping his eyes trained on the path in front of him. Behind, he heard the twang of a single bowstring.

The arrow never hit.

He didn't look back at the firestorm that erupted behind him, consuming both men and beasts. But he heard their screams, which seemed to go on far longer than they should have. Lightning struck down from the sky, summoned by the terrible wrath of his power. He fed off its electric energy, letting it invigorate him, supplementing his strength. Then he hurled it like an explosive javelin toward the group of cavalry in front of him.

This time, the screams didn't last long. He bared his sword as he strode through the inferno, but there were no enemies left to fight. A lone horse galloped past him, stirrups bouncing, its mane and tail streaming flame.

He sheathed his blade and raised his hand, dismissing the necrators.

The burning stallion reared, screaming its terror and pain. Then it stopped, appearing suddenly, inexplicably calm. It turned and sprinted back to him.

Darien reached out and caught the horse's reins. He closed his eyes and smothered the flames, healing the burns and the memories. He stroked the animal's fur, soothing the gelding with his mind. Then he climbed onto the horse's back and urged it forward. The beast leapt onto the trail, galloping with all its heart and courage toward the bottom of the pass.

He let the horse run until it tired, healed it, then let it run some more. He did that again and again, exhausting himself as much as his mount. Even at that pace, the descent into the canyon took some time. And it was unsustainable.

Eventually, the horse dropped dead beneath him.

Darien jumped clear as the gelding stumbled and rolled, coming to a rest on its side. Darien stood over it, gazing down, swaying over his feet. He turned slowly around, staggering, taking his bearings as best he could.

By the time he reached the bottom of the canyon, much of the dust had already settled. It was possible to see the devastation that had been wrought. All along the neck of the pass that extended toward the Black Lands, explosive charges had been used to bring down the side of the mountain. The entire canyon floor was filled with fresh mounds of earth. Huge chunks of stone barred the passage.

In the canyon, no one stirred. The river itself had been drowned by the rubble.

An echoing stillness hung over the pass, thundering with presence.

Darien jumped down onto the fresh-spilt earth, knowing that he walked upon a grave. They were all there, beneath his feet. The people he'd sworn to protect. The wife he'd sworn to cherish. He dropped to his knees, plunging his hands into the soil as deep as they'd go. There was only dirt to cling to. He clawed his fingers through the soil, feeling sharp rocks gouge his skin. It didn't matter; the world was gray. And Azár lay dead somewhere beneath his feet.

Eventually, he rose and wandered in the general direction of the Black Lands. As he walked, his eyes scoured the rubble, hoping in vain. But there was nothing to justify such hope; in the bottom of the pass there was no movement, no stirring of life. Nothing left to save.

He stumbled forward, picking out a treacherous path over loose rocks and jagged debris. Finally, he came to the edge of the great scree. He staggered down the slope, sliding over crumbling earth and, to his relief, encountered people.

A group of men digging in the dirt glanced up and, seeing him, dropped their shovels and bared their swords. Shaking from exhaustion, Darien raised his hands, uncertain what to do. They were Malikari soldiers: Southerners, by the uniforms. They didn't recognize him, but why should they? All they saw was an enemy.

"Demas narghul masaad," he said in their language.

The men drew up, but didn't lower their blades. They exchanged outraged glances. One growled something that Darien couldn't understand, then advanced. The others rushed forward behind him.

An arrow sliced through the air, just missing Darien's head. It buried itself in the chest of the first man, taking him to the ground.

Darien whirled to find a Greystone archer standing behind him on the lip of the scree. He didn't stop to think. He just acted. The man exploded in a shower of gore that rained down all around them. A hand tumbled through the air, falling to the ground at Darien's feet.

The Malikari soldiers faltered, looking at Darien with wide, terrified eyes. The man with the arrow in him moaned and thrashed upon the ground. Darien knelt at the warrior's side. He placed a hand on the man's heaving chest, getting a sense of the wound. The soldier gritted his teeth as Darien drew the arrow from his ribs. Then he healed the wound before the man could bleed out.

The others looked on, slowly lowering their weapons. At last, the soldiers surrounding him sheathed their blades. Darien looked from one face to the other, finally gesturing at the towering wall of rock behind them.

"How many?" he demanded.

The soldiers looked like they didn't understand.

He repeated the question in Venthic.

"Na qabir," one of the men growled. *Too many.*

Darien sagged, understanding. He gestured in vain at a shovel on the ground. "Are you finding anyone alive?"

The man looked at him then glanced down at the sleeping body of his injured comrade. He strode forward and took Darien by the arm, pulling him away.

Darien allowed the man to guide him down the riverbed, away from the killing ground. He followed the soldier without question, slogging through mucky filth.

They trudged past bodies covered in thick layers of blood and dust. Some had obviously been struck when the mountain fell. Others looked to have either been suffocated or drowned. It was hard to say. The soldier he followed skirted a pond that used to be part of the watercourse. A small child lay dead on the far side of it, face down in the mud.

Darien thought of his own son, who had died in his arms.

Then he thought of Azár.

He swallowed against a tight ball of grief. He had ordered Sayeed to get his wife through first.

He paused over the body of the child, then dropped to a crouch. Setting a hand on the boy's back, he confirmed what he already knew. There was nothing he could do. Everything had a limit, even him. The gods had seen fit to give him the power to bring death. But those same gods had denied him the power to bring life.

"Come."

He glanced up at the soldier, who motioned brusquely for him to follow. Darien heaved himself up off the ground, leaving the child where he lay. They wandered further down the riverway, past mounds of piled bodies.

Eventually, they came to a bend in the canyon where many people had gathered, most of them casualties. Men and women had been laid out in rows along the canyon walls, while others tended the injured. More victims were being carried in, as the dead were dragged away.

Darien looked around the site, at the number of wounded, and felt despair. He had already overextended himself. He didn't have much left to give. He looked at his guide, who beckoned him toward the injured.

Darien nodded wearily, and walked to the nearest victim. He knelt at the man's side, probing his body as the harsh soldier glared down at his back. He closed his eyes, resigned. He would heal as many as he could. It was all he could do. He would heal until he collapsed.

He tugged at the magic field, filling his mind, emptying his thoughts, and began.

He had no idea how long he'd been asleep. Darien awoke naked and comfortable on a soft mattress, a mass of thick covers pulled over his body. He didn't want to open his eyes. He wanted to just keep sleeping. The covers were soft, the mattress warm and comforting. He felt a light touch, a hand stroking back his hair. Darien opened his eyes and gazed upward, frozen by the vision that confronted him.

"I thought you were dead," he whispered.

Seeing him awake, Azár smiled. "I thought you were, too."

Chapter Twenty-Seven
Shahin Son of Marthax

Isle of Titherry, The Rhen

Naia gazed at Quin, considering his features. He was very obviously not a man of the Rhen. His bronze complexion and thick black hair seemed exotic to her. And yet, strangely, there were many things about Quin that didn't seem foreign at all.

"How did you come by your name?" she asked, jumping down from the counter she'd been sitting on.

Quin turned to glance up at her as he swept his pack up off the floor. "What do you mean?"

Naia shrugged, moving out of the kitchen stall. "Quinlan is a Rhenic name. You weren't born in the Rhen…So how did you come by it?"

Quin took her arm, guiding her out of the stall and back toward the entrance to the courtyard. Sunlight streamed down from a clear sky as leaves twirled from the branches above them. The walls of the castle gleamed in the light, making her squint. So much sun…on an isle encased by winter.

"Quinlan Reis was the name they gave me at the Lyceum. It wasn't my birth name."

Naia frowned at him. "What was wrong with your birth name?"

Quin thrust his hands into his pockets, explaining, "It was just something that was in fashion at the time. My brother and I were born to a nomadic culture, you see. When we were brought to the Lyceum, they gave us new names. Rhenic names."

Naia frowned harder, studying Quin's face. "That makes no sense. I thought the Lyceum was more advanced than Aerysius?"

"Oh, it was, definitely," Quin agreed. "Have no doubt! But Southern culture was something of a style that swept through Northern society for a time. Southern dress, Southern ways…Southern names. It was just something that people did, especially in the larger cities. Surnames became very popular, even though we'd never used them before. It was a way of distinguishing civil society from the 'unwashed masses' of the interior. Which was ironic, really. The people of the cities hated the nomads and their ways, but they also envied them. I think they realized, deep down inside, that it was a better way to live, both physically and spiritually. And yet they detested them just the same. It was all rather perplexing and contrived."

They reached a large door that led into the interior of the castle. Quin shoved it open with his hand, swinging it inward.

"What was your given name?" Naia asked. "Before they changed it?"

"Shahin. Shahin son of Marthax." Quin held the door open for her.

Naia smiled, liking the sound of the name. She looked Quin over closely. He looked nothing like a man of the Rhen. He didn't look like a man named Quin, she decided.

"What?" he demanded, seeming put off by her attention.

"Shahin," Naia repeated, feeling the sound of the name on her tongue. She smiled. "I like it. It suits you better."

Quin shook his head, looking regretful he had told her. "No. It's been too long. I'm not that person anymore. You see, they didn't just change my name. They took everything from me. They changed me into someone else entirely. Now I'm just Quinlan Reis. That's it. Nothing more."

The way he said it saddened Naia. It was as though he felt reduced by his Rhenic name. Or not worthy of the name his own father had bestowed upon him. The longer she knew Quin, the more she realized how broken he was. She'd never met another man who so utterly despised himself.

"Very well, then. Quin." Naia tried to smile, but couldn't make it work. The expression faltered on her face then drifted away.

Quin opened another door, standing to the side and ushering her past. They entered a spacious hall carpeted by patterned rugs, the stone walls relieved by bright streaks of woven tapestries. There was an odor to the place, like must or old neglect.

Movement from across the room caught her eye. Naia looked over to see Tsula emerging from a narrow side-corridor. The woman wore a striking robe of emerald green with a matching headwrap. She glided toward them through clusters of furniture and stopped in front of them, hands on her hips, surveying them down the length of her nose. Naia found it hard to suffer that stare, resisting the impulse to cringe away from it.

"Are you ready to begin your work?" the woman inquired of Quin, who responded only with a nod. Her eyes flicked toward Naia. "Is she going with you?"

Quin nodded again. "I told you: I need her for moral support."

Naia stood in silence, watching the conversation as much as listening to it. She considered herself fairly adept at gauging a person's emotions by the look on their face, and Tsula's was practically shouting. Naia sensed the Harbinger held a deep disdain for her. She couldn't imagine why.

"You're not an Arcanist," Quin snapped. "I don't expect you to understand."

The remark prompted Tsula to arch a quizzical eyebrow in Quin's direction. Beneath it, her gaze slid sideways to fix on Naia. At last, she issued a curt nod.

"Then let us go." She turned her back on them and retraced her steps across the room.

Naia wasn't sure what to make of the confrontation. She stood there until she felt Quin's fingers lace through her own, prompting her forward. His face was rigid with anger. He said nothing as they followed Tsula out of the hall and onto a wide balcony.

Warm sunlight slanted down on them, glaring off the stone sides of the castle. Naia had to squint, shielding her eyes with her hand. Ahead of them, Tsula paused beside a curving balustrade that edged the balcony. A breeze washed over them, fluttering Naia's hair. Despite the warmth of the sunlight, the mountain air was cold. Tsula made a sweeping gesture with her hand, inviting them to join her. Naia moved forward alongside Quin, feeling almost hesitant.

They stopped before the balustrade and looked over.

Naia's fingers tightened reflexively on Quin's. She forgot to breathe for a moment, so staggered was she by the view. Athera's Crescent stretched before her, consuming the entire valley below. It was enormous, like a concave basin of polished silver that spanned the bowl-shaped valley from mountaintop to mountaintop. Its metallic sheen seemed more liquid than solid, running in soft currents like quicksilver.

Except for the places that were dark.

Huge fragments like jagged shards of broken glass fractured the Crescent, places where the liquid texture ran black with emptiness. The Crescent was broken, Naia realized. Broken in fundamental ways. The quicksilver surface of the dish roiled with vitality, its surface dappled with energies that swarmed across it, activating other currents... Until one of the dark fragments broke the pattern. Then the dance of energy ground to a halt.

Quin dropped Naia's hand and swept his hat off his head, running a hand back through his hair, his expression vacuous. At last, he turned to Tsula with a look of gaping disbelief, gesturing downward with his hat.

"You expect me to repair *that?*"

The woman's eyebrows raised. "If you can." Her expression didn't change. "If you cannot, then the entire world is surely doomed."

Quin stood there, hat in hand, eyes studying the Crescent in frantic thought. His upper lip gave a slight twitch. At last he blinked and muttered, "Well, this is one honey of a pickle." Then he replaced his hat back on his head and adjusted the brim. He looked down at his boots. Then he glanced back up at Tsula.

"Where are the conduits?"

The fire in his eyes and the resolve in his voice filled Naia with a warm surge of pride. She realized she had faith in this man, though she didn't know why. He was quietly confident, unassuming. Nevertheless, she felt certain that if anyone could repair the Crescent, it was Quin.

"This way." Tsula turned and walked past them, making her way toward the corner of the balcony. Quin followed her, leading Naia by the hand toward a broad staircase that led down from the castle into the bowl-shaped valley.

Naia paused at the top of the steps, her hand lingering on the rough stone of the balustrade. Quin paused, his eyes following hers. There was one single flight of steps all the way down into the mouth of an enormous cave that gaped up at them from below. Many smaller caves opened up to either side.

"Lava tubes?" Quin wondered aloud. He held his hat against a sudden gust of air that whipped at them from the Crescent. There, in the shadow of the mountain, it was much colder than on the balcony. The wind carried with it an arctic chill.

"That is the entrance to the conduits," Tsula said without looking back, never pausing in her stride. Her long gown billowed behind her as she descended the relentless flight of stairs, hand trailing along the stone bannister.

Naia followed at Quin's side as the woman led them down the mountain, hugging herself against the bite of the cold. Every so often, she glanced down at Athera's Crescent, which glowed metallically beneath them like a living thing. Its features swirled and churned around the places of fractured darkness.

A shadow fell over them, the air turning chill. Naia looked up, seeing that their path had been swallowed by the jagged mouth of the cave. Goosebumps broke out across her skin. She hugged her cloak more firmly around her. A glowing white mist bloomed beneath Quin's feet, wandering ahead of them to light their way.

Up ahead, the stairs leveled out into a ramp that descended into the depths of the cavern. Quin's magelight confronted the shadows, overwhelming them. It lit the walls of the cavern before them, casting distorted streaks of light. The cave narrowed, the ceiling closing in over their heads. A narrow stream converged on their path, carving its course alongside their trail, ever downward into the depths of the earth. The sound of its trickling was the only noise in the world, other than the sounds of their own footfalls.

Abruptly, Tsula drew to a halt. She turned back around. Her eyes moved slowly from Naia to Quin.

"I will accompany you no further," she said. "Up ahead, the cavern forks. You must stay to the right. It will take you down to a chamber where you can access the conduits."

"What am I supposed to do down there?" Quin asked.

The woman shrugged dismissively. "Either fail or succeed. What will be is already written, Grand Master Quinlan."

Quin made a face. "In other words, you don't have the faintest idea what I'm supposed to do."

Tsula was unruffled by the comment. "I am a Harbinger, Quinlan Reis. I interpret readings from the Crescent. It is not my job to tinker with the bowels of it."

Quin smirked and reached out to take Naia's hand. "Very well then. Madam." He touched his hat in Tsula's direction. "I guess I'll go tinker with some bowels."

He started forward, brushing past the woman. Naia started after him but stopped, releasing Quin's hand. She turned around.

"Why do you fear me?" she asked the Harbinger.

Tsula looked at her with a sobering expression. "I do not fear you. I merely despise what you are."

"Why? What do you think I am?"

"Surely you must know."

"No. I do not." Naia clasped her hands in front of her. She glanced at Quin, who had paused and was waiting for her.

"You are a chimera," Tsula pronounced, eyes narrowing in accusation.

Naia had never heard the term before. She had no idea what it meant. "A what?"

"A portent of disaster," the woman clarified.

"Why would you say such a thing?"

"Because I know what you are, and what you've been. And what you may become." Tsula stared at her with flat black eyes that held no mercy.

"Don't say another word." Quin walked forward, one finger raised in warning. He glared at Tsula with danger in his eyes.

The woman turned to look at him. She gazed at him in contemptuous silence as he lingered with his finger held in front of her face. Under her breath, she muttered, "Peace be with you, Quinlan Reis." She swept past him, her long gown rustling as she made her way back the way they had come.

When she was gone, Naia turned to Quin. "What did she mean? About what might I become?"

Quin lowered his finger, still glaring after the woman. "I don't know, and I don't want to know. Neither do you," he snapped. He adjusted his hat. "She's a Harbinger. Her job is to sort through occurrences and possibilities. I don't know what she's seen, but whatever it is, it doesn't have to happen. She's not an oracle; she can't foretell the future."

Naia peered at him. "Is that not what a Harbinger does?"

Quin's smoldering glare flicked back in Tsula's direction. He paced away, hands in his pockets, then paced back, taking a swipe at the ground with his foot. "No. All she can do is forecast the likelihood of events. And I'm not sure how effectively she can do that, with the Crescent as broken as it is."

Naia considered his words. She couldn't help but think that there was something Quin was holding back. "What is a chimera?"

He glanced back down the slope of the cavern, his eyes bypassing her. "Another myth like Hapselon," he said. "A mismatched creature made up of the parts of many different beasts. A hybrid, of sorts."

"A hybrid," Naia said, her eyes widening in understanding. Suddenly, it made so much sense. "I'm a mage, and I'm also a priestess. Isn't that what she meant?" It had to be. It was the perfect explanation. Only…how did Tsula know? When Quin didn't say anything, Naia continued, "People keep telling me it's a dangerous thing. I'm still wondering why."

Quin looked at her then. Really looked at her, as if seeing her for the first time. Slowly, his eyes filled with wonder. "You *are* a dangerous thing," he assured her. "Have no doubt."

Naia couldn't help but smile. There was no mistaking the look of admiration in his eyes.

He blinked and took a step away. "Shall we, then?" He extended his hand toward her. She eyed his hand, then looked up and considered his face. He was a demon. He was broken. He was also the most genuine human being she had ever met in her life.

She accepted his hand and walked beside him ever deeper into the cavern. The small stream of water trickled alongside their path, a fog of steam hovering over its surface. Quin's magelight lit the way ahead, his hand guiding her forward at his side.

They came to a fork in the cave, the one Tsula had warned them about. Naia glanced warily between the two dark holes in the volcanic rock that lurked ahead of them like the open maws of a hydra. Quin's magelight didn't penetrate very deep into either shaft. Both looked equally sinister.

Quin steered her toward the opening on the right. This tube was tighter than the last had been, so narrow they couldn't walk abreast. Naia followed Quin as his magelight lit their path. The cave's ceiling was so low they had to walk stooped over. Quin led her onward, downward, still holding her hand.

The darkness and the closeness became oppressive. And the silence. That bothered her most of all. It made her feel like she was back in the warrens below Aerysius. She didn't want to think of that.

Her companion didn't seem the least troubled by their surroundings. She stared at him, musing, "Is there anything you're frightened of?"

He didn't look at her. "There is."

Naia frowned. "What is it?"

He stopped, his hand releasing hers. He took a deep breath and held it in. Then he released it with a sigh. "I was a spy," he admitted. "An assassin, actually. It's not something I'm proud of. It's just who I was, who they trained me to be. I've done things…" He shook his head with a scowl. "I'm not an honorable man, Naia. There's a special place in hell for people like me." He looked away without finishing the thought.

She couldn't blame him.

He took her hand again, his grip tighter than before. "Let's go. We're almost there."

They walked forward. The sides of the passage became gnarled, rough and irregular. Naia reached out and traced the wall with her hand. It felt odd. It wasn't rock, she realized. It felt more like bark.

"What is it?" she gasped. "It looks like tree roots."

Quin stopped and knelt down, releasing her hand.

He set both palms to the side of the passage, caressing the chitinous growth that encrusted the rock, winding along the side of their path.

"This is one of the conduits," he said, looking up at her. He scooted sideways, following the vine-like growth with his hands. Then he rose, motioning for Naia to follow as he moved forward down the passage, reinvigorated by purpose.

Naia followed as the lava tube twisted around, finally opening into a chamber filled with thread-like filaments. Naia stopped at the entrance, glancing around. The cave was aglow with a shimmering spider's web that seemed to ripple with every pulse of the magic field. All around, glowing fibers converged and twisted, interweaving in a luminous dance of color that lit the cavern.

"We'll set up here," Quin said, nodding to himself and licking his lips. He swung his pack down off his shoulder and hunkered over it. He rifled through its contents, at last producing his roll of tools, which he untied and spread out in front of him. He moved his hands over the assortment of objects, pausing now and again, lingering over some, before finally selecting an instrument.

He held up what looked like a gold necklace set with a crystal pendant. Only, instead of clasps, both ends of the chain were fastened to sharpened probes. He held one probe in each hand as his eyes scanned the chamber, taking in the glowing fibers that surrounded them.

"What is this place?" Naia whispered, her own eyes sweeping over the cavern.

"It's a nodal chamber," Quin said, running his hand along the root-like growth they had followed in the lava tube. The conduit unraveled into dozens of glowing fibers which in turn spread out into hundreds of gossamer filaments that crisscrossed the chamber.

"Where does it go?" Naia's eyes traced the conduit back toward the dark passage it had come from.

"All the way to Aerysius," Quin said. "Some come from Bryn Calazar…and all the rest of the world's vortexes. They siphon power from the Circles of Convergence and deliver it here to the Crescent. They also feed it with information from all over the world."

Naia caressed the skin of the large coil of fibers. It felt like the hard shell of an insect. She retracted her hand. "Do they run beneath the ocean?"

Quin shrugged, donning his spectacles. He held the necklace-like instrument up before him with both hands. "Something like the Catacombs, I suspect. It's got to be spelled."

He leaned forward, probing the large braid of filaments closest to him. The instrument's crystal came to life and began to glow. Appearing satisfied, Quin moved to another large braid, carefully probing it the same as he had the last.

Naia followed him at a distance. "What are they?"

Quin stood up, turning toward another bundle of glowing fibers. "This is what's known as a hyphal artifact. It's not carved or forged; it's grown. Think of it like a fungus made of thousands of tiny hairs, each hair capable of drawing tremendous amounts of power and information."

He moved down the vine-like bundle, sticking his probes deep into the chitinous flesh of the conduit. This time, the crystal failed to glow. Frowning, Quin rocked the probe back and forth, feeling deep inside the braided strand. Still, the stone failed to react.

"Here." He held the dull crystal up for Naia to see. "This is broken." He moved to the side, turning to probe another bundle of fibers. "And this one, too."

He glanced up at her. "These conduits have been severed from their Circles of Convergence. That's why Athera's Crescent is failing."

"Can you fix them?"

He licked his lips, shaking his head in an expression of uncertainty. "I'm not a hyphal architect; this isn't my area of expertise. So I really don't have a good idea of what I'm doing." He took a deep breath. "That being said…I have to try. So there's a very good chance I'm going to kill myself."

The statement sounded like his usual dry sarcasm. It took Naia a moment to realize that it wasn't.

"You're not serious," she said. The old pain came back, the same grief she had felt when Darien had left her behind in the chamber of the Well of Tears.

Quin slid the spectacles from his face, setting them aside. He reached up and rubbed his eyes. Then he looked at her, his face earnest. "I'm going to have to form a link with the conduit to repair the damage," he explained. "The problem is, the moment I fix it, the surge of power is probably going to kill me."

She stared at him in dismay. "No, Quin."

He put up a hand. "Naia, you can bring me back. The way you did with Sareen."

Naia was already shaking her head. "There's no guarantee—"

Quin's expression hardened. "I have to do this." Before she could protest, he rose to his feet. "You can bring me back. I know you can. That's why Tsula is so afraid of you."

"I can't—" Naia felt tears of frustration gathering in her eyes. They stung, hot and caustic, like the corrosive feelings eating her up inside.

Quin clenched his jaw, his eyes moving over her face. He reached up and clutched her arms. "You *can*. You're the chimera, Naia. Both priestess and mage. You didn't abandon your goddess; she just chose you for a greater purpose."

"Quin—"

He took a deep breath, eyes sad but resolute. "Just try. That's all you can do. If you can't…then I forgive you."

He released her and backed away. Despite the cold of the cavern, a trickle of sweat streaked down his face. With one last glance over his shoulder, he turned and knelt back down beside the conduit.

Her emotions numb, Naia pressed her back up against the wall. She felt like she was still in Aerysius, in the chamber of the Well of Tears. Watching Darien turn his back and leave her behind forever. Nothing had changed since then. She was still there; she'd never left.

Tears spilled down her face.

She watched Quin lean forward, reaching deep into the conduit like reaching into the innards of a body. He felt around in there for a minute. Then he stopped, motionless. He closed his eyes and bowed his head. His shoulders relaxed, his breathing slowed, becoming deep and regular. He sat like that for minutes, slouched, as if in a trance. Ever so slowly, he began to glow.

Argent light erupted from his body, saturating the chamber. Naia squinted, raising her hands against the brilliance of it. Beneath Quin's fingers, the dark conduit gave the slightest flicker of life. Then another. Soon, it pulsed like a living heartbeat. Quin's face wrinkled with concentration as the glow surrounding him strobed with the rhythm of the conduit, awakening every fiber in the braided strand. Sweat dribbled down his brow, dribbling from his nose and chin. His lips twisted, first in concentration. And then in pain. The light of the conduit swelled, the glow radiating from Quin swelled with it.

Too late, Naia realized why he wasn't moving. His body was locked rigid, his muscles paralyzed by the torrent of energy streaming through the conduit. Streaming into him. The light in the chamber became dazzling. Jaw clenched, Quin began to shake and groan, his body convulsing even as he maintained his grip on the lethal fibers of energy.

There was a brilliant flash.

Naia screamed, throwing her arms up to ward her face. When she opened her eyes, her vision swam with black motes that swirled in front of her. Her eyes stung, full of tears. Dizzy, she collapsed to a crouch, feeling around at the ground with her hands. She scrambled forward on all fours, desperately searching, her vision too distorted to see.

Her hand grasped a wad of fabric.

Scrubbing at her eyes, Naia struggled to see. She could make out only patches of light and shadow. She used her fingers instead, exploring the fabric of Quin's coat. He was lying next to her, face-down. Struggling, she rolled him over and pressed her hands against his chest, delving inside him with her mind.

Only emptiness echoed back.

Biting her lip, she probed deeper. Deep into the lifeless tissues, exploring, desperate to ascertain the type and amount of injury his ruined body had sustained. She wasted no time. Squeezing her eyes shut, she delved his flesh with all the brute diligence she could muster. She doubted if all she could do for him would come close to being enough. He'd taken so much damage.

She didn't know what to repair first. She started working furiously, first on the lifeless muscles of Quin's heart. But it was impossible. No matter what she did, she couldn't get his heart to beat. She went back and retraced her work, reexamining repairs she had already made…all for nothing.

She tossed her head back, biting her lip in frustration. Minutes passed. Sweat ran down her face. Beneath her fingers, Quin's body was still and silent. She pounded on his chest with her fists, more in anger then out of any delusion the action would help. It didn't.

Nothing did.

She probed every organ, every tissue. All were perfect; there was nothing wrong with him. Nothing left to heal. Quin's body was whole; only his soul had fled. And, no matter what she did, it wasn't coming back.

She collapsed over him and wept. She cried until there were no more tears left. Then she sat up, wiping her spilled grief off her face. She struggled to stand, blinking against the brilliant light that filled the chamber, so much stronger than it had been before. Quin had repaired the conduits before the power surge had killed him. They pulsated with a rhythmic, ethereal glow.

She knew that she should leave. There was nothing more she could do for him.

The priestess inside her wanted to turn back, to give him the proper care he deserved. To prepare his soul for its journey. But then she realized where that journey would lead him. Naia jerked to a halt, her heart wrenching. Quin wasn't destined for the Atrament. If she left his body there on the floor, his soul would never know peace.

She couldn't leave him like that.

She returned to his side.

One last time, she prodded Quin's dead heart with the power of her mind, coaxing it back to life. The heart muscle shivered and lurched in his chest. It staggered forward, settling into the semblance of a natural rhythm. Quin's staring eyes slid closed and didn't open again. His chest moved, but he didn't awaken.

At first, Naia thought it was a victory. Then she realized that it wasn't. She couldn't part the Veil of Death.

Only Xerys could help His Servant now.

Naia bowed her head and prayed for Quin's dark god to show him mercy.

No. His name wasn't Quin. It was Shahin. Shahin son of Marthax.

She leaned back against the cave wall, hugging her legs against her chest. She sat there for a long time, silently observing the rise and fall of his chest, watching his breath stir the whiskers on his face. Hours later, she fell asleep.

Naia stirred, wakening slowly. She pulled herself upright and rubbed her eyes, blinking at the brilliant light that filled the chamber. As her vision swam into focus, she realized Quin's body wasn't where she'd left it. She stood up, glancing around.

"Naia."

She whirled, flinching back before she recognized him. Quin caught her up in his arms, hugging her fiercely. Then he pulled back enough to stare into her face.

"You really are the loveliest sight I've ever seen in my whole damn life," he said.

Then he kissed her.

And she kissed him back.

Chapter Twenty-Eight
The Path of Compassion

Pass of Lor-Gamorth, The Front

Kyel crouched on the floor of the iron cage, his back pressed up against the unyielding bars. He'd been there for hours, staring down at the blackened, distorted shape that had once been Myria Anassis. No matter how hard he tried, he couldn't stop looking. The grisly remains were morbidly fascinating; it was strange how her fingers were preserved in such detail: every feature sculpted as if from black marble. He could see every crease, every fingernail, each perfectly formed and perfectly blackened. Her face had been distorted into a hideous thing, a ghastly mask of horror that gaped at him eyelessly.

The smell was sickening. The dungeon reeked of charred human.

Kyel looked to where Devlin Craig lay fallen. The commander's face was turned slightly toward him, staring with an unfocused, endless gaze into the shadows of the ceiling. A gray-fletched arrow pierced his neck, the same kind that stuck out from the back of the dead priest.

Kyel's gaze retreated to his hands, pondering them. The same hands that had nocked the arrows to the bowstring. He'd loosed them both without a second thought. It had seemed like the right thing to do.

Now he knew what a terrible choice he'd made.

The chain on his wrist was still in place, he noticed with relief. He hadn't broken his Oath of Harmony; he hadn't killed with his gift. But the conviction that held him to that Oath had eroded. He could feel it. It was like an infection, spreading like a malignancy under his skin. That was the reason why mages were forbidden weapons in the first place. Power was a temptation under the best of circumstances. Under the worst of circumstances, it was a temptation almost impossible to deny.

Holding that bow had felt so natural, so right. He'd stood there in the doorway for minutes, watching as Myria burned. When the priest had raised his torch again, Kyel had reacted. He hadn't been able to stand by and do nothing.

He'd sided with a Servant of Xerys. He'd killed his senior officer. And then he'd regretted it all a scant moment later, when he'd seen Darien finish off Craig without hesitation or remorse. And then raise the necrators. Kyel had realized he'd made a grave mistake.

Darien *was* evil. So was Craig. So was the priest. And so was Meiran. They were all evil, each in their own way. For whatever their respective reason, each had abandoned the path of compassion.

He heard a sound: the muffled echo of footsteps approaching from the corridor. Kyel stared warily at the doorway until Traver's face appeared. The man stopped between strides, staring in shock at Craig's mangled body. With a shout, he shot forward to kneel at his commander's side.

Kyel drew his knees up to his chest, tucking his head, too ashamed to look. He sat there for silent minutes, drowning in shame as Traver grieved. He only looked up when he heard the sound of footsteps approaching his cage.

"What the bloody hell happened?" Traver's voice was hoarse.

Kyel couldn't look at him. "Don't ask. Just get the keys. On the floor by Craig."

Traver looked at him sideways then glanced down at the charcoaled mass on the floor of the cage. His expression crumpled into something halfway between disgust and disbelief. He made a raspy, gagging noise way back in his throat, bringing his hand up to his mouth. Then he turned and picked his way slowly over to the body of his commander. He returned to the cage, holding his breath against the stench as he fumbled with the lock.

Kyel rose and stepped over the blackened Myriahusk, anxious to be as far away from it as he could get. He slipped out the door as soon as Traver got it open. Once outside, he bolted toward the exit, wanting nothing more than to escape the dungeon and never look back. He forced himself to stop, turning to wait for Traver.

The captain didn't follow immediately. Instead, he went back to kneel at Craig's side, bowing his head in respect. He unfastened his cloak and pulled it off his shoulders, then draped it like a shroud over the corpse. He knelt there a moment in silence. When he stood back up, Traver had a look in his eyes that Kyel had never seen before.

"Darien did this?" Traver didn't sound like he believed it. He glanced at the longbow on the floor.

Kyel didn't respond. He dropped his eyes to the ground, staring as if mesmerized by the patterns of the stonework.

Traver strode up to him, squeezing Kyel by the arm. "This is bad," he said. "But there's worse up top. You need to come see it."

Kyel nodded, too ashamed to respond. He knew Traver suspected he'd murdered Craig. The captain didn't have any proof to support his hunch, but the suspicion was there, written in his eyes. Kyel followed Traver out of the dungeon and onto the stairs, walking in silence all the way to the surface. They emerged from the stairwell into the fire-fed shadows of the courtyard.

Kyel stopped and glanced around in an attempt to get his bearings. The ward was roiling with soldiers and smoke, the garish flames of bonfires casting tortured streaks across the ground. The scene was chaotic, a turmoil of commotion. There was a lot of dead, he realized. The bodies of the fallen littered the inner ward, blood winding through channels in the cobbles. In some places, the dead were piled up on top of each other.

A gruesome corpse lay only paces from his feet. The face was locked in a rigid scream, the skin blistered and oozing. Kyel recognized the man: it was the soldier who had called him a darkmage to his face. He couldn't guess the cause of death, but he could tell it had been awful. Kyel took a step back away from the corpse. Then another.

"Kyel!"

He turned to find Meiran rushing toward him, Cadmus following as fast as his portly carriage would allow. She looked relieved to see him. "Where have you been?" she demanded, looking him over as if assessing him for injury.

Traver said warily, "I found him in the dungeon. Craig's dead. So's the priest." He shifted his weight nervously over his feet, glancing sideways at Kyel.

Meiran's face went slack. She looked from Traver to Kyel. "Are you injured?"

Kyel shook his head, looking out at the mass of bodies sprawled before him like a personal vision of hell prepared just for him. "No."

Meiran looked at Traver, demanding, "What happened?"

"Darien escaped and carved his way out of here." Traver sounded more frustrated than upset. "It's not pretty." He pointed to where gray-cloaked men were dragging corpses toward the edge of the yard, laying them out along the wall.

"Darien did this?" Kyel whispered in dismay, eyes raking over the carnage. It sunk into him then: this was all his fault. If he hadn't killed Craig and the priest, then these men would still be alive. Their deaths were on him. Aghast, he turned his back on the grisly scene, covering his mouth as he resisted the urge to vomit.

"What about the woman?" Meiran asked.

"She's dead. They burned her," Kyel responded woodenly, glancing at the nearest clump of bodies. Some of them appeared melted, as if doused with acid. Some were still smoldering.

Traver said, "I thought the magic field didn't work here. How did Darien do any of this?"

Meiran looked around, surveying the extent of the damage that surrounded her. "This wasn't the magic field that did this. Darien used the Onslaught. Maybe when he killed the priest…"

Kyel continued his relentless study of his boots as her voice trailed off.

Traver threw his hands up. "That's it, then. I can't keep either of you safe. You're both powerless here, but apparently they can come and go as they please. And after what we just did to the pass, you can expect they're going to retaliate."

"What did we do to the pass?" Kyel looked up at Traver in concern.

"We blew the powder and brought half the mountain down on top of them."

Kyel stared at the man. Then his eyes shot toward the dark ridgelines in the distance. Alarmingly, the view was very different than he remembered. The number of casualties…

Kyel spun away. He couldn't look at Traver. Darien's people had been evacuating through the canyon. He wondered how many had been buried. How many civilians. He felt betrayed. He'd given his word to Darien that his people would be safe. He'd never thought Traver or Craig would go that far, stoop to such depths of dishonor. He'd underestimated them.

"How many…?" he whispered.

"At least eight thousand casualties. More if we're lucky."

Lucky? Kyel closed his eyes as the number seeped in. He felt a numbness in his belly that clawed at his heart. So much evil. He gazed around at the corpses of the fallen. There was no right side. No good choice. It was all wrong, from every perspective. He felt sick that he'd ever been a part of any of it.

"Prime Warden, we need to get you both off the mountain," Traver said quickly. "Before they come for us."

Meiran shook her head, her face resolute. "No. We'll stand with you. But not here. Take us someplace outside the node. Somewhere we'll have a good view of the approaches."

Kyel stared after the corpses being dragged across the yard, wondering how Meiran could think they could make any bit of difference. If Darien could do this…Kyel knew there was no way they could defend against that kind of power. That kind of malice.

"I'll take you to the old keep," Traver announced. "It's far enough back behind our lines, you should be reasonably protected. Any difference you can make, well…I'd sure appreciate it."

Darien threw back the tent flap and emerged into the shadows of day. Seeing him, a score of men sitting around a coal-fire clambered to their feet. One of them was Sayeed, and the look on his face was painful to see. It rekindled the rage inside Darien, along with a profound sense of shame. He'd led Sayeed to believe that his nephew would be safely returned. He'd been wrong about that, just as he'd been wrong about everything. Darien knew that he alone was to blame.

"I'm sorry," he said. There was nothing else to say.

The Zakai officer let out a beleaguered sigh and shook his head. "Their hands are stained with blood, not yours. You are not to blame for their treachery."

Darien couldn't accept that. It was too easy; it gave none of the responsibility back to him. "I should have anticipated this. It's my fault."

"It was their fate," Sayeed insisted, laying a hand on Darien's shoulder. "Don't trouble your heart, Brother."

Hearing the man label him 'brother,' even in the face of his failure, brought Darien to new depths of shame. Anger and guilt burned together in his chest, scorching a hole right through him. "I promise you, Sayeed: Iskender will be avenged. I'll boil their blood and scatter their ashes on the winds."

Sayeed stared at him hard, a mercurial expression in his eyes. At last, he said, "There is a saying: 'Anger begins with madness, but ends in regret.'"

"Not this time," Darien disagreed. "This time, my anger has no end."

He heard a scraping noise behind him and turned to find Byron Connel standing amongst the cluster of men. The Battlemage strode up, clasped him roughly by the arm, and jerked Darien back in the direction of his tent. Darien didn't have a choice about going along with him. He glanced back at Sayeed as Connel propelled him through the flap.

Inside, Connel ripped off his shoes one at a time and threw them into a corner. Seeing him, Azár ducked through the partition. Connel sat down heavily on the floor, gesturing for Darien to follow. He seated himself across from the man.

Azár came back in with a tray in her hands, her eyes flashing in alarm. Wordlessly, she served tea.

Connel lifted his cup to his lips without a word of gratitude as Azár seated herself at Darien's side. She was keeping her gaze lowered, Darien realized. For some reason, that incensed him.

He reached up and took his wife's face in his hand. Purposefully, he lifted her chin until she was staring unblinking into his eyes. A proud smile touched her lips. With renewed confidence, she turned to stare openly at Connel.

The darkmage didn't seem to notice the interaction. Either that or he didn't care. He sat gazing down into his cup as if seeking there for insight. Without looking up, he said, "Did you really mean what you said out there?"

Darien frowned, not certain what he was referring to. Then it occurred to him: Connel had walked up just when he was avowing vendetta to Sayeed. "Every word," he said, and meant it.

"Good." Connel's eyes snapped up to lock on his own. "Because I'm going to give you the chance to scatter all the ashes you want."

Darien set his cup down, his interest piqued. "Go on."

Connel obliged him. "We're going to hit them hard. I want you and your Tanisars to spearhead the assault. Your mission will be to penetrate their lines and encircle the keep. We'll come behind you and mop up anything that's left. You're going to need to create as much shock and terror as you can. Strike enough fear into their hearts, and they'll collapse before you. Can you do that?"

"Aye." The hunger in his voice made Azár turn to stare at him.

To Darien, the plan sounded exhilarating. It was exactly the thing he needed, exactly what he craved. He wanted to plunge his sword deep into the heart of his enemy. He wanted to repay them pain for pain. He couldn't help but smile, the thrill of anticipation making his blood burn hot.

Connel set his cup down on the rugs. "Get your forces ready," he commanded, rising to his feet. "They'll be expecting us to be licking our wounds. They won't be expecting an attack."

Darien followed him to his feet, assuring him, "I'll scatter those ashes for you."

The Battlemage nodded. "I'll see you in the Rhen, Darien. Or I'll see you in hell. Whichever comes first for us."

Darien watched him leave as Azár pushed herself up off the ground. She stood gazing at him darkly, her expression resentful. She wasn't the type to stay behind and wait. He couldn't blame her.

He asked, "Would you be willing to stand and fight at my side?"

Azár's eyes widened, her cheeks flush with excitement. She gazed at him with open gratitude on her face. "I would be honored to fight at the side of my husband," she said solemnly.

Darien smiled, feeling a vast swelling of pride. "Good. Because I know exactly how to use you."

Lightning flared as their horses rounded a bend in the mountain's side. A chill gust of wind came up from the direction of the Black Lands, beating at Kyel's back. It was the same oppressive wind he remembered from the first time he'd ever looked upon the pass. Not much had changed. This was still the closest to hell he'd ever been.

He could see the foundations of the old keep above on the ridge. It was a sad and eerie sight that looked as charred and pathetic as Myria's corpse had. Below, they had a sweeping view of the canyon, and all the way out to the plains beyond. From this elevation, the landscape looked enormous, unfolding before them like a great black heaven dotted with pinpoints of light. Kyel pointed downward, uncertain what he was looking at.

"What's all that?" he asked.

Traver nodded in the direction of the grasslands. "The combined armies of Southwark and Chamsbrey."

Kyel's brow furrowed in confusion. "When did they arrive?"

"Yesterday."

He glanced back and forth between Traver, Cadmus, and Meiran, his gut tightening. "Why wasn't I told?"

"Because you're too honest, Kyel," Meiran snapped, reining in her mare and turning back to look at him pointedly.

"What does that mean?" He didn't like the look on her face, or the accusation in her voice.

"It means you wear your feelings on your face. We couldn't share our plans with you. Otherwise, we would have never gained Darien's trust. He'd have seen right through you in a heartbeat."

"So you left me in the dark on purpose." Kyel shook his head, feeling almost sorry for her. The betrayal he felt almost seemed to justify his actions back in the dungeon. Almost, but not quite. Nothing could justify that.

Meiran turned her horse, starting up the trail toward the old keep. Kyel kicked his mount forward, coming up beside her. "I'm your Sentinel, Meiran. You can't just keep me in ignorance."

"If you want to be treated like a Sentinel, then start acting like one," she snapped.

He made no attempt to mask the anger and resentment her words provoked. He'd been trying so hard for so long. But he felt hindered at every turn. Mostly by Meiran…sometimes by Cadmus. Usually by both. He was tired of the blame. Tired of the ridicule. Especially by people he felt he could no longer respect.

"I've tried, Meiran," he said. "But I've been having a hard time understanding some of the decisions you've been making lately."

The prime warden stopped her horse and cast a withering stare his way. "You don't need to understand. You don't even have to agree. All you need to do is *exactly what you're told.* Can you handle that, Grand Master?"

Kyel gritted his teeth. "Aye."

He looked at Traver, who glanced away. Then he looked at Cadmus, who returned his gaze steadily and sadly. Kyel sagged in his saddle, feeling conflicted. He'd half a mind to turn his horse around and ride back down the mountain. Only, he had no idea where he would go. He felt lost and without direction. He was embroiled in a conflict, and he didn't agree with either side.

They dismounted and led the horses the rest of the way up the slope to the ruins. The wind whipped up again, battering Kyel's cloak as he brought up the rear of their procession. Forks of lightning revealed the broken structure that awaited them. Not much was left, Kyel saw. Only two walls of the keep remained standing. The tower had collapsed entirely, now only a pile of rubble.

The wind exhaled a great, exhausted sigh.

By the time they gained the keep's ruins, Kyel's hands trembled with cold and fury. He took one last glimpse behind then followed Traver around a crumbled wall. There, he gazed down into a wide hole in the ground, what had once been the basement of the fortress. Now mostly filled in with broken rock and glistening black shafts of charred wood.

They tied the horses up along the gutted wall and made camp in a corner protected by the wind. There was no roof, no floor. Just dirt and charred embers, crumbled stone and bitter memories.

Glancing around, Kyel grumbled to no one in particular, "What good can we do here?"

Traver didn't look at him. In fact, he was making a conspicuous study of not looking at him.

Meiran did, though. She fixed him with the same, insufferable expression. "We'll do whatever we *can* do, Kyel. Defensive shielding, creating diversions, healing the wounded—whatever the moment calls for."

Kyel wondered at the wisdom of that. Their new position wasn't very defensible, and the open basement could be easily overrun. He doubted it would be wise to draw attention to their location.

They carved a firepit from the ashes and made camp around it. Cadmus rummaged through his pack, finally producing a loaf of bread and a sack of jerky, passing it around. Traver took a good-sized hunk of meat and tore off a bite with his teeth. He poked at the fire with a stick, his face hardened. He hadn't said a word since they had gained the fortress. He threw the stick down in the fire.

"I'm going to go scout around," he announced, his face grimly set. He flung his gray cloak back over his shoulder. He stabbed a glance at Kyel. "Why don't you come with me?"

"All right."

Kyel stood up, dusting his hands. He didn't like the way Traver was acting. He glanced at Meiran and, at a nod from her, started after Traver. He followed the captain out of the lee of the crumbled wall and into the infernal wind. Traver turned back, taking a quick measure of him, then motioned for Kyel to follow. They found a trail that wound around through the wreckage then cut down toward the backside of the ruin.

The wind faded as they moved behind the protection of an outcrop. Kyel walked behind Traver, taking his time about navigating the narrow path leading down the steep embankment. There, almost at the cliff's edge, was a large boulder that Kyel remembered well. He used to sit upon that rock often, just to think. Every crack and grain of its texture was familiar to him.

"I remember this place," Kyel said, reaching out to touch the worn surface of the boulder. "I used to come here with Darien."

Traver turned toward him, and Kyel saw that the hardness hadn't left his eyes. If anything, it had crystalized. Kyel drew his hand back, alarmed. He glanced at the cliff. Then he looked back at Traver, unsure of his intentions.

"I need to ask you something," Traver said, his voice more serious than Kyel had ever heard it.

"What?" Kyel sank down onto the rock, ice clawing at his chest. He thought he knew what Traver was going to say.

Traver dropped to a crouch in front of him, until he was at eye level with Kyel. He leaned forward with a hand on the pommel of his sword. "Back in the dungeon…I noticed something that struck me as odd," he said slowly.

Kyel's eyes lingered on Traver's hand. He felt a sudden, ghastly chill. The rock scarp beside them seemed altogether too close.

Peering into Kyel's eyes, Traver asked him directly, "Where did Darien Lauchlin get a longbow?"

Kyel swallowed, looking down. The world stabilized, its motion jarring to a halt. And then it condensed, contracting until the only thing left was the condemnation in Traver's stare. Kyel couldn't move. He kept his eyes fixed on Traver's hand.

"Why'd you do it?" Traver asked, picking up a fist-sized rock. He turned it over in his hands, eyes coldly examining it.

"Because they shouldn't have to die in darkness!" Kyel spat, leaping up. It was an open admission of guilt, but he didn't care anymore. He'd had enough. He wasn't the one in the wrong here. Out of all of them, he was the only one in the right.

"I disagree," Traver growled, and hurled the rock.

An explosion of sparks erupted across Kyel's vision, glittering bright.

Chapter Twenty-Nine
Xerys' Shadow

Pass of Lor-Gamorth, The Front

The demons on the wind howled like ravenous dogs, shrieking and gnashing, ripping up the topsoil and flinging it at the Spire of Orguleth. At the mountain's base, thousands of soldiers stood, overwhelming the plain, their backs to the wind, faces to their fate. At the end of the march, there would be a dawn. For most, it would be the first dawn they'd ever looked upon. For others, it would be the last. It didn't matter; the wind wailed at them all indifferently.

Darien pulled himself across the saddle of his mount as the vicious gusts tried to tear him back off again. He moved with difficulty, unused to the enameled cuirass Connel had given him. Azár mounted her own horse, armored in a similar style of plate. She glanced over at him and smiled. A proud smile, full of dark promise for their enemies.

Darien heard a low growl, distinct from the wind. Looking down, he noticed that the thanacryst had wandered out from the lee of the tent where it had been sheltering from the wind. The demon-dog paused next to him, eyes fixated on the mountains, its hackles rising. A great glob of slobber drooled from its mouth, and its eyes gleamed like hell-born embers.

The call of a war horn rose above the wind, moaning like a tortured spirit. Darien tightened the strap of his helm beneath his chin. Then he gathered the reins of his stallion and directed it forward with the pressure of his legs. The horse snorted, jerking its head, then moved forward in a swaying gait. The combined legions of Malikar advanced behind him up the incline that led into the Pass of Lor-Gamorth.

Kyel groaned, biting back the pain in his head and the bile in his throat. His eyes slit open just a crack. It was all he could manage. Through a fog of misery, he saw Meiran leaning over him. Her face looked drawn, her expression like soured wine.

"Don't try to use the magic field," she cautioned in her usual monotone. "You have a head injury."

Kyel tried to blink his vision back into focus. He gazed up at her mutely, fumbling to comprehend his situation. He was lying on his side, hands and feet trussed like a hog awaiting slaughter. Just the thought of using the magic field made his stomach rebel with a pang of nausea.

"What's going on?" he murmured, his voice just as blurry as the rest of the world.

His gaze shifted to Traver, who stood on the other side of Meiran with his hands on his hips. The look of accusation in his old friend's eyes was painful to witness. Kyel suddenly remembered the rock. And why Traver had used it on him.

Meiran said, "You admitted to being a traitor. And a murderer."

That's right. He'd killed both Craig and the priest. Kyel supposed that did make him a traitor and a murderer. Funny how he didn't feel like either.

"Then why am I still alive?" Soon, his head would be clear enough to touch the magic field again. Then all the bonds they'd tied him with wouldn't matter. He couldn't understand why they hadn't killed him already.

Meiran folded her arms, bending down until her

face was scant inches from his own. "Because their army is on the march, and they're coming here to destroy us. Despite my better judgement, *we need you.*"

Kyel's head throbbed, as much from the logic of that argument as from the injury.

"Let them through, Meiran" he said. "That way, no one needs to die. It's what you agreed to in the first place."

Meiran stood up, dusting herself off. She wore a disgusted look on her face. "They're out for blood, now. They won't just pass us by."

"And who's fault is that?"

The look in her eyes was caustic enough to corrode his confidence. Kyel closed his eyes as a fresh surge of nausea tightened his stomach. The world spun, and for a moment he thought he was going to be sick. But he spat the bile out of his mouth and swallowed the rest back down again.

He looked miserably up at Meiran. "I don't understand you. You've abandoned all sense of decency. You're just as bad as Darien. Honestly, I don't see any difference between the two of you. You've both been to hell, and you've both come back changed. Maybe there's something to that."

Meiran's face went slack, her paleness fading into whiteness. But her eyes remained hard. She whispered, "You think *I'm* the one who's corrupted?"

"I think you both are."

Meiran glanced to Cadmus, who was squatting on the other side of the dying fire. She turned back to Kyel. "It doesn't matter what you believe. I'm still the prime warden, and I'm giving you a choice. Defend me with your life. Help me get down off this mountain. Or die now on your friend's sword."

That wasn't much of an option. Kyel saw Traver's hand moving toward the hilt of his blade. His gaze traveled upward to the man's face. He saw his own fate meted out in blood in Traver's eyes.

Kyel sighed, resigned. "I'll defend you with my life. As much as my Oath will allow."

Meiran looked grimly satisfied. She said, "That chain on your wrist is the only reason you're still alive. Don't lose it. The moment that chain comes off, I'll give the order to have you slain."

Kyel nodded; he expected no less.

Meiran said to Traver, "Release him."

Kyel went rigid as both Meiran and Traver knelt beside him, one sawing through the ropes that held him, the other laying hands on his chest. Kyel stiffened, knowing exactly what was coming. But knowing didn't make it any better.

The shock of Meiran's healing swept over him, dragging him down like the suction of a whirlpool. He gasped, feeling his consciousness twist away.

The climb into the pass was slow and grueling, infinitely tedious. Rain slanted down like icy needles, buffeted by the wind. The collapse of the mountainside had buried the canyon and its approaches, which made progress even more difficult. Connel had ordered a battalion of engineers to precede them, forging a new trail and clearing debris from their path, until they reached a shallow lake that had formed behind the blockage in the stream. The walls of the canyon were too steep to bypass the lake; they would have to cross it.

Darien stared down from the top of a rock scarp at the narrow lake below, not liking the looks of the situation. The stream that fed the canyon had been blocked by the landslide. With no outlet, the water was collecting, forming a long and narrow lake that was altogether treacherous. The east edge of the lake lapped against a sheer rock precipice. The other side was overlooked by a series of low bluffs where his intuition told him Greystone archers would be stationed.

Darien didn't see any bowmen. But that didn't mean they weren't there.

He didn't trust it. The lake was a natural killing zone, a place where any advancing force would be slowed to a crawl, its defensive options limited. If Craig were still alive, he wouldn't let such an opportunity for slaughter slip him by. And even though Craig was dead, Darien guessed that his orders were still being followed. They hadn't had the time or talent to come up with something better.

Darien ordered a halt well back from the lake, out of bowshot. There was not enough room to erect tents, so he had his men camp right there on the top of the rubble, building cookfires to huddle around. If his men were going to fight, then they would fight rested, with their bodies warm and their bellies full.

"They must see us coming." Azár nodded in the direction of the cliffs above the lake, her eyes dark and shadowed with worry. "Why do we stop here and give them time to prepare?"

"Because I want them to see us coming," Darien answered, removing his helm. He pointed at the cliffs ahead with a chain-gloved hand. "I want them to watch us fill this canyon and get a good sense of our numbers."

Azár nodded, seeming to understand his intent. "Our numbers will strike fear into their hearts. Their ranks will crumble before us."

"Aye," Darien agreed. "That's the idea."

The look of excitement on Azár's face surprised him. He'd always known she was fierce; he'd admired that. But he hadn't foreseen how alive she would become at the prospect of battle.

"We will feed them their fear," she whispered.

"That will be your job. The light you'll weave will fill them with terror."

Azár's smile grew proud and ferocious. Never had Darien seen a woman more intensely beautiful than his wife was at that moment. He turned and walked away to where his officers stood gathered, the demon-hound stalking at his side. He caught Sayeed's attention with a wave of his hand, beckoning the man over.

"We'll maintain position here for a few hours," Darien instructed. "Tell the men to sharpen their tent posts at both ends. Double the fires. Burn every coal brick, if that's what it takes. I want it to look like we've got at least twice our true number."

Sayeed stared at him in incomprehension. "What do we do when we run out of coal?"

"It won't matter. After the morrow, we'll be in the Rhen. And then there'll be plenty of villages to burn."

Sayeed squeezed Darien's arm. Then he strode away to relay orders to the other officers.

Darien pulled off his gloves and turned to survey the column behind him, admiring the discipline of his men as they went about the process of setting up camp. Before arriving in the Black Lands, he never would have imagined such efficiency possible. He looked about in awe of the people he led, of the wife he'd married, of the fortunes that fate had brought him. For the first time in years, he felt worthwhile.

He realized that this must be his purpose, the reason why he had been spared when Aerysius fell, why he'd cast off the chains of his bondage. Why he had pledged his soul to two dark gods and put the Soulstone on his neck. All that had happened for a reason.

Because these people deserved to see the sun.

And Darien was determined to give it to them.

The night wore on infinitely, the way nights do before a battle. Darien had a hard time staying asleep. He kept jerking awake, gasping for air and drenched in sweat. His mind worked furiously, sifting through strategies and weighing contingencies. Minimizing casualties and maximizing assets. He knew there was no way to predict how the battle would go; the best he could do was prepare and anticipate. But battles had a way of taking on a life of their own, and that bothered him. He didn't like anything outside his control.

Darien finally gave up on sleep and rose well before the rest of the camp. He ate a quick meal then set out, intending to take one last survey of the lake and the battlefield ahead. He wore his cloak over his black cuirass. With the helm on his head, he was indistinguishable from any other officer in Bryn Calazar's legions.

No one recognized him, which was good. He walked away from the camp, following the gentle rise of the slope above the lake. Scanning the cliffs ahead, he saw no fires. But he wasn't fooled; he knew they were there. Darien knew it because that's what he would have done. And he felt certain that's what Craig would have done, too.

He marveled that he felt no compassion for the Greystone soldiers he had once fought beside, as if his death had erased all ties to his former homeland. Craig's betrayal certainly had. Men he'd once considered brothers, he now held beneath his contempt. He didn't understand the people he'd been born to, didn't want to try to understand them.

He just wanted them dead.

The fires were doused, the Tanisars formed up in a long, drawn-out column, awaiting the order to advance. Helm tucked in the crook of his arm, Darien walked with Azár toward the clump of officers standing on a long, flat ledge. Azár was wearing her armor, carrying her helm. Darien's hand rested on the hilt of the scimitar given to him by Sayeed. The blade once held by Khoresh Kateem, the only conqueror to ever successfully unite all of Caladorn.

The air was frigid, and his metal armor felt like a layer of ice. It sapped the heat right out of him, even through the thick padding he wore beneath it. Every breath formed a cloud before his face. Fingering the hilt of Kateem's sword, Darien moved into the center of the cluster of officers. He swept his gaze over them, looking into the face of each man individually. He felt a twinge of anticipation, the feeling that the future was finally forming up into something tangible. The promise of sunlight ahead didn't seem quite as surreal as it had the day before.

To the officers standing 'round him, he said, "We'll have to advance right up the center, through the middle of the lake. It's not deep, but it'll be slow going. Expect an ambush. They'll have archers stationed above you on those cliffs." He pointed at the bluffs above the water.

He continued, "There's only a thousand of us. But every one of our soldiers is worth three of theirs. Pick the fastest men and women you have. They'll need to gain the far shore as quickly as they can. They'll be under heavy fire the whole way, so tell them to keep their shields up and their heads down. Our objective is to gain and hold the shoreline. Then we'll wait for the main force to relieve us."

He turned to Azár, who stood looking up at him with a noncommittal expression. He told her, "I want you riding at my side. I'll weave shadow as we cross the lake; I want them fighting blind. You can't dodge a blade if you can't see it coming. When we reach the shoreline, that's when I'll need your light."

Azár's eyes smiled at him, proud and eager.

Darien donned his helm and mounted his armored stallion, nudging his horse toward the files of men. Azár followed on her own mare as the officers dispersed to their respective commands. He directed his mount to the front of the column, where he drew up and waited.

When the battalion was formed up behind him, Darien drew Kateem's sword. He held it over his head then brought it down decisively. The column behind him advanced. Darien kept his horse in check, allowing the warriors to pass him by as he called on the fury of the magic field, weaving shadow to cloak their intent. After the first battalion had past, he urged his mount forward, Azár at his side. The shadow he wove roiled over them like a blanket of coal-soot, covering them all in stifling darkness that muted even sound.

The infantry made their way down the rock scarp formed by the slide, then waded into the murky lake. The men moved through the water without a sound, holding their shields and weapons over their heads. Darien sent his stallion forward, wading into water almost up to its belly. Sayeed waded beside Azár's horse. A totality of silence travelled with them. No one spoke. There was no rustle of armaments or jingle of tack.

Nevertheless, a shout rang down from the heights. It was followed by the infinite quiet that only comes before the storm. Darien closed his eyes, bracing. He concentrated, thickening the shadows above Azár until they became a palpable barrier.

A whisper hissed through the darkness.

He couldn't see the arrow-cloud, so he let it descend upon them. Immediately, the silence of the canyon was assaulted by a raining clatter. Arrows clanged off shields, plunked against helms, rebounded off steel. Darien's cuirass rattled, battered by the volley coming down around him, as more arrows clanked against his stallion's armor. A man to the left of him grunted and went down, a clothyard shaft protruding from a gap between plates. Arrows collected on the surface of the water, floating like driftwood. The men around him surged forward, scrambling to reach the shoreline.

Another hiss, followed by the clamor of broadheads. There was a pause. Then more arrows came down in a constant hail as the archers began loosing their shafts at will. Darien gathered in his web of shadows further, tightening them densely around Azár while leaving his own men exposed. He heard groans and screams as more soldiers fell under the relentless barrage. But Azár remained safe, which was all that mattered. The life of one Lightweaver was worth more than a thousand warriors.

Ahead of him, the first ranks reached the shore. They were met by another cloud of arrows, this one coming from groups of bowmen stationed dead ahead against the canyon wall. At close range, the gray-fletched shafts were more effective. Instead of just plunking off armor, they began to penetrate. Screams and groans erupted all along the ranks as men began to fall with frequency. Bodies collected along the shore of the lake, creating stumbling blocks for the soldiers coming behind. Darien's horse tripped over a corpse half-submerged in the shallows, but it regained its footing quickly, surging toward the shore.

More men slumped and fell ahead of him. Darien tightened his cloak of shadows, unable to do more. Men sprinted past, rushing forward to pound the sharpened stakes they carried into the mud, creating a slanting thicket of spikes hidden by their numbers. More men screamed and fell as others set about the punishing job of resharpening the stakes after they'd been hammered in.

The barrage of arrows suddenly ceased.

Darien glanced up, knowing the reason. His body tensed in expectation.

A swelling thunder echoed off the canyon walls as a wedge of cavalry careened toward them. More Tanisars crowded the bank, a constant stream arriving from behind. The numbers amassing on the shoreline swelled, jostling the front ranks forward and pushing them toward the oncoming charge.

Darien raised his hands, reaching out from within and taking hold of the lines of power that swirled through the canyon. He drew it all in, every drop he could stand, until he was filled to the point of saturation and power bled from his body. Dropping the shadow-shield, he hurled everything he had at the incoming riders.

Horses staggered and fell, rolling as their riders flew from their backs. A few of the chargers made it as far as the front ranks, hurling onto the sharpened stakes as his own men sprang back. Animals screamed and died, spitted on shafts. Some turned and bolted back in the direction they'd come, foiling the momentum of the charge. Soon the entire beach was a gruesome tumult of confusion.

Ahead of him, Darien saw a line of Greystone infantry brandish their weapons. With a mighty warcry, they charged across the trampled beach, hoisting swords and pikes, maces and crossbows.

"Now," Darien said.

All around, Azár's magelight bloomed like glistening ribbons of dawn, so bright it made his eyes water. The golden warmth swelled, consuming the darkness in a wash of tortuous brilliance. Within it, Darien's own magelight spread forward like a molten river of bluest lava.

"Hold here!" he yelled to Sayeed and Azár as he kicked his mount through the blinding spill of light.

He could do no more with the magic field; he was already saturated to capacity and feeling the strain. So he called upon the Onslaught, sucking it into him with violent fury. Then he lashed out with everything he had, using Azár's brilliant magelight as a catalyst.

The resulting firestorm surpassed anything he could have imagined.

The screams were almost as terrible as the stench that followed. Only a few men survived long enough to engage the Tanisars. Some hit the ground, tumbling, then rose, fighting to bring their weapons up. They staggered a couple of steps before exploding. Others erupted into flame, some melting into the ground. The lucky ones just folded over and died.

The fresh corpses dissolved, searing the ground where they lay. Man-like shadows bloomed in their place. A host of necrators glided forward, disoriented. They were newborn and weak, yet uncertain of their duty. Darien looked upon his creations with a cold feeling of pride.

The Tanisars around him charged, taking advantage of the chaos. With a thundering cry, hundreds of warriors ran forward, weapons raised. The assault careened right into the center of the Greystone retreat, then continued forward as more soldiers poured through, widening the rupture.

Then the necrators swarmed in to finish off the rest.

Darien's horse reared, spooked by the presence of the shades. He was flung to the ground, the wind knocked out of him. He lay there panting as he watched his stallion bolt away. A Greystone footsoldier saw him down and raised an iron mallet to finish him off. Before the man could swing, he was hurling backward, exploding while still in the air.

Darien hauled himself to his feet, summoning the remainder of the necrators under his command: a frightful army, if ever there was one. They ranged ahead of his mortal forces, questing, seeking, terrorizing. Soldiers screamed and fled, abandoning their duties and their comrades. Those brave enough to stand their ground met terrible ends.

He followed after his creations through the blinding glare of Azár's magelight. He trudged forward, using the Onslaught to punch a wedge through a group of foot soldiers. The men shrieked as they burned, the sound of their agony grimly satisfying.

Darien continued forward into the thick of the melee, tossing would-be adversaries back away from him carelessly. Arrows and weapons didn't touch him; they were no match for the wrath of the Onslaught that surrounded him like a lethal aura. His opponents slumped to the ground or simply burned where they stood.

A squad of infantry broke out of the enemy line to assault him directly, howling and with weapons raised as they sprinted toward him. Darien closed his eyes. When he opened them again, the men were boneless globs, and he was glowing with a terrible green light.

Darien staggered back, faltering. The strain of handling the vast amounts of power he'd drawn was taking its toll. He took a lurching step forward and felt an arrow plunk against his armor. Another shaft found its way through a gap between plates.

He cried out, driven to his knees by the searing fire that erupted from his shoulder. He gritted his teeth and tugged on the arrow's shaft, wrestling the chiseled barb out from under his collar bone. Reeling from pain and on the verge of passing out, he squeezed his eyes closed and healed the injury.

He caught himself with an outstretched hand as the mending swept over him. Eventually, the world stabilized. Somehow, he managed to stay awake. Darien picked himself up off the ground, clenching his jaw against the terrible weariness that was the price of the healing. He staggered, shambling like a drunken man. The heavy armor bore down on his shoulders, pressing down on him like a giant hand trying to squash him into the grave.

Seeing his struggles, his men swept forward and formed a defensive ring around him. It wasn't necessary. Every gray-cloaked soldier that broke toward him slumped to the ground, where they lay twitching and bleeding and melting into the dirt. The more he walked, the more exhausted he became, until he staggered with every step.

A foot soldier wrapped an arm around him, supporting him as Darien sagged to the ground. He couldn't bear the weight of the armor any longer. He reached up and unlocked the rivets that held his cuirass together, letting the plates slide apart. With the Tanisar's help, he shed the heavy steel, groaning with relief when the weight was finally off him. He sat there for a moment just panting, trying desperately to catch his breath.

"Brother, are you injured?"

Suddenly, Sayeed was there, kneeling at his side. He caught Darien by the shoulders, a look of intense concern on his bearded face. Behind him came Azár, glowing with radiance brighter than the sun. The world looked smeared, like someone had swiped a cloth across wet canvas.

Darien shook his head to clear his vision. He wiped his face with his sleeve, which came away stained. Sweat and blood streamed from his brow. He felt disoriented. He glanced around, at last realizing that the fighting around him had worn itself out.

Behind Sayeed, what was left of the Greystone defenders knelt at the feet of black-mailed guards. Scattered corpses littered the landscape like fallen logs, in some places collected into heaps. Shadowy necrators roamed the battlefield, diligent in their business.

"The canyon is ours," Sayeed reported, and clapped him on the arm with a grin.

Darien stared up at him, too exhausted to smile back. He nodded instead, closing his eyes in relief.

Chapter Thirty
Battlemage

Pass of Lor-Gamorth, The Front

Darien turned at the sound of hoofbeats to find Byron Connel riding toward them along the shoreline. His courser swayed in its gait, lathered sides crusted with mud. The Battlemage reined in and dismounted, his blue robes flowing out from under an enameled breastplate. He wielded the silver talisman Thar'gon in his hand. The weapon glowed with an eldritch light, drenching Connel in a halo of radiance. He strode over to where Darien sat resting between Azár and Sayeed. Looking down, he nodded a greeting.

"That was well-executed," he said, cold eyes shifting to the grisly terrain. "We'll mop up what's left. Use the momentum we've gained to take the keep."

Sayeed glanced down at Darien, raising his eyebrows in concern. Darien shook his head and spread his fingers in a gesture of negation.

Connel mounted and rode away, awash in the argent brilliance of his weapon. Darien let his eyes follow the horse and rider across the battlefield until both were lost from sight. Then he turned to Sayeed.

"I'm tired," he admitted. "But I'm not used up. Connel's right; we need to press our advantage."

"The keep is inside a node," Azár protested, her hand on the dagger at her belt.

Darien nodded. "Aye, it is. But I've the Hellpower." He rose to his feet, working his arms to test his shoulder. It moved freely without pain, but he could still feel the effects of the healing. He tried not to let his exhaustion show on his face.

"I want you to stay here," he told Azár. "You won't be of any use up there."

But his wife lifted her chin, narrowing her eyes. She slid the dagger from its sheath, holding it up in front of him. "I fight at your side," she reminded him. "Where you go, I go."

He pulled her against his chest, dagger and all, then released her just as quickly. He motioned to his officers to gather around.

"We'll continue on to the keep," he told them. "It'll be a frontal assault straight into the teeth of their fortifications. I know of some of the traps they've rigged, so I'll go ahead of you." To Azár, he cautioned, "I won't be able to heal. The Onslaught doesn't work like that."

"Then don't get hurt."

Sayeed moved forward to help Darien back into the cuirass he'd shed. The weight of the plate immediately bore down on him. He felt a deep-seated weariness that only sleep would mend.

He gave one last glance at the fallen corpses that patterned the ground around him, most wearing gray cloaks. It occurred to him that he felt not even a scrap of compassion for the fallen. He found that odd; these men had once been under his command. Yet the only feeling he could muster was a growing sense of vindication. He stepped over the first corpse that lay sprawled in his path, the remains of a young pikeman who would move no more.

Someone brought him a captured horse, a nervous brown destrier that was rightfully skittish of him. With a word, Darien dismissed his entourage of necrators. The absence of the shades calmed the gelding somewhat, enough to tolerate him on its back. Pulling Azár up behind him, Darien gathered the reins in his hand. He grasped a fistful of the horse's mane and kicked it forward.

By the time they reached the fortress, the wind had died. The whole world seemed to be holding its breath in anticipation of the inevitable.

Darien took a good, hard look at the keep and scowled, estimating the losses they would sustain trying to penetrate its defenses. He'd already fought his way out of there, so he knew he could fight his way back in. He just dreaded doing so. He already wore enough blood on him. It coated his armor and slathered the parts of his face not shielded by his helm. He was still exhausted. And he didn't look forward to the tests he would face within those walls. Kyel might be in there somewhere. And Meiran. He wasn't sure he could bring himself to kill either one of them.

The very thought of Meiran turned his blood to ice. Her image in his mind twisted something already broken inside him. It drove all rational thought away, until all he could see was red. Darien took a deep breath and hung his head. Then he glared back up at the fortress with new resolve.

"Brother."

He looked down to find Sayeed standing alongside his mount. The officer nodded in the direction of the slopes below the fortress. Darien followed his gaze, spotting a group of men who had emerged from the dark entrance to the keep, really just a hole in the mountainside. They looked like men of rank. One of them bore a white cloth in his hand, a token of truce. To Darien's relief, he didn't see Kyel among them.

Sayeed said, "They may be wishing to discuss surrender."

Darien was not disposed to discuss surrender. Perhaps the men approaching him could tell his frame of mind; they had a nervous look about them. One man tugged at his collar as he walked. Another fidgeted with his uniform. Every face looked strained and battle-weary.

"No quarter," Darien said, his gaze tracking the approaching men. "Leave two witnesses alive to report what they've seen here. No mercy to the rest. They die here, and they die brutally. Restraint now will only cost us later."

Sayeed nodded his agreement. Then he turned and relayed Darien's orders in the language of the clans. His men raised a warcry, shaking their weapons in the air. Upon hearing it, the Greystone officers turned and fled back in the direction of the tunnel.

"Visea," Darien whispered.

Five necrators melted into existence and swept forward up the steps. From within the tunnel came frantic echoes of horror. The commotion faded quickly into a haunting silence.

Darien thrust his arm up, gripping his gloved hand into a fist. Then he brought it down.

With a cry, the Tanisar ranks burst forward, breaking like a tidal wave of wrath upon the slopes of the mountainside. Darien allowed the soldiers to charge past him. He waited, watching as his men were halted at the entrance of the fortress by the fall of an iron gate.

He dismounted stiffly and stood leaning against his horse. Azár slipped to his side, considering him with a look of concern. "This is the edge of the node," she said, reaching out and catching his hand. "Stay here, my husband. Do not enter within."

He shook his head. "I'll be fine. I want you to wait here." He stroked a thumb across her soft fingers.

"I will not—" she started to protest.

"You're more than my Lightweaver," he said. "You're my light." Then he kissed her. For the first time, he felt his wife soften in his arms, the feral tension draining out of her.

He closed his eyes and reached deep inside her, pinching something there. He caught Azár as she slumped unconscious against his chest. Darien looked to Sayeed, who stared at him with a face frozen in shock.

"Take the horse," he commanded. "Get her back down the mountain. *Now.*"

Sayeed effected a curt bow then sprang onto the back of the warhorse. Darien lifted Azár up to him, making sure she was secure in the officer's grasp. Then he slapped the horse's rump, sending it forward down the slope. He turned and mounted the steps to the keep.

Above, he could hear the sound of screams and the battering of arrows against armor as his men took fire from the arrow loops above. His assaulting force had been stopped by the sealed gate that blocked the entrance to the fortress. Without a battering ram, they could go no further.

"Stand back," he warned the Tanisars.

The men complied, backing out of his way.

Darien closed his eyes, letting the Hellpower fill him until he could feel it wriggling inside every bone, worming beneath his skin. Then he opened his eyes and hurled it all back out of him in a blast of sickening energy directed at the gate. The iron gate turned at first red and then yellow, finally heating to white before it started to slump. The whole thing melted to liquid that ran in a viscous, spreading pool down the steps toward him. Darien willed the molten iron to cool. And it did. It hardened into a cascade of gleaming metal, its leading edge a handspan away from his feet.

He didn't hesitate. He stepped forward onto it.

"Lord!" one of the officers called from behind him.

Darien turned, glancing back over his shoulder at the man, who jogged up to him and bowed.

"Give us the honor of going ahead of you!" the man gasped, his eyes wide and full of battle-rage.

Darien understood. It was a matter of *sharaq*. He nodded at the officer. "You may have the honor."

He stood on the steps, catching his breath as a regiment of Tanisars swept past him over the cooling slag that had once been the gate of the fortress. He waited until the last man entered the tunnel, then donned his helm and started after them.

A deafening thunder ripped the air. Then the shockwave hit, hurling Darien backward off his feet as the entire fortress exploded in a shower of souls and stone.

Kyel jolted awake to an intense feeling of wrongness.

He moaned, groggy, tossing his head from side to side. Blinking, he willed the world back into focus. The spinning of the universe gradually slowed. His head felt better, not so much like a gourd with all its guts scraped out of it. That was the first thought he had. The second thought made him sit bolt upright.

He scrambled to his feet. Meiran was standing with her back to him against a crumbled wall, staring out into the darkness that, for some reason, seemed less infinite than usual. In the distance, there was light. A violent, raging glow that painted her face and gleamed like blood crystals in her eyes. He took a step toward her, demanding, "What happened?"

The prime warden glanced back at him, one hand on the charred wall, her face condemning. "We brought the keep down on top of them."

Kyel felt a shiver of abject cold steel over him. He backed away from her, away from Traver's reproachful glare and Cadmus' downturned gaze. Edging backward up the dirt path, he fled the footprints of the ruin. He stopped on a lip of charred rock that was once the foundation of the fortress. He turned and gazed out across the wide ravine.

Fires burned where the new keep had once stood, their flames choked by smoke and dust. The entire stronghold had been reduced to rubble. Kyel stood there numb, gazing out upon a scene of devastation that was partially his own making.

"A lot of good people died today, Kyel." Traver's harsh words lashed out at him like a whip. Kyel jerked around to face him.

"And you blame me." He broke out in a sweat.

"I do."

Kyel clenched his hands into trembling fists. He whirled on Meiran, his eyes narrowing in cold rage. "All this could have been prevented if you'd just honored your given word. No one had to die!"

He glared back and forth between Meiran, Traver, and the fires. The graveness of their situation was starting to creep up on him. There was an entire Enemy army down there. And soon it would be marching in their direction.

"What do we do?"

"We need to go," Traver growled, gripping the pommel of his sword with his one good hand. "We can make it out of the pass by morning. Are we bringing him with us?" he asked Meiran, jerking his head at Kyel.

Meiran considered Kyel gravely, as if weighing his fate with her eyes. "Yes," she sighed finally. She started up the path toward him. But she jolted to a halt, gaping at something behind him.

Kyel whirled around. It took him precious seconds to realize what he was looking at. And precious more to react. He reached out with his mind, throwing up a golden shield between Meiran and the red-bearded darkmage striding toward them through the fog of smoke.

Traver drew his sword and stepped between them.

"NO!" Kyel shouted.

The demon didn't pause in his stride, but raised his spiked morning star over his head. He brought it down in a curving arc.

The weapon didn't connect. Yet Traver sailed backward, flung through the air as if hit by the brunt force of a hurricane. He hit the ground with a sickening noise.

Kyel gaped at the sight of Traver jerking spastically, his head leaking brains and blood onto the rocks.

The shock alone almost stunned him into inaction. But somehow, Kyel kept the golden shield up as he stood his ground between Meiran and the approaching demon. Behind him, he could hear Cadmus retching his dinner onto the ground.

The blue-robed darkmage halted in front of them, raising his accursed weapon. His eyes burned fierce, his body aglow with the argent light of the talisman. His brutal eyes locked on Kyel with a presence that was numbing in its strength.

"Surrender."

Kyel couldn't react. He was paralyzed by the demon's gaze, gripped in ice-cold shackles of terror. Out of the corner of his eye, he saw Traver still twitching on the ground. He opened his mouth, but that was the best he could do. He couldn't force a single word past his lips.

The demon took a threatening step toward him, his gaze commanding. "Drop. Your. Shield."

Kyel swallowed, finally realizing who it was that confronted him: Byron Connel, ancient Warden of Battlemages. The same man who had single-handedly decimated Caladorn's armies.

In Connel's eyes, Kyel saw the promise of his own death.

There was no reason to fight, he realized. He'd already lost. He didn't have the skills or the strength to defend against Connel's power. Nevertheless, he maintained the wavering, golden shield. He'd given Meiran his word that he'd protect her with his life.

The only thing he could do was die for her.

It was the best he could do. It was all he could do.

"Kyel..." Meiran moaned.

He held the demon's stare, clenching his jaw, and waited for the death blow to fall.

Byron Connel nodded slightly. Then he struck.

An iron fist of air slapped Kyel in the face, picking him up and flinging him to the ground. An explosion of light shocked his vision as his head struck the rocks. Somehow, he retained enough of himself to realize that he'd dropped his shield. Frantic, he rolled over just in time to see Connel disappear.

And reappear in front of Meiran.

She opened her mouth to scream but only blood came out.

Kyel lurched to his feet, clawing the dagger Craig had given him out of its scabbard as Meiran crumbled to the ground. He stared down at her face as she lay dying, gasping her last breaths through a mouthful of blood.

The darkmage whirled toward him, weapon raised.

Kyel lunged forward, plunging the dagger hilt-deep into Byron Connel's right eye.

The demon staggered, dropping his silver weapon on the rocks. He fell to his knees. Then he bowed forward to the ground, driving the dagger even deeper into his brain.

Kyel stood, gasping, numbed by shock. Shaking, he dropped to a crouch at Meiran's side, scooping her up in his arms. He sent a frantic probe into her that returned only nothingness. He threw his head back, strangling a howl.

Power surged into him, locking his muscles tight. Too late, Kyel realized what it was. He tried, but he couldn't let go. All he could do was scream as five tiers of violent power slammed into him from Meiran's corpse.

His body convulsed, his breath wrung out of him as the energies quaked his mind, wracking his brain in a firestorm of sensations. Lights exploded across his vision, a violent shower of sparks accompanied by a stabbing thrust of pain. He threw his head back and screamed his throat raw. He kept on screaming until the violent torrent of energies finally subsided, and he was left weak and shivering, dripping with sweat and drowning in tears. When it was over, Kyel collapsed on top of Meiran's limp body, spent and wrung-out. He was panting, shaking, terrified, appalled...all at the same time.

He let Meiran go, covering his face as he sucked a shuddering breath into trembling lungs. He tried to grasp the implications of what had just happened, but was beyond the capacity for coherent thought. He picked up a rock, the closest thing within reach, and flung it away from him as hard as he could, chasing after it with a howl. Then he reached for the hilt of Connel's weapon, looking for anything else to throw.

He brought the silver morning star up, drawing it back over his shoulder. He was going to hurl it off the side of the mountain like the rock. But something stopped him.

Kyel knelt on the ground, gasping, trembling, gazing at the spiked talisman in his hand. It commanded his attention, captivating him entirely.

A soothing warmth settled over him, calming his nerves and comforting his mind. Kyel let out a sigh, infused with a sense of strength and power he'd never known before. His hands stopped shaking.

All the feelings of terror eased away.

In their place, Kyel felt only a growing sense of wonder.

Darkfall

BOOK FOUR

Gannet
Wolden
Farbrook
Cerulean Plains
Creek Hollow
Vale of Amberlie
Amberlie
Glen Farquist
AERYSIUS
Orien's Finger
Auberdale
Rothscard
Covendrey
Isle of Titherry
Meridan
Southwark
THE Rhen
THE Southern Continent
c. 1749 DCE

Chapter One
Dawnbreak

Pass of Lor-Gamorth, The Front

Not all fires burn hot. The fires in Darien's heart raged like a cataclysm of ice, consuming everything he was, everything he'd been. All that he'd ever hoped to be.

He stood at the edge of the Black Lands, at the furthest extremity of the Rhen. A place where the sea of darkness behind him lapped against the promise of sunlight. As he gazed out across rolling foothills garbed in shadow, he realized the only thing left ahead of him was an end. He wasn't sure what that end would entail, or what it would look like. He only knew it would be final. And he looked forward to that finality.

Winding behind him through the Pass snaked a ragtag collection of survivors. Survivors who had, for a thousand years, forged an existence beneath the oppression of everlasting night. He wondered how they would endure under the glaring judgment of the sun. The thought bothered him, crippling his mind until it ground to a halt. He put the question aside, focusing instead on the vast, empty darkness below, a plain that stretched to the distant horizon, broader than eternity. And the spatters of light that glowed like fireflies, creeping out across the sprawling night.

The campfires of two armies awaited them below.

Darien sat down on a boulder. He looked up into the brilliant face of a full moon gliding toward the zenith of the sky, a sky more wondrous than any he remembered. No longer did the savage clouds rage and rush toward the horizon. High above stretched a starry grandeur he'd failed to appreciate until those pinpoint lights had flickered out, shadowed by the cursed darkness that plagued the world he'd left behind.

Below, the glow of campfires danced and taunted, beckoning like a siren's song. He knew better than to heed that call. It was what his enemy wanted: to lure them out from the protective walls of the canyon, to rush blindly into defeat. The Rhen's commanders had chosen their positions with slaughter in mind. Darien couldn't usher his own forces onto the plain without sacrificing the whole of his vanguard. Perhaps most of his army. Looking down, he could easily envision the mounded corpses that would collect and obstruct the mouth of the Pass. They would be forced to scale that gruesome wall. Then the enemy archers could pick them off at will.

It wouldn't even be a fight. It would be a massacre.

No, a sortie into the thick of the encampment was not an option. Without a miracle, they were pinned.

Perhaps he could provide that miracle.

The gravelly sounds of footsteps approached from behind. Darien didn't need to look to know that it was Sayeed; he had the distinct sound of the man's stride memorized. No other could replicate it; Darien would know the difference. When the officer drew up behind him, he turned and gazed up into the bearded face of his friend, his brother. The careworn look in Sayeed's eyes should have given Darien pause. But it didn't. He turned back around, looking out across the plain, considering the myriad campfires and their dire implications.

Sayeed bowed. "They have combined the armies of two nations into a single defensive force," he reported. "They have positioned archers and infantry to guard the mouth of the Pass."

"What do you need?" Darien sat gazing downward at the plain, his long hair stirring in the breeze.

There was a crunching noise as Sayeed shifted his weight. "We need a way of punching through their front ranks. Of creating a breach."

Darien nodded. He'd been thinking the same thing.

"I'll do it," he decided. With a sigh, he pushed himself up and turned to face his senior officer.

The man instantly threw his hands up as if trying to ward him off. "No, Brother. It is too dangerous—"

Darien shook his head, already moving past him. "No. It's not."

Sayeed rushed to catch up, but before he could protest further, Darien said, "I'll push their line back away from the mouth of the Pass. Send the infantry in after me. For every man that falls, have another ready to replace him."

He expected the Zakai officer to protest, but to his surprise, Sayeed didn't respond. He fell in beside Darien, matching him stride for stride as they descended the trail toward the bottom of the Pass. To where his forces huddled in the cold without enough fuel to build fires of their own, with empty bellies and determined minds, and a tenacious faith that remained unfaltering.

They reached the trail that meandered along the river bottom. On this side of the mountain divide, the flagging river trickled downhill toward the plain ahead. They followed the path along the watercourse past lines of hunkering soldiers, toward the forefront of the ranks. There Darien paused, gazing out through the narrow gap in the cliffs that formed the gateway to the Rhen. A gateway that now stood barred by forty thousand soldiers eager to deliver them to their deaths.

He pulled on his threadbare gloves, flexing his fingers. He drew the scimitar he wore at his waist, offering it to Sayeed, who received the blade gravely with both hands. Then he turned and, squaring his shoulders, strode forward.

"Husband."

Darien stopped with a sigh, closing his eyes. He didn't turn around. Instead, he bowed his head in defeat, waiting as Azár approached from behind.

"You promised. Never again." Her voice was as cold and flat as lead.

"So I did."

He turned and looked at her. His wife stood with her hands at her sides, her expression resentful. She had every right to be angry. He had betrayed Azár's trust and left her behind. It had been for her protection, but that hardly mattered. She'd made it abundantly clear that he would never repeat the mistake.

Darien had been born and raised a fighting man. He knew when he was beaten.

"Very well," he said. "I've been meaning to teach you some lessons. Perhaps now's the time for it."

He offered his hand. Azár stepped forward and took it, gazing upward into his face. The look in her eyes was fierce, daunting.

"Where you go, I go," she reminded him.

Darien nodded, internalizing her words. Turning back toward the mouth of the Pass, he started forward, hand in hand with his wife.

"Lord! Your armor!" Sayeed rushed forward.

Darien waved him away. "I don't need it. Have the infantry ready. This won't take long."

Behind him, the men were already rising to their feet, reaching for their weapons. He could feel their eyes on his back. He ignored them and kept walking. He raised his wife's soft hand to his lips, pressing a kiss against her skin.

"Feel through me," he said. "You'll have only a short while, and there's an awful lot to learn. Besides, I might need your help."

Azár looked at him and smiled, her eyes brimming with pride. "You won't need my help. My husband is the most dangerous man ever to walk the world."

"No," Darien said, softly, surely. "I'm not."

Hoyte Griswalt shivered in the cold. The small fire he'd built wasn't nearly enough to overcome the wintry chill that stiffened his joints and numbed his bones. His breath clouded the air before his face, his toes aching like open sores in his boots. It wasn't supposed to be this cold, not so far north or this late in the season. He understood weather; he'd plowed a field far more years than he'd taken coin to serve in the royal army. Weather was something he considered himself attuned to, something predictable most of the time. But this weather…it wasn't natural. Hoyte could swear there was something wrong with the wind. Or wrong with the world.

He leaned forward to warm his fingers over the dying coals of the fire, careful not to stress the longbow lying across his lap. He grimaced as feeling shot back into his hands along with a bone-throbbing ache. The fingerless gloves he wore did precious little good. He rubbed his hands together and brought his palms up to his face, blowing warmth into them.

"Fuck, it's cold," said Moss. He sat across the fire from Hoyte, hunched forward with a tattered blanket slung over his shoulders, warming his hands.

Hoyte envied Moss that blanket, just as he envied the man's thick beard. His own cheeks would only sprout a few patches of sparse whiskers, a family trait that never failed to rankle him. His boyish face had gotten him teased aplenty in his youth. It was even more of a curse now. A right good beard like Moss sported would go a long way toward warming his face. He reached up, running aching fingers over the pathetic growth on his chin.

"Damn fuckin' cold," Pinkston agreed, and spat into the fire. The glob of spittle hissed when it hit the coals. It was one of Pinkston's many talents. He could spit farther than any man in their company, and with acute precision every time. He was also the best bowman Hoyte knew. He had arms like an oak, and a calm steadiness Hoyte envied more than Moss' blanket.

"How long do you think we're gonna sit here?" Flem asked, worrying at a strip of jerky with perfect yellow teeth. He was the only man Hoyte knew with straight teeth. Even if the two front ones were big enough to remind him of a jackrabbit's grin. Flem finally tore off a bite, his jaw working slowly in a circular motion, popping as he chewed. Hoyte hated that sound. A man's jaw shouldn't pop like that. It wasn't right.

"We'll sit here however long it takes." Hoyte picked up a thatch of dry grass from a pile behind him and tossed it into the fire. The flames flared up for a moment with a puff of white smoke.

"Why'd you fuckin' do that?" Pinkston said, sitting up. "You know I fuckin' hate it."

Hoyte shrugged. He couldn't care less what Pinkston hated. He thought about tossing another handful of grass just to piss him off. Instead he turned to Moss and said, "Any more of those beans left?"

"Naw. All that's left's a few strips of meat."

"I'll take it, then. Give here."

"Tastes like dog," Flem warned, still chewing his mouthful like a cud, jaw popping with every bite.

Hoyte shot him a glare, leaning forward to snatch the leathery strip from Moss' hand. He tore off a bite and started chewing.

"I'm gonna take a piss," Pinkston said and stood up. He dusted off his pants then started walking away from the glow of the campfire. Hoyte listened to the sound of his footsteps trudging away.

The footsteps stopped abruptly.

"The fuck is that?"

Moss and Flem rose, clutching their bows. Hoyte frowned, wondering if it was worth getting up. He supposed it might be. With a groan, he pushed his stiff body off the ground, his joints popping like Flem's jaw. He worked his shoulders, trying to stretch some of the stiffness out of them. Holding his bow at his side, he walked over to where Pinkston stood staring out across the prairie with a slack mouth. He followed the man's gaze into the shadowy night. He didn't see a damn thing.

"What?"

Pinkston raised a gloved hand, pointing in the direction of the mountains. "*That.*"

Moss and Flem drew up next to them, Flem swallowing his meat noisily. Hoyte stared across the grassland, which glowed like a silver sea under the full moon. Ahead, the foothills of the Shadowspears rolled away toward a jagged wall of darkness. The mountains towered over them as if holding up the sky. Hoyte's eyes traced the slopes of the foothills before focusing on the prairie. At the forms moving toward them through the night.

"What the hell?"

A man and a woman walked through the high grass, holding hands as if out for a moonlight stroll. A stroll through a kill zone.

"The fuck," observed Moss.

He exchanged a flummoxed glance with Pinkston, who shrugged hugely, shaking his head. All around, soldiers surged to their feet, fumbled for their weapons. Hoyte calmly looped his bowstring around the notch at the end of the shaft. Then he withdrew a handful of clothyard arrows, thrusting them into the ground at his feet.

"Ready your bows!" the captain bellowed from

behind them.

Hoyte grabbed an arrow and raised his bow, angling it upward as his eyes fixed on the approaching man and woman. Neither wore armor, and they didn't appear to be armed.

What the hell?

"Hold!"

Hoyte froze, eyes fixed on the two people closing the gap of prairie toward their ranks. No, they weren't people, he chided himself. They were the Enemy.

"Emissaries?" Moss guessed.

Hoyte figured he might be right, though neither held a token of parley. It was possible they had come to negotiate. Apparently, the generals felt the same. Hoyte awaited the order to loose his shaft, but it didn't come.

The ranks bowed inward and opened up, admitting the man and woman into their midst. Archers swiveled to track their advance. Hoyte growled, realizing he now stood with his missile aimed at the company of bowmen across the gap. If the envoys proved treacherous, he was more likely to hit his own men than either of his marks. It was a bad situation, and he didn't like it.

"Hold!" the order came again.

Pinkston cursed under his breath, bow sagging at his side. Hoyte glared sidelong at him. "What?"

"It's him," Pinkston gasped, his eyes going wide. "Oh, gods, it's fucking him!"

"Who the fuck's *'him?'*" Moss demanded.

Hoyte felt his bowels loosen as he realized what Pinkston was trying to tell them. *"Lauchlin?"*

Pinkston stood there, head bobbing on his neck. Then he jerked into action, nocking an arrow as Hoyte had done. Flem stared ahead dumbly, his bow hanging slack at his waist.

"Draw!"

The shout confirmed Hoyte's worst fear. His eyes narrowed at the black-haired demon that had inserted himself into their midst. The man was still walking, deep inside their spreading ranks, holding the hand of a small woman whose eyes blazed with eager flames. Hoyte drew his bowstring back.

"Loose!"

Hoyte let the bowstring sing. He had another arrow nocked before the first had time to reach its target. He let the second missile fly as the first grouping of arrows shattered in a whiplash blast of air.

Screams and shouts drowned out bellowing orders as the ranks collapsed backward. Hoyte stooped to snatch up his remaining arrows, backing away as quickly as he could. From every side, men jostled and bumped against him in their eagerness to retreat.

A raging firestorm erupted behind them, followed by the awful sound of screams. Hoyte glanced behind to see an inferno gushing toward them from the center of the camp.

The men at his back scrambled forward in terror, shoving Hoyte against the men in front of him. Pinned on all sides, Hoyte dropped his bow and used his elbows to batter his way through the frantic mob. He glanced about desperately for Moss and Pinkston, but they were lost in the surging mass.

Another firestorm exploded only a short distance away. Hoyte felt the heat of it sear his face. Men and parts of men shot high into the air, raining down on those still fighting to escape. The roaring of flames drowned out the sound of screams, as more explosions erupted all around, guts and gore and severed limbs pelting down like battering hail.

Hoyte fought to keep his feet, terror driving him away from the exploding horror. He was shoved, punched, clawed, squeezed, and bludgeoned at every step. He fought his way forward, every inch of ground seeming a mile, as men on every side tried to push past or climb over the struggling mass ahead. Hoyte stumbled over corpses that lay trampled beneath the rage of feet. Soon he couldn't move. He couldn't breathe. The weight of soldiers around him crushed his arms against his ribs.

Hoyte would have howled in pain, but he couldn't suck enough air into his lungs to do it. He felt his ribs cracking. His legs gave out from under him. He should have fallen, but he was held upright by the sheer force of the surging masses.

A roiling furnace blasted him full in the face, ripping him out of the crowd and flinging him backward and up. He hit the ground hard, screaming in shock and pain. His arms scrambled feebly as he tried to lift himself up, but he couldn't get any traction with his legs.

He fought to raise his head from the ground and looked down at his body. At first, he couldn't understand what he was seeing. Then came understanding, along with horror. The last thing Hoyte saw as his vision dimmed was his charred backbone protruding from under his ribs, where his middle used to be.

Chapter Two
Aftermath

Pass of Lor-Gamorth, The Front

Darien glanced up at the star-scattered night that stretched on forever overhead. There were no clouds to darken the sky; it hadn't rained anytime recently. And yet, everywhere he stepped, the ground was slick with mud. He scraped the toe of his boot across the mucky soil and watched the furrow he'd created fill quickly with blood.

The smell was the worst. It rose from the mounds of smoldering corpses, borne across the battlefield by the smoke-fed air. Everywhere he looked, he saw the charred remains of fallen soldiers and horses. Some whole. Most not. The stench was nauseating. The smell of charred human was growing all too familiar. He'd smelled too much of it, too recently. It had a distinctive, sweet aroma. Roasted human smelled like roasted pork, except on a battlefield. There, mingled with the stench of blood and bowel, it was horrifically worse.

Especially when the burnt corpses were of his own making. And his own kinfolk.

The sounds of dying came from every direction and no direction, carried toward him on the air. Anguished moans and desperate weeping. All punctuated by raw, staccato shrieks, as knives worked tirelessly to open throats. His men ranged across the battlefield, sifting and prying through heaps of flesh in search of wounded. Those mortally injured were freed from their pain. Those who stood a chance of surviving were carried back to the encampment. Wounded soldiers of the Rhen were put to the knife, without exception.

Another ghastly shriek cut sharply through the smoke and stench. The sound made Darien's stomach tighten. He stood staring out across the carnage, contemplating the atrocity he had committed. He'd massacred thousands in just minutes, as he had done at Orien's Finger. Only, this time, he had slaughtered the same people he'd once sworn to defend. The thought dredged up waves of guilt he couldn't afford to feel. Guilt served no strategic purpose on a battlefield.

Azár squeezed his hand. Glancing sideways at her, he saw that his wife seemed to be weathering the carnage better than himself. She caught his stare and fixed him with a look of concern.

"This is difficult for you," she observed.

He ignored her and knelt beside a Rhenic soldier who lay moaning pitifully, clawing at his own spilled entrails as if trying to stuff them back inside. Darien stopped the man's heart then rose again. He strode forward, eyes scouring the field for other signs of life.

His gaze fell on one of his own men who lay groaning at the bottom of a heap of smoldering flesh. Darien tugged the first corpse off the top of the pile, rolling it wetly aside. Azár helped him shift the others. By the time they dug down to the wounded man, he was already dead. Frustrated, Darien cursed and whirled away.

He got only a couple of steps before he caught sight of Sayeed winding toward them through scattered piles of remains. The officer stopped in front of him, sweat mottling his brow despite the chill night air. He held his helmet tucked in the crook of his arm. His wet hair was plastered against his head, and there was a distinct line of blood around the edge of his face that resembled war paint.

He acknowledged Darien with a nod. "Lord—"

"Brother," Darien corrected.

Sayeed took a deep breath then started over. "Brother, the last of their infantry has been routed. Their officers fled on horseback at the onset of battle. We lost a little over two hundred warriors and estimate thirty-two thousand enemy casualties. We have taken over a thousand prisoners. What would you have done with them?"

Darien swept his gaze across the smoldering battlefield. There had already been too much death, and too little reason for it. At his feet lay the burnt remains of a fallen officer who wore the insignia of Chamsbrey. Two years before, he would have mourned the same man's death. Now, the only emotion he felt was anger. He despised the Rhen's generals for forcing him to resort to atrocity. Because of his past loyalties, they'd expected him to feel conflicted, to be weak. To soften the blows.

Which meant that anything short of ruthlessness would just prolong the slaughter.

Darien looked back up at Sayeed. "Spare ten prisoners and execute the remainder. Make certain those ten watch. Slay their wounded and scavenge what you can: weapons, arrows, supplies. Especially food. We need food. Slaughter any horses you find, living or dead. We need the meat."

Sayeed paled at his words. Darien could gauge the man's horror from the pallor of his complexion, which confused him. He hadn't expected such a reaction from an officer with Sayeed's discipline or experience. He shot a questioning glare at the man.

"Brother, what you ask is forbidden…"

"It doesn't matter," Darien snapped. "We can't afford to show mercy."

"I meant the horses," Sayeed corrected. "It is forbidden to eat the flesh of animals. Or to slay an animal—"

Darien barked an incredulous laugh. He'd just ordered the execution of hundreds of prisoners who had surrendered willingly. But his second-in-command was balking at the lives of a few horses. He glanced at Azár to find her nodding in agreement with Sayeed. He took a deep breath, struggling for patience. Then he fixed his gaze on both of them.

"We're not in the Black Lands anymore. We can afford to eat meat." Scoffing, he added, "Hell, we can't afford not to." He stalked away from the gaping officer, stepping over a Rhenic soldier who lay whimpering in agony. Without pausing, Darien willed the man dead.

He heard the sound of Azár's footsteps behind him, hurrying to catch up. He slowed his pace and waited for her. Together, they waded side by side through a swampy sea of blood, charred bones, and charcoaled meat.

On impulse, Darien took his wife's hand and knelt over a wounded soldier with a shattered leg. He wanted her to feel the healing process through him. The techniques he used were well beyond her ability, but he hoped she would find something in the experience that might be useful. He was surprised to see only a look of frustration on her face.

"What did you do?" Azár demanded. "I could not tell. It was too fast, and you did too much all at once."

He shrugged. "Healing's probably the hardest skill to master. That's why not every mage was trained to it."

Azár dismissed his words with a wave of her hand. "I will learn. Next time go slower."

Reaching up, Darien rubbed his eyes in weariness. "I can't heal slower. It has to happen fast, or I'll just do more damage than I'm mending. Healing's not something that can be taught overnight. It takes years."

He knelt beside a woman with a hole in her chest and lungs drowning in fluid. Taking Azár's hand, he let her feel through him as he staunched the blood flow. He worked slowly to reweave arteries and capillary beds, building the flesh around them as they grew. He drained the fluid from her lungs and engorged them with air. When it was done, he rose and left behind a soldier who lay gasping and moaning in pain. But alive.

Darien soothed the woman to sleep. Then he glared at Azár. "That's as slow as I can work. It wasn't easy on her. I won't do it again."

Azár stared at him with a hurtful look. Ripping her hand out of his grasp, she rose and stalked away. She didn't get far before she whirled back around and snarled at him angrily, "You treat me like a child!"

Darien reminded her, "That's because you are a child. At least in this." He stood up but staggered, reeling from a surge of vertigo. He closed his eyes and took a moment to steady himself. The vast amount of power he'd handled was starting to take its toll. He was exhausted, and in no shape to be arguing with his wife in the midst of a battlefield.

Rubbing his eyes, Darien said wearily, "Given enough time, I could teach you to heal. It's the time part we don't have." Seeking to mollify her, he added, "Even if I had a thousand years, I could never weave your light."

Arms crossed, Azár looked at him with an unforgiving stare. Without another word, she turned and stalked ahead of him toward the next pile of corpses. Darien stood still for a moment, watching her go. Then he forced himself to move wearily after her.

He woke up groggy. Staring up into darkness, Darien felt a moment of disorientation. He didn't know where he was. He came to the slow conclusion that he must be back in his tent. Only, he didn't remember getting there. Confused, he pushed himself upright, the motion making him groan. His head throbbed with the familiar pain that came with overexertion.

A light appeared, brightening the canvas walls of the tent. At first, he thought it was lamplight. It took him a moment to realize it was magelight.

Azár's silhouette knelt beside him and pressed a cup of tea into his hand. It was hot and minty, and felt good on his throat. Darien relaxed and drank the warm liquid slowly, hoping it would help the ache in his head that throbbed to the rhythm of his pulse.

"What happened?" he asked.

Azár looked at him flatly. "You were stupid. You killed too many, then healed too many. It was too much."

He took another sip of tea. "I didn't heal enough."

"You cannot save the world," she growled.

Darien shrugged. "Maybe not. But I need to try." He set the cup down by his side and rose from his blankets. It was dim in the tent, even with her magelight. He stared around, looking for his clothes.

"Arrogance is the hallmark of fools," his wife muttered at his back.

"Then I suppose I'm an arrogant fool." Darien rummaged through the shadows until he found a shirt. Pulling it on, he asked, "What time is it?"

"It's night. You slept through an entire day. And part of the next night. Here. Eat something, fool."

Darien smiled as he accepted a bowl from her hand. The porridge inside was a tasteless mixture of grain and something he didn't recognize. Regardless, he swallowed it thankfully. Most of the men and women in his army had nothing to eat. Their rations had been used up before the battle for the Pass, and their supply lines were becoming stretched and strained.

Azár handed him his trousers. "Get dressed. Sayeed has a report you need to hear."

Darien stabbed a glare at her even as he obeyed. "You're my wife, not my mother," he grumbled. "Why didn't you tell me about Sayeed?"

"Because you needed to eat." Her voice was matter-of-fact.

Irritated, Darien struggled into his armor. Pulling on his boots, he grabbed his sword and threw back the tent flaps. A score of officers rose to their feet at the sight of him. In deference to his authority, they had made their small camp outside his tent. Sayeed came forward through the press of men, halting in front of him.

"Lord, it is good to see you hale," he said by way of greeting.

Darien only nodded in response. "You have something to tell me?"

"Your commands were carried out. We left the bodies where they lay." Sayeed shifted uneasily. "Lord, a scout returned from the ruins of the keep. You must hear what he has to say."

Turning, Sayeed gestured behind him. A soldier scrambled forward, dropping to kneel at Darien's feet.

Darien waved his hand dismissively. "Rise. Say what you came to say."

The scout climbed to his feet. "All glory to you, Lord. I was separated from my squad during the battle. I wandered the slopes of the mountains, looking for a path down. I found myself at the ruins of the old fortress. There, I saw three corpses."

Darien frowned. "Go on."

"Lord, one of the dead was Warden Connell."

Darien stiffened, the news catching him off-guard. Byron Connell had been missing since the battle for the keep. But Darien had just assumed he had returned to his own forces, which were camped behind them in the Pass. Cold dread crept over him as the implications of the scout's words sank in.

"Are you certain?"

"I am certain, Lord."

Darien's mind went silent. He stood grappling with his frozen thoughts, uncertain what to do about them.

The soldier continued, "There was another man lying dead, and there was also a woman. The woman…Lord, I have seen her before. She was the woman imprisoned with you in Tokashi Palace."

Darien's shock crystallized. His thoughts froze, then fractured like glass.

"Meiran…?"

He felt a hand rest softly on his shoulder. The sensation jolted him, making him flinch. Turning, Darien saw that Azár had come up behind him. Ignoring her, he turned back to the soldier.

"Take me there."

It took hours on horseback to gain the trail that led to the old keep. Sayeed rode at the front of their small party. He was mounted on the back of a skittish charger whose previous rider had attempted to desert during the battle. Azár rode behind, surrounded by a capable retinue of Zakai, the only men who had any experience on horseback.

When they reached the stairs that led to the ruins, Darien dismounted and handed his reins to a soldier. Accompanied by Azár and Sayeed, he mounted the same granite steps he'd climbed hundreds of times during the two long years he'd been stationed in the Pass. His feet still remembered the path, even though the stairs were cracked and crumbling away. The wind was up, whipping his hair and stinging his cheeks. It let up as they rounded the last switchback.

There, at the top of the steps, Darien halted. He stood staring at the naked foundation of the fortress that had, for over five hundred years, guarded the Pass of Lor-Gamorth. Now only a crumble of fallen walls and charred beams remained. Darien took a step toward a scattered pile of rubble that lay ahead—all that was left of the keep's high turret. The sight of the ruin brought with it a dull ache of sentiment. Darien's thoughts turned to Devlin Craig and Sutton Royce, his brothers in arms during the two years he had served at the Front. Craig and Royce had been the best friends he'd ever known, although they had both betrayed that friendship. So many friends fallen. Most because they had the misfortune of sharing his fate.

Darien turned away from the rubble and strode over to where Sayeed waited alongside the beardless scout who served as their guide.

"Where are they?" he asked.

The soldier effected a curt bow. "Lord, I found them over there." He nodded toward a half-collapsed wall jutting up from the ground.

Darien started in the direction the man indicated. He followed a narrow trail that turned into a precipitous path leading down behind the ruin. When Darien reached the crumbled rear wall, he froze, one hand lingering on the hilt of his sword. He couldn't press himself to go any further.

Two forlorn shapes lay sprawled before him in the dirt. One was Meiran. Darien stopped breathing, overcome by emotion. But it wasn't grief he felt. Neither was it anger. Whatever it was, it was incapacitating. He drew a breath, sucking it hard into his chest. It took long seconds before he could manage another.

On legs as rigid as logs, he stumbled over to Meiran's body and sank down at her side. She had been dead awhile. Her corpse stank of rot. Darien found himself looking down at a gray face that was caked with dried blood. Sunken, milky eyes returned his stare with a look of accusation. He lifted a hand and traced Meiran's bloated face.

"Darien."

He could feel Azár lingering over him, could hear the concern in her voice. He ignored her. Staring down at Meiran, Darien didn't know what to feel. So he decided not to. He climbed to his feet and walked away, leaving Meiran in the dirt.

He went to the corpse that lay just a short distance away. The broken, gaping face looked familiar to him. It took him a moment to remember the man's name: *Traver Larsen.* He'd been Kyel Archer's friend. Darien tucked that piece of information away, saving it for later. He wandered up the slope, his eyes scanning the ground.

"The Warden is over here, Lord."

Darien turned in the direction of the scout's voice. The man stood beside the guts of a shattered wall that had disgorged its blocks over the black soil of the mountain. Darien walked to where the scout indicated, taking in the sight of Byron Connel lying face down on the path. Stooping, he rolled the man over. The stench that action provoked was nauseating. Darien winced away, fighting to keep the contents of his stomach down. It took a moment for the air to thin out enough to properly examine the corpse.

The cause of death wasn't hard to figure out. An ebony hilt protruded from Connel's eye socket. Darien gripped the handle and withdrew the blade. He held it in his hand and turned it slowly. It was the same knife that had once belonged to Garret Proctor, the Force Commander of Greystone Keep. He wiped the blade clean in the dirt, then gazed down at the corpse, speculating. Byron Connell had been one of the greatest military commanders known to history. And yet, he'd been brought down by a fragile, thin-bladed knife. It defied credulity.

But who had wielded it?

Another thought occurred to him, one far more alarming: *Thar'gon.*

Darien bolted to his feet and searched the ground around Connel. The Warden's talisman would have fallen somewhere close by. But, disturbingly, he didn't see it. Darien began pacing in a slow circle. His gaze roved over every rock, every grain of soil, every shadowed depression in the dirt.

The morning star wasn't there.

"Husband. What are you looking for?"

He'd forgotten Azár was following him. "Connel's weapon," he mumbled without pausing in his search.

A look of troubled understanding grew on Azár's face. She took a cursory glance around. "Perhaps it was looted."

Darien shook his head, growing agitated. He raked a hand through his hair. His eyes continued scouring every inch of soil. "It's designed to be wielded only by the Warden of Battlemages. I'm the only Battlemage left."

"Well, someone took it." Azár looked at him blandly. "Perhaps the weapon allowed another to carry it, someone who could pass it on to you."

Darien almost dismissed her comment as absurd...but then he realized she might be right. He stopped his pacing and halted, staring dully at the ground.

"Kyel..." he whispered, shaking his head slowly in confusion. "I don't understand. Why him?"

Sayeed strode forward to stand beside him. "Pardon, Brother," he said, looking apprehensive. "Perhaps it is because this Sentinel Kyel is alive. And you are not."

Darien hadn't thought of that. It was easy to forget that the flesh he clung to was only temporary, that he was merely a ghost in human clothing.

But even that didn't make sense. Byron Connel had been just as dead as himself. The more he thought about it, the more Azár's theory made sense. Thar'gon could have allowed the first mage who touched it to pick it up, on the chance it would be passed to its rightful master. Frustrated, Darien glared down at Connel's corpse.

"We should bury them. Help me get some rocks."

They spent the remainder of the night piling rocks to make a single burial cairn. When the last stone was laid in place, Darien stood back and bowed his head in troubled silence, battling the same conflicted emotions he'd fought earlier. He didn't know what he felt, or what he should be feeling. For so many years, Meiran had been the one thing in the world that mattered to him most. Her betrayal was like a raw wound that had never fully healed. He couldn't help the grief he felt over her death. And he also couldn't help the satisfaction.

Reaching up, he unstrapped the baldric that crossed his chest and removed his sword's harness. He drew the blade from its sheath then flung both harness and scabbard to the ground. Reversing his grip on the hilt, he used all the strength of his anger to drive the blade deeply into the ground.

He left the weapon there and walked away.

Chapter Three
The Warden's Promise

Pass of Lor-Gamorth, The Front

They rode in uneasy silence down the mountainside.

The sky rumbled and raged overhead, echoing Darien's mood. He glanced up as a streak of lightning stabbed a nearby slope, the air erupting in crackling thunder. The horse beneath him jumped sideways and tried to bolt. He pulled the reins close, fighting to calm the animal. With a defiant snort, the stallion yielded control back to him.

He was in a black mood. Too many thoughts raged in his head, warring for dominance. Each fleeting thought bubbled to the surface and then sank, tumbling back down. First Meiran's blood-crusted face gaped up at him, accompanied by an upwelling of grief and loathing. Then Kyel flashed before his mind, wielding Thar'gon in his hand—a thought so dreadful it made Darien flinch. He'd made a tremendous mistake, leaving Kyel alive. He regretted that decision now. He suspected he'd regret it even more later.

Below, the fog in the river bottom parted, and their encampment came into view. There were no lights of cookfires; there was no coal to burn. The camp was almost completely broken down. His own tent was one of the few that remained intact.

Looking at Sayeed, he asked, "How long until we march?"

"The forward camp is not yet prepared," Sayeed informed him.

"Good. That'll give me time to rest."

When they attained the camp, Darien tied his horse to the picket and returned to his tent. He threw his boots into a corner, his mail shirt following them to the ground. Feeling exhausted, he cast himself down on his pallet. He sat there until he heard Azár enter after him. She paused in the tent's entrance, one hand holding back the flap. She took a step inside, letting the canvas sway closed.

"My husband does not look well," she observed, taking another step toward him.

Darien kept his stare angled at the floor. "I'm fine."

She sat beside him and looked into his eyes. "Do you wish to speak of it?"

"No."

There was a long pause that conveyed the weight of her hesitation. After a moment, she said, "I know Meiran mattered very much to you. I know it must be hard for you to—"

"Stop." Darien jerked away from her. "You have no idea how I feel."

Azár's face hardened. She stood up, scowling. "You're right. I do not. That is because you are like a wall to me. How am I supposed to walk beside my husband, if he will not speak his heart?"

Darien glared at her through several layers of irritation. "That's your problem to figure out. When it comes to Meiran, you *will* respect my privacy. What I feel—or felt—for her is none of your damn concern. Understand?" She had no business in his feelings. His feelings were his own.

A troubled silence settled between them.

"I understand," she said at last, though he knew she didn't.

But it didn't matter. All that mattered was that she was done trying to drag his emotions out to dissect on the floor.

"I'm going to get some sleep." He lay back, tugging the blankets up, and turned away from her.

He awoke to a slobbering tongue wetting the side of his face. The sensation was accompanied by a putrid stench that was fondly familiar. Groaning, Darien reached up and pushed the weight of the demon-hound off him. The grisly thing moved back, its tail drumming against the floor.

"Theanoch."

The thanacryst obeyed with a whine, its jaw snapping shut. It stared at him dejectedly.

He rubbed his eyes. Groping at the pallet next to his, Darien found the covers empty. Azár had either awakened before him or had never slept at all. He summoned a blue glow of magelight, enough to look around. The tent was empty. Even his possessions had been packed up and carried out. Only his clothing and armor remained, piled where he'd left them in the corner.

Darien donned his boots and his mail shirt, strapping on the scimitar Sayeed had given him for a wedding gift. *Valdivora.* It had once been carried by Khoresh Kateem, the notorious conqueror who had united the tribes of Caladorn into the largest empire in history. The sword had such an important role in deciding events that had shaken the world, that Darien had been hesitant to wear it. But he didn't have a choice now. It was the only sword he had left.

He emerged from the tent and found his men forming up for the march. Frustrated, Darien wondered why no one had thought to wake him. He set out toward the horse pickets, where he found Azár untethering her mare. She saw him approaching and mounted up, kicking her horse forward and angling away from him. Darien watched her go.

He crossed the camp toward his own stallion, the demon-hound keeping pace with his strides. The soldiers paid the thanacryst no mind as he wove through their midst. It had long ago stopped being an anomaly.

Darien untied his horse and mounted up. He kicked the stallion to a canter, riding toward the front of the column. Sayeed and Azár were already there. His wife glanced his way as he drew up at her side. The anger on her face was still there, looking permanently etched into her skin. She turned away and made a conspicuous effort to avoid eye contact.

As the column moved forward, Darien found himself wondering how long his wife was going to shun him. He didn't have an answer. He didn't understand her any better than he understood himself.

As they rode out of the Pass, the clouds slowly loosened their grip on the sky. Streaks of sunlight broke through the layers, blinding rays that slanted down and dappled the slopes of the foothills. Eventually, the clouds yielded altogether, revealing a sky more furiously blue than Darien remembered. He squinted, his vision overwhelmed by the brilliant glare of sunlight. He brought a hand up to shield his face, his eyes watering. He heard gasps and cries from the soldiers behind him, many of whom had never seen the miracle of daylight.

Their joy came to a nauseating end.

Before them, stretched out across the plain, was a thick black scar where the battle had been waged. The carnage had been left untouched for two days, the dead left where they'd fallen. The air was filled with the consistent cries of birds: black ravens whose sheer numbers carpeted the battlefield and thickened the skies. Darien's stomach twisted at the sight of the birds, at the vast number of dead sprawled across the ground or collected in decomposing hummocks.

When they waded into the sea of rot, the stench became unbearable. Darien held his cloak over his face, though the thick fabric did little good. Hordes of flies bloomed up from the ground, the sound a loud, consistent drone. The stench and the noise set Darien's horse on edge. The stallion laid back its ears and tugged its head, fighting for control of the bit. Darien steadied it with a firm grip on the reins.

The sounds of their passage startled great mobs of birds, which took wing in squalling protest. They swirled in the sky, a bulbous and writhing mass, before settling back down. Looking out across the roiling sea of decay, Darien felt enraged. There was no reason for this waste. No reason why he'd had to resort to such savagery. All of this blood wasn't on his hands. It was on theirs. The commanders of the Rhen could have withdrawn their forces and let them pass. Instead, they'd ordered their soldiers to stand their ground against impossible odds. It was unsettling. And infuriating.

Clucking at his horse, Darien urged the stallion faster.

They reached the forward camp just as the sun's red disc sank beneath the grassland. The sky was a hostile red streaked with gold, an expansive display of beauty that captured Darien's gaze. It had been years since he'd last seen a sunset. He'd forgotten how powerful they were.

As they rode into the encampment, he saw that the command tent had already been raised. It was another testament to the ingenuity of the Tanisars when they were on campaign: they had a way of leapfrogging campsites to hasten the march. As the rear camp was broken down, the forward camp was already being pitched. There were actually two command tents. The one left behind in the Pass would be packed up and moved ahead of them and readied for the next day.

Sayeed set their course toward the pavilion. Darien balked, drawing back his horse's reins. He was too drained to want to deal with the clamor and challenge of the war chiefs. His emotions were too rough, too brittle. He needed time to find some clarity.

"No." He shook his head. "Not tonight. I just want to find my own tent."

Sayeed turned back to him with a confused expression. "This is your tent."

Darien opened his mouth to object, then realized he had no objection to make. With Byron Connel dead, it made sense that he would assume the Warden's command. And his tent. Darien wondered what the elders of the tribes would think about that; he was only blood of their blood through marriage. He didn't want to fight another challenge to his legitimacy.

He dismounted alongside the pavilion and handed his horse's reins to a waiting soldier. Sayeed at his side, Darien walked toward the tent on stiff legs. He stopped at the entrance, not wanting to go in. It didn't seem right. None of it felt right, like it didn't fit.

Sayeed patted his shoulder. "Go in, Brother. I will have your possessions brought to you."

Darien asked, "What about Connel's things?"

The officer shrugged. "Do with them what you will. They are yours now."

Darien followed the man's suggestion and entered the tent. The smell of incense filled his nostrils. It took a moment for his eyes to adjust to the ambient light of the interior. Hanging fabric cordoned off several rooms, and the floor was layered with overlapping rugs. Through a gap between curtains, he saw that a large table had been set up in one of the partitions. A few men were already seated on the floor in the gathering area. They looked up and frowned at the sight of him.

Darien leaned his sword against the canvas wall. Then he made his way through the cloth partition that cordoned off Byron Connel's personal quarters. Inside was a large four-poster bed with a matching wardrobe, along with cushioned chairs and an iron rack made to hold armor. Bright fabric hung from the walls and the ceiling, the floor layered with sumptuous rugs. For a moment, Darien stood staring incredulously. It all looked so surreal in the midst of a military encampment. It defied reason.

His attention was drawn to the far end of the room, where a book rested on a pedestal. The sight was so peculiar that he couldn't keep himself from wandering over to it. The tome was open, a blue silk ribbon marking the page. Darien gave the text a cursory glance, enough to see that the words were some type of poetry, perhaps an epic ballad. He read a few stanzas before deciding it was not a work he was familiar with.

He heard Azár enter and pause to stand behind him. Darien supposed he couldn't keep avoiding her. But he also didn't know what to say. So he stood there waiting, staring at everything in the tent but her. Preparing himself to weather another barrage of questions he didn't want to answer.

But instead of speaking, Azár simply drew near and wrapped her arms around him. Surprised, Darien hugged her back, wondering at her change of heart. Azár's touch felt good, comforting. Gradually, he felt the rage of emotions in his head dwindle to a manageable fury. She held him for a long time then pulled back to look into his face, her gaze wandering over his features.

Darien took her by the hand and guided her

toward the bed. This time, she let him.

He woke from sleep to a loud blur of conversation. Guessing the cause, Darien rose and dressed. Azár still slumbered in their oversized bed, one hand lingering on a pillow, fingers outstretched. The covers pulled over her body rose and fell in a gentle, consistent tide. Darien lingered for a moment, composing his thoughts, then slipped through the partition into the main gathering area of the tent.

The pavilion was crowded with people. They sat scattered in small groups across the floor. Food was arranged on long drapes of cloth that had been rolled out, covered with bowls and communal platters. There was a constant buzz of discussion, broken only by abrupt spikes of laughter. Darien looked around at the spread of food, wondering what the soldiers in the camp were eating.

The conversation died as people took notice of him. Sayeed sat close by, surrounded by a small group of Zakai. Darien recognized many of the other faces as the warlords and elders of the various clans. They were all staring at him expectantly, as if waiting for him to speak. By the wary looks he was receiving, he gathered his newfound authority was not universally accepted.

Darien decided it was time to formalize the position he'd inherited from Connel. If the war chiefs wanted to challenge him, it would be better if they did so now instead of later. He couldn't afford his orders to be questioned, and the last thing he needed was a power struggle.

Looking at the men and women seated before him, Darien said, "I'll accept your pledges of loyalty now."

Many of the faces darkened with anger. A few of the younger men threw their bowls to the floor and stood up. He knew several of them, and he also knew their temperaments. They were warriors and did not yield easily. They respected authority only when it was wielded over them like a hammer.

The leader of the Jenn Kadeesh rose and stood towering over him, looking Darien up and down as if assessing a bad piece of meat. With a heavy frown, he grumbled, "You might be a Battlemage, Darien Nach'tier. But you are not Warden. Only Zavier Renquist can name you so."

Sounds of collective agreement echoed from all around the tent. Even the elders sat nodding. Darien fumed. Apparently, nothing came without a struggle, even actions that seemed obvious and logical. He was getting tired of people pushing him further than he wanted to go. He hoped the tribal leaders would relent before things went that far.

"Zavier Renquist isn't here," he informed them. "I'm taking Byron Connel's place as Warden of the Combined Legions of Malikar. If you wish to argue, go ahead—but I'll win that argument. I have a goal. And I'll not be deterred from it."

The men stared at him with defiant faces.

Sayeed rose from the floor and whispered in his ear, "They will not give you their loyalty. You must take it."

Darien understood. He would have to prove he had the fortitude and resolve to lead Malikar's armies. In order to lead, he would first have to conquer.

He closed his eyes and reached out from within, taking hold of the magic field. Shadows bloomed within the tent as the light of the lanterns faded to darkness. He concentrated harder, feeding the air with just a trickle of power. After a moment, quiet, uncomfortable noises reached his ears. He drew harder on the magic field, applying more heat and pressure to the air, feeling it thicken around him, until the tent was filled with cries and moans.

Darien held the tormented air in the tent for a minute longer. At last, he let the light return and willed the air to cool and thin. He opened his eyes to find men and women sprawled across the floor, groaning in pain. Shaken elders, pale and trembling, turned to confer with their war chiefs.

Darien didn't wait for them to decide their positions. Stepping forward, he growled to every man and woman gathered in the tent, "Now kneel and pledge me fealty!"

There was a moment's hesitation. Then every elder in the room went to their knees, bowing forward. They were followed by the officers and then, eventually, the war chiefs.

Darien stood staring down at their backs in fury. He made them wait in the position of prostration a long time, each man and woman frozen as if carved from stone. After minutes, he walked to the back of the pavilion and claimed the bench-like chair

Connel had ruled from.

One by one, the war chiefs came forward to offer their pledge. When the last man had kissed his hand, Sayeed rose and retrieved Darien's sword. In one graceful motion, the officer bared *Valdivora* from its sheath and dropped to his knees. He bowed his head deeply and, cradling the blade in both hands, offered it to Darien.

Loudly, Sayeed proclaimed, "His Excellency, Darien Lauchlin Nach'tier, Warden of Battlemages, Last Sentinel of Aerysius, and Xerys' Shadow on Earth!"

Darien rose and accepted the sword, sweeping it around and down, parting the air with a hiss. He looked down at Sayeed.

"Sayeed son of Alborz, I name you First Among Many."

Sayeed remained frozen on his knees, absorbing his elevation in silence. But another man surged up behind him, face set in lines of outrage. Darien recognized him as Byron Connel's second-in-command.

"Warden!" the warrior cried. "By tradition, the office of the First is reserved for the general of Bryn Calazar's legions!"

"No longer." Darien glared the man back to his knees.

A cold and heavy stillness settled over the pavilion, encasing them all in silence. Long seconds wore away, each seeming to bear the weight of eternity. At last, Darien surrendered his sword into Sayeed's keeping and sank back down on the bench. He leaned back, spreading his arms as if assuming a throne. The men and women remained on their knees, eyes still fixed upon the ground.

"You may rise," Darrien allowed.

As the warlords settled back to their respective places, Darien turned his gaze to the man who had challenged him. "Make your report then leave my presence."

The general rose and, raising a hand to his chest, bowed stiffly. "Warden, the way ahead lies open and undefended before us."

Darien waved a dismissal, hastening the man out of the tent. He turned to the commanders who remained. "Advise."

There was a low murmur as the war chiefs conferred quietly. Eventually, the warlord of the Beyads rose to his feet. "Warden, we must apply our minds to the problem of logistics. As we move deeper into this land, it will become more difficult to maintain our supply lines."

"Agreed." Darien nodded. "What do you suggest?"

"We need to take care how quickly we move our civilians south of the Pass. It would not be wise to stretch our baggage train thin until we gain control of this region's food production."

Darien nodded. The words were an echo of his own thoughts. "That would be wise. What else?"

The men before him broke out in a chorus of suggestions and requests. Darien raised his hand, silencing the gathering.

"Stop. We need to provide food for our people. Until that's taken care of, no other problem exists. These are my orders: further restrict rationing. Allocate less resources to the civilians—we need our warriors strong enough to fight. We'll advance southward through the plains and scavenge food as we go."

An old woman who wore the mantle of a war chief stood and spread her arms expansively. "Forgive me, Warden, but this region appears unpopulated. Will there be food enough to sustain us all?"

Darien leaned forward in his seat, addressing not just the woman, but every chief and elder gathered in the pavilion. "We won't find enough food in the grasslands. Which is why we'll have to advance quickly. We'll go town by town, filling our stomachs as we go. Once we reach the population centers, we'll have more food than we can eat."

He paused for a moment, letting his resolve solidify. "We need more than just food. We need our own land. Our own borders. Our own sovereignty. We need everything they have, and there's only one way we'll get it. We'll take this land from them and make it our own. We'll drive them from the North."

Chapter Four
Creek Hollow

The Vale of Amberlie, The Rhen

Kyel Archer didn't like the looks of Creek Hollow. The windows of the town reflected the sunset's orange glare, a harsh intrusion into the tranquility of the forest. Craggy rooftops poked out from behind a palisade that spiked like jagged teeth out of the ridge ahead. The strong odor of wood smoke drifted toward them on the air, overwhelming the clean fragrance of the pines.

He rode alongside Cadmus on a trail that meandered through the dappled shadows of a forest. Kyel concentrated on the stillness of the grove: the faint stirring of leaves, the steady creak of his saddle, the dull plodding of his horse's hooves. The insistent hammering of a woodpecker echoed through the trees, along with the faint scampering of squirrels rummaging in the branches overhead.

"I really hope there's an inn," he commented. His voice sounded louder than he'd intended, interrupting the stillness of the grove.

"If you'd wanted an inn, then we should have taken the Northern Road," Cadmus grumbled, not for the first time.

Kyel ignored him and closed his eyes, savoring the quiet. The cleric had been complaining about his choice of route ever since they'd bypassed Wolden and headed west toward the Vale of Amberlie. Kyel had avoided the usual trade routes, desiring their passage to go as unnoticed as possible. He wanted to arrive in Glen Farquist alive, not delivered on a bier.

He reached down to grip the haft of the morning star affixed to his saddle. Instantly, he felt a soothing wash of magic flood into him from the talisman. It was as though the weapon wanted to be held and was discontent at merely riding at his side. Whenever he touched it, the artifact brought him a feeling of contentment he hadn't felt in years. It was the only thing that relieved the tension of his nerves. They had been stretched to razor-thinness ever since he'd absorbed Meiran's gift from her dying body.

Kyel shuddered, thinking of the awful amount of power contained within him. It was quiescent at the moment, though sometimes it made his blood rage as if boiling. He wondered how much longer he could stand it; he had a full eleven tiers of power ravaging his mind. Which, Kyel figured, was tantamount to a death sentence. He just didn't know how long it would take.

When they reached Creek Hollow's unguarded gate, his horse balked and tossed its head, stubbornly refusing to enter. Kyel had to dismount and lead the gelding through the gate, which seemed more than peculiar. Within the perimeter of the palisade, the town looked even more unnerving than it had from the forest below the ridge. He remounted and directed his horse down an empty boulevard lined with decrepit storefronts made of logs that seemed to sag with weariness. Many of the buildings were boarded up; some looked ready to just give up and die. There were very few people about—all men—who stopped and stared as they rode past.

A breeze kicked up, chasing leaves around the street. A faded sign creaked above a door, swaying back and forth on rusted chains. The daylight had faded to dusk by the time they drew their horses up in the center of town. Kyel looped his gelding's reins around the pommel of his saddle then climbed down, stretching his legs. He stood dusting his shirt off, staring at the one building in town that seemed intact: a river-rock inn with windows that glowed an eerie, death-pale light.

Part of him wanted to climb back on his horse and ride out of town. The last time he'd stepped foot in an inn had been with Traver. The thought brought a sharp pang of sadness along with it. Traver was dead now. And, like everything else, his death had been Kyel's fault.

He looked up at the wan light glowing through the inn's mottled glass. Leading his horse by the bridle, he followed Cadmus across the yard toward the livery stable. They handed the horses over to the hostler then made their way back toward the inn.

Kyel paused in the doorway, letting his eyes adjust to the dim interior. The common room was mostly empty, with only a few customers huddled around an enormous rock hearth. Kyel found that curious—it wasn't all that cold out. He took a step forward. A board creaked beneath his weight. Conversation died. Every stare in the room turned to fix on him.

Cadmus looked at him and shrugged. To Kyel, the reactions of the locals seemed off. They couldn't know he was a mage; the black cloak that identified him was shoved deep in the dusty saddlebag thrown over his shoulder. Kyel took another step then froze, his eyes snapping wide open.

He'd forgotten he was wearing Thar'gon strapped to his hip.

Self-conscious, Kyel reached down protectively and grasped the weapon's haft. He met the gaze of one of the men standing by the hearth, a stare that seemed absent any presence of thought. The fellow paused in the action of raising his tankard to his lips. His expression never changed.

A man behind Kyel made a gurgling sound, like a throat drowning in old phlegm. He turned to find the inn's proprietor staring at them from behind a plank bar. Kyel motioned Cadmus forward to arrange their room and meals, while he claimed a seat at a table tucked away in a corner.

Cadmus returned shortly after haggling with the innkeeper, carrying two tankards of ale. He threw his portly body down on the bench opposite Kyel, sliding a tankard across the table with a grin just as dilapidated as the town. He glanced over his shoulder at the men by the hearth.

Kyel whispered, "Why do you suppose they're staring at us?"

The cleric shrugged, taking a large swallow of ale. "Who could say? I doubt they get many wayfarers through here."

Kyel shifted uncomfortably in his seat, taking a sip from his tankard. As he did, the sight of his bare arm made him choke. His shirtsleeves had pulled back, exposing the markings of the chains on his wrists.

He looked over to the men by the fire and saw them staring at him. Kyel gave a long, troubled sigh, looking down at the rough-hewn wood of the table. He'd left his cloak off in an effort to avoid this kind of attention. He'd attracted it nonetheless.

The men by the hearth exchanged glances then turned away. Kyel settled back into his seat, frowning into his tankard as he awaited more problems. But only the sound of Cadmus slurping his ale disturbed the quiet.

Their supper was brought by a pretty serving girl with warm brown hair and a shy smile. Kyel nodded his thanks at her, noting that she was the only woman he'd seen so far in town. As she slipped away, he turned his attention to the roasted squab she'd set down in front of them.

Cadmus wasted no time tearing into his bird, pulling the flesh off the bones. He talked while he chewed. "You need to stop overthinking things. I understand—you've found yourself in an unenviable situation. But, the way I figure it, you have two choices. First, you can worry yourself into inaction trying to make sense of the senseless. Or you can accept your fate and make the most of the time you have left."

Kyel frowned. "That's not what worries me."

Cadmus harrumphed. He shoved a small wing into his mouth and stripped the meat off. "I know. You're terrified you're going to go mad, like your former master." He took a heavy sip from his tankard. "You won't. To be blunt, you're not going to have time to deteriorate that far."

"You can't know that," Kyel said. "I'm eleventh tier. Darien was only eighth tier and look how fast he declined."

"It's hard to say how much of that was power and

how much was pressure. Or personality." Cadmus shrugged. "I'll let you know if I think there's a problem. We'll worry about it when we have to."

"Can I get you more ale?"

Kyel looked up into the doll-like face of the serving girl. She stood gaping down at the chains on his wrists with moonstruck eyes. He did a double-take, eventually coming to the conclusion that she was, in fact, real. Dumbly, he offered his spent tankard to her. She accepted it with the slightest grin then set off, meandering back toward the kitchen.

"That's opportunity there."

Kyel fixed Cadmus with an irritated look. "She saw the chains. I'm surprised she wasn't terrified."

"What did I just say about making sense of the senseless?"

Kyel scoffed, pushing his platter away even though it still contained a half-eaten squab. When Cadmus raised his eyebrows and gestured at it, Kyel waved him on.

Cadmus slid the dish toward himself and picked the carcass up whole, tearing into it. Kyel's eyes roamed to the group of men by the hearth. He wondered if they were locals or just travelers passing through. Whichever, they were still shooting him glances when they thought he wasn't looking.

"Here you go."

The serving girl was back with her sweet face and starry eyes, scooting his filled tankard across the table toward him. Kyel managed to yank his gaze from her cleavage only by a heroic feat of will.

"Are you really a mage?"

Kyel gulped. "I am." He had to force himself to look at her face. From the corner of his eye, he saw Cadmus' mouth screw into a grimace of barely contained laughter. Frustrated, Kyel stabbed him a glare.

"Are you a good mage or a bad mage?"

Such an odd question, especially in light of the animosity he received anywhere else in the Rhen. This tucked-away little hamlet seemed to have missed the more condemning rumors that circulated the North. Though not all, apparently.

"I'm a good mage," he responded carefully.

The girl brightened. "That's what I thought. You look nice."

Kyel felt his ego swell with the compliment. He took a drink of ale, reminded of Cadmus' mention of opportunity. She did seem rather sweet. Her shoulder-length brown hair and pale eyes were especially to his liking. But he wasn't the type to take advantage of a mage-smitten girl he'd never see again. It just wouldn't be right.

The smile fell away from her lips, replaced by a fretful expression. "You're sworn to help people, aren't you?"

To Kyel, the question sounded like trouble. He answered guardedly, "Something like that."

"Can you help me?"

Suddenly wary, Kyel opened his mouth to discourage her, but was drowned out by a shout from the inn's proprietor. Red-faced, the girl knelt beside the table and, running nervous fingers through her hair, whispered, "Meet me out back in an hour? In the barn?"

It had sounded like a question, but she was gone before Kyel could refuse. He turned back to Cadmus, who was chuckling and shaking his head. With a frown, Kyel knocked back a large swig of ale.

"What do you think that was all about?" he asked in irritation.

Cadmus shrugged, a leering grin on his face. "If you want to know, you'd better go find out."

"'Spose she's in trouble?"

"Perhaps." Cadmus tossed the spent carcass down on the platter. "Maybe she has a sick child or a souse for a husband. Or maybe you'll get lucky, and she's just out for a romp. Whichever it is, just remember one thing: we don't have time to pick up strays. Understood?"

"Understood." Kyel felt affronted that Cadmus would even point out something so obvious. What did the man think, that he was going to fall for some starry-eyed village girl and drag her along after them? He'd never do that to any girl. Not when he had less than two months to live.

They finished their meal in silence. When Cadmus retired to their room, Kyel remained at the table, deep in thought and nursing his tankard. He'd stopped paying attention to the group by the hearth. Every once in a while, he chanced a glance at the serving girl. She was conspicuously ignoring him, taking great care to avoid eye contact. He wondered if it was because she regretted their conversation. Or an attempt to hide her interest in him from her employer.

When he'd figured about an hour had passed, Kyel slid a couple coppers to the center of the table and scooped up his saddle bags. He trudged up to the second level and left his things with a snoring Cadmus, then stole downstairs and out the front door.

The wind was up, blustery. Thankful for his coat, Kyel hugged himself as he made his way across the yard toward the stable. A tumbleweed skittered by, making him wonder what business a tumbleweed even had in a pine-forest hamlet. There were many such inconsistencies about Creek Hollow that just didn't set right with him.

He had to fight with the stable door to get it open. Then he had to struggle with it to get it closed, as if the wind was determined to rip the door from his hand. Inside, Kyel found himself accosted by the acute odor of horse manure. The only light came from a slatted window on the far wall. Kyel felt along with his hands as he made his way down the central aisle between stalls. Razor-thin streaks of moonlight slanted in through the window slats—not enough to do his vision any good. Nickers and snorts greeted him from both sides. A velvet nose shoved into him, breathing a gush of warm air against his neck.

The aisle ended at a slivery plank wall. No serving girl, for which Kyel wasn't sure he was grateful or disappointed. But then a gust of wind and moonlight erupted from a side door, startling the horses. Kyel whirled toward a hooded figure carrying a lantern who stepped inside then stopped to fight with the door. Striding forward, Kyel took the lantern, shielding its flame against the wind as he helped the girl get the door closed. Throwing off her hood, the serving girl turned and smiled at him shyly.

"You came." She beamed at him with the same starry eyes she'd had in the inn.

Kyel didn't know what to say, so he just nodded. With her hair in disarray, her cheeks reddened by the wind, she looked even prettier than before. He felt his pulse kick up as his eyes wandered over her.

"Are you really a mage?" she pressed. "Why aren't you wearing a black cloak?"

"It's in my pack."

She accepted his answer with a smile, then turned her back on him and walked away a few steps toward the nearest box stall. There, she reached her hand up and caressed a soft black nose poking out above the door.

Kyel asked, "So…why'd you ask me out here?"

She dropped her hand and turned to face him.

"I'm pregnant," she whispered.

Kyel blinked. That certainly wasn't what he'd expected to hear. "Um…aren't you supposed to tell me that *after* we've been intimate?"

She fixed him with the closest thing to a pout her pretty face could manage. "It's not like that. If my father finds out…he'll kill me."

"Well, I'm sure he won't be happy. But that's not a—"

She cut him off. "I don't think you understand. He really *will* kill me."

Kyel frowned. "You're serious."

"I am. You don't know what it's like here."

He halfway believed her. The entire town had an odd feel to it. The whole place just wasn't right. And this girl…oddly, she seemed to be the only normal person he'd seen.

Kyel's frown deepened. "So, what do you want from me?"

Emboldened, the girl took a step toward him. Looking up into his eyes, she said, "I want you to take me with you."

Kyel was already shaking his head before she got the words out. Cadmus had been right. Again. Just like he usually was about everything. "Oh, no," he muttered. "Where I'm going…no. Look, there's a war. You don't want to be anywhere near me. I can't—"

"Please! You don't understand—"

Kyel started backing away, stepping around her toward the door. "I'm sorry. There must be someone else who can help you. Where's the father?"

"He's gone! He was a patron, only here for a week. Look, you said you swore to help people!"

"It's not like that. I'd like to help you, but there's a bigger problem—"

To his horror, the girl started crying. Kyel closed his eyes, feeling his resolve washed away by the sight of her tears. He flung his hands up in frustration. "Stop! Just stop. Look, maybe we can take you as far as Amberlie. But that's it. No farther."

She gasped. "You will? You mean it?" Radiant hope beamed from her face, sparkled in her eyes.

Kyel groaned, already regretting his words. "I

can't believe I'm doing this." He rubbed his brow. "Meet us outside the gate on the morrow. An hour before dawn. You've got a horse?"

She nodded eagerly. "I can take my father's."

Before he could blink, she careened into him, catching him up in an exuberant hug as her lantern bounced against his back. He hugged her stiffly, only too aware of the feel of her breasts against him. He let her go, suddenly flustered, his hands racing to smooth his shirt.

"Thank you!" she gasped. She reached up and kissed his cheek, then was gone in a flurry of wind, fluttering hair, and moonlight.

Chapter Five
The Purge of Wolden

Wolden, The Rhen

The sound of a tolling bell woke Blake Pratson from sleep. At first, the mayor of Wolden just incorporated the sound into his dream: a distant, insignificant noise that barely registered. But the noise was insistent. He tried his best to ignore it, to fall back into the dream again. He was exasperated when it continued. He rolled over in bed, irritated that the sound wasn't going away.

He snapped awake, recognizing the warning bell for what it was.

Pratson sat up in bed, heart pounding in his chest. His brain labored to process the bell's significance. It could be a false alarm. It could be something much less dire than the horrors his mind was trying to leap to. It could be one of the town's many drunkards pulling the rope, or a scorned lover or…

The sound of distant screams shred his hopes. Pratson turned toward the window, only then noticing the dull orange glow streaming in through the tatted curtains, making the shadows dance across the walls.

Fire…

It could be a stable. An inn. It could be anything. It didn't have to be *them.*

They weren't supposed to come. Two great armies stood between Wolden and the Pass of Lor-Gamorth.

Pratson swung his feet over the side of the bed and rushed to the window. Ripping the dusty curtains aside, he pressed his palms against the cold glass and stared out into the night. He could see the outline of jagged rooftops silhouetted by the glow of fires in the distance. The sounds of screams were clearer now, heard through the glass. The scent of smoke finally reached his nostrils.

Cold terror gripped Pratson's throat. He whirled away from the window and made for the chair where he'd laid his clothes. He stumbled into his trousers then strapped his belt around his waist. He picked up his shirt, thrusting an arm into the sleeve—

The bedroom door burst open with a *crack* of shattering wood.

Pratson cried out, backing away from the lone man advancing toward him. The man shot out a hand and slammed him roughly against the wall. He started to struggle.

"They're here!" growled a low and familiar voice.

The glow of the flames revealed Broden's jagged features. The guardsman gripped Pratson by the arm and spun him around, saying, "The gate's been breached—we're overwhelmed. I'm getting you out of here."

Pratson didn't argue. He was too busy trying to keep his feet moving as the guardsman steered him out of the bed chamber. He followed Broden down a dark hallway toward a set of stairs that descended into the basement. There, they could gain access to tunnels that had been dug decades ago to escape this very threat.

As they crossed the foyer, the great double doors burst open. Armored men spilled into the room, blocking both escape and retreat. Broden shoved Pratson back and stepped in front of him, raising his blade into a warding stance.

Black-mailed soldiers fanned out from the door, shields and weapons raised. Broden stood his ground, looking determined to take down as many as he could before meeting his own end. Terrified, Pratson clung to the wall, his eyes sliding over the fearsome helms of the Enemy soldiers who confronted them.

The soldiers parted to create an opening. Pratson's eyes were drawn toward the door, then stuck there as if glued. A cold wash of air blew in, scattering leaves across the floor. The leaves whorled and fluttered, collecting in the corners.

The wind gasped its last breath and went still.

Another warrior entered, taller than the rest, all in black plate with a thick cloak furling about him. He halted in front of Broden, as if immune to the threat of the blademaster's sword. He stood there a long moment as all motion in the room ground to a halt, freezing like jammed gears. The warrior reached up and removed his helm, shaking out a dark mass of sweat-greased hair. Pratson gaped, recognition slamming into him with the force of a hammer blow.

Lauchlin.

The mage was almost unrecognizable. He'd only seen Darien Lauchlin once before, when he'd been a new Sentinel passing through town with dire warnings of invasion. Pratson had been wary of the man even then. There had been something about him. Something *tainted.* Broden had sensed it too. Even after he'd seen the markings of the chains on the man's wrists, Pratson still hadn't trusted him.

Now he understood why.

The same man stood before him. Only, now, the taint of corruption had grown too great to be bodily contained. It bled off him in waves, darkening the air around him like a vile penumbra. The eyes that locked on Broden went far beyond cold. It was as though Lauchlin's mere presence sucked all hope from the room.

Pratson's breath hitched. He stood with his back pressed against the wall, heart lurching in fear. His limbs trembled as he felt the air stagnate around him.

"Stand down," the darkmage ordered Broden. He didn't raise his voice; there was no need. Dire threat was implicit in his tone.

Pratson gaped at him in revulsion. "You were a Sentinel," he gasped. "How do you stand your own existence?"

The demon's eyes bored into him. Calmly, Lauchlin responded, "I swore to serve the land and its people. *All of its people.* I'm doing my duty—*now you do yours.* Tell the residents of Wolden to flee. Or I swear by Xerys, I'll put them all to the sword."

Adjusting his grip on his hilt, Broden growled, "I remember you. I also remember you're helpless within a vortex."

Lauchlin shook his head. "Not anymore."

Broden stood unmoving, staring into the demon's eyes as if gauging his intent.

"Ah, fuck," he whispered.

His knees buckled. Broden's sword dropped from his hands as he folded over, dead. Pratson gaped at the darkmage in horror, realizing there was nothing between him and death.

"Go do your duty," Lauchlin ordered.

Pratson bolted forward, slipping past the man out the door of the manor. He sprinted for the road, drawing up only when he reached the chaos in the street.

He gaped around in terror.

Wolden was burning. Crackling fires scorched the night, feeding roiling clouds of smoke that blotted out the stars. Screams ripped through the air as people were chased from their homes and stampeded through the streets. It took Pratson only a moment to figure out what was going on: Wolden's inhabitants were being rounded up, herded into the town square, where they were ringed by black-mailed savages brandishing torches and weapons. Women clung to their children, their men shouting in fear or defiance or both. While their homes burned behind them.

Pratson ran right up to the edge of the square and scrambled onto the back of a cart. He stood waving his hands and shouting, desperately trying to get his peoples' attention.

"Take your families and evacuate!" he bellowed. "Leave everything behind! *Run!*"

The ring of soldiers opened to allow the crowd to spill between them. Pratson jumped down from the cart and started after, but the threat of a scimitar stopped him short. He looked slowly up, his eyes meeting Darien Lauchlin's shadowed stare.

"Not you," the darkmage said, holding his blade steady.

Pratson felt all the blood leak out of his face. He

whispered, "What are you going to do?"

The demon nodded at the ground. "Kneel, and I'll make it quick."

Gripped in the claws of terror, Pratson couldn't move. A warm wetness dribbled down his leg, scarcely noticed. "No," he gasped, taking a step back and shaking his head. "No, no, please!"

"Kneel or suffer."

He didn't understand his options. They flowed over him like water. He didn't react fast enough.

Pratson screamed as his skin erupted in indescribable pain. Looking down at his hands, he saw his flesh melting, running like hot wax.

The scream that tore from his throat died just as violently as the rest of him.

Chapter Six
The Price of Arrogance

Wolden, The Rhen

Darien turned away from the gelatinous mass that had, just moments before, been Wolden's mayor. It took him a moment to realize he was surrounded by a circle of Zakai who stood staring at him warily. He hadn't bothered explaining to them about the Hellpower.

"How…?" Sayeed gasped.

Looking around for Azár, Darien answered, "I can't use the magic field in a vortex. But I can still use the Onslaught. It's ugly, but it's effective. The one drawback is, I can't heal with it."

He found Azár walking toward them, wielding a double-edged qama in her hand. He wished she had something more substantial than a short sword. She couldn't use magic in a vortex. The torrential power would kill her, just as it would kill him.

Across the street, a building gutted by fire collapsed on itself, showering glowing embers into the air. Screams came from every direction, echoing over the roar of the flames. A lone Tanisar jogged up the road and gave a concise report to Sayeed. Darien's new commander sent him off with a series of barked orders.

"The town is mostly cleared, and the fires are contained," Sayeed relayed the report. "There is only a small pocket of resistance left down by the mill."

Darien donned his helm, tightening the strap. "I'll take care of it. Round up any remaining civilians you can find—if they don't want to leave, take their heads off. Mop up, then loot what you can."

Sayeed bowed and set off with a small group of Zakai. Darien waited until Azár reached his side, then started off in the direction of the mill, surrounded by a small but formidable guard. Screaming townsfolk fled before them, some with babes in arms and children in tow. Darien took in the scene impassively, his concentration pinned on the next objective. Inflicting brutality was much easier if he didn't think about it.

They walked through the emptied streets in the direction of the flames. He had ordered the most impoverished section of Wolden put to the torch, for shock value. There were far less resources there to burn, and the housing was well-separated from the rest of town. But apparently, the tactic hadn't driven out everyone.

They found a large group of men collected in the square around the mill. Some held swords, while others were armed with axes or makeshift weapons. They stood as if guarding the mill—a pointless endeavor. They were a far inferior force than the scores of Tanisars that ringed them. The entire scene made little sense.

With a gesture of his hand, Darien ordered his guard of Zakai to stay behind. He removed his helm and strode forward, intent on a big man holding a mace who stood in front of the others, no doubt the mob's ringleader. He didn't object when Azár took his hand. She was still insistent that her place was at his side, and it wasn't worth the effort to try keeping her away from it.

He stopped in the middle of the square and confronted the ringleader.

"Tell your men to surrender," Darien advised. "If they do, I'll let them keep their lives."

Instead of complying, the bearded man spat on the ground.

His action gave Darien pause. Defiance was one thing, but the mob's behavior was suicidal. Something didn't feel right. He ran his gaze over the crowd, seeing the same confidence in the eyes of every man gathered. None of them looked prepared to die protecting a town mill.

"Go back," he ordered Azár under his breath. For once, his wife obeyed without question. She released his hand and started back across the square toward the Zakai.

He heard her fall.

All at once, a barrage of arrows rained down all around him, ricocheting off his armor. Darien dove forward and threw himself on top of Azár. He looked up to face a charging wall of men rushing toward them with weapons raised, more streaming into the square from the surrounding buildings.

Shielding his wife, Darien lashed out blindly with the Onslaught.

Ghastly screams tore through the air as the square erupted in a roiling explosion of hellish green flames. The screams didn't last long. The arrows ceased their barrage. Darien looked up to find the square covered in bodies that lay strewn like fallen trees, half-melted into the cobbles. Something—either smoke or steam—rose from the corpses.

Some of the fallen were Zakai.

Darien rolled Azár over, loosening the straps that held her breastplate, then ripped it off, casting it aside. He let out a growl at the sight of a crossbow quarrel that had slipped through a gap in Azár's armor to shatter her collar bone. His wife lay gazing up at him, eyes narrowed in pain. The bolt had penetrated deep, narrowly missing the main artery in her neck. If the shaft was jostled, even just a bit, the head might still nick it.

There was nothing Darien could do for her—he couldn't use the Onslaught to heal.

He had to get her out of the vortex.

Darien lurched to his feet, glancing around. Chaos and confusion surrounded him as some soldiers swarmed toward him while others fled back.

"I need my horse!" he bellowed.

He dropped back to Azár's side, wishing there was something, anything, he could do. As it was, he was afraid to even try stanching the flow of blood, for fear of moving the shaft. He gazed down at his wife helplessly, taking her hand. Azár stared up at him, remarkably calm.

Minutes passed. Reinforcements arrived, bolstering his guard of Zakai. All around, fires consumed the surrounding buildings. The square was eerily bright and just as eerily quiet.

From a distance, Darien heard approaching hoofbeats. He jolted to his feet, feeling infinite relief at the sight of Sayeed on his red charger, galloping across the square to draw up beside him. The officer slid from the horse's back and held the reins as Darien mounted. Two Zakai rushed forward, lifting Azár delicately and helping to settle her in his arms.

"Go, Brother!" Sayeed gasped, and swatted the horse on its flank to send it bolting forward.

Darien clutched Azár against him, clinging to the stallion with his legs. The horse raced through the streets, spurred faster by its instinctual fear of fire. Soldiers and fleeing townsfolk leaped out of their path, the sound of charging hoofbeats parting the crowd ahead.

The horse cleared the town walls and broke for the open road. But after galloping only a couple of miles, his mount began to flag. Darien pulled the stallion back to a walk, cursing the horse and cursing his luck. He shifted Azár's weight in his arms, trying to make her more comfortable. She sagged against him, her head lolling against his shoulder.

Panicked, Darien fought the urge to run the horse to death. But doing so wouldn't serve Azár, so he kept the lathered stallion alternating between a walk and a trot as they followed the road ever northward. It was still another ten or so miles before they would be clear of the vortex. And he had no idea how many of those miles Azár would last.

Darien clenched his fists in anxiety. Every minute, he felt his wife sinking lower and lower against his chest. It was a constant struggle to keep her sitting upright, keep her from slipping off the horse. Her eyes were closed, her face pale in the moonlight. He kept checking her pulse, unable to resist the compulsion. Every time he did, he was surprised to find her heart still beating. Dark blood saturated the front of her shirt. His arms were slick with it.

Darien started measuring the minutes in heartbeats, dreading the moment her pulse stopped. He felt certain that moment was coming. He didn't have the power or the luck to stop the inevitable.

He rode on, gritting his teeth and holding his

dying wife against his chest.

Eventually, the vortex above them thinned. Darien checked Azár's pulse again. It was thready and rapid, almost too weak to feel. The magic field was still too hot to handle, but he couldn't wait any longer.

Desperate, Darien pulled the horse up and slid off its back. Carrying Azár in his arms, he laid her out on the grass. He could feel the vortex still battering against the shield he'd thrown up to protect his mind from its raging torrent. It was weaker than it had been. He wasn't sure if it was weak enough.

Regardless, he had to try.

Setting his hands on Azár's chest, Darien opened his mind to the vortex. The raging cyclone of power tore through him, slamming into Azár. Every muscle in his body contracted at once, ripping a scream from his throat. He worked through the agony as fast as he could, as long as he could, throwing every effort of will into healing his wife and leaving nothing for himself.

Darien awoke hours later to the feeling of something shaking him, over and over. He groaned and shook his head, trying to rid himself of the sensation. It was more than irritating. But it continued, relentless.

"Husband!"

He gazed blearily into Azár's face. She was leaning over him, fear widening her eyes. He didn't know where he was, didn't understand why she was there.

Then he remembered.

Rage filled him.

Darien scooted away from her and staggered to his feet, fighting waves of vertigo that almost took him to his knees. Azár reached out and tried to stabilize him, but Darien jerked away. He trudged forward a few steps, fighting to contain his fury.

"What is wrong?" Azár shouted at his back. "Are you angry?"

Darien brought his hands up to clutch his throbbing temples. "Yes, I'm angry!"

She stared at him. "Why are you angry?"

Her voice was suffused with hurt and confusion. She didn't understand. How could she not understand? Her ignorance infuriated him all the more.

He whirled back to her. "Because you almost *died!"*

She stood her ground.

He moved forward and raged into her face, "Don't you understand? I couldn't heal you! *The only thing I could do was watch you die!"*

She gazed at him with mute understanding in her eyes. The look did something to him. His anger liquified, draining right out of him. He turned away.

He heard a quiet noise that sounded like a sob. Looking back, he saw that his fierce wife had tears in her eyes.

Confused, Darien gaped at her. "Why are you crying?"

She muttered something in a voice too soft to hear.

"What?"

Softly, she said, "Thank you."

Darien shook his head, baffled by her answer. "Thank you for what?"

Her eyes glistening, Azár whispered, "Thank you for caring."

It was too much. Her words tore him wide open.

He lifted Azár and lay her down on the dew-wet grass, then collapsed on top of her. His lips scoured her face, her neck, her chest. Her body moved beneath him, her lips seeking his. She wrapped her legs around him.

For one brief moment, the entire world paused and held its breath.

Chapter Seven
The Good Mage

The Vale of Amberlie, The Rhen

They left Creek Hollow as the predawn light just barely grayed the eastern horizon. The town was silent and still, its shadowed streets haunted by absence. Kyel's eyes roamed the side of the road nervously as they slipped out the gate. He hadn't liked the feel of the place the previous night. He liked it even less the next day.

There was no sign of the serving girl, for which he was grateful. He hadn't mentioned his agreement with her to Cadmus. Part of him hoped they could slip out of town ahead of her. In the fresh light of morning, he found himself doubting her story. But another part of him hoped she'd catch up. He wanted to believe her. It had been a long time since he'd met a sincerely good person. He wanted very badly for her to be as nice as she seemed.

As they rounded a switchback in the trail that led down from the ridge, he heard hoofbeats. Turning, he saw a dark horse trotting toward them up the slope, the girl on its back, her hood pulled up and cloak flapping.

Cadmus took one look at the girl then shook a finger at Kyel. "No, no, no! I told you we don't have time to take in strays. Now send her back where she came from!"

The girl reined in, a troubled frown on her face as her eyes flicked back and forth between the two of them. Exasperated, Kyel let out a heaving sigh. He'd known it would come to an argument. Only, this argument he intended to win. He was getting tired of being led around by the nose.

"I told her she could come," he stated firmly.

Cadmus snorted. "Then you can tell her she can go."

"No." Kyel felt his temper heating. "I gave my word we'd take her with us as far as Amberlie. I'm not going back on my word."

Cadmus gave a loud *harrumph* and turned to the girl. "What did you tell him? That your husband beats you? You're running away from an arranged marriage? Whichever, it must have been convincing. You play the victim well."

The girl glanced at Kyel with hurt in her eyes.

"She's pregnant," Kyel snapped. "And her life—and the child's life—are in danger. She's coming with us."

Cadmus chortled. "And what do we do when her family comes tracking us down? Or do you think they're just going to let her go? The last thing we need is a herd of fools with bent noses chasing after us."

"That won't be a problem."

"Oh, it won't? How exactly do you plan to deter them?"

Kyel glared at him. Then he reached down and patted Thar'gon's haft. "With this."

The cleric lifted a skeptical eyebrow. "What about your Oath of Harmony?"

"I'm a Sentinel." Kyel shrugged. "There's a hell of a lot I can do without breaking Oath."

Cadmus stared hard at him for a long moment, a world of skepticism in his eyes. Then he blew out a loud snort. "Let's hope so, boy. For our sake. And the world's."

"I'm not a boy," Kyel growled at him. "And I'm getting sick of being treated like one. You're not even a priest—all you are is a mouthpiece. So tell

His Eminence from now on, I'll be taking his advice under consideration, and not the other way around."

Red-faced, Cadmus glared at him. Then he wheeled his horse around, kicking it forward down the path. Kyel watched him bump along, jolting in his saddle as his stirrups flapped in time to his horse's strides.

He glanced at the girl in apology.

They rode in silence through the grove as the day dawned overhead. The chatter of birdsong filled the forest, a sound Kyel had all but forgotten during his long months in the Pass. The girl's horse plodded along behind his own, fully content to follow. She had to give it a few good kicks to make it move forward alongside his gelding.

"I'm sorry I upset your friend," she said in a lowered tone.

"He's not my friend. So don't worry." Kyel glared ahead at Cadmus.

The girl found her shy smile. "My name is Alexa. Alexa Newell."

"Kyel Archer."

Her eyebrows pinched together in a frown of confusion. "You have a longer name than that, don't you? Being a mage, and all?"

Kyel shrugged. "I have a title. But I don't like to use it." Feeling awkward, he cast his gaze back down at the road.

"Thank you for helping me, Kyel," she said after a moment. "I was right. You really are a good mage."

He managed a wan smile. "Well, I'm not a very good mage. But I'd like to think I'm a good person."

She brightened at that, gifting him with a smile that eclipsed the daylight. He couldn't help grinning back. It had been a long time since he'd been able to make a girl smile like that.

"What is that?" She pointed at the silver morning star affixed to his saddle.

"Oh, this?" He drew Thar'gon from its saddle holster, holding it up for her to see. "It's my weapon."

Alexa's brow furrowed. "I thought mages didn't carry weapons."

Feeling deflated, Kyel hung Thar'gon back in place. "Well, it's more like a talisman."

"A talisman? What does it do?" She sat up straight, her eyes teeming with interest.

It was the one question he'd rather she hadn't asked. "I haven't actually figured it out," he admitted. "I just came by it recently and haven't had a lot of time to fiddle with it."

She stared at him flatly for a moment, then turned back to the road. They rode in silence for a while. After uncomfortable minutes, Kyel glanced at Alexa and caught her staring at him. She looked away quickly. Suddenly self-conscious, he searched for something to say. The only line of conversation that came to mind was the obvious.

"I don't mean to pry," he said, "but I'd appreciate you telling me more about your ...situation."

"My situation?" She looked at him with confusion on her face.

Embarrassed, Kyel motioned toward her middle. "You know...your..."

"Oh..." Slow realization seeped onto her face. Her eyes slipped to the side, and she looked lost in thought. "There was a man who passed through town. We took a liking to each other. He said he'd take me with him, but he didn't. He left in the night and didn't come back for me."

Kyel frowned. "And what about your father?"

She pressed a finger against her lips, as if mired in deep thought. "That's just the kind of man he is. Merciless. Heartless. He has no soul..." Her voice trailed off into silence.

Ahead of them, Cadmus had drawn his horse up. When they neared, he threw a glowering stare their way. "If you two lovebirds would stop yammering for a moment, we might be able to hear if anyone's following us."

Kyel scowled, knowing the cleric was right, but nevertheless hating to admit it.

After that, they rode in silence for long hours as the gloom of the woodland creeped over them. The canopy thickened, becoming crowded by maple and birch. The grove darkened, the smell of pine replaced by the musty-damp scent of moss and detritus. All around, an eerie silence descended around them, disturbed only by the plodding of hoofbeats and the distant, trickling sounds of water.

Kyel breathed in the cold, moist air, for once wishing he'd worn his cloak. His stomach rumbled, reminding him he'd skipped breakfast. Clucking to his horse, he angled it off the road in the direction of a moss-encrusted tree that had fallen over at an angle.

"Where, pray tell, are you going?" Cadmus called at his back.

"I'm going to eat."

Ignoring the sounds of grumbling behind him, Kyel swung off his horse and tethered it to a branch. He snatched up his saddle bags then turned—

—to find himself standing nose-to-nose with Alexa. He jerked back, reflexively reaching for the magic field. He hadn't heard her coming up behind him. He held onto the field tighter as he fought to calm his racing pulse.

"How did you…" he shook his head. Staring into her doll-like face, his thoughts melted and oozed away. He let go of the field, allowing it to seep out of him slowly. He took a step back, staring questioningly into her face.

"Aren't you hungry?" she asked.

Before he could respond, she reached into her pack and removed a small burlap sack. With an angelic smile, she produced two apples, offering one to Kyel in her open palm. He accepted the apple and, lifting it to his mouth, took a bite. It was perfectly crisp and ripe, perhaps the best apple he'd ever had.

"It's delicious," he said, taking another crunching bite.

She smiled at him dearly, but instead of eating the fruit in her hand, she tucked it back away in the sack. She stood watching him with a smile on her face while Kyel finished his apple, core and all. He took a swig from his water skin and, looking up, saw her smiling at him.

Cadmus grimaced his disapproval. Turning away, he called over his shoulder, "I'm going to go find a tall bush. Don't do anything that'll get her more pregnant."

Kyel could feel himself blushing. As Cadmus' heavy footsteps retreated into the forest, he hurried toward his horse. He rifled through his saddlebags in a clumsy attempt to keep Alexa from seeing his heated cheeks. He dug his hand around, trying to find just one possession he could use to justify his action.

He felt a hand on his shoulder. He froze, uncertain what to do. He wasn't sure what to say to a pretty girl whose smile lit up the day. He turned toward her—

—and was flung backward, the forest exploding in dazzling brilliance. His body slapped hard against the ground. Kyel cried out, his mind reflexively scrambling for the magic field. He caught ahold of it and used all eleven tiers of power to strike back against the threat. Opening his eyes, he blinked against an overwhelming light that dazzled his senses. He wiped his eyes, struggling to clear his vision, then looked around.

Alexa lay on the ground in front of him, unmoving. Kyel froze halfway between breaths. Time stopped. Everything stopped.

She's dead.

Then: *I killed her…*

He scrambled forward to the girl's side, reaching out—

—another brilliant burst of light lifted him up and threw him backward. Kyel reached for Thar'gon, his hand closing on the haft—

His vision cleared. Time lurched forward. The dazzling whiteness fell away. Kyel stood up, wielding the talisman over his head as his adversary came into focus.

He gasped. Then he swung.

Thar'gon's magical strike threw the dead man away from him. Kyel swept the talisman back in an arc, repulsing the remainder of the dead things that surrounded him. Limbs flew, and corpses tumbled in a rain of decayed body parts. He felt the energy released by the morning star, an incredible surge of force. It was indomitable, unfathomable. Nothing could survive that.

But something did.

One of the corpses started crawling toward him, clawing itself over the ground, dragging the snaking ropes of its entrails behind it. Repulsed, Kyel leveled the talisman at the thing, watching it burst into pieces that showered gore all over the forest bracken.

He stood quivering, panting, his eyes ticking over the grisly scene. When he was sure the rest of the dead weren't going to get up again, he scrambled back to Alexa's side.

She was alive, but barely. He healed her injuries expertly, instantly, sucking glorious power through the talisman. He didn't have to think about what he was doing. It was as though Thar'gon sensed his need and acted of its own accord, using him as a mere conduit. When Kyel opened his eyes, Alexa lay sleeping on a bed of ferns, her head cradled in his lap. He dropped the morning star, gazing around with wide and horrified eyes.

They were surrounded by corpses and parts of corpses. He'd killed them all.

Crying out, Kyel raked back his shirtsleeve. The chain of his Oath was still intact. He looked around, taking in scattered body parts. He hadn't killed them, he decided. They weren't alive. He let out a deep, relieved, sigh.

He hadn't broken Oath.

Chapter Eight
No Mercy

The Cerulean Plains, The Rhen

Darien climbed onto his horse and, wrapping an arm around Azár, sent the animal forward at a walk, wading knee-deep through the prairie's tall grass.

To the east, the sun broke over the mountains, streaking the sky with lines of gold. Sunrise had once been his favorite time of day. The hues of the colors were different: warmer, rarer. But he could no longer take comfort in the wakening sky. Not since Orien's Finger, when he had immolated thousands and shattered the break of dawn. Now the sunrise, like everything else, was ruined for him.

"My father," he said softly, turning his face away from the sun's reproving glare.

"What?" Azár glanced back at him.

"When we first met, you asked me what I was thinking about the moment I died." He felt her body stiffen against his. The breeze chased dark strands of her hair. "I was thinking of my father."

A long silence followed his words. Darien's stare remained fixed on the sprawling prairie ahead. He remembered this place. Somewhere close by was the shrine he had entered with Naia, the one that contained an entrance to the Catacombs. There, somewhere deep in those warrens, was the chamber of souls where he'd encountered his father's spirit. Darien knew he would never see him again. His own soul was destined for a different place.

He tightened his grip around Azár, pulling her closer. He savored the scent of her hair, knowing that he didn't have much time left with her. Very soon, he'd be losing her, too.

Forever.

She said, "Tell me about your father."

Her words yanked him out of his thoughts. "His name was Gerald. He was a good Sentinel. And a great man."

Her hand found his, stroking it tenderly. "What is your best memory of him?"

Darien thumbed through his recollections, searching for the right one. Eventually, he found it. "It was the day I passed Consideration. When I became an acolyte. Instead of taking me directly up the mountain, my father led me out into the forest near Auberlie. We walked until we found a stream, then we sat down on the rocks beside it. That's all we did. For hours. We didn't talk. He never said a word to me, but I sensed he was sad. I didn't understand why at the time. Now I do. I'd never want a son of mine to follow my path."

Azár glanced back at him. "That does not sound happy. So why is it the best memory you have of him?"

Darien hung his head, ashamed to admit his feelings. He didn't like thinking about them, much less feeling them. "Because it was the last time I ever saw him."

She lifted his hand to her lips, pressing a kiss against his skin. Then she fell quiet. The horse carried them southward with a steady gait. Eventually, they came to a place he recognized.

It was the shrine.

The lone building rose out of the grassland ahead, forlorn and isolated. Darien turned the horse away from it. His memories of this place were far from comforting. The shrine led to the Catacombs. Which had led him to breaking his Oath. To his mistreatment of Naia. To the sacrifice of his soul. It led to everything that had gone wrong. He wanted nothing more to do with it.

The shrine, like his past, slipped behind him and disappeared in the distance.

It wasn't long until they came upon the encampment. They were greeted by a party of scouts, who rode out toward them on captured mounts, most looking unstable in the saddle. Darien gazed sadly at the approaching men. These were a people descended from the greatest horse culture the world had ever known. Yet they were so far removed from their origins that their blood had lost all trace of its memory.

Sayeed galloped toward them on a horse as red as Darien's, scattering soldiers out of his way. He drew his mount up and leaped to the ground, falling to his knees. He stared down at the trampled grass and, drawing his sword, offered it up.

"Lord, I have failed you twice. Please take my life."

Darien dismounted, handing the stallion's reins to Azár. He walked forward until he was standing over Sayeed. He wasn't sure what to do. This was a matter of *sharaq*, he felt certain. And he had no idea what the proper response should be that would preserve both Sayeed's life and honor. He remembered the promise he had made back at Kajiri flats, that if the Zakai ever failed him again, they would forfeit their lives. Gazing down at Sayeed, Darien now regretted those words. He would lose every drop of *sharaq* he possessed if he didn't follow through with that threat.

He had no choice. A wrong had been committed, and it would have to be redressed. Or his command—and Sayeed's life—would end here today.

Accepting the sword, he set the edge of the blade across the officer's neck. Sayeed remained motionless, frozen in his bow. He suffered the blade's touch without so much as a flinch. Darien's mind scrambled through options, finding none that were certain and safe. He decided to settle for the uncertain. And the unsafe. He widened his stance, adjusting his grip on the hilt.

"Sayeed son of Alborz, you have now failed me twice," he pronounced. "But I failed you first."

He retracted the sword and cast it to the ground. Gasps of dismay issued from the soldiers gathered around.

"I put myself in harm's way, leaving you and your men without recourse." He drew his own blade. "I dishonored you and all the Zakai. My life is yours. Take it."

He fell to his knees, offering the weapon out before him. Sayeed raised his head to gape at Darien's sword with horrified eyes. All around, soldiers looked on with faces frozen by shock.

Azár leapt from the horse with a strangled cry.

Time froze. Not a soul moved.

Sayeed lurched to his feet.

Darien felt his sword leave his hands. There was a moment's pause. Then the sharp edge of the blade kissed the skin of his neck. He closed his eyes and hoped. There was no other way. Not if he wanted to preserve Sayeed's life and honor. He hoped that by putting him in an impossible position, the soldiers couldn't blame Sayeed if he failed to strike.

Darien felt the blade's edge trembling against his neck, sending shivers down his nerves. Sayeed was Zakai—a paragon of discipline. He'd been molded from birth to remain steadfast, even in the direst of circumstances. That Sayeed couldn't maintain a steady grip on his hilt warned Darien of his danger.

In a voice fraught with dread, the officer proclaimed, "Warden Darien Lauchlin, you have failed me and all the Zakai. For that, your life is forfeit."

The pressure of the blade eased. Then it settled back down again as Sayeed adjusted his aim. Darien felt a terrible chill wash over him. He realized he'd made a fatal mistake. He had underestimated the rigidity of the Zakai's honor code.

He would have to kill Sayeed.

Darien's vision exploded as a body plowed into him, hurling him to the ground. Another soldier collapsed on top of him, knocking the wind from his lungs. Pinned to the dirt, Darien struggled as another man added his weight. Soldier after soldier fell on top of him, shielding him from Sayeed's strike with their own bodies and lives. He lay prone on the ground, gasping for air, his ribs crushing his lungs.

The weight pinning him shifted, then released.

He was jerked to his feet and held there by Sayeed. Dazed, Darien looked around to see every soldier kneeling in a great circle. Only Sayeed remained standing, his face a mask of outrage.

He let go of Darien, shoving him backward. Then

he threw the sword on the ground and stormed away.

———

"You are stupid!" Azár raged, pacing away from him.

Darien scooped up a jug then sat down on the floor, pouring himself a cup of water. His gaze tracked his wife's motion as she stalked away from him across the length of the tent.

"Stupid!"

Azár paced back toward him. She stopped, looming, her hands planted firmly on her hips. "What were you *thinking?!"*

She whirled and paced away.

"Stupid!"

She made a growling sound deep in her throat. Then she jerked back the tent's partition and tore through it. Darien listened to the sound of her footsteps stalking off, followed by one last *"Stupid!"*

He let out a sigh and leaned back against a tent post, closing his eyes in weariness. Azár was right—he had acted stupidly. He should have never confronted the townsfolk without a guard. He'd let his command of the Onslaught go to his head. And, because he had, he'd almost lost his head. He brought his hands up to rub his face, cursing his own arrogance.

"Brother."

He looked up to find Sayeed holding back the cloth partition. His commander's face had lost some of its anger, though not all of it. Darien sighed, feeling defeated. Figuring that he was due another scolding, he beckoned the man in. Sayeed claimed one of the cushions against the wall, sitting back and crossing his legs. Scowling, he dug the cushion out from under him and tossed it in front of Darien, then scrambled forward to sit on it.

Sayeed lifted a finger and opened his mouth to say something. But then he snapped his jaw shut, closing his eyes as if reconsidering his words. Then, with renewed conviction, he leaned forward and shook his finger in Darien's face.

"I would have killed you to preserve your honor!" His voice was strained with rage. "Do you understand? That is the position you put me in!"

Darien gazed at the man he had named First Among Many. He took a sip of water. "No. That's the position you put yourself in. I'm not going to murder you just because you've got a sick sense of honor. So don't ever ask me that again—or neither one of us is going to come out of it with any amount of *sharaq* left." He tossed the water out of his cup onto the rug, grumbling, "I need something stronger."

He rose and went to select one of the jugs that lined the walls of the tent: all gifts from the various clan chiefs. Unstoppering one, he took a drink that burned his throat and made his eyes water.

"This'll do."

He filled his cup and offered another to Sayeed, returning to his seat. He took another drink, making a face as the liquor went down. "What *is* this?" he gasped. It was horrifically strong—exactly what he needed.

Sayeed smelled the liquor without tasting it. "It is rika. It is served during times of celebration. Or times of woe."

Darien grunted, taking his cup back and raising it to his lips.

"Stop. Rika must be served a certain way." Before Darien could object, the man snatched the drink from his hand. "This is too much," he snapped. Sayeed returned most of the liquid back to the jug. "First, you must pour your cup into my cup," he said, performing the act. "This shares your troubles with me. Then I pour my rika back into your cup. This gives your troubles back to you, but also my understanding. Now we drink together. You must drink it all at once."

He raised his cup, gesturing for Darien to follow suit. Darien stared at the beverage warily. There was a lot more rika left in the cup than just a sip. But he followed Sayeed's prompt and drank it down, grimacing at the fire igniting in his gut.

"Now you must speak of your troubles," Sayeed said, refilling their cups.

Darien felt the magic field waver as a fiery warmth spread throughout his body. He drank the second cup that was offered, then quickly received a third.

"That is all until you speak," Sayeed told him.

Darien stared into his cup, searching for words. He was not even sure if he could put a label on his feelings. They were too muddled, too rampant. It was like mixing different textures of sand in one vessel: impossible to separate and identify. And, he had to admit, he was nervous about what the man might think of him.

He took a breath, admitting finally, "I've slain a lot of people in the past week. People who were my kin. People I'd sworn to protect."

Sayeed shrugged. "You are allowed feelings. You are allowed guilt."

"That's good, because I've a hell of a lot of it."

"Are you losing resolve?" Sayeed mixed his cup of rika with Darien's. His voice was conversational, but Darien knew better. He could sense the man's hesitance.

"No." He couldn't afford to lose resolve. Too much depended on him.

Sayeed said, "Your orders and actions have been without mercy. You have nothing to prove, Brother. You can afford to show compassion to those you have defeated."

Darien shook his head. "No. I don't want to kill any more people than I have to—killing isn't my goal. To take the North, we'll need to drive them southward. We can do that either by the sword or by fear. I choose fear. That's why I have to be ruthless. 'Compassion is like a dull blade: it might seem kinder in the moment. But in the end, it often deals more cruelty,'" he said, quoting a maxim of the Arms Guild.

He swallowed his rika, then reached up to rub his eyes. He felt enormously weary. It went much further than just the effects of the liquor. He was weary all the way to his bones.

"Be warned, Brother," Sayeed said, leaning forward. "There is no mercy for the merciless."

"Is that another one of your proverbs?"

"Perhaps. Or perhaps it is prophecy." Sayeed climbed to his feet. "You'd better find your bed, Brother."

Chapter Nine
Alexa

The Vale of Amberlie, The Rhen

Kyel lay Alexa down on a bed of oak leaves and covered her with his black cloak. He sat there for a while, making sure she was going to be all right. Then he stood up, dusted off his pants, and set off into the forest to find Cadmus.

He wandered through the dense bracken with a heavy heart. The cleric hadn't returned after the attack, which wasn't a hopeful sign. So it wasn't a surprise when he found Cadmus lying pantsless and bloodless in a ditch. Kyel stopped yet a ways back from the cleric's body, knowing there was no sense in going any further. Out of respect for the man who had helped raise his son and had followed him half the length of the continent, Kyel paused and bowed his head. He stood for a moment listening to wind whispering through the pines, his thoughts turned inward, his eyes averted.

Then he did what Cadmus would have wanted. Gripping Thar'gon's hilt, he fed energy into the corpse until the flesh ignited. He fished a rag out of his pocket and held it to his face as the smoke and stench hit him. The smell was repugnant. It brought back the vivid horror of the time he'd spent locked in a cage with Myria Anassis' charred remains. He closed his eyes, breathing through the rag's dirty fabric, until the sound of the fire died in his ears.

When he opened his eyes, Cadmus was gone. There was nothing left of him but scorched earth and gray ashes. Kyel hooked Thar'gon to his belt and turned away, walking slowly and sadly back through the thicket.

He tethered Alexa's horse to his own and climbed into the saddle, cradling her against his chest as he jabbed his heels into the gelding's flanks. She somehow remained asleep through it all. He directed his horse toward the south, deeper into the Vale of Amberlie, sticking to the lowlands and the darker thickets of trees. Always, he kept his eyes open for the reappearance of the dead.

The forest darkened as the sun sank behind the Craghorns. The shadows thickened, the birds silenced. The insects began their nightly chants. He pulled back on his horse's reins and climbed down from the saddle, carrying Alexa to a spot of ground sheltered by a rocky outcrop not too far from a small brook. There, he built a fire and tended to the horses. Then he cast his tired body down beside hers and sat worrying a strip of jerky, not really tasting it. His eyes scanned the night, not trusting it. The smallest noises set him on edge.

The shadows of the trees revolved around him, lengthening. He let the fire burn and then die a slow death.

It was morning. A new fire now crackled atop the ashes of the old. Beside Kyel, Alexa stirred. She opened her eyes and gazed loosely up at him. Stretching, she asked, "What happened?"

Kyel didn't look at her. Instead, he picked up a stick and poked a log back toward the heart of the flames. "We were attacked. By dead people." His tone conveyed the anger he felt.

Alexa sat up, drawing her knees against her chest and wrapping her arms around them. She didn't respond to his statement. To Kyel, her silence was more honest than anything she could have said.

"You're not pregnant."

She looked away into the forest. Again, her lack of response was answer enough. Kyel nodded. He'd hoped she would have an explanation he could accept. But she was damned by her own silence.

He threw the stick down. "Cadmus is dead. I almost died, too. I *would* be dead, if not for this." He brandished Thar'gon as if ready to strike her with it.

She stared at the weapon in silence. Any normal girl would have cowered in fear. Alexa didn't.

Lowering the talisman, Kyel said, "You've got one chance to convince me not to take both horses and leave you behind."

She turned away from him and fixed her gaze on the fire. He waited. She said nothing. A log popped, flinging sparks onto the ground. Alexa didn't flinch.

In a flat voice, she mumbled, "They're all dead."

"Who? Who's dead?"

"The people of Creek Hollow. They're all dead."

Kyel stared at her, digesting that information. It was the first thing she'd said that he knew he could believe. Everything about Creek Hollow had seemed wrong. Everything but Alexa.

"What about you?" he said at last.

"I was their prisoner."

He doubted that. None of her actions had seemed unwilling.

Alexa's face crumbled into a grimace of sorrow. Shaking her head, she said, "I'm so sorry Kyel. I like you. I really do. I'm sorry…"

Kyel shot to his feet, eyes scouring the shadows of the forest. He took a step back away from her, reaching out for the magic field. He dragged it into him through the talisman.

"What are you sorry about?" he demanded.

Alexa shook her head and gazed up at him sadly. "It's a trap. *I'm* a trap. He wants you. Alive or dead, he doesn't care which."

Kyel took another step back. "Who? Who wants me?"

She gazed at him flatly. "Zavier Renquist."

Kyel's eyes widened. He whirled away, striding quickly toward his horse. Behind him, he heard Alexa rushing to catch up. She caught him by the collar, tugging him around.

"He took my baby!" she shrieked, pulling on him even as he fought her off. "I didn't want to do it! He took my baby!"

Kyel tore her hand off his shoulder, flinging it away. He tied her horse to his own then turned back to her. "If Zavier Renquist took your baby, then it's already dead."

He put his foot in the stirrup and swung himself over his horse's back, kicking it forward.

"What are you doing?" Alexa screeched. "Don't leave me here!"

Kyel ignored her. He kicked his horse to a trot.

"I know how to use that talisman!"

Filled with startled rage, Kyel jerked back on the reins. He turned and cast a glare back over his shoulder. "How could you know that?"

She stood there quivering, arms folded, shaking her head.

"Answer me!"

She lowered her gaze, as if in shame.

"Because I'm a mage," she whispered.

Chapter Ten
Well of Mystery

Isle of Titherry, The Rhen

Quinlan Reis stared down from the balcony that overlooked Athera's Crescent, watching the Crescent's surface swirl and roil in patterns that looked like a boiling cauldron of quicksilver. It was mesmerizing. The dark places that had been there were now gone, the curve of its surface unbroken. A beautiful dance of energy swarmed across it, free and unconstrained.

The Crescent's power had been restored. But not without sacrifice.

Quin raised a hand to his head, massaging his temple. Ever since his near-death in the nodal chamber, his head ached from time to time. Sometimes the pain was terrible, forcing him to lie in bed in the dark, for hours at a time. It was like a migraine, only different. This pain was self-inflicted.

It was the price he paid for turning against his Master.

He had defied Xerys when he'd repaired the conduit, an act in direct contradiction with his Master's objectives. In retaliation, his connection with the Netherworld had been severed. The Onslaught was denied him now. The Soulstone was the only reason his soul hadn't been banished to Oblivion. The medallion had returned the Gift to him. He was truly alive, now, and beyond Xerys' reach.

Quin felt Naia's fingers tighten around his own. She stood next to him on the balcony, clothed in a blue gown. Her auburn hair spilled down her back, ruffled by a breeze that moved over the bowl-shaped valley. The air was warm. The curse of winter had been lifted from the isle. Athera's Crescent was sustained by its conduits now. It no longer needed to harvest energy directly from the air.

"How are you feeling?" Naia asked.

Quin smiled, turning his attention to her. "Better. I feel alive. *Really* alive."

"Which is unfortunate."

He whirled to find Tsula behind them. The Harbinger wore the same affectless look she always had. She stood with her hands clasped in front of her, a feathered turban on her head. Quin was mildly surprised to see her. She had been missing from the castle for nine days, ever since the conduits had been repaired.

"What an unpleasant thing to say," he remarked. "Does this mean you wish me to leave your ungracious hospitality?"

"It means that hope for the world has just been reduced significantly," she said.

Quin turned to Naia. "Did you hear that, darling? My very existence saps hope from the world. I believe that's rather an accomplishment, don't you think?"

The Harbinger stamped her foot on the flagstones. "It is no time for sarcasm, Quinlan Reis! There is still opportunity to recover, but it will take much sacrifice on both our parts."

"Would you rather I just jumped off the balcony?"

"If you are so inclined." Her cat-like eyes gazed at him impassively.

Letting go of his hand, Naia stepped between Quin and the Harbinger. "This is what you feared from the beginning," she accused. "Why you wanted to leave me frozen. You knew I could bring him back—and you feared that possibility."

The woman's eyebrows flicked upward in confirmation of Naia's guess. "That is part of the reason, yes."

"What's the other part?" Quin asked.

Turning to him, the Harbinger said flatly, "There is a great chance Naia will destroy the rule of the gods."

Quin blinked. That wasn't the answer he'd been expecting. He looked to Naia and smiled apologetically. "I'm sorry, darling. My penchant for disaster seems to be rubbing off."

Naia shook her head. "I don't understand."

"It is but one possibility." Tsula beckoned them toward the stairs. "Come. We have much to speak of. And you have much to learn."

Quin wasn't certain he wanted to hear anything the woman had to say. It seemed that every conversation he had with Tsula was becoming progressively grimmer. It was getting to the point he feared anything that came out of her mouth, especially now that the Crescent was fully operational. He wondered what information Tsula had managed to garner during the nine days of her absence.

She led them to the vast chamber that occupied the entire bottom floor of the castle and invited them to sit with her in a small cluster of chairs with over-stuffed cushions. Quin gazed around the enormous hall, at its hundreds of empty chairs, and felt a pang of sadness. The castle had once been bustling with mages and their attendant staff, all gathered here to serve the Crescent. All gone now. All gone because of him.

"Please, take a seat." Tsula extended her hand. "There is much for us to discuss."

With the slightest narrowing of her eyes, she ignited a fire in the hearth behind them, even though the room didn't need the warmth. Rays of sunlight glistened down from windows high above, lighting the hall and warming the air.

Quin took a seat beside Naia, holding her hand. Tsula stared down at their hands, her face darkening in irritation. It was the first emotion Quin remembered seeing on her face. He found himself enjoying it. Just to provoke her, he raised Naia's hand to his lips and kissed it, grinning in triumph at the seething look on Tsula's face.

She went deliberately about smoothing her gown, as if using the action to compose herself. Then she looked up with a flat expression and told them, "For nine days, I have been analyzing the information harvested by the Crescent. There has been much to take in."

"And what did you discover?" he asked.

"There are many things going wrong in the world, and very few going right. There are too many variables in play to guess the outcome of it all. But one thing is for certain: we must destroy the magic field. It is the only way to break the Curse over the Black Lands. And it is the only way to destroy the Well of Tears."

Quin looked at her sideways. "*Destroy* the Well of Tears. I thought that wasn't possible."

"It is possible. Difficult, but possible."

"How?" he demanded. Naia squeezed his fingers. She looked just as confused as Quin felt.

Tsula crossed her legs, folding her hands over her knees. "For you to understand, we must discuss the nature of the Well itself."

"I'm listening." Quin glanced at Naia, seeing the intense frown on her face that had to mirror his own.

The Harbinger nodded. "The Well of Tears unlocks the Gateway between worlds. Think of it as a tunnel between two realms: our realm, and the realm of Xerys."

Quin frowned. "You mean hell."

Tsula waved her hand dismissively. "Hell is a religious concept. I do not speak of religion. What you know of as the Netherworld is simply one facet of an infinite number of realms that define existence. It is the realm most closely associated with our own plane."

Her concept of the universe was so far removed from anything in Quin's experience, that her statements seemed preposterous. "I've been to the Netherworld," he reminded her. "For a thousand years, I existed there in torment. Now you're telling me I wasn't damned?"

Tsula shrugged. "Damnation is simply the consignment of a soul to the realm of Xerys. Your soul, unfortunately, was imprisoned there and subjected to torture."

He demanded, "Why? Why was I tortured?"

"Because you defied the will of Xerys."

Quin felt the heat of outrage flush his cheeks. Stewing in bitterness, he asked, "So what is the

Gateway, exactly?"

Tsula crossed her arms. "The Gateway is like a tunnel with two openings: one in our own realm, and the other in the Netherworld. It is a rip in the fabric which separates those two planes."

"How was the tunnel created?" Naia asked.

"It was created by harvesting an extraordinary amount of vitrus in the eye of a vortex, then focusing that vitrus on Xerys' plane."

Quin frowned as he thought about it. Vitrus was an archaic term used to describe the Gift that was passed from a dying mage to their successor—a mage's life force. The creation of the Well of Tears must have required the slaughter of dozens of mages.

Tsula continued, "This act opened the mouth of the tunnel in our world. The other end was bored by Xerys using the Hellpower. The manipulation of the Gateway requires tremendous amounts of vitrus. That is why a Grand Master must be sacrificed to seal the Well of Tears—the sacrifice has to be great enough; elsewise, it will fail."

"So a thousand years ago, I was the sacrifice," Quin concluded.

"Yes." Tsula nodded. "Just as Darien Lauchlin sealed it more recently."

Quin exchanged looks with Naia. Despite his reservations, he believed Tsula. She came from a perspective that contradicted every religious doctrine he had ever heard. But her explanations were too rational to deny. If she was correct, then Xerys was not necessarily a god of evil. He was merely the ruler of his own domain.

Baffled, Quin asked, "So how do we destroy the Gateway?"

"The Gateway is unstable. Its natural tendency is to collapse. It is maintained by the Well of Tears, which draws its power from the magic field. In the Netherworld, there is another Well that is powered by the Onslaught."

Tsula leaned forward, her black eyes taking in both of them with a look of grave portent. "To collapse the Gateway, we must destroy the stabilizer that holds it open: we must destroy the Well of Tears. And the only way to do that is to destroy the power that feeds it."

Quin understood. He understood completely. "Destroy the magic field," he concluded in a whisper.

"Yes."

His head spun. He felt the dizzying sensation of his headache returning. He asked, "And there's no other way?"

The Harbinger nodded. "There is no other way."

Chapter Eleven
The Naturalist

The Vale of Amberlie, The Rhen

Kyel gestured at Alexa, demanding, "Let me see your arm."

She pulled her right sleeve back, exposing the glistening mark of the Mage's Oath. Kyel glared down at the emblem, not trusting it. Perhaps Renquist had found a way to replicate it. His hand lingered on the talisman's haft while Alexa tugged her sleeve back down.

Kyel looked at her. "Start talking. Right now."

Alexa nodded, her gaze dropping to the ground. "I was away when Aerysius fell. But I returned…and I was captured."

"By Zavier Renquist?" he asked skeptically.

"No. By Cyrus Krane." She reached up and brushed a lock of hair out of her face. "They took me to Bryn Calazar and made me a slave. I was there for two years…" Her voice shook. She looked like she was close to crying.

He didn't care; she was lying to him again. "You're a mage. How could they keep you as a slave?"

She cast an injured pout his way. "They took me into the vortex. There was nothing I could do." The look on her face begged him to believe her.

He didn't. Kyel paced away, one hand on his hip, the other on Thar'gon. "So how did you end up in Creek Hollow?"

"Cyrus Krane came back. He took my baby." Her voice shook harder. "He told me he'd kill her if I didn't do what he said."

Kyel gritted his teeth. That was a lie. She couldn't possibly have a baby if she'd been a slave in the Black Lands for two years—

The thought staggered to a halt. It suddenly occurred to him how such a child could have been conceived. He turned back to her, hoping for her sake she was lying. More gently, he asked, "And what did Krane tell you to do?"

"Krane told me you were Darien's acolyte. And that Renquist wanted you. He didn't say why, but I can guess."

"Then guess!" Kyel's voice was harsher than he'd intended.

She pointed at the weapon hanging from his belt. "You're carrying the most powerful talisman in the world. I'm sure Renquist wants it. And there's only one way he can get it."

"By killing me," Kyel concluded, feeling his anger rising. Not specifically at Alexa, but at the whole situation. Almost, he thought he could believe her. Almost. But not quite. He glanced down at the ground, at the shadows of the pine trees laced with sunlight. A cool breeze swayed the branches overhead and moved the fronds of the bracken around them.

"Thar'gon binds to only one person at a time," Alexa explained. "Right now, it's bound to you. There's only two ways it could ever abandon you. First, you could die. Or if the Warden of Battlemages ever touches it, then Thar'gon will transfer to his hand."

"Byron Connel's dead," Kyel said, feeling relieved.

"Who took his place?"

Jarred, Kyel stared unblinking at Alexa. He hadn't thought of that. "There's only four Servants left. Renquist, Krane, Quin Reis…and Darien."

Alexa spread her hands. "Then you have your answer. Darien Lauchlin is the new Warden of Battlemages. And if he ever gets his hands on that weapon—"

"Oh, gods…" Kyel let out a slow sigh, realizing the likelihood of that danger. He remembered the atrocious means Darien had used to escape the dungeon of Greystone Keep. And the implacable ease with which he'd killed.

"I can't let him get it," Kyel said. No matter what. He looked at Alexa, realizing it didn't matter whether or not he trusted her. He couldn't take the risk of bringing her along. "I'm going to leave you with your horse. Don't follow me."

"I thought you—"

Kyel shook his head. "I can't trust you." He went to his mount and threw the saddle blanket over the animal's back. Alexa dashed after him, shaking her head, her eyes wide and desperate.

"I made my bargain with Krane before I ever knew you had Thar'gon!" she gasped. "Now…the stakes are too high." Her eyes fill with tears. "I'll teach you how to use it!"

Kyel paused in the action of lifting his saddle off the ground. He set it back down. "You know how it works?"

"I'm a Naturalist…pushing the boundaries of Natural Law is my area of expertise. And that talisman you're holding bends Natural Law far beyond the limits of what should ever be possible. Thar'gon is every Naturalist's dream. We studied it exhaustively, at least as much as we could from historical records."

Kyel's eyes narrowed in distrust. "Then show me something. Show me something I can do with it."

Alexa spread her hands. "What do you want to know?"

"I don't care!" He flung his arms up in frustration. "Show me anything!"

"All right." She walked away from him a few paces. Then she lifted her hand, gesturing around at the forest and the rocky outcrop behind them. "First, get a good look at your surroundings. Notice things like the horses, the rocks, these particular trees. Are you doing it?"

Kyel nodded, following her directions sourly, even though he didn't understand why he was doing any of it. For all he knew, Alexa could be tricking him into killing himself.

"Now think of somewhere nearby. Somewhere you've been and can easily visualize."

Curious now, Kyel forgot his reservations. The campsite where they'd left the remains of the dead leapt into mind. The fallen tree. The rotting body parts. Cadmus' ashes. He remembered all of it.

"Now what?" he grumbled.

Alexa approached him slowly. "Try to see it in your mind. Every detail that you can remember, as clearly as you can."

"I am." It wasn't difficult.

She stopped beside him. "I'm going to hold your hand."

He felt her fingers clasp his own. He almost flinched away. But he gripped her hand, far too curious to stop now.

"Hold your weapon," she instructed softly. "Bring it up. There. Now, say this word: *Vergis.*"

"Vergis," Kyel echoed.

The forest shivered and disappeared…and another appeared. Startled, Kyel broke away from Alexa's grip and spun in a slow circle, taking in the sight of the grove complete with its rotting smell and decomposing flesh. Lowering Thar'gon to his side, Kyel blinked, feeling dizzy.

"How is that possible?" he gasped.

"It's called transferring," Alexa informed him with a smile. "Thar'gon is imbued with several motive characters. That's one." She gestured around expansively. "Do you trust me now?"

"No."

The smile collapsed, replaced by a scowl of frustration. She stalked away through the bracken then whirled back, planting her hands on her hips.

"Use logic," she snapped. "If I was trying to hurt you, why would I be showing you how to use the most powerful talisman in the world?"

"I don't know, but I'm sure there's a reason."

Kyel moved to the nearest corpse, nudging it with his boot. Flies swarmed up to buzz him angrily before settling back down again. The stench that rose from the rotting tissue made him gag. He moved away quickly.

"What else can it do?" He set off through the trees toward the little brook he knew was there.

Alexa rushed to keep up. "Thar'gon was crafted to enhance a war mage's effectiveness in battle.

Mobility. Communication. Defense. It anticipates its master's needs and reacts accordingly."

"What else?" Kyel paused, looking around for familiar landmarks.

Alexa said to his back, "Several of its motive characters are powerful offensive strikes. It also has an amplification character I'm sure you've discovered."

"I have."

He stopped by the brook and looked down sadly at Cadmus' ashes. He turned to Alexa, gesturing with the talisman as anger tightened his throat. "This is your fault. If it wasn't for you, he'd be alive now. I needed him. And now he's dead."

A look of regret filled the woman's eyes. "I'm sorry, Kyel. It wasn't my intent to get him killed."

"No. Your intent was to get *me* killed." He glared at her. "What were those things back there? The dead people?"

She clasped her hands together. "They are the men of Creek Hollow. Or what's left of them. The women and children were carried off. I don't know what happened to them."

"They didn't look like rotten meat in Creek Hollow." The men of the town had been alive. Awkward and strange, but definitely not decomposing. But she was right; there'd been no sign of women or children. He'd thought that odd at the time.

Alexa explained, "The ward of preservation ended the moment they left the town." She lifted her arm, offering her hand out to him. "Please. Take us back."

Grudgingly, he took her hand. He looked back at Cadmus' ashes. "*Vergis.*"

The world spun and lurched. Kyel staggered as the ground stabilized beneath his feet. The horses tossed their heads, rolling their eyes at their sudden appearance. Kyel released his grip on Alexa's hand and moved to reclaim his mount. He tossed the saddle over the animal's back, then bent to tighten the girth strap.

Alexa rushed up behind him, grabbing his arm. "Please, Kyel! Take me with you! *I'm the only chance you have!*"

Kyel ripped his arm out of the woman's grasp and swung around to shout at her, "*Why?* Why are you my only chance?!"

She looked at him coldly. "Because that weapon wants to return to its rightful master. And you're not him."

Kyel held her gaze. "And what can you do about it?"

"Darien Lauchlin commands a host of necrators. They will shut you down in a heartbeat. But as you see, I have some experience with the undead." Alexa smiled slowly. "If you take me with you, we'll shut him down, instead."

Chapter Twelve
Blood Kin

The Cerulean Plains, The Rhen

Darien woke to darkness. For a moment, he thought he was back in the Black Lands. But the ubiquitous flickers of cloud-light were absent, not ribboning across the fabric of his tent. Then he remembered: he was in the Rhen, where the night sky had never been tortured by Malikar's Curse.

He put out a hand, searching next to him, but felt only empty blankets. Azár hadn't returned.

He climbed out of the covers and walked naked across the rugs to the water jug. He took a gulp of water and swished it around in his mouth. The taste was foul. Grimacing, he picked up a bristled tooth-stick and used it to scrub his teeth as he pulled on his clothes. He gathered his weapons then walked out into the gathering area.

A dozen or more men lay sleeping within, sprawled across the rugs. Darien had to pick his way carefully as he wound his way toward the door. He found his boots and pulled them on by the straps. He left the tent and walked out into the cool night, spitting the film from his teeth and pocketing the tooth-stick.

The air smelled robustly of woodsmoke. Darien breathed in deeply, filling his nostrils with the scent of it. After so many months breathing the harsh stench of burning coal, Darien relished the scent of woodfire. All across the encampment, his soldiers leaned over fires of wood and prairie dung, a first of the many bounties the Rhen had to offer.

Darien looked around for sight of his wife, wondering where she could have fled to. Azár had no immediate family to take her in. She also didn't seem to have any friends—at least, none that he was aware of. The life of a Lightweaver was a solitary existence. Searching the camp, Darien finally remembered that not all friends walked on two legs.

He found Azár by the horse pickets. She was rubbing down her mare's glossy coat, moving her hands in slow circles over the animal's neck. The horse followed her movements with its head, brushing its nose against her back. Smiling, Azár caught hold of the bridle and focused her attention on the mare's head.

A twig snapped under Darien's boot. Azár flinched then twisted around to look back at him. Her hands ceased their motion, and a scowl of anger twisted her face.

Darien halted, raising his hands. "I'm sorry. I know you're angry—"

She turned and stalked toward him, glaring at him with an alarming fury. She raised her hand as if to strike him. But instead of landing a blow, she lurched into his arms, growling, "Don't ever do something so stupid again."

Instead of responding, Darien picked her up and carried her into the shadows of the tall grass.

He woke to the sound of distant thunder. The sun was already up, its glaring light stabbing darts into his eyes. Darien sat up from the bed of grass he shared with Azár. He squinted against the light, his pulse kicking up as he recognized the earth-shaking rumble that was growing louder by the second.

Horses. Hundreds of horses. Perhaps thousands.

In the distance, he heard the encampment stirring.

At his side, Azár roused from sleep.

"Get back to the pavilion," he told her.

She glared at him reproachfully, looking ready to protest.

"We're in a *vortex,"* Darien snapped, reminding her of her vulnerability.

Azár's face softened, and she nodded. She rose and pulled on her clothes, muttering, "Don't do anything—"

"Stupid," Darien finished for her. "I know."

Confident she was on her way back, he dressed and strapped his sword on. By the time he returned to camp, the forward scouts had already reported in, and the encampment was in a state of readiness, waiting to receive an attack. The forward defenses had positioned themselves along the camp's western edge, taking cover behind earthworks and long lines of pickets. Darien looked out across the prairie in the direction of the rolling thunder, wondering what kind of horse lord would dare challenge an army of the size and capability of his own.

Seeing a cluster of Zakai, Darien sprinted toward them. He caught sight of Sayeed among their number. Halting in their midst, he demanded, "Report!"

Sayeed gestured toward the horizon. "A great many horse warriors approach from the west. They do not appear hostile, but their numbers are concerning."

Darien looked to the west and saw a brown plume of churned-up dust rising hugely into the sky. Sayeed was right to be concerned. The Jenn of the Cerulean Plains were fierce warriors who had little patience for outsiders infringing on their grazing territories. Gesturing for the demon-hound to remain behind, Darien made his way up the slope of a berm mounded to create a defiladed position. He halted on the top of the mound and gazed out across the sprawling sea of grass.

Dominating the prairie was a dark tide of horses carrying riders with dusky brown skin garbed in furs and hide. They were armed with arsenals of spears and hornbows, and their horses' blankets jingled with beads and bells. Darien stood motionless, astounded by the swirling sea of brutal weapons and flowing manes arrayed before him across the grassland.

He abandoned the berm and made his way back to Sayeed. "It's the Jenn," he said. "I don't think they'll attack."

"Why not?" The officer frowned.

"I know these people," Darien said, then corrected himself, "I don't *know* them, but I know a lot about them. I think they're here to negotiate." He glanced back over his shoulder.

"Negotiate what?" Sayeed's frown deepened.

"Our passage."

Darien started forward, ignoring Sayeed's look of incomprehension. Followed by the Zakai, he rounded the berm and strode toward a plank bridge that spanned a trench dug into the ground on the other side. He could hear the loud clatter of the officers' boots as they kept pace with him. Stepping off the planks, he made his way out across the mud-slathered kill zone.

Sayeed walked at his side, while the rest of the Zakai fanned out to stalk around them. Darien glanced around, seeing nothing but flat horizons and swarming horses in every direction.

"I thought you were going to stay out of harm's way," Sayeed growled under his breath.

"I'm not in harm's way."

Darien waded into the knee-high grass of the open prairie. Spread before him were thousands of horses clustered together in a great herd that spanned miles. They roved in circulating patterns, never still. There were men and women, even children. Horses and foals. An entire culture loomed before him.

Ahead, three horses broke off from the massive herd and trotted toward them. Darien halted, holding his ground, waiting for the riders to approach.

The man who rode in front had long black hair pulled back and tied in a topknot. He was dressed in furs and tanned leather and wore his full beard groomed to a tapering point. All three men rode without saddle or tack, using only the pressure of their legs to guide their mounts.

The strangers drew up only paces away. They didn't dismount, but sat staring down at Darien and Sayeed from their horses' backs. A tense silence clotted the air between them. Only the twitching of tails and the rippling of grass marked the passage of time. Eventually, the darkly bearded horselord nodded as if satisfied.

"Darius dreoch," he said in a rumbling voice.

Darien stood stunned at hearing those words. At

his side, Sayeed issued a sharp gasp. The man had spoken the ancient greeting of the Khazahar. Darien's brain fumbled to make connections that should have been obvious from the start. The man's olive skin. The bareback riding style. The horse blankets tinkling with tassels and bells.

The Jenn. These people call themselves the Jenn…

Stiffly, Darien returned the greeting. *"Darius dreoch,"* he said, then added, *"Sulimu kadreesh."*

The man glanced back and forth between Darien and Sayeed, his eyes widening. *"Akadreesh issulim,"* he responded, and jumped down from his horse. He strode forward with a wide smile to grasp Darien's arm in a two-handed grip. "I am Ranoch son of Tellat, warlord of the Jenn."

Sayeed stood speechless as the man clapped his arm in greeting.

Darien's mind scrambled as he realized the vast opportunity Ranoch and his people afforded them. The Jenn had been devoted allies of the Sentinels for hundreds of years. If he could harness that allegiance, the horse clans would be a formidable asset. Darien drew in a deep, steadying breath, wondering how far he dare go. With the Jenn, there could be no halfway.

"I am Grand Master Darien Lauchlin of the Order of Sentinels," he announced, claiming the title he had not worn since his death. "Warden of Battlemages and Overlord of the Khazahar."

"You are *him,"* Ranoch gasped, backing away. His men jumped off their mounts and surged forward, reaching for their weapons. Ranoch raised his hand, halting them.

Darien spread his arms, indicating the vast Malikari encampment behind him. "I've come to reunite you with your brethren."

The horse lord frowned. "I do not understand."

"What is the name of your tribe?"

Ranoch shook his head in incomprehension. "Once long ago, the Jenn were divided by clans. No longer. Now we are one tribe. One people."

"Do you know which tribe your people descend from?" Darien pressed.

The man answered slowly, "Once, my ancestors called themselves the Omeyan Jenn. But that was long ago. Now we are simply the Jenn."

It was Darien's turned to be astounded. These people were more than just a lost tribe—they were *his* tribe. His own blood. Quietly, he said, "Then you are my kin."

Ranoch shook his head. "That is not possible."

"My ancestor was Braden son of Marthax, of the Omeyan Clan of the Dur ul-Jenn."

Ranoch stared at him flatly. "You are a son of the Omeyans?"

Darien nodded.

The warlord crossed his arms, appearing greatly troubled as his eyes slipped slowly over the vast Malikari encampment. At last, he nodded.

"Then we are kin," Ranoch decided. He turned and shouted back over his shoulder, "Ride forward and welcome your lost brothers to our home!"

A deafening cry resounded across the plain. The horses of the Jenn broke forward as if sprinting into the charge. When they closed the gap, their riders abandoned their mounts and leaped to the ground. They dashed forward and embraced the Malikari soldiers like long-lost brothers in a surreal scene that transcended anything in Darien's broad experience.

"You never told me Braden Reis was your ancestor."

Darien glanced sideways at Sayeed. The man was frowning as he walked, his fingers stroking his sword's hooked pommel. It was obvious the omission hadn't pleased him. Darien glanced back to where the rest of the Zakai were clustered in the lee of the command tent. He wondered how the others would take the news.

"You never asked," Darien said, then admitted, "I figured it wouldn't go over very well."

The man nodded. Some of the tension eased from his face, though he still looked as though he held a fair bit of resentment. Darien berated himself for not being more honest from the start.

"I'm sorry, Brother," he said. "When we started down this road, I wasn't certain how far I could trust you. And I had reason not to."

Sayeed nodded thoughtfully. "It is probably for the best you kept that information to yourself. The name Braden Reis is cursed. It was he who brought about the Desecration. It is very unfortunate that this man's blood runs in your veins."

Darien was mildly surprised Sayeed didn't already know of his relation to the First Sentinel. When he'd been forced to provide his lineage to the elders of the clans, Sayeed had made him sit down and scribe a complete list of his pedigree. Braden Reis had been the last name on that long list. Apparently, the tribal elders hadn't shared that information with the Zakai.

"You have it wrong," Darien said. "It was Braden's brother who caused the Desecration. And it wasn't his fault. Braden and Quin were trying to save the people of Caladorn from the rule of Xerys. But they failed."

Sayeed looked at him, confusion carving deep furrows into his brow. "That is not the story that has been passed down."

"Then your story is wrong." Darien turned from him and shrugged. "It happens. Stories can change. Especially the stories of those who have suffered defeat. I had never heard of Braden's brother until I met him. His name had been erased entirely from our records."

Darien halted and stood looking around at the bustling encampment. To every side, soldiers were going about the labors of the day: honing weapons, repairing armor, cooking meals. At almost every fire stood men and women of the Jenn, watching the Tanisars as they worked, offering knowledge and answering questions. There were many facets of living in the land of sunlight that the Malikari people were ignorant of. He was glad to see them learning from their new allies.

Sayeed followed his gaze, his face darkening. "This man, Quin Reis—how did you meet a man who died a thousand years ago?"

"Because he is also a Servant of Xerys."

His answer appeared to have a great effect on Sayeed, who drew his pack from his shoulder and turned to Darien with concern in his eyes. "So this cursed man is a Servant? How can that be?"

Softly, Darien answered, "We are all cursed, Brother."

A long silence fell between them. Sayeed stood staring past him into the distance. At first, Darien couldn't tell what the man was looking at. Then it occurred to him: he was looking at the sun. Turning, he followed Sayeed's gaze. The sun had risen well above the Craghorns, burning fiercely in the brilliant sky. Before his death, he'd always taken the sun for granted. No longer. Darien realized that, for the rest of his time in this world, he should be thankful for every sunrise. He could only imagine what the Malikari must be feeling.

"We keep calling ourselves brothers," Sayeed said in a gruff voice. "Perhaps it is time to formalize this bond we claim to share."

Darien glanced at him sharply. "What do you mean?"

Sayeed's reply was measured and emotionless. "Among my people, there is a ritual that unites two men as kin."

"How does that work?" Darien had never heard of such a thing, although it didn't surprise him. The Malikari seemed to have a ritual for everything. For a people whose very existence was defined by chaos, such a highly methodized culture added an element of structure to their lives.

Sayeed took Darien by the arm and drew two fingers across the palm of his right hand. "Your blood and my blood would be mixed, as though we had been born of the same father."

"A blood rite," Darien concluded, not liking the sound of it. The only other blood ritual he'd experienced had ended with the chains of his Oath cleaved from his wrists. The day he'd pledged himself to the goddess of Death to become her hand of vengeance. Which brought Darien to another thought equally disturbing: he had sworn his life to a goddess and sworn his afterlife to a god. He wasn't sure how much was left of him to pledge to Sayeed.

"And what would that mean for us?" Darien asked warily.

Sayeed retracted his hand. "We would become family, in every sense of the word. Our fates and fortunes would be joined. I would support you—and your wife, and any children you might have—in all ways. I would fight at your side in every battle. I would second you in any feud. And upon your death, I would put you in your grave, and provide for your family as though they were my own. Just as you would do the same for me."

Darien dropped his gaze, feeling overwhelmed. What Sayeed was offering…it went beyond natural bonds of blood. True brothers were seldom so dedicated to each other. He felt unworthy of receiving such a commitment from another human. He couldn't fathom it.

He struggled to find words. It took him a

moment. "I had a brother once. I didn't get to choose him; I never would have. But if I'd had a choice, I would have chosen you instead." He knew his response wasn't eloquent, or even sufficient, but it was as close as he could manage.

Sayeed's smile was jubilant. He clapped Darien on the back. "We need your wife. And we need witnesses!"

Before Darien could respond, the man scooped up his pack and hauled him forward by the arm in the direction of the command tent. Darien was pressed to keep up, pulled along by Sayeed's enthusiasm. He was a little taken aback—he hadn't expected Sayeed to act on the agreement immediately.

"Can't this wait?" he gasped, thinking of the scores of other things he should be doing at the moment. He had a war council to convene, the Jenn to attend to, a land to conquer—

"These things do not wait!" his First exclaimed in a reproving tone. "We are at war, and neither one of us is guaranteed to live another day."

Darien grunted an acknowledgement. There was logic to that reasoning, he supposed. He followed Sayeed into camp along the main road that bisected the grid of tents, separating the Khazahari side of the encampment from the Calazi and Mandun armies. Banners of different colors fluttered above the tents, each emblazoned with the symbols and emblems of their units.

When they arrived at the pavilion, Darien lurched to a halt. He stood in a patch of trampled grass, staring at the sight of Azár armed with a wooden sword facing off against one of Sayeed's Zakai. They were slowly circling each other, blades poised and ready to strike. Azár lunged first, the waster in her hand parried by the officer's wooden blade. She pulled back, raising her practice sword to block the man's attack. But she moved a second too slow—the officer's wood blade connected with her chest. Azár jerked away with a growl, moving her waster back to high-ward.

Darien exchanged glances with Sayeed. Azár's movements were halting, her footwork clumsy. But her focus was intense. He had no doubt that, with time and practice, she could be quite competent with a sword. He came up behind her and grasped her sword arm, gently lowering her blade to mid-ward, and adjusted her grip.

"That's better," he said. "Otherwise, he'll just come in under your guard. Unless you're trying to feint. But I wouldn't worry about that just now."

Azár turned to him, lowering her waster to her side. She flashed him a confident smile.

"Warden." Her Zakai opponent saluted with his sword and then backed away.

Darien nodded in acknowledgement. To Azár, he said, "If you wanted to learn the dance of the blade, you could have asked me."

Azár's smile grew mischievous. "I wished to surprise my husband."

"I'm not surprised at all." His wife was the most competent woman he'd ever known. Azár had the heart and spirit of a warrior, traits he found captivating. He took her by the hand, drawing her away. "Come. I need you as a witness."

She glanced at him with a bewildered expression, then turned to look suspiciously at Sayeed. The officer walked toward them carrying a large bowl in his hands, flanked by a grave-faced group of Zakai.

"What is this?" Azár asked, tossing her practice sword on the ground.

"Sayeed asked me to become his brother by blood," Darien admitted. "I told him I'd be honored."

Azár beamed at him and kissed his cheek. "I am glad for you. You are too alone in this world."

Perhaps she was right. She usually was.

"I need your dagger," Sayeed said. He handed the bowl to a soldier at his side, then waited as his men spread out to encircle them. Darien glanced around at the ring of witnesses, feeling suddenly uncomfortable. The officers stood at attention, their faces expressionless, as if they were witnessing some formal and weighty ceremony. He hadn't realized Sayeed's ritual would amount to such a solemn ordeal.

Darien drew his dagger from its sheath and handed it to his First. Sayeed caught his forearm and forced his sleeve back to his elbow. Without hesitation, the officer drew a wide cut across Darien's palm, slicing his skin. The wound didn't bleed at first. But when the blood started, it flowed liberally down his arm.

Sayeed handed Darien back his dagger then drew his own, pressing it into his hand. Without hesitation, Darien made a similar incision in Sayeed's flesh. The officer sheathed his dagger and retrieved the bowl, which he used to collect their spilled blood. Another man stepped forward to add some wine to the pooling liquid. Darien's stomach roiled, seeing the blood swirling around in the wine. To his disgust, Sayeed raised the bowl to his lips and took a great swallow, wiping his mouth.

In a voice rigid with formality, Sayeed proclaimed, "Before the gods, I pledge my loyalty to this man, Darien Lauchlin of Amberlie, and take him into my heart as blood of my blood."

He passed the bowl to Darien. Darien stared down at the ghastly concoction, feeling his stomach tighten with nausea. Naia had forced him to drink from a chalice of his own blood to consummate his vow to her goddess. He still remembered the awful taste of it in his mouth.

Holding his breath, Darien raised the bowl and let the thick, warm liquid run into his mouth. Gagging, he forced himself to swallow it down. The wine did little to cut the sharp metallic taste of the blood.

Swallowing back bile, Darien stated gruffly, "Before the gods, I pledge my loyalty to this man, Sayeed son of Alborz, and take him into my heart as blood of my blood."

Hearing his words, the soldiers standing around finally let their discipline slip and let out a bellowing war cry. Sayeed swept forward and clapped Darien against his chest in an exuberant hug. At first, Darien recoiled from the touch. But he steadied himself and drew his wife in to include her in the embrace.

For the first time in his life, Darien felt grateful to have a family. And for the first time in a long while, he knew true happiness.

But the moment expired quickly, as he was struck by the harsh slap of reason. He pulled away, suddenly regretting his decision. He had forgotten who he was. And what he was. He hadn't been brought back into the world to form ties of kinship. He'd been brought back for a singular purpose. And when that purpose was fulfilled, any bonds he'd made along the way would shatter painfully.

Especially for those he left behind.

Chapter Thirteen
Tendrils of Portent

Isle of Titherry, The Rhen

It had been another five days with no sign of Tsula.

The Harbinger had disappeared again without warning. Naia had no idea where she had gone, though she had some idea what the woman was doing. Tsula was undoubtedly taking readings from Athera's Crescent. But where she went to do that— and how she went about it— remained a mystery. So Naia had been forced to content herself with waiting, not knowing how long that wait would last or what would come from it.

She had spent the past few days in the castle's vast library, which occupied the upper three floors. The walls were painted white, and the ceiling was a massive series of vaults covered in bright frescoes. Shelves filled with books lined the walls—all three stories—accessible by colonnaded walkways. It was the most beautiful library Naia had ever beheld, and it contained more information than she had ever seen gathered in one place.

Naia walked the long hallway back to her room with her arms full of books. She deposited her findings on the desk and then went looking for Quin. He wasn't hard to find; he'd barely ventured out of his own room in days. He'd been carving a staff out of core wood from one of the castle's many trees. It was a dark and knobby thing, roughly his own height, unadorned. Some kind of artifact, he insisted, and she believed him. She had witnessed the scope of his talents with both the Soulstone and the Crescent's conduit. Naia had no doubt he could accomplish any task he set his mind to.

She didn't bother to knock—he'd told her not to. She entered and found Quin sitting on his bed, sprawled back in a tall cushion of pillows with the staff laid across his body. He had his glasses on and was fiddling with some instrument that looked like a needle-thin probe. His roll of tools lay next to him on the bed, and an assortment of small vials was arranged beside him on a table. The vials contained a diverse collection of tiny crystals attuned to different characters of the magic field.

Lingering in the doorway, Naia asked, "How is it coming along?"

Quin raised the staff and looked down the length of it. Naia wasn't sure what he could possibly be checking for; the shaft was warped and gnarled, hardly straight.

Setting it back down, Quin shrugged and looked up at her. "Certainly not my best work, but it will have to suffice. I won't be able to give it enough time to properly season. Here, take a feel of it and tell me what you think."

He sat up and offered her the staff. Naia took it and held it vertically. The staff was taller than she was, and lighter than expected. It didn't feel like core wood.

Almost immediately, she felt the power imbued in the staff creep up her arm. It felt cold, like a reptile in the morning shade. The feel of it was unnerving, unnatural. Naia handed the staff back quickly, rubbing her hand to rid herself of the disturbing sensation.

"What's wrong with it?"

Quin grinned, obviously amused by her reaction. "It's a shadow staff," he said, laying the artifact across the bed and standing up. "Working with shadow is difficult. It's contrary to human nature."

"I should say so!" Naia thought of the times she had seen Darien weave shadow. She shivered. "I didn't realize it was so evil."

"It's not." Quin smirked. "Ever since we were children, we've learned to be afraid of the dark. It's a very primal fear. To work with shadow, you have to conquer that fear. Which is difficult, because it's very ingrained. Most mages can't tolerate it."

"I'll leave you to it." Changing the subject, she said, "I was just up in the library again. There's an awful lot of knowledge amassed there."

Quin strolled around the bed to scoop up a small cup of coffee from a bureau against the wall. "I should imagine," he said, taking a sip. "Once they were identified, apprentice Harbingers never studied in the Lyceum or Aerysius. They learned everything here."

"Why was that?"

"It was always a very secretive Order." Quin shrugged as he sat back down on the bed. "Because there is only one Crescent, it had to be shared by both the Lyceum *and* Aerysius. So the Harbingers had to go to great lengths to make certain readings from the Crescent couldn't be used for political or military gain."

He reached over to the table and picked up a leaf-wrapped cigar. He bit off the end and sent it flying across the room. He touched the other end to the shadow staff and smiled when a thin tendril of smoke appeared. Bringing the cigar up, Quin closed his eyes and drew in a long mouthful of smoke.

"I see you've been tinkering again," stated a low voice.

Naia turned to find Tsula standing in the doorway.

"Good," the Harbinger said. "We will be in need of your skills, so hone them well."

Quin puffed harder on the cigar, breathing out a great cloud of smoke. "You're assuming I still want to help you."

Tsula folded her arms, looking down the length of her nose at him. "You do not have a choice. If we destroy the magic field, then the Curse shall be lifted. Magic and mages will be gone—but our civilizations will be restored."

Quin appeared to mull over her words. "It's not going to be that easy. Even if the Curse was lifted today, there haven't been any plants growing in the Black Lands for a thousand years. There's no seeds in the dirt, and nothing to fertilize them. I don't imagine everything will come bounding back just the same as before."

"No," Tsula confirmed darkly. "It will take hundreds of years before the affected lands can be resettled. But it's the only option we have."

Quin looked sideways at her. "What if there's another option you don't know about?"

"There are no other options, Quinlan Reis. Or I would have foreseen them."

Quin's eyes narrowed. "Prove it."

Naia looked back and forth between Quin and the Harbinger, wondering who the victor of the exchange would be. Both participants seemed equally matched.

Tsula made a *tsk*ing noise with her tongue. "My readings do not work that way. You will have to trust my word."

Quin smiled sardonically around his cigar. "I learned a long time ago not to trust the word of people who tell me I have to trust their word."

Tsula paced deeper into the room. Naia moved out of her way as the Harbinger strode across the patterned rugs to stand towering before Quin, arms crossed and eyes narrowed, glaring down at him.

"The only way I could show proof of my claims is to teach you to read the Crescent yourself. Which is impossible. You are not a Harbinger."

"So make me a Harbinger."

"You know I can't do that. You are already sealed to your Order."

Quin's eyes shot to Naia. Holding his cigar between his fingers, he said, "But Naia isn't. You can teach her."

Before Naia could protest, Tsula snapped in a tone of disgust, "The magic field will reverse in two months' time. I could not possibly teach her all she would need to know in only two months."

"Who said anything about two months?" Quin ashed his cigar. "I'll be magnanimous and give you a week. After that, I'm afraid you'll have to make other arrangements, because Naia and I will be leaving."

Tsula gritted her teeth, her eyes narrowing in anger. She wrinkled her nose at a puff of smoke that drifted her way. "You cannot leave. I cannot destroy the magic field by myself!"

"Then I suppose you'd better get started." Quin smiled triumphantly, popping the cigar back into his mouth.

Naia stared at him, wide-eyed and appalled. She did not want to be trained as a Harbinger. She couldn't imagine living a life of seclusion in the castle. She had other, much more pressing things to do—

"You are a fool, Quinlan Reis," Tsula growled.

Quin blew a long trail of smoke out the side of his mouth. It curled toward Tsula's face. "Not just any fool, but a *persistent* fool. And believe me—there is no more dangerous creature on this earth."

Tsula backed away, making a face. She whirled around, snapping over her shoulder, "Come, child. Leave the fool to his foolishness."

Naia shot a glare at Quin, who responded by raising his eyebrows. She moved quickly to follow Tsula out the door and into the hallway, their steps resounding sharply off the walls.

Naia walked in silence, following Tsula through the echoing emptiness of the castle's ground floor, then out onto the long balcony that overlooked the Crescent. The air was cool but not cold, the sky clear, the surrounding mountains gleaming white. Even though the island had been freed from winter's reign, snow still lingered at the higher elevations. Tsula walked across the balcony to the stone-carved balustrade. Gripping it with her hands, she turned back to Naia.

"What I'm about to divulge to you is a secret known only to Harbingers. Think very carefully before we proceed another step. Once we start down this path, there is no turning back." She stood waiting for an answer, her eyes daring Naia to change her mind.

Naia wanted none of it. But she had a duty to the people of the Rhen. Even the people of Malikar. She had no choice but to blindly follow the woman down a road she would likely regret.

Squaring her shoulders, Naia said, "Show me what I need to know."

With one last, disparaging glance, the woman let go of the balustrade and walked *through* it. Standing on the air above the Crescent, Tsula turned and beckoned. "Then walk the path, if you dare."

Naia gazed down at Athera's Crescent then looked back up at the Harbinger. No stranger to mysteries, she wasn't disturbed by the odd circumstance of the woman standing in midair. It could be a trick, she realized. It was possible Tsula was suspended by magic, and there really was nothing beneath her feet to hold her up. Perhaps she was lingering there, taunting, hoping Naia would step off the balcony and plunge to her death.

But Naia didn't think so.

She had no reason in the world to trust Tsula.

And yet, for some reason, she did. Naia walked forward, passing through the balustrade as if it were made of gauze. She took a step off the balcony and jolted to a halt. Ahead of her appeared an arching path of glass stepping stones, carefully placed with small gaps between. Feeling a sharp twist of fear, Naia cast an accusing glare at Tsula. The woman could have warned her about the broken nature of the path. The Harbinger turned back around with a gloating smile and continued up toward what appeared to be a floating glass orb that hovered over the crescent, opalescent and gleaming in the sunlight.

"What is that?" Naia asked, staring up at their destination. A cool breeze tossed her hair about her shoulders.

Without looking back, the woman informed her, "It is the Nexus. It is where the infinite versions of the Story are read."

Naia lowered her eyes from the gleaming Nexus, taking great care in the placement of her feet. "How is it possible that I didn't notice this was here?"

"Your eyes see the Nexus," Tsula informed her, stepping onto a thin and invisible ledge that ringed the orb. "But your mind has been instructed to ignore what your eyes are telling it. It is the effect of a ward. It is a last resort, should all other means fail to protect the Crescent."

Naia stepped off the path and onto what appeared to be a glass shelf that sank slightly beneath her weight. Looking back over her shoulder, she saw the castle far below them. The path had taken them much further than it had seemed. They were hovering suspended in the air hundreds of feet above the liquid surface of the Crescent.

Gesturing for her to follow, Tsula stepped through the crystalline wall of the Nexus. Naia followed hesitantly, closing her eyes as she moved through what seemed like the thin membrane of a bubble.

She found herself standing within a spherical chamber made of shadow, interrupted by twisting tendrils of silver. The ambient light came from nowhere and everywhere. The curving walls absorbed every last drop of that light, sucking it out of the air as if feeding their hunger. Only the fine filaments of silver were visible, writhing over the curving texture of the walls. Naia realized they moved as if living things, branching and unbranching, weaving and unweaving, ambling over the walls like a living tangle of silver vines.

Tsula stopped in the center of the chamber and turned back to Naia. "The Crescent detects fluctuations in the magic field. Any disturbance of the field creates ripples in the patterns. The Crescent magnifies those ripples and interprets them. It separates the probable from the possible. We use the information it collects to read the myriad versions of the Everlasting Story."

"That is an interesting way of putting it," Naia said, moving toward Tsula and the heart of the spherical chamber.

The Harbinger opened her hands in an expansive gesture. "Every life is a chapter in the Book of All Things that tells the Everlasting Story. As a person lives their life, it is as though the mightiest of all pens is scribing their own personal Story. As long as a Story is not yet complete, it can have any number of possible endings. We call these possibilities versions. But when a Story is complete, the ending has already been written, and cannot be changed. The final version has been penned."

Naia concluded, "So a person can only see the possible versions of their own Story?"

"That is correct." The Harbinger nodded. She clasped her hands in front of her.

"But not other people's Stories?" Naia's eyes scanned the dark, curving walls, watching the thin silver vines tangle and untangle, twist and untwist. It was dizzying, mesmerizing. It made her stomach edge toward nausea.

"No," Tsula answered. "A Harbinger can only read the possible versions of their own Story. That is why Harbingers always lived apart from other mages. To read the versions of the Book of All Things, a Harbinger must be exposed to the world: living it, experiencing it. But no other person should ever know a Harbinger for what she or he is. Such would influence the versions and therefore influence the Story as it is being penned."

Naia frowned, reassessing everything she knew about the Order of Harbingers. Or thought she knew. Never was there an order of mages so cloaked in secrets and mystery. And outright misinformation. "So the Harbingers were not isolated, after all. They would have to come and go from the island frequently."

"Correct."

"But you haven't left the island in a thousand years," she protested. "Surely that must affect your Story. How much could you possibly know about the state of the world?"

Tsula narrowed her eyes, raising her chin. "Nothing about the Reversal or the magic field has changed in a thousand years. The solutions I have seen are still valid."

The silver vines twined and untwined, wove and unwove.

"How can I read my own Story?"

"When you are ready, the Crescent will show you all possible versions of your Story and separate the likely from the unlikely."

"That's all there is to it?" It was too simple. Naia's eyes wandered over the scrolling tendrils.

"Yes. The Crescent interprets the ripples in the magic field and uses those ripples to present your versions. As a Harbinger, you would merely read your own Story."

Naia turned all the way around, her mind echoing the confusion of the tendrils. "That's ridiculously simple. Why, then, would it take years of training to produce a Harbinger?"

Tsula explained, "It is not reading the Story that is difficult. What is difficult is knowing which knowledge to divulge, and which to hold back—no matter the cost. If used without wisdom and restraint, the Crescent could be made to work great evil. And a Harbinger must learn how to digest the information that is revealed without internalizing it."

"That makes sense." Naia yawned. She was becoming tired. The vines were beginning to blur and run together, weeping silver tears down the length of the curving walls. It seemed the world wept with them.

Tsula announced, "That is your lesson for the day. I want you to think very long and very hard on all I have revealed."

Naia didn't respond. She stared transfixed at the writhing tendrils.

"You have taken your first steps down the path that will make you a Harbinger. You still do not have a good understanding of which knowledge is safe to share, and which knowledge is necessary to hold back. At this point in your training, you shall share nothing. A Harbinger must remain absolutely neutral in all things. You must understand that anything you tell Quinlan Reis could have dire and everlasting consequences."

"I understand," Naia whispered.

Tsula barked, "'I understand, *Warden Renquist.*'"

Naia's attention snapped into acute focus. "I beg your pardon?"

The vines flinched all around the walls, then twinged away into nothingness. The Nexus darkened. Naia's pulse throbbed, shuddering in her ears. She stared aghast at the woman who stood before her with all the power and dignity of an empress.

The Harbinger took a step forward then informed her with a graceful sweep of her hand, "You are now my apprentice, so I expect you to address me by my proper title. I am Tsula Renquist, Warden of the Order of Harbingers. When the two of us are alone, you will address me as Warden Renquist. But when we are not alone, you are to address me simply as Tsula. Am I understood?"

Naia nodded, feeling her face whiten and her extremities go numb. She whispered, "Warden Renquist…if I may ask…?"

The woman lifted her chin and answered Naia's unspoken question, "I am the wife of Prime Warden Zavier Renquist."

Naia shook her head in confusion. It was impossible.

It is possible, the silver tendrils whispered at her from wherever they had twined away to. Or perhaps it was her own mind vining around the thought. Her heart, like the walls, wept mercurial blood.

"But how could that be?" she gasped. "Weren't you just lecturing me about the importance of neutrality? How could you be both a Harbinger and the wife of a demon?"

Tsula walked toward her until she stood only inches away, her black eyes as harsh and cold as obsidian. Folding her arms, she said carefully, "That is indeed a very important question, especially for you. I suggest you spend some time searching your own soul for the answer to it. Good day."

Naia fled the chamber of darkness and tendrils and secrets, to emerge shaken into the cruel glare of sunlight. Shielding her eyes, she hurried down the glass footpath that sloped toward the castle's balcony. Her mind reeled with an overload of information, trying to forage through tumbling thoughts and twisting fears. Nothing seemed to make sense, and yet everything did. Her footsteps rang off the walls of the castle's corridors.

As she walked, she could feel the silvery tendrils groping within her mind.

Throwing open the door to Quin's room, Naia hesitated, feeling conflicted. The Harbinger was right; she would have to be careful. She would not reveal more than she had to. Whether she liked it or not, secrets had been entrusted to her. Secrets that were dangerous to share.

But some secrets were too dangerous not to share.

Quin looked up at her, startled, and laid down his staff. He rose halfway from the bed.

"We have to kill Tsula," Naia gasped.

Quin paused in the action of standing up, straightening only slowly. His face darkened in confusion. "Why?"

Because she is Zavier Renquist's wife! The silvery tendrils in Naia's head constricted at the thought. She brought her hands up to clutch her temples.

"Because she sees only two options!" She felt the vines relax a bit. "If any other options exist, then we won't know about them unless she's dead."

Quin frowned, stroking the whiskers on his chin. "Why not?"

The tendrils tightened just a bit. Naia closed her eyes and forced the words out. "Because if any other option was part of *her* Story, she would have seen it already."

"I don't understand."

"You're not meant to understand." Naia shook her head. She was starting to feel panicked. It was as though her mind were being ripped away from her control. As if she were losing herself.

"Please trust me," she gasped. "You're an assassin—*and I need you to kill Tsula.*"

Quin regarded her a long, silent moment. His eyes roamed her face the way the harshest critic might study the work of an amateur. At last he nodded. "All right, then. I'll kill Tsula. But only because it's you doing the asking."

Chapter Fourteen
Ruthless

The Cerulean Plains, The Rhen

A cold fog descended, roiling like billowing clouds of smoke. Darien's armor was frigid, sapping the heat right out of him, and the mist collecting on his face felt like pinpricks of ice. He reined in, looking out at the muffled lights of a town visible through a tangled windbreak of trees. His horse stood on the edge of a field of winter wheat ready for the harvest: a bounty his people needed desperately.

He was determined to claim it for them.

He glanced to his right, at a mounted wedge of Zakai, their armor gleaming orange in the light of the torches they held. To his left, Azár sat mounted on a fresh courser she had claimed from the Jenn's vast herd. She looked ferocious in her black armor, her gleaming short sword in her hand. The look of eagerness on her face was chilling, and yet beautiful to behold.

"What town is this?" Sayeed asked him.

"Gannet."

The man grunted. "What kind of people live here?"

"It doesn't matter."

There came the dull thrumming of hoofbeats pounding against damp, compacted soil: their scouts returning from the town. The riders broke through the billowing mist, loping toward them across the dark field of grain. When the men drew up, they removed their helms and ducked their heads. The nearest scout, long-haired and bearded, was having a hard time holding his mount in check. It shied away from the light of the torches, dancing sideways and tugging at the reins. Of the six men who rode with him, only Sayeed was a proficient rider. That should change, though. There were many long leagues between Gannet and Rothscard.

"Warden, the town stands mostly unguarded. There are a few outlying farms, but most are empty. There is some type of festivity. Many people are gathered in a large structure on the far side of town."

"Good." Darien jerked his head, signaling the scout to join the line of men spread out at his sides. It was helpful that the townsfolk would be clustered together. That meant a more direct confrontation and less chasing about.

"Let's go."

He donned his helm then stabbed his heals into his horse's flanks. The stallion sprinted forward, the Zakai following behind. They gained the edge of the field and plunged into a snarl of willows. Whipping branches lashed at Darien's helm, reaching out for him, as if eager to tear him off his horse. The stallion hurled onto a wide road within earshot of the town's barred gate. Shouts rang out over the mist as the townsfolk responded to their attack, too late. A group of men spilled out to ward the gate, swords and shields in their hands.

Darien reined in as the Zakai charged past him, rushing the defenders. They made short work of the townsmen with their spears then pulled back from the barred gate.

Darien drew on the Hellpower. It was all he could resort to. Orien's vortex still spun the lines of the magic field into a deadly cyclone of power, so he was forced to keep his mind walled away from it. The Onslaught was slipperier than the magic field, but far more comforting, filling him with a tingling euphoria. He narrowed his eyes and focused his will on the gate.

The gate imploded, spiraling in on itself in a whirlwind of splinters, until it disappeared with a mortal groan. On the other side of the opening, a group of townsfolk stood with eyes wide and horrified. They looked up from the fallen bodies in the road, at the smoldering hole in the air that had swallowed the gate. They backed away slowly, lowering their weapons, then turned to bolt.

Darien let the Zakai enter first. They whipped their horses forward, charging down the center of the street, driving the fleeing townsfolk before them. Men and women fell beneath the thundering hooves of horses. Many fled into doorways or bolted down alleys. The charging Zakai followed in pursuit, their swords and spears inspiring panic.

The soldiers pulled up and, leaping from their mounts, began ranging house to house. They kicked in doors and shattered windows, flushing the occupants out into the streets. A few townsfolk offered resistance, only to be trampled by horses or gored by spears. The dead collected in the dirt, littering the street. The sounds of screams and the clatter of hooves grew distant as the population was herded toward the far side of town.

Darien slid from his horse's back. He stalked down the center of the road, blade drawn, stepping over bodies lying in dark pools of blood. Some still breathed. With a thought, he stopped their breathing. Fires crackled in the distance, their glows whipping the shadows. The demon-hound paced at his side, eyes gleaming with the taint of the Netherworld. Azár patrolled the side of the road, her sword bared and threatening.

The sound of a crying babe came from one of the houses. Darien started toward it, finding the door barred. He kicked it open. The wood splintered, giving way with a crack. He stepped into the gloomy interior, preceded by the haunting glow of fires. Looking around, he made out the forms of a family huddled under a table in a corner.

At his side, the thanacryst bared its teeth and emitted a low growl. A child shrieked over the sound of a baby whimpering. With a glare, Darien sent the demon-hound back outside then gestured at the doorway with his sword.

"Get out."

The woman leaped for the doorway, clutching her baby and dragging the older child behind her into the street. The man rose slowly, holding his hands up. He edged toward the door, keeping his eyes fixed on Darien's blade. When he reached the threshold, he stopped and glanced back.

Darien stepped sideways, avoiding the dagger that swept out at him. He brought his blade up in a sharp motion. The man groaned, clutching his gut as his entrails slithered out of him. He sank to his knees then collapsed to the floor.

Darien kicked the dying man out of his way and sprinted back into the street, scanning the shadows for Azár. He found her pressed up against a wall, stalking two men armed with swords who stood guarding the entrance to an alley. Darien wasn't certain she could take them both. He wasn't going to stand aside and find out.

"Visea," he whispered.

From the ground rose two living shadows that glided hellishly forward through the night. The necrators were noticed too late. The men's screams ended in sobs. The sobs ended in silence. His minions moved away, roving in a search pattern across the street. They would reap their own dark reward, ridding Gannet of any living that remained.

Darien strode to Azár and caught her by the hand. Fingers laced with hers, he walked at her side in the direction of the fires. A guard of five Zakai moved behind them, swords drawn, eyes warily scanning the rooftops.

A crossbow bolt shot past Darien's face, so close he could feel the wind of its flight. With a cry, Azár released his hand and bolted toward a building on the far side of the street. Taken off-guard, it took Darien a moment to catch up with her. He found his wife in an alley, foot planted on the chest of a man who lay dying on the ground. She twisted her sword and jerked it out of him. A repeating crossbow lay in the dirt with quarrels spilled from the magazine. Azár turned to face him, a ferocious light in her eyes.

Together with their guard of Zakai, Darien walked, holding his wife's hand, down the now-empty streets of Gannet, to a square ringed by stone houses. In the center of the square, Darien found the rest of his men gathered before a two-story inn with a shingle roof and mismatched sides. Seeing their approach, the soldiers parted to admit them into their midst. Darien drew up beside Sayeed in time to hear a report from a torch-bearing Zakai.

"Many of the townspeople have taken refuge in the building," the soldier informed them. "They braced the doors."

Darien looked over to the inn and saw the problem: the windows were set too high to break through, and there didn't seem to be another entrance. It was a problem easily solved. Darien took the torch from the Zakai and walked across the square toward the inn. He tossed the torch onto a second-floor balcony. The planks caught immediately, the fire racing up the sides of the building and across the roof.

"Either they'll come out or they won't," he said.

He made his way back through the crowd of soldiers and set off down the street without looking back. His lengthened shadow strode before him, cast by the crackling fire that consumed the inn. The sounds of screams clawed at the night, echoed through Gannet's empty streets. The demon-hound jogged up and travelled at his side, tail wagging approval, eyes glistening a hellish green.

Darien strode away from the encampment into the open prairie. As he walked, he spread his hands out at his sides, feeling the blades of grass slide over his palms. Well away from the camp, he stopped and stood gazing at the sky. The waxing moon was already making its slow descent toward the horizon. Its light spilled across the prairie, transforming the grassland into a silver ocean, its soft tides stirred by the night air. Above, the stars glittered in a sky devoid of roiling clouds. It ranged enormously above him, a vast reminder of his purpose. Even that did little to comfort him.

When he closed his eyes, he saw fires. Fires that raged within his memory, threatening to engulf him. The inn. Myria. Orien's Finger, Arden Hanna. Aerysius. Despite the cool night air, Darien broke out in a sweat. He clenched his fists at his sides, squeezing his eyes shut, grappling to smother the visions.

A scuffing noise made him flinch. Turning, he saw that Sayeed had come up behind him unnoticed. He hadn't realized the man was there, which was terrifying. So entrenched was he in his thoughts that he'd ignored the basics of self-preservation. He nodded a curt greeting, raking the sweat off his brow with a shirtsleeve. The fabric came away black with soot.

Darien asked, "Did they come out?"

"No."

He nodded and cast his stare at the ground.

Sayeed said, "What now, Brother? Can you live without mercy for your own people?"

Darien's stared at him, filled with a sudden, terrible anger. "They're not my people any longer! I can't afford to have mercy any longer! If I soften my tactics *one damn bit,* then the next town won't have forty defenders—there'll be eighty. And the next town will have two hundred! *My tactics save lives."*

"Then find your nerve, Brother," Sayeed said. "We can't afford for you to lose resolve."

His First turned and headed back toward the camp while Darien remained behind, struggling with brute self-loathing. With a growl, he raked his shirtsleeve back, exposing the bandage that encircled his palm. He tore it off, revealing the half-healed cut Sayeed had made there. He unsheathed his dagger and drew the edge of the blade across the wound. Beads of blood appeared along the cut, then ran, streaking down his arm. He closed his eyes, relishing the pain. It had an edge to it that diverted his mind from the rage of the fires. He replaced the bandage, using his teeth to pull the knot tight.

He yanked his sleeve down and strode after Sayeed. It took a while to make his way back to the encampment. There, he trudged down ordered pathways between rows of tents, until he found the command pavilion. Tugging his boots off, he tossed them aside. He batted back the flaps and ducked in, instantly confronted by a strong combination of pipe smoke and body odor. He picked his way around sleeping men and women, slipping through the tent's partition.

Azár was already in bed, asleep. He stood gazing at the curve of her body beneath the covers, outlined by the diffuse moonlight filtering through the canvas. The sight of her soothed his fury somewhat. He removed his clothes, tossed them into a corner, then sank down beside her in the bed.

Azár stirred from sleep. "Husband—"

He silenced her with a kiss, driven by a desperate need to smother his rage in her. Darien felt her stiffen beneath him. He stopped and lay unmoving, stroking her hair, until the tension eased from her body.

Kissing her softly, he took what he needed.

———

Three great bonfires crackled in the center of the camp, tongues of flame whipping at the air. Sparks showered upward, flitting like fireflies, obscured by rolling clouds of smoke. The Malikari soldiers had gathered to one side of the fires. On the other side clustered men and women of the Jenn, clothed in horse skins and dripping with armaments. War drums beat and instruments played, vying for dominance over shouts and chants in a boisterous contortion of noise.

Darien stood beside Ranoch in the center of the gathering. The war chief raised both hands above his head, calling for silence. It took a moment. But, gradually, the drums halted and the instruments tapered off. The shouts quieted to a blur of conversation. The conversation ceased. The only sound that remained was the crackle of flames. Darien turned, his eyes skimming over the hundreds of people gathered before him.

Ranoch stepped forward, raising his voice as he announced, "Darien Lauchlin, the men and women of the Jenn have gathered to hear you speak. Say what you have come to say."

Darien nodded, stepping forward. Raising his voice, he address all those gathered around. "*Darius dreoch.* My name is Grand Master Darien Lauchlin of the Order of Sentinels. I am here to ask you to lend your aid to your brothers and sisters from the north. We flee a land that has known only darkness for a thousand years. Our situation has become desperate—we have reached a crux. Either we flee the Black Lands, or we die of starvation. We no longer have a choice."

He paused, sweeping his eyes over the gathered crowd. "The monarchies of the Rhen have decided that we should perish in darkness. No people deserve that. We don't deserve that. We ask that you help us make a place for ourselves at your sides, where we can build homes and harvest food. A place where our children can grow to adulthood knowing the light of the sun.

"A thousand years ago, the horse tribes of the Khazahar formed the cavalry of Caladorn's combined legions. Today, those same legions ask that you ride with us again. Help us claim this land for ourselves. Help us *survive.* We ask this of you, not only in the name of blood, but also in the name of decency."

He backed away from the glow of the fires, while Ranoch moved forward to take his place. The war chief raised his voice and addressed his gathered people:

"The call of a Sentinel must be answered! It is our sacred duty to ride at his side! People of the Jenn, what say you?"

A thunderous cry went up as men and women surged to their feet, waving their arms and armaments in support of Ranoch's request. The war horns and drums racketed back to life, booming above the commotion. The war chief turned back to Darien with a triumphant smile on his face.

"Warden Lauchlin, your request has been heard. Your people are welcome to our food, our fires, and our protection. We will ride by your side, and your enemies shall be our enemies. Together, we will conquer the North!"

Ranoch took him by the arm and led him away from the fires and the cacophony of the celebration. Darien followed him a little ways out into the dark shadows and cool air of the grassland. They paused under a stand of oak trees.

Looking back at the fires of the gathering, Darien told the war chief, "You have my thanks. Without you, we wouldn't have received that kind of support."

The man nodded, smiling wryly. "You owe me. Someday, I'll ask you to return the favor."

"Gladly." Darien answered Ranoch's smile with his own. Then he grew serious. Now that the treaty was secured, he could waste no time in ironing out the details. He said, "I'm going to need to divide our forces. Together, there are too many people for us to feed. If we split our numbers, we split our need for resources."

Ranoch nodded. "That is wise."

Darien continued, "The army of Maridur will remain behind to defend our train. The army of Bryn Calazar will continue southward and lay siege to

Rothscard. I'll take a smaller force south through the Vale of Amberlie to assault Glen Farquist. I ask that you divide your riders and travel with our armies."

Ranoch took hold of his arm, clutching it in a two-handed grip. Solemnly, he promised, "We are yours. And you are ours, as it was a thousand years ago. The lost tribes of Caladorn have been reunited. We will always ride where you lead."

Chapter Fifteen
Versions of Calamity

Isle of Titherry, The Rhen

Naia stepped through the swirling colors of the membrane into the dark inner sphere of the Nexus. The transition reminded her of entering the Catacombs of Death: there was just a moment's disorientation, as if the world shuddered and then stabilized. The curving walls within were the quintessence of black, and they enclosed her like a womb. The silvery tendrils pulsed once as if welcoming her into their midst, twirling and untwirling.

Tsula had arrived before her. The Harbinger stood in the dim nonlight that came from everywhere and cast no shadow. Folded in a bronze kaftan and absent her signature turban, Tsula looked like a cast human sculpture, standing bald and daunting in the center of the chamber. At the sight of Naia, Tsula gestured with her hand, commanding her forward.

"Today, I will teach you how to read."

Naia knew Tsula wasn't referring to letters or words. Her stomach twinged its apprehension. The Harbinger set her hands on Naia's shoulders, turning her gently but firmly around and moving to stand behind her. Naia could feel Tsula's breath against the back of her neck as her hands slid from her shoulders to grip her arms.

"Empty your mind, child."

Naia closed her eyes and pushed her thoughts aside, until the only thing she saw within was blackness. In the absence of thought, her breathing became more relevant. Each swell and release of breath was like waves breaking and then retreating along a shoreline. She could feel her heartbeat in her temples: a serene and stately rhythm.

"Now, you must read each version of your Story in order." The Harbinger's voice was a low, whispering echo in her ear. "You cannot begin reading another version until the previous is complete. You cannot skip a version that might be painful and simply move on to the next. The Crescent will select the most probable versions first, but there can be thousands of subtle variations of each. You must learn to distinguish between them. Now. Prepare yourself. The first time is always the most difficult. For some, it is unbearable."

Naia clenched her jaw as she felt the stabilizing grip of Tsula's hands leave her arms. In her mind, there was only absence. Even the tides of her breath fell out of reach. Then, a faint glimmer of light slithered out of the blackness of nothing. A vine-like tendril uncurled before her, twisting and twining. It wound through the darkness, winding and coiling, the coils constricting around her. The darkness bled away, and her mind ran like quicksilver.

She groveled within a universe of agony, a downpour of tears raining from her eyes. Her fingers clawed at her scalp, trying to scrape away the infinite pain that seared her head. Quin clutched her tight against him, his hands running frantically over her in a vain attempt to soothe. But any comfort he could give was woefully inadequate. She was dying in agony, in terror. In futility.9

Outside, the epitome of all storms—the storm that every other storm aspired to be—raged and ripped across the atmosphere. Thunder lashed against the windows, and lightning the color of blood sliced wounds in the air. The wind howled a monstrous wail as it rampaged across the earth, terrorizing the tree limbs, which fled wildly before it. The world itself screamed in mortal anguish, and Naia screamed with it.

"I'm here! I've got you!" Quin shouted over the fury of the wind.

But he didn't have her. She was fading. The world was fading. And though it hurt, it didn't matter. All was lost—they had lost—the world was lost. It was her fault. No, Quin's fault. No, Kyel's fault for abandoning them to the violence of the Reversal. Now all the men and women of Malikar would be beaten back into the Black Lands to starve in eternal darkness. Every mage was dying in torment, and every wonder they'd ever created would be erased from the world's long memory. All was fading, all was dying. And she was dying with it.

"I can't stand it!" she shrieked to the absent gods.

She could feel the magic field stretched around her to its thin limit. It cried out in protest, in defiance, in outrage. And then it ripped. Naia screamed her life away, feeling her mind heated to boiling inside her skull.

She opened her eyes, sobbing uncontrollably. A hand reached out and collected her into a cold embrace.

"What was that?" she wailed through terror and shock and inconsolable grief.

Tsula said without emotion, "That was the most likely ending of your Story."

Naia shook her head against the woman's shoulder. "No! That can't happen! We can't let that happen!"

Tsula drew back and, reaching up, wiped Naia's tears from her eyes. Her face was as bland and expressionless as always. "Tell me what you saw."

"The Reversal was happening. All the mages were dying. Magic was ending. And we didn't break the Curse."

The Harbinger simply nodded. "That confirms what I have seen. There are other versions still available to us, but for every second that passes, the more complete our Story becomes. And the more versions will be denied us. Soon, there will be only one version left to pen."

She turned Naia back around. Taking her by the shoulders, Tsula commanded, "Try again."

Drawing a deep breath, Naia closed her eyes.

The epitome of all storms—the storm that every other storm aspired to be—raged and ripped across the atmosphere. Thunder lashed against the cliffs, and lightning the color of blood sliced wounds in the air. The wind howled a monstrous wail as it rampaged through the mountains, terrorizing the clouds, which fled wildly before it. The world screamed in mortal anguish, and Naia screamed with it.

Quin was gone. He couldn't help her anymore.

Sprawled in the center of Aerysius' great Circle of Convergence, Darien lay in an expanding pool of blood. The blood was artery-red and voluminous—far more than one human body could possibly contain. It flowed into the gaps and crevices of the Circle's rays, delineating the marble tiles with heightened contrast. The blood continued to advance, as if seeking to saturate the entire Circle. Or the entire world. Or the universe.

Zavier Renquist stood behind Naia and pushed her to her knees. In his hands, he held Quin's scimitar. His face was slicked with blood, and his eyes gleamed with triumph. He drew the sword back over his shoulder, preparing to strike the death-blow that would end her life.

"Let the reign of Xerys begin!" he snarled, and cleaved Naia's head off.

Naia opened her eyes, gasping for breath. She whirled back to Tsula. "Oh, gods! Do we have any chance at all?"

"We do," the Harbinger assured her. Reaching up, she stroked a strand of hair back from Naia's cheek. "What did you see?"

"Renquist sacrificed Darien on a Circle of Convergence. Something about his blood…He was trying to bring about the reign of Xerys. I didn't understand any of it."

"I think that is enough for one day," Tsula said and turned away, her dark eyes wandering over the walls. All around the spherical room, silver tendrils curled and uncurled in infinite variations.

Naia nodded, feeling defeated. She did not want to read another version of her Story. At least, not today.

She fled back to Quin.

He wasn't in his room. She found him in the library, sprawled across one of the sofas. He was leafing through a text with one hand, the other absently flipping a feathered quill.

"What is it?" he asked, seeing her face. He

snapped the book closed and sat upright. "Did you see something…?"

Naia drew in a deep, steadying breath. She couldn't tell him, not everything. Practically nothing. The more she thought about it, the more she wondered why she had sought him out at all. Wearily, she sank down beside him on the sofa.

He reached up and gently turned her face toward him. "Tell me what you saw."

Naia pulled back, grimacing. "I can't. If I do, then the things I saw might come to pass. And we can't let that happen."

Quin stared at her a long, hard moment, looking deeply into her eyes. At last, he nodded. "I'll kill Tsula tonight, then."

Naia gasped. "No. Not tonight—I still need her!"

Quin sucked in a cheek, looking uncertain. "But if you want to avoid the options you saw—"

"Give me one more day. I want to make certain I've learned everything I need to know from her."

He looked decisively skeptical. "Do you die in every vision you have?"

"Of course." Naia threw her hands up in exasperation. "That is the only way my own Story can end." All he ever seemed to care about was her safety. Never mind what the stakes were, or that the future of an entire population might be in jeopardy.

"What about me?" he asked. "What do I do in these visions?"

"You know I can't tell you that." Naia bent over and picked up the text Quin had been reading. She glanced down at the title, but it was written in a language of glyphs she'd never seen before. She set the book aside.

Quin grumbled, "You'd better start telling me some of the things you see, before I destroy the world all over again out of ignorance."

"I will when I find the right version for us," Naia promised. She looked at him sadly, still haunted by what she saw. "Until then, there's no sense worrying about futures that might never happen."

"Come here," he said, and pulled her down on the sofa with him. His hand rubbed her back soothingly. "You'll get through this," he assured her. "It might not seem like it now. But you will. And if you need me, I'll be here for you. Like it or not."

———

Naia rose with the dawn and made her way up the crystalline path to the Nexus. The sun had just started its climb into the sky, casting its light in vibrant hues of gold. The shadows clung to night's chill, but the sunlight felt fierce and warm on her skin. Naia smiled, looking out across the volatile beauty of Athera's Crescent, at the rippling patterns that swirled over its surface.

She wasn't surprised to find Tsula already waiting for her.

"Are you ready to read another version of your Story?" the Harbinger asked. She smiled invitingly, an expression that seemed out of place on her face. Naia was taken aback. She tried to remember another time she had ever seen the woman smile and couldn't think of one.

"I'm ready," she said, adding with a sigh, "It is daunting, though. It seems we are destined to fail."

Tsula shook her head. "There are versions still left to us, and all versions are governed by our choices. We will not run out of options until we run out of choices. And, until then, we cannot run out of hope."

She beckoned Naia closer, her face growing grim. "I was a bit disturbed by one of the versions you read yesterday."

"Which version?"

"You must remember to address me by my title," Tsula reminded her.

She'd forgotten. "Which version, Warden Renquist?"

"The version in which my husband ends your life over a spreading pool of blood. It aligns with a version of my own Story that has always been highly unlikely…until now. Now, the Crescent deems it by far the most probable."

That did worry Naia. Of the two versions she had foreseen, that was the one she feared most. She wasn't sure why. Something about the images of the blood and the sword terrified her. It was almost as though they were symbolic of something much more visceral.

"What do you think it means?" she asked.

Tsula glanced at her sharply. "It means that my husband has found a way to halt the Reversal of the magic field. Just as he tried to do a thousand years ago."

Naia stood shocked. For a moment, she couldn't

react. That had never been a possibility before, at least none she had considered. Renquist had attempted such a feat a thousand years ago and had failed then—disastrously. And he no longer had Eight Servants nor eight Circles of Convergence to accomplish the act.

"How is that possible?" she whispered.

Tsula paced away, a frown of concern on her face. "I do not know. It would take the power of eight grand masters combined to stabilize the magic field. I do not know how, but it seems that my husband has found a way around it."

Naia asked, "Pardon, but…Zavier Renquist is your husband. Do you not know his plans?"

The woman looked at her sideways, cocking an eyebrow.

Naia decided to press the issue. "To be blunt, Warden Renquist—I assume you are trying to help him."

"Pfft!" the woman spat, scrunching up her face as if tasting something awful. "Of course not! Zavier Renquist is my husband. But any love I ever had for him died the day he murdered our daughter. Ever since then, I have not once looked upon his face."

Naia gasped. "He murdered your daughter?"

Tsula regarded her flatly. "You do not know?"

"No…" Naia shook her head. "Why would I know?"

"Did Quinlan Reis never mention Amani?"

The name didn't sound familiar. Until it did. Naia blinked, suddenly remembering the story Quin had told her when they'd first met. About a woman he'd loved, who had loved him back. But she had been forced to marry his brother and had died at Braden's hand.

"Oh, gods…" Naia whispered. "Amani was your daughter?"

Tsula nodded. "It took me many years before I was able to admit the truth: that it was my own husband who had conspired to have Amani slain. Quinlan Reis and his brother were both merely pawns in Zavier's many intrigues."

Naia stared at her in horrified incomprehension. "Why would Renquist murder his own daughter?"

Tsula drew in a deep breath, face twisted into a grimace. "Because Zavier needed Braden's strength to complete his Circle of Eight. And, unfortunately for Braden, he was a man of integrity. He would never sink to the moral depths necessary to channel the Onslaught. So Zavier decided to put him in an impossible position to force the issue.

"He sent Quinlan to Aerysius under the pretense he was to assassinate Cyrus Krane. Predictably, Quinlan was captured. My husband made sure Amani knew her lover was slated to be executed unless an appropriate ransom was paid. Krane demanded documents that were in Braden's possession, and Braden was duty-bound to deny him. Amani stole the documents and delivered them to Cyrus Krane herself."

Naia shook her head, feeling sickened.

Tsula continued, "When Amani returned to the Lyceum, Zavier declared our daughter a traitor and sentenced her to death. And, for Amani's executioner, he picked Braden, who was bound by duty to murder his own wife."

The Harbinger drew in a deep, shuddering breath, bowing her head in grief. "All of this horror to corrupt the morals of one honorable mage who would never stand again at Zavier's side." She looked up then, her eyes filled with wrath. "My husband was the most despicable man the world has ever known. And now, fueled by Xerys' vast power, he is the most dangerous demon. So, no. I do not support him."

The weight of her words seemed to drag the whole world down. Naia stared at the floor in silence, respecting the doleful quiet that comes when a mother mourns her child. As a priestess, she had seen it before, many times.

Eventually, Tsula looked up and offered the smallest, strongest smile.

"There's one thing I don't understand," Naia said after a moment. "If you are Amani's mother, how could it be that Quin didn't recognize you?"

Tsula scoffed, turning away. "I never met him. I'm a Harbinger. I exist only in secrets and in shadow. Even my own daughter never knew my face… But I knew hers. I lived my entire life through her. Now, enough of this." Tsula waved her hand. "It is time to read the next possible version of your Story. Close your eyes. Now. Try again."

Naia didn't want to. But, prompted by the unyielding iron in Tsula's gaze, she collected her strength, closed her eyes, and tried again.

The epitome of all storms—the storm that every other storm aspired to be—raged and ripped across the atmosphere. Thunder lashed against the cliffs, and lightning the color of blood sliced wounds in the air. The wind howled a monstrous wail as it rampaged through the mountains, terrorizing the clouds, which fled wildly before it. The world screamed in mortal anguish, and Naia screamed with it.

Quin was below, in the chamber of the Well of Tears. Trying to wrench the portal full open before the Reversal could maximize.

In front of her, Kyel Archer advanced across the Circle of Convergence, wielding a silver morning star in his hand.

In the center of the Circle—in full command of it—Zavier Renquist swept out a fist. A blinding glare of light whiter than bright and brilliantly powerful assaulted Kyel from the sky. He brought the talisman up to deflect it, but the strike was indomitable—it impacted with all the fury of the vortex. It overwhelmed the talisman's power, hurling Kyel backward to the ground, ripping the weapon out of his hands. Another magical assault drilled down from the clouds, stabbing into him.

The blow threw Kyel across the terrace. Another strike lifted him again, slamming him against the cliff. Zavier Renquist raised his arms, summoning the energies of the vortex for one last, mortal strike.

The green pillar above them exploded in fury. A great inferno shot upward, igniting the clouds, roiling the atmosphere. Fire streamed across the sky, cauterizing the air as it scourged the magic field. The field wailed in outrage as it died. And then it went silent, its rhythmic pulse stopped forever.

Naia screamed her life away, feeling the gift inside seared out of her.

Chapter Sixteen
Farbrook

The Vale of Amberlie, The Rhen

"What town is this?"

"Farbrook," Darien responded without looking at Sayeed.

He pulled his helmet down over his head and tightened the strap under his chin. Beside him, Azár did the same, her long braid snaking down her back. Darien turned at the sound of hoofbeats approaching behind them on the road, barely visible in the light cast by the faintest sliver of moon. He turned his mount around as the scouts rode up, horses blowing hot mist into the cold air.

The lead scout, a man named Seljik, made a quick bow from his horse's back. "All appears empty, Warden."

Darien digested that information in silence. It was the fifth town since Gannet and the second they'd found deserted. It was to be expected, he supposed, with the tactics they'd been employing. He still didn't like the feel of it, all the same.

"They are starting to anticipate which towns we will hit, and when," Sayeed commented. "That can go in our favor. Or it can go very badly."

"Agreed," Darien said. He sent Seljik off with a gesture. Looking up the road toward Farbrook's jagged silhouette, he contemplated the tidings. Word had spread far ahead of them. Each town they raided was more prepared than the last.

Reaching out from within, he opened his mind to the magic field and sampled the flow of the field lines. They ran smoothly, like velvet on satin. Following the line of the mountains southward toward Aerysius. It felt good to be out from under the oppression of Orien's vortex. It felt chilling to be so close to the fallen city he'd once called home.

Darien summoned a mist of magelight that trailed out ahead of them, lighting the road with an eerie blue haze. He whistled, then waited. There was a faint rustling in the trees behind them. Then the thanacryst broke out of the shadows and bounded to his horse's side.

He said to Sayeed, "We'll split up. Take your men and go around to the south gate. I'll come in from the north. We'll meet in the middle."

Sayeed nodded and kicked his horse to a canter, followed by four dozen mounted men. Darien held his horse to a walk, following a trail of glowing mist, the remainder of his men following behind. Around them, the night was cold and still as death.

To Azár, Darien said, "Remember what I taught you about fire?"

"I do." She turned toward him, her eyes shadowed by her helm.

Darien lowered his visor. "If something attacks you, burn the hell out of it." He couldn't see the smile on her lips, but he knew it was there.

The demon-hound ranged ahead of them, nose to the ground, ears pricked. As they reached Farbrook's open gate, the beast sprang forward, working the sides of the road like a hunting dog sniffing for a trail. It zigzagged back and forth across the empty street, scenting the sides of the brick-and-lumber buildings. The thanacryst was like a fluid shadow weaving among other shadows, its eyes boring green holes through the darkness.

The sound of their horses' hooves echoed sharply off the walls of the houses, ringing through the streets. The magelight lit the path ahead of them, creeping forward like a trail of blue flames. Darien's horse snorted, shaking its head. He reached down and stroked the animal's neck, seeking to calm it. The stallion flinched at the feel of his hand.

A low growl from the thanacryst made him jerk back on the reins. His horse whinnied in protest, backing up a few steps before coming to a foot-stomping halt. Darien slid from its back, the Zakai following him to the ground. Azár moved behind him, hand resting on the hilt of her sword. The demon-hound turned back the way they had come. Hackles raised, it bared its teeth and snarled.

Darien slid his sword from its sheath.

A barrage of arrows rained down from the sky, stabbing the ground all around them. His eyes shot up to the roof of the building across the street, to the group of several archers already loosing their next volley. One of Darien's men fell with a cry. More arrows clattered down.

Darien didn't bother with the magic field. He went right to the Hellpower. The men on the rooftop dissolved into a cloud of ash that simply blew away.

He sheathed his sword and dropped to the side of the man who had fallen. An arrow had pierced his thigh. Blood spurted from the wound in time to his heart beat. With a growl, Darien set his hands on him. It took only seconds to mend the severed artery.

"Keep an eye on the rooftops," Darien ordered his men. He led his horse forward by the reins, his wife and the demon-hound stalking at his sides. He let the magelight crawl ahead of them, licking at the shadows.

All at once, a terrified-looking man burst out of an alley. Before Darien could react, the man let out a staccato scream as he erupted in flames. Shocked, Darien turned to find Azár standing beside him, hand outstretched. He could see the pride that glimmered in her eyes beneath the shadow of her helm. She had been practicing the *ruhk* attack for days.

Apparently, she'd mastered it.

Darien nodded his approval then waved his men forward, brightening the intensity of the magelight.

"Search every house," he ordered, then waited in the street as the soldiers began breaking down doors and shattering windows. He stood listening to the sounds of the town's defilement, one hand absently petting the demon-hound's head. The thing tilted its head back and licked his knuckles with a putrescent tongue. He waited for minutes. Then, taking Azár's hand, he walked calmly down the middle of the street.

They met up with Sayeed's band of raiders in the center of town. There was a large, cobbled square housing a font fed by the town's covered well. Darien led his men to where Sayeed sat his horse, scimitar in hand.

"There's nothing," the officer reported, swiping an arm across his brow. "They took everything with them. No food. They burned the granaries and drove away the livestock."

Darien cursed, turning his back on Sayeed. Farbrook was the second town they'd encountered that had either destroyed or carried off all their provisions. The situation with his own resources was becoming dire. He stared down at the ground, pondering options he didn't have.

"We captured three townsmen by an abandoned barn."

That caught Darien's attention. He turned back to Sayeed. "Take me there."

They mounted up and rode out of town, surrounded by a protective ring of Zakai. They rode past empty buildings with shattered windows and out across a harvested field.

Sayeed led them to a dilapidated barn that looked to be standing only by the grace of the gods. The leaning walls were supported by angled beams hammered into the ground. A group of Tanisars holding torches stood in the yard in front of the barn, the wavering light writhing a tortuous dance across the ground.

"They're in there." Sayeed pointed with his sword toward the entrance to the structure.

Darien dismounted and strode forward, spreading his fingers, ordering the men behind him to remain in place. Sayeed and Azár at his side, he strode toward the barn's yawning entrance. Within, a cluster of Zakai stood under the hayloft, guarding three bound men. Darien pulled his helmet off and held it dangling at his side by the chinstrap. He walked in a measured pace toward the prisoners, halting in front of them.

He looked deeply into the eyes of the eldest of the three men—a blacksmith, judging by the soot-stained apron. By his bearing, the man had probably served some time at the Front. There was no fear in his eyes. Just more scornful confidence than any man in his situation had any right to.

"Do you know who I am?" Darien asked quietly.

"I do." The smith stared at him unwaveringly. His hands were bound behind his back, his legs lashed together with strong hemp cord. All around him stood soldiers with crossbows leveled at his chest. Still, the man showed no trace of apprehension.

Darien said, "You knew we were coming. So why stay behind?"

"This is our home."

Darien shook his head. That wasn't a good enough reason to make three men eager to die. He stared harder into the smith's blue eyes, seeking there for explanation. Just in case, he reached out for the magic field and held it close. He said, "You knew you couldn't win this fight. So I'll ask you one last time: why did you remain?"

The man glared back at him with a disdainful, hard-as-stone gaze. "We heard what you did to the people of Gannet."

"That doesn't answer my question."

The smith's stare turned vengeful. "We stayed behind because we wanted to make you pay."

Something detonated in a shower of liquid. An explosion of flames erupted from the floor. Darien lashed out with his mind, beating the fire back into the ground, reversing the combustion. The flames burned back into themselves, until even the smoke curled downward. Steam rose from the fuming ground, condensing out of the now-frigid air. Darien glanced quickly to Azár, relieved to find her unharmed. There was a bitten-off scream as one of his guards shot a quarrel through a man hiding above them in the hayloft.

Darien's stare locked on the smith's.

The man's eyes now contained the fear that should have rightfully been there all along. His face had gone white beneath a thick layer of soot. His two companions stood terrified, trembling in their restraints.

Darien informed them, "You made a mistake."

He turned to Sayeed and ordered, "Let the forger go. Let him live to eat the guilt of his decisions. And tell the tale of what he's seen here tonight." To Azár, he said, "You've been wanting some practice. Go ahead. The other two are yours—make examples of them."

He strode out of the barn, taking half the Zakai with him. He didn't stay to listen to the screams.

"There was no food in all the town," Azár said, removing her helm. She released her sweat-damp hair from its braid, letting it fall in greasy waves down her back. Darien pulled her against him, squeezing her close. She smelled of smoke and sweat and was covered in grime. To Darien, she looked beautiful.

He kissed her damp hair then released her, pulling back. He knelt to rummage through a burlap sack he'd brought with him. From within, he retrieved a parcel wrapped in cloth, the one treasure he'd managed to scavenge from Farbrook. He unwrapped the loaf of bread and handed it to her.

"I saved this for you."

Her eyes widened as she stared down at the loaf hungrily. "We will share it."

Darien smiled, shaking his head. "I already ate," he lied.

He scrubbed a rough cloth over his face, wiping off most of the sooty sweat. He tossed it on the floor, then sat on their pallet watching Azár tear hungrily through the loaf. When she was done, she stood with her eyes squeezed shut in pleasure, licking the last of the crumbs off her fingertips. His own stomach tightened in envy.

"How are you faring with all this?" he asked. He wasn't speaking about hunger.

Azár's face went from blissful to ferocious in a heartbeat. "Those men tried to kill my husband. I wanted them to die slowly."

He nodded. He'd come to expect nothing less from her than cold brutality. But he wanted to be certain. He didn't want to push her past the limits of her morals.

He asked, "Which attack did you use?"

Azár smiled playfully, sitting down beside him on the pallet. "I tried something different."

"Oh?"

She leaned in close and kissed him languidly, her tongue sliding over his lips. She whispered, "It is a surprise."

He returned her kiss. Ignoring the empty ache in his belly, he pulled her on top of him.

They broke camp the next morning and headed southward into the deep forest of the Vale. As they left Farbrook, they passed a hill where a dozen long poles had been driven into the ground. On each pole, one of the town's defenders was impaled groin to neck. Two were still moving, still sobbing and moaning. Darien didn't need Azár to tell him which two they were. He was impressed. That had taken some skill, to impale men in such a way that they would remain alive to suffer the next day. He nodded his approval at his wife. Not because he took any pleasure from watching his enemies squirm on a pole, but because the people of the Vale needed a graphic demonstration of the consequences of opposition.

"Which town is next?" asked Sayeed, his face haggard.

"Kantsby."

"I hope they eat food in Kantsby."

There was nothing left of Kantsby. Just burned-out houses and watered grain—even the livestock had been slaughtered in the fields and left to rot.

There was also nothing left of Torwood.

Or Castleton. Or Glendoe.

Or Summerton.

"That was Ryloch," Darien said, even though Sayeed had stopped asking several towns and several days back.

His legs trembled as he dismounted and stood exhausted, leaning against his horse's heaving side. The wind breathed a sigh, stirring the branches of the oaks that folded over them, blocking out the starlight. He looked wearily up at Sayeed and shook his head.

"That's it, then."

Sayeed looked at him with eyes glazed and weary. He'd had that look ever since Farbrook, ever since the food had run out. Hunger had sunken his cheeks, making his angular features even more jagged. He turned and glared into the shadows of the grove, where the rest of their band had taken refuge. A form of silent protest, Darien was sure. He scuffed the leaf-laden soil with his boot, struggling to think through the fog that mired his brain.

"We can't go back," Darien grumbled. "And we can't stay here. The only thing we can do is go forward."

Sayeed didn't respond. Darien reached up and stroked the delicate head of his red stallion. The soft fur felt like velvet beneath his fingers. The horse's silken coat was the product of a thousand years of crossbreeding followed by another thousand of inbreeding. It was one of only a handful of steppe horses left alive in the entire world. With one last pat, Darien released the tasseled bridle.

"Slaughter the horses," he ordered. "We'll walk from here."

Chapter Seventeen
Tom the Smith

The Vale of Amberlie, The Rhen

A frantic thunder made Kyel twist in his saddle. Behind, three riders galloped toward them, urging their mounts faster with spurs and crops. Kyel kicked his own horse clear of the road as the riders shot past in a jarring clatter of hoofbeats. He glanced sideways at Alexa, who shrugged in reply.

"Wonder what that's about," Kyel grumbled, brushing off the dust kicked up by the galloping horses. He scanned the surrounding forest but saw nothing amiss. There was the same smell of woodfires that had dominated the air for two days, but that was all. The forest was almost unnaturally calm.

They had been riding since dawn, trying to cover as much ground as possible. Glen Farquist wasn't more than a week south of them, and Kyel was anxious. It had been months since he'd last seen his son. He'd left Gil at the Temple of Wisdom, under the tutelage of the clerics. But with recent events, Kyel had begun to fear Glen Farquist might be the most dangerous place his son could be.

Minutes later, another jarring noise disrupted the silence of the trees: this time, the juddering clatter of wagon wheels. Kyel halted his horse along the side of the road as a caravan of carts and wagons passed them by. Many of the carts were overloaded with supplies. Some only contained people. Too many people, who looked far too shocked and grieved.

"Something's wrong," Kyel muttered.

Alexa nodded, saying nothing. After the caravan passed, he nudged his horse back onto the road.

Kyel heard the commotion of the town ahead even before it came into view. The streets were swarming with people rushing in a panicked frenzy to load wagons and mules with whatever they could fit. The entire town had the look of an ant colony after a good kicking, with everyone running frantic with little mind and less direction.

"This is bad," Kyel commented, pulling his horse up.

"What do you think happened?" Alexa raised her voice to be heard over the din of the commotion.

"I think the Enemy broke through." Seeing the congestion in the streets ahead, Kyel decided against trying to wade his horse through the turmoil. He dismounted and tied the animal to a fence, then waited for Alexa to do the same.

"Isn't the Pass guarded by two armies?"

Kyel shot a glance her way. "I guess two armies weren't enough."

That silenced her.

By the time they fought their way through the crowd to the center of town, it became clear he'd been right. Scores of folk had gathered in the town square around a brick house. Two men stood on the steps: one that looked like the mayor, and another man wearing a blacksmith's apron. The smith appeared to be directing the evacuation, while the mayor stood off to the side with his hands stuffed in his pockets

"Take everything!" the blacksmith shouted. "If you can't fit it in a wagon, then burn it!"

Cries rose from the mob of panicked citizens: outrage and terror and everything in between.

The blacksmith's eyes fell on Kyel. At first, he couldn't figure out why the smith was staring at him.

Then he realized: he was wearing his mage's cloak. The man raised his hand, pointing at Kyel across the gathered crowd. Glaring him in the eye, the smith beckoned him over with a snap of his head.

Feeling more than a bit unsettled, Kyel fought his way through the jostling crowd with Alexa in tow. He mounted the steps to the porch and halted before the two men. The mayor's eyes fixed on Kyel's cloak, his cracked lips muttering words too low to hear. It was the blacksmith, though, who commanded Kyel's attention.

"Who are you?" the forger demanded, making it patently clear who wore the authority.

Before Kyel could answer, Alexa announced, "His name is Grand Master Kyel Archer. He is a Sentinel of Aerysius!"

The mayor's face ran through a range of emotions faster than a pianist's fingers flitting through scales. The smith's eyes remained cold and even, fixing Kyel with a look of distrust.

"Show us the marks of the chains," he ordered.

In the space between heartbeats, Kyel became aware that the commotion in the square had halted altogether. Glancing back, he saw that every person in the crowd had stopped moving and now stood frozen, gaping at him with fear in their eyes. With no small amount of apprehension, Kyel held his hands up one at a time, thrusting back his sleeves and baring his wrists for all to see.

The blacksmith stared hard at the markings of the chains. His gaze slid to Kyel's face. He nodded curtly.

A bottomless silence settled over the crowd. Silence and deference. At first, Kyel couldn't understand it. Then, in a flash of insight, the answer became obvious. For hundreds of years, this town had stood in the long shadow of Aerysius. None of the men and women gathered before him would dare disrespect the emblems of the chains. Kyel hadn't counted on that reaction, but that didn't make him any less relieved.

The forger thrust out his hand. "Tom Akins. I'm a smith down from Farbrook."

Kyel accepted the smith's handshake, noting the lingering doubt in the man's eyes.

Tom continued, "I'm here because, well, Farbrook doesn't exist anymore. Neither does Gannet or Castleton, or anything else north of here. The Enemy's been raiding town-to-town. Within the past week, I've witnessed atrocities that will haunt my sleep for the rest of my days. I stood in a barn and looked the demon himself in the eye. I've never seen such inhumanity. He's torched people in their own homes, crucified others. Impaled men on stakes and left them alive for the ravens to eat. He's massacred whole families: mothers, babes. He has no mercy. No respect for life."

The smith fell silent, visibly wrestling with the ghosts of the horrors he'd seen. His eyes fell on Kyel's cloak, staring at it with a peculiar mixture of revulsion and expectation.

Kyel looked at him a long moment. Tom's story was chilling. More so because his account was in line with everything Kyel had always heard about the Enemy, the kind of tales that used to terrify him as a boy. Apparently, the dark stories told to scare children were all based on truth.

The smith puffed out his cheeks in a protracted sigh. "Since Farbrook, I've made it my purpose to destroy that devil and his horde. I've been traveling south, warning the people ahead of him. Town by town, we've left them nothing. What we couldn't take, we burned. What we couldn't burn, we buried." His stare hardened, locking on Kyel's face. "Perhaps you can help us. Redeem the honor of that damn cloak you're wearing."

Kyel glanced sideways at the gathered crowd. Then he returned his stare to the blacksmith. "How hungry are they?"

"His raiders haven't had a good meal in over a week. By now, they're starving and desperate."

Kyel nodded. He'd always heard that starving men didn't think clearly. He hoped starving demons didn't, either.

"I've an idea," he said. "But it's a gamble. And I can't stay to help you pull it off."

Chapter Eighteen
Darien of Amberlie

The Vale of Amberlie, The Rhen

The cold grip of memory wound around him and constricted.

Darien gazed down at the long strip of rutted dirt and felt throttled by remembrance. He tried to maintain his focus on the road ahead, bending all his will into the effort. It was no good. He kept glancing upward. His gaze roamed over the tangle of branches overhead, desperate for just one glimpse of the mountain cliffs above. But the forest canopy refused him. So he forced his gaze back down at the dirt, plagued by emotions he couldn't name.

A town became visible through an opening in the trees. He nodded his head toward it. "That's Amberlie."

Azár and Sayeed exchanged sharp glances. Azár asked, "This is your home?"

Darien shook his head. "No. My home was up there"—he glanced up at the merciless snarl of branches— "but down here's where I grew up."

He stared harder at the road, so he wouldn't have to look up, or ahead, or back. He studied the ruts in the dirt, the pockmarked clay broken with scuffed tracks, both human and animal. At the half-buried stones. He could name most of the rocks; they were common to the area. He stepped over a pebble of gypsum. A lump of quartz protruded from the side of the road, half-covered by grass. A small chunk of granite turned under his foot. The ubiquitous river-rock, round and smooth and polished. Mica. Fool's gold. Feldspar.

"What's up there?" Azár asked softly.

He wanted to ignore her. She already knew what was up there—she had to. Flatly, he responded, "Aerysius."

"I don't see it."

Neither could he. Perhaps the thick branches were protective, like a scab over a wound.

"That's because it's gone," he answered.

Azár walked with her head craned, searching for a break in the trees. Behind them, the rhythmic clatter that accompanied a column of armed men announced their presence to the world.

A broad streak of light shot down, making him squint. Making him stop. Darien took a deep, steadying breath. Then he looked up through the trees at the soaring cliffs overhead. His eyes traveled up the sharp granite wall. And up. And up, until he couldn't tilt his head back any further.

"It was up there," he said. "Where the cliff bows inward. You can see the terraces if you look hard enough. But there's nothing else left."

He glanced back down again and started forward, his boots scuffing the dirt. Azár took his hand. He supposed it was a gesture of comfort. He didn't want it.

Two of Sayeed's scouts jogged toward them from the direction of Amberlie. The first man reported, "The town appears empty, Warden. All of the structures are intact."

"Good," Darien said. "Maybe they left some food behind."

He trained his focus on the town, visible through the trees. Out of the corner of his eye, he saw that Azár and Sayeed were still scanning the cliffs.

"It is so far up," she gasped. "How do you climb that?"

He could hear the awe in her voice. It was the same awe he used to feel as a boy, standing in that same grove, gazing up at the mountain in yearning.

"There was a lift," he said, and didn't elaborate. Ahead, the town was mercifully closer.

"It is said you fell from that mountain." There was a lightness in Sayeed's tone that made Darien realize he was trying to make a jest. Probably an attempt to buoy his mood.

"I did."

The levity melted from Sayeed's face, his eyes widening as his gaze darted back upward.

The town of Amberlie was just as Darien remembered it, only empty. Like every other town they'd come across. He stopped in the middle of the square, his eyes wandering slowly over the littered street, fighting a sharp pang of nostalgia.

Around him, Sayeed's Zakai spread out to search the structures. Darien waited with his eyes pinned on the mountain cliffs overhead. For minutes, that was all he could do. At last, the scouts reported back that the town was completely empty. Not one stubborn holdout had remained behind. Which was good. Darien hadn't wanted to kill people he'd known all his life, had grown up with. Of all the towns they'd captured in the Vale, he'd dreaded taking Amberlie the most. He'd left too many friends there. And too many memories.

"Wait here. I'll be back in a bit," he said to Azár. Ignoring her look of confusion, he walked away from her.

Turning onto a side street, Darien strode past rows of houses he remembered well, following the same old cobbled street he'd taken a thousand times before. His feet remembered where to go. He found a small dirt path just out of town that looked more like an abandoned deer trail than a footpath. He followed it anyway, aware of the crunching sounds of Azár's footsteps following behind, and the eager patter of oversized paws that trailed him everywhere he went.

Darien scowled, irritated that his desire for solitude continued to be ignored. Without looking back at his unwanted companions, he followed the path as it meandered through the trees, finally ending at a dilapidated stone-and-wattle cottage covered by gray, ancient thatch.

He paused, staring for a moment at the outside of the cottage and the glen that surrounded it. Off to the side was the covered well he used to draw water from as a boy. Across from it was the sycamore with the beehive in it. The patch of ground that had once been the widow's vegetable garden. The spot in the corner of the house where he'd buried the squirrel he'd killed with his slingshot. His brother's treehouse in the sprawling oak, now fallen. He hadn't been allowed up there. But he'd gone anyway.

Darien walked the rest of the way up the path and, motioning for the demon-hound to remain outside, entered the dark cottage. The floorboards groaned and cracked beneath his weight. Beams of light, swarming with dust, slanted down through gaping holes in the thatch. The cottage smelled of earth and mildew and abandonment. Everything inside was coated with dust. Old, tattered cobwebs sagged in the corners, looking just as neglected as the rest of the place.

He walked toward the hearth and stood looking down at the remains of the widow's bed. Mice and rats had made nests in what was left of the bedding. Water and rot had claimed the rest. On the floor beside it was a rusted rushlight holder, left behind. Everything else had been either looted or decayed.

A cracking noise told him Azár had entered the space. Without looking back at her, he said, "This is the home of the widow who raised us." He gestured at an empty corner. "We slept over there—me and my brother. She couldn't afford a bed for us, so we gathered straw and threw it down and covered it with a blanket every night. There were chinks in the walls that let the cold in. Every morning, dew collected on the ceiling and fell on us like rain."

Azár laid a hand on his back.

"We never lacked. My father made sure the widow always had food for us. He came to visit from time to time. Mother never did." He stood quietly, eyes loosely focused on the dust swirling in the air as he struggled with the decision of how much he wanted to let himself feel.

"It was a good home," Azár said, looking around.

He silently disagreed.

Footsteps on the path outside broke his attention. Sayeed burst into the cottage with an excited grin, announcing, "There's food, Brother!" He retreated out the door then turned around, beckoning.

Darien led Azár by the hand away from the

cottage, taking a shortcut he remembered. It led them under the fresh leaves of a maple grove, and down a small embankment into the outskirts of town.

Reaching the town square, Darien discovered that Sayeed's men hadn't been idle; they'd been cleaning out store houses and root cellars, stacking crates and bags of food in the center of town. Sayeed walked toward them up the main road with a broad smile on his face. "They left behind a bounty of food!" he announced. "We will feast tonight!"

Darien eyed the food stores warily. Every town they'd come to since Farbrook, without exception, had prepared in advance for their arrival. Burned to the ground, gutted. Stores depleted or destroyed. Nothing had been left to sustain a foraging army. All except this one town—a town that had special significance to him.

"No." Darien shook his head. "We can't trust this."

Sayeed's face went serious. He nodded slowly.

Darien said, "Have some of the men try it. Small portions. If they're still standing this time tomorrow, then we'll have your feast."

He looked around at the empty houses that lined the square. "Let's camp here."

They bedded down in town—at least as many as the town would yield grudging space for. The remainder of the Tanisars camped outside in a neat ring of tents. Throughout the next day, Darien paced restlessly up and down the length of Amberlie's streets, accompanied by his ever-slobbering pet. He tried to keep his eyes averted from the cliffs above, but the occasional hawk cry—or just plain distraction—inevitably turned his gaze in that direction. At last he gave in to the compulsion to acknowledge the scars raked across the cliff face above like self-inflicted wounds—and bit down on the instant pang of sorrow that shot up from some forgotten place inside.

He'd stood in this same spot as a boy, gazing up at the cliffs that loomed taller than the sky, staring in over-awed wonder at the city high above on the mountain. Dreaming of a time when he, too, could find his own place among the clouds. When he could become a Sentinel like his father and finally look upon the mother who had borne him, the woman who, for all intents and purposes, ruled the world. A time when he could at last come into his own and forge his own legend and legacy.

How naïve he had been. An ignorant boy, fool enough to hope and dream.

He shielded his eyes from the glare, focusing on a thin stream of water that plunged down the cliff in a tendril-thin cascade, never quite reaching the ground. At a point about halfway down the mountain, the waterfall dwindled to mist that was simply blown away.

He saw Azár turn a corner and angle toward him. She wore her hair unbound, which was a rare thing. It changed her appearance drastically, softening her features. He wasn't used to seeing her with her hair unconstrained outside the privacy of their own tent.

"They are hauling in wood for the fires," she announced with a smile. "It seems we will feast tonight, after all."

Darien grunted. He'd kept an eye on the men who had tested the provisions. None had fallen ill. His mouth started watering at the prospect of a full meal. Azár wrapped an arm around him and glanced upward, using the other to shield her eyes from the sun's glare.

"Tell me about the city in the sky. Speak to me of Aerysius."

He slouched under the heavy weight of the inevitable. He'd known he'd have to confront his feelings at some point. He just hadn't wanted it to be in front of her. Darien took his wife's hand and drew her over to the side of the street, where the view was better and there was a bench they could sit on. Azár lowered herself down at his side and sat looking at him expectantly. Darien didn't say anything for a while. He glanced down at her soft hand and trailed his fingers across her skin.

Indicating the cliffs, he said, "It was beautiful. It was built all on terraces, carved right out of the mountain. The towers were so elegant. It was like they floated in the clouds. The Hall of the Watchers was enormous. It was built around this giant dome. The pillars inside looked like trees. Enormous trees—far bigger than those." He gestured at the old-growth pines lurking over the rooftops. "Row upon row upon row. Scores of them. It was breathtaking. I've never felt so insignificant as I did standing under that dome."

He fell silent. Azár squeezed his hand.

"I am sorry you lost so much," she said. Then she paused. "But I am not sorry your city in the clouds perished."

He looked down regretfully. "No, I don't suppose you would be."

She reached up and turned his face toward her, forcing his eyes to meet hers. She said firmly, "If Aerysius had never fallen, then you would not have fallen. And we would not be here now. All of us—we would still be in Malikar. Waiting to die. So Aerysius had to fall. It had to fall so that we could live."

She kissed him gently, caringly. Then she rose and walked away, leaving him alone with his hound and his memories.

Somehow the anticipated meal had evolved into a full-fledged festivity. The men had found a few casks of cider and rolled them out. A great bonfire was built in the center of the square, fed with items of furniture plundered from nearby homes.

Darien felt a tug on his arm and turned to find a smiling Sayeed carrying a mug of cider. The officer forcibly planted the drink in his hands, then tugged him down the street in the direction of the fire. The odor of searing meat made Darien's stomach spasm. Tumbling smoke and waves of heat rose from the fire, the flames crackling high into the air. The sky was the bleak color of the ocean, and only one faint star braved the twilight, flickering anxiously just above the trees.

Sayeed propelled him to where a tight cluster of men and women sat on rugs thrown across the ground a little way from the fire. Azár was already there, sitting on a cushion under a cloth canopy. She sat in a ring of Zakai gathered around a cluster of dishes and bowls filled with an assortment of foods. She was laughing at a comment or joke.

When Azár looked up at him, her eyes shone joyfully. She waved him over, patting a cushion by her side. Darien sat next to her, Sayeed following right behind. The men and women acknowledged his presence with reverent bows, not going fully to the ground, but not far from it. He ignored the deference.

Darien lifted the mug to his lips and took a gulp of hard cider. He already knew what it would taste like before it reached his tongue—he'd grown up drinking Koff Tabard's favorite recipe made from local crab apples. It took just a taste to be certain the cider had come from old Koff's hoarded stash. The knowledge came with a sharp pang of guilt that didn't stop him from drinking it. Darien chugged the cider down, setting the empty mug by his side.

"Try the basha!" Azár exclaimed, scooping up some gravied vegetables with a piece of bread. She held it up before his face, grinning as he bit into it.

Immediately, Darien's hunger overrode every other impulse. He dove into the meal, unable to stuff the food into his mouth fast enough. It was a long time before he slowed his chewing enough to even taste what he was eating. Azár laughed delightfully, tearing off a slice of bread and helping herself as Darien went on to explore the numerous other offerings spread out before them.

"Whatever this is, it is very strong," Azár said, making a face and handing him her cup.

Darien accepted it with a grin. Koff's cider had been known and respected throughout the Vale. Gazing into her cup, he wondered where old Koff was now. And Koff's wife. And the rest of his family. He tossed Azár's cider down in a few swallows, feeling the magic field ebb as he did.

He stood up and wandered back through the thick smoke toward the fire, scanning for the cider cask. Night had smothered the town while he wasn't looking. The bonfire crackled at the darkness, its flames snapping at the air. The sounds of laughter and conversation rose in a dull haze of noise, punctuated by the clatter of drums and the erratic blare of a war horn. A cry went up from a ring of soldiers standing nearby—someone had won a game of cross-sticks. A group of men had formed a line beside the fire and, linking arms, began a foot-stomping dance that snaked around the gathering, picking up participants as it went.

He found one of the oak barrels and angled toward it but was intercepted by Sayeed. The officer plucked the empty mug from his hand and replaced it with a fresh one.

"Just ask, Brother," he admonished.

Darien asked, "Have you tried it?"

"Someone must have a clear head." Sayeed smiled and clapped Darien on the back. Then he took him by the arm, guiding him back across the square. Darien had the mug drained by the time he reclaimed his cushion.

"Go dance!" Azár commanded, waving him away.

Darien sat down, staring at her with a look of affronted dignity. "No."

Mischievous intent glittered in her eyes. Azár grinned at Sayeed, then leaned into Darien, nudging him forward. "Go! Just one dance!"

"Battlemages don't dance," Darien said firmly, and meant it. He reached across her for a piece of bread. The next thing he knew, he was being hauled to his feet.

"Tonight, they do!" Sayeed cried and, to Darien's horror, pulled him by the arm toward the bonfire.

He shot an outraged glare over his shoulder at Azár, who flashed him an indulgent grin. He tried to yank his arm out of Sayeed's vice-like grasp but a loud *whoop!* from the gathering stopped his squirming. Soldiers laughed and sprang back to clear a path for him. Men cheered, and women trilled their tongues, urging him forward. Before he knew it, he was standing in the line of dancers, trying to figure out when to kick and when to stomp—the whole while looking like a complete ass, he was certain.

The crowd laughed and clapped and cheered. He hadn't had near enough cider, Darien decided. He missed a step and staggered—and was caught by Sayeed, who threw his head back and burst into hearty laughter. Darien found himself grinning, finally finding some humor in the situation. He stomped and kicked and kicked and stomped, finally figuring out the pattern—and found he was able to laugh at himself when he got it wrong. The crowd roared and cheered.

Hearing the song die around him, Darien twisted out of line and fled back toward the cider cask. He stopped when he was halfway there, feeling suddenly light-headed. For just a moment, his vision blurred. The cider had been stronger than he'd thought. He decided he didn't need any more. The magic field was already a thin filament in the back of his head, scarcely tangible. He changed direction and walked back toward where Azár sat surrounded by Zakai. By the time he reached her, the exhaustion of the day had caught up with him. He sank down next to her with a full stomach and a weary sigh.

Azár threw her arms around him, squeezing him tight. "The Battlemage who dances!" she announced gleefully.

Darien feigned outrage, pulling away, trying hard not to laugh. Azár kissed him on the cheek and took his hand. Her touch sent a strange sensation shooting up his arm, like a fine needling of prickles that started in his fingertips. He let go of his wife's hand and wiggled his fingers, trying to work the sensation out of them. He felt suddenly, uncomfortably warm. A sweat broke out on his forehead.

"What is it?" Azár asked.

Darien shook his head. The prickling feeling retreated back out of his fingers. He dropped his hand to his side. "I'm just tired," he assured her. "I think I'll find my bed."

He pushed himself up off the ground.

She said, "I'll go with you."

He took her by the hand and led her through the hollering revelry back toward the mayor's home. And the mayor's bed.

Chapter Nineteen
The Sentinel's Gambit

The Vale of Amberlie, The Rhen

"Wake up!"

The voice wasn't sharp enough to cut all the way through the dense fog that smothered him, holding him down.

"Brother, wake up!"

An incessant shaking threatened to break him out of the fog. Darien groaned, willing it to stop. But it didn't. The shaking continued. He grew exasperated. He wanted to sink back down into the comfortable mist and never come up again. He lashed out with an inarticulate groan.

"He will not wake!"

The shaking stopped. A hand slapped his cheek, over and over and over again. It wouldn't let him slide back down where he wanted to go. That made him angry. He swiped out with an arm.

"Stop!" he growled and cracked open his eyes.

"Brother!"

Sayeed lifted him upright, a motion that made Darien retch. His stomach convulsed, squeezing bile into his throat. He clamped his mouth shut, trying hard not to vomit. He was still shaking, though no hands were on him. His clothing stuck to his skin, drenched in sweat. The room was dark and infinitely cold.

"What is it?" he mumbled.

"You are sick!" Azár cried. "Many are sick! You must heal yourself!"

Sick. Yes. He was sick. He supposed he could heal himself. The magic field was right there, within easy reach. He caught ahold of it—

—and jerked his mind back away.

"I can't heal myself and stay awake," he rasped. If there were others that were sick, he would have to see to their needs first, before he let the healing sleep overcome him. Gritting his teeth, Darien fought himself fully upright. Doing so made his head reel and his stomach twist. His pulse raced. He felt like he'd run miles in his sleep.

"It is poison!" Azár exclaimed, touching his cheek with the back of her hand. "It is acting fast. You do not have time to delay!"

"Not yet." Darien shook his head. "I have to stay awake. Help me up."

Azár exchanged concerned glances with Sayeed. At last, she relented. Sayeed stood and took hold of him, pulling Darien to his feet. His knees buckled, but the officer's strong grip kept him upright. Darien stood clinging to the man's shoulder until he felt stable enough to stand on his own. He took a spongy step forward. Then another. With Sayeed's help, Darien staggered down the hallway. Azár walked ahead of them, glancing back fretfully.

Darien halted in the doorway and looked out at the square, which had been turned into a makeshift campsite. Men and women lay groaning in their blankets around the still-glowing ashes of the bonfire. Others wandered as if dazed amongst the sick. The air was filled with the sounds of moans and the reek of human waste.

Sayeed shook his head. "We tested the food."

"It wasn't in the food," Darien said, cursing himself. "It was in the cider."

For the first time in a long while, he felt white-cold panic. Staring out across the devastation of his warband, he realized a very cunning mind had planned this assault—planned it well. And it wasn't over yet.

"They're going to attack," he said.

Sayeed looked at him gravely, then nodded. He shifted Darien's weight to Azár. The officer set off across the square, shouting orders at the soldiers still on their feet. All but the sickest ran to form a perimeter. Scores of men poured in from the side streets, supplementing their defenses.

Feeling suddenly weak, Darien sank down and leaned against the doorway, holding his head in his hands. Azár knelt beside him, looking at him in concern. Nothing happened for minutes. And every minute, he felt the poison gnaw a little more of him away. He stared down at the number of men who still lay on the ground, unable to stand with the rest of their comrades. He should be helping them, healing them.

But he'd been a fool. He'd lowered his guard.

"Fall back!"

Darien glanced up, peering intently out across the night. Then he heard it: the clattering sound of arrows pelting the ground, followed by the ragged sounds of his sentries dying somewhere on the outskirts of town. He pushed himself to his feet and staggered down the steps, leaning heavily on Azár. More arrows splattered the ground, this time closer. Across the square, unarmored men and women started dropping by the dozens.

Darien reached out from within and threw his will on the air, struggling to conjure a shield to protect them from the bowmen's long reach. He couldn't do it. His mind was just as feeble as the rest of him. Staggering, he trudged forward.

"What are you doing?" Azár cried. "You cannot—"

He waved her silent. "I have to get closer!"

Another cloud of arrows whispered at them from the darkness. They clattered to the earth, finding purchase in the bodies of the ill and injured. Across the square, his soldiers were dropping at an alarming rate.

Darien knew he was close enough when he felt the wind of an arrow hiss past his ear. He closed his eyes, focusing his mind as best he could. He cast a glowing shield up over the square. Arrows battered against it, ricocheting off. In the distance, he could hear shouts of frustration when the bowmen realized they were neutralized.

Knowing what was coming next, he reached to draw his sword. And cursed when it wasn't there.

"We need to flee. *Now!*" Azár jerked his arm, yanking him backward.

The shield was costing him. Darien didn't have the strength to maintain it and grapple with his wife at the same time. So he staggered after her, letting the shield thin behind him. Sweat streamed down his face, and his legs trembled beneath him. He couldn't keep up with her.

"Hurry!" Azár cried, tugging him forward.

Darien tripped and landed face down in the dirt. Azár managed to get him back on his feet, to get him moving. He could hear his soldiers engaging an assault force, the clamor of battle ringing across the square, echoing off the walls of the houses. Exhausted, Darien dropped the shield entirely. It wasn't necessary anymore.

"Back in the house!" Azár gasped, hurrying him toward the stairs. But his strength gave out. Darien sank to his knees in the dirt. The world lurched, his vision reeling. He felt like he was going to be violently ill.

"I have to help them," he gasped, trying to make the two Azárs in front of him merge into one image.

Both Azárs raised a fist as if to strike him. "You cannot help anyone dead! You need to heal yourself—*now!*"

Darien closed his eyes. The world sagged, and he sagged with it. He rolled onto his side, clutching his stomach. He felt a growing calmness, a comforting fog drifting up to claim him.

Commotion across the square made him look. A group of Valemen had broken through the perimeter and were charging their position. A few Tanisars streamed in from the alleys to attack their flanks, not fast enough to overcome them.

Azár leaped in front of him and dropped into a fighting crouch, one hand on the ground, as if readying to take them all on by herself.

Darien could do nothing to help her. He lay on his side in the dirt, watching events unfold through a bleary, tilted world. Azár held her ground as the charging men closed the distance between them.

All at once, she screamed and swept out with her hand. A whooshing gush of flames poured forth, engulfing the Valemen's front ranks. Men fled, screaming, through the street, trailing smoke behind them in a fiery wake. Others dropped and rolled in the dirt, enveloped in flames.

The last of the Valemen retreated but didn't get far. A group of Zakai rushed forward, cutting down most with swords and crossbow bolts, routing the rest.

Darien watched the last burning man flail then stop moving. He thought maybe he recognized him. Not that it mattered.

With a cry, Azár dropped back to his side.

"You are safe," she assured him, though the fear in her voice spoke otherwise. She rolled him onto his back.

Darien stared up at her blearily. He fumbled around for the magic field, grabbing the little bit he could. He drew it in and used it to look inward—

—and was horrified by what he found. His organs were shutting down, his tissues dead or dying. His heart stuttered along weakly, his lungs laboring to move air.

He closed his eyes and sucked in as much power as he could with what little he had left. He worked as quickly as he could, racing time against his own flagging consciousness. A wash of peaceful bliss swept over him, calming his heart, soothing the fire in his lungs. The fog came back and rose around him, consuming him, comforting him. Azár's face faded as the mist claimed him entirely, sucking him down. Pulling him under.

Darien awoke comfortable and warm.

The mist was gone, receded back into whatever depths it had roiled up from. Darien blinked it away.

He was back in the bedroom of the mayor's home. The mahogany bed with its over-stuffed mattress contained him, his head supported by down pillows. He was covered by a thick wool blanket that felt warm and scratchy against his skin. A tallow candle glowed from a bronze holder above the bed, the wall behind it darkened by soot.

He felt a hand squeeze his.

Darien turned his head to find Azár sitting at his bedside. She leaned forward, stroking her fingers through his hair. He couldn't tell from the expression on her face whether she was happy or angry at finding him awake.

"How many did we lose?" he asked gruffly.

"Many."

Azár continued to stroke his hair, gazing somberly down at him. Darien closed his eyes, internalizing her answer, using the knowledge to feed his self-loathing.

The deaths were on his hands.

He sat up with a struggle, swinging his legs over the side of the bed. The room wavered for a moment, then stabilized. He cast a glance around, taking in the dull, exhausted look of the bedroom. He wondered who the mayor might have been. Probably someone he knew. A tattered man with a tattered life, judging by his worn possessions.

With Azár's help, Darien rose unsteadily to his feet. He tried a step, making sure his legs could support his weight. Azár peered at him skeptically.

"I'm good," he told her.

He found his clothes draped over a shabby velvet chair. He started pulling on his shirt, but a purring noise behind made him turn. The demon-hound stood in the doorway, slobber stringing from its jowls. Darien tucked in his shirt and laced up his trousers. He walked across the room and offered out his hand. The hound licked his fingers with a festering tongue.

"Where were you last night?" he asked the detestable creature. The thing cocked its head to the side, looking fondly up at him.

"The attack was two nights ago," Azár corrected him sharply.

Darien glanced back at her, hearing the anger in her voice.

"You're unhappy."

She stood with her arms crossed, exuding rage. "You were *stupid!*"

Darien couldn't argue. He nodded in agreement, ruffling the thanacryst's fur. "I agree. I'm stupid. I shouldn't have trusted the cider. I'm sorry."

Azár made a growling noise and spun away. "I am tired of your apologies! Every day, another apology! The problem is not the cider—the problem is *you,* acting as though you are immortal!"

Darien barked a scornful laugh. "Well, I'm not mortal, either, so what does that make me?"

"It makes you a fool!"

With that, she stormed out of the room. Darien stood listening to her loud footfalls echoing down the hallway. The front door opened and slammed shut again, rattling the windows. He let out a lingering sigh, looking down at the hound.

"Never get married," he advised.

The thing looked up at him and yawned. Darien gave it one last scratch, then sat down on the bed and pulled his boots on. He fastened his sword to his waist and followed his wife out of the house.

He walked down the stone steps to the street. There, Darien paused, looking over the debris-filled square. The dead had been cleared away, but evidence of the battle lay everywhere. The dirt was ribboned with blood and scorched by fires. Pieces of armor and bloody rags lay strewn everywhere. He walked slowly across the square, watching soldiers clearing away the remaining debris. They were working hard to return the town back to the state they had found it. Not for their own sakes; their force would be moving on. They were making ready for the civilians who would be following behind to settle in this place.

Darien followed a steady stream of soldiers moving in and out through the town's main gate. He took only a few steps down the road before he slowed to a stop, too disturbed to move any further.

There, lining one of Nat Calway's grain fields, lay a long row of corpses arranged neatly side by side. Sayeed's men were laboring with shovels, digging a long trench along the far side of the field.

Darien's insides twisted up in a knot. He didn't know whether the dead were his own people…or his own people. He squeezed his eyes shut against a deluge of conflicting emotions he couldn't push aside or ignore. The one that dominated, he thought, was an intense feeling of shame.

He forced himself to walk into the field of wheat, wading through the dew-wet grass. He needed to see their faces, had to know which friends his choices had slain. Starting at the end of the row of corpses, he worked his way slowly down the line, his gaze slipping from familiar face to familiar face. They were a sad, broken mix of men and women, white and brown. He knew the names of each. By the time Darien was halfway down the line, he felt physically ill. He made himself continue, scorching each name and face into his memory. When he reached the end of the row, he stopped and stared out across the grain field, feeling suddenly, inexplicably, numb.

He stood there a good while. Then he turned his back on the people he'd failed and walked away.

He didn't know where he was going. It was almost as though he wasn't the man walking out of that field. He was someone else. And he was somewhere else, looking down at himself from some high vantage. It was all too confusing. And he was too dazed to wonder at it.

He trudged into the forest, his feet snapping twigs, crunching on pine needles and oak leaves. Somehow, he ended up on a dirt path that meandered alongside the scar of a stream. It led him deeper into the forest, through a dusty oak grove. Shadows closed in overhead, the branches thickening. Light streaked down to dapple the ground. The air was filled with the scent of forest loam and leaf litter. For some reason, those details seemed important to him.

Gradually, the forest thinned. Blinking, Darien glanced around and realized where he was. He'd journeyed much deeper into the woodland than he'd thought. He turned slowly around, as if waking from a dream, struggling to get his bearings. If he remembered right, there was another footpath just to the east, past a stand of fir trees. He started toward it as if compelled.

He found the path without difficulty. It wasn't very familiar, but he remembered clearly where it led. It ended at a small clearing surrounded by a grove of sycamores. Ahead of him sat a small cottage made of old, rotted planks and bitter memories.

Darien stopped in the clearing and stood looking at the structure for a moment. Then, with a defeated sigh, he walked toward it. He paused before entering, resting a hand on the doorframe. As though the feel of the rough, splintery pine would make the cottage seem more real.

He pushed the door open, letting it swing, moaning, on its hinges.

Immediately, he was confronted by a great heron hanging low from the ceiling on the other side. He stood still, staring at the bird sadly. It looked half-rotten. Many of its downy feathers were loose and falling out. He reached up to touch it, sending the bird spinning on its string.

He ducked under the heron and entered the cottage.

Dozens of birds hung from the ceiling, no two

alike. They spun slowly above him, wings outstretched. Sadly, more than a few had fallen to the floor. The air had a rotten smell to it he didn't remember from before. Soft feathers were scattered everywhere, collecting in the corners and captured in the cobwebs.

His eyes scanned over the Bird Man's bed, coming to rest on a chest pushed up against the far wall. The chest was covered in more birds: some upright, most not. All appeared in various stages of decomposition. Darien felt saddened, remembering how lovingly Master Edric had cared for his collection.

Curiosity impelled his feet toward the chest. He'd been too distraught to open it two years before, when he'd woken from sleep blazing with power, a dead old Master lying next to him on the floor. His only thoughts then had been of escape.

Darien knelt before the chest and lifted the first bird, setting it aside. One by one, he removed the birds from the lid, trying not to disturb the feathers. Despite his best efforts, soft down collected on the floor at his feet. The birds were far too decayed to be handled, even gently.

He removed the last small finch and, using both hands, lifted the cover of the chest. The strong smell of cedarwood jarred his nose. Darien scrubbed his shirtsleeve across his face then reached within. One item at a time, he began removing the chest's contents. An assortment of clothes was soon stacked next to him, all neatly folded. An old leather-bound tome wrapped in cloth and tied shut with hemp cord. A bone-handled knife in a leather sheath. Two chipped ceramic plates. And a folded, age-yellowed note.

Addressed to him.

The feeling left his hands as he picked the note up. He unfolded it carefully, running his fingers over the parchment to smooth out the crease.

Darien,

I hope one day you can forgive me for what I did to you. I knew that one mage could never make a difference in this war, and I was too old and weak to help you. But perhaps my legacy—and my research—can serve you better than they could ever serve me. I am leaving you my journal. Study it well. Perhaps, one day, you can realize what I never could. I did not have enough of the gift in me to bring my dreams to fruition. But now you do. I have every faith and confidence in you, just as your father always had.

Your Friend,

Edric

Darien lowered the note, setting it on the stack of clothing beside him on the floor. He knelt there for a while, staring ahead with a confused, unfocused gaze. He had never understood why Master Edric had forced more of the gift into him than one man could ever endure. It had been a death sentence. One that had never made any sense to him—it was one of the great mysteries of his life. Perhaps, now, he could finally have an explanation for it.

He reached down and lifted the cloth-wrapped tome, holding it in his hand. Delicately, he untied the hemp cord and folded back the fabric. The thick leather cover was old. Very old—far older than the normal lifespan of a man. He opened it carefully and gazed down at the first page. A single date was written there in blue ink: *1621-.*

Darien blinked. The date was over a hundred years ago. And yet it was written in the same flowing script as the Bird Man's letter. Darien turned the page and scanned the first paragraph. He dismissed it quickly—the writing was a reflective piece, nothing of importance. He opened the text to a page marked by a frayed ribbon.

On the page before him was a sketch of one of the many birds that dangled over his head, along with accompanying measurements. The same bird was sketched again at the bottom of the page, only with wings extended and feathers and skin removed—a labeled diagram showing the bird's musculature. Turning the page revealed another diagram, this one of the bird's skeleton. Then another of internal organs. Another of lace-like vascular tissues, rendered painstakingly. The next pages were devoted entirely to mathematical calculations.

He didn't understand any of it, much less why the Bird Man had gone to such lengths to explore the anatomy of a single warbler. As for the calculations…he would have to spend some time with them. Whatever problem they had been applied to solve, he couldn't determine at first glance.

He closed the book and was about ready to wrap it back up in its cloth cover. But then he paused, for the first time noticing the elegant embroidery that had been sewn into the fabric. He traced a finger over it, admiring the minute details that had been worked into the wings, the vibrant colors of the scales—

"What manner of creature is that?"

Darien flinched, almost dropping the journal. He glanced up at Sayeed. He took a deep breath, seeking to steady his nerves. Then he rose to his feet, handing the embroidered cloth to his First.

"It's a dragon," he said. "They breathe fire, slay heroes, and ravage cities."

Sayeed frowned, holding the fabric at various angles, studying the embroidered dragon with a look of grave concern.

He said, "I never knew such monsters existed."

"They don't. Except in heraldry."

Darien took the cloth back and folded it around the journal. He tied it closed then looked around, making sure there was nothing left in the cottage of any importance. He gazed upward at the twirling birds that dangled on their strings: hawks and jays, ducks and woodpeckers. A great horned owl mounted in a corner stared at him accusingly.

"Who lived here?" Sayeed asked, ducking under a peregrine falcon. He reached up and poked the wingtip, sending the bird rocking.

"The man who saved me when I fell from the mountain."

Sayeed touched another bird, making it twirl faster on its string. "A strange man."

"Aye," Darien agreed, remembering the three tiers of power the old Master had forced into him on top of the five he'd already had. "A very strange man."

"I heard you came this way," Sayeed said. He knelt and began replacing the contents of the cedar chest. "The men thought you seemed unsettled. Did you know some of the townsfolk who were slain?" He closed the lid of the chest, then set about returning the scattered birds back to their roost.

Darien nodded, feeling the shame return to clutch his throat. "Aye. Every one of them." He closed his eyes, dredging up their images in his head. "Mace Mullins taught me how to fish. He was an old farmer with six boys. Only three made it to adulthood. Lost his wife in childbirth."

He moved toward the window, looking through the uneven glass in the direction of the grove. "Nat Flannon owned a farm up the road. He was the town chandler. We always did chores for him, and he always gave us treats. Dane Tirrel was the miller's son. We used to set traps together—"

"Stop," Sayeed commanded, standing up. "There is only one man alive who can defeat you, and that man is you. Do not surrender to him."

Darien nodded, understanding. Sayeed was right. Yet he had no idea how to vanquish that particular foe.

Sayeed placed a hand on his shoulder and looked at him gravely. "Be the dragon, Darien. Breathe fire, slay heroes, and ravage cities."

Staring out the window, Darien muttered, "I told you. Dragons don't exist."

Sayeed assured him, "They do now."

Chapter Twenty
Story's End

Isle of Titherry, The Rhen

Quin inhaled the cigar deeply and, closing his eyes, let the smoke out savoringly. He lifted a cup to his lips, chasing down the taste with anise-flavored arak, swishing it around in his mouth. He smiled as the alcohol scorched his throat. Arak was supposed to be a delicate beverage, well-watered and served over ice. Quin preferred it straight from the bottle, undiluted. He smacked his lips and nestled his head back to stare directly up at a garish blue sky.

He turned at the sound of approaching footsteps, squinting through a wash of sunlight to see Naia moving toward him. Her face was set in the same, flustered scowl she had taken to wearing lately. She paused in front of his chair, hands on her hips, looking down at him with an air of disapproval. Quin adjusted his hat until the brim shielded his eyes from the sun's glare. He could see her features better, now. She was even more agitated than he'd realized.

"Whatever's the matter?" he asked. "You look like someone just pressed the ruffles out of your petticoat."

"Please, Quin." Naia sighed in exasperation. She sank down in the chair next to his. The soft breeze played with a wisp of hair that had fallen out of her braid. He leaned forward and tucked the wayward strands back behind her ear.

"I apologize for my lack of social graces. Here," he said, offering his cup to her. "This should make it all better."

Naia received the cup and brought it to her lips. Immediately, she winced, her face crumpling into a grimace.

"What *is* that?" she gasped, handing it back. "It tastes like medicine!"

Quin smiled, accepting the cup and knocking back a healthy mouthful, grinning devilishly. "Think of it as medicine for the soul."

Naia scowled. "My soul is perfectly fine, thank you. It's your own soul I'm more concerned about."

"As am I." Quin set about replenishing his cup. "Which makes finishing this bottle of paramount importance."

Quick as a snake, Naia's hand shot out and snatched the container from his hand. She turned it on end, pouring the liquor onto the flagstones in a long, thin stream. She shook the bottle to make sure every last drop had been evacuated, then clunked it down on the stones by her feet.

Watching his arak spreading across the ground, Quin sighed morosely. "I take it you have no care for my salvation."

"Please. What I need from you right now is support."

Quin couldn't ignore the weary plea in her eyes. "Come here, darling," he said, and leaned forward to embrace her with one hand, holding his cigar as far as he could away from her face. He gave her a good, tight squeeze, then kissed her forehead. He sat back in his chair, taking a few short puffs.

"More visions?" he asked.

"Versions," she corrected him, rubbing her eyes. "And yes. I mean no."

Quin cocked an eyebrow. "Do you mind clarifying?"

Naia breathed a heavy sigh. "The versions I've

been seeing just keep repeating. Over and over and over. With only minor variations in detail. In all the time I've spent reading the Crescent, I've seen only the same three outcomes." She held up a finger. "We destroy the magic field." A second finger: "Renquist halts the Reversal." And a third: "The Reversal happens and kills us all."

Quin reached over and rolled the end of his cigar against the ground to knock some of the ash off. "By 'kill us all,' you mean just us mages?"

"That's correct."

"And which outcome will free the skies over Malikar?"

Naia's gaze slipped to the side. "Destroying the magic field would break the Curse, as Tsula says. Or we could help Zavier Renquist halt the Reversal."

Probably not the best alternative, Quin decided. "I don't understand. A thousand years ago, Renquist said it would take the combined strength of eight Grand Masters to stabilize the magic field. Now he thinks he can do it all by himself?"

Naia's face became grave. "In every version of that Story, Renquist sacrifices either Darien or Kyel on a Circle of Convergence. And then he kills me."

Frowning, Quin took another puff of his cigar, giving himself time to grapple with his emotions. Out of all the terrible outcomes Naia had listed, that was the one he couldn't tolerate. He hadn't meant to fall for Naia. When it came to love, he'd had nothing but terrible experiences. He'd thought he'd learned. But he hadn't been able to help himself. Zavier Renquist had already taken Amani from him. Quin wasn't about to let him take Naia, as well.

He asked, "Is Tsula still alive in all the versions you're seeing?

Naia paused in thought before nodding. "Yes."

Quin took a few short puffs of his cigar. "So…it's possible there are still other versions of this story that are still out there. Is there some way Tsula could be blocking you from seeing them? You said her death might open up other avenues."

"Possibly."

His brain ticked through a quick checklist of reasons and rationale. When he reached the end of that list, the obvious course of action seemed like a non-decision. There were no more facts to ponder. And there was no reason to hesitate.

Quin leaned over and mashed his cigar against the ground, scrubbing it back and forth, leaving a streak of black soot on the flagstones. Flicking what was left over the side of the balcony, he rose from his chair and kissed Naia's cheek.

"Why don't you go up to the library, darling," he suggested, straightening his hat. "I think I'll go for a walk."

Naia nodded absently, gazing over the edge of the balcony in the direction of the Crescent. She didn't look up as he walked away. He wondered what she was thinking about so hard. A cool breeze came up, stirring his coat. He glanced back at Naia one last time then opened the door to the castle.

Once inside, he focused his concentration on the sound of his feet echoing sharply off the walls. The castle rang eerily, vastly empty, which worked to his advantage. The last thing he needed was distraction. As he walked, his thoughts started drifting. He battered them back into focus. Thinking led to doubt. Doubt led to hesitation.

And that was the one thing he couldn't afford.

In his profession, morality had no relevance. Right or wrong, the world—and Naia's life—depended on his decisiveness.

Quin entered the great hall and wound through the intimate clusters of furniture that filled the sprawling room. It was as though the chamber was a neglected host, waiting eternally for guests who would never arrive. He took great care to step quietly, not wanting the sounds of his footfalls to announce his presence prematurely.

He found the small room Tsula occupied at the far end of the hall.

Quin paused outside her cracked door, taking one last moment to prepare. He checked his boot knife to make sure it was loose in its sheath. He checked his pulse, checked his resolve, then reached up to push the door open.

The sound of Tsula's voice halted his motion. "Stop lurking in the doorway and come inside, Quinlan Reis."

He supposed he should have been startled. But he was unsurprised. The Harbinger seemed to have an endless supply of prescience. Quin pushed the door open and found Tsula sitting in her chair, awaiting him with hands folded on her lap. She wore an elaborate headwrap, her body swallowed by the fabric of an over-sized kaftan. She gazed up at him with eyes as dull as stone and hard as steel. Raising her hand, she indicated the chair opposite her own.

"Have a seat." Her voice was just as level as her expression. "You kept me waiting. I expected you much sooner."

Quin sat in the offered chair and stared around at the screaming colors of the cluttered room. Everywhere he looked were tapestries, knickknacks, baskets, vases, jewelry—a lifetime's worth of possessions all gathered together in one dense, claustrophobic space. It was all so distracting, he almost missed the substance of Tsula's words.

His gaze snapped toward her. "You know why I'm here?"

"Of course." She draped her hands over the armrests of her chair. "I am a Harbinger. Knowing the hour and manner of my death is just one of the many burdens those of my order must bear. At first, we see our death as only one of an infinite number of possibilities—or versions, as we like to call them. But each decision we make turns another page in the Story of our life. The longer we live, the versions of our narrative diminish before our eyes, until there is only one version left to pen. And then our life's chapter is written. I've known how my own Story ends for quite some time. And I know it will end here today."

Her words made Quin feel cold and clammy—a sensation he wasn't used to. He found himself having second thoughts.

Suspiciously, he asked, "Then why aren't you trying to stop me?"

"Because death cannot be avoided." Tsula confronted him with a relentless, deadpan stare. "Far too many times in my life, I have had to stay my hand and watch fate reap its terrible harvest. I foresaw the fall of my nation. And I foresaw my own daughter's death. Yet I could do nothing to prevent either. If I had stopped you from causing the Desecration of Caladorn, then the entire world would now be under Xerys' sway. And if I had stopped my daughter from trading her life to save your own, we would not be sitting here today. You would have never foiled my husband's plans. And now Xerys would be reigning from the throne of Isap, with the world groveling at his feet."

Quin's breath hitched. He sat frozen in his chair, shocked into rigidity. His mouth went dry. His thoughts hung suspended in the air, waiting for impact.

He whispered, "You're Amani's mother?"

"I am."

His heart broke open. Quin lurched from his chair, overcome by mindless rage. He towered over Tsula, fury sweeping away what was left of his rationality.

"And you *knew?* You knew she was going to Aerysius? *You knew she was going to be executed?"*

"I did." Tsula's expression was glacial.

Quin wanted to howl. He clenched and unclenched his fists. "Why didn't you warn her? Why didn't you stop her? *You let her die!*"

"I already told you," Tsula said, calmly. "There is a reason why all Harbingers were trained in seclusion on this isle. We are called upon to make difficult choices. Sometimes, those choices are unbearable. I knew Amani would die. And I knew her death would destroy you. And yet I could do absolutely nothing to save either of you. Otherwise, the reign of Xerys would have already come to pass."

Quin shot forward, planting both hands on the back of her chair, his face an inch away from her own. Gritting his teeth, he growled, "Amani meant everything to me! *Everything!*"

"I know."

"She didn't have to die!" His voice shook just as hard as the rest of him. His vision blurred. He pushed off from the chair, whirling away.

Almost gently, Tsula said, "I hope someday you can forgive me, Quinlan Reis. As I forgive you."

It was too much. He lashed out with the magic field, ending her life in a heartbeat.

Chapter Twenty-One
The False God

Northern Chamsbrey, The Rhen

Darien raised his practice sword, catching Azár's strike on his crossguard.

"Don't let the blade get ahead of you," he instructed. He stepped back, bringing his blade up into a high ward above his shoulder. "Again. Move together with your sword."

Azár took a step back, then repeated the action. This time, her blade impacted solidly with his.

"Like that," Darien said. "Again. This time rotate your left hand. Watch your structure."

Azár stepped back, brought her sword up, then moved forward with a downward cut. Darien moved crisply to block, noting the difference in her blade's impact. There was a lot more power behind her strike than there'd been before.

"Better."

He smiled, lowering his guard. "Why don't you practice that a few times?"

Azár grinned back, resuming her stance. Darien tossed the practice sword down on a rug beside the other dulled blades the Zakai had brought out for morning drills. He stood watching Azár rehearse her cuts, her feet now in time with the rhythm of her blade. Satisfied, he turned and strolled back across the encampment in search of Sayeed. As he walked, he realized he was smiling. He took enormous pride in his wife. He couldn't think of another woman he'd ever admired more.

He crossed the entire encampment in less time than it had taken him a week ago. The attack in Amberlie had greatly reduced their numbers. There were less soldiers, and therefore less tents. He'd healed all the men and women he could, making certain they'd suffer no further losses on the march. Even so, it had taken them longer to reach Glen Farquist than he'd anticipated.

He found Sayeed conferring with his senior officers. The men stopped talking as soon as they caught sight of him, their gazes slipping to the ground. Even after all the time he'd spent amongst the Tanisars, their eyes had never lost the formal deference that had been there from the outset.

Sayeed left his men to intercept him, guiding him away with a hand on his arm. Darien still found it peculiar, the lack of personal distance Sayeed and his people were comfortable with. He'd never liked being touched. He'd liked it less in recent months. There were only two people in the world he could endure being in close proximity to: Azár and Sayeed. Everyone else knew better and kept their distance.

At the top of a low rise, Sayeed let go of his arm and gestured downhill at the valley below. They stood in the shadow of the Craghorns, the mountain's snowy summits blocking the warm rays of the morning sun. Below, the forest thinned to grassland. Beyond the ridge, the grassland thinned to sand. The valley below was a microcosm of desert surrounded by mountains and rolling, heathered hills, protected by a horseshoe ring of golden bluffs. Highly defensible geographically. In all of recorded history, Glen Farquist had never fallen.

Sayeed asked, "What are your thoughts?"

Darien stared down at the opening between the cliffs, remembering the last time he had ridden between those sandstone walls. It had been with Naia, the same day he had forsworn his Oath of

Harmony. He still remembered the harsh face of Naia's father, the High Priest of Death, who had tried to convince him to abandon his course. Darien wondered how his life would have been different if he'd listened to the man.

"It'll be well-defended," he said. "They don't have a standing army, but they can raise a competent force of clergy and laymen. A few of the temples have monks trained in the martial arts. They're also in possession of several artifacts that might give us problems."

Sayeed's face grew very serious. "And will they yield?"

Darien shook his head. "No."

Sayeed blew out a long sigh, then bit his lip thoughtfully, his gaze travelling over the valley. His face ranged through a variety of emotions, finally settling on trepidation. "If these are men and women of the cloth, it is ill luck to strike them down."

Darien turned his back on the valley. "They struck first."

Glen Farquist, The Rhen

Kyel strode beside Alexa down a narrow tunnel that plunged beneath the cliffs rimming Glen Farquist. The silent cleric who guided them carried a flickering torch in his hand that cast a rippling plume of light. The massive expanse of rock above them seemed to bear down on the roof of the tunnel, so much so that Kyel felt like he had to duck as he walked along. The air was frigid and smelled of wet clay, an odor Kyel found nostalgic.

In the weeks before the Battle of Orien's Finger, Darien had sent him on a mission to find a way to seal the Well of Tears. There was no greater library in the world than the vast warren of Om's temple. Kyel had spent three days leafing through texts and documents in the belly of the temple, only to find out his search had been merely pretense. Darien had already known the text he needed. The search had been just another of the infuriating lessons Darien had contrived for him.

Alexa hadn't spoken a word since they'd entered the tunnels. She walked at Kyel's side looking utterly serene, as if she had been in the warrens of the temple a hundred times before. Perhaps she had. Along their journey south, she'd shared tidbits of her life, like crumbs scattered before him on the floor. But the same way crumbs did a poor job of describing the loaf they'd been broken from, Alexa's scraps of information yielded surprisingly little about her life before Aerysius' fall.

At the bottom of the tunnel, they reached a broad avenue carved from rock. There, they were passed off to another cleric, who led them along a subterranean highway past a tall water clock. They followed their guide through several corridors filled with silent men and women carrying armloads of scrolls and books. They turned down a whitewashed hallway that led to the High Priest's personal chambers.

Their brown-robed guide knocked on the door then swept it open before them. But when Kyel moved to enter the room, the cleric stepped between Alexa and himself, preventing her from following. The balding old man shook his head.

"It's all right," Kyel assured Alexa. "They're funny like this. I'll catch up with you when I'm done here."

Alexa's eyes clouded with doubt, but at last she nodded and followed their guide back in the direction they'd come from.

Kyel had good reason to trust the clerics. And good reason not to. He'd spent a lot of his time in their warrens during the past two years. They had helped him make the transition from commoner to mage, helping him locate information he so desperately needed to increase his knowledge. And they'd cared for his son and seen to Gil's education, something Kyel hadn't been able to do alone. Even after what had happened to Cadmus, he had every reason to believe the priesthood of Wisdom would still support him.

He hoped.

He entered the High Priest's chambers and found two men waiting for him within. The first was a middle-aged man Kyel had never seen before. He was slender, except for his cheeks, which looked mottled and swollen. He wore a pair of spectacles that hung off-kilter too far down his nose. But it was the man sitting beside him who commanded Kyel's attention.

Kyel moved into the room, nodding formally at the High Priest of Wisdom.

The priest returned the gesture, his long white beard dipping to brush his steepled fingers. He wore elegant robes of rich brown, along with a bronze stole draped over his shoulders. His vibrant blue gaze came to rest on Kyel's cloak.

Kyel turned to the gangly cleric sitting on the stool next to him. "I'm Kyel Archer," he introduced himself. "Pardon, but I don't believe we've met?"

The cleric's glasses slipped further down his nose. He pushed them back with a finger. "My name is Arvel. I am the Voice of His Eminence."

The man was Cadmus' replacement, Kyel realized. "Your Eminence, where did you have Alexa taken?"

It was Arvel who replied. "Your companion has been escorted to a guest room, where she may recover from her journey." He adjusted his posture on the stool, sliding his bare feet up to rest on the crossbar between the stool's legs. "We are glad you have returned. Events have transpired that—"

"I want to see my son," Kyel cut him off.

The High Priest shook his head.

Arvel stated firmly, "You may see your son after we have spoken. There are many issues that are of paramount importance, and—"

"No."

Kyel shook his head firmly. When he'd first met the High Priest of Wisdom, he had allowed the man to unsettle him, and in doing so, allowed himself to be manipulated easily. No longer. He was done with being controlled.

"Whatever you want to say, it can wait," he told the two men, pushing back his chair and standing up. "I want to see my son first."

Arvel stared at him unblinkingly. Tense moments wore by. At last, the cleric shook his head. "Our warrens extend for miles. A small child could easily get lost within," he said softly, dangerously.

Kyel froze, rooted by fear. They had anticipated his arrival and had prepared for it. He sank back into his seat, glaring at Arvel with a raptor's intensity.

"Be warned," Kyel said. "I've lost any patience I ever had with the temples of Glen Farquist. This temple, in particular. Bring my son to me. Now."

Arvel turned and looked at the High Priest. The two stared at each other a long moment. They were conferring, Kyel knew. The Vicar of Om had taken a vow of silence and could only express his thoughts through the medium of his Voice. That Voice had once been Cadmus. Apparently, it was now Arvel.

"We are willing to make a compromise," Arvel said at last. "If you address two of the issues we wish to speak of first, then your son will be brought to you. You may spend the remainder of the day in his company. Then tonight after supper, we will gather here again to address the remainder of the issues that confront us."

Kyel glared at him a moment longer, stewing. At last he nodded. The compromise was likely the best offer he'd get. He sat back in his seat and crossed his arms. "Very well."

Arvel looked pleased. He set his hands on the table, knitting his fingers with a smile. "We shall first address the abhorrent amount of power in you."

Kyel blinked. He hadn't expected that. At least, not right away. They had jumped right to the most damning subject they could confront him with. Perhaps it was an attempt to throw him off balance. If so, it was working.

"What about it?" he asked warily.

The man leaned forward in his chair, smiling at Kyel apologetically. His glasses had slipped down his nose again. This time, he didn't bother pushing them back. "Before we begin, we wish to apologize for our lack of sensitivity on these issues. However, it is not possible to discuss—"

"Just get on with it," Kyel growled.

Arvel stared at him in silence for a moment, then said with a flick of his eyebrows, "To be very blunt, you have eleven tiers of power in you. If you were any other mage, and this were any other time, we'd already have your execution prearranged. However…we wish to assure you that is not the case. We have no plans to harm you."

Kyel shrugged dismissively. "That's because you don't think I'll live long enough to be a threat."

Arvel smiled. "I'm glad you understand. Considering the situation, there can be no secrets between us." With one hand, he slid the spectacles from his face and set them on the table. Reaching up, he massaged the bridge of his nose.

When he lowered his hand, Arvel's face had transformed.

Sitting across from Kyel was a different man entirely, one of robust stature and imposing presence. Kyel stared at him in stunned silence as seconds ticked by. His eyes went to the old man. Then back to the man who had just been Arvel.

Kyel didn't know how he knew. He just *knew*.

"You are Om," he whispered.

"No." Arvel shook his head. "Om does not exist. He never has. Like almost every other deity, Om is merely an inception, an archetype of an ideal. Which explains my existence: I am the incarnation of what Om *would* be. Through my network of historians and spies, I have access to limitless knowledge and can conduct limitless surveillance. I have access to artifacts that expand my mind, my sight, and my hearing. I listen to all the mutterings and grumblings of the world. I feel the flutter of every butterfly wing. I am aware of every birth and every death. Every cry of misery and every gasp of joy. For all intents and purposes, I *am* a god. The only thing I lack is the spark of divinity."

Kyel sat back, folding his hands. Part of him felt anger, betrayal. Another part was just relieved to hear the truth. At least, now, he had something to work with.

"Why are you telling me this?" he asked. "Why now? Why me?"

Arvel stood up, turning his back on the old priest, who now sat staring at the surface of the table, looking decisively irrelevant. He said to Kyel, "All the rules have changed. We are now reaching the end game. And now, more than ever before, we must play to win. In the coming days, you will be tested more than any other mage in history. You must stand firm. It is the only way the Rhen will survive the coming crisis with any remnants of civilization intact. Unfortunately, you have no choice."

Kyel disagreed. "I do have a choice. Don't ever for a second think I don't." He narrowed his eyes. "And while we're at it, let's get one damn thing straight: I'm not on your side. I've never been. I'm on my own side—and I'm not convinced our goals are compatible."

Arvel folded his hands. Softly, he asked, "And what are your goals, Sentinel Archer?"

The man was trying to intimidate him. It wouldn't work. What Arvel didn't understand was that Kyel had already accepted the inevitability of his own death—a feeling that was oddly liberating. Very few things could scare him any longer. Certainly not the robed creature in front of him.

Kyel responded in an even tone, "My goal has never changed: to serve the land and its people."

"Ah," the false god smiled. "The Acolyte's Oath. Very noble. But very pedestrian. Even you must agree: the wording is rather vague."

"That doesn't change its intent." Kyel smiled bitterly. "What that oath means is I'm not your tool. I'm a servant of the land and the people of the land. And *I'll* be the judge as to which land that applies to, and which people that includes."

Arvel looked at him and drew in a long, expansive breath, his face menacing. "What exactly are you implying?"

Kyel sat forward, resting his arm on the table. "For a thousand years, your temple and its 'limitless knowledge' has known the truth about the Enemy. But instead of coming to their aid, you walled them away in the Black Lands and beat them back whenever they've emerged. What you've done is nothing short of genocide. I won't tolerate it anymore."

The man stiffened. "Then you have decided to align with Xerys against us?"

"No." Kyel shook his head firmly. "Not with Xerys. I'm taking the side of common sense and decency. I'll help you stand against Renquist and his Servants. I'll help you drive them from this world. But I will not help you destroy an entire population of people. I'll fight you to the death first."

Arvel cocked an eyebrow. "Are you aware there are three Enemy armies ravaging the North even as we speak? One less than a day's ride from here?"

"Of course, I'm aware of it," Kyel snapped. "I've done everything I can to slow them down and deplete their numbers. But we have to end this. We need to negotiate with them. Strike a treaty. Find a way we can peacefully coexist."

Arvel stared at him sidelong. "They're murdering and ravaging the very people you've sworn to protect."

"They're led by a demon," Kyel acknowledged. "But that doesn't make *them* demons."

Arvel slid back in his seat. He peered over the waxed table top with ice blue eyes that burned like coldfire. "So, what do you propose?"

Kyel shrugged, thinking the answer should be obvious. "I propose we get rid of the demon."

"And how do you intend to accomplish that?"

Kyel pushed himself out of his chair and stood up

from the table. He reached down and unhooked Thar'gon from his belt. He held the talisman up and, turning it slowly, watched the spikes of the morning star glisten in the candlelight.

"With this."

Chapter Twenty-Two
Hope Besieged

Northern Chamsbrey, The Rhen

Darien bit off a strip of jerky and chewed it automatically. He was engrossed in the old leather journal in his lap. He tore off another bite and flipped a page. Master Edric's notes were scrawled on papers of different sizes and weights, as if they'd been scribed loosely and then collected and bound at a later date. The journal was full of diagrams, notes, equations, and descriptions. Edric's preoccupation with birds was evident throughout. Nearly every bird species Darien knew was documented and sketched at least once. And there were many other creatures that had been the objects of intense study. Mostly reptiles: snakes and lizards. A few insects, though it seemed Edric had abandoned that line of inquiry.

Darien's finger moved over a page as he tried to follow the logic of a particularly long and complex passage. He got lost halfway through. It seemed Edric had made up his own shorthand system. Darien had tried working forward and backward to understand how the man had arrived at his conclusions, without much success. He thought he had an idea of which general directions the Bird Man's mind had wandered, but he had no idea of the exact paths.

He tore off another strip of dried horsemeat and worried it in his mouth, flipping back to the ribbon-marked page he'd started with. He studied the diagrams of the bird intensely. It was a warbler: a palm-sized bird with a sharp beak that was common throughout Amberlie Grove. There had to be some reason why Edric had bookmarked that page in particular. It had to be a starting point…but to what?

He looked up when he heard Azár's footsteps approaching. His wife sank down next to him in the grass, crossing her legs and resting her head on his shoulder.

"Have you learned anything more?" she asked, looking down at the journal.

Darien shook his head. "I think I know what he was trying to get at, but the energy transformations would be mindboggling. I don't have the faintest idea how he could get around it."

Azár sat up and took the last strip of jerky from his hand. Popping it in her mouth, she said around the bite, "What do you think he was trying to do?"

Darien hesitated, afraid to voice his thoughts for fear of sounding like a fool. "I think he was trying to turn himself into a bird."

Azár stopped chewing and looked him over with an expression that seemed to question his sanity. "How is that possible? Birds are small. How could a whole man fit into a bird's tiny body?"

Darien said, "It's a simple matter of converting the physical to energy and then converting it back again, but you'd lose a lot along the way. A better question would be, how much of the man could you get back *out* of the bird?" Darien shrugged, his shoulders vocalizing his frustration better than words ever could.

Azár swallowed her mouthful of horse meat. "Would it not be like healing? Rearrangement of the flesh?"

"It's far from rearrangement," Darien grumbled. "It's more like reinvention. I don't know how Edric could have pursued anything like this. He was only third tier. And even if he could make it work, I can't imagine he could transform himself into anything larger than a cockroach."

Azár leaned into him, her body pressed against his. "Does it say he managed to accomplish this? Or only that he tried?"

"Not that I've found. He suggests that he did, but he never comes right out and says it."

She pulled back and looked at him. "You are not thinking of trying this thing, are you?"

"No." Darien shook his head. "I don't understand even a quarter of it yet. And there's too much risk. If something went wrong, I could end up a quivering mass of goo."

Azár's face scrunched into a grimace. She held her hand up in a gesture against evil. "Ugh. No. I would not like you like that. You should put that book away."

Darien grinned, closing the journal and wrapping it back up in its cloth covering. "I thought you wanted to be rid of me."

"Not yet." Azár smiled mischievously, holding fast to the expression as she kissed him.

Glen Farquist, The Rhen

"Papa!"

Kyel laughed in joy, scooping his son off the floor. He crushed him against his chest, rocking his little body from side to side. Gil's soft curls tickled his cheek, and his sharp knees ground into Kyel's ribs.

"I've missed you!" he exclaimed into his son's golden hair.

"Missed you too, Papa!" Gil squeezed tighter, wriggling in excitement. Kyel sat down on a chair and set Gil on his lap. He had to pry Gil's arms away from his neck to keep the blood flowing to his head. Kyel held his son against his chest, never wanting to let go. When Gil had enough, he laughed and squirmed out of the embrace.

Bouncing up and down on Kyel's leg, he exclaimed, "Papa! Did you fight a war?"

Kyel shook his head. "Not really." Then he thought about it. "I don't know. Maybe I did."

His son's eyes widened like saucers, his mouth forming an enormous O. *"You fought a war?"*

Kyel ruffled Gil's hair playfully. "Something like that."

"What is that?" Gil asked, pointing at the morning star Kyel had set down by the door. It wasn't a very good place for a spiked weapon, he realized.

"It's a magic stick," he said, grinning.

Gil made a sharp, excited gasp. "Can I have it? Please?"

Kyel shook his head. "No. It's not a toy. In fact, Papa needs to find somewhere else to put it." He lifted Gil and set him on the floor, then rose to find a better home for the talisman.

"Wanna wrestle?" Gil asked, bouncing up and down.

Kyel picked up Thar'gon and glanced around for a place to put it. His eyes leaped to a book case set against the wall. He placed the weapon on top, out of reach of curious hands.

"Papa's a bit tired," he admitted.

Undeterred, Gil clung to his leg and tugged as if trying to pry Kyel's foot off the floor. Kyel pinwheeled his arms then pretend-fell and rolled onto his stomach, letting Gil clamber on top of him.

"I win!"

"Yes, you beat me!" Kyel gasped, trying to catch his breath as his son bounced up and down on his back.

Gil slid off, got down on his belly, and stared Kyel in the face. "Are you a king?"

"No, not a king," Kyel laughed, pushing himself up and leaning back against the wall. Gil wormed his way over to him, sliding into his lap. He wrapped himself in the drape of Kyel's arm.

"Uncle Arvel said you're a king."

"Oh, he did, now?" Kyel frowned, not certain how he felt about 'Uncle' Arvel. And this king business.

"Are you a prince?"

"No. Just a mage."

"Oh. Love you anyway, Papa." Gil squeezed Kyel's arm tight.

Kyel embraced his son back. "I love you too, Gil."

A knock at the door destroyed the moment.

With a sigh, Kyel set his son on the floor and rose, crossing to the door. He opened it just a crack and peered out, prepared to tell whichever cleric was there to go away. To his surprise, he found Alexa waiting in the hallway.

He'd forgotten all about her.

Feeling chagrinned, Kyel turned to Gil. "I'll be right back," he said, then slipped sideways out the door, closing it before Gil could get a look at Alexa. Or before Alexa could get a look at his son. He wasn't sure which he was trying to prevent.

"I was just coming to check on you," he lied. Then he realized he'd lied. And he didn't care, which was the strange thing. Dismissing the train of thought, he asked her, "Are they treating you well?"

Alexa regarded him with an expression that was three parts irritation and one part disbelief, no doubt over his lack of concern. "Yes, if you call ignoring me treating me well. I told them I'm a mage, but they don't seem to believe me. I can't get anyone to fetch me so much as a cup of water."

Kyel wondered why Alexa just didn't fetch her own water. Swallowing his misgivings, he tried to mollify her. "I'll talk to them. I'm going to be meeting with—err, the High Priest—after supper."

Alexa's face lit up. "Am I invited to supper?"

Kyel doubted she was. Arvel certainly hadn't requested her company. Kyel found himself lying to her again. "I assume you are. They have to feed you, don't they?" Lying was a lot easier, he realized, than telling Alexa the truth. Her feelings were fragile, he was finding out.

"Is that your son?" She leaned forward, trying to peer past him through the crack in the door.

Kyel stepped sideways to block her view, pulling the door all the way closed behind him.

"Yes," he admitted, knowing Alexa must have caught a glimpse of Gil.

"Why is he here?"

That was indeed a long story, and one Kyel deeply regretted. Trying to make it as short as possible, he told her, "Meiran had me bring him here. She was hoping he'd inherited the Potential from me. We thought it wise for Gil to receive an education, just in case. With Aerysius gone, this temple is the best center of learning in the world."

"That makes sense," Alexa said, nodding. She glanced up at Kyel, her eyes full of candid innocence. "Doesn't he miss his mum?"

Kyel sighed, nodding. "He does. It was a hard choice." Looking into her eyes, he realized how easy it could be to forget Alexa was a mage.

She looked suddenly saddened. "Poor dear. What are you going to do with him after—"

Kyel put his hand up, stopping her. He had just been holding his son after five months of being apart from him. He didn't want to be reminded that these few moments might be the last he'd ever get with him.

Alexa's gaze slid downward. Apparently, she realized she'd overstepped. She said quietly, "Maybe there's something you can do. Some way you can stay with him."

Kyel's anger flared. The last thing he needed was hope. "No," he said firmly.

"Maybe we can find a way," she insisted, her eyes brightening.

"It's impossible."

Alexa shook her head. "Nothing's impossible." She set a hand on his arm and squeezed it reassuringly. "Don't lose hope, Kyel," she said, then turned and walked back down the corridor.

Kyel stared after her, silently seething. Alexa was wrong. Hope was just a delusion people clung to in order to make life seem bearable. What they didn't understand was how much worse they'd feel when hope inevitably failed. He wasn't going to make that mistake. He wasn't going to be deluded into thinking that he'd have more time to spend with his son and show Gil how much he loved him.

To Kyel's surprise, Arvel relented and allowed Alexa to join them for supper. Not that it mattered. It was the most uncomfortable meal Kyel had ever been forced to sit through. Not a word was spoken that wasn't necessary. All parties sat on different sides of the table. Possibly different sides of the war. If Arvel and the old man next to him were conversing, Kyel couldn't tell. Both seemed just as intent on ignoring each other as they were bent on ignoring him.

When the meal was finished, Alexa pushed back her plate. "Thank you, Your Eminence, for your graceful hospitality," she said, breaking the resounding tension.

Arvel smiled at her indulgently. "His Eminence appreciates your gratitude. However, he does ask that you excuse us now. We wish to spend some time alone with Kyel."

Alexa shot Kyel a questioning look. He ignored her.

"Of course," she muttered, seeming flustered. "My apologies." She scooted her chair back and, with one last, stabbing glare at Kyel, exited the room. The door closed behind her more roughly than it should have.

Kyel took his time about folding his napkin. He set it down carefully on the table. Then he turned to look at the High Priest. Or whatever the silent old man actually was. More than a puppet but less than a figurehead, Kyel supposed. He wasn't surprised when the old man rose and followed Alexa out of the room.

Kyel watched his exit, feeling somewhat grateful for the man's departure. He turned to Arvel and spread his hands. "Well. Here I am."

"Yes," Arvel said with a condescending look. "Here you are. Let's start with that woman. Do you trust her?"

"No," Kyel said honestly.

"Interesting. And yet you travel with her."

He shrugged. "I don't distrust her, either."

Arvel planted an elbow on the table, cradling his face with his hand. "I'm aware of the peculiar way you found that woman—Cadmus was able to relay the information to us before he was slain. Let's just say…I am concerned. At the very least. You see, Alexa Newell's name was added to the List years ago."

Kyel had heard the clerics of Om referring to that List once before. He'd assumed it meant some type of catalogue of deaths.

Arvel continued, "It is possible this woman you know as Alexa is exactly what she seems. And if that's all she is, then she may be a tremendous asset. With her, there exists the possibility that together you might seal the Well of Tears before you pass from this world."

Kyel's mouth dropped open. He hadn't thought of that. Arvel was right—that would be a tremendous opportunity. Although Alexa was only a Master, not a Grand Master. They would have to find a way to Transfer her at least one more tier of power.

"There is also the chance she will betray you," Arvel continued darkly. "Be very wary of her. There is only one god who has ever returned a soul from beyond the Veil. And Xerys is very real."

Kyel nodded, pondering the implications. "Point taken."

"Now, as far as the talisman you inherited from Byron Connel—"

The man suddenly went rigid, his eyes narrowing to white slits, his lashes fluttering. The knuckles of his hands turned a milky white. He sat there tensed for a long, frightful moment. Then he opened his mouth and exhaled a great gasp, his body sagging as if melting into his seat. He opened his eyes.

"We're out of time," Arvel said, his gaze shooting up to lock on Kyel's. "Lauchlin's army has arrived and has cordoned off the entrance to the valley. For all intents and purposes, we are under siege."

"What are you going to do?" Kyel asked.

Arvel pushed his chair back and rose, tossing his napkin on the table. "We are prepared to field every able-bodied priest, monk, and layman of every temple. For the past few days, we've been fortifying the valley's mouth."

Kyel followed him to his feet. "We need to negotiate."

"There's nothing to negotiate." Arvel waved him off, making his way around the table.

Kyel moved to block him. "We don't even know what he wants."

The man studied Kyel intently, as if peering deep into his soul. "Darien Lauchlin is a Servant of Xerys who has brought an army to the Valley of the Gods. What do you think he wants?" He lifted his eyebrows.

"I'm going to talk to him," Kyel said, resolute.

Arvel stared at him flatly. "He'll kill you."

"No, he won't. He already had that chance. He didn't take it." In the dungeon of Greystone Keep, Darien had been a hairsbreadth away from ending his life, Kyel felt certain. He'd seen it in his eyes. He still wasn't sure why Darien had held back.

"How do you know he won't change his mind?" Arvel pressed.

"Because I know him."

The man fixed him with a hard-as-granite stare. "And he knows you."

"No, he doesn't. Not anymore."

Chapter Twenty-Three
Parley

Glen Farquist, The Rhen

The wind howled and shrieked like a murder. The gale battered Kyel's back, pushing him forward as he walked with Arvel and Alexa up a rise of sandstone steps that snaked upward to the crest of a low hill, the only truly defensible position on the valley floor. The steps had been worn down so much, they were almost a ramp. They led to the surface of a thick stone slab of chiseled marble: the footprint of an ancient temple, now reduced to a jumble of toppled columns.

Arvel led them across the foundation toward a group of men and women clustered at the far edge. Kyel stopped behind Arvel and watched as the man inserted himself into the group of robed priests and priestesses. He exchanged greetings and small talk, while Kyel stood on the edge of the gathering, waiting and watching, wondering how long he was going to be ignored.

After a long interval, Arvel turned and beckoned him over, the bronze sleeves of his robe billowed by the scolding wind. Kyel complied with a scowl, moving only close enough to be within earshot.

Arvel had to shout to be heard over the wind. "This is His Eminence! Ansel Stroud! The High Priest of Zephia!" He indicated a man standing next to him who wore a dark beard and a darker glower. Kyel recognized him. He'd met the man before, at a gathering of temple patriarchs. He hadn't liked Stroud then, and he liked him less now.

"I'm sure you remember Kyel Archer!" Arvel shouted at the priest, who stared at Kyel and didn't respond.

Kyel nodded a curt greeting that seemed to ruffle the man.

Arvel excused himself with a wave and a smile, moving off the foundation in a crackling ripple of oversized robes. Kyel stared after him, more unsettled than angry. He turned back to the Patriarch of Zephia, wondering who, between the two of them, was supposed to be in charge.

He leaned forward and shouted at the priest, "I'm going down there! I want to see if he'll negotiate!"

"He won't negotiate," Stroud disagreed. "We have nothing to offer him!"

Kyel thought about it. "We can tell him if he surrenders, we'll let them keep the North."

The priest took a step back, staring at Kyel with a look of gaping disbelief. "You can't just give them the North!"

Kyel shot him a disdainful glare. "They've already *taken* the North!"

With that, he swung away from the man and strode toward the stairs. The wind tore at his cloak and raked at his hair as he descended the worn steps toward the valley floor. There, a group of monks from one of the militant orders fell in around him, escorting him toward the tall cliffs that surrounded the valley.

The wind lessened as they approached the bluffs, finally giving way altogether, blocked by the walls of the bottleneck canyon that formed the valley's entrance.

Kyel followed the path through the canyon as it wound like a serpent's coils through the surrounding cliffs. The walls of the passage were high, made of stratified layers of tawny sandstone. A fast stream lined with ragged boulders ran its course along the base of the cliffs, bordered by a road only wide enough to drive a cart along.

At the mouth of the canyon, Kyel halted and looked over the temples' fortifications, in the form of mud berms, trenches, and spiked palisades warded by overlooking bluffs. The entire plain had been altered to create a narrowing path that would slow and direct the movements of an advancing army.

Kyel was impressed. He wouldn't have credited Glen Farquist's priests with that kind of tactical industry. Across the canyon's entrance, they had dug a deep trench impossible to jump across or go around. If Darien wanted his men to advance into the canyon, he would have to fill that trench with corpses.

Beyond the trench, out of bowshot of the bluffs, the Enemy army had gathered in a wedge-shaped formation. Kyel stared out at it, shielding his eyes from the sun's stabbing glare. Their numbers were far fewer than he'd anticipated. Apparently, the poisoned cider had worked even better than expected, though at enormous cost. It was just unfortunate that Darien hadn't been one of the casualties.

To his guard of armored clerics, Kyel ordered, "Wait here."

He reached down and unhooked Thar'gon from his belt. Holding the spiked artifact at his side, he walked away from the security of the earthworks and crossed the flat plain toward the trench. The wind gained strength again as he moved further from the protection of the canyon walls. But the wind was only a ghost of its former strength. The air stirred as though hesitant to add to the tension already gripping the plain.

Kyel stopped when he reached the trench. To either side of his own position, the priests had stationed foot soldiers against the canyon walls. Kyel was aware he was standing in the center of a bloodbath waiting to happen, but he wasn't afraid. With Thar'gon in his hand, he didn't have any reason to be.

Ahead, a lone figure parted off from the Enemy line and advanced toward him. Kyel knew it was Darien even before he could see his face. The darkmage had a way of moving that was unmistakable, even at a distance, like the fluid grace of a predator. Kyel held his ground, waiting as Darien approached and halted before him on the far side of the trench.

Kyel considered his adversary for a long moment, wishing he could peer into the shadows of the man's soul. When it came to Darien, he didn't know what to believe. The man seemed to be walking a thin line between reason and inhumanity. Each time Kyel saw him, Darien seemed to land with both feet planted firmly on one side or the other. Kyel wondered which side of morality Darien would be walking today.

He wouldn't know without speaking with him.

Kyel closed his eyes and, lifting Thar'gon, whispered, "*Vergis.*"

The world shivered. When he opened his eyes, Kyel found himself standing an arm's length from Darien's face.

Darien danced back, his sword already halfway out of its sheath. With a smoldering glare, he slid the blade fully back again. His eyes flicked to the talisman in Kyel's hand, which seemed to give him pause.

"You've learned how to use it," he said.

Kyel lowered Thar'gon and hooked the weapon to his belt. "Hello, Darien."

The man nodded slightly. He looked more sinister than Kyel remembered, his eyes cold and void of emotion. A dark power radiated from him, distorting the air around him. Kyel found himself scrutinizing Darien's face, trying to figure out what manner of man stood before him. If he was demon or madman. Or both.

After a moment, Kyel asked, "What are your intentions?"

"I'm here to take the valley." Darien gazed at him with a frigid expression.

"Why?"

"I think you know. The temples are a threat to us. They seek to drive us back into the Black Lands. I'm not going to let that happen."

So Darien wasn't a madman.

Kyel said, "It's not your people they fear. Only your god."

"Xerys is but one god in the pantheon."

Kyel spread his hands. "You need to be reasonable. You've taken the North. You've given your people hope and sunlight and a place to live. But in doing so, you've displaced thousands. Where are they supposed to go? What are they supposed to eat? They left everything behind—"

"They will live."

Kyel winced, shocked by the vehemence in Darien's voice. He stood regarding the darkmage warily. The power radiating from Darien's presence seemed to pulsate.

Somehow, he found the courage to glare his former master in the eye. "What about the people who *didn't* live? What about the people you killed?"

Darien shrugged coldly. "They had their chance. They didn't take it. It all boils down to this: you, Meiran, the temples—you didn't leave us any options. We threw ourselves on your mercy, and you betrayed us. Any blood that's been spilt—that's on your hands. Not ours. We tried to negotiate a peaceful solution. You wouldn't have it."

Kyel cursed Meiran. And the temples. And Darien, for always sounding rational even when trying to justify atrocity. It took him a moment to sort through the logic of it all, to come to the conclusion that just because something was rational, that didn't by default make it right.

He said, "You've already taken what you need. Any more's just greed. Work with us. We're willing to forge a treaty. We'll cede you the North, if you halt your advance and cease hostilities. Right here. Today. Otherwise, you're looking at a war of attrition that will last generations. And ultimately, we will win."

Darien stared at him for long seconds with a gaze that never wavered. At last, he said, "It's a tempting offer. Two months ago, I'd have taken it." He shook his head, stepping back. "But I'm not falling for false promises again. Tell the priests I said go fuck themselves. I'm going to turn their temples into their tombs."

Kyel gritted his teeth, his frustration on the verge of boiling over. It didn't have to be this way. If Meiran and the temples had just upheld the treaty they'd negotiated—

"Darien—"

But Darien ignored him and stalked away. Kyel growled, ripping Thar'gon off his belt. He closed his eyes, envisioning the stone foundation with its worn stairs and toppled columns. The ground shifted beneath him. He opened his eyes to find Alexa and the priest of Zephia staring at him expectantly.

"No luck." He sighed.

The priest didn't look surprised. Wind whipping his hair, he raised his voice, saying, "It doesn't matter! We have superior numbers. The terrain works in our favor, giving us great advantage. And we have a Sentinel." He stared hard at Kyel with an expression that looked almost like a threat.

"And they have a Battlemage," Kyel reminded him.

Alexa turned toward him. "It's time for you to let go of your Oath."

"No." Kyel couldn't believe she would ask that of him. She was a Master of Aerysius herself, and just as Bound as he was. He shouldn't have to argue with her about all the reasons he refused to bend on the issue.

"It doesn't matter anymore!" she pressed. "Kyel! The Oath exists to protect you from moral decay over your lifetime! But you don't have a lifetime—you have days! The Oath of Harmony doesn't apply to you!"

Her words brought Darien's image to mind, a reminder that galvanized Kyel's resolve. "I'm not turning into *him*," he snapped. "I won't do it!"

Darien dropped to a crouch beside Azár and Sayeed. He picked up a stick and drew a broad V in the dirt, then gathered a handful of rocks and took some time positioning them along the sides. He embellished his crude map with leaves and sticks, arranging them carefully.

"It's not good," he reported. He scooted a rock over, nudging it into position with his finger. "They've had time to prepare for us. They've made the entire canyon into a death trap. And they've got a Sentinel."

"Your apprentice?" Azár looked at him with confusion in her eyes. "The man who saved you from the dungeon? Will he fight against you?"

Darien scowled. "Kyel marches to the beat of his morals. He sees the value in our cause, but he disagrees with how we're going about it. He doesn't understand that sometimes you have to spill blood to save blood."

He pointed the stick at the V on the ground. "They've positioned infantry and archers along the sides of the canyon here...and here. They've left their center vulnerable. I think that's intentional.

They're going to try to draw us in, then flank us. We'll have to counter that by attacking their wings." He drew an arrow in the dirt then looked up at Sayeed, "You take the Zakai and try to roll them up on the left. I'll take the center and keep the arrows off you."

"What about your apprentice?" Azár asked with a worried frown.

Darien tapped the stick against his leg. It took him a second longer than it should have to reach a final decision. "I'll deal with Kyel."

"This Sentinel," Sayeed said slowly. "How well does he know you?"

Darien ignored him.

Sayeed reached out and caught the stick, forcing Darien to look at him.

"Take mind," Sayeed said with a sharp glare of warning. "This man is more dangerous than you think. Do not underestimate him."

"I won't," Darien said, relinquishing the stick.

Chapter Twenty-Four
The Battle of Glen Farquist

Glen Farquist, The Rhen

"Look," Sayeed said, nodding in the direction of the cliffs.

Darien removed his helm and, tucking it into the crook of his arm, peered out across the bunchgrass-cobbled plain. The militia of priests remained behind the protection of their trench: long lines of foot soldiers four to eight men deep. The wings of their army extended out along the base of the surrounding bluffs. Darien gazed ahead, uncertain what Sayeed was trying to indicate.

"What do you see?"

"The banners," Sayeed said. "They do not stir in the wind."

Darien stared harder across the plain. The wind surged in random gusts, and yet the banners of the temples remained becalmed. "He's learned control of the wind," he grumbled. "That means he can shield."

Azár asked, "How will that affect us?"

He shrugged. Kyel wielded Thar'gon, but Darien doubted he'd learned much control over it. And Kyel's hands were tied by the chains on his wrists. So was his effectiveness.

Sayeed pursed his lips in troubled thought. "It is an ill-omened day for battle. Perhaps it is best to wait."

"Ill-omened?" Darien echoed. "How so?"

"The moon is overhead in the daylight, looking down." The officer glanced upward toward the faded disk of the moon. "Many believe it is a sign of the gods' disapproval, for we make war against their home."

Darien cursed the Malikari love of superstition. "The gods don't live in Glen Farquist. As far as the moon's concerned, it's a natural cycle. We can't stand here waiting for the moon to wax."

Sayeed nodded, though he looked far from reassured. If anything, he looked resigned to a dismal end. Darien decided to let the man stew, his thoughts returning to Kyel, the one variable he couldn't predict.

He said to Azár, "I want you to stay back here, out of the battle."

His wife stabbed him with an outraged glare. "I will not stay back while my husband wages war! You promised you would never ask this—"

"I *need* you behind us," Darien snapped, more harshly than he'd intended. "If something goes wrong—if they do manage to flank us—then I'll need you in reserve at our rear. And if Kyel does give me problems, then I'll need you even more. I doubt he can manage the both of us at once, coming at him from two directions."

Her expression softened somewhat. At last, she nodded. "I will be where you need me most," she conceded. "My husband is a wise commander." Without another word, she turned and walked away from the line.

Darien heaved a sigh. The battle hadn't yet begun, and already the gods seemed against him. "All right." He tugged his helm down over his head. "Let's have at it."

Sayeed shook his head in silence, looking grim. Darien ignored him and drew his sword, the blade carried by Khoresh Kateem into the Battle of Harmudi. He hoped the sword would bring him equal success. He raised the blade high over his head.

Then he brought it down, leveling the point at his enemy.

"At them."

The lines of infantry behind him started forward, Darien striding ahead of them with Sayeed at his side, surrounded by a protective ring of elite Zakai. He drew deeply on the magic field and fed its energy. Magelight erupted beneath their feet, a blue mist that spread quickly across the ground. He increased the energy, until the magelight condensed into cobalt tongues of whipping mist that advanced beneath the feet of his army. The magelight produced the desired effect. The first ranks of defenders edged back despite their officers' commands to hold their line.

The first volley of arrows arced toward them, darkening the air. Darien waited until they reached the apex of their flight, then lashed out at them with force. The arrows shattered overhead, showering them with broken shafts. Another dark cloud met a similar fate. And another. Darien lashed out at volley after volley, knocking the arrows from the sky with furious waves of solid air.

Another arrow cloud lofted toward them, this one far larger than the rest. Darien reached out from within, summoning enough power to shatter every arrow in the sky.

The slap of air never connected.

It reversed direction and hurled back on him.

The wall of air impacted before he could react, lifting him up and slamming him to the ground. The wind knocked from his lungs, Darien lay gasping on his back, his mind struggling to make sense of what had just happened. It took him a moment to realize every man in his guard had been affected, most lying sprawled next to him in the dirt.

Darien pushed himself up, coughing and shaken. All around him, soldiers were struggling to stand, staggering back into position to reform their rank. Some of the men remained on the ground, unmoving. Darien stood blinking in a daze, his ears ringing. His mind fumbled to understand the implications of what had just occurred.

Kyel was Bound. Had he relinquished his Oath of Harmony?

Then it hit him: Kyel hadn't directly harmed a single person. He had simply deflected an oncoming assault. It was Darien's own magic that had inflicted the damage. He cursed his own arrogance. Kyel had made himself into a formidable Sentinel in only two years without tutelage. Darien hadn't thought it possible.

Another volley of arrows launched toward them. He reacted—not fast enough. The arrows peppered the ground, pelting his armor. With a growl, Darien surged forward. His men followed, covering the remaining distance under a constant barrage of arrows, the archers across the trench loosing their shafts at will.

As they closed the distance, the arrows started coming harder, no longer arcing through the air, but hurling toward them parallel to the ground. The bodkin points clanged off his armor, almost hard enough to pierce. Men to both sides started to drop. Darien threw up a shield thick enough to slow the arrows' flight—but weak enough that Kyel couldn't repurpose it into a weapon.

When they gained the trench, Darien dropped the shield and wove a web of shadow to span the gap. The web was thin as gossamer but strong enough to bear significant weight. He stood back, channeling every drop of power he could handle into maintaining it. Sayeed and the Zakai remained by his side, keeping a vigilant watch, while the rest of the Tanisars rushed forward.

When the last foot soldier cleared the bridge, Darien sprinted across the trench then dropped the shadow-bridge. He threw the shield back up. Just in time—one last volley of arrows clattered against it.

With a cry, his warriors impacted with the priests' front lines, fighting to batter their way through. Darien drew up just short of the melee, Zakai swarming into a defensive position around him. There was little he could do against the enemy as a whole. So he started attacking the priests individually.

One by one, he dropped them to the ground. Darien stood looking from face to face. Everywhere he looked, scowls of fury turned to grimaces of agony. He moved forward, wielding death to clear a path ahead of him.

He took his time, picking his way over the corpses collecting under his feet. Men and women scrambled out of his way with looks of horror.

They didn't get far. Darien pushed further into the thick of the fighting, until the bodies of the fallen became too dense an obstacle to wade through any longer.

A thundering battle cry rang across the canyon, making Darien turn. Behind, some of their men had broken away from the main force to attack the priests' left wing, charging toward the foot soldiers that lined the cliffs. And drew up short, halfway there.

Men cried out in dismay and dropped their weapons, tottering over their feet. Others fell to the ground, then tried to worm their way forward on their stomachs. Arrows rained down from the tops of the cliffs, finding easy marks.

At first, Darien couldn't understand what was happening.

It took him a moment to realize the ground beneath the troops had dissolved into a quagmire.

Kyel.

Again, the Sentinel had found a way to reap a harvest of lives without breaking his Oath.

Men screamed, lurching for firm ground and not finding it.

Priests armed with crossbows sprang forward, slaughtering the helpless soldiers mired in the mud. Soon, the ground beneath them ran red with spilt blood.

Darien broke away from the melee and started back across the canyon.

His Zakai escort swept ahead of him, slaying anyone who stood in their path. A rank of pikemen spilled forward, charging their position. Without breaking stride, Darien threw up a hand and stopped their hearts.

Kyel clenched Thar'gon so hard that his arm was shaking. The talisman glowed with a brilliant light, radiating enough power to heat the air around it. At his side, Alexa clung to his arm, her mouth open, eyes wide in an expression of awed exhilaration. Ravaged by the wind, her hair whipped against her face, giving her a wild appearance.

Kyel watched in satisfaction as the Enemy soldiers trapped in the mud were set upon by a group of warrior-priests. The sight of their slaughter chilled him, making him writhe inside his own skin. He had to keep reminding himself that he hadn't killed even one man. Not one. Yet hundreds were dying as a result of his actions. The realization made him want to vomit. With Thar'gon in his hand, he had already decimated a third of Darien's attack force. It was as though the talisman were wielding him, instead of the other way around. He was merely the weapon's conduit, nothing more.

Worse, the raw feeling of power was exhilarating, intoxicating. It was like being a god without being godly. All trace of fear inside him had been brushed aside. With the talisman in his hand, Kyel felt indomitable.

Because he was.

He saw Darien's small band of men break away from the main force, sprinting toward those being butchered in the quagmire.

"You have to stop him!" Alexa cried.

Kyel closed his eyes and tried. "I can't! He's too far away!"

Alexa tugged at his arm. "The true strength of that artifact is mobility!" she cried. "Don't stay in one place! Go where you need to be! Use it to control the field of battle!"

She was right. He wasn't using the talisman to its full potential. But if he were…

Kyel closed his eyes, visualizing the ground behind the trench.

"Vergis."

Darien staggered to a stop, realizing the only thing left ahead of him was dead warriors and blood-wet earth. Furious, he lashed out at the retreating defenders, burning the priests to char. Then burning the char to ash. The screams were satisfying. His gaze snapped back to the corpses of his men lying in a trough of oozing mud. His mouth went dry. His mind yet grappled with the concept that Kyel could pose any threat at all. Certainly nothing this devastating.

Reeling, Darien backed away from the slaughter.

He turned to find that the priests had regrouped. They had taken advantage of his absence to flank what was left of his assault force. Already, his men were nearly enveloped.

Sprinting forward, Darien pulled at the magic field, filling himself until he burned with charged power. Holding it steady, he drew next on the Onslaught, then wrapped the contradictory energies together in a knot. He launched that volatile missile at the charging priests. The hurling magic flew like a comet across the battlefield—

—and exploded in the air as if hitting a wall.

The recoil hit Darien in the face, smashing him to the ground. The world went red and then black. He blinked rapidly to clear his vision, gasping for breath.

Sayeed knelt at his side, blood running freely down the left side of his face. "Brother!"

His voice sounded strangely muffled. Darien saw that many of his Zakai lay sprawled across the ground, either dead or unconscious. The man nearest him had been dismembered. The head, still helmed, lay a good distance away.

Sayeed stood above him, repulsing the attacks of three monks who had seen Darien on the ground and were trying to exploit the opportunity. His blade wove through the air in great, slashing arcs. Kicking one man back, he drew a cut across another man's belly in time to parry an attack by the third. Sayeed brought his sword around in a diagonal slash that ended the fight.

He dropped to the ground next to Darien and hauled him upright by the arms.

"Can you walk?" he gasped.

Darien nodded. Gritting his teeth, he struggled back to his feet. He spat a mouthful of blood that stringed from his lips. Eyes searching for Kyel, he reached up and tightened his helmet's cinch, then started forward again. Ahead, his men were on the verge of being overwhelmed.

"Can you counter him?" Sayeed demanded.

Darien ignored the question. A group of priests had marked his position and were charging his way. His few remaining Zakai sprang in front of him, ready to shield him with their lives.

"Get down!" Darien shouted, forcing his way through the ring of Zakai. He dropped the magic field entirely and summoned the Onslaught, wielding the power of hell in both hands before flinging it headlong at the charging priests.

The men rushing them stumbled and fell screaming to the ground. They writhed in the dirt, wailing horrifically as their flesh began to dissolve. Their agony didn't last long.

"Narghul," Darien whispered.

A host of necrators bled up from the ground like shadowy wraiths: a hellish ring of protection. Darien's blood turned to ice. It was as though the creatures sucked the heat right out of his body to feed their own existence.

He willed them forward. The necrators obeyed, ranging out across the battlefield in search of souls to consume. They were a last resort; necrators were indiscriminate in their killing.

He turned to Sayeed.

And saw Kyel standing behind him.

Darien shouted a warning, shoving Sayeed out of the way. He lashed out viciously with the Hellpower.

Kyel merely waved his hand, deflecting the assault. Darien gaped at him in shock, taking a step backward. Then another, his mind reeling toward panic.

"Run," Darien gasped.

Sayeed and the Zakai obeyed, but Darien didn't follow. Instead, he turned back to face his adversary.

"How?" he gasped.

Kyel raised his weapon. It shimmered with power, brilliant and blinding. Darien took one, good look into Kyel's eyes. Then he turned and started running.

Kyel sensed he had one chance—one chance—to take Darien to the ground, to rid the world of him forever. He could hear Alexa's persistent voice in the back of his mind, begging him to abandon his Oath.

All it would take was one strike with the talisman. One act.

And Thar'gon was eager. He could feel its need, the weapon's desire to dominate. He swept the morning star back, preparing a strike that would send Darien's twisted soul back to his master.

Kyel growled and lowered the weapon, unable to complete the act.

His eyes tracked Darien as he sprinted away. He was losing his opportunity. His mind sifted through options.

Then it came to him. The answer was obvious.

Concentrating, Kyel willed the air to thicken around Darien. He watched the darkmage slow to a stop, stumbling, fighting to stay on his feet. Kyel tightened his grip on his weapon, concentrating harder. When Darien struck out at his invisible cage, Kyel was ready. He reflected the attack back on him. Darien staggered and fell, blood streaming down his face. He tried to get up, but Kyel thickened the air more and held him there.

He thinned the shield, allowing Darien enough air to breathe. Enemy soldiers rallied to his aid but could do nothing against the bubble of solid air that contained him. As his men watched, Darien lashed out at his prison with the magic field, with the Onslaught, with anything and everything he could throw at it.

Nothing worked.

All of Darien's demonic power was useless against Thar'gon's great might.

Kyel smiled triumphantly. He raised his hand in the air, signaling the priests to move in.

For the first time in his life, he saw real fear in Darien Lauchlin's eyes. The darkmage railed against his prison as the priests closed the distance, swords and crossbows raised. The harder Darien struggled, the stronger the shield became, absorbing his power to reinforce its structure.

Eventually, Darien gave up. He knelt on the ground, head bowed as though defeated.

Then, slowly, he looked up and locked his stare on Kyel, his eyes black pools of shadow that burned like hellish coals. He raised his hand. His lips moved silently.

A terrible chill pierced Kyel's heart. And a more terrible feeling of dread.

He whirled to find three necrators hovering behind him.

Fear clenched Kyel's throat, choking him, terrorizing him. He couldn't move, couldn't breathe. The arm that held Thar'gon sagged uselessly to his side. Like a fickle lover, the magic field abandoned him.

Wide-eyed, Kyel stared into the face of the nearest necrator and saw his own death gazing back at him. He wanted to run, but that was impossible. The fear was too raw, too paralyzing. It slithered out of his gut, tightening its grip on his chest, numbing his mind.

Kyel's hand opened reflexively, dropping the talisman.

A shadowy hand reached toward him, fingers groping to touch his face.

"Kyel!"

Something shoved him backward, hurling him away from the wraith's outstretched hand. He staggered as his mind was suddenly released from the paralyzing grip of terror. He glanced back to see Alexa standing between the necrator and himself, hands raised in the air, fingers splayed. Somehow, she was holding the demon at bay.

He couldn't leave her there. She had no chance against such a creature.

But neither did he. Kyel scooped Thar'gon off the ground and did the only thing he could do.

"*Vergis!*" he whispered.

The cage of air disappeared. Darien bellowed in rage as Kyel disappeared with it. His eyes darted toward the woman—

—but she was already gone. So were his minions. He felt their loss, as though a piece of his soul had been torn out of him. He stood rooted to the ground, crippled by shock and disbelief. He started forward toward the place where the woman had just been standing.

"No!" Sayeed bellowed. He caught Darien by the shoulder and spun him around. "Brother, we must flee!"

"That woman—" Darien began.

An explosion erupted on the far side of the battlefield. And then another. A shockwave hit, deafening. Darien could feel the thunder of it. Screams of death and terror erupted all around, ringing off the cliffs. More fires sprang out of the ground, one after another, traveling across the canyon floor in quick succession.

Everywhere Darien looked, priests were running aflame. The melee disintegrated into bedlam as screaming men and women fought and clawed and battered their way clear of the flames.

Darien stood stunned, watching it all unfold before him as if staring inward at a dream. Black smoke billowed over the battlefield, obscuring his sight. The entire scene seemed disjointed and surreal.

Before him, a lone figure emerged from the thick haze of smoke, moving toward him with a confident stride. At first, he thought it was Kyel, returned to slay him.

But it was not.
"Azár," Darien whispered in awe.

Chapter Twenty-Five
Branching and Unbranching

Isle of Titherry, The Rhen

"Are you sure you can do this by yourself?" Quin asked. "You're not a Harbinger."

Naia paused, one hand lingering on the balustrade, and looked back at him. Quin stood on the balcony overlooking the Crescent with his hat in hand, hair tousled by the wind. He was trying to look unruffled but failing miserably. He hadn't seemed right in days. Not since the morning they'd buried Tsula.

"I am the closest thing to a Harbinger there is left in the world," Naia corrected him. "I no longer need Tsula's guidance. At least, not to read the Crescent."

His brow furrowed. "In my time, it took twenty years to train a Harbinger." He bounced his hat against his leg. "Don't you think you might be getting ahead of yourself?"

Naia shot him a reproving look. "Most of the training Harbingers received went toward teaching them how to cope with their visions. Simply reading the Crescent is effortless."

Quin planted his hat squarely on his head. "Is that why Tsula had the personality of a rock?"

"Harbingers were trained to let go of all attachments and emotions. I think it was the only way they could protect themselves from going insane."

"I don't want you going up there," he said firmly, his face stern.

"I'm going up there," she insisted, and set a hand on his arm. "That's the reason why we're here. With Tsula gone, I might see new versions that were not available before. I have to try. I'm going to die, anyway, in just a few days—"

"No, you're not."

Looking suddenly more dangerous than she'd ever seen him, Quin stared at her piercingly. He held her gaze steady for a long moment, then leaned in to press a slow, lingering kiss on her lips.

"Come back to me," he ordered, his eyes still fixed on hers.

Naia swallowed, taken aback. And stunned by the bold feelings his kiss inspired. She licked her lips and turned away, feeling off-balance. This wasn't the Quin she had known, she realized. Tsula's death had changed him.

A bolt of understanding rocked her hard. This was Quin the way he used to be, she realized. This was the man he had been, before Amani's death had extinguished the spark within him. Naia turned slowly back around, searching his face for confirmation. Quin regarded her with a steady confidence she'd never seen before.

"I'll come back," she assured him.

Naia turned away and walked through the stone balustrade onto the arching path of transparent stepping stones. The breeze caressed her face and fanned her hair. It felt cool, even as the sun felt warm on her skin. She followed the invisible path out over the mercurial surface of the Crescent toward the Nexus.

Steadying herself, Naia passed through the thin membrane. Entering the room always reminded her of the way a stick can pass through the surface of a bubble without bursting it. Inside, she found herself once again within the dark, spherical chamber. The silver tendrils writhed across the walls like vines, twining and untwining, branching and unbranching. Naia moved forward until she was standing in the exact center of the sphere.

There, she closed her eyes and emptied her mind of all thought, until the only thing in the world that mattered was the sound of her own heartbeat. She stood there a moment, settling into the serene bliss of emptiness, letting her mind drift on the ebb and flow of her breath.

Then, from out of the darkness, a silvery filament emerged and uncoiled. It grew, branching and twirling, coiling and vining. It fed her with a soft luminescence that grew slowly, throbbing like a pulse. The darkness abandoned her, her mind washing after it.

———

The epitome of all storms—the storm that every other storm aspired to be—raged and ripped through the atmosphere. All was fading, all was dying. And she was dying with it.

"I can't stand it!" Naia shrieked to the absent gods.

She could feel the magic field stretched around her to its thin limit. And then it ripped. Naia screamed her life away, feeling her mind heated to boiling inside her skull.

———

With a shriek, Naia opened her eyes. All around her, the walls throbbed to the time of her heartbeat. Cold sweat dribbled down her face, and she gasped for breath. She stood there a moment, steadying herself until her pulse finally slowed. The vision had been too real.

And it was not the first time she had experienced it. That version was the most likely ending to her Story. Every time she came here, it was always the first version she was subjected to. She should be used to it by now. Desensitized. But she wasn't. It was impossible to grow accustomed to the act of dying.

She took a deep breath and closed her eyes again, letting her mind seep back into that dark and empty place.

———

The wind howled a monstrous wail as it rampaged through the mountains, terrorizing the clouds, which fled wildly before it. In front of her, Darien lay in an expanding pool of blood, more blood than any human body could possibly contain. It spread rapidly, as if seeking to saturate the entire Circle of Convergence. Or the entire world. Or the universe.

Standing behind her, Zavier Renquist lifted Quin's sword and swept it back over his shoulder. "Let the reign of Xerys begin!" he snarled, and cleaved Naia's head off.

———

Gasping a sharp hiss of breath between her teeth, Naia opened her eyes. Out of all the possible versions she'd been subjected to, she found that one the most chilling. Not only was it the most visceral, but it was also the most desperate, the most dire. She was left with the ominous feeling that the price of failure was much greater than any of the other versions. She didn't know where that future led; she couldn't read anything beyond her own death. But she knew with certainty that the resulting fate would be appalling.

With a shudder, Naia cleared her mind and, glad to be rid of that terrible image, closed her eyes.

———

Kyel advanced across the Circle of Convergence, wielding a glowing silver talisman in his hand. In the center of the Circle—in full command of it—Zavier Renquist swept out a fist. A blinding glare of light whiter than bright and brilliantly powerful assaulted Kyel from the sky. He was hurled across the terrace, the talisman flying from his hand.

The green pillar in the sky above exploded in fury. The magic field wailed in protest, in defiance, in outrage.

Then it went forever silent.

———

Naia's eyes snapped open. Inside, she roiled in a cauldron of despair and grief. That version of the future was the most painful, left her aching with a tremendous sense of loss. Every time she witnessed it, she was left heartbroken.

And that was the last version. There were never any more after that, only slight variations of those three. Those were her only possible futures, and all three were horrendous.

It was time to push beyond. With Tsula gone, it was time to forge ahead, to see if there were any more possibilities she hadn't yet encountered.

Naia closed her eyes and let the silvery tendrils uncoil. She cleared her mind and let the visions seep into her.

———

The epitome of all storms—the storm that every other storm aspired to be—raged and ripped across the atmosphere. Thunder lashed against the cliffs, and lightning the color of blood sliced wounds in the air. The wind howled a monstrous wail as it rampaged through the mountains, terrorizing the clouds, which fled wildly before it. The world screamed in mortal anguish, and Naia screamed with it.

Kyel was below them in the chamber of the Well of Tears. Wielding his silver talisman against the portal while the Reversal was still maximized.

Sprawled in the center of the Circle of Convergence, Darien lay in an expanding pool of blood. The blood was artery-red and voluminous—far more than one human body could possibly contain. It spread rapidly, as if seeking to saturate the entire Circle. Or the entire world. Or the universe.

A thunderous clap of air sent Renquist hurling to the ground. Naia looked up in terror, in hope, in desperation. She gasped in disbelief.

Blood streaming down his face, Quin stalked toward her across the glowing Circle of Convergence, Kyel's silver talisman glowing like a beacon in his hand.

"Run, Naia!" he shouted. Hefting the weapon, Quin advanced toward Renquist.

Naia froze. It was wrong. It was all terribly, terribly wrong.

"No, Quin!" she shrieked. "Leave him! Help Darien!"

Zavier Renquist rose to his feet, eyes menacing pools of shadow. He raised his hand and struck out at her with the Onslaught.

Naia screamed as the world around her broke apart, shattering like glass into a thousand tiny fragments, each with its own awful reality. She caught brief glimpses of each, each more terrible than the last.

She lived a thousand lifetimes in a heartbeat.

And a thousand deaths.

Naia collapsed to her knees, bent over in horror. Bringing her hands up to her face, she choked on tears. Quin was right: Tsula had been blocking her.

Now, her block was lifted. She realized why Tsula had placed it there in the first place: to protect her, to save her from insanity.

But she wasn't insane. Somehow, her mind had survived branching into a thousand different directions, then unbranching to become whole again. And within those myriad branches, she had caught just a glimpse of the one future they desperately needed. But that was all. Just a glimpse.

And that was all she was ever going to get. Naia felt certain she would never survive being shattered like that again.

She sucked in a deep breath through her nostrils and let it out again slowly. She waited there, kneeling, until she got her emotions back under control. Then, wiping the tears from her eyes, Naia stood up and made her way toward the tendril-encrusted wall. She took one last, stabbing glance back, then stepped out of the dark sphere, vowing to never, ever enter it again.

She could never be a Harbinger. She could never approach Tsula's courage.

Naia fled the Nexus, hardly noticing the placement of her feet as she took the glass stepping stones two at a time. She stumbled back onto the balcony of the castle, then stopped, blinking, looking around for Quin in the harsh glare of the sun.

She found him around the corner, sitting on a bench in the shade of a tree in purple bloom. He looked up, hearing her footsteps. Seeing the expression on her face, he shot out of his seat, coming toward her with his brow furrowed in concern. Naia dove into his arms, the tears already springing back into her eyes.

"I know what we have to do," she gasped, sobbing quietly against the fabric of his coat. His arms tightened around her, crushing her against his chest. His hand ran soothingly through her hair.

"What is it? What did you see?"

She pulled back and looked up at him. "We can destroy the Well of Tears without destroying the magic field."

Quin stepped back with a look of confused disbelief. "How's that possible?"

Naia shook her head as fresh tears spilled down her face. "It's possible. We can do it. But the price is so high…"

"You've seen it?" he asked. His face bled through several shades of pale before settling on gray.

She nodded. "I only saw a fragment of it. Just a glimpse. And that's all I'm going to get because the chance of it happening is so miniscule. And…" Her voice trailed off.

"And what?" he glared at her suspiciously.

"I think you're going to die, Quin," she whispered. "So will Darien. So will Kyel. Your soul will be consigned to hell. And with the Well destroyed…there'll be no coming back for you. Ever." She grimaced, bowing her head in grief.

Quin reached out and, with a finger, lifted her chin until she was gazing into his eyes.

"Do you live?" he asked.

"I think so…" she whispered.

He nodded once.

"Then it's worth it."

Chapter Twenty-Six
Gods Be Damned

The Kingdom of Emmery, The Rhen

Darien slid the oiled cloth down his sword's blade, applying all of his concentration to the effort. Not that oiling common steel was a demanding task, but it was something to divert his mind from the battle and its aftermath. All around him, tents were being broken down, fires extinguished, his soldiers going about their business with a kind of disciplined efficiency that Darien had never seen before entering the Black Lands. Even after such a harrowing defeat, his men still went about their duties with machine-like efficiency.

Darien wished he could share their focus. As it was, it was all he could do to rub his blade with the oiled rag and try not to think too much. Thinking inevitably led to remembering, and remembering was something he wanted to avoid. But there was only so much oil that could be applied to a blade without gumming it up. Darien slid *Valdivora* back into its sheath and put the cleaning kit away in his pack.

He looked up, his eyes drawn to the eastern sky, which glowed with the warmth of dawn. A breeze stirred, its breath heavy with the odor of woodsmoke and damp earth. It was a chill morning. He stood and strapped his war belt around his waist, adjusting the scabbard at his side. He scrubbed his hands together to rub the sword oil into his skin and started back to his tent.

Darien's thoughts turned to Kyel, despite his best efforts at distraction. He was tired of replaying the battle in his head, scouring his memory for things he should have done differently. After days of analyzing his strategy and actions, he kept returning to the same conclusion: that there was nothing he could have done to change the outcome.

He hadn't lost the battle because of his own lack of competence. The battle had been lost because of Kyel's superior abilities.

And that's what scared Darien most. He had control over his own actions, his own men. His own power. But there was nothing he could do to change the fact that Kyel had become far more powerful than himself. And had command of an artifact he had no hope of defending against.

Darien paused, sweeping his eyes over the encampment. He wasn't surprised when he saw Sayeed walking toward him down an aisle between tents. The man wore the same scowl he'd been wearing for the past four days.

The officer drew to a halt, looking at him critically. Appearing dissatisfied with what he saw, Sayeed made a motion with his hand, indicating a fallen tree that lay sprawled across the ground nearby. Darien took his meaning and walked over to it, lowering himself to take a seat.

Sayeed sat next to him. "Be grateful," he said. "You are alive."

Darien found the comment sadly ironic. "Am I?" he asked. His tentative existence was another source of irritation, somewhere between the world of the living and the world of the damned.

"In all ways that matter," Sayeed said. "You are a man, Brother. And, just like any man, you are fallible."

Fallible. That was not the term Darien would have used. *Ineffective* had a truer ring to it. He tossed his hands up in frustration. "I don't know how to counter him. I don't think I can."

Sayeed shrugged indifferently. "You'll find a way. He has limitations. This Oath of Harmony—that is a crippling oath. I do not understand why any mage would swear it. Especially one who is supposed to be a defender of his homeland." He reached down and scratched his leg, a quizzical expression on his face.

Darien glanced past him toward the encampment, where the last of the tents were being broken down and folded for the march. "It's supposed to prevent moral degradation. To keep someone like Kyel from becoming someone like me. It does seem limiting—yet in many ways, it's not. You saw how easily he handled me. There wasn't a thing I could do about it. Every time I attacked, he just turned my own magic against me."

"Then next time, don't attack," Sayeed suggested.

"What would you have me do?"

"The same thing he does. Think, Brother." He leaned forward, his elbows on his splayed knees. "What makes him so effective?"

Darien didn't have to think about it long. He remembered the hopeless frustration he'd felt when he realized there was nothing he could do. "He neutralizes me."

Sayeed's eyes locked on his. "Then neutralize him."

"I thought I had. With the necrators. But then…"

The Zakai officer nodded, his brow furrowing. "That woman. Was she a mage?"

"Aye." Darien stared down, absently picking at the rough bark under him. "Her name's Alexa Newell. She was a Naturalist. I didn't really know her. I just knew *of* her. She went missing a few years back. It was quite a big thing at the time. There was an enormous search. It took months. They never found a trace of her—everyone just assumed she'd died."

Sayeed grunted. "Apparently they were wrong."

"No. Not wrong."

"What do you mean?" Sayeed's brow furrowed in incomprehension.

Darien looked past him, toward the tents. He'd spent the last few days in thought, pondering Kyel's one-sided victory. Alexa's appearance at the end of the battle disturbed him most. More than anything, he feared what her presence might signify.

He said, "A mortal mage could have never confronted my necrators. Even if her soul was just as black as mine. They're *my* minions. She shouldn't have been able to command them. And she didn't just command them—she *unmade* them." It was a harrowing thought, one that smacked of forces much stronger than himself. The types of forces not Bound by the Oath of Harmony.

"Then make more necrators," Sayeed shrugged.

"I've others I can summon," Darien said absently, "but that's not the point. I need to find out what she's about and what she's doing with Kyel. I sense another hand at work here. And I don't like the implications."

Sayeed stared gravely at him, his dark eyes filled with understanding. "Whatever comes, my sword will always guard your back."

Darien appreciated that. More than Sayeed would ever know. He said with a smile he didn't feel, "Then I will never have reason to fear."

The Zakai officer ducked his head and, patting Darien on the shoulder, stood and strode back to camp. Darien remained behind on the log, watching him go. His fingers picked at the bark, peeling up thin fragments that looked like puzzle pieces. He tried fitting two together, but soon gave up and flicked the pieces away.

Darien rose and made his way toward his tent. They faced another long march that would bring them another day closer to Rothscard. At the pace he'd calculated, it would take them only three more days to reach the city and meet up with the other armies he had sent southward through the Cerulean Plains.

Reaching the tent, Darien stopped and glanced around, looking for Azár. He caught sight of her at last, a short distance away in the direction of the forest. She was kneeling on the ground, bent over her knees.

Concerned, Darien started toward her. She rose to her feet, wiping her mouth. She looked up, noticing him. A change came over her face. Her eyes widened, her jaw going slack. As he neared, she took a step back away.

"Are you ill?" Darien asked, suddenly worried. When she retreated another step, he stopped and raised his hands. He felt like he was stalking some wild creature, one prepared to bolt.

"I am fine," she said, though her voice didn't sound fine.

Hearing her tone, Darien felt genuine fear. "Come here. Let me have a look."

But his wife shook her head. She turned and walked away in haste.

"Come here!" Darien shouted at her back, starting after her.

Azár stopped. And turned around, her eyes full of misery. She bowed her head and stared at the ground instead of him. More than anything else she could have done, that one action alarmed him the most. Azár was not a submissive woman.

Darien strode toward her, fear sharpening his movements. He caught her by the shoulders and stared into her face, groping there for explanation. Azár's eyes were red and watery. As if she'd been crying. Or sick.

Darien cast his will into her, probing his wife gently with his mind. After moments, he opened his eyes, confused. His probe had returned only a strong sense of health. There was nothing wrong with her. He sagged in relief. Just to make sure, he felt her again. This time, he sensed something else, something he'd overlooked the first time.

There was another presence, deep down inside.

Darien choked, letting go of Azár and stepping back. His mind went numb. His heart stopped. The world crumbled.

"Husband—"

He backed away from her. Azár started after him, panic on her face. Darien raised his hands, fending her off. Then he whirled and strode away, moving across the camp as quickly as he could without breaking into a run. His vision swam, his thoughts paralyzed. He wasn't aware of where he was going. It didn't matter; he just needed to escape.

Darien fled the camp and followed a deer trail into the forest, moving like a man walking in his sleep. Or in a nightmare. At last, he staggered to a stop in a small clearing.

There, he fell to his knees. He brought his hands up to his face and allowed the pain to come. He wanted to throw his head back and rail at the vengeful gods.

He'd already lost one child without having the chance to know it. Now he would lose another. And the mother who bore it.

The gods were worse than cruel. They were ruthless.

It was some time before he found the courage and composure to return to camp. Darien walked automatically, striding with his head lowered, eyes locked on the ground in front of him. He couldn't look up, couldn't let the men see the defeat on his face.

He found his tent still intact. Darien batted the flap out of his way. Azár was within, sitting cross-legged in their bedding. She looked up as he entered, her face just as raw and devastated as his own.

Darien sank down beside her on the blankets and wrapped his arms around her, feeling her body shudder as she cried softly against him. He closed his eyes, reaching through her to feel the small life within. It was there: a miniscule heartbeat, faint and rapid, like the flutter of hummingbird wings. The feel of it brought a knife-sharp stab of pain. He squeezed her tighter.

"I did not know how to tell you," Azár moaned against his chest. "I did not know how to tell you that you will have another child who will not—"

"Stop," Darien growled, choking on the word. He let her go, pulling back. *"This child will live!* You will *both* live! I don't care how many eternities I spend in hell—I am *not* leaving this world until both of you are safe. Gods be damned, I'll find a way!"

Azár was sobbing. He clutched her against his chest, burying his face in her hair. He wanted to murder the gods, to take everything from them, the way they'd taken everything from him. He wanted vengeance. But the gods were out of reach, beyond his capacity to cause them pain. So he turned his attention to his wife, instead.

All he could do was hold her. And cry with her. So that's what he did.

Chapter Twenty-Seven
Sense of Purpose

Glen Farquist, The Rhen

"Papa, what's a Sentinel?"

Kyel scooped little Gil off the floor and planted him down in his lap. Smiling sadly, he said, "It's someone who stands watch. Someone who protects."

It was hard, putting the essence of who he was into words such a young child could understand. Especially a child who was losing his father. Kyel figured he had to be exceptionally careful about what was spoken and what was left unsaid. Years later, when his son thought back on him, the words said today would likely be remembered best.

"Do Sentinels have magic?"

Kyel nodded, fighting back tears. Gil was asking all the wrong questions, the kind he didn't want to answer. Or maybe they were the right questions. Regardless, they hurt.

"Yes, Gil. Sentinels have magic."

The boy's face lit up. "Do magic, Papa! Do magic!" He bounced up and down in Kyel's lap, his eagerness too great to be contained in his little body.

But it was not the time for magic.

Kyel ran his hand through his son's hair. "No, Gil. Not today. Papa's tired."

"Pleeeeease?"

"No." Kyel shook his head. He gazed into his son's face. At his warm blue eyes. At his soft skin. His full lips. Soft ringlets of hair. Gil was perfect in every way. Kyel took in each feature, one by one, trying to imprint them on his mind. Each was equally important, the most important thing in the world.

"What do you protect, Papa?"

Kyel's hand was trembling, so he clenched it into a fist. It took him a moment to answer. He knew he had to tell Gil just enough of the truth without being too candid.

"I protect you," he said finally. "And your mum. And anyone else who needs protecting."

Gil's lips twisted, his little eyes scrunching in thought. He sat there for a moment looking very skeptical. Or very concerned.

"Who protects you, Papa?"

Kyel opened his mouth. Then closed it again, not having the faintest notion how to respond. He thought hard about it. He couldn't tell Gil the truth: that no one protected him. That he was going to die in a matter of days. That Gil would never see his father again. That these scant moments would be the very last they had. Kyel swallowed back the tears that tried to come and fought the sorrow off his face. He couldn't break down. His strength was the last and best gift he could ever give his son.

"Who protects you, papa?" Gil asked again.

From some deep place of courage he didn't know he had, Kyel managed to dredge up a wavering smile. "That's what magic's for."

"Will there always be magic?"

Another unfortunate question.

"I hope so."

"I hope so, too."

With a smile, Gil threw his arms around Kyel's neck, wrapping him in a squirming bear hug. Kyel grimaced against the grief that clawed at his chest. He gathered his son in his arms and hugged him tight, cherishing the feel of him.

Into Gil's soft curls, Kyel said softly, "You need

to know how much I love you. And how proud I am of you."

The little body wriggled in his arms. In a voice muffled by Kyel's thick shirt, Gil said, "I love you too, Papa. You're the best Sentinel in the world."

———

Kyel pulled the door softly shut, cutting off the steady sounds of Gil's snoring. He squeezed his eyes closed against a stab of sorrow. It wasn't fair. A little boy shouldn't have to grow up without a father. He reached up, rubbing his eyes. He took a deep breath. Then he strode away.

He made his way through the warren of passages that formed the living quarters of Om's Temple. He rounded the last corner that led to the main entrance and there drew up. He hadn't expected Arvel to be waiting for him. But he wasn't surprised to see him, either. Avoiding eye contact, Kyel asked, "You're going to get him to his mum, right?"

The god-priest flashed Kyel a dour smile. "Of course. It is the least we can do. Don't let your thoughts be preoccupied with your son's welfare. Gil will be taken care of."

Kyel nodded, his shoulders sagging.

"Are you ready?" The smile on Arvel's face was fixed as if etched there. "The Temple of Death is expecting you."

Kyel paused. "I would like to ask a question."

Arvel's waxen smile slipped just a fraction. "You wish to know if the gods are real."

Kyel was surprised the man had anticipated his question. Nevertheless he nodded, figuring he was owed the truth. Arvel raised his hand, beckoning Kyel to follow. He led him through a doorway into a spacious chamber dominated by a table surrounded by many chairs. Kyel took a seat, while the cleric settled across from him.

Clasping his hands together, Arvel informed him, "There is only one goddess."

"Which goddess is that?" Kyel sat back in his chair, bringing a leg up.

Arvel smiled blandly. "She has gone by many names since the beginning of the world."

"So why the secrecy?" Kyel pressed.

"Because." Arvel shifted in his seat, his face becoming very serious. "The temples are not religious entities, as you've been raised to think. They are entirely political. The temples are institutions created to defend humanity against our most ancient of all adversaries."

"Mages," Kyel guessed.

Arvel nodded. "If not for the temples, mages would dominate the earth, oppressing the vulnerable masses. They've done so in the past, and they would do so again. For millennia, the temples have resorted to the one force on earth capable of challenging the power of magic: the power of faith."

Kyel frowned. "Then how do you perform your miracles?"

"Each temple was entrusted with magical artifacts. And from these artifacts, we have achieved the "miracles" that buy us the faith we need. There is only one temple that does not need to rely on artifacts of magic."

"And which temple is that?"

"The temple of the One True Goddess. The Temple of Isap." The smile on Arvel's face stagnated.

"What of the Catacombs?" Kyel pressed. "The Atrament… none of that is magically conceived?"

"All of that is Isap's domain."

It all made perfect sense, Kyel realized. Arvel's story explained so many inconsistencies he'd always wondered about. But the story did have one gaping hole. Leaning forward in his seat, Kyel pressed, "Then what of Xerys?"

Arvel slouched, his body seeming to deflate and collapse in on itself. "Xerys does, in fact, exist. But he is not a god."

Kyel frowned. "Then what is he?"

Arvel's glasses had slipped down his nose. Pushing them back up, he explained, "Xerys was the first mage, the most beloved of all of Isap's creations. He was born of magic and tasked with protecting all things magical. But Xerys became too enamored by what he guarded. He came to believe that creations born of magic were elevated above those who were born mundane. He decided it was the place of humanity to serve magic, and not the other way around. This belief was contrary to Isap's vision of her creation.

"So Xerys earned Isap's displeasure. He was banished from this world and imprisoned in another plane: what you call hell. Contrary to what you've been taught, Xerys is not the source of evil in this world. Evil is a construct, nothing more. But Xerys has no compunctions against using what we call 'evil' to his advantage, if doing so advances his own interests."

Kyel stared at Arvel, feeling physically shaken. Every tenant of faith he had ever nurtured had just been broken on the wheel of truth.

The implications were vast. They redefined his very purpose.

"So…Xerys' Servants are not demons?"

Arvel's wan smile returned. "Oh, they are most certainly demons. They are creatures of spirit who, like Xerys himself, are forbidden from ever entering Isap's domain. They have chosen to side with Xerys, so have been banished to spend eternity in the company of the master they serve."

Kyel nodded. "And what of the Hellpower?"

Arvel smiled morosely. "The Hellpower is the type of magic that exists in Xerys' realm. It is the antithesis of the magic field."

So many answers…and yet each answer spawned a host of new questions. Kyel wondered how many years it would take to get to the bottom of it all. If there was, indeed, a bottom.

He sighed wearily. "I don't understand. What are the Servants trying to accomplish? What are they looking to gain?"

Arvel shrugged, as if the answer should be obvious. "Xerys wishes to be freed from his confinement. That is the goal his Servants work toward. And that is the reason why we must oppose him. For, if Xerys is ever freed, humanity would be once again pressed into servitude by those with magic, and mages alone would rule the world."

Arvel looked down at the tabletop. "Zavier Renquist plans to halt the Reversal of the magic field using the Hellpower, just as he tried to do a thousand years ago. Only, to release enough of it, he would have to open the Gateway wide enough that it would free Xerys from the Netherworld."

Kyel stiffened as the priest's revelation sank into his chest like icy fingers groping for his heart. His first thought was of Gil. He'd told his son he was a protector. And he could think of nothing in the world more important to protect.

"What must I do?" he asked.

For the first time, Arvel's smile grew beyond bland, into something eager. Something sinister. "Stop Renquist. Stop his Servants. Before they gather enough power to release Xerys into this world."

Chapter Twenty-Eight
Transformations

Isle of Titherry, The Rhen

A bleakness encased Naia's thoughts as she stared down at the ever-changing surface of Athera's Crescent. Her gaze followed the flowing patterns that moved across it, patterns that reminded her of ripples propagating across the surface of a lake.

The day was bright, and a gentle breeze cooled her skin, but nothing could take her mind from the myriad possible destinies she had witnessed in the Nexus. Nothing could alleviate the sorrow that filled her heart. It didn't matter which future destiny held in store for her. All seemed equally bleak.

Naia sighed, pushing her hair back out of the way of her vision. Turning away from the Crescent, she made her way back into the castle. She found Quin in his room, stuffing the last of his possessions into his pack.

"Are you ready?" she asked.

He nodded, flashing her a smile that didn't quite reach his eyes.

Naia clasped her hands together as she moved across the room toward him. The new shadow staff he'd carved was leaning against the wall beside the bed. She had forgotten to ask if he'd ever finished it. Reaching out, she laid her hand upon the staff, stroking its wax-polished surface. Instantly, an ominous feeling jolted up her arm, making her flinch. Naia retracted her hand quickly. It was the same feeling she'd gotten the first time she'd touched the staff. The thing felt evil, although Quin kept insisting it wasn't.

Moving away from the staff, she asked, "Why are we going to Rothscard?"

Quin tied his pack closed, giving the cord one good, last tug. "Because you said we need to find Kyel," he said as he swung the pack over his shoulder.

Naia's brow furrowed. "And why do you think Kyel will be in Rothscard?"

Quin shrugged. "Because it's the logical place for him to be." His eyes roved quickly over the room, scanning to make certain there was nothing left behind. He took the staff into his hand. "Being a Sentinel, Kyel would want to be near the Front. But the problem is, we've been here too long. So the Front's not likely where we left it. With the Reversal so close, Darien's had no choice but to push southward. And any invading army would make Rothscard their target."

"Then the war's already begun. What are we going to do?" Naia whispered, feeling that they'd already failed before even setting off.

Quin appeared to think about it a moment. "Well, we'll just have to improvise," he said, holding the door open for her.

The Kingdom of Emmery, The Rhen

The demon-dog yawned enormously. The beast gazed across the fire at Darien with a questioning look. Its ears perked, its head whipping toward the darkness. The hound rose to its feet, emitting a low growl, intent on something outside the circle of light. Then it relaxed, apparently satisfied. The thing turned in a slow circle, then finally settled back down, closing its baneful eyes.

Darien ignored the thanacryst, his attention

riveted on the journal in his lap. He held his head in his hand, fingers clasped around a fistful of hair. His eyes scoured the page as if his life depended on the information contained there. Or another life, far more precious. All he knew was that the secrets unlocked by that journal were so important that Edric Torrence had lain down his life to pass them on.

He didn't look up at the crunch of approaching footsteps.

"Report," Darien ordered, flipping a page.

"Warden, we have only four crates of salted fish remaining and one cask of wine," his quartermaster informed him.

Darien glanced back over the last solution on the page. Absently, he said, "The fish should get us there. Ration the wine."

"Yes, Warden."

As the officer moved away, Darien tried repeating Edric's calculations in his head. He quickly found them too much to keep track of. With a grunt of frustration, he reached into the cloth sack at his side and pulled out a pot of ink and a writing stick. The *elam* wasn't sharpened, but that took only a moment's thought to fix. Unrolling a strip of parchment, he started scribbling, altering magnitudes to account for his own abilities.

The resulting number was extraordinary.

"It'll work," he muttered.

"What will work?"

Twisting, Darien looked up into Azár's face. She'd come up quietly behind him, and even the thanacryst hadn't alerted him to her presence. The beast appeared to be sleeping, its hind foot twitching just a bit. He set the parchment down and stoppered the ink pot.

"I think I know how Edric did it," Darien said, closing the journal and slipping it back into its embroidered cover.

Azár sat down beside him, her face lit by interest. "How is that?"

Darien reached up and scratched the whiskers on his jaw, wondering if he had enough understanding of Edric's methods to replicate the experiment. He decided the risk would be minimal. "It's complicated. I'm still trying to figure out why he felt flight was so important. I'm not sure what the value is, other than mobility. Still, I'd like to try it."

Azár turned away from him and gazed into the fire. The light of the flames danced across her face, tracing her features in acute contours.

"I do not like this idea," she said at last. "What if you turn yourself into a bird and cannot change back?"

That had been his first concern. Which was why he'd worked out both the forward and reverse solutions several times, just to make certain. "That wouldn't happen," Darien assured her. "The energy works out the same in both directions."

He stood up and wandered around the campfire to the demon-hound. The beast sat up on its haunches, its tail thrumming against the ground. Darien ran a hand through its matted fur, giving the thing a good scratch behind the ears.

"I could try it. See what happens," he suggested. "Master Edric obviously thought it was import—"

Azár cut him off. "This is not a good idea. It sounds dangerous."

She had made up her mind, he saw. And when Azár was adamant about something, she wasn't likely to relent. Which meant he would have to test his theory without her consent.

Darien gave the demon-hound one last, good scratch. Then he closed his eyes and wrenched as hard as he could on the magic field, forcing it in, filling himself as quickly as he could to the point of saturation.

"NO!" Azár screamed, realizing too late what was happening. All at once, a writhing mass of blue flames enveloped Darien, erupting into an inferno of blinding brilliance. She leapt to her feet, lunging for him—

A flurry of wings beat against her face, knocking her backward with a startled cry. Panicked, she screamed her husband's name.

But he was gone. Only a shimmering afterglow of his image remained in his place.

A shrill screech pierced the air. Azár's stomach lurched in fear. She scanned the line of trees, desperately seeking the source of the cry. Then she saw it. There, silhouetted against the stars, the dark form of a bird rose swiftly into the sky.

"Sayeed Zakai!" she screamed, terror in her heart.

She staggered backward over uneven ground, eyes pinned on the falcon as it darted across the thin crescent of the moon. Another shriek pierced the night.

She heard footsteps sprinting toward her. Then Sayeed was at her side, eyes wide and alarmed.

"Are you harmed? What happened?" he demanded.

"There!" Azár cried, pointing upward, her finger tracking the bird's motion. It gained height in slow circles, finally leveling out to skim gracefully overhead.

"How…?" Sayeed gasped.

The demon-hound gazed upward, cocking its head.

The falcon let out another piercing screech. It dipped its wing and veered away, soaring toward the mountains in the far distance.

"He is not coming back!" Azár cried, watching the bird flapping away.

Face aghast, Sayeed gripped her arm, his fingers biting into her skin. The cries of the falcon grew fainter. Soon its form was lost, slipping away into the shadows of the night.

Tears streaked Azár's face. A feeling of futility washed over her, weakening her knees. Sayeed caught her up, supporting her weight against him.

"He will come back," he reassured her. But she could tell by the sound of his voice that he was just as concerned as she.

"What if he doesn't remember he is a man?" she whispered.

———

They stood by the fire as the night dragged on, measured by the moon's slow progress.

They stood there until the coals grew cold and dawn broke across the horizon.

When Sayeed finally picked her up and carried her back to her tent, Azár didn't resist. She was barely aware of the officer settling her into bed, arranging her covers over her with the care and compassion of a brother. Feeling more alone than she could ever remember, she fell into a deep and troubled sleep.

———

Azár awoke to the feeling of a hand stroking her face, running tenderly through her hair. She opened her eyes and stared up through the shadows of the tent into the solemn face of her husband.

Her anger exploded. She shot bolt upright. Enraged, she swept out a hand, striking Darien in the face.

He closed his eyes, accepting the blow.

His lack of response angered her more. Azár hauled her arm back to strike him harder. This time, he caught her wrist.

"I'm sorry," he said.

Her anger melted. Sadness took its place. Exhausted, she collapsed against him.

———

Glen Farquist, The Rhen

Kyel followed the white-robed priest down the long hall toward the main sanctuary of the Temple of Death. Through the glass, he could see the temple's garden courtyard, with its long reflecting pool bordered by manicured shrubs. White and black swans plied the pool's waters and roosted along the shore. Beyond the garden rose the verdigris dome of the sanctuary, replete with its hundreds of stained-glass windows.

The sound of their footsteps rang off the walls as the gangly priest he followed turned a corner and led him down a narrow hallway that ended at a door. Kyel waited as the young man knocked twice, then opened the door and stepped back. Kyel nodded his gratitude and moved past, turning to confront the old man who sat waiting for him behind a wooden desk.

At the sight of him, Luther Penthos rose to his feet. Kyel walked forward, taking the priest's hand. Strangely, he felt none of the hesitance he'd always experienced before in the presence of this formidable man. Luther Penthos was Naia's father, as well as the High Priest of Death. Kyel's history with him had been turbulent. He had no reason to think that had changed.

"Your Eminence," he said in acknowledgement.

"Grand Master Archer." There was no trace of a smile on the priest's face. "I wish I could say it is good to see you again, but I'd be lying. Have you had word of my daughter?"

"No. Nothing." Kyel shook his head, feeling a pang of regret.

The old man nodded, slouching just a bit. "If you happen to see her before…well…" His voice trailed off. "Please tell her that I love her."

Kyel nodded. "I will, Your Eminence."

Setting his pack on the floor, he took a seat. He let his gaze travel around the room, looking over the assortment of books, tapers, lamps, and scrolls the man had amassed. The High Priest's study looked much more cluttered than the last time he'd seen it only months before. As though the man's enthusiasm for life had fled with his daughter.

"So." The old priest folded his age-spotted hands on the desk. "I hear you desire an escort through our Catacombs to Rothscard. I suppose I should warn you that Rothscard is not a safe destination at the moment. The city is under siege. We can get you in but, considering the size of the Enemy host, your sojourn may prove dangerous."

Kyel took the man's meaning. He said softly, "I'm not entirely defenseless."

Penthos raised an eyebrow. "So I've heard. I would like to thank you for a laudable defense of this valley. I fear, however, that such an outcome may not be easily replicated in Rothscard. The Enemy host is well over a hundred thousand strong, with more arriving each day. Rothscard is almost certain to fall."

Kyel glanced up at a painting that depicted one of the aspects of the goddess Isap. Remembering what Arvel had said about the goddess, Kyel stared harder at the image. In it, Isap appeared as a human woman with an elaborate headdress, holding a tall, stringed instrument. Her face, covered by an opaque veil, was unknowable. She could have been any woman, or every woman.

Looking back at Penthos, Kyel said, "I'd be grateful for help getting to Rothscard. But I'm not going there to defend the city. My goal is to destroy Xerys' Servants."

The old priest's eyes hardened to steel. "Then you will have all the aid I can give you. We no longer fight a war against the Enemy. That war is already lost. What we fight for now is the future of humanity. And that is a battle we can't afford to lose."

Kyel inclined his head. "I understand, Your Eminence."

Chapter Twenty-Nine
Every Advantage

Rothscard, The Rhen

The sound of his boots crunching on pebbles had occupied Darien's attention the entire morning. The noise grated on his nerves. He was growing fed up with it.

And with his wife's relentless silence.

Azár hadn't spoken to him all day, had made a point of showing him her back and throwing glares at him when she thought he wasn't looking. She had managed to walk at his side while successfully ignoring him for hours, her face set in a perpetual scowl. He'd had enough of it.

Darien let out a long, frustrated breath, groping for patience. "I'm sorry," he said in as gentle a tone as he could manage. "I gave you a fright. I ought to have warned you."

Azár's eyes glinted with ire. She was silent for a long minute. Then she responded, "Why did you do it?"

Darien breathed another irritated sigh. "Because I need to find an edge. Kyel handled me too well back there. With that talisman, he's stronger than I am."

Azár cast him a look of troubled doubt. "How can turning into a bird help you defeat your apprentice?"

Darien shrugged. "Mobility. Recognizance. I can go places no one could expect. Other than that…I don't know. I'm sure there are other advantages."

She tossed another glare his way. "Why didn't you return?"

"I *did* return."

"You were gone all night!"

He wanted to growl. "I told you. I'm sorry. Now, can we be done with it?"

"No," she snapped. "Tell me why you were gone so long."

He scrubbed his hands through his hair, trying to find the right words to explain his actions. It was far more difficult than it seemed. Perhaps because, at the time, he hadn't been thinking in words.

His brow furrowed. "At first, I was just taken with the feel of flying. The freedom of it. I've never known anything like that. And my thoughts were different." He struggled, searching for a way to explain it. "They were bird thoughts. Not human thoughts. All I could think about was getting away, of escaping. So that's what I did."

Azár looked appalled. She whispered, "You forgot you were a man."

Darien shook his head. He still had a hard time understanding all of it. "I didn't forget. It's just that…being a man didn't seem all that important at the time. I had other needs that were much more powerful, and I didn't know how to override them."

The look in Azár's eyes could have melted glass. "Don't *ever* do that again! What if next time, you cannot control it?"

She was being unreasonable. He had just discovered a wonderful new advantage. Darien had no idea what purpose it could be put to, but he couldn't discard it just because his wife was worried for his safety.

"Next time, I'll be stronger. I'll have more control."

"There will not *be* a next time." Her tone left no room for argument.

Darien clenched his fists. "There will. I need to find and use every advantage I can. *Every* advantage.

Don't you understand?"

He glanced significantly down at her middle. When she realized what he was staring at, her hand went immediately to her belly, as if seeking to shield the small life within.

She scowled. "How will changing into a bird save our child's life?"

"I don't know. But it might."

"You are stupid, Darien Lauchlin. I will not—"

He'd had enough. There was nothing more to be said about the issue.

Darien opened his mind to the magic field and tugged at it violently. He stumbled midstride. There was a brilliant flash. Then he was falling—

Reflexively, he shot his arms out to catch himself. But he kept falling, falling upward. Falling away from the ground, flying—

The pull of the sky…

He beat his wings, climbing higher. Below, a tangled line of people wound through the trees. He circled above them, searching for an updraft. Finding one. He relaxed and let the warm air currents lift him higher.

The feel of the wind…

Everything below was impossibly sharp, impossibly vivid. He could see every detail of every face. New colors he had never before seen. A glowing fluorescence that dappled the ground. Far away beneath a tree, something moved—

Prey…

He tucked his wings and dove toward it. Then:

War. Child…

He pulled up, reminded of his purpose. He banked sharply and set his course parallel to the river. Ahead, he could see a great black plume of smoke that resembled a bank of clouds.

The city…

Below, the forest ended, and a vast grassland began. A great mass of people spread like a dark ocean across the plain. There were horses, fires—

Danger…

He wheeled away, but not before marking the colors of the banners. He angled back toward the river, pumping his wings, soaring over the forest, to the drawn-out column of men and women—

Azár…

He skimmed lower, finding a path between the trees, lower still, meeting the ground—

He staggered and fell to his knees, roughing the heels of his palms on the pebbled surface. He glanced up—

—into Azár's startled face. Sayeed was already running toward him. People were backing away, eyes wide with fear, holding up their hands in a ward against evil.

He lurched to his feet. Sweat streamed from his brow, drained into his eyes. He swiped a sleeve across his face. He was panting. Weak. He staggered.

"I did not believe it," Sayeed gasped, putting an arm out to steady him. His face was full of wonder. Or fear. Darien couldn't tell which.

He turned to Azár. Before she could say anything, he held a hand up. "I know. I'm stupid."

To his disbelief, his wife grinned.

Isle of Titherry, The Rhen

The shrine of Death didn't look familiar, although it should have. The last time Quin had seen it had been under the spell of everlasting winter. But that spell was broken. Now the Isle of Titherry lay basking under the warm spring sun, enjoying a thaw that had been delayed for years—ever since the collapse of the Hall of the Watchers.

When Aerysius had fallen, its Circle of Convergence had died with it, its conduit severed from Athera's Crescent. Without that input, the Crescent had resorted to pulling the energy it needed directly from the air around it, encasing the isle in a winter that didn't end. Now that Quin had repaired the conduits, Athera's Crescent was functioning just as it was designed to do.

Quin turned to Naia, his eyes running over her. She was occupied with the business of lighting the shrine's assortment of tapers. It was almost like a graceful dance that swept her from one end of the room to the other. Quin watched her as she worked, lighting one taper from another by means of a wooden splint, moving in what seemed a random order back and forth across the shrine. He had a feeling there was nothing random at all about her movements. He stood back and watched, enjoying the fluid grace of her body.

"I've been thinking," he said, staring at her back.

"These visions—or versions—that you have. Is Zavier Renquist in each of them?"

"Yes," Naia responded without pausing in her candle-lighting.

Quin's eyes wandered across the walls of the shrine, taking in a series of numbered frescoes painted there. "What if Renquist was taken out of the picture? I mean, could he be blocking your ability to see past him? Like Tsula?"

Naia didn't pause. "I don't know," she said with her back to him.

"But it's possible, right?"

She turned slowly around to stare at him with a skeptical look. "I suppose. Why? What are you thinking?"

"It strikes me as odd that Renquist was Tsula's husband. It's highly irregular for Harbingers to marry anyone, much less a Prime Warden. Maybe Tsula wasn't helping him intentionally… but that doesn't mean she wasn't helping him unintentionally."

Naia frowned with a look of intense concern. "Do you think he knows what we're about?"

"I don't know," Quin muttered. It took him only a moment to arrive at a decision. "You go on ahead to Rothscard. Show me the way to Bryn Calazar. I'll meet up with you when I'm done."

"Done with what?" Naia asked, moving toward him. She extinguished the wooden splint with her fingers and set it down. She stared at him intensely.

Quin took her hand and kissed it. "There's something I need to do that I should have done a long time ago."

"And what is that?" Naia whispered with a look of dread.

Quin smiled dangerously. "I'm going to kill Zavier Renquist."

Rothscard, The Rhen

Kyel's gray stallion shied away from a street dancer's brightly colored ribbons. He reined in and brought the animal under control. He couldn't believe anyone could be dancing and flipping around ribbons in the midst of a siege. But people had to put food in their mouths, he supposed, even under the direst of circumstances. Reaching into his pocket, he pulled out a coin and tossed it to the woman, figuring she needed it more desperately than he did.

His escort of blue-cloaked guardsmen were having a difficult time holding back the crowd as they waded through Rothscard's unruly streets. The city was bursting with masses of people swarming the shops and market stalls, scrambling to find food and supplies. The city guard was hard-pressed to keep order, often resorting to bludgeons and swords to maintain some degree of civility.

Most of the markets were already emptied, the street vendors sold out of wares. The storefronts had been boarded up, the shopkeepers fled. The only commodity Rothscard seemed to have in good supply was an abundance of prostitutes and opportunists, the former touting their wares in exchange for food, the latter pushing medicinals at criminal prices. The stench of smoke and fear-sweat combined to yield a heady miasma in the air.

The gates of Emmery Palace were heavily guarded. Kyel was ushered through quickly, garnering more than his share of shocked looks and stares. The people of Rothscard were no longer used to the sight of a black cloak. Most of the population took heart in the sight of it. Others looked on in fear.

His escort led him through another gate into the Inner Ward of the palace, past fountains hedged by immaculate gardens. At the palace steps, he was relieved of his horse and greeted by a flustered-looking minister who bowed and blotted his brow with a folded kerchief.

"This way, Great Master. The Queen and Prince await you in the council chamber."

The council chamber was an upgrade, Kyel decided. The last time he'd visited Emmery Palace with Meiran, Romana had relegated them to the Blue Room. Kyel took it for a good sign; perhaps he was finally being taken more seriously. He followed the minister through a series of long hallways dripping with chandeliers to a set of double doors.

The minister pulled open the doors with a flourish and announced, "Grand Master Kyel Archer of the Distinguished Order of Sentinels."

Kyel stepped into the room, feeling irritated and rather embarrassed by the pomp and formality. He wasn't there to exchange courtesies, and he didn't care a whit about decorum. His business was far more serious in nature.

The council chamber was dominated by a long table carved from a single piece of burl wood. Queen Romana and her husband rose from their chairs, the only two people in the room. Kyel walked forward, not bothering to kneel; he was a mage, and therefore the equal of any queen. He sat next to them at the table, waving away a servant who scurried forward to offer refreshments.

Kyel's gaze travelled over the royal grandeur of the chamber, at the gilt wall panels and elaborate sconces. All eclipsed by the majesty of the Queen herself. Romana's presence saturated the room. She was no longer the young girl he remembered meeting two years before.

The Queen was staring at him expectantly, no doubt waiting for him to speak. It took Kyel a moment to form words. This was the same woman who, upon their first meeting, had ordered him arrested and had him placed in chains. He'd been completely at her mercy, and at the mercy of her husband, Nigel Swain. Kyel sat looking back and forth between the two of them. He folded his hands on the table, taking a moment to collect himself.

"Thank you for receiving me," he said at last. He was surprised by the confidence in his voice. He couldn't have managed that tone even a few months before.

"Thank you for coming, Grand Master Archer," Romana said, inclining her head.

Her husband stared at Kyel with a narrow, unblinking gaze. Swain had been Romana's captain of the guard before he had become the Prince Consort. He was also the Guild blademaster who had trained Darien in the sword. He was perhaps the most uncompromising man Kyel had ever met, and the most single-minded.

Swain said coolly, "I'm not sure how you arrived, considering our city is under siege. But we would appreciate any help you can lend us."

After two years of knowing him, Kyel still wasn't sure whether or not he liked Swain. Looking at Romana, Kyel said, "I'm sorry, Your Grace, but I'm not here to defend Rothscard. I'm here to destroy Darien Lauchlin."

Swain nodded slightly, while Romana canted her head at Kyel's words.

"A worthy goal," she pronounced with an undertone of skepticism. "However, I fear it is unachievable. And unnecessary. By all reports, the Reversal of the magic field is imminent. I am told the event will send Xerys' Servants back to whatever hell they came from."

Kyel shook his head. "There's more to it. The temples believe the Servants plan to stabilize the magic field using the Hellpower. Not only would that halt the Reversal, but it would release Xerys fully into this world. We don't know how they indent to accomplish it. But we do know it's possible."

Romana and Swain exchanged a horrified look weighed by experience and understanding. The Queen turned back to Kyel. "What do you need from us?"

Kyel said, "I need your army, Your Grace."

Romana's eyebrows shot up, her face frozen halfway between disbelief and amusement. *"Again?"*

Kyel realized he had just spoken the same words he had uttered upon their first meeting. Only, then, he had been Darien's emissary to the throne of Emmery.

"I need men behind me," he explained. "I can't bring Darien down by myself. I'm Bound by my Oath of Harmony. But I can weaken him. And I can contain him long enough for others to move in and finish him."

Romana nodded slowly, looking thoughtful. She brushed a wisp of hair out of her face, for a moment looking like the young woman Kyel remembered meeting for the first time. But the moment was fleeting, and the imposing monarch was quick to return.

Formally, she announced, "Sentinel Archer, you may have whatever resources we can spare to hunt this demon down."

"Thank you, Your Grace." Kyel said with a nod. "I will make do with whatever you can give me."

"I'll assist you personally," said Swain. "I need to finish what I started back at Orien's Finger. I should have never let Darien walk away from there alive."

Kyel remembered when Swain had stood with his sword raised over Darien, preparing to strike a blow that would have ended his misery. For some reason, the Prince had stayed his hand. Kyel wondered how events would have transpired differently if he had let the blade fall.

"There's another matter we need to speak of."

Swain's face was etched in troubled lines of concern. "Another mage arrived in the city this morning. A woman calling herself Master Alexa Newell. Do you know her?"

Kyel stared at him in shock.

"Yes, I do," he gasped. "She's here?"

When Alexa hadn't returned, he'd just assumed she'd been slain by Darien's necrators. And while he was grateful that she had saved his life, Kyel hadn't mourned her. Her appearance in Rothscard was all too coincidental and disturbing. Why hadn't she returned to him in Glen Farquist? And how had she arrived in the city ahead of him? Far too many questions still surrounded Alexa for Kyel's liking.

"She's here," Swain confirmed. "I had her arrested and taken to the Citadel. I don't like what I can't explain, and I like it even less when my city is under siege."

"I understand." Kyel said. "I would like to speak with her."

"I'll take you to her."

Kyel rose from his seat. Queen Romana stood and took him by the hand. She said with a smile, "You have grown so much since the first time we met. More than I would have ever imagined possible. You have become every inch a Sentinel, Kyel Archer."

Kyel felt certain it was by far the greatest compliment he'd ever received, and he knew he should feel proud. Two months ago, he would have. But too many events had transpired since. Instead of feeling bolstered by Romana's words, they only served to make him feel saddened.

Because the Queen was wrong. What she sensed in him was not confidence. It was simply resignation.

Chapter Thirty
Legacies

Rothscard, The Rhen

The encampment of the Malikari legions sprawled across the plains, beginning at the banks of the River Nerium and extending in every direction to the distant horizons. Thousands upon thousands of tents pitched in orderly rows radiated outward like the spokes of a wheel from the center of camp. In the far distance, the walls of Rothscard gleamed a bloody red, reflecting the saturated colors of the sunset. Black smoke billowed from the city, roiling overhead like heavy storm clouds.

Darien ordered his Tanisars to pitch their tents on the western margin of the encampment, then continued on to the command tent with Azár and a small retinue of Zakai. At the sight of their small group, men and women ran forward to line their passage, shouting and cheering and shaking weapons in the air. What surprised Darien most were the long rows of tethered horses that had been assimilated into the encampment. Apparently, the horse lords of the plains had honored their commitment.

They found the command tent abuzz with uniformed officers trickling in and out of the pavilion's entrance. A spectacularly garbed man with a tall plume on his hat intercepted them, then ducked aside to confer quietly with Sayeed in the language of the clans. After a short moment, Sayeed nodded and returned to Darien, his expression concerned.

"Your presence is requested within. You are to enter alone."

Darien frowned, wondering which warlord would be arrogant enough to greet his arrival with demands. Nevertheless, he raised his hand, cautioning Sayeed and Azár to remain outside. Whoever it was that awaited within, he wanted to confront them alone. His pregnant wife need not look on.

Darien followed the officer into the pavilion. Lining the walls were men and women who immediately clamored to their feet and, bowing, streamed out of the tent. A group of officers leaning over the map table turned and, upon marking his arrival, shifted their gazes to the floor. They filed past him, avoiding his eyes on their way out. Even Darien's plumed escort didn't remain long. The man bowed deeply then took his leave, untying the tent flaps from the support posts and letting the fabric fall. Soon, the entire pavilion stood dim and empty.

Only, it was not.

There was a rustle on the other side of the tent's partition. Darien turned, stiffening with suppressed tension. His hand moved to the hilt of his sword.

The partition was drawn back to admit two men—the only two men in the world whose very presence made Darien's nerves prickle. Without hesitation, he went to his knees and bowed forward, pressing his forehead against the rugs, his palms beside his face. He remained there, unmoving, until the rustle of robes told him both men had taken a seat. Time dribbled forward, marked only by the ebb and flow of his breath.

At last, a deep and familiar voice announced, "You may rise."

Darien pushed himself upright, feeling the blood drain from his face. He shifted into a cross-legged position, hands clasped in front of him. He raised his gaze slowly, hesitant to look Zavier Renquist in the eyes.

The Prime Warden regarded him for a long moment without moving. He was seated on a rug, wearing the formal blue robes and white cloak of his office. Beside him sat Cyrus Krane, ancient Prime Warden of Aerysius, and Renquist's second-in-command. Krane's dark eyes surveyed Darien suspiciously. The man had never liked him. He'd never thought to question why.

Renquist favored him with a fatherly smile. "Welcome, Darien. How is your health?"

Darien's eyes ranged from one man to the other. He answered guardedly, "My health is good, Prime Warden." His back remained stiff, his fingers locked together with rigid tension. He sensed danger in the air, and his muscles were responding.

Renquist nodded. "By all reports, you've done exceptionally well. You have managed to secure the whole of the North. Even the great city of Rothscard shall soon fall before us. As I predicted, you have truly become the greatest Battlemage in all of history."

Darien bowed his head, feeling a flush of humility tempered by apprehension. "Thank you, Prime Warden."

Again, Renquist supplied that same, fatherly smile. Darien didn't trust it.

"Now, let us speak of recent developments." The Prime Warden sat back and adjusted his posture. His many-stranded silver necklace shimmered in the lantern light. "I received word that Byron Connel was slain in battle. And that his talisman fell into the hands of a Sentinel. Two events which are...most unfortunate."

Darien licked his lips, a faint shiver tingling his spine. He thought perhaps Renquist blamed him for Connel's death. The man didn't say it outright. Still, there was something that hung in the air between them, like a cold and threatening undercurrent.

"The information you received is accurate." Darien looked from one Prime Warden to the other. "The Sentinel's name is Kyel Archer. He was my acolyte." He hesitated, unsure of how much information he should share. Too little could rouse suspicion. Too much might get him killed. "A woman who travels with Kyel taught him the use of the talisman. It is my suspicion he inherited Meiran's legacy, which would make him eleventh tier."

"Eleventh tier," Renquist echoed, his voice a low rumble. Almost, Darien thought he saw a fleeting smile on the man's face. The expression was there for only an instant, then was gone. If it had ever been there in the first place.

The Prime Warden said, "That would explain why this Sentinel was able to repulse your attack at Glen Farquist. So, Darien. What do you intend to do about him?"

Darien didn't answer immediately. Instead, he took a moment to think over his response carefully. "Kyel's not immune to my necrators. Or my thanacryst."

A glint of metal on Renquist's hand caught Darien's attention. The Prime Warden was wearing a ring he'd never noticed before. A silver ring set with a lapis stone. And upon that stone, depicted in gold overlay, was an ancient rune, one he knew well: *Dacros.* The first rune in the sequence that commanded the Well of Tears.

Darien frowned at the presence of the ring, uncertain of what it meant.

Renquist's face became very solemn. "There is one last matter to speak of. As you know, the Reversal of the magic field is nearly upon us. As things stand, we do not have much time left in this world."

Darien gazed at the floor, not wishing to be reminded. He'd promised Azár he would find a way to save her and the child she carried. But as the days crept by, the more it became apparent he had made a promise he couldn't keep.

"I believe there is a way to change that destiny," Zavier Renquist said softly.

Darien's eyes snapped up. Hope shot through him with the force of a lightning strike. *"How?"* he gasped.

Renquist spread his hands. "There is a way to halt the Reversal, though at great expense." His stare dug into Darien's eyes as if boring into his soul. "Tell me. How much of yourself are you willing to sacrifice in order to save your wife and unborn child?"

Darien's heart stopped. He gasped but couldn't draw breath. His mind stumbled to a standstill. *"Anything,"* he managed, surging to his feet. "What must I do?"

Zavier Renquist rose to stand in front of him. Clasping his hands behind his back, he said in a calm voice, "A thousand years ago, we had a plan to halt the Reversal. It involved combining the might of eight Grand Masters using the eight Circles of Convergence. Hence the covenant of the Eight Servants came to be. As you know, there are no longer eight Servants. Or eight Circles of Convergence."

He paced around the margin of the tent, circling Darien like a raptor. "But eight Grand Masters are not truly necessary. Only the vitrus of eight Grand Masters is needed."

Shaken, Darien looked at him in incomprehension. "So we need to combine thirty-two tiers of mage-power? How can that be done?"

Renquist stopped pacing and turned to face him. "Through the Onslaught, you already have access to eight tiers. If you are correct in your guess, then this Kyel Archer has inherited eleven. That leaves us lacking only thirteen tiers. Cyrus and Quinlan each have five. All we will need, then, is three more tiers."

Darien's heart froze. "No." He shook his head adamantly. "Not Azár."

Renquist waved his hand, dismissing the idea. "Of course not. I was thinking, rather, of the former priestess who inherited half your legacy. Together, we can save the lives of every living mage. Including the lives of your wife and child."

Darien could only stare at him, rendered speechless by a blaze of hope that was incapacitating.

Zavier Renquist smiled triumphantly. But the smile didn't last long. His face darkened again almost immediately. "I doubt your acolyte will be willing to lay down his life willingly. You will need to dispatch him and absorb his legacy. I'll take care of the others."

He took a step forward. "You will be my conduit, Darien. You will absorb all thirty-two tiers of combined vitrus. And, reaching through you, I will be able to halt the Reversal." His expression turned grim. He placed a comforting hand on Darien's shoulder. "Of course, as a consequence, you will not live to see your child born."

Even those words couldn't cool the flame of hope that had ignited inside Darien. It raged like a firestorm, consuming him utterly. He retreated a step, shaking his head. *"I don't care.* My life's not important."

Renquist gazed at him sadly. "Thank you, Darien. Know that your sacrifice will save many lives…and return the sunlight to Malikar." He hesitated then. Dropping his gaze to the floor, he spoke in a troubled voice, "You are like a son to me, Darien. Your loss will be deeply felt."

It sounded heartfelt. His own father had died long before Darien had reached adulthood, before he'd ever had a chance to make him proud. Zavier Renquist could never take his father's place. Nevertheless, he felt moved by the Prime Warden's expression of sentiment.

"Now go." Renquist dismissed him with a wave. "Find a way to strip your acolyte of his legacy."

"Aye, Prime Warden." Darien effected a formal bow, bending at the waist. He turned to leave but paused, turning back. "Prime Warden, might I ask a boon?"

Renquist nodded. "Of course."

"Please don't speak of this matter to my wife. I don't wish her to know."

Compassion filled Zavier Renquist's eyes, and he dipped his head. "Rest assured. Your wife will remain in ignorance."

Darien bowed again, lower this time. And then he left the tent.

Chapter Thirty-One
Promises and Lies

Death's Passage

Quin opened his eyes to the bleak grandeur of never-ending darkness.

Around him, a faint green light awoke and brightened gradually, until it was vibrant enough to see by. Turning, Quin found he could make out rough granite walls to either side: a passage that curved ahead of him as it sloped downward. It took him a moment to realize he was viewing the world through the hellish light of his own damnation. Looking down at his body, he could see the diffuse green aura that surrounded him. It didn't seem as potent as it had before.

There was a scuffing noise, and suddenly Naia was there with him. She drew up at his side, pausing as a mist of magelight crawled out of the shadows to linger at their feet. She placed a hand on his back and told him softly, "This is where we part."

Quin glanced at her in surprise. He'd figured he'd be journeying most of the way through the Catacombs in Naia's company. In truth, the thought of forging on alone was more than a bit unsettling.

Naia pointed to a fork in the corridor ahead that veered off to the right. "Follow that passage all the way to the end. It's long, but you shouldn't get lost. The exit will take you to a subbasement of the Temple of Death in Bryn Calazar."

Quin eyed the corridor warily. "Won't I be marked?"

Naia shrugged. "Possibly. If you are, I trust you'll know how to deal with the situation."

Quin stared at her sideways. "I do. I'm just shocked to hear you condoning such methods."

She smiled at him sadly. "We've gone far past the point where our actions can be limited by what I condone. The stakes are far too high."

Quin stared at her in admiration. Naia had come a long way from the woman who had once been defined by the chains on her wrists. She spoke from a place of calm practicality, in a way he found vastly alluring.

"Keep talking like that, darling, and I might never leave."

"Be very careful, Quinlan," she said. "That man is a monster."

"I'm a monster, too," he reminded her.

Naia shook her head. "No, Quin. You're not. Maybe you once were. But not anymore."

Looking down at the green aura that surrounded his body, Quin found himself in disagreement. But the thought fled quickly as Naia leaned in and pressed her soft lips against his. The kiss was long, and it left him dizzy and breathless.

"Go softly," Naia whispered when they parted. "Don't do anything that will get you killed. Again. Promise me you'll come back."

Quin shook his head. "I can't make that promise."

"Then promise me you'll try."

"I promise I'll try," he said, and leaned in to kiss her one last time. Then, settling his hat properly on his head, he turned and headed down the corridor.

Rothscard, The Rhen

Kyel followed Swain across the palace grounds to the sprawling hulk of the Citadel. There, the Prince led him down a flight of spiral steps into the dungeon beneath. It was not Kyel's first visit to the prison, and memories of his incarceration were bleak. They walked down a long corridor lined with wooden doors, stopping before the last.

Swain leafed through an iron ring of keys, at last settling on one, and poked it into the lock. With a click, the cell door popped outward just a crack. Swain glanced sharply at Kyel, then pulled the door open the rest of the way. Kyel stepped forward and peered within.

Alexa careened into his arms. Her body smacked against him, her arms squeezing him tight enough to choke him. Kyel reached up and, taking her by the wrists, disengaged her firmly and pushed her back. Alexa stared up at him with a wounded pout. She opened her mouth to say something.

He cut her off before she could get the words out. "Why are you here? How did you *get* here?"

Alexa's eyes darted to Swain then back to Kyel. She looked flustered, at a loss for words. "I don't know how I got here," she said frantically. "The last thing I remember was the battle. Then I woke up just outside the walls. I-I can't explain it! I know it doesn't make sense, but I don't know what to think. Kyel, I'm *scared.*"

Kyel didn't believe her. Every time he lowered his guard and started to trust her, Alexa invariably did something that made his doubt spike all over again. Frustrated, he grappled with his options. He didn't know whether to leave her in the cell or risk taking her with him. Of course, she could always get out on her own; she was a mage. If she really wanted to leave the cell, Alexa could in a heartbeat—but not without risking her Oath of Harmony.

He glanced at Swain. "Can I take her out of here?"

Swain's eyes narrowed. "How well do you know her?"

An excellent question. Kyel had to think about it hard before realizing that he really didn't know much about Alexa at all.

"I know her well enough," he lied.

The Prince stared at him. Doubt was plastered on Swain's face, and Kyel couldn't blame him. "All right," he growled. "I'll release her into your custody."

Kyel looked at Alexa, studying the expression on her face, searching for a reason to doubt her. Seeing none, he took her by the arm and let Swain guide them back out of the prison. No words were spoken as they crossed the Inner Ward back to the palace.

When they reached the entrance to the guest wing, Swain glanced at Alexa and said, "If you need me, I'll be around." His eyes stabbed one last, menacing threat before he turned and left.

It was not Kyel's first stay at Emmery palace. He remembered the opulence of the guestrooms. Nevertheless, he was surprised at the size and luxury of the eight-room suite Romana had arranged for him. Kyel waited for Alexa to enter and then caught her by the arm and spun her back toward him.

"All right," he snapped, slamming the door shut. "I want answers."

"What?" She looked at him with a fearful expression.

"The necrators," Kyel reminded her. "They didn't touch you. Well, maybe they did, but they sure didn't harm you. If anything, *you* harmed *them.* So what really happened?"

Alexa shook her head furiously. "I don't know. Honestly, I don't!" She tugged at his arm, face pale and desperate. "I saw them closing in on you. I thought if I distracted them, maybe it would give you a chance to get away. I don't remember anything after that!"

Kyel could feel a hot spark of anger igniting in his gut. Too many strange events converged around Alexa like iron filings to a lodestone. He said, "Well, you're obviously here, so how did you *get* here?"

She threw her hands up. "I don't know! That's what I'm trying to tell you! I woke up here this morning. I don't remember anything before that. I really don't. I think…"

"You think what?" Kyel demanded.

Her face went blank, her eyes slipping to the side as if in thought. Very slowly, she said, "I think I was brought here. But I don't know how."

Her explanation did nothing to ease Kyel's doubt. Rather, it had the exact opposite effect. "How could you have been brought here without knowing it? The attack on Glen Farquist was ten days ago! What have you been doing for the last *ten days?*"

Alexa staggered back. Her face was flushed, either in anger or in desperation. "I don't know! I don't remember!"

Kyel held his hand up. Thoughts tumbled around in his head then gradually began totaling themselves. The sum wasn't in Alexa's favor.

He said, "Look. It all boils down to this: can I trust you? The more I think about it, the more I think the answer is no."

She opened her mouth to speak, but he raised his hand again. "You've never told me a lie, at least none that I can verify. And you've helped me a lot, with the talisman and the necrators. But you've also never told me any truth that I can verify. Not one. Everything you say, I have to take on faith. But my faith's running out. Tell me something I can validate. Right now. Or you're going back to that cell."

Alexa shook her head in desperation, her eyes wide enough to eclipse the moon. "What am I supposed to do? I can't remember!"

Kyel could only shrug. Her response confirmed his doubts. "Then I'm sorry. I'm going to get the guards now." He started to open the door.

She shot out her hand, grasping him by the shoulder. "I banished his necrators!"

Kyel turned back around. Warily, he said, "Explain."

Tears were collecting in Alexa's eyes. "I *banished* Darien's necrators!" she repeated. "I sent them away!"

"Sent them where?"

Softly, she whispered, "I sent their souls to Oblivion."

Kyel pulled away, taken aback. "Necrators don't have souls."

She clasped her hands in front of her, shaking her head emphatically. "Necrators *are* souls! Collections of souls enslaved to the master who commands them."

"So how does this prove anything?" Kyel asked. "You're telling me you can command his minions. Wouldn't that make you a demon as well?"

"No!" Alexa shook her head furiously. "I'm a Naturalist. I'm an expert at Natural Law—that's what we do! And necrators are *unnatural.* That's why I can unmake them. If I were one of Xerys' Servants, I would have commanded those necrators to destroy you."

"All right, enough." Kyel sighed, rubbing his temples. His brain ached. And, he had to admit, what she was saying made sense. He stepped back out of the doorway.

"I'm just trying to help you, Kyel," Alexa said, her eyes pleading. "I promise."

Kyel sighed and closed the door.

The nameless Zakai officer bowed low before Darien. The man probably had a name, but he hadn't bothered to learn it. Darien realized he knew very few of the names of the men sworn to serve him. It was better that way. Better to keep a distance. He didn't want to be able to put too many names with too many faces. It made it much easier to bury a man.

He leaned forward, using a stick to probe at the fire he'd built a good distance away from camp. He'd wanted to be alone. Away from the soldiers. Away from Azár. His thoughts were rampant, like a crowd of voices all shouting in his head, drowning out the rest of the world.

"Warden, the pavilion has been made ready for your use," the nameless officer reported.

Darien glanced up, glaring at the man for disrupting his solitude. "What about Renquist?"

"Both Prime Wardens have returned to Bryn Calazar."

If the soldier was put off by the look on his face, he didn't show it. No Zakai would. Darien figured he could punch the man in the groin and the soldier would probably just thank him for it.

He gave a grunt and poked at the fire again. The officer bowed and walked back toward the heart of the encampment. Darien stared after him, his eyes tracing the rows of tents while the thoughts in his head clamored for attention.

He rose and kicked dirt into the fire, smothering it. He could have used magic—it would have been easier. But sometimes it felt better to perform a task unaided. He girded his sword belt around his hips and drew his pack on over his shoulders. Then, fingers hooked in the straps, he made his way over the trampled grass back toward the heart of the encampment.

As he moved between rows of tents, the familiar sounds and smells settled his nerves. The camp had a life and rhythm of its own. Right now it was winding down, getting ready for the smooth transition into night. The sun had already set, its light just a gray smear on the western horizon. Voices carried on the air from every direction. Laughter rose somewhere in the distance then faded again like a tide.

The smell of searing meat invaded his path, making his mouth water. In the back of his mind, his thoughts still churned, still vied for dominance. It was all he could do to ignore them.

It took him awhile to reach the command tent. Darien pushed back the flaps and entered with an intense feeling of unease, half-expecting Renquist to appear out of the shadows. But the nameless officer had been right: both Prime Wardens were truly gone. Wearily, Darien pulled off his boots and pushed back the cloth partition. He stood there a moment, just looking. The four-poster bed looked the same as he'd left it. Connel's book of poetry rested open on its pedestal. The colorful woven rugs were arrayed across the floor in the same overlapping pattern he remembered. As if the tent hadn't been packed up and moved dozens of times over hundreds of miles in his absence.

Darien's gaze travelled across the floor, coming to rest on Azár's back. He was surprised to find her kneeling on the rugs on the other side of the bed, taking items from a chest. She glanced over her shoulder at him, then rose gracefully with a smile. He slid his pack off and stood for a moment, just staring at her. Then he crossed the space and wrapped his arms around her from behind. His hands came to rest on her middle, on the slight bulge that had started to form there.

He asked, "How are you feeling?"

"Better."

He drew a deep breath, taking in the scent of her. "Your hair smells good."

"Yes, well, you stink." He could hear the smirk in her voice. It made him smile. He held her tighter.

"Do I, now?"

"You smell like that hound when it gets wet."

Darien couldn't help but grin. He released her and opened himself to the magic field, filling his mind with its sweet song. A soft blue light sprang into being around him, rippling over his body in azure waves. After a moment, he let it fade. Then he glanced down, verifying that his clothes were now just as clean as they smelled. He slipped his arms back around her.

"Better?"

"Yes." He heard the smile in her voice. "That is better."

Softly, he kissed her hair. As he did, he felt inside her, probing, exploring, until he felt her heartbeat. And beneath that sound there was another—softer and intensely faster. Darien concentrated on that sensation, bent all of his will into exploring it. At last he felt it: the faintest, tentative echo of identity.

"You carry a baby girl," he whispered, his voice full of awe.

"I know."

The smile was gone from his wife's voice. Only sadness remained. Sadness and despair. She twisted away from him. "I am going out."

He let her go, staring after her as she shrugged on a robe and fled through the partition. Darien closed his eyes and drew in a long, shuddering breath. He let it out again slowly. Collecting himself, he moved back out into the empty gathering space. Instead of following his wife, he moved to the table. He gazed down at the maps that were strewn across its surface, shoving his feelings aside. They were an unnecessary distraction.

No harm would ever come to his wife or his daughter, he decided.

He wouldn't let it.

Darien pinned his focus on the maps, studying them with an acute sense of purpose.

Chapter Thirty-Two Servants of Xerys

Bryn Calazar, The Black Lands

Quin emerged from the Catacombs into the death-dim shadows of a temple basement. The space seemed abandoned, the dark stones floured with old dust. The smell of mildew dampened the air, and the constant sound of dribbling water echoed softly through the darkness. Quin started forward, the sound of his footfalls jolting the quiet.

He walked up an aisle lined with thick, dark pillars that supported a vaulted ceiling. Overhead, the roof seemed to sag in exhaustion, burdened by weight and old age. He reached a set of stairs and paused, looking up at walls encased by shadows that convulsed with sporadic torchlight. Quin closed his eyes, taking a moment to ease himself into the old mindset of hyper-vigilance. It took longer than expected. Centuries of indifference had dulled the sharp edges of his mind.

In his former life, Quin had lived every moment in such a state. Because of his temperament, he had been identified young and trained in secret to three different orders at once, in an experiment that went far outside of ethical boundaries. He had become a perfect alloy of magical expertise: Arcanist, Empiricist, and Battlemage—an unexpectedly dark and potent combination. Quin's unique skillset made him the most dangerous kind of assassin: a mage-killer. An ambush predator capable of disappearing into the shadows or striking from a distance. And under the rule of Zavier Renquist, the need for his talents had experienced a renaissance.

No one in Aerysius had ever suspected him. Quin's victims died of natural causes: heart attacks, aneurisms, falls... The tools he'd created left no magical traces, no indications of foul play. And if a particular death seemed too coincidental, Quin had made certain he was the last person in the world anyone would suspect. He'd lived a quiet life: just an introverted, cynical artisan who never left his workshop. A talented Arcanist known throughout the world for his capacity to create. Only three men in all of history had been aware of his capacity to destroy.

One of those men was Zavier Renquist, who had commissioned his training all those years ago. Renquist called what Quin did "shadow diplomacy." Quin had found that ironic at the time, because his brother had always been the diplomat in the family. And yet it was often Quin's negotiations, more than Braden's, that had the most impact.

Beneath Quin's feet, the temple rumbled.

He paused, listening. The noise of dripping water seemed amplified in the stairwell. Above, one of the torches flared, the shadows flinching in response. Cautiously, Quin moved forward, stepping into a broad streak of torchlight.

From the corner of his eye, he caught a faint motion. His gaze ticked toward the young priest of Death who had been unfortunate enough to notice him. Quin willed the man dead then stepped over the corpse. Clutching his shadow staff close against his body, he crossed the shrine toward the door.

He peered outside, shooting a glance up and down the dark street. The ash-paved road was empty, save for one lone man who limped toward him, head wrapped in the gray scarf of Bryn Calazar's underclass. Quin stepped into the street, tipping his hat at the fellow. He caught the glint of suspicion in the man's eyes as he walked away.

Quin turned a corner and stepped into a narrow alley between the crumbling walls of two deteriorated buildings. There, he set his pack down and rifled through it. He withdrew a black vest made of a glimmering fabric that was dizzying to look at. Righting himself, Quin pulled on the vest. Immediately, the clothing he wore shimmered and blurred, distorted by a wave of magic. When he stepped out of the alley, he wore the thread-bare and soot-stained rags of a Calazari coal-digger. A mangled gray scarf hung from his shoulders, and his feet were bare and blackened. Quin wound the scarf around his head as he walked, tucking it into place.

He followed the street to its inevitable end, then turned onto a more populated thoroughfare. Adopting the bow-legged stride of a tunnel-dweller, he walked with his shoulders slumped in the general direction of the harbor. The streets became crowded—too crowded, under the circumstances. Looking around at the intersections teeming with foot traffic, Quin began to wonder if Bryn Calazar had ever been evacuated.

As he walked, he was constantly jostled by citizens in too much of a hurry to dodge him properly. Cadak was the busiest quarter of the city, and the most impoverished. Most people scurried about wrapped in throws and blankets, their skin unwashed, open wounds festering on their legs. Gas lanterns bordered the street, hazy orbs of light that faded in and out, at the mercy of roving clouds of coal-smoke. Quin followed the street as it curved, rising, to the top of a low hill.

At the summit, he paused and caught his breath. Below, at the bottom of the cliff, a broad expanse of ocean unfurled before him. He could hear the crash of the waves as they broke against an offshore reef, could feel the thick humidity in the air. But there was no scent to the ocean. The miasma of coal-smoke overwhelmed even the taste of salt in the air. Quin stood there for a long time, listening to the gentle rhythm of the waves, remembering the myriad gulls and sails that had once bobbed on the surface of the crystalline water.

Gazing out across the harbor, Quin realized how much he missed Bryn Calazar. Not this decapitated and resurrected monster of a city—he missed Bryn Calazar as it had been a thousand years ago, as it would never be again.

Across the harbor, overlooking the ocean, limestone cliffs capped by a modest-sized temple drew his attention. In that spot, the Lyceum had once stood, its arching domes and graceful minarets a wonder of the ancient world. The Lyceum had survived wars, dynasties, millennia…

…until his own choices had destroyed it.

A low rumble overhead echoed Quin's mood. He glanced up at the sky. The black clouds above looked even more volatile than usual, racing toward the horizon. The lights within their murky depths strobed as if incensed. Every once in a while, the lights would flare in unison, sending branches of lightning spiderwebbing across the sky. The sight was chilling. He knew what he was witnessing, for he had seen it before: the first throes of the magic field, as it cringed in anticipation of the Reversal.

Quin thrust his hands deep into his pockets and turned away from his memories. Keeping the harbor on his right, he set his course for the ziggurat.

———

Rothscard, The Rhen

Darien folded his arms, looking around at the tight circle of war chiefs gathered in the command tent. Of them all, the general of Bryn Calazar's army stared back at him the hardest. Masil ul-Calazi resented him and made no effort to hide it. Darien didn't care. The man was capable and efficient. He'd secured the whole of the western plains while Darien's Tanisars had been raiding down the far side of the Craghorns. Ul-Calazi commanded the largest professional fighting force in the world. It would be foolish not to take him seriously.

Speaking with his hands as much as his mouth, the general explained, "When we first arrived, the defenders would ride out from their gates in groups of roughly two hundred and attack our flanks. They would hit us quickly and then flee back behind their walls. Since then, they have engaged in no offensive maneuvers."

Darien nodded, taking in the information and saying nothing. His gaze was focused on the general's eyes, which stared back at him flatly. He was beginning to get the impression that, to ul-Calazi, war was only about numbers, timing, and probability. Darien found himself in agreement.

"Have you met any magical defenses?" he asked.

The general scratched the side of his nose, his mouth pursing. "There has been no magic used against us."

Which was well. Darien had been hoping Kyel wouldn't follow them to Rothscard. Or worse—arrive ahead of them. Resting his hands on his thighs, he nodded thoughtfully. He swept his gaze around the circle of officers, then directed his response to ul-Calazi.

"Prepare your men for an assault. We'll attack the Lion's Gate at dawn. While you've got their attention, I'll create a breach in the eastern wall…here." He planted a finger on one of the maps spread out on the floor between them. "As soon as I do, abandon the gate and make for the breach."

Ul-Calazi glanced down at the map, dropping his hand. "What opposition should we expect within the walls?"

Darien tapped on the map, indicating a dense section of the city snug up against the eastern wall. "This quarter's called the Regret. It's mostly peasant shacks and fishmonger huts. It's also about as far away from the Citadel as you can get. They won't be guarding it. Just get there quickly, before they have time to plug the hole. We'll be fighting in the streets, house-to-house. It's going to get bloody."

The general waved his hand, as though dismissing Darien's concerns as trivial. He inclined his head stiffly. "Is that all, Warden?"

"That's all."

As the men and women rose from the floor, Darien commanded, "Sayeed. Remain."

His First turned back toward him, lingering on his feet as the other war chiefs cleared the tent. When they were alone, Darien gestured for him to sit, then rose and replaced the various maps he'd been using back on the table. He fetched a jug and two tin cups from an assortment of supplies stashed along the wall, then took a seat on the spread of rugs. Guessing his intent, Sayeed's eyebrows rose in question, even as his expression tightened with worry.

Very deliberately, Darien set the cups down between them and unstoppered the jar. He poured enough rika into each cup to fill it halfway. He then lifted his cup and emptied the contents into Sayeed's. As he did, the man's eyes snapped up to lock on him. Keeping to the ritual, Sayeed gave Darien back his share and, watching him drink it down, followed suit.

Darien refilled both cups then sat back, resting his hands on his knees. He said, "I've a favor to ask of you."

Sayeed's gaze never left his own. "You may ask me anything, Brother."

Darien warned him, "It's an awfully big favor."

He drew in a deep, troubled breath, feeling his emotions squirm inside him. He didn't like letting them out; admitting his fears made him feel wretchedly uncomfortable. He knew the rika was meant to help with that but, of course, it didn't. Nothing could.

He poured Sayeed another cup, then filled his own to the brim, knocking the liquor back in one swallow. "The magic field will reverse its polarity in two days. Then I'll be returning to the Netherworld."

Sayeed stared at him in silence a long minute before pouring them both another round. He said softly, "And your wife carries your child in her womb."

Darien froze, pausing in the motion of lifting his drink. For a moment, he sat still and silent, gazing down at the scrollwork pattern of the rug. "How did you know?"

Sayeed's whole body appeared to deflate. "She is sick every morning. Brother…I have no words…"

Darien set his cup down hard. "Forget words. I've a problem to solve. And I need you to help me solve it." He didn't want the man's pity. That was the last thing in the world he needed.

Sayeed nodded, his face hardening. "Of course. Forgive me."

"There's a way to stop this," Darien said. "To stop the Reversal."

"*Ishilzeri!* How? What must we do?"

Darien raised his hand. "Stop. You can do nothing—it's all on me. And I won't survive, so I need you to—"

Sayeed shook his head vehemently. "You have no way of knowing that—"

"I do," Darien insisted. "Remember when you swore to be my brother? You told me that, if I should ever fall, you'd provide for my family. Tell me those weren't just words. Tell me you meant it." He pinned his stare on Sayeed's face as he waited for a response. It took long seconds to come.

"Of course I meant it." Sayeed's voice sounded hoarse. He stared past Darien at the wall of the tent, looking deeply troubled. Darien hoped it wasn't because the man had changed his mind.

"Then would you do that for me, Brother? Will you care for my wife and daughter after I'm gone?"

Sayeed placed his cup upside down on the rug, then firmly clasped Darien's arm with both hands. He said gravely, "I swear I will guard your family with my life and provide for their needs. And I will make certain your daughter grows to womanhood knowing of the man her father was. It is far more than my obligation. It is my honor."

Darien nodded, feeling suddenly incapable of trusting his voice. To cover, he lifted the jug and poured each of them a fresh cup. He drank his down, listening to the great, brooding silence that had settled between them. He felt comforted by Sayeed's pledge. But at the same time, he felt disturbed by his own reaction to it. He had expected to feel the sadness, the frustration, the grief.

He just hadn't expected to feel the envy.

Naia stared out through the curtained window of the carriage that carried her, rattling along, toward Emmery Palace. The city teemed with panicked residents who filled the streets, shouting and shoving their way through the bedlam.

By the time her carriage drew up in the manicured courtyard of the palace, Naia was already on edge. Athera's Crescent had shown her visions of Rothscard under siege, and those visions had always led to dark and uncertain futures.

A group of blue-cloaked guardsmen rushed forward to attend her. One man with captain's bars peered in through the carriage window. His face had been scarred by the pox, his hair white and peppered with gray.

"Come on out," he ordered. "What business have you?"

Naia threw open the carriage door and hopped to the ground without waiting for a footman. She informed the captain, "I am Master Naia Seleni of the Order of Harbingers. I am here to request an audience with the Queen."

"You claim to be a mage?" The captain sounded skeptical, looking her up and down intently. "Let's see the chains on your wrists."

Naia froze. She hadn't anticipated such a question. She had lost the markings of her Oath before her journey to Titherry. Her mind searched frantically for excuses—anything to distract from the glaring absence of the chains.

The captain's eyes narrowed. In a rigid voice tempered by ice, he said, "Bare your arms. If you like, you can do it away from my men. But unless you've got the marks of the Oath on your wrists, you won't be going anywhere near the Queen."

Naia stared at the captain in dismay, having no idea how to react. If Romana found out she'd given up her Oath, the Queen might go so far as to order her execution. Staring at the captain fixedly, she said, "You wish me to prove that I'm a mage? There are other ways."

A blue mist of magelight appeared at her feet. Startled, the captain stepped back with a look of alarm.

"I am a Master of Aerysius," Naia proclaimed. "Do you still doubt?"

The captain stared at her hard, unblinking. A small drop of sweat dribbled down his brow. His hand tensed and then untensed on the hilt of his sword. His lips compressed to a fine line, his jaw tightening. He took another step back.

"Run, Jeffers!" he growled.

The captain drew his sword, his men fanning out behind him. One of the guards turned and lit out across the courtyard.

Something struck Naia from behind.

Her knees buckled, her vision erupting in a shower of sparks.

Chapter Thirty-Three
The Pain of Truth

Rothscard, The Rhen

Kyel Archer stood on a turret overlooking the Lion's Gate, the banners of Emmery Palace fluttering behind him. A breeze stirred the air, moving in from the river delta. Kyel stared off in that direction, hoping for a glimpse of the ocean. But Rothscard was still a good distance from the shore, and the tower wasn't tall enough to offer a view of it.

A different kind of ocean spread out from the base of Rothscard's walls. The Enemy encampment extended to the horizon, arranged in perfect geometric patterns. There were so many more tents than he had expected. Kyel tried not to let the numbers intimidate him, but it was hard not to. His hand tightened around Thar'gon's haft, seeking and finding comfort in the weapon's extraordinary might.

He turned away from the parapets. As he did, a jolting shock seared down his nerves, making him reel. He shot his hand out and caught himself on the coarse stone of a merlon. All around him, the lines of the magic field stretched and then recoiled as if bludgeoned. The aftershocks continued for a while, the field lines convulsing spastically before evening out again.

Kyel stood panting, taking a moment to collect himself. He knew exactly what had happened, and it scared the hell out of him. The Reversal was imminent, and the magic field was already cringing in anticipation.

Filled with dread, he fled the ramparts and turned his attention to navigating the escalating confusion of Rothscard's streets. Even the black cloak on his back didn't spare him from being pushed and jostled, shoved and elbowed. A climate of panic had infested the city, which was getting worse as the siege dragged on. By the time he gained the palace grounds, Kyel felt as though he'd been on the receiving side of a tavern brawl. The streets were becoming dangerous, nearly impossible to negotiate.

As he crossed the Inner Ward, a commotion across the courtyard caught his attention. Near the Citadel, a group of guards had a woman on the ground. Two men had thrown their weight on top of her, pinning her down, while another man struggled to lock a set of manacles around her wrists. To Kyel, the entire scene looked brutal and irregular. There were far more guards than it should take to arrest one woman who wasn't resisting. Concerned, he hastened toward her, wondering what she had done to deserve such treatment.

They rolled the woman over, and Kyel got a glimpse of her face.

Recognition slapped him in the stomach, tearing a gasp from his lips. He lurched forward, shoving his way through the cluster of shocked guards.

The woman on the ground peered up at him, squinting, as though staring into the sun. Her face was streaked with bloody grime, her dress torn and filthy.

"Kyel?" she muttered.

A grizzled captain with a pox-scarred face shot between them, waving him away. Seeing the color of Kyel's cloak, the guardsman's face twisted into a grimace.

"Do you know this woman?"

"I know her," Kyel growled, dodging past him. He dropped down to Naia's side and, setting a hand on her back, healed the cut on her scalp before the man could protest.

The captain caught his arm, trying to pull him away. "This woman's a darkmage! She admitted it freely!"

Kyel jerked his arm out of the man's grip. He looked down at Naia, suddenly troubled. Her wrists were bound by wide iron bands that hid the presence of any markings that might be there. Or any scars. Remembering the body of Sareen Qadir lying dead on the floor of the shrine, Kyel had to admit that the guards might be right.

His eyes went back to Naia's face, searching there for answers. But her eyes were closed; she'd fallen into the healing sleep. He wasn't going to get any information from her. So he went with his gut.

Kyel stared flatly at the officer. "I'm not asking. I'm telling. Get the damn restraints off her."

The guard captain didn't move. The man stood frozen as his men looked nervously on. Frustrated, Kyel reached out from within and tore Naia's shackles off himself. They opened of their own accord, slipping to the ground with a metallic clink. The guards surged back, hands darting for their weapons.

Kyel's stare remained fixed on Naia, at the set of awful scars that encircled both her wrists. A feeling of profound sadness crept over him. Anger followed quickly. With a disgusted growl, he heaved Naia into his arms and lifted her from the ground.

The captain bellowed after him, "She's a gods-damned darkmage! And you're one, too, for helping her!"

Ignoring him, Kyel carried Naia toward the palace, mired in his own turbulent outrage.

Bryn Calazar, The Black Lands

The dark avenue Quin followed split into two smaller avenues, forking around a short temple that squatted like an abandoned god in the midst of the intersection. The temple's walls leaned drunkenly to one side, its parallel columns bent at a painful angle. The entire structure looked ready to fall over. It was a miracle it already hadn't.

The city streets still buzzed with people who, for whatever reason, had chosen to ignore the order to evacuate. Tall-wheeled rickshaws sped by, pulled by bone-thin youths, while merchants dragged carts behind them laden with trade goods. Quin walked down the center of the street, careful to maintain the shambling stride of the city's malnourished underclass. A peddler, mummified in cloth, noticed him and sprang forward, thrusting a skewer of roasted vegetables under his nose.

"Five darham!" the peddler shouted in the Calazi dialect, waving the skewer. "Five darham! Delicious!"

"No thank you," Quin said, pushing the skewer out of his way.

The man was undeterred. He jogged after Quin, waving his skewer. "Four darham! Very fresh! You should taste!"

Quin waved him away, quickening his pace. A woman ahead of him carried a howling baby strapped to her back, its thin legs kicking in exclamation. Quin veered around her, almost tripping over a broken cobble in the street. Up ahead, he could see the tall, step-sided ziggurat thrusting its weight above the skyline. He set his course toward it, boring his way against the flow of foot traffic. Vexed pedestrians dodged and jostled him, raining him with curses and threats. Quin ignored them all and shambled onward.

The avenue narrowed abruptly, tall walls erupting on both sides of the street. Quin turned onto a winding alley lined with merchant stalls, each stuffed with odd assortments of pottery, textiles, and iron-forged wares. Eventually, the cobbles ran out. The street continued on, paved with tarry mud that reeked of stale urine.

Quin halted at the base of the ziggurat. His eyes traced the long, ramp-like steps that slanted upward at an intimidating angle. There were no guards stationed around the temple's base, at least none visible. He paused long enough to make certain the fabric of his head scarf was tucked in tight, then started up the stairs.

The steps were grueling and precarious, much taller than they were narrow. His legs burned by the time he reached the temple entrance only midway up. There, recessed in a split in the rise of steps, two black-mailed sentries warded the entrance to the Grand Temple of Xerys. Though they remained thoroughly motionless, Quin knew the sentries had marked his approach.

Which was why they slumped dead, like toppled suits of armor.

Unwinding the scarf, Quin stepped around the bodies and slipped into the dim corridor beyond. A narrow passage led straight back into the temple's dark interior, lit at long intervals by lanterns ensconced along the walls. Quin moved forward cautiously, using just a dribble of magic to soften the sounds of his footfalls. A little ways in, he found an opening in the wall that led to a side passage. He turned onto it, finding himself in a short corridor that led to a series of rooms partitioned by brightly colored fabric. Quin stopped at the first drape of gauzy cloth and, pulling the fabric aside, slipped through the doorway.

Warm light greeted him within, along with the heady odor of perfume. Sounds of conversation and laughter drifted from an adjoining chamber. Backing against a wall, Quin wove a web of shadow and tightened it around his body. Within the shadow-web, he could go unremarked by the casual observer, nothing more than a fuzzy distortion in the air. He moved toward the light and the laughter, stopping before a thin drape of turquoise gauze.

He pushed the curtain aside just a fraction and peered within. The chamber on the other side was ornately tiled and contained a luxurious octagonal bath ringed by pillowed sofas. Men and women lounged in and around the water, in various stages of undress. Judging by their well-nourished bodies, the men were most likely priests of Xerys. Which would make the women attending them either acolytes or slaves, if there truly was a distinction.

He let the fabric sway closed then retraced his steps, taking a moment to tighten his shadow-web.

Back out in the hallway, Quin moved to the next fabric-draped doorway. He parted the curtain and slipped into a long, dim chamber lit only by the glow of a single lantern. He stood quietly for a moment, just listening to the sound of the room's emptiness, assessing his surroundings. Dark silhouettes of furniture lined the walls. The oil lantern sat on the floor in the corner behind him, casting a timid glow. He crept further in, drawn toward an unlit doorway at the far end of the room.

"Your hatred is so loud, I could hear it echoing from Titherry."

Quin squeezed his eyes shut as a feeling of defeat seeped through the pores in his skin. He released the shadow-web, since it no longer served a purpose.

If it ever had.

He turned slowly around to confront the dark figure that moved forward to eclipse the lantern light.

"You knew I'd come," Quin surmised.

The shadow nodded. "Of course I did. In truth, I was counting on it."

Quin groaned. Renquist must be a sensitive—and a damn powerful one, to feel his emotions across such a broad expanse of ocean. He hadn't suspected that. But there was so much that revelation explained. Suddenly, a thousand different things made a thousand different kinds of sense.

Quin asked, "What do you want from me?"

He leaned his staff against the wall and curled his fingers around the hilt of his sword, the one artifact in the world capable of dampening a mage's gift. He could feel Renquist's strength from across the room, a dark and potent energy that exuded from his presence to oppress the air. Renquist's power had grown tremendously since the last time Quin had seen him, making him wonder if the Prime Warden had been sitting in Bryn Calazar drinking in mage power. And mage lives.

Renquist took a step deeper into the pool of light. The wavering glow of the lantern defined his face in jagged angles and sharp planes. His eyes burned through the shadows like glowing embers.

He said, "You have something I deeply desire."

Quin drew his sword with a metallic hiss, holding the tip leveled at the demon's heart. Or where his heart should have been. Quin doubted Renquist had ever had one.

"I didn't think you had such confidence in my abilities."

He was awarded with a condescending smile. "It's not your abilities I have confidence in, Quinlan. It's your stupidity. You have defied me twice. Once with Braden. And now with Darien. You have a knack for leading my most talented pupils astray."

Quin scoffed. "Darien isn't like Braden."

"No," Renquist agreed. "He's not. Darien is much more competent and powerful than your brother ever was. Which is why I need your assistance."

Quin felt his heart pounding against his ribs. With every word, Renquist's voice clawed deeper into his chest. "What makes you think I'll help you?"

The demon smiled. "You'll help me because Darien is determined to do exactly what you and your brother gave your lives to prevent all those years ago. You see, Darien knows a way to halt the Reversal. And he is willing to open the floodgates of hell to accomplish it."

"No." Quin shook his head. "Darien wouldn't do that."

Renquist took a step toward him, smiling kindly. "Wouldn't he? Perhaps you don't know him as well as you think."

"I know him well enough." Quin drew the sword back over his shoulder, winding his arms as he backed away. He didn't get far.

A noise behind him made him turn. Cyrus Krane stood in the doorway, flanked by three of his sinister pets. The necrators glided silently forward like obsidian death. Quin backed away until he found himself pinned against the wall. He didn't know if Krane's necrators could harm him, but he didn't want to find out.

Renquist continued, "If you know Darien, then you know he already lost one child. How must he feel, knowing he is about to lose another?"

Quin lowered his sword, his arms sagging to his sides. He opened his mouth to deny the man's words but then stopped himself. Zavier Renquist never lied. He never had to. The truth was always much more painful.

Quin swallowed heavily. "Who's the mother?"

"Darien's wife. The Lightweaver, Azár."

Quin glared his hatred at Renquist, shaking his head in disgust. "You really are a demon, aren't you? It's not good enough for you to destroy a man. You have to destroy all that he is and all that he loves. And even then, you're still not satisfied." He regarded Renquist a long, searching moment. "You still haven't explained why you need me."

"I don't need you at all," the Prime Warden responded in an ice-calm voice. "The strength of the gift inside you will be enough to suffice."

Quin's stomach froze like a block of ice. He pressed himself against the wall as close as he could.

The light of the lantern winked out. An encompassing blackness settled thickly around him, cold and terrifying. Quin couldn't see the necrators, but he could feel them there, just on the edge of his senses. Gliding toward him through the darkness.

Rothscard, The Rhen

Kyel's hand trembled as he offered Naia a glass of water. She sat on a sofa, rubbing her temples, looking up at him with dark eyes that bore no degree of malice. Still, Kyel couldn't drag his gaze away from the scars on her wrists, repulsed by the sight of them.

"Explain yourself," he said, crossing his arms.

Naia took a sip of water then smiled patiently. "I'm not a darkmage, Kyel. I'm just a mage." Her eyes were kind, compassionate. Just the way he remembered. "Bound or Unbound, it makes no difference. I'm still the same person you've always known. I haven't changed."

"You broke Oath!" he growled, filled with both anger and fear. When—not if—Romana found out about her, the Queen would order Naia put to death. Kyel knew he couldn't argue with that decision. The thought made him want to retch.

Naia raised her eyebrows, fixing him with a disappointed look. "I did it to save you. Sareen was killing you—"

Kyel raised his hand, cutting her off. She had condemned herself by her own words. The realization made him feel intensely sad. He blew out a protracted sigh, resenting the hell out of her. He would have to tell Swain. Sooner, rather than later.

Naia was a mage, so the Citadel couldn't contain her if she decided to walk out.

Swain and Romana wouldn't want to take that risk.

Chapter Thirty-Four
The Regret

Rothscard, The Rhen

Darien sat his horse, Sayeed and his Zakai at his side, watching the gray light of dawn bleed slowly across the horizon.

The morning was cold; he could feel the chill of his armor even through his padded gambeson. Dark clouds had moved in sometime during the night. Deep within their depths, Darien could see swarms of flickering lights. The lights seemed to wince in time to the pulsations of the magic field. The disturbances were entirely unnatural. The feel of them grated like sandpaper down his nerves.

He stared out across the wide swath of denuded ground that stood between their ranks and Rothscard's high walls. To the left of his Tanisars, the army of Bryn Calazar was amassed before Rothscard's north gate, spread out across the grassland like a tumultuous black sea. At their rear, the horse warriors of the Jenn had collected in a vast, milling horde.

Thin columns of smoke rose at intervals from Rothscard's crenelated ramparts, from fires lit to heat oil and pitch and add an element of horror to the missiles of the trebuchets. Rothscard's commanders had positioned the bulk of their defenses along the north wall in anticipation of an attack on the Lion's Gate. The rest of the city's battlements remained relatively undermanned. So far, his feint was working.

A sonorous horn cry rose over the plain, followed by a disciplined stillness no army of the Rhen could ever rival. Amongst the Malikari legions, not a soul moved. There was no clatter of weapons, no rustle of armor.

Just an unnerving silence that clung like a pall over an army of one hundred thousand men, a silence that thundered louder than any war drum ever could.

The general of Bryn Calazar's legions raised his sword. Upon his signal, every throat in the ranks behind him bellowed a whip-crack war cry.

There was a pause.

Then, faintly at first, deep-throated drums began tapping out a measured cadence. The drums gradually increased in tempo and intensity, the resonant booms rising in crescendo over the plain. The pulse of the drums continued, relentless and precise, rattling the air until Darien could feel their rumble in his chest. Another staccato shout bellowed from thousands of throats, then another, just off-beat. The resounding noise swelled to a climax, sustained there for minutes, then ceased with a final, thundering *BOOM*.

Stillness followed.

A lone war horn brayed languorously.

Then, with a tremendous cry, the whole of the Malikari army broke forward at a run.

The thunder of their charge was deafening. As the front ranks came within bowshot of the walls, dark arrow clouds began arcing downward, dropping soldiers at random. Trebuchets mounted to the ramparts joined in, hurling projectiles coated with Hell's Fire that blazed like long-tailed comets across the sky, tearing great swaths through the advancing army. Men and women were set ablaze with sticky flames that spread quickly to devour anyone nearby.

Ul-Calazi's men raised ladders against the walls that were immediately flung back, only to be raised again. All the while the trebuchets worked tirelessly, hurling their blazing payloads at the attacking army. One of the siege engines erupted in flames, the men tending it hurled from the battlements. Another trebuchet exploded seconds later, taking its attending crew with it.

A great cry rose from the battlefield, and then the dark host parted to admit an armored battering ram, covered and shielded. It was drawn by many teams of horses that were then unhitched before they were brought within bowshot. From there, men ran forward to push the ram up against the gate. Hot oil and flaming arrows flooded down from above like scalding rain. For every man that dropped, another took his place, the ram moving inexorably forward.

Darien swept his gaze over the fortifications, noting the lack of soldiers on the eastern side of the city. As predicted, Swain had pulled the bulk of his forces from that section of wall, leaving its defenders spread few and thin.

A resounding shout brought his attention back to the Lion's Gate. A brilliant gold shield had insinuated itself between the ram and the gate, repulsing their efforts. The ram battered futilely against the shield, while Malikari infantry screamed their frustration at the unyielding walls. Flights of arrows splattered the ground, felling men like trees.

Seeing that golden shield, Darien swore a curse. He'd hoped they'd left Kyel behind in Glen Farquist.

His eyes scoured the battlements, searching. But the city was too far away to make out the faces of the men defending it. His frustration mounded by the second. It felt like the battle had reached a critical climax and was ready to implode. He looked at Sayeed.

"Are you ready, Brother?" he asked.

His First nodded. "We are ready."

"Then let's have at it."

He kicked his boots into his horse's sides, clutching the stallion's mane in his fist. The animal surged forward, moving quickly up to speed, its hooves tearing up the grassland as it raced toward the city's eastern wall. Sayeed's horse labored alongside his own, his men fanned out behind them.

Ahead, the few soldiers guarding the east gate noticed their approach and started scrambling. A few panicked and loosed their shafts early, which fell well short of hitting their marks. Darien drew his mount up and motioned his men to move into position at his sides. He glanced up and down the face of the wall, getting a better idea of the defenses. Urging his stallion into motion, he veered the horse toward the gate.

As they came within range, groupings of arrows began arcing down from the walls. Darien deflected the shafts before they could find purchase. When they neared the gate, he slid off his horse, then sent the beast on its way with a slap on the hindquarters.

He opened his mind to the magic field, gathering it in and holding it at ready. The field thrashed wildly, already tormented by the coming Reversal. He tightened his grip on it, despite its protest. The feel of it rubbed his nerves wrong, made his skin crawl.

Darien concentrated on the masonry that lined the gate, feeling inside the stones and applying pressure to the weakest joints. Fine cracks erupted all along the wall, racing outward like spiders' veins. Flakes of granite showered down. Above on the battlements, the soldiers realized their danger and retreated to the towers. Darien concentrated harder, bending all the brute force of his will into the effort. Chunks of stone sprayed from deep fissures, and a terrible groaning noise rumbled from deep within.

Still, the wall stood.

Darien reached for the Onslaught and used the Hellpower to augment his strength. Within seconds, he felt the blocks surrounding the gate start to *shift*. Huge chunks shivered and disappeared, leaving gaps in the stone arch. More stones shivered and then gave way, raining shards of crumbled rock onto the ground. Then, with a deafening roar, the entirety of the wall collapsed into a mounded berm of jagged stone.

Darien's men scrambled forward, leaping onto the rubble as arrows pelted down from the towers still standing. Darien deflected the arrows and scrambled after Sayeed into the breach. The debris shifted beneath him, the stones turning underfoot. It was harrowing minutes before he followed the Zakai off the scree. Skidding down the last few crumbling steps, Darien stumbled to a stop, then glanced around to get his bearings.

They had breached the wall in a remote section of the city called the Regret. The quarter was populated mostly by criminals and unfortunates, its slums and back-waters burgeoning with black-market trade. Ahead, his Zakai patrolled the street, moving in zig-zag patterns from one side to the other, crossbows cocked, swords held ready. Darien walked behind them, his eyes scanning the long, dilapidated layers of shanties stacked one atop the other. Drying laundry flapped like colorful banners above the street, hanging from clothes lines that crisscrossed above. The smell of the place was a cloying combination of mold, wood smoke, and rot.

Ahead, a disjointed collection of slum dwellers had amassed at the end of the street, armed with a variety of impromptu weapons. Seeing the advancing Zakai, the mob broke toward them.

"No mercy," Darien ordered. The Zakai sprinted forward. He ran after them, sword in hand, bringing the Onslaught to bear against Rothscard's luckless defenders.

Kyel tightened his grip on Thar'gon, nervous sweat trickling from his brow. Alexa stood at his side, clinging to his arm. He wasn't sure whether she sought to steady him or steady herself. He was starting to have a hard time keeping focus. The power Thar'gon channeled was wild and difficult to control in the amounts Kyel found himself wielding. With the talisman's aide, he'd been able to force the massive battering ram back from the gate, but only at great risk to his Oath. He hadn't killed any of the attackers directly, but it had been too close for Kyel's liking. He'd narrowly avoided immolating a siege engine, along with all of the men tending it.

At his side, Nigel Swain stood shouting orders at the top of his lungs. There was frenzied fighting all along the battlements. Ladders were being raised from below, more and more each minute—too many to deal with all at once. Little by little, the Enemy was making their way onto the walls and expanding the footholds they gained. Up and down the ramparts, Enemy warriors were capturing the wall-mounted trebuchets and turning them against the city's own defenses. Soon, Kyel found his attention pulled away from the gate, forced to defend Rothscard against flaming projectiles hurled from its own walls.

A concussive blast exploded against the tower behind him.

Kyel threw a ward up—probably the only thing that saved his life—but couldn't expand it in time to save the soldiers on the tower who fell, engulfed in roiling flames. Kyel extinguished the flames but not the pain. The men continued to writhe and scream, while Kyel looked helplessly on. He couldn't heal them without physical contact, and he was too occupied trying to prevent another such catastrophe.

Alexa tugged harder on his arm. "It's not enough!" she cried. "We are losing this battle! You must make a choice—between preserving your Oath or preserving the Rhen!"

Angered, Kyel waved her off. She could be doing a lot more than she was, he thought, watching another tower erupt in flames, men thrown from its walls. Kyel cursed in frustration. He'd let that one get by him.

At his side, Swain stiffened. "Something's wrong," he said, his voice barely audible over the rage of the battle

Kyel shouted, "What?"

Reaching up, the Prince ripped his helm off and moved to a crenel overlooking the plain. His face was covered in soot, except for branching streaks where sweat had eroded the grime. He finished his study of the battlefield, then turned back to Kyel with a look of alarm. "They're not using Darien."

Kyel froze. He hadn't noticed Darien's glaring absence from the battle. The thought made his stomach wrench. "Then where is he?"

"Gods be damned!"

A merlon exploded beside him, flinging them backward. Swain recovered quickly, blood leaking from a gash over his eye.

Another, larger, explosion rocked the city.

Kyel stared out across the skyline, to where a wide plume of smoke rose and was spreading swiftly.

Swain started swearing fluently. He shouted at his officers, "Pull everyone you can off the gate and get them down to the Regret! Gods' whoring mother, they've already breached the fucking wall!"

Darien backed away from the fires consuming the Regret's layered shanties and turned to follow Sayeed into a narrow alley. The fires were spreading hungrily, leaping from rooftop to rooftop, much faster than he'd expected. Panicked residents fled before the roiling heat of the flames, taking to the streets—sometimes through doors, more often through windows. The morning had gone dark, the sky blackened by billowing smoke swarming with embers. The air was filled with horrendous shrieks, the kind that only came from the throats of the dying.

A window broke overhead, raining shards of glass down right in front of him. A woman followed, streaming fire behind her and screaming all the way to the ground. Darien lurched backward, filled with revulsion, then turned to jog after Sayeed toward the street.

At the intersection, Sayeed caught him by the arm and nodded toward another group of men collecting a ways up the street, a combination of city regulars and armed citizens. Darien wrapped a glowing shield around himself and motioned for Sayeed and his men to remain behind. Drinking in the Onslaught, he strode alone up the center of the street toward the gathered resistance. Seeing him haloed by an aura of green energy, the mob became chaotic. Most of the men started backing away. Others turned and bolted. Darien summoned a mist of magelight and sent it slithering ahead of him. More men fled. The rest broke toward him.

Something *cracked* against his shield. Darien whirled to see a soldier reloading an arbalest, in the process of fighting with the crank. He threw the Hellpower mindlessly at the man. The soldier melted, dissolving with a sizzling hiss.

Darien turned back to face the charging militia.

Sayeed sprang in front of him and struck out at the first man, slicing his head off, then kicked another man back against the side of a building. He ducked an oncoming strike, then whirled to thrust his sword into his opponent's chest.

The rest of the attackers exploded in a rain of gore.

Sayeed whirled to look at Darien with startled eyes.

"Where is ul-Calazi?" Darien growled.

He kicked the severed head out of his path, then glanced back in the direction of the breach. The Calazari reinforcements should have arrived minutes ago. Ahead, more blue-cloaked soldiers poured into the end of the street. Defenders worked feverishly to seal them off, erecting a barricade that consisted of any lose items they could scavenge from the surrounding buildings. Already, in the span of minutes, hundreds of soldiers had collected behind that barricade. Very soon, there would be thousands. For the first time, Darien started to doubt. He had brought only his warband to capture the Regret, but it would take more than that to keep control of it.

He wondered if Ul-Calazi had abandoned him intentionally.

Growing nervous, Darien scanned his surroundings, searching for a good defensive position they could retreat to. As an extra precaution, he summoned his array of necrators and sent them ranging ahead. He wasn't sure they would be enough. But they were all he had.

Kyel pulled his horse to a halt and swung down from its back, striding across the street toward the lowered portcullis that sealed off the Regret Quarter. Swain tossed his horse's reins to a soldier and then ran over to take reports from a cluster of officers. Kyel slowed to a stop, daunted by the mayhem that reigned on the other side of the gate.

Through the portcullis' rusted bars, he could see that a large section of the Regret was already enveloped in flames, the smoke so thick it was impossible to estimate the extent of the destruction. A terrified mob had gathered on the other side of the portcullis. People were struggling to reach a small sally port beside the gate. The crowd surged violently. Panicked residents shoved and fought their way forward. People were starting to get trampled, while others were desperate enough to try climbing the portcullis despite iron spikes meant to discourage such activity.

Outraged, Kyel crossed back toward Alexa and said to her, "We have to stop this here. Can you banish his necrators?"

Alexa nodded. "If I get close enough."

Kyel bit his lip, trying to think of the best way to proceed. "Stay by me," he ordered. He crossed the street toward Swain.

"This is a godsdamn disaster," the Prince growled.

Glaring in rage at the gate, Kyel said, "I'll control him. Have your men finish him off."

Swain flashed him a devil grin and freed his longsword from its wooden sheath. He waved Kyel and Alexa back against the wall, then shouted the order to raise the portcullis. There was a groaning shriek of fatigued gears and clattering chain. The portcullis shuddered upward to admit a frantic hoard of rampaging people who streamed past them out of the Regret. It was minutes before the flood drained to a trickle. When it did, Swain ordered his men forward. They moved through the gate at a dogtrot, faces pale and rigid. Kyel couldn't blame them. They knew exactly what they advanced toward.

Side-by-side with Alexa and Swain, Kyel followed the soldiers into the Regret.

Chapter Thirty-Five
Duel with a Devil

Rothscard, The Rhen

Darien led his men across a war-torn square that had, only minutes before, been part of the Rhen's largest covered market. The slatted roof had burned away, leaving only the scorched bricks of merchant stalls intact. Darien swiped his hand out, throwing a concussive blast that sent a group of city regulars hurling to the ground. Only a few managed to get back up again. By the time the Zakai arrived, most of the survivors had fled. His warriors dispatched the rest

Looking back, Darien saw that an entire company of Bluecloaks had flanked them and were closing on their rear. He recalled his necrators to his aid. They rose around him, shadowed wraiths that served with mindless hunger. With a whispered word, he sent them gliding toward the encroaching soldiers.

A shout from Sayeed made him whirl back around. Dozens more guardsmen were pouring into the other side of the market. His necrators weren't done eliminating the threat behind. Darien drew in the exhilarating taint of the Onslaught, wielding it against the men-at-arms ahead.

Immediately as he struck, a group of his own warriors were lifted off their feet and thrown brutally backward. They collided with the sides of the tall brick buildings, their skulls and spines shattering on impact. Darien froze in place, numbed by shock. Sayeed started forward, but Darien threw a hand up, stopping him.

"It's Kyel." He swore a curse.

Sayeed hissed in frustration, raising his sword. "Can you counter him?"

"We're about to find out."

Darien intensified the glowing shield that warded them, reinforcing it with the Onslaught. He scanned the way ahead, searching rooftop to rooftop, window by window. Confounded, he moved warily forward, Sayeed at his side, a half-dozen injured Zakai behind them. They were all that was left of his warband. The remainder of his men lay dead and broken in the street behind them.

The market square was eerily quiet, save for the crackle of flames still gnawing at the bones of the surrounding district. Ash drifted through the air like snowflakes, borne on a wicked-hot breeze.

Darien tried to swallow, but his throat was too dry to perform the action. He turned slowly around, scanning the alleys, seeing nothing. The day had become eclipsed, a totality of smoke that darkened the sun.

A distant clattering echoed toward them, sharp noises ringing off the surrounding walls: the sound of hoofbeats. Darien whirled toward the end of the street, bringing his sword back. Sayeed moved into position at his side, his blade held ready, glancing up and down the street.

All at once, a lone horse erupted from a side street, careening toward them at full gallop, empty stirrups bouncing at its sides. Startled, Darien lowered his sword and backed away. The horse didn't slow its charge, but angled toward them as if aiming to run them down. Darien leaped out of the way, Sayeed throwing himself in the other direction. Before Darien could recover, scores of soldiers spilled into the market, converging on them from all sides.

The Zakai leaped forward to ring them defensively. Sayeed raised his sword, his fingers flexing and unflexing their grip on the hilt. Blood and grimy sweat ran down his cheeks, dripped from his chin. His lips drew back in the rictus of a snarl. He stepped behind Darien, turning to ward his back.

The Bluecloaks closed the distance and engaged with fury. Darien seized the magic field, lashing out with it violently. A roiling conflagration of flames consumed the center of the square, devouring everything in its path. Soldiers screamed and fell, thrashing on the ground before quickly succumbing. Those who tried to outrun the flames didn't get far. The entire market was ablaze with whipping whirlwinds of fire that twisted high in the air.

When there was nothing left to consume, the flames died down. It took Darien a moment to realize that only Sayeed and himself remained alive in the square, crouching in a perfect ring of uncharred cobbles.

Trembling, Darien pushed himself to his feet. His anger burned raw, hotter than the flames.

"Visea," he whispered, recalling his necrators.

———

Swain cursed and ordered his reinforcements into the market. Kyel stood glaring at the black smoke that rolled from the center of the square ahead, wondering how many soldiers had been devoured by Darien's assault.

Suddenly, a terrible feeling overcame him, making the hairs on the back of his neck stand on end. A ghastly chill seeped through his skin, freezing his heart in a thick layer of ice. The cold was insidious and complete, terrifying. He'd felt that feeling before and knew exactly what it meant.

He wasn't surprised when the song of the magic field died inside him.

From out of the ground, shadowy forms rose to encircle them. The necrators made no move to advance, but lingered, wavering, as if uncertain of their purpose. Kyel turned slowly, raising the talisman. He was cut off from the field, but he could still feel magic in the weapon. Considering the number of shades surrounding him, Kyel figured it wouldn't be enough. But perhaps he could take a few of the demons out with him.

"You can't fight them, Kyel," Alexa said with calm resolve. "But I can."

Walking forward, she moved toward the nearest living shadow. The necrator's ebony form rotated slowly, centering on her. Alexa muttered a phrase in a language Kyel didn't recognize. The necrator immediately vanished.

As Kyel looked on, Alexa moved toward the next demonic shadow, dismissing it casually. Then she went on to the next, making a slow circuit of their position. One by one, Darien's necrators popped out of existence, until only one remained. Alexa halted in front of it. With a smile, she waved her hand.

The necrator steamed and hissed as it dissolved.

———

Darien staggered, the pain of loss slamming into him like a sword thrust, tearing the breath out of him.

"Brother!" Sayeed cried. "Are you wounded?"

It was all Darien could do to shake his head. His screaming nerves were like phantom pains from a lost limb. His minions were gone. All of them. Unmade.

He wavered, feeling unstable, then took a step forward.

An invisible wall of air slammed over him, imprisoning him. He brought his hands up, testing the limits of a cage he couldn't see. He couldn't penetrate it, not with his hands, not with magic. He groped at it frantically, nervous sweat streaming down his face.

The square around them erupted in fire. Shattered cobblestones rained down on their heads like falling hail. Darien dropped to the ground beside Sayeed as another fiery explosion scorched the air around them. The intensity of the heat nearly overwhelmed his shield. At first, Darien thought it was Kyel attacking them. Then he realized it wasn't.

"They've turned the trebuchets on us," he rasped. The first two projectiles coated with Hell's Fire had missed them, but the soldiers tending the siege weapons would be recalculating their aim.

Another flaming missile arced toward them from the ramparts, trailing a tail of smoke behind it. Darien closed his eyes and put everything he had into an absorption shield strong enough to cover both himself and Sayeed. The missile hit, its flames gushing in a whooshing fireball that overwhelmed his shield. The searing heat scorched Darien's skin even as he fought to heal himself. At his side, Sayeed screamed in agony. Darien dropped to the ground, holding the man who called him brother, healing Sayeed as he burned.

Another flaring missile hit, disgorging its payload of flames. This time, Darien diverted the heat from the air and channeled it into the ground, a reservoir big enough to absorb the energy. Another projectile exploded around them, followed by another. Each time, he diverted the heat of the flames into the ground.

But the street was starting to heat up. His tactic wouldn't save them much longer. Trembling, he held Sayeed clutched against him and fought with all his might to keep ahead of the flames.

He was starting to panic. The nightmares that plagued him endlessly, of being roasted alive, were no longer just torturous memories—they were quickly becoming reality. With every shuddering attack, his defenses slipped another crack. He could no longer keep the agony of the flames at bay. Waves of heat roiling off the ground distorted his vision. And still the trebuchets thundered, wearing him down a little more with each strike.

He knew he was at his end when he could no longer feel the pain. He clenched his teeth and held Sayeed tighter.

All at once, the bombardment stopped.

Darien remained hunkered down, waiting for the barrage of flames to resume. When they didn't, he chanced a glance up at the battlements and saw that every last trebuchet was on fire. Ul-Calazi's men had finally overrun the walls.

In his arms, Sayeed lay limp, but alive.

The world reeled around Kyel. He gasped, filled with a euphoric excitement he couldn't explain. Before him, crouched on the ground, Darien knelt in a blackened ring of smoldering bricks that glowed red at the edges. Even though the city was falling around him, Kyel felt triumphant.

He felt a tug on his sleeve. Alexa stared up at him, her eyes wide and feverish. "You have him down!" she exclaimed. "Now end this!"

Kyel shook his head, wishing he could.

Her face flushed brightly. "You are dead in two days! What does your Oath matter?"

"It matters!" Kyel jerked his arm out of her grasp. He didn't have the energy or the desire to argue with her. He was still maintaining the cage of air around Darien, and the effort was taxing.

At his side, Swain growled. "I've had enough of this."

He reached behind his back and tugged at the cinch straps of the harness that anchored his armor. His breastplate slid off, falling to the ground. Swain trudged forward, armored only by his chain hauberk and gambeson.

"Release him," he shouted over his shoulder.

To Kyel's dismay, Swain drew his sword and stalked down the street in the direction of the market. Kyel stared after him, incredulous. He thought he could guess the man's intent, and it scared the hell out of him. Even so, he released the prison of air around Darien.

Kyel strode forward, Alexa at his side, trailing Swain down the street. He stopped at the edge of the square, silently absorbing the devastation.

Darien still crouched in a smoldering ring of blackened stone, while all around him the remains of collapsed buildings yet smoldered. Corpses lay sprawled across the ground, most reduced to charred skeletons. The smell was ghastly, a combination of sulphur and roasted flesh. Kyel brought his hand up to his mouth, fighting back bile.

Ahead, Swain approached Darien cautiously, blade drawn and carried downward at his side. Darien stared reproachfully up at him from the ground, his face a mixture of rage and pain and some other emotion Kyel couldn't identify.

Darien lay the man in his lap down on the cobbles, then rose unsteadily to his feet. Dark power seethed from his body, bleeding into the air in distorted waves. He was drawing hard on the Onslaught, Kyel realized. Preparing for a strike. Wary, Kyel tightened the protective shield around Swain.

The Prince halted. He stood hefting the hilt of his sword in his hand, as if testing the weight of it. He acknowledged Darien with a nod, and said in a calm voice, "Just you and me, like the old days. But this time, only one of us walks away."

Kyel felt his stomach clench. Darien was the best swordsman he'd ever known, but Swain was a blademaster, the man who had trained him.

Darien stood motionless in the street, eyes fixed

on the slow motion of the Prince's blade. His gaze slid slowly upward to lock on Swain's eyes. He nodded slightly.

Reaching up, Darien unbuckled his chinstrap. He tugged his helmet off and tossed it on the ground, shaking out a mane of sweat-matted hair. His face was darkened by sooty grime that left a perfect delineation where the protection of his helm had ended. The look in his eyes was cold as death.

Swain took a step forward, his eyebrows raised in question. Darien glowered at him for a moment then reached up and unfastened the buckles of his harness, dropping his armor to the ground. His hand traveled to the hilt of his sword and drew the weapon from its sheath. It wasn't the same sword Kyel remembered; it was a scimitar. Kyel didn't know much about the mechanics of swordplay, but he couldn't help wondering if Darien's training with the longsword would translate well to this curved, sleeker blade.

Swain approach slowly, his weapon extended in front of him. Darien brought his sword up, lightly tapping Swain's blade.

The Prince exploded into motion.

He swept forward with a lightning series of attacks that sent Darien retreating.

Swain's sword moved so quickly, so precisely, that Kyel's eyes couldn't keep up with it. The violent hammering of steel against steel rang sharply off the walls, echoing through the square.

Behind Darien, the Enemy soldier he'd been protecting stirred, leveraging his torso off the ground. Seeing Darien circling Swain, the man's eyes went wide, first in surprise. Then in fear.

Kyel understood why. Darien was at a clear disadvantage. The sword in his hand was shorter than Swain's. The Prince had a much longer reach, and Darien was forced to keep dodging and retreating. While Swain's motions were crisp and precise, Darien moved his scimitar in great, sweeping arcs.

He swept out with a feint. Swain dodged, rotating his blade and deflecting the blow. He brought his sword up and held it out in front of him, keeping Darien at a distance. Then he brought the blade back over his shoulder and swept it down. Darien ducked under the attack and used his momentum to shove Swain forcefully aside.

The Prince whirled around, scoring a cut across Darien's back. Then he launched a crisp sequence of attacks that battered him to the ground. Overwhelmed, Darien raised his sword over his head to fend off Swain's hacking cuts.

He struck out with a foot, taking the Prince behind the knees and sweeping his legs out from under him. Swain hit the ground and rolled, somehow ending up on his feet. He sprang back, then whirled, delivering a slice that cut through Darien's gambeson, drawing a line of blood across his ribs as he rose from the ground.

Kyel gasped, appalled by the sheer brutality of it all. The harsh clangs of steel impacting with steel drove home the viciousness of the fight. It was starting to sink in that one of the two men before him was going to die a brutal death. Kyel dreaded that moment.

Swain struck again, batting Darien's sword aside. Darien danced back, drawing his long dagger from his belt. Crossing both dagger and sword, he interrupted Swain's next strike with a scissoring motion. The two men circled slowly, each waiting for an opening.

All at once, Darien lunged. Moving both dagger and sword together, he parried Swain's attack with the dagger while throwing a high cut with the sword. The curved blade took the Prince in the neck, continuing its slice down through tissue and bone. Darien tore the sword out, fanning the cobblestones with blood. He stepped back, weapons held ready, even as Swain fell.

Chest heaving, Darien stood over the Prince and watched him bleed out. Callously, he wiped his blade clean on the fabric of Swain's leggings. Then he returned both weapons to their sheathes and turned to fix his stare on Kyel.

"Your turn," he said.

Kyel understood. There was nothing more he could do. The city had fallen and would soon be overrun. He couldn't stop Darien, not by himself.

Darien glared at him hard, his expression going from dark to demonic. A terrible green light suffused him, pulsating, sucking the light from the day. The shadows of the square deepened, the air growing fiercely chill. It was terrifying to behold, especially since Kyel knew what was happening: Darien was filling himself to saturation with the combined might of both the Onslaught and the magic field.

Preparing a strike that Kyel couldn't deflect, not even with Thar'gon's great aide.

"Darien, no!"

Naia hurled past Kyel, inserting her own body between the darkmage and himself. Darien's expression changed, fading through various degrees of rage into something that looked like regret. The green aura around him slowly waned but didn't fade completely.

Naia took a step toward him. "Please, Darien. You need Kyel to destroy the Well of Tears."

Darien recoiled as if struck.

The glow around him winked out. He looked back and forth between Naia and Kyel with the haunted face of a condemned man. He shook his head. "That's not possible."

"It *is* possible!" Naia insisted, closing the gap between them. "Come away and listen. You sent Quin to Titherry for a reason. We have your answer, Darien! The answer you wanted us to find!"

Darien looked dazed, as if the sight of her was like venom, paralyzing his ability to react or comprehend. His mouth moved, fumbling silently, at last forming words. "Quin? You came with Quin?"

She halted before him, commanding, "Afford him clemency!"

To Kyel's disbelief, Darien obeyed. Nodding, the darkmage turned to address him. "A truce, then. Your life is under my protection." He turned back to Naia, his face telling a dismal story of boundless guilt. He said softly, "Naia. I don't know what to say…I don't have the words…"

Naia stared at him a long, hard moment. "Then don't speak."

Chapter Thirty-Six
Freedom of Will

Rothscard, The Rhen

Darien closed his eyes as Azár fell into his arms. He sagged against her while she hugged him tight, maybe tighter than ever before. She sighed happily against his ear. "Thank the gods you are safe. Did you take the city?"

"Aye, we did," he said, letting go.

"Ishilzeri! My husband is a great commander!"

"Your husband is exhausted."

Darien turned and started pulling off his armor, tossing it piece by piece on a rug laid out on the ground. When he was down to just his leggings, he strode over to a cask of water standing upright against the side of the command tent. He plunged his head in, then righted himself with a great gasp, whipping his hair back and spraying water everywhere. Azár brought her hands up, shielding her face. There was laughter in her eyes. Darien bent to pick his shirt back up, using it to wipe the wet grime from his face. Shoulders sagging, he walked toward the tent's entrance.

"You should lie down," Azár said, plucking the dirty cloth out of his hands.

He'd forgotten he was holding it; his mind felt dazed. He was battle-weary. No, it was more than that. He was grieving, Darien realized. He'd killed his mentor. No matter what else Nigel Swain had become to him, he would always be that.

He paused and turned back to the soldiers lingering behind him. "A moment, Sayeed."

His First hurried over, concern on his face. He had been acting odd, ever since the battle. Darien didn't understand why. Sayeed had begun treating him as though he'd taken a mortal wound. His apprehension was almost palpable.

And irritating.

"We'll need some fresh horses for the morrow," Darien said. "And round up what's left of the Zakai. It'd be wise to enter the city by procession, to demonstrate our strength. I want the Zakai to ride at my side. I'll need a guard of honor."

Sayeed stared at him blankly, as though he hadn't understood a word.

Darien raised a weary eyebrow. "Horses. Zakai."

The man ducked his head more deferentially than he ever should have. "Of course."

Darien clapped him on the back and sent him off. Then he ducked into the dim interior of the tent and trudged wearily through the cloth partition. He stripped and sank into bed, falling instantly to sleep.

When Darien open his eyes, he found Azár lying soft and naked at his side, her body only half-covered in blankets. It was night, but the ambient light was enough to reveal her features. Darien traced the gentle curve of her body with his gaze. She was beautiful. Perhaps the most beautiful thing he'd ever seen. She stirred, her eyes blinking open enough to look at him.

"You're awake," she said groggily, stretching. "You slept through dinner."

Which explained his vast hunger. Darien sat up, letting the covers fall off him, and rubbed his eyes. He wondered what time it was. He still felt bone-weary.

"How does one become a Servant?" Azár asked, setting a hand on him. "Is there some vow or ritual?"

The question came out of nowhere and caught Darien by surprise. Rubbing his eyes, he answered guardedly, "There's a vow."

"And did you speak this vow?"

He frowned, not liking this peculiar line of questioning. At best, it brought on feelings of shame. "I did," he admitted.

"Will you teach it to me, so that I might speak it also?"

Darien winced, shocked by the question. Azár was beautiful and good. Unblemished. The thought of her becoming a creature such as himself was horrifying. Shaking his head in dismay, he asked, "Why would you wish that?"

She sat up and set her hand on his own, gazing into his eyes. "Because our time in this world grows short. And I am scared. I have only just found my husband. I do not wish to lose him." She leaned into him, kissing his cheek. "Where you go, I go."

"No."

Appalled, Darien jerked back from her. He threw off the covers and stood up.

Confusion rampant on her face, Azár asked, "Why not?" She drew her knees against her chest.

Darien stood gaping down at her, not knowing what to say. Hoarsely, he whispered, "Because where I'm going, you can't follow."

Azár's face darkened, her eyes narrowing. "Why not?"

He hung his head, feeling suddenly sad. He wanted to stay with her. To grow old with her. To love and raise his daughter. He sank back into bed and, with a sigh, pulled her close.

"You don't belong there," he said softly.

"Neither do you."

He breathed a sigh and assured her, "You have me now. And when I move on, you'll have my memory. Keep me alive in your heart."

"You already live in my heart."

Darien took a long, steadying breath, trying to stuff his emotions back down deep where they belonged. He couldn't afford to acknowledge them. He owed her that much. He wanted to tell his wife he loved her but couldn't bring himself to speak the words.

He knew that saying them would only hurt her more.

———

Somehow, he'd fallen back to sleep.

Darien woke to empty blankets and a devil-dog licking his face with a sticky tongue. Groaning, he raised his hands up to fend the damn thing off. He squirmed his head from side to side, trying to escape its fetid breath.

"All right! Enough!"

The hound drew back and stared down at him with hollow eyes. He snapped his fingers and pointed to the corner. But the thing disobeyed him, instead trotting out through the cloth partition. Darien ran his arm over his face, then grabbed a handful of blankets to wipe off his arm.

The partition flapped open, and Azár stepped through. A warm smile brightened her face. "It is good you are awake. Your Zakai and horses await you outside. And you have a visitor."

Darien grunted and pushed himself out of bed. He started toward his wooden chest, but Azár's hand on his arm stopped him.

"I brought out the outfit you wore at our wedding." She motioned toward a chair.

There, laid out neatly, was the embroidered black tunic the tailors of the Jenn Asyaadi had made for him. He'd forgotten he owned it. He moved to the chair and held it up, then pulled on the pants. He had to rely on Azár to help him with the tunic. He couldn't button the sleeves on his own.

When she was done, he tied back his hair then turned toward her. He brought a hand up to trace her cheek. "You should wear your red gown."

Her eyes widened in surprise even as her hands went to her belly. "You wish me to come with you?

Darien nodded, smiling. "I'm not entering our new capital without my wife."

Azár glowed with excitement. While he collected his weapons, she produced the red gown she'd worn the day he'd proposed marriage to her. He watched her pull it on, then took a step back, admiring. Pregnancy suited her, he decided. Azár's olive skin seemed even softer than usual, her hair lustrous and sleek. Her dark eyes glowed with excitement and affection.

Offering his arm, Darien led her through the partition into the gathering area of the tent. So intent was he on his wife, that he almost didn't notice the lone figure in the corner. He glanced up and froze.

Naia stood with her hands clasped in front of her. Her gaze trailed from Darien to Azár, then back again with a questioning look.

Composing himself, Darien led Azár forward. Very rigidly, he said, "Azár, this is Master Naia Seleni. Without Naia, I couldn't have sealed the Well of Tears." He turned to Naia. "I would like to introduce to you Lightweaver Azár." He added, "My wife."

Naia blinked her shock but recovered quickly. She put on a welcoming smile and took Azár's hands into her own. "I am most honored to meet you, Lightweaver Azár. Congratulations on your nuptials. I wish you both much joy and happiness."

Darien shifted his weight from one foot to the other, and stood fidgeting with the collar of his tunic. Beneath the thick fabric, he was already breaking a sweat.

"Thank you for receiving me," Naia said. "I have come to accompany you to the palace. But first, I need you to do something for me." She lifted her hands, offering an object out to him. "I'm going to ask you to put this on."

When he saw what she was holding, Darien's breath clotted like blood.

Fear clenched his chest in an iron fist and *squeezed.* His heart terrorized his rib cage, his mind staggering toward panic. Reflexively, he reached out and groped for the Onslaught, wrenching it into him.

"Get that thing away from me!"

"Stop!" Naia held up the Soulstone before his eyes. "Quin repaired it—it can't harm you."

"How could you? You know what that damn thing did to me!"

Naia dropped her hand, the medallion dangling from her fingers. Her face set in patient lines, she moved toward him, speaking calmly, "You know me, Darien. I would never ask this of you unless I thought it truly imperative. And it *is* imperative."

She raised the Soulstone again, offering it out to him in her palm. "Take it. It can't harm you again. You're dead; there is no gift left within you. Nothing to fear."

Darien looked back and forth between Naia's face and the medallion in her hand. Little by little, reason returned to him. He let go of the Onslaught, letting most of it drain away, holding back just a little. His eyes ticked down to the glowing stone, then back up to Naia's face.

At his side, Azár snarled, "Is that the thing that killed my husband? Are you a witch, come to claim his soul? I will—"

"No." Darien shook his head, eyes transfixed on the stone. "I trust her."

"Take it," Naia urged. "Take it and put it on."

He looked at her sideways. "Why?"

Naia met his gaze unflinchingly. "Because that is what you are destined to do."

Darien nodded, at last understanding. Naia had journeyed to Athera's Crescent with Quin. She must have gained some knowledge he wasn't privy to.

He reached out and grabbed the glowing medallion. As his fingers closed around it, the feel of the cool stone shot fear into his chest. His mouth went dry, his heart thundering. He clenched his jaw, fighting against panic as he brought the thick bands of the silver collar up and wrapped them around his neck.

"Azár," he said. "Fasten it for me."

"Husband—"

"Do it."

For the second time in his life, he heard the horrifying sound of the Soulstone's clasp snapping closed.

Darien cried out as the stone's power raged into him. He sagged to his knees, folding forward. A savage torrent of energy streaked up his nerves and assaulted his mind. The violence of it was appalling. Recognizing the feeling for what it was, he didn't struggle against it. He could feel the power within the stone pour into him, filling his mind with a warm, wonderous feeling he'd entirely forgotten.

The Transference ended as abruptly as it had begun. Darien knelt trembling and gasping on the rugs, staring up at Naia's face in outright amazement. He reached up and uncinched the clasp, letting the collar slip off his neck. His mind raced frantically to understand the implications of what had just happened.

Through shivering breaths, he demanded, "Why?"

Naia bent over, a warm smile on her face. "Don't you understand? *You're alive.*"

Darien stared at her numbly.

It took him a moment to realize she was right.

Then another moment to see the irony.

That was the one thing he'd been lacking, the only thing separating him from life. It was the spark of the gift that had been ripped out of him upon his death, now given back to him by the very object that had stolen it in the first place.

"I don't understand," he whispered.

Azár dropped to his side and hugged him protectively.

Naia smiled to reassure her, then said to Darien, "You lost the legacy of power within you when you died. Since then, your link with Xerys has been the only thing keeping you in the flesh. Your gift has now been restored. You no longer need to fear your Master—Xerys has no power over you anymore. Your destiny is your own, to do with as you wish."

Darien struggled to his feet, panting to catch his breath and leaning heavily on Azár. He was filled with a numbing euphoria.

He took Naia's hand and gasped, "I don't know how to thank you."

But Naia shook her head, retracting her hand. "Don't thank me, Darien. This is no gift."

"What do you mean?" He stared at her in incomprehension.

"Trust me. You will understand."

Frowning, Darien nodded. He closed his eyes, fighting to calm his breath and steady his mind. Azár drew him aside, shooting a sharp glare at Naia. Rubbing his back, she whispered something in his ear that fled right by him. He wasn't paying attention. His head still reeled from the Transference, and he was still struggling to make sense of this new position he found himself in. He was still a Servant of Xerys. But he no longer had to be his Master's slave.

"Are you able to continue?" Azár asked gently. "Or should I tell the Zakai to stand down?"

Struggling out of his thoughts, Darien shook his head. "No. This should be done now, not later."

He swiped his sleeve across his brow, wiping off at least some of the sweat. He paused for a moment to collect himself. Then, taking Azár by the hand, he walked on unsteady legs out of the command tent and into the cool morning air. He had to squint against the sun; it seemed enormous and far brighter than ever before. Darien looked around in amazement, at a world saturated with color. He'd forgotten what it was like, to have his senses augmented by a mage's gift burning inside him. An entire division of cavalry stood arrayed before him, brilliant banners flapping in the breeze. Darien paused, allowing himself just a moment to marvel at the sight.

The silhouette of a man, backlit by the rising sun, approached leading a horse. As he neared, Darien recognized Ranoch, the clan chief of the grasslands Jenn. The stallion behind him was tall and fine, its black coat sleek and gleaming in the sun, its bridle quaking with jewels and tassels. A richly embroidered blanket had been draped over its back, sewn with tassels that reached almost to the ground.

Ranoch halted before him. He offered the horse's reins to Darien. "This is Turtak, the finest stallion of my herd. He is a gift."

Darien looked upon his new mount in admiration. He raised his hand and stroked the silken fur of the stallion's neck. He said in wonder, "He is a tremendous gift. You have my gratitude."

He moved to mount the horse, but a low growl from behind him made him turn. Behind him, the demon-hound stood, feet spread widely apart, its hindquarters raised as if ready to spring. The beast's gleaming eyes were trained on him, its lips drawn back to reveal a mouth full of heinous teeth. The thanacryst's growl deepened, became threatening.

"Theanoch," Darien ordered it, feeling suddenly unsure.

The hound sprang.

The beast slammed into him, hurling him backward to the ground and knocking the air from his lungs. Stunned, Darien groped for the magic field but couldn't catch hold of it.

The hound clamped its jaws around his thigh and began to maul him. Darien howled in pain, kicking and beating his fists against the creature, trying frantically to dislodge it. He rolled away, feeling the teeth rip the flesh of his leg.

Desperate, he reached for the Onslaught. But the power of hell was useless against hell's minions.

The demon-dog sprang on top of him, pressing him against the ground. Its maw closed around his shoulder, its teeth sinking deep into the tissues. The hound shook him violently, thrashing him back and forth across the ground, as his blood sprayed the grass.

A terrible agony took hold of him as the hungering beast began to feed off his newfound power. The jaws released his shoulder and closed on his neck.

Darien caught hold of the magic field and speared it into the creature with all the vast strength of his mind. The hound flinched but didn't let go. If anything, it clamped down harder.

Hot blood drained from his neck, saturating his tunic. Darien was vaguely aware of Sayeed standing over him, thrusting his sword into the demon-hound over and over, to no effect. Darien's vision went dim. His breathing became gurgling.

As a last resort, Darien used the last scrap of his failing power on himself.

The jaws released him. He sprang up from the ground and twisted, snarling in outrage. His adversary's gleaming eyes narrowed. The beast drew back, preparing to spring. Darien didn't give it the chance.

He launched himself at the creature, tearing a long gash in its neck. The demon-hound yelped in pain, twisting away. Darien stalked the creature in a slow circle, growling menacingly. For the first time, there was fear in the thanacryst's eyes. Darien wondered why. Then, looking back at himself, he realized with shock:

He was no longer human.

He was a hell-hound.

Darien lunged, his jaws snapping closed around the beast's head. He twisted, his teeth sinking deep into the animal's flesh as he fought to wrestle it to the ground. The hound resisted, thrashing about and whining in pain. He locked his jaws, digging deep into the dirt for leverage. The delicious taste of demon-blood filled his mouth. He clamped down harder as the beast's struggles became desperate, then gradually weakened.

The thanacryst's legs beat against him, over and over. The struggling slowed. Then, with one last, forlorn whimper, the demon-hound went limp. Darien waited, his teeth sunk deeply into its flesh, until he was certain the thing was dead. He unlocked his jaws and released it.

And released the magic that sustained him.

He sank to his knees, his strength draining from him. Blood saturated his tunic, gushed from the wound in his neck. He healed the injury, but then exhaustion hit him like a hammer blow. Sayeed caught him before he could fall and eased him the rest of the way to the ground.

Darien lay in the blood-wet grass, gaping up at the sky as the rest of the world blurred around him.

"Rest," his brother commanded. Darien obeyed, closing his eyes.

Chapter Thirty-Seven
The Price of Betrayal

Rothscard, The Rhen

The western sky was the faded yellow of an old bruise. Darien stared out at the sunset and cursed himself, regretting how long he'd slept while letting the daylight go to waste. Zakai moved immediately to cluster about him, much more protective than they had ever been before. The carcass of the thanacryst had been dragged away, but there was still a dark stain in the grass where the beast had fallen. Demon blood. Too dark to be human. He stopped and stood there still, gazing down at the place where the hound had fallen, a deep sadness working its way into his bones. He hadn't realized how much the beast had wormed its way into his heart. It felt like a little piece of him was gone, bled away into the grass.

Darien lifted Azár onto her horse, a golden palomino with a silvery mane. Moving to his own mount, he climbed onto Turtak's back. He took the braided reins in his hand and directed the horse forward with the pressure of his legs. The stallion snorted and moved into a trot, head and tail carried proudly high. Darien guided the animal into a gap in the long column of soldiers, behind a small vanguard of Zakai. There, he pulled the horse to a halt and waited for his wife to draw up at his side.

On his signal, the soldiers started forward. Their column marched to a cadence tapped out by a single drum, an irregular pattern that had a rustic wildness about it. To Darien, it seemed an odd rhythm to march to. Nevertheless, the horses and men seemed born to it.

The procession moved forward as a unit, moving off the grass and onto a wide and rutted road. Darien stared in front of him at the mangled city ahead. The victory they had won felt more bitter than sweet. Rothscard as he had grown up knowing it was no more. The city once heralded as unconquerable had fallen under his sword.

The procession reached the remains of the Lion's Gate. The arch above the gate had fallen, the rubble already cleared away. On the other side of the walls, he could hear the sounds of the city, a restless and growing panic. The air moving toward them carried with it a malodorous blend of smoke, death, and spilled sewage. Their assault had crippled parts of the city's infrastructure. It would have to be rebuilt.

Above them rose a pair of limestone turrets that looked gnawed by the teeth of a monster. Remains of the portcullis had been pushed aside, its lattice grate bent into a distorted, crosshatch pattern. The gate itself had been shattered, its wood carried away to be used to fuel Malikari fires. Beyond the wall, the sounds of a terrified populace grew boisterous and frantic.

At the sight of their vanguard, the crowds erupted into a collective outcry of terror and fury. Darien's stallion tossed its head, spooked by the thunderous clamor. They processed down a broad avenue lined with mailed sentries who were hard-pressed to restrain the surging masses. The entire crowd behind them churned like a boiling pot as individuals vied for a better view.

Until they caught sight of him.

It was like a strange ripple that passed through the crowd, flowing behind Darien as he passed. People stilled and fell quiet, their eyes filling with awe and horror.

Silence trembled in his wake.

Darien's ears rang with the hollow sound of his horse's hooves striking the blood-stained cobbles. The animal lifted its legs smartly, as if purposefully strutting to impress the crowd. To his left, Sayeed fought to keep his spirited mount in check. And on his right, Azár rode straight-backed and elegant, her red gown flowing over the sides of her golden mare.

They rode along the wide boulevard that paralleled the Grand Canal. The avenue they followed led through the center of the city, under the shadows of tall, sloped-roof buildings joined together in long rows. All along their path, the crowds remained dense and frantic. Only the threat of the soldiers' weapons prevented the populace from spilling into the street. The avenue ended at a large, tree-covered hill that contained the palace grounds.

They were met at the gate by a company of Tanisars, while the rest of the procession continued on through the city. Riding within a tight guard of Zakai, Darien entered the grounds of Emmery Palace. He directed his horse around the girth of the Citadel, through acres of torn-up gardens and trampled lawns. Ahead, above the substantial wall that curtained the Inner Ward, the towers of the castle came into view, high turrets of white limestone capped by crenelated ramparts. Smoke yet billowed from the eastern wing, and one of the turrets was partially collapsed. Emmery Palace had not fallen easily.

Their party gained the courtyard, where they were met by a small group of elite Zakai who took the reins of their mounts. Darien dismounted and helped his wife climb down from her horse's back. Together they strode, arm in arm, up a wide span of steps to where a group of the city's former ministers awaited them under the castle's broad portico.

Darien stopped at the top of the steps, hand resting on the hilt of his sword, his gaze sliding from one horrified face to the next. The ministers stood sweating and fidgeting, as if too fearful to act. At last, a balding man in a rumpled suit walked pale-faced toward him. Halting a good distance from Darien, he went to his knees then bowed forward to the ground.

There was a rustle of nervous motion. Then the other ministers followed suit, abasing themselves on the ground, granting him the obeisance usually reserved for a Prime Warden.

Darien stared down at them, coolly considering the gesture, giving them ample time for the humility of the act to sink in. His mother had sometimes waited minutes before acknowledging a petitioner. Darien had learned many things from Emelda Lauchlin, not the least of which was how to intimidate.

He'd learned that lesson well.

After long minutes, he uttered, "You may rise."

The group of ministers regained their feet, more than a few tottering dizzily. The balding man came forward, wringing his hands nervously.

"Welcome to Emmery Palace, my Lord."

"I'm not a lord," Darien snapped. "Where's Romana?"

"My Lo…" The minister's voice trailed off as he visibly struggled to find a more suitable honorific. He finally settled on "Great Master," a generic title that could be applied to any mage. When Darien didn't correct him, he stumbled on, "The Queen awaits you in her throne room."

"*Former* Queen."

The man paled even whiter. Swallowing heavily, he bobbed his head. "The former Queen awaits you."

The minister turned and beckoned their party forward. Offering his arm to Azár, Darien strode beside the man into the guts of the palace. The tiled floor of the foyer was sticky with blood. The room reeked a strong metallic odor, which combined with the choking smell of smoke. As they crossed the wide room, Darien had to watch his step, picking his way over the wreckage of a chandelier that had fallen from the ceiling, its crystalline remains scattered across the floor. A wide smear of blood streaked the tiles where a corpse had been dragged away.

The minister turned and led them down a wood-paneled hallway that ended at a set of double doors. The man paused for a moment, then pulled both doors open with a flourish. Darien guided his wife through without sparing the minister a glance, his eyes fixed on the pair of chairs sitting on a dais at the far end of the hall. Emmery's throne was a tall, elaborately carved piece of rosewood, set with velvet cushions. To its right sat a similar throne, smaller and less ornate.

Darien's eyes were drawn to the group of people clustered together on the far end of the dais. Romana Norengail stood with one hand draped over a wood banister. The look on her face could have curdled milk. Beside her stood Kyel and the woman who had banished his necrators. Her presence in the throne room troubled Darien more than anything else.

A terrified servant lingered off to the side, holding a trembling platter laden with filled wine glasses. None of the Queen's company seemed to be partaking.

Letting go of his wife's arm, Darien climbed the steps of the dais and approached the Queen. But instead of halting before Romana, he angled toward the servant and scooped a wine glass off the tray. He slung himself down on the Queen's throne, slouching back with deliberate arrogance. He drained the wine in one swallow.

To Romana, he said, "My condolences on the death of your husband." He opened his hand and let the spent glass fall from his fingers. It shattered on the tiles.

The Queen shot him a hateful glare. "My condolences on the death of your soul."

Ignoring her, Darien beckoned his wife forward, motioning her toward the smaller throne. With a calm and regal grace she'd never shown before, Azár flowed across the dais and assumed her place at his side. Darien smiled at Romana.

He nodded toward the doors. "If you leave now, you leave with your head." Thinking on it, he corrected himself. "Well, you'll be leaving either way. I'd just prefer you not bloody up my throne room."

Romana shot him one last, vicious glare, then turned and moved with an unhurried stride out of the hall, her life and dignity intact.

When the doors closed behind her, Darien allowed himself a smirk. He beckoned the servant with the wine forward, claiming a glass for his wife and another for himself. He looked up to find Naia gaping at him, her face aghast. He didn't care. With a toss of his head, he commanded her:

"Talk. Start with the Soulstone."

Naia shared a nervous glance with Kyel, then stepped forward. For once, she seemed at a loss for words. After a moment, she said, "The Soulstone was created by Quinlan Reis."

Darien blinked. The revelation was both surprising and disturbing.

Naia went on, "Quin did what he could to fix the medallion's gemstone. The stone now functions better than he ever intended. So well, in fact, it can create new legacies by drawing vitrus directly from the magic field itself. With it, we have the ability to recover our lost numbers—conceivably, anyone with the slightest scrap of the Potential can be imbued with the gift."

Darien sat quietly, letting the information sink in. When it had, he needed another glass of wine. He motioned the servant with the tray back and helped himself.

"Why was it necessary I put it on?"

Spreading her hands, Naia explained, "I needed to be able to speak freely about what Quin and I discovered. And you need to be able to act on that knowledge, even if it contradicts Xerys' interests."

Darien set the empty glass down on the floor. "Then speak."

Naia nodded. "On Titherry, we found one last Harbinger who taught me how to read Athera's Crescent. With the Crescent, I saw there are only three possible futures still available to us. There are an infinite number of variations of those futures, but it boils down to this: we must destroy the Well of Tears."

"How is that possible?" he whispered.

Naia turned to look at Kyel over her shoulder. "We need Kyel's talisman. He can use it to shatter the Well of Tears, but it needs to be done at just the right time. The magic field will fail completely before it flips. Most of the Well's defenses rely on magic—when the magic field falters, the Well will be vulnerable."

Kyel stared at her sideways, looking intensely skeptical. "I can't shatter anything without magic."

Naia insisted, "Somehow it works. In my visions of this future, you always wield the talisman successfully, even in the absence of the magic field."

Darien realized he already knew the answer to that problem. "Thar'gon is a magical reservoir," he said. "It'll work."

Naia turned back to Darien. "If we destroy the Well, then the portal between worlds will collapse. And the recoil will knock the magic field back into its proper alignment."

Darien gnawed on that for a moment. It was an enticing alternative to Renquist's dire strategy…too enticing. There had to be a reason why Renquist had chosen to ignore that option. He took another glass of wine, drank it down in one swallow, then replaced the spent glass on the servant's tray.

"What are the risks?"

"If we fail, then Renquist will bring Xerys fully into this world."

Darien nodded slowly. Naia had seen Renquist's plan in the mirror of Athera's Crescent. He couldn't help wondering if she had seen his own part in it. He studied her eyes, looking for sign of doubt. But in Naia's dark eyes, he saw only hope.

False hope, he felt certain.

"And why would releasing Xerys be so terrible?" he asked.

Naia's mouth dropped open. The hope in her eyes chilled to icy dismay. "Did you truly just ask that question?"

Darien sat forward. "I did. Xerys is not evil. He has been tasked with the preservation of the magic field. He is simply carrying out his duty. But, then, aren't we all?"

Naia shook her head slowly, as if dazed. After a long moment, she breathed, "No, Darien. Not at that price."

He shrugged. She still embraced the false narrative that Xerys was an evil god. That Chaos was malevolent by nature. She didn't understand that the magic field was born of Chaos, that Chaos itself birthed every destiny.

But he understood part of Naia's hesitance. Xerys was, at best, a callous and indifferent master without compassion for the masses. If Xerys was allowed to cross into the world, it would precipitate a purging of the temples and risked a genocidal war that could last generations. Thousands would die. Perhaps hundreds of thousands. And, yet, it was conceivably worth the price. How much was the existence of magic worth? Could anyone put a value to it?

"What are our chances of success?"

"Not good," Naia admitted in a dismal tone. "Quin went to Bryn Calazar to try to assassinate Renquist and Krane. He hasn't come back."

Which meant Quin was dead. He would have no chance against Renquist. Darien couldn't imagine what the man had been thinking. He sagged, collapsing back into the throne. He shook his head, feeling an aching grief as familiar as breathing. He'd lost enough kin in his life that he should be used to the ache of it by now.

But he wasn't.

Forcing his emotions aside, he looked back up at Naia and started weighing his options. Renquist's plan had a much higher chance of success. But a success that came at tremendous cost. Naia's proposal had a great risk of failure, and that failure would mean the death of all mages.

Including Azár. And their child.

But perhaps he could hedge his bets. Darien's gaze slipped to Kyel and the woman from Aerysius he had taken up company with. It was Renquist's will that he absorb Kyel's power along with Naia's. Darien didn't know how that made him feel. Kyel's opposition had hurt—hurt with the bitter ache of betrayal. But Darien respected it. Through all that had transpired, Kyel's chains and integrity had remained intact. Not like his own. In the end, Darien decided that Kyel's life was worth something, worth enough to give him a chance. Naia's life, as well. And if her plan failed, then there would still be time to carry out Renquist's command.

Darien gave a slight nod. "You have my support."

As soon as the words were out, a terrible feeling of loss welled within him. It was a harrowing feeling. A life-twisting feeling. Suddenly ill, Darien broke into a clammy sweat, clenching the armrests of the throne. Rocked to his core, he sat upright with a gasp of understanding.

He had betrayed his Master, so his Master had betrayed him.

He had lost the Onslaught again, just as he had in Tokashi's dungeons. Only, this time, he'd lost it permanently.

He leaned forward, hands on his knees, and sat there panting, sweat streaming down his face. Azár leaned into him, setting a hand on his back, her face full of concern. Kyel started forward, his companion moving alongside him. Darien looked up, feeling a lightning-like stab of fear.

"Don't bring that woman near me," he snarled.

Kyel halted and threw his hand up, blocking the woman from moving forward. He stared a question at Darien.

Darien rose to his feet, feeling besieged. "Her

name is Alexa Newell. She was a Master who disappeared from Aerysius four years ago. She's not on your side."

"I have no reason to doubt her," Kyel said.

"Then let me give you one." Darien paced forward, skirting their position. "She banished my necrators. Only a darkmage could do that. And not just any darkmage—only one with the talent to command the undead."

Kyel's stare shot to Alexa. A peculiar smile formed on her face. A knowing smile, full of confidence and audacity. She trained that smile on Darien like a weapon.

"Where is your hound, Darien?" she asked. Her smile became a gloating sneer. "Where are your necrators? Why don't you summon them?"

Darien's insides twisted as he realized his danger. He closed his eyes, his shoulders sagging under the heavy burden of defeat. She had him, and she knew it.

Azár rose from her seat and moved to stand at his side. The fear in her eyes told him she understood every nuance of his plight. She set a hand on his back. He barely felt the touch. His mind and senses stood frozen.

The woman's eyes widened, her smile triumphant. She whispered a word. And with that whisper, commanded shadow. All around the room, necrators bloomed upward from the floor, coalescing into obsidian forms.

Darien's heart chilled with terror—a primal, feral emotion unlike any other. At his sides, his hands grew cold and started trembling.

The woman spun to Kyel. "Look at him—he's defenseless! Kill him now and absorb his gift—then even Renquist himself will not have the might to oppose us! We will destroy the Well of Tears together. Act now and rid the world of this monster!"

Kyel stepped back away from her, his face gripped in a war of conflicted emotions. Darien could see the struggle in him. It was brutal.

The woman reached out and tugged on Kyel's arm. "Listen to me! Your Oath doesn't matter anymore! This is your chance! You can slay him right here!"

In defiance of the necrators, Darien mustered the last, fraying thread of his courage. He taunted Alexa, "Why don't you do it? I'm here. Take my soul."

He spread his arms, inviting her to attack. The woman narrowed her eyes, visibly seething. But she did nothing.

"You can't, can you? That's why you need him." Darien dropped his arms and said to Kyel, "She's Renquist's insurance, should I turn against him. He needs one of us dead."

He turned his glare back to Alexa. Staring at her and her only, Darien pronounced with confidence, "She's not living, Kyel. She's like a necrator herself. She's Renquist's minion."

Kyel backed slowly away. "Then why didn't she just kill me herself?"

Darien stood focused on Alexa. "She's a conduit. A soul-siphon. She needs us together, in close proximity. That's the only way she can wrench the gift out of one of us and Transfer it to the other."

The woman's smile grew slowly exultant. "So you found me out, fool. I applaud you. Only, you're wrong about one thing."

"What is that?" Darien asked.

She scoffed. Then she spread her hands. "I *can* kill you myself."

The ring of necrators swept forward. Darien threw his hands out to stop them—a futile effort. There was nothing he could do. But they didn't touch him. Instead they surrounded him, containing him.

The woman walked toward him, confident, triumphant.

She parted the ring of shadows and stepped inside the circle.

She raised her hand.

Darien doubled over as vicious agony clawed at him from the inside, tearing rapidly through every fiber of his being. He knew what it was—and the terror of that knowledge was incapacitating. The woman had captured him in a terrible link that was ripping his newfound gift out of his soul. Darien dropped to the floor, howling in mortal anguish as he thrashed in his death throes.

With a cry, Azár sprang in front of him. A wave of Alexa's arm sent her flying backward.

A jarring thump was followed by a shrieking scream.

Life and power crashed back into him. The song of the magic field surged, soaring with fury in his head. He was filled to bursting with power, but it wasn't a power he could use. It collapsed into silence as swiftly as it rose, held in check by the presence of the necrators.

Darien lay twitching as the pain slowly released its grip. At last, his body relaxed, and air returned to his lungs. He thrust out a hand and pushed himself upright.

He sat blinking, too shocked and too weakened to move. It took him long seconds to realize what had happened. The woman knelt on the floor, her fingers groping at the hilt of Sayeed's sword, sunken like a lance through the center of her chest. Alexa's face went slowly slack, her eyes rolling back. She slumped forward, driving the blade in further.

Still, the necrators remained. She hadn't commanded them to leave.

"Darien..."

It was the smallest, weakest sound. He turned and glanced behind him.

Azár lay sprawled on the floor, her lids heavy, her eyes staring upward. She wasn't moving.

"No."

Darien shook his head in denial even as he scrambled toward her. He collapsed at her side, pulling his wife into his arms. She was alive, but barely. Blood drained from her scalp, her nose, her mouth. Her eyes stared up at him, her lips moving wordlessly. He had no idea what she was trying to say. All he knew was that she was dying. And there was nothing he could do about it.

He was losing his wife. He was losing his daughter. He was losing them both.

Darien lifted Azár's head until her face was pressed against his. He closed his eyes and silently begged her not to go.

But she was going. He could feel her dying.

So he did the one thing he could. He kissed her softly and told her he loved her.

His voice was the last sound she heard. A slight smile touched Azár's lips as she died.

Immediately, Darien felt the stir of energy in his arms as the conduit of Transference between them opened. Power gushed into him from his wife's broken body, invading his own. Darien's muscles locked rigid—he couldn't let go—as Azár's body shed its two tiers of power like a parting gift.

He screamed in outrage, in defiance, in futility.

When it was done, he collapsed on top of her, weeping scalding tears of grief. He clutched her tight in his arms and pressed his face against hers.

"Brother. Come away."

Hands encircled him, tugging at him gently. He jerked away. He wasn't ready to let her go.

"I'm so sorry, Darien."

That was Naia's voice.

His tears flowed freely, wetting his wife's soft cheeks.

"Take him somewhere he can mourn," Naia whispered.

Hands encircled him again.

"Leave me alone," he rasped, and clutched Azár harder.

Naia sank down beside him and set a comforting hand on his shoulder. Her touch was a rude invasion. He tried shrugging it off.

"Let me care for her, Darien," Naia said in the compassionate and composed voice of a priestess.

For some reason, her words made him weep harder.

"Come away, Brother," Sayeed said.

Darien didn't fight him. With one last kiss, he let his wife's body slide out of his arms and settle on the floor. Then he rose from the ground, trembling and broken, a thin fragment of the man he'd been just moments before.

Leaning heavily on Sayeed, he let his brother guide him out of the ring of necrators.

Chapter Thirty-Eight
Broken

Rothscard, The Rhen

Kyel took a step into the shrine.

Beneath his feet, the floorboards gave an exhausted groan. The sound startled him. He jerked to a halt, planting a hand on the cold stone wall. Standing rigid in the doorway, he gazed straight ahead into the dimly lit shrine, a small room with oppressive walls, not much more than a niche carved out of the temple's long nave. The shrine was filled with a gloomy light shed from dozens of small candles spread across the floor. Kyel lingered in the doorway, a silent and uninvited spectator, not wanting to infringe on the privacy of the scene playing out within.

"You can come in, Kyel."

He winced at the sound of Naia's voice. Swallowing, he moved hesitantly toward her, stepping with care through a meandering forest of flickering candleflame. Naia knelt at the far end of the shrine over the body of the dead woman. With the patient care of a sister, she fussed over every detail: smoothing fabric, arranging hair, painstakingly composing every feature. Kyel stood in awe of Naia's talents. In a short span of time, the former priestess had transformed a broken and bloodied corpse into an exotic beauty that seemed reposed in peaceful slumber.

"Who was she?" he asked, watching Naia stroke a silken lock of hair into place.

"His wife."

"I know that," Kyel grumbled. "But who *was* she?"

Naia didn't respond immediately. Her hand stopped moving. She knelt quietly, gazing down at the woman with a whimsical expression on her face. "I don't know," she said at last. "Someone very special, I think."

Kyel believed that. He knelt beside Naia, pondering the woman laid out before them. She was small, even dainty. But there was something about her face that hinted at something stronger within. He thought Naia might be right. Darien had chosen an exceptional woman to love.

He sat down on the floor. "I've been thinking," he said. "About Alexa. She was killing him, and Darien couldn't do anything about it. Her necrators had him paralyzed. I wonder if that means...?"

"That he's not evil anymore?" Naia shook her head. "It's not that simple. Darien's the same man you met at Greystone Keep, the same man I fell in love with. In all this time, he's never changed. The only thing that's different are the circumstances surrounding him. Darien has pulled his support from Xerys. Nothing more. And now his master has abandoned him."

Kyel looked back down at the dead woman. He sat there in silence for a long time, contemplating Naia's words. Pondering his own emotions, which surprised him. He realized there was still a small part of him that held out hope for Darien. He wasn't sure if that made him feel better or worse about himself.

Suddenly, the floor beneath him lurched.

Kyel started, groping at the wall for stability. Naia pushed herself off the ground. She stood glancing about, her face paling.

Kyel could feel the entire magic field quaking, like a powerful aftershock. He rose to his feet, his hands clutching his head. The field lines grated against each other, raking like a dull knife down his nerves.

"It's getting bad," he gasped.

Beside him, Naia turned in a slow circle, staring up at the ceiling. "It is. We need to be getting up the mountain. I fear our time is running short."

Kyel was thinking the same thing. "I hope Darien is up for this."

She shrugged dismissively. "He doesn't have a choice." Her gaze trailed over the dead woman. "She's ready. I'll go get him."

———

Darien stared at the passionless flames in the hearth, feeling trapped in a universe of nothingness. The nothingness was like a thick cotton blanket that enveloped him, encasing him completely, muffling out the world. He was dimly aware of time sliding past him. But it had nothing to do with him, so he paid it no mind. He thought perhaps he might be cold but couldn't tell for sure. He could feel the creeping fingers of madness groping over him, and welcomed them in.

"Darien."

A hand settled on his shoulder. He resented the feel of it. The touch was an invasion he couldn't bear and couldn't ignore. He moved slightly, pulling away from it.

"It's time." It was Naia's voice, knifing through the comforting layers of detachment. "We have to be going. Would you like to say goodbye first?"

Hurt stabbed through him. He wanted to retreat back into the world of nothingness and dancing flame.

"Come, Darien. Let me help you up."

Hands eased him to his feet. He followed where those hands led, lacking the will to resist. He let Naia guide him away from the hearth and back through the sitting area of the suite. Vaguely, he was aware of Sayeed standing and moving toward him, a deep scowl of concern on his face. But Naia shook her head, and the officer came no closer. Darien gazed at him dully, as if through a thick screen of lead.

The door closed behind them softly.

Naia's hand on his arm kept him moving. It was the only thing that did. Darien followed her along corridors and down flights of stairs. Out into a dark and blustery night. Wind raked his hair, clawed tears from his eyes. Or maybe it wasn't the wind. He didn't know. Smoke rode the scourging currents of air, thick and caustic. He thought perhaps the city burned. He hoped it did.

The wind whipped his senses back into focus, and he became slowly aware of his surroundings. He realized Naia had led him out of the palace grounds, that they were moving through the city streets. Frantic citizens hastened by, their children and possessions in their arms. In the distance glowed a luminous orange cloud. He could hear the sounds of screams.

Naia swept a door open and closed it behind them. Darkness settled around him, lit only by a soft, wavering light. And silence. Darien closed his eyes, savoring the quiet. Naia led him forward, moving through a gauzy haze of muted light.

Her hand released him.

"I'll wait here," she said softly.

Darien could feel her moving away. He knew what lay before him. He didn't want to look. But he did anyway.

Azár lay on the floor, surrounded by a sea of candles glowing with a timid light. At once, his shield of detachment fell away, and he was instantly engulfed in a holocaust of grief. Darien sank to his knees, taking his wife's limp hand into his own. He sent his will plummeting into her, probing, seeking, to find only emptiness. An emptiness more eternal than the world that imprisoned him.

He closed his eyes and let the despair come. But it was fleeting, replaced quickly by rage. A savage anger consumed him, burning away reason.

Growling, Darien clenched Azár's hand and sent a violent deluge of healing energies flooding into her body. He forced his will into her, prying and tunneling into every sinew and tissue, assaulting her violently. He pulled with all his great might at the magic field, filling himself to the point of pain, channeling every last drop of power he could wrest into her. Until she glowed with brilliant energies that streamed off her in sad, radiant waves.

"Stop, Darien!"

He ignored the command, intensifying his efforts, until the pain became excruciating. With a cry, he released the magic field and slumped forward.

"You have to let her go." Naia's voice was filled with compassion and good sense.

He knew she was right. The knowledge defeated him, forcing him to give in to the futility of it all. Darien released Azár, laying her down to rest. Then he turned and glared up at Naia with wrath in his eyes.

"I'm so tired of this world," he grated. "I want nothing more to do with it. People say hell is a place of torment. Well, I've been there. And believe me, hell's a much kinder place."

He surged to his feet and made for the door of the shrine. But he halted as something caught his attention: a frieze of the Goddess of Death, carved into the wall beside the doorway. The sight of it tore him wide open.

"Damn you, bitch," he snarled as he fled.

It took Naia long minutes and many steps to catch up with him. She wove through Rothscard's frantic streets, dodging panicked mobs of citizens. Ahead of her, Darien carved his way through the densely packed avenues. His very presence radiated dark power, inspiring enough fear to clear a path ahead of him. Naia jogged in his wake, at last closing the distance to walk at his side.

Darien didn't appear to notice her. His long, forceful strides propelled him toward the castle, while Naia had to jog to keep up. Seeing their approach, a group of Tanisars guarding the gates rushed forward. Darien stormed through their ranks without acknowledging them. He didn't slow until he reached the courtyard of the palace. Then he finally relented and looked at her.

"Do you have a plan?" he demanded, angling toward the steps.

"We'll use the Rothscard portal to transfer north to Orien's finger," she informed him, hurrying to keep up. "From there, we'll take the stairs into the warrens, just as we did before."

"What then?"

They entered the castle and crossed the foyer. "Then Kyel destroys the Well."

"And what about Renquist and Krane?"

Feeling a terrible, sinking ache, Naia halted in her tracks. Darien continued on a few steps before stopping to turn back. Choking on sorrow, Naia shrugged helplessly. "Quin never returned," she whispered. She had foreseen Quin's death in one variation of this future. They still had a chance of success. A chance that would have to be purchased with blood.

"Your plan isn't going to work," Darien grumbled. "Without the magic field, we're defenseless. But Renquist will still have the Hellpower."

Of course, he was right. She'd put so much faith in her vision, she hadn't thought of that.

"You're a darkmage," she said at last. "What do you suggest?"

Pacing slowly back and forth, Darien stared at the ground with a relentless scowl. "We need to distract them long enough for Kyel to reach the Well." Continuing to pace, he went silent for a long moment. Then he halted and said without looking at her, "I think I can manage that."

Naia felt a surge of hope. "How?"

Darien's expression collapsed into something that looked an awful lot like shame. He admitted, "Before you arrived, I agreed to help Renquist with a proposal."

"What proposal?" Naia asked warily.

He turned away. "I agreed to help him stabilize the magic field by absorbing enough power to release Xerys from the Netherworld. I was supposed to start with Kyel."

Naia stood speechless, staring at him in revulsion. "And you thought this was a good idea?" she finally managed. She felt throttled by disappointment. Like Kyel, she had allowed herself to hope Darien's soul might be salvageable. But his admission was a painful reminder of his nature. A reminder she dared not ignore.

He glowered at her. "At the time, yes. I thought it was a good idea, considering the alternatives."

"And have you changed your mind?" Naia pressed, angry now.

"I have. But Renquist doesn't know that. I'll tell him I killed Kyel and absorbed his gift. He will have no reason to doubt me, so he won't be guarding the Well. I'll keep his attention focused on me. That should give Kyel time to act."

Naia felt somewhat reassured. "Then this is the version I saw. We're on the right path with this plan."

"That's well and good." Darien's gaze drifted back down the hallway.

Just then, the magic field sprang taut, making the

world teeter. Naia's stomach took a downward plunge. Her gaze shot to Darien.

"It's now or never," she warned.

He nodded. "I'll meet you down by the Citadel. There's something I have to do first."

He turned and strode away. Naia stood watching him go, daring to hope.

Darien retrieved the small bronze cylinder from the desk and, pocketing it, left the steward's office. He walked up the stairs to the guestrooms and found Sayeed's door. He entered without knocking.

Startled, the officer bolted out of his chair. He crossed the floor in three great strides, catching Darien up in a crushing embrace.

Darien stiffened. But then he relented, taking what comfort he could from the gesture. After a long moment, Sayeed let him go, and stepping back, regarded him with an expression of boundless sympathy.

Darien ignored the man's unspoken question.

Reaching down, he removed the two sheathed blades that hung from their belt-hoops at his waist. He unbuckled his war belt, the one he'd inherited from his ancestor, Braden Reis. The belt came off with a clatter of steel rings, heavy with the combined weights of the implements it bore. Very deliberately, Darien wound the leather strap around both scabbards. Then he offered the weapons and belt to Sayeed.

The officer's face went slack. He accepted the gift with great hesitance, opening his mouth to say something. But then he closed it again. He stood staring down at the jewel-encrusted hilts with a look of stricken awe.

"I want you to have them," Darien said, gazing down at *Valdivora,* the legendary sword of Khoresh Kateem, and its matching dagger. "They belong to the clans. I won't be needing them any longer."

Sayeed looked up with a frozen expression.

Darien continued, "The people of Malikar now have a land to call their own. And a capital to rule it from. Sayeed son of Alborz, when I became Warden, I named you First Among Many. Now I name you Sultan of the Malikari Empire."

Reaching into the pocket of his cloak, he retrieved the small bronze cylinder that was no bigger than his index finger. He handed it to Sayeed, watching the man's face as he opened the end of the tube and removed the thin scroll within. Sayeed's skin went pale as his eyes scanned over the curling parchment. When he reached the bottom of the page, he rolled the scroll back up and replaced it in its container, letting his hand drop limply to his side.

"Brother…" He shook his head, visibly groping for words. "I do not have the ability to express my gratitude. But only the Prime Warden has the authority to elevate me to such a high position."

Darien gestured dismissively. "After I kill Renquist, I will be Prime Warden. For a short while, at least."

Sayeed stared at him blankly for another minute. Then, very formally, he went to his knees. He took the hem of Darien's cloak and brought it up to his face, pressing the fabric to his lips. Darien frowned down at him, feeling repulsed by the gesture.

"Stand," he commanded.

Sayeed rose from the floor with grace and stood before him, his gaze lowered to the ground—another unwanted sign of deference. Darien reached up and firmly lifted the man's chin until he was forced to look him in the eyes.

"Never lower your gaze, Sayeed. And never kneel before another man again." Darien brushed past him, moving toward the hallway. Opening the door, he paused and turned back.

"Thank you for being my brother," he said.

And left.

Chapter Thirty-Nine
The Waking Storm

Rothscard, The Rhen

Naia stood in the courtyard, ringed by soldiers and horses. Overhead, dark clouds tumbled toward the horizon. Eerie colors erupted within their depths, spreading quickly across the sky. Jagged forks of lightning speared the ground, followed by rolling thunder that rattled the earth. All around them, the entire magic field lurched and writhed as if in pain.

The horse she was holding crabstepped, looking ready to bolt. Naia ran a hand over the gelding's quivering neck, attempting to sooth it. It did little good. The beast could sense her anxiety.

The ring of soldiers parted to admit a lone man into the ragged pool of torchlight: Kyel Archer. Naia sighed in relief. She had been beginning to fret he wouldn't show at all. Now they only waited on Darien. Looking up at the tortured sky, Naia silently willed him to hurry. They hadn't much time.

Kyel drew up in front of her, a scowl of irritation on his face. The silver weapon at his side shimmered with a kaleidoscope of colors reflected from the cloud-light.

"How is he?" Kyel asked, just loud enough to be heard over the whistling wind.

"As good as can be expected."

"Is he coming?"

"Oh, yes." Naia sighed. "He wants revenge. And he needs closure. This is the only way he'll get either."

She thought of the look on Darien's face when he'd cursed the image of her goddess. She couldn't blame him for his anger, though he had directed his wrath at the wrong deity.

"I hope he finds what he seeks," he said softly.

The magic field spasmed violently. Kyel winced, and Naia felt the shock of it all the way to her core. The Zakai around them appeared thoroughly unaffected. She glanced back apprehensively at the palace steps.

The magic field quieted, but still trembled on the far edge of normal. The night was cooling around them, and there was still no sign of Darien.

She turned to Kyel. "What about you? What do you seek?"

He stared at the ground. After a long moment, he responded, "I just want this to be over."

"That's all? No more?"

Kyel smiled regretfully. "I have eleven tiers of power in me."

Naia blinked in shock, feeling intense sympathy. She whispered, "I'm so sorry, Kyel."

He shrugged. "I'm already coming undone. You have no idea how close I came to killing Darien today. No idea."

"And what if you had?"

Kyel looked away. He stood in silence as the wind rolled over him, whipping his cloak. She waited for him to reply. Eventually, she realized he wasn't going to.

She asked, "Do you think me evil, Kyel? Because I killed in your defense?"

He looked at her, his eyes studying her face as if seeking there for the answer to her question. "No. Not evil. But you weren't in the right, either." He sighed heavily. "There must be some middle ground. I just don't know where it is or what it would look like."

"I think I know," Naia said. "And it has nothing to do with oaths, and everything to do with what's inside. Our decisions define us. Not our chains."

The ring of soldiers parted again, this time admitting Darien into their midst. He stalked toward them with the dangerous grace of a predator, his body emanating a penumbra of dark power. His black cloak rippled behind him in the wind, and his long, black hair lashed his face. When he reached them, he drew to a halt and stood staring into the distance.

Kyel shot a meaningful glance at Naia, one that seemed to question the man's sanity. To Darien, he said, "I'm very sorry about your wife."

The darkmage cast him a leaden stare and said nothing in reply.

"Where's your sword?" Naia asked, noting the blade's conspicuous absence.

Darien shrugged. "It was time to give it up."

A soldier led his horse forward. Another took Naia's reins and held her gelding for her to mount. She twisted in the saddle, waiting for Darien and Kyel, then clucked her horse forward.

Darien sent his stallion trotting after Naia's mare. The horses were skittish as they made their way across the palace grounds, perhaps sensing the tension in the air.

Ringed by a squad of Zakai, they turned onto the canal road. As it turned out, the escort was unnecessary. It was past the curfew the occupying military had imposed throughout the city. Rothscard's streets were eerily empty. During the long ride to the Lion's Gate, Darien saw very few people about, mostly soldiers. Many of the city's inhabitants had already fled, leaving their possessions behind. Signs of their passage were strewn everywhere in the streets: scraps of garments and shoes, housewares and children's toys. Stray dogs and rats rifled through the scattered garbage, emboldened by the absence of humans.

The wind had died down, though the clouds still roiled overhead. Their party rode in silence out the gate and into the thick of the Malikari encampment. Campfires marched toward the northern horizon in perfect, geometric patterns. Beyond them, Darien knew, stretched a struggling train of refugees filing down from the mountains to the north. They would find new homes and new lives, even new customs. It would be a very different society than the one they had left behind. But they would live. Darien felt no small amount of gratitude for that.

They rode for a long time in silence, past the encampment's long rows of tents bordered by lines of pickets and earthworks. Overhead, the lights within the clouds strobed in time to the pulse of the magic field. An erratic pulse, like a failing heartbeat.

Darien was surprised when Naia brought her horse abreast of his. He glanced over at her, unsure of her purpose. She rode for a moment in silence, her body moving with the slow rhythm of her horse's swaying strides.

"Tell me about your wife," she said at last. "Did she make you happy?"

The question caught Darien off-guard. He glanced down, fumbling for the right words to express his feelings. "She did. I didn't expect her to. She was the singular, most beautiful thing in my life. I ought to have told her that."

"I'm sure she knew what you felt for her," Naia said after a moment.

He shrugged. It wasn't a response. More of an attempt to dismiss her concern.

"Darien."

The way she said his name made him glance at her sharply.

"In my visions…I've seen what happens to you." She was looking at him with vast amounts of sympathy.

Darien shrugged again, letting her words slide off him. He had no interest in his future.

Naia said, "The most important part of my training as a Harbinger had to be skipped because we simply didn't have the time. I never learned how much of what I see is safe to reveal …and how much is best held back."

"Then don't tell me anything," he snapped, more sharply than he intended. He already knew what she was going to say, and truthfully didn't care.

"I think you need to know," she pressed, reining her mount closer to his. "There are now only two possible versions of the future left to us. And in both versions, Renquist spills your blood in sacrifice. In one version, your death is the catalyst that brings Xerys fully into this world. In the other, it is our only chance to prevail against him.

"But Darien," she paused, fixing him with a penetrating stare. "I feel certain it will be up to you—and only you—to determine which future comes to pass. All of us—and all the world—will be at the mercy of your decision. You *must* make the right choice."

Darien rode in silence for a time, head bowed against the occasional gusts of wind. Eventually, he asked, "So today's my last day in this world?"

"I believe so," Naia answered, her expression compassionate.

Darien allowed himself a dark and fleeting grin. "Good."

She stared at him flatly. It was a long time before she looked away.

The sound of the horses' hooves became muffled as they transitioned from the packed dirt of the road onto the spongy loam of the prairie. His stallion fought the reins, wanting to stretch its neck down to graze. He had to keep urging it forward. Kyel trailed behind them with the rest of the Zakai, either in a sulk or a gloom—Darien couldn't tell which.

"What about you?" he asked Naia after a long interval of silence. "Have you foreseen your own death?"

"I have seen my own death countless times. That doesn't bother me in the least. It's the loss of others I've cared about that saddens me."

"Quin," Darien guessed. He knew Naia and Quin had spent time together at the Crescent. He hadn't realized their relationship had progressed into something more. "I'm sorry, Naia. The gods are brutal, aren't they?"

"Don't blame the gods, Darien. That's too easy. And it minimizes our own responsibility."

He couldn't deny the logic of her words. He pulled back on the reins, drawing his horse to a halt. He let Kyel pass him by, then kicked his stallion after him. He followed at the end of their small column the rest of the way, flanked by two Zakai.

They rode in silence for hours.

Eventually, they came to a long line of serrated hills that marched in darkness toward the foothills of the Craghorns. They pulled their horses up just outside the opening of a large gash cut into a jagged hill. A small stream trickled out, feeding a willow grove downslope. There, they dismounted and, unloading their packs, handed their horses over to the Zakai. At Darien's directive, their silent guard bowed from their horses' backs and rode away, trailing the spare mounts behind.

"The transfer portal is this way," Naia said, indicating a deep fissure in the cliffs ahead.

Darien studied the cut warily. He'd been through these same foothills several times and couldn't remember seeing it before. He asked, "How did you know this was here?"

"I used it when Quin and I left Titherry." Naia shouldered her pack and set off toward it.

The crevasse slanted uphill at a sharp angle, bordered on both sides by fractured granite. Small, sharp rocks that had crumbled from the eroded cliffs provided an unstable footpath. Naia mounted the slope gamely, leaning forward under the weight of her pack. She was wearing a pair of men's breeches and a good pair of serviceable boots. Darien was surprised he hadn't noticed that before. She'd planned ahead.

At the top of the cleft, they came to a water-carved bow in the cliff face. There, Naia waved her hand and muttered a soft string of words. Instantly, the granite wall dissolved to reveal an opening. Darien followed behind Kyel into a dimly lit chamber carved into the cliff itself, taking note of the cross-vaulted arch perched in the center of the room.

"For a thousand years, no one remembered this was here," he commented wonderingly, shaking his head.

Without pausing for the others, Darien strode forward into the portal arch. Immediately, the world around him shivered and disappeared in a brilliant gush of light.

Orien's Finger, The Rhen

Darien stumbled out from under the arch, finding himself in a different chamber entirely. Gazing upward, he took in the sight of a dark ceiling riddled with tiny pinpricks of light. He recognized the place. He had been there before, with Azár. It had been the first time he'd ever held her hand.

There was another flash, and both Naia and Kyel appeared at his side. Kyel gazed around, blinking, looking thoroughly disoriented.

This time, it was Darien's own whispered words that unlocked the doorway. He stepped out into a horseshoe-shaped canyon surrounded by charred cliffs that still bore the scars of his own insanity.

He strode out from the portal chamber then turned back to gaze up at the tall spire of Orien's Finger. It was from that high vantage he had summoned a fiery holocaust that had immolated Malikar's armies—men and women of the nation he would later come to defend. With a sigh, he turned his back on the monolith, too weary to confront its silent recrimination.

"This looks too familiar," Kyel grumbled.

Darien set off across the curved valley, outpacing the others by design. He remembered exactly where the entrance to the hidden stair was, beneath a spelled set of runic numerals. Fortunately, he knew the Word of Command that unlocked them. The numerals awakened, gleaming with an inner light. A dark opening appeared in the scorched rock beneath, revealing a set of dim stairs that climbed upward into darkness.

Darien looked back over his shoulder at the others. "Remember. Shield yourselves. We'll be walking into the vortex that surrounds Aerysius."

Naia dropped her pack on the ground, then knelt to rifle through it. She withdrew two short branches and a sealed earthen jug. Unstoppering the jug, she produced long, oil-soaked strips of cloth and began winding them around the ends of the shafts.

"This time, I thought to bring torches." She smiled up at him. The torch in her hand burst aflame.

Darien accepted the other torch with a feeling of appreciation. Too many times in his life, he had taken too many people for granted. Naia's name was at the top of his long list of regrets.

"You first," he said, moving behind her.

The Craghorns, The Rhen

The stairway was steep and brutal. Even with the torchlight, Darien found it hard to keep his footing. The pool of light they moved within extended only a short distance, enough to see the steps ahead, but not enough to see where they led. The stairs were broken intermittently by short landings, where their party halted to catch their breath. Over the edge was only a vast maw of emptiness. Darien had no idea what manner of death a fall would bring.

His mind wandered rampantly as he climbed. His thoughts turned to Azár, his beautiful wife. He tried picturing her in his mind. But, to his irritation, every image he summoned was out of focus, as though it had been years since he'd last looked upon her face. Perhaps it was just his mind's way of coping. If so, it was a cruel trick.

A ghastly roar shook the mountain beneath their feet, rattling the stair. Jagged fissures raced across their path, fracturing the steps. Kyel staggered and fell to his knees. He glanced up, eyes wide and startled.

"What was that?" he gasped.

Staring upward into darkness, Darien responded, "I think we're running out of time."

Chapter Forty
The Demon's Pawn

Aerysius, The Rhen

Naia tripped.

Darien reached out to catch her but was a fraction too slow. She hit the floor of the landing with a grunt and a splash. He reached down and helped her back to her feet, stabilizing her until she could find her balance.

"The floor is wet!" Naia exclaimed through chattering teeth.

Darien moved past her, his feet splashing through pools of water on the floor. The flame of his torch reflected in a distorted pattern off the surface of the water. Despite the light, he could see only a short distance ahead. But it was enough to make him feel certain they had finally come to the end of the stairs.

"We've reached the bottom of the warrens," he said.

"The Well's up three levels, isn't it?" Kyel asked. He mounted the last step and stopped beside Darien, his face a jagged dance of shadow in the flickering torchlight. At Darien's nod, he strode forward a few steps before turning back. "We have to keep moving. Can't you feel it?"

"I feel it," Darien growled.

He tossed his torch on the ground. The flame hissed out as it struck the water. In its place, he conjured a mist of magelight that trailed ahead of them, lighting their path with a silvery glow. Kyel stared at the magelight with a look of speculation on his face, then turned to glare back at Darien. He flung his own torch over the edge of the landing.

They followed Darien's magelight down a long tunnel. Naia trailed after him, while Kyel brought up the rear. Their feet splashed through water that pooled on the floor and wept like blood down the walls. The warrens were humid and cold, smelling sharply of loamy mildew. It wasn't long until they reached a series of adjoining chambers Darien remembered well.

They pressed on until they came to a winding stair that led precipitously upward.

Suddenly, the entire magic field wrenched and groaned, gasping like a dying thing. The field lines oscillated wildly, sending a sharp pain lancing through Darien's skull. He brought his arms up to cover his head, but the gesture did little good. It wasn't something that could be muffled or blocked out. It was more like something that was trapped within, clawing to escape.

Eventually it passed. But not without leaving Darien feeling shaken and fatigued.

He stopped for a moment, collecting himself, and then started forward again. The stairs ended in a long, mist-lit corridor that seemed to waver around them. Ahead, there was an intersection that looked familiar. Darien brought his hand up, signaling a halt. He groped along the slimy, spring-fed rock until he found a small button. He pushed it. The trap built into the wall gave a small click. Straightening, he turned and started forward—

—and jolted to a stop.

His magelight collapsed into darkness.

The air around him cooled to a glacial chill.

Utter blackness caved in on top of them, complete in its totality. Cold terror stabbed into Darien's gut like barbed crystals of ice. He didn't need to see to recognize the threat. Necrators. He could feel them there, lingering in the shadows. Waiting for their master's command.

From out of the chill emptiness, he heard the swishing sounds of footsteps. They paced slowly, relentlessly nearer, stopping just ahead. There was a long gap of silence. Then a malevolent voice pierced the darkness like a knife.

"I warned him not to trust you. He wouldn't listen to me. It took Alexa's death to convince him otherwise."

A sinister gleam of crimson magelight slithered toward them from out of the darkness. By its glow, Darien could make out the owner of the voice. Cyrus Krane strode forward to stand in front of him, gazing into Darien's face with a strange, mercurial expression that seemed stuck somewhere between contempt and regret. Krane's necrators glided smoothly forward, ringing them in like a shadow-woven cage.

Leaning closer, Krane asked in a taunting voice, "Has there ever been an oath you haven't broken?"

"No," Darien answered honestly.

Krane sneered. He turned away and, with a wave of his hand, beckoned them to follow. "Come. We haven't much time."

The ring of necrators constricted, herding them forward. Naia winced as one of the shadows reached out to touch her. Darien pulled her close against him, out of the demon's reach. With a hand on Naia's shoulder, he moved after Krane. The unnatural terror provoked by the necrators lessoned, slowly displaced by anger.

Chaperoned by their demonic guard, they had no choice but to follow the ancient darkmage up long flights of steps that wept running water in an unnatural cascade. As they neared the surface, the magic field wrenched atrociously, sending a shockwave through Darien that shook him all the way to his bones. He reached out and caught himself on the wall, his knees turning to jelly.

Krane glanced back at him and smirked.

Darien scowled his anger at Krane's back, but even that small token of resistance sapped his strength. A chill breeze fanned the magelight ahead. The crimson mist crept forward again only hesitantly. Ahead, the corridor ended at a steep flight of steps that angled through the roof of the tunnel. The stairs were illuminated by an awful green light that flickered and strobed, as if lit by a thousand jabs of lightning.

Another gust whipped Darien's hair and billowed his cloak. It brought with it a sharp, pungent odor, like the smell of clay after a heavy rain. He recognized the scent and knew the origin. The Gateway stood just above them, feeding the air with the Netherworld's taint.

They ascended through the roof of the warrens, buffeted by gusts of wind. All around them, the magic field shuddered and winced. It was growing fainter, Darien realized, its struggles weak and exhausted. The rock walls strobed with a hellish light. Rumbling crackles of thunder shook the entire mountain to its core.

Darien paused at the top of the stairs, reluctant to take the last step. The empty terraces of dead Aerysius still haunted his memories. He had no desire to look upon them, to be reminded of the majesty of the city that had been his home and heritage. It took every last drop of resolve he had left to will his feet forward after Krane.

They emerged into a ghastly world of buffeting winds and tormented skies. Darien narrowed his eyes against the raging gale. His gaze was drawn upward to a towering pillar of green light that pierced the heavens high above. Surging clouds circulated the spire like a vortex. The sight of it, the smell of it, made his stomach clench in dread. It was an abomination, a malevolent lance that pierced the sky and impaled the earth. At his side, Naia issued a sharp gasp of horror.

"This way," Krane commanded, impelling them forward.

They had no choice but to obey. The ancient darkmage led them across the remains of the Grand Square's once-elaborate tiles, now broken and scattered. Ahead through the shrieking wind, Darien could make out a glowing orb of light where the enormous Hall of the Watchers had once stood. Now, only the bared footprint remained, jagged shards of broken stone jutting upward from the ground. The rubble of the hall had been cleared away, leaving behind only a half-buried foundation.

The ring of necrators constricted again, now little more than an arm span away. Darien could no longer ignore the fear inspired by their influence. It was too encompassing, eating away at his courage and resolve until very little remained. Staggering against the rage of the wind, he stumbled forward into the circle of light.

And stopped, frozen between strides.

He stood on the margin of Aerysius' Circle of Convergence. Its power had been quenched the night the city had fallen.

Somehow, impossibly, the Circle had been restored.

Silver light shone from its rock-hewn lines, bright enough to chase back the night. A liquid radiance delineated the Circle's rays, which converged to form an enormous eight-pointed star. The Circle hummed eagerly, already awakened and primed. Darien stared at it in awe, rocked by the sheer impossibility of what he was seeing. There was only one man who had the skill and knowledge to repair such an evolved artifact of magic.

Darien's stomach sank like a lead weight. He raised his eyes to look across the Circle of Convergence. What he saw confirmed his fear. Restrained by bonds of light, Quinlan Reis knelt, hunched in defeat, on the broken ground at Renquist's feet. The Prime Warden stood over him, wielding Quin's own sword in his hand. The sight was chilling.

Darien knew exactly what it meant.

He had failed utterly.

No. It was worse than that. He'd allowed himself to be manipulated from the very beginning. By Renquist's design, he had betrayed every person he'd ever loved. Every value he held sacred. Every cause he'd ever championed, every commitment he'd ever made. And he had done it all willingly, deluded into thinking he was in command of his own destiny. He had been Renquist's puppet all along, and too arrogant to recognize it.

The weight of that realization was crushing. It nearly drove him to his knees.

Beneath him, the Circle of Convergence throbbed in time to his own heartbeat.

Slowly, inexorably, Zavier Renquist crossed the pulsating Circle, leading Quin by a leash woven of magic. He drew to a halt before Darien, gazing upon him with the saddened face of a father sorely disappointed in a son. There was no air of triumph about him, and there should have been. Darien wondered at that. Summoning his courage, he lifted his eyes to meet Renquist's gaze. It was like looking into the depths of the abyss. There was nothing remotely human in that stare.

Zavier Renquist informed him, "It is time for you to complete your purpose, your final duty to our Master. Thank you, Darien, for your sacrifice."

He lifted the sword. At first, Darien thought he was going to strike him down. But instead, Renquist handed the blade to Cyrus Krane. Then he stepped back out of the Circle's pulsating light.

Krane stared down at the hilt of the sword in his hand as if unsure what to do with it. A slow smile formed on his lips. He turned to Quin, raising the blade. "I've waited a thousand years to gut you with this."

Quin stared at him blandly. "That's an awfully long time. You must be fantastically incompetent."

The blade jerked upward, slicing a cut across Quin's cheek.

"No!" Naia sprang forward, dodging a necrator.

Renquist waved his hand casually. With a startled scream, Naia staggered and collapsed. Instantly, Quin was in motion, throwing himself at Cyrus Krane.

He was knocked to the ground as if smacked by a god-sized hammer. He rolled over and groaned, coming to rest against Naia.

Krane swung his attention to Kyel. With a jerk of his head, he summoned the Sentinel forward. "We need your talisman."

Impelled by the threat of the necrators, Kyel had no choice but to do as directed. Darien finally realized Renquist's strategy: he was gathering them together in one place. He intended to kill them all, then use Krane as a conduit to store their combined power. For Renquist's plan to work, Krane would have to be touching all three of them when they died.

The way Darien saw it, they had only one chance.

"Stop," he commanded. Reaching into the pocket of his cloak, he withdrew the Soulstone. He held it up in front of him, swaying by the band, the red stone glowing brilliantly.

"With this, you'll only need one of us," he informed Krane. "I'm holding your thirty-two tiers of power in my hand. Quin fixed it. Now it draws vitrus right out of the magic field itself."

Staring at the medallion, Krane's eyes brightened for a fleeting second. But then he shook his head. "Even if you are correct, you can't know its capacity."

"I do," Quin growled. "I'm the one who created it. It can draw any amount of vitrus you need."

Darien glanced at Naia, remembering her warning. About the decision he would have to make, the one choice that would determine the world's destiny. He felt it in his gut: that decision was upon him. The most important choice he would ever make.

He looked back at Krane. "I'll be your conduit. If I can spare even one of them, I'll do it gladly."

Krane glanced at Renquist, who shrugged noncommittally. Then he looked at the medallion in Darien's hand, his eyes cool and considering. He nodded slightly.

Darien brought the necklace up and wrapped the silver bands of the collar around his neck. He closed his eyes and opened the clasp.

"Darien, don't!" Naia screamed, her voice shrill with panic.

But there was no other choice to make.

This was the one chance they had.

He filled his mind with a singular thought: *Thirty-two.*

Then he let the clasp spring closed.

The world went brilliantly, atrociously white. Then there was silence, complete and perfect, soon broken by a high-pitched ringing in his ears. From somewhere very distant, Darien was vaguely aware of pain. But the pain wasn't part of him. The world had stopped. Time had stopped. The motion of the universe had frozen to a standstill.

Then, all at once, it all came crashing back at a harrowing speed.

Darien screamed as all the vast agony in the world slammed into him.

Chapter Forty-One
Born in Blood

Aerysius, The Rhen

Quin sprang to his feet and wrenched Naia off the ground, hauling her after him toward the stairs. But she jerked her arm away, twisting out of his grasp.

"Get Kyel!" she cried and ran back toward where Darien lay writhing and screaming in an inferno of raging power.

Quin growled in frustration and fear. He turned back, searching frantically for Kyel. He found him at last, pinned by three necrators against a toppled column. Quin gasped, recognizing the danger: if the shades touched Kyel, they'd lose the talisman and their last hope of success. Quin knew he'd never reach him in time.

So he flung himself at Cyrus Krane instead.

He took the darkmage by surprise, knocking him off his feet and jarring the sword from his hand. Quin rolled, snatching the weapon off the ground. He brought the blade around in a sweeping arc, slashing Krane's neck.

Blood sprayed, and the demon slumped to the ground. Quin whirled, looking desperately for Naia. He didn't see her. Across the Circle, Darien lay still, most likely dead. Quin hoped, for all their sakes, he was.

Overhead, the magic field trembled. It shuddered violently, quaking the mountainside. Quin was knocked off his feet. He lost his grip on *Zanikar*. The sword flew from his hand and tumbled, skittering across the ground, sliding to a halt at Renquist's feet.

Across the glowing Circle, Kyel sidled out of the ring of necrators. The shadowy forms remained frozen in place, obeying the last command of their master.

"Hurry!" Quin shouted, spurring Kyel faster. He turned and looked frantically for Naia, but she was nowhere. He had no choice—they were out of time. He turned and dashed for the stairs.

Kyel caught up to him, and together they raced for the opening to the warrens. The Sentinel held his gleaming talisman in his hand, using its radiance to light their way. Quin followed him down the stairs and through a series of winding passages.

"Stop!" Kyel shouted.

Quin halted in his tracks.

Kyel pressed a button on the wall then stepped back, heaving a sigh. "The Well's just around that corner. I need you to guard the door."

Quin looked at him skeptically. "What exactly do you expect me to do?"

"Whatever you *can* do!" Hefting the talisman, Kyel strode away down the corridor. Quin traipsed after him, casting a frantic glance back over his shoulder.

He found himself in a dim passage filled with an appalling green light. The light poured from a doorway just ahead, streaming out in ghastly rays, brilliant and blinding. Kyel didn't hesitate. Gripping his weapon, he strode forward into the light. Quin stopped, holding his hand up to shield his eyes from the glare.

The magic field winced painfully. And then it died.

"Damn," Quin muttered, knowing exactly what that meant.

Clenching his jaw in determination, he followed

Kyel through the opening.

And stopped, too paralyzed to move a step further.

The Well of Tears stood before them, a waist-high ring of granite stone. Around its circumference, sinister markings glowed malevolently. A violent column of energy erupted from the Well's bore, piercing the ceiling overhead. Quin knew where it went. It shot up through the rock, thrusting upward from the mountain to impale the sky.

Kyel stood staring at the crackling pillar of light, his cloak rippled by a wind of displaced air. He hesitated for a moment, unmoving. Then he raised the morning star over his head and brought it down with all his might, striking the Well's rim.

The weapon didn't impact. But the force of its magic did. Fragments of stone shot out, flying in all directions.

Somehow, the Well fought back.

Kyel was hurled backward, impacting with the wall behind him. Shaking his head as if dazed, he picked himself up off the ground. A thin stream of blood leaked from his nostrils. His face grimly resolute, he approached the Well and, raising the morning star over his head, brought it down with all the force in his body.

Naia knelt on the edge of the Circle of Convergence, constrained by bonds of light. But Zavier Renquist paid her no mind; his attention was focused on Darien.

Holding Quin's sword, Renquist strode across the Circle to where Darien lay on his back. Naia couldn't tell whether he was stunned or dead. Twenty-two tiers of power had slammed into him from the stone, on top of the ten he already had. Enough to kill him, she felt certain. She just didn't know how fast.

Renquist drew to a stop and lingered over Darien for a moment, gazing somberly down. Almost, Naia thought, the Prime Warden's face held an expression of regret. Gritting his teeth, he reversed his grip on *Zanikar's* hilt. Then he plunged the blade into Darien's chest.

As Naia looked on in horror, Darien's blood ran freely, spreading outward over the Circle of Convergence in an ever-enlarging pool.

Kyel howled in pain as jagged blocks of stone cracked and fell away from the Well's girth. Again, he was thrown back against the wall, this time sagging to his knees. Blood flowed in thick ropes from his nose, trickled from his ears. Like a drunken man, he hauled himself upright and lurched sideways. Then he lifted his weapon and threw himself at the Well again.

Stone rained. Kyel screamed. He brought the talisman up and slammed it down again and again, fracturing block after block. He reeled, stumbling backward, catching himself on the wall. He pushed himself off and staggered around the Well's circumference to attack the other side. Again and again, he brought the talisman down against the Well with all the strength he had, raining shards of granite all over the chamber.

Blood sprayed. Kyel dropped, moaning, to his knees. Thar'gon fell from his hands.

Quin looked on in horror. Without the magic field, there was nothing he could do. There was nothing to shield Kyel from the terrible force of the Well's backlash.

With a growl, Kyel grabbed the weapon off the ground and heaved himself back to his feet. He teetered and almost fell. Streams of blood rolled down his face, leaking like tears. The front of his shirt was saturated. The Well had been reduced to a pile of broken stone, only the blocks of its foundation yet remaining. But the portal was still full-open, the gush of energy still raging furiously upward from the bore.

Kyel heaved the weapon over his head and brought it down again with a furious shout. Chips of rock ricocheted off the walls, striking Quin in the face. Kyel screamed in agony, and Thar'gon flew from his hands. He wavered for a moment, off-balanced. Then he collapsed, falling forward toward the gaping bore of the Well of Tears.

"NO!" Quin shouted. He caught Kyel by the cloak and jerked him back. His momentum carried him to the floor, Kyel falling on top of him.

Quin rolled him over and sat up.

Kyel stared up at him with a loose, unfocused gaze, his face a glistening mask of blood. More blood ran from his nose in a viscous stream that drained down his cheeks.

Panicked, Quin glanced back at the ruin of the Well. There were still blocks remaining. Kyel needed to get up, needed to finish the job. Only he could wield the talisman.

Quin growled in desperation. He had to find a way to get Kyel back on his feet. Frantic, he grasped him by the shoulders, ready to try shaking him back to his senses. But then he stopped himself. It wouldn't do any good, he realized with a stab of desperation that felt like a gut punch.

Kyel wouldn't be getting up again.

Quin looked down at the glowing morning star that lay on the floor next to him. He glanced back at the Well. Then he looked down at Kyel. The Sentinel's lips were moving, struggling to form words Quin couldn't make out. He leaned closer, straining to hear.

"Take it," Kyel whispered in a gurgling breath. "Finish it."

Kyel's fingers groped for the silver talisman that lay just out of reach.

Drowning in uncertainty, Quin shook his head. "I can't. I can't lift it."

Kyel whispered, "You can if I'm dead."

Quin froze, gripped by cold revulsion as he realized what the Sentinel was asking. He shook his head in an attempt to deny him. But one glance back at the pillar of energy told him he didn't have a choice. He reached for his boot knife.

With a growl, Quin drove the knife as hard as he could between Kyel's ribs, burying it up to the hilt.

Kyel flinched. Then he blinked. And that was all.

Quin sagged back on his haunches, watching as waves of power gushed from Kyel's body in distorted waves, lost to the air. Quin threw his head back and screamed. Balling his fist, he smacked his hand against the ground in rage.

Across the room, the surge of energy yet surged from the Well's gaping bore.

Trembling, Quin reached for Thar'gon. But he stopped himself, suddenly mired in doubt. The talisman was designed to be wielded only by the Warden of Battlemages. And he wasn't a Battlemage.

But, then, Kyel hadn't been either.

With conviction, Quin closed his fingers around the weapon's haft and lifted the talisman from the floor. Immediately, warmth and solace flowed into him along with a newfound strength he'd never known. Filled with a blissful sense of euphoria, Quin rose from the ground.

He glanced back at Kyel and whispered his gratitude to the fallen Sentinel.

Then he raised the weapon over his head and, with all his might, brought the talisman smashing down.

The Well fought back.

Quin screamed.

The Gateway was still open. It shot upward into the sky, spearing the heavens.

Naia struggled against her bonds, trying desperately to escape the advancing demon. Across from her, sprawled in the center of the Circle of Convergence, Darien lay dying in an expanding pool of blood. It flowed into the gaps and crevices of the Circle's rays, outlining the marble tiles with heightened contrast. The blood continued to advance, as if seeking to saturate the entire Circle.

Zavier Renquist pushed Naia to her knees, positioning himself behind her. He drew the sword back over his shoulder, preparing to strike.

A thunderous clap of air sent him hurling backward. Naia looked up in terror, in hope, in desperation. She gasped in disbelief. Blood streaming down his face, Quin stalked toward her across the glowing Circle, the talisman Thar'gon glowing like a beacon in his hand.

"Run, Naia!"

Naia froze. Renquist was already pushing himself to his feet.

"Run!" Quin commanded again, raising the morning star.

He swung the weapon at Renquist, creating a concussive blast of air that knocked the Prime Warden back to the ground. Hefting the weapon, Quin advanced.

"No," Naia whispered, shaking her head. This was wrong. It was all terribly, terribly wrong.

"No, Quin!" she shrieked. *"Leave him! Help Darien!"*

Quin froze in the action of drawing the weapon back for another blow. He growled in frustration. Then he whirled and ran back across the Circle of Convergence.

He dropped to Darien's side and lay a hand on his

chest. He closed his eyes, gripping the talisman. The silver artifact glowed, swelling with a powerful brilliance.

Darien gasped. Then he opened his eyes.

Behind Naia, Renquist was moving. He rose to his feet, eyes menacing pools of shadow. He raised his hand and struck out at her with the Onslaught. Naia was lifted from the ground and hurled through the air.

Her body impacted with the rock, cutting short her scream.

"Naia!" Quin bellowed.

He bolted toward her but halted as Zavier Renquist stepped between them.

Spreading his arms, Renquist began to glow with the vile light of the Gateway. It was then that Quin saw it: a streaking ribbon of energy arcing from the pillar to Renquist, as though he were drawing power from it.

Hellpower.

Quin realized that ribbon of corrupt energy was the reason why the portal hadn't collapsed. Renquist was drinking in the Onslaught, sustaining the Gateway by keeping the Hellpower flowing through it.

With a great, thunderous growl, Zavier Renquist changed. Before Quin's eyes, he swelled to enormous size, his arms growing and spreading into heinous, bat-like wings. Quin cried out, scrambling away from the twisted beast. Its head seemed all teeth, its eyes infinite pools of darkness. The demon gave a shrill screech, spread its leathery wings, and launched into the air.

Quin struggled to help Darien gain his feet. Darien wavered, his eyes sliding shut. Overhead, the demon emitted a piercing shriek. Quin looked up. His mouth fell open, his eyes going wide.

"Give it to me," Darien whispered.

It took Quin a moment to realize what he meant. He pressed the morning star's haft into Darien's hand and squeezed his fingers closed around it. A bloom of silver radiance erupted from the talisman, overwhelming his vision. Quin whirled away, throwing his hands up to shield his eyes.

Recovering, he sprinted toward Naia. He ran off the Circle, falling down at her side and turning her over. She was unconscious. Blood ran from a wound over her eye, streaking her face. Without the magic field, he couldn't heal her. So he did the only thing he could do: he wrapped his arms around her and held her tight.

An explosive crackle of thunder rocked the mountain.

Quin looked back and squinted through the glare. Across the Circle, Darien was on his feet, surrounded by a sphere of dazzling light. Above him, the creature disgorged a stream of flame that gushed against Darien's brilliant shield, unable to penetrate. Darien danced back, raised his weapon, and swung it around in a great arc. A compressed wave of solid air slammed into the demon, knocking it from the sky and hurling it to the ground with a furious shriek.

The monster recovered quickly. It took to the air again then spun on wing, turning to retaliate. It opened its mouth and belched forth a roiling inferno of flames. Darien staggered, holding the talisman up defensively as a torrent of fire streamed over him. He fell to his knees, holding the glowing talisman over his head and straining with all his might to keep the shield of argent light in place.

The demon landed, spewing gouts of flame into the air. Its tail cracked into Darien, knocking him to the ground. He lost his grip on the morning star, and it flew away from him. He scrambled after it, snatching the talisman up and rolling onto his back just in time, as the demon landed on top of him. He used the weapon to bludgeon the monster's head, sending the creature cringing back in a showering spray of ink-dark blood. The demon flapped into the air with a cry of outrage, then banked sharply back toward the Circle, streaming fire in its wake.

The creature attacked, throwing itself against Darien's shield and sending him hurling backward. Overhead, the clouds thundered their fury. Bleeding and dazed, Darien fought his way back to his feet. But the argent brilliance of his weapon was dimming, his arms sagging to his sides.

The demon let out a hungering screech, then turned to attack. This time, it penetrated Darien's weakened defenses. The beast's mouth closed on his chest. Darien howled, flailing in the demon's grasp. Bringing the morning star up, he battered it against the monster's leathery hide.

The creature tossed him into the air, flinging him

across the tiles of the square.

Darien rolled to a stop at the edge of the cliff. He pushed himself up and stood, swaying, his back against the cliff's harrowing edge.

The demon took flight, circling upward over the terrace. It opened its jaws, baring a mouthful of chiseled teeth.

Fire gushed from the creature's mouth. Darien threw himself sideways in an attempt to dodge. He wasn't fast enough.

The blast of flames swept Darien off his feet, hurling him over the cliff's edge.

"NO!" Quin screamed.

Overhead, the skies strobed and rumbled their fury.

The demon alighted on the terrace and, noticing Quin, stalked forward. Quin set Naia on the ground and rose, stepping between her and the monster. The demon opened its mouth, smoke trailing from its nostrils. Its sides expanded as it filled its bellows with a great chestful of air.

Quin threw his hands up.

There was a violent gush of wind, the crackling sound of flapping wings.

The demon shrieked as it was snatched into the air by a pair of enormous talons. It writhed and twisted, squirming to break free, finally dislodging itself from the dark-scaled creature that veered upward into the sky.

Quin threw himself to the ground.

Overhead, a tremendous dragon unfurled wings large enough to dominate the sky. It banked gracefully, circling the turbulent pillar of light. Its obsidian scales looked blacker than the abyss against the awful glow of the Gateway.

Quin gawked up at the sky, shaking his head in mute denial, jaw slack in disbelief.

Darien.

The dragon tucked its wings and plunged into a steep dive. With a deafening roar, it opened its mouth and flooded the Circle with flames. The demon was thrown across the ground, rolling to a stop. It lay still for a moment, singed and smoldering.

The dragon alighted on the Circle with a graceful backstroking of wings, the wind of its landing whipping Quin's hair like a gale. The beast advanced, stalking forward, head lowered and nostrils flaring. Cowering before it, the demon scrambled back. There was a brilliant flash of light.

The demon was gone.

In its place reared another dragon, larger than the first, its scales a dark emerald green. It took fluidly to the air, the obsidian dragon vaulting after it.

The sky thundered as the two beasts collided overhead, a writhing tangle of wings and talons and gushing streaks of flame. Both creatures screamed their rage, their claws raking scales, serrated teeth shredding wings. The ferocity of their battle trembled the clouds and shook the very roots of the mountain. Their dark blood fell from the sky like rain.

The monsters broke apart. The emerald dragon beat the air furiously to gain height, while the other soared low, favoring an injured wing. It banked over the terrace and angled sharply downward toward the valley.

The green dragon roared, wingtips parting the clouds, then threw itself into a plummeting dive. Its talons outstretched, it scooped its enemy out of the sky, dashing the black dragon hard against the cliff face.

Rock fractured. Part of the cliffside gave way, raining stone down onto the valley floor. Recovering, the black dragon roared a challenge. It pushed off from the cliff with a powerful thrust of its hindquarters, slithering after its adversary.

The beasts crashed together and locked in the air, a mass of spewing flames and clashing wings. Together, the dragons grappled with claws and teeth. Twined together in a deadly knot, each strove to rip the throat out of the other. Locked in a death-spiral, the two creatures plummeted down the face of the mountain, ragged wings outstretched, helpless to break their fall.

Quin sprang toward the cliff's edge, halting just in time to witness the dragons break apart. The black dragon tumbled away, coming to a rolling stop on the ground. The emerald dragon slammed against a rock outcrop then dropped, broken and lifeless, to the valley floor.

Above, a horrendous grating noise filled the night. The mountains lurched as if convulsed.

The spear of light erupted violently. The pillar shivered and distorted, caving in on itself. The green spire roiled like a frothing geyser, collapsing into the mountainside. The clouds above it slammed together with a shocking fury that showered the night with jagged streaks of lightning.

Shaking, Quin pushed himself back from the cliff's edge and stumbled back to Naia's side. He dropped down next to her and pulled her into his arms, clutching her tight.

"It's over," he assured her, stroking his fingers through her hair.

Chapter Forty-Two
Damned

Glen Farquist, The Rhen

Darien hadn't expected to wake.

He had a feeling he'd been floating somewhere between full sleep and full wakefulness for quite some time, like a man drowning in the ocean, groping for the surface. He cracked open his eyes, blinking against a riotous glare of light that stung his vision. He was shivering. Shaking. He couldn't control it. The air was stale. Cold. He burned from within. Beyond the light, the world was an obscure haze, as though he were looking out a window through a pane of mottled glass.

Something wet touched his face. A rag. It made him shiver harder.

"Where…" he whispered. It was all he could do to get that one syllable past his throat.

"You're in Glen Farquist. You've been unconscious for ten days."

He licked his parched lips. His eyelids felt too heavy to hold open any longer. He closed his eyes and drifted back under.

———

The next time he surfaced, he felt a bit better. He opened his eyes. He was still shivering, just not as violently as before. There was movement. And a voice. He tried to focus.

"Naia…"

"I'm here," she said. She was holding his hand. "Quin's here, too."

The room was so cold. So bright. A raging fire burned inside him, greater than he could ever endure.

"Try to stay awake," she urged.

He couldn't. It was too hard. He was too tired.

———

He drifted for a long time, floating on a tide of muddled dreams. The next time he awoke, he felt stronger. The room wasn't so bright, the air not so cold and stale. He'd stopped shivering. But the fire within him still raged.

He fought to sit up.

"Careful. You are still very weak."

Hands caught him and helped him upright. Someone stuffed a pillow behind his back. Darien looked around, squinting, at last recognizing where he was. In the Temple of Death. In the same room they'd lent him two years before.

"Here." Naia draped a blanket over him, her face tight with concern.

"What happened?" he asked in a raspy voice.

She glanced back over her shoulder. Looking past her, Darien saw Quin lingering in the doorway. Holding his hat in his hands, he approached the bed and sat down in a chair beside Naia. He kept his eyes averted and didn't say a word.

"Kyel and Quin destroyed the Well of Tears," Naia informed him gently. "You killed Zavier Renquist. The portal collapsed."

The flood of relief Darien felt almost washed him away. He closed his eyes. "Where's Kyel?"

"I'm sorry, Darien. He didn't survive."

That hurt. It hurt deeper than he'd thought it would. Darien took a deep breath, feeling a knot tighten in his throat. Kyel had been more than just his acolyte. He'd been someone Darien respected and admired, the most honorable man he'd ever known.

Naia patted his hand. "You need food. I'll bring you some."

Darien shook his head. "I'm not hungry."

"You must eat." she insisted. "You need to get your strength back."

"For what?"

Darien saw in her face that Naia didn't have an answer to that question. Neither did he. He could feel all thirty-two tiers of power raging inside him, burning him up from within. He couldn't survive that kind of assault, and she knew it. He saw the pity written in her eyes, and even Quin couldn't look at him. They both knew as well as he did that there was no point.

Naia said softly, "There might be something we can do."

"No." Darien shook his head. "Whatever it is, I don't want it."

Naia squeezed his hand. In the consoling tones of a priestess, she said, "It is your choice, of course, how you wish to die. I do understand the predicament you're in. It's not enviable. But you do have options."

Darien looked up at her uncertainly.

"You can stay here," she told him. "The priests of Death would care for you the rest of your days. They would be honored to do so, for the great service you rendered their goddess. Or you can come with Quin and me. We are going to Rothscard to build a school for mages. Nothing like Aerysius. But we could certainly use your knowledge and experience, as long as you are able to provide it."

It was a worthwhile endeavor, and it made Darien glad to hear. But he knew he wouldn't be around long enough to make a difference. He shook his head.

Quin blew out a heavy sigh, then finally turned to face him. "What are you going to do?" he asked in a dismal tone.

Darien shrugged. "I'm damned," he said, stating the obvious. "I don't want to go back to the Netherworld, and I'm denied the Atrament. My only recourse is Oblivion."

Naia bowed her head. Softly, she whispered, "Perhaps we can help with that."

Her words filled Darien with hope. Oblivion wasn't as simple a choice as it had once been. He'd lost his link with Xerys, the only god he knew who would be willing to cast his soul to the winds.

He whispered, "Tell me how."

Naia glanced down, looking hesitant. "Do you remember when you travelled with me into the Catacombs? We were separated. You wandered into a chamber where you were greeted by your dead. There, you met the shade of your father. He told you that you didn't belong there."

Darien nodded. He remembered that encounter well. It was one of the most painful moments of his life.

"Your father was right." Naia sighed. "You *don't* belong there. That hall is a very sacred place to the goddess. Damned as you are, Isap would shred your soul if you stepped foot back in there. There would be nothing left of you. You would be unmade."

Darien sagged back into the pillows, feeling the tension drain from his body. He closed his eyes and took a deep breath, savoring an intense feeling of relief.

"Then that's perfect."

"Are you very certain, Darien?" she asked.

He nodded wearily. "Aye. More certain than I've ever been of anything."

Naia leaned forward and kissed him on the forehead. Then, with a glance at Quin, she rose from her chair. "Wait here. Rest for a while. I'll go make arrangements."

Feeling content, Darien lay back into his pillows and closed his eyes.

When he awoke again, he felt stronger. Better. Hopeful. The fire still blazed within, consuming a bit more of him every moment. Darien felt glad he wouldn't have to linger, waiting for that fire to consume him utterly. He opened his eyes to find that Naia had returned to his side.

"Are you ready?" she asked.

Darien nodded without speaking.

Naia and Quin helped him out of bed. The act of standing took every last bit of strength he possessed. Once they had him dressed, Darien sagged back down on the bed and sat there, cradling his head in his hands. The room seemed unstable, rocking gently. The sensation made him queasy. Inside his head, the fire raged hotter.

"Wait here. I'll be right back," Naia said and left the room. He didn't ask why.

Quin sat down beside him, looking wretched. He was absent his hat, which Darien thought strange. Squinting against the motion of the world, Darien frowned up at him.

He asked, "What will you do, Quin? At the end? Do you want to go back?"

Quin shook his head. "Things are different for me. I struck the last blow that destroyed the Well of Tears. For some reason I'll never fathom, the goddess has forgiven me."

Darien was glad for him. Despite his propensity for disaster, Quin's heart was true.

A motion drew his attention to the doorway. Naia entered the room, a sympathetic smile on her face. She carried a white bundle in her hands, holding it before her reverently.

"The priests had this made for you," she said, offering the parcel to Darien. "They want you to wear it."

Darien started to reach for it. But then, realizing what it was, his hand froze. It was a white cloak, folded so that the Silver Star faced upward, glittering in the candlelight. Feeling a sudden gush of shame, Darien withdrew his hand.

"I can't wear that."

Naia's smile didn't falter. "You can. And you will."

Despite his protestations, they helped him to his feet and draped the thick cloak over his shoulders. Naia adjusted the lay of the fabric down his back, smoothing out the folds. Straightening, she took a step back and nodded her approval. "You look respectable."

Darien felt patently uncomfortable, knowing that his touch soiled the honor of that cloak. Before he could object further, Naia took his hand and led him out the door, Quin following behind. It felt strange to walk. His legs were weak, spongy. He leaned heavily on Naia, her strength keeping him upright. Keeping him moving. They turned a corner into a wide hallway.

Darien halted midstride.

The entire corridor was lined with priests and priestesses wearing stoles of various colors. Seeing him, they dropped to their knees in unison, bowing forward in the traditional obeisance reserved only for a Prime Warden. Darien caught his breath, stunned by the gesture. He groped for words.

"Why are they doing this?" he finally managed to gasp. "I led an army against them."

Naia turned to fix him with a proud smile. "Because they owe you their lives, Darien. If Renquist had succeeded, then every last temple would have been destroyed and the priests put to death. You saved not only their lives, but all their work and all their heritage."

It was too much. He didn't deserve it. Couldn't accept it. "Tell them to stop," he whispered.

Naia's smile only deepened. "If I did, they wouldn't listen to me."

Taking his hand, she guided him forward.

Chapter Forty-Three
Last of the Light

Glen Farquist, The Rhen

A diffuse glow filtered down from the ceiling. In the warmth of that surreal haze, the shrine of the Goddess of the Eternal Requiem seemed rendered from a dream, as though seen through the fog of awakening.

Naia clutched Quin's arm, watching Darien move ahead of them, his gaze wandering over the satin walls of the shrine. Naia's own attention was drawn to an alcove in the far corner. There, a life-size statue of her goddess awaited, one marble hand extended as though beckoning them near.

Darien appeared to be obeying her silent gesture. He gazed up into the goddess' face as he approached, pausing only when he stood at the statue's base. There, he reached out and touched her tapering fingers, caressing her stone skin.

Shoulders sagging, he let his hand drop to his side. He stood forlorn at the goddess' feet, bowing his head as if offering a prayer.

Or offering up his soul.

Whichever it was, Naia couldn't know, but the sight of him made her heart ache.

Quin released her hand and strode forward, his heavy footfalls disrupting the tension of the shrine. Reaching Darien, he clutched him in a tight embrace and kissed his cheek. Then he let him go.

Quin turned and hastened from the shrine, departing without a glance back. Naia knew he wouldn't return. She understood. And she knew Darien understood also. His eyes followed after Quin, lingering on the doorway even after the man was gone.

Silence echoed.

Darien turned toward her. He still lingered at the feet of the goddess who had propelled his fate toward this end. And yet, he didn't appear to harbor resentment. Naia was grateful for that. Swallowing her feelings, she crossed the shrine toward him. She reached up and cupped his face in her hands.

"Are you ready?" she whispered.

Darien nodded. "I'm tired, Naia."

She took him by the hand. "Then come with me. I'll show you to a place where you can rest."

Gently, she guided him away from the statue's base. She led him across the shrine to a passage that opened into darkness. There, Naia paused and murmured a soft prayer. With a hesitant step, she crossed the threshold. For a moment, the world shivered, filling her with a sudden surge of vertigo. Then the darkness fell away and the floor steadied. The shadows parted to reveal a dim corridor lit by putrid green light.

Naia drew up, startled by the color. It took her a moment to realize its origin. Turning back, she took in the sight of the green aura that emanated from Darien's body, a ghastly symptom of his damnation. It had grown so much brighter than the last time she'd seen it. Looking at him, Naia felt her chest tighten. The aura was a dreadful reminder of the urgency of her task.

Darien gazed down at himself, studying the terrible light that rippled over him, his eyes darkened by shame. Naia felt a cold sense of resolve creep over her. She clutched Darien's hand and urged him forward, the awful glow of his aura illuminating their path.

The passage led to the doorway of a large

chamber that stood cloaked in silence and shadow. Naia stopped at the opening, dreading what awaited within. She closed her eyes, summoning the last of her courage. It took everything she had to turn and face him.

"I hope you find what you're looking for," she said.

Darien nodded, gazing into her eyes with a sad smile. "I'll be fine. This is what I want, Naia. I won't miss this world."

"But this world will miss you," she whispered.

She took him into her arms and held him close one last time. It hurt to let him go. She remained behind as Darien strode alone into the darkness of the chamber. He didn't turn to say goodbye.

She watched from the doorway as he crossed to the center of the wide hall, drawn as if by a summons only he could hear. He gazed upward into the shadows of the ceiling, his attention captivated by something high above. Following his gaze, Naia saw a wrought-iron chandelier that hung from the ceiling. Six orbs hovered above it, glowing with a rich golden light.

As Darien neared, the dim light of the hall wavered and began to fade, diminishing into darkness. There was a great gap of silence, as if time itself had paused and stood waiting. Then, subtly, the orbs began to rotate. They spun slowly at first, then faster, picking up speed, the glows within them swelling to brilliance.

A tremendous deluge of light gushed from the chandelier, a torrent of radiance that consumed Darien entirely. The light savaged him, battering at his corrupted aura as if warring with it for mastery. The brutality of the light was appalling to behold. It was ferocious, a radiant inferno that ravaged his skin like searing flames. It clawed at him, burning away the Netherworld's taint and replacing it with an argent brilliance that streamed outward in glimmering rays.

High above, the orbs slowed and began to dim, losing the violence of their fury, eventually giving way to darkness.

Below in the shadows, Darien remained, the light of his presence fading to a soft azure glow. He turned toward her.

Naia gasped. Darien stood in front of her, just as he had before. But his flesh was gone, seared away by the goddess' grace. What remained was a luminous memory of the man she had known, glowing softly with the miracle of redemption.

Darien's shade raised his hands before his face, gazing at them, through them, as if confused by their significance. Naia looked on, her heart quietly breaking as she watched his eyes widen and fill with wonder. He shot a glance her way, his expression full of amazed disbelief.

From out of the darkness, delicate shapes began to emerge. They crept silently forward, their pale glimmers closing in to surround him: dozens of fragile wights that shone with ethereal glows. Naia was filled with a terrified sense of awe, knowing that she gazed upon the dead of fallen Aerysius. All of the people Darien had ever known, had ever loved, had ever lost. There were so many faces Naia recognized, and so many she did not. Dozens. Perhaps hundreds. Their myriad glows saturated the hall.

The host surrounding Darien parted to admit a gentle shape that squeezed forward through the pressing crowd.

Naia gasped as she witnessed the joy on Azár's face as she swept forward into the arms of the husband who loved her.

More spirits emerged, filling the hall until their combined lights swelled into one all-consuming flame that defeated the shadows and then, eventually, diminished. Gradually, the host of wights drifted away, receding back into the walls from whence they came. One by one, their soft glows faded and winked out, until only Darien remained. He started after the others, but then paused. He turned back, fixing Naia with a look of heartfelt gratitude that lasted only a moment. Then he, too, was gone.

Naia stared after him with gladness in her heart.

The Last Sentinel of Aerysius had finally won his war.

Epilogue

A warm breeze sighed through the quiet of the morning, trailing leaves across the courtyard of Emmery Palace. Captured by a gust, the leaves tumbled along, carried upward and over the city walls. They lofted on an updraft, fluttering and spinning, before floating back down to scatter across the grasslands.

The wind swept briskly through the Malikari encampment, billowing the banners, flaring the cook fires, ruffling the horses' long manes. Gaining energy, the air sped over the plains, rippling the tall grasses, gusting past a long, winding column of refugees. The wind blew across the foothills, sweeping up the naked slopes of the Shadowspears.

The gusts howled and twisted, funneled through the ridges and canyons of the Pass of Lor-Gamorth, past the remains of two shattered strongholds that would soon be lost to memory. The wind raged across the black desert beyond, taking hold of a bank of flickering clouds and hurling them furiously at the horizon.

But then the impetus behind the wind lost its urgency.

At first, the change was subtle. The gusts faded to a breeze that slowly exhausted itself, dying peacefully somewhere in the dark hills above the desert. The tumbling cloudbank lost its inertia and slowed, coasting to a standstill. In the haunting stillness that followed, the vast entirety of the Black Lands seemed to pause in anticipation.

The black clouds lightened to gray, their soft edges brightening until they gleamed with a silvery glow. For long minutes, they held steady in defiance of the sun, as if determined to maintain their tyranny.

But they couldn't hold forever against the conquering dawn.

The skies opened, shedding brilliant rays that angled down to splatter the earth with sunlight.

In the east, dawn broke over the horizon, more welcome than any sunrise that had ever come before.

THE END

Darkstorm

PREQUEL

Alandan
Khazahar Steppe
Vintgar
Dhural Uplands
Caladorn
BRYN CALAZAR
Skara
Desert of Maridur
Cerulean Plains
AERYSIUS
Glen Farquist
Xerys' Pedestal
Auburn Dale
THE Rhen
Isle of Titherry
Southwark
THE Southern Continent
c. 1623 DCE

Prologue

Bryn Calazar, Caladorn
A thousand years ago…

"Braden Reis."

He didn't look up at the sound of his own name being spoken from the doorway. Instead, he swallowed, squeezing his eyes shut as he ran his tongue across his parched lips. The sound of his own breath was a turbulent noise in his ears. He forced himself to concentrate on that sound, focusing his mind on every sharp hiss of air he sucked into his chest.

The sound of approaching footsteps made him flinch. Try as he might, he couldn't stop his hands from trembling.

"On your feet."

Braden ignored the command, knowing there would be a penalty for his defiance. He squeezed his hands into fists in anticipation of the pain. For heartbeats, he waited. When nothing happened, he allowed himself to relax a bit.

The pain hit with force.

Molten-silver lightning raged like a firestorm through his mind. He threw his head back, clenching his teeth. Slumping to the floor, Braden convulsed as liquid energies seared through his body. Bile rose in his throat, choking him as he writhed on the floor.

The pain lessened only gradually, taking a long time to completely go away. He lay on his back on the cold stone, staring upward, spent and gasping.

A different voice, soft and repulsively familiar, addressed him from the doorway. "Think very carefully, Ambassador Reis. There are many kinds of deaths, some much worse than others."

He shuddered at the sound of that voice. It was despicably seductive, stroking like soft velvet down the length of his nerves. Braden kept his eyes squeezed closed, so loath was he to gaze upon that face.

He could feel her moving toward him across the cell. Her hands brushed his skin, a silken caress as she slid her arms around his torso. With gentle pressure she compelled him to his feet. He stood, swaying, naked from the waist up, arms chained behind his back. His breath still came in gasps.

"It doesn't have to be this way," she whispered gently in his ear as her soft fingertips stroked the skin of his back. "You can still choose to make a difference. Think of the lives you could save. It's the right thing to do."

His eyes shot open, glaring his contempt at her.

"Don't lecture me on morals, woman," he grated. "You have no idea what they are."

The smile that bloomed on her lovely face was only a dim reflection of the delight that filled her eyes. His response had pleased her. It sickened him, knowing that he had given her exactly what she'd wanted.

"I want you to die knowing that they chose me to inherit your legacy," she informed him with a grin. "One way or another, your gift will be put to the service of Xerys. With your power inside me, *I* will be the one destined for greatness. And you?" She looked at him sadly and scoffed with a shrug. "You'll just be dead."

Hearing her words, Braden Reis closed his eyes and bowed his head in acceptance of defeat. Never before in his life had he felt so utterly powerless.

The sound of her slippered footsteps moved away from him across the floor. Then hands were upon him, wrenching him forward. Braden allowed his guards to escort him out of the cell.

The despair that gripped him dulled his senses. It

was as though he moved through a dim and murky haze, the world around him distant and strangely muted. They ushered him up many flights of stairs toward the floor of the Lyceum. The dance of magelight that churned at their feet only served to confound his senses all the more.

Braden gazed ahead with bleary eyes at the woman who strode before him. She glided in a sway of blue silks, platinum curls spiraling to her waist. She moved with an easy grace, every motion poised, every step a deliberate, calculated seduction. Arden Hannah was just as alluring as she was vile. It was a powerful and frightening dichotomy. She gazed back at him and smiled, her wide eyes glistening in the magelight.

He dropped his stare back to the floor.

They reached the level of the Assembly. There, his guards wrenched back on Braden's arms, forcing him to a halt. The sound of a staff rapping thrice upon wood resounded throughout the hall. There was a pause. Then the knocks were answered in kind, echoing from the other side of the barred doorway.

The bars were thrown from the inside, the enormous double doors cast open, shuddering on their hinges with a throaty groan. Braden avoided Arden's eyes as his guards forced him forward. He could see very little, only shadowy silhouettes of people gathered above in the galleries. Within, the room was completely dark save for a single sphere of brilliant light in the center of the hall. It was toward that orb of light that he was made to walk.

Braden forced himself to hold his head up despite the chill fingers of dread that caressed his bare skin. Nervous sweat trickled down his brow. He couldn't help trembling as he stepped within that sphere of light. There he paused, hands bound behind him, completely blinded by the dazzling brilliance. That was the purpose of the light: to protect the anonymity of those gathered above in the galleries.

The doors slammed closed, sealing the chamber with a resounding *thud.* An awful, gaping silence struck the room. The silence lingered, long moments stretching on and on. Braden continued to stand, blinking against the glare, eyes groping desperately for the sight of just one face he could recognize. But he could make out nothing; the thick wall of light was dense and unyielding.

A deep and resonant voice addressed him:

"Braden Reis, you have been convicted, attainted, and condemned of high treason committed against the state of Caladorn and the Lyceum of Bryn Calazar. A sentence of death has been pronounced against you. May the gods have mercy on your soul."

Braden bowed his head under the sheer weight of the words. A paralyzing numbness overcame him. He stood there shaking, withered by the miserable knowledge that he had failed so utterly in his purpose.

Slithering ropes of energy twined around him, restraining him completely as they forced him roughly to his knees in the circle of light. He fought to draw breath, but succeeded only in producing a strangled wheeze.

The Prime Warden himself stepped forward into the wash of light to carry out his sentence. Panic seized Braden at the sight of the object displayed in Zavier Renquist's hands: a stone of many facets, lifeless, dull and black. It hung from the bands of a silver collar that shone like satin in the light.

The sight of the Soulstone was ghastly, terrifying.

Braden's eyes shot up, groping at Renquist's face. But in the gaze of his executioner, he found no trace of mercy.

Chapter One
Jumping at Shadows

Aerysius, The Rhen
Three weeks prior...

Rain pelted the dark streets of Aerysius as thunder rolled expansively across the cloud-choked night. Merris Bryar shivered as her feet splashed through growing rivulets in the street, hugging her black cloak tightly against her body. She was drenched, her toes almost numb in her wet slippers. It was a terrible storm, the worst yet of the season. There was really no good reason for anyone to be moving about the city streets on such a night.

Which was exactly why Merris stalked the man who walked ahead of her through the storm.

Of all the people in Aerysius, the person Merris followed had the least excuse to be skulking through the shadows of the city. Merris hung well back from him, relying on the cloak she wore to obscure her features in the darkness. Her quest was dangerous, but that did little to daunt her. Rather, the thrill of the risk she was taking urged her forward.

Merris was no stranger to the night. She knew perfectly well how to navigate the city streets unseen. Her father had been a cutpurse, her mother a sot and a swindler. Their combined examples had served Merris well in her youth. This was not the first time she had tracked a mark through the city streets under the cover of darkness.

It was just the first time she had done so since becoming an acolyte mage.

And back when Merris had forged a living on the streets, she would never, ever, have considered selecting Cyrus Krane himself, the Prime Warden of Aerysius, as her quarry.

Merris moved as silently as she could, keeping at least a block's distance between herself and Cyrus Krane. She kept to the shadows, moving low, using the pillars of balconies and the arches of doorways as concealment. The rattle of the downpour covered any noise her slippered feet might have possibly made. Merris smiled slightly. She knew exactly what she was doing; she was in her element.

She watched as Krane turned and crossed the cobbled street toward the opening of an alleyway. Tonight, the Prime Warden wore just the thick, black cloak of a common mage rather than the white cloak with the Silver Star that was the emblem of his office.

As Krane disappeared around the corner, Merris dashed forward. She didn't dare take the chance of losing him in the darkness. Ducking down behind a large bin, she wedged her body behind it and peered around the edge of a building. By the light of a street lamp, she could barely make out Krane's shadowy figure. The Prime Warden had stopped, glancing around as he reached for the handle of a door. He cracked the door open. Into that opening Cyrus Krane quietly slipped, pulling the door closed after him.

Merris pulled back behind the bin, pressing up against the cold stone wall. She sat hugging her knees against her chest, shivering, wondering what she should do. She bit her lip, considering. She knew better than to follow her quarry inside the building. The right thing would be to turn back and return to the Hall of the Watchers. But she had no proof to validate her suspicions. Without proof, she would be sorely punished, most likely expelled from

Aerysius for sure.

There really was no decision to be made. She rose from her hiding place behind the bin and slipped quietly into the alley. Here, the cobblestones ran with icy rainwater that flowed over the tops of her slippers. She splashed across the street through fast-moving rivulets, pausing beside the building Krane had disappeared into.

She stood there considering the door as the rain came down steadily, plastering her hair against her face. The wood was made of age-grayed pine, reinforced with iron bands. It looked like any other back-alley door in the heart of Aerysius.

Merris gripped the rusted metal handle. She started to pull it open but stopped herself, taking a deep breath and holding it in. Then, with gentle pressure, she pulled the door open just a fraction. Leaning forward, she glanced within then stole quietly inside.

She found herself in some type of storage cellar or undercroft. The room was very dim, lit only by two tapers that glowed from sconces on opposing walls. All around the room were stacked row upon row of wooden crates, the floor littered with straw. The only exit was another door at the far end.

The cellar appeared empty, but anyone could be hiding within those rows of crates. Merris strained to listen. All she could hear was the sound of pattering rain. She considered the door on the opposite wall. Krane must have gone through there ahead of her. Merris did not want to follow him into the guts of the building; she had pushed her luck already.

But she had come this far. Gathering her courage, she took a step forward into the cellar. Then another.

Merris reached the door and pressed an ear up against the wood, straining to listen. There were no sounds coming from the other side. Her hand trembled as she reached for the handle, depressing the latch. The door swung inward, revealing dark depths beyond.

The corridor ahead was lightless, narrow, and empty.

Merris moved forward into the shadows, pulling the door closed behind her. She lingered there for a moment, uncertain, trailing her hand along the cold wall. The stone was rough and uneven, carved by the harsh strokes of tools. This building was old, she surmised, possibly as old as Aerysius itself. So unlike the rest of the structures in the city, which had been seamlessly wrought by magecraft.

Merris stepped into the darkness, using her hands to grope along the walls to either side. She strained to hear the sound of footsteps that might be following. Her fingers traced the stone, searching for a doorway. Ten paces. Fifteen. Twenty. Still no sign of either door or passage leading off. The narrow corridor led straight ahead into the dark bowels of the ancient structure.

When her next footstep felt only air, Merris drew up short. She reached down ahead with her foot, finally encountering stone.

Stairs. Leading downward into blackness.

She shivered, knowing in her heart that she should turn around and go back. Merris forced herself to press forward anyway. It was imperative that she follow through with this plan, despite the risk.

She had discovered a letter in Cyrus Krane's office which professed his disappointment with her character and noted his intent to have Merris removed. Her entire existence in Aerysius depended on finding something she could use against him: some secret, some evidence of treachery. If she didn't, then the Prime Warden would proceed with her expulsion.

Merris was not about to let that happen; she couldn't go back to life on the streets. She had to find something, anything she could use as leverage. Some token, some bargaining chip that would persuade the Prime Warden to let her remain and pursue her studies.

He'd had no business testing her character in the first place. Krane had meddled where he didn't belong....

Merris followed the stairs cautiously as they curved around and down into darkness, arguing with herself at every step. She shouldn't be here—this was becoming too dangerous. She greatly feared what she would find at the bottom of those stairs. Or, worse, what would find her. In the darkness, Merris' imagination ran rampant. She wished for magelight or even a taper to light her path.

A loud, metallic *clank* resounded from far below.

Merris startled, flinching to a crouch. Another noise echoed up the stairwell. Trembling, she regained her feet and turned, ready to flee. From the depths below came the sound of voices.

Merris stopped in her tracks, straining to listen. The voices were distant, too indistinct to make out words. They did not seem to be coming any closer.

She bit her lip, trembling, glancing behind and ahead in desperate indecision. Her foot kept wanting to slide back up the stair behind her. She willed it forward instead. Courage nearly spent, Merris continued down the stairs in the direction of the voices.

She moved slowly, cautiously, creeping forward as silently as she could. There was another sharp, metallic groan. The sound of the voices ceased.

Then came another noise: that of approaching footsteps.

Merris turned and ran. Dizzy with fear, she was not at all careful about her retreat. She took the stairs two at a time, curving back upward in the direction she had come. She staggered and almost fell as she gained the top of the steps, catching herself on the rough stone of the passage. Then she was sprinting forward again on unstable legs down the corridor in the direction of the cellar.

She spilled through the cellar door, throwing it closed behind her and pulling it firmly shut. Wondrous light confronted her vision. She started toward the outer door, but brute stubbornness made her turn back.

Determined to glean some answers from this harrowing night, Merris dropped to her knees and squirmed herself into a corner between two stacks of wooden crates. She wriggled her body between them as far as she could, pressing herself tightly against them and pulling the cowl of her black cloak down to conceal her face. She fought for control over her panting breath, willing the speed of her heart to slow its frenzied pace.

Confident as she could be in her hiding spot, Merris waited as long moments dragged by. She strained to listen. Outside, there was the constant sound of the rain hitting the cobbled street. Inside the cellar, she could hear the faintest noise of soft, scurrying feet. Mice, or even rats, were about their business among the crates.

Abruptly, the cellar door creaked open.

Merris could see nothing; her eyes were veiled behind her cowl. The sound of voices only paces away made her flinch.

"All seems to be progressing well," echoed the familiar voice of Cyrus Krane. "Have Master Remzi keep working on the cipher. There's not much time; we have little more than a fortnight."

"All shall be made ready," responded the voice of another man. That voice Merris did not know. It was calmly authoritative, resonant and deep. Softly, Merris tried pulling back the lip of her cowl just enough to try to get a glimpse of the speaker. It was useless; the stack of crates in front of her blocked her view completely.

Merris realized that the air around her was starting to feel atrociously cold. The fear in her gut was like a tight knot that slowly writhed, working its way upward to choke her throat. She shivered, hugging her arms tightly about herself. The dread within her grew along with the cold, condensing into icy panic. The panic swelled, evolving gradually into terror.

Merris' eyes widened with realization: there was…something else…in the cellar. Something in there with them. Something *wrong.*

"I'm still working on the required payment," Krane's voice continued evenly, as if the Prime Warden himself sensed nothing at all out of sorts. "I have someone in mind, but nothing definitive as yet."

"Be certain there is no deviation from the covenant," the deep voice responded. "Failure is greatly misliked by our Master."

Merris chewed her lip on the edge of panic, the terrible feeling of dread becoming almost unbearable.

Movement stirred in front of her. Something streaked across her vision, coming to a rest on top of the stack of crates. A hand. A man's hand with thick fingers relaxed against the edge of the crate in front of her. A wide, silver band encircled the third finger. Merris shirked back away from the sight of that hand, her eyes welling with tears as she struggled to keep from crying out.

"There will be no failure," Krane's voice echoed, his tone full of dire promise.

Merris heard the sound of the outer door creaking open and then closing once again as the Prime Warden took his leave. The other man yet remained behind, his hand still resting on top of the crate.

The loss of Krane's familiar presence came almost as a blow to Merris. She resisted a powerful urge to bolt out of her hiding place and run for the door.

There was a rustle of fabric as the hand withdrew.

The sound of footsteps, walking away.

Then came the noise of the inner door shivering open and then closed.

Merris lingered, trembling violently, not daring yet to move. The awful fear within her refused to subside. Moments crept by, painfully slow. She strained to listen, hearing nothing. Even the scurrying of the rats had ceased.

Just then, a blur of dark motion streaked across the edge of her vision. The form of a man, all in black, faceless and in shadow.

———

Sephana Clemley rolled over in bed, groaning in her sleep. She had been tossing fitfully most of the night. The sound of the rain needling the panes of her leaded-glass window had been keeping her awake. Normally, she would have found the sound of the raindrops soothing. But there was something different about this night. Even the cadence of the rain seemed charged with tension.

Sephana's hand groped blindly across the mattress, exploring, but finding only empty space at her side. Her groggy mind fumbled toward the vague rudiments of a question. But before the thought could even halfway form, an urgent clatter jolted her sharply out of sleep.

Sephana jerked upright, throwing off her covers. Her eyes quickly scanned the dark interior of her bedchamber as another round of boisterous knocking echoed from the hallway.

Her eyes darted to the empty mattress beside her as she reached for the cloak she always kept hanging from the poster of her bed. She pulled the black wool cloak on over her shoulders, holding it closed as she fumbled her way out into the dark hallway of her suite.

"I'm coming," she growled at the door, which was fairly shuddering from the abuse it was taking. Sephana paused, warily contemplating the door. Then she threw back the bolt and swept it open, glaring her ire at the person on the other side.

Sephana blinked in shock at the wet, bedraggled woman who stood shivering on her threshold.

"*Merris?*" she gasped, peering intently into the girl's face.

Her young acolyte's skin was pale as chalk, her brown hair falling in wet disarray about her face. Her cloak dripped rainwater all over the freshly polished floor tiles. Merris' usual composure was thoroughly shattered. She stood trembling, furiously wringing her hands, her blue eyes haunted by fear.

"The Prime Warden is a traitor!" Merris exclaimed, sweeping past her into the room.

Sephana closed the door to her chambers firmly, considering her acolyte with a vexed expression. Merris was dripping rainwater onto her costly Tiborian rug, she noted with a flare of annoyance. Sephana reached a hand out and guided the girl back onto the tile, pulling her in almost conversationally.

"Be still," she commanded, placing a steadying hand on the younger woman's shoulder. "Come, now. First things first. Let's get you out of these wet clothes."

She led Merris to her bedchamber and threw open the door of her wardrobe. Then she left the girl alone to dress. Sephana wandered out into the sitting room and made her way toward the hearth, her eyes narrowing slightly. The gray andirons that held the logs began to darken, taking on a deep-red glow. Within seconds, the hearth was ablaze with a lively dance of flame.

Sephana busied herself by pouring a cup of wine from a wineskin that hung from a peg on the wall. Upon second thought, she poured another. Then she took a seat in one of the high-backed chairs before the fire, sipping her wine and observing the flames grow and spread throughout the kindling.

Reaching out with her mind, Sephana tasted the flow of the magic field that moved like a swift current through the heart of Aerysius. It felt like a soothing cadence in the back of her head, like the soft tempo of a waltz. She grasped ahold of it, taking in just a small fraction and savoring its comforting presence.

When Merris returned, Sephana noted with a flare of irritation that her acolyte had managed to select one of her own favorite gowns from the wardrobe, a yellow dress with a flowing skirt. It looked better on Merris, she noted.

"Wine?" Sephana offered, extending her hand toward the second cup she'd poured while forcing a smile to her face.

Merris approached slowly, timidly, at last

dropping into the chair across from Sephana. Her hand trembled slightly as she raised the wine to her lips. Sephana studied her acolyte's face as Merris closed her eyes and drank deeply from the cup. She looked back up with obvious reluctance.

Brushing back a lock of burnished-gold hair, Sephana invited her, "Now, why don't you tell me what's troubling you, dear."

Merris squeezed her eyes shut, her hand coming up to rub her temple. "I followed the Prime Warden tonight," she admitted in a tremulous voice that was little more than a whisper.

Sephana's mouth dropped open, her stomach twisting into knots. Merris was the Prime Warden's own personal secretary, a highly coveted position. It was an honor reserved only for acolytes of the most unblemished reputation. That Merris might have abused her position troubled Sephana deeply; she was the girl's own sworn mentor. Ultimately, Sephana herself was responsible for Merris' actions. Or crimes.

"I'm afraid I don't understand." Deceptively calm, Sephana's words were carefully phrased to hide her ire. "Could you please explain to me what, exactly, made you think that it would be wise to shadow *the Prime Warden of Aerysius*?"

"Please, hear me out," the young woman begged, a note of panic cracking her voice. "He's been meeting with strange people lately and receiving messages that are written in some sort of code. It's all very irregular! And every time I turn around he's—"

Sephana threw her hands up in exasperation. "We are on the brink of *war* with Caladorn, Merris! Surely a few encrypted communiqués are not too far out of the realm of possibility?"

"Not like this," Merris insisted, leaning forward in her chair. "Please, just listen! I've never seen runes like these before. And every time he receives one of these notes, the Prime Warden tells me he's feeling ill and has me cancel all of his appointments for the remainder of the day. Then he just leaves. Every time! I always thought he was just retiring to his chambers. But then this evening I actually caught him slipping out."

The sound of her door creaking open made Sephana startle. She sprang to her feet, nearly losing her grip on her cup of wine. Whirling, she brought her hand up to her chest in relief as she recognized the face of the man who entered. Closing her eyes, Sephana heaved a long sigh. Then she rounded on Merris, blaming the fool girl for inspiring such fear in the first place.

"Now you have me jumping at shadows," Sephana snapped as she rushed forward to greet their guest.

Braden Reis paused in the act of closing the door as his eyes slid slowly from Sephana to Merris.

"I wasn't aware that you were expecting company," he said in a questioning voice, eyebrows raised. He pushed the door the rest of the way closed behind him, latching it quietly. His eyes never left Merris.

"Ambassador Reis," Merris exclaimed, hastening to her feet with a look of dismay. "What are you doing here?"

Sephana paused in mid-stride, turning back to her wayward acolyte with a seething expression on her face. "I'm afraid I am going to have to trust you with one of my own secrets for a change."

A frown of consternation nettled Merris' brow before her eyes widened in sudden insight. "You're lovers," she gasped in realization. Her tone betrayed more than a trace of disapproval. "Master Sephana, I don't understand… How can you be sure he's not a spy for the Lyceum? I mean… *how could you?* He's the enemy!"

"I am *not* the enemy," Braden assured her quickly, taking a step forward and drawing himself up. "At least, not yet, anyway. And not if I can help it."

"He's been working night and day to forestall a war," Sephana argued defensively.

Without taking his eyes off Merris, Braden slipped an arm around Sephana. He was a tall man, muscular enough to fill out the indigo robes of the Lyceum better than most mages of his stature. He was the Ambassador of Bryn Calazar, and the blood of Caladorn was very obvious in his appearance. His skin was tanned olive, his hair thick and black. He had the characteristic full lips and almond eyes of a Northerner. A closely trimmed beard lent a chiseled look to his features.

Sephana could tell by the wary expression on his face that Braden was anything but comfortable with the situation. They had worked hard to keep their relationship a secret, especially from other members of the Assembly.

"Braden, you've met my acolyte, Merris Bryar," Sephana offered curtly.

Braden nodded stiffly. "Of course." His dark eyes were clouded with concern.

Sephana nodded. Braden met often with Prime Warden Krane in his capacity as the Lyceum's ambassador. More than once he had been forestalled by Merris while seeking an audience unannounced. He could be rather brazen when he wanted to be, one of the myriad qualities that Sephana found so compelling about him.

"Why don't you have a seat, Braden," Sephana sighed, stepping away from him. "Grab some wine for yourself. Merris has quite a story to share with us."

Braden's confusion was obvious as he complied, helping himself to the wineskin. When they were all gathered in the chairs before the hearth, Sephana leaned forward in her seat and directed Merris firmly:

"Now, start over from the beginning. This time, take your time and try to elaborate as much as you possibly can. Details, my dear. As many details as you can remember."

Merris swallowed. Then she obeyed. Sephana sat back and listened carefully as Merris unfolded her story for them, relaying all of the events she had experienced earlier that night. Sephana often found herself trading startled glances with Braden, who was listening attentively, broad shoulders tight with concern. By the end of Merris' account, Braden's look of concern had become eclipsed by an expression of incredulity. Sephana herself felt slightly nauseous. She regretted ever drinking the wine.

"And then I fled," Merris finished with a shrug. "I ran all the way back to the Hall. I didn't dare return to my cell; the man in black saw me. He might know who I am."

Sephana turned to Braden. He was no longer looking at Merris, just staring down into the embers of the hearth. His hand scratched absently at the dark whiskers on his chin.

"What do you make of all this?" she asked him.

Braden threw back his head and swallowed the remainder of the wine in his cup. He looked almost dumbfounded as he shrugged, shaking his head. In a voice colored by a slight Northern accent, he responded, "I'm not sure what I *can* make of it. It could be anything…or nothing." Narrowing his eyes, he turned to Merris. "This ring you saw. Can you describe it?"

Merris nodded eagerly. "It was a silver ring. It had a blue stone. I think it might have been lapis. There was a rune overlaid in gold, but I didn't recognize it."

"Do you think you could draw it?"

Merris nodded. "I think so."

Sephana stood and went to her writing desk, retrieving parchment, ink, and quill. She handed them over to Merris and then sat back down again. As her acolyte sketched, Sephana felt Braden's hand on hers, massaging her fingers with his thumb. The sensation was comforting, easing the tension within her. When Merris finished, she handed her sketch over to Braden.

He squinted down at the parchment, studying it for seconds. Sephana peered at it over his shoulder, her eyes narrowing.

Frowning in consternation, she wondered, "Do you recognize it?"

"No," he responded, still staring at the marks Merris had made. Slowly, he rotated the drawing first one direction then the other. He ran a hand through his tousled hair. Then he reached out, plucking the quill from Merris' hand. He added two strokes to what was already there, tracing the ink boldly down at a curving angle.

"Are you sure it didn't look more like this?" he prodded her, handing it back.

Merris stared for a moment at her altered sketch with a frown. At last, she nodded and looked back up at him with excitement in her eyes. "Yes—that's it!"

Braden's somber gaze latched on to Merris', capturing her stare with rigid intensity. "I cannot emphasize enough how important this is, Merris. Don't just guess. I need you to be certain."

Merris paled, her eyes ticking upward to Sephana and then back again to Braden. She licked her lips. "I'm certain," she whispered. "That's what I saw."

Sephana looked back and forth between her acolyte and her lover. Braden was a mage of the Order of Chancellors, well-schooled in the history and lore of his culture. He did not look pleased with Merris' confirmation.

"What is it?" Sephana pressed, gazing down at the completed rune.

"It's Venthic," Braden explained, handing the parchment over to her as he rose to his feet. He paced away toward the hearth. "An ancient dialect of my people. It's almost a dead language now, used only by a few of the original clans. This particular rune is *dacros*. It's used as a symbol for the cult of Xerys."

Sephana found herself scowling. Turning to the young woman beside her, she tried to form her words as carefully as she could. "Merris, I'm not trying to scare you, but I do have to ask you one question. This man in black you spoke of—are you certain that it *was* a man? Or is it possible that it was not a man at all?"

From his position by the hearth, Braden stiffened at the import of her words.

Merris bit her lip. "He…looked like a man made of shadow. He terrified me."

"A necrator!" Sephana gasped.

"What's a necrator?" Merris wondered, looking suddenly very frail.

Braden spun around, eyes wide with stark realization. He turned to Sephana. "We have to get her out of Aerysius. *Tonight.*"

Chapter Two
What Lies Beneath

Aerysius, The Rhen

Braden scrubbed his hands through his hair, fuming as he paced the length of the chamber. A dozen or more jumbled thoughts churned in his head, making it all but impossible to chase any single one of them. He glanced sideways at Merris, who sat across the room from him busily scribing away at the writing desk. She sat hunched over, thoroughly engrossed in her task.

Braden swirled the wine in his cup absently. His eyes darted to Sephana, who stood gazing out the window into the dark, rain-clad night. Her hand lingered beside her face, absently stroking a lock of her red-gold hair between her fingers. She had changed into a pale green dress with rose embroidery, the affair covered by her black Master's cloak with the Silver Star of Aerysius embroidered on the back.

"Merris, if you please…" Sephana groaned, eyes sparkling with irritation.

"Almost done," the girl muttered, not bothering to look up from her work.

Braden tossed his head back and downed a mouthful of wine.

"There," Merris announced, setting her quill down on the writing table with finality.

Braden crossed the room toward her in two large strides. He scooped the parchment she had been working on up in his hand and held it before his face. His eyes hastily scanned the lavish, flowing script of the message, lingering for a moment on the signature at the bottom, then read back over the whole affair one more time.

"Remarkable," he muttered at last. The letter could have been written by the Prime Warden's own hand. The signature was a perfect forgery. Braden had carried enough of Cyrus Krane's letters back to the Lyceum to know that Merris was a marvel.

"The Prime Warden is too busy to sign every slip of parchment that crosses his desk," the young woman explained. "I've been rendering his signature for months, but recently he's had me drafting most of his official documents, as well. He's scarcely ever in his office of late."

Braden scanned the letter one last time, just to be sure. "This will do," he assured her. He rolled the parchment up into a scroll. "We should try to copy his seal."

"There's no time," Sephana hissed from the window. A flash of lightning briefly illuminated her face, making her eyes gleam from the shadows. "She has to go *now*."

Braden nodded. He handed Merris back the scroll along with three other documents he had drafted earlier. "The first letter is for the guard on the Lyceum side of the portal," he explained to her hastily. "Without that introduction, you'll likely end up dead or in a cell. The second letter is for Grand Master Quinlan Reis, my brother. Ask for him the moment you arrive. The third letter is for Prime Warden Renquist. Use it only as a last resort. Give it to Quin, and he'll know when it's time to pass it along."

Merris' eyes darkened with uncertainty as she received the scrolls into her hand, glancing quickly at Sephana in concern. "I didn't realize that I'd be asked to commit treason."

"Oh, do shut up, Merris," Sephana growled irritably. "Just pass the damn letters. If Prime Warden Krane is compromised, then don't you suppose Renquist has a right to know before he commits his mages to a war?"

"Yes, I suppose…" Merris said, sounding altogether unconvinced. She shoved Braden's letters into the inside pocket of her cloak, retaining only the one scroll she had forged in her grasp.

"Then let's be about it." Braden set his empty cup down on the writing desk. He was already halfway to the door when Sephana's voice stopped him in his tracks.

"Wait."

He turned, brows raised in question.

"Go softly," she muttered. "You have no idea what they already suspect. I'll meet you by the fountain."

Braden acknowledged her only with a troubled nod.

He cracked the door open and peered out, glancing up and down the length of the hallway. It was empty; most of the Masters were asleep in their beds at this hour of the night. Beckoning to Merris, he strolled casually out of Sephana's suite toward a wide spiral stair.

It was a long way down to the Chamber of Egress in the lowest subbasement below the Hall of the Watchers. Braden trailed his hand along the wooden rail as he hurried down the stairs, Merris following behind in his wake. They made no attempt at conversation; the descent was taxing.

Braden loathed the way Aerysius was spread out so vertically; the spire of the Hall was just an acute exaggeration of the rest of the city. Aerysius was built into the granite face of a mountain precipice, its towers and arches sequestered high in the clouds. Its streets were often switchbacks, contorted with many bridges and sky ramps that spanned the mountainside.

Braden longed for the sprawling balconies of the Lyceum that overlooked the dark waters of the sea. He missed Caladorn, missed the expansive openness of the plains, its fragrant gardens and fertile orchards. In Bryn Calazar, his spirit had always felt free and unconfined, so unlike the imprisoning embrace of mountain-born Aerysius, where he had spent the past nine years of his life.

Wistfully, Braden mused that his time in Aerysius was most likely coming to an end.

His thoughts drifted to Sephana as his feet continued to carry him, spiraling, down the stairs. Both of them had known from the beginning that their affair was destined to be but a temporary thing. But that didn't mean that he had to be happy about leaving. His feelings for Sephana ran far deeper than he cared to admit.

Braden glanced back at Merris. She was nimbly following behind without complaint, having no trouble keeping up. She was strong and vigorous with youth. She would have need of both those qualities in the very near future. Life for a young woman in Caladorn was extremely different from anything she was used to. Merris had grown up sheltered by the coddling ways of the Rhen. In the Lyceum, she would be forced to explore facets of herself she had never yet encountered. Either she would survive and flourish or she would fail; either way, she would be empowered. Her destiny would be completely in her own hands.

The stairs finally ended in a wide hallway at a level below the ground floor. Here, Merris pulled up short, as if hesitant to move off the last marble step. Braden turned back to her, seeing how her eyes darted nervously up and down the corridor. He understood her agitation; that same hallway led to the Prime Warden's own solar. Placing a steadying hand on her shoulder, Braden guided her down the passage in the opposite direction.

"Keep your mind focused," he advised under his breath. "We're almost there."

Merris nodded, biting her lip. "Will it hurt?"

Braden shook his head. "No. There will be no pain. It's actually very quick."

Again, Merris nodded. Her brow was furrowed with doubt.

As they turned a corner, he leaned into her and whispered, "Remember my brother. Ask for him first, before anything else. The Lyceum is not Aerysius; you will be in need of his guidance. You don't want to be snatched up by just any passing mage. In fact, I'd advise you not to speak with anyone at all until you find Quin."

They rounded a corner and were confronted by a closed door ahead. Braden shoved it open, allowing Merris to pass through before he followed. "If you get into trouble, I mean real trouble, find the biggest man around and ask him to take you under his protection," Braden advised as he guided Merris toward the opening of another stair. "He'll have no choice but to defend you. It's a matter of *sharaq,* what we call honor. If you can get his word, any man will defend you to the death."

Braden continued to guide Merris forward with the pressure of his hand on her back. He could feel the tension in her shoulders; she was frightened. Perhaps even frightened enough to balk. They were well below the Hall of the Watchers, in the levels carved out of the mountain centuries before the Hall was ever built or even imagined. This room, as well as those beneath it, had been cut out of solid rock by the first mages who had come to dwell in this high place. It was ancient, almost as ancient as the mountain itself.

He took her hand, squeezing her fingers in reassurance, and led her down another flight of stairs. At the base of the steps, he guided her across a dim foyer to a large door, feeling Merris' hand trembling in his grasp.

"This is it," he told her gently. "You have nothing to fear. It's not as bad as you're imagining."

"I'm scared," she whispered.

Braden nodded, knowing she had every right to be. He placed a comforting hand on her arm. "This is as far as I go. I'm sorry, but I can't take the risk of being seen with you."

Merris nodded. Then, perhaps on impulse, she leaned forward and pressed a kiss against the whiskers of his cheek.

"Thank you, Ambassador," she said, smiling shyly. "I really do appreciate all you've done. And don't worry; I will deliver your letters. Is there anything else you'd like me to tell your brother for you?"

Braden shook his head with a scowl. "No. Absolutely nothing. And don't worry; you'll do just fine."

He drew himself up and offered her a formal bow. Then he turned and strode away.

Merris stared after him, her eyes following the sway of his indigo robes as he disappeared back up the stairs. She felt suddenly very alone. Clutching the scroll she had prepared, Merris pushed open the shod door and started forward. A frown troubled her features as her eyes took in the large room on the other side.

The Chamber of Egress was a wide, natural cavern. In the midst of the room were two concentric rings of freestanding arches. Stationed beside each individual arch was an armed guardsman. All of the sentries in the chamber wore the black uniform of Aerysius with the emblem of the Silver Star embroidered on their chests. But these guardsmen were altogether different from any Merris had ever seen. Every man within the Chamber of Egress was heavily armed and well armored. And the discipline of these men was absolute; each stood with spear and shield in hand, back straight in a stance of rigid attention beside the portal he warded. Not one face so much as swiveled in her direction at the sound of Merris' entrance.

Which do I choose? she wondered as she scanned the many arching doorways before her in consternation. Each portal must lead somewhere different in the Rhen. Perhaps some even led to lands far more distant. Some might lead nowhere at all.

Clutching the scroll against her chest, Merris wandered toward the nearest arch. The portal's sentry made no sign that he even took notice of her approach. Trembling, Merris moistened her lips before daring to address the stony figure.

"Is this the way to Bryn Calazar?" she inquired timidly.

At first, the portal's guardian showed no sign that he had heard her. But then his arm shifted slightly. The spear in his grip now pointed across the room in the direction of another archway. Merris allowed her gaze to follow the direction indicated by the spear, her eyes widening in understanding.

"Thank you," she whispered and, gathering her skirts, made her way across the chamber.

As she approached the second cross-vaulted arch, its guardian took one step forward, lowering his spear and barring her path.

Swallowing, Merris looked down at the scroll in her hand. She extended it toward the sentry, announcing, "By order of the Prime Warden, you are commanded to let me pass."

The guardsman appeared to take no notice of the scroll. Merris frowned, her eyes darting around the room in confusion. There was no one else to give the letter to. Completely befuddled by what she was supposed to do, Merris took a guess. She held the scroll up before her face and delicately unrolled it. She read the contents aloud in a firm voice that miraculously did not falter:

"'The acolyte Merris Bryar is granted passage to Bryn Calazar through the Portal of Egress.' The scroll is signed, 'Cyrus Krane, Prime Warden of Aerysius, Guardian of the Eightfold Light.'"

She turned the scroll around, showing the guardian her perfect forgery of Cyrus Krane's bold signature. There was a pause of five slow heartbeats. Then the man raised his spear and stepped back, returning to his station beside the arch. Merris rolled the scroll back up, unable to contain the sigh of relief that escaped her chest.

She nodded her gratitude at the guardsman as she tucked the scroll back under her arm. She took one last glance around the chamber then moved forward under the cross-vaulted arch, positioning herself right in the center between all four columns.

Merris closed her eyes and held her breath.

A sudden gush of light surrounded her as the world shifted and lurched beneath her feet.

The rain had stopped. For now, at least. In its place, a murky layer of fog had descended to enshroud Aerysius in a pall of gloom. The lights from the oil lamps that hedged the avenues formed diffuse, yellow orbs. The fog was almost palpably thick; it was impossible to make out even the outline of structures just across the street.

Sephana only knew she was standing beside Regent Font because of the trickling sound made by the water. The soft gurgling noise it produced was the only evidence that the fountain even existed at all.

She paced away and then retraced her steps back again slowly. Glancing over her shoulder, Sephana regarded the gray entrance to Torte Street. No one had come from that direction in minutes. Aerysius seemed like a city deserted; it was as though she was alone in the chill thickness of night. It was either very late or already very early. Even the bakers had not yet risen to prepare the morning dough.

A distant clop-clopping noise echoed from far away. A coach was moving through the cobbled streets somewhere high above on an upper terrace of the city. Sephana's eyes darted in the direction of the sound.

A hand on her shoulder made her flinch.

Sephana whirled, gasping, her heart leaping from her chest into her throat. She had to choke back a sigh of relief when her eyes took in Braden's familiar features. Her glare shot daggers at him; Sephana did not like being startled. She liked it even less when her nerves were already affray.

"What took you so long?" she hissed, swiping a golden curl back away from her face. Her eyes squinted as they raked sharply over him. He was dressed in the same deep-indigo robes he always wore, the Silver Star of the Lyceum embroidered on his breast. His expression was careworn, but otherwise he looked hale. Relieved, she collapsed against him.

Braden put an arm around her, rubbing her back and replying gently, "I came as quickly as I could."

Sephana pulled away enough to stare up into his face. "I was worried," she admitted, although it sounded more like an accusation.

He scowled, reaching up to rub the back of his neck. "I still am. You'll be the first person they come looking for once Merris turns up missing."

Sephana dismissed his statement with a wave of her hand. "Then let them come. I have a few questions myself for Prime Warden Krane. And I'm certain the Assembly would be very interested to hear his answers."

"I'm certain they would," Braden agreed stiffly. "But you're going to need evidence. You can't just accuse the Prime Warden of Aerysius of conspiring with cultists without evidence, Seph."

"Then let's go get some," she announced, already walking away from him, black cloak flapping in her wake. Behind her, she could hear him jogging to catch up. He grabbed her arm, pulling her to a stop.

"Wait."

She looked up into Braden's gentle eyes and was troubled by what she saw there. Worry was written in them, and something else, as well. Troubled shadows of fear darkened his expression.

Sephana couldn't think of another time when she had ever seen Braden Reis afraid. He was one of the bravest men she knew. He was no Battlemage; he had never wielded his power in the taking of a life.

His was a different kind of courage entirely. Braden was the lead negotiator between two rampantly hostile nations on the eve of war. That took more nerve than Sephana knew she could ever possess.

"I don't think this is a good idea," Braden muttered, running a hand through the dark strands of his hair. "Why don't you go back to the Hall and wait for me."

Sephana couldn't help the grin that sprang instantly to her lips. "It would seem, Ambassador Reis, that you don't know me well at all."

He sucked in a cheek and shook his head, thoroughly indifferent to her attempt at levity. "I'm going alone, Seph. It won't do us any good if we both get discovered. I want you to go back to the Hall and wait."

"No," Sephana insisted doggedly. Despite the cold logic of his argument, she was having none of it. "You need me, Braden. You may have knowledge that I lack, but the one thing I do know better than you is Aerysius itself. And if we do run into trouble down there, then you really *will* need me by your side." She was referring to the fact that she was trained to the Order of Querers, schooled in a far broader range of magical applications. As a Chancellor, Braden would lack many of Sephana's talents. He would be easy prey if he were assaulted; his specialties lay in other areas.

Braden just stared at her blandly for a long moment. Then he sighed. "'Easier to teach a fish to fly than a woman to use reason.'"

She glared at him in feigned outrage. "There *are* fish that can fly, you ignorant boor."

"Thank you for proving my point," he retorted gallantly. Before she could react, he gestured forward with his hand. "Lead the way, my dear. Before the sun comes up, if you please."

Sephana wanted to growl in frustration, but instead she found herself smirking as she followed his directive. She set out through the foggy night, Braden sauntering along at her side as if out for a leisurely stroll. He walked with one hand tucked behind his back, the other guiding her arm. At the corner of Torte and High Street, they passed by a lone constable standing in the murky yellow glow of an oil lamp.

Braden gave a curt nod in the man's direction. "Good evening, officer," he said by way of greeting.

At the sight of Sephana's black cloak, the constable tipped his hat in her direction. "Evenin', Great Lady."

Sephana dipped her chin regally, noting as she did that Braden's presence by her side had gone completely unremarked. The constable probably had no idea what his dark-blue robes even signified. They marked him as a full Master of the Lyceum, the equivalent of the ceremonial black robes worn by the mages of Aerysius. The only difference was the color and the position of the embroidered Silver Star. Braden wore his star over his heart, while Sephana wore hers on the back of her cloak. The sight of a mage of the Lyceum was not common on the streets of Aerysius, even in good times. The hostility that existed between Caladorn and the Rhen was not a recent inception, but rather the culmination of conflicting interests and ideologies that spanned millennia.

Sephana led Braden around a corner and onto a cobbled side street. Here, the fog was thickly nestled between buildings. She paused, eyes scanning through the mist until at last she found the landmark she was searching for. Walking toward it, Sephana bent down to examine a wooden bin near the entrance to an alleyway.

She placed a hand on the container's lid, using her other hand to grope into the empty space behind it. There was just enough room there, she figured, for someone slight of frame.

"This must be it," Braden whispered at her side, his breath warm against her neck.

Sephana nodded as she withdrew her hand. Straightening, she peered into the alley. So heavy was the fog that she could make out nothing. She started forward into the thick grayness, but Braden's firm grip on her arm stopped her short. The acrid look he shot her was enough to remind her of his peculiar Northern sentiments when it came to gender roles. Sephana knew better than to argue with him.

So she followed Braden into the mist. He walked cautiously forward, splashing through puddles that had gathered on the cobbled street. His shoulders were rigid with tension, fists balled at his sides. There was nothing soft or gentle about his face anymore; his lips were compressed in a straight line, his brow deeply furrowed.

Reaching the other side of the alley, he drew up and raised his hand to signal a halt. Slowing, he pulled open a door that Sephana hadn't even noticed was there. Her eyes widened as she watched him step inside, the door swinging closed behind him. She made no move to follow; she was fighting a strong impulse to run the other way. Instead she waited, nerves on edge, eyes intently focused on the handle of the door. After only moments, the door cracked open again, enough to admit Sephana through the opening.

The cellar she found herself within was exactly the way Merris had described, complete with rows of stacked crates and straw-covered floor. But it was to the door at the far end of the room that Sephana's eyes were immediately drawn as if compelled. That door now stood closed. For a moment, she forgot to breathe. She stood transfixed by the sight of it, completely rooted in place.

Braden moved forward, but Sephana could not force herself to do more than track his motion with her eyes. She watched as if from a distance as he rested his palm against the door's rough texture as if trying to get a feel for what might be lingering on the other side of it. For seconds, he just stood there, hand planted squarely in the center of the wood. His fingers went to fumble with the rusty knob. He set his shoulder against the door and gave a push. With a shudder, the tired oak gave way beneath the weight of his body.

Beyond, a dark passage was revealed.

Braden glanced back at Sephana with eyes that seemed more saddened than worried.

She forced herself to cross the cellar floor toward him. As she walked past him through the doorway, he caught her by the hand and stopped her short.

Gazing adamantly into her eyes, his voice grated in a near-whisper, "Last chance. There's really no sense in risking us both."

Sephana scowled. Then she kissed him.

Hand in hand, they entered the lightless corridor together, allowing the door to swing fully closed behind them. Sephana winced as darkness enveloped them. She stopped, unable to make out Braden's outline even though he stood only a pace away. She couldn't even see his hand in hers; the blackness of the passage was too complete.

This would never do, she decided. She opened her mind to the magic field, allowing its rhythmic cadence to soothe her. Awash in the soft comfort of the field, Sephana produced a glow of magelight at their feet.

The mist she summoned flowed out ahead of them, a churning blue incandescence that writhed across the floor, lighting their way. In its glow, Braden's image sprang into lurid focus. His features had the appearance of a portrait rendered by a novice's crude hand: all harsh strokes punctuated by bold contrasts.

He nodded his head in wary approval of her use of the magelight. Sephana could almost sense the conflict that seethed just below the patient expression on his face. The light could easily give away their presence, but it was necessary. Without it, they would only fumble blindly in the dark. He took her by the hand and together they made their way down the narrow passage, the dim tendrils of her magelight groping vaporously ahead.

The walls of the corridor were narrow, carved from the dark granite of the mountainside. The passage before them led straight ahead. Her magelight served only to illuminate the stone right beneath their feet; it did nothing to drive back the darkness either ahead or behind.

The corridor they travelled became a treacherous, narrow stair that angled sharply downward. There, they paused. Sephana closed her eyes, straining to listen into the black depths below. But there was nothing; only the distant sound of trickling water broke the gaping silence that surrounded them. They descended the stairs together, hand in hand, her magelight like roiling fog cascading down the steps.

"This is as far as Merris got," Braden whispered at her side.

Sephana nodded her agreement. She looked up and noticed a rock archway overhead. A symbol was carved into the keystone of the arch: the Silver Star. She could feel Braden's fingers tightening on her own.

The sound of dribbling water was louder now and seemed to be coming from all directions at once. It was as though the very walls of the mountain were weeping. It was much colder down here than it had been at the top of the stairs, a damp and penetrating chill.

The steps came to an end at a narrow, rock-encrusted passage.

Sephana let the magelight that guided their path fade quietly away. The corridor ahead was lit by fiery torches ensconced upon the walls. Sephana swallowed a nervous lump in her throat as she wondered who the torches were meant for.

"Let me go first," Braden whispered against her ear.

Numb, Sephana could only nod in response as Braden started down the passage ahead of her. The floor was sloped, leading them further down into the bedrock of the mountainside. All around them the flickering light of torches cast a lurid shadow play on the stone. The walls themselves were wet, oozing dark water that dribbled down their rough faces to gather in stagnant pools on the floor.

The passage made a sharp turn, doubling back upon itself, then angled steeply downward.

Braden stopped and pressed his body up against the wall. He peered around a corner ahead. He then pulled back, casting a troubled glance her way.

"There's an intersection just ahead," he whispered. "I thought I heard something. I can't be sure. Just be ready."

Sephana nodded her understanding. She felt for the pulse of the magic field and took ahold of it. She would keep it there, just at the edge of her mind, within easy reach.

Swallowing, Sephana followed Braden as he edged forward, rounding the corner. Ahead, she could make out the intersection he had spoken of. Another corridor crossed their path.

"Stop," Braden hissed sharply.

He ran his hand down the wall beside him, feeling its damp, rough texture. His fingers paused at a circular indentation in the rock. Frowning, he reached for the torch on the wall opposite and took it into his hand, holding the crackling flame up as he bent forward to examine the small depression in the wall.

"Smart," he muttered. "Whoever they are, these people certainly don't want any visitors."

Sephana frowned, wordlessly pressing him to elaborate. He indicated what looked like a small button recessed into the stone. She could make out some sort of glyph that had been carved into the center of it. The markings looked fresh and precisely wrought; it was a recent addition to the ancient wall.

"This symbol is *callebra*," Braden whispered, his fingers tracing over the small circle. "The hunter's horn. It's a trap; walking through the intersection probably sounds an alarm somewhere."

"How do you know?" Sephana demanded.

"I've seen its like before," he explained. "In the Lyceum. We use devices such as these to control access to certain critical areas."

"Interesting," Sephana muttered, gazing up into her lover's face in wordless speculation. "So why do we find one here beneath Aerysius?"

Braden shook his head with a troubled shrug. With his finger, he depressed the button on the wall. There was a small clicking noise.

Sephana jerked back, glancing at him sharply in alarm. "What was that?"

"I think I disarmed it," he informed her. "But let's hurry—for all I know, I might have just set the damned thing off."

He replaced the torch in its sconce and led her forward through the intersection ahead. Their feet splashed through pools of water. The walls themselves were weeping crusted minerals down their faces.

Suddenly, Braden's fingers clamped down hard on her hand. He stopped so fast that Sephana almost ran into the back of him. He turned and threw an arm across her chest, forcing her back against the wall.

Sephana gaped at the sight of a man crossing the corridor just ahead. He was there for only a second and then was gone again, disappearing through a passage on the right. The sound of his footsteps continued on, the noise slowly receding.

"This is getting too dangerous," Braden grumbled. "We need to turn back."

"No," Sephana insisted stubbornly. "We've come this far."

"It's a warren down here," he argued. "We could get lost. Or what if I miss one of those traps? It's no good, Seph. We need to go back and report what we've already found. Let the Assembly deal with these people."

But she was adamant. "Just a little further. You said so yourself: I need evidence, Braden. I'm not leaving here until I get some."

Braden glared at her hard for a long moment. In

the wavering glow of the torchlight, he looked subtly older, subtly more dangerous. Finally he released a beleaguered sigh, shaking his head.

"I'll give you five minutes," he allowed. "Then we leave."

Ahead, the corridor widened, the walls rounding, until it looked more like a natural cave than it did any human-carved passage. The torches here were spaced out at much greater intervals, creating long stretches of darkness between pools of wavering torchlight. The tunnel was icy and wet, the water beneath their feet stagnant and foul smelling.

Before them, the passage came to a sudden end.

They both drew up to stare at a wide doorway that was carved into the wall just ahead. There was no light at all beyond. The opening in the rock was little more than a gaping hole that led straight ahead into blackness.

Glancing at Braden, Sephana quickly produced another glow of magelight at their feet. To this he added his own, a golden-amber shade that mingled with Sephana's mist, became a churning fog of roiling colors. The magelight trailed ahead of them through the opening in the wall, illuminating a dark chamber just ahead.

Through the glowing fog they walked hand in hand, their shadows cast in tormented display upon the walls to either side.

As they stepped into the chamber, Braden pulled up short.

Sephana shivered, feeling as if a cold wash of water had been poured over her head, running down her neck and trickling down her back.

The room they entered was just as dark and wet as the rest of the warren of passageways they had traversed. On one side of the floor was a large slab of granite, waist-high. It had the look of a table or altar, hewn from a single slab of rock. A foul, dark liquid oozed down its sides, congealing on its surface.

To the other side of the chamber was a circular well made of staggered granite blocks.

It was toward the stone table that Braden moved first. He paused beside it, eyes contemplating the rough surface. Slowly, he extended his hand and dipped a finger into the dark liquid pooled on its surface. His finger came away coated with thick, coagulated blood.

Sephana recoiled with a gasp. The sheer amount of blood was appalling. It collected on the surface of the table, running in thick rivulets to the floor. She was standing in it. The blood had mixed with the water at her feet, rendering it impossible to tell how much there actually was.

She shook her head and whispered, "Animal sacrifice? To what purpose?"

"No."

Braden's voice was empty and hollow, completely drained of all emotion. The sound of it chilled her heart. He lifted something from the floor next to the slab of rock. It took Sephana a moment to recognize the object in his hand: a thick iron shackle anchored by a heavy chain to the side of the granite block.

"*Human*," she whispered.

She covered her mouth with her hand as Braden cast the chain away from him, repulsed. The iron shackle slapped hard against the slab with a sharp ring of metal.

Sephana flinched at the harsh sound. Braden hardly seemed to care if anyone heard. With a grimace of contempt, he wrenched himself back away from the altar, swinging around to face the well. He stalked across the floor toward it, kneeling down beside the granite ring. His hand rose, tracing over a series of vile-looking markings that were carved into the well's rim. They looked more like claw marks raked into the stone by some ghastly creature than any language Sephana knew.

She crept up beside him and observed Braden's study of the gruesome marks.

"I want to go," she insisted, voice quavering.

But he didn't act as though he even heard her. He was kneeling beside the well, inching his way slowly around its circumference, eyes and fingers exploring the hideous markings all around the rim.

At last, Braden finished his scrutiny of the well's texture and pushed himself to his feet. His gaze remained fixed on the sinister markings, stare narrowed in thought. He brought his hand up to his face, absently stroking his thumb over the whiskers on his chin. He rested his other hand on the well's cover, a thick slab of granite stone.

"This is a portal," he said finally. His voice was cold and dispassionate. Utterly flat. He didn't look up at her; his eyes remained captured by the cruel markings of the well's rim. "They're boring a gateway to the Netherworld. And they're using human sacrifice to finish the job."

Sephana could only stare vacantly ahead, mouth agape.

"They call it the Well of Tears," Braden continued impassively, indicating an inscription set into the very base of the well itself. "If they succeed—if this gateway is ever opened—then more than just Aerysius will be in danger. They will unleash the powers of Chaos across the world."

The sound of a loud, metallic *crash* rang out across the chamber. And then another noise: a distant thundering sound, low and throbbing, echoing up from the depths.

"They know we're here," Sephana gasped.

Chapter Three
The Enemy

Bryn Calazar, Caladorn

Merris spilled forward through the portal, body slapping hard against stone. Hands were suddenly upon her, lifting her up and dragging her forward over the ground. There was no point in struggling; the thick arms that encircled her chest felt like the hard trunks of oaks. She was heaved onto her feet, those strong arms stabilizing her enough to stand, swaying in their rigid embrace.

Merris raised her head enough to peer through the brown strands of her matted hair into the face of the man who held her upright. The sight of him made her flinch.

The man's face was grizzly and scarred, eyes dark and fiercely intense. They bored into her like twin wooden spears. She turned her face away, seeking refuge behind the length of her hair. The man reached up with callused fingers and cupped her cheek, forcefully directing her stare back up into his own.

The guard was tall, almost looming over her. He was dressed in leather breeches with two woven straps that crossed his bare chest. He carried two swords at his back, their hilts visible over his wide shoulders. He was dreadful to behold, all thick muscle and angry scars. His coarse black hair was drawn back into a top braid.

"By whose authority do you come here?" he growled, lips barely moving over clenched teeth. His eyes looked particularly murderous.

Merris glanced around frantically, realizing that she had arrived in another chamber full of arches. Only, the arches in this place were absent their posted sentries. Instead, there was only a pack of rough-looking men seated on rugs around a flaming brazier at the far end of the room. They didn't have the appearance of stationed guardsmen. They looked rather like a pack of brutes.

Merris swallowed hard before answering in a quavering voice, "Ambassador Braden Reis sent me with dispatches from Aerysius. Please, I need to deliver them to his brother, Grand Master Quinlan."

The guardsman's hand swept down and caught her left arm in his grasp. He brought it up before his face, grimacing at the sight of the chain-like markings that encircled her left wrist. He threw her arm back away from him as if affronted.

"Your very presence here breaks the treaty," he snarled. "Do the witches of Aerysius really desire war this desperately?"

"No!" Merris cried out, retreating away from him a step while reaching into the pocket of her cloak. She fished out the introduction Braden had written for her, wielding it like a scepter in her hand. "I mean, I wasn't *sent!* They don't even know I'm here—read this! It's from Ambassador Braden!"

Glaring at her sideways, the grizzly man snatched Braden's letter right out of her hand. Tearing through the wax seal, his face remained rigid as his eyes scanned over the scroll. Merris stood as if rooted in place, mouth open, her hand still extended before her.

The guardsman finally lowered the letter and wadded it up in his hand. His expression had changed somewhat; he appeared to be appraising her. His eyes roamed savagely over her body, lingering for a moment on her hips. At last he nodded slightly.

"Welcome to Bryn Calazar," he all but growled.

He took a lock of her rain-dampened hair into his hand, bringing it up before his face to consider. He fingered it for a moment before tossing the strands aside. "I am Cael Stinar of the Areshi Jenn. I do not know what your life was worth in the Rhen, but here you have very little status. If you ever have need of protection, I will let you share my bed."

Merris gasped, appalled by his base assessment of her worth. Red heat rose to her cheeks. But before she could say a word to deny him, he went on:

"You've lost the right to that cloak you wear. Remove it. Only then will I take you to the Grand Master."

Merris didn't want to, but she obeyed his command. She retrieved the last two scrolls Braden had given her from the inside pocket and then let the black cloak of Aerysius fall from her shoulders, spilling to the ground around her feet.

Cael picked the cloak up in his big hands, wadding it into a ball. Then he strode over to the wall and removed a torch from its brace. He held it up to Merris' cloak until the fabric caught, orange-red flames spreading quickly in his hand. He let the burning cloak fall to the stone floor, stepping back as the flames blossomed to engulf it.

"You are of Aerysius no longer," the guard pronounced ominously. His eyes went to the chain on her wrist.

Merris couldn't take her eyes from her burning cloak as a tear rolled softly down her cheek. She had worked very hard for many years for the right to wear it. She had been only an acolyte, had never had the chance to become a full Master. Now that dream would probably remain forever unfulfilled. Cael was right; she was no longer of Aerysius. At least she still bore the chain on her left wrist; she doubted they could take that from her.

"Come," he grated, striding away a few steps before turning to look back.

Merris didn't follow, instead lingering where she was, transfixed by the smoldering remains of her cloak. It took a great effort of will to turn away from it. She brought her watery gaze up to Cael's. She swallowed what seemed like the last bit of resolve that yet remained to her. Feeling completely numb in every way possible, Merris moved to follow after him.

He waited as she approached, watching her with brown eyes full of disdain. When she reached him, he put a hand on her back and pressed her forward toward a doorway. Her mind was swimming, mired in a dark haze. She could only stare ahead blearily as the guard propelled her forward.

"Lower your gaze," he commanded sternly. "Lower it! Did they teach you no manners in the Rhen?"

"I don't know your ways," she reminded him tartly, lowering her eyes to the ground.

He glared at her sideways but said nothing. They walked in silence as the guardsman led her down an exceptionally long and narrow corridor that descended gradually over a very long distance.

After minutes of walking, they finally arrived at a thick iron door. Cael used a key to unlock it, shoving the door open before them. They emerged onto a tiled walkway that led out of a hillside into a star-filled, cloudless night. Merris kept her gaze trained on the tiles under her feet, observing her surroundings only with her peripheral vision.

They had emerged onto a massive terrace. The stones that made up the wall beside her were lightly colored, having the texture of porous sandstone. Vines with pink flowers meandered across their surface. The air felt warm, summery. It had a thick and salty taste to it.

"You must learn your place if you wish to live," Cael informed her, striding ahead. "You project far too much confidence for a woman of your status. You'd better tame it before it tames you."

"What is my status?" Merris wondered sourly, keeping her eyes fixed on the ground just ahead of her feet.

"You are clanless, old, and very plain, so you have very little status," the burly man responded matter-of-factly.

"*Old*?" Merris gasped. "I'm only twenty-four! And I have never been considered plain."

"Plain," Cael repeated. "Your breasts are small, you have the hips of a boy, and your hair is the color of a mouse. Did your mother never teach you how to walk?"

Merris felt warmth flush her cheeks, surprised by her own reaction to his brutal assessment. "Well, I couldn't be all that plain," she snapped, positively seething. "After all, you offered to share your bed with me."

"Out of pity," he growled at her. "Eyes to the ground!"

Merris fumed in silence as he pressed her ahead down a flight of broad stairs. Somehow, she managed to keep her eyes lowered. Her barbarous companion frightened her just as much as he infuriated her. Not for the first time, she berated herself for having the temerity to follow the Prime Warden into that cellar. It had been such a rash thing to do. She wished to the gods she could take that decision back.

Chancing a glance up, she realized they had entered a wide courtyard. Merris lowered her eyes again quickly, but not before noticing the few people that were about. There were two women crossing the courtyard toward them, along with another man walking ahead. The women were robed in brightly colored dresses of a very fine material that rippled about them as they moved. Merris couldn't help but stare at the pair of them, one woman in orange and gold, the other in emerald green.

She whispered disdainfully under her breath, "*They're* not staring at the ground."

Beside her, Cael made a scoffing noise. "They are mages of the Lyceum. They are women of high status."

"And I'm an *acolyte* of *Aerysius*," Merris countered obstinately. "I am the Prime Warden's personal secretary!"

The brutish guardsman halted in mid-stride and turned to fix her with a toxic sneer. "I told you: you are no longer *of* Aerysius. Neither are you an apprentice of the Lyceum. You are a clanless, wedless, ignorant and boyish woman. You are nothing."

Merris whirled on him in defiance. "I am not *nothing*. I am strong in the potential, and I have all the knowledge and training I need to become a full Master; the only thing I lack is the Transference! I don't know about Caladorn, but back in the Rhen people like me are considered very rare. And I will *not* continue to go about staring at the ground!"

"May I inquire what's going on here?"

Merris whirled to find herself confronted by the self-same women she had just been comparing herself to. The one standing nearest her had lustrous ebony hair that fell down her back to her waist. A gown of bright-orange silk was elegantly draped over her statuesque figure.

The other woman was exceptionally tall and lithe, waves of cinnamon hair curling about her olive complexion. She was wearing a gossamer-fine gown of emerald green that glistened as it was stirred by a breeze. There was something about her; perhaps it was the confidence she projected or the sinuous way she moved. Maybe it was the child-like glint in her eyes. Or a combination of everything. Whichever it was, Merris had no doubt: this was the most beautiful woman she had ever seen in her life.

And probably the most dangerous.

"Great Lady," Cael addressed her, dropping immediately to his knees and bowing his head, eyes trained on the ground at her feet.

Merris moved to emulate him, falling quickly into her deepest curtsey and spreading wide the simple gown Sephana had lent her. No Master of Aerysius had ever demanded such a display of deference from her. In the Rhen, people did not bow or scrape before any mage; only the office of the Prime Warden demanded such a humbling display.

The chestnut-haired woman nodded slightly. Cael rose to his full height, drawing himself up and squaring his shoulders. But he still did not meet the woman's gaze, keeping his eyes respectfully lowered. Apparently, these women had more status than he did.

"Great Ladies," he addressed them, "I am escorting this courier to Grand Master Quinlan Reis."

"Are you, now?" the red-haired woman responded in a sultry voice, gaze flicking toward Merris. Those confident eyes wandered over her, taking in every feature about her from her shoes to the top of her head. They traveled down her arm, halting at the markings of the chain upon her wrist. Her gaze snapped instantly back to Merris' face, locking on her eyes.

"Your presence here is an act of war," the woman said almost conversationally in a thick, melodic accent. She took a step forward and reached up, stroking her fingers down the side of Merris' face. "Explain to me, my dear, how does an acolyte of Aerysius come to be a courier for the Lyceum?"

Merris swallowed, deeply disturbed by the feel of the woman's touch. "I beg your pardon, Great Lady," she responded, choosing her words as carefully as she could. "I was sent here by Ambassador Braden Reis with dispatches for his brother."

"Truly?" The raven-haired woman wandered forward, raising a pair of perfectly arched eyebrows. "And what prevented Ambassador Reis from simply bearing the dispatches himself?"

Merris felt beads of perspiration beginning to gather on her forehead. She didn't know what to say. She had taken Braden's warning to heart, and she certainly did not want to reveal the nature of her mission to these two vipers. She glanced nervously at the guardsman.

"Do you still have the letter I gave you?" she asked.

Cael frowned, but produced the crumpled-up parchment from a small leather pouch attached to his belt. He handed it across to the red-haired woman, avoiding her stare. The woman took the note into her delicate hand and smoothed it with a graceful motion of her fingers. Merris studied her as her eyes scanned over the letter, noting her posture, the careful way she centered her weight over one foot, which lent a gentle curve to her hipline. Every action she performed was a study in deliberate seduction.

Status, Merris thought. She understood now. She understood why the guardsman had considered her to be so plain. Compared to these women, she *was* plain.

"Welcome to the Lyceum, my dear." The chestnut-haired creature smiled, glancing up from the note. She was staring now at Merris with unabashed interest in her eyes. "It would seem that Grand Master Braden has found us a very talented turncoat."

Her smile broadened. "You will be tested, of course, to be certain that Braden's assessment of you is accurate. I'm quite positive that you will pass our testing. Tell me, my sweet, how did he ever convince you to abandon Aerysius? Is he really that good in bed?"

Merris' mouth dropped open in shock. She began to form a denial, but couldn't make the words move past her lips. She closed her mouth, completely uncertain of how to respond. *Status,* her mind echoed. Apparently a woman's status in Caladorn was tied to her perceived sensuality. If she was going to remain here, she figured, she had better learn how to emulate their ways.

Merris shrugged, assuming the most confident posture she could muster. "Braden has a few talents, I suppose. Not enough for my taste."

The red-haired woman's eyes sparkled with amusement. "My name is Sareen Qadir," she introduced herself as she smoothed a strand of Merris' hair back behind her ear. "You will soon be in need of a mentor, I think. I will be happy to help you fill in any gaps in your knowledge." She bent forward and pressed a soft kiss against Merris' cheek. She let her lips trail lightly over the girl's skin as she moved to whisper in her ear, "It would please me to teach you everything I know."

With that, she handed Braden's note back to Cael and strolled away, her raven-haired companion following with a mischievous glance back over her shoulder. Merris turned to gape at the guardsman in frank disbelief; she could barely make sense of the exchange that had just occurred.

Cael's gaze still lingered on the red-haired woman's back as she moved away across the courtyard. He explained softly, "Of all the women of the Lyceum, Sareen Qadir has the greatest status. It would be a great honor for you to be chosen as her apprentice."

Merris turned to eye him with a look of speculation. "Tell me, Guardsman Cael," she asked, "how do the men of Caladorn measure their status?"

Cael's gaze was still fixed on the sway of Sareen's hips as he responded, "We measure our worth by the number of enemies we have vanquished."

To Merris, that seemed rather impossible. After all, not every man of Cael's bizarre society could be a murderous warrior. "What about Braden Reis?" she wondered. "He seems to have a great deal of status, and yet I sincerely doubt he has ever killed a man."

Cael shrugged as he turned and strode away. "There are more ways to defeat an enemy than by putting him to the sword. Be assured, Ambassador Reis did not arrive at his position without conquering a great many foes. And if you truly doubt that he has ever killed a man, think again. Battlemages live and die by his command."

Merris frowned. "But he's a Chancellor," she protested, taking quick strides to catch up. "He's just a diplomat."

The guardsman shrugged. "Chancellors are masters of tactics, both at the negotiating table and in the command tent," he argued. "When talk fails and the fighting starts, it will be the Order of Chancellors that decides our strategy on the field of battle. It is they who command Caladorn's legions."

Merris frowned in consternation. "So Braden is some sort of... field commander?"

"You do not understand." Cael shook his head. "Braden Reis is Warden of the Order of Chancellors. If his negotiations in Aerysius fail, it will be he who leads Caladorn's armies into battle."

Merris' eyes slipped slowly to the side, her mouth going slack.

"Come."

Cael was already moving forward across the dark courtyard. Merris started after him. Resolved, she returned her gaze to the ground and followed Cael's long strides into a large building constructed of many layers of soaring balconies. The entrance was a wide arch that looked to be made of braided stone.

Within, Merris found herself in a large hall. The floor was covered by dozens of patterned rugs, the walls draped with silks and tapestries. Small trees grew out of colored pots spaced closely together around the room. The sound of trickling water was easy on the ears, coming from small fonts built into the walls themselves. It was a warm and intimate setting, casual and comforting. So unlike the stark and formal grandeur of Aerysius.

Cael led her out of the hall and into a series of corridors broken by outdoor patios, at last arriving at a door at the far end of a balcony. The guardsman rapped twice upon the door with his knuckles then shifted into a wide stance with both hands tucked behind his back.

As she waited, Merris wandered a few steps away to a stone balustrade and leaned over, looking out into the night. A warm breeze stirred her hair as she contemplated the view before her. There was only blackness below that stretched out to the far horizon, a wide expanse of star-filled sky overhead. A crescendoing noise came from below, like a gust of wind swelling to a gale and then gradually dissipating. Merris leaned further over, peering straight down the rocky cliff. Waves. She realized with a shiver that she was listening to the sound of the ocean.

She heard Cael rap upon the door again, much louder this time.

The door swung open. But it was not a man that greeted them.

It was a woman with kohl-darkened eyes, wearing only a blanket that was loosely draped around her naked body. Her hair was so matted that it must have been days since she had last combed it. Her dark eyes focused on them blearily as she swayed over her feet, clutching at the door for stability.

"What do you want?" she demanded in a slurred and thickly accented voice.

Merris shot a glance at Cael, but the burly guardsman seemed thoroughly unaffected. "We seek Grand Master Quinlan," he announced stiffly. "Go tell him he has company."

The girl glared at Cael, taking a staggering step backward. Then she turned and called over her shoulder, "You have visitors, my love."

"Tell them I'm out," came the reply from within.

The woman simply shrugged at Cael. "He's not home," she said, swinging the door shut.

The guardsman reached out and caught the door, thrusting it open again forcefully. The girl tottered backward into the room as Cael pushed his way past her, dragging Merris in after him.

Merris glanced around, taking in the interior that might once have been lavish, but was littered with trash and rotten food, piles of clothes and overturned furniture. A haze of white smoke filled the air. Merris coughed, waving the fumes away from her face as she gazed around in disgruntled astonishment.

Cael caught the girl by the arm and, ripping the blanket off her torso, firmly escorted her out of the residence. He slammed the door closed behind her then turned to confront the filthy quarters with a look of disdain.

He grabbed Merris by the hand and dragged her forward down a short hallway strewn with clothing and litter. Merris had to almost jog to keep up with him, stumbling over filth. He led her through a doorway created by a drape of beads that hung from floor to ceiling, pushing them back out of his way with a tinkling clatter.

Merris stopped in her tracks, appalled at the sight of a man who lay sprawled in the midst of a mass of blankets, cushions and assorted garbage. Only his lower body was covered by a careless drape of cloth, his torso completely exposed. He was exceptionally thin. His sallow skin seemed almost stretched over bone and protruding ribs. It was impossible to tell if his dark hair was either very wet or very oily. The unkempt growth of whiskers on his face was too short to be properly called a beard and yet far too long to be considered stubble. He was staring at the two of them with an expression of dazed befuddlement.

"Oh, my, isn't this awkward," the naked man announced in a thick and garbled voice. "My apologies, guardsman, but I do regret that I'm rather indisposed." His red and watery eyes glanced toward Merris. "Unless you come bearing gifts, of course. Always room for one more, I say. Hop on in, darling," he invited, patting the cushions beside him.

Cael drew himself up to his full height, face grimacing in disgust. "Grand Master Quinlan Reis, I present to you Merris Bryar, an acolyte of Aerysius. She is here at the bequest of your brother, Ambassador Braden."

Grand Master Quinlan stared at Cael and then stared at Merris, his forehead creased in obvious bewilderment. At last, he nodded. "So it is my intractable brother who seeks to indulge me with exotic pleasures from afar? Even better, I say. What are you waiting for, my dear? I am anxious to explore how the delicate flowers of the Rhen compare to those of Bryn Calazar." Then he paused, frowning uncertainly as his gaze struggled over the dim interior of the room.

"Where did you put my whore?"

Merris slammed the door shut behind her as she ran after the guardsman's burly form.

"Where are you going?" she demanded, shouting after him. "You can't just *leave* me with that man!"

Cael cast her a sidelong glare over his shoulder, not slowing his long, brisk strides. Without looking back, he assured her confidently, "Yes, I can."

Merris found herself having to jog to keep up. "Wait!" she shrieked, reaching out to catch his arm. "*Please*! Please, take me back!"

Thankfully, Cael stopped walking. He rounded on her with a thoroughly exasperated expression on his face. *"Take you back where?"*

He flung his arms open wide, indicating the broad expanse of city around them, a city that was altogether foreign to Merris in every conceivable way. He was right, of course. And he knew it. She had absolutely nowhere else to go and knew nothing of Bryn Calazar or its ways.

She didn't want to start crying, but she couldn't help herself. The tears gathering in her eyes managed to slip down her cheeks right in front of him. Angry, she scrubbed them away with the back of her hand. *"I just want to go home."*

Cael gazed at her with a flat expression, absolutely indifferent to the sight of her tears. "This *is* your home now," he insisted. "You'd better start getting used to it." Then he turned away.

"Stop!" Merris called after him. "Take me under your protection!"

Her words halted him mid-stride. The guardsman turned slowly back around, eyes squinting against the glare of the rising sun.

"What?" His mouth formed the word slowly, incredulously. Then he just stood looking at her, hands resting on the pair of baldrics crossed over his massive chest.

"I said take me under your protection!" Merris insisted.

Cael gave her one last, vindictive glare. Then he turned his head to the side and spat upon the ground.

"I can't do that," he said quietly.

Merris took a bold step toward him. "Why can't you?" she demanded. "Won't you lose honor if you don't?"

"I will lose some *sharaq,*" he agreed, appearing none too happy about it. "But Quinlan Reis has first claim on you."

He started forward again, this time in the opposite direction. She realized he was trudging back the way they had come, the twin scabbards slapping hard against his back with every stride.

"Then you're not going to help me?" Merris all but shrieked. She didn't even bother jogging after him. She just stood there, arms locked at her sides, hands balled into fists, looking thoroughly pitiful.

Cael growled back at her, "What does it look like I'm doing?"

"I don't know!"

"I *am* helping you," he snapped, not even bothering to look at her. "I'm going to take you back there. I'll help you start sobering him up. But that's as far as my obligation goes. After that, you're on your own."

Merris tilted the stoneware pitcher in her hand, allowing its contents to pour slowly over the unconscious man's head in a thin but merciless stream. The water splattered off the mage's face, thoroughly wetting the haphazard collection of bedding and scattered refuse that lay jumbled about him.

"Wake. Up."

Merris tilted the pitcher further, allowing the stream of water to continue relentlessly.

"Wake. Up."

Beneath her, the subject of her ministrations groaned and thrashed, almost squirming out from under the covers she had flung over him to cover his indecency. The mage brought his arm up and tried to protect his face from her watery assault, but to no avail. Merris followed his every motion with the pitcher.

Sputtering for air, Quinlan Reis raised his hand and gasped, "Enough! I surrender! No more water, I beg you! Unless it's in a cup. It seems that I've sweat out quite a thirst."

Merris glanced across at Cael, who was standing there watching her with stoic approval. He offered her the slightest nod. Merris righted the pitcher in her hand and lowered it, halting the flow of water.

She placed the pitcher on a table, picking up a cup of tea she had brewed using petrified herbs she'd found in the mage's unserviceable kitchen. She offered the cup to him.

"Drink this," she commanded without the slightest trace of compassion in her tone.

The wet and bedraggled mage propped himself up on an elbow as he accepted the offered cup. He stared blearily into her eyes, a flustered expression on his face. He raised the tea to his lips and took a sip.

Immediately he winced, grimacing as if in pain, and waved the tea away from him. "If Xerys himself ever pissed into a cup, it would hardly taste as noxious a brew."

"Drink it," Merris insisted, handing the cup back to him. "I need you sober."

He shook his head, setting the tea firmly down. "I've managed to successfully refrain from sobriety for the past nine years," he explained in a lecturing tone. "Doesn't agree with my constitution, you see. If temperance is truly what you value, then I'm afraid you've got the wrong mage."

The smell of his breath was repugnant. Merris blinked, turning her face away with a scowl. "It had better start agreeing with your constitution," she warned him sincerely. "I need your mind sound."

The man wriggled up into a reclining position on a stack of pillows. From somewhere in the bedding he produced a folded handkerchief and used it to dab at the water beading on his brow. He gazed up at her for a moment with reddened eyes before inquiring, "And whom, exactly, am I addressing? I regret that our previous introduction seems to have slipped my mind."

She drew herself up before him formally. "My name is Merris Bryar, acolyte of Aerysius," she said as she offered him the slightest curtsey. "Former acolyte, that is. At your service."

Quinlan Reis blinked. "*Former* acolyte of Aerysius?" he pressed, cocking his head to the side. "How interesting. The plot thickens relentlessly."

Merris ignored him and continued, raising a scroll in her hand. "I have a letter here for you from your brother, Ambassador Braden—"

He frowned at her as if disappointed. "You could have just delivered it and spared me the intrigue. By all means, hand it over, dear." He extended his hand toward it.

Merris snatched the scroll back out of his reach. "Not so fast. Swear you'll take me under your protection."

The look offered her by Quinlan Reis was one of profound skepticism. "And why, exactly, would I want to do that?"

Merris allowed herself the smug rudiments of a smile. "Because if you don't, I'll torch this letter right here in front of you. Then I'll march into Prime Warden Renquist's office and offer him proof that your brother, Braden Reis, is a traitor to Caladorn."

The mage sat straight up with a frown as his saucy countenance faltered. "What evidence do you have against my brother?" His words were suddenly, threateningly, direct.

Merris remained undaunted. She continued confidently, "I can personally bear witness that Ambassador Braden Reis is the secret lover of Master

Sephana Clemley, First Minister of the Assembly of the Hall."

The mage raised his eyebrows as the implications of her words slowly penetrated his liquor-induced fog. He sucked in a mouthful of air, allowing his cheeks to expand, before blowing it back out again with an exasperated sigh. He sank back against his pillows, eyes wandering sightlessly upward.

Staring up at the ceiling, he muttered quietly, "Well, isn't that just a honey of a pickle."

Merris nodded her agreement, feeling confident in her victory.

"Such news would hardly go over well with the Lyceum, I'm afraid," he continued without looking at her. "If this news is truly as factual as you say it is."

"Oh, it's factual, all right," Merris assured him. "Now swear."

His eyes squinted in her direction with obvious confusion. "Swear?"

"Swear you'll take me under your protection," she reminded him, leaning forward with arms crossed, her posture overbearing.

The mage appeared to be considering. Frowning, he wondered, "And what, exactly, do I gain from this arrangement?"

Merris chortled. "Well, I'm certainly not going to sleep with you, if that's what you're asking!" She flung her hands out in exasperation.

The man just shrugged. "We don't have to sleep, darling. Sex is all I really had in mind."

Merris' mouth dropped open. She glanced helplessly across the room to Cael, shaking her head in astonishment. "This is impossible," she confessed to the guardsman, eyes imploring.

Cael contemplated her for a long moment, face utterly impassive. Then he trudged around the bed toward her. Without a word he reached up and plucked the scroll she was holding out of her hand and offered it across to Quinlan Reis. Before she could stop him, the mage snatched it up with a look of affronted gratitude.

"What are you doing?" Merris gasped at Cael, appalled.

When he glared her into silence, all she could do was stand there and helplessly watch as the mage's eyes scanned the letter written to him by his brother. He lay there for minutes, eyes tracing back and forth across the scroll as he read, then reread, the words it contained. Merris realized with a sinking feeling that she had no idea what the letter even said.

The mage lowered the scroll, allowing it to curl back up as he set the parchment down at his side. His eyes wandered up once again in grim contemplation of the ceiling. "Yes, indeed. A honey of a pickle," he sighed. "What time is it, love?"

"Sunrise," Merris heard herself responding automatically, the will to argue with him evaporated.

"You'd better give me that other letter, then." He didn't look at her as he stated the request. Instead, his attention remained focused on the roof above his bed, eyes vacant in thought.

Merris didn't move. She clutched the last letter Braden had given her protectively against her chest.

Quinlan Reis grimaced. "Oh, do calm down," he insisted. "Of course I will extend my protection to you. For whatever it is worth—which is not much, I assure you."

"Good," Cael announced, promptly turning away from his position beside Merris. "Then I guess I'm not needed anymore." Without another word, the guardsman made his way briskly toward the door.

"You're right," Quinlan Reis agreed to Cael's retreating back. "You're not."

His eyes narrowed slightly.

The guardsman faltered in mid-stride. His hands came up, flailing for a second in the air. Then he slumped quietly forward.

Merris gaped in shock even as she bolted toward him. She reached Cael before he made it all the way to the ground, but it was already too late. As she caught his head in her hands, she found his mouth hanging slack, eyes wide open and staring up at her. The skin of his face was completely devoid of color.

"You *killed* him!" she accused as she turned to stare in shock at the man still reclined upon the cushions.

"Oh, dear. Why, I suppose I did," Quin admitted in a voice suffused with exaggerated dismay. "How unseemly of me."

"Why?" Merris demanded, her expression utterly bewildered.

Before her disbelieving eyes the mage rose naked from his bed and stalked forward to kneel in front of her on the other side of the corpse. His face scant inches away, his gaze shot up and locked on Merris' with rigid intensity.

"You shouldn't have called my brother a traitor in front of him."

Chapter Four
Already Damned

Aerysius, The Rhen

Sephana let the magelight go entirely, allowing the shadows to reclaim the chamber. The Well of Tears was consumed by darkness, its terrible features obscured from sight. Which was better. The Well was appalling on such a primal level; the sight of it filled her with an urgent sense of dread. She wanted away from it, as far away from it as she could get.

She took a step backward in the darkness.

"This way."

It was Braden's voice, disembodied and lost in shadow. She felt him take her hand firmly, guiding her forward through absolute darkness. Her slippered feet splashed through stagnant pools of water mixed with blood as he hurried her out of the chamber, one hand entwined with her own, compelling her forward with urgent pressure.

The thrumming sounds from below were growing louder, motivating her stride.

"They're almost here," she whispered, caught off-guard by the panicked sound of her own voice. "We can't outrun them."

"No, we can't," Braden responded simply.

She wished she could see his features in the darkness. The pressure of his hand eased as he brought them both to a halt. She had no idea where they even were in the warren of passages below Aerysius. A cold stirring of breeze rose up from the depths, the only telltale sign that the corridor they traversed actually went somewhere and didn't just lead to a dead end.

She glanced around, both forward and behind, eyes scouring the shadows. She could make out nothing in the darkness. Nothing except Braden.

Sephana winced, recoiling from the sight of her lover silhouetted by a golden aura of energies that rippled over his body like lustrous ribbons, diffusing into the air around him. Braden had saturated himself with the magic field, letting its power completely suffuse him, filling him, the way Battlemages were trained to do in preparation for a strike.

Sephana felt ire flush her cheeks as she realized what the sight of those energies implied. She found herself standing in the center of the dark and eerie passage, warily reassessing the man next to her.

"Are you sure you're a Chancellor?" she asked him slowly, guardedly. Her words were so soft that they were almost inaudible. "Because, in Aerysius at least, saturation with the field is a technique taught only to Battlemages."

Instantly, Braden released his grip on the field. She could feel the powerful energies draining out of him, dispelling back into the air. The darkness returned again quickly; she could no longer make out his features in the absence of light.

She heard Braden explain in a weary, leaden voice, "In the Lyceum, the orders aren't quite as cut-and-dried as they are in the Rhen. Once we become full Masters, we are allowed to choose a minor course of study. I am a Chancellor, Sephana. I didn't lie to you about that. But I am also Battlemage-trained."

"To what purpose?" she demanded, the angry heat of betrayal rising to her cheeks. "Why would a Chancellor with purely political ambitions have need for that kind of study?"

She was suddenly glad that she couldn't see his face.

"Sephana," he began. There was sadness in his voice.

That was all he said; Braden didn't get a chance to finish.

The air in the passage turned suddenly, atrociously cold. As it did, Sephana was filled with an appalling sense of dread.

Desperate, her mind groped for the magic field and found nothing there.

"*Don't let them touch you!*" Braden gasped.

She turned and fled.

Groping ahead, Sephana made her way as fast as she could manage through the darkness. She felt along the walls of the passage with her hands, turning always to the right at every doorway she encountered. Filled with a mind-numbing terror that knew nothing of reason, Sephana had no idea what was following her through the darkness.

She turned a corner and found herself in the passageway lit by torches. She gasped at the disorientation that came to her with the sudden return of vision. Behind, she could hear the ringing sounds of metal against metal. Ahead, the way they had come lay open before her.

Almost, she turned back for Braden. She actually paused. She closed her eyes and argued silently with herself. In the end, it was not distrust of the man she loved that turned Sephana away from him. It was fear.

Fear inspired by the pair of necrators that melted up from the ground six paces away.

The necrators were vaguely human in shape, but utterly featureless. Like twin, twisted figures of charred mist. Sephana's eyes widened as her throat spasmed in terror. She tried to breathe, but all she could produce was a choking whimper. She took a fumbling step backward.

The touch of a necrator was not death; it was something much, much worse.

She tried one last time to reach for the comfort of the magic field, but it was gone. In its place was only emptiness.

"Turn around slowly."

Sephana almost screamed at the sound of Braden's voice. Somehow, he was behind her. Though her nerves shrieked in panic, she obeyed him, turning her back on the appalling pair of shadows.

He brought his hand up to her cheek, his touch a gentle caress that directed her attention fully into his eyes. He was saturated with the field again, amber ribbons of energy roving like a glorious web over his body. The look in his eyes was dark and dangerously intense.

"Get behind me. When I say so, I want you to close your eyes and run as fast as you can." His voice was absolutely calm and suffused with authority. "Back the way we came. Don't stop. No matter what. Don't turn around. Stop only when you reach the Hall of the Watchers."

Some reflex within her wanted to argue with him. But her will was silenced by the awful influence of the necrators. She stepped behind him.

He grabbed her arm in a vise-like grip, forcing her backward with him. Two more necrators rose up from the ground to join the others. There were now four of them, dark and featureless shadows moving inexorably toward them.

A man and a woman entered the corridor wearing the same indigo robes as Braden. Sephana gasped at the sight of them. The pair strode confidently forward through their escort of necrators, unaffected by their demonic influence.

"Careful," Sephana heard the man whisper to his companion. "He's still holding the field."

Sephana's eyes went wide as she realized exactly what that meant. She gawked at Braden, appalled to find the golden aura still surrounding him despite the presence of the necrators.

She felt Braden's hand upon her back, his touch a lingering caress. "It's time," he told her calmly. "Remember what I told you. Close your eyes. Now, *run!*"

She didn't obey him fast enough. Her eyes were still open when a brilliant glare exploded in the passage, completely overwhelming her vision. But Sephana didn't need to see; her mind had already mapped out the path of the corridor behind her. Her vision blinded, she ran back the way they had come.

Behind her, she could hear frantic sounds of struggle. She ignored the noises, her fingers trailing along the rough walls of the passage as her feet propelled her forward. She couldn't see anything. Her foot smacked hard against stone and she tripped, falling to her knees.

The pain was intense, but she forced herself to stand anyway. Shaking, overcome by fear, she felt around in the space ahead of her and realized she had come to the stairs. Tears streaked her face, falling like rain from her light-blistered eyes.

Limping, she staggered up the steps until she came to a landing. There, she stopped, scrubbing at her eyes with the palms of her hands, trying in vain to clear her vision. Sephana let out a gasping cry of frustration. She needed healing badly. She needed the magic field.

But the cadence of the field was still just the dimmest echo in her memory, chased away by the influence of the necrators. Choking on fear, Sephana brought her hands up again to grope at her eyes.

"It's really quite a shame," uttered a voice right beside her.

Sephana flinched backward with a cry.

Vintgar, Caladorn

The first thing Braden felt was pain. His head throbbed with each pulse of his heartbeat, his body aching at every joint. He closed his eyes with a groan, bringing his hands up to his temples.

"I know it hurts," a soft, feminine voice whispered in his ear. "Go back to sleep. It will pass soon."

The sound of that voice was vaguely familiar, like the dimmest recollection of a dream. Braden tried to open his eyes again, but the throbbing ache in his head prevented him. Instead, he found himself doing exactly what the voice suggested. He lowered his hands back to his sides and relaxed, letting sleep deliver him from the pain.

When he opened his eyes again, his head felt better. He was still far from hale, but the improvement was vast. He tried to sit up but couldn't. It took him a moment to realize that they had him tightly bound.

He started to reach for the magic field.

"*Don't*," a man's voice commanded severely. "Shield yourself; you are deep within a vortex."

Braden closed his eyes against a surge of panic that was almost overwhelming. Never before in his life had he come so unwittingly close to death. Instantly, he threw up a shield between his mind and the dangerous flux of power that surrounded him, balling his fists in rage and fear.

Whoever these people were, they had come damned close to killing him.

A vortex was a place of power where the lines of the magic field swirled and converged with hurricane force, like a great cyclone of energy. No Master could tame such a torrent of raw power; merely touching the magic field here would liquefy his brain.

Within the energies of a vortex, he was utterly powerless. Which was probably why they had brought him here. Braden tested his strength against the bonds that held him, finding them secure.

The room they had him in was cold, cold enough for his breath to form a mist before his face. He glanced around, trying to get a sense of the nature of his surroundings. The walls were grayish blue and glistening, crystalline-solid. He was in some kind of cell made completely of ice.

Vintgar.

The realization that they had moved him to northern Caladorn was startling.

He turned to glance at the man standing beside him, the same man who had bested him in the warren beneath Aerysius. Nashir Arman was a mage Braden had grown up with, studied with, had worked with all his life. Nashir was neither friend nor foe; rather, more of a rival than anything else. Nashir was second-in-command of the Order of Battlemages. He was also one of the most powerful Grand Masters the Lyceum had in its arsenal.

"What have you done with Sephana?" Braden demanded of the quietly arrogant mage. "And why am I being held?" He spoke in the language of the clans, the same Northern dialect that Nashir spoke, as well. It was something that the two of them shared in common, distinct from the more conventional Rhenic tongue that had invaded Caladorn from the south.

Nashir's face remained stoically placid. He was dressed in the same indigo robes as Braden, the Silver Star of the Lyceum embroidered upon his breast. He was darker in complexion than Braden, his angular face clean shaven, his hair a thick and lustrous black. Nashir's eyes were a striking hazel.

"Sephana remains unharmed," Nashir answered

matter-of-factly. "As far as I know, your fate remains undecided." He spread his hands apologetically. The expression on his face was not unkindly. He stood up, hands moving to smooth his robe. "I'll go inform Krane and the others that you have awakened."

Braden gazed after him as Nashir exited the ice cell. Cyrus Krane, then, was with them at Vintgar. There was no logic to that. To any of this. *Why would the Prime Warden of Aerysius be working with Nashir?* The absurdity of the thought made Braden's mind want to scream in frustration. Caladorn and the Rhen were all but at war. No one knew this better than Braden himself, whose job it was to lead the hostile negotiations ongoing between their two nations.

That Nashir Arman and Cyrus Krane could have forged some sort of secret alliance was inconceivable.

Braden didn't have long to wonder about it. Nashir reappeared quickly in the doorway. The Battlemage was accompanied by two guards in leather gear. The men swept forward into the cell and began loosening his bindings.

They led him out into a hallway. There, Braden realized that his previous guess was confirmed: they truly were at Vintgar.

The legendary ice fortress in the far north of Caladorn was well-known to him. The stronghold of Vintgar had been constructed from preexisting natural caverns. It was a living, breathing, dynamic cave system formed entirely of rock and ice. Vintgar's galleries were decorated by spectacular ice sculptures and strange formations, all formed by water dripping in through fissures in the rocks.

They led Braden down a wide, ice-encrusted corridor. The walls of the passage were crystalline blue and iridescent. Braden could see through the walls all the way down to the bottom of the cavern. There, the blue-green waters of the River Nym flowed at the bottom of a great chasm, the start of their long journey to the sea.

His guards guided Braden to a large gallery thrust out over the gorge, overlooking the headwaters of the Nym. The air here was slightly warmer, the walls hewn from limestone but for a room-length window made of ice that looked down upon the sacred river. The floor was covered with finely woven carpets, the air thickly scented with incense. In the center of the chamber was a large, circular table surrounded by eight wrought iron chairs.

Braden's guards gestured for him to take a seat and then bowed and left the room. He did as they bid, seating himself across the table from Nashir. He sat without speaking, absently rubbing at the depressions the restraints had made in his wrists.

Presently, a door at the far end of the room swung open.

Cyrus Krane still wore the white cloak of a Prime Warden, which rippled behind him as he moved across the chamber and took his place at the table beside Nashir. He was a tall man, dark of hair but pale of complexion, his features fine boned and aristocratic, distinctive of the people of the Rhen. Even after years of negotiations, Braden had never become immune to the formidable presence of Aerysius' Prime Warden. He clenched his jaw, following Krane's movements distrustfully with his eyes.

"I'm told that you discovered my little secret," Krane remarked ominously.

Braden decided not to dignify the man's comment with a response. Instead, he folded his hands in front of him and stared flatly across the length of the table at his adversary.

"And you are involved with Master Sephana Clemley," the Prime Warden accused. "I was greatly displeased to hear that."

Still, Braden refrained from comment. So deep was his contempt for this man that he didn't trust himself to speak.

The slightest trace of a smile formed on Krane's thin lips. "In all our years of negotiations, I've never known Braden Reis to be at a loss for words."

If it was an attempt at humor, then Braden was thoroughly unamused. He moved his hand to a crack in the table, catching his thumbnail in the groove and rubbing it slowly back and forth along the crevice.

"I have nothing to say," he muttered quietly, eyes studying the motion of his nail against the wood.

The Prime Warden considered him for a moment. He adjusted his posture in his seat. "I am told that my necrators have no effect on you."

Braden seemed completely engrossed with the table's surface, brazenly ignoring the man's comment.

Krane appeared not to notice the slight. Instead, he continued darkly, "Your immunity to my necrators speaks volumes about your character. And it actually works to our advantage. You see, we need your help, Braden."

"I have absolutely no interest in helping you with anything." Braden's response was immediate and decisive. It was spoken without a glance at Cyrus Krane.

The Prime Warden's voice was almost gentle as he argued, "I think you might change your mind after hearing me out."

"I doubt it. Not unless I can gain some type of assurance that Sephana has been released. *Unharmed.*"

Krane turned to nod once in the direction of the wall behind him. Immediately, the door to the room cracked open. Braden looked up from his study of the table's texture just as a woman appeared in the doorway, one he immediately recognized. His jaw went slack at the sight of her.

"How have you been, Braden? I've missed you." Sareen Qadir smiled sweetly as she swept into the room, the chestnut waves of her hair flowing behind her as she moved.

Another woman familiar to Braden entered on her heels: Myria Anassis. She was beautiful, dark and statuesque, with sleek raven hair. Myria was both confident and intelligent, well-respected by her peers. Braden tensed at the sight of her; back in the warrens, it had been Myria who had helped Nashir take him down.

"Good to see you, Braden," a masculine voice greeted him.

Braden's attention was drawn to the bearded man with red hair who entered behind the others, his astonishment growing. Byron Connel was Warden of the Order of Battlemages and was the greatest contemporary strategist Braden knew. He carried a spiked silver morning star in his hand, the iconic badge of his office. On his face he wore an amiable grin.

Cyrus Krane nodded curtly. "Well, it seems that we all know each other. I gather we can skip the introductions?"

Sareen smiled sweetly as she claimed a chair next to Braden, brushing up against his arm as she situated herself in her seat. "I believe we're all very well acquainted." She turned to Braden with a conspiratorial grin. "I just met the acolyte you sent us. Thank you, by the way! She is simply adorable."

Hearing that, Braden's stomach sank along with the remainder of his hopes. Somehow, they had found out about Merris. If they knew about Merris, then they likely knew about his attempt to involve Quin. He wondered if the two of them were even still alive.

Braden took a deep breath and closed his eyes, trying to regain what little composure he had left. He sat there for a moment. Then he fixed his stare on Cyrus Krane and stated in a gravelly voice, "Why don't you start by telling me what this is all about."

The Prime Warden of Aerysius nodded, knitting his fingers together in front of him. "Very well," he allowed. "The mages that you see around this table have agreed to work together, to stand united for a common purpose. It is our goal to combine the strength of Aerysius with that of Bryn Calazar to avert a very credible threat that has the potential to destroy us all."

Braden let his eyes wander around the table, taking in every face in the room one by one. There were five of them in all: Cyrus Krane, Nashir Arman, Byron Connel, Sareen Qadir, Myria Anassis. Curiously, there were two empty chairs at the table. Braden's eyes lingered for a moment upon those chairs, wondering for whom they were intended.

"If that's true, then why the need for subterfuge?" he demanded of Krane. "Why not just present the problem before both Assemblies?"

Myria Anassis looked almost disappointed with him as she responded, "You already know the answer to that, Braden. There's too much bad blood between Bryn Calazar and Aerysius. The Lyceum and the Hall will never work together willingly. At least, not in the foreseeable future."

Byron Connell grimaced. "And there's another problem," he said with obvious reluctance. "I'm afraid that our methods would be considered…too unorthodox."

Braden glared scathingly in Connel's direction. "From what I've seen, 'unorthodox' doesn't *begin* to describe what you're doing."

Myria sighed, looking impatient. "Braden, please hear us out."

Braden shrugged then gestured brusquely at

Krane, urging him to continue.

Aerysius' Prime Warden nodded graciously. "Are you aware of Master Devrim Remzi?"

Braden frowned, nettled by confusion. "Remzi? Sure, I've met him once or twice."

Krane continued, "Master Remzi stumbled across a rather disturbing find while doing research above Skara a few years ago."

"Is that why Remzi and his whole team went missing?"

Myria made a petulant face, obviously frustrated by his reaction. "They never 'went missing,'" she chided him. "That was just the story we put out. Actually, Master Remzi is still very much alive and working for us."

Braden gestured around the table. "By 'us' you are referring to the five of you?"

"There are six of us, actually," Cyrus Krane corrected him.

Braden sneered as his eyes slipped to the table's two empty chairs. *Whom are they meant for?* "Of course. Please. Go on."

Myria continued patiently, "Master Remzi was trying to find a more accurate way to map the lines of the magic field. His methodology involved looking at the alignment of certain minerals found in volcanic rock. What he found instead was evidence of an approaching catastrophe.

"Remzi's rocks contain evidence that the entire magic field of our planet reverses in polarity every ten thousand years. He calls it a 'geotheurgic reversal.'"

Braden nodded slowly, his mind chewing on the information.

Krane told him, "We have corroborated Master Remzi's findings several times since. All of the data support his conclusions."

Myria added quickly, "These events appear to occur with predictable regularity."

Byron Connel nodded. "That's the problem. According to the model Remzi came up with, the magic field is going to reverse itself again sometime within the next few weeks.

"Do you understand what this means, Braden?" Connel asked. "A Reversal such as this would be utterly catastrophic. Every mage on the planet will most likely die. We'll lose anything ever wrought by magic. The entire heritage of both Aerysius and the Lyceum would be completely destroyed."

Myria said, "The Circles of Convergence, Athera's Crescent, the transfer portals…everything would be gone. The might of the temples—"

Braden raised his hand in the air to stop her. "I get it," he said. Then he turned to cast a glare at Cyrus Krane. "What I don't understand is how boring a gateway to Hell is supposed to improve the situation."

He heard a rustle of silk as Sareen moved to set a hand lightly on his arm. "We've found a way to reinforce the magic field and postpone the Reversal for a thousand years," she explained to him, her breath a gentle whisper in his ear. "Our plan involves linking together the eight Circles of Convergence. Then, when the magic field begins to collapse, we will stabilize it by using a different kind of power source entirely."

What different kind of power source? Braden wanted to scream at her. Then, suddenly, he was hit with a flash of startling insight. In that moment, everything became shockingly very clear. He felt his stomach turn sour, the hair on the back of his neck standing upright. A slithering feeling of dread curled up around his insides, constricting his chest like the cold embrace of a serpent.

"By all the gods," Braden whispered, patently appalled. "*You're planning to use the power of the Onslaught to stabilize the magic field.*"

That explained the inception of the Well of Tears. Cyrus Krane was opening a gateway to Hell in order to harvest the corrupt power of the Netherworld to stabilize the magic field. He was hoping to prevent the Reversal by bolstering the magic field with the tainted power of damnation: Hellpower, they called it. The Onslaught. There were other terms, but it didn't matter. Braden couldn't fathom what these mages were even thinking, seriously considering such a perilous endeavor.

Cyrus Krane nodded sagaciously at Braden's perception. "That's right. It is the only alternative available to us."

Myria smiled across the table at Braden. "You guessed our purpose. What are your thoughts?"

Braden could only stare at her, aghast. "You really want my opinion?" Glancing around the table, he spared none of them his ire. "I think that all of you are completely insane."

He pressed on, "It's a no-win situation any way you look at it. The best outcome you could possibly hope for would be to trade one disaster for another, potentially much worse. You can't be sure that you could even control the Onslaught. You risk reducing the entire planet to a chunk of cinder."

Cyrus Krane responded to his words with absolute conviction. "That is a risk we are all willing to take to preserve our lives, our heritage, and our future."

"The alternative is to just sit back and wait for our own annihilation," Byron Connel said. "I, for one, can't do that."

Sareen's hand came to rest on Braden's arm as she leaned into him, urging him in an imploring tone, "This can only work with all eight Circles of Convergence tied in together. As it stands right now, there are only six of us. We need you, Braden. You are a gifted Grand Master and the Warden of Chancellors. You have the strength to command the greater circle here at Vintgar. We need you to harness the might of this vortex for us."

"And you're immune to the influence of my necrators," Krane reminded him ominously. "Which means that your soul is already corrupt enough to channel the power of the Onslaught."

Sareen smiled, the light of excitement dazzling in her eyes. "That's what makes you so perfect," she insisted. "You've already sold your own soul; you've got nothing more to lose."

Cyrus Krane nodded in agreement. "She's right, Braden. Whether you want to admit it or not, your soul is already damned. You're one of us already, even if you just haven't realized it yet."

Chapter Five
An Unfortunate Revelation

Bryn Calazar, Caladorn

The light of the setting sun coming in through an open window wakened Merris from sleep. She stretched, enjoying the comforting warmth of the rays. She could hear the faint tinkling sounds made by many strings of colored beads that lined the windowsill. The beads were stirred by the same soft breeze that toyed with the wispy strands of her hair.

Her stomach growled. Looking up from the pile of assorted fabrics she had thrown together to form a makeshift bed, Merris squinted against the light coming in through the window in golden streams.

"I'm starving," she complained to her inhospitable host. She had no idea whether the man was anywhere within earshot. "Let me guess: you don't have any food around here, do you?"

She rubbed her eyes then let her stare wander across the floor, taking in the assorted piles of garbage that lay strewn about. She frowned, nudging something half-buried beneath a pile of clothing with her toe. Was that a chicken bone?

Revolted, she jerked her foot back away.

"I try not to eat if I can help it. Food sours my stomach."

She turned to find Quinlan Reis standing behind her, leaning with his elbow resting against the wall, gazing out the window toward the sunset. He was still shirtless, but had mercifully managed to find a pair of trousers that looked a few sizes too big for him. Beneath his skin, she could make out the outline of every rib etched into his sallow flesh. The man was more than just gaunt; it was as though he had some kind of wasting sickness.

"How do you *live* like this?" Merris grumbled as she stood up, gesturing broadly at the array of filth that surrounded her.

Keeping his gaze upon the window, Quin responded to her question miserably, "My home was a much happier place before your arrival."

With a sigh, he paced away toward a small wooden cabinet set against the wall. Opening the cabinet's door, he produced a painted ceramic jar and proceeded to pour himself a drink from it.

"Oh, no, you don't!" Merris cried, lunging toward him from across the room. She snatched the cup out of his hand just before the liquor reached his mouth. "That is the *last* thing you need right now!"

Setting the jar down firmly on top of the cabinet, Quin glared sideways at her in reproach. "Kindly remove your claws from my beverage," he directed her in a tone that brooked no argument. He raised his eyebrows expectantly, waiting for her to let go. When she released her hold, he threw his head back and downed all of the liquor in one swallow.

Then he went on to explain, "And I beg to differ with you, but this is *exactly* what I need right now. Unless you want me to succumb to a fit of the shakes before the Prime Warden of the Lyceum."

Merris bit her lip to keep herself from saying anything as she gazed into the man's sad, skeletal features. He appeared to be somewhere in his late thirties or early forties, although with mages it could be hard to tell. It defied belief that this man was Ambassador Braden's own brother. Try as she might, she could find no resemblance at all between the two men. Quin's red and watery eyes held no trace of the strength and integrity she had envied in his brother. Instead of envy, the only emotion she could dredge up for Quinlan Reis was pity.

"I thought Masters couldn't drink to excess," Merris sighed in frustration as she turned away from him, giving up the fight.

"Let me assure you, I can drink *well* beyond excess," he responded tartly as he moved to pour himself another cup. Gazing down at the amber liquid, he swirled the fluid around with his hand. "Strong liquor dulls the perception of the magic field," he explained quietly. "Most mages don't appreciate the loss of that sensation."

Merris narrowed her eyes in suspicion. "But you do. Why?"

He downed the liquid in one swallow. Then he moved away from her back toward the window. Merris allowed her eyes to follow his gaze. Through the many-colored beads, she could make out the orange glow of sunset streaking the western sky.

Softly, he asked her, "How well do you know my brother?"

Merris frowned, turning her attention back to him. "Your brother? Not very well at all, I'm afraid."

He was still staring out the window, watching the slow changes that were taking place across the sky. The shadows were lengthening, orange and golden hues giving way to streaks of pink and vermillion.

"Oh, hell." Quin set his cup down with an air of finality, turning his stare toward the wall. "It's time to deliver that last letter you carry."

Merris' eyes widened with understanding. The third letter Braden had given her was addressed to Prime Warden Zavier Renquist. He had called it a last resort.

"Something's gone wrong, hasn't it?" she asked.

Quin nodded, then muttered ruefully, "I suppose I should go try to make myself look presentable."

He started to wander toward the bedchamber but then stopped and turned back around. His hand came up to his chin as he stood there, gazing at Merris appraisingly. He slowly shook his head.

"Oh, my. That's never going to do, is it?"

His eyes moved over the floor in a searching pattern. It took him a while to find whatever he was looking for in the pile of fabric Merris had gathered for a bed. Reaching down, he scooped up a handful of rumpled garments and practically dumped them into her hands.

"Wear this," he advised her.

Merris had no idea what he was talking about. Perplexed, she stared down at the bright wad of fabric he had shoved her way. Fingering the silk, it took her a moment to realize that what she was holding was a thin but elegant dress. There were also pants, as well as a shawl-like wrap. It finally dawned on her: these must be the clothes that the whore had left behind. Merris' mouth dropped open in dismay.

"You can't be serious," she started to protest, shaking her head and offering the clothes back toward him.

Apparently he was. Quin raised his hands in the air in a gesture of refusal. "Well, it's not like she's coming back for them," he argued spiritedly. "You may as well." In response to the look on her face, he pressed, "You certainly can't go out in what you're currently wearing. You'd look ridiculous."

"Ridiculous?" Merris echoed, feeling honestly offended. The dress she wore, though slept in, had been one of Master Sephana's finest gowns. The woman actually had taste. "You'd rather me dress as a *prostitute?"*

"An *expensive* prostitute," Quinlan Reis corrected her acidly. "Just do us both a favor and wear the damned clothes."

He turned and headed back in the direction of the bedroom, picking his way carefully over piles of filth.

Merris waited for a moment to make certain that he was gone, then slipped quickly out of Sephana's yellow dress and donned the outfit he'd given her, running her fingers through her hair.

The new dress was actually very beautiful. It was sleeveless and flowing. The colors were brilliant: saffron at the top fading to turquoise at the bottom of the skirt, embroidered with a pattern of blue branches full of leaves. The pants were made of bright-blue silk.

Merris could not figure out what to do with the other piece of fabric, a wide strip of royal blue that was longer than she was tall. It was too long to be draped like a scarf, and she had no idea how to wear it. She tried to wrap it a couple of different ways, eventually giving up.

The sound of Quin's laughter behind her made her startle. Whirling, she found him staring at her from the doorway. "Never wrapped a dupatta before?" he wondered with a roguish grin.

Merris was stricken speechless. With clothes on, Grand Master Quinlan Reis was actually almost handsome. He was wearing the standard indigo robe of the Lyceum, the same as Merris had seen his brother wear on countless occasions. But over the robe, Quin had donned an embroidered vest girthed by a sash of golden silk. In his hand he held a black felt hat of a style inspired by the Rhen. He had actually washed up, even shaved his beard into a well-groomed mustache. His cheeks still looked flushed from the passage of the blade. His dark hair was wet, combed back away from his face. He was still quite gaunt; no amount of grooming could fix that. But to Merris, the improvement was vast.

"You look…respectable." Merris attempted a smile in his direction as he strolled forward.

He relieved her of the long strip of fabric, spreading it out before him in his hands. He then proceeded to drape the long material over her shoulder, letting it fall down across the front of her body before bringing it up again from behind to achieve a crisscross effect.

"What is it for, exactly?" Merris tried to clarify, spreading the fabric out by extending her arm away from her body.

"How the hell should I know?" He shrugged, stepping back with a critical stare. "That looks about right. Are you ready, then?"

"I'm *hungry,*" Merris admitted plaintively. "Is there any way we could get something to eat along the way?"

Quin sucked in a cheek, nodding thoughtfully. "I suppose we could," he allowed. He offered his hand to Merris. "Shall we, then?"

She accepted his offered hand and allowed him to lead her toward the door, picking her way carefully. Once outside, Merris pulled up short, halting on his doorstep.

She closed her eyes and breathed in the heady scent of the city. The smell of the ocean was strong in her nostrils, the warm night air thick with salt and humidity. It was like nothing she had ever experienced before. And all around her, surrounding them on every side, were the walls and towers of Bryn Calazar, the brightly lit terraces draped with hanging vines and greenery.

"It's amazing," she whispered. She wandered away toward a low wall and gazed over the balustrade. Far below, an ocean wave broke against the seawall, sending spray high enough for her to feel the mist.

"I never knew that a place like this could even exist."

Quin took her by the arm and maneuvered her away from the edge. "You're hungry, remember?"

"I am," she sighed as she let him lead her forward down a tiled walkway. They turned a corner then emerged onto a busy thoroughfare.

Merris allowed Quin to guide her out into the bustling city street. There were crowds of people moving by, walking every which direction, and yet somehow a bubble of space seemed to just open up around them and let them pass. To Merris' amazement, she saw that people were actually stopping at the sight of Quin's robes and moving backward out of his way, yielding him room to pass.

Quin tipped his hat at the occasional passerby, but otherwise moved through the streets without any acknowledgement of the deference being paid to him by the citizens of Bryn Calazar. Merris could only gaze in wonder at the scene unfolding around her; it was so distinctively foreign. She had never seen the like, not in Aerysius, not anywhere.

"It's almost as if you're a prince," she said wonderingly, staring around in amazement.

He shook his head dismissively. "It's status," Quin corrected her. "This entire society is utterly obsessed by it. It's like a caste system, only you're not born into it. You can fight and claw your way to the top if you have it within you. Or you can just put on one of these wretched robes."

"So being a mage of the Lyceum confers its own status?"

He grinned at her wryly. "There's only two classes of people in Caladorn: those who have the potential to sense the magic field and those who can't. Those who can't serve those who can. People like you and I, we are the royalty here. Caladorn knows nothing of kings and queens, pawns and princes." He gestured around expansively with his hand. "The heroes of this land are warriors and magicians, whether real or imagined."

He drew her toward the side of the boulevard and stopped at the stall of a street vendor that had skewers of meat roasting over a woodfire grill. Quin spent a good amount of time haggling with the woman tending the meat, at last procuring two skewers of lamb. He took one for himself and handed the other over to Merris. She bit into the lamb gratefully, to her delight finding the meat savory and delicious.

"Is there anything in this city that's not exquisite?" She laughed with a surge of joy. They strolled onward through the market, Merris taking in the vibrant colors and energy of Bryn Calazar as she dined. And then, as they rounded a corner, she saw a sight so spectacular that it stopped her in her tracks.

Up ahead on the cliffs overlooking the ocean rose a massive stone structure, a palace of such majesty and vastness that Merris had never before imagined its equivalent. Not even the Hall of the Watchers in Aerysius could rival it. It was a massive edifice, a glorious cascade of domes flanked by tall minarets, one at every corner. Each of the domes was spectacularly wrought and looked to have been tiled in purest gold. Its curvaceous walls were lit with many-colored tendrils of magelight writhing upward from the ground.

"Is that…?" Merris gasped.

Quin nodded. "The Lyceum of Bryn Calazar."

Merris stared, stricken speechless by the view. Strangely, the sight of the Lyceum filled her with only confusion. Merris glanced again at the man beside her, then let her gaze wander back to the stately domed structure with its fragile arcades and graceful minarets. She shook her head, unable to understand how one could ever be a product of the other.

"Tell me," she pressed at last. "How did you end up…the way you ended up?"

Beside her, Quinlan stopped in his tracks, sucking in a deep breath as his eyes rose musingly toward the imposing walls of the Lyceum.

He said quietly, "Since I can remember, I've always had a problem avoiding temptation. It's a character defect, I suppose. A flaw in my personality. There's just something about the forbidden that I find unbearably seductive."

Merris frowned. "I don't understand. What did you do?"

Quin spread his hands as if for once at a complete loss for words. After a long moment of searching, he finally managed to admit, "I simply can't resist the irresistible."

Then he was moving again, guiding Merris by the arm toward the billowing array of domes as the citizens of Bryn Calazar backed deferentially out of his path.

The road that they traveled took them up the hill toward the cliffs overlooking the ocean. For the first time, Merris had a good view of the harbor and the sea. The broad expanse of ocean was calm and black, unfolding before them toward the horizon. An exceptionally bright star glowed low overhead in the eastern sky, larger than all the others.

As they passed through the tall gateway into the Lyceum's outer courtyard, Merris was reminded of the Arches of Aerysius that guarded the entry to the Hall of the Watchers. The Lyceum's portal consisted of a carved, horseshoe-shaped arch that was held aloft by a matching set of carved marble pillars. Like the Arches of Aerysius, the Lyceum's outer gate was more than just ornamentation; it was a ward. No person insensitive to the pulse of the magic field could enter through that doorway.

Merris felt a familiar prickling sensation as she passed across the threshold of the portal. The brightly lit courtyard beyond was flanked by grand successions of arcaded walkways. No one appeared to be about; for all its splendor, the Lyceum appeared starkly empty.

"Where are we going?" Merris whispered as Quin led her through a side door almost hidden in the forest of columns.

"The office of the Prime Warden is this way. It's not under the Grand Dome," Quin explained.

"Then what is?" Merris wondered.

"The Lyceum's Circle of Convergence," he answered matter-of-factly.

Merris nodded. The eight Circles of Convergence were the strongest objects of power that existed anywhere in the world. Within each circle were lines of power that formed two four-pointed stars, one offset against the other. Together, the twin stars of a Circle of Convergence formed what was known throughout the world as the Silver Star.

The rays of a Silver Star worked like a giant magical focus, collecting the vast power of a vortex into one single point at the center. At such a place, all of the energy of a vortex could be harnessed by one single Master, one strong enough to control such a vast well of power. Some circles were inherently stronger than others; these were the greater circles. The greater circles of Aerysius, Bryn Calazar and Vintgar were the most powerful foci of magic anywhere in the world.

"Is it…Quinlan Reis…?"

Merris turned toward the sound of a female voice and found an elegant, middle-aged woman striding toward them across the hallway.

"That's *Grand Master* Quinlan Reis," Quin corrected the woman with a sardonic grin. "How have you been, Gertris? I just need a quick audience with the Prime Warden, if you don't mind—nothing that will take too much of his time, I assure you."

The woman frowned, shaking her head. "The Prime Warden is quite busy—"

Somehow, Quin managed to retain his smile without faltering. "It's a matter of terrible urgency, you see."

The woman appeared suddenly flustered. Instead of waiting for her to respond, Quin started forward, brushing past her. "Actually, if he's in there right now, I'll just go on ahead—"

"You know better than that, Quinlan Reis, Grand Master or no!" the woman's voice called after them as Merris jogged to catch up.

Quin didn't slow his pace at all. Leaning into her, he whispered in Merris' ear, "Trust me."

Despite the woman's loud objections, Quin strode across the hallway and thrust open a door in the wall, leading her through by the wrist. Inside, Merris found herself in a dimly lit corridor. Quin paused, his finger pointing from one door to the next as if trying to remember which was the one he wanted. At last, he nodded to himself and moved forward.

Merris found herself being propelled through a doorway by the force of his hand on her shoulder. Then Quin caught her arm, dragging her downward with him toward the ground.

It took her a moment of disorientation before Merris could figure out what he was doing. Quin was forcing them both to the floor to assume the mandatory position of abasement that was required before any Prime Warden. Merris' body knew instantly what to do; she dropped to her knees and bent forward until her forehead brushed against the floor. There was a long moment of silence while they both held their positions.

She dared not move. She dared not look up or even glance around. She wasn't even certain that there was anyone else with them in the room. But by the unspoken rules of protocol, there was nothing else she could do. Merris had no choice but to kneel there, abased with her palms and head resting against the floor, for however long it took to be acknowledged.

It took a long time. For over a minute she remained in that position, listening to the echoing sounds of her own heartbeat.

Finally, a deep and authoritative voice resonated throughout the chamber:

"You may rise."

The sound of that voice was disturbingly familiar. Merris found herself complying automatically with the directive, rising first to her knees, then to her feet. She took a step backward behind Quin. Her eyes wandered around the chamber in subtle confusion, scanning the shadows of the dimly lit room for the face of the man who had addressed them.

At first glance, the room appeared to be empty. But then the Prime Warden of the Lyceum, Zavier Renquist, stood up and approached.

"Grand Master Quinlan Reis," resonated the deeply baritone voice that was so oddly familiar. "It is good to see you again; you have been away from us far too long this time."

Merris watched with a sensation akin to awe as Prime Warden Renquist reached out a hand and clasped her companion's forearm in a warm gesture. Renquist was a tall man with long brown hair that he wore pulled back sharply from his face. Like Quin, he wore the indigo robes of the Lyceum. But from Renquist's broad shoulders hung the white cloak that was the emblem of his office. A brace of tapers high above on the wall cast a dance of shadow across the angular planes of his face.

Quin cleared his throat, eyes apparently unable to meet the harsh intensity of Renquist's gaze. "I apologize for my dereliction of duty, Prime Warden," he said, staring down at the ground. "I am afraid that my health has been somewhat compromised of late."

The thin smile that appeared on Zavier Renquist's lips was almost fatherly. "But you're here now.

That's all that matters."

Quinlan shifted his weight from one foot to the other. "Yes, I suppose you're correct," he nodded, holding his hat in his hands. He turned, gesturing toward Merris. "Please allow me to introduce my lovely companion, Merris Bryar. Merris was an acolyte of Aerysius until just yesterday. She was witness to an unfortunate incident that has caused her to rethink her allegiance."

Renquist's eyes shot instantly toward Merris. His stare was hawk-like and intense, fiercely inquisitive. Merris felt like her every nuance was being probed by the harsh severity of that gaze.

Zavier Renquist said, "I take it that your presence here is without the knowledge or consent of your own Prime Warden."

It was not a question, but rather a statement of plain, simple fact. Merris couldn't tell whether the man was pleased or displeased. His expression gave away absolutely nothing of his emotions or intent.

"I apologize, Prime Warden Renquist, for the nature of my arrival," Merris told him with the slightest dip of a curtsey. "I hope that my actions have not put you in a difficult position."

Renquist merely waved his hand in the air dismissively. "Save your apologies," he rumbled. "The only person you are capable of putting in a difficult position is yourself." A knowing smile formed slowly on his lips as he reached out and clasped her hand. "Welcome to the Lyceum of Bryn Calazar, acolyte Merris Bryar. May the grace and blessings of the gods be upon you."

"And also upon you, Prime Warden," Merris spoke through a daze of nervous fog in her head. She tried to keep the tremor out of her voice, but it was there despite her best efforts.

Renquist must have sensed her anxiety.

"Please. Be at ease." He set his hand lightly upon her shoulder. He leaned forward ever so slightly, gazing into her eyes with a penetrating stare. "You must have quite a story to share," he said softly. "I would be very interested to hear it."

Merris ran her tongue across her lips, buying herself time to work up enough nerve to speak. "Actually, I'd rather that you read it, Prime Warden."

She extended the last of the scrolls she carried toward him, offering it up in the palm of her hand.

"What is this?" he wondered, the expression on his face suddenly uncertain.

Gathering her courage, Merris answered in a steady voice, "A letter addressed to you from Grand Master Braden Reis. He put his own life at risk to make certain that you received this."

Renquist took the letter from her hand, gripping the scroll in his fist.

It was then that she noticed the ring that he wore on the third finger of his right hand. A silver band set with a lapis stone. She realized with dread that she had seen such a ring before.

It was the same ring she had seen only yesterday on the finger of the man in the cellar.

Merris' eyes went wide, her heart plunging deeply into her stomach. Upon the lapis stone was inlaid the same image she had drawn for Braden in Sephana's sitting room. The unholy rune *dacros,* the symbol of Xerys, God of Chaos and Lord of the Netherworld.

A bone-numbing chill slipped over her. Merris shuddered, realizing where she had heard that voice before.

If Renquist had any way of sensing her fear, he didn't let on about it. He went deliberately about breaking the wax seal and unrolling the scroll. Merris stared on in silent horror, eyes locked on the lapis ring as the Prime Warden's gaze traced slowly across the parchment. All the while he was reading, she could feel the dread within her swelling, changing, evolving into something much more sinister.

She realized that she was utterly terrified. Like a mouse frozen in the shadow of a raptor.

Zavier Renquist rolled the scroll back up and carefully set it aside. Then, clenching his hands together behind his back, he strode away from them. The white cloak he wore with its embroidered Silver Star rippled behind him as he walked, swaying with the motion of his gait.

"You have earned my gratitude, acolyte Merris. The sound of his voice was throaty and resonant. "Unfortunately, you will not be returning to Aerysius. Not now, at least, and probably not ever. I will do everything in my power to make your life at the Lyceum fulfilling. If there is ever anything you require, please don't hesitate to ask."

She could tell by his tone that their audience with the Prime Warden was over.

Quin stepped forward, furiously shaking his head.

"But Prime Warden, my brother…" He spread his hands beseechingly. "I've had no word…"

"Your brother is a very capable man, Quinlan Reis," Renquist asserted, still with his back to them. "Who else knows about this?"

"Just us. But these allegations are very concerning," Quin pressed him, stepping forward. "You need to bring this matter before the Assembly."

Zavier Renquist turned back to glare at him with dark and derisive eyes. "To what end?" he demanded. "Perhaps you've forgotten that the bulk of our armed forces are already deployed along our southern border. If I were to even mention the contents of this letter before the Assembly, our invasion of the Rhen would be all but insured."

"But Prime Warden—"

Zavier Renquist raised a hand, firmly cutting off his words. "Tread softly, Quinlan Reis," he uttered ominously. "The hawks are already circling. Let me handle this. If I need your help with this matter, please be assured: *I'll ask for it.*"

Merris effected the scantest curtsey as she fled the chamber, waiting only for the sound of the door closing behind them before whirling to confront Quin.

"He's the man from the cellar!" she gasped in a whimper, latching on to the lapels of his vest with both hands. "He's wearing the ring!"

"Renquist?" Quin gasped in a voice that sounded utterly bewildered. Then he grimaced, squeezing his eyes shut.

Merris nodded urgently, pressing her lips together in frantic dismay. "We just gave your brother away!"

Quin shook his head, sucking in a cheek. "No, we didn't," he disagreed ominously. "He already knew about Braden. We just gave *ourselves* away."

Chapter Six
The Silver Star

Vintgar, Caladorn

Braden let his gaze wander around the circular table, taking in the faces of the five mages that surrounded him. No; not mages. Darkmages. *Nach'tieri,* in the language of the clans. Each person gathered in the room with him already had a soul so terribly black that they were each capable of wielding the Onslaught, the infernal power of the Netherworld. Every mage seated around the table...including himself. Cyrus Krane had been right; Braden was already one of them, whether he wanted to be or not. He had already made that decision nine years before. There was no going back from it now.

But that didn't mean he had to like it. Or go along with it.

Braden leaned back in his chair and folded his hands in his lap. He allowed his gaze to drift slowly toward Byron Connel, lingering on the silver morning star that the man had carried in with him, now resting on the tabletop in front of him. Thar'gon was its name, the Silver Star of Battle, renowned heirloom of the Warden of Battlemages. It was a handsome weapon, the haft short and wrought completely of beaten silver. A long spike extended straight up from the top of its mace-like head, girthed by many smaller spikes. The haft was wrapped in black leather strapping, which was looped at the end so that the morning star could be hung from a belt or peg. It was far more than just a mere weapon; Thar'gon was a legendary talisman endowed with a rich compliment of arcane abilities.

"It's a lot to take in," Braden said finally, his eyes sliding away from Connel's weapon. "I'll need a while to think on it. But you're not going to hear my answer until you can prove to me that Sephana Clemley remains alive and unharmed."

"You have my assurance that Master Sephana has not been harmed in any way," Krane asserted.

Braden glared his contempt at the man. "Let me make myself absolutely clear: *I don't trust you.* I never have. Tell me, where did all the shades come from in that warren of yours beneath Aerysius? The creation of just *one* necrator requires twenty human deaths. How many lives have you already sacrificed?"

He shifted his gaze to Byron Connel, who was seated to Krane's right. "Bring me Sephana. Right here, right now. This negotiation is over until I see her with my own eyes."

"Sephana is still in Aerysius," Myria admitted with a look of concern, glancing back and forth between Connel and Cyrus Krane. "It will take us some time to accommodate your request."

Braden dismissed her concern with a wave of his hand. "Then use the damned transfer portal. Whatever you have to do—just get her here. *Expeditiously.*"

Myria leaned into Krane, setting her hand on his arm as she conferred with him quietly. The Prime Warden of Aerysius at last issued a stilted nod.

"Byron, you may remain," he commanded.

Myria Anassis stood up from her seat. As she did, Sareen and Nashir rose with her and followed her around the table and out of the room. Sareen glanced back over her shoulder, casting a smug grin at Braden as she disappeared through the doorway. Only Cyrus Krane and Byron Connel remained with him in the chamber.

Braden turned his gaze toward the window-wall of ice, staring down into the depths of the chasm below. The sacred river Nym churned in its course, turquoise blue and softly glowing with a quiet iridescence. He wondered what gave the river its characteristic color and radiance. Magelight, perhaps. He frowned, considering the implications. That would mean that the bottom of the gorge would have to be outside of the torrent of Vintgar's power vortex.

"While we wait, there are a few details that I would like to clarify," Byron Connel said. "Not a negotiation. Call it simply a gesture of goodwill." He leaned back in his chair and absently stroked the wrapped haft of his weapon.

Still staring at the gorge below, Braden nodded his permission.

Connel straightened in his seat, steepling his hands before him on the table. When he spoke, his voice was gentle, even frank. "As you've probably guessed, the recent escalation in tensions between Aerysius and Bryn Calazar has been nothing more than fabrication. A smokescreen. We created the crisis in order to turn attention away from our own operations."

Braden turned to glare at him, seething in silence. He didn't respond to Connel's admission. He was too afraid of what would come out of his mouth. His eyes darted to the man's silver weapon, imagining what it would feel like in his own hand.

"As I'm sure you've probably guessed, your work in Aerysius has failed. As we speak, Caladorn's armies are mounting a large-scale offensive, invading the Rhen through the Pass of Lor-Gamorth. Within two weeks, both the Hall of the Watchers and the Lyceum will be all but emptied, allowing us access to those two Circles of Convergence. The other six circles are already under our control."

Braden remained completely impassive as he listened to the unfolding of Connel's strategy. Outwardly, his face was a study in utter indifference. On the inside, Braden was silently raging. Connel's words explained why his own work in Aerysius had been such a vexingly uphill struggle, why his every attempt at compromise had been met with resistance and delay.

"What about the mages who remain behind?" Braden demanded. "They're not going to just surrender the circles to you freely. If you go through with this, you're going to have a lot of innocent blood on your hands."

Connel replied, "We will have safeguards in place to insure that no one will interfere with our purpose."

"A lot of good people are going to die, Byron. And you can give me no guarantee that your plan is even going to work."

"Nothing in life is ever guaranteed," Cyrus Krane interrupted. "You should understand that better than anyone, Ambassador Reis. 'The brave act. Only cowards ever yield,'" Krane quoted. "I know you, Braden. And I know you are no coward."

Braden turned to Aerysius' Prime Warden with an incredulous sneer. "If that's what you think, then you really don't know me well at all."

Bryn Calazar, Caladorn

Merris took a step back away from Quin as she realized they were not alone in the hallway. She whirled to find herself confronted by the same flustered woman who had tried to divert them from Renquist's office in the first place. The woman stood now with hands on her hips, face set in livid irritation. Quin took Merris by the hand and hurried her past the woman, pausing just a moment as they crossed in front of her.

"It's been a pleasure to see you again, Gertris," he said, reaching up to tip the brim of his hat in her direction. "I'm truly sorry the years haven't been kinder to you."

Merris gasped as she felt Quin's hand on her back, hurrying her forward. She had to struggle to keep up with him as he directed her toward the end of the hallway. "Why are we walking so fast?" she whispered.

Quin leaned in close, muttering into her ear without slowing his pace a fraction, "Because Renquist knows we haven't told anyone."

Merris' eyes went wide in understanding as she struggled to hurry. Quin directed her away from the forecourt, ushering her through another doorway that took them into the dark interior of the Lyceum itself.

"Where are we going?" Merris wondered, gazing around nervously. They had entered a large domed chamber with intricate tiles lining the walls. The high glass windows let in only starlight.

"We need to find another way out," Quin explained as he directed her across the carpeted floor to the opposite end of the room. "The problem is, our options are a bit limited."

They stepped through a door that led to an arcaded walkway with a ceiling of domed vaults. Here, their path was dimly lit by widely spaced braziers that glowed softly with magelight.

A man stepped out from behind a pillar in front of them, cutting off their route.

At the sight of him, Merris halted in mid-stride. She felt her chest tighten as she stood there, glancing frantically around, waiting as her companion appeared to be taking his time about assessing the situation. At last, the sallow mage beside her sucked in a cheek and muttered softly:

"Yes, indeed. A honey of a pickle."

Merris blinked at the remark, feeling her stomach lurch.

From the pocket of his vest, Quinlan Reis produced a small bronze flask and went unhurriedly about the business of removing the stopper. He brought the container up to his lips and, throwing his head back, took a rather large swallow of the contents. He then replaced the stopper and tucked the container neatly back into the pocket of his vest.

A confident smile erupted on his face.

"Why, look here, darling. It's Rustin Taman," Quin announced spectacularly. "Merris, please allow me to introduce you to Master Rustin."

Merris swallowed, her eyes widening in alarm as she took in the threatening presence of the mage who confronted them. The man was dressed all in dark leathers rather than the ceremonial robes that Merris had become accustomed to seeing. His face was dark and bearded, black hair pulled back into a topknot. His eyes were piercingly narrow and intense, fixed on Quin's face.

"Hello," Merris muttered as she moved to put her protector between herself and the threatening mage.

"Step away from the girl, Quin." Rustin's voice was rigid and cold, absolutely flat.

The side of Quin's mouth jerked upward into the crooked resemblance of a grin. "Now, Rustin, didn't your mother ever teach you how to be cordial? Say hello to Merris."

The dangerous-looking man before them only shook his head. "I think we both know that I'm not here to be cordial. I'm going to say this one last time: step away from the girl."

A sound from behind her made Merris startle. Whirling, she saw that two silk-clad women had come up behind them from out of the shadows of the cloistered walkway. Merris moved back to Quin's side, clinging tightly to his arm with both hands.

Quin glanced over his shoulder at the two newcomers, taking note of their presence. He turned back to the mage in front of him with an amused grin. "Why, Rusty, you flatter me. You think it will take all three of you to bring me down?"

Rustin Taman brought his hand up to scratch the side of his face. "No, Quin. I think I can handle you just fine all by myself. From what I've heard, your brain's got to be so pickled by now that you probably couldn't light a candle with it."

Quin cocked an eyebrow, nodding back over his shoulder. "Then why are they here?"

"They're here for her." The man's gaze ticked toward Merris.

At his words, Quin chortled his disbelief. "For her? Truly?" He turned toward Merris with a delighted grin. "Did you hear that, darling? Apparently Master Rustin here believes you are more dangerous than I am. What do you think? Should I trouble myself to correct him or leave him wallowing in his ignorance?"

Merris at last realized the dangerous nature of the game Quinlan Reis was playing. They were outnumbered, outmaneuvered, and trapped. She had no idea whether or not Braden's brother was a gambler, but at that moment it seemed only too obvious he was bluffing.

She just hoped it wasn't as obvious to Rustin Taman and his companions as it was to her. She had to find a way to help him seem more believable. Merris brought her hand up, caressing the side of Quin's face as she gazed up at him.

"I think you should make him scream for a long time before he dies," she suggested in a mild voice, smiling sweetly.

"Isn't she adorable?" Quin laughed, stroking his

hand through Merris' hair, continuing the motion all the way down her back. "What do you say, Rusty? Are you in or are you out? Or do you need a moment to think about it?"

The mage shook his head, eyes narrowing. "I'm about—"

His words were cut off as the expression on his face suddenly froze. A thick stream of blood dribbled out of his left nostril, running over his lips and streaming down his chin. As Merris watched in amazement, the man appeared to totter on his feet and then leaned over, slumping sideways to the ground.

From behind, she could hear the shrill sound of a woman's scream.

Merris whirled in the direction of the sound, bringing a finger up to point first at one woman then the other. Taking in their horrified expressions, she felt a rush of exhilaration.

"Which one of you sweetlings would like to be next?" Merris inquired with a grin.

Both women turned and fled. Merris laughed as she watched them run, feeling almost giddy with the intoxicating illusion of power, something altogether different from anything she had ever felt before. The feel of it was thrilling, liberating. For the first time in her life, Merris felt firmly in command of her own destiny.

When she turned back to Quin, she found him staring at her in astonished bewilderment. Merris giggled, throwing her arms around him, in awe of the sinister elegance of his power.

Vintgar, Caladorn

Braden looked up at the sound of the door opening. He immediately rose to his feet as Sephana entered the long rectangular chamber made of rock and ice, flanked closely by Myria Anassis and Sareen Qadir. She moved forward with a calm, dignified poise, still enveloped in her black Master's cloak. The embroidered Silver Star of Aerysius rode between her shoulder blades.

Braden's eyes scoured over her for signs of injury. To his relief, Sephana seemed hale. Her red-gold curls spilled down around her face, only slightly disarrayed. For just a moment their eyes met, but Sephana's gaze moved away again quickly, betraying nothing of her emotions. Her expression maintained an air of cool composure.

Braden swept forward around the table to intercept her before she reached the middle of the room. He took her fingers into his own and brought them up to his lips, kissing them gently. "I trust you are well?" he asked.

Sephana turned away from him, plucking her hand back out of his grasp. She glared her reproach at Cyrus Krane, who remained in his seat at the table next to Byron Connel.

"Prime Warden Krane," she remarked dryly. "Why am I not surprised?"

She turned to glance around the cold chamber, her gaze lingering on the window-wall and its sweeping view of the gorge hundreds of feet below.

"And you, Ambassador Reis," she spat vindictively. Her eyes narrowed as she glared at him. "Or is it Battlemage Reis?"

"Braden Reis is Warden of Chancellors," Byron Connel corrected her astutely. "I, actually, have the singular honor of being Warden of Battlemages."

"Which makes him your superior, does it not?" Sephana retorted.

Braden frowned, shocked that she could possibly know such a detail. The hierarchy of orders within the ranks of the Lyceum had always been kept a closely guarded secret from the mages of Aerysius.

Byron Connel stared long and hard at Braden, obviously just as shaken as he was at Sephana's knowledge. And obviously blaming Braden for Sephana coming by that knowledge. At last, the red-bearded man responded, "You are correct, actually. But only during time of war. Otherwise, our two orders remain completely autonomous." An easy smile spread across his lips. "Why do I get the feeling that the two of you know each other better than you reasonably should?"

"Because we're lovers, you moron," Sephana admonished him dryly. "At least, we were." She glared at Braden in disdain. "You shouldn't have lied to me," she hissed at him under her breath.

"I didn't lie to you, my dear," Braden corrected her mildly, wrapping a possessive hand around her shoulders. "I simply omitted a piece of information. I hope you can forgive me."

"Enough," spat Cyrus Krane. "I have honored

your request, Ambassador Reis. Master Sephana has arrived before you, alive and unharmed. Now, let us resume our conversation."

Braden nodded slightly, his gaze momentarily falling on the silver morning star that gleamed up at him from the table in front of Byron Connel.

The Prime Warden continued, "Sephana, I will ask that you wait in another area of the fortress while I continue my discussion with Ambassador Reis. When this is over, I desire the opportunity to speak with you before our return to Aerysius." He didn't pause for her acquiescence before turning to the two women behind her. "Escort Master Sephana to the holding area and remain with her until I send word."

Both Sareen and Myria bowed their heads in deference to Cyrus Krane, a Prime Warden that was not even their own. Myria stepped forward out of the chamber first, gesturing for Sephana to follow as Sareen lingered behind to bring up the rear.

"Stop," Braden called out as Sephana passed by Connel's chair.

She turned to glance back at him with an inquiring expression on her face. He strode around the table toward her, taking her suddenly into his arms and kissing her full on the lips. His mouth explored hers, his right hand sliding up to caress the side of her face.

With his left hand, he reached down by his side and grasped the haft of Connel's spiked weapon.

Braden jerked Sephana roughly backward, propelling her bodily away from the table as he launched himself toward the window-wall with the full weight of his body behind the morning star's weighted strike. The head bit deeply into the ice and stuck there, deep cracks radiating outward to compromise the structure of the window. Braden struggled to dislodge the weapon, having to use his foot to leverage it out of the ice and, spinning around, struck the window again with all of his strength.

The window-wall caved away, raining sharp fragments of ice down into the gorge below. A frigid wind gusted into the chamber as he scrambled back away from the edge.

"Braden!" Sephana screamed.

Whirling, he saw that Byron Connel had her by the hair. The other mages had fanned out in a half-circle behind them. The fury of the surrounding vortex shielded them from the magic field just as much as it did himself. But that would not stop them from overwhelming him with sheer numbers.

"Drop the weapon," Connel barked, jerking Sephana's head backwards. He had a knife in his hand and was brandishing it against her throat. The blade's sharp tip had already scored her flesh; a thin trickle of blood ran down Sephana's neck. Connel maneuvered her closer to the edge of the floor where the window-wall had been, threatening to send her bodily over.

Braden reacted immediately, holding Thar'gon out away from his body. He tossed the weapon up, catching it again crisply near the end of the shaft and offering it haft-first to Byron Connel.

"Drop it," the Battlemage rasped, nodding his head in the direction of the floor.

Braden sneered, shaking his head emphatically as he retracted the offered haft.

"You're killing her, Braden," Connel growled, pressing the tip of the knife deeper into Sephana's throat. "I know you murdered the last woman who made the mistake of falling in love with you. Are you going to watch this one die, as well?"

Sephana whimpered as the knife blade sawed wickedly against the skin of her throat. The thin trickle of blood running down her neck became a stream. Fear and betrayal consumed her tear-filled eyes.

Braden's expression became deadly serious. "If you kill her, what's there to stop me from taking you over that edge with me?" The look in his eyes was dangerous, almost a dare.

For just a moment, doubt clouded Connel's eyes as his gaze ticked toward the gaping chasm. The knifepoint eased just a fraction from Sephana's throat.

"Don't be a fool, Byron," Cyrus Krane growled. "He's not going to choose suicide over the chance to aid Bryn Calazar."

"Really?" Braden demanded of him, looping the leather cords of the morning star's shaft around his belt and tying it there. "I warned you before, Krane. You don't know me half as well as you think you do."

He charged at Sephana and Connel, shoving them both forcefully over the edge. He could hear Sephana scream as she went over.

And then he was falling after them.

Sephana broke away from Connel's hold, shrieking as she flailed her arms desperately in the air. Braden struggled to catch her hand, but she was too far away. He looked down. Hundreds of feet below, the River Nym ran its course, glowing bright with blue-green magelight from deep within its depths.

The cold embrace of the Nym seemed like it was rushing up to meet them.

Right before they hit the water's surface, Braden opened himself to the magic field, allowing its wild energies to rage across his mind. This close to the vortex, the field was a torrent of molten power. It quickly overwhelmed him, the pain excruciating.

Braden retained just enough of himself to use the power of his mind to disrupt the river's surface right before they hit.

The impact of his body with the water still felt like a powder keg exploding right in front of him. It knocked the breath out of him, his consciousness dimming toward darkness. Vaguely, Braden was aware of the feeling of the icy current grabbing him up, his body being spun like a leaf in the wind. He opened his eyes but saw only a bright, diffuse glow all around him. He couldn't even tell which direction the surface lay.

His lungs were already burning.

Desperate, Braden clawed at the water with his hands. The current was deceptively stronger than it looked from above and shockingly cold. Beneath its smooth surface the River Nym was a nimble giant, its blue-green waters swift and turbulent. Braden found himself spun first one direction then another, at last breaking through the river's surface.

He sucked in a great chestful of air right before the current dragged him back under again. The river had its way with him as it surged ahead in its course. Braden struggled toward the bank, but the current was too strong. The channel was narrowing, forming white-capped rapids that churned and punished him, beating his flailing limbs against the rocks that lined the bottom of the gorge.

Ahead, he could see a large boulder directly in his path. He struggled to propel his body away from it, but then he thought better of it and instead swam toward the massive rock. He put his hand out, trying to catch the boulder. His fingers slipped along its surface, finding no purchase on the stone. His body was hurled once again into the thick of the whitewater.

Something came down from out of nowhere, delivering a crushing blow to his head.

Braden was forced under as he sucked in a mouthful of water. His vision exploded in streaks of red, his lungs spasming in his chest. He almost lost consciousness. Then a hand was on him, jerking him roughly upward by the collar of his robe.

His head broke through the surface and he sputtered, gasping, trying desperately to expel the water from his lungs before he went under again. He opened his eyes long enough to get a glimpse of Byron Connel just before the man forced him back below the surface. Braden struggled futilely against the Battlemage's brute strength. The big warrior was holding him down with a vise-like grip that he had no hope of breaking free of.

Braden's lungs screamed, his mind edging towards panic. He flailed wildly against Connel's hold on him. The urge to breathe was becoming too powerful to resist.

Then Braden remembered the magic field. Frantic, he lashed out with it.

Byron Connel screamed loud enough for Braden to hear him underwater. Released suddenly from the man's powerful grip, Braden struggled back to the surface, sucking in desperate gulps of air.

Somehow, he managed to hook on to a large rock thrusting out of the river. He used the last of his strength to haul his body up onto the boulder's wet surface. He lay there, spent and gasping, his heart thundering as it struggled to make up for lack of air. He couldn't feel the tips of his fingers. His whole body was trembling violently.

Braden opened his eyes and glanced around to get an idea of his circumstances. He was on a boulder toward the side of the churning river. Swift rapids swirled by on both sides of the rock. The shore wasn't far away, but in order to reach it he would have to get back into the turbulent river and swim.

Something floating by caught his attention.

Braden forced his body into motion. He rolled forward, spilling off the rock into the icy water. His feet reached the bottom and he stood, splashing forward against the current. He staggered, almost falling, at last reaching out and catching the edge of Sephana's black cloak with fingers so numb they almost didn't work.

He pulled her toward him by the fabric of her cloak, turning her over and hauling her up into his arms. Her eyes were closed, her face devoid of color.

"No," Braden whispered, hugging her close against him. He stood there in the water as despair got the better of him, trying to find enough presence of mind to act.

Desperate, he reached out from within and let the magic field rampage across his brain. Through the agony in his head, Braden got a vague sense of Sephana's condition. Her heart was stilled, her blood cold and stalled in her veins. But she was still there, somewhere, deep down inside. Her soul had not yet fled her body.

There was still time.

Crying out in frustration, Braden sent a confused and desperate torrent of healing energies coursing through her body. In the chaos of his anguish, his attempt at a probe had returned precious little information about what was actually wrong with her, and he had no idea how to go about fixing it. The only thing he could do was try to start her heart again and pray that would be enough.

He could feel warmth returning to Sephana's cold limbs. Her nostrils quivered as she drew in a breath of air and life. Braden held her close as she sputtered and choked up the water from her lungs, maintaining the flow of healing despite the harsh toll the magic field was taking on his mind. He could feel his strength waning, his vision starting to ebb.

Braden struggled toward the shore, half carrying, half dragging Sephana in his arms. He cast himself down upon the rocks and pulled her close, hoping to revive her with the warmth of his body.

The flesh of her neck was still bleeding from the bite of Connel's knife. With a thought, Braden staunched the flow of blood. He reached up to stroke a finger down her soft, pale cheek.

"I'm sorry, darling," he confessed to her, resting his forehead against the gentle curve of her shoulder. His head was throbbing with every pulse, the exhaustion becoming more than he could stand. He didn't have the strength to fight it anymore.

Braden wrapped his arms tightly around Sephana and held her close. Then he closed his eyes and allowed his mind to drift away.

Chapter Seven
A Broken Vow

Bryn Calazar, Caladorn

Merris giggled in delight as she threw her arms around Quin, catching him up in an exuberant hug. Then she pulled away with a giddy little whirl of excitement. The colorful silks that draped her body shimmered in the glow reflected off the walls of the Lyceum. The entire city lay unfolded before her, shining like a jewel beside the black waters of the ocean.

"I thought we were dead!" she exclaimed in wonderment. "I can't believe you saved us! Did you see the looks on the faces of those women? They were *terrified* of us!"

Quin's eyes held a trace of concern as he stood considering Merris, head canted to one side, hand fumbling in the pocket of his vest. "Are you certain you're feeling quite well?" he asked slowly, fishing out his flask of liquor and unstoppering it. "You look a bit flushed, I'm afraid." He downed a healthy draught from the container before extending it in her direction.

Merris broke into an endearing smile. "You're such a sweetling. Thank you, but I shouldn't."

Quin shrugged indifferently, withdrawing the offer of the flask. "Suit yourself. Although if there was ever an occasion to drink, tonight might be it. Or any other night, for that matter. I was wondering…do you have any questions for me? About what happened with Master Rustin, I mean? Or anything else?"

"No." Merris shook her head, eyes bright and glistening with exhilaration. Her heart pounded with what felt like the hooves of a hundred galloping horses, circulating the rush of excitement throughout her eager body. She had never felt a sensation so enthralling, so intoxicating, ever before in her life. The thrill of Quin's power was euphoric. It was almost as though she could sense it radiating from his body just standing there next to him.

"What do we do now?" Merris wondered, her voice a bit breathless. She leaned into him, placing one hand possessively on his shoulder.

Quin took another gulp from his flask then carefully stoppered the container and stowed it back away in the pocket of his vest. "Now we split up," he responded matter-of-factly. He took a step forward. "I need to find out what has become of my brother. And I need you to go do some research for us."

"Research?" Merris gasped with a frown. "But I don't want to be apart from you. I don't know what I'd do if—"

He cut her off with a finger pressed against her lips. He brought the finger back up to his own mouth, cautioning her to be more quiet. "You'll do just fine," he assured her softly. "You're going to pay a little visit to Om's temple. You'll be safe there. We need to find out why both Renquist and Krane are conspiring with the Priesthood of Xerys."

"When I was in the cellar, I heard something about a cipher," Merris told him, straining to remember the words she'd heard Renquist utter the previous night beneath Aerysius.

Quin nodded sagely. "I'll be willing to bet that *dacros* plays some part in that cipher. Start with researching the symbology of ancient Venthic. There has to be some reason why they've taken that particular rune to use as their standard."

Merris nodded then, on impulse, reached up to press a kiss against his cheek. "Where do I find the Temple of Wisdom in this city?"

Quin brought a hand up to touch his fingers against the place where Merris' kiss had brushed his face. He lowered his hand again slowly, frowning down at his fingers as if considering the moisture her lips had left behind on his skin.

"Go east following this road," he told her, still staring down at his fingers. "You'll come across an intersection with a statue of an elephant. Turn to the left and the Temple of Wisdom will be directly before you. You should know it when you see it."

He brought his hand down slowly again to his side, his expression still tangibly confused. "If all goes well, I'll meet you back here at sunrise."

Merris paid no attention to Quin's troubled visage. She was too distracted by the nagging suspicion that he was trying to abandon her in this strange city. Without Quin and his potent strength, she would be weak and helpless, utterly alone. Powerless.

Her mind was panicking, trying to figure out what she had done to make him wish to be rid of her. Maybe Quin was just like all the others, the long list of men who had used her and then abandoned her throughout her life. She didn't understand why both friends and lovers always seemed to want to shy away eventually. All Merris knew was that there must be something wrong with her, something other people could sense. She had never been able to figure out what it was, or what she needed to change to make them stay.

"Did I do something wrong?" she finally asked, giving fragile voice to her fears.

Quin frowned, his eyes finally able to meet her gaze. "No, no. You did nothing wrong." He moved forward to cup her face with a hand, seeming troubled by her anxiety. "Please don't take it that way. I'm not upset with you at all."

"Then why are you leaving me?" she pressed.

Quin traced the side of her cheek with his thumb. "I have to find out what's happened to Braden," he explained, staring into her eyes as if ensnarled by her gaze. "There's risk involved. You'll be safer at the Temple of Wisdom."

But his words failed to console her. Merris paled as she wondered, "What do I do if you don't come back for me?"

Quin could only offer her a beleaguered shrug. He licked his lips, looking completely befuddled. "Then ask the clerics of Om for sanctuary and pray that Renquist never finds you. But that won't happen. I'll be back for you, I promise."

Merris nodded, somewhat mollified, and turned to pace away from him a few steps. Passersby gazed at her with curiosity in their eyes. She could tell by their faces that they didn't quite know what to make of her. In the silken dress her status was ambiguous, she supposed. Most of the people on the street were disinclined to make eye contact with her, glancing down the very moment their eyes found hers. They directed their stares toward the ground as they drifted by, deferentially keeping themselves at a distance.

Status, Merris realized. In Quin's presence, she felt her status uplifted tremendously. Recalling the harsh treatment she had received from the brusque guardsman the previous night, she marveled at how much her status had improved within the span of just a single day. It was not only because of Quin, she realized, watching the people of Bryn Calazar conspicuously avoiding her gaze. She was learning how to carry herself, how to project the kind of confidence conveyed by the women of the Lyceum. She was blossoming.

"I don't understand," she remarked. "All of these people act as though I'm already a Master. Why?"

"Because there is no reason in the world for them to suspect otherwise," Quin said softly, looking at her as if seeing her for the very first time. "You are a chameleon, Merris. Very beautiful, very intelligent…very talented. A dangerous combination, if I might venture. Absolutely beguiling."

Merris turned to smile at him, basking in the warm flush brought on by his compliments. The wind whipped at the long spirals of her hair, sending it tumbling around her face. She could tell by the look in his eyes that she already had him captivated.

She had seen the same look before in the eyes of many other men, men from the dim and distant past of her youth. The old Merris was coming back, she realized. The girl she used to be before she became an acolyte was reemerging, was beginning to assert herself again.

She realized that her rough start in life was not the

disadvantage here in Bryn Calazar that it had been in the Rhen. Here, the lessons she had learned on the streets of Aerysius gave her an advantage.

Merris drew herself up, trying to replicate the poise and grace she had seen in the women she had met the previous night. Offering a last, radiant smile at Quin, she turned away from him and moved off down the street in the direction he had indicated. She could feel his eyes on her back, following her as she made her way down the busy avenue. The crowd opened up and parted, letting her pass.

Merris chuckled softly, reveling in the exhilaration of her own innate power.

Quin allowed his eyes to follow Merris until the sight of her was completely absorbed by the city. Then he sighed and drew himself up, turning reluctantly away. He was having a hard time reconciling the woman before him with the one he had met just that morning. It was almost as though he was witnessing some rare and wondrous metamorphosis. Before his eyes, Merris was evolving from a timid and frightened child into a self-confident and beguiling young woman.

"Have a care, Quinlan," he muttered to himself. But he knew that it was already too late.

He turned and sauntered off in the opposite direction, tipping his hat in apology at a woman who had to avoid his sudden change of direction. Then he set off down the street. The avenues of Bryn Calazar were crowded, but much less so than they had been. The city streets were already beginning to empty for the night.

He walked crisply, turning a corner and crossing a narrow bridge into the Lantern District. Here the streets were aglow, lit by many strings of colored lanterns that crisscrossed overhead, suspended from layered ropes that spanned the streets from the windows of tall buildings. The district was a chiaroscuro of noise, commotion and color. The air was fairly saturated with music and incense, the swell of laughter and the din of revelry.

He passed before a balcony that contained a throng of brightly clad women. One of the girls whistled at him as he strode by. Any other night, he would have engaged them in flirtatious banter, or at the very least offered the prettiest one a coin from his purse.

But this night Quin ignored them, his mind on another woman entirely.

"What are you doing to me?" he wondered at the air, shaking his head and frowning in troubled concern. Quin reached into his vest and produced his bronze flask of liquor, taking a heavy pull from it before stoppering the container and returning it again to his pocket.

He crossed another bridge over the wide span of the River Nym, its waters aglow with the scattered light of the full moon. He ignored the frequent pairs of lovers that strolled by holding hands or stood embracing in the shadows by the railing. One young woman glanced up at him from the arms of the man she was with, her eyes darting quickly away as Quin strode by.

On the far side of the river, he turned onto a broad avenue and then rounded a corner onto his own street. His residence was a good place to start looking, Quin figured. If Braden was trying to get word to him, that's where he would attempt to make contact.

In the middle of the street, Quin pulled up short.

Something wasn't right.

The hair on his arms and the back of his neck stood upright. He could almost feel the lines of the magic field crawling over his skin.

He didn't hesitate another second. Quin turned and ran.

He got only two steps before a thunderous explosion picked him up and hurled him across the street. His head hit the brick wall, stars exploding across his vision as he was thrown again by another discharge of violent energy. Quin staggered forward, having a hard time keeping his legs underneath him. He half stumbled, half careened into a narrow alley, using his hands to pull himself forward along the walls.

A familiar face stepped out of the shadows before him. Quin sneered at the sight of his former apprentice, raking blood out of his eyes with a shirtsleeve.

"Why, congratulations, Tarik. It looks like you've found me," he commented dryly, struggling to stand upright without falling over.

The man moved his lips, but Quin's ears were still ringing from the violence of the blast.

He spat a mouthful of blood onto the pavement

of the alley. "I'm sorry, but you'll have to speak up if you have anything worthwhile to say."

A sinuous rope of light snaked around him, constricting Quin's arms against his body. At the same time, the pulse of the magic field in his head suddenly vanished. His eyes widened in alarm.

Trying not to let the panic he felt show on his face, Quin tested the strength of his arms against the bonds of light. "Why, Tarik, I'm truly impressed," he remarked. "Did someone actually trust you enough to loan you a field damper?"

The ringing in his ears prevented him from hearing the man's response. Tarik moved forward, reaching out and catching him by the collar of his robe. Quin grunted, flinching away. As he did, he lashed out with his foot, taking Tarik in the side of the knee.

The man howled, staggering backwards. Quin took advantage of his distraction and kicked him full in the face.

The pulse of the magic field came flooding back. Sparing his adversary hardly a thought, Quin caused an artery to burst in the man's brain.

"I taught you better than that, Tarik," Quin criticized the corpse as the bonds of energy evaporated from around him. "It's a pity your attention span wasn't nearly as big as your ego."

Tipping his hat at his former apprentice, Quin slipped away into the shadows of the night.

Merris gazed up at the façade of the small building before her, wondering how in the world such a structure could possibly contain an entire library of information. The Temple of Wisdom was little more than a stone house with a sloping tiled roof, the image of a bearded man with a laureled head engraved in bas-relief above the door. She raised her hand up to knock.

The door cracked open almost immediately. Merris peered within, her eyes searching through the shadows of the small room. Not seeing anyone, she took a hesitant step inside.

"Greetings, Great Lady. May the light of wisdom shine upon you."

Merris whirled to find herself confronted by a small man standing in the corner of the room behind her. He was smiling jovially, hands clasped together before his chest. The man was very short, little more than the size of a child. A loose woven cloth was draped about his body, hanging from one shoulder.

"Thank you," Merris responded guardedly. "But I'm afraid you mistake me; I'm not a Master of the Lyceum."

The bizarre little man blinked, appearing to be taking a moment to reassess her. "Then I apologize for my presumption. May I inquire your name and clan?"

Merris pulled the door fully closed behind her. "Merris Bryar," she uttered with a slight bob. "Acolyte of Aerysius. I regret that I have no clan affiliation."

The man absorbed this information with seeming indifference. He stood there for a moment, staring at her blankly. Then his mouth jerked into a grin. "Welcome, Merris Bryar of Aerysius to Om's temple in Bryn Calazar. My name is Abir," he introduced himself with a bow. "I serve as the Voice of His Reverence, the priest who ministers to this temple. He would greatly desire a word with you."

Merris nodded, a slight frown worrying her forehead. "That would be fine," she agreed. She glanced around, seeing no other doors leading from the room. It took her a moment to realize that Abir was actually standing at the top of a stairwell that spiraled downward into the ground.

"Would you follow me, please?" he invited her, extending a hand.

Merris accepted his offer, allowing him to clench her fingers and lead her forward down the winding stairs. She followed, lifting her skirt. The stairs were made of clay bricks built on to an iron scaffold that wound around and down through the wooden floor. Below the small room was another, just as empty as the first. The stairs continued spiraling downward through the floor of that level, as well.

The room below was furnished, having the appearance of a waiting area. It was lit with the glow of twin sconces attached to smooth, whitewashed walls. A door was set into the far wall. Two high-backed chairs faced each other from opposite ends of the room.

Merris allowed Abir to guide her toward the door, which he opened and graciously held for her as she stepped within. On the other side of the doorway, she found herself in what appeared to be a small office.

A man was waiting for them, seated behind a wooden desk. He was robed in rough fabric and wore a stole of rich bronze silk set about his shoulders. He was of middle age with thinning brown hair combed back primly from a high forehead. His complexion was dark, which contrasted acutely with his pale-blue eyes. He smiled at her in silent greeting.

Abir beckoned Merris to take a seat across the desk, making a place for himself on a stool in the corner of the room.

"May I present to you His Reverence, Kaz Kirmani, Vicar of Om's temple in Bryn Calazar," Abir said by way of introduction. "Your Reverence, please allow me to introduce the acolyte Merris Bryar of Aerysius. Merris, you must forgive His Reverence, for, as all of Om's clerics, Vicar Kirmani has taken a vow of silence."

Merris raised her eyebrows in surprise, glancing back and forth between Abir and the stoic cleric seated beside him. The vicar nodded formally in her direction. A greeting, perhaps.

"Please," Abir continued, "His Reverence would like to learn the nature of your visit. What brings you to Om's temple, acolyte Merris?"

Merris swallowed, unsure of exactly where to start. "Well," she began, taking a breath, "I am here to do some research at the bequest of Grand Master Quinlan Reis."

The two men on the other side of the desk exchanged a lengthy stare. At last, Abir turned back to Merris. "His Reverence would like to know the topic of your research. He would furthermore like to understand the nature of your relationship to the Grand Master. You are, after all, an acolyte of Aerysius and not an apprentice of the Lyceum. Considering the times that are now upon us, your presence here is a matter of some concern."

Merris nodded, fully appreciating the cleric's apprehension. "I was sent to Grand Master Quinlan by his brother, Ambassador Braden," she explained. "I was witness to some troubling events back in Aerysius."

"What troubling events?" Abir asked, his easy smile urging her gently to continue.

"I would love to explain," Merris confided with a smile of her own. "But I'm afraid I must ask for some assurances first."

Abir leaned forward on his stool, adjusting his seat as he glanced at the balding cleric beside him. "What kind of assurances?"

Merris folded her hands on the desk and leaned forward, responding in a firm voice, "I want His Reverence's word that I will be allowed access to the information I require. I furthermore want His Reverence to guarantee my safety whilst I remain within the confines of this temple. Only then will I feel confident enough to share my story."

Abir's eyes widened at the boldness of her request. He glanced at the man seated beside him and, as Merris watched, the two of them seemed to be staring at each other for a lengthy period of time. Fleeting expressions seemed to be crossing their faces as they gazed into one another's eyes.

"Are you…communicating?" Merris wondered in astonishment. They had to be. That was the only explanation for the silent discourse taking place across the desk from her.

After a moment, Abir sat upright on his stool, turning in her direction. He folded his hands in his lap. There was no trace of a smile on his face anymore. "That is indeed a lot to ask," he said. "Might I inquire what you can offer us in return?"

"I can give you information," Merris responded without hesitation. "I will tell you everything I've learned about a conspiracy that exists between Prime Warden Renquist and Prime Warden Krane…who are both in collusion with the Priesthood of Xerys."

Abir's stare darted quickly to the side, confronting the widened gaze of the cleric sitting beside him. "Can you, now?" he uttered in a voice that sounded almost like a whispered hiss. "That would indeed prove worthwhile."

Merris stepped out of the stairwell and glanced around at the dark vault that surrounded her. Her nose was immediately confronted by the familiar scent of mildew, dust and ancient leather. It was a comforting smell, one she had grown quite fond of from the years she had spent in the libraries of Aerysius. She gazed around, noting that the shelves that lined the small chamber were loaded with the weight of scores of books. She clutched the oil lamp she bore more tightly in her hand, afraid of the damage its flickering flame could do in here.

A movement out of the corner of her eye made her turn.

Searching the shadows of the vault, Merris discovered that she was not alone in the dim room. There was someone else in there with her. A man, seated in the far corner at a small writing desk. He appeared to be scribing notes into the margin of a text. At the sight of Merris, the man closed the book and immediately tucked it away into a shelf beside him.

"Peace! How long have you been there?" His voice was deep and thickly accented.

"My apologies," Merris fumbled, holding her hand up as a stir of air from the stairwell played with the delicate flame of her lamp, threatening to blow it off its wick. "I didn't know anyone else would be down here."

The man rose from his writing desk, his hands going to smooth the lay of his robe. She could tell he was a Master of the Lyceum by the Silver Star emblazoned upon his breast. Older, with gray hair and beard, brows thick and wiry over dark and penetrating eyes. He stood beside his chair, regarding her cautiously.

"I'm used to working alone in this particular vault," his voice rumbled through the chamber. "Company is actually rather hard to come by down here. If you don't mind me asking, what is the nature of your research?"

Merris took a step toward him, raising her lamp to allow its glow to illuminate her face. "I'm trying to find information about the cult of Xerys."

The old Master harrumphed, crossing his arms before his chest. "Are you, now? Might I inquire as to what inspired your interest in such a darkly peculiar topic?"

Merris swallowed. She had just spent the last hour or more mired in the very same conversation with Abir and his silent companion. "I'm really not at liberty to say," she answered guardedly.

The old man seemed disappointed, but accepting, of her answer. "That's unfortunate, for you have certainly piqued my curiosity." He strode toward her, bringing his hand up to his chest. "Please allow me to introduce myself. Devrim Remzi, First Tier Master of the Order of Empiricists."

Merris blinked; she had heard that name before. She smiled as she imitated his gesture, trying very hard to keep the surprise she felt from reaching her face. "I'm just Merris," she introduced herself. "Nobody special, I mean."

The aged Master smiled. "It is truly a pleasure to meet you, 'Just Merris'. Although I can see with my own eyes that you are far more than what you claim to be. At the very least, you are an acolyte of Aerysius. So forgive me if I dispute the fact that you are nobody special."

Merris gazed down at the symbol of the Acolyte's Oath upon her left wrist, realizing that the marking had given her away. It was wrapped around her arm like a sinuous iron chain, its metallic sheen very visible in the lantern light.

"I am no longer an acolyte of anything," Merris disagreed darkly, staring down at the markings of the oath set into her skin. She wondered, "What do I have to do to get rid of it?"

"Why, that should be obvious," Master Remzi said, gazing at her sideways in confusion. "Should you wish to be rid of the oath, you must simply disavow it."

It was now Merris' turn to be perplexed; she had never heard of such a thing. Many an acolyte had been released from their oath; it was far more common to fail in the Hall than it was to actually succeed. But never before in her life had she ever heard of anyone giving up the oath voluntarily.

"How do I disavow it?" she wondered.

Master Remzi glowered at the markings on her arm, finally raising his eyes to stare at her from beneath his unkempt brows. "I think the far more pressing question is, why do you feel the need to disavow it in the first place? You are obviously more than qualified to become a Master. I can sense how strong the potential is in you. You must have years of training behind you already. What could possibly motivate you to want to give all that up?"

Merris shook her head. She didn't want to explain herself again. "I'm looking for something," she redirected the conversation testily. "Maybe you can help me. What do you know about the rune *dacros?*"

The Master's eyes widened as he took a step backward away from her. "I'm sorry, but the Venthic language is not my area of expertise." He reached down and extinguished the light of the oil lamp on the desk he had been working at. "Perhaps you should consult a text on the subject."

Merris took a step toward him, blocking off his path of retreat. She could tell that her question had agitated him, but she was determined to find out what he knew. It had to be no coincidence that she had walked in on him in this particular vault.

Remzi.

That was the name she had overheard spoken by Prime Warden Renquist in the cellar. Remzi was the name of the man he had working on the cipher.

"Master Remzi," she stated firmly, "I don't believe a text is going to help me, and I think you know that. I need to find out why Prime Warden Renquist wears a ring with the rune *dacros* set into the stone. And why both Prime Wardens, Renquist and Krane, are convening secret meetings beneath Aerysius."

The aged Master's eyes narrowed. He stood there cornered against his writing desk. He looked rather like an animal trapped in its own den. Even with so decisive a parallel, Merris lacked the good sense to be afraid.

This time when Remzi opened his mouth to address her, his tone was very cold and very flat. "I feel I must warn you, 'Just Merris', that the path you tread is fraught with danger. And I'm not entirely convinced that you will be happy with the places it might lead you. If I may be so bold to suggest, you would be wise to abandon your present course and search instead for safe harbor."

Merris glared at him. "And do what?" she demanded icily.

Remzi shrugged as he returned her glare right back at her. "Survive," he responded. "Now, please excuse me."

Merris stepped aside and allowed him to pass. She watched as the old man ascended the spiral stair into shadow. When he was gone, she wandered over to the writing desk Remzi had occupied and set her oil lamp down upon its surface. She brushed her hand across the desk's smooth grain then trailed her fingers up the bookcase beside it. Her fingers went to the text he had set there when she had first interrupted him.

Using her index finger, Merris pressed down and tilted the thin, leather-bound manuscript out toward her. She grabbed ahold of the binding between her thumb and middle finger, wriggling it the rest of the way out. She held the book in her hands, admiring the ancient leather cover as she traced her fingers over the title:

She bent the binding back and opened the text to the first page. The entire manuscript was written in a language she had never seen before. She turned the page, passing her eyes over more runes she did not understand. She turned to the next page, accidentally skipping a whole section at once. The binding bent back to reveal a page with notes written in the margin. The script was Rhenic, written in a delicate and precise hand.

Merris whispered, *"Calebra, metha, benthos, noctua, ledros, dacros . . ."* She drew in a quick intake of breath. "It's the cipher."

It was very early and Quinlan Reis was very tired. More than tired. He'd healed the injuries he had sustained during the attack at his residence, but now what he needed most was sleep. Either that or a good amount of drink. Unfortunately, it didn't look like he was likely to come by either. At least, not anytime soon.

He leaned back against the bark of a date palm, eyes searching the faces of the passersby that drifted in front of him on the street. The crowd had thinned substantially since the previous night. It was early; almost sunrise, he supposed. He was growing nervous. Merris should be back by now.

"Quin!"

He whirled and already had a shield ready to throw up before he saw that it was actually her. He released the magic field, dispelling the energies he had conjured as he caught Merris up in his arms. She fell against him with the soft weight of her body, her hands wrapping around his back as she squeezed him enthusiastically.

"Look what I found!"

Her voice was full of joyous elation. Quin pulled back just enough to see what she had in her hand: a thin strip of parchment with writing scrawled across it. He fought to keep his mind on what she was trying to show him, but really all he could pay attention to was her. His eyes raked over every inch of Merris as he reassured himself that she was alive and whole, standing right there beside him.

"You're safe," he gasped, gaze loosely focused on her radiant features. "What's this?" He glanced down at the note she had shoved into his hand, spreading it open with his fingers.

"I think I found Remzi's cipher," Merris gushed excitedly, smiling at him.

"Remzi?" Quinlan frowned, still gazing down at the thin strip of parchment in his hand, turning it first one direction then the other. "As in Master *Devrim* Remzi? How peculiar; I thought he was dead."

"Apparently not." Her voice was almost giddy with excitement. "I met him in the vaults under Om's temple. Isn't that wonderful?"

"Why, yes, that's wonderful, but—"

Quin found his words cut off by the feel of her lips against his. For a full moment, nothing else mattered in the world. Only Merris, the feel of her touch, the sweet fragrance of her hair. She slid her arms around his back, pulling him even closer.

Then she jerked away, giggling with excitement. Quin was left staring slack-jawed into the space where she had just been, completely dumbfounded. He breathed in a large chestful of air, then pursed his lips as he blew the air back out again slowly.

"That was…unexpected…"

He stared at her in open-mouthed astonishment as she grinned up at him adorably. "You're such a sweetling," she said with a grin. "Quin, I want you to help me disavow the Acolyte's Oath."

Quin winced, taken completely aback by her statement and wondering if he had even heard her right. He found himself more confused than before, unable to do more than reach up and rub his temple with a fist.

She wanted *what?*

Merris smiled then, the look in her eyes bewitching him completely. "I want you to make me your apprentice, Quin. I want to learn from you. I want you to teach me everything you know."

Quinlan Reis shook his head, not even sure if he had just heard her right. "That wouldn't be very much, I assure you," he finally managed to say, thinking of the corpse of the last apprentice he had mentored, which had been left lying in a puddle in the alleyway outside his home. He felt suddenly, terribly awkward. "Look, darling, you don't know anything about me. You don't even know which order I belong to."

"I just assumed you were a Battlemage," Merris admitted.

Quin couldn't suppress a grin as he reached up and swept his hat off his head. With a flourish, he bowed low before her. "Grand Master Quinlan Reis of the Order of Arcanists at your service."

"You're an *Arcanist?*" Merris exclaimed. "How is that even possible? You killed a Battlemage!"

Quin shrugged, straightening himself as he replaced his hat back on his head. "Battlemages do tend to be an insufferably arrogant lot, but they're not particularly well suited to the fine art of assassination," he explained. "If what you need is massive numbers of casualties, then a Battlemage is the natural choice. But if the job requires any element of sophistication or subtlety, then setting a Battlemage to the task would be like turning a bull loose in a porcelain shop."

Merris was shaking her head in disbelief. "But I thought Arcanists just engineered objects of power."

"So says the charter of our order," Quin agreed. He reached down and took her hand in his, guiding her forward down the avenue. "But our particular skill set lends itself well to a wide variety of dedicated tasks. Arcanists are masters of minutiae. If you don't mind me asking, what order were you preferenced to back in Aerysius?"

"I was preferenced to the Order of Querers."

Quin said, "Then it would certainly do you little good to become my apprentice. My particular knowledge base is far too narrow to be of any use to a Querer prospect. And, to be perfectly honest, I'm not certain we'd be very compatible."

Merris appeared to scoff at his words. "Why not? We seem to work very well together." The sound of her voice was low and flirtatious. Her hand tugged at his own, trying to pull him in closer.

But Quin refused to budge. He suddenly had a very bad feeling. There was something wrong about this situation; something about it just didn't feel right. He tried to put a finger on exactly what the problem was, but couldn't. He squirmed internally, writhing in consternation.

"Well, for one thing, my services have not exactly been in very high demand lately," he explained, doing his best to put his apprehensions into words. "It would seem that my reputation has sustained a substantial amount of tarnish. Forgive me for saying this, but you seem to be rather ambitious. I think you'd be far happier with a master of much greater status."

Merris appeared crestfallen, as if shocked and hurt that he would even suggest such a thing. "I am *not* ambitious," she maintained. "I just want to continue my training. And I want to continue it with you."

Quin swallowed. His mind was suddenly panicking, his mouth completely dry. "Why me?" he heard himself whisper.

Then she was kissing him again, this time much more adamantly. He felt her tongue caress his lips, her hands sliding up his neck and running down his back. He couldn't stop himself; he kissed her back, long and hard, his hands stroking through the rich curls of her hair.

"Why not you?" she whispered against his ear after they had finally parted. Her arms were still around his back, her breath warm against the side of his face. "Despite what you think, you're every bit the man your brother is."

Quin felt himself stiffen at the mention of his brother. But her next words took away any last amount of resistance he might have had left:

"And besides, I want you, Quin. Not him."

He could only stare at her, completely at a loss for words. He was not sure if he was even able to breathe.

"Give me your left hand," Quin directed her hoarsely. He was barely aware of what he was doing or why he was even doing it. As if from a great distance, he heard himself say:

"Now, repeat after me:

> *I swear to serve the Lyceum of Bryn Calazar.*
> *I will obey all commands given me by my master without question or hesitation.*
> *May my life be forfeit if either my service or my ability is ever found wanting."*

He waited, holding his breath, listening as Merris repeated the words exactly as he had spoken them. When she was done, he opened his hand, releasing the fingers he had used to encircle her left wrist.

The mark of the Acolyte's Oath was gone from her flesh. In its place was a red and textured scar.

Merris gazed up at him, her eyes moist with a quagmire of emotion. Quin swallowed, unable to break away from the compulsion of her stare.

"Kiss me," was his first command to his new apprentice. "And this time, please don't stop."

Chapter Eight
The Sentinel

Vintgar, Caladorn

Braden awoke to a jarring kaleidoscope of pain. "Come on, come on!" someone was shouting over him, though the sound of the voice seemed to be echoing from very far away.

Braden opened his eyes, peering blearily up into Sephana's panicked features.

"Wake up!" she hissed at him, shaking him urgently.

The motion brought such an explosion of pain and nausea that Braden rolled onto his side, retching as his stomach emptied its contents onto the rocks beside him.

"They're coming!" Sephana whimpered against his ear.

Braden forced himself to his hands and knees, glancing up. Through the mist of the grotto he could see dark forms approaching along the rocks above the river. He couldn't make out faces in the shadows, but he didn't have to. He already knew exactly who they would send.

"Can you stand?"

Braden feared he could not. The raging power of the vortex had exacted too great a toll on him, both mentally and physically. No amount of healing could fix what ailed him; sleep was the only cure for an overtaxed mind.

He reached down at his side and fumbled at the leather straps that secured Thar'gon to his belt. It was still amazing to him that the weapon would even suffer his touch at all. The talisman had been forged with a singular purpose: to be wielded only by the hand of the Warden of Battlemages.

When he had reached for the morning star on the table, Braden had known he was taking a risk. Normally, Thar'gon would have never allowed itself to be lifted by any hand other than Byron Connel's. But Sephana had been right—during time of war, Braden's own authority superseded that of even Connel. It was a technicality he had gambled on.

The moment Braden's hand had closed around Thar'gon's silver haft, the weapon's allegiance had shifted to him. The talisman now recognized Braden as its master.

Which could only mean one thing: war with the Rhen had already begun.

Braden raised Thar'gon in his hand, wielding the short-hafted morning star like a club. Immediately, a flood of invigorating warmth rushed up his arm and into his core, lending his frail body the weapon's own strength. The iconic talisman was sensing its master's need and responding with arcane purpose.

Bolstered by the weapon's vitality, Braden rose trembling to his feet. "Get behind me," he ordered Sephana.

His eyes searched through the shadows of the rocks, at last recognizing the features of Byron Connel. At his side strode Nashir Arman and Myria Anassis. And they were not alone; two dark creatures the size of large wolves stalked menacingly behind them, eyes aglow with a piercing, ethereal light.

They were thanacrysts, demonic hounds that fed solely on the life force of a mage.

"Legend comes to life," Braden muttered in wonderment. The sight of the demon-dogs did not scare him nearly as much as it should have. Rather, it had entirely the opposite effect on him. The spectacle of the thanacrysts only lent strength to Braden's convictions.

He raised Thar'gon up before him, brandishing the talisman in the air.

"Don't come any closer," he admonished the approaching figures. "With this, I have the advantage this close to a vortex."

The three darkmages stopped before him, the thanacrysts bounding to Myria's side. The beasts sat back on their haunches, tilting their heads up to lick the tips of their mistress' fingers with fetid black tongues.

"What are you going to do, Braden?" Byron Connel shouted from across the rocky span between them. "There's nowhere to go."

"I'm not going to let you do this," Braden assured him. "I'll find a way to stop you."

"Why?" Myria demanded, moving forward a step. One of the beasts at her side growled, thick slaver oozing from its mouth. "Why would you want to stop us? Everything you've spent your entire life working toward lies threatened."

"Because what you're doing is *wrong,*" Braden responded emphatically. He gestured at the thanacrysts. "This—this is evil. I will not be part of it."

Byron Connel took another step toward him. "Our plan is going to move forward with or without your help," he explained pragmatically. "If you refuse to aid us, then we'll just find someone else to take your place. Look, Braden. I respect you. I do. But I also have a family. And I won't hesitate to kill you if that's what it takes to save the lives of my children."

Braden gazed at Connel and nodded thoughtfully. He understood. He empathized with the man's situation, even though he didn't have children of his own. But even though he understood, he simply didn't agree. There was only one option, the way he saw things.

"Take my hand," he told Sephana, extending his palm out toward her. He felt her warm fingers clasp around his own.

He closed his eyes and envisioned a place outside of the cavern and yet not terribly far away, a red bottleneck canyon near the entrance to Vintgar he had visited many times before in the very distant past. In his mind, he remembered in great detail exactly what the rocks of the canyon looked like this time of year.

"Vergis," he commanded the silver talisman in his hand.

The grotto of the Nym shivered and then disappeared around them completely. In its place appeared tall sandstone bluffs.

Beside him, Sephana cried out in pain. Glancing down, Braden saw the white fletching of an arrow that had embedded itself in her shoulder.

"Gods be damned!" he swore as Sephana collapsed against him. He caught her up, struggling to ease her to the ground as he quickly mended her wound with the power of his mind. With the aid of the silver morning star, healing such an injury required very little effort; it was exactly what the talisman had been designed to do.

He caressed Sephana's face and then brought the weapon up to confront their attacker.

"Al'thartier!" a bearded man cried out, throwing his bow and quiver to the ground before prostrating himself in the dirt.

Braden stared at the man in shock as waves of anger gradually dissipated from his body. The man was probably a stationed sentry who had merely reacted to their sudden appearance. The man remained in the position of prostration, forehead to the ground, absolutely still. Finally reassured that he no longer posed a threat, Braden set the morning star down at his side.

As soon as the weapon left his hand, the strength lent to him by Thar'gon drained entirely from his body. It had been the only thing keeping him standing. Braden sagged forward, unconscious before he hit the ground.

The Khazahar Steppe, Caladorn

He awoke to a heady blend of fragrances: the sweet scent of horse manure mingled with wood smoke, leather and wormwood. It was an earthy and altogether agreeable odor, not unpleasant in the least. The smell was comforting, bringing back memories of a childhood spent roaming the vast expanse of grassland known as the Khazahar Steppe.

Braden had grown up on the sprawling immensity of the prairie, the youngest son of a warrior-chieftain. He had been raised to follow the same harsh way of life as the rest of his clan, a roguish band of nomadic horse lords who drank hard, fought hard and often died even harder. It was a ruthless and uncompromising existence, brutal from the very beginning.

Braden's mother had died bringing him into the world, and his father had followed her to the grave shortly after, victim of his own indulgences. Orphaned and alone, Braden and his older siblings had been fostered out to other families of the clan.

Braden and Quin had been taken in by one of their various uncles, a hardened old warrior affluent with many horses, wagons and women, but cruel of temperament. He was just as quick with his whip as he was with his bow, and just as likely to strike a maiming blow as to inflict pain. He had taken the two boys into his household as servants, kept them fed and saw to it that their earliest education was provided for. It had been a harsh and bitter upbringing.

Braden remembered well the day he and Quin had left the forest steppe. A robed Master of the Lyceum had shown up among the tents riding an exquisite white stallion of a foreign bloodline. Never had Braden seen a horse so fine of bone, so elegant in pace and conformation. The Master had tested the children of the clan, first the girls and then the boys, gazing deeply into their eyes one by one as they stood together in a makeshift line down the center of the camp. One at a time, the children were dismissed back to their families.

But not Quin. And not Braden.

It had been explained to their uncle that both boys carried within them a spark, something called the potential, a seed so special and so unique that it would only germinate away from the Khazahar Steppe. Because of that one rare trait, both boys were immediately claimed as the property of the Lyceum of Bryn Calazar. Braden's uncle hadn't objected; his life would be easier with two less mouths to feed. And he was well compensated for the loss of his young servants with two colts of the same bloodline as the Master's elegant steed.

Thus, Braden's people had sent him and Quin off to the Lyceum with nothing more than the shirt and trousers they had been wearing at the time. He remembered his uncle standing against the sunset in the waves of thigh-high grass, holding the twin bridles of his two new colts as darkness stole across the prairie behind him. That vision of his uncle was the last sight Braden had ever seen of a man of his own clan other than Quin.

Until now.

Braden struggled upright, realizing that he was the object of attention of a particularly cruel-looking man who sat only paces away, cross-legged on a braided wool rug. A curved short sword was held in his lap, the oiled steel bared from its scabbard. The man was slowly caressing the edge of the blade with a whetstone in smooth, deliberate strokes. He paused in his motion, testing his thumb against the hone of the edge. Then he carefully set the weapon down by his side, hanging the whetstone from a hook at his belt.

"Darius dreoch, Al'thartier," the man pronounced, raising his right hand solemnly to his chest in an expression of greeting. Then the man abased himself on the floor of his tent, kneeling with his face pressed against the carpets.

"Darius dreoch," Braden responded, the customary greeting of the horse folk rolling fluently off his tongue. It was an elegant salutation, one he had not heard spoken aloud in over thirty years.

But then Braden winced, suddenly realizing the significance of the man's gesture.

The warrior had just referred to him as Al'thartier, a Venthic title that could only be translated as Greatest Battlemage. By naming him that, the horselord was honoring Braden's command of Thar'gon. In a society that revered nothing so highly as courage and fighting ability, the man who wielded Thar'gon was the embodiment of the warrior archetype. And now that onus had fallen to him.

Braden winced, suddenly realizing the remarkable position he found himself in. The Jenn, the ancient horse culture of the Khazahar Steppe and Braden's own people by blood, were prepared to recognize him as their overlord.

Braden was rendered speechless, thoroughly overcome. When he had left the forest steppe as a child, he had been among the most humble of its servants: horseless, kinless, penniless, a child slave; nothing more than a liability. When he had become a Master of the Lyceum, his status had increased. But now with Thar'gon his to command, the great horse culture of the Khazahar would be duty-bound to respond to his call.

Thoroughly moved, Braden was so shaken that at first he could find no words to utter.

"Rise," was the only thing he could finally manage to say.

The man complied instantly, returning to his cross-legged position on the braided rug. Braden guessed that he was an elder of his clan, probably a war chief, judging by the rich embroidery on the collar and the sleeves of his tunic. The man's face was sun-worn and deeply wrinkled. His dark and narrow eyes betrayed nothing of his emotions.

Braden regarded him silently for a long moment before wondering, "The woman I came with. Where is she?"

"We preserved the life of the witch from Aerysius," the old clansman pronounced as he resheathed the blade he'd just been honing. "It was obvious that she belongs to you. She is resting now in the tent of my third wife. My name is Elessar. I am warlord of this encampment."

He rose and strode a few paces away to the tent's stone hearth, where he poked around at the graying coals with a stick. Bending over, he set a bronze kettle to heat over the flames. Braden's eyes cautiously tracked the fellow's motions.

"My name is now Braden Reis," he introduced himself. "But I was born Berkant son of Marthax, warlord of the Omeyan Clan."

"I know," the old man responded without looking at him. "I was once a friend of your uncle." Elessar brought his hand up, gripping an object that hung by a thin sinew from a tent pole. He plucked the item down, turning it over in his fingers, at last holding the object out for Braden to inspect. It was a small, whittled carving of a horse.

"You may not remember, but you made this for me," Elessar remarked musingly, "before the *dakura* stole you away."

Braden stared down at the carving, which looked utterly unfamiliar. "I'm sorry," he said whimsically. "I don't remember."

"Of course you don't." Elessar scowled, dropping the small object into the palm of Braden's hand. "You were very young. But you are not so young anymore. And you are no longer Berkant son of Marthax, warlord of the Omeyans. That boy is dead. More than just dead; it is as though he never existed at all. So, tell me, who is the man that addresses me now?"

Braden stared down at the small wooden horse in his hand, marveling at its features. It didn't look at all like the work of a young child. The horse was completely accurate, delicately carved and carefully polished; it even wore a blanket and bridle, both intricately wrought in every painstaking detail. Braden knew enough, now, to recognize the work for what it was: a sign of the potential within him, discovered later by the Master who had taken him and his brother away to the Lyceum. Even then, he had been different. He would always be different. His ability had always been both his strength and his curse.

"My name is Braden Reis, Grand Master of the Sixth Tier and Warden of the Order of Chancellors." He could not look the old man in the eye as he said the long chain of words that formed the imposing syllables of his title.

"You are no Battlemage," Elessar observed, dark eyes filling with ire. "How is it that you come to us bearing the Silver Star of Battle?"

"You're right." Braden shook his head. "I am not a Battlemage. But I'm Battlemage-trained." He struggled to his feet, gripping a tent post for support. "During time of war, my authority supersedes all others, save only for the Prime Warden of the Lyceum. When our legions march to war, it will be I who leads Caladorn's warriors into battle. Thar'gon, ancient weapon of our ancestors, has chosen me as her bearer."

The grizzled old warlord seemed to be looking him over, running his eyes over Braden from his feet to his head, as if assessing the truth of his claim. At last, almost grudgingly, he gave the slightest, most cursory nod.

"I offer my food, my fire, and my protection for both you and your woman," the old man pronounced at last, finally extending to Braden the sacred status of a guest. "Please feel free to walk among my herds choose whichever horses you wish. I will see to it that both arms and armor are delivered to you. In return, I ask but one favor: that you look in upon my son. He has sustained a grievous wound, and your witch-woman could do little for him. I only ask that you try to do what you can.

If nothing else can be done, I would rather it be your own hand that delivers Nerus from his pain."

Braden nodded somberly as he tucked the little horse carving into the pocket of his trousers. "I'll do everything in my power to help your son," he assured Elessar. "And after I tend to him, I'll make myself available to anyone else in the camp that requires mending. But I need you to do something for me. The cry must be raised across the plains. War is coming to Caladorn, and I need the might of the horse lords at my side. I will need riders sent out as fast as possible in every direction to assemble the hordes from across the steppe."

Elessar looked away, allowing his gaze to wander over the felt siding of his tent. "It is your right as Al'thartier to raise the cry. But first I would ask that you speak to the war council of the Omeyans. It would be better to obtain their support."

Braden nodded. "I will speak to the council, as you suggest. Now, please, Elessar. Show me to your son's bedside."

The old man made a motion with his hand, gesturing for Braden to follow him out of the circular lodge. Shirtless, Braden fell in behind him, treading carefully across the carpets. His strength was back, but his legs were stiff after days of bedrest.

Outside the tent, Braden allowed his eyes to wander over the encampment. It was dark; the sun had already set, though the gray glow of twilight still lit the western sky above the bluffs. The red box canyon in the hills below Vintgar was the winter home of the Omeyan Clan. The plainspeople spent the spring and summer months following their grazing herds. But winter came swiftly and cruelly to the steppe, and the Omeyans had learned to seek refuge during the coldest months of the year. A light dusting of snow was already upon the ground, rendering the encampment white except for muddy trails between tents.

As Braden followed Elessar across the camp, he took quiet note of the familiar bustle of life within the city of tents. Everywhere he looked people were busily occupied with the tasks of daily life: women tending cook fires, bowyers and armorers plying their crafts. Sheep and dogs milled about the tents, as often as not followed by a wandering child carrying a stick. A group of men looked up at him from a game of bones as he passed, their faces stern and severe. The men nodded his way in deference. Some stared in outright interest, as if debating whether it would be worth the risk to challenge him to a fight. One small boy came out of a tent and stopped dead in his tracks, gaping up at the sight of Braden. Before the mage could conjure up a smile, the child turned and ran away.

"I am sorry our clan does not remember you," Elessar said, his eyes sadly surveying the people of the encampment. "They will, after this day. Never before has a child stolen by the *dakura* ever been returned to us."

Dakura was the name the clans used to describe the people of the cities, especially Bryn Calazar. The term had a derogatory connotation; the people of the Jenn had a low opinion of any stationary group that subsisted on agriculture.

"This is the yurt of my son, Nerus," Elessar announced, indicating the broad, felt-covered tent ahead of them. He pushed back the flap that formed the tent's doorway and gestured for Braden to enter ahead of him.

Within, Braden found the interior of the yurt dark. A terrible odor hit him strong in the face. The stench sent him reeling; the smell was sweet and sickening, like corpses moldering in a fetid grave. Quiet mewling noises could be heard coming from the far side of a dividing curtain that cut the tent neatly in half. His eyes took a moment to adjust to the darkness. When they did, Braden scowled, swallowing against the urge to retch.

He could understand why Sephana had been unable to help Nerus.

"I'm going to need Thar'gon," he whispered, turning and ducking back outside the tent. On the threshold, he paused and took a deep breath of fresh air. But even that did little to allay the scent of corruption in his nostrils.

"The wound has festered," Elessar explained, spreading his hands.

Braden regarded the stern warrior for a long moment. "I don't know how much of your son there is left to work with. But to have any chance at all, I'll need the talisman."

The horselord nodded. "The weapon remains where you dropped it. Not a hand has been able to lift it, although many have tried."

Braden nodded. "Take me there."

He followed Elessar up a path away from the camp toward the bottleneck canyon where they had first appeared. The old horselord was right; the silver talisman was exactly where Braden had left it. Many tracks encircled the weapon in the snow, and yet the morning star remained exactly where Braden's hand had last set it down. He wrapped his fingers around its leather-wrapped haft and lifted it easily.

The old man nodded once, acknowledging Braden's command of the weapon, then turned his back and walked ahead of him back down the path. Braden strode with Thar'gon at his side back through the center of the camp, doing his best to ignore the stares of the clanspeople.

As they approached the tent of Nerus, he recognized Sephana moving toward him through tight clusters of people. She was still wearing her black Master's cloak, the cowl pulled up over her head as she hurried in his direction. The emotion on her face was impossible to decipher; he couldn't tell if she was more relieved or more angry to see him.

Braden strode over to her, a questioning look on his face. To his relief, Sephana threw her arms around him, collapsing against his bare chest.

"I was so worried about you," she whispered against his ear. Braden put his arms around her and held her close for a moment before pulling back just enough to press a kiss against her forehead.

"I'm fine," he reassured her as his hand caressed a lock of her golden hair. "Everything's fine now." Taking her by the hand, he turned to face Elessar. "I assume that the two of you have been introduced?"

The old man nodded stiffly.

"We have met," Sephana clarified rigidly. Braden could tell by her tone that she did not consider the manner of their meeting an appropriate introduction. He couldn't help the small smile that chased across his face. Sephana was Aerysius-born and -bred, thoroughly out of place on the Khazahar Steppe.

"Elessar has asked me to have a look at his son," Braden informed her. "I hear you were unsuccessful at a mending?"

Sephana nodded, her face going taut. She glanced back and forth between Braden and the old warrior, obviously struggling to frame her words as judiciously as possible. "The arrow was poisoned," she explained carefully. "A mixture of snake venom, horse dung, and putrefied human blood. I couldn't get past the venom. I'm sorry; I'm skilled at healing, but there was just not enough left to work with."

Braden sighed, shaking his head sadly. The usage of such vile concoctions was a common practice across the steppe. It was custom for the warriors of the clans to soak the shafts of their weapons in such filth before riding into battle. The use of such bitter toxins ensured that even the slightest wounds would fester and turn fatal.

"The venom is depressing his breathing," Sephana continued grimly. "I didn't think he would survive the mending."

"I'll see what I can do," Braden said. He glanced over at Elessar for approval and, receiving a nod of permission from the old man, led Sephana into the darkened tent.

He made his way to the bedside of Elessar's son. The young man was lying on a straw-stuffed mattress in the middle of the tent surrounded by three women that Braden took to be Nerus' wives. All three of them were weeping quietly, wringing their hands and clutching one against the other. At Braden's arrival they fled together to the far side of the tent, yielding space so he could work.

The odor was even stronger than it had been before, especially this far away from the entrance. Braden fought against the urge to be sick as he bent over his unconscious patient. He took note of the mottled pallor of the young man's skin, the way the damp flesh seemed to sag against the bones of the face, the man's cracked and peeling lips. Nerus was only hours, if not minutes, from riding the endless plains of the Atrament.

Gripping the talisman in his left hand, Braden set his right hand upon the dying man's chest. The impression that was returned to him was discouraging. Nerus' organs had already begun to fail, his blood teeming with poisons and accumulated toxins. The snake venom had already digested much of his tissues and was now affecting his capacity to draw breath. Elessar's son was all but a corpse, literally rotting from within.

Closing his eyes, Braden did what he had been trained to do by the Battlemages of Bryn Calazar: he opened his mind to the magic field, channeling its energies into Nerus' failing body, using the silver talisman to guide his efforts. He started with the organs that were the most severely damaged then used the argent fire of healing to burn the poisons from Nerus' blood. He left the snake venom and the damage it had wrought for last.

When it was done, Braden opened his eyes and rose to his feet, feeling suddenly, terribly weak. From behind him he could hear the sobs and cries of Nerus' wives. He backed away, catching himself on a pole of the tent.

"I tried," he muttered as he staggered toward the opening. Disoriented, he stumbled and nearly fell. Sephana caught his arm and guided him the rest of the way out through the doorway into the brisk evening air.

"You did more than try." Her voice was hoarse and adamant as she wrapped her arms around him in support. "That man will live, Braden. You accomplished the impossible."

She took him by the hand, guiding him to the nearest campfire and easing him down beside it on a log. She knelt down next to him and, taking his face in her hands, peered at him anxiously. "You're dehydrated," she muttered. "And you haven't eaten anything in days. What are you thinking, Braden?"

"I'm thinking about Cyrus Krane," he stated bleakly. "And Byron Connel…and all the others. We don't even know if Merris was able to warn the Lyceum. Renquist still might be completely oblivious to all that's been going on."

She drew her cowl back, moving to sit down alongside him on the log. Braden took her hand into his own. He traced his fingers along the back of her hand, admiring the softness of her skin.

"We need to talk," he told her gently in a lowered voice. "I need to tell you everything I know, what I found out back there. It's important."

He stopped, realizing that they were not alone at the campfire. A young woman with plaited dark hair was tending to a heavy bronze cauldron. She had ceased her ministrations of the kettle to stare across the fire at them pointedly. At her side, a small toddler clung to her quilted tunic, peering out at them with widened eyes from behind his mother's shawl.

"You can talk to me later tonight," Sephana told Braden, giving his hand a squeeze of reassurance. "In the meantime, let's get some food and drink into you."

The woman across the campfire gestured invitingly at her cook pot. "*Darius dreoch,* Al'thartier. You are welcome to our food, our fire, and our protection."

Braden managed to conjure up something resembling a smile of thanks, humbly accepting her offer. "Some water would be appreciated," he admitted. The inside of his mouth was dry, his lips terribly parched.

"And food," Sephana insisted. "You need to keep up your strength."

"And food," Braden agreed.

The dark-haired woman quickly produced a waterskin made from a sheep's bladder, handing it across the hearth over to Braden. He accepted it from her hand, raising it to his lips and drinking down the cool water in thirsty gulps. In seconds, he had the contents emptied. He brought his arm up to wipe his face.

"Slow down," Sephana admonished him, leaning in to kiss him softly on the cheek.

The clanswoman looked up from the bowl she was filling and smiled at Sephana's gesture.

"Your wife is very beautiful," she commented to Braden as she handed the bowl across to him. At her side, her young son grinned up at Sephana and then squealed in delight when she grinned back.

Braden glanced over at Sephana, a half-hearted smile on his lips. He had never, would never, ask her to become his wife. He had already been married once, a long time ago. He would never make that mistake again.

He would not take the chance that he might hurt Sephana the way he'd hurt his wife.

Braden ate in troubled silence, not really tasting the stew that he spooned into his mouth. When the bowl was drained, he threw his head back and drank the dregs, finally handing it back to the woman across the hearth.

"My thanks," he said to her, unable to look her in the eye as he pushed himself up off the log and started out across the camp.

"Braden," Sephana called after him as she jogged to catch up. "Is everything all right?"

"I'm fine," he muttered as his fingers worked to tie Thar'gon's leather straps to his belt. He tried to change the subject. "I promised Elessar I would make myself available to his people."

"Stop." Sephana's hand on his shoulder drew him up short. She tilted her head to the side, raising her brows as her stare smoldered in frustration. "I'm the Querer, remember?" she reminded him acerbically. "You're not in any condition to see to the needs of this camp. Let me do my job. You go and do yours."

Braden gazed at her levelly, his mouth drawn into a scowl. "And what, exactly, is my job, Sephana?" he demanded of her.

She brought her hands up to her face, rubbing her eyes in obvious exasperation. He could tell that she had been too long without sleep; the strain was starting to catch up with her. She took a deep breath to steady herself, closing her eyes before replying.

"I'm trying," she reminded him. "I really am. I'm doing my best, Braden, but it's hard. The only thing I know is that you need me. And whatever it is you're up against, you shouldn't have to face it alone. I want to be here for you. Please allow me to be."

Braden turned away from the heartfelt tension of her words. He couldn't force himself to look at her; it was too painful.

For the second time in his life, Braden held the fate of a woman he loved in his hands, to save or damn as he saw fit.

And, for the second time in his life, he knew for a bitter fact that he couldn't do anything to save her.

———

Braden stared out at the assemblage of faces gathered around the bonfire built in the center of the camp. The proud warriors of the Omeyan Clan were turned out in a spectacular display of armaments, both the men and the women alike. The neighing of nervous horses and the clink of scale mail could be heard over the sputtering noise of the flames. The air was redolent with a potent mixture of smoke, sweat, searing meat and burning hemp. A cacophony of flutes and lyre music played above the spirited cadence of war drums.

In his right hand Braden fingered the small carving of the stallion he had made in his youth, the one Elessar had returned to him. He clutched it in his palm, the fingernail of his thumb absently scraping along the thin notch between the stallion's tiny ears.

Over his indigo robes he wore a new vest of bronze scales sewn over leather in overlapping rows. Elessar had also fitted him with a warrior's belt, complete with an intricately wrought golden buckle that depicted a horse bent over backwards, as if trying to eat its own tail. Many leather thongs and hooks were attached to the belt, from which Braden had hung Thar'gon and the small arsenal of weapons his benefactor had presented him with: lances, knives, a whip, a pair of short swords, even a whetstone to hone his new collection.

He sat by Sephana's side, listening to Elessar address the gathered war council, as was the custom of the clan. He watched, shoulders tense, and waited his turn. His eyes were trained on the snaking orange flames of the bonfire, watching as a procession of sparks exploded up into the air and then came raining back down again like darting fireflies. As Elessar spoke, a gradual hush descended over the gathered crowd. The drums ceased their beating, the horses quieted, the minstrels laid their instruments aside. A slow tension crept inexorably over the camp, like the anxious quiet before a storm.

"Al'thartier," Elessar finally turned to address him. "The men and women of the Omeyan Clan have gathered to hear you speak. Take up the cry. Say what you have come to say."

Braden nodded and stood up, Sephana rising to stand by his side. In his hand, he still fingered the small wooden horse. He gazed around, taking in the sea of faces before him. With his left hand he held aloft the silver morning star he had taken from Byron Connel, displaying it before the gathered crowd. Then he raised his voice to be heard over the wind-whipped crackling of flames:

"*Darius dreoch,* my people. I was born Berkant son of Marthax, warlord of the Omeyan Clan. But that was many years ago. That was before I was taken away by the *dakura*, who raised me up and trained me to be what I am today. Tonight I stand before you a different man than the one my father intended me to be. I am no longer Berkant of the Omeyans.

"My name is Grand Master Braden Reis, Warden of Chancellors and wielder of Thar'gon, the Silver Star of Battle. War is coming to the plains. I have come to you to ask that the cry be raised that gathers our warriors from across the far distances. The Jenn have always formed the cavalry of Caladorn's combined legions. I would not think of riding into battle without the might of the horse lords at my side."

Of the people gathered around the bonfire, Braden demanded, "Will the hordes of the Khazahar ride with me?"

There was a tense moment of silence. No one responded to his request. A quiet muttering formed from deep within the gathered crowd, gradually rising over the crackling of the flames. Then:

"The call of the Al'thartier must be answered," an old warrior finally stood and spoke up. "It is our sacred duty to heed the cry." Others responded to his words by nodding their agreement. There was a swell of discussion followed by a boisterous chorus of assent.

"Al'thartier!" another man shouted, and the shout was taken up across the gathering.

"No!" Braden admonished them harshly. "Never call me that again. I am no Battlemage."

His words immediately silenced the gathering. He could feel the stares of the warriors on him, wordlessly demanding explanation. He could almost feel the heat of their rising anger. The fingers of his right hand continued stroking the polished wood carving of the horse. The grip of his left hand tightened on Thar'gon.

"*Darius dreoch,* Braden Reis of the Lyceum. What would you have us call you, then?" the patient voice of an old man inquired of him at last.

Darius dreoch. The words echoed in Braden's head, the ancient formal greeting of the horse lords. "May you offer protection," was the phrase in Rhenic. The sound of the words resonated in Braden's mind, slowly taking on new significance, evolving into the solemn onus of duty. With that phrase in mind, Braden responded to the old man's question, addressing the gathered crowd.

"I've come to protect, not to destroy." He raised his voice, staring at each man and each woman in turn as he paced in a circle around the fire. "I've come to stand guard against a storm of darkness that threatens to destroy our people. I can no longer afford to be just a Chancellor, and yet I have no desire to be a Battlemage.

"Call me a Sentinel," he asserted, lowering Thar'gon back down to his side. "A protector, whose duty it is to keep watch and defend against the encroaching darkness that threatens to consume our lives, our liberty, and our lands."

His words caused an emotional stir around the fire as men and women voiced their eager support. Braden turned to find that Elessar had come up quietly to his side, extending toward him the offering of a thin dagger with a slender, ebony hilt. Braden accepted the offer of the blade gravely, fully appreciating the significance of the gesture.

"Which direction would you have us ride?" Elessar wondered, fingers stroking the hilt of the dagger one last time as he released it into Braden's care. "Southward to Lor-Gamorth or westward to Glen Farquist?"

Braden looked down, sliding the blade into a loop of his war belt. With a sigh he brought his eyes back up past the flames, staring out across the mouth of the canyon. Toward the east. Toward the dawn.

"Neither," he responded ominously. "This time, our fight isn't with the Rhen. What threatens our homeland doesn't invade from without; it festers from within. This time, the war we fight is against our own.

"We march on Bryn Calazar."

Chapter Nine
A Shift in Perspective

Bryn Calazar, Caladorn

Merris collapsed on top of Quin, panting in breathless exhilaration. Her cheeks were flushed red, a glistening sheen of perspiration frosting her body. Beneath her, Quin lay with eyes wide open but staring sightlessly up at the ceiling. Every so often he gave a faint shiver.

Merris trailed her lips against the side of his neck, squirming her soft body against him.

"I think you've got some more in there," she urged in a sweet whisper. "I bet I know where to find it."

Quin reached up to pat her consolingly on the back, furrowing his brow and shaking his head slowly from side to side. "Mercy, no," he whispered. "I'm afraid you have vanquished me entirely. I am utterly defeated, madam."

Merris giggled, rolling off him onto the straw-stuffed mattress. She lay her head against his lanky frame, tracing a line down his chest with a finger. "I suppose I should allow you some time to recuperate," she mused with a smile. "Tonight I want you to do that thing that you do to me again."

"That thing that I do to you?" Quin smiled innocently.

"You know exactly what I mean." She grinned, a mischievous glint in her eye.

Quin snaked an arm around her and pulled her in for a kiss. "So you like that thing that I do to you?" he teased, lips exploring the delicate curve of her collarbone.

"Oh, yes," she murmured, closing her eyes at the memory of the last time he allowed the power of his mind to flow through her like an exhilarating torrent of carnal energy.

"I do believe you're going to be the death of me," Quin muttered sagely. "I swear you're more obsessed with lovemaking than the average man."

Merris grinned broadly at him. "Then you're lucky I'm not the average man."

He raised his eyebrows, nodding in easy agreement. "Yes, actually, in that respect I am quite fortunate." Then he was all seriousness, squinting down at her in appraisal as he ran a hand through her long, tousled hair. "You know, I think I prefer you as a blonde."

"Do you, now?" she muttered, lifting a soft platinum curl before her face, twining it about her fingertips. She had discovered that she actually liked the change. When the decision had first been made to hide in plain sight in the Lantern District, Merris had suggested darkening her hair in order to disguise her appearance. The platinum blonde had been Quin's idea. Easier to subtract than to add pigment, he'd argued, although Merris suspected he simply had a preference for the color.

"I think it suits me," she mused, then reached up to stroke the backs of her fingers through Quin's full growth of beard. "I fancy your new whiskers."

He smiled, rolling over onto his side. "Be a darling and fetch me a drink?"

Merris kissed him on the neck as she swung her legs over the edge of the bed. "I'll do you one better. I'll fetch the whole bottle."

Sounding already half asleep, Quin muttered, "That's my lovely girl."

Merris slipped a thin silk robe over her shoulders, tying it closed about her willowy figure. She combed her fingers through her hair swiftly then let herself out into the narrow hallway. From behind the next door, she could hear the muffled sounds of love-making.

She wandered down the hallway in the direction of the inn's common area. It was mostly empty with only a few patrons seated on rugs and cushions spread out across the floor. Silk curtains draped down from the ceiling, partitioning off small sections of the room, allowing space for privacy and talk of trade. Most of the ambient lighting came from a diverse assortment of colored lanterns that hung suspended by long chains from the ceiling, shedding surreal patterns of dappled light and shadow across the floor.

A storm was coming. Merris could already hear the howling of the wind as it gusted through the streets outside. Seen through the glass above the door, the afternoon sky looked dark and ominous, illuminated by the occasional flicker of lightning.

The dark-haired and bearded owner looked up from where he stood with a towel in his hand, rubbing it over a collection of copper trays with a scowl of concentration on his face. She was not the only girl wandering about the inn in a thin silk robe; Quin had picked the establishment with a keen eye for camouflage. Merris was posing as one of the inn's servant girls who offered the customers food and drink or whatever they had an appetite for at the moment.

The owner tossed his head at Merris as she approached, extending a palmful of coins out toward him.

"There's my newest ripe and pretty flower," he greeted her without looking up from his task. "How is that wealthy merchant you're with? I hope he is still paying well. He is certainly taking advantage of my generous hospitality."

He chortled as he reached up, ignoring the coins in her hand, and trailed his fingers down the silken length of her torso.

"My client desires another bottle of wine," Merris informed him flatly, standing there with her hand extended as he ran his hand along the curve of her hips. "Make that two bottles," she amended, glaring down at the offending hand.

"You're a soft little flower," he whispered under his breath, withdrawing his hand. He chortled noisily, bursting into a wheezy coughing spasm. Merris stared at him, jingling the coins around in her hand.

"My client prefers a red vintage," she reminded him.

He grunted and turned abruptly away, clawing the coppers out of her hand and then disappearing through a doorway. He returned after a moment, handing Merris a pair of wine bottles corked with rags that had been rolled up and stuffed down their necks.

Merris gazed at him dully as she accepted the bottles from him and turned away, striding back out of the common area. Once back in the narrow hallway, she stopped, leaning against the bricks of the wall as she adjusted her robe. She didn't want Quin finding out what the inn's owner had been up to every time she left the room to fetch a new bottle of wine. They were supposed to be blending in and avoiding notice. Merris didn't know for certain what Quin would do if he found out, but she was fairly sure that his reaction would probably cost them their hiding place.

The sound of thunder echoed from without. It was followed by the harsh noise of pattering rain.

Once back in the room with Quin, Merris slipped back underneath the covers of the bed. "Your wine, my sweet," she giggled, plucking the rag out from the bottle's neck.

Quin sat up, accepting her offer of the bottle and, tossing his head back, downed a large draught of wine. "You are such a lovely dear," he commended her. "I am very fortunate indeed to have an apprentice so devoted to fulfilling my every whim."

Merris smiled, leaning in to kiss him on his whiskered cheek. "I'm the one who is lucky to have such a shrewd and clever master so willing to share his knowledge. So what lesson are you planning to teach me tonight, my mighty stallion of a man?"

Quin tilted his head back for another gulp of wine that ended in an abrupt fit of coughing. "'Stallion of a man', now, is it? Darling, I'm not usually one to dodge a compliment, but I beg you to at least try to conceive of some endearment that I have a prayer of living up to."

Merris giggled, running her hand down the side of his face. "I have no complaints," she whispered.

Quin leered at her sideways from around the neck

of his wine bottle. "Do you want me to teach you or make love to you?"

"Both," she challenged.

He shrugged helplessly, shaking his head. "I'm sorry, darling, but you've just about broken this stallion's wind."

Merris swirled a finger around in his hair. "Then show me something new. Show me something about healing."

Quin sat up, allowing the covers to fall off his emaciated chest. He took a last pull off the wine bottle before setting it down on the floor on his side of the bed. His dark hair was rumpled, but he still looked far better than he had when Merris first met him. The new beard did something to fill in the skeletal gauntness of his features. Even his color had improved somewhat in the past two weeks they had spent at the inn.

"Here, give me your hands."

She sat up, her hair spilling in platinum curls down her back as she offered her hands out toward him, palms up. The pink scar that encircled her left wrist was very visible even in the dim lighting. Quin had tried to heal it, to no avail. The awful thing was carved permanently into her flesh, a constant reminder of the oath she had abandoned. No amount of wishing or even magic would ever make it go away.

"Now, pay attention," Quin ordered, suddenly businesslike, without any trace of his previous levity. "I'm going to teach you how to detect the amount of air in a person's blood. It's a good indicator of their condition. Close your eyes and try to feel your body through me."

Merris obeyed, squeezing her eyes shut. Immediately, she could feel the link he established with her, like a conduit opening up between the two of them. She became aware of herself through Quin's magically enhanced perceptions. The feeling was disorienting, like staring at a mirror's reflection in another mirror set slightly off-angle, creating a series of endless reflections, each slightly more distant. She could pick which image she chose to focus on, but then became confused, unsure of which point of view she had just selected. Was it her own perception of her body, or was it Quin's perception of her? Or was it Quin's sense of his own self? It took her a moment of adjustment to focus on the perspective she thought was the correct one.

"Is it getting any easier?" he asked.

"Somewhat," Merris acknowledged, her eyes closed in concentration. "But it still makes me queasy."

"It'll improve with time and practice. Now, I want you to keep your focus on my perspective. Don't let your attention drift back to your own sense of self; you're going to want it to, and you need to resist the impulse."

"I won't," Merris assured him.

"Now…hold your breath," he directed her. "Don't breathe until I tell you to."

Merris complied, concentrating on feeling her own body through Quin's link, through his perception of her. At first, there was no change that she could sense. Then, gradually, she could feel something begin to diverge.

There was an insistent tug in the back of her mind, a desire to change perspectives back to her own sense of self. She refused to acknowledge the urge, instead concentrating harder on that strange sense of something moving further away from its set point. The further apart it grew, the greater the need became to switch back to her own perspective. The need intensified, becoming an overwhelming desire.

"Breathe," Quin commanded, his voice insistent as he released the conduit between them.

Suddenly confronted with her own awareness, Merris sucked in a great gasp, dizzy from lack of air. She lay back against the pillows, panting, her eyes sparkling in excited wonder. She bolted upright, hugging him as she exclaimed breathlessly:

"I felt it! Quin, that was marvelous! Can such a technique be used offensively?"

"Certainly it can," he said, "with just a little modification. Like this."

Suddenly, Merris wasn't breathing again. Only, this time, it wasn't by choice. Her throat hadn't closed and there was no gasping or wheezing. Her lungs had simply ceased to function. Moreover, she could feel through Quin her state of unbreathing. It was that same sense of divergence she had felt before, only this time she knew it was being inflicted upon her.

He quickly released his hold on her lungs, allowing her chest to resume its natural rhythm. Instead of the panic she should have felt, Merris experienced a thrill of exhilaration. She flung her arms around him.

"So simple," she exclaimed. "I can't believe it's that easy to kill someone."

Quin reached down by the bedside, scooping up his wine bottle by the neck. "Killing someone is easy, darling. All it takes is a little knowledge and a robust sense of moral depravity. Keeping someone alive takes far more effort."

He took a long pull off the wine bottle then just kept swallowing until most of the liquid was gone. He brought his hand up to rake across his lips. He then set the near-empty bottle down beside him, cradling it in the crook of his arm.

He was getting that dazed look in his eyes again. It was not the first bottle of wine Quin had consumed that afternoon. Merris smiled when she saw that expression in his eyes; he was feeling his liquor more than usual. Sometimes he opened up more in such a state. Sometimes, but not always. She liked him better when he was in a mood to be talkative.

Merris leaned forward, cradling her head in her hand with her elbow settled deeply into the pillow alongside him. "Tell me, Quin. How is it that you know so much about killing people?"

He took another swig of wine. "Because inventing new ways to kill people used to be what kept me employed."

"Really?" Merris pressed, "What kind of job did you have?"

Quin shrugged, lifting the bottle for another swallow. "I'm an Arcanist. I'm trained in the making of things, trinkets and suchlike. Objects of power. My specialty was making dangerous trinkets."

Merris smiled slyly. This was a side of Quin she hadn't expected. "How intriguing. Why? I mean, why would you choose such employment?"

"Because I was good at it," he stated with a whimsical smirk on his lips. He stared off blankly into the dim shadows of the room, eyes focused loosely on somewhere in the past. "More than good, really. I was a master of my craft. My mind is sadistically warped in an artistic sort of way."

Merris kissed him on the forehead, stroking a finger through his dark and wiry beard. "What happened?" she prodded. "What made you stop inventing things?"

He looked down. "Because one of my trinkets was used to kill someone very dear to me." Upending the bottle, he finished the last of the wine. Then he set the container down beside the bed, giving it a little push to send it over.

Merris sat up, drawing her knees against her chest. "Really? Who?"

Quin was still staring down at the mattress beside him, conspicuously avoiding her eyes. "The woman I loved. Unfortunately, my brother had already married her."

"You killed your brother's *wife?"* Merris gasped.

"No. Braden killed her." Quin sucked in a cheek, obviously uncomfortable with the topic of conversation. "I simply provided the motivation. And the means."

Merris stared at him wide-eyed, absolutely transfixed. "What *happened?"* she all but exclaimed.

"More wine, I think, will be required," he stated.

Merris nodded. "Of course."

She reached down by the bedside and produced the second bottle she had fetched, now glad she'd had the foresight to acquire it. Quin had a habit of running out of dialog the moment the liquor ran dry. This was not a topic of conversation that Merris was willing to miss out on for lack of enough wine to sustain it.

She removed the rag from the bottle's neck and handed the wine over. Quin grasped the bottle with a fist around the neck, upending it thirstily.

"Her name was Amani," he said in a voice low and gruff as he lowered the bottle back down to his side. "Braden and I were both in love with her. I think everyone was. She was the sort of person who could light up a whole room with just one smile. She was the most gentle and kindhearted person I've ever met.

"We both wanted her. Had we been raised with the clans, we probably would have fought to the death over her. As it was, Braden and I decided that the most judicious thing would be to appear together and present our mutual suits before her father.

"Of course, Amani's father picked Braden over me." Quin glowered as he took a large gulp of wine. "My brother was always the one with all the accolades, all the titles...all the panache. How could I hope to compete with that? Next to Braden's glittering accomplishments, my own resume appears quite lackluster, I assure you."

"So Braden and Amani were married," Merris prompted him, attempting to move the conversation forward.

"Yes, they were. And, as one might expect, he made her thoroughly miserable." Quin shook his head, his face growing quite somber. His eyes finally lifted to consider Merris' face. "Braden is many things, but romantic is not one of his qualities," he assured her. "Don't get me wrong; he tried his best to make her happy. He bought Amani anything she could possibly desire. Clothing, gifts, power, friends…" His voice trailed off as he shook his head sadly. "He just never understood that the one thing she desired most from him was his time. And time was the one thing Braden would never give her."

He took a quick nip off the bottle. "So I took it upon myself to offer Amani some companionship from time to time."

Merris' jaw dropped open in disbelief. "You slept with your brother's *wife?*"

Quin emitted a slight shrug, canting the bottle in his hand lazily to the side. "Oh, it probably wasn't very smart. But I'd be lying if I told you it was the basest thing I've ever done in my life. Believe me, my morals have been compromised so far and so often, you'd swear I was the politician in the family. Amani needed me, so I was there for her. It's really just that simple. Braden never once suspected us. He never cast a shadow of doubt her way.

"Then one night, things went sideways."

His tone had suddenly darkened. Merris detected the change immediately. She placed a steadying hand on Quin's arm, wordlessly urging him to continue.

"I was on an assignment down in the south. There was a man—a mark. I got careless; I let them catch me off-guard. Aerysius offered to hand me over in exchange for a ransom, but Renquist refused to pay up. I suppose my life just wasn't worth it to him."

Quin took a deep drag off the wine bottle before lowering it back down again. He sat there on the bed, twirling the bottle around by its neck as he swirled the liquid up the sides of the container.

"In the end, Amani was the only one who came to my rescue. She stole some documents from Braden's desk, the kind of papers she had no business even knowing existed. She handed them over to the enemy in exchange for my life.

"I was released," he said, scowling. "But by the time I got back to the Lyceum, Amani had already been charged with treason. The penalty for treason in Bryn Calazar is death."

Merris stroked her fingers down his arm to his hand, squeezing his fingers with her own. "What did Braden do?" she wondered softly.

Quinlan shrugged. His voice cracked as he responded pragmatically, "What else could he do? He did his duty. He used an artifact of my own creation to execute her, a silver medallion I called the Soulstone." There was a deep, festering anger in his eyes that Merris found fascinating.

He continued gruffly, "Braden fastened the clasp around his own wife's neck and then watched Amani die. It was horrible: slow, agonizing. He just held her as she writhed on the floor, screaming as her life was sucked right out of her."

Merris gaped at him as she shook her head, trying in vain to reconcile the image just provided by Quin with the Braden she had met back in Aerysius. The two visions just didn't seem to want to resolve in her head. "Why would he do such a thing?" she wondered, failing completely to comprehend.

Quin raised his eyebrows, taking another large swallow of wine. "Because, in Braden's mind, it was the right thing to do," he explained matter-of-factly. "He was even awarded a promotion for his cooperation in the matter."

Merris narrowed her eyes in consternation. She couldn't help the next thought that sprang to her mind. It slipped right out of her lips before she could stop it:

"What would you have done?"

"Put in the same position? I would have used the damned thing on myself."

He lifted his bottle toward her as if proffering a toast. On his face he wore a vile and sardonic grin. "My dear, let us drink to the perils of love."

The Dhural Uplands, Caladorn

Braden gazed out across the undulating terrain that sprawled out before them to the far distant horizons. Above, flocks of eagles flew across the cloud-filled skies or wheeled high overhead, riding the updrafts. The vast herds of the Jenn waded up to their knees in a sea of silkweed, oats and einkorn.

"I can't believe so many actually came," Sephana remarked from the back of the sorrel mare she rode at his side.

Braden couldn't help the smile that came to his lips. After traveling for two weeks among the warriors of the Omeyan Clan, Sephana's appreciation for the horse culture had increased, but she still vastly underestimated the competence of the Khazahar's warrior tribes. If nothing else, the sight before them should be evidence enough to convince her.

From over the great distances of the eastern steppe, the tribes had come to converge at this place, every warrior of every clan, every nation of the Khazahar hordes. As was their custom, the Jenn had sent their women and children far away to the south, to the elder forests of the Sajar-Asharu, the Mountains of Cedar. There, they would remain in relative security, waiting for word that all was safe to return again.

The herds had made good time. In only two weeks, the Omeyan people had traveled from their winter home in the canyon near Vintgar all the way to the eastern edge of the steppe, almost to the dark waters of the sea. The walls of Bryn Calazar would be within sight tomorrow evening if they kept going at their present pace. The hordes travelled swiftly, leaving behind a vast swathe of trampled ground behind their fast-ranging herds that numbered in the tens of thousands.

Beneath him, Braden's horse danced impatiently. He reached down and ran his hand along the stallion's neck and scratched its short-cropped mane. The flame-colored stallion was an exquisite creature of a proud bloodline, the product of thousands of years of expert husbandry and meticulous breeding. But it was spirited, eager for the thrill of the gallop or the heat of a fight.

At a signal from its rider, the stallion knelt forward to the ground, allowing Braden to slide easily from its back. He removed the embroidered riding blanket and slipped the bridle off over the horse's ears. He stroked the animal's velvety nose, murmuring a quiet word of thanks. Then he released the stallion back to the herd for the night. Braden watched as the chestnut darted off, tail carried high and neck arched, anxious for the company of its own kind.

He looked to Elessar, who remained mounted on his own dark bay. "We'll make camp here for the night," Braden explained to him. "Then tomorrow we'll go down into the valley and make preparations for a siege."

Elessar commanded his own horse to kneel, slipping agilely off its back. His darkly bearded face looked even more severe than usual as he stepped forward. He appeared to be mulling the implications of Braden's words. After a long moment of silence, he voiced his concern:

"Grand Master Braden, of course you understand that we lack the means of laying an effective siege to a port city the size of Bryn Calazar."

Braden nodded, placing a hand upon Elessar's shoulder in reassurance. "I am aware of that. It doesn't matter, to be frank. The point is, you'll be there, threatening their walls. I just need you to get their attention. Get their attention and *keep* their attention."

The warlord nodded thoughtfully. "I understand. The siege is a feint. We are meant only to distract."

Braden frowned, hearing the disappointment in the warlord's voice. He felt suddenly uncertain. "I'm sorry, Elessar. I hope that doesn't lessen the honor or the glory for your warriors. If the darkmages are focused on you, then I'll be able to strike them where they are most vulnerable: in the heart of the Lyceum itself."

The old man's gaze lowered to Thar'gon, the silver talisman of war that hung at Braden's side. In his age-strained voice, he assured him, "There is no lessening of glory. It remains an honor to ride at the side of our Sentinel, a mage whose blood is our own blood."

Braden smiled, releasing his shoulder. "Believe me, the honor is mine, Elessar." He took a step away then turned back again, as if in afterthought. "We'll be riding out tomorrow. Sephana and I are going ahead into the city to implement our part in all this. We will talk more tonight."

At a stiff nod from Elessar, Braden turned away. He walked over to where Sephana sat astride her sorrel mare.

"Walk with me?" he invited her.

She dismounted and, with Braden's help, released

her mare back into the herd. He took the bridle from her, hanging it in his hand along with his own, tossing her riding blanket over his shoulder.

"You know, I'm perfectly capable of carrying my own tack," she chided him.

Braden nodded with a smile. "I know. And I could let you do it. But I won't."

Sephana shook her head with a wry grin, falling into step beside him as he wandered toward a low hill. He took her hand in his, feeling the straw of the steppe grass brush softly against his knuckles. He led her up the rise of the hill and, at the summit, tossed down the horses' tack, spreading out the blankets for a place to sit upon. Overhead, storm clouds gathered to darken the western horizon.

Braden brought Sephana's hand up to his lips, pressing it with a tender kiss. "I've always wanted to show you Bryn Calazar," he told her softly. "I just never thought it would be like this."

An expansive peal of thunder rolled toward them from the distance. Looking up, Braden saw strange, flickering lights that seemed to come from deep within the churning layer of clouds. The magic field itself felt a little strange. He reached out with his mind, sampling the flow of the lines of power in this place. The feel of it made his skin itch, raising goosebumps on his flesh.

"What is it?" Sephana wondered beside him.

Braden continued to stare upward at the strange flickering lights in the clouds. A streak of lightning forked upward from the ground.

Grimly, he informed her, "It's been happening on and off for the past couple of days. I didn't want to say anything. I was almost hoping you wouldn't notice."

She turned toward him, obviously troubled. "What is it, Braden?"

He gazed into her eyes, observing the fear that was already there. He could tell that she already knew. "It's beginning," he informed her. "The magic field is starting to destabilize."

Sephana turned and took a step away as lightning crackled overhead. He wished that he could see her face. He wanted to know what emotions were there.

"You're doing the right thing, Braden," she said at last, still with her back to him.

Deeply troubled, Braden focused his stare downward at the ground. "Is it really the right thing? Because I'm not so sure anymore."

"Of course it is." She turned and strode back toward him, catching him up in her arms, running a hand through his hair. Gazing into his eyes, she insisted, "What Krane is doing is wrong from so many different perspectives. The mages he has surrounded himself with are only acting in their own interest. There's a whole world out there that knows nothing of magecraft or magic fields or any of that nonsense. Those are the people who will suffer the most if Krane goes through with his plan. It's always been the responsibility the mage class to protect the weak, lend strength to the powerless. Cyrus Krane and his kind have forgotten that."

Braden drew in a deep breath, letting it out again slowly. He couldn't help but glance back up at the strange, ominous lights in the clouds. "I know we're in the right. But that doesn't make it any easier."

A terrible, sickening feeling twinged across the inside of his skull. Overhead, the clouds fairly spasmed with a rippling burst of luminescent color. Wincing, Braden started to bring his hands up. But the sensation was gone almost as soon as it began. The magic field yet resonated around him, swirling like eddies in a stream current.

"I felt that." Sephana's voice was low, devoid of all emotion.

Braden swallowed. "I know. I felt it, too."

She brought her hand up to the side of his face, directing his stare into her own. "Are you scared, Braden?"

He pulled back, taking long strides away from her. He didn't want her to see his face.

He was confronted with the sudden, overwhelming impulse to turn and just walk away, just leave her standing there on the hillside. It would be so easy to save her life; all he had to do was nothing.

He didn't know if he could go through with it. He didn't know if he had the strength to condemn another woman to death.

Chapter Ten
A Step Away from Hell

Bryn Calazar, Caladorn

The crackling noise of thunder jarred Merris wide awake. She pushed back her thin blanket, sitting straight up in bed and glancing around in apprehension at the darkness.

Something in the world seemed terribly out of sorts. There was no other way to describe the feeling that clawed at the back of her neck, grated down her spine. Beside her, the sound of Quin's snoring continued unbroken. Merris didn't understand how the man could remain asleep despite the lingering tension in the air. But Quin had so thoroughly drowned himself in wine over the past two weeks that Merris doubted he could sense much of anything anymore.

She pulled her embroidered silk robe on over her shoulders, tying the sash firmly into place. Opening the door of their small room, she let herself out into the dim hallway. The ringing swells of laughter echoing from down the hall seemed distant and muted.

Merris stopped at the entrance to the common area. She peered around the corner, scanning her eyes over the faces in the crowd. It was late, but the flow of customers had been steady throughout the evening. The common area was almost full, patrons reclining in rings of conversation upon the rugs or huddled up in tight clusters beside flaming braziers. The sounds of boisterous laughter filled Merris' ears. Silk-robed serving girls wove in and out about the room, carrying trays of food or pitchers of drink.

Merris frowned, staring out at the animated scene. No one in the room appeared bothered or disturbed in the least. No one seemed to so much as sense the strange tension in the air. She lingered in the doorway another minute before finally turning away.

As she did, a hand caught her shoulder.

Merris whirled, startled, to find herself enveloped by Sephana's soft embrace.

"Merris."

She recognized the voice instantly, but the shock of actually hearing it prevented her from reacting. Dazed, Merris pulled back away from her former mentor, gazing with shock into the woman's beleaguered features. Sephana's eyes were troubled, trailing over her with obvious concern. Blinking, Merris took in the sight of the tall and bearded man standing behind Sephana, garbed in travel-stained robes covered with a vest of barbarian scale. It took her a long moment to recognize Braden's unkempt features.

Rendered speechless, Merris could only gaze back and forth between the two of them in mute astonishment. Slowly, her senses returned to acuity. Taking Sephana by the hand, she pulled her forward and guided them both down the length of the hallway to the room she shared with Quin. She glanced around to make sure no one was watching. Then she quickly opened the door and ushered them both inside.

Darkness covered them with the closing of the door, but the amber glow of Braden's magelight spread out to illuminate the room in a soft radiance. Behind her, a copper lantern flared to life.

Merris glanced toward the bed where Quin lay sleeping, his naked body barely covered by a corner of the blanket. The sound of his snoring was loud and abrasive. Merris caught a glimpse of the bitter scowl that passed over Braden's face at the first sight of his brother. For just a moment, there was an almost murderous glint in his dark eyes. He glanced sideways at Merris.

"I had given you credit for better taste," he commented, striding toward the bed.

Merris immediately found herself back in Sephana's arms, the irritating woman stroking through her hair in a vexing attempt to offer comfort. Merris wanted to pull away; Sephana fairly reeked of sweat and horse. She forced herself to smile instead.

"Thank the gods you are safe," Sephana muttered, pushing Merris' platinum locks back away from her face. She took a seat on the floor, urging Merris to follow suit. Two embroidered cushions were the only decorations in the room except for the carpets and the bed.

Merris finally trusted her voice enough to speak. "We feared you were dead," she explained. Her fingers traced over the silken folds of her robe, adjusting the lay of the fabric over her chest.

"Came damned close," was Braden's grated response. He was trying to shake his brother awake. "Quin. *Quin.*"

A low groan issued from the direction of the bed.

"Why am I surprised?" Braden sounded exasperated. As Merris watched, he closed his eyes and placed an outstretched hand on his brother's chest. After only a moment he opened his eyes again, withdrawing.

Quin stirred, groaning, then slowly cracked open his eyes and gazed around in confusion. At the sight of his brother, his mouth dropped open. His hand shot down to his side, pulling the blanket further up his chest. His eyes wandered from Braden across the room to Sephana. He sat up, his expression brightening.

"Why, I'll be damned if it isn't Braden." He regarded his brother with a wry grin. "I don't quite believe I'm saying this, but I think I might actually be glad to see you."

Braden stared flatly ahead for a long moment, at last acknowledging him with a nod. "It's been a long time, Quin. Maybe even long enough. I see Merris found you."

A grin sprang instantly to Quin's bearded face as his eyes flicked across the room to where Merris reclined on a cushion beside Sephana. "Yes, she certainly did find me. Thank you, by the way, for the gift of her company. She's been a rare glimmer of sunlight."

"Yes, she certainly looks like a rare glimmer of sunlight," Sephana remarked dryly.

Merris shifted uncomfortably on her cushion, her hand moving upward to attend to the gape of her cleavage. On the inside, she was seething. On her face, though, she managed a shy smile.

"Please forgive my appearance, Master Sephana," she apologized. "I was only trying to fit in."

Sephana cast a withering glance in her direction. "I'm sure you were, dear," she responded dismissively before turning to Quin. "I'm so very sorry to have stumbled in upon you like this. You must be terribly uncomfortable. Why don't we all go out for a while and give you some space to clean up a bit?"

Quin shook his head, raising his hand up as if warding off the thought. "Thank you, no. Too much going in and coming out will attract the kind of attention we don't need. And, at any rate, I've never been exactly prudish. Darling," he called over to Merris, "would you mind fetching my clothes up off the floor? I can't seem to recall where I put them last. That's a good dear."

Merris smiled politely as she moved to comply, noticing out of the corner of her eye the looks exchanged between Braden and Sephana. She located Quin's robe and vest at the bottom of a rumpled pile of filth. She tried to think back to the last time she'd actually seen him wearing clothing at all. She didn't think he had put on so much as a stitch since the day they'd first arrived at the inn.

She handed the clothes over to Quin with a sweet smile on her face, bending down to brush the side of his cheek with a dutiful kiss. The smile on her face remained a fixed thing as she sat beside him on the bed.

Ignoring Sephana's astonished reaction, Merris busied herself with helping Quin pull his indigo robes on over his head. When at last she had him fully dressed, Quin immediately rose to his feet and affected a formal bow in the direction of Sephana.

"May the peace and blessings of the gods be with you, Great Lady," he announced splendidly. "You truly are just as gracious as Merris has described. Quinlan Reis, Fifth Tier Grand Master, at your service."

Sephana acknowledged him with an almost regal nod. "Please. Let us dispense with such formalities. It is very much an honor, Quinlan. I never thought that I would ever have the opportunity to meet a member of Braden's family. You have no idea how much this means to me."

She rose from her cushion and strode across the room with the grace and dignity of a queen despite the tattered green dress that stirred around her. She embraced Quin warmly, softly kissing him on both cheeks before pulling away. He smiled shyly, looking patently uncomfortable.

"That's enough," Braden barked tersely. "Were you able to pass my message along to Renquist?"

Quin nodded, sucking in his lip as he sank back down onto the bed next to Merris. "Unfortunately, we did," he muttered. "We discovered that Prime Warden Renquist was the man Merris saw that night in the cellar."

Merris nodded adamantly, wringing her hands in her lap. "It was him," she affirmed. "It was his voice I heard. He was wearing the ring."

She gazed up at Braden, watching with fascination the slow progression of emotions that evolved gradually across his face. At first, there was only confusion followed by doubt. Then his eyes slowly widened as realization hit home. Fear came next. She could practically map the connections his brain was making as he groped toward full understanding of the magnitude of Quin's revelation. Despair was slow to come, but come it finally did.

"You are certain?" he demanded at last in a hollow-sounding voice.

Merris nodded without looking at him. She was watching Sephana's hand moving up to cover her mouth as she shook her head slowly in denial. It was an intriguing reaction, quite different than Braden's had been.

Braden sagged back against the mud bricks of the wall, allowing his body to slump down into a crouch, resting his elbows against his knees. He brought his hands up to his forehead, raking back his dark hair.

"Then we're completely on our own," he whispered. "The entire Lyceum will stand barred against us. It's over. There is nothing we can do if Renquist has allied with the rest."

Sephana shook her head, eyes adamant. "All is not lost," she rebuked her lover confidently. "There is still hope to be had. We have each other. And, together, our combined strength is not insignificant."

Gazing at her former mentor, Merris was reminded of exactly why she had never liked the woman. Sephana had a way of positively exuding competence; it was a trait that made others trust her and turn to her for guidance. It lent credence to her gentle arguments and weight to her quiet authority.

Braden stared miserably upward, eyes wide and wandering the ceiling, mouth open and agape. "It's happening again," he whispered. The sound of despair in his voice was chilling.

Merris concentrated, reaching out from within to sample the pulse of the magic field as she had been taught to do since the first days of her training. The field was still tangibly hostile, its normally tame currents flowing unbridled across the city. Again, she had the gnawing feeling that something in the world had gone terribly wrong.

She opened her eyes, suddenly afraid. "I don't understand. What's happening?"

"The cipher," Quin exclaimed, changing topics as if he hadn't even felt the spike in the magic field or noticed his brother's reaction to it. "Merris, where did you put the parchment?"

Merris wanted to gape at the man, that or slap him for being so oblivious. Had he really drunk his senses so utterly dull that he couldn't even sense what was happening? With the strength of his power and the rarity of his talents, Quinlan Reis could have been one of the greatest mages in the history of the Lyceum. To see him so thoroughly reduced by his own fallibilities was repulsive.

Merris forced a smile and leaned against him, stroking a soothing hand through his hair. "Don't worry, darling, I have the parchment right here."

She pressed a kiss against his cheek, rising from the bed to walk halfway across the room. There, she stopped, using her foot to roll an empty wine bottle out of the way. Stooping down, she found the brick she was looking for in the flooring, hooking the nail of her index finger on it. At first, the brick didn't want to come up; it slipped away from her twice, falling from her grasp and sinking back down into place.

After some struggle, she finally got it. Lifting the

loose brick enough to grab ahold of it with her other hand, Merris moved it aside to reveal the small hiding place she had discovered.

She smiled up at Quin, lifting the folded note up for him to see. "Here it is, my sweet," she reassured him, rising to her feet. She offered the parchment across to Braden.

Quin's brother frowned as he accepted the note into his hand and unfolded it. Merris watched with a self-satisfied smirk as Braden's eyes scanned over the strip of parchment she had torn from the book in Om's temple, the page with Remzi's notes scribed in the margin.

"You're right," Braden said at last. "It's an encryption of some sort, and a dark one at that. There might be a method of decoding it, but we lack the key. Look at these runes. They're Venthic, but ancient. This could be the sequence that unlocks the Well of Tears. How did you come by this?"

Hearing him talk, Quin rolled his eyes and muttered derisively, "Braden, you are a tin god of frivolous knowledge. When you're done parading your intellect, would you mind please explaining what the hell is going on?"

Braden stared down at his upturned hands. The sleeves of his robe had pulled back, exposing his arms. He contemplated the smooth texture of his skin, so very much different from the mages of Aerysius who wore the mark of the Acolyte's Oath upon their left wrists like a thick iron shackle. He let his gaze wander over to Sephana, to the markings of the oath engraved into her own flesh. It looked very much like a lustrous metallic chain, glimmering gently in the candlelight. The markings looked very lovely, a sinuous band of grace and courage. He found himself rather envious of them.

Before him on the bed, Quin still sat staring straight ahead with a look of brazen disbelief on his face. Braden had stopped speaking minutes before. He was still waiting to hear his brother's response. Quin seemed be groping for words.

"Let me make sure my understanding of this situation is accurate," he said finally. "You want to kill us all—literally bring an end to the world as we know it—and you're asking me to *help* you?"

Sephana leaned forward, burnished ringlets spilling forward over her shoulders. Clasping her hands in her lap, she assured him, "Quinlan, the world as we know it is already coming to an end. There's nothing we can do to stop that. The best we can hope to accomplish is to minimize the extent of the damage. And if we can contain the casualties to the mageclass while shielding the common citizens, then that has to be our duty. Possibly our highest duty."

Quin sucked in a cheek, grimacing at her words. "I understand your line of reasoning," he allowed cautiously. "I'm just quite certain I don't agree with it."

Braden glanced up from his position against the wall. Glowering across the room at his brother, he remarked with a voice full of brittle contempt, "Of course you don't agree with it. That's because you've never had any honor."

His statement made his brother sit straight upright. Quin's face turned pale, his cheek twitching the way it did when he was very angry. "Who are you to dare lecture me about honor, Braden?" he demanded in a composed voice seething with injury. "I'm not the brother who killed his own wife."

The insult of his words sent Braden reeling. He shook his head, glaring up at Quin with scalding hatred in his eyes.

"That's where you're wrong," he snarled. "It is not my fault Amani's dead; it's *your* fault. First you seduced her, then you plagued her with guilt until she mortgaged your life at the expense of her own. If you had just one scrap of moral decency, my wife would still be alive today. *You* were the one who should have been executed that day, not her. If you had any shame at all, you'd understand that."

Quin merely shrugged. "That's your way of looking at it, Braden. Not mine." He gathered his hat in his hand as he rose from the bed. Placing it on his head, he adjusted the brim carefully. "I wish you both the best of luck, but I want no part in any of this."

He extended his hand toward Merris, who accepted his invitation and rose to follow him toward the door. Her eyes were wide and deeply unsettled.

Braden called after him, "Integrity comes from doing what you know is right, no matter how much you despise doing it. You're still one step away from Hell, Quin. It's not too late to turn back."

At his brother's words, Quin drew to a halt and glared back at him over his shoulder. "I might be just a step away from Hell, Braden, but you've already thrown yourself in."

He reached out to open the door.

Feeling utterly besieged, Braden rose to his feet, resigned, running his hands back through his hair. "I need you, Quin."

His brother finally turned completely back around to face him. Quin was actually chuckling, a wry and scornful sneer on his face. "You've got to be kidding me. When have you ever needed me before in your life?"

Braden lowered his head, gazing down at the floor. He swallowed the emotions gathered in his throat.

"I've always needed you," he explained in all honesty. "You were just never there for me. And now I need you more than ever. This is our last chance to be brothers, Quinlan. It won't make up for all the bad blood between us, but it will sure make up for a lot of it. Now, I'm asking you: will you be there for me, Brother?"

It was Quin's turn to look down. His gaze dropped to Braden's waist, coming to rest on the silver talisman that hung from his war belt. Quin's eyes slowly widened as it dawned on him what Braden's possession of the ancient heirloom implied.

He brought his hand up to rub his eyes in weary resignation. "Please tell me that isn't Thar'gon."

"Of course it is."

Quin dropped his hand, tilting back his head to stare upward at the ceiling. "Oh, gods, we really do actually have a chance, don't we?" He did not sound pleased about it at all.

Braden nodded, running his hand down Thar'gon's leather-wrapped haft. "Yes, we do have a chance. We have a very good chance, actually."

Quin drew in a deep breath and held it for a long moment. Then he blew it out, puffing out his cheeks and muttering, "What a honey of a pickle."

He raised Merris' hand to his lips, pressing a gentle kiss against her knuckles. "Wait for me here, darling," he directed her. "I have to go collect some things."

He tipped his hat. Then he turned and strode out of the room.

Merris flinched at the sound of the closing door, dropping back down onto the bedside. Alone in the room with both Braden and Sephana, she felt suddenly very uncomfortable. Both Masters intimidated her terribly, making her skin fairly crawl with the degree of power they were both capable of wielding. Especially Sephana. She didn't trust the woman. She might be able to manipulate Braden if necessary; he was male, after all. But Merris knew from experience that her former mentor was thoroughly immune to her influence.

"Come now, dear," Sephana beckoned, moving to sit beside her on the bed. She took Merris' hands into her own, caressing her thumbs against her wrists.

She inhaled sharply. "You disavowed the Acolyte's Oath?"

Sephana's voice sounded horrified. Merris felt a numbing stab of fear. She had forgotten all about the damning absence of the chain from her flesh.

"Quin made me his apprentice!" Merris gasped defensively, glancing back and forth between Braden and Sephana. "We didn't think I'd ever be going back!"

"Quin?" Braden gasped, his face a mask of incomprehension. "You traded your allegiance to *Quin* over Aerysius? This is all my fault," he insisted to Sephana. "I should have explained things better before sending her off."

Sephana dismissed him with a curt wave of her hand. "What's done is done. It doesn't matter anyway," she sighed, turning back to Merris. "I guess all that matters is this: are you happy?"

Merris frowned, blinking in consternation. She really didn't understand Sephana's reaction at all. Why would the woman care whether or not she was happy?

"I'm...very happy," she responded quietly before admitting, "I'm also scared."

Sephana nodded in understanding. "Of course you are, dear. We all are. Listen. I'm not going to promise you anything, but there is a chance that you might survive this. You are not a Master, after all. There is no gift yet in you. You can sense the magic field, but you have no power to influence it. That might make all the difference between life and death for you."

Merris stared at her dully, not really listening to any of Sephana's words. She wanted to leave. She *needed* to leave. She was starting to feel very claustrophobic in the small room.

"So, tell me, how did you come by that sequence?" Braden inquired of her.

Merris turned toward him, running a hand through the platinum spirals of her hair. She explained, "I met a Master by the name of Devrim Remzi in the vaults under Om's temple. I got the sequence from him."

Braden frowned, eyes sliding to the side in thought. "Devrim Remzi." He seemed as though he might know the man. Merris figured he probably did; they were both colleagues of the Lyceum, after all.

He continued almost to himself, "Remzi would know the Empirical side of this situation better than anyone else. He might even be able to help us destroy the Well of Tears." To Merris, he wondered, "Did you get the impression that Remzi might aid us? Or is he thoroughly their man?"

Merris shrugged, realizing this might be her one opportunity to escape their tense presence. "I couldn't say for certain," she responded. "If I could talk to him again, I could find out. He seems easy enough to find; I think he spends a great deal of time in the temple. He may even be living there."

Braden and Sephana exchanged a long look. At last, Braden nodded. He put his hand on Merris' shoulder. "I want you to go back to the Temple of Wisdom. Find Remzi and bring him here if you can. I need you back here by second watch. Do you think you can do that?"

Merris nodded eagerly. "Oh, yes!" she exclaimed. "Anything I can do to help. I'll hurry back."

She sprang up from the bed and then paused, realizing that she couldn't run out into the streets in the silken robe of a serving girl. Somewhere on the dirty floor of the room was the elegant wrap she'd worn on the first day of her arrival.

Glancing up at Braden, she wondered self-consciously, "Would you mind turning your back for a moment?"

As he complied, Merris allowed Sephana to help dress her, assembling all the pieces from off the floor into a rumpled but serviceable garment. She donned the dupatta last, draping it gracefully over her shoulder and fixing it in place.

"You look beautiful," Sephana smiled, stroking her cheek. "Doesn't she, Braden?"

Braden nodded once without looking as he strode over to a cushion and dropped down upon it. He pulled out a knife from his belt and began using the tip to scrape at the dirt under his nails.

Merris glared at him in disdain, feeling thoroughly insulted by his lack of response. Red heat rushed to her cheeks, her nails digging into the flesh of her palms. She swallowed, feeling the anger slide like a lump of poorly chewed food down her throat and into her stomach. She took a deep breath, inhaling fresh air while exhaling the remainder of her ire. She looked back up at Braden with a grin on her face and hatred in her eyes.

She ran her fingers through her curls then offered Sephana a warm hug. "Thank you again. I'll do my very best," she promised, smiling with as much affection as she could muster.

Merris could not bring herself to say anything to Braden. As far as she was concerned, the man was utterly contemptible. Pulling back from Sephana's embrace, she opened the door and let herself out.

Once outside the inn, Merris smiled triumphantly. Away from Braden and Sephana, away from Quin's suffocating presence, she felt a sudden, remarkable thrill. She started down the city street with a smile of delight on her face, noticing how people dodged quickly out of her way in deference, clearing a path before her. She did not understand how or why, but her mage training was somehow obvious to the common folk that walked Bryn Calazar's crowded streets. There was no longer any hesitation or indecision in their eyes. When they looked at her, when they saw her gaze, they just knew. They could sense the potential within her. It was in the way she carried herself, the grace with which she moved. The confidence projected from her face.

Merris giggled and spun around in the street, the sound of her laughter like ringing silver bells. People darted back away from her, their faces clouded with confusion. The looks in their eyes made Merris smile even more.

She crossed the bridge over the River Nym out of the Lantern District, turning onto a broad avenue. Overhead, on the cliff above the sea, sprawled the

Lyceum's cascading domes. The Lyceum's grand structure stood watch above the harbor, its tall minarets and golden domes drawing Merris toward it like a moth to a candle flame. She desperately desired to be a part of that splendor, to take her place within those lofty walls. She had come so far and was now so very close.

All she needed was the gift. But the only way she could acquire power of her own was to have it Transferred to her upon the death of another mage.

"Turn and look at me, love."

Merris whirled at the sound of a stranger's voice, redirecting her attention from the Lyceum's shining walls. Behind her stood an exceptionally attractive man with dark-olive skin and piercing hazel eyes. There was something about his eyes, far more intriguing than just the color, that Merris found immediately captivating.

"Yes, it is true," the man said with a charming grin, nodding in a satisfied way. "You are even more beautiful than I believed. I must know your name."

His words brought a smile to Merris' lips. He held her eyes entranced by his gaze.

"Merris," she offered.

"Merris," the darkly handsome man spoke her name as if savoring the sound of it on his tongue. "You intrigue me, Merris."

Merris blinked. There was something about him. Too late, she noticed the shadows that consumed his eyes.

Merris recoiled, backing away from the man as a chilling fear drove deep into the pit of her stomach. She turned to flee—

—and ran right into the chest of another man standing right behind her.

"Nooo..."

It was really more of a moan than a word. But it was the last word ever spoken by Merris Bryar.

Chapter Eleven
The Monster Within

Bryn Calazar, Caladorn

Braden held Sephana's hand in his own, messaging the markings on her arm gently with his thumb. The silvery luster of the chain on her wrist glimmered in the flickering light of the lantern. The intricate design looked very much real, not at all like a tattoo or sketch, but rather with an illusion of depth and realism that was remarkable.

Braden invited her, "Tell me again how you came by this marking."

Sephana graced him with a patient smile, obviously pleased by his interest in the symbol. She explained, "When an acolyte is first brought before the Assembly of the Hall, they are made to swear the Acolyte's Oath. The vow pledges us to a far higher duty than what we may have served previously. The mark of the chain reminds us of our obligation to that duty."

Braden nodded thoughtfully, still caressing the pad of his thumb over the beguiling and intricate design. He was vaguely surprised that there was no texture to the image at all; despite appearances, the skin of Sephana's wrist beneath the chain was just as smooth and soft as the rest of her arm.

"What were the words of the vow that marked you with such a fetter?" he wondered.

She drew herself up on the side of the bed, withdrawing her hand from his grasp but leaving the markings uncovered by the sleeve of her gown. Holding his gaze, she recited formally:

> "I swear to exist only to serve the land and its people.
> With my life, if possible. If not, then by death."

Braden nodded, looking down. "That's really quite profound," he said finally. "And remarkable, when you think about it. That vow seems to be the embodiment of our own purpose. I mean, that is our goal, is it not? To live up to the letter of that oath?"

Sephana seemed to be gazing at him with a newfound respect, appearing to weigh his words carefully, considering their implications. "Indeed, it is," she finally agreed.

He reached out and took her hand in his. "I want you to help me say the Acolyte's Oath. I want to make sure I get the words right."

Sephana frowned, staring at him skeptically for a long moment as if expecting him to change his mind. At last, when it became obvious that his motives were pure and unwavering, she nodded and muttered solemnly, "All right, Braden."

She took his left arm into her hand and encircled her thumb and fingers about his wrist. "Repeat after me," she directed him firmly.

Braden closed his eyes as he solemnly uttered the phrases of the vow, repeating them exactly as Sephana instructed. When he finished, she released her grip upon his arm.

He opened his eyes, looking down. The sight of the fresh markings on his wrist didn't surprise him in the least. What was shocking was how the emblem of the chain looked so natural against his own flesh, already seeming so much a part of him. He rotated his arm, allowing the intricate pattern to glimmer metallically in the light of the tapers as he inspected the fresh design.

He felt awestruck, rendered thoroughly speechless by the beauty of the symbol. Very seldom in his life had he ever acted on impulse—doing so had never seemed to work out very well. Nevertheless, Braden was glad he had chosen to take this leap of faith. It seemed very right.

He grinned up at Sephana, feeling somewhat euphoric. "This doesn't mean I'm bound to serve Aerysius now, does it?" he asked in jest.

"It does not," she assured him with a smile. Then she bent forward, wrapping her arms around him. "I don't know if I've ever told you how much I admire you," she whispered in his ear. "You're the kind of person that I've always aspired to be. I want you to know that. And I also want to tell you how much I love you."

Braden stiffened in her arms, her confession bringing him only pain instead of gladness. He squeezed his eyes shut, wishing with all his soul that he could actually be the man she thought he was. He wished he was worthy of such praise.

"You honor me too much," he cautioned her. "You are an amazing woman, Sephana. You deserve far better than I can ever give you."

Then he kissed her slowly, drawing her down onto the bed with him as his hand went with purpose to the fastenings of her gown.

That was how Quin found them hours later. Drawing the large pack he was carrying off his shoulder, he dropped it to the floor. On top of it he tossed down a jumble of assorted items he'd been carrying in his arms. He stared in astonishment at the sight of his brother and Sephana lying entwined in his own bed. After a moment, he remarked:

"They say that a man is not made by clothes and manners alone. Which is a good thing, Braden, because I see you have neither."

He sank down onto a patterned rug, reclining with an elbow on a cushion, chin propped in the cup of his hand. "Would it truly have put you out so much to rent a room of your own?"

Braden cast a weary grin in his direction. He lay with his arms folded around Sephana, who was somehow still managing to stay asleep, head cradled against his chest.

Braden responded with quiet aplomb, "In the future, I will try harder to retain both my manners and my clothing in your company."

Quin grinned, always glad to have his own sarcasm returned in kind. "That's all I dare ask. Here, why don't you put these on instead of those horse-smelling rags you wore in? And I have something for Sephana, as well."

Sitting up, he fished around in his leather pack, producing a stack of folded garments. He laid them out on the fringed rug beside him. Then he stood up and walked toward the door, announcing, "It seems I've worked up quite a thirst. I'll just go grab a bottle of wine. Where is Merris?"

Braden's eyes slid to the side. Quinlan frowned, knowing well that reaction and not liking it in the least. He had seen that look on his brother's face too many times before. Usually right before Braden explained why he had made some decision that Quin knew he wasn't going to like but had better start getting used to.

Quin lifted a finger, shaking his head as he took a step toward the bed. "Oh, don't you start, Braden. Don't lay there scheming up justifications before you even tell me what you've gone and already done. Now, where did you send her off to?"

Sephana roused from sleep, bringing a hand up to rub at her eyes as she squinted up at Quin blearily.

"Go back to sleep, my dear. I very much doubt you had any part in this," Quin told her brusquely. Then he glared down at his brother with his arms crossed over his chest.

Braden squirmed himself into a reclining position against the pillows, pulling the covers up to cover Sephana's shoulders and most of his own chest. He glanced sideways at Quin with an irritated scowl.

Reluctantly, he admitted, "I sent her back to the Temple of Wisdom."

Quin's mouth dropped open, eyes widening. *"Why would you do that?"* he demanded. "Master Remzi surely reported her presence there the moment she left! That's the first place they'll be looking for her to show back up!"

"It's possible," his brother agreed. "But there is also a very good chance she can win Remzi over to our cause. The man's reasonable, Quin, and we need him. I thought it worth the risk."

Quin raked his hair back away from his face

before scrubbing his hand over his darkly whiskered chin. "This is unbelievable. The way you treat me is appalling, Braden. I would never disrespect you so."

Braden frowned up at him, a look of incomprehension clouding his face. "Disrespect you?" he repeated. "Quin, she's just an acolyte."

Quin drew himself up very formally, holding his hat before his chest with both of his hands. Rigidly, he stated, "Merris is my apprentice now, Braden. And I'm in love with her." At the look of astonishment on his brother's face, he continued defensively. "Look, I didn't mean to have feelings for her, but that doesn't change the fact that I do. And it doesn't excuse your actions."

Clinging to the blankets, Sephana sat upright on the bed, pulling the covers tightly around her body. She gazed up at Quin with eyes full of honest sympathy.

Braden bowed his head, finally nodding in resignation. "Then I'm sorry, Quinlan. I didn't know. I mean, you've only known her for, what? Two weeks?"

Quin sucked at his lip, staring down at his hat in his hands. He was fingering the brim, rotating it slowly in his grip. "I understand, Braden," he acknowledged somberly without looking up. "You couldn't have known. But next time, please trouble yourself to ask."

"I will. I'll go out and look for her."

"No. That won't help at all." Avoiding his brother's eyes, Quin turned toward the door, replacing his hat on his head and muttering, "Merris is a resourceful girl. She'll come back." He reached for the door handle. "I believe I'll just help myself to a spot of wine. Why don't the two of you get dressed."

Merris gazed up at the high vaulted ceiling graced with a colorful tile mosaic. Soft magelight glowed from the four corners of the room, illuminating the walls and the columns with a diffuse and scintillating glow. Merris marveled at the elegant sophistication of the chamber, every detail meticulously presented to emphasize the majesty and splendor of the Lyceum and yet subtly reduce the status of the visitor.

The man standing behind Merris placed his hands upon her shoulders and applied a gentle but consistent pressure, forcing her downward to her knees. She complied, lowering herself to kneel upon the chamber's sumptuous woven carpets. Her hands were bound behind her back, rendering the action a bit awkward. She gazed ahead, eyes wide with a heady excitement laced with fear.

The man who entered the vaulted chamber was not at all who she'd been expecting.

Merris shivered, a feeling of dread overcoming her as she stared up into the ominous face of Cyrus Krane. The Prime Warden of Aerysius stopped in the doorway of the room, pausing there to consider her with an expression of distaste. Oddly, he was wearing the indigo robes of the Lyceum in place of the black robes of Aerysius that were his custom. Over the whole affair he retained the white cloak of a Prime Warden. Merris wondered what the change in wardrobe might signify.

He strode toward her, reaching out his hand and taking her by the hair, wrenching her neck back until Merris was forced to stare upward into his sinister black eyes. She gasped at the lack of humanity in Krane's stare. He looked utterly different from the last time she had seen him, the day she had followed him down into the tunnels beneath the cellar. Krane no longer carried himself with the dignity and composure of a Prime Warden.

He looked rather like a demon, eyes sinister pools of shadow.

Krane coldly examined her, taking in the features of Merris' face. He did not appear pleased at all with what he was seeing. Still with his hand entwined in her hair, he spoke down into her upturned face:

"You've always had such a high opinion of yourself. It amazes me; your audacity knows no bounds."

He tightened his grip on her hair, leaning forward until his face was scant inches away from her own. "Somehow you found out that I'd discovered the little secret you've been hiding. That's why you followed me that night. You must have come across the order I'd signed to have you dismissed. Were you going to try to blackmail me into letting you remain in Aerysius? Was that your plan? As if I would ever let a child as damaged as yourself accept the Transference."

Merris swallowed, perspiration beading on her

brow. She could do nothing but gaze up into his cruel eyes, mouth open and panting. A chill fear crawled over the exposed surfaces of her body, raising goose pimples on her flesh. She wanted to turn away, hide her eyes from the terrible intent written in Krane's shadowed visage. But he had her too tightly by the hair; she had no choice but to confront the sinister fury of his gaze.

"I only need one last sacrifice to unseal the Well of Tears. I will enjoy harvesting your blood. The service brought about by your death might be enough to justify the miserable burden of your life."

He smiled cruelly as he released her with a shove, spilling her backward to the ground. Merris collapsed upon the rug, tears welling in her eyes. She opened her mouth to beg for mercy, but the words would not form in her throat. Only silence escaped her quivering lips; it was not his will to let her speak.

Tears spilled freely down her cheeks, raining from her chin. She had come so close to fulfilling her dreams. The power she had always aspired to had been practically within her grasp. She could feel it, stirring through her, filling her with its promise, every time she lay with Quinlan Reis. She had every right to make it hers.

But now those dreams would be forever lost.

Cyrus Krane had seen through her, seen through to the gaping hole where her heart should have been. He had discovered the monster that lived inside her, the darkness of her soul that she had labored a lifetime to conceal from the eyes of others.

Merris remembered well the night the monster had come to dwell within her. She had been only a little girl at the time, living on the streets of Aerysius. She had been made to look on as her mother had been savagely raped and then bludgeoned to death. Then her attacker had turned his attention to Merris. He had taken her back with him, had kept her locked away like a special trophy, exacting pleasure from her pain for a very long time.

The monster within had been spawned during those months of torture. It had been nursed on the blood of her innocence, weaned by the death of her childhood. Its coils had wrapped tightly about her soul, clutching and constricting, squeezing out the pain of emotions until only a comforting numbness had instilled itself in their place. It was a monster condemned to be forever greedy, forever hungering, with an appetite for power and control that could never be satisfied.

Somehow, Cyrus Krane had found out about her inner monster. He had conspired to send Merris away down the mountain, to dismiss her from Aerysius altogether. So Merris had decided to follow him, to find out something she could use against him as a bargaining chip. Something that would force him to allow her to remain.

How foolish she had been.

Merris bowed her head and cried in desperation, unable to do anything more.

"Don't be so quick to rush to judgment, old friend."

Merris whirled at the sound of the voice coming from behind. Gaping, she found herself staring up into the imposing face of Zavier Renquist. She tried to scuttle away from him as he strode briskly toward her, but her bonds prevented her from moving out of his way. He stopped in front of her, lowering himself to a crouch until he was at eye level with her face.

She stared up at him with wide and fearful eyes. Prime Warden Renquist was an imposing man, broad of shoulder, with long brown hair pulled back and gathered in a braid at the crown of his head. He wore the same white cloak as did Krane over the flowing blue robes of the Lyceum.

He leaned ominously forward, examining her closely in the harsh glare of the chamber's magelight. His shadowy eyes stared deeply into her, down into the very depths of Merris' tormented soul. He seemed to approve of what he discovered there; the corners of his mouth drew upwards into the faintest hint of a smile.

"You lust for power of your own," he murmured after a long moment of consideration. "I can sense the hunger for it within you. I can satiate that desire."

Behind him, Cyrus Krane growled, "Merris Bryar is an acolyte of Aerysius. She is my responsibility to dispose of as I see fit."

Zavier Renquist did not remove his eyes from Merris. He reached up, caressing her cheek, drying her tears with the palm of his hand. "She is an acolyte of Aerysius no longer, my friend," he uttered with his back yet to Cyrus Krane. His hand moved to the other side of Merris' face, stroking away the dampness left behind by her tears. His hand then went to Merris' arm, tracing the red, textured scar that encircled her left wrist.

"This woman before you is an apprentice of the Lyceum," he stated with confidence. "She is under my own jurisdiction. And believe me, Cyrus, I am more than pleased with what I see here."

Zavier Renquist smiled down upon her in an almost fatherly sort of way. He then leaned forward to press a gentle kiss against her forehead.

"You are Merris Bryar, acolyte of Aerysius, no longer," he pronounced ominously. "You have become an apprentice of the Lyceum. Upon the death of your current master, I will find you another. In return, I only ask that you agree to two very simple terms. Does that condition sound agreeable to you?"

Merris nodded eagerly, her eyes glistening with gratitude.

Zavier Renquist smiled, patting her hand. "Very good. By what name shall you be called?"

Merris swallowed, gazing up into the Prime Warden's trenchant face with a newfound sense of wonderment. She drew in a deep breath, finding strength in her voice at last. The thrill of excitement that stirred within her veins made the sound of her tone almost breathless.

"I am…Arden Hannah."

The Prime Warden smiled, obviously pleased with her selection. "Arden. That means 'passion' in the language of my own people. From this day forth, you will be known to the world as Arden Hannah, apprentice mage of the Lyceum. Now, my darling, let us talk about preparing you for the Rite of Transference."

"Rite of Transference?" she gasped, a sharp thrill of excitement surging through her veins. "Prime Warden, I don't understand. Who will I be receiving the Transference from?"

"Quinlan Reis," Zavier Renquist responded with a shrug. "Or Braden Reis; whichever brother I fail to sway. Remember those simple terms you agreed to?"

The woman named Arden Hannah could only nod, stricken speechless with euphoric desire.

Zavier Renquist unmade her bonds, taking her hand into his own and lifting it up to her lips. He allowed her to press a kiss against the knuckles of his right hand, smiling warmly into her lovely face.

"The first of my terms is this: you shall betray your friends. After you receive the Transference, you will commit your soul to Xerys. You will then join the alliance I have forged and help us save our world with the power of the Onslaught."

Arden's eyes gleamed in the warm glow of the magelight that scintillated along the walls of the chamber. She ran her hand through her hair, taking up a platinum curl and twirling it between her fingers. Tears of gratitude gathered in her eyes.

"I don't know how to thank you," she whispered in response.

Chapter Twelve
Of Light and Shadow

Bryn Calazar, Caladorn

Braden examined the garments his brother had left behind for him on the carpet. He held up the first article, a thigh-length black tunic. Beneath it was a pair of worn but serviceable trousers and a patterned *kafyah*, a type of traditional scarf donned by warriors of the clans before going into battle.

There were also items for Sephana's use that would render her less conspicuous on the streets of Bryn Calazar. The thick wool dress she wore marked her too obviously as a woman of the Rhen. Quin had provisioned her with a short silk gown that was at once both practical and lovely, matched with a pair of bright leggings. The combination would free up her legs and allow her to blend in with the local populace.

They donned the new clothes, Braden slipping on the scale male vest over his tunic, girdling the whole affair with the war belt Elessar had given him. In a leather pouch attached to it, he discovered the small wooden horse he'd carved as a child, yet another gift from the clan chief. He held the tiny stallion in his hand, smiling down at it sadly before tucking it back into the pouch at his waist. Then he wrapped the *kafyah* about his neck, tying it in place.

Turning, he caught sight of Sephana slipping into the turquoise dress of gauzy silk. Seeing her in the sleeveless gown with its vibrant hues, Braden couldn't help but stare. In the fashion of his homeland, Sephana looked radiant, her beauty unbridled and enriched.

"Gods, woman," he muttered, staring at her in open admiration. "You never stop reminding me of how lucky I am."

Sephana smiled at him gratefully. "You look…fierce." She somehow managed to make the statement sound more like a question than a compliment.

Braden grinned wryly. "That's rather the point, actually. A little intimidation is never a bad thing."

"I suppose it's not," she agreed just as the sound of the door opening made them turn to look.

Quin entered the room, hefting a wine bottle in his fist in a gesture of greeting. Braden nodded indifferently in his direction, all trace of his prior levity gone, sapped away by the sudden appearance of his brother.

"How much have you had to drink?" he wondered testily, staring down at the new chain upon his wrist as a means of avoiding eye contact.

"Not nearly enough, I assure you," was Quin's saucy response. "Surely you can't fault my lack of sobriety while facing the end of the world?"

"It's not the end of the world," Sephana corrected him mildly. "Just *our* world."

Braden blew out a heavy sigh, exasperated by his brother's flaws. "I told you that I need you, Quin. That means all of you."

"You'll have all that's left of me, Brother," Quin assured him. He strode forward into the room, throwing his head back and draining the last dregs in the bottle. He then tossed the container down on the floor and flopped down onto a carpet.

Braden stared at the bottle rolling noisily across the bricks, following it with his eyes until it finally came to a rest against the wall. He shifted his gaze back to Quinlan. For the first time he realized that his brother had changed into a different outfit, as well. No longer was he clothed in the stained and rumpled robes of the Lyceum. Instead, he was garbed in the rich silks of a nobleman.

He wore a black kaftan longcoat over a pristine white tunic, silk trousers and a long vest of gold damask. He still retained his Rhenic-style hat, though. He had even shaved; the wiry and unkempt beard was gone, replaced by a well-groomed mustache. He wore his dark hair oiled back, curling neatly over his collar.

"You cleaned up," Braden remarked. "Thank you. It's an improvement."

Quin merely shrugged. "I had to find something suitable to be buried in."

His voice was absent its normal wry undertones of wit. It took Braden a moment to realize that, for once, his brother was being absolutely serious.

"What do you think?" Quin asked, indicating Braden's new garments with a resentful nod. "Good enough for your own funeral? I had a hard time picking those out, you know. It's a dreadful thing, actually, dressing your own brother for his grave."

Braden winced, casting an anxious glance back over his shoulder at Sephana. "It'll do me just fine," he managed stiffly.

"Don't be cruel, Quinlan," Sephana admonished, looking pale.

Quin dismissed her with a grunt, moving to kneel down beside the pile of items he'd tossed down on the floor earlier. Braden scowled, trying to make sense of the jumble of clutter as he watched his brother rummage through the diverse collection.

Gradually, he found his consternation replaced by a growing sense of wonder. "Are all those artifacts?" he breathed, dropping down to crouch by his brother's side.

He reached down, picking up the first object that caught his eye: a silver rod ending in a wolf's head. Quin nodded in response to his question. He was still sorting through his collection, appearing to be grouping objects by category.

Sephana sank down to sit on the edge of the bed. "I don't believe it," she marveled. "Where did you get all this?"

Quin just shrugged without looking up at her. "I'm an Arcanist. Making artifacts used to be my passion. I'm just glad I had the common sense to hide most of my collection in a place where they'd never think to look for it."

"What place was that?" Braden wondered.

"The Lyceum," Quin smiled proudly. He pointed at Thar'gon, which Braden wore hanging from his war belt. "That talisman's the greatest asset we have, actually. Almost like carrying a Circle of Convergence around in your pocket. I don't have anything nearly so powerful or so versatile. But I do have these."

Loosening a leather cord, he unrolled a long, quiver-like case. From within its folds he produced two wooden staves, which he held crossed before him, one in each hand. The staff in his right hand was thin and black, longer than he was tall. The staff in his left hand was much shorter and squat, made of golden wood polished to a glossy sheen.

"Light or shadow?" he inquired of Sephana.

"Light," she responded without hesitation. She had to reach up fast, barely managing to catch the golden staff he tossed her way.

"It's a light staff," Quin explained in answer to Braden's unspoken question. "It's also imbued with amplification and shielding characters."

Braden nodded, feeling somewhat comforted. Between the three of them, Sephana was the weakest member of their group. It was good that she was a Querer, but she was still only third tier. She would need all of the help she could get.

"Is that your old shadow staff?" Braden wondered, indicating the tall ebony staff Quin retained in his own hands.

Quin shook his head. "I made a new one," he admitted. "This one has a few extra tricks the other didn't have."

Braden picked up one of many palm-sized copper cubes worked with detailed geometric designs that had spilled from Quin's leather pack. They were surprisingly light. "What are these?" he wondered.

"Disruption charges," Quin replied. He tossed another over to Braden. "Here, take a few of them. They come in handy."

He then picked up a black leather scabbard and strapped it on around his waist. Braden recognized the ivory hilt of his brother's sword immediately. It was a long scimitar with a gracefully thin blade. Known as Zanikar, the blade was wickedly curved. The shape rendered it unwieldy to use, difficult to even draw from its scabbard. But it was infused with dampening, the rarest and most difficult character to imbue. Of all the items in Quin's collection, Zanikar was by far the most invaluable. It was unique, the only dampening sword in existence.

Loosening Zanikar's hilt in its scabbard, Quin leaned forward and demanded of his brother, "So what, exactly, is going to be our strategy?"

Braden rose from a crouch, still holding the two disruption charges in his hand. He slid them both into a pocket as he paced away a few steps. He leaned back against the mud bricks of the wall, one finger hooked around his belt.

"Our mission is to prevent Renquist and his associates from unsealing the Well of Tears and unleashing the power of the Onslaught," he explained rigidly. "Our best chance for success is to impede their mobility. They've been relying heavily on the transfer portal system. If we can destroy the Chamber of Egress, then that should prevent them from achieving both their primary and secondary objectives."

Still leaning against his knee, Quin stared at him blankly. "You do realize there's no way to collapse the Chamber of Egress without bringing down the whole Lyceum?"

Braden shook his head. "Not the whole Lyceum. Just the Grand Dome."

"And the Circle of Convergence beneath it," Quin reminded him, obviously disapproving of the idea.

Braden pushed his weight off the wall, pacing away from Quinlan. "But that works to our advantage, don't you see?" he insisted, gesturing with his hands. "They will need all eight Circles of Convergence tied in together in order to stabilize the magic field. If they lose even one of the circles, there won't be a reason to open the Well of Tears. They'll have already lost."

Quin stood up straight to confront his brother. "Braden, there are only three greater circles left in the entire world. You are talking about destroying one of them."

"I know I am," Braden assured him. "Believe me, I've thought about it long and hard. It's not like it's going to matter, anyway. Nobody left alive after today is going to know or care what a Circle of Convergence even is. You're the Arcanist, Quin. So answer me this: is it even possible?"

Quin narrowed his eyes, looking almost ready to turn his back on his brother and stalk out of the room again. Fortunately, he didn't. He took a few deep breaths, striving for composure. With his hands in the pockets of his black coat, he informed them:

"The Circle of Convergence is built over a series of barrel vaults supported by load-bearing columns. If we can damage enough of the columns, then the whole circle will give way. It should even take out the Chamber of Egress below it."

Braden nodded, his dark eyes gazing up and to the side in thought. He shifted his weight, bringing a hand up to scratch the whiskers on his face as he asked, "How do you propose we destroy the columns?"

Quin indicated Braden's weapon with a wave of his hand. "Thar'gon has a strong motive character. It was designed to level walls, so it should make short work of a few columns. We could also use the disruption charges to try to buy us time to get out from underneath it. It would really help if the circle was already in play before we activate the charges. It would be like using its own resonance against it."

Braden nodded his agreement. "I already took care of that. With luck, the circle should already be in use by the time we arrive."

From her seat on the bed, Sephana sat bolt upright. "You're talking about the horse clans, aren't you?"

"What about the Jenn?" Quin demanded, whirling to face his brother with unrestrained aggression in his eyes. "Braden, tell me you didn't involve our people."

Braden glared his brother in the eye, his stare firm and unwavering. "By sunset tonight, Bryn Calazar will be besieged by fifty thousand clansmen. With the regular army already deployed against the Rhen, they will have no choice but to use the Circle of Convergence to defend the walls."

Quinlan growled, raising his hand in a fist as he swiped out at the air. "*Why?*" he all but shouted. "They'll be defenseless against the kind of power the circle is capable of throwing at them—it will be genocide!"

"Would they really do that?" Sephana wondered with a horrified expression on her face. "Use the Circle of Convergence against their own people?"

Braden grimaced. "It's been done before in the past."

"That's barbaric," she maintained.

"It's what I'm counting on," Braden assured her. "We need their attention focused away from us. That's the only way we'll be able to penetrate far enough into the Lyceum to do any good."

A deep and rolling thunder emanating from outside resonated within his chest, trembling the very foundations of the inn. At the same time every line of the magic field seemed to writhe and distort. The roaring sound of thunder swelled, lingering in the air, far longer than it reasonably should have. The normally peaceful song of the magic field became a tortuous standing wave that wracked the inside of Braden's head.

"What is that?" Sephana cried out in pain.

Braden took Sephana by the arm and guided her out the door and into the hallway, which was filled with patrons fleeing their rooms in panic. The terrible thundering noise continued as Braden fought his way through the commotion of the crowd, jostling past people toward the back door of the inn. Throwing it open, he staggered out into the yard, gazing up.

An expansive layer of clouds choked the sky overhead, though unlike any storm clouds Braden had ever seen. These were atrociously dark, churning across the sky as they raced to cover the eastern horizon. Brief flashes of light seemed to emanate from deep within the dark bank of clouds. An icy wind had picked up ahead of the storm, tossing dust and debris about the yard of the inn.

A tongued fork of lightning streaked upward from the ground. The crackling noise of thunder followed immediately, rattling the air. The magic field oscillated for a moment, finally restoring itself. It never quite returned to normal, though. Subtle vibrations in the field lines yet remained, like quavering aftershocks.

Braden lowered his hands from his head, turning slowly as his eyes took in the entire blackened expanse of sky. The wind howled in his ears, tossing his hair forward and tugging at his clothes. He glanced to Sephana, making certain she was all right.

Over the noise of the scolding wind he could hear the ominous tones of his brother's voice. "We'd better make a good account of ourselves today. It seems we'll be sleeping in Hell tonight." Another harsh stab of lightning seemed to punctuate his words.

Braden turned to face his companions. Scowling, he uttered, "Let's go get our things."

Once back in the room, they gathered up the remainder of Quin's trinkets from off the floor. Sephana took the light staff into her hand, holding it up before her face as she rotated it slowly in admiration. She closed her eyes. A diffuse glow brightened above the end of the staff, like a flickering flame in the shape of an upturned crescent moon.

"That's good," Quin praised her with a nod. "Do you feel the amplification?"

"I do." She smiled, her eyes on the glowing end of the staff. The flickering brilliance increased until it chased away the shadows of the room, bathing them all in a dazzling golden glow. Sephana let the light diminish, allowing the staff to go once again dormant.

Quin clapped her on the back. Braden regarded the two of them with a smile of his own. But then the door to the room opened, and the expression on his face instantly faltered.

Merris stood in the doorway.

Only, it wasn't the Merris he remembered.

Immediately, Braden opened his mind to the magic field and saturated himself with it, drawing violently upon that well of power until his mind was filled with its raging intensity. Amber ripples of energy coruscated over his body, bleeding away the excess energies his flesh could not contain. He already had a shield thrown up and an attack at ready by the time Sephana's shrill cry stopped him short:

"Braden, no!"

"Release!" Quin bellowed, slamming Braden back against the wall with the full force of his body.

Shaken, Braden severed his connection with the magic field, allowing the turbulent energies to drain slowly away. Drawing himself upright, he fought to stop shaking. He gazed back at Merris with eyes wide with panic, mind reeling in confusion.

"It's just Merris!" Quin shouted at him. "What the hell's wrong with you? You could have killed her!"

Braden looked back and forth between the woman and his brother, blinking as if bludgeoned.

Quin was right; it was just Merris. But there was something very different about the girl.

"It's not just Merris," he insisted. "Quin, it's not!" He turned to confront the woman standing in the doorway. "What happened?" he demanded. "What did they do to you?"

The woman who used to be Merris glided casually forward into the room, a confident smile on her face. The smile widened as she passed by Braden, trailing a finger over his cheek as she brushed by. The creature paused before Quin, smiling as she gazed up endearingly into his eyes. Then she leaned forward and kissed him full on the mouth.

Quin was panting and breathless by the time he pulled back away from her. His face had gone very pale, eyes clouded with concern.

Braden opened himself again to the field. But this time he pulled at the energies more slowly, saturating himself cautiously, instead of trying to take it in all at once.

"What did they do to you?" he repeated.

The woman who used to be Merris slowly turned to regard him, eyebrows raised. The smile on her face was a haughty, self-satisfied smirk.

"My name isn't Merris," she informed him, her voice low and husky. She giggled, reveling in his puzzlement.

"Then who are you?" Braden insisted. He took a step to the left, circling away from her, holding her pale blue eyes severely with his own.

"I go by a different name now." She took a step forward, closing the distance between them. "Call me Arden Hannah."

Braden frowned, his hand going to his side to finger Thar'gon's leather-wrapped haft. "What do you want?"

The woman who had once been Merris Bryar smirked, her face radiant with delight. "I want what you have," she informed him bluntly. "What's inside you. I want your power, Braden. And I'm going to take it."

Braden raised the morning star up before him, holding the weapon in a warding stance. "I don't think I'm going to let you do that," he assured the malicious creature before him. "Tell me, Arden, if that really is your name, why are you here?"

The woman who called herself Arden Hannah grinned as she entwined her fingers around a lock of her long, spiraling hair, twisting it slowly around her fingertips.

"I've been sent to deliver a message." The expression on her face was something akin to a challenge or even a dare. Or a cold and sinister seduction. He wasn't sure which one. Regardless, it sent icy shivers through his nerves, raking down his spine. The hungering look in her eyes made him feel like he'd never been so defiled in all his life.

"What's the message?" Braden held Thar'gon up before him as he slowly circled around her, trying to put his back to the open doorway while keeping Arden between his brother and himself.

The woman reached out toward him, the smile on her face playful and eager. She caressed the side of his face with the back of her hand. "Master Devrim Remzi has agreed to meet with you, Braden. Only you. He will be waiting in the forecourt under the Fountain House in one hour's time."

"What makes you think I would do that?" Braden demanded softly, his gaze unwavering from the pale intensity of her eyes. "I don't understand."

"Because if you don't, Renquist promises to kill him instead of you."

Arden grinned up at him triumphantly, excitement shimmering in her eyes. "Think about it, my sweet. You have no idea how the sequence works; you have no way to seal the Well of Tears once it's opened. But Master Remzi does."

She leaned forward, kissing Braden softly on the cheek. Then she turned her back to him and glided smoothly toward the door.

Braden almost formed a thought that would have killed her. Almost. He came very close to actually doing it.

But then he thought better of it and stayed his hand.

"What happened to Merris?" he called after her.

She turned back around with a small, amused grin. "I've always been Arden Hannah," she informed him. "Merris was just a figment of my imagination."

Chapter Thirteen
Assault on the Lyceum

Bryn Calazar, Caladorn

"Tell me you're not seriously considering this, Braden." Sephana was livid, her cheeks reddened with anger.

Braden shrugged, reminding her, "We'll need Master Remzi alive if they open the Well of Tears."

He paced over to the wall and leaned with his back up against it, slouching. His body still felt a little unsteady from drawing so strongly on the magic field. With the field as unpredictable as it was, his action had been downright dangerous. Especially here in the eye of Bryn Calazar's vortex, where the lines of power converged, greatly magnifying the field's intensity.

"We won't need Remzi at all if we stop them before they can open it," Quin remarked dismally. He was sitting against a wall on the opposite side of the room, holding his hat in his hands. It was the first thing he'd spoken since Merris had left.

Braden pointed out, "We have no way of knowing they haven't opened the Well of Tears already."

Quin frowned, seeming to mull Braden's remark in his head. "I think we'd know it if they did. I mean, something like that…we would feel it, don't you think?"

Braden could only offer him a shrug. "I honestly don't know," he admitted.

Staring down at his hat in his hands, Quin shook his head and muttered, "I miss Merris."

Braden felt profoundly saddened for his brother. For just a little while, Quin had been living under the illusion that he had stumbled on to something actually good, had found new reason to enjoy living. That reason had turned out to be nothing more than a mirage of false hopes and manipulation.

Braden told him sincerely, "I'm sorry, Quin."

His brother gazed drearily off to the side, eyes introspective in thought. "I didn't see that coming. There was just something about her that I found irresistibly attractive. Funny, how the very thing that I found most beguiling about her was the fact that she reminded me…of *me*. Indeed, I wonder what that says about my own character," he mused.

Just then, the entire magic field seemed to spasm, the lines of the field folding as if jostled by a tremor.

"We need to get out of here," Braden growled.

Quin and Sephana swept quickly into motion, gathering their things. Quin caught his leather pack up in his hand, commenting as he did, "I wonder what Hell feels like this time of year. Do you suppose I should bring along a jacket?"

Braden held open the door to the room, hardly sparing him a glance as he let Sephana out into the hallway. "Bring it along, Quin."

Quin tossed his head, drawing his black longcoat on over his body. He then shouldered his pack and grabbed his staff, carrying it in the crook of his arm. He trotted forward out the door, sidling past Braden as he hurried to catch up with Sephana.

Braden let the door swing closed behind them then followed his brother down the dim hallway. Stepping outside, he glanced up and took in the dark expanse of cloud cover that now completely obscured the sky. Strange lights flickered deep within the bank of clouds, almost like lightning, but colorful and more diffuse. The entire magic field was off kilter, timid one moment and then hostile the next. The wind was up, rippling Quin's coat out before him and crackling the skirt of Sephana's dress.

A general feeling of panic consumed the streets of Bryn Calazar. Citizens scurried by, jostling others out of their way, heedless of anything but the path before them. Most seemed to be rushing toward the center of the city in the direction of the harbor and the Lyceum. Braden noticed that most of the men wearing state livery appeared to be headed in the opposite direction. It was hard to walk; the streets were in chaotic turmoil. The wind carried toward them the sound of distant screams.

An echoing thunder rumbled from the west. It didn't come from the storm clouds. Braden instantly recognized the din of hundreds of war drums.

Jogging ahead of the others, he hurried toward a narrow staircase protruding from the side of a nearby building. He took the steps two at a time, rushing up onto a tiled balcony, where he leaned out to peer westward toward the horizon.

From that vantage, Braden had a sweeping view of most of the city and the rolling countryside beyond. A choking sea of men and horses churned like a dark tide that frothed with banners and spears, breaking like waves against the fortifications of the city walls. Braden felt a thrill of excitement at the sight; thousands more warriors than he'd anticipated had responded to his summons. The sight was awe-inspiring, even humbling. In the rear of the turbulent ranks he could see siege engines being readied, arbalests and ballistae preparing to fling munitions at the walls. Elessar had heeded him well.

Overhead in the sky, the flickering lights in the clouds resembled a sickened aurora.

"I'll be damned," Quin muttered beside him.

He looked over at his brother and, to his surprise, saw that Quin's attention wasn't focused on the besieging army at all. Instead, he was gazing upward at the Lyceum's graceful domes. The magelight that illuminated its walls was tinted a murky blood-red hue. It was a signal, one that Braden had never actually witnessed before in his life. He understood its purpose immediately with a sharp wrench of his stomach.

Quin remarked with trepidation, "They're summoning the full Assembly."

Braden stared upward at the scintillating magelight that bathed the walls of the Lyceum, rendering the gilt domes a rich and coppery bronze. "Good," he commented coldly. "We'll want them all inside."

"Why?" Sephana wondered, a hand going up to push a lock of hair back out of her face.

Still gazing up at the ominous portent of the blood-red domes, Braden answered her, "When the magic field destabilizes, it will reverse the polarity of the arches that ward the entrance to the Lyceum. Instead of barring the gates against intruders, anyone sensitive to the magic field will be stuck inside. If we can destroy the Chamber of Egress, then Renquist's darkmages will be trapped."

"Along with everyone else," Sephana observed softly, her eyes full of sadness.

At Braden's side, Quin drew in a deep breath. He uttered portentously, "'From the Atrament we all come, and back to the Atrament we all return.'"

He was quoting from the *Dhummad,* the book of the dead. Braden stared hard at his brother, trying to put a finger on his emotions. With Quin, it was often hard to tell exactly what he was feeling. Quin stood leaning with his elbows against the stone balustrade, hat cradled in his hands. He was gazing outward across the city, surveying the prevailing tides of battle beyond the walls with narrowed eyes. His expression remained distant and enigmatic.

Sephana glanced at Braden with a somber smile, entwining her fingers with his own. He squeezed her hand gently, caressing her soft skin with his thumb.

A trail of fire streaked by overhead from the direction of the Lyceum, passing right over them with a terrible crackling sound. All three of them ducked as the balcony they stood upon shook with the thunder of its impact. A rumbling explosion brightened the shadows beyond the city walls, the sounds of screams both terrible and terrifying.

Another flaming volley shot out from the Grand Dome, arcing across the sky before dropping down onto the besieging army of the Jenn. The fire spread outward upon impact, liquid tongues of flame ravaging everything in their path, leaving only a charred swath of ground and the anguished shrieks of dying men and beasts. Two large ballistae erupted into flames, quickly consumed along with the men who tended them.

Braden felt his stomach sickened by the violence of the assault. A terrible chill settled into his bones, along with a profound sadness. He forced himself to turn away from the edge of the balcony, disengaging his senses from the horror. Voice gruff with emotion, he informed the others, "That's our cue."

Quin spun immediately to face him, raising a finger up before his face. "Stop right there," he commanded his brother, voice quavering in revulsion. His face was milky pale, eyes moist and bloodshot. "You're the one who brought this all down upon them. You'd better figure out a way of making it count."

Braden turned his back on him and started walking away. Jogging, Quin caught up to him immediately, catching him by the shoulder and wrenching him forcibly back around. Quin leaned forward into his brother's face until the brim of his hat was pressed against Braden's forehead.

"What are you going to do?" he demanded with a snarl. "Whatever it is, Brother, you'd better act fast. *Our people are dying.*"

Braden's gaze was resolute. "I'm going to spring their trap."

Sephana's mouth dropped open in shock. To Braden, she inquired softly, "Are you completely certain that's a good idea?"

Braden wasn't looking at her. He kept his eyes fixed on Quin as he responded, "I am."

Quin drew back away from Braden's face, adjusting his hat and grumbling, "In my experience, only fools and fanatics are ever completely certain. Which one are you?"

Braden shook his head as another flaming lance darted across the sky above them. His face was illuminated briefly in the flare of light from the explosion as the missile shattered against the Jenn army below.

"Probably both," he grated, turning away from the horror of the screams and moving in the direction of the steps.

At the bottom of the stairs they found the streets a chaotic frenzy. People were running, panicking, racing about without aim or direction. Braden stepped out first into the frenzied commotion, flanked closely by Quin and Sephana walking side by side, staffs in hand.

At the sight of the three mages, some folk stopped and stared, others scurried back out of their way. Quin stalked behind Braden, carrying his staff crossed diagonally in front of his torso. Sephana kept her staff held straight upright and tight against her side, glancing around apprehensively at the surging crowd of onlookers. Overhead, fiery arcs of flame lanced across the darkened sky, raining down death and terror upon the clans.

As they mounted the path up the hill toward the Lyceum, Braden reached down and unhooked Thar'gon from his belt, carrying it downward by his side. He glanced up at the crimson-hued domes on the cliffs above them, feeling the weight of trepidation slowly sink into his chest. He swallowed against the dryness in his throat.

He raised his fist, calling for the others to halt. "This is as close as we dare," he told them. "I'm going to use Thar'gon to transfer us up to the rooftop above the forecourt. From there, we'll split up. Sephana, I want you to go with Quin. Get under the dome, to the room below the circle. Start laying out the disruption charges at the base of the columns. I'm going to spring their trap and try to draw their attention off you. I'll catch up when I can."

Quin fixed him with a sidelong glare. "And what, exactly, are we supposed to do when you don't just 'catch up?'"

Braden spread his hands. "Then you improvise."

At that, his brother rolled his eyes, muttering, "Braden, you are a wellspring of inspiration."

Braden ignored the comment, extending his arm to Sephana with a smile. "Take my hand," he directed her. "Quin, link in."

Quin nodded once, grasping Braden's wrist.

Braden raised the silver morning star against his chest and closed his eyes, envisioning the Lyceum's forecourt with its marching colonnades.

"Vergis," he whispered.

The path up the cliffs under his feet shifted and was immediately replaced by the pumice bricks that formed the roof of one of the courtyard's long covered walkways. Braden instantly felt a jar of disorientation as his stomach plunged from the transfer.

No sooner had they arrived then a lance of flame streaked out from the Lyceum's dome right over their heads, leaving a fiery trail of smoke across the sky. The sound of the crackling firestorm was deafening. He could actually feel the heat coming off of it. In reflex, Braden brought Thar'gon up to ward his face.

He released his grip on Sephana then backed up as far as he could go against the edge of the rooftop with his back to the sea cliff. Then, slowly, he stepped cautiously forward to get a glimpse of the courtyard below. The others moved forward with him, Sephana on his right and Quin on his left.

At the edge of the rooftop, all three of them drew up short, gazing down.

"Well, damn," Quin remarked.

Directly below, the Lyceum's forecourt was writhing with the bodies and armaments of hundreds of liveried warriors. At the forefront of the throng, blue-robed mages stood in a line gazing up at them, both men and women alike.

The sound of Quin's voice prompted Braden into motion.

"Run!" he shouted as the host below them surged forward with a thunderous war cry.

Braden brought Thar'gon up just in time to block the first magical assaults that were hurled against them by the mages on the ground. A spear of light shattered into crystalline fragments that fell harmlessly about them, another absorbed by a shadow shield thrown up by Quin.

Braden shouted back over his shoulder, "Get to the dome!"

Wielding the silver morning star like a club, he turned and sprinted across the vaulted rooftop toward the stairs. As he moved, he sucked in the turbulence of the magic field, filling himself completely to the threshold of his tolerance until liquid energies bled off his body in amber waves.

He met the swarming rush of warriors at the top of the stairs, swinging Thar'gon out before him in great, sweeping arcs. Mangled bodies were flung backwards out of his way, hurled in all directions by the force of the talisman's concussive impact. Braden conjured an absorption shield that surrounded his body, a gleaming nimbus that countered the magical assaults that rained down upon him. The mighty talisman glowed argent in his hands.

He pushed forward, forcing a wedge deep into the writhing ranks, overpowering their assault and beating them backwards, down and off the stairs. With the might of the legendary artifact in his hands, Braden didn't have to fight individual warriors. Instead, he used Thar'gon's imbued motive force to create concussion waves that sent broken bodies exploding backward into the surging turmoil.

Reaching the base of the steps, Braden realized that he could go no further. Confronted from every direction with a battering confusion of conventional and magical attacks, his absorption shield was starting to falter. Braden limped backward, bringing Thar'gon up and closing his eyes.

"*Vergis*," he commanded the weapon.

Beneath his feet, the staircase shivered and shifted.

Quin leaped over a gap between two domes then caught Sephana as she followed behind him, helping her keep her feet as she came down hard on the rooftop. The gilt tiles were sharply angled and slippery. His feet lost traction. Sephana reached out and steadied him and, together, they sprinted forward toward the entrance to the Lyceum.

They chased around the circumference of the dome then leaped, dropping down to the roof of a cupola below. Behind them, the sun was starting to set, illuminating the dark bank of cloud cover. Against the light of the setting sun, their bodies were reduced to featureless silhouettes as they crossed the portico above the entrance.

From the edge of the roof, Quin leaped over to the balcony of an adjacent minaret. Then he leaned his staff against the wall, beckoning for Sephana to follow.

"Come on!" he urged her.

Sephana looked ready to balk. But then she gathered her courage and made the leap. Quin caught her in his arms, gently lowering her to the floor of the balcony with a cavalier grin on his face.

"Are you actually *enjoying* this?" Sephana gasped, leaning forward over her knees to catch her breath.

Quin shrugged, reclaiming his staff. "It sure beats death and boredom," came his indifferent response.

He led her down the winding stairs within the minaret. Halfway down, they met a guardsman charging up the steps toward them with weapons drawn. Quin brought his staff up in his hands, holding it like a javelin, and dispatched the man with one quick thrust to the head.

At the base of the tower, they ran out through a narrow doorway into the interior under the dome.

There, Quin put out his arm, stopping Sephana in her tracks and pressing her back up against the wall. He brought his hand up to cover her own, silencing the glow of her staff.

"Don't move," he whispered.

Beneath the Lyceum's central dome, the Circle of Convergence had been put into play. Lines of power pulsated across the floor, uniting at one point in the center of the eight-pointed Silver Star. All around the perimeter of the circle, cyclone gusts of wind swirled and rotated, distributing the energies harvested from the vortex up through the hundreds of open windows at the base of the dome.

Quin squinted, staring through the rotating column of air at the man who stood at the center of it all, commanding the Lyceum's circle. Quin recognized the profile immediately. The man responsible for using the energies of Bryn Calazar's vortex to fling lances of flame at the Jenn was Byron Connel, the Warden of Battlemages.

Quin's eyes narrowed in revulsion as he stared at the arrogant darkmage before him. He felt a strong compulsion to just stride out across the floor and take on Connel right there, just the two of them. But common sense got the better of him; he had no chance against a mage already saturated in the energies focused by an entire Circle of Convergence.

Quin turned his head and spat upon the tiled floor. Then he took Sephana by the hand and strode forward along the walls around the perimeter of the room. The opening to a stairwell gaped from out of the floor in front of them, beckoning. He jogged toward it.

Braden reappeared next to the fountain—behind the mob still trying to charge his last position on the stairs. He whirled, bringing Thar'gon violently down. A mage collapsed under the force of the blow, blood splattering the columns and the fountain.

Braden glanced up at Devrim Remzi, who stood next to the fountain, gaping into his face with terrified astonishment. Braden reached up, catching the man's wrist in his hand.

"Do you serve Xerys?" he demanded.

The aged Empiricist stared at him, wide-eyed, taking a step backward and slowly blinking as if grappling for understanding. Adamantly, he shook his head from side to side.

That was enough for Braden.

He brought Thar'gon up in a backhand strike, swatting away the first group of warriors who had turned back to retake the fountain. The atrocious force of the weapon's discharge sent limbs and torsos hurling away across the courtyard. Braden raised Thar'gon high over his head.

"*Vergis.*"

The fountain and the forecourt shivered and disappeared.

Quin jumped, landing hard on the stone floor at the base of the stairs, and brought his staff around to shatter the skull of the first guard who came forward to attack them. At his side, Sephana raised her light staff, its glow inspired to brilliance with the power she wielded through it. She held it forward in a walking stance, fending off the ring of guards who rushed forward from the walls of the chamber to confront them.

Quin raised his own staff, crossing it over Sephana's. Together, light and shadow intermixed to weave a devastating attack. A streak of writhing darkness and light came forth from the ends of their combined staves, undulating across the chamber. Men screamed in agony, their ranks turning to flee before the writhing mass of conflicting energies.

Quin advanced across the vaulted room, taking advantage of the guardsmen's retreat. Reaching into the leather pack he wore hanging from one shoulder, he pulled out a disruption charge and flung it toward a nearby column. It rolled like a molded copper die across the floor, coming to rest at the base of a scalloped pillar.

He withdrew a second charge, flinging it across the room in the opposite direction. He reached deep within his pack, pulling out more of the charged cubes. He ran forward, dropping them one at a time at intervals all around the chamber.

"*Quin!*"

The urgency in Sephana's voice made him turn toward the stairs. Quin's jaw dropped at the sight of at least a dozen blue-robed mages swarming down the steps and spreading out across the room toward them. He stopped and confronted them, holding his staff horizontal to the floor.

"Come on," he dared the first man who approached in front of the others. Quin smiled, raising his staff. "I'll be your pallbearer."

Braden's stomach felt ill from the disorientation caused by the rapid use of transfers. He swayed for a moment over his feet, struggling to get his bearings. Devrim Remzi disengaged from his grip, backing away.

It took Braden only a moment to confirm that the last transfer had shifted them under the dome of the Lyceum, to the arched gallery above the Circle of Convergence. A great wind rose from the floor below, circulating throughout the dome, charged energies creating a crackling of static discharge against the tiled ceiling above.

"What is your intent?" Devrim Remzi bellowed at him over the angry howl of the gale.

Braden turned toward him, lowering the silver morning star back down to his side. He glanced downward at the circle, to where Byron Connel stood commanding the pulsating energies of the vortex.

"I have to stop them." Braden hoped that somehow the man would understand.

The aged Master raised his eyebrows, eyes fixed on the iconic talisman in Braden's hand. "There's nothing you can do," Remzi assured him. "Don't you think I would have stopped them if I could? They're too powerful, too well connected. They've come too far."

"I won't accept that," Braden snarled.

Below them, the doors of the Lyceum were thrust open, soldiers and mages spilling in in droves. Hundreds of men fanned out, making their way around the Circle of Convergence toward the stairs to the gallery. Braden watched them come, knowing there was nowhere else to go. All he really had to do was buy Quin enough time to plant the charges. He just had to hold them off as long as he could.

"Get down," he ordered Remzi.

The old man complied as Braden raised Thar'gon in a warding stance over both of them.

The first magical attacks came, zealous energies shattering against his amber shield of light. The shield absorbed most of the damage, reflecting the rest. It shuddered, taking a tremendous battering. Braden struck out with the morning star, knocking the first ranks of soldiers off the balcony.

A vicious magical assault bore down against Braden's shield. This time, the shield was incapable of absorbing anything but the brunt of the force. Braden was beaten to his knees, using every bit of the power he drew through the talisman just to keep from going down completely. He struggled to lash back against the attack, but to no avail. All of his strength was committed to defense.

More mages swarmed onto the gallery, surrounding him, the sum of their combined power overwhelming even Thar'gon's great might. He had no choice but to transfer out of there again. Braden staggered to his feet and raised the talisman above his head.

Glancing down, he noticed that the Circle of Convergence stood abandoned.

Braden whirled around in a moment of sudden panic, desperately trying to locate Byron Connel. Turning back, he found himself confronted by the unpredictable Battlemage standing right in front of his face. Connel launched himself at Braden, knocking him out of his stance and capturing Thar'gon's haft above his grip.

"You're done," Connel growled.

Braden's eyes widened in shocked understanding. "*Vergis,*" he gasped.

Absolutely nothing happened. He realized too late that the jaws of the trap had decisively closed.

Thar'gon's allegiance had shifted back to Byron Connel.

Braden's hand went limp, opening reflexively as Thar'gon surrendered itself back to its former master. Byron Connel snatched the morning star away from him, wielding it back over his shoulder with both hands. Then he brought the talisman forward and viciously down.

A concussive force of power hit Braden full in the face, hurling him backward against the wall. His body slapped hard against the patterned tiles, his vision exploding in sparks and then going dark. A thick stream of blood drained from his mouth and nose.

Braden sagged to the ground as a surge of warriors spilled over the sides of the gallery toward him.

Quin stood with staff in hand, the smile on his face daring the man in front of him to strike. But instead of lashing out at the mage, Quin whirled and struck at the scalloped column beside him. The column exploded, collapsing to a mess of rubble on the floor.

"Anyone so much as flinches and I'll ignite them all," Quin threatened, indicating with his eyes the disruption charges scattered about the floor of the chamber. He raised his staff, angling it back over his head, ready to strike the column on his left.

"No, you won't."

He recognized that deep and resonant voice immediately. Glancing up to the top of the stairs, Quin felt a numbing paralysis sink deep into his bones as he raised his eyes to confront Zavier Renquist. The Prime Warden was flanked by a row of four mages, all of whom Quin recognized. Behind them strode Byron Connel himself, hauling behind him another man, unconscious, dragging him down the stairs by the scruff of the collar.

Quin grimaced, squeezing his eyes shut at the horrific sight of his own brother, badly beaten, at the mercy of Byron Connel.

"It's over," Renquist promised.

Quin froze, unsure of what, if anything, he could do. He was afraid Renquist was right.

Then he felt Sephana's fingers entwine about his own. She squeezed his hand in comforting reassurance.

"Blow the columns," she urged quietly into his ear. Her voice sounded absolutely resolute, content with her decision. "Bring it all down. Finish it."

Quin swallowed. His grip tightened on the shadow staff as he steeled himself, trying to gather the kind of courage he'd never had.

He gazed at Braden, unconscious and bloodied at Connel's feet. His eyes shifted back to Renquist. Then another movement behind them all caught his attention.

His mouth opened at the sight of Merris—Arden—descending the stairs toward them. She wore a new dress made entirely of thin layers of silver-blue silk that surrounded her body like a cloud. Her platinum hair flowed to her waist in perfect, spiraling ringlets. In all his life, Quin had never seen a woman look so desirable, so vulnerable. He stared up at her in open, unabashed wonder.

"Don't do it, Quin," she implored him, eyes sad and sweet and so very fragile.

She was everything he had ever wanted in life.

Quin grimaced, throwing his head back and squeezing his eyes shut.

Then he lashed out, flinging the ebony staff away as hard as he could. It exploded into shattering fractals of shadow against the wall as he turned his back on them all and took a staggering step away.

Quin covered his face with his hands, unable to bring himself to face the consequences of his own decision.

Chapter Fourteen
Rites of the Fallen

Bryn Calazar, Caladorn

Quin gazed miserably around the dark dungeon, his eyes finally coming to rest on the silver talisman that hung at Byron Connel's side. Strange; he hadn't noticed it there before on the long walk down the stairs to this sublevel below the Lyceum. The sight of the spiked morning star filled Quin with a sinking feeling of desperation.

He commented, "I thought Thar'gon only suffered one master at a time."

Byron Connel glanced downward to the weapon at his waist, patting the leather-wrapped haft possessively. "The Assembly voted to formally declare your brother a traitor. He is no longer Warden of Chancellors." There was no malice in his voice; he stated only the plain and simple facts. For a darkmage, Byron Connel was almost affable.

They moved through a pool of violet magelight produced by Nashir Arman, who strode before them, illuminating their path. Quin wished he could summon a light of his own. But he could not; they had spent a great deal of effort shielding his mind, making certain his connection with the magic field was quite thoroughly dampened. He couldn't even sense the field any longer. The conspicuous absence of its comfort was like an open sore, a constant and insistent irritation.

Bryon Connel continued almost amiably, "That was quite a feat you pulled off, just you and the girl. You made a good account of yourself today. You've nothing to be ashamed of."

Quin frowned back at him. "Ashamed? Quite the contrary. You and I are both entirely beneath shame. Shame is an emotion reserved only for those with an actual conscience."

Molten energies raged like an electrical storm through his mind. Quin sank to the ground, moaning as he brought his shackled hands up to ward against the pain. When it was over, he remained in a crouch on the floor, trembling violently. He lowered his hands back down in front of him.

"You will learn to show respect for your betters," Nashir growled, glaring down at him derisively.

Quin rose unsteadily to his feet. His body was still shaking from the man's excruciating assault.

He narrowed his eyes, glaring his hatred. "You've never been my better, Nashir, so let's make certain we have that straight. The truth is, I should have put you down years ago like the rabid dog you are."

Nashir's eyes narrowed in malice.

"Don't," Byron Connel commanded, stepping between Nashir and their prisoner. "Let him be. He'll see reason soon enough."

Connel unlocked one of several oaken doors that lined the passage, swinging it wide and gesturing for him to enter. Quin went into the cell complacently, having no desire to be taught another lesson by Nashir. The interior of the cell was indeed quite small. There was a rusted iron cot at one end with only a little space to stand in front of it.

Quin turned at the sound of a commotion outside. Another group of mages had entered the dungeon. He got a quick glimpse of Sephana and another of Braden being half dragged, half carried into a cell across from his own. Eyes filled with concern, he demanded of his jailor, "Aren't you going to heal him?"

Byron Connel took a step back out of the

doorway, saying in a voice suffused with compassion, "Better start praying for your brother. I don't think he has much time left."

Quin grimaced as the door of his cell was firmly closed, encasing him in darkness.

Braden clung tenuously to consciousness as they laid him out on the cot in his cell. He lay there shivering as layers of armor and clothing were stripped away from his body. At last they had him down to his trousers, naked and bloody from the waist up.

A woman came in with a washrag and bucket. She went efficiently about the task of sponging him off. Braden flinched away from her touch as she went to dab at his face. She reached up, running a hand through his hair in an effort to soothe him, continuing with her ministrations much more delicately.

When the woman was finally gone, Braden laid his head back, closing his eyes and allowing his mind to fade quietly toward sleep. His mouth felt horribly dry; if he could wish for anything in the world, it would be for a cup of water.

He heard a movement in the cell and opened his eyes to gaze up blearily into the face of Byron Connel. The man had wandered in through the open doorway and stood, arms crossed, leaning over him.

The red-bearded Battlemage told him gruffly, "I've never liked you. You've always been a constant thorn in my side, and I find you arrogant and insufferable. But I do want you to know that I take no pleasure from any of this."

Braden somehow managed to find his voice, though it was raspy and very weak. "Go to hell."

His mind exploded in pain. It chased him downward toward unconsciousness. Mercifully, the torture was short-lived.

"That's enough," Connel barked. He placed a hand on Braden's chest and appeared to be concentrating for just a moment. Then he turned to a woman standing behind him. "He's worse for wear. I think I need to heal him."

"We were told not to offer him clemency of any kind."

Braden recognized the voice of Myria Anassis. The last he'd seen of Myria had been in the gorge below Vintgar.

"I know," said Byron Connel. "But at this point, I don't think it really matters, do you?"

Braden felt hands upon him, then the warm surge of security that always seemed to accompany a healing. He gasped, feeling the terrible ache in his head dissolve, melting right away. Greatly comforted, he closed his eyes and let his mind drift toward sleep.

An insistent shaking jostled him awake.

Braden opened his eyes, struggling to sit up. His head no longer hurt, but his mind was working as if through a thick blanket of fog. He still felt terribly weak. They had not given him enough time to fully recuperate from the healing. His mouth was horribly parched; if only they would give him just one sip of water. But after hearing Myria's comment about clemency, he knew better than to ask.

"The Prime Warden is ready."

Braden recognized Nashir's voice. He nodded, standing up. The sinister-looking mage strode forward to inspect Braden's shackles very carefully, yanking at the links to make certain they still held. Tugging roughly on his chains, he forced Braden to walk forward, hastening him out of the cell.

In the dark corridor outside, Braden could make out the form of Byron Connel standing in a toxic-looking pool of magelight. The Battlemage was standing beside Quin, one fist entwined around the iron chains that bound him.

"Hello, Brother," Quin greeted him cautiously. Like himself, Quin's wrists were tightly bound with iron manacles. More chains draped downward to both ankles, making it impossible for him to do more than shamble forward. Quin looked sickly pale, his face glistening with perspiration.

Braden greeted him with a weary nod of his head.

"I tried," Quin said in a ragged voice. "I did my best." He looked earnestly saddened. "I failed you, Brother."

Braden assured him, "You didn't fail me. Your intentions were pure. That's all that matters."

"Enough."

Nashir jerked on Braden's chains to quiet him down and get him moving. They started forward down the lightless corridor, Nashir walking beside him with a painfully firm grip on his arm. Their feet trudged through foggy pools of glowing magelight encased by absolute darkness.

They took the stairs up several floors. Braden kept his eyes fixed on the wooden railing to avoid Nashir's unfeeling gaze. He noticed that, with each successive level, the workmanship of the railing became somehow less ascetic. By the time they arrived at the level of the main floor, the wooden rail had been entirely replaced by rose-colored marble held in place by chiseled corbels.

How strange; he had traversed those self-same stairs thousands of times before in his life and had never once paid attention to the workmanship of the railing. He mused at how odd were the things one notices at such a time.

The stairwell opened up out of the ground onto the floor of the Lyceum complex, to a wide hall several stories tall. It was crowded with mages who stood gathered about in tight clusters, some dressed in formal indigo robes, others wearing a great variety of assorted fabrics and colors. The din of the room was almost palpable with so many people talking all together at once, their voices raised in tension.

At the sight of their small party, the fragile order of the room quickly disintegrated into chaos. Men and women rushed forward to surround them, faces hostile, brandishing arms and fists in the air and shouting despicable, hostile things. Braden bowed his head, fixing his stare on the ground just before his feet, unable to confront the brazen hatred in the eyes of his former peers.

A contingent of guards swept forward, forcing back the surging throng. Despite the presence of the guards, Braden was repeatedly slapped and cuffed. A young woman in a bright-red dress ducked and slipped past the wall of guards, approaching close enough to spray a wad of spittle into his face. Braden did his best to wipe the offensive fluid off with his shoulder.

They reached the end of the paneled hall and were propelled forcibly forward through a set of double doors. The doors were then thrown shut and barred against the crowd. Braden could hear the jarring thunder of people pounding with their fists from the other side, rattling the doors violently on their hinges.

"Keep going."

Nashir jerked him forward by the chains, impelling him in the direction of a plain white door at the far end of the room. Braden struggled to keep up, his stride compromised by the length of the chain between his feet.

They were led through the door into a modest-sized room beyond. Within, Braden stopped and peered around, his face a mask of confusion. The room was completely empty, save for patterned carpets laid out on the floor and many embroidered cushions upon which to sit. The walls were draped with silk in a variety of colors. An exquisite tea set of beaten copper was laid out upon a short-legged table in the midst of the room.

Braden's eyes darted to Quin with a questioning look. His brother returned his befuddled stare, shrugging helplessly. The room was a conference chamber. Not at all what he had been expecting.

Braden was led to one corner of the room, Quin to another. There, he was made to kneel upon the floor while Nashir unlocked his shackles long enough to lace the chain through an iron ring affixed to the wall behind him. He settled down upon a cushion, leaning with his back up against the wall.

Byron Connel stood in the front of the room, hands on his hips, glancing back and forth between the two brothers. Then he called back over his shoulder to Nashir:

"Go convene the Assembly."

Upon hearing that, Braden felt his stomach tighten.

Connel remained standing as Nashir left to follow his directive. His gaze was stern but not cruel. He was merely waiting, one hand upon Thar'gon's silver haft.

Braden caught Quin's gaze and held it meaningfully. He didn't have any last words he wanted to say, or even felt he could say. He hoped that one look would be enough.

Quin swallowed, his stare faltering. He broke eye contact, bowing his head and lowering his gaze to the floor.

The door opened. Prime Warden Renquist strode forward into the room, hands clasped behind his back, white cloak billowing out behind him. He stopped beside Byron Connel, who went instantly to his knees, bending forward until his forehead touched the floor. It was protocol to offer obeisance in the presence of a Prime Warden. Braden ignored that deference deliberately. He was not about to abase himself before any darkmage.

Renquist appeared not to notice the slight. He gazed down for a long, searching moment, first at Braden and then at Quin, jaw squared and fists set against his hips. Then he dropped into a cross-legged position upon the floor as Connel drew himself back upright.

With deliberate, careful motions, Renquist poured himself a cup of tea from the copper kettle. He raised the cup to his lips and took a long, savoring taste.

Braden swallowed against the aching dryness in his throat.

"I'm going to make this short, because I don't have much time." Renquist lowered the cup away from his mouth, setting it down on the carpet by his side. "The Reversal of the magic field is already well underway. I need eight mages tending eight Circles of Convergence within the hour. All must be Grand Masters, and that's very hard to come by. Right now I have only six. So I will not mince words: I need both of you."

"Prime Warden Krane has already heard my answer," Braden informed him. The sound of his voice was coarse and gravelly.

Renquist raised the cup for another long sip, holding Braden's eyes with his own. "I'm the one asking this time, Braden, out of respect for the friendship we once enjoyed."

He set the cup back down, adjusting the lay of his robe. His face was very angular, his nose hawk-like. The age-inscribed lines beneath his eyes cast harsh shadows in the light.

He continued, "You've always been the very best of us, Braden. In so many ways, you have exemplified everything it means to be a Master of the Lyceum of Bryn Calazar. I have always been able to depend upon you to do what you deem is right. There has only been one other issue that has ever come between us, and I forgave you for that a long time ago."

Braden bowed his head, knowing exactly what the Prime Warden was referring to.

He told Renquist sincerely, "I apologize that my actions have ever brought you grief. You and I, we both come from two very different places on these issues. Just like last time, this situation is no different."

Zavier Renquist shook his head, eyes narrowing. "I disagree. We have so much in common, you and I. If you will just hear me out, I think you will come to understand what I mean. Would you do that for me? Hear me out? For the sake of the bonds of kinship we once shared?"

Braden clenched his teeth at that painful reminder, but forced himself to nod anyway. "I will."

Zavier Renquist smiled. It was a chill smile, one with very little true emotion behind it. "I think we can both agree that all of us have a moral obligation to strive for the best possible outcomes in any given situation. Where you and I differ is that I believe some outcomes are so important that they must be achieved at all cost, no matter the price. Even if the actions we must perform to accomplish our goals do not sit very well with our conscience. Motives, intentions…none of those things ever matter in the end. The results of our actions are the only things that truly count, for that is the only part of us that has any real impact upon the world. Good intentions, empty of results, don't count for much. They don't count for anything at all, really."

He shifted his weight on the cushions before continuing. "Far more than just our own lives are at stake in this matter. At stake is our entire legacy, our history, our heritage, and our future. I'm not asking this only for the benefit of magekind. Magic is an asset to all of humanity. As a civilization, we define ourselves by our achievements, and only through magic have mankind's greatest accomplishments ever been rendered possible."

Braden shook his head in disagreement. "The common folk won't bat an eye if all of magekind passes on," he stated pragmatically. "It would be far better for them to lose all memory and trace of us than to do as you suggest: to open the floodgates of Hell and allow Xerys free reign to subjugate humanity."

Renquist pursed his lips, shaking his head. "You're wrong, Braden. The common folk *do* need us. Without the guidance of the Masters, civilization as we know it will cease to exist. The temples will be abandoned, entire cities will decline into decay. Eventually, everything we have achieved, everything we have built, it will all collapse. A dark and unenlightened age will be thrust upon the world.

"I want you to understand that the world under

the reign of Xerys will not be as intolerable as you imagine or fear," the Prime Warden reassured him. "All it will involve is a slight change in ideology for most people. The addition of a temple to the skyline. A different altar to worship at. A new face to add to the pantheon. Most citizens, so caught up in their own lives, will never even realize they have become the ignorant subjects of a different kind of tyranny. They will go about their lives completely oblivious and unaffected.

"And, in appreciation for our service, Xerys has generously agreed to allow the eight of us, His Chosen Servants, to exercise His rule over the world. You and I, Braden, we will be the overlords of His dominion, to govern our territories as we see fit. It is part of the covenant we have struck with Him. We can each make of our own nations whatever we desire, to be as great or as modest as we please."

Braden tried unsuccessfully to wet his parched lips with his tongue. Staring down at the cup on the floor, he responded softly, "I am sorry, Prime Warden. I just don't see it working out that way. I'm afraid I don't share your optimism. Or your ambitions."

He drew himself up, raising his troubled eyes to meet Renquist's gaze. "I beg you not to do this, Prime Warden. If we do what is right and pass without struggle from this world, then humanity will soon forget we ever existed. They will move on. Given time, they will eventually prosper. Someday, their achievements may even grow to surpass our own. All I ask is that you give them that chance. Give them the opportunity to prove you wrong."

Zavier Renquist shook his head. In his eyes was a deep and profound sadness, the first trace of true emotion Braden had seen since the conversation began. Very softly, even gently, he uttered:

"You've fallen into the trap of shallow thinking, Braden, the kind that brings only enslavement to moral principles. There is no room there for shades of gray; it paints the world only in broad strokes of black and white. Life, very fortunately, cannot be reduced to such simplicity."

Braden bowed his head. "Then I'm sorry, Prime Warden. I've heard you out, but I'm afraid I still can't help you. It goes against every principle I have."

Zavier Renquist threw his head back and downed the remainder of his tea. Then, very firmly, he set the small brass cup upside down upon the tray it had come from. He turned to Byron Connel and nodded once.

Immediately, the red-bearded Battlemage rose and strode over to the door, rapping twice upon the wood. The door cracked open, slowly at first. Then it swung open broadly.

Braden winced, turning away from the sight of Sephana being led forward into the room. Her face was streaked with tears, her dress blood-stained and rumpled. Her eyes sought Braden's, full of sorrow and sympathy.

Very softly, Zavier Renquist asked of Braden, "Which one, do you think, should die first? You or her?"

Hearing that question, Braden grimaced and threw his head back.

Renquist pressed on, voice urgent and relentless, "Should I force her to look on as I take your life slowly? Or should I make you watch your lover suffer the consequences of your decision?"

Braden opened his eyes, shaking his head and gazing imploringly at the Prime Warden. He couldn't help the tears that gathered in his eyes. He couldn't bring himself to look at Sephana as he whispered in a barren voice:

"Kill her first. Just, please…do it *quickly.*"

His voice broke with emotion. He lowered his head to his chest as silent sobs wracked his frame. He brought his hands up to cover his face.

"No, Brother. I can't let you do this again."

It was Quin's voice. Braden glanced up, eyes wide and horrified, in time to watch Quin turn to look at Renquist with a feverish intensity. "If I do as you ask, will you promise to spare her?"

"Quin, no!" Sephana cried out, her arms crossed around her chest as she hugged herself desperately. Her face glistened with tears. "Please, no! *Don't do it!"*

"You have my word," Zavier Renquist responded gravely.

Quin nodded, rising to his knees. "What do I say?"

As Braden looked on in abject horror, his brother was guided through the ritual that would render him a darkmage. *Nach'tier,* in the language of the clans. He repeated the words exactly as Renquist pronounced them:

I commit my soul to Chaos. From this day forth,
I will be the obedient servant of Xerys.
I will serve faithfully all the days of my life…
and may not even death itself release me.

When it was over, the Prime Warden nodded once. Very formally, he uttered, "Thank you, Quinlan."

Then he turned to Braden, eyes simmering shadows of glaring intensity. "You have only this one last chance. Commit your soul to Xerys or Transfer your gift to someone who will."

Quin tried to jerk himself erect but was prevented by the constraints that held him. *"No!"* he shouted, flailing against his bonds, "You can't do this! *We had an agreement, damn you!"*

Zavier Renquist turned to regard him coolly, eyebrows raised, the expression on his face indifferent. "Your brother's life was not part of that agreement," he reminded Quin smoothly.

Braden knew he had to end this, one way or another.

Following Quin's example, he rose to his knees, palms resting on his thighs, and bowed his head deeply. His whole body shaking, he uttered solemnly the first words that came to mind, a vow that seemed to be born of desperation:

I swear to live in harmony with all of creation,
To use my gift with temperance and wisdom;
Always to heal and never to harm,
Or my life will be righteously forfeit.

When he opened his eyes, he saw that another metallic chain had appeared of its own accord, this time on his right wrist, identical to the one he had gained from the Acolyte's Oath. Now both of his wrists were thus marked. He caught his breath as he stared down at the silvery emblem of the chains. They were beautiful, seamless and flawless, indelible and perfect in every way.

Zavier Renquist glowered down at the twin set of markings engraved into the flesh of Braden's wrists. His mouth curled into a grimace of distaste. Slowly, he gathered up his robes and drew himself to his feet.

"Unfortunate," he pronounced, voice gruff and resolute. "Now that you are well and truly shackled to your morals, your life is worthless to me." To Connel, he commanded, "Take him back to his cell. I'll have Arden prepared for the Rite of Transference."

He turned toward the door.

Braden called after him, "I won't willingly Transfer my gift to that woman."

Renquist paused, fingers on the handle of the door. He turned to glance back, the look in his eyes hateful and terrifying.

"You won't have to," he assured Braden with a snarl. "I'll rip the gift right out of you just like you tore my daughter's soul from her living body."

Chapter Fifteen
Damn the Consequences

Bryn Calazar, Caladorn

Quin leaned his head back against the wall, arms folded across his chest, rocking himself ever so slightly. His eyes wandered upward to gaze at the ceiling.

They had just taken Braden and Sephana away.

His brother had never once looked back at him again; he had kept his stare lowered, eyes trained on the ground at his feet. Quin brought his knees up to his chest, clenching his jaw, all the while trying very hard not to weep.

Standing before him, Byron Connel shifted his weight over his feet. The motion made his long robes sway. Thar'gon gleamed coldly in the lantern light.

"I'm sorry," Connel stated in an attempt to console. "If it helps at all, you saved the one person whose life mattered more to him than his own. He'd thank you for it if he could."

Quin's view of the ceiling blurred as tears welled in his eyes.

"It doesn't help." His voice was ragged and drained of emotion. "All I've ever desired is for Braden to know how terribly proud—and how very grateful—I've always been to have him as a brother. But instead of being there for him whenever he needed me, all I've ever been is the architect of his pain. There truly is no end to my duplicity."

Byron Connel paced away, hands on his hips, moving his boot to swipe at a spilled teacup on the floor. "That has to hurt. Unfortunately, there is no way of going back and changing what's already been done, of making things right by him. The only thing you can do now is to try to keep Braden's interests at heart going forward. At least, in that, there is yet something you can still accomplish."

Quin scrubbed at his eyes with the back of his hand. "What is that?"

"Protect Sephana. Make sure you live up to your end of the bargain. Keep her safe."

Quin raised his eyebrows, pondering the idea. "Is that truly what Braden would wish?" The question was rhetorical, addressed more to himself rather than Connel.

"I believe so. What do you think?"

Quin frowned, still gazing up at the ceiling. He deliberated the answer for a moment. At length, he responded with an element of certainty:

"I think he'd want me to destroy you all and damn the consequences."

The Battlemage jerked his head around, hand moving to the haft of his weapon. He was ready to act, should Quin decide to try and deliver on his brother's legacy.

Byron Connel reminded him, "You couldn't rise to that challenge before. I don't think you can bring yourself to do it now."

Quin swallowed, realizing the man was absolutely right. "No," he agreed. "I could not. And I'm far too much of a coward to attempt it by myself."

Connel's hand relaxed at his side, slipping away from his weapon. He gave a curt nod. "Very well. At least we both know where you stand."

Quin sucked in a sharp breath, biting his lip against the feeling of despair that came with acceptance of Connel's logic. There was no further struggle left within him; he had been too thoroughly defeated.

"It's time for us to go," Connel announced, turning back toward the door. "I'm going to release the field damper on you now. I trust you won't do anything stupid?"

Quin scowled. "I assure you, I've already used up all the stupid left within me today."

He drew himself up away from the wall, rising uncertainly to his feet. He offered his manacled wrists out in front of him.

"Fair enough," uttered the Battlemage.

With the power of his mind, Byron Connel released the locks holding Quin's shackles in place. The manacles on his wrists and ankles opened of their own accord, falling away and dropping to the ground. Quin gazed down at the flesh of his wrists, reddened and raw and chafed from the weight of the bonds.

Connel closed his eyes and unmade the ward that had been used to shield Quin's mind from the magic field. The glorious power of the field flooded into him like a river surging back into its course, at first offering Quin a gentle and comforting security. He closed his eyes, savoring the sweet sensation he had gone so long without.

But it wasn't right. It wasn't right at all.

Indeed, it was all sorts of wrong.

Quin reached out with his mind, testing the capricious energies of the field, only to find his gesture rebuffed by its strange and peculiar tension. Quin's mind flinched back away from the field's acrid touch. He turned back to Connel with a look of alarm.

"You feel that?" demanded the red-bearded Battlemage. "That's our death riding toward us on the wings of apocalypse unless we do something to stop it. Follow me."

He turned and stalked out of the room, gloved hands clenched into fists. Quin followed after him, having to jog to catch up. He held on to his hat with his hand, falling into step and trying to match Connel's long strides.

He was led down long flights of stairs to one of the war rooms below the Grand Assembly. Connel threw open the door, sweeping it back and holding it open for him. Quin paused in the threshold, uncertain, eyes scanning over the chamber.

A dark-haired woman whirled to confront him, eyes startled. A look of recognition slowly dawned on her face. Four other mages in the room stopped what they were doing and turned to stare, fixing Quin with questioning looks. He knew them all, of course, every face in the room.

He swallowed, trying hard not to look away, feeling a profound sense of shame.

From over his shoulder, Connel announced, "Let me introduce our newest associate, Quinlan Reis."

The dark-haired woman smirked, her eyes considering him dubiously. "I'm sorry, Quin, I almost didn't recognize you. I forgot what you look like sober."

Reaching up, Quin carefully drew his hat off his head, holding it in his hands against his chest. "Why, thank you, Myria. I almost didn't recognize you, either. You look so much better when I'm drunk."

The woman chortled, rolling her eyes. With a quirk of her brow, she commented, "Welcome to the Servants, Quin. It's good to see you haven't lost your spark."

Quin drew himself up formally, addressing her, "If only my 'spark' was the only thing in jeopardy here today. As it is, I gravely fear you'll be stuck with my catalytic disposition until Hell freezes over."

Byron Connel smiled wanly, shaking his head. "Quin, this is Myria Anassis."

"We've met. Unfortunately." Quin replaced his hat back on his head with a nod in Myria's direction. "Madam."

She turned away with a look of exasperation. "Your dog needs a muzzle, Connel."

The Battlemage put an arm around Quin's shoulders, drawing him near as he strolled back with him in the direction of the door. He whispered in a lowered voice, "I understand you've suffered a loss today. But you need to tread more carefully. These people are your allies now. And there are still a lot of ruffled feathers to go around."

Quin nodded, taking the warning to heart. Byron Connel turned back toward Myria. "Would you please brief Quin about his part in our undertaking?"

"I will if he minds his manners," she simpered. Myria turned back to Quin with a grudging smile on her lips. But when she actually started talking, her face became a mask of cool, businesslike efficiency.

"The Reversal is already underway," she explained in curt, professional tones. "Right now its effects are being felt further to the north, directly over Aeridor. But as the night lengthens, the field will depolarize progressively further toward the south.

"Quin, you will be operating the Circle of Convergence at Vintgar," she informed him. "That will be the first circle under the effects of the Reversal. You will have to create and maintain a resonance to stabilize the magic field as it weakens. Then, at the moment of oscillation, the field strength will be reduced to null. When that happens, you will have to rely on the power of the Onslaught to maintain the circle's acceleration."

Quin stared at her blankly, feeling suddenly weak and very dizzy, his insides going completely numb. Deep down in his chest, his heart despaired. His soul felt brittle, fragile and cold.

He nodded absently when she finished talking. He heard the words she was saying, even understood what she was asking of him. But, somehow, it all just seemed remote and unimportant. Like it didn't pertain to him at all.

It didn't; his mind was entirely somewhere else.

Not sensing his mood, Myria pressed on, "For the first hour, it will be entirely up to you, Quin. No other circle will be tied in, yet. You must maintain the resonance. If something goes wrong and you drop your circle, we could lose control of the entire Onslaught. I don't think I need to emphasize how devastating that would be."

Once again, Quin could only nod. He really had heard very little of what was being said. He turned toward Byron Connel, a profound and weary sadness in his eyes.

"Is my brother dead yet?" he wondered in morbid speculation.

Connel compressed his lips together, eyes full of compassion. He reached out, laying a comforting hand on Quin's shoulder. "Not yet. Soon, though. Quin, you have to let this go. There's nothing you can do. It is out of your hands."

Quin drew in a deep breath, swallowing against a bitter lump of grief in his throat.

He felt completely at a loss.

He had no idea how to follow the man's advice.

The woman named Arden Hannah smiled up into the angular planes of Nashir Arman's chiseled face. Of all the Servants she had met so far, he was the most self-assured, the most mysterious, the most dangerous and fascinating. She found his sinister charisma enticingly desirable.

Gazing down at her with his hazel eyes, Nashir asked of her with a smile, "Arden, you are glowing. Are you so very eager for the Transference?"

She smiled and glanced shyly at the two guardsmen that stood stone-faced at the bottom of the stairs, double swords crossed behind their backs. She despised their presence, but knew there was nothing to be done about them. So she decided to ignore them completely, acting as though they weren't even there.

Arden grinned, smirking playfully up at Nashir, twirling her fingers around in her hair.

"I am," she admitted sincerely. "I've been waiting for this moment most of my life."

He raised his thick eyebrows, nodding in understanding. "What of Braden Reis? Do you not harbor any feelings of remorse for him? He was your friend once…was he not?"

Arden scoffed. She drew closer to him, reaching out and trailing her hand along the rise of his broad chest. "You are far more of a man than Braden ever was," she assured him with confidence, her eyes intent upon the texture of his muscles beneath her fingers. She lifted her gaze to meet his. "No. I feel no remorse at all. I feel only…*vindication.*"

She leaned forward to whisper that last word in his ear. Her eyes lingered on him longingly, her lips parted and inviting. He placed a firm hand behind her head, drawing her toward him.

Arden moaned softly as his lips pressed against her own, his tongue exploring the inside of her mouth. She ran her fingers through his hair.

When they parted, Nashir stood there for a moment gazing hungrily into her eyes. At last, he informed her in a breathless whisper, "It is time."

Arden's eyes widened in anticipation.

She walked forward beside Nashir, who strode down the stairs with cat-like grace, wielding an ironwood staff that was taller than he was and shod with elaborate gold end caps. They followed the guards down the lightless corridor, walking through a churning trail of amethyst magelight. They paused before a thick oaken door approximately halfway down the passage. Arden waited behind as Nashir undid the lock with his mind, letting the door sway open on its hinges.

"Braden Reis," he called within. "On your feet."

Arden moved forward, peering around Nashir's tall frame into the cell. She found Braden sitting hunched over on the floor, arms bound behind his back, head bowed forward against his chest. He showed no sign whatsoever that he was even aware of their presence. He just sat there, gaze fixed somewhere on the floor between his feet. His hands were trembling.

Noticing his discomfort, Arden couldn't help but smile.

Nashir stroked her cheek, indicating Braden with his eyes.

Arden turned to look.

Braden lurched suddenly upright, throwing his head back and groaning through clenched teeth. He fell sideways to the floor, limbs flailing in anguished torment. Arden watched, startled, but otherwise completely mesmerized by the brazen display of torture. She trailed her tongue across her lips, wetting them.

"Still feeling vindicated?"

Arden glanced upward at Nashir, breath coming in gasps, face flushed with excitement.

"Very much," she whispered.

———

Vintgar, Caladorn

Quin staggered, catching himself from falling but roughing the palms of his hands on the coarse stones of the floor. He righted himself, gazing around. The room he was standing in now was different from the one he had just been walking through only moments before. He instantly recognized the stark bleakness of the walls and the cross-vaulted arch behind him.

He had arrived in the portal chamber at Vintgar.

Here in the eye of Vintgar's vortex, at the bottom of the ice chasm, he knew it would be safe enough to open his mind to sample the flavor of the magic field.

Only, he wasn't nearly prepared for what he'd find.

The magic field itself was keening, wailing like the howls of a thousand tortured spirits. Quin cried out, wincing back from the frenzied disquiet of the field. The eye of the vortex was contorting, shuddering as if in violent distress. It pained his head to open his mind enough to sense it.

He knew what he had to do, although his heart was not really in it. Looking around, he gathered his thoughts, his feelings. What little courage he had left. And then he compelled himself to walk out the door of the room, leaving the portal chamber behind.

As he strode through the halls of glowing ice toward the hall where Vintgar's Circle of Convergence lay dormant, there was only one subject of thought on his mind: was his brother already dead, or was he yet still alive?

The thought plagued him utterly; he dwelled upon it, and upon it only. Despite his every attempt, he could not get the topic out of his head. Dark, morose thoughts churned around in his brain, frothing with morbid conjecture.

Was the bond of brotherhood between them strong enough to allow him to feel the moment when Braden died? Would he even be aware of his passing?

Would Braden's last thoughts be warm memories of the love and joy he had known? Or would his final moments be full of despair and pain?

Would there be anyone there with him at the end, someone to offer him comfort? Or would he die alone and in misery, with no friend to ease his passing?

Quin clenched his jaw, scrubbing at his eyes with his sleeve. He swallowed heavily against the sorrow that plagued his heart. He shook his head violently and drew up, determined to cast the tormented images from his mind.

Before him, quiescent in the shadows and dormant from a long period of sleep, lay Vintgar's Circle of Convergence.

Quin stepped out into the room, placing his feet timidly between the axes of power on the floor. Engraved into the basalt rock at his feet was a larger copy of the Silver Star that Braden had always worn embroidered over his heart. The pattern was far more than mere ornamentation; it was the focus of the Circle of Convergence.

All he had to do was awaken it.

Quin strode over to the tip of the nearest ray and

drew deeply on the power of the magic field. At first, the field did not respond to his call. Like a skittish foal, the magic field resisted his touch, flinching away from the caress of his mind. Quin closed his eyes, concentrating harder, and commanded it again. This time, he mustered much more authority, summoning that great well of power through the lines at his feet.

The Circle of Convergence at last responded, hearkening to his call. The ancient, stone-carved lines awakened, beginning to glow with argent intensity. A graceful trickle of light traveled outward from his boots, running like liquid silver from a blacksmith's forge, trailing outwards to ignite the tips of all eight rays. Quin walked forward, taking up position at the circle's center, closing his eyes as he exerted his dominance over the vortex.

Then:

Another feeling enveloped him, one so consummate, so penetrating, so encompassing, that it wracked his mind in molten ecstasy.

Quin's mouth fell agape, eyes springing wide open, as he gasped for air. His emotions jolted in a rhapsody of spiraling sensations.

He realized with a fragmented, scattered thought:

The Well of Tears has been opened.

Consumed by the euphoric power of the Onslaught, Quinlan Reis writhed in the center of Vintgar's power vortex, drowning in smothering tidal waves of rapture.

———

Bryn Calazar, Caladorn

Arden grinned at Braden, reveling in the pleasure she was taking from his pain. She pressed her soft body up against his as she gazed up into his eyes with a smile.

"I want you to die knowing that they chose me to inherit your legacy," she whispered into his ear. "One way or another, your gift will be put to the service of Xerys. With your power inside me, *I* will be the one destined for greatness. And you?" She fixed him with a pout, then scoffed with a shrug. "You'll just be dead."

She stepped back away to observe his reaction.

Braden bowed his head, his whole body seeming to sag. The gentle confidence she had once admired in him was now completely gone from his eyes. In its place was only weary acceptance.

Arden couldn't help the smile of triumph that sprang to her lips. Glancing behind her at Nashir, she saw the darkmage return her expression with a look of satisfied esteem.

She turned her back on Braden and stepped out into the corridor. She left him at the mercy of the guards, who swept forward to claim him.

———

Vintgar, Caladorn

Quin gazed up at the black dome above the circle, mouth agape, eyes widened by a mixture of horror and euphoria. Through perceptions extended by his connection with the Onslaught, he could sense the effects of the circle's acceleration.

Far above, in the rolling hills above the ice chasms, the swirling mass of midnight cloud cover was starting to give way.

High above in the sky, the powerful energies of the vortex were hurling against the forces driving the Reversal. It was an ever-evolving battle that spanned the entire length of the sky, both terrible and awe-inspiring. Arcs of wild lightning licked across the atmosphere, nebulous auroras flickering brilliantly before collapse. Thunderheads clashed, colliding, showering cascades of sparks that rained down upon the hills from the heavens above.

Quin's heightened perceptions confirmed what his senses were already telling him: in this place, the magic field was beginning to stabilize.

It was truly magnificent. And it was also terrifying.

Quin beheld it all through a suffocating veil of tormented anguish.

As he watched the ongoing battle ensuing across the sky, his mind kept drifting back toward his brother.

Why was he even here? What purpose did it even serve?

I'm here for Sephana. No; not for her. For Braden.

Would his brother even have wanted this?

No, he wouldn't. Not at all.

Quin cried out in a rage of conflicted emotions. This is not what Braden would have wanted, he realized tragically. Never in a thousand years.

Is it over for you yet, Brother?

Quin's eyes shot wide open. It had taken this, the torrent of the Onslaught, to make him realize the magnitude of his own hypocrisy, the terrible extent of his betrayal. All along, Quin had thought he was doing something to honor his brother's memory. Instead, Quin realized in horror, he had been working to destroy everything Braden considered worth dying for.

When had he ever been there for his brother? Never before in his life.

I am the architect of his pain.

Quin staggered backwards, tormented by feelings of guilt and despair. With a cry, he let go of his command of the Circle of Convergence, dropping the energies to the floor like a sack of spilt grain. He staggered toward the door, covering his ears against the wailing backlash of the magic field.

Reaching within, he drove a mental barrier between his mind and the Onslaught, railing against that terrible power and battering it away.

Then he was running as fast as he could in the direction of the transfer portal.

Maybe, just perhaps, there was still yet time…

Back in the circle's chamber, the Onslaught assumed its own sinister domination over the vortex, filling the power vacuum that Quin had left behind.

Chapter Sixteen
Atonement

Bryn Calazar, Caladorn

Arden watched Nashir raise his staff, using its gilt end cap to rap three times upon the enormous double doors that warded the entrance to the Grand Assembly. The resounding noise of his strikes echoed throughout the tall chamber.

There was a pause.

Then the knocks were answered in kind, the sound emanating from within.

The doors of the Assembly were thrust open, their ancient hinges groaning in rusty protest. Arden stepped to the side as she coldly observed Braden's guards impelling him forward. He staggered, seeming to have a hard time moving in their iron clasp. He didn't fight, but he did not go quietly, either. To Arden, Braden Reis appeared a reluctant but active participant in his own execution.

The double doors were closed, the bar thrown down to seal them shut. The doors would not be opened again until Braden's fate was resolved to the satisfaction of the Assembly.

Nashir draped his arm around Arden's shoulders possessively.

"I'll take you up to the second gallery." He pressed a kiss against her cheek. "When it is done, the Prime Warden will call you down. Make certain to offer him the appropriate obeisance."

Suddenly uncertain, Arden wondered, "Am I going to be required to say any words as part of the ritual?"

Nashir shook his head, stroking a finger over her chin. "No. Not in this situation. This is not the way it typically works." His voice was calm and reassuring.

He kissed her again, slowly, cupping her face.

"I should warn you," he whispered, still holding her face in his dark hands, "this is not going to be like any Transference you've ever witnessed. It is going to hurt. A lot."

Arden blinked. "Him? Or me?"

"Both," Nashir answered ominously. "But mostly him."

"Good."

"You'll do just fine." Nashir held her gaze steady with her chin between his thumb and forefinger. "I'll be waiting for you when it's over."

Vintgar, Caladorn

Quin ran through the deserted halls of ancient Vintgar, dodging falling bricks and shifting floor tiles. The ground shook beneath his feet, heaving in seething turmoil from the violence of the Onslaught. Huge fragments of ice rained down from above in the chasm, bounding like hail upon the lower caverns. Down in the gorge, the River Nym was hurled from its course, spilling chill floodwaters into the halls of the ice fortress.

Dodging a boulder that was only just moments ago part of the ceiling, Quin sprinted across the threshold of the portal chamber. To his relief, the cross-vaulted arch remained intact, the warm glow between its columns beckoning like a promise. Quin threw himself headfirst into the transfer portal just as the raging waters of the Nym spilled into the chamber behind him.

Bryn Calazar, Caladorn

Arden stepped out onto the second-floor gallery, moving toward the chairs Nashir had reserved for them. Her eyes swept across the dimly lit hall, widening with amazement. There, in the Grand Assembly of the Lyceum, were gathered more mages than she had ever known even existed in all the world. They were seated in rows on terraced galleries, level upon level of cascading rings encompassing the entire height of the dome.

The Assembly was filled with the drone of conversation, a compressed and uneasy tension filling the air.

As Arden seated herself, she could feel her eyes tear up in gratitude that she was finally, actually, *here,* ready to take her own place as a member of this great body.

She had waited so many years. So much struggle. So much effort. So much pain. She had come so close to losing everything so many times.

It had always been possible, but always a distant dream, tangible, but ever just out of reach. And now that dream was about to be hers to grasp in her hands and claim as she pleased.

Deeply moved, Arden brought her fingers up to cover her mouth as all across the chamber the drone of conversation faltered.

An anxious silence settled gradually over the hall.

A large orb of light appeared on the floor of the chamber. It was brilliant, intense. All around, the ambient lighting slowly dimmed. The effect was hypnotic, mesmerizing. Her gaze was directed at the sphere of light on the floor, forsaking all else.

She watched as Braden was brought forward by his guards into that argent glow. They positioned him there in the center, one man to either side. He was made to stand there, shirtless, blinking against the brilliance that surrounded him.

Arden's pulse lurched in anticipation as she stared down at the man who was about to surrender to her his legacy and life. Braden did not go to his death with defiance or pride, nor did he rail in panic against his fate. There was no fight left within him at all.

She closed her eyes, savoring the sweet exhilaration brought about by that insight.

Quin rolled as he landed on the other side of the portal, hauling himself up off the ground and staggering forward at a run. He ignored the shouts of the guards behind him as he outdistanced them, launching his body in the direction of the stairwell.

He ran down flights of stairs, taking two and three steps at a time, finally spilling out into the darkness of the dungeon. Quickly, he produced a glowing mass of magelight, sending it spreading forward ahead of him over the ground.

He jogged up the narrow hallway between cells, trying to remember which one they had put his brother in. Picking a door he thought was the right one, he threw it open with both hands.

The cell was empty.

He tried the one across from it.

It, too, was empty.

He tried another door. And another.

The next cell was not empty. But it also did not contain Braden.

What it did contain was important enough to stop Quin in his tracks. He paused, groping forward through his burgundy glow of magelight.

In a pile scattered carelessly across the floor were all of the things that had been taken from them. His pack was there, along with his sword, Zanikar, still in its scabbard. Sephana's light staff lay beneath a pile of blood-soaked rags.

Wincing, Quin reached down and plucked his sword up from the ground. He strapped the scabbard around his hips. He shouldered his pack and took up the staff.

And then he paused.

On the floor, half hidden by the pile of clothing they had stripped from his brother, was the war belt given to Braden by the clan chief of the Omeyan Jenn. Still attached to it were all of the weapons and tools that had been affixed to it when Braden had worn it last. Quin drew the belt on over his own waist, tying it in place before ducking out the door.

"Braden!" he shouted, slapping his hand on the wooden door of the cell across from him. *"Sephana!"*

He went door to door down the passage, thrusting open random doors, pounding on the walls until his knuckles were torn and bloodied.

And then he found someone.

Tearing open a door, Quin flinched back at the

sight of an old and sickly looking man with thinning white hair, face quilted by wrinkles. Quin pulled up short, recognition dawning in his eyes.

"I thought you were one of them," he said of Devrim Remzi.

The aged Empiricist rose to his feet, spreading out his shackled hands as far as his bonds would allow. Quin released him from his manacles, turning the locks with the power of his mind.

Then he assaulted Remzi, grabbing the old man by the shoulders. "Please," he begged him. "Tell me, have you seen my brother? Or Sephana?"

The old Master took a step back away from him and sat back down upon his cot, gazing up into Quin's face suspiciously. He raised his hand to his nose, wiping away a fresh drop of blood. The old Master had not been treated kindly, Quin surmised.

"You will find the woman two cells down on the right," Remzi informed him, still glaring him cautiously in the eye. His gaze was intense, and intensely distrustful. "If you're looking for your brother, then I'm afraid you are already too late."

Upon hearing his words, Quin felt an awful, chilling weakness in his joints. He shook his head, unwilling to believe such dreadful tidings.

"No," he gasped, whirling back out of the cell. With his shoulder, he shoved at the door the old man had indicated. It was locked.

He pounded on the wood, rattling it against its hinges.

He shattered the locking mechanism with the power of his mind. The door sprang open a narrow inch. He kicked it open the rest of the way.

Sephana careened toward him, falling into Quin's arms, clinging to him desperately. She was crying, the abundance of her tears wetting his neck and cheek.

"*They took him away*," she sobbed against his chest.

At first, all Quin could do was stare at her mutely. But then he clenched his jaw, rallying his strength.

"Then let's go get him back," he challenged her, tossing Sephana her staff.

She caught it up in her hand, eyes brimming with grief mixed with hope as they sprinted out of the dungeon and raced together toward the stairs.

In the hall of the Grand Assembly, the sound of a deep and resonant voice interrupted the silence:

"Braden Reis, you have been convicted, attainted, and condemned of high treason committed against the state of Caladorn and the Lyceum of Bryn Calazar. A sentence of death has been pronounced against you. May the gods have mercy on your soul."

Hearing that verdict, Arden leaned forward on the edge of her seat, hands gripping the railing in front of her.

Down on the floor in the circle of light, ropes of energy materialized to entwine tightly about Braden's body. His guards forced him roughly to his knees, one man leveraging him down by the shoulders, the other taking him by the hair, jerking his head forward and forcing his chin against his chest.

Nashir tried to take hold of her hand. Arden ignored his touch, too entranced was she by the pathos of the scene unfolding before her. It was enthralling, intoxicating, wondrously stimulating. It excited her desperately. Her heart thrummed, her head dizzy with the thrill of expectation.

She watched as, down on the floor, Zavier Renquist strode forward into the glowing sphere of light. From his hands swayed a large pendant that hung from a thick silver band, the medallion's stone faceted, dull and black.

Seeing that dark stone held before him, Braden Reis at last looked properly afraid.

The Prime Warden moved to stand behind him, pausing there for a moment, raising the pendant up over his head. He gazed up solemnly, perhaps even sadly, at the artifact in his hands. Then he was bending over, draping the bands of the silver collar around Braden's neck.

In the silence that encased the chamber, Arden actually heard the *click* of the metallic clasp.

The sound made her flinch.

Braden cringed forward, his body held upright only by the considerable strength of the guards. He struggled against their grip, shuddering violently. On his chest, the black medallion began to glow, dark facets filling with a terrible inner fire.

They released his bonds of light, the guards stepping back away. Braden spilled forward to the floor, writhing and moaning in tormented anguish.

When he finally began to scream, Arden sucked in a sharp hiss of air. She was trembling all over, jaw slack and shivering, breath ragged and panting. Her fingers clenched the arms of her chair until her knuckles turned white.

The sound of Braden's screams became desperate, horrific. Arden moaned, caught up in the throes of an exhilarated climax unlike anything she had ever felt before in her life.

Quin staggered out of the stairwell and out into the wide hall, his eyes making a quick survey of the room. It was the same place where the crowd had assaulted Braden and himself just hours before.

The wide hall was now completely empty. Scattered trash strewn across the tiles was the only reminder that so many people had even been there.

Frowning in incomprehension, Quin drew Zanikar from its scabbard and rushed forward across the hall, Sephana right behind him. He made toward an enormous set of double doors set into the end of a vaulted transept. One of the doors was already ajar, cracked partially open.

Quin began to raise his hand but then paused. He closed his eyes, steeling himself before asserting his weight against the door.

Sephana at his side, Quin stepped forward into the Grand Assembly. Terraced galleries soared upward along the walls of the massive dome.

The chamber was dim and empty. Completely deserted.

Only silence greeted their arrival.

Numb with fear and trepidation, Quin's legs trembled as he moved forward down the aisle and out into the center of the floor. He sheathed his sword. His eyes scanned the painted tiles for evidence that his brother had ever been there.

There was nothing to find. No blood. No signs of struggle.

A fragile sound came echoing from somewhere down below.

Quin's eyes darted to Sephana, questioning, then trailed back again across the floor. It took him a moment to notice the gaping entrance to a stairway set behind the lower gallery.

Quin surged toward it, his breath ragged, desperate thoughts wildly flailing through his head. Sephana by his side, he clung to her arm as he staggered down the steps.

Halfway down, he drew up short.

Quin's heart stalled in his chest. For a moment all he could do was stand there, unable to draw breath. Pressed up against him, he could feel Sephana's body stiffen.

Below him on the floor, a woman in white was tending to his brother's corpse. She was in the process of composing him on a bier. The woman glanced up, gazing at them through a sheer veil of white.

Quin groaned, turning away. He enfolded Sephana in his arms. Closing his eyes, he held her close, letting her spill her grief against his chest.

The priestess of Death paused in her ministrations, looking on with face full of sympathy.

Chapter Seventeen
Architect of Pain

Bryn Calazar, Caladorn

The white-veiled priestess withdrew to the side, yielding them space to grieve. Quin remained behind on the stairs as Sephana swept forward to kneel at Braden's side. She took his limp hand into her own, caressing it tenderly.

Quin wandered slowly forward, dropping to the floor. Blinking back scalding tears, he gazed down upon his brother. Braden's dark eyes were open and staring, but they were dull and empty. Nothing of his character yet remained; the spirit inside had fled.

Quin bent down to press a kiss against his brother's forehead. At the same time, he drew his hand down over Braden's face, closing his eyes. He remained that way for a little while, just to be certain.

He sat back up, comforted to discover his brother appeared much more at peace.

He glanced over to Sephana. She was still grieving, shoulders quivering as she clung desperately to Braden's hand. She was running her thumb back and forth over the interlaced markings on his wrist. The emblem of the chain shimmered coldly in her magelight.

Quin started to pull away, but hesitated as a metallic glint caught his eye. There, dropped carelessly on the floor beside the corpse, was the Soulstone medallion.

Quin's breath hitched in his throat as fresh, hot tears spilled down his cheeks. No longer would he have to morbidly speculate how Braden had spent the last moments of his life. He knew exactly the manner of death inflicted by that artifact.

After all, the medallion was his own creation.

When Quin had first conceived the notion of the Soulstone, he had envisioned a benevolent talisman, a gentle means of Transferring the gift from a dying mage to an apprentice if the two were separated by distance or by time.

In his youth, Quin had been considered something of a protégé, the foremost master of his craft at a very young age. He had intended the Soulstone medallion to be his masterpiece, his opus, his crowning achievement. A precious heirloom that would endure long after he was gone, preserving magical legacies that might otherwise have been lost due to circumstance or atrophy.

It was never his intent to create such a malevolent device.

He hadn't known about the flaw. Not until he had been forced to witness Amani's execution. Quin had been made to sit there and watch as Amani died in agony, writhing and screaming in Braden's arms.

Her death should have been a peaceful one. Quin had personally assured his brother that it would be.

Which was the only reason Braden had chosen to use the Soulstone in the first place.

Amani's father, Prime Warden Renquist, had refused to recuse himself from the case when his own daughter had been brought forward for Inquiry. Amani had been condemned to death by her father's pronounced judgment. And it was by Renquist's command that Braden was forced to administrate his own wife's execution.

Braden had not chosen to use the Soulstone out of malice or any kind of thirst for revenge. Not for justice or jealousy. No; he had made that choice out of compassion. Out of mercy. Because he had, once again, made the mistake of trusting Quin's advice.

Quin swallowed heavily against bitter tears of self-hatred. He fully understood the enormity of his guilt.

If he hadn't rushed to finish the Soulstone, Amani wouldn't have suffered.

His brother, as well, need not have suffered.

At least, he could spare Sephana from knowing what manner of death Braden had been subjected to. Far better for her if she never knew.

Quin shifted his weight, letting the hem of his coat fall forward to cover the medallion on the floor. He slipped it away before she could see it, dropping the vile thing into the pocket of his vest. He leaned forward, brushing a kiss against her cheek.

"Take as long as you need," he whispered.

Sephana nodded, grimacing against her tears.

He rose, hand in his pocket, and shambled away like a sad and abject man lost in a wilderness of regret.

It was to the priestess of Death that Quin wandered first. The woman was biding her time in an adjacent room, giving them space to be alone with their dead. The priestess rose to her feet when she noticed Quin's presence in the doorway.

He gazed into the woman's veiled face, not fully trusting his voice. He fished the silver medallion out of his pocket and extended it out toward her in his hand.

"I named this talisman the Soulstone," he managed raggedly, his voice hoarse with misery. "It's an artifact…a holding vessel for a mage's legacy, but one entirely despicable. I created it, " he admitted wretchedly, holding her dark eyes through her veil. "But I can't destroy it.

"So please," he begged of her, "take this back with you to your high temple and seal it away in your deepest vaults. Keep it there. Never allow knowledge of its existence to pass to the mages of Aerysius. Please, if you fear Xerys, you will do this for me."

The woman gazed at him with compassionate understanding in her eyes. She nodded once. Then she reached out and withdrew the medallion from his hand, holding it cautiously by its silver band.

Quin turned and stalked away, not wanting to look back to see what she did with it. He had no interest in ever seeing it again.

Arden Hannah glanced upward at the sky from her perch on a high balcony overlooking the Lyceum. What she saw terrified her.

Black thunderheads churned across the night, flickering lights strobing deep within their depths. Every so often an arcing fork of lightning would crackle overhead, followed instantly by a rolling peal of thunder.

The turmoil in the sky was mirrored by the chaos beneath in the city. Arden gazed out across Bryn Calazar and wondered what could have gone so terribly wrong in such a short amount of time.

Outside the city gates, the rolling landscape was blackened, charred and empty. The besieging army of the horse lords no longer assailed the city gates. Their remains had been cremated by Connel's assault with the Circle of Convergence, their ashes strewn across the ground by the careless fingers of the wind.

Below her feet, Bryn Calazar was dying. Citizens ran panicked through the streets as the city crumbled all around them. Everywhere she looked, walls were giving way, buildings toppled, bridges collapsing into rubble.

Arden turned to Nashir, her eyes deeply troubled. "How can this be happening?" she wondered. "What went wrong?"

He was gazing down at the fires that had ignited below in the courtyard, their orange reflection smoldering in his eyes. "It is the fault of Quinlan Reis," he acknowledged at last. "He let go of Vintgar's circle too soon. The Onslaught has escaped our control."

Arden turned to stare at him, wide eyes full of concern. "What can we do?"

He shrugged. "We can still try to stabilize the magic field with the other Circles of Convergence. It might not work. But that is all that can be done at this time."

"Is there hope?" she wondered.

The cruelly handsome darkmage turned to gaze at her. He brought his hand up, stroking the back of his fingers gently down her cheek. With a sad smile on his lips, he whispered, "Maybe. If not, I look forward to spending an eternity in the Netherworld with you."

Quin glanced through the doorway to Sephana, still keeping watch at Braden's side. He looked down. For the first time, he realized that he was still wearing his brother's war belt.

He considered leaving it behind to be buried with the corpse, but he couldn't bring himself to do it. It was the only thing he had left of Braden.

Curious, he stuffed his fingers inside a pouch and, fishing around, withdrew a small object. He held the item up in his hand, frowning down at it. It only took him a moment to recognize what it was.

"I'll be damned," he whispered.

Quin remembered the day Braden had carved the wooden horse. Gazing down at the tiny stallion, he couldn't help the small, sad grin that worked its way to his lips.

A hand squeezed his shoulder. Sephana had retired from her watch.

Quin realized it was time to go.

He wandered back in the direction of the stairs, kneeling one last time at Braden's side.

"Goodbye, little brother," he whispered. "I'll never forget you. Never in a thousand years."

Into Braden's flaccid hand he pressed the tiny wooden horse, squeezing the fingers closed around it.

"'From the Atrament we all come, and back to the Atrament we all return,'" he whispered as he rose. He turned to leave.

"Pardon, Great Master."

He glanced back, an unspoken question on his face as he regarded the dark-haired priestess behind him. She nodded in his direction, a somber but compassionate expression on her face.

"I'm sorry to intrude, but…I do need to know his name."

Sephana strode forward, drawing herself up nobly. To the priestess she announced in unfaltering tones, "His name was Braden Reis, Grand Master of the Sixth Tier, First of the Sentinels. He was the very best of us. So, please, lay him out properly."

The priestess of Death dropped instantly into a low and formal curtsey. "He will be well cared for, Great Lady."

Arden Hannah leaned forward, intent on the deep and velvety tones of Nashir's clanborn accent. It was much thicker than either Quin's or Braden's had been, harsher and more difficult to follow unless she was paying very close attention.

"How does it feel?" he probed her, stroking the side of her face with a finger. "Is there still any pain?"

Arden stretched languidly, luxuriating in the strength of her newfound abilities. She drew in a small taste of the magic field, sampling its profound energies. "I feel…*empowered.*" She shook her head, at a complete loss for words. "I can't describe it."

"And vindicated?" Nashir pressed with an amused grin.

Arden smiled. "Yes. And vindicated."

She closed her eyes, savoring the vibrant thrill of the fierce inheritance she had received from Braden through the Soulstone. The feel of it was intoxicating, prodigious, eclipsing anything she had ever dreamed or expected it would be like. She'd had no idea the man had been endowed with so much raw, terrifying power. Braden Reis had been sixth tier, the most vested mage in all of history. And now his great and potent legacy had fallen to her.

"It doesn't hurt anymore," she informed Nashir.

"Good," the darkmage smiled, gazing deeply into her eyes. "We are sending you to Xerys' Pedestal on the edge of the Cerulean Plains." His eyes were full of malevolent confidence, holding no scrap of doubt for her newfound abilities. "There's still a chance to stabilize the magic field. You must use the circle there then transfer to Aerysius to assist Prime Warden Krane."

Nashir smiled at her reassuringly. Then he leaned forward to whisper in her ear, "Come. I have something for you."

He led her back into the shadows of his quarters, to a dark and narrow hallway. There, he opened a door at the far end. Arden peered into the shadows, eyes searching. She heard the sound of it before she saw anything.

A creature padded toward her from out of the darkness, eyes glowing with a menacing green intensity. Arden flinched back away from the appalling beast. It resembled a black wolfhound with crusted fur and a great, cavernous mouth. But it was not a dog; indeed, not any living animal. It looked like evil incarnate.

Nashir smiled affectionately, extending his hand toward his vile pet. It sniffed his fingers loudly, oozing great globs of slaver from its jowls.

"He's a loyal beast," the darkmage commented, ruffling the thing's wet and matted fur. "He is yours. Take him with you for protection."

"What is it?" she gasped, drawing away.

"A thanacryst." Nashir took her hand into his own and guided her toward the beast. "A creature that feeds on the life force of a mage."

The thing sniffed twice at her hand, the sound of its breath like the gasp of air from a grave. Arden had to fight the impulse to pull away.

"How dreadful," she whispered, staring down at the creature in revulsion. "Won't it harm me?"

Nashir smiled, crouching down beside his pet, ruffling the fur of its withers with his hands. "It shouldn't," he reassured her. "Such beasts have been known to turn against their masters, but the blackness of your soul should quiet its appetite."

Arden raised her eyebrows at his remark. She had never thought of it that way before. Was her soul so very black? She gazed back down at the foul creature, bending forward to scratch it behind the ears.

The thanacryst sounded almost like it was purring.

Arden Hannah smiled. Her soul *was* very black.

Of that fact she was rather proud.

Quin wandered the halls of the Lyceum, numb and dazed by loss. He had no idea where he was going, letting his feet carry him forward without purpose or direction. Sephana was at his side, but she, too, seemed similarly affected. Neither said a word.

A sudden tremor in the floor jolted Quin's senses back into focus. Above, suspended from the tiled ceiling, an enormous chandelier began to sway side to side like a pendulum on its iron chain. Another quake jolted the ground beneath their feet.

"What is that?" Sephana gasped.

Quin glanced around, eyes wide and fearful.

He took her by the wrist and rushed her forward toward an exit. Bursting through the door, he ran halfway out into the courtyard, head craned back, gazing up into the sky with mouth agape. He took in the fearsome aspect of the clouds overhead, of the surging clash of energies within them.

Immediately, he understood: the disturbance in the skies over Vintgar had swept southeast to threaten Bryn Calazar.

He brought his hand up to cover his mouth in agonized despair.

"This is my fault," he admitted over the howl of the raging winds. "I dropped the circle—I left the vortex exposed to the Onslaught! I stabilized the field there, but the Onslaught has gotten out of hand!"

Beside him, Sephana was regarding him very seriously. Over the sound of the rumbling thunder she called out to him, "Can you pick the circle back up again?"

He shook his head, holding his hat against the wind as his coat was crackled out behind him. "No. It's too late! Vintgar has fallen."

He turned to look behind them, to the Grand Dome of the Lyceum. Within, someone was commanding Bryn Calazar's Circle of Convergence. He could see the acceleration rings coming off from it, masses of air that churned, rotating in the sky over the dome. It created a column of swirling clouds that fought for dominance against the Onslaught.

"What they're trying it won't work," came a gruff voice from behind them.

Quin whirled to find Devrim Remzi standing there, quietly gazing up into the sky. The aged Master drew toward them, staring upward as he took in the vision of the resonance driving the swirling masses of air high overhead.

"Why won't it work?" Quin demanded, holding his hat against his head.

Still peering at the circle's acceleration, the old man explained, "They're still trying to save themselves—they're still working to stabilize the magic field. What they should be doing instead is trying to contain the Onslaught before it blackens the entire world."

Quin hung his head, lowering his hat against his chest. "This is my fault," he repeated, admitting his failure to the old man.

"Even if it is, it makes little difference," Remzi shrugged. "What matters now is whether you have the courage to right what you have wronged."

Quin frowned, prodding him, "What do you mean?"

The old man turned toward him. "Already, most of Caladorn has been charred to ash. The cataclysm is advancing toward the south, and will soon begin consuming the Rhen. There is nothing you can do to save our homeland. But you still have a chance to save hers." He indicated Sephana with a glance.

Quin gawked at him, open-mouthed and incredulous. He looked around, blinking furiously, unable to fully process the tidings he'd just heard.

Caladorn, destroyed. By him.

His fault.

"How?" he whispered, heart writhing in anguished torment.

"You must seal the Well of Tears," commanded Remzi. "Cut the Onslaught off from its source. Let your brother's vision come to pass."

"But what if they can stabilize it in time?" Sephana whispered. "If we seal the Well of Tears after the Reversal has been neutralized, then wouldn't that deny Xerys power over this world?"

"It might break their covenant," Remzi agreed guardedly. "At the very least, it's worth a try."

Appalled, Quin shuddered, "Can it even be done? I don't know how…"

"I do," the aged Empiricist insisted. "But I can't do it alone. The sealing of the Well requires a Grand Master, someone of at least fourth tier. You must enter the gateway that has been forged between worlds. There, you must offer yourself in sacrifice to mend the seal on the side of the Netherworld."

Quin stared at him a long, hard moment, eyes feverish with intensity. *"Show me how."*

"Quin—" Sephana began, but he was already stalking away.

He strode back toward the Lyceum, feet moving with determined purpose.

Xerys' Pedestal, The Rhen

Arden Hannah stepped out of the portal chamber at the base of the rock formation known as Xerys' Pedestal on the edge of the Cerulian Plains. She muttered a Word of Command as she moved across the threshold of the chamber. The dark basalt rock surrounding the door filled in the gap where the opening had just been.

She stepped out into the bleak grayness of night, alarmed by the sight of gathering cloud cover overhead. A wind was picking up, ruffling her hair. The Reversal was not yet here, but it was certainly on its way. To the northwest, she could see the dark peaks of the Craghorns encased in a thick fogbank that writhed and churned, incensed by violent forks of lightning.

Mounting the man-carved steps that wrapped, spiraling, around the thick column of rock, Arden ascended the narrow path toward the summit of the crag. At her side paced the terrible creature Nashir had given her. The thanacryst trotted dutifully ahead, its black tongue slavering fetid droplets as it sniffed the way.

She climbed, spiraling, hundreds of feet above the horseshoe-shaped valley that surrounded the pedestal. After long minutes, she gained the summit and stepped out onto the flattened vista.

Arden smiled, staring down at the lines of the small Circle of Convergence that was there, carved into the polished surface of the summit itself. This circle had been dormant a very long time, she surmised, tracing one of the focus lines with a slippered foot. She was excited, anticipating the thrill of power that would be hers to command when the circle awakened. Xerys' Vortex awaited her, its lines of charged power already beginning to cringe in anticipation of the oncoming Reversal.

Moving to the circle's center, Arden summoned the vortex's power through her feet. All around her, energies shivered as the circle responded. The focus lines shimmered, aglow with liquid metallic light. The image of the Silver Star appeared, awakening out of the black rock of the summit. All around a wind kicked up, rotating, increasing in fury.

Bryn Calazar, Caladorn

Quin stared up at the transfer portal to Aerysius, feeling a surge of trepidation. Sephana drew up to stand at his side, face drawn and grimly set. Behind her walked Devrim Remzi, ambling forward with a limp.

Quin positioned himself in the center of the tall, cross-vaulted arch. He put his hand out to Sephana. She stared at his offered hand for a long moment, considering it with a disdainful expression as though it were something diseased. Her gaze ticked upward to examine his face. Then something in her expression subtly changed, her eyes visibly softening.

Sephana accepted Quin's offered hand, lifting his arm along with hers as she stepped forward into the glow of the transfer portal.

There was a blinding flash of light as the world lurched beneath their feet.

Xerys' Pedestal, The Rhen

Above Arden's head, black clouds raced to confront the circle's resonance. She could feel the magic field destabilizing around her. Containing it was like trying to hold back a cup of spilt milk that just kept running through her fingers.

And then, suddenly, the song of the magic field went abruptly silent.

The field's absence was shocking in its totality.

But she had expected this.

Arden smiled and drew heavily on the rapturous power of the Onslaught. The circle's resonance rallied, the magic field surging back to life with brilliant intensity. The skies above thundered, the field lines wailing like a threnody. She flung her mind out on waves of light, searching for confirmation of what she already knew:

In this place, at least, the magic field was stable.

Her work here was complete.

Smiling in victory, Arden Hannah sprinted toward the flight of spiraling stairs.

Aerysius, The Rhen

Quin and Sephana spilled out of the portal into the Chamber of Egress beneath the Hall of the Watchers. Devrim Remzi came through directly after, collapsing to his knees. A guard rushed forward to confront them, halted by Sephana. She strode toward the man, brandishing the chain on her left wrist like an emblem before her face.

"Clear the chamber!" she commanded in a voice that rang with authority.

All of the men who guarded the portals turned as one then jogged together toward the exit.

Quin reached down, offering to help Remzi to his feet. The old Empiricist just batted his hand away with a scowl, pushing himself unsteadily to his feet.

Quin looked to Sephana in askance, wondering what her intentions were with the removal of the guards.

"We have to destroy the Egress," she explained, walking toward the nearest cross-vaulted arch. "Do you have any disruption charges left?"

Quin immediately nodded. He tossed open his pack, verifying that indeed they were all still accounted for, even the ones he had spilled out across the floor beneath the Lyceum. Someone had gathered them all up and replaced them back into his pack.

"Sephana…are you certain?" he asked her. "There's no coming back from this."

"Very certain," Sephana told him levelly. "We can't risk exposure at our rear."

Quin grudgingly agreed. He fished his arm deep within his pack, pulling out a handful of the small copper cubes. Four he tossed to Sephana. Then he ran to the first portal and began laying down the rest.

Chapter Eighteen
Cataclysm

Bryn Calazar, Caladorn

Zavier Renquist stared down from the balcony of a minaret high above the Lyceum's golden dome. Unfurling before him was an apocalyptic vision of his own inception. Below, the city of Bryn Calazar burned. Even the tall ships in the harbor were ablaze, their sails black and curling, fragmenting into ash. The night sky was adrift with glowing cinders that wafted gently to the ground, drifting like snowflakes. Black, acrid smoke roved over the city in great plumes, lingering close to the ground in some places or swept high up into the air, gathering in ominous pillars.

Renquist's predator-like gaze remained intent upon the scene of devastation unfolding below. He stood against the balcony wall with feet apart, cradling a cup in his hands. To the man standing behind him, he commanded:

"Evacuate the Lyceum."

There was a pause. The response was timorous when it came:

"I am sorry, Prime Warden. That is not possible."

Renquist turned to glare his contempt at the man, his stare dispassionate and intense. "What do you mean?"

The young mage before him swallowed, fidgeting. "It is the Onslaught. The transfer portals are no longer safe. We already tried sending a few people through… It did not turn out well, Prime Warden."

Renquist glowered. "Then evacuate to the city."

There was another long gap of silence. Then:

"The arches warding the gates have malfunctioned. Their polarity has been reversed. Anyone can enter the Lyceum…but no mage can leave."

Zavier Renquist turned his back on the man to consider the apocalyptic panorama below. He took a sip from the cup he was holding in his hand, a spiced wine fermented from mare's milk.

To the young man behind him, he wondered, "Then why are you still here? Go home. Make love to your wife. Then make your peace with the gods."

The Prime Warden continued to gaze down from the heights long after the other man had gone. The air was terrible, chokingly thick and filled with the acrid taste of wood smoke and defeat.

Glowing embers continued to shower down from the midnight sky, falling everywhere, wafting down to cover Bryn Calazar in drifting blankets of smothering ash.

It seemed the whole world was on fire.

Aerysius, The Rhen

Quin covered his ears and threw himself down, shielding Sephana with his own body.

There was a noise like deafening thunder followed by a concussion wave so intense it battered him against the ground. A thick cloud of fine, gray dust billowed toward them.

Choking, Quin held the fabric of his coat up over his mouth. Beside him, Devrim Remzi made a retching noise. Quin locked his hand on the mage's collar, pulling him along after him as he struggled to his feet.

One hand on Remzi, the other around Sephana's shoulders, Quin steered them back down the hallway. They jogged forward, finding a set of winding stairs that led upward. Here, Quin let Sephana go first. She knew this place far better than he.

"Well, that was one way to announce our arrival," he muttered.

Sephana led them to the top of the stairs and out across the tiled floor of the Hall of the Watchers. There, Aerysius' Circle of Convergence lay quiescent. Quin considered the circle carefully, distrusting it. Crouching down, he spread his hand upon the red marble of its surface.

"It's been in use," he observed. "And it's been used hard."

He rose, turning to stare upward into the shadows of the dome above. A gnawing feeling of trepidation crept over him. He retreated a step, then another, eyes scouring the forest of stone columns that supported the roof as he turned slowly around. A terrible feeling of cold shivered across his nerves.

All around the Hall of the Watchers, a host of necrators rose upward from the ground. They seemed nebulous, like demonic silhouettes constructed of living shadow. Quin froze, knowing very well what the touch of just one of those creatures could do.

He reached down to his side, drawing his scimitar.

"That sword will do you little good."

Quin glanced up and found himself gaping into the eyes of Cyrus Krane. The Prime Warden of Aerysius was glowering arrogantly down from a balcony high above the floor. He appeared completely at ease, master of his own dominion.

Quin slowly circled his companions, holding Zanikar up before him. A necrator glided toward them from its position along the wall.

Quin pushed Sephana back, inserting himself between her and the living shadow. He brought the sword up, tip pointed at the necrator's chest. To his horror, the blade penetrated the creature harmlessly, as if the necrator was nothing more than animated mist.

He glanced around. More shadows were gliding toward them, streaming forward from the walls, herding them toward the center of the Hall. Quin allowed himself to be forced backward with Sephana.

"Can either of you sense the field?" he inquired of both his companions.

"No," Remzi responded.

Sephana silently shook her head.

All around, the ring of necrators was drawing inexorably closer, little by little tightening the noose around them.

Quin froze; he didn't know what to do. Slowly, he eased Zanikar back into its scabbard. He looked around at the constricting ring of shadows. He was immune to the necrators' awful influence because of his covenant with evil, but there was nothing he could do to stop them; they were not his minions to command.

He paced slowly in a circle around Sephana and Remzi, arms spread out at his sides, warding them both with his body. Suddenly, he stopped in his tracks.

"How ironic," Quin muttered, one corner of his mouth twitching upward into the slightest hint of a grin. "I just remembered something." His eyes narrowed at Cyrus Krane. "I'm a darkmage."

He reached back, plucking Sephana's light staff out of her hand. At the same time, he opened his mind to the power of the Onslaught.

"*No!*" shouted Krane.

Quin smiled as he channeled the malevolent power of the Netherworld into the ring of necrators around him. Dazzling rays of unholy light blossomed from the end of the staff, shining out in every direction at once. All around the room necrators withered and died, impaled by spears of light, consumed by licking tongues of putrid flame.

Quin raised the staff up over his head and then brought it down with force against the ground. The Hall of the Watchers went absolutely dark and then erupted into a dim glow of ethereal green light. The world seemed rendered in a monochromatic pallet of pestilence and decay.

"That was impressive," Krane commended him as he descended the curving staircase toward the floor. "But it was also stupid." His face was a lurid chiaroscuro of shadow.

Krane paused at the bottom of the stairs, one hand lingering on the rail, white cloak swaying behind him. He took a step out onto the tiled floor. It seemed as though he oozed arrogance from every pore.

"Xerys is your Master now," he explained to Quin in a lecturing tone, eyes only for him. "Every move you make in opposition to His will brings you closer to His judgment. Only torment shall await you should you betray the covenant you made."

All the while he was speaking, Krane was slowly inching forward, closing the distance between them. His piercing black eyes glowed with malevolent intensity fraught with shadow. Quin found himself forced gradually backward as he attempted to draw Krane toward himself and away from the others. The Prime Warden pressed forward, cornering him against the far wall near the stairs. A disdainful sneer contorted his features.

Quin leaned the light staff against the corner of the wall. Carefully, he withdrew Zanikar from its scabbard, holding the thin-bladed scimitar out in front of him.

Krane scoffed at the blade, indifferent to Quin's threat. "Such resistance will not serve you. Every act of virtue you commit renders you more vulnerable to my pets."

Quin sneered, shaking his head. "It doesn't matter," he spat. "After today, I could stand here exuding virtue the rest of my life and still have evil left to burn."

He lunged forward, swiping Zanikar up in a backhanded arc that scored a ragged gash across the Prime Warden's face. With a cry, Cyrus Krane flinched back, blood welling from the wound. He brought his hands up to cover his face.

His entire body jerked.

Krane brought his hands down, eyes wide and horrified.

Quin grinned at him, stepping back with Zanikar raised. "The sword's a dampener," he informed Krane, hatred gloating in his eyes. "Now, isn't that a honey of a pickle?"

He raised the sword, focusing his mind for a killing strike.

"No!" he heard Sephana shout from behind him. "Don't do it, Quin!"

Suddenly, she was behind him, hands around his chest, grappling with him for command of the blade. At first he resisted her. But, grudgingly, he lowered Zanikar back down to his side.

He turned to glare at her. *"Why not?"*

She shook her head, eyes wild and tormented. "You have enough blood on your hands today," she scolded him in a near-whisper. "Think of your soul, Quinlan. You are going to *need* to start exuding virtue to have any hope of salvation. He's not worth it, Quin. Let him live to face the justice of the Assembly."

Quin grimaced, knowing she was right. He slammed Zanikar back into its scabbard, turning away as he used the power of his mind to bind his enemy with fetters born of shadow.

He left the Prime Warden there on the floor of his own Hall, bound and gagged, face battered and bloodied. He left him kneeling before the judgmental eyes of the stone Watchers on the walls.

He strode away from the man, walking back toward Remzi. The Empiricist was resting at the base of the staircase, leaning with his back against the rail. He appeared very old and very weary. When he looked up at Quin, his eyes were full of disgust.

"I was afraid you were one of them," Remzi muttered in a tone full of contempt. "I didn't know for certain…I just had a feeling. It made sense." He turned his head and spat upon the ground. "Your brother would turn over in his grave."

Quin stared down at the old Empiricist for a long moment. Softly, he assured him, "There is no way I could possibly be more of a disappointment to my brother than I already am. But, for some reason beyond my capacity to fathom, he always still loved me."

He knelt down before Remzi, one hand on Zanikar's hilt. "Now. Tell me what we have to do to close this Well of your creation."

"I didn't create it," the old man argued defensively. "It was always just a theory. Research I was dabbling in. Renquist stole my notes, all my journals. He brought my work to life, unearthed the Well against my better judgment. Then he leveraged my cooperation."

Quin couldn't help the smirk that came to his face. "It would seem that you and I have more in common than you'd care to admit." He reached up and adjusted his hat. "Now, what do we do to destroy it?"

"You can't destroy it." The old man shook his head with confidence. "You can only seal it. We will have to split up. Only a Grand Master can enter the gateway that has opened to the Netherworld. But someone else must venture below and erase the rune sequence on the Well itself."

"I can do that," Sephana assured him, kneeling at his side. "But I will need your help; I don't understand the cipher."

Devrim Remzi nodded solemnly. "I will guide you."

Quin frowned in consternation, not fully understanding his role. "So the gateway is something different from the Well itself? Where do I find it?"

The old man stated tightly, "The Well of Tears is the lock that opens the door. The gateway is the path to that door. You'll find it most accessible in the square beneath the Hall of the Watchers. Take some courage along with you, Grand Master Quinlan. You won't be walking back out again."

Quin supplied a small, sad grin. "I've never had any courage, I'm afraid. What I do have is an unending supply of indifference and audacity. It will have to suffice."

He rose and turned to Sephana. He gazed into her eyes for a long moment. Then he took her hand and pressed a kiss against her fingers. "I would tell you that I'm truly sorry for all the pain I've caused, but I doubt that would do much, if anything, to ease your sorrow. I fear it would only add to the greatness of my hypocrisy."

Sephana's eyes filled with tears. "Gods' mercy, Quinlan."

He shook his head with a scowl. "I'm well beneath their mercy."

She caught him as he turned away, scooping him up in her arms and embracing him fiercely. He returned the gesture awkwardly, hugging her back.

Into his ear, she whispered, "Thank you, Quin."

Holding her gaze solemnly, he told her, "Enjoy your life, Sephana. Do it for Braden. And for me. Live every minute to its very fullest, but never do one damn thing that you'll ever regret. Please, Sephana. Sleep well at night."

With that he turned and walked away.

Sephana stared after Quin long after he was gone. She wrapped her arms around her chest, her shoulders shaking with muted grief.

She heard a soft noise, turning to find that Devrim Remzi had risen to console her. The old man put a hand on her shoulder, patting her gently and bowing his head.

"Don't mourn him, my dear. Quinlan Reis is no hero."

Sephana turned to glare at him, angered by his coldness. "You judge too harshly," she snapped.

The old man shook his head, disagreeing. "I don't think so."

He gestured with his hand toward the enormous doors that guarded the entrance to the Hall of the Watchers. "Shall we go?"

She started forward but then turned back to consider Cyrus Krane. Frowning, she wondered, "Do you suppose it's safe to leave him here?"

"Absolutely," Remzi asserted, his gaze travelling up the walls to the severe faces of the Watchers. "Let him wait for his hour of reckoning under the censure of his own paragons."

Sephana scooped up the light staff Quin had left for her. Then she guided Remzi out the doors and into the cool night air.

The urgent peal of a tolling bell rang out across the city. They followed the same path she had tread the evening she and Braden had fled the Hall in pursuit of Merris' story. It seemed like such a long time ago.

As they passed by the font on the corner of Torte and Regent, Sephana felt an unexpected stab of sentiment. She had waited by that font for Braden to catch up with her.

Swallowing, she clenched Quin's staff tighter in her hand.

She found the alley without any problem. Holding the staff gripped in her hands, she guided Remzi toward the door of the cellar.

Quin strolled down the street toward the square below the Hall of the Watchers. The avenue ahead was empty; indeed, the entire city seemed deserted. Odd. In the distance, the sound of a tolling bell rang out across the night.

The sound of the bell was a warning, he surmised. *Where are you?* he wondered of the mages of Aerysius, conspicuously absent in their own desperate hour of need.

Then he remembered who their leader was.

Cyrus Krane had no doubt contrived a means of keeping his own people at bay while he was about his own malevolent purpose. Quin clenched his hands into fists, cracking the knuckles of his fingers.

He turned a corner onto the square and stopped.

Gazing up, his eyes went wide.

"Mother of the gods," he whispered.

Ahead, piercing up into the sky from the center of the square, was a towering spire of sickly green light. The air around it contorted, shivering, writhing as if taxed by waves of heat. Lightning licked down from the sky around it, exploding against that awful pillar. There was an odor to the air, a sharp and pungent smell.

Gazing up at that column of energy, Quin almost lost his nerve. Reflexively, he reached into the silk pocket of his vest. He pulled his hand back out again—empty. His bronze flask of alcohol had been drained a long time ago.

"Damn," he muttered.

———

Sephana knelt down beside the Well of Tears in black pools of stagnant water mixed with the blood of victims spilled by sacrifice. The thick, gray blocks of the Well felt rough and cold beneath her hand. Around its rim glowed runes of power, shining with a putrescent inner light. The entire chamber was swathed in a malignant glare that issued forth from the shivering column of energy that spilled upward from the Well's depths.

The sight of it made her want to retch, filling her with a gut-penetrating cold. Somehow, Sephana knew exactly what she was looking at. She knew she was staring at a portal to the Netherworld. And it was appalling.

Thinking of Quin, she shivered in horror.

"Peace," the aged Master whispered, laying a steadying hand upon her shoulder. "Concentrate. Do exactly what I say. The first rune of the sequence is *dacros*. There. Use fire. You must clean the stain of blood that feeds each rune and gives it life."

Sephana gazed at the rune *dacros,* raising her hand. With her finger, she traced above the glowing symbol in the air. Then, determined, she focused her mind and drew deeply on the power of the magic field through the staff of light.

———

"What are you doing here, Quin?"

He squeezed his eyes shut at the sound of that soft and silky voice. He didn't turn, just brought his hand up to rub his eyes. He searched his feelings, not knowing how to react. He hadn't anticipated this confrontation.

"Hello, Merris," Quin muttered wearily, still with his back to her.

He didn't want to look at her. Just hearing the sound of her voice turned his stomach sour. He swallowed heavily against the bitter aftertaste of her betrayal.

He asked of her, "Are you enjoying the sweet legacy you plundered from my brother's corpse?"

He stood there, shoulders tense, eyes closed. Waiting to hear her response.

"That's not very nice," she admonished him in low and sultry tones. "Did your mother not teach you how to be cordial?"

"It wasn't meant to be cordial," Quin informed her stiffly. His eyes were open now, gazing up at the glowing pillar of energy thrusting upward into the sky. Far easier to look upon the promise of his own damnation than subject himself to the alluring manipulation of her eyes.

"Did it hurt very much," he wondered, "receiving the Transference through the Soulstone?" He was deliberately baiting her. He needed to hear her admit her part in his brother's murder.

Smiling darkly, he went on, "It's a beautiful artifact, the Soulstone. Especially when it's full of its own inner life. Beckoning. Alluring. It just…begs for your attention. Entices you with its vitality, its facets, its promises…its lies.

"But it has a flaw in it, you know, hidden very deep inside. One that's impossible to detect until you actually put it on. Of course, by that time, it's simply too late." Quin smiled morbidly. "Maybe you really were fated to wear the Soulstone, Arden. You're just like it."

There was a long, gaping silence that could be measured by the echoing cadence of his heartbeat. Then:

"The Transference did hurt, Quinlan. Dreadfully. But what I went through was nothing compared to your brother's torment. I wish you could have been there to see his face, to hear the sound of his screams. They went on and on until he was too hoarse to scream anymore. And even then…he still tried. Braden was a strong man. It took him a very long time to die. And I enjoyed *every…single…agonized…scream.*"

Quin whirled toward her, lashing out viciously with a thought designed to rip her blackened heart to shreds in her chest.

Casually, she blocked his strike.

Laughing in delight, Arden Hannah strode toward him, gesturing with her hand in the air. A shield of amber light appeared about her, nebulous, golden and scintillating. Quin cringed back as he took in the characteristic color of the vibrant energies that sustained her.

Each magical lineage was distinguishable by its own unique color. That shade of amber had been his brother's signature. Seeing such obvious evidence of Braden's legacy wielded by Arden Hannah was too much for him to stand.

With a howl that seemed ripped right out of his battered soul, Quin drew his sword and lunged toward her. But before he could land the strike, something tackled him to the ground from behind.

Quin rolled out from under the thanacryst's attack, wiping its fetid slobber off his face. Staggering to his feet, he lifted his sword to ward the beast away. It stood there growling, hackles raised, eyes fiercely menacing.

"Do you like my new pet?" Arden inquired with a grin. "I think it's hungry."

Quin edged away from the creature, backing up toward the pulsating light of the Gateway. With a sinking feeling, he realized that her own strength by far exceeded his own. Arden was sixth tier, just as Braden had been. Never in all of history had there ever been a mage more powerful. Added to that was the sinister threat of the thanacryst.

Quin glanced up into the sky, knowing there was very little he could do. There was nowhere to go. She had him cornered against the shivering energies of the gateway.

"You can't win." The silken texture of her voice was full of confident satisfaction. "So tell me, Quinlan Reis, are you ready to die?"

Quin grimaced. Then he smirked, startled by a moment of insight. To Arden, he observed, "Yes, remarkably, I believe I am."

He didn't have to win, he realized. He didn't even have to fight. All he had to do was turn and walk away. He smiled, a toxic sneer that emphasized the harsh angles of his face.

He tipped his hat in her direction. "Madam, I will see you in Hell."

The confidence in her expression faltered as she guessed his purpose too late.

The sound of her piercing scream was the last thing Quin heard as he stepped into the gateway. The column of energy collapsed behind him, delivering Arden and the rest of her kind to their Master in the Netherworld.

Epilogue

Aerysius, The Rhen

Inside the Hall of the Watchers, a forest of stone pillars chiseled into the semblances of massive trees spread their branches in support of the vaulted ceiling. All across the floor were gathered hundreds of mages in formal black robes, assembled together in ordered ranks across the lines of power of Aerysius' great Circle of Convergence.

A clanking noise echoed loudly as one of the enormous doors shuddered open, admitting a brilliant sliver of sunlight into the dim chamber beyond. From out of that harsh glare emerged the figure of Sephana Clemley, moving at the head of a long train of attendants. Throughout the Hall, the gathered onlookers receded toward the walls, clearing a path before her.

Sephana moved with a dignified grace as she mounted the sweeping curve of marble steps. Her face was blank and without expression, eyes trained straight ahead. She wore a flowing gown of purest white, golden hair adorned with sprigs of floral herbs. Arriving at the mezzanine balcony, she took her place at the edge of the balustrade. There, Sephana paused, gazing solemnly out over the gathered crowd of onlookers.

Two women in formal black robes approached from behind, bearing between them a thick cloak of white embroidered with the image of the Silver Star, renowned vestment of the Prime Warden. Together in unison, the women spread the fabric out between them and ceremoniously drew the cloak of office over Sephana's frame, securing it in place with a silver brooch. They dropped to their knees at her sides, carefully arranging the drape of cloth.

A white mantle of luxurious ermine was spread across her shoulders, the signet of office thrust onto her finger. Into Sephana's hands were placed the traditional regalia of Aerysius: a tapering rod made of crystal and a lapis orb topped with the image of the Silver Star.

There, standing on the balcony before the faces of the Watchers of the Hall, Prime Warden Sephana Clemley swore her oath of office. After she pledged her vows, there was a momentary gap of silence. Then, together as one, every Master of Aerysius dropped to the floor in a great wave that spread throughout the entire crowd, falling forward over their knees with heads and palms pressed against the ground in a humbling display of deference.

When all had risen from their homage, Sephana gave a nod, gazing down upon her subjects. Then she turned, replacing the rod and orb back onto their cushion.

A murmuring tension swept throughout the Hall as mages reacted to her break with time-honored tradition. Sephana glared down upon them, her face severe and authoritative, aware that what she was about to do next went far beyond any action ever taken by a Prime Warden to come before her.

Above the gathered mages, Sephana raised her naked hands, shaking back the wide sleeves of her gown. She rotated her arms slowly until the palms of her hands faced toward her, spreading her fingers wide.

"I, Sephana Clemley, Prime Warden of Aerysius, hereby institute an Oath of Harmony, decreeing this pledge obligatory upon all Masters from this day forward unto the end of time. Please repeat each word I say exactly as I say it:

> "I swear to live in harmony with all of creation."

She paused then, listening with a sense of triumph as her words were echoed back to her from the gathered mages, the sound of their voices resonating in choral unison off the high dome of the Hall.

> "To use my gift with temperance and wisdom;
> Always to heal and never to harm,
> Or my life will be righteously forfeit."

As she completed the oath, Sephana paused to listen as the voices of the crowd beneath her faded away into silence.

Then she glanced up, rotating her arms before her face. On both of her wrists now glimmered a matching set of metallic chains, binding her and all of Aerysius firmly to the constraints of Braden's Oath.

She allowed herself a smile of satisfaction, gazing down at a hall full of mages who, spreading their hands before them, stared with wonder and curiosity at the fresh set of markings that would forever remain an indelible reminder of the vow they had collectively taken.

Sephana wondered what Braden would be feeling if he could be here with her now, staring out at such a sight. She suspected he would be very humbled and very gladdened at the same time. Sephana reached down, caressing the slight swelling in her middle where their baby had taken root and was growing deep inside. It was greatly comforting to know that something of him would yet remain in this world, a child of Braden's lineage that could carry on his legacy. Sephana smiled, blinking back tears of grief and gratitude that tried to fill her eyes.

She wiped the tears away; this was no time for mourning. She wasn't done yet. There was still one last hurdle to overcome. Sephana had to insure that what had happened to Caladorn could never happen to the Rhen. She had to guarantee that there would never be another Cyrus Krane or Zavier Renquist. To the gathered Assembly, she continued:

"Let it be known that, by my own decree and proclamation, the Order of Battlemages is hereby forever disbanded and dissolved. In its place, I formally institute the Order of Sentinels, to be chartered with the solemn duty to watch over, defend, and protect the nations of the Rhen in a manner consistent with the moral principles and imperatives of the Oath of Harmony."

THE END

Glossary

acolyte: apprentice mage who has passed the Trial of Consideration and sworn the Acolyte's Oath.

Acolyte's Oath: first vow taken by every acolyte of Aerysius to serve the land and its people, symbolized by a chain-like marking on the left wrist.

Aerysius: ancient city where the Masters of Aerysius dwell.

Akins, Tom: blacksmith from Farbrook.

Al'thartier: Venthic title that means Greatest Battlemage.

Amani: wife of Braden Reis who was executed for treason against the Assembly of the Lyceum.

Amberlie: town in the Vale of Amberlie below Aerysius.

amplification: character of increasing a mage's permeability to the magic field.

Anassis, Myria: ancient Querer of the Lyceum, now a Servant of Xerys.

apprentice: mage in training in the Lyceum who has passed the Trial of Consideration and sworn the oath of apprenticeship.

Archer, Amelia: wife of Kyel Archer.

Archer, Gilroy: baby son of Kyel Archer.

Archer, Kyel: apprentice merchant of Coventry Township.

Arches: enchanted monuments that guard the Hall of the Watchers and the Lyceum, allowing only mages access.

Arman, Nashir: ancient Battlemage and Servant of Xerys.

Arms Guild: institution for the study of blademastery. Also called the School of Arms.

artifact: heirloom of power that has been imbued with magical characters or properties.

Arvel: Voice of the High Priest of Wisdom.

Assembly: the Masters of Aerysius or the Lyceum, as a collective entity.

Asyaadi Clan: group of kinsfolk who live in the village of Qul in the Black Lands.

Athera's Crescent: Mysterious and ancient artifact on the Isle of Titherry.

Atrament: the realm of Death, ruled by the goddess Isap.

Auberdale: capital city of Chamsbrey.

Azár ni Suam: Lightweaver of the Asyaadi Clan.

Battle of Meridan: famous battle in which the Enemy was turned back in large part due to the efforts of the Sentinels.

Battlemage: order of mages who accompanied armies into battle in ancient times before the Oath of Harmony.

Black Lands: what was once Caladorn, now the desecrated home of the Enemy.

Black Solstice: The battle that ended the Fifth Invasion.

blademaster: title awarded to graduates of the Arms Guild.

Blandford, General: general of the Emrish Army.

Bloodquest: ancient rite of vengeance condoned by the goddess Isap for righteous causes.

Bluecloaks: slang for the Rothscard city guard.

Book of All Things: book in which the Everlasting Story is said to be scribed by the mightiest of all pens.

Book of the Dead: ancient text wherein the Strictures of Death are inscribed.

Bound: describes a mage who has sworn the Oath of Harmony.

Broden: Guild blademaster employed by the Mayor of Wolden.

Bryar, Merris: ancient acolyte of Aerysius mentored by Master Sephana Clemley.
Bryn Calazar: ancient capital of Caladorn.
Cadmus: Voice of the High Priest of Wisdom.
Caladorn: ancient empire to the north, now known only as the Black Lands.
caravansary: in the Black Lands, a large courtyard with attached rooms built for the purposes of accommodating caravans resting overnight.
Catacombs: place of burial that exists partly in the Atrament.
Cerulean Plains: large grassland region in the North.
Chamber of Egress: rooms containing transfer portals between both Aerysius and the Lyceum. Relics left behind of an ancient past when the two schools of magic enjoyed better relations.
Chamsbrey: Northern kingdom ruled by Godfrey Faukravar.
Circle of Convergence: focus of magic designed to draw on the vast power of a vortex.
clan: in the Black Lands, a kin-based group of close, interrelated families.
Clemley, Sephana: ancient Prime Warden of Aerysius and lover of Braden Reis.
colleges of magic: the Hall of the Watchers in Aerysius and the Lyceum in Bryn Calazar.
Connel, Byron: ancient Battlemage of the Lyceum, now a Servant of Xerys.
Corlan, Finneus: first tier Master of the Order of Sentinels.
Covendrey: town in the kingdom of Lynnley.
Craghorns: mountains that border the Vale of Amberlie.
Craig, Devlin: captain of Greystone Keep.
Creek Hollow: town in the Vale of Amberlie.
Cromm, Cedric: author of *The Mysteries of Aerysius.*
Cummings, Chadwick: advisor to the King of Chamsbrey.
Curse, the: term used to describe the darkening of the skies and earth of the Black Lands, as well as for the unusual weather patterns and electrical storms experienced in the region.
dakura: ancient derogatory term used by the Jenn for the city-dwelling people of Caladorn.
dampen: to shield a mage from sensing the magic field.
damper: an object that has the ability to dampen a mage from sensing the magic field.
darkmage: a mage who has made a compact with Xerys.
Death's Passage: *see* **Catacombs**.
Desco: priest of Deshari.
Desecration, the: the apocalyptic event that destroyed Caladorn by blackening the skies and the earth.
destrier: various breeds of large warhorse.
Eight, the: the Eight Servants of Xerys.
elam: a writing stick
Elessar: ancient warlord of the Omeyan Jenn.
Emmery: Northern kingdom of the Rhen.
Emmery Palace: the Queen's palace in Rothscard.
Enemy, the: collective name for inhabitants of the Black Lands.
Everlasting Story: according to Harbingers, the ever-evolving story that chronicles all the events in the world.
eye: area at the heart of a vortex where the lines of the magic field run almost parallel.
Farbrook: town in the Vale of Amberlie.
Faukravar, Godfrey: King of Chamsbrey, also known as the Vile Prince.
field lines: currents of the magic field.
Field of Tol-Ranier: ancient battle site near Auberdale.
First Sentinel, the: *see* **Braden Reis**.
First Among Many: in the combined legions of Malikar, second-in-command to the Warden of Battlemages. The highest ranking officer who is not a mage.
Flynn, Tyrius: fourth tier Grand Master of the Order of Sentinels.
Front, the: area bordering the Black Lands.
Gannet: town in the Vale below Aerysius.
Gateway: portal to the Netherworld.
Glen Farquist: holy city in the Valley of the Gods.
Goddess of the Eternal Requiem: statue of an aspect of the Goddess of Death; her face of Righteous Vengeance.
Grand Master: any mage of the fourth tier or higher.
Grand Resonance: theoretical acceleration of the magic field that produces a cataclysmic chain reaction.
Great Lady: title of honor applied to any female Master or Grand Master.
Great Master: title of honor applied to any male Master or Grand Master.

Great Schism: separation between the Assemblies of mages and the ruling bodies of the temples.

Greystone Keep: legendary fortress in the Pass of Lor-Gamorth.

Hall of the Watchers: Stronghold of the mages of Aerysius, where exists Aerysius' Circle of Convergence.

Hannah, Arden: ancient Querer, now a Servant of Xerys.

Hellpower: *see* **Onslaught**.

Henley, Corban: formerly of the Vale, now a soldier of Greystone Keep.

High Priest: title of the religious leader of one of the ten Holy Temples.

hyphal artifact: an artifact that is grown instead of wrought.

Ironguard Pass: passage from the Black Lands into the Rhen created by Aiden Lauchlin.

Isap: Goddess of Death.

Ishara: border town in the Black Lands, in the region once known as Skara.

Isle of Titherry: Isle off the coast of the Rhen where exists the artifact known as Athera's Crescent.

Jenn: nomadic horse culture of the Cerulean Plains.

Kateem, Khoresh: infamous Emperor who united all of Caladorn under a singular rule before the Desecration.

Kayna: woman of the Jenn, wife of Ranoch.

Khazahar Desert: arid region in the Black Lands that was once an expansive grassland.

Krane, Cyrus: ancient Prime Warden of Aerysius, now a Servant of Xerys.

Landry, Clement: Minister of State to the King of Chamsbrey.

Larsen, Ellen: wife of Traver Larsen.

Larsen, Traver: friend of Kyel Archer.

Lauchlin, Aidan: first tier Master of the Order of Empiricists. Firstborn son of Gerald and Emelda Lauchlin.

Lauchlin, Darien: second son of Gerald and Emelda Lauchlin.

Lauchlin, Emelda: Prime Warden of Aerysius. First tier Master of the Order of Chancellors.

Lauchlin, Gerald: father of Aidan and Darien Lauchlin, fourth tier Grand Master of the Order of Sentinels. Murdered by ritual immolation during the Battle of Meridan *(deceased).*

lightfields: in the Black Lands, places where food is grown using light produced by mages called Lightweavers.

Lightweaver: in the Black Lands, mages who have the ability to produce a color of magelight that mimics the full spectrum of the sun.

Lyceum: ancient stronghold of the mages of Bryn Calazar.

Lynnley: Kingdom of the Rhen.

Mage's Oath: *see* **Oath of Harmony**.

magelight: magical illumination that takes on the hue of the mage's signature color.

magic field: source of magical energy that runs in lines of power over the earth.

Maidenclaw: one of the two mountains that mark the entrance of the Black Lands.

Malikar: modern name of the nation that was once Caladorn.

Master: any mage; more specifically, a mage of the first through third tier.

Meridan: *see* **Battle of Meridan**.

motive character: in an artifact, the ability to create a force that produces motion.

Mountains of Cedar: ancient name for the Shadowspear Mountains, before the Desecration. *Sajar-Asharu* in Venthic.

Mysteries of Aerysius, The: authoritative text on the subject of the Masters of Aerysius.

***nach'tier*:** word for darkmage in the language of the Enemy.

Natural Law: law that governs the workings of the universe that can be strained by the application of magic, but never broken.

necrator: demonic creature that renders a mage powerless in its presence.

Nelle, Lynnea: first tier Master of the Order of Querers.

Netherworld: realm of Xerys, God of Chaos.

Newell, Alexa: serving girl in Creek Hollow.

node: place where the lines of the magic field come together in parallel direction but opposite in energy and cancel out.

Nordric, Ezras: fifth tier Grand Master of the Order of Sentinels.

Norengail, Romana: Queen of Emmery.

North, the: the Northern kingdoms of the Rhen, including Emmery, Chamsbrey and Lynnley.

Nym: ancient river in the Black Lands once considered sacred.

Oath of Harmony: oath taken by every Master of Aerysius to do no harm, symbolized by a chain-like marking on the right wrist.

Oblivion: outcome for a soul who is denied entry into both the Atrament and the Netherworld, which results in the complete destruction of that soul and the denial of eternity.

Omeyan Clan: ancient clan of the Jenn led by Elessar.

Onslaught: the corrupt power of the netherworld, also known as the Hellfire.

orders: different schools of magic.

Orguleth: one of the two mountains that mark the entrance to the Black Lands. Also called the Spire of Orguleth.

Orien Oathbreaker: infamous Grand Master who used the Circle of Convergence on Orien's Finger to turn back the Third Invasion almost single-handedly.

Orien's Finger: crag on the edge of the Cerulean Plains where Orien Oathbreaker made his stand.

Qadir, Sareen: ancient Querer and one the Eight Servants of Xerys .

Qul: village in the Khazahar Desert in the Black Lands.

Pass of Lor-Gamorth: pass through the Shadowspear Mountains that guards the border of the Black Lands.

Penthos, Luther: High Priest of the Temple of Death.

potential: ability in a person to sense the magic field.

Pratson, Blake: Mayor of Wolden.

Prime Warden: leader of the Assembly of the Hall. Literally, the 'First Guardian' of the Rhen.

Proctor, Garret: legendary Force Commander of Greystone Keep.

Raising: Rite of Transference, during which an acolyte inherits the legacy of power from another mage.

Rakkah: the final test of an apprentice Battlemage

Ranoch: man of the Jenn, husband of Kayna.

Reis, Braden: ancient Caladornian Battlemage who was executed for treason against the Assembly of the Lyceum. Founder of the Oath of Harmony and the Order of Sentinels.

Reis, Quinlan: ancient Arcanist and brother of Braden Reis. One of the Eight Servants of Xerys.

Remzi, Devrim: ancient first tier Master of the Order of Empiricists who wrote *Treatise on the Well of Tears.*

Renquist, Zavier: ancient Prime Warden of the Lyceum, now a Servant of Xerys.

Rhen: name of the collective kingdoms south of the Black Lands.

Rhenic: common language spoken throughout the kingdoms of the Rhen.

rika: ceremonial beverage served by the people of the Khazahar during times of celebration or times of woe.

Rothscard: capital city of Emmery.

Royce, Sutton: captain of Greystone Keep and Guild blademaster.

saturation: Battlemage tactic of overloading with magical power in anticipation of creating an enormous discharge of force.

Sayeed son of Alborz: Zakai of the Tanisar corps at Tokashi Palace.

School of Arms: *see* **Arms Guild**.

Seleni, Naia: priestess of Death.

sensitive: ability in some people to detect the emotions of others. Not dependent on the magic field, and not limited to mages.

Sentinels: order of mages chartered with the defense of the Rhen.

Shadowspears: mountains that border the Black Lands.

sharaq: ancient system of honor code of the Black Lands.

Silver Star: symbol of the Masters of Aerysius, indicative of the focus lines of the Circles of Convergence.

Skara: ancient city in the Black Lands that was destroyed during the Desecration.

Soulstone: ancient artifact that is a storage receptacle for a dying mage's legacy.

South, the: Southern kingdoms of the Rhen, including Creston, Gandrish, and Farley.

Spire of the Hall: tower of the Hall of the Watchers where the Masters keep their residence.

Strictures of Death: laws of Death.

Structural Resonance: acceleration of the magic field that produces a harmonic instability in the field capable of destroying large structures.

Superposition: within a vortex, where several lines of the magic field combine and produce a vast well of power.

Swain, Nigel: Guild blademaster, formerly Captain of the Guard in Aerysius, currently Captain of the Guard in Rothscard.

Tanisar corps: legions of highly disciplined elite infantry units of the Khazahar.

Tarkendar: breed of destrier, or warhorse.

Tarpen, Wade: soldier of Greystone Keep.

temples: various sects of worship. Each temple is devoted to a particular deity of the pantheon.

thanacryst: demonic creature that feeds off a mage's gift.

thar'tier: word for Battlemage in the language of the Enemy.

Thar'gon: magical talisman carried by Byron Connel that is the symbol of the Warden of Battlemages of the Lyceum.

tier: additive levels of power among Masters. The higher a Master's tier, the greater that person's ability to strain the limits of Natural Law.

Tokashi Palace: fortress in the north of the Black Lands.

Torrence, Edric: third tier Master, also known as the Bird Man to the local peasants.

transfer portal: ancient system of artifacts capable of transferring a person to various locations.

Transference: process by which an acolyte inherits the legacy of power from another mage, resulting in the death of the Master who gives up his or her ability.

Treaton, Lance: Minister of the Treasury to the King of Chamsbrey.

Trial of Consideration: rite by which the potential to perceive the magic field is tested in a person.

Tsula daughter of Mundi: ancient Warden of Harbingers.

Ul-Calazi, Masil: general of the army of Bryn Calazar.

Ulric: soldier of Greystone Keep.

Unbinding: the act of forswearing the Oath of Harmony.

Valdivora: blade carried by Khoresh Kateem in the Battle of Harmudi.

Vale of Amberlie: long, narrow valley in the North.

Valley of the Gods: valley where exists the holy city of Glen Farquist.

Venthic: the language of the Enemy.

versions: according to Harbingers, possibilities of the future, as read by Athera's Crescent.

Vile Prince: *see* **Faukravar, Godfrey**.

Vintgar: ancient ice fortress and source of the River Nym.

vortex: cyclone of power where the lines of the magic field superimpose and become vastly intense.

Well of Tears: well that unlocks the gateway to the Netherworld.

Wellingford, Malcolm: soldier of the Northern Army of Chamsbrey.

Withersby, Meiran: sixth tier Grand Master of the Order of Querers.

Wolden: town in the North, in the Kingdom of Emmery.

Xerys: God of Chaos and Lord of the Netherworld.

Xerys' Pedestal: ancient name of Orien's Finger.

yurt: a portable, round lodge or tent covered in felt used as dwellings by the Jenn.

Zakai: officers of the Tanisar corps that form their own distinctive social class.

Zanikar: magical sword and artifact created by Quinlan Reis.

The Orders of Mages

Order of Arcanists: order of mages chartered with the study and creation of artifacts and heirlooms of power.

Order of Architects: order of mages chartered with the construction of magical infrastructure.

Order of Battlemages: order of mages chartered with martial applications of the magic field.

Order of Chancellors: order of mages chartered with the governance of the Assembly.

Order of Empiricists: order of mages chartered with the theoretical study of the magic field, its laws and principles.

Order of Harbingers: order of mages chartered with maintaining watch over Athera's Crescent.

Order of Naturalists: order of mages chartered with the study of Natural Law.

Order of Querers: order of mages chartered with practical applications of the magic field.

Order of Sentinels: order of mages chartered with watching over and protecting the Rhen in a manner consistent with the Oath of Harmony.

www.ingramcontent.com/pod-product-compliance
Lightning Source LLC
Chambersburg PA
CBHW081133300726
48982CB00005B/948
* 9 7 8 0 9 9 9 7 8 2 5 7 6 *